Selected Works of D. H. Lawrence

Selected Works of
D. H. Lawrence

NOVELS

Sons and Lovers

Women in Love

Lady Chatterley's Lover

SHORT NOVELS

The Captain's Doll

The Fox

The Ladybird

St Mawr

The Princess

The Virgin and the Gipsy

The Escaped Cock

Wordsworth Editions

1

Readers who are interested in other titles from
Wordsworth Editions are invited to visit out website at
www.wordsworth-editions.com

For our latest list and a full mail-order service contact
Bibliophile Books, 5 Thomas Road, London E14 7BN
Tel: +44 0207 515 9222   Fax: +44 0207 538 4115
e-mail: orders@bibliophilebooks.com

This edition published 2006 by Wordsworth Editions Limited
8B East Street, Ware, Hertfordshire SG12 9HJ

ISBN 1 84022 494 0

Typeset in Great Britain by Antony Gray
Printed by Clays Ltd, St Ives plc

CONTENTS

SONS AND LOVERS

looked out, from the attic windows at least, on the slow climb of the valley towards Selby.

The houses themselves were substantial and very decent. One could walk all round, seeing little front gardens with auriculas and saxifrage in the shadow of the bottom block, sweet-williams and pinks in the sunny top block; seeing neat front windows, little porches, little privet hedges, and dormer windows for the attics. But that was outside; that was the view on to the uninhabited parlours of all the colliers' wives. The dwelling-room, the kitchen, was at the back of the house, facing inward between the blocks, looking at a scrubby back garden, and then at the ash-pits. And between the rows, between the long lines of ash-pits, went the alley, where the children played and the women gossiped and the men smoked. So, the actual conditions of living in the Bottoms, that was so well built and that looked so nice, were quite unsavoury because people must live in the kitchen, and the kitchens opened on to that nasty alley of ash-pits.

Mrs Morel was not anxious to move into the Bottoms, which was already twelve years old and on the downward path, when she descended to it from Bestwood. But it was the best she could do. Moreover, she had an end house in one of the top blocks, and thus had only one neighbour; on the other side an extra strip of garden. And, having an end house, she enjoyed a kind of aristocracy among the other women of the 'between' houses, because her rent was five shillings and sixpence instead of five shillings a week. But this superiority in station was not much consolation to Mrs Morel.

She was thirty-one years old, and had been married eight years. A rather small woman, of delicate mould but resolute bearing, she shrank a little from the first contact with the Bottoms women. She came down in the July, and in the September expected her third baby.

Her husband was a miner. They had only been in their new home three weeks when the wakes, or fair, began. Morel, she knew, was sure to make a holiday of it. He went off early on the Monday morning, the day of the fair. The two children were highly excited. William, a boy of seven, fled off immediately after breakfast, to prowl round the wakes ground, leaving Annie, who was only five, to whine all morning to go also. Mrs Morel did her work. She scarcely knew her neighbours yet, and knew no one with whom to trust the little girl. So she promised to take her to the wakes after dinner.

William appeared at half-past twelve. He was a very active lad, fair-haired, freckled, with a touch of the Dane or Norwegian about him.

'Can I have my dinner, mother?' he cried, rushing in with his cap on. ''Cause it begins at half-past one, the man says so.'

'You can have your dinner as soon as it's done,' replied the mother.

'Isn't it done?' he cried, his blue eyes staring at her in indignation. 'Then I'm goin' be-out it.'

'You'll do nothing of the sort. It will be done in five minutes. It is only half-past twelve.'

'They'll be beginnin',' the boy half cried, half shouted.

PART ONE

CHAPTER I

The Early Married Life of the Morels

THE BOTTOMS' succeeded to 'Hell Row'. Hell Row was a block of thatched, bulging cottages that stood by the brookside on Greenhill Lane. There lived the colliers who worked in the little gin-pits two fields away. The brook ran under the alder trees, scarcely soiled by these small mines, whose coal was drawn to the surface by donkeys that plodded wearily in a circle round a gin. And all over the countryside were these same pits, some of which had been worked in the time of Charles II, the few colliers and the donkeys burrowing down like ants into the earth, making queer mounds and little black places among the cornfields and the meadows. And the cottages of these coal-miners, in blocks and pairs here and there, together with odd farms and homes of the stockingers, straying over the parish, formed the village of Bestwood.

Then, some sixty years ago, a sudden change took place. The gin-pits were elbowed aside by the large mines of the financiers. The coal and iron field of Nottinghamshire and Derbyshire was discovered. Carston, Waite and Co. appeared. Amid tremendous excitement, Lord Palmerston formally opened the company's first mine at Spinney Park, on the edge of Sherwood Forest.

About this time the notorious Hell Row, which through growing old had acquired an evil reputation, was burned down, and much dirt was cleansed away.

Carston, Waite and Co. found they had struck on a good thing, so, down the valleys of the brooks from Selby and Nuttall, new mines were sunk, until soon there were six pits working. From Nuttall, high up on the sandstone among the woods, the railway ran, past the ruined priory of the Carthusians and past Robin Hood's Well, down to Spinney Park then on to Minton, a large mine among cornfields; from Minton across the farmlands of the valleyside to Bunker's Hill, branching off there, and running north to Beggarlee and Selby, that looks over at Crich and the hills of Derbyshire; six mines like black studs on the countryside, linked by a loop of fine chain, the railway.

To accommodate the regiments of miners, Carston, Waite and Co. built the Squares, great quadrangles of dwellings on the hillside of Bestwood, and then, in the brook valley, on the site of Hell Row, they erected the Bottoms.

The Bottoms consisted of six blocks of miners' dwellings, two rows of three, like the dots on a blank-six domino, and twelve houses in a block. This double row of dwellings sat at the foot of the rather sharp slope from Bestwood, and

CONTENTS

PART ONE

PART TWO

'You won't die if they do,' said the mother. 'Besides, it's only half-past twelve, so you've a full hour.'

The lad began hastily to lay the table, and directly the three sat down. They were eating batter-pudding and jam, when the boy jumped off his chair and stood perfectly still. Some distance away could be heard the first small braying of a merry-go-round, and the tooting of a horn. His face quivered as he looked at his mother.

'I told you!' he said, running to the dresser for his cap.

'Take your pudding in your hand – and it's only five past one, so you were wrong – you haven't got your twopence,' cried the mother in a breath.

The boy came back, bitterly disappointed, for his twopence; then went off without a word.

'I want to go, I want to go,' said Annie, beginning to cry.

'Well, and you shall go, whining, wizening little stick!' said the mother. And later in the afternoon she trudged up the hill under the tall hedge with her child. The hay was gathered from the fields, and cattle were turned on to the eddish. It was warm, peaceful.

Mrs Morel did not like the wakes. There were two sets of horses, one going by steam, one pulled round by a pony; three organs were grinding, and there came odd cracks of pistol-shots, fearful screeching of the coconut man's rattle, shouts of the Aunt Sally man, screeches from the peep-show lady. The mother perceived her son gazing enraptured outside the Lion Wallace booth, at the pictures of this famous lion that had killed a negro and maimed for life two white men. She left him alone, and went to get Annie a spin of toffee. Presently the lad stood in front of her, wildly excited.

'You never said you was coming – isn't the' a lot of things? – that lion's killed three men – I've spent my tuppence – an' look here.'

He pulled from his pocket two egg-cups, with pink moss-roses on them.

'I got these from that stall where y'ave ter get them marbles in them holes. An' I got these two in two goes – 'aepenny a go – they've got moss-roses on, look here. I wanted these.'

She knew he wanted them for her.

'I I'm!' she said, pleased. 'They are pretty!'

'Shall you carry 'em, 'cause I'm frightened o' breakin' 'em?'

He was tipful of excitement now she had come, led her about the ground, showed her everything. Then, at the peep-show, she explained the pictures, in a sort of story, to which he listened as if spellbound. He would not leave her. All the time he stuck close to her, bristling with a small boy's pride of her. For no other woman looked such a lady as she did, in her little black bonnet and her cloak. She smiled when she saw women she knew. When she was tired she said to her son, 'Well, are you coming now, or later?'

'Are you goin' a'ready?' he cried, his face full of reproach.

'Already? It is past four, I know.'

'What are you goin' a'ready for?' he lamented.

'You needn't come if you don't want,' she said.

And she went slowly away with her little girl, whilst her son stood watching her, cut to the heart to let her go, and yet unable to leave the wakes. As she crossed the open ground in front of the Moon and Stars she heard men shouting, and smelled the beer, and hurried a little, thinking her husband was probably in the bar.

At about half-past six her son came home, tired now, rather pale, and somewhat wretched. He was miserable, though he did not know it, because he had let her go alone. Since she had gone, he had not enjoyed his wakes.

'Has my dad been?' he asked.

'No,' said the mother.

'He's helping to wait at the Moon and Stars. I seed him through that black tin stuff wi' holes in, on the window, wi' his sleeves rolled up.'

'Ha!' exclaimed the mother shortly. 'He's got no money. An' he'll be satisfied if he gets his 'lowance, whether they give him more or not.'

When the light was fading, and Mrs Morel could see no more to sew, she rose and went to the door. Everywhere was the sound of excitement, the restlessness of the holiday, that at last infected her. She went out into the side garden. Women were coming home from the wakes, the children hugging a white lamb with green legs, or a wooden horse. Occasionally a man lurched past, almost as full as he could carry. Sometimes a good husband came along with his family, peacefully. But usually the women and children were alone. The stay-at-home mothers stood gossiping at the corners of the alley, as the twilight sank, folding their arms under their white aprons.

Mrs Morel was alone, but she was used to it. Her son and her little girl slept upstairs; so, it seemed, her home was there behind her, fixed and stable. But she felt wretched with the coming child. The world seemed a dreary place, where nothing else would happen for her – at least until William grew up. But for herself, nothing but this dreary endurance – till the children grew up. And the children! She could not afford to have this third. She did not want it. The father was serving beer in a public-house, swilling himself drunk. She despised him, and was tied to him. This coming child was too much for her. If it were not for William and Annie, she was sick of it, the struggle with poverty and ugliness and meanness.

She went into the front garden, feeling too heavy to take herself out, yet unable to stay indoors. The heat suffocated her. And looking ahead, the prospect of her life made her feel as if she were buried alive.

The front garden was a small square with a privet hedge. There she stood, trying to soothe herself with the scent of flowers and the fading, beautiful evening. Opposite her small gate was the stile that led uphill, under the tall hedge, between the burning glow of the cut pastures. The sky overhead throbbed and pulsed with light. The glow sank quickly off the field; the earth and the hedges smoked dusk. As it grew dark, a ruddy glare came out on the hilltop, and out of the glare the diminished commotion of the fair.

Sometimes, down the trough of darkness formed by the path under the hedges, men came lurching home. One young man lapsed into a run down the steep bit that ended the hill, and went with a crash into the stile. Mrs Morel shuddered. He picked himself up, swearing viciously, rather pathetically, as if he thought the stile had wanted to hurt him.

She went indoors, wondering if things were never going to alter. She was beginning by now to realise that they would not. She seemed so far away from her girlhood, she wondered if it were the same person walking heavily up the back garden at the Bottoms as had run so lightly on the breakwater at Sheerness ten years before.

'What have *I* to do with it?' she said to herself. 'What have I to do with all this? Even the child I am going to have! It doesn't seem as if *I* were taken into account.'

Sometimes life takes hold of one, carries the body along, accomplishes one's history, and yet is not real, but leaves oneself as it were slurred over.

'I wait,' Mrs Morel said to herself – 'I wait, and what I wait for can never come.'

Then she straightened the kitchen, lit the lamp, mended the fire, looked out the washing for the next day, and put it to soak. After which she sat down to her sewing. Through the long hours her needle flashed regularly through the stuff. Occasionally she sighed, moving to relieve herself. And all the time she was thinking how to make the most of what she had, for the children's sakes.

At half-past eleven her husband came. His cheeks were very red and very shiny above his black moustache. His head nodded slightly. He was pleased with himself.

'Oh! Oh! waitin' for me, lass? I've bin 'elpin' Anthony, an' what's think he's gen me? Nowt b'r a lousy hae'fcrown, an' that's ivry penny – '

'He thinks you've made the rest up in beer,' she said shortly.

'An' I 'aven't – that I 'aven't. You b'lieve me, I've 'ad very little this day, I have an' all.' His voice went tender. 'Here, an' I browt thee a bit o' brandy-snap, an' a coconut for th' children.' He laid the gingerbread and the coconut, a hairy object, on the table. 'Nay, tha niver said thankyer for nowt i' thy life, did ter?'

As a compromise, she picked up the coconut and shook it, to see if it had any milk.

'It's a good 'un, you may back yer life o' that. I got it fra' Bill Hodgkisson. "Bill," I says, "tha non wants them three nuts, does ter? Arena ter for gi'ein' me one for my bit of a lad an' wench?" "I ham, Walter, my lad," 'e says; "ta'e which on 'em ter's a mind." An' so I took one, an' thanked 'im. I didn't like ter shake it afore 'is eyes, but 'e says, "Tha'd better ma'e sure it's a good un, Walt." An' so, yer see, I knowed it was. He's a nice chap, is Bill Hodgkisson, 'e 's a nice chap!'

'A man will part with anything so long as he's drunk, and you're drunk along with him,' said Mrs Morel.

'Eh, tha mucky little 'ussy, who's drunk, I sh'd like ter know?' said Morel. He was extraordinarily pleased with himself, because of his day's helping to wait in the Moon and Stars. He chattered on.

Mrs Morel, very tired, and sick of his babble, went to bed as quickly as possible, while he raked the fire.

Mrs Morel came of a good old burgher family, famous independents who had fought with Colonel Hutchinson, and who remained stout Congregationalists. Her grandfather had gone bankrupt in the lace-market at a time when so many lace manufacturers were ruined in Nottingham. Her father, George Coppard, was an engineer – a large, handsome, haughty man, proud of his fair skin and blue eyes, but more proud still of his integrity. Gertrude resembled her mother in her small build. But her temper, proud and unyielding, she had from the Coppards.

George Coppard was bitterly galled by his own poverty. He became foreman of the engineers in the dockyard at Sheerness. Mrs Morel – Gertrude – was the second daughter. She favoured her mother, loved her mother best of all; but she had the Coppards' clear, defiant blue eyes and their broad brow. She remembered to have hated her father's overbearing manner towards her gentle, humorous, kindly-souled mother. She remembered running over the break-water at Sheerness and finding the boat. She remembered to have been petted and flattered by all the men when she had gone to the dockyard, for she was a delicate, rather proud child. She remembered the funny old mistress, whose assistant she had become, whom she had loved to help in the private school. And she still had the Bible that John Field had given her. She used to walk home from chapel with John Field when she was nineteen. He was the son of a well-to-do tradesman, had been to college in London, and was to devote himself to business.

She could always recall in detail a September Sunday afternoon, when they had sat under the vine at the back of her father's house. The sun came through the chinks in the vine-leaves and made beautiful patterns, like a lace scarf, falling on her and on him. Some of the leaves were clean yellow, like yellow flat flowers.

'Now sit still,' he had cried. 'Now your hair, I don't know what it *is* like! It's as bright as copper and gold, as red as burnt copper, and it has gold threads where the sun shines on it. Fancy their saying it's brown. Your mother calls it mouse-colour.'

She had met his brilliant eyes, but her clear face scarcely showed the elation which rose within her.

'But you say you don't like business,' she pursued.

'I don't. I hate it!' he cried hotly.

'And you would like to go into the ministry,' she half implored.

'I should. I should love it, if I thought I could make a first-rate preacher.'

'Then why don't you – why *don't* you?' Her voice rang with defiance. 'If I were a man, nothing would stop me.'

She held her head erect. He was rather timid before her.

'But my father's so stiff-necked. He means to put me into the business, and I know he'll do it.'

'But if you're a *man*?' she had cried.

'Being a man isn't everything,' he replied, frowning with puzzled helplessness.

Now, as she moved about her work at the Bottoms, with some experience of what being a man meant, she knew that it was *not* everything.

At twenty, owing to her health, she had left Sheerness. Her father had retired home to Nottingham. John Field's father had been ruined, the son had gone as a teacher in Norwood. She did not hear of him until, two years later, she made determined enquiry. He had married his landlady, a woman of forty, a widow with property.

And still Mrs Morel preserved John Field's Bible. She did not now believe him to be – Well, she understood pretty well what he might or might not have been. So she preserved his Bible, and kept his memory intact in her heart, for her own sake. To her dying day, for thirty-five years, she did not speak of him.

When she was twenty-three years old, she met, at a Christmas party, a young man from the Erewash Valley. Morel was then twenty-seven years old. He was well set-up, erect, and very smart. He had wavy black hair that shone again, and a vigorous black beard that had never been shaved. His cheeks were ruddy, and his red, moist mouth was noticeable because he laughed so often and so heartily. He had that rare thing, a rich, ringing laugh. Gertrude Coppard had watched him, fascinated. He was so full of colour and animation, his voice ran so easily into comic grotesque, he was so ready and so pleasant with everybody. Her own father had a rich fund of humour, but it was satiric. This man's was different: soft, non-intellectual, warm, a kind of gambolling.

She herself was opposite. She had a curious, receptive mind, which found much pleasure and amusement in listening to other folk. She was clever in leading folk on to talk. She loved ideas, and was considered very intellectual. What she liked most of all was an argument on religion or philosophy or politics with some educated man. This she did not often enjoy. So she always had people tell her about themselves, finding her pleasure so.

In her person she was rather small and delicate, with a large brow, and dropping bunches of brown silk curls. Her blue eyes were very straight, honest, and searching. She had the beautiful hands of the Coppards. Her dress was always subdued. She wore dark blue silk, with a peculiar silver chain of silver scallops. This, and a heavy brooch of twisted gold, was her only ornament. She was still perfectly intact, deeply religious, and full of beautiful candour.

Walter Morel seemed melted away before her. She was to the miner that thing of mystery and fascination, a lady. When she spoke to him, it was with a southern pronunciation and a purity of English which thrilled him to hear. She watched him. He danced well, as if it were natural and joyous in him to dance. His grandfather was a French refugee who had married an English barmaid – if it had been a marriage. Gertrude Coppard watched the young miner as he danced, a certain subtle exultation like glamour in his movement, and his face the flower of his body, ruddy, with tumbled black hair, and laughing alike whatever partner he bowed above. She thought him rather wonderful, never having met anyone like him. Her father was to her the type of all men. And George Coppard, proud in his bearing, handsome, and rather bitter; who preferred theology in reading, and who drew near in sympathy only to one man, the Apostle Paul; who was harsh in government, and in familiarity ironic; who ignored all sensuous pleasure – he was very different from the miner. Gertrude herself was rather contemptuous of dancing; she had not the slightest inclination towards that accomplishment, and had never learned even a Roger de Coverley. She was a puritan, like her father, high-minded, and really stern. Therefore the dusky, golden softness of this man's sensuous flame of life, that flowed off his flesh like the flame from a candle, not baffled and gripped into incandescence by thought and spirit as her life was, seemed to her something wonderful, beyond her.

He came and bowed above her. A warmth radiated through her as if she had drunk wine.

'Now do come and have this one wi' me,' he said caressingly. 'It's easy, you know. I'm pining to see you dance.'

She had told him before she could not dance. She glanced at his humility and smiled. Her smile was very beautiful. It moved the man so that he forgot everything.

'No, I won't dance,' she said softly. Her words came clean and ringing.

Not knowing what he was doing – he often did the right thing by instinct – he sat beside her, inclining reverentially.

'But you mustn't miss your dance,' she reproved.

'Nay, I don't want to dance that – it's not one as I care about.'

'Yet you invited me to it.'

He laughed very heartily at this.

'I never thought o' that. Tha'rt not long in taking the curl out of me.'

It was her turn to laugh quickly.

'You don't look as if you'd come much uncurled,' she said.

'I'm like a pig's tail, I curl because I canna help it,' he laughed, rather boisterously.

'And you are a miner!' she exclaimed in surprise.

'Yes. I went down when I was ten.'

She looked at him in wondering dismay.

'When you were ten! And wasn't it very hard?' she asked.

'You soon get used to it. You live like th' mice, an' you pop out at night to see what's going on.'

'It makes me feel blind,' she frowned.

'Like a moudiwarp!' he laughed. 'Yi, an' there's some chaps as does go round like moudiwarps.' He thrust his face forward in the blind, snout-like way of a mole, seeming to sniff and peer for direction. 'They dun though!' he protested naïvely. 'Tha niver seed such a way they get in. But tha mun let me ta'e thee down some time, an' tha can see for thysen.'

She looked at him, startled. This was a new tract of life suddenly opened before her. She realised the life of the miners, hundreds of them toiling below earth and coming up at evening. He seemed to her noble. He risked his life daily, and with gaiety. She looked at him, with a touch of appeal in her pure humility.

'Shouldn't ter like it?' he asked tenderly. ' 'Appen not, it 'ud dirty thee.'

She had never been 'thee'd' and 'thou'd' before.

The next Christmas they were married, and for three months she was perfectly happy: for six months she was very happy.

He had signed the pledge, and wore the blue ribbon of a teetotaller: he was nothing if not showy. They lived, she thought, in his own house. It was small, but convenient enough, and quite nicely furnished, with solid, worthy stuff that suited her honest soul. The women, her neighbours, were rather foreign to her, and Morel's mother and sisters were apt to sneer at her ladylike ways. But she could perfectly well live by herself, so long as she had her husband close.

Sometimes, when she herself wearied of love-talk, she tried to open her heart seriously to him. She saw him listen deferentially, but without understanding. This killed her efforts at a finer intimacy, and she had flashes of fear. Sometimes he was restless of an evening: it was not enough for him just to be near her, she realised. She was glad when he set himself to little jobs.

He was a remarkably handy man – could make or mend anything. So she would say, 'I do like that coal-rake of your mother's – it is small and natty.'

'Does ter, my wench? Well, I made that, so I can make thee one.'

'What! why, it's a steel one!'

'An' what if it is! Tha s'it ha'e one very similar, if not exactly same.'

She did not mind the mess, nor the hammering and noise. He was busy and happy.

But in the seventh month, when she was brushing his Sunday coat, she felt papers in the breast-pocket, and, seized with a sudden curiosity, took them out to read. He very rarely wore the frock-coat he was married in: and it had not occurred to her before to feel curious concerning the papers. They were the bills of the household furniture, still unpaid.

'Look here,' she said at night, after he was washed and had had his dinner. 'I found these in the pocket of your wedding-coat. Haven't you settled the bills yet?'

'No. I haven't had a chance.'

'But you told me all was paid. I had better go into Nottingham on Saturday and settle them. I don't like sitting on another man's chairs and eating from an unpaid table.'

He did not answer.

'I can have your bankbook, can't I?'

'Tha can ha'e it, for what good it'll be to thee.'

'I thought – ' she began. He had told her he had a good bit of money left over. But she realised it was no use asking questions. She sat rigid with bitterness and indignation.

The next day she went down to see his mother.

'Didn't you buy the furniture for Walter?' she asked.

'Yes, I did,' tartly retorted the elder woman.

'And how much did he give you to pay for it?'

The elder woman was stung with fine indignation.

'Eighty pound, if you're so keen on knowin',' she replied.

'Eighty pounds! But there are forty-two pounds still owing!'

'I can't help that.'

'But where has it all gone?'

'You'll find all the papers, I think, if you look – beside ten pound as he owed me, an' six pound as the wedding cost down here.'

'Six pounds!' echoed Gertrude Morel. It seemed to her monstrous that, after her own father had paid so heavily for her wedding, six pounds more should have been squandered in eating and drinking at Walter's parents' house, at his expense.

'And how much has he sunk in his houses?' she asked.

'His houses – which houses?'

Gertrude Morel went white to the lips. He had told her the house he lived in, and the next one, was his own.

'I thought the house we live in –' she began.

'They're my houses, those two,' said the mother-in-law. 'And not clear either. It's as much as I can do to keep the mortgage interest paid.'

Gertrude sat white and silent. She was her father now.

'Then we ought to be paying you rent,' she said coldly.

'Walter is paying me rent,' replied the mother.

'And what rent?' asked Gertrude.

'Six-and-six a week,' retorted the mother.

It was more than the house was worth. Gertrude held her head erect, looked straight before her.

'It is lucky to be you,' said the elder woman, bitingly, 'to have a husband as takes all the worry of the money, and leaves you a free hand.'

The young wife was silent.

She said very little to her husband, but her manner had changed towards him. Something in her proud, honourable soul had crystallised out hard as rock.

When October came in, she thought only of Christmas. Two years ago, at Christmas, she had met him. Last Christmas she had married him. This Christmas she would bear him a child.

'You don't dance yourself, do you, missis?' asked her nearest neighbour, in October, when there was great talk of opening a dancing-class over the Brick and Tile Inn at Bestwood.

'No – I never had the least inclination to,' Mrs Morel replied.

'Fancy! An' how funny as you should ha' married your Mester. You know he's quite a famous one for dancing.'

'I didn't know he was famous,' laughed Mrs Morel.

'Yea, he is though! Why, he run that dancing-class in the Miners' Arms club-room for over five year.'

'Did he?'

'Yes, he did.' The other woman was defiant. 'An' it was thronged every Tuesday, and Thursday, an' Sat'day – an' there *was* carryin's-on, accordin' to all accounts.'

This kind of thing was gall and bitterness to Mrs Morel and she had a fair share of it. The women did not spare her, at first, for she was superior, though she could not help it.

He began to be rather late in coming home.

'They're working very late now, aren't they?' she said to her washerwoman.

'No later than they allers do, I don't think. But they stop to have their pint at Ellen's, an' they get talkin', an' there you are! Dinner stone cold – an' it serves 'em right.'

'But Mr Morel does not take any drink.'

The woman dropped the clothes, looked at Mrs Morel, then went on with her work, saying nothing.

Gertrude Morel was very ill when the boy was born. Morel was good to her, as good as gold. But she felt very lonely, miles away from her own people. She felt lonely with him now, and his presence only made it more intense.

The boy was small and frail at first, but he came on quickly. He was a beautiful child, with dark gold ringlets, and dark blue eyes which changed gradually to a clear grey. His mother loved him passionately. He came just when her own bitterness of disillusion was hardest to bear; when her faith in life was shaken, and her soul felt dreary and lonely. She made much of the child, and the father was jealous.

At last Mrs Morel despised her husband. She turned to the child; she turned from the father. He had begun to neglect her; the novelty of his own home was gone. He had no grit, she said bitterly to herself. What he felt just at the minute, that was all to him. He could not abide by anything. There was nothing at the back of all his show.

There began a battle between the husband and wife – a fearful, bloody battle that ended only with the death of one. She fought to make him undertake his own responsibilities, to make him fulfil his obligations. But he was too different from her. His nature was purely sensuous, and she strove to make him moral, religious. She tried to force him to face things. He could not endure it – it drove him out of his mind.

While the baby was still tiny, the father's temper had become so irritable that it was not to be trusted. The child had only to give a little trouble when the man began to bully. A little more, and the hard hands of the collier hit the baby. Then Mrs Morel loathed her husband, loathed him for days; and he went out and drank; and she cared very little what he did. Only, on his return, she scathed him with her satire.

The estrangement between them caused him, knowingly or unknowingly, grossly to offend her where he would not have done.

William was only one year old, and his mother was proud of him, he was so pretty. She was not well off now, but her sisters kept the boy in clothes. Then, with his little white hat curled with an ostrich feather, and his white coat, he was a joy to her, the twining wisps of hair clustering round his head. Mrs Morel lay listening, one Sunday morning, to the chatter of the father and child downstairs. Then she dozed off. When she came downstairs, a great fire glowed in the grate, the room was hot, the breakfast was roughly laid, and seated in his armchair, against the chimney-piece, sat Morel, rather timid; and standing between his legs, the child – cropped like a sheep, with such an odd round poll – looking wondering at her; and on a newspaper spread out upon the hearthrug, a myriad of crescent-shaped curls, like the petals of a marigold scattered in the reddening firelight.

Mrs Morel stood still. It was her first baby. She went very white, and was unable to speak.

'What dost think o' 'im?' Morel laughed uneasily.

She gripped her two fists, lifted them, and came forward. Morel shrank back.

'I could kill you, I could!' she said. She choked with rage, her two fists uplifted.

'Yer non want ter make a wench on 'im,' Morel said, in a frightened tone, bending his head to shield his eyes from hers. His attempt at laughter had vanished.

The mother looked down at the jagged, close-clipped head of her child. She put her hands on his hair, and stroked and fondled his head.

'Oh – my boy!' she faltered. Her lip trembled, her face broke, and, snatching up the child, she buried her face in his shoulder and cried painfully. She was one of those women who cannot cry; whom it hurts as it hurts a man. It was like ripping something out of her, her sobbing.

Morel sat with his elbows on his knees, his hands gripped together till the knuckles were white. He gazed in the fire, feeling almost stunned, as if he could not breathe.

Presently she came to an end, soothed the child and cleared away the breakfast-table. She left the newspaper, littered with curls, spread upon the hearthrug. At last her husband gathered it up and put it at the back of the fire. She went about her work with closed mouth and very quiet. Morel was subdued. He crept about wretchedly, and his meals were a misery that day. She spoke to him civilly, and never alluded to what he had done. But he felt something final had happened.

Afterwards she said she had been silly, that the boy's hair would have had to be cut, sooner or later. In the end, she even brought herself to say to her husband it was just as well he had played barber when he did. But she knew, and Morel knew, that that act had caused something momentous to take place in her soul. She remembered the scene all her life, as one in which she had suffered the most intensely.

This act of masculine clumsiness was the spear through the side of her love for Morel. Before, while she had striven against him bitterly, she had fretted after him, as if he had gone astray from her. Now she ceased to fret for his love; he was an outsider to her. This made life much more bearable.

Nevertheless, she still continued to strive with him. She still had her high moral sense inherited from generations of Puritans. It was now a religious instinct, and she was almost a fanatic with him, because she loved him, or had loved him. If he sinned, she tortured him. If he drank, and lied, was often a poltroon, sometimes a knave, she wielded the lash unmercifully.

The pity was, she was too much his opposite. She could not be content with the little he might be; she would have him the much that he ought to be. So, in seeking to make him nobler than he could be she destroyed him. She injured and hurt and scarred herself, but she lost none of her worth. She also had the children.

He drank rather heavily, though not more than many miners, and always beer, so that whilst his health was affected it was never injured. The weekend was his chief carouse. He sat in the Miners' Arms until turning-out time every Friday, every Saturday, and every Sunday evening. On Monday and Tuesday he had to get up and reluctantly leave towards ten o'clock. Sometimes he stayed at home on Wednesday and Thursday evenings, or was only out for an hour. He practically never had to miss work owing to his drinking.

But although he was very steady at work, his wages fell off. He was blab-mouthed, a tongue-wagger. Authority was hateful to him, therefore he could only abuse the pit-managers. He would say, in the Palmerston, 'Th' gaffer come down to our stall this morning, an' 'e says, "You know, Walter, this 'ere'll not do. What about these props?" An' I says to him, "Why, what art talkin' about? What d'st mean about th' props?" "It'll never do, this 'ere," 'e says. "You'll be havin' th' roof in, one o' these days." An' I says, "Tha'd better stan' on a bit o' clunch, then, an' hold it up wi' thy 'ead." So 'e wor that mad, 'e cossed an' 'e swore, an' t'other chaps they did laugh.' Morel was a good mimic. He imitated the manager's fat, squeaky voice, with its attempt at good English.

' "I shan't have it, Walter. Who knows more about it, me or you?" So I says, "I've niver fun out how much tha' knows, Alfred. It'll 'appen carry thee ter bed an' back." '

So Morel would go on to the amusement of his boon companions. And some of this would be true. The pit-manager was not an educated man. He had been a boy along with Morel, so that, while the two disliked each other, they more or less took each other for granted. But Alfred Charlesworth did not forgive the butty these public-house sayings. Consequently, although Morel was a good miner, sometimes earning as much as five pounds a week when he married, he came gradually to have worse and worse stalls, where the coal was thin, and hard to get, and unprofitable.

Also, in summer, the pits are slack. Often, on bright sunny mornings, the men are seen trooping home again at ten, eleven, or twelve o'clock. No empty trucks stand at the pit-mouth. The women on the hillside look across as they shake the hearthrug against the fence, and count the waggons the engine is taking along the line up the valley. And the children, as they come from school at dinner-time, looking down the fields and seeing the wheels on the headstocks standing, say, 'Minton's knocked off. My dad'll be at home.'

And there is a sort of shadow over all, women and children and men, because money will be short at the end of the week.

Morel was supposed to give his wife thirty shillings a week, to provide everything – rent, food, clothes, clubs, insurance, doctors. Occasionally, if he were flush, he gave her thirty-five. But these occasions by no means balanced those when he gave her twenty-five. In winter, with a decent stall, the miner might earn fifty or fifty-five shillings a week. Then he was happy. On Friday night, Saturday, and Sunday, he spent royally, getting rid of his sovereign or thereabouts. And out of so much, he scarcely spared the children an extra penny or bought them a pound of apples. It all went in drink. In the bad times, matters were more worrying, but he was not so often drunk, so that Mrs Morel used to say, 'I'm not sure I wouldn't rather be short, for when he's flush, there isn't a minute of peace.'

If he earned forty shillings he kept ten; from thirty-five he kept five; from thirty-two he kept four; from twenty-eight he kept three; from twenty-four he kept two; from twenty he kept one-and-six; from eighteen he kept a shilling; from sixteen he kept sixpence. He never saved a penny, and he gave his wife no opportunity of saving; instead, she had occasionally to pay his debts; not public-house debts, for those never were passed on to the women, but debts when he had bought a canary, or a fancy walking-stick.

At the wakes time, Morel was working badly, and Mrs Morel was trying to save against her confinement. So it galled her bitterly to think he should be out taking his pleasure and spending money, whilst she remained at home, harassed. There were two days' holiday. On the Tuesday morning Morel rose early. He was in good spirits. Quite early, before six o'clock, she heard him whistling away to himself downstairs. He had a pleasant way of whistling, lively and musical. He nearly always whistled hymns. He had been a choirboy with a beautiful voice, and had taken solos in Southwell cathedral. His morning whistling alone betrayed it.

His wife lay listening to him tinkering away in the garden, his whistling ringing out as he sawed and hammered away. It always gave her a sense of warmth and peace to hear him thus as she lay in bed, the children not yet awake, in the bright early morning, happy in his man's fashion.

At nine o'clock, while the children with bare legs and feet were sitting playing on the sofa, and the mother was washing up, he came in from his carpentry, his sleeves rolled up, his waistcoat hanging open. He was still a good-looking man with black, wavy hair, and a large black moustache. His face was perhaps too much inflamed, and there was about him a look almost of peevishness. But now he was jolly. He went straight to the sink where his wife was washing up.

'What, are thee there!' he said boisterously. 'Sluther off an' let me wesh mysen.'

'You may wait till I've finished,' said his wife.

'Oh, mun I? An' what if I shonna?'

This good-humoured threat amused Mrs Morel.

'Then you can go and wash yourself in the soft-water tub.'

'Ha! I can an' a', tha mucky little 'ussy.'

With which he stood watching her a moment, then went away to wait for her. When he chose he could still make himself again a real gallant. Usually he preferred to go out with a scarf round his neck.

Now, however, he made a toilet. There seemed so much gusto in the way he puffed and swilled as he washed himself, so much alacrity with which he hurried to the mirror in the kitchen, and, bending because it was too low for him, scrupulously parted his wet black hair, that it irritated Mrs Morel. He put on a turn-down collar, a black bow, and wore his Sunday tail-coat. As such, he looked spruce, and what his clothes would not do, his instinct for making the most of his good looks would.

At half-past nine Jerry Purdy came to call for his pal. Jerry was Morel's bosom friend, and Mrs Morel disliked him. He was a tall, thin man, with a rather foxy face, the kind of face that seems to lack eyelashes. He walked with a stiff brittle dignity, as if his head were on a wooden spring. His nature was cold and shrewd. Generous where he intended to be generous, he seemed to be very fond of Morel, and more or less to take charge of him.

Mrs Morel hated him. She had known his wife, who had died of consumption, and who had, at the end, conceived such a violent dislike of her husband, that if he came into her room it caused her to haemorrhage. None of which Jerry had seemed to mind. And now his eldest daughter, a girl of fifteen, kept a poor house for him, and looked after the two younger children.

'A mean, wizen-hearted stick!' Mrs Morel said of him.

'I've never known Jerry mean in *my* life,' protested Morel. 'A opener-handed and more freer chap you couldn't find anywhere, accordin' to my knowledge.'

'Open-handed to you,' retorted Mrs Morel. 'But his fist is shut tight enough to his children, poor things.'

'Poor things! And what for are they poor things, I should like to know.'

But Mrs Morel would not be appeased on Jerry's score.

The subject of argument was seen, craning his thin neck over the scullery curtain. He caught Mrs Morel's eye.

'Mornin', missis! Mester in?'

'Yes – he is.'

Jerry entered unasked, and stood by the kitchen doorway. He was not invited to sit down, but stood there, coolly asserting the rights of men and husbands.

'A nice day,' he said to Mrs Morel.

'Yes.'

'Grand out this morning – grand for a walk.'

'Do you mean *you're* going for a walk?' she asked.

'Yes. We mean walkin' to Nottingham,' he replied.

'H'm!'

The two men greeted each other, both glad: Jerry, however, full of assurance, Morel rather subdued, afraid to seem too jubilant in presence of his wife. But he laced his boots quickly, with spirit. They were going for a ten-mile walk across the fields to Nottingham. Climbing the hillside from the Bottoms, they mounted gaily into the morning. At the Moon and Stars they had their first drink, then on to the Old Spot. Then a long five miles of drought to carry them into Bulwell to a glorious pint of bitter. But they stayed in a field with some haymakers whose gallon bottle was full, so that, when they came in sight of the city, Morel was sleepy. The town spread upwards before them, smoking vaguely in the midday glare, fringing the crest away to the south with spires and factory bulks and chimneys. In the last field Morel lay down under an oak tree and slept soundly for over an hour. When he rose to go forward he felt queer.

The two had dinner in the Meadows, with Jerry's sister, then repaired to the Punch Bowl, where they mixed in the excitement of pigeon-racing. Morel never in his life played cards, considering them as having some occult, malevolent power – 'the devil's pictures', he called them! But he was a master of skittles and of dominoes. He took a challenge from a Newark man, on skittles. All the men in the old, long bar took sides, betting either one way or the other. Morel took off his coat. Jerry held the hat containing the money. The men at the tables watched. Some stood with their mugs in their hands. Morel felt his big wooden ball carefully, then launched it. He played havoc among the ninepins, and won half a crown, which restored him to solvency.

By seven o'clock the two were in good condition. They caught the 7.30 train home.

In the afternoon the Bottoms was intolerable. Every inhabitant remaining was out of doors. The women, in twos and threes, bareheaded and in white aprons, gossiped in the alley between the blocks. Men, having a rest between drinks, sat on their heels and talked. The place smelled stale; the slate roofs glistered in the arid heat.

Mrs Morel took the little girl down to the brook in the meadows, which were not more than two hundred yards away. The water ran quickly over stones and broken pots. Mother and child leaned on the rail of the old sheep-bridge, watching. Up at the dipping-hole, at the other end of the meadow, Mrs Morel could see the naked forms of boys flashing round the deep yellow water, or an occasional bright figure dart glittering over the blackish stagnant meadow. She knew William was at the dipping-hole, and it was the dread of her life lest he should get drowned. Annie played under the tall old hedge picking up alder cones, that she called currants. The child required much attention, and the flies were teasing.

The children were put to bed at seven o'clock. Then she worked awhile.

When Walter Morel and Jerry arrived at Bestwood they felt a load off their minds; a railway journey no longer impended, so they could put the finishing touches to a glorious day. They entered the Nelson with the satisfaction of returned travellers.

The next day was a workday, and the thought of it put a damper on the men's spirits. Most of them, moreover, had spent their money. Some were already rolling dismally home, to sleep in preparation for the morrow. Mrs Morel, listening to their mournful singing, went indoors. Nine o'clock passed and ten, and still 'the pair' had not returned. On a doorstep somewhere a man was singing loudly, in a drawl, 'Lead, kindly Light'. Mrs Morel was always indignant with the drunken men that they must sing that hymn when they got maudlin.

'As if "Genevieve" weren't good enough,' she said.

The kitchen was full of the scent of boiled herbs and hops. On the hob a large black saucepan steamed slowly. Mrs Morel took a panchion, a great bowl of thick red earth, streamed a heap of white sugar into the bottom, and then, straining herself to the weight, was pouring in the liquor.

Just then Morel came in. He had been very jolly in the Nelson, but coming home had grown irritable. He had not quite got over the feeling of irritability and pain, after having slept on the ground when he was so hot; and a bad conscience afflicted him as he neared the house. He did not know he was angry. But when the garden gate resisted his attempts to open it, he kicked it and broke the latch. He entered just as Mrs Morel was pouring the infusion of herbs out of the saucepan. Swaying slightly, he lurched against the table. The boiling liquor pitched. Mrs Morel started back.

'Good gracious,' she cried, 'coming home in his drunkenness!'

'Comin' home in his what?' he snarled, his hat over his eye.

Suddenly her blood rose in a jet

'Say you're *not* drunk!' she flashed.

She had put down her saucepan, and was stirring the sugar into the beer. He dropped his two hands heavily on the table, and thrust his face forward at her.

' "Say you're not drunk," ' he repeated. 'Why, nobody but a nasty little bitch like you 'ud 'ave such a thought.'

He thrust his face forward at her.

'There's money to bezzle with, if there's money for nothing else.'

'I've not spent a two-shillin' bit this day,' he said.

'You don't get as drunk as a lord on nothing,' she replied. 'And,' she cried, flashing into sudden fury, 'if you've been sponging on your beloved Jerry, why, let him look after his children, for they need it.'

'It's a lie, it's a lie. Shut your face, woman.'

They were now at battle-pitch. Each forgot everything save the hatred of the other and the battle between them. She was fiery and furious as he. They went on till he called her a liar.

'No,' she cried, starting up, scarce able to breathe. 'Don't call me that – you, the most despicable liar that ever walked in shoe-leather.' She forced the last words out of suffocated lungs.

'You're a liar!' he yelled, banging the table with his fist. 'You're a liar, you're a liar.'

She stiffened herself, with clenched fists.

'The house is filthy with you,' she cried.

'Then get out on it – it's mine. Get out on it!' he shouted. 'It's me as brings th' money whoam, not thee. It's my house, not thine. Then get out on't – get out on't!'

'And I would,' she cried, suddenly shaken into tears of impotence. 'Ah, wouldn't I, wouldn't I have gone long ago, but for those children. Ay, haven't I repented not going years ago, when I'd only the one' – suddenly drying into rage. 'Do you think it's for *you* I stop – do you think I'd stop one minute for *you*?'

'Go, then,' he shouted, beside himself. 'Go!'

'No!' she faced round. 'No,' she cried loudly, 'you shan't have it *all* your own way; you shan't do *all* you like. I've got those children to see to. My word,' she laughed, 'I should look well to leave them to you.'

'Go,' he cried thickly, lifting his fist. He was afraid of her. 'Go!'

'I should be only too glad. I should laugh, laugh, my lord, if I could get away from you,' she replied.

He came up to her, his red face, with its bloodshot eyes, thrust forward, and gripped her arms. She cried in fear of him, struggled to be free. Coming slightly to himself, panting, he pushed her roughly to the outer door, and thrust her forth, slotting the bolt behind her with a bang. Then he went back into the kitchen, dropped into his armchair, his head, bursting full of blood, sinking between his knees. Thus he dipped gradually into a stupor, from exhaustion and intoxication.

The moon was high and magnificent in the August night. Mrs Morel, seared with passion, shivered to find herself out there in a great white light, that fell cold on her, and gave a shock to her inflamed soul. She stood for a few moments helplessly staring at the glistening great rhubarb leaves near the door. Then she got the air into her breast. She walked down the garden path, trembling in every limb, while the child boiled within her. For a while she could not control her consciousness; mechanically she went over the last scene, then over it again, certain phrases, certain moments coming each time like a brand red-hot down on her soul; and each time she enacted again the past hour, each time the brand came down at the same points, till the mark was burnt in and the pain burnt out, and at last she came to herself. She must have been half an hour in this delirious condition. Then the presence of the night came again to her. She glanced round in fear. She had wandered to the side garden, where she was walking up and down the path beside the currant bushes under the long wall. The garden was a narrow strip, bounded from the road, that cut transversely between the blocks, by a thick thorn hedge.

She hurried out of the side garden to the front, where she could stand as if in an immense gulf of white light, the moon streaming high in face of her, the moonlight standing up from the hills in front, and filling the valley where the Bottoms crouched, almost blindingly. There, panting and half weeping in reaction from the stress, she murmured to herself over and over again: 'The nuisance! the nuisance!'

She became aware of something about her. With an effort she roused herself to see what it was that penetrated her consciousness. The tall white lilies were reeling in the moonlight and the air was charged with their perfume, as with a presence. Mrs Morel gasped slightly in fear. She touched the big, pallid flowers on their petals, then shivered. They seemed to be stretching in the moonlight. She put her hand into one white bin: the gold scarcely showed on her fingers by moonlight. She bent down to look at the binful of yellow pollen; but it only appeared dusky. Then she drank a deep draught of the scent. It almost made her dizzy.

Mrs Morel leaned on the garden gate, looking out, and she lost herself awhile. She did not know what she thought. Except for a slight feeling of sickness, and her consciousness in the child, herself melted out like scent into the shiny, pale air. After a time the child, too, melted with her in the mixing-pot of moonlight, and she rested with the hills and lilies and houses, all swum together in a kind of swoon.

When she came to herself she was tired for sleep. Languidly she looked about her; the clumps of white phlox seemed like bushes spread with linen; a moth ricocheted over them and right across the garden. Following it with her eye roused her. A few whiffs of the raw, strong scent of phlox invigorated her. She passed along the path, hesitating at the white rose bush. It smelled sweet and simple. She touched the white ruffles of the roses. Their fresh scent and cool, soft leaves reminded her of the morning-time and sunshine. She was very fond of them. But she was tired, and wanted to sleep. In the mysterious out-of-doors she felt forlorn.

There was no noise anywhere. Evidently the children had not been wakened, or had gone to sleep again. A train, three miles away, roared across the valley. The night was very large, and very strange, stretching its hoary distances infinitely. And out of the silver-grey fog of darkness came sounds vague and hoarse: a corncrake not far off, sound of a train like a sigh, and distant shouts of men.

Her quietened heart beginning to beat quickly again, she hurried down the side garden to the back of the house. Softly she lifted the latch; the door was still bolted, shut hard against her. She rapped gently, waited, then rapped again. She must not rouse the children, nor the neighbours. He must be asleep, and he would not wake easily. Her heart began to burn to be indoors. She clung to the door-handle. Now it was cold; she would take a chill, and in her present condition!

Putting her apron over her head and her arms, she hurried again to the side garden, to the window of the kitchen. Leaning on the sill, she could just see, under the blind, her husband's arms spread out on the table, and his black head on the board. He was sleeping with his face lying on the table. Something in his attitude made her feel tired of things. The lamp was burning smokily; she could tell by the copper colour of the light. She tapped at the window more and more noisily.

Almost it seemed as if the glass would break. Still he did not wake up.

After vain efforts, she began to shiver, partly from contact with the stone, and from exhaustion. Fearful always for the unborn child, she wondered what she could do for warmth. She went down to the coal-house, where there was an old hearthrug she had carried out for the rag-man the day before. This she wrapped over her shoulders. It was warm, if grimy. Then she walked up and down the garden path, peeping every now and then under the blind, knocking, and telling herself that in the end the very strain of his position must wake him.

At last, after about an hour, she rapped long and low at the window. Gradually the sound penetrated to him. When, in despair, she had ceased to tap, she saw him stir, then lift his face blindly. The labouring of his heart hurt him into consciousness. She rapped imperatively at the window. He started awake. Instantly she saw his fists set and his eyes glare. He had not a grain of physical fear. If it had been twenty burglars, he would have gone blindly for them. He glared round, bewildered, but prepared to fight.

'Open the door, Walter,' she said coldly.

His hands relaxed. It dawned on him what he had done. His head drooped, sullen and dogged. She saw him hurry to the door, heard the bolt chock. He tried the latch. It opened – and there stood the silver-grey night, fearful to him, after the tawny light of the lamp. He hurried back.

When Mrs Morel entered, she saw him almost running through the door to the stairs. He had ripped the collar off his neck in his haste to be gone ere she came in, and there it lay with bursten buttonholes. It made her angry.

She warmed and soothed herself. In her weariness forgetting everything, she moved about at the little tasks that remained to be done, set his breakfast, rinsed his pit-bottle, put his pit-clothes on the hearth to warm, set his pit-boots beside them, put him out a clean scarf and snap-bag and two apples, raked the fire, and went to bed. He was already dead asleep. His narrow black eyebrows were drawn up in a sort of peevish misery into his forehead, while his cheeks' downstrokes, and his sulky mouth, seemed to be saying: 'I don't care who you are nor what you are, I *shall* have my own way.'

Mrs Morel knew him too well to look at him. As she unfastened her brooch at the mirror, she smiled faintly to see her face all smeared with the yellow dust of lilies. She brushed it off, and at last lay down. For some time her mind continued snapping and jetting sparks, but she was asleep before her husband awoke from the first sleep of his drunkenness.

CHAPTER 2

The Birth of Paul, and Another Battle

After such a scene as the last, Walter Morel was for some days abashed and ashamed, but he soon regained his old bullying indifference. Yet there was a slight shrinking, a diminishing in his assurance. Physically even, he shrank, and his fine full presence waned. He never grew in the least stout, so that, as he sank from his erect, assertive bearing, his physique seemed to contract along with his pride and moral strength.

But now he realised how hard it was for his wife to drag about at her work, and, his sympathy quickened by penitence, hastened forward with his help. He came straight home from the pit, and stayed in at evening till Friday, and then he could not remain at home. But he was back again by ten o'clock, almost quite sober.

He always made his own breakfast. Being a man who rose early and had plenty of time he did not, as some miners do, drag his wife out of bed at six o'clock. At five, sometimes earlier, he woke, got straight out of bed, and went downstairs. When she could not sleep, his wife lay waiting for this time, as for a period of peace. The only real rest seemed to be when he was out of the house.

He went downstairs in his shirt and then struggled into his pit-trousers, which were left on the hearth to warm all night. There was always a fire, because Mrs Morel raked. And the first sound in the house was the bang, bang of the poker against the raker, as Morel smashed the remainder of the coal to make the kettle, which was filled and left on the hob, finally boil. His cup and knife and fork, all he wanted except just the food, was laid ready on the table on a newspaper. Then he got his breakfast, made the tea, packed the bottom of the doors with rugs to shut out the draught, piled a big fire, and sat down to an hour of joy. He toasted his bacon on a fork and caught the drops of fat on his bread; then he put the rasher on his thick slice of bread, and cut off chunks with a clasp-knife, poured his tea into his saucer, and was happy. With his family about, meals were never so pleasant. He loathed a fork; it is a modern introduction which has still scarcely reached common people. What Morel preferred was a clasp-knife. Then, in solitude, he ate and drank, often sitting, in cold weather, on a little stool with his back to the warm chimney-piece, his food on the fender, his cup on the hearth. And then he read the last night's newspaper – what of it he could – spelling it over laboriously. He preferred to keep the blinds down and the candle lit even when it was daylight; it was the habit of the mine.

At a quarter to six he rose, cut two thick slices of bread and butter, and put them in the white calico snap-bag. He filled his tin bottle with tea. Cold tea without milk or sugar was the drink he preferred for the pit. Then he pulled off his shirt, and put on his pit-singlet, a vest of thick flannel cut low round the neck, and with short sleeves like a chemise.

Then he went upstairs to his wife with a cup of tea because she was ill, and because it occurred to him.

'I've brought thee a cup o' tea, lass,' he said.

'Well, you needn't, for you know I don't like it,' she replied.

'Drink it up; it'll pop thee off to sleep again.'

She accepted the tea. It pleased him to see her take it and sip it.

'I'll back my life there's no sugar in,' she said.

'Yi – there's one big un,' he replied, injured.

'It's a wonder,' she said, sipping again.

She had a winsome face when her hair was loose. He loved her to grumble at him in this manner. He looked at her again, and went, without any sort of leave-taking. He never took more than two slices of bread and butter to eat in the pit, so an apple or an orange was a treat to him. He always liked it when she put one out for him. He tied a scarf round his neck, put on his great, heavy boots, his coat, with the big pocket, that carried his snap-bag and his bottle of tea, and went forth into the fresh morning air, closing, without locking, the door behind him. He loved the early morning, and the walk across the fields. So he appeared at the pit-top, often with a stalk from the hedge between his teeth, which he chewed all day to keep his mouth moist, down the mine, feeling quite as happy as when he was in the field.

Later, when the time for the baby grew nearer, he would bustle round in his slovenly fashion, poking out the ashes, rubbing the fireplace, sweeping the house before he went to work. Then, feeling very self-righteous, he went upstairs.

'Now I'm cleaned up for thee; tha's no 'casions ter stir a peg all day, but sit and read thy books.'

Which made her laugh, in spite of her indignation.

'And the dinner cooks itself?' she answered.

'Eh, I know nowt about th' dinner.'

'You'd know if there weren't any.'

'Ay, 'appen so,' he answered, departing.

When she got downstairs, she would find the house tidy, but dirty. She could not rest until she had thoroughly cleaned; so she went down to the ash-pit with her dust-pan. Mrs Kirk, spying her, would contrive to have to go to her own coal-place at that minute. Then, across the wooden fence, she would call, 'So you keep wagging on, then?'

'Ay,' answered Mrs Morel deprecatingly. 'There's nothing else for it.'

'Have you seen Hose?' called a very small woman from across the road. It was Mrs Anthony, a black-haired, strange little body, who always wore a brown velvet dress, tight fitting.

'I haven't,' said Mrs Morel.

'Eh, I wish he'd come. I've got a copperful of clothes an' I'm sure I heered his bell.'

'Hark! He's at the end.'

The two women looked down the alley. At the end of the Bottoms a man stood in a sort of old-fashioned trap, bending over bundles of cream-coloured stuff; while a cluster of women held up their arms to him, some with bundles. Mrs Anthony herself had a heap of creamy, undyed stockings hanging over her arm.

'I've done ten dozen this week,' she said proudly to Mrs Morel.

'T–t–t!' went the other. 'I don't know how you can find time.'

'Eh!' said Mrs Anthony. 'You can find time if you make time.'

'I don't know how you do it,' said Mrs Morel. 'And how much shall you get for those many?'

'Tuppence-ha'penny a dozen,' replied the other.

'Well,' said Mrs Morel, 'I'd starve before I'd sit down and seam twenty-four stockings for twopence-ha'penny.'

'Oh, I don't know,' said Mrs Anthony. 'You can rip along with 'em.'

Hose was coming along, ringing his bell. Women were waiting at the yard-ends with their seamed stockings hanging over their arms. The man, a common fellow, made jokes with them, tried to swindle them, and bullied them. Mrs Morel went up her yard disdainfully.

It was an understood thing that if one woman wanted her neighbour, she should put the poker in the fire and bang at the back of the fireplace, which, as the fires were back to back, would make a great noise in the adjoining house. One morning Mrs Kirk, mixing a pudding, nearly started out of her skin as she heard the thud, thud, in her grate. With her hands all floury, she rushed to the fence.

'Did you knock, Mrs Morel?'

'If you wouldn't mind, Mrs Kirk.'

Mrs Kirk climbed on to her copper, got over the wall on to Mrs Morel's copper, and ran in to her neighbour.

'Eh, dear, how are you feeling?' she cried in concern.

'You might fetch Mrs Bower,' said Mrs Morel.

Mrs Kirk went into the yard, lifted up her strong, shrill voice, and called, 'Ag–gie – Ag–gie!'

The sound was heard from one end of the Bottoms to the other. At last Aggie came running up, and was sent for Mrs Bower, whilst Mrs Kirk left her pudding and stayed with her neighbour.

Mrs Morel went to bed. Mrs Kirk had Annie and William for dinner. Mrs Bower, fat and waddling, bossed the house.

'Hash some cold meat up for the master's dinner, and make him an apple-charlotte pudding,' said Mrs Morel.

'He may go without pudding *this* day,' said Mrs Bower.

Morel was not as a rule one of the first to appear at the bottom of the pit, ready to come up. Some men were there before four o'clock, when the whistle blew loose-all; but Morel, whose stall, a poor one, was at this time about a mile and a half away from the bottom, worked usually till the first mate stopped, then he finished also. This day, however, the miner was sick of the work. At two o'clock he looked at his watch, by the light of the green candle – he was in a safe working – and again at half-past two. He was hewing at a piece of rock that was in the way for the next day's work. As he sat on his heels, or kneeled, giving hard blows with his pick, 'Uszza – uszza!' he went.

'Shall ter finish, Sorry?'* cried Barker, his fellow butty.

'Finish? Niver while the world stands!' growled Morel.

And he went on striking. He was tired.

'It's a heart-breaking job,' said Barker.

But Morel was too exasperated, at the end of his tether, to answer. Still he struck and hacked with all his might.

'Tha might as well leave it, Walter,' said Barker. 'It'll do tomorrow, without thee hackin' thy guts out.'

'I'll lay no b— finger on this tomorrow, Isr'el!' cried Morel.

'Oh, well, if tha wunna, someb'dy else'll ha'e to,' said Israel.

Then Morel continued to strike.

'Hey-up there – *loose-a*'!' cried the men, leaving the next stall.

Morel continued to strike.

'Tha'll happen catch me up,' said Barker, departing.

When he had gone, Morel, left alone, felt savage. He had not finished his job. He had overworked himself into a frenzy. Rising, wet with sweat, he threw his tool down, pulled on his coat, blew out his candle, took his lamp, and went. Down the main road the lights of the other men went swinging. There was a hollow sound of many voices. It was a long, heavy tramp underground.

He sat at the bottom of the pit, where the great drops of water fell plash. Many colliers were waiting their turns to go up, talking noisily. Morel gave his answers short and disagreeable.

'It's rainin', Sorry,' said old Giles, who had had the news from the top.

Morel found one comfort. He had his old umbrella, which he loved, in the lamp cabin. At last he took his stand on the chair, and was at the top in a moment. Then he handed in his lamp and got his umbrella, which he had bought at an auction for one-and-six. He stood on the edge of the pit-bank for a moment, looking out over the fields; grey rain was falling. The trucks stood full of wet, bright coal. Water ran down the sides of the waggons, over the white 'C. W. and Co.' Colliers, walking indifferent to the rain, were streaming down the line and up the field, a grey, dismal host. Morel put up his umbrella, and took pleasure from the peppering of the drops thereon.

All along the road to Bestwood the miners tramped, wet and grey and dirty, but their red mouths talking with animation. Morel also walked with a gang, but he said nothing. He frowned peevishly as he went. Many men passed into the Prince of Wales or into Ellen's. Morel, feeling sufficiently disagreeable to resist

* 'Sorry' is a common form of address. It is, perhaps, a corruption of 'sirrah'.

temptation, trudged along under the dripping trees that overhung the park wall, and down the mud of Greenhill Lane.

Mrs Morel lay in bed, listening to the rain, and the feet of the colliers from Minton, their voices, and the bang, bang of the gates as they went through the stile up the field.

'There's some herb beer behind the pantry-door,' she said. 'Th' master'll want a drink, if he doesn't stop.'

But he was late, so she concluded he had called for a drink, since it was raining. What did he care about the child or her?

She was very ill when her children were born.

'What is it?' she asked, feeling sick to death.

'A boy.'

And she took consolation in that. The thought of being the mother of men was warming to her heart. She looked at the child. It had blue eyes, and a lot of fair hair and was bonny. Her love came up hot, in spite of everything. She had it in bed with her.

Morel, thinking nothing, dragged his way up the garden path, wearily and angrily. He closed his umbrella, and stood it in the sink; then he sluthered his heavy boots into the kitchen. Mrs Bower appeared in the inner doorway.

'Well,' she said, 'she's about as bad as she can be. It's a boy child.'

The miner grunted, put his empty snap-bag and his tin bottle on the dresser, went back into the scullery and hung up his coat, then came and dropped into his chair.

'Han yer got a drink?' he asked.

The woman went into the pantry. There was heard the pop of a cork. She set the mug, with a little, disgusted rap, on the table before Morel. He drank, gasped, wiped his big moustache on the end of his scarf, drank, gasped, and lay back in his chair. The woman would not speak to him again. She set his dinner before him, and went upstairs.

'Was that the master?' asked Mrs Morel.

'I've gave him his dinner,' replied Mrs Bower.

After he had sat with his arms on the table – he resented the fact that Mrs Bower put no cloth on for him, and gave him a little plate, instead of a full-sized dinner-plate – he began to eat. The fact that his wife was ill, that he had another boy, was nothing to him at that moment. He was too tired; he wanted his dinner; he wanted to sit with his arms lying on the board; he did not like having Mrs Bower about. The fire was too small to please him.

After he had finished his meal, he sat for twenty minutes; then he stoked up a big fire. Then, in his stockinged feet, he went reluctantly upstairs. It was a struggle to face his wife at this moment, and he was tired. His face was black, and smeared with sweat. His singlet had dried again, soaking the dirt in. He had a dirty woollen scarf round his throat. So he stood at the foot of the bed.

'Well, how are ter, then?' he asked.

'I s'll be all right,' she answered.

'H'm!'

He stood at a loss what to say next. He was tired, and this bother was rather a nuisance to him, and he didn't quite know where he was.

'A lad, tha says,' he stammered.

She turned down the sheet and showed the child.

'Bless him!' he murmured. Which made her laugh, because he blessed by rote – pretending paternal emotion, which he did not feel just then.

'Go now,' she said.

'I will, my lass,' he answered, turning away.

Dismissed, he wanted to kiss her, but he dared not. She half wanted him to kiss her, but could not bring herself to give any sign. She only breathed freely when he was gone out of the room again, leaving behind him a faint smell of pit-dirt.

Mrs Morel had a visit every day from the Congregational clergyman. Mr Heaton was young, and very poor. His wife had died at the birth of his first baby, so he remained alone in the manse. He was a Bachelor of Arts of Cambridge, very shy, and no preacher. Mrs Morel was fond of him, and he depended on her. For hours he talked to her, when she was well. He became the godparent of the child.

Occasionally the minister stayed to tea with Mrs Morel. Then she laid the cloth early, got out her best cups, with a little green rim, and hoped Morel would not come too soon; indeed, if he stayed for a pint, she would not mind this day. She had always two dinners to cook because she believed children should have their chief meal at midday, whereas Morel needed his at five o'clock. So Mr Heaton would hold the baby, whilst Mrs Morel beat up a batter-pudding or peeled the potatoes, and he, watching her all the time, would discuss his next sermon. His ideas were quaint and fantastic. She brought him judiciously to earth. It was a discussion of the wedding at Cana.

'When He changed the water into wine at Cana,' he said, 'that is a symbol that the ordinary life, even the blood, of the married husband and wife, which had before been uninspired, like water, became filled with the Spirit, and was as wine because, when love enters, the whole spiritual constitution of a man changes, is filled with the Holy Ghost, and almost his form is altered.'

Mrs Morel thought to herself, 'Yes, poor fellow, his young wife is dead; that is why he makes his love into the Holy Ghost.'

They were halfway down their first cup of tea when they heard the sluther of pit-boots.

'Good gracious!' exclaimed Mrs Morel, in spite of herself.

The minister looked rather scared. Morel entered. He was feeling rather savage. He nodded a 'How d'yer do' to the clergyman, who rose to shake hands with him.

'Nay,' said Morel, showing his hand, 'look thee at it! Tha niver wants ter shake hands wi' a hand like that, does ter? There's too much pick-haft and shovel-dirt on it.'

The minister flushed with confusion, and sat down again. Mrs Morel rose, carried out the steaming saucepan. Morel took off his coat, dragged his armchair to table, and sat down heavily.

'Are you tired?' asked the clergyman.

'Tired? I ham that,' replied Morel. '*You* don't know what it is to be tired, as *I'm* tired.'

'No,' replied the clergyman.

'Why, look yer 'ere,' said the miner, showing the shoulders of his singlet. 'It's a bit dry now, but it's wet as a clout with sweat even yet. Feel it.'

'Goodness!' cried Mrs Morel. 'Mr Heaton doesn't want to feel your nasty singlet.'

The clergyman put out his hand gingerly.

'No, perhaps he doesn't,' said Morel; 'but it's all come out of *me*, whether or not. An' iv'ry day alike my singlet's wringin' wet. 'Aven't you got a drink, Missis, for a man when he comes home barkled up from the pit?'

'You know you drank all the beer,' said Mrs Morel, pouring out his tea.

'An' was there no more to be got?' Turning to the clergyman – 'A man gets that caked up wi' th' dust, you know – that clogged up down a coal-mine, he *needs* a drink when he comes home.'

'I am sure he does,' said the clergyman.

'But it's ten to one if there's owt for him.'

'There's water – and there's tea,' said Mrs Morel.

'Water! It's not water as'll clear his throat.'

He poured out a saucerful of tea, blew on it, and sucked it up through his great black moustache, sighing afterwards. Then he poured out another saucerful, and stood his cup on the table.

'My cloth!' said Mrs Morel, putting it on a plate.

'A man as comes home as I do 's too tired to care about cloths,' said Morel.

'Pity!' exclaimed his wife, sarcastically.

The room was full of the smell of meat and vegetables and pit-clothes.

He leaned over to the minister, his great moustache thrust forward, his mouth very red in his black face.

'Mr Heaton,' he said, 'a man as has been down the black hole all day, dingin' away at a coal face, yi, a sight harder than that wall – '

'Needn't make a moan of it,' put in Mrs Morel.

She hated her husband because, whenever he had an audience, he whined and played for sympathy. William, sitting nursing the baby, hated him, with a boy's hatred for false sentiment, and for the stupid treatment of his mother. Annie had never liked him; she merely avoided him.

When the minister had gone, Mrs Morel looked at her cloth.

'A fine mess!' she said.

'Dos't think I'm goin' to sit wi' my arms danglin', cos tha's got a parson for tea wi' thee?' he bawled.

They were both angry, but she said nothing. The baby began to cry, and Mrs

Morel, picking up a saucepan from the hearth, accidentally knocked Annie on the head, whereupon the girl began to whine, and Morel to shout at her. In the midst of this pandemonium, William looked up at the big glazed text over the mantelpiece and read distinctly, 'God Bless Our Home!'

Whereupon Mrs Morel, trying to soothe the baby, jumped up, rushed at him, boxed his ears, saying, 'What are you putting in for?'

And then she sat down and laughed, till tears ran over her cheeks, while William kicked the stool he had been sitting on, and Morel growled, 'I canna see what there is so much to laugh at.'

One evening, directly after the parson's visit, feeling unable to bear herself after another display from her husband, she took Annie and the baby and went out. Morel had kicked William, and the mother would never forgive him.

She went over the sheep-bridge and across a corner of the meadow to the cricket-ground. The meadows seemed one space of ripe, evening light, whispering with the distant mill-race. She sat on a seat under the alders in the cricket-ground, and fronted the evening. Before her, level and solid, spread the big green cricket-field, like the bed of a sea of light. Children played in the bluish shadow of the pavilion. Many rooks, high up, came cawing home across the softly-woven sky. They stooped in a long curve down into the golden glow, concentrating, cawing, wheeling, like black flakes on a slow vortex, over a tree-clump that made a dark boss among the pasture.

A few gentlemen were practising, and Mrs Morel could hear the chock of the ball, and the voices of men suddenly roused; could see the white forms of men shifting silently over the green, upon which already the under shadows were smouldering. Away at the grange, one side of the haystacks was lit up, the other sides blue-grey. A waggon of sheaves rocked small across the melting yellow light.

The sun was going down. Every open evening, the hills of Derbyshire were blazed over with red sunset. Mrs Morel watched the sun sink from the glistening sky, leaving a soft flower-blue overhead, while the western space went red, as if all the fire had swum down there, leaving the bell cast flawless blue. The mountain-ash berries across the field stood fierily out from the dark leaves, for a moment. A few shocks of corn in a corner of the fallow stood up as if alive; she imagined them bowing; perhaps her son would be a Joseph. In the east, a mirrored sunset floated pink opposite the west's scarlet. The big haystacks on the hillside, that butted into the glare, went cold.

With Mrs Morel it was one of those still moments when the small frets vanish, and the beauty of things stands out, and she had the peace and the strength to see herself. Now and again, a swallow cut close to her. Now and again, Annie came up with a handful of alder-currants. The baby was restless on his mother's knee, clambering with his hands at the light.

Mrs Morel looked down at him. She had dreaded this baby like a catastrophe, because of her feeling for her husband. And now she felt strangely towards the infant. Her heart was heavy because of the child, almost as if it were unhealthy, or malformed. Yet it seemed quite well. But she noticed the peculiar knitting of the baby's brows, and the peculiar heaviness of its eyes, as if it were trying to understand something that was pain. She felt, when she looked at her child's dark, brooding pupils, as if a burden were on her heart.

'He looks as if he was thinking about something – quite sorrowful,' said Mrs Kirk.

Suddenly, looking at him, the heavy feeling at the mother's heart melted into passionate grief. She bowed over him, and a few tears shook swiftly out of her very heart. The baby lifted his fingers.

'My lamb!' she cried softly.

And at that moment she felt, in some far inner place of her soul, that she and her husband were guilty.

The baby was looking up at her. It had blue eyes like her own, but its look was heavy, steady, as if it had realised something that had stunned some point of its soul.

In her arms lay the delicate baby. Its deep blue eyes, always looking up at her unblinking, seemed to draw her innermost thoughts out of her. She no longer loved her husband; she had not wanted this child to come, and there it lay in her arms and pulled at her heart. She felt as if the navel string that had connected its frail little body with hers had not been broken. A wave of hot love went over her to the infant. She held it close to her face and breast. With all her force, with all her soul she would make up to it for having brought it into the world unloved. She would love it all the more now it was here, carry it in her love. Its clear, knowing eyes gave her pain and fear. Did it know all about her? When it lay under her heart, had it been listening then? Was there a reproach in the look? She felt the marrow melt in her bones, with fear and pain.

Once more she was aware of the sun lying red on the rim of the hill opposite. She suddenly held up the child in her hands.

'Look!' she said. 'Look, my pretty!'

She thrust the infant forward to the crimson, throbbing sun, almost with relief. She saw him lift his little fist. Then she put him to her bosom again, ashamed almost of her impulse to give him back again whence he came.

'If he lives,' she thought to herself, 'what will become of him – what will he be?'

Her heart was anxious.

'I will call him "Paul",' she said suddenly; she knew not why.

After a while she went home. A fine shadow was flung over the deep green meadow, darkening all.

As she expected, she found the house empty. But Morel was home by ten o'clock, and that day, at least, ended peacefully.

Walter Morel was, at this time, exceedingly irritable. His work seemed to exhaust him. When he came home he did not speak civilly to anybody. If the fire were rather low he bullied about that – he grumbled about his dinner; if the children made a chatter he shouted at them in a way that made their mother's blood boil, and made them hate him.

On the Friday, he was not home by eleven o'clock. The baby was unwell, and was restless, crying if he were put down. Mrs Morel, tired to death, and still weak, was scarcely under control.

'I wish the nuisance would come,' she said wearily to herself.

The child at last sank down to sleep in her arms. She was too tired to carry him to the cradle.

'But I'll say nothing, whatever time he comes,' she said. 'It only works me up; I won't say anything. But I know if he does anything it'll make my blood boil,' she added to herself.

She sighed, hearing him coming, as if it were something she could not bear. He, taking his revenge, was nearly drunk. She kept her head bent over the child as he entered, not wishing to see him. But it went through her like a flash of hot fire when, in passing, he lurched against the dresser, setting the tins rattling, and clutched at the white pot knobs for support. He hung up his hat and coat, then returned, stood glowering from a distance at her, as she sat bowed over the child.

'Is there nothing to eat in the house?' he asked, insolently, as if to a servant. In certain stages of his intoxication he affected the clipped, mincing speech of the towns. Mrs Morel hated him most in this condition.

'You know what there is in the house,' she said, so coldly it sounded impersonal.

He stood and glared at her without moving a muscle.

'I asked a civil question, and I expect a civil answer,' he said affectedly.

'And you got it,' she said, still ignoring him.

He glowered again. Then he came unsteadily forward. He leaned on the table with one hand, and with the other jerked at the table drawer to get a knife to cut bread. The drawer stuck because he pulled sideways. In a temper he dragged it, so that it flew out bodily, and spoons, forks, knives, a hundred metallic things, splashed with a clatter and a clang upon the brick floor. The baby gave a little convulsed start.

'What are you doing, clumsy, drunken fool?' the mother cried.

'Then tha should get the flamin' thing thysen. Tha should get up, like other women have to, an' wait on a man.'

'Wait on you – wait on you?' she cried. 'Yes, I see myself.'

'Yis, an' I'll learn thee tha's got to. Wait on *me*, yes, tha sh'lt wait on me – '

'Never, milord. I'd wait on a dog at the door first.'

'What – what?'

He was trying to fit in the drawer. At her last speech he turned round. His face was crimson, his eyes bloodshot. He stared at her one silent second in threat.

'P–h!' she went quickly, in contempt.

He jerked at the drawer in his excitement. It fell, cut sharply on his shin, and on the reflex he flung it at her.

One of the corners caught her brow as the shallow drawer crashed into the fireplace. She swayed, almost fell stunned from her chair. To her very soul she was sick; she clasped the child tightly to her bosom. A few moments elapsed; then, with an effort, she brought herself to. The baby was crying plaintively. Her left brow was bleeding rather profusely. As she glanced down at the child, her brain reeling, some drops of blood soaked into its white shawl; but the baby was at least not hurt. She balanced her head to keep equilibrium, so that the blood ran into her eye.

Walter Morel remained as he had stood, leaning on the table with one hand, looking blank. When he was sufficiently sure of his balance, he went across to her, swayed, caught hold of the back of her rocking-chair, almost tipping her out; then, leaning forward over her, and swaying as he spoke, he said, in tone of wondering concern, 'Did it catch thee?'

He swayed again, as if he would pitch on to the child. With the catastrophe he had lost all balance.

'Go away,' she said, struggling to keep her presence of mind.

He hiccoughed. 'Let's – let's look at it,' he said, hiccoughing again.

'Go away!' she cried.

'Lemme – lemme look at it, lass.'

She smelled him of drink, felt the unequal pull of his swaying grasp on the back of her rocking-chair.

'Go away,' she said, and weakly she pushed him off.

He stood, uncertain in balance, gazing upon her. Summoning all her strength she rose, the baby on one arm. By a cruel effort of will, moving as if in sleep, she went across to the scullery, where she bathed her eye for a minute in cold water; but she was too dizzy. Afraid lest she should swoon, she returned to her rocking-chair, trembling in every fibre. By instinct, she kept the baby clasped.

Morel, bothered, had succeeded in pushing the drawer back into its cavity, and was on his knees, groping, with numb paws, for the scattered spoons.

Her brow was still bleeding. Presently Morel got up and came craning his neck towards her.

'What has it done to thee, lass?' he asked, in a very wretched, humble tone.

'You can see what it's done,' she answered.

He stood, bending forward, supported on his hands, which grasped his legs just above the knee. He peered to look at the wound. She drew away from the thrust of his face with its great moustache, averting her own face as much as possible. As he looked at her, who was cold and impassive as stone, with mouth shut tight, he sickened with feebleness and hopelessness of spirit. He was turning drearily away, when he saw a drop of blood fall from the averted wound into the baby's fragile, glistening hair. Fascinated, he watched the heavy dark drop hang in the glistening cloud, and pull down the gossamer. Another drop fell. It would soak through to the baby's scalp. He watched, fascinated, feeling it soak in; then, finally, his manhood broke.

'What of this child?' was all his wife said to him. But her low, intense tones brought his head lower. She softened: 'Get me some wadding out of the middle drawer,' she said.

He stumbled away very obediently, presently returning with a pad, which she singed before the fire, then put on her forehead, as she sat with the baby on her lap.

'Now that clean pit-scarf.'

Again he rummaged and fumbled in the drawer, returning presently with a red, narrow scarf. She took it, and with trembling fingers proceeded to bind it round her head.

'Let me tie it for thee,' he said humbly.

'I can do it myself,' she replied. When it was done she went upstairs, telling him to rake the fire and lock the door.

In the morning Mrs Morel said, 'I knocked against the latch of the coal-place, when I was getting a raker in the dark, because the candle blew out.' Her two small children looked up at her with wide, dismayed eyes. They said nothing, but their parted lips seemed to express the unconscious tragedy they felt.

Walter Morel lay in bed next day until nearly dinner-time.

He did not think of the previous evening's work. He scarcely thought of anything, but he would not think of that. He lay and suffered like a sulking dog. He had hurt himself most; and he was the more damaged because he would never say a word to her, or express his sorrow. He tried to wriggle out of it. 'It was her own fault,' he said to himself. Nothing, however, could prevent his inner consciousness inflicting on him the punishment which ate into his spirit like rust, and which he could only alleviate by drinking.

He felt as if he had not the initiative to get up, or to say a word, or to move, but could only lie like a log. Moreover, he had himself violent pains in the head. It was Saturday. Towards noon he rose, cut himself food in the pantry, ate it with his head dropped, then pulled on his boots, and went out, to return at three o'clock slightly tipsy and relieved; then once more straight to bed. He rose again at six in the evening, had tea and went straight out.

Sunday was the same: bed till noon, the Palmerston Arms till 2.30, dinner, and bed; scarcely a word spoken. When Mrs Morel went upstairs, towards four o'clock, to put on her Sunday dress, he was fast asleep. She would have felt sorry for him, if he had once said, 'Wife, I'm sorry.' But no; he insisted to himself it was her fault. And so he broke himself. So she merely left him alone. There was this deadlock of passion between them, and she was stronger.

The family began tea. Sunday was the only day when all sat down to meals together.

'Isn't my father going to get up?' asked William.

'Let him lie,' the mother replied.

There was a feeling of misery over all the house. The children breathed the air that was poisoned, and they felt dreary. They were rather disconsolate, did not know what to do, what to play at.

Immediately Morel woke he got straight out of bed. That was characteristic of him all his life. He was all for activity. The prostrated inactivity of two mornings was stifling him.

It was near six o'clock when he got down. This time he entered without hesitation, his wincing sensitiveness having hardened again. He did not care any longer what the family thought or felt.

The tea-things were on the table. William was reading aloud from 'The Child's Own', Annie listening and asking eternally 'Why?' Both children hushed into silence as they heard the approaching thud of their father's stockinged feet, and shrank as he entered. Yet he was usually indulgent to them.

Morel made the meal alone, brutally. He ate and drank more noisily than he had need. No one spoke to him. The family life withdrew, shrank away, and became hushed as he entered. But he cared no longer about his alienation.

Immediately he had finished tea he rose with alacrity to go out. It was this alacrity, this haste to be gone, which so sickened Mrs Morel. As she heard him sousing heartily in cold water, heard the eager scratch of the steel comb on the side of the bowl, as he wetted his hair, she closed her eyes in disgust. As he bent over, lacing his boots, there was a certain vulgar gusto in his movement that divided him from the reserved, watchful rest of the family. He always ran away from the battle with himself. Even in his own heart's privacy, he excused himself, saying, 'If she hadn't said so-and-so, it would never have happened. She asked for what she's got.' The children waited in restraint during his preparations. When he had gone, they sighed with relief.

He closed the door behind him, and was glad. It was a rainy evening. The Palmerston would be the cosier. He hastened forward in anticipation. All the slate roofs of the Bottoms shone black with wet. The roads, always dark with coal-dust, were full of blackish mud. He hastened along. The Palmerston windows were steamed over. The passage was paddled with wet feet. But the air was warm, if foul, and full of the sound of voices and the smell of beer and smoke.

'What shollt ha'e, Walter?' cried a voice, as soon as Morel appeared in the doorway.

'Oh, Jim, my lad, wheriver has thee sprung frae?'

The men made a seat for him, and took him in warmly. He was glad. In a minute or two they had thawed all responsibility out of him, all shame, all trouble, and he was clear as a bell for a jolly night.

On the Wednesday following, Morel was penniless. He dreaded his wife. Having hurt her, he hated her. He did not know what to do with himself that evening, having not even twopence with which to go to the Palmerston, and being already rather deeply in debt. So, while his wife was down the garden with the child, he hunted in the top drawer of the dresser where she kept her purse, found it, and looked inside. It contained a half-crown, two halfpennies, and a sixpence. So he took the sixpence, put the purse carefully back, and went out.

The next day, when she wanted to pay the greengrocer, she looked in the purse for her sixpence, and her heart sank to her shoes. Then she sat down and thought: '*Was* there a sixpence? I hadn't spent it, had I? And I hadn't left it anywhere else?'

She was much put about. She hunted round everywhere for it. And, as she sought, the conviction came into her heart that her husband had taken it. What she had in her purse was all the money she possessed. But that he should sneak it from her thus was unbearable. He had done so twice before. The first time she had not accused him, and at the weekend he had put the shilling again into her purse. So that was how she had known he had taken it. The second time he had not paid back.

This time she felt it was too much. When he had had his dinner – he came home early that day – she said to him coldly, 'Did you take sixpence out of my purse last night?'

'Me!' he said, looking up in an offended way. 'No, I didna! I niver clapped eyes on your purse.'

But she could detect the lie.

'Why, you know you did,' she said quietly.

'I tell you I didna,' he shouted. 'Yer at me again, are yer? I've had about enough on't.'

'So you filch sixpence out of my purse while I'm taking the clothes in.'

'I'll make yer pay for this,' he said, pushing back his chair in desperation. He bustled and got washed, then went determinedly upstairs. Presently he came down dressed, and with a big bundle in a blue-checked, enormous handkerchief.

'And now,' he said, 'you'll see me again when you do.'

'It'll be before I want to,' she replied; and at that he marched out of the house with his bundle. She sat trembling slightly, but her heart brimming with contempt. What would she do if he went to some other pit, obtained work, and got in with another woman? But she knew him too well – he couldn't. She was dead sure of him. Nevertheless her heart was gnawed inside her.

'Where's my dad?' said William, coming in from school.

'He says he's run away,' replied the mother.

'Where to?'

'Eh, I don't know. He's taken a bundle in the blue handkerchief, and says he's not coming back.'

'What shall we do?' cried the boy.

'Eh, never trouble, he won't go far.'

'But if he doesn't come back,' wailed Annie.

And she and William retired to the sofa and wept. Mrs Morel sat and laughed.

'You pair of gabeys!' she exclaimed. 'You'll see him before the night's out.'

But the children were not to be consoled. Twilight came on. Mrs Morel grew anxious from very weariness. One part of her said, it would be a relief to see the last of him, another part fretted because of keeping the children, and inside her, as yet, she could not quite let him go. At the bottom, she knew very well he could *not* go.

When she went down to the coal-place at the end of the garden, however, she felt something behind the door. So she looked. And there in the dark lay the big blue bundle. She sat on a piece of coal in front of the bundle and laughed. Every time she saw it, so fat and yet so ignominious, slunk into its corner in the dark, with its ends flopping like dejected ears from the knots, she laughed again. She was relieved.

Mrs Morel sat waiting. He had not any money, she knew, so if he stopped he was running up a bill. She was very tired of him – tired to death. He had not even the courage to carry his bundle beyond the yard end.

As she meditated at about nine o'clock, he opened the door and came in, slinking, and yet sulky. She said not a word. He took off his coat, and slunk to his armchair, where he began to take off his boots.

'You'd better fetch your bundle before you take your boots off,' she said quietly.

'You may thank your stars I've come back tonight,' he said, looking up from under his dropped head, sulkily, trying to be impressive.

'Why, where should you have gone? You daren't even get your parcel through the yard-end,' she said.

He looked such a fool she was not even angry with him. He continued to take his boots off and prepare for bed.

'I don't know what's in your blue handkerchief,' she said. 'But if you leave it the children shall fetch it in the morning.'

Whereupon he got up and went out of the house, returning presently and crossing the kitchen with averted face, hurrying upstairs. As Mrs Morel saw him slink quickly through the inner doorway, holding his bundle, she laughed to herself; but her heart was bitter, because she had loved him.

CHAPTER 3

The Casting off of Morel – the Taking on of William

During the next week Morel's temper was almost unbearable. Like all miners, he was a great lover of medicines, which, strangely enough, he would often pay for himself.

'You mun get me a drop o' laxy vitral,' he said. 'It's a winder as we canna ha'e a sup i' th' 'ouse.'

So Mrs Morel bought him elixir of vitriol, his favourite first medicine. And he made himself a jug of wormwood tea. He had hanging in the attic great bunches of dried herbs: wormwood, rue, horehound, elder-flowers, parsley-purt, marshmallow, hyssop, dandelion, and centuary. Usually there was a jug of one or other decoction standing on the hob, from which he drank largely.

'Grand!' he said, smacking his lips after wormwood. 'Grand!' And he exhorted the children to try.

'It's better than any of your tea or your cocoa stews,' he vowed. But they were not to be tempted.

This time, however, neither pills nor vitriol nor all his herbs would shift the 'nasty peens in his head'. He was sickening for an attack of an inflammation of the brain. He had never been well since his sleeping on the ground when he went with Jerry to Nottingham. Since then he had drunk and stormed. Now he fell seriously ill, and Mrs Morel had him to nurse. He was one of the worst patients imaginable. But, in spite of all, and putting aside the fact that he was breadwinner, she never quite wanted him to die. Still there was one part of her wanted him for herself.

The neighbours were very good to her: occasionally some had the children in to meals, occasionally some would do the downstairs work for her, one would mind the baby for a day. But it was a great drag, nevertheless. It was not every day the neighbours helped. Then she had nursing of baby and husband, cleaning and cooking, everything to do. She was quite worn out, but she did what was wanted of her.

And the money was just sufficient. She had seventeen shillings a week from clubs, and every Friday Barker and the other butty put by a portion of the stall's profits for Morel's wife. And the neighbours made broths, and gave eggs, and such invalids' trifles. If they had not helped her so generously in those times, Mrs Morel would never have pulled through, without incurring debts that would have dragged her down.

The weeks passed. Morel, almost against hope, grew better. He had a fine constitution, so that, once on the mend, he went straight forward to recovery. Soon he was pottering about downstairs. During his illness his wife had spoilt him a little. Now he wanted her to continue. He often put his hand to his head, pulled down the corners of his mouth, and shammed pains he did not feel. But there was no deceiving her. At first she merely smiled to herself. Then she scolded him sharply.

'Goodness, man, don't be so lachrymose.'

That wounded him slightly, but still he continued to feign sickness.

'I wouldn't be such a mardy baby,' said his wife shortly.

Then he was indignant, and cursed under his breath, like a boy. He was forced to resume a normal tone, and to cease to whine.

Nevertheless, there was a state of peace in the house for some time. Mrs Morel was more tolerant of him, and he, depending on her almost like a child, was rather happy. Neither knew that she was more tolerant because she loved him less. Up till this time, in spite of all, he had been her husband and her man. She had felt that, more or less, what he did to himself he did to her. Her living depended on him. There were many, many stages in the ebbing of her love for him, but it was always ebbing.

Now, with the birth of this third baby, her self no longer set towards him, helplessly, but was like a tide that scarcely rose, standing off from him. After this she scarcely desired him. And, standing more aloof from him, not feeling him so much part of herself, but merely part of her circumstances, she did not mind so much what he did, could leave him alone.

There was the halt, the wistfulness about the ensuing year, which is like autumn in a man's life. His wife was casting him off, half regretfully, but relentlessly; casting him off and turning now for love and life to the children. Henceforward he was more or less a husk. And he half acquiesced, as so many men do, yielding their place to their children.

During his recuperation, when it was really over between them, both made an effort to come back somewhat to the old relationship of the first months of their marriage. He sat at home and, when the children were in bed, and she was sewing – she did all her sewing by hand, made all shirts and children's clothing – he would read to her from the newspaper, slowly pronouncing and delivering the words like a man pitching quoits. Often she hurried him on, giving him a phrase in anticipation. And then he took her words humbly.

The silences between them were peculiar. There would be the swift, slight 'cluck' of her needle, the sharp 'pop' of his lips as he let out the smoke, the warmth, the sizzle on the bars as he spat in the fire. Then her thoughts turned to William. Already he was getting a big boy. Already he was top of the class, and the master said he was the smartest lad in the school. She saw him a man, young, full of vigour, making the world glow again for her.

And Morel sitting there, quite alone, and having nothing to think about, would be feeling vaguely uncomfortable. His soul would reach out in its blind way to her and find her gone. He felt a sort of emptiness, almost like a vacuum in his soul. He was unsettled and restless. Soon he could not live in that atmosphere, and he affected his wife. Both felt an oppression on their breathing when they were left together for some time. Then he went to bed and she settled down to enjoy herself alone, working, thinking, living.

Meanwhile another infant was coming, fruit of this little peace and tenderness between the separating parents. Paul was seventeen months old when the new baby was born. He was then a plump, pale child, quiet, with heavy blue eyes, and still the peculiar slight knitting of the brows. The last child was also a boy, fair and bonny. Mrs Morel was sorry when she knew she was with child, both for economic reasons and because she did not love her husband; but not for the sake of the infant.

They called the baby Arthur. He was very pretty, with a mop of gold curls, and he loved his father from the first. Mrs Morel was glad this child loved the father. Hearing the miner's footsteps, the baby would put up his arms and crow.

And if Morel were in a good temper, he called back immediately, in his hearty, mellow voice, 'What then, my beauty? I sh'll come to thee in a minute.'

And as soon as he had taken off his pit-coat, Mrs Morel would put an apron round the child, and give him to his father.

'What a sight the lad looks!' she would exclaim sometimes, taking back the baby, that was smutted on the face from his father's kisses and play. Then Morel laughed joyfully.

'He's a little collier, bless his bit o' mutton!' he exclaimed.

And these were the happy moments of her life now, when the children included the father in her heart.

Meanwhile William grew bigger and stronger and more active, while Paul, always rather delicate and quiet, got slimmer, and trotted after his mother like her shadow. He was usually active and interested, but sometimes he would have fits of depression. Then the mother would find the boy of three or four crying on the sofa.

'What's the matter?' she asked, and got no answer.

'What's the matter?' she insisted, getting cross.

'I don't know,' sobbed the child.

So she tried to reason him out of it, or to amuse him, but without effect. It made her feel beside herself. Then the father, always impatient, would jump from his chair and shout, 'If he doesn't stop, I'll smack him till he does.'

'You'll do nothing of the sort,' said the mother coldly. And then she carried the child into the yard, plumped him into his little chair, and said: 'Now cry there, Misery!'

And then a butterfly on the rhubarb-leaves perhaps caught his eye, or at last he cried himself to sleep. These fits were not often, but they caused a shadow in Mrs Morel's heart, and her treatment of Paul was different from that of the other children.

Suddenly one morning as she was looking down the alley of the Bottoms for the barm-man, she heard a voice calling her. It was the thin little Mrs Anthony in brown velvet.

'Here, Mrs Morel, I want to tell you about your Willie.'

'Oh, do you?' replied Mrs Morel. 'Why, what's the matter?'

'A lad as gets 'old of another an' rips his clothes off'n 'is back,' Mrs Anthony said, 'wants showing something.'

'Your Alfred's as old as my William,' said Mrs Morel.

' 'Appen 'e is, but that doesn't give him a right to get hold of the boy's collar, an' fair rip it clean off his back.'

'Well,' said Mrs Morel, 'I don't thrash my children and even if I did, I should want to hear their side of the tale.'

'They'd happen be a bit better if they did get a good hiding,' retorted Mrs Anthony. 'When it comes ter rippin' a lad's clean collar off'n 'is back a-purpose – '

'I'm sure he didn't do it on purpose,' said Mrs Morel.

'Make me a liar!' shouted Mrs Anthony.

Mrs Morel moved away and closed her gate. Her hand trembled as she held her mug of barm.

'But I s'll let your mester know,' Mrs Anthony cried after her.

At dinner-time, when William had finished his meal and wanted to be off again – he was then eleven years old – his mother said to him, 'What did you tear Alfred Anthony's collar for?'

'When did I tear his collar?'

'I don't know when, but his mother says you did.'

'Why – it was yesterday – an' it was torn a'ready.'

'But you tore it more.'

'Well, I'd got a cobbler as 'ad licked seventeen – an' Alfy Ant'ny 'e says:

> "Adam an' Eve an' pinch-me,
> Went down to a river to bade.
> Adam an' Eve got drownded,
> Who do yer think got saved?"

'An' so I says, "Oh, Pinch-*you*," an' so I pinched 'im, an' 'e was mad, an' so he snatched my cobbler an' run off with it. An' so I run after 'im, an' when I was gettin' hold of him, 'e dodged, an' it ripped 'is collar. But I got my cobbler – '

He pulled from his pocket a black old horse-chestnut hanging on a string. This old cobbler had 'cobbled' – hit and smashed – seventeen other cobblers on similar strings. So the boy was proud of his veteran.

'Well,' said Mrs Morel, 'you know you've got no right to rip his collar.'

'Well, our mother!' he answered. 'I never meant tr'a done it – an' it was on'y an old india-rubber collar as was torn a'ready.'

'Next time,' said his mother, '*you* be more careful. I shouldn't like it if you came home with *your* collar torn off.'

'I don't care, our mother; I never did it a-purpose.'

The boy was rather miserable at being reprimanded.

'No – well, you be more careful.'

William fled away, glad to be exonerated. And Mrs Morel, who hated any bother with the neighbours, thought she would explain to Mrs Anthony, and the business would be over.

But that evening Morel came in from the pit looking very sour. He stood in the kitchen and glared round, but did not speak for some minutes. Then, 'Wheer's that Willy?' he asked.

'What do you want *him* for?' asked Mrs Morel, who had guessed.

'I'll let 'im know when I get him,' said Morel, banging his pit-bottle on to the dresser.

'I suppose Mrs Anthony's got hold of you and been yarning to you about their Alfy's collar,' said Mrs Morel, rather sneering.

'Niver mind who's got hold of me,' said Morel. 'When I get hold of '*im* I'll make his bones rattle.'

'It's a poor tale,' said Mrs Morel, 'that you're so ready to side with any snipey vixen who likes to come telling tales against your own children.'

'I'll learn 'im!' said Morel. 'It none matters to me whose lad 'e is; 'e's none goin' rippin' an' tearin' about just as he's a mind.'

' "Ripping and tearing about"! ' repeated Mrs Morel. 'He was running after that Alfy, who'd taken his cobbler, and he accidentally got hold of his collar, because the other dodged – as an Anthony would.'

'I know!' shouted Morel threateningly.

'You would, before you're told,' replied his wife bitingly.

'Niver you mind,' stormed Morel. 'I know my business.'

'That's more than doubtful,' said Mrs Morel, 'supposing some loud-mouthed creature had been getting you to thrash your own children.'

'I know,' repeated Morel.

And he said no more, but sat and nursed his bad temper. Suddenly William ran in, saying, 'Can I have my tea, mother?'

'Tha can ha'e more than that!' shouted Morel.

'Hold your noise, man,' said Mrs Morel; 'and don't look so ridiculous.'

'He'll look ridiculous before I've done wi' him!' shouted Morel, rising from his chair and glaring at his son.

William, who was a tall lad for his years, but very sensitive, had gone pale, and was looking in a sort of horror at his father.

'Go out!' Mrs Morel commanded her son.

William had not the wit to move. Suddenly Morel clenched his fist, and crouched.

'I'll gi'e him "go out"! ' he shouted like an insane thing.

'What!' cried Mrs Morel, panting with rage. 'You shall not touch him for her telling, you shall not!'

'Shonna I?' shouted Morel. 'Shonna I?'

And, glaring at the boy, he ran forward. Mrs Morel sprang in between them, with her fist lifted.

'Don't you dare!' she cried.

'What!' he shouted, baffled for the moment. 'What!'

She spun round to her son.

'Go out of the house!' she commanded him in fury.

The boy, as if hypnotised by her, turned suddenly and was gone. Morel rushed to the door, but was too late. He returned, pale under his pit-dirt with fury. But now his wife was fully roused.

'Only dare!' she said in a loud, ringing voice. 'Only dare, milord, to lay a finger on that child! You'll regret it for ever.'

He was afraid of her. In a towering rage, he sat down.

When the children were old enough to be left, Mrs Morel joined the Women's Guild. It was a little club of women attached to the Co-operative Wholesale Society, which met on Monday night in the long room over the grocery shop of the Bestwood 'Co-op'. The women were supposed to discuss the benefits to be derived from co-operation, and other social questions. Sometimes Mrs Morel read a paper. It seemed queer to the children to see their mother, who was always busy about the house, sitting writing in her rapid fashion, thinking, referring to books, and writing again. They felt for her on such occasions the deepest respect.

But they loved the Guild. It was the only thing to which they did not grudge their mother – and that partly because she enjoyed it, partly because of the treats they derived from it. The Guild was called by some hostile husbands, who found their wives getting too independent, the 'clat-fart' shop – that is, the gossip-shop. It is true, from off the basis of the Guild, the women could look at their homes, at the conditions of their own lives, and find fault. So the colliers found their women had a new standard of their own, rather disconcerting. And also, Mrs Morel always had a lot of news on Monday nights, so that the children liked William to be in when their mother came home, because she told him things.

Then, when the lad was thirteen, she got him a job in the Co-op office. He was a very clever boy, frank, with rather rough features and real Viking blue eyes.

'What dost want ter ma'e a stool-harsed Jack on 'im for?' said Morel. 'All he'll do is to wear his britches behind out, an' earn nowt. What's 'e startin' wi'?'

'It doesn't matter what he's starting with,' said Mrs Morel.

'It wouldna! Put 'im i' th' pit wi' me, an' 'e'll earn a easy ten shillin' a wik from th' start. But six shillin' wearin' his truck-end out on a stool's better than ten shillin' i' th' pit wi' me, I know.'

'He is not going in the pit,' said Mrs Morel, 'and there's an end of it.'

'It wor good enough for me, but it's non good enough for 'im.'

'If your mother put you in the pit at twelve, it's no reason why I should do the same with my lad.'

'Twelve! It wor a sight afore that!'

'Whenever it was,' said Mrs Morel.

She was very proud of her son. He went to the night-school, and learned shorthand, so that by the time he was sixteen he was the best shorthand clerk and bookkeeper on the place, except one. Then he taught in the night-schools. But he was so fiery that only his good-nature and his size protected him.

All the things that men do – the decent things – William did. He could run like the wind. When he was twelve he won a first prize in a race; an inkstand of glass, shaped like an anvil. It stood proudly on the dresser, and gave Mrs Morel a keen pleasure. The boy only ran for her. He flew home with his anvil, breathless, with a 'Look, mother!' That was the first real tribute to herself. She took it like a queen.

'How pretty!' she exclaimed.

Then he began to get ambitious. He gave all his money to his mother. When he earned fourteen shillings a week, she gave him back two for himself, and, as he never drank, he felt himself rich. He went about with the bourgeois of Bestwood. The townlet contained nothing higher than the clergyman. Then came the bank manager, then the doctors, then the tradespeople, and after that the hosts of colliers. William began to consort with the sons of the chemist, the schoolmaster, and the tradesmen. He played billiards in the Mechanics Hall. Also he danced – this in spite of his mother. All the life that Bestwood offered he enjoyed, from the sixpenny-hops down Church Street, to sports and billiards.

Paul was treated to dazzling descriptions of all kinds of flower-like ladies, most of whom lived like cut blooms in William's heart for a brief fortnight.

Occasionally some flame would come in pursuit of her errant swain. Mrs Morel would find a strange girl at the door, and immediately she sniffed the air.

'Is Mr Morel in?' the damsel would ask appealingly.

'My husband is at home,' Mrs Morel replied.

'I – I mean *young* Mr Morel,' repeated the maiden painfully.

'Which one? There are several.'

Whereupon much blushing and stammering from the fair one.

'I – I met Mr Morel – at Ripley,' she explained.

'Oh – at a dance!'

'Yes.'

'I don't approve of the girls my son meets at dances. And he is *not* at home.'

Then he came home angry with his mother for having turned the girl away so rudely. He was a careless, yet eager-looking fellow, who walked with long strides, sometimes frowning, often with his cap pushed jollily to the back of his head. Now he came in frowning. He threw his cap on to the sofa, and took his strong jaw in his hand, and glared down at his mother. She was small, with her hair taken straight back from her forehead. She had a quiet air of authority, and yet of rare warmth. Knowing her son was angry, she trembled inwardly.

'Did a lady call for me yesterday, mother?' he asked.

'I don't know about a lady. There was a girl came.'

'And why didn't you tell me?'

'Because I forgot, simply.'

He fumed a little.

'A good-looking girl – seemed a lady?'

'I didn't look at her.'

'Big brown eyes?'

'I did *not* look. And tell your girls, my son, that when they're running after you, they're not to come and ask your mother for you. Tell them that – brazen baggages you meet at dancing-classes.'

'I'm sure she was a nice girl.'

'And I'm sure she wasn't.'

There ended the altercation. Over the dancing there was a great strife between the mother and the son. The grievance reached its height when William said he was going to Hucknall Torkard – considered a low town – to a fancy-dress ball. He was to be a Highlander. There was a dress he could hire, which one of his friends had had, and which fitted him perfectly. The Highland suit came home. Mrs Morel received it coldly and would not unpack it.

'My suit come?' cried William.

'There's a parcel in the front-room.'

He rushed in and cut the string.

'How do you fancy your son in this!' he said, enraptured, showing her the suit.

'You know I don't want to fancy you in it.'

On the evening of the dance, when he had come home to dress, Mrs Morel put on her coat and bonnet.

'Aren't you going to stop and see me, mother?' he asked.

'No; I don't want to see you,' she replied.

She was rather pale, and her face was closed and hard. She was afraid of her son's going the same way as his father. He hesitated a moment, and his heart stood still with anxiety. Then he caught sight of the Highland bonnet with its ribbons. He picked it up gleefully, forgetting her. She went out.

When he was nineteen he suddenly left the Co-op office and got a situation in Nottingham. In his new place he had thirty shillings a week instead of eighteen. This was indeed a rise. His mother and his father were brimmed up with pride. Everybody praised William. It seemed he was going to get on rapidly. Mrs Morel hoped, with his aid, to help her younger sons. Annie was now studying to be a teacher. Paul, also very clever, was getting on well, having lessons in French and German from his godfather, the clergyman who was still a friend to Mrs Morel. Arthur, a spoilt and very good-looking boy, was at the Board-school, but there was talk of his trying to get a scholarship for the High School in Nottingham.

William remained a year at his new post in Nottingham. He was studying hard, and growing serious. Something seemed to be fretting him. Still he went out to the dances and the river parties. He did not drink. The children were all rabid teetotallers. He came home very late at night, and sat yet longer studying. His mother implored him to take more care, to do one thing or another.

'Dance, if you want to dance, my son; but don't think you can work in the office, and then amuse yourself, and then study on top of all. You can't; the human frame won't stand it. Do one thing or the other – amuse yourself or learn Latin; but don't try to do both.'

Then he got a place in London, at a hundred and twenty a year. This seemed a fabulous sum. His mother doubted almost whether to rejoice or to grieve.

'They want me in Lime Street on Monday week, mother,' he cried, his eyes blazing as he read the letter. Mrs Morel felt everything go silent inside her. He read the letter: ' "And will you reply by Thursday whether you accept. Yours faithfully — " They want me, mother, at a hundred and twenty a year, and don't even ask to see me. Didn't I tell you I could do it! Think of me in London! And I can give you twenty pounds a year, mater. We s'll all be rolling in money.'

'We shall, my son,' she answered sadly.

It never occurred to him that she might be more hurt at his going away than glad of his success. Indeed, as the days drew near for his departure, her heart began to close and grow dreary with despair. She loved him so much! More than that, she hoped in him so much. Almost she lived by him. She liked to do things for him: she liked to put a cup for his tea and to iron his collars, of which he was so proud. It was a joy to her to have him proud of his collars. There was no laundry. So she used to rub away at them with her little convex iron, to polish them, till they shone from the sheer pressure of her arm. Now she would not do it for him. Now he was going away. She felt almost as if he were going as well out of her heart. He did not seem to leave her inhabited with himself. That was the grief and the pain to her. He took nearly all himself away.

A few days before his departure – he was just twenty – he burned his love-letters. They had hung on a file at the top of the kitchen cupboard. From some of them he had read extracts to his mother. Some of them she had taken the trouble to read herself. But most were too trivial.

Now, on the Saturday morning he said, 'Come on, Postle, let's go through my letters, and you can have the birds and flowers.'

Mrs Morel had done her Saturday's work on the Friday, because he was having a last day's holiday. She was making him a rice cake, which he loved, to take with him. He was scarcely conscious that she was so miserable.

He took the first letter off the file. It was mauve-tinted, and had purple and green thistles. William sniffed the page.

'Nice scent! Smell.'

And he thrust the sheet under Paul's nose.

'Um!' said Paul, breathing in. 'What d'you call it? Smell, mother.'

His mother ducked her small, fine nose down to the paper.

'I don't want to smell their rubbish,' she said, sniffing.

'This girl's father,' said William, 'is as rich as Croesus. He owns property without end. She calls me Lafayette, because I know French. "You will see, I've forgiven you" – I like *her* forgiving me. "I told mother about you this morning, and she will have much pleasure if you come to tea on Sunday, but she will have to get father's consent also. I sincerely hope he will agree. I will let you know how it transpires. If, however, you – "'

'Let you know how it what?' interrupted Mrs Morel.

' "Transpires" – oh yes!'

' "Transpires!" ' repeated Mrs Morel mockingly. 'I thought she was so well educated!'

William felt slightly uncomfortable, and abandoned this maiden, giving Paul the corner with the thistles. He continued to read extracts from his letters, some of which amused his mother, some of which saddened her and made her anxious for him.

'My lad,' she said, 'they're very wise. They know they've only got to flatter your vanity, and you press up to them like a dog that has its head scratched.'

'Well, they can't go on scratching for ever,' he replied. 'And when they've done, I trot away.'

'But one day you'll find a string round your neck that you can't pull off,' she answered.

'Not me! I'm equal to any of 'em, mater, they needn't flatter themselves.'

'You flatter *yourself*,' she said quietly.

Soon there was a heap of twisted black pages, all that remained of the file of scented letters, except that Paul had thirty or forty pretty tickets from the corners of the notepaper – swallows and forget-me-nots and ivy sprays. And William went to London, to start a new life.

CHAPTER 4

The Young Life of Paul

Paul would be built like his mother, slightly and rather small. His fair hair went reddish, and then dark brown; his eyes were grey. He was a pale, quiet child, with eyes that seemed to listen, and with a full, dropping underlip.

As a rule he seemed old for his years. He was so conscious of what other people felt, particularly his mother. When she fretted he understood, and could have no peace. His soul seemed always attentive to her.

As he grew older he became stronger. William was too far removed from him to accept him as a companion. So the smaller boy belonged at first almost entirely to Annie. She was a tomboy and a 'flybie-skybie', as her mother called her. But she was intensely fond of her second brother. So Paul was towed round at the heels of Annie, sharing her game. She raced wildly at lerky with the other young wild cats of the Bottoms. And always Paul flew beside her, living her share of the game, having as yet no part of his own. He was quiet and not noticeable. But his sister adored him. He always seemed to care for things if she wanted him to.

She had a big doll of which she was fearfully proud, though not so fond. So she laid the doll on the sofa, and covered it with an antimacassar, to sleep. Then she forgot it. Meantime Paul must practise jumping off the sofa arm. So he jumped crash into the face of the hidden doll. Annie rushed up, uttered a loud wail, and sat down to weep a dirge. Paul remained quite still.

'You couldn't tell it was there, mother; you couldn't tell it was there,' he repeated over and over. So long as Annie wept for the doll he sat helpless with misery. Her grief wore itself out. She forgave her brother – he was so much upset. But a day or two afterwards she was shocked.

'Let's make a sacrifice of Arabella,' he said. 'Let's burn her.'

She was horrified, yet rather fascinated. She wanted to see what the boy would do. He made an altar of bricks, pulled some of the shavings out of Arabella's body, put the waxen fragments into the hollow face, poured on a little paraffin, and set the whole thing alight. He watched with wicked satisfaction the drops of wax melt off the broken forehead of Arabella, and drop like sweat into the flame. So long as the stupid big doll burned he rejoiced in silence. At the end he poked among the embers with a stick, fished out the arms and legs, all blackened, and smashed them under stones.

'That's the sacrifice of Missis Arabella,' he said. 'An' I'm glad there's nothing left of her.'

Which disturbed Annie inwardly, although she could say nothing. He seemed to hate the doll so intensely, because he had broken it.

All the children, but particularly Paul, were peculiarly *against* their father, along with their mother. Morel continued to bully and to drink. He had periods, months at a time, when he made the whole life of the family a misery. Paul never forgot coming home from the Band of Hope one Monday evening and finding his mother with her eye swollen and discoloured, his father standing on the hearthrug, feet astride, his head down, and William, just home from work, glaring at his father. There was a silence as the young children entered, but none of the elders looked round.

William was white to the lips, and his fists were clenched. He waited until the children were silent, watching with children's rage and hate; then he said, 'You coward, you daren't do it when I was in.'

But Morel's blood was up. He swung round on his son. William was bigger, but Morel was hard-muscled, and mad with fury.

'Dossn't I?' he shouted. 'Dossn't I? Ha'e much more o' thy chelp, my young jockey, an' I'll rattle my fist about thee. Ay, an' I sholl that, dost see.'

Morel crouched at the knees and showed his fist in an ugly, almost beast-like fashion. William was white with rage.

'Will yer?' he said, quiet and intense. 'It 'ud be the last time, though.'

Morel danced a little nearer, crouching, drawing back his fist to strike. William put his fists ready. A light came into his blue eyes, almost like a laugh. He watched his father. Another word, and the men would have begun to fight. Paul hoped they would. The three children sat pale on the sofa.

'Stop it, both of you,' cried Mrs Morel in a hard voice. 'We've had enough for *one* night. And *you*,' she said, turning on to her husband, 'look at your children!'

Morel glanced at the sofa.

'Look at the children, you nasty little bitch!' he sneered. 'Why, what have *I* done to the children, I should like to know? But they're like yourself; you've put 'em up to your own tricks and nasty ways – you've learned 'em in it, you 'ave.'

She refused to answer him. No one spoke. After a while he threw his boots under the table and went to bed.

'Why didn't you let me have a go at him?' said William, when his father was upstairs. 'I could easily have beaten him.'

'A nice thing – your own father,' she replied.

'*Father!*' repeated William. 'Call *him my* father?'

'Well, he is – and so – '

'But why don't you let me settle him? I could do, easily.'

'The idea!' she cried. 'It hasn't come to *that* yet.'

'No,' he said, 'it's come to worse. Look at yourself. *Why* didn't you let me give it him?'

'Because I couldn't bear it, so never think of it,' she cried quickly.

And the children went to bed, miserably.

When William was growing up, the family moved from the Bottoms to a house on the brow of the hill, commanding a view of the valley, which spread out like a convex cockleshell, or a clamp-shell, before it. In front of the house was a huge old ash tree. The west wind, sweeping from Derbyshire, caught the houses with full force, and the tree shrieked again. Morel liked it.

'It's music,' he said. 'It sends me to sleep.'

But Paul and Arthur and Annie hated it. To Paul it became almost a demoniacal noise. The winter of their first year in the new house their father was very bad. The children played in the street, on the brim of the wide, dark valley, until eight o'clock. Then they went to bed. Their mother sat sewing below. Having such a great space in front of the house gave the children a feeling of night, of vastness, and of terror. This terror came in from the shrieking of the tree and the anguish of the home discord. Often Paul would wake up, after he had been asleep a long time, aware of thuds downstairs. Instantly he was wide awake. Then he heard the booming shouts of his father, come home nearly drunk, then the sharp replies of his mother, then the bang, bang of his father's fist on the table, and the nasty snarling shout as the man's voice got higher. And then the whole was drowned in a piercing medley of shrieks and cries from the great, windswept ash tree. The children lay silent in suspense, waiting for a lull in the wind to hear what their father was doing. He might hit their mother again. There was a feeling of horror, a kind of bristling in the darkness, and a sense of blood. They lay with their hearts in the grip of an intense anguish. The wind came through the tree fiercer and fiercer. All the cords of the great harp hummed, whistled, and shrieked. And then came the horror of the sudden silence, silence everywhere, outside and downstairs. What was it? Was it a silence of blood? What had he done?

The children lay and breathed the darkness. And then, at last, they heard their father throw down his boots and tramp upstairs in his stockinged feet. Still they listened. Then at last, if the wind allowed, they heard the water of the tap drumming into the kettle, which their mother was filling for morning, and they could go to sleep in peace.

So they were happy in the morning – happy, very happy playing, dancing at night round the lonely lamp-post in the midst of the darkness. But they had one tight place of anxiety in their hearts, one darkness in their eyes, which showed all their lives.

Paul hated his father. As a boy he had a fervent private religion.

'Make him stop drinking,' he prayed every night. 'Lord, let my father die,' he prayed very often. 'Let him not be killed at pit,' he prayed when, after tea, the father did not come home from work.

That was another time when the family suffered intensely. The children came from school and had their teas. On the hob the big black saucepan was simmering, the stew-jar was in the oven, ready for Morel's dinner. He was expected at five o'clock. But for months he would stop and drink every night on his way from work.

In the winter nights, when it was cold, and grew dark early, Mrs Morel would put a brass candlestick on the table, light a tallow candle to save the gas. The children finished their bread-and-butter, or dripping, and were ready to go out to play. But if Morel had not come they faltered. The sense of his sitting in all his pit-dirt, drinking, after a long day's work, not coming home and eating and washing, but sitting, getting drunk, on an empty stomach, made Mrs Morel unable to bear herself. From her the feeling was transmitted to the other children. She never suffered alone any more; the children suffered with her.

Paul went out to play with the rest. Down in the great trough of twilight, tiny clusters of lights burned where the pits were. A few last colliers straggled up the dim field-path. The lamp-lighter came along. No more colliers came. Darkness shut down over the valley; work was gone. It was night.

Then Paul ran anxiously into the kitchen. The one candle still burned on the table, the big fire glowed red. Mrs Morel sat alone. On the hob the saucepan steamed; the dinner-plate lay waiting on the table. All the room was full of the sense of waiting, waiting for the man who was sitting in his pit-dirt, dinnerless, some mile away from home, across the darkness, drinking himself drunk. Paul stood in the doorway.

'Has my dad come?' he asked.

'You can see he hasn't,' said Mrs Morel, cross with the futility of the question.

Then the boy dawdled about near his mother. They shared the same anxiety. Presently Mrs Morel went out and strained the potatoes.

'They're ruined and black,' she said; 'but what do I care?'

Not many words were spoken. Paul almost hated his mother for suffering because his father did not come home from work.

'What do you bother yourself for?' he said. 'If he wants to stop and get drunk, why don't you let him?'

'Let him!' flashed Mrs Morel. 'You may well say "let him".'

She knew that the man who stops on the way home from work is on a quick way to ruining himself and his home. The children were yet young, and depended on the breadwinner. William gave her the sense of relief, providing her at last with someone to turn to if Morel failed. But the tense atmosphere of the room on these waiting evenings was the same.

The minutes ticked away. At six o'clock still the cloth lay on the table, still the dinner stood waiting, still the same sense of anxiety and expectation in the room. The boy could not stand it any longer. He could not go out and play. So he ran in to Mrs Inger, next door but one, for her to talk to him. She had no children. Her husband was good to her, but was in a shop, and came home late. So, when she saw the head at the door, she called, 'Come in, Paul.'

The two sat talking for some time, when suddenly the boy rose, saying, 'Well, I'll be going and seeing if my mother wants an errand doing.'

He pretended to be perfectly cheerful, and did not tell his friend what ailed him. Then he ran indoors.

Morel at these times came in churlish and hateful.

'This is a nice time to come home,' said Mrs Morel.

'Wha's it matter to yo' what time I come whoam?' he shouted.

And everybody in the house was still, because he was dangerous. He ate his food in the most brutal manner possible, and, when he had done, pushed all the pots in a heap away from him, to lay his arms on the table. Then he went to sleep.

Paul hated his father so. The collier's small, mean head, with its black hair slightly soiled with grey, lay on the bare arms, and the face, dirty and inflamed, with a fleshy nose and thin, paltry brows, was turned sideways, asleep with beer and weariness and nasty temper. If anyone entered suddenly, or a noise were made, the man looked up and shouted, 'I'll lay my fist about thy y'ead, I'm tellin' thee, if tha doesna stop that clatter! Dost hear?'

And the two last words, shouted in a bullying fashion, usually at Annie, made the family writhe with hate of the man.

He was shut out from all family affairs. No one told him anything. The children, alone with their mother, told her all about the day's happenings, everything. Nothing had really taken place in them until it was told to their mother. But as soon as the father came in, everything stopped. He was like the scotch in the smooth, happy machinery of the home. And he was always aware of this fall of silence on his entry, the shutting off of life, the unwelcome. But now it was gone too far to alter.

He would dearly have liked the children to talk to him, but they could not. Sometimes Mrs Morel would say, 'You ought to tell your father.'

Paul won a prize in a competition in a child's paper. Everybody was highly jubilant.

'Now you'd better tell your father when he comes in,' said Mrs Morel. 'You know how he carries on and says he's never told anything.'

'All right,' said Paul. But he would almost rather have forfeited the prize than have to tell his father.

'I've won a prize in a competition, dad,' he said.

Morel turned round to him.

'Have you, my boy? What sort of a competition?'

'Oh, nothing – about famous women.'

'And how much is the prize, then, as you've got?'

'It's a book.'

'Oh, indeed!'

'About birds.'

'Hm – hm!'

And that was all. Conversation was impossible between the father and any other member of the family. He was an outsider. He had denied the God in him.

The only times when he entered again into the life of his own people was when he worked, and was happy at work. Sometimes, in the evening, he cobbled the boots or mended the kettle or his pit-bottle. Then he always wanted several attendants, and the children enjoyed it. They united with him in the work, in the actual doing of something, when he was his real self again.

He was a good workman, dexterous, and one who, when he was in a good humour, always sang. He had whole periods, months, almost years, of friction and nasty temper. Then sometimes he was jolly again. It was nice to see him run with a piece of red-hot iron into the scullery, crying, 'Out of my road – out of my road!'

Then he hammered the soft, red-glowing stuff on his iron goose, and made the shape he wanted. Or he sat absorbed for a moment, soldering. Then the children watched with joy as the metal sank suddenly molten, and was shoved about against the nose of the soldering-iron, while the room was full of a scent of burnt resin and hot tin, and Morel was silent and intent for a minute. He always sang when he mended boots because of the jolly sound of hammering. And he was rather happy when he sat putting great patches on his moleskin pit-trousers, which he would often do, considering them too dirty, and the stuff too hard, for his wife to mend.

But the best time for the young children was when he made fuses. Morel fetched a sheaf of long sound wheat-straws from the attic. These he cleaned with his hand, till each one gleamed like a stalk of gold, after which he cut the straws into lengths of about six inches, leaving, if he could, a notch at the bottom of each piece. He always had a beautifully sharp knife that could cut a straw clean without hurting it. Then he set in the middle of the table a heap of gunpowder, a little pile of black grains upon the white-scrubbed board. He made and trimmed the straws while Paul and Annie filled and plugged them. Paul loved to see the black grains trickle down a crack in his palm into the mouth of the straw, peppering jollily downwards till the straw was full. Then he bunged up the mouth with a bit of soap – which he got on his thumbnail from a pat in a saucer – and the straw was finished.

'Look dad!' he said.

'That's right, my beauty,' replied Morel, who was peculiarly lavish of endearments to his second son. Paul popped the fuse into the powder-tin, ready for the morning, when Morel would take it to the pit, and use it to fire a shot that would blast the coal down.

Meantime Arthur, still fond of his father, would lean on the arm of Morel's chair, and say, 'Tell us about down pit, daddy.'

This Morel loved to do.

'Well, there's one little 'oss – we call 'im Taffy,' he would begin. 'An' he's a fawce un!'

Morel had a warm way of telling a story. He made one feel Taffy's cunning.

'He's a brown un,' he would answer, 'an' not very high. Well, he comes i' th' stall wi' a rattle, an' then yo' 'ear 'im sneeze.

' " 'Ello, Taff," you say, "what art sneezin' for? Bin ta'ein' some snuff?"

'An' 'e sneezes again. Then he slives up an' shoves 'is 'ead on yer, that cadin'.

' "What's want, Taff?" yo' say.'

'And what does he?' Arthur always asked.

'He wants a bit o' bacca, my duckey.'

This story of Taffy would go on interminably, and everybody loved it.

Or sometimes it was a new tale.

'An' what dost think, my darlin'? When I went to put my coat on at snap-time, what should go runnin' up my arm but a mouse.

' "Hey up, theer!" I shouts.

'An' I wor just in time ter get 'im by th' tail.'

'And did you kill it?'

'I did, for they're a nuisance. The place is fair snied wi' 'em.'

'An' what do they live on?'

'The corn as the 'osses drops – an' they'll get in your pocket an' eat your snap, if you'll let 'em – no matter where yo' hing your coat – the slivin', nibblin' little nuisances, for they are.'

These happy evenings could not take place unless Morel had some job to do. And then he always went to bed very early, often before the children. There was nothing remaining for him to stay up for, when he had finished tinkering, and had skimmed the headlines of the newspaper.

And the children felt secure when their father was in bed. They lay and talked softly awhile. Then they started as the lights went suddenly sprawling over the ceiling from the lamps that swung in the hands of the colliers tramping by outside, going to take the nine o'clock shift. They listened to the voices of the men, imagined them dipping down into the dark valley. Sometimes they went to the window and watched the three or four lamps growing tinier and tinier, swaying down the fields in the darkness. Then it was a joy to rush back to bed and cuddle closely in the warmth.

Paul was rather a delicate boy, subject to bronchitis. The others were all quite strong; so this was another reason for his mother's difference in feeling for him. One day he came home at dinner-time feeling ill. But it was not a family to make any fuss.

'What's the matter with *you*?' his mother asked sharply.

'Nothing,' he replied.

But he ate no dinner.

'If you eat no dinner, you're not going to school,' she said.

'Why?' he asked.

'That's why.'

So after dinner he lay down on the sofa, on the warm chintz cushions the children loved. Then he fell into a kind of doze. That afternoon Mrs Morel was ironing. She listened to the small, restless noise the boy made in his throat as she worked. Again rose in her heart the old, almost weary feeling towards him. She had never expected him to live. And yet he had a great vitality in his young body. Perhaps it would have been a little relief to her if he had died. She always felt a mixture of anguish in her love for him.

He, in his semi-conscious sleep, was vaguely aware of the clatter of the iron on the iron-stand, of the faint thud, thud on the ironing-board. Once roused, he opened his eyes to see his mother standing on the hearthrug with the hot iron near her cheek, listening, as it were, to the heat. Her still face, with the mouth closed tight from suffering and disillusion and self-denial, and her nose the smallest bit on one side, and her blue eyes so young, quick, and warm, made his heart contract with love. When she was quiet, so, she looked brave and rich with life, but as if she had been done out of her rights. It hurt the boy keenly, this feeling about her that she had never had her life's fulfilment: and his own incapability to make up to her hurt him with a sense of impotence, yet made him patiently dogged inside. It was his childish aim.

She spat on the iron, and a little ball of spit bounded, raced off the dark, glossy surface. Then, kneeling, she rubbed the iron on the sack lining of the hearthrug vigorously. She was warm in the ruddy firelight. Paul loved the way she crouched and put her head on one side. Her movements were light and quick. It was always a pleasure to watch her. Nothing she ever did, no movement she ever made, could have been found fault with by her children. The room was warm and full of the scent of hot linen. Later on the clergyman came and talked softly with her.

Paul was laid up with an attack of bronchitis. He did not mind much. What happened happened, and it was no good kicking against the pricks. He loved the evenings, after eight o'clock, when the light was put out, and he could watch the fire-flames spring over the darkness of the walls and ceiling; could watch huge shadows waving and tossing, till the room seemed full of men who battled silently.

On retiring to bed, the father would come into the sick-room. He was always very gentle if anyone were ill. But he disturbed the atmosphere for the boy.

'Are ter asleep, my darlin'?' Morel asked softly.

'No; is my mother comin'?'

'She's just finishin' foldin' the clothes. Do you want anything?' Morel rarely 'thee'd' his son.

'I don't want nothing. But how long will she be?'

'Not long, my duckie.'

The father waited undecidedly on the hearthrug for a moment or two. He felt his son did not want him. Then he went to the top of the stairs and said to his wife, 'This childt's axin' for thee; how long art goin' to be?'

'Until I've finished, good gracious! Tell him to go to sleep.'

'She says you're to go to sleep,' the father repeated gently to Paul.

'Well, I want *her* to come,' insisted the boy.

'He says he can't go off till you come,' Morel called downstairs.

'Eh, dear! I shan't be long. And do stop shouting downstairs. There's the other children –'

Then Morel came again, and crouched before the bedroom fire. He loved a fire dearly.

'She says she won't be long,' he said.

He loitered about indefinitely. The boy began to get feverish with irritation. His father's presence seemed to aggravate all his sick impatience. At last Morel, after having stood looking at his son awhile, said softly, 'Good-night, my darling.'

'Good-night,' Paul replied, turning round in relief to be alone.

Paul loved to sleep with his mother. Sleep is still most perfect, in spite of hygienists, when it is shared with a beloved. The warmth, the security and peace of soul, the utter comfort from the touch of the other, knits the sleep, so that it takes the body and soul completely in its healing. Paul lay against her and slept, and got better; whilst she, always a bad sleeper, fell later on into a profound sleep that seemed to give her faith.

In convalescence he would sit up in bed, see the fluffy horses feeding at the troughs in the field, scattering their hay on the trodden yellow snow; watch the miners troop home – small, black figures trailing slowly in gangs across the white field. Then the night came up in dark blue vapour from the snow.

In convalescence everything was wonderful. The snowflakes, suddenly arriving on the window-pane, clung there a moment like swallows, then were gone, and a drop of water was crawling down the glass. The snowflakes whirled round the corner of the house, like pigeons dashing by. Away across the valley the little black train crawled doubtfully over the great whiteness.

While they were so poor, the children were delighted if they could do anything to help economically. Annie and Paul and Arthur went out early in the morning, in summer, looking for mushrooms, hunting through the wet grass, from which the larks were rising, for the white-skinned, wonderful naked bodies crouched secretly in the green. And if they got half a pound they felt exceedingly happy: there was the joy of finding something, the joy of accepting something straight from the hand of Nature, and the joy of contributing to the family exchequer.

But the most important harvest, after gleaning for frumenty, was the black-berries. Mrs Morel must buy fruit for puddings on the Saturdays; also she liked blackberries. So Paul and Arthur scoured the coppices and woods and old quarries, so long as a blackberry was to be found, every weekend going on their search. In that region of mining villages blackberries became a comparative rarity. But Paul hunted far and wide. He loved being out in the country, among the bushes. But he also could not bear to go home to his mother empty. That, he felt, would disappoint her, and he would have died rather.

'Good gracious!' she would exclaim as the lads came in late, and tired to death, and hungry, 'wherever have you been?'

'Well,' replied Paul, 'there wasn't any, so we went over Misk Hills. And look here, our mother!'

She peeped into the basket.

'Now, those are fine ones!' she exclaimed.

'And there's over two pounds – isn't there over two pounds?'

She tried the basket.

'Yes,' she answered doubtfully.

Then Paul fished out a little spray. He always brought her one spray, the best he could find.

'Pretty!' she said, in a curious tone, of a woman accepting a love-token.

The boy walked all day, went miles and miles, rather than own himself beaten and come home to her empty-handed. She never realised this, whilst he was young. She was a woman who waited for her children to grow up. And William occupied her chiefly.

But when William went to Nottingham, and was not so much at home, the mother made a companion of Paul. The latter was unconsciously jealous of his brother, and William was jealous of him. At the same time, they were good friends.

Mrs Morel's intimacy with her second son was more subtle and fine, perhaps not so passionate as with her eldest. It was the rule that Paul should fetch the money on Friday afternoons. The colliers of the five pits were paid on Fridays, but not individually. All the earnings of each stall were put down to the chief butty, as contractor, and he divided the wages again, either in the public-house or in his own home. So that the children could fetch the money, school closed early on Friday afternoons. Each of the Morel children – William, then Annie, then Paul – had fetched the money on Friday afternoons, until they went themselves to work. Paul used to set off at half-past three, with a little calico bag in his pocket. Down all the paths, women, girls, children, and men were seen trooping to the offices.

These offices were quite handsome: a new, red-brick building, almost like a mansion, standing in its own well-kept grounds at the end of Greenhill Lane. The waiting-room was the hall, a long, bare room paved with blue brick, and having a seat all round, against the wall. Here sat the colliers in their pit-dirt. They had come up early. The women and children usually loitered about on the red gravel paths. Paul always examined the grass border, and the big grass bank, because in it grew tiny pansies and tiny forget-me-nots. There was a sound of many voices. The women had on their Sunday hats. The girls chattered loudly. Little dogs ran here and there. The green shrubs were silent all around.

Then from inside came the cry, 'Spinney Park – Spinney Park'. All the folk for Spinney Park trooped inside. When it was time for Bretty to be paid, Paul went in among the crowd. The pay-room was quite small. A counter went across, dividing it into half. Behind the counter stood two men – Mr Braithwaite and his clerk, Mr Winterbottom. Mr Braithwaite was large, somewhat of the stern patriarch in appearance, having a rather thin white beard. He was usually muffled in an enormous silk neckerchief, and right up to the hot summer a huge fire burned in the open grate. No window was open. Sometimes in winter the air scorched the throats of the people, coming in from the freshness. Mr Winterbottom was rather small and fat, and very bald. He made remarks that were not witty, whilst his chief launched forth patriarchal admonitions against the colliers.

The room was crowded with miners in their pit-dirt, men who had been home and changed, and women, and one or two children, and usually a dog. Paul was quite small, so it was often his fate to be jammed behind the legs of the men, near the fire which scorched him. He knew the order of the names – they went according to stall number.

'Holliday,' came the ringing voice of Mr Braithwaite. Then Mrs Holliday stepped silently forward, was paid, drew aside.

'Bower – John Bower.'

A boy stepped to the counter. Mr Braithwaite, large and irascible, glowered at him over his spectacles.

'John Bower!' he repeated.

'It's me,' said the boy.

'Why, you used to 'ave a different nose than that,' said glossy Mr Winterbottom, peering over the counter. The people tittered, thinking of John Bower senior.

'How is it your father's not come?' said Mr Braithwaite, in a large and magisterial voice.

'He's badly,' piped the boy.

'You should tell him to keep off the drink,' pronounced the great cashier.

'An' niver mind if he puts his foot through yer,' said a mocking voice from behind.

All the men laughed. The large and important cashier looked down at his next sheet.

'Fred Pilkington!' he called, quite indifferent.

Mr Braithwaite was an important shareholder in the firm.

Paul knew his turn was next but one, and his heart began to beat. He was pushed against the chimney-piece. His calves were burning. But he did not hope to get through the wall of men.

'Walter Morel!' came the ringing voice.

'Here!' piped Paul, small and inadequate.

'Morel – Walter Morel!' the cashier repeated, his finger and thumb on the invoice, ready to pass on.

Paul was suffering convulsions of self-consciousness, and could not or would not shout. The backs of the men obliterated him. Then Mr Winterbottom came to the rescue.

'He's here. Where is he? Morel's lad?'

The fat, red, bald little man peered round with keen eyes. He pointed at the fireplace. The colliers looked round, moved aside, and disclosed the boy.

'Here he is!' said Mr Winterbottom.

Paul went to the counter.

'Seventeen pounds, eleven and fivepence. Why don't you shout up when you're called?' said Mr Braithwaite. He banged on to the invoice a five-pound bag of silver, then, in a delicate and pretty movement, picked up a little ten-pound column of gold, and plumped it beside the silver. The gold slid in a bright stream over the paper. The cashier finished counting off the money; the boy dragged the whole down the counter to Mr Winterbottom, to whom the stoppages for rent and tools must be paid. Here he suffered again.

'Sixteen-an'-six,' said Mr Winterbottom.

The lad was too much upset to count. He pushed forward some loose silver and half a sovereign.

'How much do you think you've given me?' asked Mr Winterbottom.

The boy looked at him, but said nothing. He had not the faintest notion.

'Haven't you got a tongue in your head?'

Paul bit his lip, and pushed forward some more silver.

'Don't they teach you to count at the Board-school?' he asked.

'Nowt but Algibbra an' French,' said a collier.

'An' cheek an' impidence,' said another.

Paul was keeping someone waiting. With trembling fingers he got his money into the bag and slid out. He suffered the tortures of the damned on these occasions.

His relief, when he got outside, and was walking along the Mansfield Road, was infinite. On the park wall the mosses were green. There were some gold and some white fowls pecking under the apple trees of an orchard. The colliers were walking home in a stream. The boy went near the wall, self-consciously. He knew many of the men, but could not recognise them in their dirt. And this was a new torture to him.

When he got down to the New Inn, at Bretty, his father was not yet come. Mrs Wharmby, the landlady, knew him. His grandmother, Morel's mother, had been Mrs Wharmby's friend.

'Your father's not come yet,' said the landlady, in the peculiar half-scornful, half-patronising voice of a woman who talks chiefly to grown men. 'Sit you down.'

Paul sat down on the edge of the bench in the bar. Some colliers were 'reckoning' – sharing out their money – in a corner; others came in. They all glanced at the boy without speaking. At last Morel came; brisk, and with something of an air, even in his blackness.

'Hello!' he said rather tenderly to his son. 'Have you bested me? Shall you have a drink of something?'

Paul and all the children were bred up fierce anti-alcoholists, and he would have suffered more in drinking a lemonade before all the men than in having a tooth drawn.

The landlady looked at him *de haut en bas*, rather pitying, and at the same time resenting, his clear, fierce morality. Paul went home, glowering. He entered the house silently. Friday was baking day, and there was usually a hot bun. His mother put it before him.

Suddenly he turned on her in a fury, his eyes flashing, 'I'm *not* going to the office any more,' he said.

'Why, what's the matter?' his mother asked in surprise. His sudden rages rather amused her.

'I'm *not* going any more,' he declared.

'Oh, very well, tell your father so.'

He chewed his bun as if he hated it.

'I'm not – I'm not going to fetch the money.'

'Then one of Carlin's children can go; they'd be glad enough of the sixpence,' said Mrs Morel.

This sixpence was Paul's only income. It mostly went in buying birthday presents; but it was an income, and he treasured it. But – !

'They can have it, then!' he said. 'I don't want it.'

'Oh, very well,' said his mother. 'But you needn't bully me about it.'

'They're hateful, and common, and hateful, they are, and I'm not going any more. Mr Braithwaite drops his "h's", an' Mr Winterbottom says "You was". '

'And is that why you won't go any more?' smiled Mrs Morel.

The boy was silent for some time. His face was pale, his eyes dark and furious. His mother moved about at her work, taking no notice of him.

'They always stan' in front of me, so's I can't get out,' he said.

'Well, my lad, you've only to ask them,' she replied.

'An' then Alfred Winterbottom says, "What do they teach you at the Board-school?" '

'They never taught *him* much,' said Mrs Morel, 'that is a fact – neither manners nor wit – and his cunning he was born with.'

So, in her own way, she soothed him. His ridiculous hypersensitiveness made her heart ache. And sometimes the fury in his eyes roused her, made her sleeping soul lift up its head a moment, surprised.

'What was the cheque?' she asked.

'Seventeen pounds, eleven and fivepence, and sixteen-and-six stoppages,' replied the boy. 'It's a good week; and only five shillings stoppages for my father.'

So she was able to calculate how much her husband had earned, and could call him to account if he gave her short money. Morel always kept to himself the secret of the week's amount.

Friday was the baking night and market night. It was the rule that Paul should stay at home and bake. He loved to stop in and draw or read; he was very fond of drawing. Annie always 'gallivanted' on Friday nights; Arthur was enjoying himself as usual. So the boy remained alone.

Mrs Morel loved her marketing. In the tiny market-place on the top of the hill, where four roads, from Nottingham and Derby, Ilkeston and Mansfield, meet, many stalls were erected. Brakes ran in from surrounding villages. The market-place was full of women, the streets packed with men. It was amazing to see so many men everywhere in the streets.

Mrs Morel usually quarrelled with her lace woman, sympathised with her fruit man – who was a gabey, but his wife was a bad un – laughed with the fish man – who was a scamp but so droll – put the linoleum man in his place, was cold with the odd-wares man, and only went to the crockery man when she was driven – or drawn by the cornflowers on a little dish; then she was coldly polite.

'I wondered how much that little dish was,' she said.

'Sevenpence to you.'

'Thank you.'

She put the dish down and walked away; but she could not leave the market-place without it. Again she went by where the pots lay coldly on the floor, and she glanced at the dish furtively, pretending not to.

She was a little woman, in a bonnet and a black costume. Her bonnet was in its third year; it was a great grievance to Annie.

'Mother!' the girl implored, 'don't wear that nubbly little bonnet.'

'Then what else shall I wear?' replied the mother tartly. 'And I'm sure it's right enough.'

It had started with a tip; then had had flowers; now was reduced to black lace and a bit of jet.

'It looks rather come down,' said Paul. 'Couldn't you give it a pick-me-up?'

'I'll jowl your head for impudence,' said Mrs Morel, and she tied the strings of the black bonnet valiantly under her chin.

She glanced at the dish again. Both she and her enemy, the pot man, had an uncomfortable feeling, as if there were something between them. Suddenly he shouted, 'Do you want it for fivepence?'

She started. Her heart hardened; but then she stooped and took up her dish.

'I'll have it,' she said.

'Yer'll do me the favour, like?' he said. 'Yer'd better spit in it, like yer do when y'ave something give yer.'

Mrs Morel paid him the fivepence in a cold manner.

'I don't see you give it me,' she said. 'You wouldn't let me have it for fivepence if you didn't want to.'

'In this flamin', scrattlin' place you may count yerself lucky if you can give your things away,' he growled.

'Yes; there are bad times, and good,' said Mrs Morel.

But she had forgiven the pot man. They were friends. She dare now finger his pots. So she was happy.

Paul was waiting for her. He loved her home-coming. She was always her best so – triumphant, tired, laden with parcels, feeling rich in spirit. He heard her quick, light step in the entry and looked up from his drawing.

'Oh!' she sighed, smiling at him from the doorway.

'My word, you *are* loaded!' he exclaimed, putting down his brush.

'I am!' she gasped. 'That brazen Annie said she'd meet me. *Such* a weight!'

She dropped her string bag and her packages on the table.

'Is the bread done?' she asked, going to the oven.

'The last one is soaking,' he replied. 'You needn't look, I've not forgotten it.'

'Oh, that pot man!' she said, closing the oven door. 'You know what a wretch I've said he was? Well, I don't think he's quite so bad.'

'Don't you?'

The boy was attentive to her. She took off her little black bonnet.

'No. I think he can't make any money – well, it's everybody's cry alike nowadays – and it makes him disagreeable.'

'It would *me*,' said Paul.

'Well, one can't wonder at it. And he let me have – how much do you think he let me have *this* for?'

She took the dish out of its rag of newspaper, and stood looking on it with joy.

'Show me!' said Paul.

The two stood together gloating over the dish.

'I *love* cornflowers on things,' said Paul.

'Yes, and I thought of the teapot you bought me – '

'One-and three,' said Paul.

'Fivepence!'

'It's not enough, mother.'

'No. Do you know, I fairly sneaked off with it. But I'd been extravagant, I couldn't afford any more. And he needn't have let me have it if he hadn't wanted to.'

'No, he needn't, need he,' said Paul, and the two comforted each other from the fear of having robbed the pot man.

'We c'n have stewed fruit in it,' said Paul.

'Or custard, or a jelly,' said his mother.

'Or radishes and lettuce,' said he.

'Don't forget that bread,' she said, her voice bright with glee.

Paul looked in the oven; tapped the loaf on the base.

'It's done,' he said, giving it to her.

She tapped it also.

'Yes,' she replied, going to unpack her bag. 'Oh, and I'm a wicked, extravagant woman. I know I s'll come to want.'

He hopped to her side eagerly, to see her latest extravagance. She unfolded another lump of newspaper and disclosed some roots of pansies and of crimson daisies.

'Four penn'orth!' she moaned.

'How *cheap*!' he cried.

'Yes, but I couldn't afford it *this* week of all weeks.'

'But lovely!' he cried.

'Aren't they!' she exclaimed, giving way to pure joy. 'Paul, look at this yellow one, isn't it – and a face just like an old man!'

'Just!' cried Paul, stooping to sniff. 'And smells that nice! But he's a bit splashed.'

He ran in the scullery, came back with the flannel, and carefully washed the pansy.

'*Now* look at him now he's wet!' he said.

'Yes!' she exclaimed, brimful of satisfaction.

The children of Scargill Street felt quite select. At the end where the Morels lived there were not many young things. So the few were more united. Boys and girls played together, the girls joining in the fights and the rough games, the boys taking part in the dancing games and rings and make-believe of the girls.

Annie and Paul and Arthur loved the winter evenings, when it was not wet. They stayed indoors till the colliers were all gone home, till it was thick dark, and the street would be deserted. Then they tied their scarves round their necks, for they scorned overcoats, as all the colliers' children did, and went out. The entry was very dark, and at the end the whole great night opened out, in a hollow, with a little tangle of lights below where Minton pit lay, and another far away opposite for Selby. The farthest tiny lights seemed to stretch out the darkness for ever. The children looked anxiously down the road at the one lamp-post which stood at the end of the field-path. If the little, luminous space were deserted, the two boys felt genuine desolation. They stood with their hands in their pockets under the lamp, turning their backs on the night, quite miserable, watching the dark houses. Suddenly a pinafore under a short coat was seen, and a long-legged girl came flying up.

'Where's Billy Pillins an' your Annie an' Eddie Dakin?'

'I don't know.'

But it did not matter so much – there were three now. They set up a game round the lamp-post, till the others rushed up, yelling. Then the play went fast and furious.

There was only this one lamp-post. Behind was the great scoop of darkness, as if all the night were there. In front, another wide, dark way opened over the hill brow. Occasionally somebody came out of this way and went into the field down the path. In a dozen yards the night had swallowed them. The children played on.

They were brought exceedingly close together owing to their isolation. If a quarrel took place, the whole play was spoilt. Arthur was very touchy, and Billy Pillins – really Philips – was worse. Then Paul had to side with Arthur, and on Paul's side went Alice, while Billy Pillins always had Emmie Limb and Eddie Dakin to back him up. Then the six would fight, hate with a fury of hatred, and flee home in terror. Paul never forgot, after one of these fierce internecine fights, seeing a big red moon lift itself up, slowly, between the waste road over the hilltop, steadily, like a great bird. And he thought of the Bible, that the moon should be turned to blood. And the next day he made haste to be friends with Billy Pillins. And then the wild, intense games went on again under the lamp-post, surrounded by so much darkness. Mrs Morel, going into her parlour, would hear the children singing away:

> 'My shoes are made of Spanish leather
> My socks are made of silk
> I wear a ring on every finger
> I wash myself in milk.'

They sounded so perfectly absorbed in the game as their voices came out of the night, that they had the feel of wild creatures singing. It stirred the mother; and she understood when they came in at eight o'clock, ruddy, with brilliant eyes, and quick, passionate speech.

They all loved the Scargill Street house for its openness, for the great scallop of the world it had in view. On summer evenings the women would stand against the field fence, gossiping, facing the west, watching the sunsets flare quickly out, till the Derbyshire hills ridged across the crimson far away, like the black crest of a newt.

In this summer season the pits never turned full time, particularly the soft coal. Mrs Dakin, who lived next door to Mrs Morel, going to the field fence to shake her hearthrug, would spy men coming slowly up the hill. She saw at once they were colliers. Then she waited, a tall, thin, shrew-faced woman, standing on the hill brow, almost like a menace to the poor colliers who were toiling up. It was only eleven o'clock. From the far-off wooded hills the haze that hangs like fine black crape at the back of a summer morning had not yet dissipated. The first man came to the stile. 'Chock-chock!' went the gate under his thrust.

'What, han' yer knocked off?' cried Mrs Dakin.

'We han, missis.'

'It's a pity as they letn yer goo,' she said sarcastically.

'It is that,' replied the man.

'Nay, you know you're flig to come up again,' she said.

And the man went on. Mrs Dakin, going up her yard, spied Mrs Morel taking the ashes to the ash-pit.

'I reckon Minton's knocked off, missis,' she cried.

'Isn't it sickenin'!' exclaimed Mrs Morel in wrath.

'Ha! But I'n just seed Jont Hutchby.'

'They might as well have saved their shoe-leather,' said Mrs Morel. And both women went indoors disgusted.

The colliers, their faces scarcely blackened, were trooping home again. Morel hated to go back. He loved the sunny morning. But he had gone to pit to work, and to be sent home again spoilt his temper.

'Good gracious, at this time!' exclaimed his wife, as he entered.

'Can I help it, woman?' he shouted.

'And I've not done half enough dinner.'

'Then I'll eat my bit o' snap as I took with me,' he bawled pathetically. He felt ignominious and sore.

And the children, coming home from school, would wonder to see their father eating with his dinner the two thick slices of rather dry and dirty bread-and-butter that had been to pit and back.

'What's my dad eating his snap for now?' asked Arthur.

'I should ha'e it holled at me if I didna,' snorted Morel.

'What a story!' exclaimed his wife.

'An' is it goin' to be wasted?' said Morel. 'I'm not such a extravagant mortal as you lot, with your waste. If I drop a bit of bread at pit, in all the dust an' dirt, I pick it up an' eat it.'

'The mice would eat it,' said Paul. 'It wouldn't be wasted.'

'Good bread an' butter's not for mice, either,' said Morel. 'Dirty or not dirty, I'd eat it rather than it should be wasted.'

'You might leave it for the mice and pay for it out of your next pint,' said Mrs Morel.

'Oh, might I?' he exclaimed.

They were very poor that autumn. William had just gone away to London, and his mother missed his money. He sent ten shillings once or twice, but he had many things to pay for at first. His letters came regularly once a week. He wrote a good deal to his mother, telling her all his life, how he made friends, and was exchanging lessons with a Frenchman, how he enjoyed London. His mother felt again he was remaining to her just as when he was at home. She wrote to him every week her direct, rather witty letters. All day long, as she cleaned the house, she thought of him. He was in London: he would do well. Almost, he was like her knight who wore *her* favour in the battle.

He was coming at Christmas for five days. There had never been such preparations. Paul and Arthur scoured the land for holly and evergreens. Annie made the pretty paper loops in the old-fashioned way. And there was unheard-of extravagance in the larder. Mrs Morel made a big and magnificent cake. Then, feeling queenly, she showed Paul how to blanch almonds. He skinned the long nuts reverently, counting them all, to see not one was lost. It was said that eggs whisked better in a cold place. So the boy stood in the scullery, where the temperature was nearly at freezing-point, and whisked and whisked, and flew in excitement to his mother as the white of egg grew stiffer and more snowy.

'Just look, mother! Isn't it lovely?'

And he balanced a bit on his nose, then blew it in the air.

'Now, don't waste it,' said the mother.

Everybody was mad with excitement. William was coming on Christmas Eve. Mrs Morel surveyed her pantry. There was a big plum cake, and a rice cake, jam tarts, lemon tarts, and mince-pies – two enormous dishes. She was finishing cooking Spanish tarts and cheese-cakes. Everywhere was decorated. The kissing bunch of berried holly hung with bright and glittering things, spun slowly over Mrs Morel's head as she trimmed her little tarts in the kitchen. A great fire roared. There was a scent of cooked pastry. He was due at seven o'clock, but he would be late. The three children had gone to meet him. She was alone. But at a quarter to seven Morel came in again. Neither wife nor husband spoke. He sat in his armchair, quite awkward with excitement, and she quietly went on with her baking. Only by the careful way in which she did things could it be told how much moved she was. The clock ticked on.

'What time dost say he's coming?' Morel asked for the fifth time.

'The train gets in at half-past six,' she replied emphatically.

'Then he'll be here at ten past seven.'

'Eh, bless you, it'll be hours late on the Midland,' she said indifferently. But she hoped, by expecting him late, to bring him early. Morel went down the entry to look for him. Then he came back.

'Goodness, man!' she said. 'You're like an ill-sitting hen.'

'Hadna you better be gettin' him summat t'eat ready?' asked the father.

'There's plenty of time,' she answered.

'There's not so much as I can see on,' he answered, turning crossly in his chair. She began to clear her table. The kettle was singing. They waited and waited.

Meantime the three children were on the platform at Sethley Bridge, on the

Midland main line, two miles from home. They waited one hour. A train came – he was not there. Down the line the red and green lights shone. It was very dark and very cold.

'Ask him if the London train's come,' said Paul to Annie, when they saw a man in a tip cap.

'I'm not,' said Annie. 'You be quiet – he might send us off.'

But Paul was dying for the man to know they were expecting someone by the London train: it sounded so grand. Yet he was much too much scared of broaching any man, let alone one in a peaked cap, to dare to ask. The three children could scarcely go into the waiting-room for fear of being sent away, and for fear something should happen whilst they were off the platform. Still they waited in the dark and cold.

'It's an hour an' a half late,' said Arthur pathetically.

'Well,' said Annie, 'it's Christmas Eve.'

They all grew silent. He wasn't coming. They looked down the darkness of the railway. There was London! It seemed the uttermost of distance. They thought anything might happen if one came from London. They were all too troubled to talk. Cold, and unhappy, and silent, they huddled together on the platform.

At last, after more than two hours, they saw the lights of an engine peering round, away down the darkness. A porter ran out. The children drew back with beating hearts. A great train bound for Manchester drew up. Two doors opened, and from one of them, William. They flew to him. He handed parcels to them cheerily, and immediately began to explain that this great train had stopped for *his* sake at such a small station as Sethley Bridge: it was not booked to stop.

Meanwhile the parents were getting anxious. The table was set, the chop was cooked, everything was ready. Mrs Morel put on her black apron. She was wearing her best dress. Then she sat, pretending to read. The minutes were a torture to her.

'H'm!' said Morel. 'It's an hour an' a ha'ef.'

'And those children waiting!' she said.

'Th' train canna ha' come in yet,' he said.

'I tell you, on Christmas Eve they're *hours* wrong.'

They were both a bit cross with each other, so gnawed with anxiety. The ash tree moaned outside in a cold, raw wind. And all that space of night from London home! Mrs Morel suffered. The slight click of the works inside the clock irritated her. It was getting so late; it was getting unbearable.

At last there was a sound of voices, and a footstep in the entry.

'Ha's here!' cried Morel, jumping up.

Then he stood back. The mother ran a few steps towards the door and waited. There was a rush and a patter of feet, the door burst open. William was there. He dropped his Gladstone bag and took his mother in his arms.

'Mater!' he said.

'My boy!' she cried.

And for two seconds, no longer, she clasped him and kissed him. Then she withdrew and said, trying to be quite normal, 'But how late you are!'

'Aren't I!' he cried, turning to his father. 'Well, dad!'

The two men shook hands.

'Well, my lad!'

Morel's eyes were wet.

'We thought tha'd niver be commin',' he said.

'Oh, I'd come!' exclaimed William.

Then the son turned round to his mother.

'But you look well,' she said proudly, laughing.

'Well!' he exclaimed. 'I should think so – coming home!'

He was a fine fellow, big, straight, and fearless-looking. He looked round at the evergreens and the kissing bunch, and the little tarts that lay in their tins on the hearth.

'By jove! mother, it's not different!' he said, as if in relief.

Everybody was still for a second. Then he suddenly sprang forward, picked a tart from the hearth, and pushed it whole into his mouth.

'Well, did iver you see such a parish oven!' the father exclaimed.

He had brought them endless presents. Every penny he had he had spent on them. There was a sense of luxury overflowing in the house. For his mother there was an umbrella with gold on the pale handle. She kept it to her dying day, and would have lost anything rather than that. Everybody had something gorgeous, and besides, there were pounds of unknown sweets: Turkish delight, crystallised pineapple, and suchlike things which, the children thought, only the splendour of London could provide. And Paul boasted of these sweets among his friends.

'Real pineapple, cut off in slices, and then turned into crystal – fair grand!'

Everybody was mad with happiness in the family. Home was home, and they loved it with a passion of love, whatever the suffering had been. There were parties, there were rejoicings. People came in to see William, to see what difference London had made to him. And they all found him 'such a gentleman, and *such* a fine fellow, my word!'

When he went away again the children retired to various places to weep alone. Morel went to bed in misery, and Mrs Morel felt as if she were numbed by some drug, as if her feelings were paralysed. She loved him passionately.

He was in the office of a lawyer connected with a large shipping firm, and at the midsummer his chief offered him a trip in the Mediterranean on one of the boats, for quite a small cost. Mrs Morel wrote: 'Go, go, my boy. You may never have a chance again, and I should love to think of you cruising there in the Mediterranean almost better than to have you at home.' But William came home for his fortnight's holiday. Not even the Mediterranean, which pulled at all his young man's desire to travel, and at his poor man's wonder at the glamorous south, could take him away when he might come home. That compensated his mother for much.

CHAPTER 5

Paul Launches into Life

Morel was rather a heedless man, careless of danger. So he had endless accidents.
Now, when Mrs Morel heard the rattle of an empty coal-cart cease at her entry-
end, she ran into the parlour to look, expecting almost to see her husband seated
in the waggon, his face grey under his dirt, his body limp and sick with some hurt
or other. If it were he, she would run out to help.

About a year after William went to London, and just after Paul had left
school, before he got work, Mrs Morel was upstairs and her son was painting in
the kitchen – he was very clever with his brush – when there came a knock at the
door. Crossly he put down his brush to go. At the same moment his mother
opened a window upstairs and looked down.

A pit-lad in his dirt stood on the threshold.

'Is this Walter Morel's?' he asked.

'Yes,' said Mrs Morel. 'What is it?'

But she had guessed already.

'Your mester's got hurt,' he said.

'Eh, dear me!' she exclaimed. 'It's a wonder if he hadn't, lad. And what's he
done this time?'

'I don't know for sure, but it's 'is leg somewhere. They ta'ein' 'im ter th'
'ospital.'

'Good gracious me!' she exclaimed. 'Eh, dear, what a one he is! There's not
five minutes of peace, I'll be hanged if there is! His thumb's nearly better, and
now – Did you see him?'

'I seed him at th' bottom. An' I seed 'em bring 'im up in a tub, an' 'e wor in a
dead faint. But he shouted like anythink when Doctor Fraser examined him i'
th' lamp cabin – an' cossed an' swore, an' said as 'e wor goin' to be ta'en
whoam – 'e worn't goin' ter th' 'ospital.'

The boy faltered to an end.

'He *would* want to come home, so that I can have all the bother. Thank you,
my lad. Eh, dear, if I'm not sick – sick and surfeited, I am!'

She came downstairs. Paul had mechanically resumed his painting.

'And it must be pretty bad if they've taken him to the hospital,' she went on.
'But what a *careless* creature he is! *Other* men don't have all these accidents. Yes,
he *would* want to put all the burden on me. Eh, dear, just as we *were* getting easy
a bit at last. Put those things away, there's no time to be painting now. What
time is there a train? I know I s'll have to go trailing to Keston. I s'll have to leave
that bedroom.'

'I can finish it,' said Paul.

'You needn't. I shall catch the seven o'clock back, I should think. Oh, my blessed heart, the fuss and commotion he'll make! And those granite setts at Tinder Hill – he might well call them kidney pebbles – they'll jolt him almost to bits. I wonder why they can't mend them, the state they're in, an' all the men as go across in that ambulance. You'd think they'd have a hospital here. The men bought the ground, and, my sirs, there'd be accidents enough to keep it going. But no, they must trail them ten miles in a slow ambulance to Nottingham. It's a crying shame! Oh, and the fuss he'll make! I know he will! I wonder who's with him. Barker, I s'd think. Poor beggar, he'll wish himself anywhere rather. But he'll look after him, I know. Now there's no telling how long he'll be stuck in that hospital – and won't he hate it! But if it's only his leg it's not so bad.'

All the time she was getting ready. Hurriedly taking off her bodice, she crouched at the boiler while the water ran slowly into her lading-can.

'I wish this boiler was at the bottom of the sea!' she exclaimed, wriggling the handle impatiently. She had very handsome, strong arms, rather surprising on a smallish woman.

Paul cleared away, put on the kettle, and set the table.

'There isn't a train till four-twenty,' he said. 'You've time enough.'

'Oh no I haven't!' she cried, blinking at him over the towel as she wiped her face.

'Yes you have. You must drink a cup of tea at any rate. Should I come with you to Keston?'

'Come with me? What for, I should like to know? Now, what have I to take him? Eh, dear! His clean shirt – and it's a blessing it is clean. But it had better be aired. And stockings – he won't want them – and a towel, I suppose; and handkerchiefs. Now what else?'

'A comb, a knife and fork and spoon,' said Paul. His father had been in the hospital before.

'Goodness knows what sort of state his feet were in,' continued Mrs Morel, as she combed her long brown hair, that was fine as silk, and was touched now with grey. 'He's very particular to wash himself to the waist, but below he thinks doesn't matter. But there, I suppose they see plenty like it.'

Paul had laid the table. He cut his mother one or two pieces of very thin bread-and-butter.

'Here you are,' he said, putting her cup of tea in her place.

'I can't be bothered!' she exclaimed crossly.

'Well, you've got to, so there, now it's put out ready,' he insisted.

So she sat down and sipped her tea, and ate a little, in silence. She was thinking.

In a few minutes she was gone, to walk the two and a half miles to Keston Station. All the things she was taking him she had in her bulging string bag. Paul watched her go up the road between the hedges – a little, quick-stepping figure, and his heart ached for her, that she was thrust forward again into pain and trouble. And she, tripping so quickly in her anxiety, felt at the back of her her son's heart waiting on her, felt him bearing what part of the burden he could, even supporting her. And when she was at the hospital, she thought: 'It *will* upset that lad when I tell him how bad it is. I'd better be careful.' And when she was trudging home again, she felt he was coming to share her burden.

'Is it bad?' asked Paul, as soon as she entered the house.

'It's bad enough,' she replied.

'What?'

She sighed and sat down, undoing her bonnet-strings. Her son watched her face as it was lifted, and her small, work-hardened hands fingering at the bow under her chin.

'Well,' she answered, 'it's not really dangerous, but the nurse says it's a dreadful smash. You see, a great piece of rock fell on his leg – here – and it's a compound fracture. There are pieces of bone sticking through – '

'Ugh – how horrid!' exclaimed the children.

'And,' she continued, 'of course he says he's going to die – it wouldn't be him if he didn't. "I'm done for, my lass!" he said, looking at me. "Don't be so silly," I said to him. "You're not going to die of a broken leg, however badly it's smashed," "I s'll niver come out of 'ere but in a wooden box," he groaned. "Well," I said, "if you want them to carry you into the garden in a wooden box, when you're better, I've no doubt they will." "If we think it's good for him," said the Sister. She's an awfully nice Sister, but rather strict.'

Mrs Morel took off her bonnet. The children waited in silence.

'Of course, he is bad,' she continued, 'and he will be. It's a great shock, and he's lost a lot of blood; and, of course, it is a very dangerous smash. It's not at all sure that it will mend so easily. And then there's the fever and the mortification if it took bad ways he'd quickly be gone. But there, he's a clean-blooded man, with wonderful healing flesh, and so I see no reason why it *should* take bad ways. Of course there's a wound – '

She was pale now with emotion and anxiety. The three children realised that it was very bad for their father, and the house was silent, anxious.

'But he always gets better,' said Paul after a while.

'That's what I tell him,' said the mother.

Everybody moved about in silence.

'And he really looked nearly done for,' she said. 'But the Sister says that is the pain.'

Annie took away her mother's coat and bonnet.

'And he looked at me when I came away! I said: "I s'll have to go now, Walter, because of the train – and the children." And he looked at me. It seems hard.'

Paul took up his brush again and went on painting. Arthur went outside for some coal. Annie sat looking dismal. And Mrs Morel, in her little rocking-chair that her husband had made for her when the first baby was coming, remained motionless, brooding. She was grieved, and bitterly sorry for the man who was hurt so much. But still, in her heart of hearts, where the love should have burned, there was a blank. Now, when all her woman's pity was roused to its full extent, when she would have slaved herself to death to nurse him and to save him, when she would have taken the pain herself, if she could, somewhere far away inside her, she felt indifferent to him and to his suffering. It hurt her most of all, this failure to love him, even when he roused her strong emotions. She brooded awhile.

'And there,' she said suddenly, 'when I'd got halfway to Keston, I found I'd come out in my working-boots – and *look* at them.' They were an old pair of Paul's, brown and rubbed through at the toes. 'I didn't know what to do with myself, for shame,' she added.

In the morning, when Annie and Arthur were at school, Mrs Morel talked again to her son, who was helping her with her housework.

'I found Barker at the hospital. He did look bad, poor little fellow! "Well," I said to him, "what sort of a journey did you have with him?" "Dunna ax me, missis!" he said. "Ay," I said, "I know what he'd be." "But it *wor* bad for him, Mrs Morel, it *wor* that!" he said. "I know," I said. "At ivry jolt I thought my 'eart would ha' flown clean out o' my mouth," he said. "An' the scream 'e gives sometimes! Missis, not for a fortune would I go through wi' it again." "I can quite understand it," I said. "It's a nasty job though," he said, "an' one as'll be a long while afore it's right again." "I'm afraid it will," I said. I like Mr Barker – I *do* like him. There's something so manly about him.'

Paul resumed his task silently.

'And of course,' Mrs Morel continued, 'for a man like your father, the hospital is hard. He *can't* understand rules and regulations. And he won't let anybody else touch him, not if he can help it. When he smashed the muscles of his thigh, and it had to be dressed four times a day, *would* he let anybody but me or his mother do it? He wouldn't. So, of course, he'll suffer in there with the nurses. And I didn't like leaving him. I'm sure, when I kissed him an' came away, it seemed a shame.'

So she talked to her son, almost as if she were thinking aloud to him, and he took it in as best he could, by sharing her trouble to lighten it. And in the end she shared almost everything with him without knowing.

Morel had a very bad time. For a week he was in a critical condition. Then he began to mend. And then, knowing he was going to get better, the whole family sighed with relief, and proceeded to live happily.

They were not badly off whilst Morel was in the hospital. There were fourteen shillings a week from the pit, ten shillings from the sick club, and five shillings from the Disability Fund; and then every week the butties had something for Mrs Morel – five or seven shillings – so that she was quite well to do. And whilst Morel was progressing favourably in the hospital, the family was extraordinarily happy and peaceful. On Saturdays and Wednesdays Mrs Morel went to Nottingham to see her husband. Then she always brought back some little thing: a small tube of paints for Paul, or some thick paper; a couple of postcards for Annie, that the whole family rejoiced over for days before the girl was allowed to send them away; or a fret-saw for Arthur, or a bit of pretty wood. She described her adventures into the big shops with joy. Soon the folk in the picture-shop knew her and knew about Paul. The girl in the bookshop took a keen interest in her, Mrs Morel was full of information when she got home from Nottingham. The three sat round till bedtime, listening, putting in, arguing. Then Paul often raked the fire.

'I'm the man in the house now,' he used to say to his mother with joy. They learned how perfectly peaceful the home could be. And they almost regretted – though none of them would have owned to such callousness – that their father was soon coming back.

Paul was now fourteen, and was looking for work. He was a rather small and rather finely-made boy, with dark brown hair and light blue eyes. His face had already lost its youthful chubbiness, and was becoming somewhat like William's – rough-featured, almost rugged – and it was extraordinarily mobile. Usually he looked as if he saw things, was full of life, and warm; then his smile, like his mother's, came suddenly and was very lovable; and then, when there was any clog in his soul's quick running, his face went stupid and ugly. He was the sort of boy that becomes a clown and a lout as soon as he is not understood, or feels himself held cheap; and, again, is adorable at the first touch of warmth.

He suffered very much from the first contact with anything. When he was seven, the starting school had been a nightmare and a torture to him. But afterwards he liked it. And now that he felt he had to go out into life, he went through agonies of shrinking self-consciousness. He was quite a clever painter for a boy of his years, and he knew some French and German and mathematics that Mr Heaton had taught him. But nothing he had was of any commercial value. He was not strong enough for heavy manual work, his mother said. He did not care for making things with his hands, preferred racing about, or making excursions into the country, or reading, or painting.

'What do you want to be?' his mother asked.

'Anything.'

'That is no answer,' said Mrs Morel.

But it was quite truthfully the only answer he could give. His ambition as far as this world's gear went, was quietly to earn his thirty or thirty-five shillings a week somewhere near home, and then, when his father died, have a cottage with his mother, paint and go out as he liked, and live happy ever after. That was his programme as far as doing things went. But he was proud within himself, measuring people against himself, and placing them, inexorably. And he thought that *perhaps* he might also make a painter, the real thing. But that he left alone.

'Then,' said his mother, 'you must look in the paper for the advertisements.'

He looked at her. It seemed to him a bitter humiliation and an anguish to go through. But he said nothing. When he got up in the morning, his whole being was knotted up over this one thought, 'I've got to go and look for advertisements for a job.'

It stood in front of the morning, that thought, killing all joy and even life, for him. His heart felt like a tight knot.

And then, at ten o'clock, he set off. He was supposed to be a queer, quiet child. Going up the sunny street of the little town, he felt as if all the folk he met said to themselves: 'He's going to the Co-op reading-room to look in the papers for a place. He can't get a job. I suppose he's living on his mother.' Then he crept up the stone stairs behind the drapery shop at the Co-op, and peeped in the reading-room. Usually one or two men were there, either old, useless fellows, or colliers 'on the club'. So he entered, full of shrinking and suffering when they looked up, seated himself at the table, and pretended to scan the news. He knew they would think, 'What does a lad of thirteen want in a reading-room with a newspaper?' and he suffered.

Then he looked wistfully out of the window. Already he was a prisoner of industrialism. Large sunflowers stared over the old red wall of the garden opposite, looking in their jolly way down on the women who were hurrying with something for dinner. The valley was full of corn, brightening in the sun. Two collieries, among the fields, waved their small white plumes of steam. Far off on the hills were the woods of Annesley, dark and fascinating. Already his heart went down. He was being taken into bondage. His freedom in the beloved home valley was going now.

The brewers' waggons came rolling up from Keston with enormous barrels, four a side, like beans in a burst bean-pod. The waggoner, throned aloft, rolling massively in his seat, was not so much below Paul's eye. The man's hair on his small, bullet head, was bleached almost white by the sun, and on his thick red arms, rocking idly on his sack apron, the white hairs glistened. His red face shone and was almost asleep with sunshine. The horses, handsome and brown, went on by themselves, looking by far the masters of the show.

Paul wished he were stupid. 'I wish,' he thought to himself, 'I was fat like him, and like a dog in the sun. I wish I was a pig and a brewer's waggoner.'

Then, the room being at last empty, he would hastily copy an advertisement on a scrap of paper, then another, and slip out in immense relief. His mother would scan over his copies.

'Yes,' she said, 'you may try.'

William had written out a letter of application, couched in admirable business language, which Paul copied, with variations. The boy's handwriting was execrable, so that William, who did all things well, got into a fever of impatience.

The elder brother was becoming quite swanky. In London he found that he could associate with men far above his Bestwood friends in station. Some of the clerks in the office had studied for the law, and were more or less going through a kind of apprenticeship. William always made friends among men wherever he went, he was so jolly. Therefore he was soon visiting and staying in houses of men who, in Bestwood, would have looked down on the unapproachable bank manager, and would merely have called indifferently on the Rector. So he began to fancy himself as a great gun. He was, indeed, rather surprised at the ease with which he became a gentleman.

His mother was glad, he seemed so pleased. And his lodging in Walthamstow was so dreary. But now there seemed to come a kind of fever into the young man's letters. He was unsettled by all the change, he did not stand firm on his own feet, but seemed to spin rather giddily on the quick current of the new life. His mother was anxious for him. She could feel him losing himself. He had danced and gone to the theatre, boated on the river, been out with friends; and she knew he sat up afterwards in his cold bedroom grinding away at Latin, because he intended to get on in his office, and in the law as much as he could. He never sent his mother any money now. It was all taken, the little he had, for his own life. And she did not want any, except sometimes, when she was in a tight corner, and when ten shillings would have saved her much worry. She still dreamed of William, and of what he would do, with herself behind him. Never for a minute would she admit to herself how heavy and anxious her heart was because of him.

Also he talked a good deal now of a girl he had met at a dance, a handsome brunette, quite young, and a lady, after whom the men were running thick and fast.

'I wonder if you would run, my boy,' his mother wrote to him, 'unless you saw all the other men chasing her too. You feel safe enough and vain enough in a crowd. But take care, and see how you feel when you find yourself alone, and in triumph.'

William resented these things, and continued the chase. He had taken the girl on the river. 'If you saw her, mother, you would know how I feel. Tall and elegant, with the clearest of clear, transparent olive complexions, hair as black as jet, and such grey eyes – bright, mocking, like lights on water at night. It is all very well to be a bit satirical till you see her. And she dresses as well as any woman in London. I tell you your son doesn't half put his head up when she goes walking down Piccadilly with him.'

Mrs Morel wondered, in her heart, if her son did not go walking down Piccadilly with an elegant figure and fine clothes, rather than with a woman who was near to him. But she congratulated him in her doubtful fashion. And, as she stood over the washing-tub, the mother brooded over her son. She saw him saddled with an elegant and expensive wife, earning little money, dragging along and getting draggled in some small, ugly house in a suburb. 'But there,' she told herself, 'I am very likely a silly – meeting trouble halfway.' Nevertheless, the load of anxiety scarcely ever left her heart lest William should do the wrong thing by himself.

Presently, Paul was bidden call upon Thomas Jordan, Manufacturer of Surgical Appliances, at 21, Spaniel Row, Nottingham. Mrs Morel was all joy.

'There, you see!' she cried, her eyes shining. 'You've only written four letters, and the third is answered. You're lucky, my boy, as I always said you were.'

Paul looked at the picture of a wooden leg, adorned with elastic stockings and other appliances, that figured on Mr Jordan's notepaper, and he felt alarmed. He had not known that elastic stockings existed. And he seemed to feel the business world, with its regulated system of values, and its impersonality, and he dreaded it. It seemed monstrous also that a business could be run on wooden legs.

Mother and son set off together one Tuesday morning. It was August and blazing hot. Paul walked with something screwed up tight inside him. He would have suffered much physical pain rather than this unreasonable suffering at being exposed to strangers, to be accepted or rejected. Yet he chattered away with his mother. He would never have confessed to her how he suffered over these things, and she only partly guessed. She was gay, like a sweetheart. She stood in front of the ticket-office at Bestwood, and Paul watched her take from her purse the money for the tickets. As he saw her hands in their old black kid gloves getting the silver out of the worn purse, his heart contracted with pain of love of her.

She was quite excited, and quite gay. He suffered because she *would* talk aloud in presence of the other travellers.

'Now look at that silly cow!' she said, 'careering round as if it thought it was a circus.'

'It's most likely a bottfly,' he said very low.

'A what?' she asked brightly and unashamed.

They thought awhile. He was sensible all the time of having her opposite him. Suddenly their eyes met, and she smiled to him – a rare, intimate smile, beautiful with brightness and love. Then each looked out of the window.

The sixteen slow miles of railway journey passed. The mother and son walked down Station Street, feeling the excitement of lovers having an adventure together. In Carrington Street they stopped to hang over the parapet and look at the barges on the canal below.

'It's just like Venice,' he said, seeing the sunshine on the water that lay between high factory walls.

'Perhaps,' she answered, smiling.

They enjoyed the shops immensely.

'Now you see that blouse,' she would say, 'wouldn't that just suit our Annie? And for one-and-eleven-three. Isn't that cheap?'

'And made of needlework as well,' he said.

'Yes.'

They had plenty of time, so they did not hurry. The town was strange and delightful to them. But the boy was tied up inside in a knot of apprehension. He dreaded the interview with Thomas Jordan.

It was nearly eleven o'clock by St Peter's Church. They turned up a narrow street that led to the Castle. It was gloomy and old-fashioned, having low dark shops and dark green house-doors with brass knockers, and yellow-ochred doorsteps projecting on to the pavement; then another old shop whose small window looked like a cunning, half-shut eye. Mother and son went cautiously, looking everywhere for 'Thomas Jordan and Son'. It was like hunting in some wild place. They were on tiptoe of excitement.

Suddenly they spied a big, dark archway, in which were names of various firms, Thomas Jordan among them.

'Here it is!' said Mrs Morel. 'But now where is it?'

They looked round. On one side was a queer, dark, cardboard factory, on the other a Commercial Hotel.

'It's up the entry,' said Paul.

And they ventured under the archway, as into the jaws of the dragon. They emerged into a wide yard, like a well, with buildings all round. It was littered with straw and boxes, and cardboard. The sunshine actually caught one crate whose straw was streaming on to the yard like gold. But elsewhere the place was like a pit. There were several doors, and two flights of steps. Straight in front, on a dirty glass door at the top of a staircase, loomed the ominous words 'Thomas Jordan and Son – Surgical Appliances'. Mrs Morel went first, her son followed her. Charles I mounted his scaffold with a lighter heart than had Paul Morel as he followed his mother up the dirty steps to the dirty door.

She pushed open the door, and stood in pleased surprise. In front of her was a big warehouse, with creamy paper parcels everywhere, and clerks, with their shirt-sleeves rolled back, were going about in an at-home sort of way. The light was subdued, the glossy cream parcels seemed luminous, the counters were of dark brown wood. All was quiet and very homely. Mrs Morel took two steps forward, then waited. Paul stood behind her. She had on her Sunday bonnet and a black veil; he wore a boy's broad white collar and a Norfolk suit.

One of the clerks looked up. He was thin and tall, with a small face. His way of looking was alert. Then he glanced round to the other end of the room, where was a glass office. And then he came forward. He did not say anything, but leaned in a gentle, enquiring fashion towards Mrs Morel.

'Can I see Mr Jordan?' she asked.

'I'll fetch him,' answered the young man.

He went down to the glass office. A red-faced, white-whiskered old man looked up. He reminded Paul of a Pomeranian dog. Then the same little man came up the room. He had short legs, was rather stout, and wore an alpaca jacket. So, with one ear up, as it were, he came stoutly and enquiringly down the room.

'Good-morning!' he said, hesitating before Mrs Morel, in doubt as to whether she were a customer or not.

'Good-morning. I came with my son, Paul Morel. You asked him to call this morning.'

'Come this way,' said Mr Jordan, in a rather snappy little manner intended to be businesslike.

They followed the manufacturer into a grubby little room, upholstered in black American leather, glossy with the rubbing of many customers. On the table was a pile of trusses, yellow wash-leather hoops tangled together. They looked new and living. Paul sniffed the odour of new wash-leather. He wondered what the things were. By this time he was so much stunned that he only noticed the outside things.

'Sit down!' said Mr Jordan, irritably pointing Mrs Morel to a horsehair chair. She sat on the edge in an uncertain fashion. Then the little old man fidgeted and found a paper.

'Did you write this letter?' he snapped, thrusting what Paul recognised as his own notepaper in front of him.

'Yes,' he answered.

At that moment he was occupied in two ways: first, in feeling guilty for telling a lie, since William had composed the letter; second, in wondering why his letter seemed so strange and different, in the fat, red hand of the man, from what it had been when it lay on the kitchen table. It was like part of himself, gone astray. He resented the way the man held it.

'Where did you learn to write?' said the old man crossly.

Paul merely looked at him shamedly, and did not answer.

'He is a bad writer,' put in Mrs Morel apologetically. Then she pushed up her veil. Paul hated her for not being prouder with this common little man, and he loved her face clear of the veil.

'And you say you know French?' enquired the little man, still sharply.

'Yes,' said Paul.

'What school did you go to?'

'The Board-school.'

'And did you learn it there?'

'No – I – ' The boy went crimson and got no further.

'His godfather gave him lessons,' said Mrs Morel, half pleading and rather distant.

Mr Jordan hesitated. Then, in his irritable manner – he always seemed to keep his hands ready for action – he pulled another sheet of paper from his pocket, unfolded it. The paper made a crackling noise. He handed it to Paul.

'Read that,' he said.

It was a note in French, in thin, flimsy foreign handwriting that the boy could not decipher. He stared blankly at the paper.

' "Monsieur," ' he began; then he looked in great confusion at Mr Jordan. 'It's the – it's the – '

He wanted to say 'handwriting', but his wits would no longer work even sufficiently to supply him with the word. Feeling an utter fool, and hating Mr Jordan, he turned desperately to the paper again.

' "Sir, – Please send me" – er – er – I can't tell the – er – "two pairs – *gris fil bas* – grey thread stockings" – er – er – "*sans* – without" – er – I can't tell the words – er – "*doigts* – fingers" – er – I can't tell the – '

He wanted to say 'handwriting', but the word still refused to come. Seeing him stuck, Mr Jordan snatched the paper from him.

' "Please send by return two pairs grey thread stockings without *toes*." '

'Well,' flashed Paul, ' "*doigts*" means "fingers" – as well – as a rule – '

The little man looked at him. He did not know whether '*doigts*' meant 'fingers'; he knew that for all *his* purposes it meant 'toes'.

'Fingers to stockings!' he snapped.

'Well, it *does* mean fingers,' the boy persisted.

He hated the little man, who made such a clod of him. Mr Jordan looked at the pale, stupid, defiant boy, then at the mother, who sat quiet and with that peculiar shut-off look of the poor who have to depend on the favour of others.

'And when could he come?' he asked.

'Well,' said Mrs Morel, 'as soon as you wish. He has finished school now.'

'He would live in Bestwood?'

'Yes; but he could be in – at the station – at quarter to eight.'

'H'm!'

It ended by Paul's being engaged as junior spiral clerk at eight shillings a week. The boy did not open his mouth to say another word, after having insisted that '*doigts*' meant 'fingers'. He followed his mother down the stairs. She looked at him with her bright blue eyes full of love and joy.

'I think you'll like it,' she said.

' "*Doigts*" does mean "fingers", mother, and it was the writing. I couldn't read the writing.'

'Never mind, my boy. I'm sure he'll be all right, and you won't see much of him. Wasn't that first young fellow nice? I'm sure you'll like them.'

'But wasn't Mr Jordan common, mother? Does he own it all?'

'I suppose he was a workman who has got on,' she said. 'You mustn't mind people so much. They're not being disagreeable to *you* – it's their way. You always think people are meaning things for you. But they don't.'

It was very sunny. Over the big desolate space of the market-place the blue sky shimmered, and the granite cobbles of the paving glistened. Shops down the Long Row were deep in obscurity, and the shadow was full of colour. Just where the horse trams trundled across the market was a row of fruit stalls, with fruit blazing in the sun – apples and piles of reddish oranges, small greengage plums and bananas. There was a warm scent of fruit as mother and son passed. Gradually his feeling of ignominy and of rage sank.

'Where should we go for dinner?' asked the mother.

It was felt to be a reckless extravagance. Paul had only been in an eating-house once or twice in his life, and then only to have a cup of tea and a bun. Most of the people of Bestwood considered that tea and bread-and-butter, and perhaps potted-beef, was all they could afford to eat in Nottingham. Real cooked dinner was considered great extravagance. Paul felt rather guilty.

They found a place that looked quite cheap. But when Mrs Morel scanned the bill of fare, her heart was heavy, things were so dear. So she ordered kidney pies and potatoes as the cheapest available dish.

'We oughtn't to have come here, mother,' said Paul.

'Never mind,' she said. 'We won't come again.'

She insisted on his having a small currant tart, because he liked sweets.

'I don't want it, mother,' he pleaded.

'Yes,' she insisted; 'you'll have it.'

And she looked round for the waitress. But the waitress was busy, and Mrs Morel did not like to bother her then. So the mother and son waited for the girl's pleasure, whilst she flirted among the men.

'Brazen hussy!' said Mrs Morel to Paul. 'Look now, she's taking that man his pudding, and he came long after us.'

'It doesn't matter, mother,' said Paul.

Mrs Morel was angry. But she was too poor, and her orders were too meagre, so that she had not the courage to insist on her rights just then. They waited and waited.

'Should we go, mother?' he said.

Then Mrs Morel stood up. The girl was passing near.

'Will you bring one currant tart?' said Mrs Morel clearly.

The girl looked round insolently.

'Directly,' she said.

'We have waited quite long enough,' said Mrs Morel.

In a moment the girl came back with the tart. Mrs Morel asked coldly for the bill. Paul wanted to sink through the floor. He marvelled at his mother's hardness. He knew that only years of battling had taught her to insist even so little on her rights. She shrank as much as he.

'It's the last time I go *there* for anything!' she declared, when they were outside the place, thankful to be clear.

'We'll go,' she said, 'and look at Keep's and Boot's, and one or two places, shall we?'

They had discussions over the pictures, and Mrs Morel wanted to buy him a little sable brush that he hankered after. But this indulgence he refused. He stood in front of milliners' shops and drapers' shops almost bored, but content for her to be interested. They wandered on.

'Now, just look at those black grapes!' she said. 'They make your mouth water. I've wanted some of those for years, but I s'll have to wait a bit before I get them.'

Then she rejoiced in the florists, standing in the doorway sniffing.

'Oh! oh! Isn't it simply lovely!'

Paul saw, in the darkness of the shop, an elegant young lady in black peering over the counter curiously.

'They're looking at you,' he said, trying to draw his mother away.

'But what is it?' she exclaimed, refusing to be moved.

'Stocks!' he answered, sniffing hastily. 'Look, there's a tubful.'

'So there is – red and white. But really, I never knew stocks to smell like it!' And, to his great relief, she moved out of the doorway, but only to stand in front of the window.

'Paul!' she cried to him, who was trying to get out of sight of the elegant young lady in black – the shop-girl. 'Paul! Just look here!'

He came reluctantly back.

'Now, just look at that fuchsia!' she exclaimed, pointing.

'H'm!' He made a curious, interested sound. 'You'd think every second as the flowers was going to fall off, they hang so big an' heavy.'

'And such an abundance!' she cried.

'And the way they drop downwards with their threads and knots!'

'Yes!' she exclaimed. 'Lovely!'

'I wonder who'll buy it!' he said.

'I wonder!' she answered. 'Not us.'

'It would die in our parlour.'

'Yes, beastly cold, sunless hole; it kills every bit of a plant you put in, and the kitchen chokes them to death.'

They bought a few things, and set off towards the station. Looking up the canal, through the dark pass of the buildings, they saw the Castle on its bluff of brown, green-bushed rock, in a positive miracle of delicate sunshine.

'Won't it be nice for me to come out at dinner-times?' said Paul. 'I can go all round here and see everything. I s'll love it.'

'You will,' assented his mother.

He had spent a perfect afternoon with his mother. They arrived home in the mellow evening, happy, and glowing, and tired.

In the morning he filled in the form for his season-ticket and took it to the station. When he got back, his mother was just beginning to wash the floor. He sat crouched up on the sofa.

'He says it'll be here by Saturday,' he said.

'And how much will it be?'

'About one pound eleven,' he said.

She went on washing her floor in silence.

'Is it a lot?' he asked.

'It's no more than I thought,' she answered.

'An' I s'll earn eight shillings a week,' he said

She did not answer, but went on with her work. At last she said, 'That William promised me, when he went to London, as he'd give me a pound a month. He has given me ten shillings – twice; and now I know he hasn't a farthing if I asked him. Not that I want it. Only just now you'd think he might be able to help with this ticket, which I'd never expected.'

'He earns a lot,' said Paul.

'He earns a hundred and thirty pounds. But they're all alike. They're large in promises, but it's precious little fulfilment you get.'

'He spends over fifty shillings a week on himself,' said Paul.

'And I keep this house on less than thirty,' she replied; 'and am supposed to find money for extras. But they don't care about helping you, once they've gone. He'd rather spend it on that dressed-up creature.'

'She should have her own money if she's so grand,' said Paul.

'She should, but she hasn't. I asked him. And I know he doesn't buy her a gold bangle for nothing. I wonder whoever bought *me* a gold bangle.'

William was succeeding with his 'Gypsy', as he called her. He asked the girl – her name was Louisa Lily Denys Western – for a photograph to send to his mother. The photo came – a handsome brunette, taken in profile, smirking slightly – and, it might be, quite naked, for on the photograph not a scrap of clothing was to be seen, only a naked bust.

'Yes,' wrote Mrs Morel to her son, 'the photograph of Louisa is very striking, and I can see she must be attractive. But do you think, my boy, it was very good taste of a girl to give her young man that photo to send to his mother – the first? Certainly the shoulders are beautiful, as you say. But I hardly expected to see so much of them at the first view.'

Morel found the photograph standing on the chiffonier in the parlour. He came out with it between his thick thumb and finger.

'Who dost reckon this is?' he asked of his wife.

'It's the girl our William is going with,' replied Mrs Morel.

'H'm! 'Er's a bright spark, from th' look on 'er, an' one as wunna do him owermuch good neither. Who is she?'

'Her name is Louisa Lily Denys Western.'

'An' come again tomorrer!' exclaimed the miner. 'An' is 'er an actress?'

'She is not. She's supposed to be a lady.'

'I'll bet!' he exclaimed, still staring at the photo. 'A lady, is she? An' how much does she reckon ter keep up this sort o' game on?'

'On nothing. She lives with an old aunt, whom she hates, and takes what bit of money's given her.'

'H'm!' said Morel, laying down the photograph. 'Then he's a fool to ha' ta'en up wi' such a one as that.'

'Dear Mater,' William replied. 'I'm sorry you didn't like the photograph. It never occurred to me when I sent it, that you mightn't think it decent. However, I told Gyp that it didn't quite suit your prim and proper notions, so she's going to send you another, that I hope will please you better. She's always being photographed; in fact, the photographers *ask* her if they may take her for nothing.'

Presently the new photograph came, with a little silly note from the girl. This time the young lady was seen in a black satin evening bodice, cut square, with little puff sleeves, and black lace hanging down her beautiful arms.

'I wonder if she ever wears anything except evening clothes,' said Mrs Morel sarcastically. 'I'm sure I ought to be impressed.'

'You are disagreeable, mother,' said Paul. 'I think the first one with bare shoulders is lovely.'

'Do you?' answered his mother. 'Well, I don't.'

On the Monday morning the boy got up at six to start work. He had the season-ticket, which had cost such bitterness, in his waistcoat pocket. He loved it with its bars of yellow across. His mother packed his dinner in a small, shut-up basket, and he set off at a quarter to seven to catch the 7.15 train. Mrs Morel came to the entry-end to see him off.

It was a perfect morning. From the ash tree the slender green fruits that the children call 'pigeons' were twinkling gaily down on a little breeze, into the front gardens of the houses. The valley was full of a lustrous dark haze, through which the ripe corn shimmered, and in which the steam from Minton pit melted swiftly. Puffs of wind came. Paul looked over the high woods of Aldersley, where the country gleamed, and home had never pulled at him so powerfully.

'Good-morning, mother,' he said, smiling, but feeling very unhappy.

'Good-morning,' she replied cheerfully and tenderly.

She stood in her white apron on the open road, watching him as he crossed the field. He had a small, compact body that looked full of life. She felt, as she saw him trudging over the field, that where he determined to go he would get. She thought of William. He would have leaped the fence instead of going round to the stile. He was away in London, doing well. Paul would be working in Nottingham. Now she had two sons in the world. She could think of two places, great centres of industry, and feel that she had put a man into each of them, that these men would work out what she wanted; they were derived from her, they were of her, and their works also would be hers. All the morning long she thought of Paul.

At eight o'clock he climbed the dismal stairs of Jordan's Surgical Appliance Factory, and stood helplessly against the first great parcel-rack, waiting for somebody to pick him up. The place was still not awake. Over the counters were great dust sheets. Two men only had arrived, and were heard talking in a corner, as they took off their coats and rolled up their shirt-sleeves. It was ten past eight. Evidently there was no rush of punctuality. Paul listened to the voices of the two clerks. Then he heard someone cough, and saw in the office at the end of the room an old decaying clerk, in a round smoking-cap of black velvet embroidered with red and green, opening letters. He waited and waited. One of the junior clerks went to the old man, greeted him cheerily and loudly. Evidently the old 'chief' was deaf. Then the young fellow came striding importantly down to his counter. He spied Paul.

'Hello!' he said. 'You the new lad?'

'Yes,' said Paul.

'H'm! What's your name?'

'Paul Morel.'

'Paul Morel? All right, you come on round here.'

Paul followed him round the rectangle of counters. The room was second storey. It had a great hole in the middle of the floor, fenced as with a wall of counters, and down this wide shaft the lifts went, and the light for the bottom storey. Also there was a corresponding big, oblong hole in the ceiling, and one could see above, over the fence of the top floor, some machinery; and right away overhead was the glass roof, and all light for the three storeys came downwards, getting dimmer, so that it was always night on the ground floor and rather gloomy on the second floor. The factory was the top floor, the warehouse the second, the storehouse the ground floor. It was an insanitary, ancient place.

Paul was led round to a very dark corner.

'This is the "Spiral" corner,' said the clerk. 'You're Spiral, with Pappleworth. He's your boss, but he's not come yet. He doesn't get here till half-past eight. So you can fetch the letters, if you like, from Mr Melling down there.'

The young man pointed to the old clerk in the office.

'All right,' said Paul.

'Here's a peg to hang your cap on. Here are your entry ledgers. Mr Pappleworth won't be long.'

And the thin young man stalked away with long, busy strides over the hollow
wooden floor.

After a minute or two Paul went down and stood in the door of the glass
office. The old clerk in the smoking-cap looked down over the rim of his
spectacles.

'Good-morning,' he said, kindly and impressively. 'You want the letters for
the Spiral department, Thomas?'

Paul resented being called 'Thomas'. But he took the letters and returned to
his dark place, where the counter made an angle, where the great parcel-rack
came to an end, and where there were three doors in the corner. He sat on a
high stool and read the letters – those whose handwriting was not too difficult.
They ran as follows, 'Will you please send me at once a pair of lady's silk spiral
thigh-hose, without feet, such as I had from you last year; length, thigh to knee,
etc.' Or, 'Major Chamberlain wishes to repeat his previous order for a silk non-
elastic suspensory bandage.'

Many of these letters, some of them in French or Norwegian, were a great
puzzle to the boy. He sat on his stool nervously awaiting the arrival of his 'boss'.
He suffered tortures of shyness when, at half-past eight, the factory girls for
upstairs trooped past him.

Mr Pappleworth arrived, chewing a chlorodyne gum, at about twenty to
nine, when all the other men were at work. He was a thin, sallow man with a red
nose, quick, staccato, and smartly but stiffly dressed. He was about thirty-six
years old. There was something rather 'doggy', rather smart, rather cute and
shrewd, and something warm, and something slightly contemptible about him.

'You my new lad?' he said.

Paul stood up and said he was.

'Fetched the letters?'

Mr Pappleworth gave a chew to his gum.

'Yes.'

'Copied 'em?'

'No.'

'Well, come on then, let's look slippy. Changed your coat?'

'No.'

'You want to bring an old coat and leave it here.' He pronounced the last
words with the chlorodyne gum between his side teeth. He vanished into
darkness behind the great parcel-rack, reappeared coatless, turning up a smart
striped shirt-cuff over a thin and hairy arm. Then he slipped into his coat. Paul
noticed how thin he was, and that his trousers were in folds behind. He seized a
stool, dragged it beside the boy's, and sat down.

'Sit down,' he said.

Paul took a seat.

Mr Pappleworth was very close to him. The man seized the letters, snatched a long entry-book out of a rack in front of him, flung it open, seized a pen, and said, 'Now look here. You want to copy these letters in here.' He sniffed twice, gave a quick chew at his gum, stared fixedly at a letter, then went very still and absorbed, and wrote the entry rapidly, in a beautiful flourishing hand. He glanced quickly at Paul.

'See that?'

'Yes.'

'Think you can do it all right?'

'Yes.'

'All right then, let's see you.'

He sprang off his stool. Paul took a pen. Mr Pappleworth disappeared. Paul rather liked copying the letters but he wrote slowly, laboriously, and exceedingly badly. He was doing the fourth letter, and feeling quite busy and happy, when Mr Pappleworth reappeared.

'Now then, how'r' yer getting on? Done 'em?'

He leaned over the boy's shoulder, chewing, and smelling of chlorodyne.

'Strike my bob, lad, but you're a beautiful writer!' he exclaimed satirically. 'Ne'er mind, how many h'yer done? Only three! I'd 'a eaten 'em. Get on, my lad, an' put numbers on 'em. Here, look! Get on!'

Paul ground away at the letters, whilst Mr Pappleworth fussed over various jobs. Suddenly the boy started as a shrill whistle sounded near his ear. Mr Pappleworth came, took a plug out of a pipe, and said, in an amazingly cross and bossy voice, 'Yes?'

Paul heard a faint voice, like a woman's, out of the mouth of the tube. He gazed in wonder, never having seen a speaking-tube before.

'Well,' said Mr Pappleworth disagreeably into the tube, 'you'd better get some of your back work done, then.'

Again the woman's tiny voice was heard, sounding pretty and cross.

'I've not time to stand here while you talk,' said Mr Pappleworth, and he pushed the plug into the tube.

'Come, my lad,' he said imploringly to Paul, 'there's Polly crying out for them orders. Can't you buck up a bit? Here, come out!'

He took the book, to Paul's immense chagrin, and began the copying himself. He worked quickly and well. This done, he seized some strips of long yellow paper, about three inches wide, and made out the day's orders for the work-girls.

'You'd better watch me,' he said to Paul, working all the while rapidly. Paul watched the weird little drawings of legs, and thighs, and ankles, with the strokes across and the numbers, and the few brief directions which his chief made upon the yellow paper. Then Mr Pappleworth finished and jumped up.

'Come on with me,' he said, and the yellow papers flying in his hands, he dashed through a door and down some stairs, into the basement where the gas was burning. They crossed the cold, damp storeroom, then a long, dreary room with a long table on trestles, into a smaller, cosy apartment, not very high, which had been built on to the main building. In this room a small woman with a red serge blouse, and her black hair done on top of her head, was waiting like a proud little bantam.

'Here y'are!' said Pappleworth.

'I think it is "here you are!" ' exclaimed Polly. 'The girls have been here nearly half an hour waiting. Just think of the time wasted!'

'*You* think of getting your work done and not talking so much,' said Mr Pappleworth. 'You could ha' been finishing off.'

'You know quite well we finished everything off on Saturday!' cried Polly, flying at him, her dark eyes flashing.

'Tu–tu–tu–tu–terterter!' he mocked. 'Here's your new lad. Don't ruin him as you did the last.'

' "As we did the last!" ' repeated Polly. 'Yes, *we* do a lot of ruining, we do. My word, a lad would *take* some ruining after he'd been with you.'

'It's time for work now, not for talk,' said Mr Pappleworth severely and coldly.

'It was time for work some time back,' said Polly, marching away with her head in the air. She was an erect little body of forty.

In that room were two round spiral machines on the bench under the window. Through the inner doorway was another longer room, with six more machines. A little group of girls, nicely dressed and in white aprons, stood talking together.

'Have you nothing else to do but talk?' said Mr Pappleworth.

'Only wait for you,' said one handsome girl, laughing.

'Well, get on, get on,' he said. 'Come on, my lad. You'll know your road down here again.'

And Paul ran upstairs after his chief. He was given some checking and invoicing to do. He stood at the desk, labouring in his execrable handwriting. Presently Mr Jordan came strutting down from the glass office and stood behind him, to the boy's great discomfort. Suddenly a red and fat finger was thrust on the form he was filling in.

'*Mr* J. A. Bates, Esquire!' exclaimed the cross voice just behind his ear.

Paul looked at 'Mr J. A. Bates, Esquire' in his own vile writing, and wondered what was the matter now.

'Didn't they teach you any better than *that* while they were at it? If you put "Mr" you don't put "Esquire" – a man can't be both at once.'

The boy regretted his too-much generosity in disposing of honours, hesitated, and with trembling fingers, scratched out the 'Mr'. Then all at once Mr Jordan snatched away the invoice.

'Make another! Are you going to send *that* to a gentleman?' And he tore up the blue form irritably.

Paul, his ears red with shame, began again. Still Mr Jordan watched.

'I don't know what they *do* teach in school. You'll have to write better than that. Lads learn nothing nowadays, but how to recite poetry and play the fiddle. Have you seen his writing?' he asked of Mr Pappleworth.

'Yes; prime, isn't it?' replied Mr Pappleworth indifferently.

Mr Jordan gave a little grunt, not unamiable. Paul divined that his master's bark was worse than his bite. Indeed, the little manufacturer, although he spoke bad English, was quite gentleman enough to leave his men alone and to take no notice of trifles. But he knew he did not look like the boss and owner of the show, so he had to play his role of proprietor at first, to put things on a right footing.

'Let's see, *what's* your name?' asked Mr Pappleworth of the boy.

'Paul Morel.'

It is curious that children suffer so much at having to pronounce their own names.

'Paul Morel, is it? All right, you Paul-Morel through them things there, and then – '

Mr Pappleworth subsided on to a stool, and began writing. A girl came up from out of a door just behind, put some newly pressed elastic web appliances on the counter, and returned. Mr Pappleworth picked up the whitey-blue knee-band, examined it, and its yellow order-paper quickly, and put it on one side. Next was a flesh-pink 'leg'. He went through the few things, wrote out a couple of orders, and called to Paul to accompany him. This time they went through the door whence the girl had emerged. There Paul found himself at the top of a little wooden flight of steps, and below him saw a room with windows round two sides, and at the farther end half a dozen girls sitting bending over the benches in the light from the window, sewing. They were singing together 'Two Little Girls in Blue'. Hearing the door opened, they all turned round, to see Mr Pappleworth and Paul looking down on them from the far end of the room. They stopped singing.

'Can't you make a bit less row?' said Mr Pappleworth. 'Folk'll think we keep cats.'

A hunchback woman on a high stool turned her long, rather heavy face towards Mr Pappleworth, and said, in a contralto voice, 'They're all tom-cats then.'

In vain Mr Pappleworth tried to be impressive for Paul's benefit. He descended the steps into the finishing-off room, and went to the hunchback Fanny. She had such a short body on her high stool that her head, with its great bands of bright brown hair, seemed over-large, as did her pale, heavy face. She wore a dress of green-black cashmere, and her wrists, coming out of the narrow cuffs, were thin and flat, as she put down her work nervously. He showed her something that was wrong with a kneecap.

'Well,' she said, 'you needn't come blaming it on to me. It's not my fault.' Her colour mounted to her cheek.

'I never said it *was* your fault. Will you do as I tell you?' replied Mr Pappleworth shortly.

'You don't say it's my fault, but you'd like to make out as it was,' the hunchback woman cried, almost in tears. Then she snatched the kneecap from her 'boss', saying: 'Yes, I'll do it for you, but you needn't be snappy.'

'Here's your new lad,' said Mr Pappleworth.

Fanny turned, smiling very gently on Paul.

'Oh!' she said.

'Yes; don't make a softy of him between you.'

'It's not us as 'ud make a softy of him,' she said indignantly.

'Come on then, Paul,' said Mr Pappleworth.

'*Au revoy*, Paul,' said one of the girls.

There was a titter of laughter. Paul went out, blushing deeply, not having spoken a word.

The day was very long. All morning the work-people were coming to speak to Mr Pappleworth. Paul was writing or learning to make up parcels, ready for the midday post. At one o'clock, or, rather, at a quarter to one, Mr Pappleworth disappeared to catch his train: he lived in the suburbs. At one o'clock, Paul, feeling very lost, took his dinner-basket down into the stockroom in the basement, that had the long table on trestles, and ate his meal hurriedly, alone in that cellar of gloom and desolation. Then he went out of doors. The brightness and the freedom of the streets made him feel adventurous and happy. But at two o'clock he was back in the corner of the big room. Soon the work-girls went trooping past, making remarks. It was the commoner girls who worked upstairs at the heavy tasks of truss-making and the finishing of artificial limbs. He waited for Mr Pappleworth, not knowing what to do, sitting scribbling on the yellow order-paper. Mr Pappleworth came at twenty minutes to three. Then he sat and gossiped with Paul, treating the boy entirely as an equal, even in age.

In the afternoon there was never very much to do, unless it were near the weekend, and the accounts had to be made up. At five o'clock all the men went down into the dungeon with the table on trestles, and there they had tea, eating bread-and-butter on the bare, dirty boards, talking with the same kind of ugly haste and slovenliness with which they ate their meal. And yet upstairs the atmosphere among them was always jolly and clear. The cellar and the trestles affected them.

After tea, when all the gases were lighted, *work* went more briskly. There was the big evening post to get off. The hose came up warm and newly pressed from the workrooms. Paul had made out the invoices. Now he had the packing up and addressing to do, then he had to weigh his stock of parcels on the scales. Everywhere voices were calling weights, there was the chink of metal, the rapid snapping of string, the hurrying to old Mr Melling for stamps. And at last the postman came with his sack, laughing and jolly. Then everything slacked off, and Paul took his dinner-basket and ran to the station to catch the eight-twenty train. The day in the factory was just twelve hours long.

His mother sat waiting for him rather anxiously. He had to walk from Keston, so was not home until about twenty past nine. And he left the house before seven in the morning. Mrs Morel was rather anxious about his health. But she herself had had to put up with so much that she expected her children to take the same odds. They must go through with what came. And Paul stayed at Jordan's, although all the time he was there his health suffered from the darkness and lack of air and the long hours.

He came in pale and tired. His mother looked at him. She saw he was rather pleased, and her anxiety all went.

'Well, and how was it?' she asked.

'Ever so funny, mother,' he replied. 'You don't have to work a bit hard, and they're nice with you.'

'And did you get on all right?'

'Yes; they only say my writing's bad. But Mr Pappleworth – he's my man – said to Mr Jordan I should be all right. I'm Spiral, mother; you must come and see. It's ever so nice.'

Soon he liked Jordan's. Mr Pappleworth, who had a certain 'saloon bar' flavour about him, was always natural, and treated him as if he had been a comrade. Sometimes the 'Spiral boss' was irritable, and chewed more lozenges than ever. Even then, however, he was not offensive, but one of those people who hurt themselves by their own irritability more than they hurt other people.

'Haven't you done that *yet*?' he would cry. 'Go on, be a month of Sundays.'

Again, and Paul could understand him least then, he was jocular and in high spirits.

'I'm going to bring my little Yorkshire terrier bitch tomorrow,' he said jubilantly to Paul.

'What's a Yorkshire terrier?'

'*Don't* know what a Yorkshire terrier is? *Don't know a Yorkshire* – ' Mr Pappleworth was aghast.

'Is it a little silky one – colours of iron and rusty silver?'

'That's it, my lad. She's a gem. She's had five pounds' worth of pups already, and she's worth over seven pounds herself; and she doesn't weigh twenty ounces.'

The next day the bitch came. She was a shivering, miserable morsel. Paul did not care for her; she seemed so like a wet rag that would never dry. Then a man called for her, and began to make coarse jokes. But Mr Pappleworth nodded his head in the direction of the boy, and the talk went on *sotto voce*.

Mr Jordan only made one more excursion to watch Paul, and then the only fault he found was seeing the boy lay his pen on the counter.

'Put your pen in your ear, if you're going to be a clerk. Pen in your ear!' And one day he said to the lad, 'Why don't you hold your shoulders straighter? Come down here,' when he took him into the glass office and fitted him with special braces for keeping the shoulders square.

But Paul liked the girls best. The men seemed common and rather dull. He liked them all, but they were uninteresting. Polly, the little brisk overseer downstairs, finding Paul eating in the cellar, asked him if she could cook him anything on her little stove. Next day his mother gave him a dish that could be heated up. He took it into the pleasant, clean room to Polly. And very soon it grew to be an established custom that he should have dinner with her. When he came in at eight in the morning he took his basket to her, and when he came down at one o'clock she had his dinner ready.

He was not very tall, and pale, with thick chestnut hair, irregular features, and a wide, full mouth. She was like a small bird. He often called her a 'robinet'. Though naturally rather quiet, he would sit and chatter with her for hours telling her about his home. The girls all liked to hear him talk. They often gathered in a little circle while he sat on a bench, and held forth to them, laughing. Some of them regarded him as a curious little creature, so serious, yet so bright and jolly, and always so delicate in his way with them. They all liked him, and he adored them. Polly he felt he belonged to. Then Connie, with her mane of red hair, her face of apple-blossom, her murmuring voice, such a lady in her shabby black frock, appealed to his romantic side.

'When you sit winding,' he said, 'it looks as if you were spinning at a spinning-wheel – it looks ever so nice. You remind me of Elaine in the "Idylls of the King". I'd draw you if I could.'

And she glanced at him blushing shyly. And later on he had a sketch he prized very much: Connie sitting on the stool before the wheel, her flowing mane of red hair on her rusty black frock, her red mouth shut and serious, running the scarlet thread off the hank on to the reel.

With Louisa, handsome and brazen, who always seemed to thrust her hip at him, he usually joked.

Emma was rather plain, rather old, and condescending. But to condescend to him made her happy, and he did not mind.

'How do you put needles in?' he asked.

'Go away and don't bother.'

'But I ought to know how to put needles in.'

She ground at her machine all the while steadily.

'There are many things you ought to know,' she replied.

'Tell me, then, how to stick needles in the machine.'

'Oh, the boy, what a nuisance he is! Why, *this* is how you do it.'

He watched her attentively. Suddenly a whistle piped. Then Polly appeared, and said in a clear voice, 'Mr Pappleworth wants to know how much longer you're going to be down here playing with the girls, Paul.'

Paul flew upstairs, calling 'Goodbye!' and Emma drew herself up.

'It wasn't *me* who wanted him to play with the machine,' she said.

As a rule, when all the girls came back at two o'clock he ran upstairs to Fanny, the hunchback, in the finishing-off room. Mr Pappleworth did not appear till twenty to three and he often found his boy sitting beside Fanny, talking, or drawing, or singing with the girls.

Often, after a minute's hesitation, Fanny would begin to sing. She had a fine contralto voice. Everybody joined in the chorus, and it went well. Paul was not at all embarrassed, after a while, sitting in the room with the half a dozen work-girls.

At the end of the song Fanny would say, 'I know you've been laughing at me.'

'Don't be so soft, Fanny!' cried one of the girls.

Once there was mention of Connie's red hair.

'Fanny's is better, to my fancy,' said Emma.

'You needn't try to make a fool of me,' said Fanny, flushing deeply.

'No, but she has, Paul; she's got beautiful hair.'

'It's a treat of a colour,' said he. 'That coldish colour like earth, and yet shiny. It's like bog-water.'

'Goodness me!' exclaimed one girl, laughing.

'How I do but get criticised,' said Fanny.

'But you should see it down, Paul,' cried Emma earnestly. 'It's simply beautiful. Put it down for him, Fanny, if he wants something to paint.'

Fanny would not, and yet she wanted to.

'Then I'll take it down myself,' said the lad.

'Well, you can if you like,' said Fanny.

And he carefully took the pins out of the knot, and the rush of hair, of uniform dark brown, slid over the humped back.

'What a lovely lot!' he exclaimed.

The girls watched. There was silence. The youth shook the hair loose from the coil.

'It's splendid!' he said, smelling its perfume. 'I'll bet it's worth pounds.'

'I'll leave it you when I die, Paul,' said Fanny, half joking.

'You look just like anybody else, sitting drying their hair,' said one of the girls to the long-legged hunchback.

Poor Fanny was morbidly sensitive, always imagining insults. Polly was curt and businesslike. The two departments were for ever at war, and Paul was always finding Fanny in tears. Then he was made the recipient of all her woes, and he had to plead her cause with Polly.

So the time went along happily enough. The factory had a homely feel. No one was rushed or driven. Paul always enjoyed it when the work got faster, towards post-time, and all the men united in labour. He liked to watch his fellow clerks at work. The man was the work and the work was the man, one thing, for the time being. It was different with the girls. The real woman never seemed to be there at the task, but as if left out, waiting.

From the train going home at night he used to watch the lights of the town, sprinkled thick on the hills, fusing together in a blaze in the valleys. He felt rich in life and happy. Drawing farther off, there was a patch of lights at Bulwell like myriad petals shaken to the ground from the shed stars; and beyond was the red glare of the furnaces, playing like hot breath on the clouds.

He had to walk two and more miles from Keston home, up two long hills, down two short hills. He was often tired, and he counted the lamps climbing the hill above him, how many more to pass. And from the hilltop, on pitch-dark nights, he looked round on the villages five or six miles away, that shone like swarms of glittering living things, almost a heaven against his feet. Marlpool and

Heanor scattered the far-off darkness with brilliance. And occasionally the black valley space between was traced, violated by a great train rushing south to London or north to Scotland. The trains roared by like projectiles level on the darkness, fuming and burning, making the valley clang with their passage. They were gone, and the lights of the towns and villages glittered in silence.

And then he came to the corner at home, which faced the other side of the night. The ash tree seemed a friend now. His mother rose with gladness as he entered. He put his eight shillings proudly on the table.

'It'll help, mother?' he asked wistfully.

'There's precious little left,' she answered, 'after your ticket and dinners and such are taken off.'

Then he told her the budget of the day. His life-story, like an Arabian Nights, was told night after night to his mother. It was almost as if it were her own life.

CHAPTER 6

Death in the Family

Arthur Morel was growing up. He was a quick, careless, impulsive boy, a good deal like his father. He hated study, made a great moan if he had to work, and escaped as soon as possible to his sport again.

In appearance he remained the flower of the family, being well made, graceful, and full of life. His dark brown hair and fresh colouring, and his exquisite dark blue eyes shaded with long lashes, together with his generous manner and fiery temper, made him a favourite. But as he grew older his temper became uncertain. He flew into rages over nothing, seemed unbearably raw and irritable.

His mother, whom he loved, wearied of him sometimes. He thought only of himself. When he wanted amusement, all that stood in his way he hated, even if it were she. When he was in trouble he moaned to her ceaselessly.

'Goodness, boy!' she said, when he groaned about a master who, he said, hated him, 'if you don't like it, alter it, and if you can't alter it, put up with it.'

And his father, whom he had loved and who had worshipped him, he came to detest. As he grew older Morel fell into a slow ruin. His body, which had been beautiful in movement and in being, shrank, did not seem to ripen with the years, but to get mean and rather despicable. There came over him a look of meanness and of paltriness. And when the mean-looking elderly man bullied or ordered the boy about, Arthur was furious. Moreover, Morel's manners got worse and worse, his habits somewhat disgusting. When the children were growing up and in the crucial stage of adolescence, the father was like some ugly irritant to their souls. His manners in the house were the same as he used among the colliers down pit.

'Dirty nuisance!' Arthur would cry, jumping up and going straight out of the house when his father disgusted him. And Morel persisted the more because his children hated it. He seemed to take a kind of satisfaction in disgusting them, and driving them nearly mad, while they were so irritably sensitive at the age of fourteen or fifteen. So that Arthur, who was growing up when his father was degenerate and elderly, hated him worst of all.

Then, sometimes, the father would seem to feel the contemptuous hatred of his children.

'There's not a man tries harder for his family!' he would shout. 'He does his best for them, and then gets treated like a dog. But I'm not going to stand it, I tell you!'

But for the threat and the fact that he did not try so hard as he imagined, they would have felt sorry. As it was, the battle now went on nearly all between father and children, he persisting in his dirty and disgusting ways, just to assert his independence. They loathed him.

Arthur was so inflamed and irritable at last, that when he won a scholarship for the Grammar School in Nottingham, his mother decided to let him live in town, with one of her sisters, and only come home at weekends.

Annie was still a junior teacher in the Board-school, earning about four shillings a week. But soon she would have fifteen shillings, since she had passed her examination, and there would be financial peace in the house.

Mrs Morel clung now to Paul. He was quiet and not brilliant. But still he stuck to his painting, and still he stuck to his mother. Everything he did was for her. She waited for his coming home in the evening, and then she unburdened herself of all she had pondered, or of all that had occurred to her during the day. He sat and listened with his earnestness. The two shared lives.

William was engaged now to his brunette, and had bought her an engagement ring that cost eight guineas. The children gasped at such a fabulous price.

'Eight guineas!' said Morel. 'More fool him! If he'd gen me some on't, it 'ud ha' looked better on 'im.'

'Given *you* some of it!' cried Mrs Morel. 'Why give *you* some of it!'

She remembered *he* had bought no engagement ring at all, and she preferred William, who was not mean, if he were foolish. But now the young man talked only of the dances to which he went with his betrothed, and the different resplendent clothes she wore; or he told his mother with glee how they went to the theatre like great swells.

He wanted to bring the girl home. Mrs Morel said she should come at the Christmas. This time William arrived with a lady, but with no presents. Mrs Morel had prepared supper. Hearing footsteps, she rose and went to the door. William entered.

'Hello, mother!' He kissed her hastily, then stood aside to present a tall, handsome girl, who was wearing a costume of fine black-and-white check, and furs.

'Here's Gyp!'

Miss Western held out her hand and showed her teeth in a small smile.

'Oh, how do you do, Mrs Morel!' she exclaimed.

'I am afraid you will be hungry,' said Mrs Morel.

'Oh no, we had dinner in the train. Have you got my gloves, Chubby?'

William Morel, big and raw-boned, looked at her quickly.

'How should I?' he said.

'Then I've lost them. Don't be cross with me.'

A frown went over his face, but he said nothing. She glanced round the kitchen. It was small and curious to her, with its glittering kissing-bunch, its evergreens behind the pictures, its wooden chairs and little deal table. At that moment Morel came in.

'Hello, dad!'

'Hello, my son! Tha's let on me!'

The two shook hands, and William presented the lady. She gave the same smile that showed her teeth.

'How do you do, Mr Morel?'

Morel bowed obsequiously.

'I'm very well, and I hope so are you. You must make yourself very welcome.'

'Oh, thank you,' she replied, rather amused.

'You will like to go upstairs,' said Mrs Morel.

'If you don't mind; but not if it is any trouble to you.'

'It is no trouble. Annie will take you. Walter, carry up this box.'

'And don't be an hour dressing yourself up,' said William to his betrothed.

Annie took a brass candlestick, and, too shy almost to speak, preceded the young lady to the front bedroom, which Mr and Mrs Morel had vacated for her. It, too, was small and cold by candlelight. The colliers' wives only lit fires in bedrooms in case of extreme illness.

'Shall I unstrap the box?' asked Annie.

'Oh, thank you very much!'

Annie played the part of maid, then went downstairs for hot water.

'I think she's rather tired, mother,' said William. 'It's a beastly journey, and we had such a rush.'

'Is there anything I can give her?' asked Mrs Morel.

'Oh no, she'll be all right.'

But there was a chill in the atmosphere. After half an hour Miss Western came down, having put on a purplish-coloured dress, very fine for the collier's kitchen.

'I told you you'd no need to change,' said William to her.

'Oh, Chubby!' Then she turned with that sweetish smile to Mrs Morel. 'Don't you think he's always grumbling, Mrs Morel?'

'Is he?' said Mrs Morel. 'That's not very nice of him.'

'It isn't, really!'

'You are cold,' said the mother. 'Won't you come near the fire?'

Morel jumped out of his armchair.

'Come and sit you here!' he cried. 'Come and sit you here!'

'No, dad, keep your own chair. Sit on the sofa, Gyp,' said William.

'No, no!' cried Morel. 'This cheer's warmest. Come and sit here, Miss Weston.'

'Thank you so much,' said the girl, seating herself in the collier's armchair, the place of honour. She shivered, feeling the warmth of the kitchen penetrate her.

'Fetch me a hanky, Chubby dear!' she said, putting up her mouth to him, and using the same intimate tone as if they were alone; which made the rest of the family feel as if they ought not to be present. The young lady evidently did not realise them as people: they were creatures to her for the present. William winced.

In such a household, in Streatham, Miss Western would have been a lady condescending to her inferiors. These people were, to her, certainly clownish – in short, the working classes. How was she to adjust herself?

'I'll go,' said Annie.

Miss Western took no notice, as if a servant had spoken. But when the girl came downstairs again with the handkerchief, she said, 'Oh, thank you!' in a gracious way.

She sat and talked about the dinner on the train, which had been so poor; about London, about dances. She was really very nervous, and chattered from fear. Morel sat all the time smoking his thick twist tobacco, watching her, and listening to her glib London speech, as he puffed. Mrs Morel, dressed up in her best black silk blouse, answered quietly and rather briefly. The three children sat round in silence and admiration. Miss Western was the princess. Everything of the best was got out for her: the best cups, the best spoons, the best tablecloth, the best coffee-jug. The children thought she must find it quite grand. She felt strange, not able to realise the people, not knowing how to treat them. William joked, and was slightly uncomfortable.

At about ten o'clock he said to her, 'Aren't you tired, Gyp?'

'Rather, Chubby,' she answered, at once in the intimate tones and putting her head slightly on one side.

'I'll light her the candle, mother,' he said.

'Very well,' replied the mother.

Miss Western stood up, held out her hand to Mrs Morel.

'Good-night, Mrs Morel,' she said.

Paul sat at the boiler, letting the water run from the tap into a stone beer-bottle. Annie swathed the bottle in an old flannel pit-singlet, and kissed her mother good-night. She was to share the room with the lady, because the house was full.

'You wait a minute,' said Mrs Morel to Annie. And Annie sat nursing the hot-water bottle. Miss Western shook hands all round, to everybody's discomfort, and took her departure, preceded by William. In five minutes he was downstairs again. His heart was rather sore; he did not know why. He talked very little till everybody had gone to bed, but himself and his mother. Then he stood with his legs apart, in his old attitude on the hearthrug, and said hesitatingly, 'Well, mother?'

'Well, my son?'

She sat in the rocking-chair, feeling somehow hurt and humiliated, for his sake.

'Do you like her?'

'Yes,' came the slow answer.

'She's shy yet, mother. She's not used to it. It's different from her aunt's house, you know.'

'Of course it is, my boy; and she must find it difficult.'

'She does.' Then he frowned swiftly. 'If only she wouldn't put on her *blessed* airs!'

'It's only her first awkwardness, my boy. She'll be all right.'

'That's it, mother,' he replied gratefully. But his brow was gloomy. 'You know, she's not like you, mother. She's not serious, and she can't think.'

'She's young, my boy.'

'Yes; and she's had no sort of show. Her mother died when she was a child. Since then she's lived with her aunt, whom she can't bear. And her father was a rake. She's had no love.'

'No! Well, you must make up to her.'

'And so – you have to forgive her a lot of things.'

'*What* do you have to forgive her, my boy?'

'I dunno. When she seems shallow, you have to remember she's never had anybody to bring her deeper side out. And she's *fearfully* fond of me.'

'Anybody can see that.'

'But you know, mother – she's – she's different from us. Those sort of people, like those she lives amongst, they don't seem to have the same principles.'

'You mustn't judge too hastily,' said Mrs Morel.

But he seemed uneasy within himself.

In the morning, however, he was up singing and larking round the house.

'Hello!' he called, sitting on the stairs. 'Are you getting up?'

'Yes,' her voice called faintly.

'Merry Christmas!' he shouted to her.

Her laugh, pretty and tinkling, was heard in the bedroom. She did not come down in half an hour.

'Was she *really* getting up when she said she was?' he asked of Annie.

'Yes, she was,' replied Annie.

He waited awhile, then went to the stairs again.

'Happy New Year,' he called.

'Thank you, Chubby dear!' came the laughing voice, far away.

'Buck up!' he implored.

It was nearly an hour, and still he was waiting for her. Morel, who always rose before six, looked at the clock.

'Well, it's a winder!' he exclaimed.

The family had breakfasted, all but William. He went to the foot of the stairs.

'Shall I have to send you an Easter egg up there?' he called, rather crossly. She only laughed. The family expected, after that time of preparation, something like magic. At last she came, looking very nice in a blouse and skirt.

'Have you *really* been all this time getting ready?' he asked.

'Chubby dear! That question is not permitted, is it, Mrs Morel?'

She played the grand lady at first. When she went with William to chapel, he in his frock-coat and silk hat, she in her furs and London-made costume, Paul and Arthur and Annie expected everybody to bow to the ground in admiration. And Morel, standing in his Sunday suit at the end of the road, watching the gallant pair go, felt he was the father of princes and princesses.

And yet she was not so grand. For a year now she had been a sort of secretary or clerk in a London office. But while she was with the Morels she queened it. She sat and let Annie or Paul wait on her as if they were her servants. She treated Mrs Morel with a certain glibness and Morel with patronage. But after a day or so she began to change her tune.

William always wanted Paul or Annie to go along with them on their walks. It was so much more interesting. And Paul really *did* admire 'Gypsy' whole-heartedly; in fact, his mother scarcely forgave the boy for the adulation with which he treated the girl.

On the second day, when Lily said, 'Oh, Annie, do you know where I left my muff?' William replied, 'You know it is in your bedroom. Why do you ask Annie?'

And Lily went upstairs with a cross, shut mouth. But it angered the young man that she made a servant of his sister.

On the third evening William and Lily were sitting together in the parlour by the fire in the dark. At a quarter to eleven Mrs Morel was heard raking the fire. William came out to the kitchen, followed by his beloved.

'Is it as late as that, mother?' he said. She had been sitting alone.

'It is not late, my boy, but it is as late as I usually sit up.'

'Won't you go to bed, then?' he asked.

'And leave you two? No, my boy, I don't believe in it.'

'Can't you trust us, mother?'

'Whether I can or not, I won't do it. You can stay till eleven if you like, and I can read.'

'Go to bed, Gyp,' he said to his girl. 'We won't keep mater waiting.'

'Annie has left the candle burning, Lily,' said Mrs Morel; 'I think you will see.'

'Yes, thank you. Good-night, Mrs Morel.'

William kissed his sweetheart at the foot of the stairs, and she went. He returned to the kitchen.

'Can't you trust us, mother?' he repeated, rather offended.

'My boy, I tell you I don't *believe* in leaving two young things like you alone downstairs when everyone else is in bed.'

And he was forced to take this answer. He kissed his mother good-night.

At Easter he came over alone. And then he discussed his sweetheart endlessly with his mother.

'You know, mother, when I'm away from her I don't care for her a bit. I shouldn't care if I never saw her again. But, then, when I'm with her in the evenings I am awfully fond of her.'

'It's a queer sort of love to marry on,' said Mrs Morel, 'if she holds you no more than that!'

'It is funny!' he exclaimed. It worried and perplexed him. 'But yet – there's so much between us now I couldn't give her up.'

'You know best,' said Mrs Morel. 'But if it is as you say, I wouldn't call it *love* – at any rate, it doesn't look much like it.'

'Oh, I don't know, mother. She's an orphan, and – '

They never came to any sort of conclusion. He seemed puzzled and rather fretted. She was rather reserved. All his strength and money went in keeping this girl. He could scarcely afford to take his mother to Nottingham when he came over.

Paul's wages had been raised at Christmas to ten shillings, to his great joy. He was quite happy at Jordan's, but his health suffered from the long hours and the confinement. His mother, to whom he became more and more significant, thought how to help.

His half-day holiday was on Monday afternoon. On a Monday morning in May, as the two sat alone at breakfast, she said, 'I think it will be a fine day.'

He looked up in surprise. This meant something.

'You know Mr Leivers has gone to live on a new farm. Well, he asked me last week if I wouldn't go and see Mrs Leivers, and I promised to bring you on Monday if it's fine. Shall we go?'

'I say, little woman, how lovely!' he cried. 'And we'll go this afternoon?'

Paul hurried off to the station jubilant. Down Derby Road was a cherry tree that glistened. The old brick wall by the Statutes ground burned scarlet, spring was a very flame of green. And the steep swoop of highroad lay, in its cool morning dust, splendid with patterns of sunshine and shadow, perfectly still. The trees sloped their great green shoulders proudly; and inside the warehouse all the morning, the boy had a vision of spring outside.

When he came home at dinner-time his mother was rather excited.

'Are we going?' he asked.

'When I'm ready,' she replied.

Presently he got up.

'Go and get dressed while I wash up,' he said.

She did so. He washed the pots, straightened, and then took her boots. They were quite clean. Mrs Morel was one of those naturally exquisite people who can walk in mud without dirtying their shoes. But Paul had to clean them for her. They were kid boots at eight shillings a pair. He, however, thought them the most dainty boots in the world, and he cleaned them with as much reverence as if they had been flowers.

Suddenly she appeared in the inner doorway rather shyly.

She had got a new cotton blouse on. Paul jumped up and went forward.

'Oh, my stars!' he exclaimed. 'What a bobby-dazzler!'

She sniffed in a little haughty way, and put her head up.

'It's not a bobby-dazzler at all!' she replied. 'It's very quiet.'

She walked forward, whilst he hovered round her.

'Well,' she asked, quite shy, but pretending to be high and mighty, 'do you like it?'

'Awfully! You *are* a fine little woman to go jaunting out with!'

He went and surveyed her from the back.

'Well,' he said, 'if I was walking down the street behind you, I should say, "Doesn't that little person fancy herself!"'

'Well, she doesn't,' replied Mrs Morel. 'She's not sure it suits her.'

'Oh no! she wants to be in dirty black, looking as if she was wrapped in burnt paper. It *does* suit you, and *I* say you look nice.'

She sniffed in her little way, pleased, but pretending to know better.

'Well,' she said, 'it's cost me just three shillings. You couldn't have got it ready-made for that price, could you?'

'I should think you couldn't,' he replied.

'And, you know, it's good stuff.'

'Awfully pretty,' he said.

The blouse was white, with a little sprig of heliotrope and black.

'Too young for me, though, I'm afraid,' she said.

'Too young for you!' he exclaimed in disgust. 'Why don't you buy some false white hair and stick it on your head?'

'I s'll soon have no need,' she replied. 'I'm going white fast enough.'

'Well you've no business to,' he said. 'What do I want with a white-haired mother?'

'I'm afraid you'll have to put up with one, my lad,' she said rather strangely.

They set off in great style, she carrying the umbrella William had given her, because of the sun. Paul was considerably taller than she, though he was not big. He fancied himself.

On the fallow land the young wheat shone silkily. Minton pit waved its plumes of white steam, coughed, and rattled hoarsely.

'Now look at that!' said Mrs Morel. Mother and son stood on the road to watch. Along the ridge of the great pit-hill crawled a little group in silhouette against the sky, a horse, a small truck, and a man. They climbed the incline against the heavens. At the end the man tipped the waggon. There was an undue rattle as the waste fell down the sheer slope of the enormous bank.

'You sit a minute, mother,' he said, and she took a seat on a bank, whilst he sketched rapidly. She was silent whilst he worked, looking round at the afternoon, the red cottages shining among their greenness.

'The world is a wonderful place,' she said, 'and wonderfully beautiful.'

'And so's the pit,' he said. 'Look how it heaps together, like something alive almost – a big creature that you don't know.'

'Yes,' she said. 'Perhaps!'

'And all the trucks standing waiting, like a string of beasts to be fed,' he said.

'And very thankful I am they *are* standing,' she said, 'for that means they'll turn middling time this week.'

'But I like the feel of *men* on things, while they're alive. There's a feel of men about trucks, because they've been handled with men's hands, all of them.'

'Yes,' said Mrs Morel.

They went along under the trees of the highroad. He was constantly informing her, but she was interested. They passed the end of Nethermere, that was tossing its sunshine like petals lightly in its lap. Then they turned on a private road, and in some trepidation approached a big farm. A dog barked furiously. A woman came out to see.

'Is this the way to Willey Farm?' Mrs Morel asked.

Paul hung behind in terror of being sent back. But the woman was amiable, and directed them. The mother and son went through the wheat and oats, over a little bridge into a wild meadow. Peewits, with their white breasts glistening, wheeled and screamed about them. The lake was still and blue. High overhead a heron floated. Opposite, the wood heaped on the hill, green and still.

'It's a wild road, mother,' said Paul. 'Just like Canada.'

'Isn't it beautiful!' said Mrs Morel, looking round.

'See that heron – see – see her legs?'

He directed his mother, what she must see and what not. And she was quite content.

'But now,' she said, 'which way? He told me through the wood.'

The wood, fenced and dark, lay on their left.

'I can feel a bit of a path on this road,' said Paul. 'You've got town feet, somehow or other, you have.'

They found a little gate, and soon were in a broad green alley of the wood, with a new thicket of fir and pine on one hand, an old oak glade dipping down on the other. And among the oaks, the bluebells stood in pools of azure, under the new green hazels, upon a pale fawn floor of oak-leaves. He found flowers for her.

'Here's a bit of new-mown hay,' he said; then, again, he brought her forget-me-nots. And again, his heart hurt with love, seeing her hand, used with work, holding the little bunch of flowers he gave her. She was perfectly happy.

But at the end of the riding was a fence to climb. Paul was over in a second.

'Come,' he said, 'let me help you.'

'No, go away. I will do it in my own way.'

He stood below with his hands up ready to help her. She climbed cautiously.

'What a way to climb!' he exclaimed scornfully, when she was safely to earth again.

'Hateful stiles!' she cried.

'Duffer of a little woman,' he replied, 'who can't get over 'em.'

In front, along the edge of the wood, was a cluster of low red farm buildings. The two hastened forward. Flush with the wood was the apple orchard, where blossom was falling on the grindstone. The pond was deep under a hedge and overhanging oak trees. Some cows stood in the shade. The farm and buildings, three sides of a quadrangle, embraced the sunshine towards the wood. It was very still.

Mother and son went into the small railed garden, where was a scent of red gillivers. By the open door were some floury loaves, put out to cool. A hen was just coming to peck them. Then, in the doorway suddenly appeared a girl in a dirty apron. She was about fourteen years old, had a rosy dark face, a bunch of short black curls, very fine and free, and dark eyes; shy, questioning, a little resentful of the strangers, she disappeared. In a minute another figure appeared, a small, frail woman, rosy, with great dark brown eyes.

'Oh!' she exclaimed, smiling with a little glow, 'you've come, then. I *am* glad to see you.' Her voice was intimate and rather sad.

The two women shook hands.

'Now are you sure we're not a bother to you?' said Mrs Morel. 'I know what a farming life is.'

'Oh no! We're only too thankful to see a new face, it's so lost up here.'

'I suppose so,' said Mrs Morel.

They were taken through into the parlour – a long, low room, with a great bunch of guelder roses in the fireplace. There the women talked, whilst Paul went out to survey the land. He was in the garden smelling the gillivers and looking at the plants, when the girl came out quickly to the heap of coal which stood by the fence.

'I suppose these are cabbage-roses?' he said to her, pointing to the bushes along the fence.

She looked at him with startled, big brown eyes.

'I suppose they are cabbage-roses when they come out?' he said.

'I don't know,' she faltered. 'They're white with pink middles.'

'Then they're maiden-blush.'

Miriam flushed. She had a beautiful warm colouring.

'I don't know,' she said.

'You don't have *much* in your garden,' he said.

'This is our first year here,' she answered, in a distant, rather superior way, drawing back and going indoors. He did not notice, but went his round of exploration. Presently his mother came out, and they went through the buildings. Paul was hugely delighted.

'And I suppose you have the fowls and calves and pigs to look after?' said Mrs Morel to Mrs Leivers.

'No,' replied the little woman. 'I can't find time to look after cattle, and I'm not used to it. It's as much as I can do to keep going in the house.'

'Well, I suppose it is,' said Mrs Morel.

Presently the girl came out.

'Tea is ready, mother,' she said in a musical, quiet voice.

'Oh, thank you, Miriam, then we'll come,' replied her mother, almost ingratiatingly. 'Would you *care* to have tea now, Mrs Morel?'

'Of course,' said Mrs Morel. 'Whenever it's ready.'

Paul and his mother and Mrs Leivers had tea together. Then they went out into the wood that was flooded with bluebells, while furry forget-me-nots were in the paths. The mother and son were in ecstasy together.

When they got back to the house, Mr Leivers and Edgar, the eldest son, were in the kitchen. Edgar was about eighteen. Then Geoffrey and Maurice, big lads of twelve and thirteen, were in from school. Mr Leivers was a good-looking man in the prime of life, with a golden-brown moustache, and blue eyes screwed up against the weather.

The boys were condescending, but Paul scarcely observed it. They went round for eggs, scrambling into all sorts of places. As they were feeding the fowls Miriam came out. The boys took no notice of her. One hen, with her yellow chickens, was in a coop. Maurice took his hand full of corn and let the hen peck from it.

'Durst you do it?' he asked of Paul.

'Let's see,' said Paul.

He had a small hand, warm, and rather capable-looking. Miriam watched. He held the corn to the hen. The bird eyed it with her hard, bright eye, and suddenly made a peck into his hand. He started, and laughed. 'Rap, rap, rap!' went the bird's beak in his palm. He laughed again, and the other boys joined.

'She knocks you, and nips you, but she never hurts,' said Paul, when the last corn had gone.

'Now, Miriam,' said Maurice, 'you come an' 'ave a go.'

'No,' she cried, shrinking back.

'Ha! baby. The mardy-kid!' said her brothers.

'It doesn't hurt a bit,' said Paul. 'It only just nips rather nicely.'

'No,' she still cried, shaking her black curls and shrinking.

'She dursn't,' said Geoffrey. 'She niver durst do anything except recite poitry.'

'Dursn't jump off a gate, dursn't tweedle, dursn't go on a slide, dursn't stop a girl hittin' her. She can do nowt but go about thinkin' herself somebody. "The Lady of the Lake". Yah!' cried Maurice.

Miriam was crimson with shame and misery.

'I dare do more than you,' she cried. 'You're never anything but cowards and bullies.'

'Oh, cowards and bullies!' they repeated, mincingly, mocking her speech.

> 'Not such a clown shall anger me,
> A boor is answered silently,'

he quoted against her, shouting with laughter.

She went indoors. Paul went with the boys into the orchard, where they had rigged up a parallel bar. They did feats of strength. He was more agile than strong, but it served. He fingered a piece of apple-blossom that hung low on a swinging bough.

'I wouldn't get the apple-blossom,' said Edgar, the eldest brother, 'There'll be no apples next year.'

'I wasn't going to get it,' replied Paul, going away.

The boys felt hostile to him; they were more interested in their own pursuits. He wandered back to the house to look for his mother. As he went round the back, he saw Miriam kneeling in front of the hen coop, some maize in her hand, biting her lip, and crouching in an intense attitude. The hen was eyeing her wickedly. Very gingerly she put forward her hand. The hen bobbed for her. She drew back quickly with a cry, half of fear, half of chagrin.

'It won't hurt you,' said Paul.

She flushed crimson and started up.

'I only wanted to try,' she said in a low voice.

'See, it doesn't hurt,' he said, and, putting only two corns in his palm, he let the hen peck, peck, peck at his bare hand. 'It only makes you laugh,' he said.

She put her hand forward, and dragged it away, tried again, and started back with a cry. He frowned.

'Why, I'd let her take corn from my face,' said Paul, 'only she bumps a bit. She's ever so neat. If she wasn't, look how much ground she'd peck up every day.'

He waited grimly, and watched. At last Miriam let the bird peck from her hand. She gave a little cry – fear, and pain because of fear – rather pathetic. But she had done it, and she did it again.

'There, you see,' said the boy. 'It doesn't hurt, does it?'

She looked at him with dilated dark eyes.

'No,' she laughed, trembling.

Then she rose and went indoors. She seemed to be in some way resentful of the boy.

'He thinks I'm only a common girl,' she thought, and she wanted to prove she was a grand person like the 'Lady of the Lake'.

Paul found his mother ready to go home. She smiled on her son. He took the great bunch of flowers. Mr and Mrs Leivers walked down the fields with them. The hills were golden with evening; deep in the wood showed the darkening purple of bluebells. It was everywhere perfectly still, save for the rustling of leaves and birds.

'But it is a beautiful place,' said Mrs Morel.

'Yes,' answered Mr Leivers; 'it's a nice little place, if only it weren't for the rabbits. The pasture's bitten down to nothing. I dunno if ever I s'll get the rent off it.'

He clapped his hands, and the field broke into motion near the woods, brown rabbits hopping every-where.

'Would you believe it!' exclaimed Mrs Morel.

She and Paul went on alone together.

'Wasn't it lovely, mother?' he said quietly.

A thin moon was coming out. His heart was full of happiness till it hurt. His mother had to chatter, because she, too, wanted to cry with happiness.

'Now *wouldn't* I help that man!' she said. '*Wouldn't* I see to the fowls and the young stock! And *I'd* learn to milk, and *I'd* talk with him, and *I'd* plan with him. My word, if I were his wife, the farm would be run, I know! But there, she hasn't the strength – she simply hasn't the strength. She ought never to have been burdened like it, you know. I'm sorry for her, and I'm sorry for him too. My word, if *I'd* had him, I shouldn't have thought him a bad husband! Not that she does either; and she's very lovable.'

William came home again with his sweetheart at the Whitsuntide. He had one week of his holidays then. It was beautiful weather. As a rule, William and Lily and Paul went out in the morning together for a walk. William did not talk to his beloved much, except to tell her things from his boyhood. Paul talked endlessly to both of them. They lay down, all three, in a meadow by Minton Church. On one side, by the Castle Farm, was a beautiful quivering screen of poplars. Hawthorn was dropping from the hedges; penny daisies and ragged robin were in the field, like laughter. William, a big fellow of twenty-three, thinner now and even a bit gaunt, lay back in the sunshine and dreamed, while she fingered with his hair. Paul went gathering the big daisies. She had taken off her hat; her hair was black as a horse's mane. Paul came back and threaded daisies in her jet-black hair – big spangles of white and yellow, and just a pink touch of ragged robin.

'Now you look like a young witch-woman,' the boy said to her. 'Doesn't she, William?'

Lily laughed. William opened his eyes and looked at her. In his gaze was a certain baffled look of misery and fierce appreciation.

'Has he made a sight of me?' she asked, laughing down on her lover.

'That he has!' said William, smiling.

He looked at her. Her beauty seemed to hurt him. He glanced at her flower-decked head and frowned.

'You look nice enough, if that's what you want to know,' he said.

And she walked without her hat. In a little while William recovered, and was rather tender to her. Coming to a bridge, he carved her initials and his in a heart.

L. L. W.
W. M.

She watched his strong, nervous hand, with its glistening hairs and freckles, as he carved, and she seemed fascinated by it.

All the time there was a feeling of sadness and warmth, and a certain tenderness in the house, whilst William and Lily were at home. But often he got irritable. She had brought, for an eight-days' stay, five dresses and six blouses.

'Oh, would you mind,' she said to Annie, 'washing me these two blouses, and these things?'

And Annie stood washing when William and Lily went out the next morning.

Mrs Morel was furious. And sometimes the young man, catching a glimpse of his sweetheart's attitude towards his sister, hated her.

On Sunday morning she looked very beautiful in a dress of foulard, silky and sweeping, and blue as a jay-bird's feather, and in a large cream hat covered with many roses, mostly crimson. Nobody could admire her enough. But in the evening, when she was going out, she asked again, 'Chubby, have you got my gloves?'

'Which?' asked William.

'My new black *suéde*.'

'No.'

There was a hunt. She had lost them.

'Look here, mother,' said William, 'that's the fourth pair she's lost since Christmas – at five shillings a pair!'

'You only gave me *two* of them,' she remonstrated.

And in the evening, after supper, he stood on the hearthrug whilst she sat on the sofa, and he seemed to hate her. In the afternoon he had left her whilst he went to see some old friend. She had sat looking at a book. After supper William wanted to write a letter.

'Here is your book, Lily,' said Mrs Morel. 'Would you care to go on with it for a few minutes?'

'No, thank you,' said the girl. 'I will sit still.'

'But it is so dull.'

William scribbled irritably at a great rate. As he sealed the envelope he said, 'Read a book! Why, she's never read a book in her life.'

'Oh, go along!' said Mrs Morel, cross with the exaggeration.

'It's true, mother – she hasn't,' he cried, jumping up and taking his old position on the hearthrug. 'She's never read a book in her life.'

''Er's like me,' chimed in Morel. ''Er canna see what there is i' books, ter sit borin' your nose in 'em for, nor more can I.'

'But you shouldn't say these things,' said Mrs Morel to her son.

'But it's true, mother – she *can't* read. What did you give her?'

'Well, I gave her a little thing of Annie Swan's. Nobody wants to read dry stuff on Sunday afternoon.'

'Well, I'll bet she didn't read ten lines of it.'

'You are mistaken,' said his mother.

All the time Lily sat miserably on the sofa. He turned to her swiftly.

'*Did* you read any?' he asked.

'Yes, I did,' she replied.

'How much?'

'I don't know how many pages.'

'Tell me *one thing* you read.'

She could not.

She never got beyond the second page. He read a great deal, and had a quick, active intelligence. She could understand nothing but love-making and chatter.

He was accustomed to having all his thoughts sifted through his mother's mind; so, when he wanted companionship, and was asked in reply to be the billing and twittering lover, he hated his betrothed.

'You know, mother,' he said, when he was alone with her at night, 'she's no idea of money, she's so wessel-brained. When she's paid, she'll suddenly buy such rot as *marrons glacés*, and then *I* have to buy her season-ticket, and her extras, even her underclothing. And she wants to get married, and I think myself we might as well get married next year. But at this rate – '

'A fine mess of a marriage it would be,' replied his mother. 'I should consider it again, my boy.'

'Oh, well, I've gone too far to break off now,' he said, 'and so I shall get married as soon as I can.'

'Very well, my boy. If you will, you will, and there's no stopping you; but I tell you, I can't sleep when I think about it.'

'Oh, she'll be all right, mother. We shall manage.'

'And she lets you buy her underclothing?' asked the mother.

'Well,' he began apologetically, 'she didn't ask me; but one morning – and it *was* cold – I found her on the station shivering, not able to keep still; so I asked her if she was well wrapped up. She said: "I think so." So I said: "Have you got warm underthings on?" And she said No, they were cotton. I asked her why on earth she hadn't got something thicker on in weather like that, and she said because she *had* nothing. And there she is – a bronchial subject! I *had* to take her and get some warm things. Well, mother, I shouldn't mind the money if we had any. And, you know, she *ought* to keep enough to pay for her season-ticket; but no, she comes to me about that, and I have to find the money.'

'It's a poor lookout,' said Mrs Morel bitterly.

He was pale, and his rugged face, that used to be so perfectly careless and laughing, was stamped with conflict and despair.

'But I can't give her up now; it's gone too far,' he said. 'And, besides, for *some* things I couldn't do without her.'

'My boy, remember you're taking your life in your hands,' said Mrs Morel. '*Nothing* is as bad as a marriage that's a hopeless failure. Mine was bad enough, God knows, and ought to teach you something; but it might have been worse by a long chalk.'

He leaned with his back against the side of the chimney-piece, his hands in his pockets. He was a big, raw-boned man, who looked as if he would go to the world's end if he wanted to. But she saw the despair on his face.

'I couldn't give her up now,' he said.

'Well,' she said, 'remember there are worse wrongs than breaking off an engagement.'

'I can't give her up *now*,' he said.

The clock ticked on; mother and son remained in silence, a conflict between them; but he would say no more. At last she said, 'Well, go to bed, my son. You'll feel better in the morning, and perhaps you'll know better.'

He kissed her, and went. She raked the fire. Her heart was heavy now as it had never been. Before, with her husband, things had seemed to be breaking down in her, but they did not destroy her power to live. Now her soul felt lamed in itself. It was her hope that was struck.

And so often William manifested the same hatred towards his betrothed. On the last evening at home he was railing against her.

'Well,' he said, 'if you don't believe me, what she's like, would you believe she has been confirmed three times?'

'Nonsense!' laughed Mrs Morel.

'Nonsense or not, she has! That's what confirmation means for her – a bit of a theatrical show where she can cut a figure.'

'I haven't, Mrs Morel!' cried the girl – 'I haven't! it is not true!'

'What!' he cried, flashing round on her. 'Once in Bromley, once in Beckenham, and once somewhere else.'

'Nowhere else!' she said, in tears – 'nowhere else!'

'It *was*! And if it wasn't, why were you confirmed *twice*?'

'Once I was only fourteen, Mrs Morel,' she pleaded, tears in her eyes.

'Yes,' said Mrs Morel; 'I can quite understand it, child. Take no notice of him. You ought to be ashamed, William, saying such things.'

'But it's true. She's religious – she had blue velvet Prayer-Books – and she's not as much religion, or anything else, in her than that table-leg. Gets confirmed three times for show, to show herself off, and that's how she is in *everything – everything*!'

The girl sat on the sofa, crying. She was not strong.

'As for *love*!' he cried, 'you might as well ask a fly to love you! It'll love settling on you – '

'Now, say no more,' commanded Mrs Morel. 'If you want to say these things, you must find another place than this. I am ashamed of you, William! Why don't you be more manly. To do nothing but find fault with a girl, and then pretend you're engaged to her!'

Mrs Morel subsided in wrath and indignation.

William was silent, and later he repented, kissed and comforted the girl. Yet it was true, what he had said. He hated her.

When they were going away, Mrs Morel accompanied them as far as Nottingham. It was a long way to Keston station.

'You know, mother,' he said to her, 'Gyp's shallow. Nothing goes deep with her.'

'William, I *wish* you wouldn't say these things,' said Mrs Morel, very uncomfortable for the girl who walked beside her.

'But it doesn't, mother. She's very much in love with me *now*, but if I died she'd have forgotten me in three months.'

Mrs Morel was afraid. Her heart beat furiously, hearing the quiet bitterness of her son's last speech.

'How do you know?' she replied. 'You *don't* know, and therefore you've no right to say such a thing.'

'He's always saying these things!' cried the girl.

'In three months after I was buried you'd have somebody else, and I should be forgotten,' he said. 'And that's your love!'

Mrs Morel saw them into the train in Nottingham, then she returned home. 'There's one comfort,' she said to Paul – 'he'll never have any money to marry on, that I *am* sure of. And so she'll save him that way.'

So she took cheer. Matters were not yet very desperate. She firmly believed William would never marry his Gypsy. She waited, and she kept Paul near to her.

All summer long William's letters had a feverish tone; he seemed unnatural and intense. Sometimes he was exaggeratedly jolly, usually he was flat and bitter in his letter.

'Ay,' his mother said, 'I'm afraid he's ruining himself against that creature, who isn't worthy of his love – no, no more than a rag doll.'

He wanted to come home. The midsummer holiday was gone; it was a long while to Christmas. He wrote in wild excitement, saying he could come for Saturday and Sunday at Goose Fair, the first week in October.

'You are not well, my boy,' said his mother, when she saw him.

She was almost in tears at having him to herself again.

'No, I've not been well,' he said. 'I've seemed to have a dragging cold all the last month, but it's going, I think.'

It was sunny October weather. He seemed wild with joy, like a schoolboy escaped; then again he was silent and reserved. He was more gaunt than ever, and there was a haggard look in his eyes.

'You are doing too much,' said his mother to him.

He was doing extra work, trying to make some money to marry on, he said. He only talked to his mother once on the Saturday night; then he was sad and tender about his beloved.

'And yet, you know, mother, for all that, if I died she'd be broken-hearted for two months, and then she'd start to forget me. You'd see, she'd never come home here to look at my grave, not even once.'

'Why, William,' said his mother, 'you're not going to die, so why talk about it?'

'But whether or not – ' he replied.

'And she can't help it. She is like that, and if you choose her – well, you can't grumble,' said his mother.

On the Sunday morning, as he was putting his collar on, 'Look,' he said to his mother, holding up his chin, 'what a rash my collar's made under my chin!'

Just at the junction of chin and throat was a big red inflammation.

'It ought not to do that,' said his mother. 'Here, put a bit of this soothing ointment on. You should wear different collars.'

He went away on Sunday midnight, seeming better and more solid for his two days at home.

On Tuesday morning came a telegram from London that he was ill. Mrs Morel got off her knees from washing the floor, read the telegram, called a neighbour, went to her landlady and borrowed a sovereign, put on her things, and set off. She hurried to Keston, caught an express for London in Nottingham. She had to wait in Nottingham nearly an hour. A small figure in her black bonnet, she was anxiously asking the porters if they knew how to get to Elmers End. The journey was three hours. She sat in her corner in a kind of stupor, never moving. At King's Cross still no one could tell her how to get to Elmers End. Carrying her string bag, that contained her nightdress, comb and brush, she went from person to person. At last they sent her underground to Cannon Street.

It was six o'clock when she arrived at William's lodging. The blinds were not down.

'How is he?' she asked.

'No better,' said the landlady.

She followed the woman upstairs. William lay on the bed, with bloodshot eyes, his face rather discoloured. The clothes were tossed about, there was no fire in the room, a glass of milk stood on the stand at his bedside. No one had been with him.

'Why, my son!' said the mother bravely.

He did not answer. He looked at her, but did not see her. Then he began to say, in a dull voice, as if repeating a letter from dictation, 'Owing to a leakage in the hold of this vessel, the sugar had set, and become converted into rock. It needed hacking –'

He was quite unconscious. It had been his business to examine some such cargo of sugar in the Port of London.

'How long has he been like this?' the mother asked the landlady.

'He got home at six o'clock on Monday morning, and he seemed to sleep all day; then in the night we heard him talking, and this morning he asked for you. So I wired, and we fetched the doctor.'

'Will you have a fire made?'

Mrs Morel tried to soothe her son, to keep him still.

The doctor came. It was pneumonia, and, he said, a peculiar erysipelas, which had started under the chin where the collar chafed, and was spreading over the face. He hoped it would not get to the brain.

Mrs Morel settled down to nurse. She prayed for William, prayed that he would recognise her. But the young man's face grew more discoloured. In the night she struggled with him. He raved, and raved, and would not come to consciousness. At two o'clock, in a dreadful paroxysm, he died.

Mrs Morel sat perfectly still for an hour in the lodging bedroom; then she roused the household.

At six o'clock, with the aid of the charwoman, she laid him out; then she went round the dreary London village to the registrar and the doctor.

At nine o'clock to the cottage on Scargill Street came another wire, 'William died last night. Let father come, bring money.'

Annie, Paul, and Arthur were at home; Mr Morel was gone to work. The three children said not a word. Annie began to whimper with fear; Paul set off for his father.

It was a beautiful day. At Brinsley pit the white steam melted slowly in the sunshine of a soft blue sky; the wheels of the headstocks twinkled high up; the screen, shuffling its coal into the trucks, made a busy noise.

'I want my father; he's got to go to London,' said the boy to the first man he met on the bank.

'Tha wants Walter Morel? Go in theer an' tell Joe Ward.'

Paul went into the little top office.

'I want my father; he's got to go to London.'

'Thy feyther? Is he down? What's his name?'

'Mr Morel.'

'What, Walter? Is owt amiss?'

'He's got to go to London.'

The man went to the telephone and rang up the bottom office.

'Walter Morel's wanted. Number 42, Hard. Summat's amiss; there's his lad here.'

Then he turned round to Paul.

'He'll be up in a few minutes,' he said.

Paul wandered out to the pit-top. He watched the chair come up, with its waggon of coal. The great iron cage sank back on its rest, a full carfle was hauled off, an empty tram run on to the chair, a bell ting'ed somewhere, the chair heaved, then dropped like a stone.

Paul did not realise William was dead; it was impossible, with such a bustle going on. The puller-off swung the small truck on to the turntable, another man ran with it along the bank down the curving lines.

'And William is dead and my mother's in London, and what will she be doing?' the boy asked himself, as if it were a conundrum.

He watched chair after chair come up, and still no father. At last, standing beside a waggon, a man's form! The chair sank on its rests, Morel stepped off. He was slightly lame from an accident.

'Is it thee, Paul? Is 'e worse?'

'You've got to go to London.'

The two walked off the pit-bank, where men were watching curiously. As they came out and went along the railway, with the sunny autumn field on one side and a wall of trucks on the other, Morel said in a frightened voice, "E's niver gone, child?'

'Yes.'

'When wor't?'

The miner's voice was terrified.

'Last night. We had a telegram from my mother.'

Morel walked on a few strides, then leaned up against a truck side, his hand over his eyes. He was not crying. Paul stood looking round, waiting. On the weighing-machine a truck trundled slowly. Paul saw everything, except his father leaning against the truck as if he were tired.

Morel had only once before been to London. He set off, scared and peaked, to help his wife. That was on Tuesday. The children were left alone in the house. Paul went to work, Arthur went to school, and Annie had in a friend to be with her.

On Saturday night, as Paul was turning the corner, coming home from Keston, he saw his mother and father, who had come to Sethley Bridge Station. They were walking in silence in the dark, tired, straggling apart. The boy waited.

'Mother!' he said, in the darkness.

Mrs Morel's small figure seemed not to observe. He spoke again.

'Paul!' she said, uninterestedly.

She let him kiss her, but she seemed unaware of him.

In the house she was the same – small, white, and mute. She noticed nothing, she said nothing, only, 'The coffin will be here tonight, Walter. You'd better see about some help.' Then, turning to the children: 'We're bringing him home.'

Then she relapsed into the same mute looking into space, her hands folded on her lap. Paul, looking at her, felt he could not breathe. The house was dead silent.

'I went to work, mother,' he said plaintively.

'Did you?' she answered, dully.

After half an hour Morel, troubled and bewildered, came in again.

'Wheer s'll we ha'e him when he *does* come?' he asked his wife.

'In the front room.'

'Then I'd better shift th' table?'

'Yes.'

'An' ha'e him across th' chairs?'

'You know there – Yes, I suppose so.'

Morel and Paul went, with a candle, into the parlour. There was no gas there. The father unscrewed the top of the big mahogany oval table, and cleared the middle of the room; then he arranged six chairs opposite each other, so that the coffin could stand on their beds.

'You niver seed such a length as he is!' said the miner, and watching anxiously as he worked.

Paul went to the bay window and looked out. The ash tree stood monstrous and black in front of the wide darkness. It was a faintly luminous night. Paul went back to his mother.

At ten o'clock Morel called, 'He's here!'

Everyone started. There was a noise of unbarring and unlocking the front door, which opened straight from the night into the room.

'Bring another candle,' called Morel.

Annie and Arthur went. Paul followed with his mother. He stood with his arm round her waist in the inner doorway. Down the middle of the cleared room waited six chairs, face to face. In the window, against the lace curtains, Arthur held up one candle, and by the open door, against the night, Annie stood leaning forward, her brass candlestick glittering.

There was the noise of wheels. Outside in the darkness of the street below

Paul could see horses and a black vehicle, one lamp, and a few pale faces; then some men, miners, all in their shirt-sleeves, seemed to struggle in the obscurity. Presently two men appeared, bowed beneath a great weight. It was Morel and his neighbour.

'Steady!' called Morel, out of breath.

He and his fellow mounted the steep garden step, heaved into the candlelight with their gleaming coffin-end. Limbs of other men were seen struggling behind. Morel and Burns, in front, staggered, the great dark weight swayed.

'Steady, steady!' cried Morel, as if in pain.

All the six bearers were up in the small garden, holding the great coffin aloft. There were three more steps to the door. The yellow lamp of the carriage shone alone down in the black road.

'Now then!' said Morel.

The coffin swayed, the men began to mount the three steps with their load. Annie's candle flickered, and she whimpered as the first men appeared, and the limbs and bowed heads of six men struggled to climb into the room, bearing the coffin that rode like sorrow on their living flesh.

'Oh, my son – my son!' Mrs Morel sang softly, and each time the coffin swung to the unequal climbing of the men: 'Oh, my son – my son – my son!'

'Mother!' Paul whimpered, his hand round her waist. 'Mother!'

She did not hear.

'Oh, my son – my son!' she repeated.

Paul saw drops of sweat fall from his father's brow. Six men were in the room – six coatless men, with yielding, struggling limbs, filling the room and knocking against the furniture. The coffin veered, and was gently lowered on to the chairs. The sweat fell from Morel's face on its boards.

'My word, he's a weight!' said a man, and the five miners sighed, bowed, and, trembling with the struggle, descended the steps again, closing the door behind them.

The family was alone in the parlour with the great polished box. William, when laid out, was six feet four inches long. Like a monument lay the bright brown, ponderous coffin. Paul thought it would never be got out of the room again. His mother was stroking the polished wood.

They buried him on the Monday in the little cemetery on the hillside that looks over the fields at the big church and the houses. It was sunny, and the white chrysanthemums frilled themselves in the warmth.

Mrs Morel could not be persuaded, after this, to talk and take her old bright interest in life. She remained shut off. All the way home in the train she had said to herself: 'If only it could have been me!'

When Paul came home at night he found his mother sitting, her day's work done, with hands folded in her lap upon her coarse apron. She always used to have changed her dress and put on a black apron, before. Now Annie set his supper, and his mother sat looking blankly in front of her, her mouth shut tight. Then he beat his brains for news to tell her.

'Mother, Miss Jordan was down today, and she said my sketch of a colliery at work was beautiful.'

But Mrs Morel took no notice. Night after night he forced himself to tell her things, although she did not listen. It drove him almost insane to have her thus. At last, 'What's a-matter, mother?' he asked.

She did not hear.

'What's a-matter?' he persisted. 'Mother, what's a-matter?'

'You know what's the matter,' she said irritably, turning away.

The lad – he was sixteen years old – went to bed drearily. He was cut off and wretched through October, November, and December. His mother tried, but she could not rouse herself. She could only brood on her dead son; he had been let to die so cruelly.

At last, on December 23, with his five shillings Christmas-box in his pocket, Paul wandered blindly home. His mother looked at him, and her heart stood still.

'What's the matter?' she asked.

'I'm badly, mother!' he replied. 'Mr Jordan gave me five shillings for a Christmas-box!'

He handed it to her with trembling hands. She put it on the table.

'You aren't glad!' he reproached her; but he trembled violently.

'Where hurts you?' she said, unbuttoning his overcoat.

It was the old question.

'I feel badly, mother.'

She undressed him and put him to bed. He had pneumonia dangerously, the doctor said.

'Might he never have had it if I'd kept him at home, not let him go to Nottingham?' was one of the first things she asked.

'He might not have been so bad,' said the doctor.

Mrs Morel stood condemned on her own ground.

'I should have watched the living, not the dead,' she told herself.

Paul was very ill. His mother lay in bed at nights with him; they could not afford a nurse. He grew worse, and the crisis approached. One night he tossed into consciousness in the ghastly, sickly feeling of dissolution, when all the cells in the body seem in intense irritability to be breaking down, and consciousness makes a last flare of struggle, like madness.

'I s'll die, mother!' he cried, heaving for breath on the pillow.

She lifted him up, crying in a small voice, 'Oh, my son – my son!'

That brought him to. He realised her. His whole will rose up and arrested him. He put his head on her breast, and took ease of her for love.

'For some things,' said his aunt, 'it was a good thing Paul was ill that Christmas. I believe it saved his mother.'

Paul was in bed for seven weeks. He got up white and fragile. His father had bought him a pot of scarlet and gold tulips. They used to flame in the window in the March sunshine as he sat on the sofa chattering to his mother. The two knitted together in perfect intimacy. Mrs Morel's life now rooted itself in Paul.

William had been a prophet. Mrs Morel had a little present and a letter from Lily at Christmas. Mrs Morel's sister had a letter at the New Year.

'I was at a ball last night. Some delightful people were there, and I enjoyed myself thoroughly,' said the letter. 'I had every dance – did not sit out one.'

Mrs Morel never heard any more of her.

Morel and his wife were gentle with each other for some time after the death of their son. He would go into a kind of daze, staring wide-eyed and blank across the room. Then he got up suddenly and hurried out to the Three Spots, returning in his normal state. But never in his life would he go for a walk up Shepstone, past the office where his son had worked, and he always avoided the cemetery.

PART TWO

CHAPTER 7

Lad-and-Girl Love

Paul had been many times up to Willey Farm during the autumn. He was friends with the two youngest boys. Edgar, the eldest, would not condescend at first. And Miriam also refused to be approached. She was afraid of being set at nought, as by her own brothers. The girl was romantic in her soul. Everywhere was a Walter Scott heroine being loved by men with helmets or with plumes in their caps. She herself was something of a princess turned into a swine-girl in her own imagination. And she was afraid lest this boy, who, nevertheless, looked something like a Walter Scott hero, who could paint and speak French, and knew what algebra meant, and who went by train to Nottingham every day, might consider her simply as the swine-girl, unable to perceive the princess beneath; so she held aloof.

Her great companion was her mother. They were both brown-eyed and inclined to be mystical, such women as treasure religion inside them, breathe it in their nostrils, and see the whole of life in a mist thereof. So to Miriam, Christ and God made one great figure, which she loved tremblingly and passionately when a tremendous sunset burned out the western sky, and Ediths, and Lucys, and Rowenas, Brian de Bois Guilberts, Rob Roys, and Guy Mannerings, rustled the sunny leaves in the morning, or sat in her bedroom aloft, alone, when it snowed. That was life to her. For the rest, she drudged in the house, which work she would not have minded had not her clean red floor been mucked up immediately by the trampling farm-boots of her brothers. She madly wanted her little brother of four to let her swathe him and stifle him in her love; she went to church reverently, with bowed head, and quivered in anguish from the vulgarity of the other choirgirls and from the common-sounding voice of the curate; she fought with her brothers, whom she considered brutal louts; and she held not her father in too high esteem because he did not carry any mystical ideals cherished in his heart, but only wanted to have as easy a time as he could, and his meals when he was ready for them.

She hated her position as swine-girl. She wanted to be considered. She wanted to learn, thinking that if she could read, as Paul said he could read, 'Colomba', or the 'Voyage autour de ma Chambre', the world would have a different face for her and a deepened respect. She could not be princess by wealth or standing. So she was mad to have learning whereon to pride herself.

For she was different from other folk, and must not be scooped up among the common fry. Learning was the only distinction to which she thought to aspire.

Her beauty – that of a shy, wild, quiveringly sensitive thing – seemed nothing to her. Even her soul, so strong for rhapsody, was not enough. She must have something to reinforce her pride, because she felt different from other people. Paul she eyed rather wistfully. On the whole, she scorned the male sex. But here was a new specimen, quick, light, graceful, who could be gentle and who could be sad, and who was clever, and who knew a lot, and who had a death in the family. The boy's poor morsel of learning exalted him almost sky-high in her esteem. Yet she tried hard to scorn him, because he would not see in her the princess but only the swine-girl. And he scarcely observed her.

Then he was so ill, and she felt he would be weak. Then she would be stronger than he. Then she could love him. If she could be mistress of him in his weakness, take care of him, if he could depend on her, if she could, as it were, have him in her arms, how she would love him!

As soon as the skies brightened and plum-blossom was out, Paul drove off in the milkman's heavy float up to Willey Farm. Mr Leivers shouted in a kindly fashion at the boy, then clicked to the horse as they climbed the hill slowly, in the freshness of the morning. White clouds went on their way, crowding to the back of the hills that were rousing in the springtime. The water of Nethermere lay below, very blue against the seared meadows and the thorn trees.

It was four and a half miles' drive. Tiny buds on the hedges, vivid as copper-green, were opening into rosettes; and thrushes called, and blackbirds shrieked and scolded. It was a new, glamorous world.

Miriam, peeping through the kitchen window, saw the horse walk through the big white gate into the farmyard that was backed by the oak-wood, still bare. Then a youth in a heavy overcoat climbed down. He put up his hands for the whip and the rug that the good-looking, ruddy farmer handed down to him.

Miriam appeared in the doorway. She was nearly sixteen, very beautiful, with her warm colouring, her gravity, her eyes dilating suddenly like an ecstasy.

'I say,' said Paul, turning shyly aside, 'your daffodils are nearly out. Isn't it early? But don't they look cold?'

'Cold!' said Miriam, in her musical, caressing voice.

'The green on their buds – ' and he faltered into silence timidly.

'Let me take the rug,' said Miriam over-gently.

'I can carry it,' he answered, rather injured. But he yielded it to her.

Then Mrs Leivers appeared.

'I'm sure you're tired and cold,' she said. 'Let me take your coat. It is heavy. You mustn't walk far in it.'

She helped him off with his coat. He was quite unused to such attention. She was almost smothered under its weight.

'Why, mother,' laughed the farmer as he passed through the kitchen, swinging the great milk-churns, 'you've got almost more than you can manage there.'

She beat up the sofa cushions for the youth.

The kitchen was very small and irregular. The farm had been originally a labourer's cottage. And the furniture was old and battered. But Paul loved it – loved the sack-bag that formed the hearthrug, and the funny little corner under the stairs, and the small window deep in the corner, through which, bending a little, he could see the plum trees in the back garden and the lovely round hills beyond.

'Won't you lie down?' said Mrs Leivers.

'Oh no, I'm not tired,' he said. 'Isn't it lovely coming out, don't you think? I saw a sloe-bush in blossom and a lot of celandines. I'm glad it's sunny.'

'Can I give you anything to eat or to drink?'

'No, thank you.'

'How's your mother?'

'I think she's tired now. I think she's had too much to do. Perhaps in a little while she'll go to Skegness with me. Then she'll be able to rest. I s'll be glad if she can.'

'Yes,' replied Mrs Leivers. 'It's a wonder she isn't ill herself.'

Miriam was moving about preparing dinner. Paul watched everything that happened. His face was pale and thin, but his eyes were quick and bright with life as ever. He watched the strange, almost rhapsodic way in which the girl moved about, carrying a great stew-jar to the oven, or looking in the saucepan. The atmosphere was different from that of his own home, where everything seemed so ordinary. When Mr Leivers called loudly outside to the horse, that was reaching over to feed on the rose-bushes in the garden, the girl started, looked round with dark eyes, as if something had come breaking in on her world. There was a sense of silence inside the house and out. Miriam seemed as in some dreamy tale, a maiden in bondage, her spirit dreaming in a land far away and magical. And her discoloured old blue frock and her broken boots seemed only like the romantic rags of King Cophetua's beggar-maid.

She suddenly became aware of his keen blue eyes upon her, taking her all in. Instantly her broken boots and her frayed old frock hurt her. She resented his seeing everything. Even he knew that her stocking was not pulled up. She went into the scullery, blushing deeply. And afterwards her hands trembled slightly at her work. She nearly dropped all she handled. When her inside dream was shaken, her body quivered with trepidation. She resented that he saw so much.

Mrs Leivers sat for some time talking to the boy, although she was needed at her work. She was too polite to leave him. Presently she excused herself and rose. After a while she looked into the tin saucepan.

'Oh *dear*, Miriam,' she cried, 'these potatoes have boiled dry!'

Miriam started as if she had been stung.

'*Have* they, mother?' she cried.

'I shouldn't care, Miriam,' said the mother, 'if I hadn't trusted them to you.' She peered into the pan.

The girl stiffened as if from a blow. Her dark eyes dilated; she remained standing in the same spot.

'Well,' she answered, gripped tight in self-conscious shame, 'I'm sure I looked at them five minutes since.'

'Yes,' said the mother, 'I know it's easily done.'

'They're not much burned,' said Paul. 'It doesn't matter, does it?'

Mrs Leivers looked at the youth with her brown, hurt eyes.

'It wouldn't matter but for the boys,' she said to him. 'Only Miriam knows what a trouble they make if the potatoes are "caught".'

'Then,' thought Paul to himself, 'you shouldn't let them make a trouble.'

After a while Edgar came in. He wore leggings and his boots were covered with earth. He was rather small, rather formal, for a farmer. He glanced at Paul, nodded to him distantly, and said, 'Dinner ready?'

'Nearly, Edgar,' replied the mother apologetically.

'I'm ready for mine,' said the young man, taking up the newspaper and reading. Presently the rest of the family trooped in. Dinner was served. The meal went rather brutally. The over-gentleness and apologetic tone of the mother brought out all the brutality of manners in the sons. Edgar tasted the potatoes, moved his mouth quickly like a rabbit, looked indignantly at his mother, and said, 'These potatoes are burnt, mother.'

'Yes, Edgar. I forgot them for a minute. Perhaps you'll have bread if you can't eat them.'

Edgar looked in anger across at Miriam.

'What was Miriam doing that she couldn't attend to them?' he said.

Miriam looked up. Her mouth opened, her dark eyes blazed and winced, but she said nothing. She swallowed her anger and her shame, bowing her dark head.

'I'm sure she was trying hard,' said the mother.

'She hasn't got sense even to boil the potatoes,' said Edgar. 'What is she kept at home for?'

'On'y for eating everything that's left in th' pantry,' said Maurice.

'They don't forget that potato-pie against our Miriam,' laughed the father.

She was utterly humiliated. The mother sat in silence, suffering, like some saint out of place at the brutal board.

It puzzled Paul. He wondered vaguely why all this intense feeling went running because of a few burnt potatoes.

The mother exalted everything – even a bit of housework – to the plane of a religious trust. The sons resented this; they felt themselves cut away underneath, and they answered with brutality and also with a sneering superciliousness.

Paul was just opening out from childhood into manhood. This atmosphere, where everything took a religious value, came with a subtle fascination to him. There was something in the air. His own mother was logical. Here there was something different, something he loved, something that at times he hated.

Miriam quarrelled with her brothers fiercely. Later in the afternoon, when they had gone away again, her mother said, 'You disappointed me at dinner-time, Miriam.'

The girl dropped her head.

'They are such *brutes*!' she suddenly cried, looking up with flashing eyes.

'But hadn't you promised not to answer them?' said the mother. 'And I believed in you. I *can't* stand it when you wrangle.'

'But they're so hateful!' cried Miriam, 'and – and low.'

'Yes, dear. But how often have I asked you not to answer Edgar back? Can't you let him say what he likes?'

'But why should he say what he likes?'

'Aren't you strong enough to bear it, Miriam, if even for my sake? Are you so weak that you must wrangle with them?'

Mrs Leivers stuck unflinchingly to this doctrine of 'the other cheek'. She could not instil it at all into the boys. With the girls she succeeded better, and Miriam was the child of her heart. The boys loathed the other cheek when it was presented to them. Miriam was often sufficiently lofty to turn it. Then they spat on her and hated her. But she walked in her proud humility, living within herself.

There was always this feeling of jangle and discord in the Leivers family. Although the boys resented so bitterly this eternal appeal to their deeper feelings of resignation and proud humility, yet it had its effect on them. They could not establish between themselves and an outsider just the ordinary human feeling and unexaggerated friendship; they were always restless for the something deeper. Ordinary folk seemed shallow to them, trivial and inconsiderable. And so they were unaccustomed, painfully uncouth in the simplest social intercourse, suffering, and yet insolent in their superiority. Then beneath was the yearning for the soul-intimacy to which they could not attain because they were too dumb, and every approach to close connection was blocked by their clumsy contempt of other people. They wanted genuine intimacy, but they could not get even normally near to anyone, because they scorned to take the first steps, they scorned the triviality which forms common human intercourse.

Paul fell under Mrs Leivers's spell. Everything had a religious and intensified meaning when he was with her. His soul, hurt, highly developed, sought her as if for nourishment. Together they seemed to sift the vital fact from an experience.

Miriam was her mother's daughter. In the sunshine of the afternoon mother and daughter went down the fields with him. They looked for nests. There was a jenny wren's in the hedge by the orchard.

'I *do* want you to see this,' said Mrs Leivers.

He crouched down and carefully put his finger through the thorns into the round door of the nest.

'It's almost as if you were feeling inside the live body of the bird,' he said, 'it's so warm. They say a bird makes its nest round like a cup with pressing its breast on it. Then how did it make the ceiling round, I wonder?'

The nest seemed to start into life for the two women. After that, Miriam came to see it every day. It seemed so close to her. Again, going down the hedge-side with the girl, he noticed the celandines, scalloped splashes of gold, on the side of the ditch.

'I like them,' he said, 'when their petals go flat back with the sunshine. They seem to be pressing themselves at the sun.'

And then the celandines ever after drew her with a little spell. Anthropo morphic as she was, she stimulated him into appreciating things thus, and then they lived for her. She seemed to need things kindling in her imagination or in her soul before she felt she had them. And she was cut off from ordinary life by her religious intensity which made the world for her either a nunnery garden or a paradise where sin and knowledge were not, or else an ugly, cruel thing.

So it was in this atmosphere of subtle intimacy, this meeting in their common feeling for something in Nature, that their love started.

Personally, he was a long time before he realised her. For ten months he had to stay at home after his illness. For a while he went to Skegness with his mother, and was perfectly happy. But even from the seaside he wrote long letters to Mrs Leivers about the shore and the sea. And he brought back his beloved sketches of the flat Lincoln coast, anxious for them to see. Almost they would interest the Leiverses more than they interested his mother. It was not his art Mrs Morel cared about; it was himself and his achievement. But Mrs Leivers and her children were almost his disciples. They kindled him and made him glow to his work, whereas his mother's influence was to make him quietly determined, patient, dogged, unwearied.

He soon was friends with the boys, whose rudeness was only superficial. They had all, when they could trust themselves, a strange gentleness and lovableness.

'Will you come with me on to the fallow?' asked Edgar, rather hesitatingly.

Paul went joyfully, and spent the afternoon helping to hoe or to single turnips with his friend. He used to lie with the three brothers in the hay piled up in the barn and tell them about Nottingham and about Jordan's. In return they taught him to milk, and let him do little jobs – chopping hay or pulping turnips – just as much as he liked. At midsummer he worked all through hay-harvest with them, and then he loved them. The family was so cut off from the world actually. They seemed, somehow, like 'les derniers fils d'une race épuisée'. Though the lads were strong and healthy, yet they had all that over-sensitiveness and hanging-back which made them so lonely, yet also such close, delicate friends once their intimacy was won. Paul loved them dearly, and they him.

Miriam came later. But he had come into her life before she made any mark on his. One dull afternoon, when the men were on the land and the rest at school, only Miriam and her mother at home, the girl said to him, after having hesitated for some time, 'Have you seen the swing?'

'No,' he answered. 'Where?'

'In the cowshed,' she replied.

She always hesitated to offer or to show him anything. Men have such different standards of worth from women, and her dear things – the valuable things to her – her brothers had so often mocked or flouted.

'Come on, then,' he replied, jumping up.

There were two cowsheds, one on either side of the barn. In the lower, darker shed there was standing for four cows. Hens flew scolding over the manger-wall as the youth and girl went forward for the great thick rope which hung from the beam in the darkness overhead, and was pushed back over a peg in the wall.

'It's something like a rope!' he exclaimed appreciatively; and he sat down on it, anxious to try it. Then immediately he rose.

'Come on, then, and have first go,' he said to the girl.

'See,' she answered, going into the barn, 'we put some bags on the seat'; and she made the swing comfortable for him. That gave her pleasure. He held the rope.

'Come on, then,' he said to her.

'No, I won't go first,' she answered.

She stood aside in her still, aloof fashion.

'Why?'

'You go,' she pleaded.

Almost for the first time in her life she had the pleasure of giving up to a man, of spoiling him. Paul looked at her.

'All right,' he said, sitting down. 'Mind out!'

He set off with a spring, and in a moment was flying through the air, almost out of the door of the shed, the upper half of which was open, showing outside the drizzling rain, the filthy yard, the cattle standing disconsolate against the black cart-shed, and at the back of all the grey-green wall of the wood. She stood below in her crimson tam-o'-shanter and watched. He looked down at her, and she saw his blue eyes sparkling.

'It's a treat of a swing,' he said.

'Yes.'

He was swinging through the air, every bit of him swinging, like a bird that swoops for joy of movement. And he looked down at her. Her crimson cap hung over her dark curls, her beautiful warm face, so still in a kind of brooding, was lifted towards him. It was dark and rather cold in the shed. Suddenly a swallow came down from the high roof and darted out of the door.

'I didn't know a bird was watching,' he called.

He swung negligently. She could feel him falling and lifting through the air, as if he were lying on some force.

'Now I'll die,' he said, in a detached, dreamy voice, as though he were the dying motion of the swing. She watched him, fascinated. Suddenly he put on the brake and jumped out.

'I've had a long turn,' he said. 'But it's a treat of a swing – it's a real treat of a swing!'

Miriam was amused that he took a swing so seriously and felt so warmly over it.

'No; you go on,' she said.

'Why, don't you want one?' he asked, astonished.

'Well, not much. I'll have just a little.'

She sat down, whilst he kept the bags in place for her.

'It's so ripping!' he said, setting her in motion. 'Keep your heels up, or they'll bang the manger-wall.'

She felt the accuracy with which he caught her, exactly at the right moment, and the exactly proportionate strength of his thrust, and she was afraid. Down to her bowels went the hot wave of fear. She was in his hands. Again, firm and inevitable came the thrust at the right moment. She gripped the rope, almost swooning.

'Ha!' she laughed in fear. 'No higher!'

'But you're not a *bit* high,' he remonstrated.

'But no higher.'

He heard the fear in her voice, and desisted. Her heart melted in hot pain when the moment came for him to thrust her forward again. But he left her alone. She began to breathe.

'Won't you really go any farther?' he asked. 'Should I keep you there?'

'No; let me go by myself,' she answered.

He moved aside and watched her.

'Why, you're scarcely moving,' he said.

She laughed slightly with shame, and in a moment got down.

'They say if you can swing you won't be seasick,' he said, as he mounted again. 'I don't believe I should ever be seasick.'

Away he went. There was something fascinating to her in him. For the moment he was nothing but a piece of swinging stuff; not a particle of him that did not swing. She could never lose herself so, nor could her brothers. It roused a warmth in her. It were almost as if he were a flame that had lit a warmth in her whilst he swung in the middle air.

And gradually the intimacy with the family concentrated for Paul on three persons – the mother, Edgar, and Miriam. To the mother he went for that sympathy and that appeal which seemed to draw him out. Edgar was his very close friend. And to Miriam he more or less condescended, because she seemed so humble.

But the girl gradually sought him out. If he brought up his sketchbook, it was she who pondered longest over the last picture. Then she would look up at him. Suddenly, her dark eyes alight like water that shakes with a stream of gold in the dark, she would ask, 'Why do I like this so?'

Always something in his breast shrank from these close, intimate, dazzled looks of hers.

'Why *do* you?' he asked.

'I don't know. It seems so true.'

'It's because – it's because there is scarcely any shadow in it; it's more shimmery, as if I'd painted the shimmering protoplasm in the leaves and everywhere, and not the stiffness of the shape. That seems dead to me. Only this shimmeriness is the real living. The shape is a dead crust. The shimmer is inside really.'

And she, with her little finger in her mouth, would ponder those sayings. They gave her a feeling of life again, and vivified things which had meant nothing to her. She managed to find some meaning in his struggling, abstract speeches. And they were the medium through which she came distinctly at her beloved objects.

Another day she sat at sunset whilst he was painting some pine trees which caught the red glare from the west. He had been quiet.

'There you are!' he said suddenly. 'I wanted that. Now, look at them and tell me, are they pine-trunks or are they red coals, standing-up pieces of fire in that darkness? There's God's burning bush for you, that burned not away.'

Miriam looked, and was frightened. But the pine-trunks were wonderful to her, and distinct. He packed his box and rose. Suddenly he looked at her.

'Why are you always sad?' he asked her.

'Sad!' she exclaimed, looking up at him with startled, wonderful brown eyes.

'Yes,' he replied. 'You are always, always sad.'

'I am not – oh, not a bit!' she cried.

'But even your joy is like a flame coming off of sadness,' he persisted. 'You're never jolly, or even just all right.'

'No,' she pondered. 'I wonder – why.'

'Because you're not; because you're different inside, like a pine tree, and then you flare up; but you're not just like an ordinary tree, with fidgety leaves and jolly – '

He got tangled up in his own speech; but she brooded on it, and he had a strange, roused sensation, as if his feelings were new. She got so near him. It was a strange stimulant.

Then sometimes he hated her. Her youngest brother was only five. He was a frail lad, with immense brown eyes in his quaint fragile face – one of Reynolds's 'Choir of Angels', with a touch of elf. Often Miriam kneeled to the child and drew him to her.

'Eh, my Hubert!' she sang, in a voice heavy and surcharged with love. 'Eh, my Hubert!'

And, folding him in her arms, she swayed slightly from side to side with love, her face half lifted, her eyes half closed, her voice drenched with love.

'Don't!' said the child, uneasy – 'don't, Miriam!'

'Yes; you love me, don't you?' she murmured deep in her throat, almost as if she were in a trance, and swaying also as if she were swooned in an ecstasy of love.

'Don't!' repeated the child, a frown on his clear brow.

'You love me, don't you?' she murmured.

'What do you make such a *fuss* for?' cried Paul, all in suffering because of her extreme emotion. 'Why can't you be ordinary with him?'

She let the child go and rose, and said nothing. Her intensity, which would leave no emotion on a normal plane, irritated the youth into a frenzy. And this fearful, naked contact of her on small occasions shocked him. He was used to his mother's reserve. And on such occasions he was thankful in his heart and soul that he had his mother, so sane and wholesome.

All the life of Miriam's body was in her eyes, which were usually dark as a dark church, but could flame with light like a conflagration. Her face scarcely ever altered from its look of brooding. She might have been one of the women who went with Mary when Jesus was dead. Her body was not flexible and living. She walked with a swing, rather heavily, her head bowed forward, pondering. She was not clumsy, and yet none of her movements seemed quite *the* movement. Often, when wiping the dishes, she would stand in bewilderment and chagrin because she had pulled in two halves a cup or a tumbler. It was as if, in her fear and self-mistrust, she put too much strength into the effort. There was no looseness or abandon about her. Everything was gripped stiff with intensity, and her effort, overcharged, closed in on itself.

She rarely varied from her swinging, forward, intense walk. Occasionally she ran with Paul down the fields. Then her eyes blazed naked in a kind of ecstasy that frightened him. But she was physically afraid. If she were getting over a stile, she gripped his hands in a little hard anguish, and began to lose her presence of mind. And he could not persuade her to jump from even a small height. Her eyes dilated, became exposed and palpitating.

'No!' she cried, half laughing in terror – 'no!'

'You shall!' he cried once, and, jerking her forward, he brought her falling from the fence. But her wild 'Ah!' of pain, as if she were losing consciousness, cut him. She landed on her feet safely, and afterwards had courage in this respect.

She was very much dissatisfied with her lot.

'Don't you like being at home?' Paul asked her, surprised.

'Who would?' she answered, low and intense. 'What is it? I'm all day cleaning what the boys make just as bad in five minutes. I don't *want* to be at home.'

'What do you want, then?'

'I want to do something. I want a chance like anybody else. Why should I, because I'm a girl, be kept at home and not allowed to be anything? What chance *have* I?'

'Chance of what?'

'Of knowing anything – of learning, of doing anything. It's not fair, because I'm a woman.'

She seemed very bitter. Paul wondered. In his own home Annie was almost glad to be a girl. She had not so much responsibility; things were lighter for her. She never wanted to be other than a girl. But Miriam almost fiercely wished she were a man. And yet she hated men at the same time.

'But it's as well to be a woman as a man,' he said, frowning.

'Ha! Is it? Men have everything.'

'I should think women ought to be as glad to be women as men are to be men,' he answered.

'No!' she shook her head – 'no! Everything the men have.'

'But what do you want?' he asked.

'I want to learn. Why *should* it be that I know nothing?'

'What! such as mathematics and French?'

'Why *shouldn't* I know mathematics? Yes!' she cried, her eye expanding in a kind of defiance

'Well, you can learn as much as I know,' he said. 'I'll teach you, if you like.'

Her eyes dilated. She mistrusted him as a teacher.

'Would you?' he asked.

Her head had dropped, and she was sucking her finger broodingly.

'Yes,' she said hesitatingly.

He used to tell his mother all these things.

'I'm going to teach Miriam algebra,' he said.

'Well,' replied Mrs Morel, 'I hope she'll get fat on it.'

When he went up to the farm on the Monday evening, it was drawing twilight. Miriam was just sweeping up the kitchen, and was kneeling at the hearth when he entered. Everyone was out but her. She looked round at him, flushed, her dark eyes shining, her fine hair falling about her face.

'Hello!' she said, soft and musical. 'I knew it was you.'

'How?'

'I knew your step. Nobody treads so quick and firm.'

He sat down, sighing.

'Ready to do some algebra?' he asked, drawing a little book from his pocket.

'But –'

He could feel her backing away.

'You said you wanted,' he insisted.

'Tonight, though?' she faltered.

'But I came on purpose. And if you want to learn it, you must begin.'

She took up her ashes in the dustpan and looked at him, half tremulously, laughing.

'Yes, but tonight! You see, I haven't thought of it.'

'Well, my goodness! Take the ashes and come.'

He went and sat on the stone bench in the back-yard, where the big milk-cans were standing, tipped up, to air. The men were in the cowsheds. He could hear the little singsong of the milk spurting into the pails. Presently she came, bringing some big greenish apples.

'You know you like them,' she said.

He took a bite.

'Sit down,' he said, with his mouth full.

She was short-sighted, and peered over his shoulder. It irritated him. He gave her the book quickly.

'Here,' he said. 'It's only letters for figures. You put down "a" instead of "2" or "6".'

They worked, he talking, she with her head down on the book. He was quick and hasty. She never answered. Occasionally, when he demanded of her, 'Do you see?' she looked up at him, her eyes wide with the half-laugh that comes of fear. 'Don't you?' he cried.

He had been too fast. But she said nothing. He questioned her more, then got hot. It made his blood rouse to see her there, as it were, at his mercy, her mouth open, her eyes dilated with laughter that was afraid, apologetic, ashamed. Then Edgar came along with two buckets of milk.

'Hello!' he said. 'What are you doing?'

'Algebra,' replied Paul.

'Algebra!' repeated Edgar curiously. Then he passed on with a laugh. Paul took a bite at his forgotten apple, looked at the miserable cabbages in the garden, pecked into lace by the fowls, and he wanted to pull them up. Then he glanced at Miriam. She was poring over the book, seemed absorbed in it, yet trembling lest she could not get at it. It made him cross. She was ruddy and beautiful. Yet her soul seemed to be intensely supplicating. The algebra-book she closed, shrinking, knowing he was angered; and at the same instant he grew gentle, seeing her hurt because she did not understand.

But things came slowly to her. And when she held herself in a grip, seemed so utterly humble before the lesson, it made his blood rouse. He stormed at her, got ashamed, continued the lesson, and grew furious again, abusing her. She listened in silence. Occasionally, very rarely, she defended herself. Her liquid dark eyes blazed at him.

'You don't give me time to learn it,' she said.

'All right,' he answered, throwing the book on the table and lighting a cigarette. Then, after a while, he went back to her repentant. So the lessons went. He was always either in a rage or very gentle.

'What do you tremble your *soul* before it for?' he cried. 'You don't learn algebra with your blessed soul. Can't you look at it with your clear simple wits?'

Often, when he went again into the kitchen, Mrs Leivers would look at him reproachfully, saying, 'Paul, don't be so hard on Miriam. She may not be quick, but I'm sure she tries.'

'I can't help it,' he said rather pitiably. 'I go off like it.'

'You don't mind me, Miriam, do you?' he asked of the girl later.

'No,' she reassured him in her beautiful deep tones – 'no, I don't mind.'

'Don't mind me; it's my fault.'

But, in spite of himself, his blood began to boil with her. It was strange that no one else made him in such fury. He flared against her. Once he threw the pencil in her face. There was a silence. She turned her face slightly aside.

'I didn't – ' he began, but got no farther, feeling weak in all his bones. She never reproached him or was angry with him. He was often cruelly ashamed. But still again his anger burst like a bubble surcharged; and still, when he saw her eager, silent, as it were, blind face, he felt he wanted to throw the pencil in it; and still, when he saw her hand trembling and her mouth parted with suffering, his heart was scalded with pain for her. And because of the intensity to which she roused him, he sought her.

Then he often avoided her and went with Edgar. Miriam and her brother were naturally antagonistic. Edgar was a rationalist, who was curious, and had a sort of scientific interest in life. It was a great bitterness to Miriam to see herself deserted by Paul for Edgar, who seemed so much lower. But the youth was very happy with her elder brother. The two men spent afternoons together on the land or in the loft doing carpentry, when it rained. And they talked together, or Paul taught Edgar the songs he himself had learned from Annie at the piano. And often all the men, Mr Leivers as well, had bitter debates on the nationalising of the land and similar problems. Paul had already heard his mother's views, and as these were as yet his own, he argued for her. Miriam attended and took part, but was all the time waiting until it should be over and a personal communication might begin.

'After all,' she said within herself, 'if the land were nationalised, Edgar and Paul and I would be just the same.' So she waited for the youth to come back to her.

He was studying for his painting. He loved to sit at home, alone with his mother, at night, working and working. She sewed or read. Then, looking up from his task, he would rest his eyes for a moment on her face, that was bright with living warmth, and he returned gladly to his work.

'I can do my best things when you sit there in your rocking-chair, mother,' he said.

'I'm sure!' she exclaimed, sniffing with mock scepticism. But she felt it was so, and her heart quivered with brightness. For many hours she sat still, slightly conscious of him labouring away, whilst she worked or read her book. And he, with all his soul's intensity directing his pencil, could feel her warmth inside him like strength. They were both very happy so, and both unconscious of it. These times, that meant so much, and which were real living, they almost ignored.

He was conscious only when stimulated. A sketch finished, he always wanted to take it to Miriam. Then he was stimulated into knowledge of the work he had produced unconsciously. In contact with Miriam he gained insight; his vision went deeper. From his mother he drew the life-warmth, the strength to produce; Miriam urged this warmth into intensity like a white light.

When he returned to the factory the conditions of work were better. He had Wednesday afternoon off to go to the Art School – Miss Jordan's provision – returning in the evening. Then the factory closed at six instead of at eight on Thursday and Friday evenings.

One evening in the summer Miriam and he went over the fields by Herod's Farm on their way from the library home. So it was only three miles to Willey Farm. There was a yellow glow over the mowing-grass, and the sorrel-heads burned crimson. Gradually, as they walked along the high land, the gold in the west sank down to red, the red to crimson, and then the chill blue crept up against the glow.

They came out upon the highroad to Alfreton, which ran white between the darkening fields. There Paul hesitated. It was two miles home for him, one mile forward for Miriam. They both looked up the road that ran in shadow right under the glow of the north-west sky. On the crest of the hill, Selby, with its stark houses and the up-pricked headstocks of the pit, stood in black silhouette small against the sky.

He looked at his watch.

'Nine o'clock!' he said.

The pair stood, loth to part, hugging their books.

'The wood is so lovely now,' she said. 'I wanted you to see it.'

He followed her slowly across the road to the white gate.

'They grumble so if I'm late,' he said.

'But you're not doing anything wrong,' she answered impatiently.

He followed her across the nibbled pasture in the dusk. There was a coolness in the wood, a scent of leaves, of honeysuckle, and a twilight. The two walked in silence. Night came wonderfully there, among the throng of dark tree-trunks. He looked round, expectant.

She wanted to show him a certain wild-rose bush she had discovered. She knew it was wonderful. And yet, till he had seen it, she felt it had not come into her soul. Only he could make it her own, immortal. She was dissatisfied.

Dew was already on the paths. In the old oak-wood a mist was rising, and he hesitated, wondering whether one whiteness were a strand of fog or only campion flowers pallid in a cloud.

By the time they came to the pine trees Miriam was getting very eager and very tense. Her bush might be gone. She might not be able to find it; and she wanted it so much. Almost passionately she wanted to be with him when he stood before the flowers. They were going to have a communion together – something that thrilled her, something holy. He was walking beside her in silence. They were very near to each other. She trembled, and he listened, vaguely anxious.

Coming to the edge of the wood, they saw the sky in front, like mother-of-pearl, and the earth growing dark. Somewhere on the outermost branches of the pine-wood the honeysuckle was streaming scent.

'Where?' he asked.

'Down the middle path,' she murmured, quivering.

When they turned the corner of the path she stood still. In the wide walk between the pines, gazing rather frightened, she could distinguish nothing for some moments; the greying light robbed things of their colour. Then she saw her bush.

'Ah!' she cried, hastening forward.

It was very still. The tree was tall and straggling. It had thrown its briers over a hawthorn-bush, and its long streamers trailed thick, right down to the grass, splashing the darkness everywhere with great spilt stars, pure white. In bosses of ivory and in large splashed stars the roses gleamed on the darkness of foliage and stems and grass. Paul and Miriam stood close together, silent, and watched. Point after point the steady roses shone out to them, seeming to kindle something in their souls. The dusk came like smoke around, and still did not put out the roses.

Paul looked into Miriam's eyes. She was pale and expectant with wonder, her lips were parted, and her dark eyes lay open to him. His look seemed to travel down into her. Her soul quivered. It was the communion she wanted. He turned aside, as if pained. He turned to the bush.

'They seem as if they walk like butterflies, and shake themselves,' he said.

She looked at her roses. They were white, some incurved and holy, others expanded in an ecstasy. The tree was dark as a shadow. She lifted her hand impulsively to the flowers; she went forward and touched them in worship.

'Let us go,' he said.

There was a cool scent of ivory roses – a white, virgin scent. Something made him feel anxious and imprisoned. The two walked in silence.

'Till Sunday,' he said quietly, and left her; and she walked home slowly, feeling her soul satisfied with the holiness of the night. He stumbled down the path. And as soon as he was out of the wood, in the free open meadow, where he could breathe, he started to run as fast as he could. It was like a delicious delirium in his veins.

Always when he went with Miriam, and it grew rather late, he knew his mother was fretting and getting angry about him – why, he could not understand. As he went into the house, flinging down his cap, his mother looked up at the clock. She had been sitting thinking, because a chill to her eyes prevented her reading. She could feel Paul being drawn away by this girl. And she did not care for Miriam. 'She is one of those who will want to suck a man's soul out till he has none of his own left,' she said to herself; 'and he is just such a gaby as to let himself be absorbed. She will never let him become a man; she never will.' So, while he was away with Miriam, Mrs Morel grew more and more worked up.

She glanced at the clock and said, coldly and rather tired, 'You have been far enough tonight.'

His soul, warm and exposed from contact with the girl, shrank.

'You must have been right home with her,' his mother continued.

He would not answer. Mrs Morel, looking at him quickly, saw his hair was damp on his forehead with haste, saw him frowning in his heavy fashion, resentfully.

'She must be wonderfully fascinating, that you can't get away from her, but must go trailing eight miles at this time of night.'

He was hurt between the past glamour with Miriam and the knowledge that his mother fretted. He had meant not to say anything, to refuse to answer. But he could not harden his heart to ignore his mother.

'I *do* like to talk to her,' he answered irritably.

'Is there nobody else to talk to?'

'You wouldn't say anything if I went with Edgar.'

'You know I should. You know, whoever you went with, I should say it was too far for you to go trailing, late at night, when you've been to Nottingham.

Besides' – her voice suddenly flashed into anger and contempt – 'it is disgusting – bits of lads and girls courting.'

'It is *not* courting,' he cried.

'I don't know what else you call it.'

'It's not! Do you think we *spoon* and do? We only talk.'

'Till goodness knows what time and distance,' was the sarcastic rejoinder.

Paul snapped at the laces of his boots angrily.

'What are you so mad about?' he asked. 'Because you don't like her.'

'I don't say I don't like her. But I don't hold with children keeping company, and never did.'

'But you don't mind our Annie going out with Jim Inger.'

'They've more sense than you two.'

'Why?'

'Our Annie's not one of the deep sort.'

He failed to see the meaning of this remark. But his mother looked tired. She was never so strong after William's death; and her eyes hurt her.

'Well,' he said, 'it's so pretty in the country. Mr Sleath asked about you. He said he'd missed you. Are you a bit better?'

'I ought to have been in bed a long time ago,' she replied.

'Why, mother, you know you wouldn't have gone before quarter-past ten.'

'Oh yes, I should!'

'Oh, little woman, you'd say anything now you're disagreeable with me, wouldn't you?'

He kissed her forehead that he knew so well: the deep marks between the brows, the rising of the fine hair, greying now, and the proud setting of the temples. His hand lingered on her shoulder after his kiss. Then he went slowly to bed. He had forgotten Miriam; he only saw how his mother's hair was lifted back from her warm, broad brow. And somehow, she was hurt.

Then the next time he saw Miriam he said to her, 'Don't let me be late tonight – not later than ten o'clock. My mother gets so upset.'

Miriam dropped her head, brooding.

'Why does she get upset?' she asked.

'Because she says I oughtn't to be out late when I have to get up early.'

'Very well!' said Miriam, rather quietly, with just a touch of a sneer.

He resented that. And he was usually late again.

That there was any love growing between him and Miriam neither of them would have acknowledged. He thought he was too sane for such sentimentality, and she thought herself too lofty. They both were late in coming to maturity, and psychical ripeness was much behind even the physical. Miriam was exceedingly sensitive, as her mother had always been. The slightest grossness made her recoil almost in anguish. Her brothers were brutal, but never coarse in speech. The men did all the discussing of farm matters outside. But, perhaps, because of the continual business of birth and of begetting which goes on upon every farm, Miriam was the more hypersensitive to the matter, and her blood was chastened almost to disgust of the faintest suggestion of such intercourse. Paul took his pitch from her, and their intimacy went on in an utterly blanched and chaste fashion. It could never be mentioned that the mare was in foal.

When he was nineteen, he was earning only twenty shillings a week, but he was happy. His painting went well, and life went well enough. On the Good Friday he organised a walk to the Hemlock Stone. There were three lads of his own age, then Annie and Arthur, Miriam and Geoffrey. Arthur, apprenticed as an electrician in Nottingham, was home for the holiday. Morel, as usual, was up early, whistling and sawing in the yard. At seven o'clock the family heard him buy threepennyworth of hot-cross buns; he talked with gusto to the little girl who brought them, calling her 'my darling'. He turned away several boys who came with more buns, telling them they had been 'kested' by a little lass. Then Mrs Morel got up, and the family straggled down. It was an immense luxury to everybody, this lying in bed just beyond the ordinary time on a weekday. And Paul and Arthur read before breakfast, and had the meal unwashed, sitting in their shirt-sleeves. This was another holiday luxury. The room was warm. Everything felt free of care and anxiety. There was a sense of plenty in the house.

While the boys were reading, Mrs Morel went into the garden. They were now in another house, an old one, near the Scargill Street home, which had been left soon after William had died. Directly came an excited cry from the garden, 'Paul, Paul! come and look!'

It was his mother's voice. He threw down his book and went out. There was a long garden that ran to a field. It was a grey, cold day, with a sharp wind blowing out of Derbyshire. Two fields away Bestwood began, with a jumble of roofs and red house-ends, out of which rose the church tower and the spire of the Congregational Chapel. And beyond went woods and hills, right away to the pale grey heights of the Pennine Chain.

Paul looked down the garden for his mother. Her head appeared among the young currant-bushes.

'Come here!' she cried.

'What for?' he answered.

'Come and see.'

She had been looking at the buds on the currant trees. Paul went up.

'To think,' she said, 'that here I might never have seen them!'

Her son went to her side. Under the fence, in a little bed, was a ravel of poor grassy leaves, such as come from very immature bulbs, and three scyllas in bloom. Mrs Morel pointed to the deep blue flowers.

'Now, just see those!' she exclaimed. 'I was looking at the currant-bushes, when, thinks I to myself, "There's something very blue; is it a bit of sugar-bag?" and there, behold you! Sugar-bag! Three glories of the snow, and *such* beauties! But where on earth did they come from?'

'I don't know,' said Paul.

'Well, that's a marvel, now! I *thought* I knew every weed and blade in this garden. But *haven't* they done well? You see, that gooseberry-bush just shelters them. Not nipped, not touched!'

He crouched down and turned up the bells of the little blue flowers.

'They're a glorious colour!' he said.

'Aren't they!' she cried. 'I guess they come from Switzerland, where they say they have such lovely things. Fancy them against the snow! But where have they come from? They can't have *blown* here, can they?'

Then he remembered having set here a lot of little trash of bulbs to mature.

'And you never told me,' she said.

'No; I thought I'd leave it till they might flower.'

'And now, you see! I might have missed them. And I've never had a glory of the snow in my garden in my life.'

She was full of excitement and elation. The garden was an endless joy to her. Paul was thankful for her sake at last to be in a house with a long garden that went down to a field. Every morning after breakfast she went out and was happy pottering about in it. And it was true, she knew every weed and blade.

Everybody turned up for the walk. Food was packed, and they set off, a merry, delighted party. They hung over the wall of the mill-race, dropped paper in the water on one side of the tunnel and watched it shoot out on the other. They stood on the footbridge over Boathouse Station and looked at the metals gleaming coldly.

'You should see the Flying Scotchman come through at half-past six!' said Leonard, whose father was a signalman. 'Lad, but she doesn't half buzz!' and the little party looked up the lines one way, to London, and the other way, to Scotland, and they felt the touch of these two magical places.

In Ilkeston the colliers were waiting in gangs for the public-houses to open. It was a town of idleness and lounging. At Stanton Gate the iron foundry blazed. Over everything there were great discussions. At Trowell they crossed again from Derbyshire into Nottinghamshire. They came to the Hemlock Stone at dinner-time. Its field was crowded with folk from Nottingham and Ilkeston.

They had expected a venerable and dignified monument. They found a little, gnarled, twisted stump of rock, something like a decayed mushroom, standing out pathetically on the side of a field. Leonard and Dick immediately proceeded to carve their initials, 'L. W.' and 'R. P.', in the old red sandstone; but Paul desisted, because he had read in the newspaper satirical remarks about initial-carvers, who could find no other road to immortality. Then all the lads climbed to the top of the rock to look round.

Everywhere in the field below, factory girls and lads were eating lunch or sporting about. Beyond was the garden of an old manor. It had yew-hedges and thick clumps and borders of yellow crocuses round the lawn.

'See,' said Paul to Miriam, 'what a quiet garden!'

She saw the dark yews and the golden crocuses, then she looked at him gratefully. He had not seemed to belong to her among all these others; he was different then – not her Paul, who understood the slightest quiver of her innermost soul, but something else, speaking another language than hers. How it hurt her, and deadened her very perceptions. Only when he came right back to her, leaving his other, his lesser self, as she thought, would she feel alive again. And now he asked her to look at this garden, wanting the contact with her again. Impatient of the set in the field, she turned to the quiet lawn, surrounded by sheaves of shut-up crocuses. A feeling of stillness, almost of ecstasy, came over her. It felt almost as if she were alone with him in this garden.

Then he left her again and joined the others. Soon they started home. Miriam loitered behind, alone. She did not fit in with the others; she could very rarely get into human relation with anyone: so her friend, her companion, her lover, was Nature. She saw the sun declining wanly. In the dusky, cold hedgerows were some red leaves. She lingered to gather them, tenderly, passionately. The love in her fingertips caressed the leaves; the passion in her heart came to a glow upon the leaves.

Suddenly she realised she was alone in a strange road, and she hurried forward. Turning a corner in the lane, she came upon Paul, who stood bent over something, his mind fixed on it, working away steadily, patiently, a little hopelessly. She hesitated in her approach, to watch.

He remained concentrated in the middle of the road. Beyond, one rift of rich gold in that colourless grey evening seemed to make him stand out in dark relief. She saw him, slender and firm, as if the setting sun had given him to her. A deep pain took hold of her, and she knew she must love him. And she had discovered him, discovered in him a rare potentiality, discovered his loneliness. Quivering as at some 'annunciation', she went slowly forward.

At last he looked up.

'Why,' he exclaimed gratefully, 'have you waited for me!'

She saw a deep shadow in his eyes.

'What is it?' she asked.

'The spring broken here'; and he showed her where his umbrella was injured.

Instantly, with some shame, she knew he had not done the damage himself, but that Geoffrey was responsible.

'It is only an old umbrella, isn't it?' she asked.

She wondered why he, who did not usually trouble over trifles, made such a mountain of this molehill.

'But it was William's, an' my mother can't help but know,' he said quietly, still patiently working at the umbrella.

The words went through Miriam like a blade. This, then, was the confirmation of her vision of him. She looked at him. But there was about him a certain reserve, and she dared not comfort him, not even speak softly to him.

'Come on,' he said. 'I can't do it'; and they went in silence along the road.

That same evening they were walking along under the trees by Nether Green. He was talking to her fretfully, seemed to be struggling to convince himself.

'You know,' he said, with an effort, 'if one person loves, the other does.'

'Ah!' she answered. 'Like mother said to me when I was little, "Love begets love." '

'Yes, something like that, I think it *must* be.'

'I hope so, because, if it were not, love might be a very terrible thing,' she said.

'Yes, but it is – at least with most people,' he answered.

And Miriam, thinking he had assured himself, felt strong in herself. She always regarded that sudden coming upon him in the lane as a revelation. And this conversation remained graven in her mind as one of the letters of the law.

Now she stood with him and for him. When, about this time, he outraged the family feeling at Willey Farm by some overbearing insult, she stuck to him, and believed he was right. And at this time she dreamed dreams of him, vivid, unforgettable. These dreams came again later on, developed to a more subtle psychological stage.

On the Easter Monday the same party took an excursion to Wingfield Manor. It was great excitement to Miriam to catch a train at Sethley Bridge, amid all the bustle of the Bank Holiday crowd. They left the train at Alfreton. Paul was interested in the street and in the colliers with their dogs. Here was a new race of miners. Miriam did not live till they came to the church. They were all rather timid of entering, with their bags of food, for fear of being turned out. Leonard, a comic, thin fellow, went first; Paul, who would have died rather than be sent back, went last. The place was decorated for Easter. In the font hundreds of white narcissi seemed to be growing. The air was dim and coloured from the windows, and thrilled with a subtle scent of lilies and narcissi. In that atmosphere Miriam's soul came into a glow. Paul was afraid of the things he mustn't do; and he was sensitive to the feel of the place. Miriam turned to him. He answered. They were together. He would not go beyond the Communion-rail. She loved him for that. Her soul expanded into prayer beside him. He felt the strange fascination of shadowy religious places. All his latent mysticism quivered into life. She was drawn to him. He was a prayer along with her.

Miriam very rarely talked to the other lads. They at once became awkward in conversation with her. So usually she was silent.

It was past midday when they climbed the steep path to the manor. All things shone softly in the sun, which was wonderfully warm and enlivening. Celandines and violets were out. Everybody was tip-top full with happiness. The glitter of the ivy, the soft, atmospheric grey of the castle walls, the gentleness of everything near the ruin, was perfect.

The manor is of hard, pale grey stone, and the outer walls are blank and calm. The young folk were in raptures. They went in trepidation, almost afraid that the delight of exploring this ruin might be denied them. In the first courtyard, within the high broken walls, were farm-carts, with their shafts lying idle on the ground, the tyres of the wheels brilliant with gold-red rust. It was very still.

All eagerly paid their sixpences, and went timidly through the fine clean arch

of the inner courtyard. They were shy. Here on the pavement, where the hall
had been, an old thorn tree was budding. All kinds of strange openings and
broken rooms were in the shadow around them.

After lunch they set off once more to explore the ruin. This time the girls
went with the boys, who could act as guides and expositors. There was one tall
tower in a corner, rather tottering, where they say Mary Queen of Scots was
imprisoned.

'Think of the Queen going up here!' said Miriam in a low voice, as she
climbed the hollow stairs.

'If she could get up,' said Paul, 'for she had rheumatism like anything. I
reckon they treated her rottenly.'

'You don't think she deserved it?' asked Miriam.

'No, I don't. She was only lively.'

They continued to mount the winding staircase. A high wind, blowing
through the loopholes, went rushing up the shaft, and filled the girl's skirts like a
balloon, so that she was ashamed, until he took the hem of her dress and held it
down for her. He did it perfectly simply, as he would have picked up her glove.
She remembered this always.

Round the broken top of the tower the ivy bushed out, old and handsome.
Also, there were a few chill gillivers, in pale cold bud. Miriam wanted to lean
over for some ivy, but he would not let her. Instead, she had to wait behind him,
and take from him each spray as he gathered it and held it to her, each one
separately, in the purest manner of chivalry. The tower seemed to rock in the
wind. They looked over miles and miles of wooded country, and country with
gleams of pasture.

The crypt underneath the manor was beautiful, and in perfect preservation.
Paul made a drawing: Miriam stayed with him. She was thinking of Mary Queen
of Scots looking with her strained, hopeless eyes, that could not understand
misery, over the hills whence no help came, or sitting in this crypt, being told of
a God as cold as the place she sat in.

They set off again gaily, looking round on their beloved manor that stood so
clean and big on its hill.

'Supposing you could have *that* farm,' said Paul to Miriam.

'Yes!'

'Wouldn't it be lovely to come and see you!'

They were now in the bare country of stone walls, which he loved, and
which, though only ten miles from home, seemed so foreign to Miriam. The
party was straggling. As they were crossing a large meadow that sloped away
from the sun, along a path embedded with innumerable tiny glittering points,
Paul, walking alongside, laced his fingers in the strings of the bag Miriam was
carrying, and instantly she felt Annie behind, watchful and jealous. But the
meadow was bathed in a glory of sunshine, and the path was jewelled, and it was
seldom that he gave her any sign. She held her fingers very still among the
strings of the bag, his fingers touching; and the place was golden as a vision.

At last they came into the straggling grey village of Crich, that lies high. Beyond the village was the famous Crich Stand that Paul could see from the garden at home. The party pushed on. Great expanses of country spread around and below. The lads were eager to get to the top of the hill. It was capped by a round knoll, half of which was by now cut away, and on the top of which stood an ancient monument, sturdy and squat, for signalling in old days far down into the level lands of Nottinghamshire and Leicestershire.

It was blowing so hard, high up there in the exposed place, that the only way to be safe was to stand nailed by the wind to the wall of the tower. At their feet fell the precipice where the limestone was quarried away. Below was a jumble of hills and tiny villages – Matlock, Ambergate, Stoney Middleton. The lads were eager to spy out the church of Bestwood, far away among the rather crowded country on the left. They were disgusted that it seemed to stand on a plain. They saw the hills of Derbyshire fall into the monotony of the Midlands that swept away South.

Miriam was somewhat scared by the wind, but the lads enjoyed it. They went on, miles and miles, to Whatstandwell. All the food was eaten, everybody was hungry, and there was very little money to get home with. But they managed to procure a loaf and a currant-loaf, which they hacked into pieces with shut-knives, and ate sitting on the wall near the bridge, watching the bright Derwent rushing by, and the brakes from Matlock pulling up at the inn.

Paul was now pale with weariness. He had been responsible for the party all day, and now he was done. Miriam understood, and kept close to him, and he left himself in her hands.

They had an hour to wait at Ambergate Station. Trains came, crowded with excursionists returning to Manchester, Birmingham, and London.

'We might be going there – folk easily might think we're going that far,' said Paul.

They got back rather late. Miriam, walking home with Geoffrey, watched the moon rise big and red and misty. She felt something was fulfilled in her.

She had an elder sister, Agatha, who was a schoolteacher. Between the two girls was a feud. Miriam considered Agatha worldly. And she wanted herself to be a schoolteacher.

One Saturday afternoon Agatha and Miriam were upstairs dressing. Their bedroom was over the stable. It was a low room, not very large, and bare. Miriam had nailed on the wall a reproduction of Veronese's 'St Catherine'. She loved the woman who sat in the window, dreaming. Her own windows were too small to sit in. But the front one was dripped over with honeysuckle and virginia creeper, and looked upon the tree-tops of the oak-wood across the yard, while the little back window, no bigger than a handkerchief, was a loophole to the east, to the dawn beating up against the beloved round hills.

The two sisters did not talk much to each other. Agatha, who was fair and small and determined, had rebelled against the home atmosphere, against the doctrine of 'the other cheek'. She was out in the world now, in a fair way to be independent. And she insisted on worldly values, on appearance, on manners, on position, which Miriam would fain have ignored.

Both girls liked to be upstairs, out of the way, when Paul came. They preferred to come running down, open the stair-foot door, and see him watching, expectant of them. Miriam stood painfully pulling over her head a rosary he had given her. It caught in the fine mesh of her hair. But at last she had it on, and the red-brown wooden beads looked well against her cool brown neck. She was a well-developed girl, and very handsome. But in the little looking-glass nailed against the whitewashed wall she could only see a fragment of herself at a time. Agatha had bought a little mirror of her own, which she propped up to suit herself. Miriam was near the window. Suddenly she heard the well-known click of the chain, and she saw Paul fling open the gate, push his bicycle into the yard. She saw him look at the house, and she shrank away. He walked in a nonchalant fashion, and his bicycle went with him as if it were a live thing.

'Paul's come!' she exclaimed.

'Aren't you glad?' said Agatha cuttingly.

Miriam stood still in amazement and bewilderment.

'Well, aren't you?' she asked.

'Yes, but I'm not going to let him see it, and think I wanted him.'

Miriam was startled. She heard him putting his bicycle in the stable underneath, and talking to Jimmy, who had been a pit-horse and who was seedy.

'Well, Jimmy my lad, how are ter? Nobbut sick an' sadly, like? Why, then, it's a shame, my owd lad.'

She heard the rope run through the hole as the horse lifted its head from the lad's caress. How she loved to listen when he thought only the horse could hear. But there was a serpent in her Eden. She searched earnestly in herself to see if she wanted Paul Morel. She felt there would be some disgrace in it. Full of twisted feeling, she was afraid she did want him. She stood self-convicted. Then came an agony of new shame. She shrank within herself in a coil of torture. Did she want Paul Morel, and did he know she wanted him? What a subtle infamy upon her! She felt as if her whole soul coiled into knots of shame.

Agatha was dressed first, and ran downstairs. Miriam heard her greet the lad gaily, knew exactly how brilliant her grey eyes became with that tone. She herself would have felt it bold to have greeted him in such wise. Yet there she stood under the self-accusation of wanting him, tied to that stake of torture. In bitter perplexity she kneeled down and prayed, 'O Lord, let me not love Paul Morel. Keep me from loving him, if I ought not to love him.'

Something anomalous in the prayer arrested her. She lifted her head and pondered. How could it be wrong to love him? Love was God's gift. And yet it caused her shame. That was because of him, Paul Morel. But, then, it was not his affair, it was her own, between herself and God. She was to be a sacrifice. But it was God's sacrifice, not Paul Morel's or her own. After a few minutes she hid her face in the pillow again, and said, 'But, Lord, if it is Thy will that I should love him, make me love him – as Christ would, who died for the souls of men. Make me love him splendidly, because he is Thy son.'

She remained kneeling for some time, quite still, and deeply moved, her black hair against the red squares and the lavender-sprigged squares of the patchwork-quilt. Prayer was almost essential to her. Then she fell into that rapture of self-sacrifice, identifying herself with a God who was sacrificed, which gives to so many human souls their deepest bliss.

When she went downstairs Paul was lying back in an armchair, holding forth with much vehemence to Agatha, who was scorning a little painting he had brought to show her. Miriam glanced at the two, and avoided their levity. She went into the parlour to be alone.

It was tea-time before she was able to speak to Paul, and then her manner was so distant he thought he had offended her.

Miriam discontinued her practice of going each Thursday evening to the library in Bestwood. After calling for Paul regularly during the whole spring, a number of trifling incidents and tiny insults from his family awakened her to their attitude towards her, and she decided to go no more. So she announced to Paul one evening she would not call at his house again for him on Thursday nights.

'Why?' he asked, very short.

'Nothing. Only I'd rather not.'

'Very well.'

'But,' she faltered, 'if you'd care to meet me, we could still go together.'

'Meet you where?'

'Somewhere – where you like.'

'I shan't meet you anywhere. I don't see why you shouldn't keep calling for me. But if you won't, I don't want to meet you.'

So the Thursday evenings which had been so precious to her, and to him, were dropped. He worked instead. Mrs Morel sniffed with satisfaction at this arrangement

He would not have it that they were lovers. The intimacy between them had been kept so abstract, such a matter of the soul, all thought and weary struggle into consciousness, that he saw it only as a platonic friendship. He stoutly denied there was anything else between them. Miriam was silent, or else she very quietly agreed. He was a fool who did not know what was happening to himself. By tacit agreement they ignored the remarks and insinuations of their acquaintances.

'We aren't lovers, we are friends,' he said to her. '*We* know it. Let them talk. What does it matter what they say?'

Sometimes, as they were walking together, she slipped her arm timidly into his. But he always resented it, and she knew it. It caused a violent conflict in him. With Miriam he was always on the high plane of abstraction, when his natural fire of love was transmitted into the fine stream of thought. She would have it so. If he were jolly and, as she put it, flippant, she waited till he came back to her, till the change had taken place in him again, and he was wrestling with his own soul, frowning, passionate in his desire for understanding. And in this passion for understanding her soul lay close to his; she had him all to herself. But he must be made abstract first.

Then, if she put her arm in his, it caused him almost torture. His consciousness seemed to split. The place where she was touching him ran hot with friction. He was one internecine battle, and he became cruel to her because of it.

One evening in midsummer Miriam called at the house, warm from climbing. Paul was alone in the kitchen; his mother could be heard moving about upstairs. 'Come and look at the sweet-peas,' he said to the girl.

They went into the garden. The sky behind the townlet and the church was orange-red; the flower-garden was flooded with a strange warm light that lifted every leaf into significance. Paul passed along a fine row of sweet-peas, gathering a blossom here and there, all cream and pale blue. Miriam followed, breathing the fragrance. To her, flowers appealed with such strength she felt she must make them part of herself. When she bent and breathed a flower, it was as if she and the flower were loving each other. Paul hated her for it. There seemed a sort of exposure about the action, something too intimate.

When he had got a fair bunch, they returned to the house. He listened for a moment to his mother's quiet movement upstairs, then he said, 'Come here, and let me pin them in for you.' He arranged them two or three at a time in the bosom of her dress, stepping back now and then to see the effect. 'You know,' he said, taking the pin out of his mouth, 'a woman ought always to arrange her flowers before her glass.'

Miriam laughed. She thought flowers ought to be pinned in one's dress without any care. That Paul should take pains to fix her flowers for her was his whim.

He was rather offended at her laughter.

'Some women do – those who look decent,' he said.

Miriam laughed again, but mirthlessly, to hear him thus mix her up with women in a general way. From most men she would have ignored it. But from him it hurt her.

He had nearly finished arranging the flowers when he heard his mother's footstep on the stairs. Hurriedly he pushed in the last pin and turned away.

'Don't let mater know,' he said.

Miriam picked up her books and stood in the doorway looking with chagrin at the beautiful sunset. She would call for Paul no more, she said.

'Good-evening, Mrs Morel,' she said, in a deferential way. She sounded as if she felt she had no right to be there.

'Oh, is it you, Miriam?' replied Mrs Morel coolly.

But Paul insisted on everybody's accepting his friendship with the girl, and Mrs Morel was too wise to have any open rupture.

It was not till he was twenty years old that the family could ever afford to go away for a holiday. Mrs Morel had never been away for a holiday, except to see her sister, since she had been married. Now at last Paul had saved enough money, and they were all going. There was to be a party: some of Annie's friends, one friend of Paul's, a young man in the same office where William had previously been, and Miriam.

It was great excitement writing for rooms. Paul and his mother debated it endlessly between them. They wanted a furnished cottage for two weeks. She thought one week would be enough, but he insisted on two.

At last they got an answer from Mablethorpe, a cottage such as they wished for thirty shillings a week. There was immense jubilation. Paul was wild with joy for his mother's sake. She would have a real holiday now. He and she sat at evening picturing what it would be like. Annie came in, and Leonard, and Alice, and Kitty. There was wild rejoicing and anticipation. Paul told Miriam. She seemed to brood with joy over it. But the Morels' house rang with excitement.

They were to go on Saturday morning by the seven train. Paul suggested that Miriam should sleep at his house, because it was so far for her to walk. She came down for supper. Everybody was so excited that even Miriam was accepted with warmth. But almost as soon as she entered the feeling in the family became close and tight. He had discovered a poem by Jean Ingelow which mentioned Mable-thorpe, and so he must read it to Miriam. He would never have got so far in the direction of sentimentality as to read poetry to his own family. But now they condescended to listen. Miriam sat on the sofa absorbed in him. She always seemed absorbed in him, and by him, when he was present. Mrs Morel sat jealously in her own chair. She was going to hear also. And even Annie and the father attended, Morel with his head cocked on one side, like somebody listening to a sermon and feeling conscious of the fact. Paul ducked his head over the book. He had got now all the audience he cared for. And Mrs Morel and Annie almost contested with Miriam who should listen best and win his favour. He was in very high feather.

'But,' interrupted Mrs Morel, 'what *is* the "Bride of Enderby" that the bells are supposed to ring?'

'It's an old tune they used to play on the bells for a warning against water. I suppose the Bride of Enderby was drowned in a flood,' he replied. He had not the faintest knowledge what it really was, but he would never have sunk so low as to confess that to his womenfolk. They listened and believed him. He believed himself.

'And the people knew what that tune meant?' said his mother.

'Yes – just like the Scotch when they heard "The Flowers o' the Forest" – and when they used to ring the bells backward for alarm.'

'How?' said Annie. 'A bell sounds the same whether it's rung backwards or forwards.'

'But,' he said, 'if you start with the deep bell and ring up to the high one – der – der – der – der – der – der – der – der!'

He ran up the scale. Everybody thought it clever. He thought so too. Then, waiting a minute, he continued the poem.

'Hm!' said Mrs Morel curiously, when he finished. 'But I wish everything that's written weren't so sad.'

'I canna see what they want drownin' theirselves for,' said Morel.

There was a pause. Annie got up to clear the table.

Miriam rose to help with the pots.

'Let *me* help to wash up,' she said.

'Certainly not,' cried Annie. 'You sit down again. There aren't many.'

And Miriam, who could not be familiar and insist, sat down again to look at the book with Paul.

He was master of the party; his father was no good. And great tortures he suffered lest the tin box should be put out at Firsby instead of at Mablethorpe. And he wasn't equal to getting a carriage. His bold little mother did that.

'Here!' she cried to a man. 'Here!'

Paul and Annie got behind the rest, convulsed with shamed laughter.

'How much will it be to drive to Brook Cottage?' said Mrs Morel.

'Two shillings.'

'Why, how far is it?'

'A good way.'

'I don't believe it,' she said.

But she scrambled in. There were eight crowded in one old seaside carriage.

'You see,' said Mrs Morel, 'it's only threepence each, and if it were a tramcar – '

They drove along. Each cottage they came to, Mrs Morel cried, 'Is it this? Now, this is it!'

Everybody sat breathless. They drove past. There was a universal sigh.

'I'm thankful it wasn't that brute,' said Mrs Morel. 'I *was* frightened.' They drove on and on.

At last they descended at a house that stood alone over the dyke by the highroad. There was wild excitement because they had to cross a little bridge to get into the front garden. But they loved the house that lay so solitary, with a sea-meadow on one side, and immense expanse of land patched in white barley, yellow oats, red wheat, and green root-crops, flat and stretching level to the sky.

Paul kept accounts. He and his mother ran the show. The total expenses – lodging, food, everything – was sixteen shillings a week per person. He and Leonard went bathing in the morning. Morel was wandering abroad quite early.

'You, Paul,' his mother called from the bedroom, 'eat a piece of bread-and-butter.'

'All right,' he answered.

And when he got back he saw his mother presiding in state at the breakfast-table. The woman of the house was young. Her husband was blind, and she did laundry work. So Mrs Morel always washed the pots in the kitchen and made the beds.

'But you said you'd have a real holiday,' said Paul, 'and now you work.'

'Work!' she exclaimed. 'What are you talking about!'

He loved to go with her across the fields to the village and the sea. She was afraid of the plank bridges, and he abused her for being a baby. On the whole he stuck to her as if he were her man.

Miriam did not get much of him, except, perhaps, when all the others went to the 'Coons'. Coons were insufferably stupid to Miriam, so he thought they were to himself also, and he preached priggishly to Annie about the fatuity of listening to them. Yet he, too, knew all their songs, and sang them along the roads roisterously. And if he found himself listening, the stupidity pleased him very much. Yet to Annie he said, 'Such rot! there isn't a grain of intelligence in it. Nobody with more gumption than a grasshopper could go and sit and listen.' And to Miriam he said, with much scorn of Annie and the others: 'I suppose they're at the "Coons".'

It was queer to see Miriam singing coon songs. She had a straight chin that went in a perpendicular line from the lower lip to the turn. She always reminded Paul of some sad Botticelli angel when she sang, even when it was:

> 'Come down lovers' lane
> For a walk with me, talk with me.'

Only when he sketched, or at evening when the others were at the 'Coons', she had him to herself. He talked to her endlessly about his love of horizontals: how they, the great levels of sky and land in Lincolnshire, meant to him the eternality of the will, just as the bowed Norman arches of the church, repeating themselves, meant the dogged leaping forward of the persistent human soul, on and on, nobody knows where; in contradiction to the perpendicular lines and to the Gothic arch, which, he said, leapt up at heaven and touched the ecstasy and lost itself in the divine. Himself, he said, was Norman, Miriam was Gothic. She bowed in consent even to that.

One evening he and she went up the great sweeping shore of sand towards Theddlethorpe. The long breakers plunged and ran in a hiss of foam along the coast. It was a warm evening. There was not a figure but themselves on the far reaches of sand, no noise but the sound of the sea. Paul loved to see it clanging at the land. He loved to feel himself between the noise of it and the silence of the sandy shore. Miriam was with him. Everything grew very intense. It was quite dark when they turned again. The way home was through a gap in the sand-hills, and then along a raised grass road between two dykes. The country was black and still. From behind the sand-hills came the whisper of the sea. Paul and Miriam walked in silence. Suddenly he started. The whole of his blood seemed to burst into flame, and he could scarcely breathe. An enormous orange moon was staring at them from the rim of the sand-hills. He stood still, looking at it.

'Ah!' cried Miriam, when she saw it.

He remained perfectly still, staring at the immense and ruddy moon, the only thing in the far-reaching darkness of the level. His heart beat heavily, the muscles of his arms contracted.

'What is it?' murmured Miriam, waiting for him.

He turned and looked at her. She stood beside him, for ever in shadow. Her face, covered with the darkness of her hat, was watching him unseen. But she was brooding. She was slightly afraid – deeply moved and religious. That was her best state. He was impotent against it. His blood was concentrated like a flame in his chest. But he could not get across to her. There were flashes in his blood. But somehow she ignored them. She was expecting some religious state in him. Still yearning, she was half aware of his passion, and gazed at him, troubled.

'What is it?' she murmured again.

'It's the moon,' he answered, frowning.

'Yes,' she assented. 'Isn't it wonderful?' She was curious about him. The crisis was past.

He did not know himself what was the matter. He was naturally so young, and their intimacy was so abstract, he did not know he wanted to crush her on to his breast to ease the ache there. He was afraid of her. The fact that he might want her as a man wants a woman had in him been suppressed into a shame. When she shrank in her convulsed, coiled torture from the thought of such a thing, he had winced to the depths of his soul. And now this 'purity' prevented even their first love-kiss. It was as if she could scarcely stand the shock of physical love, even a passionate kiss, and then he was too shrinking and sensitive to give it.

As they walked along the dark fen-meadow he watched the moon and did not speak. She plodded beside him. He hated her, for she seemed in some way to make him despise himself. Looking ahead – he saw the one light in the darkness, the window of their lamp-lit cottage.

He loved to think of his mother, and the other jolly people.

'Well, everybody else has been in long ago!' said his mother as they entered.

'What does that matter!' he cried irritably. 'I can go a walk if I like, can't I?'

'And I should have thought you could get in to supper with the rest,' said Mrs Morel.

'I shall please myself,' he retorted. 'It's not *late*. I shall do as I like.'

'Very well,' said his mother cuttingly, 'then *do* as you like.'

And she took no further notice of him that evening. Which he pretended neither to notice nor to care about, but sat reading. Miriam read also, obliterating herself. Mrs Morel hated her for making her son like this. She watched Paul growing irritable, priggish, and melancholic. For this she put the blame on Miriam. Annie and all her friends joined against the girl. Miriam had no friend of her own, only Paul. But she did not suffer so much, because she despised the triviality of these other people.

And Paul hated her because, somehow, she spoilt his ease and naturalness. And he writhed himself with a feeling of humiliation.

CHAPTER 8

Strife in Love

Arthur finished his apprenticeship, and got a job on the electrical plant at Minton Pit. He earned very little, but had a good chance of getting on. But he was wild and restless. He did not drink or gamble. Yet he somehow contrived to get into endless scrapes, always through some hot-headed thoughtlessness. Either he went rabbiting in the woods, like a poacher, or he stayed in Nottingham all night instead of coming home, or he miscalculated his dive into the canal at Bestwood, and scored his chest into one mass of wounds on the raw stones and tins at the bottom.

He had not been at his work many months when again he did not come home one night.

'Do you know where Arthur is?' asked Paul at breakfast.

'I do not,' replied his mother.

'He is a fool,' said Paul. 'And if he *did* anything I shouldn't mind. But no, he simply can't come away from a game of whist, or else he must see a girl home from the skating-rink – quite proprietously – and so can't get home. He's a fool.'

'I don't know that it would make it any better if he did something to make us all ashamed,' said Mrs Morel.

'Well, *I* should respect him more,' said Paul.

'I very much doubt it,' said his mother coldly.

They went on with breakfast.

'Are you fearfully fond of him?' Paul asked his mother.

'What do you ask that for?'

'Because they say a woman always likes the youngest best.'

'She may do – but I don't. No, he wearies me.'

'And you'd actually rather he was good?'

'I'd rather he showed some of a man's common sense.'

Paul was raw and irritable. He also wearied his mother very often. She saw the sunshine going out of him, and she resented it.

As they were finishing breakfast came the postman with a letter from Derby. Mrs Morel screwed up her eyes to look at the address.

'Give it here, blind eye!' exclaimed her son, snatching it away from her.

She started, and almost boxed his ears.

'It's from your son, Arthur,' he said.

'What now!' cried Mrs Morel.

' "My dearest Mother," ' Paul read, ' "I don't know what made me such a fool. I want you to come and fetch me back from here. I came with Jack Bredon yesterday, instead of going to work, and enlisted. He said he was sick of wearing the seat of a stool out, and, like the idiot you know I am, I came away with him."

' "I have taken the King's shilling, but perhaps if you came for me they would let me go back with you. I was a fool when I did it. I don't want to be in the army. My dear mother, I am nothing but a trouble to you. But if you get me out of this, I promise I will have more sense and consideration ... " '

Mrs Morel sat down in her rocking-chair.

'Well, *now*,' she cried, 'let him stop!'

'Yes,' said Paul, 'let him stop.'

There was silence. The mother sat with her hands folded in her apron, her face set, thinking.

'If I'm not *sick*!' she cried suddenly. 'Sick!'

'Now,' said Paul, beginning to frown, 'you're not going to worry your soul out about this, do you hear?'

'I suppose I'm to take it as a blessing,' she flashed, turning on her son.

'You're not going to mount it up to a tragedy, so there,' he retorted.

'The *fool*! – the young fool!' she cried.

'He'll look well in uniform,' said Paul irritatingly.

His mother turned on him like a fury.

'Oh, will he!' she cried. 'Not in my eyes!'

'He should get in a cavalry regiment; he'll have the time of his life, and will look an awful swell.'

'Swell! – *swell*! – a mighty swell indeed! – a common soldier!'

'Well,' said Paul, 'what am I but a common clerk?'

'A good deal, my boy!' cried his mother, stung.

'What?'

'At any rate, a *man*, and not a thing in a red coat.'

'I shouldn't mind being in a red coat – or dark blue, that would suit me better – if they didn't boss me about too much.'

But his mother had ceased to listen.

'Just as he was getting on, or might have been getting on, at his job – a young nuisance – here he goes and ruins himself for life. What good will he be, do you think, after *this*?'

'It may lick him into shape beautifully,' said Paul.

'Lick him into shape! – lick what marrow there *was* out of his bones. A *soldier*! – a common *soldier*! – nothing but a body that makes movements when it hears a shout! It's a fine thing!'

'I can't understand why it upsets you,' said Paul.

'No, perhaps you can't. But *I* understand'; and she sat back in her chair, her chin in one hand, holding her elbow with the other, brimmed up with wrath and chagrin.

'And shall you go to Derby?' asked Paul.

'Yes.'

'It's no good.'

'I'll see for myself.'

'And why on earth don't you let him stop? It's just what he wants.'

'Of course,' cried the mother, '*you* know what he wants!'

She got ready and went by the first train to Derby, where she saw her son and the sergeant. It was, however, no good.

When Morel was having his dinner in the evening, she said suddenly, 'I've had to go to Derby today.'

The miner turned up his eyes, showing the whites in his black face.

'Has ter, lass. What took thee there?'

'That Arthur!'

'Oh – an' what's agate now?'

'He's only enlisted.'

Morel put down his knife and leaned back in his chair.

'Nay,' he said, 'that he niver 'as!'

'And is going down to Aldershot tomorrow.'

'Well!' exclaimed the miner. 'That's a winder.' He considered it a moment, said 'H'm!' and proceeded with his dinner. Suddenly his face contracted with wrath. 'I hope he may never set foot i' my house again,' he said.

'The idea!' cried Mrs Morel. 'Saying such a thing!'

'I do,' repeated Morel. 'A fool as runs away for a soldier, let 'im look after 'issen; I s'll do no more for 'im.'

'A fat sight you have done as it is,' she said.

And Morel was almost ashamed to go to his public-house that evening.

'Well, did you go?' said Paul to his mother when he came home.

'I did.'

'And could you see him?'

'Yes.'

'And what did he say?'

'He blubbered when I came away.'

'H'm!'

'And so did I, so you needn't "h'm!" '

Mrs Morel fretted after her son. She knew he would not like the army. He did not. The discipline was intolerable to him.

'But the doctor,' she said with some pride to Paul, 'said he was perfectly proportioned – almost exactly – all his measurements were correct. He's good-looking, you know.'

'He's awfully nice-looking. But he doesn't fetch the girls like William, does he?'

'No; it's a different character. He's a good deal like his father, irresponsible.'

To console his mother, Paul did not go much to Willey Farm at this time. And in the autumn exhibition of students' work in the Castle he had two studies, a landscape in watercolour and a still life in oil, both of which had first-prize awards. He was highly excited.

'What do you think I've got for my pictures, mother?' he asked, coming home one evening. She saw by his eyes he was glad. Her face flushed.

'Now, how should I know, my boy!'

'A first prize for those glass jars – '

'H'm!'

'And a first prize for that sketch up at Willey Farm.'

'Both first?'

'Yes.'

'H'm!'

There was a rosy, bright look about her, though she said nothing.

'It's nice,' he said, 'isn't it?'

'It is.'

'Why don't you praise me up to the skies?'

She laughed.

'I should have the trouble of dragging you down again,' she said.

But she was full of joy, nevertheless. William had brought her his sporting trophies. She kept them still, and she did not forgive his death. Arthur was handsome – at least, a good specimen – and warm and generous, and probably would do well in the end. But Paul was going to distinguish himself. She had a great belief in him, the more because he was unaware of his own powers. There was so much to come out of him. Life for her was rich with promise. She was to see herself fulfilled. Not for nothing had been her struggle.

Several times during the exhibition Mrs Morel went to the Castle unknown to Paul. She wandered down the long room looking at the other exhibits. Yes, they were good. But they had not in them a certain something which she demanded for her satisfaction. Some made her jealous, they were so good. She looked at them a long time trying to find fault with them. Then suddenly she had a shock that made her heart beat. There hung Paul's picture! She knew it as if it were printed on her heart.

'Name – Paul Morel – First Prize.'

It looked so strange, there in public, on the walls of the Castle gallery, where in her lifetime she had seen so many pictures. And she glanced round to see if anyone had noticed her again in front of the same sketch.

But she felt a proud woman. When she met well-dressed ladies going home to the Park, she thought to herself, 'Yes, you look very well – but I wonder if *your* son has two first prizes in the Castle.'

And she walked on, as proud a little woman as any in Nottingham. And Paul felt he had done something for her, if only a trifle. All his work was hers.

One day, as he was going up Castle Gate, he met Miriam. He had seen her on the Sunday, and had not expected to meet her in town. She was walking with a rather striking woman, blonde, with a sullen expression, and a defiant carriage. It was strange how Miriam, in her bowed, meditative bearing, looked dwarfed beside this woman with the handsome shoulders. Miriam watched Paul searchingly. His gaze was on the stranger, who ignored him. The girl saw his masculine spirit rear its head.

'Hello!' he said, 'you didn't tell me you were coming to town.'

'No,' replied Miriam, half apologetically. 'I drove in to Cattle Market with father.'

He looked at her companion.

'I've told you about Mrs Dawes,' said Miriam huskily; she was nervous. 'Clara, do you know Paul?'

'I think I've seen him before,' replied Mrs Dawes indifferently, as she shook hands with him. She had scornful grey eyes, a skin like white honey, and a full mouth, with a slightly lifted upper lip that did not know whether it was raised in scorn of all men or out of eagerness to be kissed, but which believed the former. She carried her head back, as if she had drawn away in contempt, perhaps from men also. She wore a large, dowdy hat of black beaver, and a sort of slightly affected simple dress that made her look rather sacklike. She was evidently poor, and had not much taste. Miriam usually looked nice.

'Where have you seen me?' Paul asked of the woman.

She looked at him as if she would not trouble to answer. Then, 'Walking with Louie Travers,' she said.

Louie was one of the 'spiral' girls.

'Why, do you know her?' he asked.

She did not answer. He turned to Miriam.

'Where are you going?' he asked.

'To the Castle.'

'What train are you going home by?'

'I am driving with father. I wish you could come too. What time are you free?'

'You know not till eight tonight, damn it!'

And directly the two women moved on.

Paul remembered that Clara Dawes was the daughter of an old friend of Mrs Leivers. Miriam had sought her out because she had once been spiral overseer at Jordan's, and because her husband, Baxter Dawes, was smith for the factory, making the irons for cripple instruments, and so on. Through her Miriam felt she got into direct contact with Jordan's, and could estimate better Paul's position. But Mrs Dawes was separated from her husband, and had taken up Women's Rights. She was supposed to be clever. It interested Paul.

Baxter Dawes he knew and disliked. The smith was a man of thirty-one or thirty-two. He came occasionally through Paul's corner – a big, well-set man, also striking to look at, and handsome. There was a peculiar similarity between himself and his wife. He had the same white skin, with a clear golden tinge. His hair was of soft brown, his moustache was golden. And he had a similar defiance in his bearing and manner. But then came the difference. His eyes, dark brown and quick-shifting, were dissolute. They protruded very slightly, and his eyelids hung over them in a way that was half hate. His mouth, too, was sensual. His whole manner was of cowed defiance, as if he were ready to knock anybody down who disapproved of him – perhaps because he really disapproved of himself.

From the first day he had hated Paul. Finding the lad's impersonal, deliberate gaze of an artist on his face, he got into a fury.

'What are yer lookin' at?' he sneered, bullying.

The boy glanced away. But the smith used to stand behind the counter and talk to Mr Pappleworth. His speech was dirty, with a kind of rottenness. Again he found the youth with his cool, critical gaze fixed on his face. The smith started round as if he had been stung.

'What'r yer lookin' at, three hap'orth o' pap?' he snarled.

The boy shrugged his shoulders slightly.

'Why yer – !' shouted Dawes.

'Leave him alone,' said Mr Pappleworth, in that insinuating voice which means, 'he's only one of your good little sops who can't help it'.

Since that time the boy used to look at the man every time he came through with the same curious criticism, glancing away before he met the smith's eye. It made Dawes furious. They hated each other in silence.

Clara Dawes had no children. When she had left her husband the home had been broken up, and she had gone to live with her mother. Dawes lodged with his sister. In the same house was a sister-in-law, and somehow Paul knew that this girl, Louie Travers, was now Dawes's woman. She was a handsome, insolent hussy, who mocked at the youth, and yet flushed if he walked along to the station with her as she went home.

The next time he went to see Miriam it was Saturday evening. She had a fire in the parlour, and was waiting for him. The others, except her father and mother and the young children, had gone out, so the two had the parlour together. It was a long, low, warm room. There were three of Paul's small sketches on the wall, and his photo was on the mantelpiece. On the table and on the high old rosewood piano were bowls of coloured leaves. He sat in the armchair, she crouched on the hearthrug near his feet. The glow was warm on her handsome, pensive face as she kneeled there like a devotee.

'What did you think of Mrs Dawes?' she asked quietly.

'She doesn't look very amiable,' he replied.

'No, but don't you think she's a fine woman?' she said, in a deep tone.

'Yes – in stature. But without a grain of taste. I like her for some things. Is she disagreeable?'

'I don't think so. I think she's dissatisfied.'

'What with?'

'Well – how would you like to be tied for life to a man like that?'

'Why did she marry him, then, if she was to have revulsions so soon?'

'Ay, why did she!' repeated Miriam bitterly.

'And I should have thought she had enough fight in her to match him,' he said.

Miriam bowed her head.

'Ay?' she queried satirically. 'What makes you think so?'

'Look at her mouth – made for passion – and the very setback of her throat –'

He threw his head back in Clara's defiant manner.

Miriam bowed a little lower.

'Yes,' she said.

There was a silence for some moments, while he thought of Clara.

'And what were the things you liked about her?' she asked.

'I don't know – her skin and the texture of her – and her – I don't know – there's a sort of fierceness somewhere in her. I appreciate her as an artist, that's all.'

'Yes.'

He wondered why Miriam crouched there brooding in that strange way. It irritated him.

'You don't really like her, do you?' he asked the girl.

She looked at him with her great, dazzled dark eyes.

'I do,' she said.

'You don't – you can't – not really.'

'Then what?' she asked slowly.

'Eh, I don't know – perhaps you like her because she's got a grudge against men.'

That was more probably one of his own reasons for liking Mrs Dawes, but this did not occur to him. They were silent. There had come into his forehead a knitting of the brows which was becoming habitual with him, particularly when he was with Miriam. She longed to smooth it away, and she was afraid of it. It seemed the stamp of a man who was not her man in Paul Morel.

There were some crimson berries among the leaves in the bowl. He reached over and pulled out a bunch.

'If you put red berries in your hair,' he said, 'why would you look like some witch or priestess, and never like a reveller?'

She laughed with a naked, painful sound. 'I don't know,' she said.

His vigorous warm hands were playing excitedly with the berries.

'Why can't you laugh?' he said. 'You never laugh laughter. You only laugh when something is odd or incongruous, and then it almost seems to hurt you.'

She bowed her head as if he were scolding her.

'I wish you could laugh at me just for one minute – just for one minute. I feel as if it would set something free.'

'But' – and she looked up at him with eyes frightened and struggling – 'I do laugh at you – I *do*.'

'Never! There's always a kind of intensity. When you laugh I could always cry; it seems as if it shows up your suffering. Oh, you make me knit the brows of my very soul and cogitate.'

Slowly she shook her head despairingly.

'I'm sure I don't want to,' she said.

'I'm so damned spiritual with *you* always!' he cried.

She remained silent, thinking, 'Then why don't you be otherwise?' But he saw her crouching, brooding figure, and it seemed to tear him in two.

'But, there, it's autumn,' he said, 'and everybody feels like a disembodied spirit then.'

There was still another silence. This peculiar sadness between them thrilled her soul. He seemed so beautiful with his eyes gone dark, and looking as if they were deep as the deepest well.

'You make me so spiritual!' he lamented. 'And I don't want to be spiritual.'

She took her finger from her mouth with a little pop, and looked up at him almost challenging. But still her soul was naked in her great dark eyes, and there was the same yearning appeal upon her. If he could have kissed her in abstract purity he would have done so. But he could not kiss her thus – and she seemed to leave no other way. And she yearned to him.

He gave a brief laugh.

'Well,' he said, 'get that French and we'll do some – some Verlaine.'

'Yes,' she said in a deep tone, almost of resignation. And she rose and got the books. And her rather red, nervous hands looked so pitiful, he was mad to comfort her and kiss her. But then he dared not – or could not. There was something prevented him. His kisses were wrong for her. They continued the reading till ten o'clock, when they went into the kitchen, and Paul was natural and jolly again with the father and mother. His eyes were dark and shining; there was a kind of fascination about him.

When he went into the barn for his bicycle he found the front wheel punctured.

'Fetch me a drop of water in a bowl,' he said to her. 'I shall be late, and then I s'll catch it.'

He lighted the hurricane lamp, took off his coat, turned up the bicycle, and set speedily to work. Miriam came with the bowl of water and stood close to him, watching. She loved to see his hands doing things. He was slim and vigorous, with a kind of easiness even in his most hasty movements. And busy at his work he seemed to forget her. She loved him absorbedly. She wanted to run her hands down his sides. She always wanted to embrace him, so long as he did not want her.

'There!' he said, rising suddenly. 'Now, could you have done it quicker?'

'No!' she laughed.

He straightened himself. His back was towards her. She put her two hands on his sides, and ran them quickly down.

'You are so *fine*!' she said.

He laughed, hating her voice, but his blood roused to a wave of flame by her hands. She did not seem to realise *him* in all this. He might have been an object. She never realised the male he was.

He lighted his bicycle-lamp, bounced the machine on the barn floor to see that the tyres were sound, and buttoned his coat.

'That's all right!' he said.

She was trying the brakes, that she knew were broken.

'Did you have them mended?' she asked.

'No!'

'But why didn't you?'

'The back one goes on a bit.'

'But it's not safe.'

'I can use my toe.'

'I wish you'd had them mended,' she murmured.

'Don't worry – come to tea tomorrow, with Edgar.'

'Shall we?'

'Do – about four. I'll come to meet you.'

'Very well.'

She was pleased. They went across the dark yard to the gate. Looking across, he saw through the uncurtained window of the kitchen the heads of Mr and Mrs Leivers in the warm glow. It looked very cosy. The road, with pine trees, was quite black in front.

'Till tomorrow,' he said, jumping on his bicycle.

'You'll take care, won't you?' she pleaded.

'Yes.'

His voice already came out of the darkness. She stood a moment watching the light from his lamp race into obscurity along the ground. She turned very slowly indoors. Orion was wheeling up over the wood, his dog twinkling after him, half smothered. For the rest the world was full of darkness, and silent, save for the breathing of cattle in their stalls. She prayed earnestly for his safety that night. When he left her, she often lay in anxiety, wondering if he had got home safely.

He dropped down the hills on his bicycle. The roads were greasy, so he had to let it go. He felt a pleasure as the machine plunged over the second, steeper drop in the hill. 'Here goes!' he said. It was risky, because of the curve in the darkness at the bottom, and because of the brewers' waggons with drunken waggoners asleep. His bicycle seemed to fall beneath him, and he loved it. Recklessness is almost a man's revenge on his woman. He feels he is not valued, so he will risk destroying himself to deprive her altogether.

The stars on the lake seemed to leap like grasshoppers, silver upon the blackness, as he spun past. Then there was the long climb home.

'See, mother!' he said, as he threw her the berries and leaves on to the table.

'H'm!' she said, glancing at them, then away again. She sat reading, alone, as she always did.

'Aren't they pretty?'

'Yes.'

He knew she was cross with him. After a few minutes he said, 'Edgar and Miriam are coming to tea tomorrow.'

She did not answer.

'You don't mind?'

Still she did not answer.

'Do you?' he asked.

'You know whether I mind or not.'

'I don't see why you should. I have plenty of meals there.'

'You do.'

'Then why do you begrudge them tea?'

'I begrudge whom tea?'

'What are you so horrid for?'

'Oh, say no more! You've asked her to tea, it's quite sufficient. She'll come.'

He was very angry with his mother. He knew it was merely Miriam she objected to. He flung off his boots and went to bed.

Paul went to meet his friends the next afternoon. He was glad to see them coming. They arrived home at about four o'clock. Everywhere was clean and still for Sunday afternoon. Mrs Morel sat in her black dress and black apron. She rose to meet the visitors. With Edgar she was cordial, but with Miriam cold and rather grudging. Yet Paul thought the girl looked so nice in her brown cashmere frock.

He helped his mother to get the tea ready. Miriam would have gladly proffered, but was afraid. He was rather proud of his home. There was about it now, he thought, a certain distinction. The chairs were only wooden, and the sofa was old. But the hearthrug and cushions were cosy; the pictures were prints in good taste; there was a simplicity in everything, and plenty of books. He was never ashamed in the least of his home, nor was Miriam of hers, because both were what they should be, and warm. And then he was proud of the table; the china was pretty, the cloth was fine. It did not matter that the spoons were not silver nor the knives ivory-handled; everything looked nice. Mrs Morel had managed wonderfully while her children were growing up, so that nothing was out of place.

Miriam talked books a little. That was her unfailing topic. But Mrs Morel was not cordial, and turned soon to Edgar.

At first Edgar and Miriam used to go into Mrs Morel's pew. Morel never went to chapel, preferring the public-house. Mrs Morel, like a little champion, sat at the head of her pew, Paul at the other end; and at first Miriam sat next to him. Then the chapel was like home. It was a pretty place, with dark pews and slim, elegant pillars, and flowers. And the same people had sat in the same places ever since he was a boy. It was wonderfully sweet and soothing to sit there for an hour and a half, next to Miriam, and near to his mother, uniting his two loves under the spell of the place of worship. Then he felt warm and happy and religious at once. And after chapel he walked home with Miriam, whilst Mrs Morel spent the rest of the evening with her old friend, Mrs Burns. He was keenly alive on his walks on Sunday nights with Edgar and Miriam. He never went past the pits at night, by the lighted lamp-house, the tall black head-stocks and lines of trucks, past the fans spinning slowly like shadows, without the feeling of Miriam returning to him, keen and almost unbearable.

She did not very long occupy the Morels' pew. Her father took one for themselves once more. It was under the little gallery, opposite the Morels'.

When Paul and his mother came in the chapel the Leiverses' pew was always empty. He was anxious for fear she would not come: it was so far, and there were so many rainy Sundays. Then, often very late indeed, she came in, with her long stride, her head bowed, her face hidden under her hat of dark green velvet. Her face, as she sat opposite, was always in shadow. But it gave him a very keen feeling, as if all his soul stirred within him, to see her there. It was not the same glow, happiness, and pride, that he felt in having his mother in charge: something more wonderful, less human, and tinged to intensity by a pain, as if there were something he could not get to.

At this time he was beginning to question the orthodox creed. He was twenty-one, and she was twenty. She was beginning to dread the spring: he became so wild, and hurt her so much. All the way he went cruelly smashing her beliefs. Edgar enjoyed it. He was by nature critical and rather dispassionate. But Miriam suffered exquisite pain, as, with an intellect like a knife, the man she loved examined her religion in which she lived and moved and had her being. But he did not spare her. He was cruel. And when they went alone he was even more fierce, as if he would kill her soul. He bled her beliefs till she almost lost consciousness.

'She exults – she exults as she carries him off from me,' Mrs Morel cried in her heart when Paul had gone. 'She's not like an ordinary woman, who can leave me my share in him. She wants to absorb him. She wants to draw him out and absorb him till there is nothing left of him, even for himself. He will never be a man on his own feet – she will suck him up.' So the mother sat, and battled and brooded bitterly.

And he, coming home from his walks with Miriam, was wild with torture. He walked biting his lips and with clenched fists, going at a great rate. Then, brought up against a stile, he stood for some minutes, and did not move. There was a great hollow of darkness fronting him, and on the black up-slopes patches of tiny lights, and in the lowest trough of the night, a flare of the pit. It was all weird and dreadful. Why was he torn so, almost bewildered, and unable to move? Why did his mother sit at home and suffer? He knew she suffered badly. But why should she? And why did he hate Miriam, and feel so cruel towards her, at the thought of his mother? If Miriam caused his mother suffering, then he hated her – and he easily hated her. Why did she make him feel as if he were uncertain of himself, insecure, an indefinite thing, as if he had not sufficient sheathing to prevent the night and the space breaking into him? How he hated her! And then, what a rush of tenderness and humility!

Suddenly he plunged on again, running home. His mother saw on him the marks of some agony, and she said nothing. But he had to make her talk to him. Then she was angry with him for going so far with Miriam.

'Why don't you like her, mother?' he cried in despair.

'I don't know, my boy,' she replied piteously. 'I'm sure I've tried to like her. I've tried and tried, but I can't – I can't!'

And he felt dreary and hopeless between the two.

Spring was the worst time. He was changeable, and intense and cruel. So he decided to stay away from her. Then came the hours when he knew Miriam was expecting him. His mother watched him growing restless. He could not go on with his work. He could do nothing. It was as if something were drawing his soul out towards Willey Farm. Then he put on his hat and went, saying nothing. And his mother knew he was gone. And as soon as he was on the way he sighed with relief. And when he was with her he was cruel again.

One day in March he lay on the bank of Nethermere, with Miriam sitting beside him. It was a glistening, white-and-blue day. Big clouds, so brilliant, went by overhead, while shadows stole along on the water. The clear spaces in the sky were of clean, cold blue. Paul lay on his back in the old grass, looking up. He could not bear to look at Miriam. She seemed to want him, and he resisted. He resisted all the time. He wanted now to give her passion and tenderness, and he could not. He felt that she wanted the soul out of his body, and not him. All his strength and energy she drew into herself through some channel which united them. She did not want to meet him, so that there were two of them, man and woman together. She wanted to draw all of him into her. It urged him to an intensity like madness, which fascinated him, as drug-taking might.

He was discussing Michelangelo. It felt to her as if she were fingering the very quivering tissue, the very protoplasm of life, as she heard him. It gave her her deepest satisfaction. And in the end it frightened her. There he lay in the white intensity of his search, and his voice gradually filled her with fear, so level it was, almost inhuman, as if in a trance.

'Don't talk any more,' she pleaded softly, laying her hand on his forehead.

He lay quite still, almost unable to move. His body was somewhere discarded.

'Why not? Are you tired?'

'Yes, and it wears you out.'

He laughed shortly, realising.

'Yet you always make me like it,' he said.

'I don't wish to,' she said, very low.

'Not when you've gone too far, and you feel you can't bear it. But your unconscious self always asks it of me. And I suppose I want it.'

He went on, in his dead fashion, 'If only you could want *me*, and not want what I can reel off for you!'

'I!' she cried bitterly – 'I! Why, when would you let me take you?'

'Then it's my fault,' he said, and, gathering himself together, he got up and began to talk trivialities. He felt insubstantial. In a vague way he hated her for it. And he knew he was as much to blame himself. This, however, did not prevent his hating her.

One evening about this time he had walked along the home road with her. They stood by the pasture leading down to the wood, unable to part. As the stars came out the clouds closed. They had glimpses of their own constellation, Orion, towards the west. His jewels glimmered for a moment, his dog ran low, struggling with difficulty through the spume of cloud.

Orion was for them chief in significance among the constellations. They had gazed at him in their strange, surcharged hours of feeling, until they seemed themselves to live in every one of his stars. This evening Paul had been moody and perverse. Orion had seemed just an ordinary constellation to him. He had fought against his glamour and fascination. Miriam was watching her lover's mood carefully. But he said nothing that gave him away, till the moment came to part, when he stood frowning gloomily at the gathered clouds, behind which the great constellation must be striding still.

There was to be a little party at his house the next day, at which she was to attend.

'I shan't come and meet you,' he said.

'Oh, very well; it's not very nice out,' she replied slowly.

'It's not that – only they don't like me to. They say I care more for you than for them. And you understand, don't you? You know it's only friendship.'

Miriam was astonished and hurt for him. It had cost him an effort. She left him, wanting to spare him any further humiliation. A fine rain blew in her face as she walked along the road. She was hurt deep down; and she despised him for being blown about by any wind of authority. And in her heart of hearts, unconsciously, she felt that he was trying to get away from her. This she would never have acknowledged. She pitied him.

At this time Paul became an important factor in Jordan's warehouse. Mr Pappleworth left to set up a business of his own, and Paul remained with Mr Jordan as spiral overseer. His wages were to be raised to thirty shillings at the year-end, if things went well.

Still on Friday night Miriam often came down for her French lesson. Paul did not go so frequently to Willey Farm, and she grieved at the thought of her education's coming to an end; moreover, they both loved to be together, in spite of discords. So they read Balzac, and did compositions, and felt highly cultured.

Friday night was reckoning night for the miners. Morel 'reckoned' – shared up the money of the stall – either in the New Inn at Bretty or in his own house, according as his fellow-butties wished. Barker had turned a non-drinker, so now the men reckoned at Morel's house.

Annie, who had been teaching away, was at home again. She was still a tomboy; and she was engaged to be married. Paul was studying design.

Morel was always in good spirits on Friday evening, unless the week's earnings were small. He bustled immediately after his dinner, prepared to get washed. It was decorum for the women to absent themselves while the men reckoned. Women were not supposed to spy into such a masculine privacy as the butties' reckoning, nor were they to know the exact amount of the week's earnings. So, whilst her father was spluttering in the scullery, Annie went out to spend an hour with a neighbour. Mrs Morel attended to her baking.

'Shut that doo–er!' bawled Morel furiously.

Annie banged it behind her, and was gone.

'If tha oppens it again while I'm weshin' me, I'll ma'e thy jaw rattle,' he threatened from the midst of his comrades. Paul and the mother frowned to hear him.

Presently he came running out of the scullery with the soapy water dripping from him, dithering with cold.

'Oh, my sirs!' he said. 'Wheer's my towel?'

It was hung on a chair to warm before the fire, otherwise he would have bullied and blustered. He squatted on his heels before the hot baking-fire to dry himself.

'F–ff–f!' he went, pretending to shudder with cold.

'Goodness, man, don't be such a kid!' said Mrs Morel. 'It's *not* cold.'

'Thee strip thysen stark nak'd to wesh thy flesh i' that scullery,' said the miner, as he rubbed his hair; 'nowt b'r a ice-'ouse!'

'And I shouldn't make that fuss,' replied his wife.

'No, tha'd drop down stiff, as dead as a doorknob, wi' thy nesh sides.'

'Why is a doorknob deader than anything else?' asked Paul, curious.

'Eh, I dunno; that's what they say,' replied his father. 'But there's that much draught i' yon scullery, as it blows through your ribs like through a five-barred gate.'

'It would have some difficulty in blowing through yours,' said Mrs Morel.

Morel looked down ruefully at his sides.

'Me!' he exclaimed. 'I'm nowt b'r a skinned rabbit. My bones fair juts out on me.'

'I should like to know where,' retorted his wife.

'Iv'ry-wheer! I'm nobbut a sack o' faggots.'

Mrs Morel laughed. He had still a wonderfully young body, muscular, without any fat. His skin was smooth and clear. It might have been the body of a man of twenty-eight, except that there were, perhaps, too many blue scars, like tattoo-marks, where the coal-dust remained under the skin, and that his chest was too hairy. But he put his hand on his sides ruefully. It was his fixed belief that, because he did not get fat, he was as thin as a starved rat.

Paul looked at his father's thick, brownish hands all scarred, with broken nails, rubbing the fine smoothness of his sides, and the incongruity struck him. It seemed strange they were the same flesh.

'I suppose,' he said to his father, 'you had a good figure once.'

'Eh!' exclaimed the miner, glancing round, startled and timid, like a child.

'He had,' exclaimed Mrs Morel, 'if he didn't hurtle himself up as if he was trying to get in the smallest space he could.'

'Me!' exclaimed Morel – 'me a good figure! I wor niver much more n'r a skeleton.'

'Man!' cried his wife, 'don't be such a pulamiter!'

'Strewth!' he said. 'Tha's niver knowed me but what I looked as if I wor goin' off in a rapid decline.'

She sat and laughed.

'You've had a constitution like iron,' she said; 'and never a man had a better start, if it was body that counted. You should have seen him as a young man,' she cried suddenly to Paul, drawing herself up to imitate her husband's once handsome bearing.

Morel watched her shyly. He saw again the passion she had had for him. It blazed upon her for a moment. He was shy, rather scared, and humble. Yet again he felt his old glow. And then immediately he felt the ruin he had made during these years. He wanted to bustle about, to run away from it.

'Gi'e my back a bit of a wesh,' he asked her.

His wife brought a well-soaped flannel and clapped it on his shoulders. He gave a jump.

'Eh, tha mucky little 'ussy!' he cried. 'Cowd as death!'

'You ought to have been a salamander,' she laughed, washing his back. It was very rarely she would do anything so personal for him. The children did those things.

'The next world won't be half hot enough for you,' she added.

'No,' he said; 'tha'lt see as it's draughty for me.'

But she had finished. She wiped him in a desultory fashion, and went upstairs, returning immediately with his shifting-trousers. When he was dried he struggled into his shirt. Then, ruddy and shiny, with hair on end, and his flannelette shirt hanging over his pit-trousers, he stood warming the garments he was going to put on. He turned them, he pulled them inside out, he scorched them.

'Goodness, man!' cried Mrs Morel; 'get dressed!'

'Should thee like to clap thysen into britches as cowd as a tub o' water?' he said.

At last he took off his pit-trousers and donned decent black. He did all this on the hearthrug, as he would have done if Annie and her familiar friends had been present.

Mrs Morel turned the bread in the oven. Then from the red earthenware panchion of dough that stood in a corner she took another handful of paste, worked it to the proper shape, and dropped it into a tin. As she was doing so Barker knocked and entered. He was a quiet, compact little man who looked as if he would go through a stone wall. His black hair was cropped short, his head was bony. Like most miners, he was pale, but healthy and taut.

'Evenin', missis,' he nodded to Mrs Morel, and he seated himself with a sigh.

'Good-evening,' she replied cordially.

'Tha's made thy heels crack,' said Morel.

'I dunno as I have,' said Barker.

He sat, as the men always did in Mrs Morel's kitchen, effacing himself rather.

'How's missis?' she asked of him.

He had told her some time back, 'We're expectin' us third just now, you see.'

'Well,' he answered, rubbing his head, 'she keeps pretty middlin', I think.'

'Let's see – when?' asked Mrs Morel.

'Well, I shouldn't be surprised any time now.'

'Ah! And she's kept fairly?'

'Yes, tidy.'

'That's a blessing, for she's none too strong.'

'No. An' I've done another silly trick.'

'What's that?'

Mrs Morel knew Barker wouldn't do anything very silly. 'I'm come be-out th' market-bag.'

'You can have mine.'

'Nay, you'll be wantin' that yourself.'

'I shan't. I take a string bag always.'

She saw the determined little collier buying in the week's groceries and meat on the Friday nights, and she admired him.

'Barker's little, but he's ten times the man you are,' she said to her husband.

Just then Wesson entered. He was thin, rather frail-looking, with a boyish ingenuousness and a slightly foolish smile, despite his seven children. But his wife was a passionate woman.

'I see you've kested me,' he said, smiling rather vapidly.

'Yes,' replied Barker.

The newcomer took off his cap and his big woollen muffler. His nose was pointed and red.

'I'm afraid you're cold, Mr Wesson,' said Mrs Morel.

'It's a bit nippy,' he replied.

'Then come to the fire.'

'Nay, I s'll do where I am.'

Both colliers sat away back. They could not be induced to come on to the hearth. The hearth is sacred to the family.

'Go thy ways i' th' armchair,' cried Morel cheerily.

'Nay, thank yer; I'm very nicely here.'

'Yes, come, of course,' insisted Mrs Morel.

He rose and went awkwardly. He sat in Morel's armchair awkwardly. It was too great a familiarity. But the fire made him blissfully happy.

'And how's that chest of yours?' demanded Mrs Morel.

He smiled again, with his blue eyes rather sunny.

'Oh, it's very middlin',' he said.

'Wi' a rattle in it like a kettle-drum,' said Barker shortly.

'T–t–t–t!' went Mrs Morel rapidly with her tongue. 'Did you have that flannel singlet made?'

'Not yet,' he smiled.

'Then, why didn't you?' she cried.

'It'll come,' he smiled.

'Ah, an' Doomsday!' exclaimed Barker.

Barker and Morel were both impatient of Wesson. But, then, they were both as hard as nails, physically.

When Morel was nearly ready he pushed the bag of money to Paul.

'Count it, boy,' he asked humbly.

Paul impatiently turned from his books and pencil, tipped the bag upside down on the table. There was a five-pound bag of silver, sovereigns and loose money. He counted quickly, referred to the checks – the written papers giving amount of coal – put the money in order. Then Barker glanced at the checks.

Mrs Morel went upstairs, and the three men came to table. Morel, as master of the house, sat in his armchair, with his back to the hot fire. The two butties had cooler seats. None of them counted the money.

'What did we say Simpson's was?' asked Morel; and the butties cavilled for a minute over the dayman's earnings. Then the amount was put aside.

'An' Bill Naylor's?'

This money also was taken from the pack.

Then, because Wesson lived in one of the company's houses, and his rent had been deducted, Morel and Barker took four-and-six each. And because Morel's coals had come, and the leading was stopped, Barker and Wesson took four shillings each. Then it was plain sailing. Morel gave each of them a sovereign till there were no more sovereigns; each half a crown till there were no more half-crowns; each a shilling till there were no more shillings. If there was anything at the end that wouldn't split, Morel took it and stood drinks.

Then the three men rose and went. Morel scuttled out of the house before his wife came down. She heard the door close, and descended. She looked hastily at the bread in the oven. Then, glancing on the table, she saw her money lying. Paul had been working all the time. But now he felt his mother counting the week's money, and her wrath rising.

'T–t–t–t–t!' went her tongue.

He frowned. He could not work when she was cross. She counted again.

'A measly twenty-five shillings!' she exclaimed. 'How much was the cheque?'

'Ten pounds eleven,' said Paul irritably. He dreaded what was coming.

'And he gives me a scrattlin' twenty-five, an' his club this week! But I know him. He thinks because *you're* earning he needn't keep the house any longer. No, all he has to do with his money is to guttle it. But I'll show him!'

'Oh, mother, don't!' cried Paul.

'Don't what, I should like to know?' she exclaimed.

'Don't carry on again. I can't work.'

She went very quiet.

'Yes, it's all very well,' she said; 'but how do you think I'm going to manage?'

'Well, it won't make it any better to whittle about it.'

'I should like to know what you'd do if you had it to put up with.'

'It won't be long. You can have my money. Let him go to hell.'

He went back to his work, and she tied her bonnet-strings grimly. When she was fretted he could not bear it. But now he began to insist on her recognising him.

'The two loaves at the top,' she said, 'will be done in twenty minutes. Don't forget them.'

'All right,' he answered; and she went to market.

He remained alone working. But his usual intense concentration became unsettled. He listened for the yard-gate. At a quarter-past seven came a low knock, and Miriam entered.

'All alone?' she said.

'Yes.'

As if at home, she took off her tam-o'-shanter and her long coat, hanging them up. It gave him a thrill. This might be their own house, his and hers. Then she came back and peered over his work.

'What is it?' she asked.

'Still design, for decorating stuffs, and for embroidery.'

She bent short-sightedly over the drawings.

It irritated him that she peered so into everything that was his, searching him out. He went into the parlour and returned with a bundle of brownish linen. Carefully unfolding it, he spread it on the floor. It proved to be a curtain or *portière*, beautifully stencilled with a design of roses.

'Ah, how beautiful!' she cried.

The spread cloth, with its wonderful reddish roses and dark green stems, all so simple, and somehow so wicked-looking, lay at her feet. She went on her knees before it, her dark curls dropping. He saw her crouched voluptuously before his work, and his heart beat quickly. Suddenly she looked up at him.

'Why does it seem cruel?' she asked.

'What?'

'There seems a feeling of cruelty about it,' she said.

'It's jolly good, whether or not,' he replied, folding up his work with a lover's hands.

She rose slowly, pondering.

'And what will you do with it?' she asked.

'Send it to Liberty's. I did it for my mother, but I think she'd rather have the money.'

'Yes,' said Miriam. He had spoken with a touch of bitterness, and Miriam sympathised. Money would have been nothing to her.

He took the cloth back into the parlour. When he returned, he threw to Miriam a smaller piece. It was a cushion cover with the same design.

'I did that for you,' he said.

She fingered the work with trembling hands, and did not speak. He became embarrassed.

'By Jove, the bread!' he cried.

He took the top loaves out, tapped them vigorously. They were done. He put them on the hearth to cool. Then he went to the scullery, wetted his hands, scooped the last white dough out of the punchion, and dropped it in a baking-tin. Miriam was still bent over her painted cloth. He stood rubbing the bits of dough from his hands.

'You do like it?' he asked.

She looked up at him, with her dark eyes one flame of love. He laughed uncomfortably. Then he began to talk about the design. There was for him the most intense pleasure in talking about his work to Miriam. All his passion, all his wild blood, went into this intercourse with her, when he talked and conceived his work. She brought forth to him his imaginations. She did not understand, any more than a woman understands when she conceives a child in her womb. But this was life for her and for him.

While they were talking, a young woman of about twenty-two, small and pale, hollow-eyed, yet with a relentless look about her, entered the room. She was a friend at the Morels'.

'Take your things off,' said Paul.

'No, I'm not stopping.'

She sat down in the armchair opposite Paul and Miriam, who were on the sofa. Miriam moved a little farther from him. The room was hot, with a scent of new bread. Brown, crisp loaves stood on the hearth.

'I shouldn't have expected to see you here tonight, Miriam Leivers,' said Beatrice wickedly.

'Why not?' murmured Miriam huskily.

'Why, let's look at your shoes.'

Miriam remained uncomfortably still.

'If tha doesna tha durs'na,' laughed Beatrice.

Miriam put her feet from under her dress. Her boots had that queer, irresolute, rather pathetic look about them, which showed how self-conscious and self-mistrustful she was. And they were covered with mud.

'Glory! You're a positive muck-heap,' exclaimed Beatrice. 'Who cleans your boots?'

'I clean them myself.'

'Then you wanted a job,' said Beatrice. 'It would ha' taken a lot of men to ha' brought me down here tonight. But love laughs at sludge, doesn't it, 'Postle my duck?'

'*Inter alia*,' he said.

'Oh, Lord! are you going to spout foreign languages? What does it mean, Miriam?'

There was a fine sarcasm in the last question, but Miriam did not see it.

' "Among other things," I believe,' she said humbly.

Beatrice put her tongue between her teeth and laughed wickedly.

' "Among other things," 'Postle?' she repeated. 'Do you mean love laughs at mothers, and fathers, and sisters, and brothers, and men friends, and lady friends, and even at the b'loved himself?'

She affected a great innocence.

'In fact, it's one big smile,' he replied.

'Up its sleeve, 'Postle Morel – you believe me,' she said; and she went off into another burst of wicked, silent laughter.

Miriam sat silent, withdrawn into herself. Everyone of Paul's friends delighted in taking sides against her, and he left her in the lurch seemed almost to have a sort of revenge upon her then.

'Are you still at school?' asked Miriam of Beatrice.

'Yes.'

'You've not had your notice, then?'

'I expect it at Easter.'

'Isn't it an awful shame, to turn you off merely because you didn't pass the exam?'

'I don't know,' said Beatrice coldly.

'Agatha says you're as good as any teacher anywhere. It seems to me ridiculous. I wonder why you didn't pass.'

'Short of brains, eh 'Postle?' said Beatrice briefly.

'Only brains to bite with,' replied Paul, laughing.

'Nuisance!' she cried; and, springing from her seat, she rushed and boxed his ears. She had beautiful small hands. He held her wrists while she wrestled with him. At last she broke free, and seized two handfuls of his thick, dark brown hair, which she shook.

'Beat!' he said, as he pulled his hair straight with his fingers. 'I hate you!'

She laughed with glee.

'Mind!' she said. 'I want to sit next to you.'

'I'd as lief be neighbours with a vixen,' he said, nevertheless making place for her between him and Miriam.

'Did it ruffle his pretty hair, then!' she cried; and, with her hair-comb, she combed him straight. 'And his nice little moustache!' she exclaimed. She tilted his head back and combed his young moustache. 'It's a wicked moustache, 'Postle,' she said. 'It's a red for danger. Have you got any of those cigarettes?'

He pulled his cigarette-case from his pocket. Beatrice looked inside it.

'And fancy me having Connie's last cig,' said Beatrice, putting the thing between her teeth. He held a lit match to her, and she puffed daintily.

'Thanks so much, darling,' she said mockingly.

It gave her a wicked delight.

'Don't you think he does it nicely, Miriam?' she asked.

'Oh, very!' said Miriam.

He took a cigarette for himself

'Light, old boy?' said Beatrice, tilting her cigarette at him.

He bent forward to her to light his cigarette at hers. She was winking at him as he did so. Miriam saw his eyes trembling with mischief, and his full, almost sensual, mouth quivering. He was not himself, and she could not bear it. As he was now, she had no connection with him; she might as well not have existed. She saw the cigarette dancing on his full red lips. She hated his thick hair for being tumbled loose on his forehead.

'Sweet boy!' said Beatrice, tipping up his chin and giving him a little kiss on the cheek.

'I s'll kiss thee back, Beat,' he said.

'Tha wunna!' she giggled, jumping up and going away. 'Isn't he shameless, Miriam?'

'Quite,' said Miriam. 'By the way, aren't you forgetting the bread?'

'By Jove!' he cried, flinging open the oven door.

Out puffed the bluish smoke and a smell of burned bread.

'Oh, golly!' cried Beatrice, coming to his side. He crouched before the oven, she peered over his shoulder. 'This is what comes of the oblivion of love, my boy.'

Paul was ruefully removing the loaves. One was burnt black on the hot side; another was hard as a brick.

'Poor mater!' said Paul.

'You want to grate it,' said Beatrice. 'Fetch me the nutmeg-grater.'

She arranged the bread in the oven. He brought the grater, and she grated the bread on to a newspaper on the table. He set the doors open to blow away the smell of burned bread. Beatrice grated away, puffing her cigarette, knocking the charcoal off the poor loaf.

'My word, Miriam! you're in for it this time,' said Beatrice.

'I!' exclaimed Miriam in amazement.

'You'd better be gone when his mother comes in. I know why King Alfred burned the cakes. Now I see it! 'Postle would fix up a tale about his work making him forget, if he thought it would wash. If that old woman had come in a bit sooner, she'd have boxed the brazen thing's ears who made the oblivion, instead of poor Alfred's.'

She giggled as she scraped the loaf. Even Miriam laughed in spite of herself. Paul mended the fire ruefully.

The garden-gate was heard to bang.

'Quick!' cried Beatrice, giving Paul the scraped loaf. 'Wrap it up in a damp towel.'

Paul disappeared into the scullery. Beatrice hastily blew her scrapings into the fire, and sat down innocently. Annie came bursting in. She was an abrupt, quite smart young woman. She blinked in the strong light.

'Smell of burning!' she exclaimed.

'It's the cigarettes,' replied Beatrice demurely.

'Where's Paul?'

Leonard had followed Annie. He had a long comic face and blue eyes, very sad.

'I suppose he's left you to settle it between you,' he said. He nodded sympathetically to Miriam, and became gently sarcastic to Beatrice.

'No,' said Beatrice, 'he's gone off with number nine.'

'I just met number five enquiring for him,' said Leonard.

'Yes – we're going to share him up like Solomon's baby,' said Beatrice. Annie laughed.

'Oh, ay,' said Leonard. 'And which bit should you have?'

'I don't know,' said Beatrice. 'I'll let all the others pick first.'

'An' you'd have the leavings, like?' said Leonard, twisting up a comic face.

Annie was looking in the oven. Miriam sat ignored. Paul entered.

'This bread's a fine sight, our Paul,' said Annie.

'Then you should stop an' look after it,' said Paul.

'You mean *you* should do what you're reckoning to do,' replied Annie.

'He should, shouldn't he!' cried Beatrice.

'I s'd think he'd got plenty on hand,' said Leonard.

'You had a nasty walk, didn't you, Miriam?' said Annie.

'Yes – but I'd been in all week – '

'And you wanted a bit of a change, like,' insinuated Leonard kindly.

'Well, you can't be stuck in the house for ever,' Annie agreed. She was quite amiable. Beatrice pulled on her coat, and went out with Leonard and Annie. She would meet her own boy.

'Don't forget that bread, our Paul,' cried Annie. 'Good-night, Miriam. I don't think it will rain.'

When they had all gone, Paul fetched the swathed loaf, unwrapped it, and surveyed it sadly.

'It's a mess!' he said.

'But,' answered Miriam impatiently, 'what is it, after all – twopence ha'penny.'

'Yes, but – it's the mater's precious baking, and she'll take it to heart. However, it's no good bothering.'

He took the loaf back into the scullery. There was a little distance between him and Miriam. He stood balanced opposite her for some moments considering, thinking of his behaviour with Beatrice. He felt guilty inside himself, and yet glad. For some inscrutable reason it served Miriam right. He was not going to repent. She wondered what he was thinking of as he stood suspended. His thick hair was tumbled over his forehead. Why might she not push it back for him, and remove the marks of Beatrice's comb? Why might she not press his body with her two hands? It looked so firm, and every whit living. And he would let other girls, why not her?

Suddenly he started into life. It made her quiver almost with terror as he quickly pushed the hair off his forehead and came towards her.

'Half-past eight!' he said. 'We'd better buck up. Where's your French?'

Miriam shyly and rather bitterly produced her exercise-book. Every week she wrote for him a sort of diary of her inner life, in her own French. He had found this was the only way to get her to do compositions. And her diary was mostly a love-letter. He would read it now; she felt as if her soul's history were going to be desecrated by him in his present mood. He sat beside her. She watched his hand, firm and warm, rigorously scoring her work. He was reading only the French, ignoring her soul that was there. But gradually his hand forgot its work. He read in silence, motionless. She quivered.

' "*Ce matin les oiseaux m'ont éveillé,*" ' he read. ' "*Il faisait encore un crépuscule. Mais la petite fenêtre de ma chambre était blême, et puis, jaune, et tous les oiseaux du bois éclatèrent dans un chanson vif et résonnant. Toute l'aube tressaillit. J'avais revé de vous. Est-ce que vous voyez aussi l'aube? Les oiseaux m'éveillent presque tous les matins, et toujours il y a quelque chose de terreur dans le cri des grives. Il est si clair –*" '

Miriam sat tremulous, half ashamed. He remained quite still, trying to under-stand. He only knew she loved him. He was afraid of her love for him. It was too good for him, and he was inadequate. His own love was at fault, not hers. Ashamed, he corrected her work, humbly writing above her words.

'Look,' he said quietly, 'the past participle conjugated with *avoir* agrees with the direct object when it precedes.'

She bent forward, trying to see and to understand. Her free, fine curls tickled his face. He started as if they had been red hot, shuddering. He saw her peering forward at the page, her red lips parted piteously, the black hair springing in fine strands across her tawny, ruddy cheek. She was coloured like a pomegranate for richness. His breath came short as he watched her. Suddenly she looked up at him. Her dark eyes were naked with their love, afraid, and yearning. His eyes, too, were dark, and they hurt her. They seemed to master her. She lost all her self-control, was exposed in fear. And he knew, before he could kiss her, he must drive something out of himself. And a touch of hate for her crept back again into his heart. He returned to her exercise.

Suddenly he flung down the pencil, and was at the oven in a leap, turning the bread. For Miriam he was too quick. She started violently, and it hurt her with real pain. Even the way he crouched before the oven hurt her. There seemed to be something cruel in it, something cruel in the swift way he pitched the bread out of the tins, caught it up again. If only he had been gentle in his movements she would have felt so rich and warm. As it was, she was hurt.

He returned and finished the exercise.

'You've done well this week,' he said.

She saw he was flattered by her diary. It did not repay her entirely.

'You really do blossom out sometimes,' he said. 'You ought to write poetry.'

She lifted her head with joy, then she shook it mistrustfully.

'I don't trust myself,' she said.

'You should try!'

Again she shook her head.

'Shall we read, or is it too late?' he asked.

'It is late – but we can read just a little,' she pleaded.

She was really getting now the food for her life during the next week. He made her copy Baudelaire's 'Le Balcon'. Then he read it for her. His voice was soft and caressing, but growing almost brutal. He had a way of lifting his lips and showing his teeth, passionately and bitterly, when he was much moved. This he did now. It made Miriam feel as if he were trampling on her. She dared not look at him, but sat with her head bowed. She could not understand why he got into such a tumult and fury. It made her wretched. She did not like Baudelaire, on the whole – nor Verlaine.

> 'Behold her singing in the field
> Yon solitary highland lass.'

That nourished her heart. So did 'Fair Ines'. And –

'It was a beauteous evening, calm and pure,
And breathing holy quiet like a nun.'

These were like herself. And there was he, saying in his throat bitterly:

'Tu te rappelleras la beauté des caresses.'

The poem was finished; he took the bread out of the oven, arranging the burnt loaves at the bottom of the panchion, the good ones at the top. The desiccated loaf remained swathed up in the scullery.

'Mater needn't know till morning,' he said. 'It won't upset her so much then as at night.'

Miriam looked in the bookcase, saw what postcards and letters he had received, saw what books were there. She took one that had interested him. Then he turned down the gas and they set off. He did not trouble to lock the door.

He was not home again until a quarter to eleven. His mother was seated in the rocking-chair. Annie, with a rope of hair hanging down her back, remained sitting on a low stool before the fire, her elbows on her knees, gloomily. On the table stood the offending loaf unswathed. Paul entered rather breathless. No one spoke. His mother was reading the little local newspaper. He took off his coat, and went to sit down on the sofa. His mother moved curtly aside to let him pass. No one spoke. He was very uncomfortable. For some minutes he sat pretending to read a piece of paper he found on the table. Then –

'I forgot that bread, mother,' he said.

There was no answer from either woman.

'Well,' he said, 'it's only twopence ha'penny. I can pay you for that.'

Being angry he put three pennies on the table, and slid them towards his mother. She turned away her head. Her mouth was shut tightly.

'Yes,' said Annie, 'you don't know how badly my mother is!'

The girl sat staring glumly into the fire.

'Why is she badly?' asked Paul, in his overbearing way.

'Well!' said Annie. 'She could scarcely get home.'

He looked closely at his mother. She looked ill.

'*Why* could you scarcely get home?' he asked her, still sharply. She would not answer.

'I found her as white as a sheet sitting here,' said Annie, with a suggestion of tears in her voice.

'Well, *why*?' insisted Paul. His brows were knitting, his eyes dilating passionately.

'It was enough to upset anybody,' said Mrs Morel, 'hugging those parcels – meat, and greengroceries, and a pair of curtains – '

'Well, why *did* you hug them; you needn't have done.'

'Then who would?'

'Let Annie fetch the meat.'

'Yes, and I *would* fetch the meat, but how was I to know. You were off with Miriam, instead of being in when my mother came.'

'And what was the matter with you?' asked Paul of his mother.

'I suppose it's my heart,' she replied. Certainly she looked bluish round the mouth.

'And have you felt it before?'

'Yes – often enough.'

'Then why haven't you told me? – and why haven't you seen a doctor?'

Mrs Morel shifted in her chair, angry with him for his hectoring.

'You'd never notice anything,' said Annie. 'You're too eager to be off with Miriam.'

'Oh, am I – and any worse than you with Leonard?'

'*I* was in at a quarter to ten.'

There was silence in the room for a time.

'I should have thought,' said Mrs Morel bitterly, 'that she wouldn't have occupied you so entirely as to burn a whole ovenful of bread.'

'Beatrice was here as well as she.'

'Very likely. But we know why the bread is spoilt.'

'Why?' he flashed.

'Because you were engrossed with Miriam,' replied Mrs Morel hotly.

'Oh, very well – then it was *not*!' he replied angrily.

He was distressed and wretched. Seizing a paper, he began to read. Annie, her blouse unfastened, her long ropes of hair twisted into a plait, went up to bed, bidding him a very curt good-night.

Paul sat pretending to read. He knew his mother wanted to upbraid him. He also wanted to know what had made her ill, for he was troubled. So, instead of running away to bed, as he would have liked to do, he sat and waited. There was a tense silence. The clock ticked loudly.

'You'd better go to bed before your father comes in,' said the mother harshly. 'And if you're going to have anything to eat, you'd better get it.'

'I don't want anything.'

It was his mother's custom to bring him some trifle for supper on Friday night, the night of luxury for the colliers. He was too angry to go and find it in the pantry this night. This insulted her.

'If I *wanted* you to go to Selby on Friday night, I can imagine the scene,' said Mrs Morel. 'But you're never too tired to go if *she* will come for you. Nay, you neither want to eat nor drink then.'

'I can't let her go alone.'

'Can't you? And why does she come?'

'Not because I ask her.'

'She doesn't come without you want her –'

'Well, what if I *do* want her –' he replied.

'Why, nothing, if it was sensible or reasonable. But to go traipsing up there miles and miles in the mud, coming home at midnight, and got to go to

Nottingham in the morning – '

'If I hadn't, you'd be just the same.'

'Yes, I should, because there's no sense in it. Is she so fascinating that you must follow her all that way?' Mrs Morel was bitterly sarcastic. She sat still, with averted face, stroking with a rhythmic, jerked movement, the black sateen of her apron. It was a movement that hurt Paul to see.

'I do like her,' he said, 'but – '

'*Like* her!' said Mrs Morel, in the same biting tones. 'It seems to me you like nothing and nobody else. There's neither Annie, nor me, nor anyone now for you.'

'What nonsense, mother – you know I don't love her – I – I tell you I *don't* love her – she doesn't even walk with my arm, because I don't want her to.'

'Then why do you fly to her so often!'

'I do like to talk to her – I never said I didn't. But I *don't* love her.'

'Is there nobody else to talk to?'

'Not about the things we talk of. There's lots of things that you're not interested in, that – '

'What things?'

Mrs Morel was so intense that Paul began to pant.

'Why – painting – and books. *You* don't care about Herbert Spencer.'

'No,' was the sad reply. 'And you won't at my age.'

'Well, but I do now – and Miriam does – '

'And how do you know,' Mrs Morel flashed defiantly, 'that *I* shouldn't? Do you ever try me?'

'But you don't, mother, you know you don't care whether a picture's decorative or not; you don't care what *manner* it is in.'

'How do you know I don't care? Do you ever try me? Do you ever talk to me about these things, to try?'

'But it's not that that matters to you, mother, you know it's not.'

'What is it, then – what is it, then, that matters to me?' she flashed. He knitted his brows with pain.

'You're old, mother, and we're young.'

He only meant that the interests of *her* age were not the interests of his. But he realised the moment he had spoken that he had said the wrong thing.

'Yes, I know it well – I am old. And therefore I may stand aside; I have nothing more to do with you. You only want me to wait on you – the rest is for Miriam.'

He could not bear it. Instinctively he realised that he was life to her. And, after all, she was the chief thing to him, the only supreme thing.

'You know it isn't, mother, you know it isn't!'

She was moved to pity by his cry.

'It looks a great deal like it,' she said, half putting aside her despair.

'No, mother – I really *don't* love her. I talk to her, but I want to come home to you.'

He had taken off his collar and tie, and rose, bare-throated, to go to bed. As he stooped to kiss his mother, she threw her arms round his neck, hid her face on his shoulder, and cried, in a whimpering voice, so unlike her own that he writhed in agony, 'I can't bear it. I could let another woman – but not her. She'd leave me no room, not a bit of room – '

And immediately he hated Miriam bitterly.

'And I've never – you know, Paul – I've never had a husband – not really – '

He stroked his mother's hair, and his mouth was on her throat.

'And she exults so in taking you from me – she's not like ordinary girls.'

'Well, I don't love her, mother,' he murmured, bowing his head and hiding his eyes on her shoulder in misery. His mother kissed him a long, fervent kiss.

'My boy!' she said, in a voice trembling with passionate love.

Without knowing, he gently stroked her face.

'There,' said his mother, 'now go to bed. You'll be so tired in the morning.' As she was speaking she heard her husband coming. 'There's your father – now go.' Suddenly she looked at him almost as if in fear. 'Perhaps I'm selfish. If you want her, take her, my boy.'

His mother looked so strange, Paul kissed her, trembling.

'Ha – mother!' he said softly.

Morel came in, walking unevenly. His hat was over one corner of his eye. He balanced in the doorway.

'At your mischief again?' he said venomously.

Mrs Morel's emotion turned into sudden hate of the drunkard who had come in thus upon her.

'At any rate, it is sober,' she said.

'H'm – h'm! h'm – h'm!' he sneered. He went into the passage, hung up his hat and coat. Then they heard him go down three steps to the pantry. He returned with a piece of pork pie in his fist. It was what Mrs Morel had bought for her son.

'Nor was that bought for you. If you can give me no more than twenty-five shillings, I'm sure I'm not going to buy you pork pie to stuff, after you've swilled a bellyful of beer.'

'Wha-at – wha-at!' snarled Morel, toppling in his balance. 'Wha-at – not for me?' he looked at the piece of meat and crust, and suddenly, in a vicious spurt of temper, flung it into the fire.

Paul started to his feet.

'Waste your own stuff!' he cried.

'What – what!' suddenly shouted Morel, jumping up and clenching his fist. 'I'll show yer, yer young jockey!'

'All right!' said Paul viciously, putting his head on one side. 'Show me!'

He would at that moment dearly have loved to have a smack at something. Morel was half crouching, fists up, ready to spring. The young man stood, smiling with his lips.

'Ussha!' hissed the father, swiping round with a great stroke just past his son's face. He dared not, even though so close, really touch the young man, but swerved an inch away.

'Right!' said Paul, his eyes upon the side of his father's mouth, where in another instant his fist would have hit. He ached for that stroke. But he heard a faint moan from behind. His mother was deadly pale, and dark at the mouth. Morel was dancing up to deliver another blow.

'Father!' said Paul, so that the word rang.

Morel started, and stood at attention.

'Mother!' moaned the boy. 'Mother!'

She began to struggle with herself. Her open eyes watched him, although she could not move. Gradually she was coming to herself. He laid her down on the sofa, and ran upstairs for a little whisky, which at last she could sip. The tears were hopping down his face. As he kneeled in front of her he did not cry, but the tears ran down his face quickly. Morel, on the opposite side of the room, sat with his elbows on his knees glaring across.

'What's a-matter with 'er?' he asked.

'Faint!' replied Paul.

'H'm!'

The elderly man began to unlace his boots. He stumbled off to bed. His last fight was fought in that home.

Paul kneeled there, stroking his mother's hand.

'Don't be poorly, mother – don't be poorly!' he said time after time.

'It's nothing, my boy,' she murmured.

At last he rose, fetched in a large piece of coal, and raked the fire. Then he cleared the room, put everything straight, laid the things for breakfast, and brought his mother's candle.

'Can you go to bed, mother?'

'Yes, I'll come.'

'Sleep with Annie, mother, not with him.'

'No. I'll sleep in my own bed.'

'Don't sleep with him, mother.'

'I'll sleep in my own bed.'

She rose, and he turned out the gas, then followed her closely upstairs, carrying her candle. On the landing he kissed her close.

'Good-night, mother.'

'Good-night!' she said.

He pressed his face upon the pillow in a fury of misery. And yet, somewhere in his soul, he was at peace because he still loved his mother best. It was the bitter peace of resignation.

The efforts of his father to conciliate him next day were a great humiliation to him.

Everybody tried to forget the scene.

CHAPTER 9

Defeat of Miriam

Paul was dissatisfied with himself and with everything. The deepest of his love belonged to his mother. When he felt he had hurt her, or wounded his love for her, he could not bear it. Now it was spring, and there was battle between him and Miriam. This year he had a good deal against her. She was vaguely aware of it. The old feeling that she was to be a sacrifice to this love, which she had had when she prayed, was mingled in all her emotions. She did not at the bottom believe she ever would have him. She did not believe in herself primarily: doubted whether she could ever be what he would demand of her. Certainly she never saw herself living happily through a lifetime with him. She saw tragedy, sorrow, and sacrifice ahead. And in sacrifice she was proud, in renunciation she was strong, for she did not trust herself to support everyday life. She was prepared for the big things and the deep things, like tragedy. It was the sufficiency of the small day-life she could not trust.

The Easter holidays began happily. Paul was his own frank self. Yet she felt it would go wrong. On the Sunday afternoon she stood at her bedroom window, looking across at the oak trees of the wood, in whose branches a twilight was tangled, below the bright sky of the afternoon. Grey-green rosettes of honey-suckle leaves hung before the window, some already, she fancied, showing bud. It was spring, which she loved and dreaded.

Hearing the clack of the gate she stood in suspense. It was a bright grey day. Paul came into the yard with his bicycle, which glittered as he walked. Usually he rang his bell and laughed towards the house. Today he walked with shut lips and cold, cruel bearing, that had something of a slouch and a sneer in it. She knew him well by now, and could tell from that keen-looking, aloof young body of his what was happening inside him. There was a cold correctness in the way he put his bicycle in its place, that made her heart sink.

She came downstairs nervously. She was wearing a new net blouse that she thought became her. It had a high collar with a tiny ruff, reminding her of Mary, Queen of Scots, and making her, she thought, look wonderfully a woman, and dignified. At twenty she was full-breasted and luxuriously formed. Her face was still like a soft rich mask, unchangeable. But her eyes, once lifted, were wonderful. She was afraid of him. He would notice her new blouse.

He, being in a hard, ironical mood, was entertaining the family to a description of a service given in the Primitive Methodist Chapel, conducted by one of the well-known preachers of the sect. He sat at the head of the table, his mobile face, with the eyes that could be so beautiful, shining with tenderness or dancing with laughter, now taking on one expression and then another, in imitation of various people he was mocking. His mockery always hurt her; it was too near the reality. He was too clever and cruel. She felt that when his eyes were like this, hard with mocking hate, he would spare neither himself nor anybody else. But Mrs Leivers was wiping her eyes with laughter, and Mr Leivers, just awake from his Sunday nap, was rubbing his head in amusement. The three brothers sat with ruffled, sleepy appearance in their shirt-sleeves, giving a guffaw from time to time. The whole family loved a 'take-off' more than anything.

He took no notice of Miriam. Later, she saw him remark her new blouse, saw that the artist approved, but it won from him not a spark of warmth. She was nervous, could hardly reach the teacups from the shelves.

When the men went out to milk, she ventured to address him personally.

'You were late,' she said.

'Was I?' he answered.

There was silence for a while.

'Was it rough riding?' she asked.

'I didn't notice it.'

She continued quickly to lay the table. When she had finished –

'Tea won't be for a few minutes. Will you come and look at the daffodils?' she said.

He rose without answering. They went out into the back garden under the budding damson trees. The hills and the sky were clean and cold. Everything looked washed, rather hard. Miriam glanced at Paul. He was pale and impassive. It seemed cruel to her that his eyes and brows, which she loved, could look so hurting.

'Has the wind made you tired?' she asked. She detected an underneath feeling of weariness about him.

'No, I think not,' he answered.

'It must be rough on the road – the wood moans so.'

'You can see by the clouds it's a south-west wind; that helps me here.'

'You see, I don't cycle, so I don't understand,' she murmured.

'Is there need to cycle to know that?' he said.

She thought his sarcasms were unnecessary. They went forward in silence. Round the wild, tussocky lawn at the back of the house was a thorn hedge, under which daffodils were craning forward from among their sheaves of grey-green blades. The cheeks of the flowers were greenish with cold. But still some had burst, and their gold ruffled and glowed. Miriam went on her knees before one cluster, took a wild-looking daffodil between her hands, turned up its face of gold to her, and bowed down, caressing it with her mouth and cheeks and brow. He stood aside, with his hands in his pockets, watching her. One after another she turned up to him the faces of the yellow, bursten flowers appealingly, fondling them lavishly all the while.

'Aren't they magnificent?' she murmured.

'Magnificent! it's a bit thick – they're pretty!'

She bowed again to her flowers at his censure of her praise. He watched her crouching, sipping the flowers with fervid kisses.

'Why must you always be fondling things!' he said irritably.

'But I love to touch them,' she replied, hurt.

'Can you never like things without clutching them as if you wanted to pull the heart out of them? Why don't you have a bit more restraint, or reserve, or something?'

She looked up at him full of pain, then continued slowly to stroke her lips against a ruffled flower. Their scent, as she smelled it, was so much kinder than he; it almost made her cry.

'You wheedle the soul out of things,' he said. 'I would never wheedle – at any rate, I'd go straight.'

He scarcely knew what he was saying. These things came from him mechanically. She looked at him. His body seemed one weapon, firm and hard against her.

'You're always begging things to love you,' he said, 'as if you were a beggar for love. Even the flowers, you have to fawn on them – '

Rhythmically, Miriam was swaying and stroking the flower with her mouth, inhaling the scent which ever after made her shudder as it came to her nostrils.

'You don't want to love – your eternal and abnormal craving is to be loved. You aren't positive, you're negative. You absorb, absorb, as if you must fill yourself up with love, because you've got a shortage somewhere.'

She was stunned by his cruelty, and did not hear. He had not the faintest notion of what he was saying. It was as if his fretted, tortured soul, run hot by thwarted passion, jetted off these sayings like sparks from electricity. She did not grasp anything he said. She only sat crouched beneath his cruelty and his hatred of her. She never realised in a flash. Over everything she brooded and brooded.

After tea he stayed with Edgar and the brothers, taking no notice of Miriam. She, extremely unhappy on this looked-for holiday, waited for him. And at last he yielded and came to her. She was determined to track this mood of his to its origin. She counted it not much more than a mood.

'Shall we go through the wood a little way?' she asked him, knowing he never refused a direct request.

They went down to the warren. On the middle path they passed a trap, a narrow horseshoe hedge of small fir-boughs, baited with the guts of a rabbit. Paul glanced at it frowning. She caught his eye.

'Isn't it dreadful?' she asked.

'I don't know! Is it worse than a weasel with its teeth in a rabbit's throat? One weasel or many rabbits? One or the other must go!'

He was taking the bitterness of life badly. She was rather sorry for him.

'We will go back to the house,' he said. 'I don't want to walk out.'

They went past the lilac tree, whose bronze leaf-buds were coming unfastened. Just a fragment remained of the haystack, a monument squared and brown, like a pillar of stone. There was a little bed of hay from the last cutting.

'Let us sit here a minute,' said Miriam.

He sat down against his will, resting his back against the hard wall of hay. They faced the amphitheatre of round hills that glowed with sunset, tiny white farms standing out, the meadows golden, the woods dark and yet luminous, tree-tops folded over tree-tops, distinct in the distance. The evening had cleared, and the east was tender with a magenta flush under which the land lay still and rich.

'Isn't it beautiful?' she pleaded.

But he only scowled. He would rather have had it ugly just then.

At that moment a big bull-terrier came rushing up, open-mouthed, pranced his two paws on the youth's shoulders, licking his face. Paul drew back, laughing. Bill was a great relief to him. He pushed the dog aside, but it came leaping back.

'Get out,' said the lad, 'or I'll dot thee one.'

But the dog was not to be pushed away. So Paul had a little battle with the creature, pitching poor Bill away from him, who, however, only floundered tumultuously back again, wild with joy. The two fought together, the man laughing grudgingly, the dog grinning all over. Miriam watched them. There was something pathetic about the man. He wanted so badly to love, to be tender. The rough way he bowled the dog over was really loving. Bill got up, panting with happiness, his brown eyes rolling in his white face, and lumbered back again. He adored Paul. The lad frowned.

'Bill, I've had enough o' thee,' he said.

But the dog only stood with two heavy paws, that quivered with love, upon his thigh, and flickered a red tongue at him. He drew back.

'No,' he said – 'no – I've had enough.'

And in a minute the dog trotted off happily, to vary the fun.

He remained staring miserably across at the hills, whose still beauty he begrudged. He wanted to go and cycle with Edgar. Yet he had not the courage to leave Miriam.

'Why are you sad?' she asked humbly.

'I'm not sad; why should I be?' he answered. 'I'm only normal.'

She wondered why he always claimed to be normal when he was disagreeable.

'But what is the matter?' she pleaded, coaxing him soothingly.

'Nothing!'

'Nay!' she murmured.

He picked up a stick and began to stab the earth with it.

'You'd far better not talk,' he said.

'But I wish to know – ' she replied.

He laughed resentfully.

'You always do,' he said.

'It's not fair to me,' she murmured.

He thrust, thrust, thrust at the ground with the pointed stick, digging up little clods of earth as if he were in a fever of irritation. She gently and firmly laid her hand on his wrist.

'Don't!' she said. 'Put it away.'

He flung the stick into the currant-bushes, and leaned back. Now he was bottled up.

'What is it?' she pleaded softly.

He lay perfectly still, only his eyes alive, and they full of torment.

'You know,' he said at length, rather wearily – 'you know – we'd better break off.'

It was what she dreaded. Swiftly everything seemed to darken before her eyes.

'Why!' she murmured. 'What has happened?'

'Nothing has happened. We only realise where we are. It's no good – '

She waited in silence, sadly, patiently. It was no good being impatient with him. At any rate, he would tell her now what ailed him.

'We agreed on friendship,' he went on in a dull, monotonous voice. 'How often *have* we agreed for friendship! And yet – it neither stops there, nor gets anywhere else.'

He was silent again. She brooded. What did he mean? He was so wearying. There was something he would not yield. Yet she must be patient with him.

'I can only give friendship – it's all I'm capable of – it's a flaw in my make-up. The thing overbalances to one side – I hate a toppling balance. Let us have done.'

There was warmth of fury in his last phrases. He meant she loved him more than he her. Perhaps he could not love her. Perhaps she had not in herself that which he wanted. It was the deepest motive of her soul, this self-mistrust. It was so deep she dared neither realise nor acknowledge it. Perhaps she was deficient. Like an infinitely subtle shame, it kept her always back. If it were so, she would do without him. She would never let herself want him. She would merely see.

'But what has happened?' she said.

'Nothing – it's all in myself – it only comes out just now. We're always like this towards Easter-time.'

He grovelled so helplessly, she pitied him. At least she never floundered in such a pitiable way. After all, it was he who was chiefly humiliated.

'What do you want?' she asked him.

'Why – I mustn't come often – that's all. Why should I monopolise you when I'm not – You see, I'm deficient in something with regard to you – '

He was telling her he did not love her, and so ought to leave her a chance with another man. How foolish and blind and shamefully clumsy he was! What were other men to her! What were men to her at all! But he, ah! she loved his soul. Was he deficient in something? Perhaps he was.

'But I don't understand,' she said huskily. 'Yesterday – '

The night was turning jangled and hateful to him as the twilight faded. And she bowed under her suffering.

'I know,' he cried, 'you never will! You'll never believe that I can't – can't physically, any more than I can fly up like a skylark – '

'What?' she murmured. Now she dreaded.

'Love you.'

He hated her bitterly at that moment because he made her suffer. Love her! She knew he loved her. He really belonged to her. This about not loving her, physically, bodily, was a mere perversity on his part, because he knew she loved him. He was stupid like a child. He belonged to her. His soul wanted her. She guessed somebody had been influencing him. She felt upon him the hardness, the foreignness of another influence.

'What have they been saying at home?' she asked.

'It's not that,' he answered.

And then she knew it was. She despised them for their commonness, his people. They did not know what things were really worth.

He and she talked very little more that night. After all he left her to cycle with Edgar.

He had come back to his mother. Hers was the strongest tie in his life. When he thought round, Miriam shrank away. There was a vague, unreal feel about her. And nobody else mattered. There was one place in the world that stood solid and did not melt into unreality: the place where his mother was. Everybody else could grow shadowy, almost non-existent to him, but she could not. It was as if the pivot and pole of his life, from which he could not escape, was his mother.

And in the same way she waited for him. In him was established her life now. After all, the life beyond offered very little to Mrs Morel. She saw that our chance for doing is here, and doing counted with her. Paul was going to prove that she had been right; he was going to make a man whom nothing should shift off his feet; he was going to alter the face of the earth in some way which mattered. Wherever he went she felt her soul went with him. Whatever he did she felt her soul stood by him, ready, as it were, to hand him his tools. She could not bear it when he was with Miriam. William was dead. She would fight to keep Paul.

And he came back to her. And in his soul was a feeling of the satisfaction of self-sacrifice because he was faithful to her. She loved him first; he loved her first. And yet it was not enough. His new young life, so strong and imperious, was urged towards something else. It made him mad with restlessness. She saw this, and wished bitterly that Miriam had been a woman who could take this new life of his, and leave her the roots. He fought against his mother almost as he fought against Miriam.

It was a week before he went again to Willey Farm. Miriam had suffered a great deal, and was afraid to see him again. Was she now to endure the ignominy of his abandoning her? That would only be superficial and temporary. He would come back. She held the keys to his soul. But meanwhile, how he would torture her with his battle against her. She shrank from it.

However, the Sunday after Easter he came to tea. Mrs Leivers was glad to see him. She gathered something was fretting him, that he found things hard. He seemed to drift to her for comfort. And she was good to him. She did him that great kindness of treating him almost with reverence.

He met her with the young children in the front garden.

'I'm glad you've come,' said the mother, looking at him with her great appealing brown eyes. 'It is such a sunny day. I was just going down the fields for the first time this year.'

He felt she would like him to come. That soothed him. They went, talking simply, he gentle and humble. He could have wept with gratitude that she was deferential to him. He was feeling humiliated.

At the bottom of the Mow Close they found a thrush's nest.

'Shall I show you the eggs?' he said.

'Do!' replied Mrs Leivers. 'They seem *such* a sign of spring, and so hopeful.'

He put aside the thorns, and took out the eggs, holding them in the palm of his hand.

'They are quite hot – I think we frightened her off them,' he said.

'Ay, poor thing!' said Mrs Leivers.

Miriam could not help touching the eggs, and his hand which, it seemed to her, cradled them so well.

'Isn't it a strange warmth!' she murmured, to get near him.

'Blood heat,' he answered.

She watched him putting them back, his body pressed against the hedge, his arm reaching slowly through the thorns, his hand folded carefully over the eggs. He was concentrated on the act. Seeing him so, she loved him; he seemed so simple and sufficient to himself. And she could not get to him.

After tea she stood hesitating at the bookshelf. He took *Tartarin de Tarascon*. Again they sat on the bank of hay at the foot of the stack. He read a couple of pages, but without any heart for it. Again the dog came racing up to repeat the fun of the other day. He shoved his muzzle in the man's chest. Paul fingered his ear for a moment. Then he pushed him away.

'Go away, Bill,' he said. 'I don't want you.'

Bill slunk off, and Miriam wondered and dreaded what was coming. There was a silence about the youth that made her still with apprehension. It was not his furies, but his quiet resolutions that she feared.

Turning his face a little to one side, so that she could not see him, he began, speaking slowly and painfully, 'Do you think – if I didn't come up so much – you might get to like somebody else – another man?'

So this was what he was still harping on.

'But I don't know any other men. Why do you ask?' she replied, in a low tone that should have been a reproach to him.

'Why,' he blurted, 'because they say I've no right to come up like this – without we mean to marry –'

Miriam was indignant at anybody's forcing the issues between them. She had been furious with her own father for suggesting to Paul, laughingly, that he knew why he came so much.

'Who says?' she asked, wondering if her people had anything to do with it. They had not.

'Mother – and the others. They say at this rate everybody will consider me engaged, and I ought to consider myself so, because it's not fair to you. And I've tried to find out – and I don't think I love you as a man ought to love his wife. What do *you* think about it?'

Miriam bowed her head moodily. She was angry at having this struggle. People should leave him and her alone.

'I don't know,' she murmured.

'Do you think we love each other enough to marry?' he asked definitely. It made her tremble.

'No,' she answered truthfully. 'I don't think so – we're too young.'

'I thought perhaps,' he went on miserably, 'that you, with your intensity in things, might have given me more – than I could ever make up to you. And even now – if you think it better – we'll get engaged.'

Now Miriam wanted to cry. And she was angry, too. He was always such a child for people to do as they liked with.

'No, I don't think so,' she said firmly.

He pondered a minute.

'You see,' he said, 'with me – I don't think one person would ever monopolise me – be everything to me – I think never.'

This she did not consider.

'No,' she murmured. Then, after a pause, she looked at him, and her dark eyes flashed.

'This is your mother,' she said. 'I know she never liked me.'

'No, no, it isn't,' he said hastily. 'It was for your sake she spoke this time. She only said, if I was going on, I ought to consider myself engaged.' There was a silence. 'And if I ask you to come down any time, you won't stop away, will you?'

She did not answer. By this time she was very angry.

'Well, what shall we do?' she said shortly. 'I suppose I'd better drop French. I was just beginning to get on with it. But I suppose I can go on alone.'

'I don't see that we need,' he said. 'I can give you a French lesson, surely.'

'Well – and there are Sunday nights. I shan't stop coming to chapel, because I enjoy it, and it's all the social life I get. But you've no need to come home with me. I can go alone.'

'All right,' he answered, rather taken aback. 'But if I ask Edgar, he'll always come with us, and then they can say nothing.'

There was silence. After all, then, she would not lose much. For all their talk down at his home there would not be much difference. She wished they would mind their own business.

'And you won't think about it, and let it trouble you, will you?' he asked.

'Oh no,' replied Miriam, without looking at him.

He was silent. She thought him unstable. He had no fixity of purpose, no anchor of righteousness that held him.

'Because,' he continued, 'a man gets across his bicycle – and goes to work – and does all sorts of things. But a woman broods.'

'No, I shan't bother,' said Miriam. And she meant it.

It had gone rather chilly. They went indoors.

'How white Paul looks!' Mrs Leivers exclaimed. 'Miriam, you shouldn't have let him sit out of doors. Do you think you've taken cold, Paul?'

'Oh, no!' he laughed.

But he felt done up. It wore him out, the conflict in himself. Miriam pitied him now. But quite early, before nine o'clock, he rose to go.

'You're not going home, are you?' asked Mrs Leivers anxiously.

'Yes,' he replied. 'I said I'd be early.' He was very awkward.

'But this is early,' said Mr Leivers.

Miriam sat in the rocking-chair, and did not speak. He hesitated, expecting her to rise and go with him to the barn as usual for his bicycle. She remained as she was. He was at a loss.

'Well – good-night all!' he faltered.

She spoke her good-night along with all the others. But as he went past the window he looked in. She saw him pale, his brows knit slightly in a way that had become constant with him, his eyes dark with pain.

She rose and went to the doorway to wave goodbye to him as he passed through the gate. He rode slowly under the pine trees, feeling a cur and a miserable wretch. His bicycle went tilting down the hills at random. He thought it would be a relief to break one's neck.

Two days later he sent her up a book and a little note, urging her to read and be busy.

At this time he gave all his friendship to Edgar. He loved the family so much, he loved the farm so much; it was the dearest place on earth to him. His home was not so lovable. It was his mother. But then he would have been just as happy with his mother anywhere. Whereas Willey Farm he loved passionately. He loved the little pokey kitchen, where men's boots tramped, and the dog slept with one eye open for fear of being trodden on; where the lamp hung over the table at night, and everything was so silent. He loved Miriam's long, low parlour, with its atmosphere of romance, its flowers, its books, its high rose-wood piano. He loved the gardens and the buildings that stood with their scarlet roofs on the naked edges of the fields, crept towards the wood as if for cosiness, the wild country scooping down a valley and up the uncultured hills of the other side. Only to be there was an exhilaration and a joy to him. He loved Mrs Leivers, with her unworldliness and her quaint cynicism; he loved Mr Leivers so warm and young and lovable; he loved Edgar, who lit up when he came, and the boys and the children and Bill – even the sow Circe and the Indian gamecock called Tippoo. All this besides Miriam. He could not give it up.

So he went as often, but he was usually with Edgar. Only all the family, including the father, joined in charades and games at evening. And later, Miriam drew them together, and they read *Macbeth* out of penny books, taking parts. It was great excitement. Miriam was glad, and Mrs Leivers was glad, and Mr Leivers enjoyed it. Then they all learned songs together from tonic sol-fa, singing in a circle round the fire. But now Paul was very rarely alone with

Miriam. She waited. When she and Edgar and he walked home together from chapel or from the literary society in Bestwood, she knew his talk, so passionate and so unorthodox nowadays, was for her. She did envy Edgar, however, his cycling with Paul, his Friday nights, his days working in the fields. For her Friday nights and her French lessons were gone. She was nearly always alone, walking, pondering in the wood, reading, studying, dreaming, waiting. And he wrote to her frequently.

One Sunday evening they attained to their old rare harmony. Edgar had stayed to Communion – he wondered what it was like – with Mrs Morel. So Paul came on alone with Miriam to his home. He was more or less under her spell again. As usual, they were discussing the sermon. He was setting now full sail towards Agnosticism, but such a religious Agnosticism that Miriam did not suffer so badly. They were at the Renan 'Vie de Jésus' stage. Miriam was the threshing-floor on which he threshed out all his beliefs. While he trampled his ideas upon her soul, the truth came out for him. She alone was his threshing-floor. She alone helped him towards realisation. Almost impassive, she submitted to his argument and expounding. And somehow, because of her, he gradually realised where he was wrong. And what he realised, she realised. She felt he could not do without her.

They came to the silent house. He took the key out of the scullery window, and they entered. All the time he went on with his discussion. He lit the gas, mended the fire, and brought her some cakes from the pantry. She sat on the sofa, quietly, with a plate on her knee. She wore a large white hat with some pinkish flowers. It was a cheap hat, but he liked it. Her face beneath was still and pensive, golden-brown and ruddy. Always her ears were hid in her short curls. She watched him.

She liked him on Sundays. Then he wore a dark suit that showed the lithe movement of his body. There was a clean, clear-cut look about him. He went on with his thinking to her. Suddenly he reached for a Bible. Miriam liked the way he reached up – so sharp, straight to the mark. He turned the pages quickly, and read her a chapter of St John. As he sat in the armchair reading, intent, his voice only thinking, she felt as if he were using her unconsciously as a man uses his tools at some work he is bent on. She loved it. And the wistfulness of his voice was like a reaching to something, and it was as if she were what he reached with. She sat back on the sofa away from him, and yet feeling herself the very instrument his hand grasped. It gave her great pleasure.

Then he began to falter and to get self-conscious. And when he came to the verse, 'A woman, when she is in travail, hath sorrow because her hour is come', he missed it out. Miriam had felt him growing uncomfortable. She shrank when the well-known words did not follow. He went on reading, but she did not hear. A grief and shame made her bend her head. Six months ago he would have read it simply. Now there was a scotch in his running with her. Now she felt there was really something hostile between them, something of which they were ashamed.

She ate her cake mechanically. He tried to go on with his argument, but could not get back the right note. Soon Edgar came in. Mrs Morel had gone to her friends'. The three set off to Willey Farm.

Miriam brooded over his split with her. There was something else he wanted. He could not be satisfied; he could give her no peace. There was between them now always a ground for strife. She wanted to prove him. She believed that his chief need in life was herself. If she could prove it, both to herself and to him, the rest might go, she could simply trust to the future.

So in May she asked him to come to Willey Farm and meet Mrs Dawes. There was something he hankered after. She saw him, whenever they spoke of Clara Dawes, rouse and get slightly angry. He said he did not like her. Yet he was keen to know about her. Well, he should put himself to the test. She believed that there were in him desires for higher things, and desires for lower, and that the desire for the higher would conquer. At any rate, he should try. She forgot that her 'higher' and 'lower' were arbitrary.

He was rather excited at the idea of meeting Clara at Willey Farm. Mrs Dawes came for the day. Her heavy, dun-coloured hair was coiled on top of her head. She wore a white blouse and navy skirt, and somehow, wherever she was, seemed to make things look paltry and insignificant. When she was in the room, the kitchen seemed too small and mean altogether. Miriam's beautiful twilightly parlour looked stiff and stupid. All the Leiverses were eclipsed like candles. They found her rather hard to put up with. Yet she was perfectly amiable, but indifferent, and rather hard.

Paul did not come till afternoon. He was early. As he swung off his bicycle, Miriam saw him look round at the house eagerly. He would be disappointed if the visitor had not come. Miriam went out to meet him, bowing her head because of the sunshine. Nasturtiums were coming out crimson under the cool green shadow of their leaves. The girl stood, dark-haired, glad to see him.

'Hasn't Clara come?' he asked.

'Yes,' replied Miriam in her musical tone. 'She's reading.'

He wheeled his bicycle into the barn. He had put on a handsome tie, of which he was rather proud, and socks to match.

'She came this morning?' he asked.

'Yes,' replied Miriam, as she walked at his side. 'You said you'd bring me that letter from the man at Liberty's. Have you remembered?'

'Oh dash, no!' he said. 'But nag at me till you get it.'

'I don't like to nag at you.'

'Do it whether or not. And is she any more agreeable?' he continued.

'You know I always think she is quite agreeable.'

He was silent. Evidently his eagerness to be early today had been the new-comer. Miriam already began to suffer. They went together towards the house. He took the clips off his trousers, but was too lazy to brush the dust from his shoes, in spite of the socks and tie.

Clara sat in the cool parlour reading. He saw the nape of her white neck, and the fine hair lifted from it. She rose, looking at him indifferently. To shake hands she lifted her arm straight, in a manner that seemed at once to keep him at a distance, and yet to fling something to him. He noticed how her breasts swelled inside her blouse, and how her shoulder curved handsomely under the thin muslin at the top of her arm.

'You have chosen a fine day,' he said.

'It happens so,' she said.

'Yes,' he said; 'I am glad.'

She sat down, not thanking him for his politeness.

'What have you been doing all morning?' asked Paul of Miriam.

'Well, you see,' said Miriam, coughing huskily, 'Clara only came with father – and so – she's not been here very long.'

Clara sat leaning on the table, holding aloof. He noticed her hands were large, but well kept. And the skin on them seemed almost coarse, opaque, and white, with fine golden hairs. She did not mind if he observed her hands. She intended to scorn him. Her heavy arm lay negligently on the table. Her mouth was closed as if she were offended, and she kept her face slightly averted.

'You were at Margaret Bonford's meeting the other evening,' he said to her.

Miriam did not know this courteous Paul. Clara glanced at him.

'Yes,' she said.

'Why,' asked Miriam, 'how do you know?'

'I went in for a few minutes before the train came,' he answered.

Clara turned away again rather disdainfully.

'I think she's a lovable little woman,' said Paul.

'Margaret Bonford!' exclaimed Clara. 'She's a great deal cleverer than most men.'

'Well, I didn't say she wasn't,' he said, deprecating. 'She's lovable for all that.'

'And, of course, that is all that matters,' said Clara witheringly.

He rubbed his head, rather perplexed, rather annoyed.

'I suppose it matters more than her cleverness,' he said; 'which, after all, would never get her to heaven.'

'It's not heaven she wants to get – it's her fair share on earth,' retorted Clara. She spoke as if he were responsible for some deprivation which Miss Bonford suffered.

'Well,' he said, 'I thought she was warm, and awfully nice – only too frail. I wished she was sitting comfortably in peace –'

' "Darning her husband's stockings," ' said Clara scathingly.

'I'm sure she wouldn't mind darning even my stockings,' he said. 'And I'm sure she'd do them well. Just as I wouldn't mind blacking her boots if she wanted me to.'

But Clara refused to answer this sally of his. He talked to Miriam for a little while. The other woman held aloof.

'Well,' he said, 'I think I'll go and see Edgar. Is he on the land?'

'I believe,' said Miriam, 'he's gone for a load of coal. He should be back directly.'

'Then,' he said, 'I'll go and meet him.'

Miriam dared not propose anything for the three of them. He rose and left them.

On the top road, where the gorse was out, he saw Edgar walking lazily beside the mare, who nodded her white-starred forehead as she dragged the clanking load of coal. The young farmer's face lighted up as he saw his friend. Edgar was good-looking, with dark, warm eyes. His clothes were old and rather disreputable, and he walked with considerable pride.

'Hello!' he said, seeing Paul bareheaded. 'Where are you going?'

'Came to meet you. Can't stand "Nevermore".'

Edgar's teeth flashed in a laugh of amusement.

'Who is "Nevermore"?' he asked.

'The lady – Mrs Dawes – it ought to be Mrs The Raven that quothed "Nevermore".'

Edgar laughed with glee.

'Don't you like her?' he asked.

'Not a fat lot,' said Paul. 'Why, do you?'

'No!' The answer came with a deep ring of conviction. 'No!' Edgar pursed up his lips. 'I can't say she's much in my line.' He mused a little. Then: 'But why do you call her "Nevermore"?' he asked.

'Well,' said Paul, 'if she looks at a man she says haughtily "Nevermore", and if she looks at herself in the looking-glass she says disdainfully "Nevermore", and if she thinks back she says it in disgust, and if she looks forward she says it cynically.'

Edgar considered this speech, failed to make much out of it, and said, laughing, 'You think she's a man-hater?'

'*She* thinks she is,' replied Paul.

'But you don't think so?'

'No,' replied Paul.

'Wasn't she nice with you, then?'

'Could you imagine her *nice* with anybody?' asked the young man.

Edgar laughed. Together they unloaded the coal in the yard. Paul was rather self-conscious, because he knew Clara could see if she looked out of the window. She didn't look.

On Saturday afternoons the horses were brushed down and groomed. Paul and Edgar worked together, sneezing with the dust that came from the pelts of Jimmy and Flower.

'Do you know a new song to teach me?' said Edgar.

He continued to work all the time. The back of his neck was sun-red when he bent down, and his fingers that held the brush were thick. Paul watched him sometimes.

' "Mary Morrison"?' suggested the younger.

Edgar agreed. He had a good tenor voice, and he loved to learn all the songs his friend could teach him, so that he could sing whilst he was carting. Paul had a very indifferent baritone voice, but a good ear. However, he sang softly, for fear of Clara. Edgar repeated the line in a clear tenor. At times they both broke off to sneeze, and first one, then the other, abused his horse.

Miriam was impatient of men. It took so little to amuse them – even Paul. She thought it anomalous in him that he could be so thoroughly absorbed in a triviality.

It was teatime when they had finished.

'What song was that?' asked Miriam.

Edgar told her. The conversation turned to singing.

'We have such jolly times,' Miriam said to Clara.

Mrs Dawes ate her meal in a slow, dignified way. Whenever the men were present she grew distant.

'Do you like singing?' Miriam asked her.

'If it is good,' she said.

Paul, of course, coloured.

'You mean if it is high-class and trained?' he said.

'I think a voice needs training before the singing is anything,' she said.

'You might as well insist on having people's voices trained before you allowed them to talk,' he replied. 'Really, people sing for their own pleasure, as a rule.'

'And it may be for other people's discomfort.'

'Then the other people should have flaps to their ears,' he replied.

The boys laughed. There was a silence. He flushed deeply, and ate in silence.

After tea, when all the men had gone but Paul, Mrs Leivers said to Clara, 'And you find life happier now?'

'Infinitely.'

'And you are satisfied?'

'So long as I can be free and independent.'

'And you don't *miss* anything in your life?' asked Mrs Leivers gently.

'I've put all that behind me.'

Paul had been feeling uncomfortable during this discourse. He got up.

'You'll find you're always tumbling over the things you've put behind you,' he said. Then he took his departure to the cowsheds. He felt he had been witty, and his manly pride was high. He whistled as he went down the brick track.

Miriam came for him a little later to know if he would go with Clara and her for a walk. They set off down to Strelley Mill Farm. As they were going beside the brook, on the Willey Water side, looking through the brake at the edge of the wood, where pink campions glowed under a few sunbeams, they saw, beyond the tree-trunks and the thin hazel bushes, a man leading a great bay horse through the gullies. The big red beast seemed to dance romantically through that dimness of green hazel drift, away there where the air was shadowy, as if it were in the past, among the fading bluebells that might have bloomed for Deidre or Iseult.

The three stood charmed.

'What a treat to be a knight,' he said, 'and to have a pavilion here.'

'And to have us shut up safely?' replied Clara.

'Yes,' he answered, 'singing with your maids at your broidery. I would carry your banner of white and green and heliotrope. I would have "W.S.P.U." emblazoned on my shield, beneath a woman rampant.'

'I have no doubt,' said Clara, 'that you would much rather fight for a woman than let her fight for herself.'

'I would. When she fights for herself she seems like a dog before a looking-glass, gone into a mad fury with its own shadow.'

'And *you* are the looking-glass?' she asked, with a curl of the lip.

'Or the shadow,' he replied.

'I am afraid,' she said, 'that you are too clever.'

'Well, I leave it to you to be *good*,' he retorted, laughing. 'Be good, sweet maid, and just let *me* be clever.'

But Clara wearied of his flippancy. Suddenly, looking at her, he saw that the upward lifting of her face was misery and not scorn. His heart grew tender for everybody. He turned and was gentle with Miriam, whom he had neglected till then.

At the wood's edge they met Limb, a thin, swarthy man of forty, tenant of Strelley Mill, which he ran as a cattle-raising farm. He held the halter of the powerful stallion indifferently, as if he were tired. The three stood to let him pass over the stepping-stones of the first brook. Paul admired that so large an animal should walk on such springy toes, with an endless excess of vigour. Limb pulled up before them.

'Tell your father, Miss Leivers,' he said, in a peculiar piping voice, 'that his young beas'es 'as broke that bottom fence three days an' runnin'.'

'Which?' asked Miriam, tremulous.

The great horse breathed heavily, shifting round its red flanks, and looking suspiciously with its wonderful big eyes upwards from under its lowered head and falling mane.

'Come along a bit,' replied Limb, 'an' I'll show you.'

The man and the stallion went forward. It danced sideways, shaking its white fetlocks and looking frightened, as it felt itself in the brook.

'No hanky-pankyin',' said the man affectionately to the beast.

It went up the bank in little leaps, then splashed finely through the second brook. Clara, walking with a kind of sulky abandon, watched it half-fascinated, half-contemptuous. Limb stopped and pointed to the fence under some willows.

'There, you see where they got through,' he said. 'My man's druv 'em back three times.'

'Yes,' answered Miriam, colouring as if she were at fault.

'Are you comin' in?' asked the man.

'No, thanks; but we should like to go by the pond.'

'Well, just as you've a mind,' he said.

The horse gave little whinneys of pleasure at being so near home.

'He is glad to be back,' said Clara, who was interested in the creature.

'Yes – 'e's been a tidy step today.'

They went through the gate, and saw approaching them from the big farm-house a smallish, dark, excitable-looking woman of about thirty-five. Her hair was touched with grey, her dark eyes looked wild. She walked with her hands behind her back. Her brother went forward. As it saw her, the big bay stallion whinneyed again. She came up excitedly.

'Are you home again, my boy!' she said tenderly to the horse, not to the man. The great beast shifted round to her, ducking his head. She smuggled into his mouth the wrinkled yellow apple she had been hiding behind her back, then she kissed him near the eyes. He gave a big sigh of pleasure. She held his head in her arms against her breast.

'Isn't he splendid!' said Miriam to her.

Miss Limb looked up. Her dark eyes glanced straight at Paul.

'Oh, good-evening, Miss Leivers,' she said. 'It's ages since you've been down.' Miriam introduced her friends.

'Your horse *is* a fine fellow!' said Clara.

'Isn't he!' Again she kissed him. 'As loving as any man!'

'More loving than most men, I should think,' replied Clara.

'He's a nice boy!' cried the woman, again embracing the horse.

Clara, fascinated by the big beast, went up to stroke his neck.

'He's quite gentle,' said Miss Limb. 'Don't you think big fellows are?'

'He's a beauty!' replied Clara.

She wanted to look in his eyes. She wanted him to look at her.

'It's a pity he can't talk,' she said.

'Oh, but he can – all but,' replied the other woman.

Then her brother moved on with the horse.

'Are you coming in? *Do* come in, Mr – I didn't catch it.'

'Morel,' said Miriam. 'No, we won't come in, but we should like to go by the mill-pond.'

'Yes – yes, do. Do you fish, Mr Morel?'

'No,' said Paul.

'Because if you do you might come and fish any time,' said Miss Limb. 'We scarcely see a soul from week's end to week's end. I should be thankful.'

'What fish are there in the pond?' he asked.

They went through the front garden, over the sluice, and up the steep bank to the pond, which lay in shadow, with its two wooded islets. Paul walked with Miss Limb.

'I shouldn't mind swimming here,' he said.

'Do,' she replied. 'Come when you like. My brother will be awfully pleased to talk with you. He is so quiet because there is no one to talk to. Do come and swim.'

Clara came up.

'It's a fine depth,' she said, 'and so clear.'

'Yes,' said Miss Limb.

'Do you swim?' said Paul. 'Miss Limb was just saying we could come when we liked.'

'Of course there's the farm-hands,' said Miss Limb.

They talked a few moments, then went on up the wild hill, leaving the lonely, haggard-eyed woman on the bank.

The hillside was all ripe with sunshine. It was wild and tussocky, given over to rabbits. The three walked in silence. Then, 'She makes me feel uncomfortable,' said Paul.

'You mean Miss Limb?' asked Miriam. 'Yes.'

'What's a matter with her? Is she going dotty with being too lonely?'

'Yes,' said Miriam. 'It's not the right sort of life for her. I think it's cruel to bury her there. I really ought to go and see her more. But – she upsets me.'

'She makes me feel sorry for her – yes, and she bothers me,' he said.

'I suppose,' blurted Clara suddenly, 'she wants a man.'

The other two were silent for a few moments.

'But it's the loneliness sends her cracked,' said Paul.

Clara did not answer, but strode on uphill. She was walking with her head hanging, her legs swinging as she kicked through the dead thistles and the tussocky grass, her arms hanging loose. Rather than walking, her handsome body seemed to be blundering up the hill. A hot wave went over Paul. He was curious about her. Perhaps life had been cruel to her. He forgot Miriam, who was walking beside him talking to him. She glanced at him, finding he did not answer her. His eyes were fixed ahead on Clara.

'Do you still think she is disagreeable?' she asked.

He did not notice that the question was sudden. It ran with his thoughts.

'Something's the matter with her,' he said.

'Yes,' answered Miriam.

They found at the top of the hill a hidden wild field, two sides of which were backed by the wood, the other sides by high loose hedges of hawthorn and elder-bushes. Between these overgrown bushes were gaps that the cattle might have walked through had there been any cattle now. There the turf was smooth as velveteen, padded and holed by the rabbits. The field itself was coarse, and crowded with tall, big cowslips that had never been cut. Clusters of strong flowers rose everywhere above the coarse tussocks of bent. It was like a road-stead crowded with tall, fairy shipping.

'Ah!' cried Miriam, and she looked at Paul, her dark eyes dilating. He smiled. Together they enjoyed the field of flowers. Clara, a little way off, was looking at the cowslips disconsolately. Paul and Miriam stayed close together, talking in subdued tones. He kneeled on one knee, quickly gathering the best blossoms, moving from tuft to tuft restlessly, talking softly all the time. Miriam plucked the flowers lovingly, lingering over them. He always seemed to her too quick and almost scientific. Yet his bunches had a natural beauty more than hers. He loved them, but as if they were his and he had a right to them. She had more reverence for them: they held something she had not.

The flowers were very fresh and sweet. He wanted to drink them. As he gathered them, he ate the little yellow trumpets. Clara was still wandering about disconsolately. Going towards her, he said, 'Why don't you get some?'

'I don't believe in it. They look better growing.'

'But you'd like some?'

'They want to be left.'

'I don't believe they do.'

'I don't want the corpses of flowers about me,' she said.

'That's a stiff, artificial notion,' he said. 'They don't die any quicker in water than on their roots. And besides they *look* nice in a bowl – they look jolly. And you only call a thing a corpse because it looks corpse-like.'

'Whether it is one or not?' she argued.

'It isn't one to me. A dead flower isn't a corpse of a flower.'

Clara now ignored him.

'And even so – what right have you to pull them?' she asked.

'Because I like them, and want them – and there's plenty of them.'

'And that is sufficient?'

'Yes. Why not? I'm sure they'd smell nice in your room in Nottingham.'

'And I should have the pleasure of watching them die.'

'But then – it does not matter if they do die.'

Whereupon he left her, and went stooping over the clumps of tangled flowers which thickly sprinkled the field like pale luminous foam-clots. Miriam had come close. Clara was kneeling, breathing some scent from the cowslips.

'I think,' said Miriam, 'if you treat them with reverence you don't do them any harm. It is the spirit you pluck them in that matters.'

'Yes,' he said. 'But no, you get 'em because you want 'em, and that's all.' He held out his bunch.

Miriam was silent. He picked some more.

'Look at these!' he continued; 'sturdy and lusty like little trees and like boys with fat legs.'

Clara's hat lay on the grass not far off. She was kneeling, bending forward still to smell the flowers. Her neck gave him a sharp pang, such a beautiful thing, yet not proud of itself just now. Her breasts swung slightly in her blouse. The arching curve of her back was beautiful and strong; she wore no stays. Suddenly, without knowing, he was scattering a handful of cowslips over her hair and neck, saying:

> 'Ashes to ashes and dust to dust,
> If the Lord won't have you the devil must.'

The chill flowers fell on her neck. She looked up at him, with almost pitiful, scared grey eyes, wondering what he was doing. Flowers fell on her face, and she shut her eyes.

Suddenly, standing there above her, he felt awkward.

'I thought you wanted a funeral,' he said, ill at ease.

Clara laughed strangely, and rose, picking the cowslips from her hair. She took up her hat and pinned it on. One flower had remained tangled in her hair. He saw, but would not tell her. He gathered up the flowers he had sprinkled over her.

At the edge of the wood the bluebells had flowed over into the field and stood there like flood water. But they were fading now. Clara strayed up to them. He wandered after her. The bluebells pleased him.

'Look how they've come out of the wood!' he said.

Then she turned with a flash of warmth and of gratitude.

'Yes,' she smiled.

His blood beat up.

'It makes me think of the wild men of the woods, how terrified they would be when they got breast to breast with the open space.'

'Do you think they were?' she asked.

'I wonder which was more frightened among old tribes – those bursting out of their darkness of woods upon all the space of light, or those from the open tip-toeing into the forests.'

'I should think the second,' she answered.

'Yes, you *do* feel like one of the open space sort, trying to force yourself into the dark, don't you?'

'How should I know?' she answered queerly.

The conversation ended there.

The evening was deepening over the earth. Already the valley was full of shadow. One tiny square of light stood opposite at Crossleigh Bank Farm. Brightness was swimming on the tops of the hills. Miriam came up slowly, her face in her big, loose bunch of flowers, walking ankle-deep through the scattered froth of the cowslips. Beyond her the trees were coming into shape, all shadow.

'Shall we go?' she asked.

And the three turned away. They were all silent. Going down the path they could see the light of home right across, and on the ridge of the hill a thin dark outline with little lights, where the colliery village touched the sky.

'It has been nice, hasn't it?' he asked.

Miriam murmured assent. Clara was silent.

'Don't you think so?' he persisted.

But she walked with her head up, and still did not answer. He could tell by the way she moved, as if she didn't care, that she suffered.

At this time Paul took his mother to Lincoln. She was bright and enthusiastic as ever, but as he sat opposite her in the railway carriage, she seemed to look frail. He had a momentary sensation as if she were slipping away from him. Then he wanted to get hold of her, to fasten her, almost to chain her. He felt he must keep hold of her with his hand.

They drew near to the city. Both were at the window looking for the cathedral.

'There she is, mother!' he cried.

They saw the great cathedral lying couchant above the plain

'Ah!' she exclaimed. 'So she is!'

He looked at his mother. Her blue eyes were watching the cathedral quietly. She seemed again to be beyond him. Something in the eternal repose of the uplifted cathedral, blue and noble against the sky, was reflected in her, something of the fatality. What was, *was*. With all his young will he could not alter it. He saw her face, the skin still fresh and pink and downy, but crow's-feet near her eyes, her eyelids steady, sinking a little, her mouth always closed with disillusion; and there was on her the same eternal look, as if she knew fate at last. He beat against it with all the strength of his soul.

'Look, mother, how big she is above the town! Think, there are streets and streets below her! She looks bigger than the city altogether.'

'So she does!' exclaimed his mother, breaking bright into life again. But he had seen her sitting, looking steady out of the window at the cathedral, her face and eyes fixed, reflecting the relentlessness of life. And the crow's-feet near her eyes, and her mouth shut so hard, made him feel he would go mad.

They ate a meal that she considered wildly extravagant.

'Don't imagine I like it,' she said, as she ate her cutlet. 'I *don't* like it, I really don't! Just *think* of your money wasted!'

'You never mind my money,' he said. 'You forget I'm a fellow taking his girl for an outing.'

And he bought her some blue violets.

'Stop it at once, sir!' she commanded 'How can I do it?'

'You've got nothing to do. Stand still!'

And in the middle of High Street he stuck the flowers in her coat.

'An old thing like me!' she said, sniffing.

'You see,' he said, 'I want people to think we're awful swells. So look ikey.'

'I'll jowl your head,' she laughed.

'Strut!' he commanded. 'Be a fantail pigeon.'

It took him an hour to get her through the street. She stood above Glory Hole, she stood before Stone Bow, she stood everywhere, and exclaimed.

A man came up, took off his hat, and bowed to her.

'Can I show you the town, madam?'

'No, thank you,' she answered. 'I've got my son.'

Then Paul was cross with her for not answering with more dignity.

'You go away with you!' she exclaimed. 'Ha! that's the Jew's House. Now, do you remember that lecture, Paul – ?'

But she could scarcely climb the cathedral hill. He did not notice. Then suddenly he found her unable to spek. He took her into a little public-house, where she rested.

'It's nothing,' she said. 'My heart is only a bit old; one must expect it.'

He did not answer, but looked at her. Again his heart was crushed in a hot grip. He wanted to cry, he wanted to smash things in fury.

They set off again, pace by pace, so slowly. And every step seemed like a weight on his chest. He felt as if his heart would burst. At last they came to the top. She stood enchanted, looking at the castle gate, looking at the cathedral front. She had quite forgotten herself.

'Now *this* is better than I thought it could be!' she cried.

But he hated it. Everywhere he followed her, brooding. They sat together in the cathedral. They attended a little service in the choir. She was timid.

'I suppose it is open to anybody?' she asked him.

'Yes,' he replied. 'Do you think they'd have the damned cheek to send us away?'

'Well, I'm sure,' she exclaimed, 'they would if they heard your language.'

Her face seemed to shine again with joy and peace during the service. And all the time he was wanting to rage and smash things and cry.

Afterwards, when they were leaning over the wall, looking at the town below, he blurted suddenly, 'Why can't a man have a *young* mother? What is she old for?'

'Well,' his mother laughed, 'she can scarcely help it.'

'And why wasn't I the oldest son? Look – they say the young ones have the advantage – but look, *they* had the young mother. You should have had me for your eldest son.'

'I didn't arrange it,' she remonstrated. 'Come to consider, you're as much to blame as me.'

He turned on her, white, his eyes furious.

'What are you old for?' he said, mad with his impotence. '*Why* can't you walk? *Why* can't you come with me to places?'

'At one time,' she replied, 'I could have run up that hill a good deal better than you.'

'What's the good of that to me?' he cried, hitting his fist on the wall. Then he became plaintive. 'It's too bad of you to be ill, Little, it is – '

'Ill!' she cried. 'I'm a bit old, and you'll have to put up with it, that's all.'

They were quiet. But it was as much as they could bear. They got jolly again over tea. As they sat by Brayford watching the boats, he told her about Clara. His mother asked him innumerable questions.

'Then who does she live with?'

'With her mother, on Bluebell Hill.'

'And have they enough to keep them?'

'I don't think so. I think they do lace work.'

'And wherein lies her charm, my boy?'

'I don't know that she's charming, mother. But she's nice. And she seems straight, you know – not a bit deep, not a bit.'

'But she's a good deal older than you.'

'She's thirty, I'm going on twenty-three.'

'You haven't told me what you like her for.'

'Because I don't know – a sort of defiant way she's got – a sort of angry way.'

Mrs Morel considered. She would have been glad now for her son to fall in love with some woman who would – she did not know what. But he fretted so, got so furious suddenly, and again was melancholic. She wished he knew some nice woman – She did not know what she wished, but left it vague. At any rate she was not hostile to the idea of Clara.

Annie, too, was getting married. Leonard had gone away to work in Birmingham. One weekend when he was home she had said to him, 'You don't look very well, my lad.'

'I dunno,' he said. 'I feel anyhow or nohow, ma.'

He called her 'ma' already in his boyish fashion.

'Are you sure they're good lodgings?' she asked.

'Yes – yes. Only – it's a winder when you have to pour your own tea out – an' nobody to grouse if you teem it in your saucer and sup it up. It somehow takes a' the taste out of it.'

Mrs Morel laughed.

'And so it knocks you up!' she said.

'I dunno. I want to get married,' he blurted, twisting his fingers and looking down at his boots. There was a silence.

'But,' she exclaimed, 'I thought you said you'd wait another year.'

'Yes, I did say so,' he replied stubbornly.

Again she considered.

'And you know,' she said, 'Annie's a bit of a spendthrift. She's saved no more than eleven pounds. And I know, lad, you haven't had much chance.'

He coloured up to the ears.

'I've got thirty-three quid,' he said.

'It doesn't go far,' she answered.

He said nothing, but twisted his fingers.

'And you know,' she said, 'I've nothing – '

'I didn't want, ma!' he cried, very red, suffering and remonstrating.

'No, my lad, I know. I was only wishing I had. And take away five pounds for the wedding and things – it leaves twenty-nine pounds. You won't do much on that.'

He twisted still, impotent, stubborn, not looking up.

'But do you really want to get married?' she asked. 'Do you feel as if you ought?'

He gave her one straight look from his blue eyes.

'Yes,' he said.

'Then,' she replied, 'we must all do the best we can for it, lad.'

The next time he looked up there were tears in his eyes.

'I don't want Annie to feel handicapped,' he said, struggling.

'My lad,' she said, 'you're steady – you've got a decent place. If a man had *needed* me I'd have married him on his last week's wages. She may find it a bit hard to start humbly. Young girls *are* like that. They look forward to the fine home they think they'll have. But I had expensive furniture. It's not everything.'

So the wedding took place almost immediately. Arthur came home, and was splendid in uniform. Annie looked nice in a dove-grey dress that she could take for Sundays. Morel called her a fool for getting married, and was cool with his son-in-law. Mrs Morel had white tips in her bonnet, and some white on her blouse, and was teased by both her sons for fancying herself so grand. Leonard was jolly and cordial, and felt a fearful fool. Paul could not quite see what Annie wanted to get married for. He was fond of her, and she of him. Still, he hoped rather lugubriously that it would turn out all right. Arthur was astonishingly handsome in his scarlet and yellow, and he knew it well, but was secretly ashamed of the uniform. Annie cried her eyes out in the kitchen, on leaving her mother. Mrs Morel cried a little, then patted her on the back and said, 'But don't cry, child, he'll be good to you.'

Morel stamped and said she was a fool to go and tie herself up. Leonard looked white and overwrought. Mrs Morel said to him, 'I s'll trust her to you, my lad, and hold you responsible for her.'

'You can,' he said, nearly dead with the ordeal. And it was all over.

When Morel and Arthur were in bed, Paul sat talking, as he often did, with his mother.

'You're not sorry she's married, mother, are you?' he asked.

'I'm not sorry she's married – but – it seems strange that she should go from me. It even seems to me hard that she can prefer to go with her Leonard. That's how mothers are – I know it's silly.'

'And shall you be miserable about her?'

'When I think of my own wedding day,' his mother answered, 'I can only hope her life will be different.'

'But you can trust him to be good to her?'

'Yes, yes. They say he's not good enough for her. But I say if a man is *genuine*, as he is, and a girl is fond of him – then – it should be all right. He's as good as she.'

'So you don't mind?'

'I would *never* have let a daughter of mine marry a man I didn't *feel* to be genuine through and through. And yet, there's a gap now she's gone.'

They were both miserable, and wanted her back again. It seemed to Paul his mother looked lonely, in her new black silk blouse with its bit of white trimming.

'At any rate, mother, I s'll never marry,' he said.

'Ay, they all say that, my lad. You've not met the one yet. Only wait a year or two.'

'But I shan't marry, mother. I shall live with you, and we'll have a servant.'

'Ay, my lad, it's easy to talk. We'll see when the time comes.'

'What time? I'm nearly twenty-three.'

'Yes, you're not one that would marry young. But in three years' time –'

'I shall be with you just the same.'

'We'll see, my boy, we'll see.'

'But you don't want me to marry?'

'I shouldn't like to think of you going through your life without anybody to care for you and do – no.'

'And you think I ought to marry?'

'Sooner or later every man ought.'

'But you'd rather it were later.'

'It would be hard – and very hard. It's as they say:

> "A son's my son till he takes him a wife,
> But my daughter's my daughter the whole of her life." '

'And you think I'd let a wife take me from you?'

'Well, you wouldn't ask her to marry your mother as well as you,' Mrs Morel smiled.

'She could do what she liked; she wouldn't have to interfere.'

'She wouldn't – till she'd got you – and then you'd see.'

'I never will see. I'll never marry while I've got you – I won't.'

'But I shouldn't like to leave you with nobody, my boy,' she cried.

'You're not going to leave me. What are you? Fifty-three! I'll give you till seventy-five. There you are, I'm fat and forty-four. Then I'll marry a staid body. See!'

His mother sat and laughed.

'Go to bed,' she said – 'go to bed.'

'And we'll have a pretty house, you and me, and a servant, and it'll be just all right. I s'll perhaps be rich with my painting.'

'Will you go to bed!'

'And then you s'll have a pony carriage. See yourself – a little Queen Victoria trotting round.'

'I tell you to go to bed,' she laughed.

He kissed her and went. His plans for the future were always the same.

Mrs Morel sat brooding – about her daughter, about Paul, about Arthur. She fretted at losing Annie. The family was very closely bound. And she felt she must live now, to be with her children. Life was so rich for her. Paul wanted her, and so did Arthur. Arthur never knew how deeply he loved her. He was a creature of the moment. Never yet had he been forced to realise himself. The army had disciplined his body, but not his soul. He was in perfect health and very handsome. His dark, vigorous hair sat close to his smallish head. There was something childish about his nose, something almost girlish about his dark blue eyes. But he had the full red mouth of a man under his brown moustache, and his jaw was strong. It was his father's mouth; it was the nose and eyes of her own mother's people – good-looking, weak-principled folk. Mrs Morel was anxious about him. Once he had really run the rig he was safe. But how far would he go?

The army had not really done him any good. He resented bitterly the authority of the petty officers. He hated having to obey as if he were an animal. But he had too much sense to kick. So he turned his attention to getting the best out of it. He could sing, he was a boon-companion. Often he got into scrapes, but they were the manly scrapes that are easily condoned. So he made a good time out of it, whilst his self-respect was in suppression. He trusted to his good looks and handsome figure, his refinement, his decent education to get him most of what he wanted, and he was not disappointed. Yet he was restless. Something seemed to gnaw him inside. He was never still, he was never alone. With his mother he was rather humble. Paul he admired and loved and despised slightly. And Paul admired and loved and despised him slightly.

Mrs Morel had had a few pounds left to her by her father, and she decided to buy her son out of the army. He was wild with joy. Now he was like a lad taking a holiday.

He had always been fond of Beatrice Wyld, and during his furlough he picked up with her again. She was stronger and better in health. The two often went long walks together, Arthur taking her arm in soldier's fashion, rather stiffly. And she came to play the piano whilst he sang. Then Arthur would unhook his tunic collar. He grew flushed, his eyes were bright, he sang in a manly tenor. Afterwards they sat together on the sofa. He seemed to flaunt his body: she was aware of him so – the strong chest, the sides, the thighs in their close-fitting trousers.

He liked to lapse into the dialect when he talked to her. She would sometimes smoke with him. Occasionally she would only take a few whiffs at his cigarette.

'Nay,' he said to her one evening, when she reached for his cigarette. 'Nay, tha doesna. I'll gi'e thee a smoke kiss if ter's a mind.'

'I wanted a whiff, no kiss at all,' she answered.

'Well, an' tha s'lt ha'e a whiff,' he said, 'along wi' t' kiss.'

'I want a draw at thy fag,' she cried, snatching for the cigarette between his lips.

He was sitting with his shoulder touching her. She was small and quick as lightning. He just escaped.

'I'll gi'e thee a smoke kiss,' he said.

'Tha'rt a knivey nuisance, Arty Morel,' she said, sitting back.

'Ha'e a smoke kiss?'

The soldier leaned forward to her, smiling. His face was near hers.

'Shonna!' she replied, turning away her head.

He took a draw at his cigarette, and pursed up his mouth, and put his lips close to her. His dark-brown cropped moustache stood out like a brush. She looked at the puckered crimson lips, then suddenly snatched the cigarette from his fingers and darted away. He, leaping after her, seized the comb from her back hair. She turned, threw the cigarette at him. He picked it up, put it in his mouth, and sat down.

'Nuisance!' she cried. 'Give me my comb!'

She was afraid that her hair, specially done for him, would come down. She stood with her hands to her head. He hid the comb between his knees.

'I've non got it,' he said.

The cigarette trembled between his lips with laughter as he spoke.

'Liar!' she said.

''S true as I'm here!' he laughed, showing his hands.

'You brazen imp!' she exclaimed, flushing and scuffling for the comb, which he had under his knees. As she wrestled with him, pulling at his smooth, tight-covered knees, he laughed till he lay back on the sofa shaking with laughter. The cigarette fell from his mouth, almost singeing his throat. Under his delicate tan the blood flushed up, and he laughed till his blue eyes were blinded, his throat swollen almost to choking. Then he sat up. Beatrice was putting in her comb.

'Tha tickled me, Beat,' he said thickly.

Like a flash her small white hand went out and smacked his face. He started up, glaring at her. They stared at each other. Slowly the flush mounted her cheek, she dropped her eyes, then her head. He sat down sulkily. She went into the scullery to adjust her hair. In private there she shed a few tears, she did not know what for.

When she returned she was pursed up close. But it was only a film over her fire. He, with ruffled hair, was sulking upon the sofa. She sat down opposite, in the armchair, and neither spoke. The clock ticked in the silence like blows.

'You are a little cat, Beat,' he said at length, half apologetically.

'Well, you shouldn't be brazen,' she replied.

There was again a long silence. He whistled to himself, like a man much agitated but defiant. Suddenly she went across to him and kissed him.

'Did it, pore fing!' she mocked.

He lifted his face, smiling curiously.

'Kiss?' he invited her.

'Daren't I?' she asked.

'Go on!' he challenged, his mouth lifted to her.

Deliberately, and with a peculiar quivering smile that seemed to overspread her whole body, she put her mouth on his. Immediately his arms folded round her. As soon as the long kiss was finished she drew back her head from him, put her delicate fingers on his neck, through the open collar. Then she closed her eyes, giving herself up again in a kiss.

She acted of her own free will. What she would do she did, and made nobody responsible.

Paul felt life changing around him. The conditions of youth were gone. Now it was a home of grown-up people. Annie was a married woman, Arthur was following his own pleasure in a way unknown to his folk. For so long they had all lived at home, and gone out to pass their time. But now, for Annie and Arthur, life lay outside their mother's house. They came home for holiday and for rest. So there was that strange, half-empty feeling about the house, as if the birds had flown. Paul became more and more unsettled. Annie and Arthur had gone. He was restless to follow. Yet home was for him beside his mother. And still there was something else, something outside, something he wanted.

He grew more and more restless. Miriam did not satisfy him. His old mad desire to be with her grew weaker. Sometimes he met Clara in Nottingham, sometimes he went to meetings with her, sometimes he saw her at Willey Farm. But on these last occasions the situation became strained. There was a triangle of antagonism between Paul and Clara and Miriam. With Clara he took on a smart, worldly, mocking tone very antagonistic to Miriam. It did not matter what went before. She might be intimate and sad with him. Then as soon as Clara appeared, it all vanished, and he played to the newcomer.

Miriam had one beautiful evening with him in the hay. He had been on the horse-rake, and, having finished, came to help her to put the hay in cocks. Then he talked to her of his hopes and despairs, and his whole soul seemed to lie bare before her. She felt as if she watched the very quivering stuff of life in him. The moon came out: they walked home together: he seemed to have come to her because he needed her so badly, and she listened to him, gave him all her love and her faith. It seemed to her he brought her the best of himself to keep, and that she would guard it all her life. Nay, the sky did not cherish the stars more surely and eternally than she would guard the good in the soul of Paul Morel. She went on home alone, feeling exalted, glad in her faith.

And then, the next day, Clara came. They were to have tea in the hayfield. Miriam watched the evening drawing to gold and shadow. And all the time Paul was sporting with Clara. He made higher and higher heaps of hay that they were jumping over. Miriam did not care for the game, and stood aside. Edgar and Geoffrey and Maurice and Clara and Paul jumped. Paul won, because he was light. Clara's blood was roused. She could run like an Amazon. Paul loved the determined way she rushed at the haycock and leaped, landed on the other side, her breasts shaken, her thick hair coming undone.

'You touched!' he cried. 'You touched!'

'No!' she flashed, turning to Edgar. 'I didn't touch, did I? Wasn't I clear?'

'I couldn't say,' laughed Edgar.

None of them could say.

'But you touched,' said Paul. 'You're beaten.'

'I did *not* touch!' she cried.

'As plain as anything,' said Paul.

'Box his ears for me!' she cried to Edgar.

'Nay,' Edgar laughed. 'I daren't. You must do it yourself.'

'And nothing can alter the fact that you touched,' laughed Paul.

She was furious with him. Her little triumph before these lads and men was gone. She had forgotten herself in the game. Now he was to humble her.

'I think you are despicable!' she said.

And again he laughed, in a way that tortured Miriam.

'And I *knew* you couldn't jump that heap,' he teased.

She turned her back on him. Yet everybody could see that the only person she listened to, or was conscious of, was he, and he of her. It pleased the men to see this battle between them. But Miriam was tortured.

Paul could choose the lesser in place of the higher, she saw. He could be unfaithful to himself, unfaithful to the real, deep Paul Morel. There was a danger of his becoming frivolous, of his running after his satisfactions like any Arthur, or like his father. It made Miriam bitter to think that he should throw away his soul for this flippant traffic of triviality with Clara. She walked in bitterness and silence, while the other two rallied each other, and Paul sported.

And afterwards, he would not own it, but he was rather ashamed of himself, and prostrated himself before Miriam. Then again he rebelled.

'It's not religious to be religious,' he said. 'I reckon a crow is religious when it sails across the sky. But it only does it because it feels itself carried to where it's going, not because it thinks it is being eternal.'

But Miriam knew that one should be religious in everything, have God, whatever God might be, present in everything.

'I don't believe God knows such a lot about Himself,' he cried. 'God doesn't *know* things, He *is* things. And I'm sure He's not soulful.'

And then it seemed to her that Paul was arguing God on to his own side, because he wanted his own way and his own pleasure. There was a long battle between him and her. He was utterly unfaithful to her even in her own presence; then he was ashamed, then repentant; then he hated her, and went off again. Those were the ever-recurring conditions.

She fretted him to the bottom of his soul. There she remained – sad, pensive, a worshipper. And he caused her sorrow. Half the time he grieved for her, half the time he hated her. She was his conscience; and he felt, somehow, he had got a conscience that was too much for him. He could not leave her, because in one way she did hold the best of him. He could not stay with her because she did not take the rest of him, which was three-quarters. So he chafed himself into rawness over her.

When she was twenty-one he wrote her a letter which could only have been written to her.

> May I speak of our old, worn love, this last time. It, too, is changing, is it not? Say, has not the body of that love died, and left you its invulnerable soul? You see, I can give you a spirit love, I have given it you this long, long time; but not embodied passion. See, you are a nun. I have given you what I would give a holy nun – as a mystic monk to a mystic nun. Surely you esteem it best. Yet you regret – no, have regretted – the other. In all our relations no body enters. I do not talk to you through the senses – rather through the spirit. That is why we cannot love in the common sense. Ours is not an everyday affection. As yet we are mortal, and to live side by side with one another would be dreadful, for somehow with you I cannot long be trivial, and, you know, to be always beyond this mortal state would be to lose it. If people marry, they must live together as affectionate humans, who may be commonplace with each other without feeling awkward – not as two souls. So I feel it.
>
> Ought I to send this letter – I doubt it. But there – it is best to understand. *Au revoir.*

Miriam read this letter twice, after which she sealed it up. A year later she broke the seal to show her mother the letter.

'You are a nun – you are a nun.' The words went into her heart again and again. Nothing he ever had said had gone into her so deeply, fixedly, like a mortal wound.

She answered him two days after the party.

' "Our intimacy would have been all-beautiful but for one little mistake," ' she quoted. 'Was the mistake mine?'

Almost immediately he replied to her from Nottingham, sending her at the same time a little *Omar Khayyám*.

'I am glad you answered; you are so calm and natural you put me to shame. What a ranter I am! We are often out of sympathy. But in fundamentals we may always be together I think.

'I must thank you for your sympathy with my painting and drawing. Many a sketch is dedicated to you. I do look forward to your criticisms, which, to my shame and glory, are always grand appreciations. It is a lovely joke, that. *Au revoir*.'

This was the end of the first phase of Paul's love-affair. He was now about twenty-three years old, and, though still virgin, the sex instinct that Miriam had over-refined for so long now grew particularly strong. Often, as he talked to Clara Dawes, came that thickening and quickening of his blood, that peculiar concentration in the breast, as if something were alive there, a new self or a new centre of consciousness, warning him that sooner or later he would have to ask one woman or another. But he belonged to Miriam. Of that she was so fixedly sure that she allowed her right.

CHAPTER 10

Clara

When he was twenty-three years old Paul sent in a landscape to the winter exhibition at Nottingham Castle. Miss Jordan had taken a good deal of interest in him, had invited him to her house, where he met other artists. He was beginning to grow ambitious.

One morning the postman came just as he was washing in the scullery. Suddenly he heard a wild noise from his mother. Rushing into the kitchen, he found her standing on the hearthrug wildly waving a letter and crying 'Hurrah!' as if she had gone mad. He was shocked and frightened.

'Why, mother!' he exclaimed.

She flew to him, flung her arms round him for a moment, then waved the letter, crying, 'Hurrah, my boy! I knew we should do it!'

He was afraid of her – the small, severe woman with greying hair suddenly bursting out in such frenzy. The postman came running back, afraid something had happened. They saw his tipped cap over the short curtain. Mrs Morel rushed to the door.

'His picture's got first prize, Fred,' she cried, 'and is sold for twenty guineas.'

'My word, that's something like!' said the young postman, whom they had known all his life.

'And Major Moreton has bought it!' she cried.

'It looks like meanin' something, that does, Mrs Morel,' said the postman, his blue eyes bright. He was glad to have brought such a lucky letter. Mrs Morel went indoors and sat down, trembling. Paul was afraid lest she might have misread the letter, and might be disappointed after all. He scrutinised it once, twice. Yes, he became convinced it was true. Then he sat down, his heart beating with joy.

'Mother!' he exclaimed.

'Didn't I *say* we should do it!' she said, pretending she was not crying.

He took the kettle off the fire and mashed the tea.

'You didn't think, mother – ' he began tentatively.

'No, my son – not so much – but I expected a good deal.'

'But not so much,' he said.

'No – no – but I knew we should do it.'

And then she recovered her composure, apparently at least. He sat with his shirt turned back, showing his young throat almost like a girl's, and the towel in his hand, his hair sticking up wet.

'Twenty guineas, mother! That's just what you wanted to buy Arthur out. Now you needn't borrow any. It'll just do.'

'Indeed, I shan't take it all,' she said.

'But why?'

'Because I shan't.'

'Well – you have twelve pounds, I'll have nine.'

They cavilled about sharing the twenty guineas. She wanted to take only the five pounds she needed. He would not hear of it. So they got over the stress of emotion by quarrelling.

Morel came home at night from the pit, saying, 'They tell me Paul's got first prize for his picture, and sold it to Lord Henry Bentley for fifty pound.'

'Oh, what stories people do tell!' she cried.

'Ha!' he answered. 'I said I wor sure it wor a lie. But they said tha'd told Fred Hodgkisson.'

'As if I would tell him such stuff!'

'Ha!' assented the miner.

But he was disappointed nevertheless.

'It's true he has got the first prize,' said Mrs Morel.

The miner sat heavily in his chair.

'Has he, beguy!' he exclaimed.

He stared across the room fixedly.

'But as for fifty pounds – such nonsense!' She was silent awhile. 'Major Moreton bought it for twenty guineas, that's true.'

'Twenty guineas! Tha niver says!' exclaimed Morel.

'Yes, and it was worth it.'

'Ay!' he said. 'I don't misdoubt it. But twenty guineas for a bit of a paintin' as he knocked off in an hour or two!'

He was silent with conceit of his son. Mrs Morel sniffed, as if it were nothing.

'And when does he handle th' money?' asked the collier.

'That I couldn't tell you. When the picture is sent home, I suppose.'

There was silence. Morel stared at the sugar-basin instead of eating his dinner. His black arm, with the hand all gnarled with work, lay on the table. His wife pretended not to see him rub the back of his hand across his eyes, nor the smear in the coal-dust on his black face.

'Yes, an' that other lad 'ud 'a done as much if they hadna ha' killed 'im,' he said quietly.

The thought of William went through Mrs Morel like a cold blade. It left her feeling she was tired, and wanted rest.

Paul was invited to dinner at Mr Jordan's. Afterwards he said, 'Mother, I want an evening suit.'

'Yes, I was afraid you would,' she said. She was glad. There was a moment or two of silence. 'There's that one of William's,' she continued, 'that I know cost four pounds ten and which he'd only worn three times.'

'Should you like me to wear it, mother?' he asked.

'Yes. I think it would fit you – at least the coat. The trousers would want shortening.'

He went upstairs and put on the coat and vest. Coming down, he looked strange in a flannel collar and a flannel shirt-front, with an evening coat and vest. It was rather large.

'The tailor can make it right,' she said, smoothing her hand over his shoulder. 'It's beautiful stuff. I never could find in my heart to let your father wear the trousers, and very glad I am now.'

And as she smoothed her hand over the silk collar she thought of her eldest son. But this son was living enough inside the clothes. She passed her hand down his back to feel him. He was alive and hers. The other was dead.

He went out to dinner several times in his evening suit that had been William's. Each time his mother's heart was firm with pride and joy. He was started now. The studs she and the children had bought for William were in his shirt-front; he wore one of William's dress shirts. But he had an elegant figure. His face was rough, but warm-looking and rather pleasing. He did not look particularly a gentleman, but she thought he looked quite a man.

He told her everything that took place, everything that was said. It was as if she had been there. And he was dying to introduce her to these new friends who had dinner at seven-thirty in the evening.

'Go along with you!' she said. 'What do they want to know me for?'

'They do!' he cried indignantly. 'If they want to know me – and they say they do – then they want to know you, because you are quite as clever as I am.'

'Go along with you, child!' she laughed.

But she began to spare her hands. They, too, were work-gnarled now. The skin was shiny with so much hot water, the knuckles rather swollen. But she began to be careful to keep them out of soda. She regretted what they had been – so small and exquisite. And when Annie insisted on her having more stylish blouses to suit her age, she submitted. She even went so far as to allow a black velvet bow to be placed on her hair. Then she sniffed in her sarcastic manner, and was sure she looked a sight. But she looked a lady, Paul declared, as much as Mrs Major Moreton, and far, far nicer. The family was coming on. Only Morel remained unchanged, or rather, lapsed slowly.

Paul and his mother now had long discussions about life. Religion was fading into the background. He had shovelled away all the beliefs that would hamper him, had cleared the ground, and come more or less to the bedrock of belief that one should feel inside oneself for right and wrong, and should have the patience to gradually realise one's God. Now life interested him more.

'You know,' he said to his mother, 'I don't want to belong to the well-to-do middle class. I like my common people best. I belong to the common people.'

'But if anyone else said so, my son, wouldn't you be in a tear. *You* know you consider yourself equal to any gentleman.'

'In myself,' he answered, 'not in my class or my education or my manners. But in myself I am.'

'Very well, then. Then why talk about the common people?'

'Because – the difference between people isn't in their class, but in themselves. Only from the middle classes one gets ideas, and from the common people – life itself, warmth. You feel their hates and loves.'

'It's all very well, my boy. But, then, why don't you go and talk to your father's pals?'

'But they're rather different.'

'Not at all. They're the common people. After all, whom do you mix with now – among the common people? Those that exchange ideas, like the middle classes. The rest don't interest you.'

'But – there's the life –'

'I don't believe there's a jot more life from Miriam than you could get from any educated girl – say Miss Moreton. It is *you* who are snobbish about class.'

She frankly *wanted* him to climb into the middle classes, a thing not very difficult, she knew. And she wanted him in the end to marry a lady.

Now she began to combat him in his restless fretting. He still kept up his connection with Miriam, could neither break free nor go the whole length of engagement. And this indecision seemed to bleed him of his energy. Moreover, his mother suspected him of an unrecognised leaning towards Clara, and, since the latter was a married woman, she wished he would fall in love with one of the girls in a better station of life. But he was stupid, and would refuse to love or even to admire a girl much, just because she was his social superior.

'My boy,' said his mother to him, 'all your cleverness, your breaking away from old things, and taking life in your own hands, doesn't seem to bring you much happiness.'

'What is happiness!' he cried. 'It's nothing to me! How *am* I to be happy?'

The plump question disturbed her.

'That's for you to judge, my lad. But if you could meet some *good* woman who would *make* you happy – and you began to think of settling your life – when you have the means – so that you could work without all this fretting – it would be much better for you.'

He frowned. His mother caught him on the raw of his wound of Miriam. He pushed the tumbled hair off his forehead, his eyes full of pain and fire.

'You mean easy, mother,' he cried. 'That's a woman's whole doctrine for life – ease of soul and physical comfort. And I do despise it.'

'Oh, do you!' replied his mother. 'And do you call yours a divine discontent?'

'Yes. I don't care about its divinity. But damn your happiness! So long as life's full, it doesn't matter whether it's happy or not. I'm afraid your happiness would bore me.'

'You never give it a chance,' she said. Then suddenly all her passion of grief over him broke out. 'But it does matter!' she cried. 'And you *ought* to be happy, you ought to try to be happy, to live to be happy. How could I bear to think your life wouldn't be a happy one!'

'Your own's been bad enough, mater, but it hasn't left you so much worse off than the folk who've been happier. I reckon you've done well. And I am the same. Aren't I well enough off?'

'You're not, my son. Battle – battle – and suffer. It's about all you do, as far as I can see.'

'But why not, my dear? I tell you it's the best – '

'It isn't. And one *ought* to be happy, one *ought*.'

By this time Mrs Morel was trembling violently. Struggles of this kind often took place between her and her son, when she seemed to fight for his very life against his own will to die. He took her in his arms. She was ill and pitiful.

'Never mind, Little,' he murmured. 'So long as you don't feel life's paltry and a miserable business, the rest doesn't matter, happiness or unhappiness.'

She pressed him to her.

'But I want you to be happy,' she said pathetically.

'Eh, my dear – say rather you want me to live.'

Mrs Morel felt as if her heart would break for him. At this rate she knew he would not live. He had that poignant carelessness about himself, his own suffering, his own life, which is a form of slow suicide. It almost broke her heart. With all the passion of her strong nature she hated Miriam for having in this subtle way undermined his joy. It did not matter to her that Miriam could not help it. Miriam did it, and she hated her.

She wished so much he would fall in love with a girl equal to be his mate – educated and strong. But he would not look at anybody above him in station. He seemed to like Mrs Dawes. At any rate that feeling was wholesome. His mother prayed and prayed for him, that he might not be wasted. That was all her prayer – not for his soul or his righteousness, but that he might not be wasted. And while he slept, for hours and hours she thought and prayed for him.

He drifted away from Miriam imperceptibly, without knowing he was going. Arthur only left the army to be married. The baby was born six months after his wedding. Mrs Morel got him a job under the firm again, at twenty-one shillings a week. She furnished for him, with the help of Beatrice's mother, a little cottage of two rooms. He was caught now. It did not matter how he kicked and struggled, he was fast. For a time he chafed, was irritable with his young wife, who loved him; he went almost distracted when the baby, which was delicate, cried or gave trouble. He grumbled for hours to his mother. She only said, 'Well, my lad, you did it yourself, now you must make the best of it.' And then the grit came out in him. He buckled to work, undertook his responsibilities, acknowledged that he belonged to his wife and child, and did make a good best of it. He had never been very closely inbound into the family. Now he was gone altogether.

The months went slowly along. Paul had more or less got into connection with the Socialist, Suffragette, Unitarian people in Nottingham, owing to his acquaintance with Clara. One day a friend of his and of Clara's, in Bestwood, asked him to take a message to Mrs Dawes. He went in the evening across Sneinton Market to Bluebell Hill. He found the house in a mean little street paved with granite cobbles and having causeways of dark blue, grooved bricks. The front door went up a step from off this rough pavement, where the feet of the passers-by rasped and clattered. The brown paint on the door was so old that the naked wood showed between the rents. He stood on the street below and knocked. There came a heavy footstep; a large, stout woman of about sixty towered above him. He looked up at her from the pavement. She had a rather severe face.

She admitted him into the parlour, which opened on to the street. It was a small, stuffy, defunct room, of mahogany, and deathly enlargements of photographs of departed people done in carbon. Mrs Radford left him. She was stately, almost martial. In a moment Clara appeared. She flushed deeply, and he was covered with confusion. It seemed as if she did not like being discovered in her home circumstances.

'I thought it couldn't be your voice,' she said.

But she might as well be hung for a sheep as for a lamb. She invited him out of the mausoleum of a parlour into the kitchen.

That was a little, darkish room too, but it was smothered in white lace. The mother had seated herself again by the cupboard, and was drawing thread from a vast web of lace. A clump of fluff and ravelled cotton was at her right hand, a heap of three-quarter-inch lace lay on her left, whilst in front of her was the mountain of the lace web, piling the hearthrug. Threads of curly cotton, pulled out from between the lengths of lace, strewed over the fender and the fireplace. Paul dared not go forward, for fear of treading on piles of white stuff.

On the table was a jenny for carding the lace. There was a pack of brown cardboard squares, a pack of cards of lace, a little box of pins, and on the sofa lay a heap of drawn lace.

The room was all lace, and it was so dark and warm that the white, snowy stuff seemed the more distinct.

'If you're coming in you won't have to mind the work,' said Mrs Radford. 'I know we're about blocked up. But sit you down.'

Clara, much embarrassed, gave him a chair against the wall opposite the white heaps. Then she herself took her place on the sofa, shamedly.

'Will you drink a bottle of stout?' Mrs Radford asked. 'Clara, get him a bottle of stout.'

He protested, but Mrs Radford insisted.

'You look as if you could do with it,' she said. 'Haven't you never any more colour than that?'

'It's only a thick skin I've got that doesn't show the blood through,' he answered.

Clara, ashamed and chagrined, brought him a bottle of stout and a glass. He poured out some of the black stuff.

'Well,' he said, lifting the glass, 'here's health!'

'And thank you,' said Mrs Radford.

He took a drink of stout.

'And light yourself a cigarette, so long as you don't set the house on fire,' said Mrs Radford.

'Thank you,' he replied.

'Nay, you needn't thank me,' she answered. 'I s'll be glad to smell a bit of smoke in th' 'ouse again. A house o' women is as dead as a house wi' no fire, to my thinkin'. I'm not a spider as likes a corner to myself. I like a man about, if he's only something to snap at.'

Clara began to work. Her jenny spun with a subdued buzz; the white lace hopped from between her fingers on to the card. It was filled; she snipped off the length, and pinned the end down to the banded lace. Then she put a new card in her jenny. Paul watched her. She sat square and magnificent. Her throat and arms were bare. The blood still mantled below her ears; she bent her head in shame of her humility. Her face was set on her work. Her arms were creamy and full of life beside the white lace; her large, well-kept hands worked with a balanced movement, as if nothing would hurry them. He, not knowing, watched her all the time. He saw the arch of her neck from the shoulder, as she bent her head; he saw the coil of dun hair; he watched her moving, gleaming arms.

'I've heard a bit about you from Clara,' continued the mother. 'You're in Jordan's, aren't you?' She drew her lace unceasing.

'Yes.'

'Ay, well, and I can remember when Thomas Jordan used to ask *me* for one of my toffies.'

'Did he?' laughed Paul. 'And did he get it?'

'Sometimes he did, sometimes he didn't – which was latterly. For he's the sort that takes all and gives naught, he is or used to be.'

'I think he's very decent,' said Paul.

'Yes; well, I'm glad to hear it.'

Mrs Radford looked across at him steadily. There was something determined about her that he liked. Her face was falling loose, but her eyes were calm, and there was something strong in her that made it seem she was not old; merely her wrinkles and loose cheeks were an anachronism. She had the strength and sang-froid of a woman in the prime of life. She continued drawing the lace with slow, dignified movements. The big web came up inevitably over her apron; the length of lace fell away at her side. Her arms were finely shapen, but glossy and yellow as old ivory. They had not the peculiar dull gleam that made Clara's so fascinating to him.

'And you've been going with Miriam Leivers?' the mother asked him.

'Well – ' he answered.

'Yes, she's a nice girl,' she continued. 'She's very nice, but she's a bit too much above this world to suit my fancy.'

'She is a bit like that,' he agreed.

'She'll never be satisfied till she's got wings and can fly over everybody's head, she won't,' she said.

Clara broke in, and he told her his message. She spoke humbly to him. He had surprised her in her drudgery. To have her humble made him feel as if he were lifting his head in expectation.

'Do you like jennying?' he asked.

'What can a woman do!' she replied bitterly.

'Is it sweated?'

'More or less. Isn't *all* woman's work? That's another trick the men have played, since we force ourselves into the labour market.'

'Now then, you shut up about the men,' said her mother. 'If the women wasn't fools, the men wouldn't be bad uns, that's what I say. No man was ever that bad wi' me but what he got it back again. Not but what they're a lousy lot, there's no denying it.'

'But they're all right really, aren't they?' he asked.

'Well, they're a bit different from women,' she answered.

'Would you care to be back at Jordan's?' he asked Clara.

'I don't think so,' she replied.

'Yes, she would!' cried her mother; 'thank her stars if she could get back. Don't you listen to her. She's for ever on that 'igh horse of hers, an' it's back's that thin an' starved it'll cut her i' two one of these days.'

Clara suffered badly from her mother. Paul felt as if his eyes were coming very wide open. Wasn't he to take Clara's fulminations so seriously, after all?

She spun steadily at her work. He experienced a thrill of joy, thinking she might need his help. She seemed denied and deprived of so much. And her arm moved mechanically, that should never have been subdued to a mechanism, and her head was bowed to the lace, that never should have been bowed. She seemed to be stranded there among the refuse that life has thrown away doing her jennying. It was a bitter thing to her to be put aside by life, as if it had no use for her. No wonder she protested.

She came with him to the door. He stood below in the mean street, looking up at her. So fine she was in her stature and her bearing, she reminded him of Juno dethroned. As she stood in the doorway, she winced from the street, from her surroundings.

'And you will go with Mrs Hodgkisson to Hucknall?'

He was talking quite meaninglessly, only watching her. Her grey eyes at last met his. They looked dumb with humiliation, pleading with a kind of captive misery. He was shaken and at a loss. He had thought her high and mighty.

When he left her, he wanted to run. He went to the station in a sort of dream, and was at home without realising he had moved out of her street.

He had an idea that Susan, the overseer of the spiral girls, was about to be married. He asked her the next day.

'I say, Susan, I heard a whisper of your getting married. What about it?'

Susan flushed red.

'Who's been talking to you?' she replied.

'Nobody. I merely heard a whisper that you *were* thinking – '

'Well, I am, though you needn't tell anybody. What's more, I wish I wasn't!'

'Nay, Susan, you won't make me believe that.'

'Shan't I? You *can* believe it, though. I'd rather stop here a thousand times.'

Paul was perturbed.

'Why, Susan?'

The girl's colour was high, and her eyes flashed.

'That's why!'

'And must you?'

For answer, she looked at him. There was about him a candour and gentleness which made the women trust him. He understood.

'Ah, I'm sorry,' he said.

Tears came to her eyes.

'But you'll see it'll turn out all right. You'll make the best of it,' he continued rather wistfully.

'There's nothing else for it.'

'Yea, there's making the worst of it. Try and make it all right.'

He soon made occasion to call again on Clara.

'Would you,' he said, 'care to come back to Jordan's?'

She put down her work, laid her beautiful arms on the table, and looked at him for some moments without answering. Gradually the flush mounted her cheek.

'Why?' she asked.

Paul felt rather awkward.

'Well, because Susan is thinking of leaving,' he said.

Clara went on with her jennying. The white lace leaped in little jumps and bounds on to the card. He waited for her. Without raising her head, she said at last, in a peculiar low voice, 'Have you said anything about it?'

'Except to you, not a word.'

There was again a long silence.

'I will apply when the advertisement is out,' she said.

'You will apply before that. I will let you know exactly when.'

She went on spinning her little machine, and did not contradict him.

Clara came to Jordan's. Some of the older hands, Fanny among them, remembered her earlier rule, and cordially disliked the memory. Clara had always been 'ikey', reserved, and superior. She had never mixed with the girls as one of themselves. If she had occasion to find fault, she did it coolly and with perfect politeness, which the defaulter felt to be a bigger insult than crossness. Towards Fanny, the poor, overstrung hunchback, Clara was unfailingly compassionate and gentle, as a result of which Fanny shed more bitter tears than ever the rough tongues of the other overseers had caused her.

There was something in Clara that Paul disliked, and much that piqued him. If she were about, he always watched her strong throat or her neck, upon which the blonde hair grew low and fluffy. There was a fine down, almost invisible, upon the skin of her face and arms, and when once he had perceived it, he saw it always.

When he was at his work, painting in the afternoon, she would come and stand near to him, perfectly motionless. Then he felt her, though she neither spoke nor touched him. Although she stood a yard away he felt as if he were in contact with her. Then he could paint no more. He flung down the brushes, and turned to talk to her.

Sometimes she praised his work; sometimes she was critical and cold.

'You are affected in that piece,' she would say; and, as there was an element of truth in her condemnation, his blood boiled with anger.

Again: 'What of this?' he would ask enthusiastically.

'H'm!' She made a small doubtful sound. 'It doesn't interest me much.'

'Because you don't understand it,' he retorted.

'Then why ask me about it?'

'Because I thought you would understand.'

She would shrug her shoulders in scorn of his work. She maddened him. He was furious. Then he abused her, and went into passionate exposition of his stuff. This amused and stimulated her. But she never owned that she had been wrong.

During the ten years that she had belonged to the women's movement she had acquired a fair amount of education, and having had some of Miriam's passion to be instructed, had taught herself French, and could read in that language with a struggle. She considered herself as a woman apart, and particularly apart, from her class. The girls in the spiral department were all of good homes. It was a small, special industry, and had a certain distinction. There was an air of refinement in both rooms. But Clara was aloof also from her fellow-workers.

None of these things, however, did she reveal to Paul. She was not the one to give herself away. There was a sense of mystery about her. She was so reserved, he felt she had much to reserve. Her history was open on the surface, but its inner meaning was hidden from everybody. It was exciting. And then sometimes he caught her looking at him from under her brows with an almost furtive, sullen scrutiny which made him move quickly. Often she met his eyes. But then her own were, as it were, covered over, revealing nothing. She gave him a little, lenient smile. She was to him extraordinarily provocative, because of the knowledge she seemed to possess, and gathered fruit of experience he could not attain.

One day he picked up a copy of *Lettres de mon Moulin* from her workbench.

'You read French, do you?' he cried.

Clara glanced round negligently. She was making an elastic stocking of heliotrope silk, turning the spiral machine with slow, balanced regularity, occasionally bending down to see her work or to adjust the needles; then her magnificent neck, with its down and fine pencils of hair, shone white against the lavender, lustrous silk. She turned a few more rounds, and stopped.

'What did you say?' she asked, smiling sweetly.

Paul's eyes glittered at her insolent indifference to him.

'I did not know you read French,' he said, very polite.

'Did you not?' she replied, with a faint, sarcastic smile.

'Rotten swank!' he said, but scarcely loud enough to be heard.

He shut his mouth angrily as he watched her. She seemed to scorn the work she mechanically produced; yet the hose she made were as nearly perfect as possible.

'You don't like spiral work,' he said.

'Oh, well, all work is work,' she answered, as if she knew all about it.

He marvelled at her coldness. He had to do everything hotly. She must be something special.

'What would you prefer to do?' he asked.

She laughed at him indulgently, as she said, 'There is so little likelihood of my ever being given a choice, that I haven't wasted time considering.'

'Pah!' he said, contemptuous on his side now. 'You only say that because you're too proud to own up what you want and can't get.'

'You know me very well,' she replied coldly.

'I know you think you're terrific great shakes, and that you live under the eternal insult of working in a factory.'

He was very angry and very rude. She merely turned away from him in disdain. He walked whistling down the room, flirted and laughed with Hilda.

Later on he said to himself, 'What was I so impudent to Clara for?' He was rather annoyed with himself, at the same time glad. 'Serve her right; she stinks with silent pride,' he said to himself angrily.

In the afternoon he came down. There was a certain weight on his heart which he wanted to remove. He thought to do it by offering her chocolates.

'Have one?' he said. 'I bought a handful to sweeten me up.'

To his great relief, she accepted. He sat on the workbench beside her machine, twisting a piece of silk round his finger. She loved him for his quick, unexpected movements, like a young animal. His feet swung as he pondered. The sweets lay strewn on the bench. She bent over her machine, grinding rhythmically, then stooping to see the stocking that hung beneath, pulled down by the weight. He watched the handsome crouching of her back, and the apron-strings curling on the floor.

'There is always about you,' he said, 'a sort of waiting. Whatever I see you doing you're not really there: you are waiting – like Penelope when she did her weaving.' He could not help a spurt of wickedness. 'I'll call you Penelope,' he said.

'Would it make any difference?' she said, carefully removing one of her needles.

'That doesn't matter, so long as it pleases me. Here, I say you seem to forget I'm your boss. It just occurs to me.'

'And what does that mean?' she asked coolly.

'It means I've got a right to boss you.'

'Is there anything you want to complain about?'

'Oh, I say, you needn't be nasty,' he said angrily.

'I don't know what you want,' she said, continuing her task.

'I want you to treat me nicely and respectfully.'

'Call you "sir", perhaps?' she asked quietly.

'Yes, call me "sir". I should love it.'

'Then I wish you would go upstairs, sir.'

His mouth closed, and a frown came on his face. He jumped suddenly down.

'You're too blessed superior for anything,' he said.

And he went away to the other girls. He felt he was being angrier than he had any need to be. In fact, he doubted slightly that he was showing off. But if he were, then he would. Clara heard him laughing, in a way she hated, with the girls down the next room.

When at evening he went through the department after the girls had gone, he saw his chocolates lying untouched in front of Clara's machine. He left them. In the morning they were still there, and Clara was at work. Later on Minnie, a little brunette they called Pussy, called to him, 'Hey, haven't you got a chocolate for anybody?'

'Sorry, Pussy,' he replied. 'I meant to have offered them; then I went and forgot 'em.'

'I think you did,' she answered.

'I'll bring you some this afternoon. You don't want them after they've been lying about, do you?'

'Oh, I'm not particular,' smiled Pussy.

'Oh no,' he said. 'They'll be dusty.'

He went up to Clara's bench.

'Sorry I left these things littering about,' he said.

She flushed scarlet. He gathered them together in his fist.

'They'll be dirty now,' he said. 'You should have taken them. I wonder why you didn't. I meant to have told you I wanted you to.'

He flung them out of the window into the yard below. He just glanced at her. She winced from his eyes.

In the afternoon he brought another packet.

'Will you take some?' he said, offering them first to Clara. 'These are fresh.'

She accepted one, and put it on to the bench.

'Oh, take several – for luck,' he said.

She took a couple more, and put them on the bench also. Then she turned in confusion to her work. He went on up the room.

'Here you are, Pussy,' he said. 'Don't be greedy!'

'Are they all for her?' cried the others, rushing up.

'Of course they're not,' he said.

The girls clamoured round. Pussy drew back from her mates.

'Come out!' she cried. 'I can have first pick, can't I, Paul?'

'Be nice with 'em,' he said, and went away.

'You are a dear,' the girls cried.

'Tenpence,' he answered.

He went past Clara without speaking. She felt the three chocolate creams would burn her if she touched them. It needed all her courage to slip them into the pocket of her apron.

The girls loved him and were afraid of him. He was so nice while he was nice, but if he were offended, so distant, treating them as if they scarcely existed, or not more than the bobbins of thread. And then, if they were impudent, he said quietly: 'Do you mind going on with your work,' and stood and watched.

When he celebrated his twenty-third birthday, the house was in trouble. Arthur was just going to be married. His mother was not well. His father, getting an old man, and lame from his accidents, was given a paltry, poor job. Miriam was an eternal reproach. He felt he owed himself to her, yet could not give himself. The house, moreover, needed his support. He was pulled in all directions. He was not glad it was his birthday. It made him bitter.

He got to work at eight o'clock. Most of the clerks had not turned up. The girls were not due till 8.30. As he was changing his coat, he heard a voice behind him say, 'Paul, Paul, I want you.'

It was Fanny, the hunchback, standing at the top of her stairs, her face radiant with a secret. Paul looked at her in astonishment.

'I want you,' she said.

He stood, at a loss.

'Come on,' she coaxed. 'Come before you begin on the letters.'

He went down the half-dozen steps into her dry, narrow, 'finishing-off' room. Fanny walked before him; her black bodice was short – the waist was under her armpits – and her green-black cashmere skirt seemed very long, as she strode with big strides before the young man, himself so graceful. She went to her seat at the narrow end of the room, where the window opened on to chimney-pots. Paul watched her thin hands and her flat red wrists as she excitedly twitched her white apron, which was spread on the bench in front of her. She hesitated.

'You didn't think we'd forgot you?' she asked, reproachful.

'Why?' he asked. He had forgotten his birthday himself.

' "Why," he says! "Why!" Why, look here!' She pointed to the calendar, and he saw, surrounding the big black number '21', hundreds of little crosses in blacklead.

'Oh, kisses for my birthday,' he laughed. 'How did you know?'

'Yes, you want to know, don't you?' Fanny mocked, hugely delighted. 'There's one from everybody – except Lady Clara – and two from some. But I shan't tell you how many *I* put.'

'Oh, I know, you're spooney,' he said.

'There you *are* mistaken!' she cried indignant. 'I could never be so soft.' Her voice was strong and contralto.

'You always pretend to be such a hard-hearted hussy,' he laughed. 'And you know you're as sentimental – '

'I'd rather be called sentimental than frozen meat,' Fanny blurted. Paul knew she referred to Clara, and he smiled.

'Do you say such nasty things about me?' he laughed.

'No, my duck,' the hunchback woman answered, lavishly tender. She was thirty-nine. 'No, my duck, because you don't think yourself a fine figure in marble and us nothing but dirt. I'm as good as you, aren't I, Paul?' and the question delighted her.

'Why, we're not better than one another, are we?' he replied.

'But I'm as good as you, aren't I, Paul?' she persisted daringly.

'Of course you are. If it comes to goodness, you're better.'

She was rather afraid of the situation. She might get hysterical.

'I thought I'd get here before the others – won't they say I'm deep! Now shut your eyes – ' she said.

'And open your mouth, and see what God sends you,' he continued, suiting action to words, and expecting a piece of chocolate. He heard the rustle of the apron, and a faint clink of metal. 'I'm going to look,' he said.

He opened his eyes. Fanny, her long cheeks flushed, her blue eyes shining, was gazing at him. There was a little bundle of paint-tubes on the bench before him. He turned pale.

'No, Fanny,' he said quickly.

'From us all,' she answered hastily.

'No, but – '

'Are they the right sort?' she asked, rocking herself with delight.

'Jove! they're the best in the catalogue.'

'But they're the right sorts?' she cried.

'They're off the little list I'd made to get when my ship came in.' He bit his lip.

Fanny was overcome with emotion. She must turn the conversation.

'They was all on thorns to do it; they all paid their shares, all except the Queen of Sheba.'

The Queen of Sheba was Clara.

'And wouldn't she join?' Paul asked.

'She didn't get the chance; we never told her; we wasn't going to have *her* bossing *this* show. We didn't *want* her to join.'

Paul laughed at the woman. He was much moved. At last he must go. She was very close to him. Suddenly she flung her arms round his neck and kissed him vehemently.

'I can give you a kiss today,' she said apologetically. 'You've looked so white, it's made my heart ache.'

Paul kissed her, and left her. Her arms were so pitifully thin that his heart ached also.

That day he met Clara as he ran downstairs to wash his hands at dinner-time.

'You have stayed to dinner!' he exclaimed. It was unusual for her.

'Yes; and I seem to have dined on old surgical-appliance stock. I *must* go out now, or I shall feel stale india-rubber right through.'

She lingered. He instantly caught at her wish.

'You are going anywhere?' he asked.

They went together up to the Castle. Outdoors she dressed very plainly, down to ugliness; indoors she always looked nice. She walked with hesitating steps alongside Paul, bowing and turning away from him. Dowdy in dress, and drooping, she showed to great disadvantage. He could scarcely recognise her strong form, that seemed to slumber with power. She appeared almost insignificant, drowning her stature in her stoop, as she shrank from the public gaze.

The Castle grounds were very green and fresh. Climbing the precipitous ascent, he laughed and chattered, but she was silent, seeming to brood over something. There was scarcely time to go inside the squat, square building that crowns the bluff of rock. They leaned upon the wall where the cliff runs sheer down to the Park. Below them, in their holes in the sandstone, pigeons preened themselves and cooed softly. Away down upon the boulevard at the foot of the rock, tiny trees stood in their own pools of shadow, and tiny people went scurrying about in almost ludicrous importance.

'You feel as if you could scoop up the folk like tadpoles, and have a handful of them,' he said.

She laughed, answering, 'Yes; it is not necessary to get far off in order to see us proportionately. The trees are much more significant.'

'Bulk only,' he said.

She laughed cynically.

Away beyond the boulevard the thin stripes of the metals showed upon the railway track, whose margin was crowded with little stacks of timber, beside which smoking toy engines fussed. Then the silver string of the canal lay at random among the black heaps. Beyond, the dwellings, very dense on the river flat, looked like black, poisonous herbage, in thick rows and crowded beds, stretching right away, broken now and then by taller plants, right to where the river glistened in a hieroglyph across the country. The steep scarp cliffs across the river looked puny. Great stretches of country darkened with trees and faintly brightened with cornland spread towards the haze, where the hills rose blue beyond grey.

'It is comforting,' said Mrs Dawes, 'to think the town goes no farther. It is only a *little* sore upon the country yet.'

'A little scab,' Paul said.

She shivered. She loathed the town. Looking drearily across at the country which was forbidden her, her impassive face, pale and hostile, she reminded Paul of one of the bitter, remorseful angels.

'But the town's all right,' he said, 'it's only temporary. This is the crude, clumsy makeshift we've practised on, till we find out what the idea is. The town will come all right.'

The pigeons in the pockets of rock, among the perched bushes, cooed comfortably. To the left the large church of St Mary rose into space, to keep close company with the Castle, above the heaped rubble of the town. Mrs Dawes smiled brightly as she looked across the country.

'I feel better,' she said.

'Thank you,' he replied. 'Great compliment!'

'Oh, my brother!' she laughed.

'H'm! that's snatching back with the left hand what you gave with the right, and no mistake,' he said.

She laughed in amusement at him.

'But what was the matter with you?' he asked. 'I know you were brooding something special. I can see the stamp of it on your face yet.'

'I think I will not tell you,' she said.

'All right, hug it,' he answered.

She flushed and bit her lip.

'No,' she said, 'it was the girls.'

'What about 'em?' Paul asked.

'They have been plotting something for a week now, and today they seem particularly full of it. All alike; they insult me with their secrecy.'

'Do they?' he asked in concern.

'I should not mind,' she went on, in the metallic, angry tone, 'if they did not thrust it into my face – the fact that they have a secret.'

'Just like women,' said he.

'It is hateful, their mean gloating,' she said intensely.

Paul was silent. He knew what the girls gloated over. He was sorry to be the cause of this new dissension.

'They can have all the secrets in the world,' she went on, brooding bitterly; 'but they might refrain from glorying in them, and making me feel more out of it than ever. It is – it is almost unbearable.'

Paul thought for a few minutes. He was much perturbed.

'I will tell you what it's all about,' he said, pale and nervous. 'It's my birthday, and they've bought me a fine lot of paints, all the girls. They're jealous of you' – he felt her stiffen coldly at the word 'jealous' – 'merely because I sometimes bring you a book,' he added slowly. 'But, you see, it's only a trifle. Don't bother about it, will you – because' – he laughed quickly – 'well, what would they say if they saw us here now, in spite of their victory?'

She was angry with him for his clumsy reference to their present intimacy. It was almost insolent of him. Yet he was so quiet, she forgave him, although it cost her an effort.

Their two hands lay on the rough stone parapet of the Castle wall. He had inherited from his mother a fineness of mould, so that his hands were small and vigorous. Hers were large, to match her large limbs, but white and powerful-looking. As Paul looked at them he knew her. 'She is wanting somebody to take her hands – for all she is so contemptuous of us,' he said to himself. And she saw nothing but his two hands, so warm and alive, which seemed to live for her. He was brooding now, staring out over the country from under sullen brows. The little, interesting diversity of shapes had vanished from the scene; all that remained was a vast, dark matrix of sorrow and tragedy, the same in all the houses and the river-flats and the people and the birds, they were only shapen differently. And now that the forms seemed to have melted away, there remained the mass from which all the landscape was composed, a dark mass of struggle and pain. The factory, the girls, his mother, the large, uplifted church, the thicket of the town, merged into one atmosphere – dark, brooding, and sorrowful, every bit.

'Is that two o'clock striking?' Mrs Dawes said in surprise.

Paul started, and everything sprang into form, regained its individuality, its forgetfulness, and its cheerfulness.

They hurried back to work.

When he was in the rush of preparing for the night's post, examining the work up from Fanny's room, which smelt of ironing, the evening postman came in.

' "Mr Paul Morel",' he said, smiling, handing Paul a package. 'A lady's handwriting! Don't let the girls see it.'

The postman, himself a favourite, was pleased to make fun of the girls' affection for Paul.

It was a volume of verse with a brief note: 'You will allow me to send you this, and so spare me my isolation. I also sympathise and wish you well. – C. D.' Paul flushed hot.

'Good Lord! Mrs Dawes. She can't afford it. Good Lord, who ever'd have thought it!'

He was suddenly intensely moved. He was filled with the warmth of her. In the glow he could almost feel her as if she were present – her arms, her shoulders, her bosom, see them, feel them, almost contain them.

This move on the part of Clara brought them into closer intimacy. The other girls noticed that when Paul met Mrs Dawes his eyes lifted and gave that peculiar bright greeting which they could interpret. Knowing he was unaware, Clara made no sign, save that occasionally she turned aside her face from him when he came upon her.

They walked out together very often at dinner-time; it was quite open, quite frank. Everybody seemed to feel that he was quite unaware of the state of his own feeling, and that nothing was wrong. He talked to her now with some of the old fervour with which he had talked to Miriam, but he cared less about the talk; he did not bother about his conclusions.

One day in October they went out to Lambley for tea. Suddenly they came to a halt on top of the hill. He climbed and sat on a gate, she sat on the stile. The afternoon was perfectly still, with a dim haze, and yellow sheaves glowing through. They were quiet.

'How old were you when you married?' he asked quietly.

'Twenty-two.'

Her voice was subdued, almost submissive. She would tell him now.

'It is eight years ago?'

'Yes.'

'And when did you leave him?'

'Three years ago.'

'Five years! Did you love him when you married him?'

She was silent for some time; then she said slowly, 'I thought I did – more or less. I didn't think much about it. And he wanted me. I was very prudish then.'

'And you sort of walked into it without thinking?'

'Yes. I seemed to have been asleep nearly all my life.'

'Somnambule? But – when did you wake up?'

'I don't know that I ever did, or ever have – since I was a child.'

'You went to sleep as you grew to be a woman? How queer! And he didn't wake you?'

'No; he never got there,' she replied, in a monotone.

The brown birds dashed over the hedges where the rose-hips stood naked and scarlet.

'Got where?' he asked.

'At me. He never really mattered to me.'

The afternoon was so gently warm and dim. Red roofs of the cottages burned among the blue haze. He loved the day. He could feel, but he could not understand, what Clara was saying.

'But why did you leave him? Was he horrid to you?'

She shuddered lightly.

'He – he sort of degraded me. He wanted to bully me because he hadn't got me. And then I felt as if I wanted to run, as if I was fastened and bound up. And he seemed dirty.'

'I see.'

He did not at all see.

'And was he always dirty?' he asked.

'A bit,' she replied slowly. 'And then he seemed as if he couldn't get *at* me, really. And then he got brutal – he *was* brutal!'

'And why did you leave him finally?'

'Because – because he was unfaithful to me – '

They were both silent for some time. Her hand lay on the gatepost as she balanced. He put his own over it. His heart beat quickly.

'But did you – were you ever – did you ever give him a chance?'

'Chance? How?'

'To come near to you.'

'I married him – and I was willing – '

They both strove to keep their voices steady.

'I believe he loves you,' he said.

'It looks like it,' she replied.

He wanted to take his hand away, and could not. She saved him by removing her own. After a silence, he began again, 'Did you leave him out of count all along?'

'He left me,' she said.

'And I suppose he couldn't *make* himself mean everything to you?'

'He tried to bully me into it.'

But the conversation had got them both out of their depth. Suddenly Paul jumped down.

'Come on,' he said. 'Let's go and get some tea.'

They found a cottage, where they sat in the cold parlour. She poured out his tea. She was very quiet. He felt she had withdrawn again from him. After tea, she stared broodingly into her teacup, twisting her wedding ring all the time. In her abstraction she took the ring off her finger, stood it up, and spun it upon the table. The gold became a diaphanous, glittering globe. It fell, and the ring was quivering upon the table. She spun it again and again. Paul watched, fascinated.

But she was a married woman, and he believed in simple friendship. And he considered that he was perfectly honourable with regard to her. It was only a friendship between man and woman, such as any civilised persons might have.

He was like so many young men of his own age. Sex had become so complicated in him that he would have denied that he ever could want Clara or Miriam or any woman whom he *knew*. Sex desire was a sort of detached thing, that did not belong to a woman. He loved Miriam with his soul. He grew warm at the thought of Clara, he battled with her. He knew the curves of her breast and shoulders as if they had been moulded inside him; and yet he did not positively desire her. He would have denied it for ever. He believed himself really bound to Miriam. If ever he should marry, sometime in the far future, it would be his duty to marry Miriam. That he gave Clara to understand, and she said nothing, but left him to his courses. He came to her, Mrs Dawes, whenever he could 'Then he wrote frequently to Miriam, and visited the girl occasionally. So he went on through the winter; but he seemed not so fretted. His mother was easier about him. She thought he was getting away from Miriam.

Miriam knew now how strong was the attraction of Clara for him; but still she was certain that the best in him would triumph. His feeling for Mrs Dawes – who, moreover, was a married woman – was shallow and temporal, compared with his love for herself. He would come back to her, she was sure with some of his young freshness gone, perhaps, but cured of his desire for the lesser things which other women than herself could give him. She could bear all if he were inwardly true to her and must come back.

He saw none of the anomaly of his position. Miriam was his old friend, lover, and she belonged to Bestwood and home and his youth. Clara was a newer friend, and she belonged to Nottingham, to life, to the world. It seemed to him quite plain.

Mrs Dawes and he had many periods of coolness, when they saw little of each other; but they always came together again.

'Were you horrid with Baxter Dawes?' he asked her. It was a thing that seemed to trouble him.

'In what way?'

'Oh, I don't know. But weren't you horrid with him? Didn't you do something that knocked him to pieces?'

'What, pray?'

'Making him feel as if he were nothing – *I* know,' Paul declared.

'You are so clever, my friend,' she said coolly.

The conversation broke off there. But it made her cool with him for some time.

She very rarely saw Miriam now. The friendship between the two women was not broken off, but considerably weakened.

'Will you come into the concert on Sunday afternoon?' Clara asked him just after Christmas.

'I promised to go up to Willey Farm,' he replied.

'Oh, very well.'

'You don't mind, do you?' he asked.

'Why should I?' she answered.

Which almost annoyed him.

'You know,' he said, 'Miriam and I have been a lot to each other ever since I was sixteen – that's seven years now.'

'It's a long time,' Clara replied.

'Yes; but somehow she – it doesn't go right – '

'How?' asked Clara.

'She seems to draw me and draw me, and she wouldn't leave a single hair of me free to fall out and blow away – she'd keep it.'

'But you like to be kept.'

'No,' he said, 'I don't. I wish it could be normal, give and take – like me and you. I want a woman to keep me, but not in her pocket.'

'But if you love her, it couldn't be normal, like me and you.'

'Yes; I should love her better then. She sort of wants me so much that I can't give myself.'

'Wants you how?'

'Wants the soul out of my body. I can't help shrinking back from her.'

'And yet you love her!'

'No, I don't love her. I never even kiss her.'

'Why not?' Clara asked.

'I don't know.'

'I suppose you're afraid,' she said.

'I'm not. Something in me shrinks from her like hell – she's so good, when I'm not good.'

'How do you know what she is?'

'I do! I know she wants a sort of soul union.'

'But how do you know what she wants?'

'I've been with her for seven years.'

'And you haven't found out the very first thing about her.'

'What's that?'

'That she doesn't want any of your soul communion. That's your own imagination. She wants you.'

He pondered over this. Perhaps he was wrong.

'But she seems – ' he began.

'You've never tried,' she answered.

CHAPTER 11

The Test on Miriam

With the spring came again the old madness and battle. Now he knew he would have to go to Miriam. But what was his reluctance? He told himself it was only a sort of over-strong virginity in her and him which neither could break through. He might have married her; but his circumstances at home made it difficult, and, moreover, he did not want to marry. Marriage was for life, and because they had become close companions, he and she, he did not see that it should inevitably follow they should be man and wife. He did not feel that he wanted marriage with Miriam. He wished he did. He would have given his head to have felt a joyous desire to marry her and to have her. Then why couldn't he bring it off? There was some obstacle; and what was the obstacle? It lay in the physical bondage. He shrank from the physical contact. But why? With her he felt bound up inside himself. He could not go out to her. Something struggled in him, but he could not get to her. Why? She loved him. Clara said she even wanted him; then why couldn't he go to her, make love to her, kiss her? Why, when she put her arm in his, timidly, as they walked, did he feel he would burst forth in brutality and recoil? He owed himself to her; he wanted to belong to her. Perhaps the recoil and the shrinking from her was love in its first fierce modesty. He had no aversion for her. No, it was the opposite; it was a strong desire battling with a still stronger shyness and virginity. It seemed as if virginity were a positive force, which fought and won in both of them. And with her he felt it so hard to overcome; yet he was nearest to her, and with her alone could he deliberately break through. And he owed himself to her. Then, if they could get things right, they could marry; but he would not marry unless he could feel strong in the joy of it – never. He could not have faced his mother. It seemed to him that to sacrifice himself in a marriage he did not want would be degrading, and would undo all his life, make it a nullity. He would try what he *could* do.

And he had a great tenderness for Miriam. Always, she was sad, dreaming her religion; and he was nearly a religion to her. He could not bear to fail her. It would all come right if they tried.

He looked round. A good many of the nicest men he knew were like himself, bound in by their own virginity, which they could not break out of. They were so sensitive to their women that they would go without them for ever rather than do them a hurt, an injustice. Being the sons of mothers whose husbands had blundered rather brutally through their feminine sanctities, they were themselves too diffident and shy. They could easier deny themselves than incur any reproach from a woman; for a woman was like their mother, and they were full of the sense of their mother. They preferred themselves to suffer the misery of celibacy, rather than risk the other person.

He went back to her. Something in her, when he looked at her, brought the tears almost to his eyes. One day he stood behind her as she sang. Annie was playing a song on the piano. As Miriam sang her mouth seemed hopeless. She sang like a nun singing to heaven. It reminded him so much of the mouth and eyes of one who sings beside a Botticelli Madonna, so spiritual. Again, hot as steel, came up the pain in him. Why must he ask her for the other thing? Why was there his blood battling with her? If only he could have been always gentle, tender with her, breathing with her the atmosphere of reverie and religious dreams, he would give his right hand. It was not fair to hurt her. There seemed an eternal maidenhood about her; and when he thought of her mother, he saw the great brown eyes of a maiden who was nearly scared and shocked out of her virgin maidenhood, but not quite, in spite of her seven children. They had been born almost leaving her out of count, not of her, but upon her. So she could never let them go, because she never had possessed them.

Mrs Morel saw him going again frequently to Miriam, and was astonished.

He said nothing to his mother. He did not explain nor excuse himself. If he came home late, and she reproached him, he frowned and turned on her in an overbearing way, 'I shall come home when I like,' he said; 'I am old enough.'

'Must she keep you till this time?'

'It is I who stay,' he answered.

'And she lets you? But very well,' she said.

And she went to bed, leaving the door unlocked for him; but she lay listening until he came, often long after. It was a great bitterness to her that he had gone back to Miriam. She recognised, however, the uselessness of any further interference. He went to Willey Farm as a man now, not as a youth. She had no right over him. There was a coldness between him and her. He hardly told her anything. Discarded, she waited on him, cooked for him still, and loved to slave for him; but her face closed again like a mask. There was nothing for her to do now but the housework; for all the rest he had gone to Miriam. She could not forgive him. Miriam killed the joy and the warmth in him. He had been such a jolly lad, and full of the warmest affection; now he grew colder, more and more irritable and gloomy. It reminded her of William; but Paul was worse. He did things with more intensity, and more realisation of what he was about. His mother knew how he was suffering for want of a woman, and she saw him going to Miriam. If he had made up his mind, nothing on earth would alter him. Mrs Morel was tired. She began to give up at last; she had finished. She was in the way.

He went on determinedly. He realised more or less what his mother felt. It only hardened his soul. He made himself callow towards her; but it was like being callous to his own health. It undermined him quickly; yet he persisted.

He lay back in the rocking-chair at Willey Farm one evening. He had been talking to Miriam for some weeks, but had not come to the point. Now he said suddenly, 'I am twenty-four, almost.'

She had been brooding. She looked up at him suddenly in surprise.

'Yes. What makes you say it?'

There was something in the charged atmosphere that she dreaded.

'Sir Thomas More says one can marry at twenty-four.'

She laughed quaintly, saying, 'Does it need Sir Thomas More's sanction?'

'No; but one ought to marry about then.'

'Ay,' she answered broodingly; and she waited.

'I can't marry you,' he continued slowly, 'not now, because we've no money, and they depend on me at home.'

She sat half guessing what was coming.

'But I want to marry now –'

'You want to marry?' she repeated.

'A woman – you know what I mean.'

She was silent.

'Now, at last, I must,' he said.

'Ay,' she answered.

'And you love me?'

She laughed bitterly.

'Why are you ashamed of it?' he answered. 'You wouldn't be ashamed before your God, why are you before people?'

'Nay,' she answered deeply, 'I am not ashamed.'

'You are,' he replied bitterly; 'and it's my fault. But you know I can't help being – as I am – don't you?'

'I know you can't help it,' she replied.

'I love you an awful lot – then there is something short.'

'Where?' she answered, looking at him.

'Oh, in me! It is I who ought to be ashamed – like a spiritual cripple. And I am ashamed. It is misery. Why is it?'

'I don't know,' replied Miriam.

'And I don't know,' he repeated. 'Don't you think we have been too fierce in our what they call purity? Don't you think that to be so much afraid and averse is a sort of dirtiness?'

She looked at him with startled dark eyes.

'You recoiled away from anything of the sort, and I took the motion from you, and recoiled also, perhaps worse.'

There was silence in the room for some time.

'Yes,' she said, 'it is so.'

'There is between us,' he said, 'all these years of intimacy. I feel naked enough before you. Do you understand?'

'I think so,' she answered.

'And you love me?'

She laughed.

'Don't be bitter,' he pleaded.

She looked at him and was sorry for him; his eyes were dark with torture. She was sorry for him; it was worse for him to have this deflected love than for herself, who could never be properly mated. He was restless, for ever urging forward and trying to find a way out. He might do as he liked, and have what he liked of her.

'Nay,' she said softly, 'I am not bitter.'

She felt she could bear anything for him; she would suffer for him. She put her hand on his knee as he leaned forward in his chair. He took it and kissed it; but it hurt to do so. He felt he was putting himself aside. He sat there sacrificed to her purity, which felt more like nullity. How could he kiss her hand passionately, when it would drive her away, and leave nothing but pain? Yet slowly he drew her to him and kissed her.

They knew each other too well to pretend anything. As she kissed him, she watched his eyes; they were staring across the room, with a peculiar dark blaze in them that fascinated her. He was perfectly still. She could feel his heart throbbing heavily in his breast.

'What are you thinking about?' she asked.

The blaze in his eyes shuddered, became uncertain.

'I was thinking, all the while, I love you. I have been obstinate.'

She sank her head on his breast.

'Yes,' she answered.

'That's all,' he said, and his voice seemed sure, and his mouth was kissing her throat.

Then she raised her head and looked into his eyes with her full gaze of love. The blaze struggled, seemed to try to get away from her, and then was quenched. He turned his head quickly aside. It was a moment of anguish.

'Kiss me,' she whispered.

He shut his eyes, and kissed her, and his arms folded her closer and closer.

When she walked home with him over the fields, he said, 'I am glad I came back to you. I feel so simple with you – as if there was nothing to hide. We will be happy?'

'Yes,' she murmured, and the tears came to her eyes.

'Some sort of perversity in our souls,' he said, 'makes us not want, get away from, the very thing we want. We have to fight against that.'

'Yes,' she said, and she felt stunned.

As she stood under the drooping thorn tree, in the dark by the roadside, he kissed her, and his fingers wandered over her face. In the darkness, where he could not see her but only feel her, his passion flooded him. He clasped her very close.

'Sometime you will have me?' he murmured, hiding his face on her shoulder. It was so difficult.

'Not now,' she said.

His hopes and his heart sunk. A dreariness came over him.

'No,' he said.

His clasp of her slackened.

'I love to feel your arm *there*!' she said, pressing his arm against her back, where it went round her waist. 'It rests me so.'

He tightened the pressure of his arm upon the small of her back to rest her.

'We belong to each other,' he said.

'Yes.'

'Then why shouldn't we belong to each other altogether?'

'But – ' she faltered.

'I know it's a lot to ask,' he said; 'but there's not much risk for you really – not in the Gretchen way. You can trust me there?'

'Oh, I can trust you.' The answer came quick and strong. 'It's not that – it's not that at all – but – '

'What?'

She hid her face in his neck with a little cry of misery.

'I don't know!' she cried.

She seemed slightly hysterical, but with a sort of horror. His heart died in him.

'You don't think it ugly?' he asked.

'No, not now. You have *taught* me it isn't.'

'You are afraid?'

She calmed herself hastily.

'Yes, I am only afraid,' she said.

He kissed her tenderly.

'Never mind,' he said. 'You shall please yourself.'

Suddenly she gripped his arms round her, and clenched her body stiff.

'You *shall* have me,' she said, through her shut teeth.

His heart beat up again like fire. He folded her close, and his mouth was on her throat. She could not bear it. She drew away. He disengaged her.

'Won't you be late?' she asked gently.

He sighed, scarcely hearing what she said. She waited, wishing he would go. At last he kissed her quickly and climbed the fence. Looking round he saw the pale blotch of her face down in the darkness under the hanging tree. There was no more of her but this pale blotch.

'Goodbye!' she called softly. She had no body, only a voice and a dim face. He turned away and ran down the road, his fists clenched; and when he came to the wall over the lake he leaned there, almost stunned, looking up the black water.

Miriam plunged home over the meadows. She was not afraid of people, what they might say; but she dreaded the issue with him. Yes, she would let him have her if he insisted; and then, when she thought of it afterwards, her heart went down. He would be disappointed, he would find no satisfaction, and then he would go away. Yet he was so insistent; and over this, which did not seem so all-important to her, was their love to break down. After all, he was only like other men, seeking his satisfaction. Oh, but there was something more in him, something deeper! She could trust to it, in spite of all desires. He said that possession was a great moment in life. All strong emotions concentrated there. Perhaps it was so. There was something divine in it; then she would submit, religiously, to the sacrifice. He should have her. And at the thought her whole body clenched itself involuntarily, hard, as if against something; but Life forced her through this gate of suffering, too, and she would submit. At any rate, it would give him what he wanted, which was her deepest wish. She brooded and brooded and brooded herself towards accepting him.

He courted her now like a lover. Often, when he grew hot, she put his face from her, held it between her hands, and looked in his eyes. He could not meet her gaze. Her dark eyes, full of love, earnest and searching, made him turn away. Not for an instant would she let him forget. Back again he had to torture himself into a sense of his responsibility and hers. Never any relaxing, never any leaving himself to the great hunger and impersonality of passion; he must be brought back to a deliberate, reflective creature. As if from a swoon of passion she called him back to the littleness, the personal relationship. He could not bear it.

'Leave me alone – leave me alone!' he wanted to cry; but she wanted him to look at her with eyes full of love. His eyes, full of the dark, impersonal fire of desire, did not belong to her.

There was a great crop of cherries at the farm. The trees at the back of the house, very large and tall, hung thick with scarlet and crimson drops, under the dark leaves. Paul and Edgar were gathering the fruit one evening. It had been a hot day, and now the clouds were rolling in the sky, dark and warm. Paul climbed high in the tree, above the scarlet roofs of the buildings. The wind, moaning steadily, made the whole tree rock with a subtle, thrilling motion that stirred the blood. The young man, perched insecurely in the slender branches, rocked till he felt slightly drunk, reached down the boughs, where the scarlet beady cherries hung thick underneath, and tore off handful after handful of the sleek, cool-fleshed fruit. Cherries touched his ears and his neck as he stretched forward, their chill fingertips sending a flash down his blood. All shades of red, from a golden vermilion to a rich crimson, glowed and met his eyes under a darkness of leaves.

The sun, going down, suddenly caught the broken clouds. Immense piles of gold flared out in the south-east, headed in soft, glowing yellow right up the sky. The world, till now dusk and grey, reflected the gold glow, astonished. Everywhere the trees, and the grass, and the far-off water, seemed roused from the twilight and shining.

Miriam came out wondering.

'Oh!' Paul heard her mellow voice call, 'isn't it wonderful?'

He looked down. There was a faint gold glimmer on her face, that looked very soft, turned up to him.

'How high you are!' she said.

Beside her, on the rhubarb leaves, were four dead birds, thieves that had been shot. Paul saw some cherry-stones hanging quite bleached, like skeletons, picked clear of flesh. He looked down again to Miriam.

'Clouds are on fire,' he said.

'Beautiful!' she cried.

She seemed so small, so soft, so tender, down there. He threw a handful of cherries at her. She was startled and frightened. He laughed with a low, chuckling sound, and pelted her. She ran for shelter, picking up some cherries. Two fine red pairs she hung over her ears; then she looked up again.

'Haven't you got enough?' she asked.

'Nearly. It is like being on a ship up here.'

'And how long will you stay?'

'While the sunset lasts.'

She went to the fence and sat there, watching the gold clouds fall to pieces, and go in immense, rose-coloured ruin towards the darkness. Gold flamed to scarlet, like pain in its intense brightness. Then the scarlet sank to rose, and rose to crimson, and quickly the passion went out of the sky. All the world was dark grey. Paul scrambled quickly down with his basket, tearing his shirt-sleeve as he did so.

'They are lovely,' said Miriam, fingering the cherries.

'I've torn my sleeve,' he answered.

She took the three-cornered rip, saying, 'I shall have to mend it,' It was near the shoulder. She put her fingers through the tear. 'How warm!' she said.

He laughed. There was a new, strange note in his voice, one that made her pant.

'Shall we stay out?' he said.

'Won't it rain?' she asked.

'No, let us walk a little way.'

They went down the fields and into the thick plantation of fir trees and pines.

'Shall we go in among the trees?' he asked.

'Do you want to?'

'Yes.'

It was very dark among the firs, and the sharp spines pricked her face. She was afraid. Paul was silent and strange.

'I like the darkness,' he said. 'I wish it were thicker – good, thick darkness.'

He seemed to be almost unaware of her as a person: she was only to him then a woman. She was afraid.

He stood against a pine-tree trunk and took her in his arms. She relinquished herself to him, but it was a sacrifice in which she felt something of horror. This thick-voiced, oblivious man was a stranger to her.

Later it began to rain. The pine trees smelled very strong.

Paul lay with his head on the ground, on the dead pine-needles, listening to the sharp hiss of the rain – a steady, keen noise. His heart was down, very heavy. Now he realised that she had not been with him all the time, that her soul had stood apart, in a sort of horror. He was physically at rest, but no more. Very dreary at heart, very sad, and very tender, his fingers wandered over her face pitifully. Now again she loved him deeply. He was tender and beautiful.

'The rain!' he said.

'Yes – is it coming on you?'

She put her hands over him, on his hair, on his shoulders, to feel if the raindrops fell on him. She loved him dearly. He, as he lay with his face on the dead pine-leaves, felt extraordinarily quiet. He did not mind if the raindrops came on him: he would have lain and got wet through: he felt as if nothing mattered, as if his living were smeared away into the beyond, near and quite lovable. This strange, gentle reaching-out to death was new to him.

'We must go,' said Miriam.

'Yes,' he answered, but did not move.

To him now, life seemed a shadow, day a white shadow; night, and death, and stillness, and inaction, this seemed like *being*. To be alive, to be urgent and insistent – that was *not-to-be*. The highest of all was to melt out into the darkness and sway there, identified with the great Being.

'The rain is coming in on us,' said Miriam.

He rose, and assisted her.

'It is a pity,' he said.

'What?'

'To have to go. I feel so still.'

'Still!' she repeated.

'Stiller than I have ever been in my life.'

He was walking with his hand in hers. She pressed his fingers, feeling a slight fear. Now he seemed beyond her; she had a fear lest she should lose him.

'The fir trees are like presences on the darkness: each one only a presence.'

She was afraid, and said nothing.

'A sort of hush: the whole night wondering and asleep: *I* suppose that's what we do in death – sleep in wonder.'

She had been afraid before of the brute in him: now of the mystic. She trod beside him in silence. The rain fell with a heavy 'Hush!' on the trees. At last they gained the cart-shed.

'Let us stay here awhile,' he said.

There was a sound of rain everywhere, smothering everything.

'I feel so strange and still,' he said, 'along with everything.'

'Ay,' she answered patiently.

He seemed again unaware of her, though he held her hand close.

'To be rid of our individuality, which is our will, which is our effort – to live effortless, a kind of conscious sleep – that is very beautiful, I think; that is our afterlife – our immortality.'

'Yes?'

'Yes – and very beautiful to have.'

'You don't usually say that.'

'No.'

In a while they went indoors. Everybody looked at them curiously. He still kept the quiet, heavy look in his eyes, the stillness in his voice. Instinctively, they all left him alone.

About this time Miriam's grandmother, who lived in a tiny cottage in Woodlinton, fell ill, and the girl was sent to keep house. It was a beautiful little place. The cottage had a big garden in front, with red-brick walls, against which the plum trees were nailed. At the back another garden was separated from the fields by a tall old hedge. It was very pretty. Miriam had not much to do, so she found time for her beloved reading, and for writing little introspective pieces which interested her.

At the holiday-time her grandmother, being better, was driven to Derby to stay with her daughter for a day or two. She was a crotchety old lady, and might return the second day or the third; so Miriam stayed alone in the cottage, which also pleased her.

Paul used often to cycle over, and they had as a rule peaceful and happy times. He did not embarrass her much; but then on the Monday of the holiday he was to spend a whole day with her.

It was perfect weather. He left his mother, telling her where he was going. She would be alone all the day. It cast a shadow over him; but he had three days that were all his own, when he was going to do as he liked. It was sweet to rush through the morning lanes on his bicycle.

He got to the cottage at about eleven o'clock. Miriam was busy preparing dinner. She looked so perfectly in keeping with the little kitchen, ruddy and busy. He kissed her and sat down to watch. The room was small and cosy. The sofa was covered all over with a sort of linen in squares of red and pale blue, old, much washed, but pretty. There was a stuffed owl in a case over a corner cupboard. The sunlight came through the leaves of the scented geraniums in the window. She was cooking a chicken in his honour. It was their cottage for the day, and they were man and wife. He beat the eggs for her and peeled the potatoes. He thought she gave a feeling of home almost like his mother; and no one could look more beautiful, with her tumbled curls, when she was flushed from the fire.

The dinner was a great success. Like a young husband, he carved. They talked all the time with unflagging zest. Then he wiped the dishes she had washed, and they went out down the fields. There was a bright little brook that ran into a bog at the foot of a very steep bank. Here they wandered, picking still a few marsh-marigolds and many big blue forget-me-nots. Then she sat on the bank with her hands full of flowers, mostly golden water-blobs. As she put her face down into the marigolds, it was all overcast with a yellow shine.

'Your face is bright,' he said, 'like a transfiguration.'

She looked at him, questioning. He laughed pleadingly to her, laying his hand on hers. Then he kissed her fingers, then her face.

The world was all steeped in sunshine, and quite still, yet not asleep, but quivering with a kind of expectancy.

'I have never seen anything more beautiful than this,' he said. He held her hand fast all the time.

'And the water singing to itself as it runs – do you love it?' She looked at him full of love. His eyes were very dark, very bright.

'Don't you think it's a great day?' he asked.

She murmured her assent. She was happy, and he saw it.

'And our day – just between us,' he said.

They lingered a little while. Then they stood up upon the sweet thyme, and he looked down at her simply.

'Will you come?' he asked.

They went back to the house, hand-in-hand, in silence. The chickens came scampering down the path to her. He locked the door, and they had the little house to themselves.

He never forgot seeing her as she lay on the bed, when he was unfastening his collar. First he saw only her beauty, and was blind with it. She had the most beautiful body he had ever imagined. He stood unable to move or speak, looking at her, his face half smiling with wonder. And then he wanted her, but as he went forward to her, her hands lifted in a little pleading movement, and he looked at her face, and stopped. Her big brown eyes were watching him, still and resigned and loving; she lay as if she had given herself up to sacrifice: there was her body for him; but the look at the back of her eyes, like a creature awaiting immolation, arrested him, and all his blood fell back.

'You are sure you want me?' he asked, as if a cold shadow had come over him.

'Yes, quite sure.'

She was very quiet, very calm. She only realised that she was doing something for him. He could hardly bear it. She lay to be sacrificed for him because she loved him so much. And he had to sacrifice her. For a second, he wished he were sexless or dead. Then he shut his eyes again to her, and his blood beat back again.

And afterwards he loved her – loved her to the last fibre of his being. He loved her. But he wanted, somehow, to cry. There was something he could not bear for her sake. He stayed with her till quite late at night. As he rode home he felt that he was finally initiated. He was a youth no longer. But why had he the dull pain in his soul? Why did the thought of death, the afterlife, seem so sweet and consoling?

He spent the week with Miriam, and wore her out with his passion before it was gone. He had always, almost wilfully, to put her out of count, and act from the brute strength of his own feelings. And he could not do it often, and there remained afterwards always the sense of failure and of death. If he were really with her, he had to put aside himself and his desire. If he would have her, he had to put her aside.

'When I come to you,' he asked her, his eyes dark with pain and shame, 'you don't really want me, do you?'

'Ah, yes!' she replied quickly.

He looked at her.

'Nay,' he said.

She began to tremble.

'You see,' she said, taking his face and shutting it out against her shoulder – 'you see – as we are – how can I get used to you? It would come all right if we were married.'

He lifted her head and looked at her.

'You mean, now, it is always too much shock?'

'Yes – and –'

'You are always clenched against me.'

She was trembling with agitation.

'You see,' she said, 'I'm not used to the thought –'

'You are lately,' he said.

'But all my life. Mother said to me, "There is one thing in marriage that is always dreadful, but you have to bear it." And I believed it.'

'And still believe,' he said.

'No!' she cried hastily. 'I believe, as you do, that loving, even in *that* way, is the high-water mark of living.'

'That doesn't alter the fact that you never *want* it.'

'No,' she said, taking his head in her arms and rocking in despair. 'Don't say so! You don't understand.' She rocked with pain. 'Don't I want your children?'

'But not me.'

'How can you say so? But we must be married to have children – '

'Shall we be married, then? I want you to have my children.'

He kissed her hand reverently. She pondered sadly, watching him.

'We are too young,' she said at length.

'Twenty-four and twenty-three – '

'Not yet,' she pleaded, as she rocked herself in distress.

'When you will,' he said.

She bowed her head gravely. The tone of hopelessness in which he said these things grieved her deeply. It had always been a failure between them. Tacitly, she acquiesced in what he felt.

And after a week of love he said to his mother suddenly one Sunday night, just as they were going to bed, 'I shan't go so much to Miriam's, mother.'

She was surprised, but she would not ask him anything.

'You please yourself,' she said.

So he went to bed. But there was a new quietness about him which she had wondered at. She almost guessed. She would leave him alone, however. Precipitation might spoil things. She watched him in his loneliness, wondering where he would end. He was sick, and much too quiet for him. There was a perpetual little knitting of his brows, such as she had seen when he was a small baby, and which had been gone for many years. Now it was the same again. And she could do nothing for him. He had to go on alone, make his own way.

He continued faithful to Miriam. For one day he had loved her utterly. But it never came again. The sense of failure grew stronger. At first it was only a sadness. Then he began to feel he could not go on. He wanted to run, to go abroad, anything. Gradually he ceased to ask her to have him. Instead of drawing them together, it put them apart. And then he realised, consciously, that it was no good. It was useless trying: it would never be a success between them.

For some months he had seen very little of Clara. They had occasionally walked out for half an hour at dinner-time. But he always reserved himself for Miriam. With Clara, however, his brow cleared, and he was gay again. She treated him indulgently, as if he were a child. He thought he did not mind. But deep below the surface it piqued him.

Sometimes Miriam said, 'What about Clara? I hear nothing of her lately.'

'I walked with her about twenty minutes yesterday,' he replied.

'And what did she talk about?'

'I don't know. I suppose I did all the jawing – I usually do. I think I was telling her about the strike, and how the women took it.'

'Yes.'

So he gave the account of himself.

But insidiously, without his knowing it, the warmth he felt for Clara drew him away from Miriam, for whom he felt responsible, and to whom he felt he belonged. He thought he was being quite faithful to her. It is not easy to estimate exactly the strength and warmth of one's feelings for a woman till they have run away with one.

He began to give more time to his men friends. There was Jessop, at the Art School; Swain, who was chemistry demonstrator at the University; Newton, who was a teacher; besides Edgar and Miriam's younger brothers. Pleading work, he sketched and studied with Jessop. He called in the University for Swain, and the two went 'down town' together. Having come home in the train with Newton, he called and had a game of billiards with him in the Moon and Stars. If he gave to Miriam the excuse of his men friends, he felt quite justified. His mother began to be relieved. He always told her where he had been.

During the summer Clara wore sometimes a dress of soft cotton stuff with loose sleeves. When she lifted her hands, her sleeves fell back, and her beautiful strong arms shone out.

'Half a minute,' he cried. 'Hold your arm still.'

He made sketches of her hand and arm, and the drawings contained some of the fascination the real thing had for him. Miriam, who always went scrupulously through his books and papers, saw the drawings.

'I think Clara has such beautiful arms,' he said.

'Yes! When did you draw them?'

'On Tuesday, in the workroom. You know, I've got a corner where I can work. Often I can do every single thing they need in the department, before dinner. Then I work for myself in the afternoon, and just see to things at night.'

'Yes,' she said, turning the leaves of his sketchbook.

Frequently he hated Miriam. He hated her as she bent forward and pored over his things. He hated her way of patiently casting him up, as if he were an endless psychological account. When he was with her, he hated her for having got him, and yet not got him, and he tortured her. She took all and gave nothing, he said. At least, she gave no living warmth. She was never alive, and giving off life. Looking for her was like looking for something which did not exist. She was only his conscience, not his mate. He hated her violently, and was more cruel to her. They dragged on till the next summer. He saw more and more of Clara.

At last he spoke. He had been sitting working at home one evening. There was between him and his mother a peculiar condition of people frankly finding fault with each other. Mrs Morel was strong on her feet again. He was not going to stick to Miriam. Very well; then she would stand aloof till he said something. It had been coming a long time, this bursting of the storm in him, when he would come back to her. This evening there was between them a peculiar condition of suspense. He worked feverishly and mechanically, so that he could escape from himself. It grew late. Through the open door, stealthily, came the scent of madonna lilies, almost as if it were prowling abroad. Suddenly he got up and went out of doors.

The beauty of the night made him want to shout. A half-moon, dusky gold, was sinking behind the black sycamore at the end of the garden, making the sky dull purple with its glow. Nearer, a dim white fence of lilies went across the garden, and the air all round seemed to stir with scent, as if it were alive. He went across the bed of pinks, whose keen perfume came sharply across the rocking, heavy scent of the lilies, and stood alongside the white barrier of flowers. They flagged all loose, as if they were panting. The scent made him drunk. He went down to the field to watch the moon sink under.

A corncrake in the hay-close called insistently. The moon slid quite quickly downwards, growing more flushed. Behind him the great flowers leaned as if they were calling. And then, like a shock, he caught another perfume, something raw and coarse. Hunting round, he found the purple iris, touched their fleshy throats and their dark, grasping hands. At any rate, he had found something. They stood stiff in the darkness. Their scent was brutal. The moon was melting down upon the crest of the hill. It was gone; all was dark. The corncrake called still.

Breaking off a pink, he suddenly went indoors.

'Come, my boy,' said his mother. 'I'm sure it's time you went to bed.'

He stood with the pink against his lips.

'I shall break off with Miriam, mother,' he answered calmly.

She looked up at him over her spectacles. He was staring back at her, unswerving. She met his eyes for a moment then took off her glasses. He was white. The male was up in him, dominant. She did not want to see him too clearly.

'But I thought – ' she began.

'Well,' he answered, 'I don't love her. I don't want to marry her – so I shall have done.'

'But,' exclaimed his mother, amazed, 'I thought lately you had made up your mind to have her, and so I said nothing.'

'I had – I wanted to – but now I don't want. It's no good. I shall break off on Sunday. I ought to, oughtn't I?'

'You know best. You know I said so long ago.'

'I can't help that now. I shall break off on Sunday.'

'Well,' said his mother, 'I think it will be best. But lately I decided you had made up your mind to have her, so I said nothing, and should have said nothing. But I say as I have always said, I *don't* think she is suited to you.'

'On Sunday I break off,' he said, smelling the pink. He put the flower in his mouth. Unthinking, he bared his teeth, closed them on the blossom slowly, and had a mouthful of petals. These he spat into the fire, kissed his mother, and went to bed.

On Sunday he went up to the farm in the early afternoon. He had written Miriam that they would walk over the fields to Hucknall. His mother was very tender with him. He said nothing. But she saw the effort it was costing. The peculiar set look on his face stilled her.

'Never mind, my son,' she said. 'You will be so much better when it is all over.'

Paul glanced swiftly at his mother in surprise and resentment. He did not want sympathy.

Miriam met him at the lane-end. She was wearing a new dress of figured muslin that had short sleeves. Those short sleeves, and Miriam's brown-skinned arms beneath them – such pitiful, resigned arms – gave him so much pain that they helped to make him cruel. She had made herself look so beautiful and fresh for him. She seemed to blossom for him alone. Every time he looked at her – a mature young woman now, and beautiful in her new dress – it hurt so much that his heart seemed almost to be bursting with the restraint he put on it. But he had decided, and it was irrevocable.

On the hills they sat down, and he lay with his head in her lap, whilst she fingered his hair. She knew that 'he was not there', as she put it. Often, when she had him with her, she looked for him, and could not find him. But this afternoon she was not prepared.

It was nearly five o'clock when he told her. They were sitting on the bank of a stream, where the lip of turf hung over a hollow bank of yellow earth, and he was hacking away with a stick, as he did when he was perturbed and cruel.

'I have been thinking,' he said, 'we ought to break off.'

'Why?' she cried in surprise.

'Because it's no good going on.'

'Why is it no good?'

'It isn't. I don't want to marry. I don't want ever to marry. And if we're not going to marry, it's no good going on.'

'But why do you say this now?'

'Because I've made up my mind.'

'And what about these last months, and the things you told me then?'

'I can't help it; I don't want to go on.'

'You don't want any more of me?'

'I want us to break off – you be free of me, I free of you.'

'And what about these last months?'

'I don't know. I've not told you anything but what I thought was true.'

'Then why are you different now?'

'I'm not – I'm the same – only I know it's no good going on.'

'You haven't told me why it's no good.'

'Because I don't want to go on – and I don't want to marry.'

'How many times have you offered to marry me, and I wouldn't?'

'I know; but I want us to break off.'

There was silence for a moment or two, while he dug viciously at the earth. She bent her head, pondering. He was an unreasonable child. He was like an infant which, when it has drunk its fill, throws away and smashes the cup. She looked at him, feeling she could get hold of him and *wring* some consistency out of him. But she was helpless. Then she cried, 'I have said you were only fourteen – you are only *four*!'

He still dug at the earth viciously. He heard.

'You are a child of four,' she repeated in her anger.

He did not answer, but said in his heart: 'All right; if I'm a child of four, what do you want me for? I don't want another mother.' But he said nothing to her, and there was silence.

'And have you told your people?' she asked.

'I have told my mother.'

There was another long interval of silence.

'Then what do you *want?*' she asked.

'Why, I want us to separate. We have lived on each other all these years; now let us stop. I will go my own way without you, and you will go your way without me. You will have an independent life of your own then.'

There was in it some truth that, in spite of her bitterness, she could not help registering. She knew she felt in a sort of bondage to him, which she hated because she could not control it. She had hated her love for him from the moment it grew too strong for her. And, deep down, she had hated him because she loved him and he dominated her. She had resisted his domination. She had fought to keep herself free of him in the last issue. And she *was* free of him, even more than he of her.

'And,' he continued, 'we shall always be more or less each other's work. You have done a lot for me, I for you. Now let us start and live by ourselves.'

'What do you want to do?' she asked.

'Nothing – only be free,' he answered.

She, however, knew in her heart that Clara's influence was over him to liberate him. But she said nothing.

'And what have I to tell my mother?' she asked.

'I told my mother,' he answered, 'that I was breaking off – clean and altogether.'

'I shall not tell them at home,' she said.

Frowning, 'You please yourself,' he said.

He knew he had landed her in a nasty hole, and was leaving her in the lurch. It angered him.

'Tell them you wouldn't and won't marry me, and have broken off,' he said. 'It's true enough.'

She bit her finger moodily. She thought over their whole affair. She had known it would come to this; she had seen it all along. It chimed with her bitter expectation.

'Always – it has always been so!' she cried. 'It has been one long battle between us – you fighting away from me.'

It came from her unawares, like a flash of lightning. The man's heart stood still. Was this how she saw it?

'But we've had *some* perfect hours, *some* perfect times, when we were together!' he pleaded.

'Never!' she cried; 'never! It has always been you fighting me off.'

'Not always – not at first!' he pleaded.

'Always, from the very beginning – always the same!'

She had finished, but she had done enough. He sat aghast. He had wanted to say, 'It has been good, but it is at an end.' And she – she whose love he had believed in when he had despised himself – denied that their love had ever been love. 'He had always fought away from her?' Then it had been monstrous. There had never been anything really between them; all the time he had been imagining something where there was nothing! And she had known. She had known so much, and had told him so little. She had known all the time. All the time this was at the bottom of her!

He sat silent in bitterness. At last the whole affair appeared in a cynical aspect to him. She had really played with him, not he with her. She had hidden all her condemnation from him, had flattered him, and despised him. She despised him now. He grew intellectual and cruel.

'You ought to marry a man who worships you,' he said; 'then you could do as you liked with him. Plenty of men will worship you, if you get on the private side of their natures. You ought to marry one such. They would never fight you off.'

'Thank you!' she said. 'But don't advise me to marry someone else any more. You've done it before.'

'Very well,' he said; 'I will say no more.'

He sat still, feeling as if he had had a blow, instead of giving one. Their eight years of friendship and love, *the* eight years of his life, were nullified.

'When did you think of this?' she asked.

'I thought definitely on Thursday night.'

'I knew it was coming,' she said.

That pleased him bitterly. 'Oh, very well! If she knew then it doesn't come as a surprise to her,' he thought.

'And have you said anything to Clara?' she asked.

'No; but I shall tell her now.'

There was a silence.

'Do you remember the things you said this time last year, in my grand-mother's house – nay last month even?'

'Yes,' he said; 'I do! And I meant them! I can't help that it's failed.'

'It has failed because you want something else.'

'It would have failed whether or not. You never believed in me.'

She laughed strangely.

He sat in silence. He was full of a feeling that she had deceived him. She had despised him when he thought she worshipped him. She had let him say wrong things, and had not contradicted him. She had let him fight alone. But it stuck in his throat that she had despised him whilst he thought she worshipped him. She should have told him when she found fault with him. She had not played fair. He hated her. All these years she had treated him as if he were a hero, and thought of him secretly as an infant, a foolish child. Then why had she left the foolish child to his folly? His heart was hard against her.

She sat full of bitterness. She had known – oh, well she had known! All the time he was away from her she had summed him up, seen his littleness, his meanness, and his folly. Even she had guarded her soul against him. She was not overthrown, nor prostrated, not even much hurt. She had known. Only why, as he sat there, had he still this strange dominance over her? His very movements fascinated her as if she were hypnotised by him. Yet he was despicable, false, inconsistent, and mean. Why this bondage for her? Why was it the movement of his arm stirred her as nothing else in the world could? Why was she fastened to him? Why, even now, if he looked at her and commanded her, would she have to obey? She would obey him in his trifling commands. But once he was obeyed, then she had him in her power, she knew, to lead him where she would. She was sure of herself. Only, this new influence! Ah, he was not a man! He was a baby that cries for the newest toy. And all the attachment of his soul would not keep him. Very well, he would have to go. But he would come back when he had tired of his new sensation.

He hacked at the earth till she was fretted to death. She rose. He sat flinging lumps of earth in the stream.

'We will go and have tea here?' he asked.

'Yes,' she answered.

They chattered over irrelevant subjects during tea. He held forth on the love of ornament – the cottage parlour moved him thereto – and its connection with aesthetics.

She was cold and quiet. As they walked home, she asked, 'And we shall not see each other?'

'No – or rarely,' he answered.

'Nor write?' she asked, almost sarcastically.

'As you will,' he answered. 'We're not strangers – never should be, whatever happened. I will write to you now and again. You please yourself.'

'I see!' she answered cuttingly.

But he was at that stage at which nothing else hurts. He had made a great cleavage in his life. He had had a great shock when she had told him their love had been always a conflict. Nothing more mattered. If it never had been much, there was no need to make a fuss that it was ended.

He left her at the lane-end. As she went home, solitary, in her new frock, having her people to face at the other end, he stood still with shame and pain in the highroad, thinking of the suffering he caused her.

In the reaction towards restoring his self-esteem, he went into the Willow Tree for a drink. There were four girls who had been out for the day, drinking a modest glass of port. They had some chocolates on the table. Paul sat near with his whisky. He noticed the girls whispering and nudging. Presently one, a bonny dark hussy, leaned to him and said, 'Have a chocolate?'

The others laughed loudly at her impudence.

'All right,' said Paul. 'Give me a hard one – nut. I don't like creams.'

'Here you are, then,' said the girl; 'here's an almond for you.'

She held the sweet between her fingers. He opened his mouth. She popped it in, and blushed.

'You *are* nice!' he said.

'Well,' she answered, 'we thought you looked overcast, and they dared me offer you a chocolate.'

'I don't mind if I have another – another sort,' he said.

And presently they were all laughing together.

It was nine o'clock when he got home, falling dark. He entered the house in silence. His mother, who had been waiting, rose anxiously.

'I told her,' he said.

'I'm glad,' replied the mother, with great relief.

He hung up his cap wearily.

'I said we'd have done altogether,' he said.

'That's right, my son,' said the mother. 'It's hard for her now, but best in the long run. I know. You weren't suited for her.'

He laughed shakily as he sat down.

'I've had such a lark with some girls in a pub,' he said. His mother looked at him. He had forgotten Miriam now. He told her about the girls in the Willow Tree. Mrs Morel looked at him. It seemed unreal, his gaiety. At the back of it was too much horror and misery.

'Now have some supper,' she said very gently.

Afterwards he said wistfully, 'She never thought she'd have me, mother, not from the first, and so she's not disappointed.'

'I'm afraid,' said his mother, 'she doesn't give up hopes of you yet.'

'No,' he said, 'perhaps not.'

'You'll find it's better to have done,' she said.

'I don't know,' he said desperately.

'Well, leave her alone,' replied his mother.

So he left her, and she was alone. Very few people cared for her, and she for very few people. She remained alone with herself, waiting.

CHAPTER 12

Passion

He was gradually making it possible to earn a livelihood by his art. Liberty's had taken several of his painted designs on various stuffs, and he could sell designs for embroideries for altar-cloths, and similar things, in one or two places It was not very much he made at present, but he might extend it. He had also made friends with the designer for a pottery firm, and was gaining some knowledge of his new acquaintance's art. The applied arts interested him very much. At the same time he laboured slowly at his pictures. He loved to paint large figures, full of light, but not merely made up of lights and cast shadows, like the impressionists; rather definite figures that had a certain luminous quality, like some of Michelangelo's people. And these he fitted into a landscape, in what he thought true proportion. He worked a great deal from memory, using everybody he knew. He believed firmly in his work, that it was good and valuable. In spite of fits of depression, shrinking, everything, he believed in his work.

He was twenty-four when he said his first confident thing to his mother.

'Mother,' he said, 'I s'll make a painter that they'll attend to.'

She sniffed in her quaint fashion. It was like a half-pleased shrug of the shoulders.

'Very well, my boy, we'll see,' she said.

'You shall see, my pigeon! You see if you're not swanky one of these days!'

'I'm quite content, my boy,' she smiled.

'But you'll have to alter. Look at you with Minnie!'

Minnie was the small servant, a girl of fourteen.

'And what about Minnie?' asked Mrs Morel, with dignity.

'I heard her this morning: "Eh, Mrs Morel! I was going to do that," when you went out in the rain for some coal,' he said. 'That looks a lot like your being able to manage servants!'

'Well, it was only the child's niceness,' said Mrs Morel.

'And you apologising to her: "You can't do two things at once, can you?" '

'She *was* busy washing up,' replied Mrs Morel.

'And what did she say? "It could easy have waited a bit. Now look how your feet paddle!" '

'Yes – brazen young baggage!' said Mrs Morel, smiling.

He looked at his mother, laughing. She was quite warm and rosy again with love of him. It seemed as if all the sunshine were on her for a moment. He continued his work gladly. She seemed so well when she was happy that he forgot her grey hair.

And that year she went with him to the Isle of Wight for a holiday. It was too exciting for them both, and too beautiful. Mrs Morel was full of joy and wonder. But he would have her walk with him more than she was able. She had a bad fainting bout. So grey her face was, so blue her mouth! It was agony to him. He felt as if someone were pushing a knife in his chest. Then she was better again, and he forgot. But the anxiety remained inside him, like a wound that did not close.

After leaving Miriam he went almost straight to Clara. On the Monday following the day of the rupture he went down to the workroom. She looked up at him and smiled. They had grown very intimate unawares. She saw a new brightness about him.

'Well, Queen of Sheba!' he said, laughing.

'But why?' she asked.

'I think it suits you. You've got a new frock on.'

She flushed, asking, 'And what of it?'

'Suits you – awfully! *I* could design you a dress.'

'How would it be?'

He stood in front of her, his eyes glittering as he expounded. He kept her eyes fixed with his. Then suddenly he took hold of her. She half started back. He drew the stuff of her blouse tighter, smoothed it over her breast.

'More *so*!' he explained.

But they were both of them flaming with blushes, and immediately he ran away. He had touched her. His whole body was quivering with the sensation.

There was already a sort of secret understanding between them. The next evening he went into the cinematograph with her for a few minutes before train-time. As they sat, he saw her hand lying near him. For some moments he dared not touch it. The pictures danced and dithered. Then he took her hand in his. It was large and firm; it filled his grasp. He held it fast. She neither moved nor made any sign. When they came out his train was due. He hesitated.

'Good-night,' she said. He darted away across the road.

The next day he came again, talking to her. She was rather superior with him.

'Shall we go a walk on Monday?' he asked.

She turned her face aside.

'Shall you tell Miriam?' she replied sarcastically.

'I have broken off with her,' he said.

'When?'

'Last Sunday.'

'You quarrelled?'

'No! I had made up my mind. I told her quite definitely I should consider myself free.'

Clara did not answer, and he returned to his work. She was so quiet and so superb!

On the Saturday evening he asked her to come and drink coffee with him in a restaurant, meeting him after work was over. She came, looking very reserved and very distant. He had three-quarters of an hour to train-time.

'We will walk a little while,' he said.

She agreed, and they went past the Castle into the Park. He was afraid of her. She walked moodily at his side, with a kind of resentful, reluctant, angry walk. He was afraid to take her hand.

'Which way shall we go?' he asked as they walked in darkness.

'I don't mind.'

'Then we'll go up the steps.'

He suddenly turned round. They had passed the Park steps. She stood still in resentment at his suddenly abandoning her. He looked for her. She stood aloof. He caught her suddenly in his arms, held her strained for a moment, kissed her. Then he let her go.

'Come along,' he said, penitent.

She followed him. He took her hand and kissed her fingertips. They went in silence. When they came to the light, he let go her hand. Neither spoke till they reached the station. Then they looked each other in the eyes.

'Good-night,' she said.

And he went for his train. His body acted mechanically. People talked to him.

He heard faint echoes answering them. He was in a delirium. He felt that he would go mad if Monday did not come at once. On Monday he would see her again. All himself was pitched there, ahead. Sunday intervened. He could not bear it. He could not see her till Monday. And Sunday intervened – hour after hour of tension. He wanted to beat his head against the door of the carriage. But he sat still. He drank some whisky on the way home, but it only made it worse. His mother must not be upset, that was all. He dissembled, and got quickly to bed. There he sat, dressed, with his chin on his knees, staring out of the window at the far hill, with its few lights. He neither thought nor slept, but sat perfectly still, staring. And when at last he was so cold that he came to himself, he found his watch had stopped at half-past two. It was after three o'clock. He was exhausted, but still there was the torment of knowing it was only Sunday morning. He went to bed and slept. Then he cycled all day long, till he was fagged out. And he scarcely knew where he had been. But the day after was Monday. He slept till four o'clock. Then he lay and thought. He was coming nearer to himself – he could see himself, real, somewhere in front. She would go a walk with him in the afternoon. Afternoon! It seemed years ahead.

Slowly the hours crawled. His father got up; he heard him pottering about. Then the miner set off to the pit, his heavy boots scraping the yard. Cocks were still crowing. A cart went down the road. His mother got up. She knocked the fire. Presently she called him softly. He answered as if he were asleep. This shell of himself did well.

He was walking to the station – another mile! The train was near Nottingham. Would it stop before the tunnels? But it did not matter; it would get there before dinner-time. He was at Jordan's. She would come in half an hour. At any rate, she would be near. He had done the letters. She would be there. Perhaps she had not come. He ran downstairs. Ah! he saw her through the glass door. Her shoulders stooping a little to her work made him feel he could not go forward; he could not stand. He went in. He was pale, nervous, awkward, and quite cold. Would she misunderstand him? He could not write his real self with this shell.

'And this afternoon,' he struggled to say. 'You will come?'

'I think so,' she replied, murmuring.

He stood before her, unable to say a word. She hid her face from him. Again came over him the feeling that he would lose consciousness. He set his teeth and went upstairs. He had done everything correctly yet, and he would do so. All the morning things seemed a long way off, as they do to a man under chloroform. He himself seemed under a tight band of constraint. Then there was his other self, in the distance, doing things, entering stuff in a ledger, and he watched that far-off him carefully to see he made no mistake.

But the ache and strain of it could not go on much longer. He worked incessantly. Still it was only twelve o'clock. As if he had nailed his clothing against the desk, he stood there and worked, forcing every stroke out of himself. It was a quarter to one; he could clear away. Then he ran downstairs.

'You will meet me at the Fountain at two o'clock,' he said.

'I can't be there till half-past.'

'Yes!' he said.

She saw his dark, mad eyes.

'I will try at a quarter past.'

And he had to be content. He went and got some dinner. All the time he was still under chloroform, and every minute was stretched out indefinitely. He walked miles of street. Then he thought he would be late at the meeting-place. He was at the Fountain at five past two. The torture of the next quarter of an hour was refined beyond expression. It was the anguish of combining the living self with the shell. Then he saw her. She came! And he was there.

'You are late,' he said.

'Only five minutes,' she answered.

'I'd never have done it to you,' he laughed.

She was in a dark blue costume. He looked at her beautiful figure.

'You want some flowers,' he said, going to the nearest florists.

She followed him in silence. He bought her a bunch of scarlet, brick-red carnations. She put them in her coat, flushing.

'That's a fine colour!' he said.

'I'd rather have had something softer,' she said.

He laughed.

'Do you feel like a blot of vermilion walking down the street?' he said.

She hung her head, afraid of the people they met. He looked sideways at her as they walked. There was a wonderful close down on her face near the ear that he wanted to touch. And a certain heaviness, the heaviness of a very full ear of corn that dips slightly in the wind, that there was about her, made his brain spin. He seemed to be spinning down the street, everything going round.

As they sat in the tramcar, she leaned her heavy shoulder against him, and he took her hand. He felt himself coming round from the anaesthetic, beginning to breathe. Her ear, half hidden among her blonde hair, was near to him. The temptation to kiss it was almost too great. But there were other people on top of the car. It still remained to him to kiss it. After all, he was not himself, he was some attribute of hers, like the sunshine that fell on her.

He looked quickly away. It had been raining. The big bluff of the Castle rock was streaked with rain, as it reared above the flat of the town. They crossed the wide, black space of the Midland Railway, and passed the cattle enclosure that stood out white. Then they ran down sordid Wilford Road.

She rocked slightly to the tram's motion, and as she leaned against him, rocked upon him. He was a vigorous, slender man, with exhaustless energy. His face was rough, with rough-hewn features, like the common people's; but his eyes under the deep brows were so full of life that they fascinated her. They seemed to dance, and yet they were still, trembling on the finest balance of laughter. His mouth, the same, was just going to spring into a laugh of triumph, yet did not. There was a sharp suspense about him. She bit her lip moodily. His hand was hard clenched over hers.

They paid their two halfpennies at the turnstile and crossed the bridge. The Trent was very full. It swept silent and insidious under the bridge, travelling in a soft body. There had been a great deal of rain. On the river levels were flat gleams of flood water. The sky was grey, with glisten of silver here and there. In Wilford Churchyard the dahlias were sodden with rain – wet black-crimson balls. No one was on the path that went along the green river meadow, along the elm-tree colonnade.

There was the faintest haze over the silvery-dark water and the green meadow-banks, and the elm trees that were spangled with gold. The river slid by in a body, utterly silent and swift, intertwining among itself like some subtle, complex creature. Clara walked moodily beside him.

'Why,' she asked at length, in rather a jarring tone, 'did you leave Miriam?'

He frowned.

'Because I *wanted* to leave her,' he said.

'Why?'

'Because I didn't want to go on with her. And I didn't want to marry.'

She was silent for a moment. They picked their way down the muddy path. Drops of water fell from the elm trees.

'You didn't want to marry Miriam, or you didn't want to marry at all?' she asked.

'Both,' he answered – 'both!'

They had to manoeuvre to get to the stile, because of the pools of water.

'And what did she say?' Clara asked.

'Miriam? She said I was a baby of four, and that I always *had* battled her off.'

Clara pondered over this for a time.

'But you have really been going with her for some time?' she asked.

'Yes.'

'And now you don't want any more of her?'

'No. I know it's no good.'

She pondered again.

'Don't you think you've treated her rather badly?' she asked.

'Yes; I ought to have dropped it years back. But it would have been no good going on. Two wrongs don't make a right.'

'How old *are* you?' Clara asked.

'Twenty-five.'

'And I am thirty,' she said.

'I know you are.'

'I shall be thirty-one – or *am* I thirty-one?'

'I neither know nor care. What does it matter!'

They were at the entrance to the Grove. The wet, red track, already sticky with fallen leaves, went up the steep bank between the grass. On either side stood the elm trees like pillars along a great aisle, arching over and making high up a roof from which the dead leaves fell. All was empty and silent and wet. She stood on top of the stile, and he held both her hands. Laughing, she looked down into his eyes. Then she leaped. Her breast came against his; he held her, and covered her face with kisses.

They went on up the slippery, steep red path. Presently she released his hand and put it round her waist.

'You press the vein in my arm, holding it so tightly,' she said.

They walked along. His fingertips felt the rocking of her breast. All was silent and deserted. On the left the red wet plough-land showed through the doorways between the elm-boles and their branches. On the right, looking down, they could see the tree-tops of elms growing far beneath them, hear occasionally the gurgle of the river. Sometimes there below they caught glimpses of the full, soft-sliding Trent, and of water-meadows dotted with small cattle.

'It has scarcely altered since little Kirke White used to come,' he said.

But he was watching her throat below the ear, where the flush was fusing into the honey-white, and her mouth that pouted disconsolate. She stirred against him as she walked, and his body was like a taut string.

Halfway up the big colonnade of elms, where the Grove rose highest above the river, their forward movement faltered to an end. He led her across to the grass, under the trees at the edge of the path. The cliff of red earth sloped swiftly down, through trees and bushes, to the river that glimmered and was dark between the foliage. The far-below water-meadows were very green. He and she stood leaning against one another, silent, afraid, their bodies touching all along. There came a quick gurgle from the river below.

'Why,' he asked at length, 'did you hate Baxter Dawes?'

She turned to him with a splendid movement. Her mouth was offered him, and her throat; her eyes were half shut; her breast was tilted as if it asked for him. He flashed with a small laugh, shut his eyes, and met her in a long, whole kiss. Her mouth fused with his; their bodies were sealed and annealed. It was some minutes before they withdrew. They were standing beside the public path.

'Will you go down to the river?' he asked.

She looked at him, leaving herself in his hands. He went over the brim of the declivity and began to climb down.

'It is slippery,' he said.

'Never mind,' she replied.

The red clay went down almost sheer. He slid, went from one tuft of grass to the next, hanging on to the bushes, making for a little platform at the foot of a tree. There he waited for her, laughing with excitement. Her shoes were clogged with red earth. It was hard for her. He frowned. At last he caught her hand, and she stood beside him. The cliff rose above them and fell away below. Her colour was up, her eyes flashed. He looked at the big drop below them.

'It's risky,' he said; 'or messy, at any rate. Shall we go back?'

'Not for my sake,' she said quickly.

'All right. You see, I can't help you; I should only hinder. Give me that little parcel and your gloves. Your poor shoes!'

They stood perched on the face of the declivity, under the trees.

'Well, I'll go again,' he said.

Away he went, slipping, staggering, sliding to the next tree, into which he fell with a slam that nearly shook the breath out of him. She came after cautiously, hanging on to the twigs and grasses. So they descended, stage by stage, to the river's brink. There, to his disgust, the flood had eaten away the path, and the red decline ran straight into the water. He dug in his heels and brought himself up violently. The string of the parcel broke with a snap; the brown parcel bounded down, leaped into the water, and sailed smoothly away. He hung on to his tree.

'Well, I'll be damned!' he cried crossly. Then he laughed. She was coming perilously down.

'Mind!' he warned her. He stood with his back to the tree, waiting. 'Come now,' he called, opening his arms.

She let herself run. He caught her, and together they stood watching the dark water scoop at the raw edge of the bank. The parcel had sailed out of sight.

'It doesn't matter,' she said.

He held her close and kissed her. There was only room for their four feet.

'It's a swindle!' he said. 'But there's a rut where a man has been, so if we go on I guess we shall find the path again.'

The river slid and twined its great volume. On the other bank cattle were feeding on the desolate flats. The cliff rose high above Paul and Clara on their right hand. They stood against the tree in the watery silence.

'Let us try going forward,' he said; and they struggled in the red clay along the groove a man's nailed boots had made. They were hot and flushed. Their barkled shoes hung heavy on their steps. At last they found the broken path. It was littered with rubble from the water, but at any rate it was easier. They cleaned their boots with twigs. His heart was beating thick and fast.

Suddenly, coming on to the little level, he saw two figures of men standing silent at the water's edge. His heart leaped. They were fishing. He turned and put his hand up warningly to Clara. She hesitated, buttoned her coat. The two went on together.

The fishermen turned curiously to watch the two intruders on their privacy and solitude. They had had a fire, but it was nearly out. All kept perfectly still. The men turned again to their fishing, stood over the grey glinting river like statues. Clara went with bowed head, flushing; he was laughing to himself. Directly they passed out of sight behind the willows.

'Now, they ought to be drowned,' said Paul softly.

Clara did not answer. They toiled forward along a tiny path on the river's lip. Suddenly it vanished. The bank was sheer red solid clay in front of them, sloping straight into the river. He stood and cursed beneath his breath, setting his teeth.

'It is impossible!' said Clara.

He stood erect, looking round. Just ahead were two islets in the stream, covered with osiers. But they were unattainable. The cliff came down like a sloping wall from far above their heads. Behind, not far back, were the fishermen.

Across the river the distant cattle fed silently in the desolate afternoon. He cursed again deeply under his breath. He gazed up the great steep bank. Was there no hope but to scale back to the public path?

'Stop a minute,' he said, and, digging his heels sideways into the steep bank of red clay, he began nimbly to mount. He looked across at every tree-foot. At last he found what he wanted. Two beech trees side by side on the hill held a little level on the upper face between their roots. It was littered with damp leaves, but it would do. The fishermen were perhaps sufficiently out of sight. He threw down his rainproof and waved to her to come.

She toiled to his side. Arriving there, she looked at him heavily, dumbly, and laid her head on his shoulder. He held her fast as he looked round. They were safe enough from all but the small, lonely cows over the river. He sunk his mouth on her throat, where he felt her heavy pulse beat under his lips. Everything was perfectly still. There was nothing in the afternoon but themselves.

When she arose, he, looking on the ground all the time, saw suddenly sprinkled on the black wet beech-roots many scarlet carnation petals, like splashed drops of blood; and red, small splashes fell from her bosom, streaming down her dress to her feet.

'Your flowers are smashed,' he said.

She looked at him heavily as she put back her hair. Suddenly he put his fingertips on her cheek.

'Why dost look so heavy?' he reproached her.

She smiled sadly, as if she felt alone in herself. He caressed her cheek with his fingers, and kissed her.

'Nay!' he said. 'Never thee bother!'

She gripped his fingers tight, and laughed shakily. Then she dropped her hand. He put the hair back from her brows, stroking her temples, kissing them lightly.

'But tha shouldna worrit!' he said softly, pleading.

'No, I don't worry!' she laughed tenderly and resigned.

'Yea, tha does! Dunna thee worrit,' he implored, caressing.

'No!' she consoled him, kissing him.

They had a stiff climb to get to the top again. It took them a quarter of an hour. When he got on to the level grass, he threw off his cap, wiped the sweat from his forehead, and sighed.

'Now we're back at the ordinary level,' he said.

She sat down, panting, on the tussocky grass. Her cheeks were flushed pink. He kissed her, and she gave way to joy.

'And now I'll clean thy boots and make thee fit for respectable folk,' he said.

He kneeled at her feet, worked away with a stick and tufts of grass. She put her fingers in his hair, drew his head to her, and kissed it.

'What am I supposed to be doing,' he said, looking at her laughing; 'cleaning shoes or dibbling with love? Answer me that!'

'Just whichever I please,' she replied.

'I'm your boot-boy for the time being, and nothing else!' But they remained looking into each other's eyes and laughing. Then they kissed with little nibbling kisses.

'T–t–t–t!' he went with his tongue, like his mother. 'I tell you, nothing gets done when there's a woman about.'

And he returned to his boot-cleaning, singing softly. She touched his thick hair, and he kissed her fingers. He worked away at her shoes. At last they were quite presentable.

'There you are, you see!' he said. 'Aren't I a great hand at restoring you to respectability? Stand up! There, you look as irreproachable as Britannia herself!'

He cleaned his own boots a little, washed his hands in a puddle, and sang. They went on into Clifton village. He was madly in love with her; every movement she made, every crease in her garments, sent a hot flash through him and seemed adorable.

The old lady at whose house they had tea was roused into gaiety by them.

'I could wish you'd had something of a better day,' she said, hovering round.

'Nay!' he laughed. 'We've been saying how nice it is.'

The old lady looked at him curiously. There was a peculiar glow and charm about him. His eyes were dark and laughing. He rubbed his moustache with a glad movement.

'Have you been saying *so*!' she exclaimed, a light rousing in her old eyes.

'Truly!' he laughed.

'Then I'm sure the day's good enough,' said the old lady.

She fussed about, and did not want to leave them.

'I don't know whether you'd like some radishes as well,' she said to Clara; 'but I've got some in the garden and a cucumber.'

Clara flushed. She looked very handsome.

'I should like some radishes,' she answered.

And the old lady pottered off gleefully.

'If she knew!' said Clara quietly to him.

'Well, she doesn't know; and it shows we're nice in ourselves, at any rate. You look quite enough to satisfy an archangel, and I'm sure I feel harmless – so – if it makes you look nice, and makes folk happy when they have us, and makes us happy – why, we're not cheating them out of much!'

They went on with the meal. When they were going away, the old lady came timidly with three tiny dahlias in full blow, neat as bees, and speckled scarlet and white. She stood before Clara, pleased with herself, saying, 'I don't know whether – ' and holding the flowers forward in her old hand.

'Oh, how pretty!' cried Clara, accepting the flowers.

'Shall she have them all?' asked Paul reproachfully of the old woman.

'Yes, she shall have them all,' she replied, beaming with joy. 'You have got enough for your share.'

'Ah, but I shall ask her to give me one!' he teased.

'Then she does as she pleases,' said the old lady, smiling. And she bobbed a little curtsey of delight.

Clara was rather quiet and uncomfortable. As they walked along, he said, 'You don't feel criminal, do you?'

She looked at him with startled grey eyes.

'Criminal!' she said. 'No.'

'But you seem to feel you have done a wrong?'

'No,' she said. 'I only think, "If they knew!"'

'If they knew, they'd cease to understand. As it is, they do understand, and they like it. What do they matter? Here, with only the trees and me, you don't feel not the least bit wrong, do you?'

He took her by the arm, held her facing him, holding her eyes with his. Something fretted him.

'Not sinners, are we?' he said, with an uneasy little frown.

'No,' she replied.

He kissed her, laughing.

'You like your little bit of guiltiness, I believe,' he said. 'I believe Eve enjoyed it, when she went cowering out of Paradise.'

But there was a certain glow and quietness about her that made him glad. When he was alone in the railway-carriage, he found himself tumultuously happy, and the people exceedingly nice, and the night lovely, and everything good.

Mrs Morel was sitting reading when he got home. Her health was not good now, and there had come that ivory pallor into her face which he never noticed, and which afterwards he never forgot. She did not mention her own ill-health to him. After all, she thought, it was not much.

'You are late!' she said, looking at him.

His eyes were shining; his face seemed to glow. He smiled to her.

'Yes; I've been down Clifton Grove with Clara.'

His mother looked at him again.

'But won't people talk?' she said.

'Why? They know she's a suffragette, and so on. And what if they do talk!'

'Of course, there may be nothing wrong in it,' said his mother. 'But you know what folk are, and if once she gets talked about –'

'Well, I can't help it. Their jaw isn't so almighty important, after all.'

'I think you ought to consider *her*.'

'So I *do*! What can people say? – that we take a walk together. I believe you're jealous.'

'You know I should be *glad* if she weren't a married woman.'

'Well, my dear, she lives separate from her husband, and talks on platforms; so she's already singled out from the sheep, and, as far as I can see, hasn't much to lose. No; her life's nothing to her, so what's the worth of nothing? She goes with me – it becomes something. Then she must pay – we both must pay! Folk are so frightened of paying; they'd rather starve and die.'

'Very well, my son. We'll see how it will end.'

'Very well, my mother. I'll abide by the end.'

'We'll see!'

'And she's – she's *awfully* nice, mother; she is really! You don't know!'

'That's not the same as marrying her.'

'It's perhaps better.'

There was silence for a while. He wanted to ask his mother something, but was afraid.

'Should you like to know her?' he hesitated.

'Yes,' said Mrs Morel coolly. 'I should like to know what she's like.'

'But she's nice, mother, she is! And not a bit common!'

'I never suggested she was.'

'But you seem to think she's – not as good as – She's better than ninety-nine folk out of a hundred, I tell you! She's *better*, she is! She's fair, she's honest, she's straight! There isn't anything underhand or superior about her. Don't be mean about her!'

Mrs Morel flushed.

'I am sure I am not mean about her. She may be quite as you say, but – '

'You don't approve,' he finished.

'And do you expect me to?' she answered coldly.

'Yes! – yes! – if you'd anything about you, you'd be glad! Do you *want* to see her?'

'I said I did.'

'Then I'll bring her – shall I bring her here?'

'You please yourself.'

'Then I *will* bring her here – one Sunday – to tea. If you think a horrid thing about her, I shan't forgive you.'

His mother laughed.

'As if it would make any difference!' she said. He knew he had won.

'Oh, but it feels so fine, mother, when she's there! She's such a queen in her way.'

Occasionally he still walked a little way from chapel with Miriam and Edgar. He did not go up to the farm. She, however, was very much the same with him, and he did not feel embarrassed in her presence. One evening she was alone when he accompanied her. They began by talking books: it was their unfailing topic. Mrs Morel had said that his and Miriam's affair was like a fire fed on books – if there were no more volumes it would die out. Miriam, for her part, boasted that she could read him like a book, could place her finger any minute on the chapter and the line. He, easily taken in, believed that Miriam knew more about him than anyone else. So it pleased him to talk to her about himself, like the simplest egoist. Very soon the conversation drifted to his own doings. It flattered him immensely that he was of such supreme interest.

'And what have you been doing lately?'

'I – oh, not much! I made a sketch of Bestwood from the garden, that is nearly right at last. It's the hundredth try.'

So they went on. Then she said, 'You've not been out, then, lately?'

'Yes; I went up Clifton Grove on Monday afternoon with Clara.'

'It was not very nice weather,' said Miriam, 'was it?'

'But I wanted to go out, and it was all right. The Trent is full.'

'And did you go to Barton?' she asked.

'No; we had tea in Clifton.'

'*Did* you! That would be nice.'

'It was! The jolliest old woman! She gave us several pom-pom dahlias, as pretty as you like.'

Miriam bowed her head and brooded. He was quite unconscious of concealing anything from her.

'What made her give them you?' she asked.

He laughed.

'Because she liked us – because we were jolly, I should think.'

Miriam put her finger in her mouth.

'Were you late home?' she asked.

At last he resented her tone.

'I caught the seven-thirty.'

'Ha!'

They walked on in silence, and he was angry.

'And how *is* Clara?' asked Miriam.

'Quite all right, I think.'

'That's good!' she said, with a tinge of irony. 'By the way, what of her husband? One never hears anything of him.'

'He's got some other woman, and is also quite all right,' he replied. 'At least, so I think.'

'I see – you don't know for certain. Don't you think a position like that is hard on a woman?'

'Rottenly hard!'

'It's so unjust!' said Miriam. 'The man does as he likes – '

'Then let the woman also,' he said.

'How can she? And if she does, look at her position!'

'What of it?'

'Why, it's impossible! You don't understand what a woman forfeits – '

'No, I don't. But if a woman's got nothing but her fair fame to feed on, why, it's thin tack, and a donkey would die of it!'

So she understood his moral attitude, at least, and she knew he would act accordingly.

She never asked him anything direct, but she got to know enough.

Another day, when he saw Miriam, the conversation turned to marriage, then to Clara's marriage with Dawes.

'You see,' he said, 'she never knew the fearful importance of marriage. She thought it was all in the day's march – it would have to come – and Dawes – well, a good many women would have given their souls to get him; so why not him? Then she developed into the *femme incomprise*, and treated him badly, I'll bet my boots.'

'And she left him because he didn't understand her?'

'I suppose so. I suppose she had to. It isn't altogether a question of under-standing; it's a question of living. With him, she was only half alive; the rest was dormant, deadened. And the dormant woman was the *femme incomprise* and she *had* to be awakened.'

'And what about him?'

'I don't know. I rather think he loves her as much as he can, but he's a fool.'

'It was something like your mother and father,' said Miriam.

'Yes; but my mother, I believe, got *real* joy and satisfaction out of my father at first. I believe she had a passion for him; that's why she stayed with him. After all, they were bound to each other.'

'Yes,' said Miriam.

'That's what once I must *have*, I think,' he continued – 'the real, real flame of feeling through another person – once, only once, if it only lasts three months. See, my mother looks as if she'd *had* everything that was necessary for her living and developing. There's not a tiny bit of a feeling of sterility about her.'

'No,' said Miriam.

'And with my father, at first, I'm sure she had the real thing. She knows; she has been there. You can feel it about her, and about him, and about hundreds of people you meet every day; and, once it has happened to you, you can go on with anything and ripen.'

'What has happened, exactly?' asked Miriam.

'It's so hard to say, but the something big and intense that changes you when you really come together with somebody else. It almost seems to fertilise your soul and make it that you can go on and mature.'

'And you think your mother had it with your father?'

'Yes; and at the bottom she feels grateful to him for giving it her, even now, though they are miles apart.'

'And you think Clara never had it?'

'I'm sure.'

Miriam pondered this. She saw what he was seeking – a sort of baptism of fire in passion, it seemed to her. She realised that he would never be satisfied till he had it. Perhaps it was essential to him, as to some men, to sow wild oats; and afterwards, when he was satisfied, he would not rage with restlessness any more, but could settle down and give her his life into her hands. Well, then, if he must go, let him go and have his fill – something big and intense, he called it. At any rate, when he had got it, he would not want it – that he said himself; he would want the other thing that she could give him. He would want to be owned, so that he could work. It seemed to her a bitter thing that he must go, but she could let him go into an inn for a glass of whisky, so she could let him go to Clara, so long as it was something that would satisfy a need in him, and leave him free for herself to possess.

'Have you told your mother about Clara?' she asked.

She knew this would be a test of the seriousness of his feeling for the other woman; she knew he was going to Clara for something vital, not as a man goes for pleasure to a prostitute, if he told his mother.

'Yes,' he said, 'and she is coming to tea on Sunday.'

'To your house?'

'Yes; I want mater to see her.'

'Ah!'

There was a silence. Things had gone quicker than she thought. She felt a sudden bitterness that he could leave her so soon and so entirely. And was Clara to be accepted by his people, who had been so hostile to herself?

'I may call in as I go to chapel,' she said. 'It is a long time since I saw Clara.'

'Very well,' he said, astonished, and unconsciously angry.

On the Sunday afternoon he went to Keston to meet Clara at the station. As he stood on the platform he was trying to examine in himself if he had a premonition.

'Do I *feel* as if she'd come?' he said to himself, and he tried to find out. His heart felt queer and contracted. That seemed like foreboding. Then he had a foreboding she would not come! Then she would not come, and instead of taking her over the fields home, as he had imagined, he would have to go alone. The train was late; the afternoon would be wasted, and the evening. He hated her for not coming. Why had she promised, then, if she could not keep her promise? Perhaps she had missed her train – he himself was always missing trains, but that was no reason why she should miss this particular one. He was angry with her; he was furious.

Suddenly he saw the train crawling, sneaking round the corner. Here, then, was the train, but of course she had not come. The green engine hissed along the platform, the row of brown carriages drew up, several doors opened. No; she had not come! No! Yes; ah, there she was! She had a big black hat on! He was at her side in a moment.

'I thought you weren't coming,' he said.

She was laughing rather breathlessly as she put out her hand to him; their eyes met. He took her quickly along the platform, talking at a great rate to hide his feeling. She looked beautiful. In her hat were large silk roses, coloured like tarnished gold. Her costume of dark cloth fitted so beautifully over her breast and shoulders. His pride went up as he walked with her. He felt the station people, who knew him, eyed her with awe and admiration.

'I was sure you weren't coming,' he laughed shakily.

She laughed in answer, almost with a little cry.

'And I wondered, when I was in the train, what*ever* I should do if you weren't there!' she said.

He caught her hand impulsively, and they went along the narrow twitchel. They took the road into Nuttall and over the Reckoning House Farm. It was a blue, mild day. Everywhere the brown leaves lay scattered; many scarlet hips stood upon the hedge beside the wood. He gathered a few for her to wear.

'Though, really,' he said, as he fitted them into the breast of her coat, 'you ought to object to my getting them, because of the birds. But they don't care much for rose-hips in this part, where they can get plenty of stuff. You often find the berries going rotten in the springtime.'

So he chattered, scarcely aware of what he said, only knowing he was putting berries in the bosom of her coat, while she stood patiently for him. And she watched his quick hands, so full of life, and it seemed to her she had never *seen* anything before. Till now, everything had been indistinct.'

They came near to the colliery. It stood quite still and black among the cornfields, its immense heap of slag seen rising almost from the oats.

'What a pity there is a coal-pit here where it is so pretty!' said Clara.

'Do you think so?' he answered. 'You see, I am so used to it I should miss it. No; and I like the pits here and there. I like the rows of trucks and the head-stocks, and the steam in the daytime, and the lights at night. When I was a boy, I always thought a pillar of cloud by day and a pillar of fire by night was a pit, with its steam, and its lights, and the burning bank – and I thought the Lord was always at the pit-top.'

As they drew near home she walked in silence, and seemed to hang back. He pressed her fingers in his own. She flushed, but gave no response.

'Don't you want to come home?' he asked.

'Yes, I want to come,' she replied.

It did not occur to him that her position in his home would be rather a peculiar and difficult one. To him it seemed just as if one of his men friends were going to be introduced to his mother, only nicer.

The Morels lived in a house in an ugly street that ran down a steep hill. The street itself was hideous. The house was rather superior to most. It was old, grimy, with a big bay window, and it was semi-detached; but it looked gloomy. Then Paul opened the door to the garden, and all was different. The sunny afternoon was there, like another land. By the path grew tansy and little trees. In front of the window was a plot of sunny grass, with old lilacs round it. And away went the garden, with heaps of dishevelled chrysanthemums in the sunshine, down to the sycamore tree, and the field, and beyond one looked over a few red-roofed cottages to the hills with all the glow of the autumn afternoon.

Mrs Morel sat in her rocking-chair, wearing her black silk blouse. Her grey-brown hair was taken smooth back from her brow and her high temples; her face was rather pale. Clara, suffering, followed Paul into the kitchen. Mrs Morel rose. Clara thought her a lady, even rather stiff. The young woman was very nervous. She had almost a wistful look, almost resigned.

'Mother – Clara,' said Paul.

Mrs Morel held out her hand and smiled.

'He has told me a good deal about you,' she said.

The blood flamed in Clara's cheek.

'I hope you don't mind my coming,' she faltered.

'I was pleased when he said he would bring you,' replied Mrs Morel.

Paul, watching, felt his heart contract with pain. His mother looked so small, and sallow, and done-for beside the luxuriant Clara.

'It's such a pretty day, mother!' he said. 'And we saw a jay.'

His mother looked at him; he had turned to her. She thought what a man he seemed, in his dark, well-made clothes. He was pale and detached-looking; it would be hard for any woman to keep him. Her heart glowed; then she was sorry for Clara.

'Perhaps you'll leave your things in the parlour,' said Mrs Morel nicely to the young woman.

'Oh, thank you,' she replied.

'Come on,' said Paul, and he led the way into the little front-room, with its old piano, its mahogany furniture, its yellowing marble mantelpiece. A fire was burning; the place was littered with books and drawing-boards. 'I leave my things lying about,' he said. 'It's so much easier.'

She loved his artist's paraphernalia, and the books, and the photos of people. Soon he was telling her: this was William, this was William's young lady in the evening dress, this was Annie and her husband, this was Arthur and his wife and the baby. She felt as if she were being taken into the family. He showed her photos, books, sketches, and they talked a little while. Then they returned to the kitchen. Mrs Morel put aside her book. Clara wore a blouse of fine silk chiffon, with narrow black-and-white stripes; her hair was done simply, coiled on top of her head. She looked rather stately and reserved.

'You have gone to live down Sneinton Boulevard?' said Mrs Morel. 'When I was a girl – girl, I say! – when I was a young woman *we* lived in Minerva Terrace.'

'Oh, did you!' said Clara. 'I have a friend in Number 6.'

And the conversation had started. They talked Nottingham and Nottingham people; it interested them both. Clara was still rather nervous; Mrs Morel was still somewhat on her dignity. She clipped her language very clear and precise. But they were going to get on well together, Paul saw.

Mrs Morel measured herself against the younger woman, and found herself easily stronger. Clara was deferential. She knew Paul's surprising regard for his mother, and she had dreaded the meeting, expecting someone rather hard and cold. She was surprised to find this little interested woman chatting with such readiness; and then she felt, as she felt with Paul, that she would not care to stand in Mrs Morel's way. There was something so hard and certain in his mother, as if she never had a misgiving in her life.

Presently Morel came down, ruffled and yawning, from his afternoon sleep. He scratched his grizzled head, he plodded in his stocking feet, his waistcoat hung open over his shirt. He seemed incongruous.

'This is Mrs Dawes, father,' said Paul.

Then Morel pulled himself together. Clara saw Paul's manner of bowing and shaking hands.

'Oh, indeed!' exclaimed Morel. 'I am very glad to see you – I am, I assure you. But don't disturb yourself. No, no; make yourself quite comfortable, and be very welcome.'

Clara was astonished at this flood of hospitality from the old collier. He was so courteous, so gallant! She thought him most delightful.

'And may you have come far?' he asked.

'Only from Nottingham,' she said.

'From Nottingham! Then you have had a beautiful day for your journey.'

Then he strayed into the scullery to wash his hands and face, and from force of habit came on to the hearth with the towel to dry himself.

At tea Clara felt the refinement and sang-froid of the household. Mrs Morel was perfectly at her ease. The pouring out the tea and attending to the people went on unconsciously, without interrupting her in her talk. There was a lot of room at the oval table; the china of dark blue willow pattern looked pretty on the glossy cloth. There was a little bowl of small, yellow chrysanthemums. Clara felt she completed the circle, and it was a pleasure to her. But she was rather afraid of the self-possession of the Morels, father and all. She took their tone; there was a feeling of balance. It was a cool, clear atmosphere, where everyone was himself, and in harmony. Clara enjoyed it, but there was a fear deep at the bottom of her.

Paul cleared the table whilst his mother and Clara talked. Clara was conscious of his quick, vigorous body as it came and went, seeming blown quickly by a wind at its work. It was almost like the hither and thither of a leaf that comes unexpected. Most of herself went with him. By the way she leaned forward, as if listening, Mrs Morel could see she was possessed elsewhere as she talked, and again the elder woman was sorry for her.

Having finished, he strolled down the garden, leaving the two women to talk. It was a hazy, sunny afternoon, mild and soft. Clara glanced through the window after him as he loitered among the chrysanthemums. She felt as if something almost tangible fastened her to him; yet he seemed so easy in his graceful, indolent movement, so detached as he tied up the too-heavy flower-branches to their stakes, that she wanted to shriek in her helplessness.

Mrs Morel rose.

'You will let me help you wash up,' said Clara.

'Eh, there are so few, it will only take me a minute,' said the other.

Clara, however, dried the tea-things, and was glad to be on such good terms with his mother, but it was torture not to be able to follow him down the garden. At last she allowed herself to go; she felt as if a rope were taken off her ankle.

The afternoon was golden over the hills of Derbyshire. He stood across in the other garden, beside a bush of pale Michaelmas daisies, watching the last bees crawl into the hive. Hearing her coming, he turned to her with an easy motion, saying, 'It's the end of the run with these chaps.'

Clara stood near him. Over the low red wall in front was the country and the far-off hills, all golden dim.

At that moment Miriam was entering through the garden door. She saw Clara go up to him, saw him turn, and saw them come to rest together. Something in their perfect isolation together made her know that it was accomplished between them, that they were, as she put it, married. She walked very slowly down the cinder-track of the long garden.

Clara had pulled a button from a hollyhock spire, and was breaking it to get the seeds. Above her bowed head the pink flowers stared, as if defending her. The last bees were falling down to the hive.

'Count your money,' laughed Paul, as she broke the flat seeds one by one from the roll of coin. She looked at him.

'I'm well off,' she said, smiling.

'How much? Pf!' He snapped his fingers. 'Can I turn them into gold?'

'I'm afraid not,' she laughed.

They looked into each other's eyes, laughing. At that moment they became aware of Miriam. There was a click, and everything had altered.

'Hello, Miriam!' he exclaimed. 'You said you'd come!'

'Yes. Had you forgotten?'

She shook hands with Clara, saying, 'It seems strange to see you here.'

'Yes,' replied the other; 'it seems strange to be here.'

There was a hesitation.

'It is pretty, isn't it?' said Miriam.

'I like it very much,' replied Clara.

Then Miriam realised that Clara was accepted as she had never been.

'Have you come down alone?' asked Paul.

'Yes; I went to Agatha's to tea. We are going to chapel. I only called in for a moment to see Clara.'

'You should have come in here to tea,' he said.

Miriam laughed shortly, and Clara turned impatiently aside.

'Do you like the chrysanthemums?' he asked.

'Yes; they are very fine,' replied Miriam.

'Which sort do you like best?' he asked

'I don't know. The bronze, I think.'

'I don't think you've seen all the sorts. Come and look. Come and see which are your favourites, Clara.'

He led the two women back to his own garden, where the tousled bushes of flowers of all colours stood raggedly along the path down to the field. The situation did not embarrass him, to his knowledge.

'Look, Miriam; these are the white ones that came from your garden. They aren't so fine here, are they?'

'No,' said Miriam.

'But they're hardier. You're so sheltered; things grow big and tender, and then die. These little yellow ones I like. Will you have some?'

While they were out there the bells began to ring in the church, sounding loud across the town and the field. Miriam looked at the tower, proud among the clustering roofs, and remembered the sketches he had brought her. It had been different then, but he had not left her even yet. She asked him for a book to read. He ran indoors.

'What! is that Miriam?' asked his mother coldly.

'Yes; she said she'd call and see Clara.'

'You told her, then?' came the sarcastic answer.

'Yes; why shouldn't I?'

'There's certainly no reason why you shouldn't,' said Mrs Morel, and she returned to her book. He winced from his mother's irony, frowned irritably, thinking: 'Why can't I do as I like?'

'You've not seen Mrs Morel before?' Miriam was saying to Clara.

'No; but she's *so* nice!'

'Yes,' said Miriam, dropping her head; 'in some ways she's very fine.'

'I should think so.'

'Had Paul told you much about her?'

'He had talked a good deal.'

'Ha!'

There was silence until he returned with the book.

'When will you want it back?' Miriam asked.

'When you like,' he answered.

Clara turned to go indoors, whilst he accompanied Miriam to the gate.

'When will you come up to Willey Farm?' the latter asked.

'I couldn't say,' replied Clara.

'Mother asked me to say she'd be pleased to see you any time, if you cared to come.'

'Thank you; I should like to, but I can't say when.'

'Oh, very well!' exclaimed Miriam rather bitterly, turning away.

She went down the path with her mouth to the flowers he had given her.

'You're sure you won't come in?' he said.

'No, thanks.'

'We are going to chapel.'

'Ha, I shall see you, then!' Miriam was very bitter.

'Yes.'

They parted. He felt guiltily towards her. She was bitter, and she scorned him. He still belonged to herself, she believed; yet he could have Clara, take her home, sit with her next his mother in chapel, give her the same hymn-book he had given herself years before. She heard him running quickly indoors.

But he did not go straight in. Halting on the plot of grass, he heard his mother's voice, then Clara's answer, 'What I hate is the bloodhound quality in Miriam.'

'Yes,' said his mother quickly, 'yes; *doesn't* it make you hate her, now?'

His heart went hot, and he was angry with them for talking about the girl. What right had they to say that? Something in the speech itself stung him into a flame of hate against Miriam. Then his own heart rebelled furiously at Clara's taking the liberty of speaking so about Miriam. After all, the girl was the better woman of the two, he thought, if it came to goodness. He went indoors. His mother looked excited. She was beating with her hand rhythmically on the sofa-arm, as women do who are wearing out. He could never bear to see the movement. There was a silence; then he began to talk.

In chapel Miriam saw him find the place in the hymn-book for Clara, in exactly the same way as he used for herself. And during the sermon he could see the girl across the chapel, her hat throwing a dark shadow over her face. What did she think, seeing Clara with him? He did not stop to consider. He felt himself cruel towards Miriam.

After chapel he went over Pentrich with Clara. It was a dark autumn night. They had said goodbye to Miriam, and his heart had smitten him as he left the girl alone. 'But it serves her right,' he said inside himself, and it almost gave him pleasure to go off under her eyes with this other handsome woman.

There was a scent of damp leaves in the darkness. Clara's hand lay warm and inert in his own as they walked. He was full of conflict. The battle that raged inside him made him feel desperate.

Up Pentrich Hill Clara leaned against him as he went. He slid his arm round her waist. Feeling the strong motion of her body under his arm as she walked, the tightness in his chest because of Miriam relaxed, and the hot blood bathed him. He held her closer and closer.

Then: 'You still keep on with Miriam,' she said quietly.

'Only talk. There never *was* a great deal more than talk between us,' he said bitterly.

'Your mother doesn't care for her,' said Clara.

'No, or I might have married her. But it's all up, really!'

Suddenly his voice went passionate with hate.

'If I was with her now, we should be jawing about the "Christian Mystery", or some such tack. Thank God, I'm not!'

They walked on in silence for some time.

'But you can't really give her up,' said Clara.

'I don't give her up, because there's nothing to give,' he said.

'There is for her.'

'I don't know why she and I shouldn't be friends as long as we live,' he said. 'But it'll only be friends.'

Clara drew away from him, leaning away from contact with him.

'What are you drawing away for?' he asked.

She did not answer, but drew farther from him.

'Why do you want to walk alone?' he asked.

Still there was no answer. She walked resentfully, hanging her head.

'Because I said I would be friends with Miriam!' he exclaimed.

She would not answer him anything.

'I tell you it's only words that go between us,' he persisted, trying to take her again.

She resisted. Suddenly he strode across in front of her, barring her way.

'Damn it!' he said. 'What do you want now?'

'You'd better run after Miriam,' mocked Clara.

The blood flamed up in him. He stood showing his teeth. She drooped sulkily. The lane was dark, quite lonely. He suddenly caught her in his arms, stretched forward, and put his mouth on her face in a kiss of rage. She turned frantically to avoid him. He held her fast. Hard and relentless his mouth came for her. Her breasts hurt against the wall of his chest. Helpless, she went loose in his arms, and he kissed her, and kissed her.

He heard people coming down the hill.

'Stand up! stand up!' he said thickly, gripping her arm till it hurt. If he had let go, she would have sunk to the ground.

She sighed and walked dizzily beside him. They went on in silence.

'We will go over the fields,' he said; and then she woke up.

But she let herself be helped over the stile, and she walked in silence with him over the first dark field. It was the way to Nottingham and to the station, she knew. He seemed to be looking about. They came out on a bare hilltop where stood the dark figure of the ruined windmill. There he halted. They stood together high up in the darkness, looking at the lights scattered on the night before them, handfuls of glittering points, villages lying high and low on the dark, here and there.

'Like treading among the stars,' he said, with a quaky laugh.

Then he took her in his arms, and held her fast. She moved aside her mouth to ask, dogged and low, 'What time is it?'

'It doesn't matter,' he pleaded thickly.

'Yes it does – yes! I must go!'

'It's early yet,' he said.

'What time is it?' she insisted.

All round lay the black night, speckled and spangled with lights.

'I don't know.'

She put her hand on his chest, feeling for his watch. He felt the joints fuse into fire. She groped in his waistcoat pocket, while he stood panting. In the darkness she could see the round, pale face of the watch, but not the figures. She stooped over it. He was panting till he could take her in his arms again.

'I can't see,' she said.

'Then don't bother.'

'Yes; I'm going!' she said, turning away.

'Wait! I'll look!' But he could not see. 'I'll strike a match.'

He secretly hoped it was too late to catch the train. She saw the glowing lantern of his hands as he cradled the light; then his face lit up, his eyes fixed on the watch. Instantly all was dark again. All was black before her eyes; only a glowing match was red near her feet. Where was he?

'What is it?' she asked, afraid.

'You can't do it,' his voice answered out of the darkness.

There was a pause. She felt in his power. She had heard the ring in his voice. It frightened her.

'What time is it?' she asked, quiet, definite, hopeless.

'Two minutes to nine,' he replied, telling the truth with a struggle.

'And can I get from here to the station in fourteen minutes?'

'No. At any rate – '

She could distinguish his dark form again a yard or so away. She wanted to escape.

'But can't I do it?' she pleaded.

'If you hurry,' he said brusquely. 'But you could easily walk it, Clara; it's only seven miles to the tram. I'll come with you.'

'No; I want to catch the train.'

'But why?'

'I do – I want to catch the train.'

Suddenly his voice altered.

'Very well,' he said, dry and hard. 'Come along, then.'

And he plunged ahead into the darkness. She ran after him, wanting to cry. Now he was hard and cruel to her. She ran over the rough, dark fields behind him, out of breath, ready to drop. But the double row of lights at the station drew nearer. Suddenly, 'There she is!' he cried, breaking into a run.

There was a faint rattling noise. Away to the right the train, like a luminous caterpillar, was threading across the night. The rattling ceased.

'She's over the viaduct. You'll just do it.'

Clara ran, quite out of breath, and fell at last into the train. The whistle blew. He was gone. Gone! – and she was in a carriage full of people. She felt the cruelty of it.

He turned round and plunged home. Before he knew where he was he was in the kitchen at home. He was very pale. His eyes were dark and dangerous-looking, as if he were drunk. His mother looked at him.

'Well, I must say your boots are in a nice state!' she said.

He looked at his feet. Then he took off his overcoat. His mother wondered if he were drunk.

'She caught the train, then?' she said.

'Yes.'

'I hope *her* feet weren't so filthy. Where on earth you dragged her I don't know!'

He was silent and motionless for some time.

'Did you like her?' he asked grudgingly at last.

'Yes, I liked her. But you'll tire of her, my son; you know you will.'

He did not answer. She noticed how he laboured in his breathing.

'Have you been running?' she asked.

'We had to run for the train.'

'You'll go and knock yourself up. You'd better drink hot milk.'

It was as good a stimulant as he could have, but he refused and went to bed. There he lay face down on the counterpane, and shed tears of rage and pain. There was a physical pain that made him bite his lips till they bled, and the chaos inside him left him unable to think, almost to feel.

'This is how she serves me, is it?' he said in his heart over and over, pressing his face in the quilt. And he hated her. Again he went over the scene, and again he hated her.

The next day there was a new aloofness about him. Clara was very gentle, almost loving. But he treated her distantly, with a touch of contempt. She sighed, continuing to be gentle. He came round.

One evening of that week Sarah Bernhardt was at the Theatre Royal in Nottingham, giving 'La Dame aux Camélias'. Paul wanted to see this old and famous actress, and he asked Clara to accompany him. He told his mother to leave the key in the window for him.

'Shall I book seats?' he asked of Clara.

'Yes. And put on an evening suit, will you? I've never seen you in it.'

'But, good Lord, Clara! Think of *me* in evening suit at the theatre!' he remonstrated.

'Would you rather not?' she asked.

'I will if you *want* me to; but I s'll feel a fool.'

She laughed at him.

'Then feel a fool for my sake, once, won't you?'

The request made his blood flush up.

'I suppose I s'll have to.'

'What are you taking a suitcase for?' his mother asked.

He blushed furiously.

'Clara asked me,' he said.

'And what seats are you going in?'

'Circle – three-and-six each!'

'Well, I'm sure!' exclaimed his mother sarcastically.

'It's only once in the bluest of blue moons,' he said.

He dressed at Jordan's, put on an overcoat and a cap, and met Clara in a café. She was with one of her suffragette friends. She wore an old long coat, which did not suit her, and had a little wrap over her head, which he hated. The three went to the theatre together.

Clara took off her coat on the stairs, and he discovered she was in a sort of semi-evening dress, that left her arms and neck and part of her breast bare. Her hair was done fashionably. The dress, a simple thing of green crape, suited her.

She looked quite grand, he thought. He could see her figure inside the frock, as if that were wrapped closely round her. The firmness and the softness of her upright body could almost be felt as he looked at her. He clenched his fists.

And he was to sit all the evening beside her beautiful naked arm, watching the strong throat rise from the strong chest, watching the breasts under the green stuff, the curve of her limbs in the tight dress. Something in him hated her again for submitting him to this torture of nearness. And he loved her as she balanced her head and stared straight in front of her, pouting, wistful, immobile, as if she yielded herself to her fate because it was too strong for her. She could not help herself; she was in the grip of something bigger than herself. A kind of eternal look about her, as if she were a wistful sphinx, made it necessary for him to kiss her. He dropped his programme, and crouched down on the floor to get it, so that he could kiss her hand and wrist. Her beauty was a torture to him. She sat immobile. Only, when the lights went down, she sank a little against him, and he caressed her hand and arm with his fingers. He could smell her faint perfume. All the time his blood kept sweeping up in great white-hot waves that killed his consciousness momentarily.

The drama continued. He saw it all in the distance, going on somewhere; he did not know where, but it seemed far away inside him. He was Clara's white heavy arms, her throat, her moving bosom. That seemed to be himself. Then away somewhere the play went on, and he was identified with that also. There was no himself. The grey-and-black eyes of Clara, her bosom coming down on him, her arm that he held gripped between his hands, were all that existed. Then he felt himself small and helpless, her towering in her force above him.

Only the intervals, when the lights came up, hurt him expressibly. He wanted to run anywhere, so long as it would be dark again. In a maze, he wandered out for a drink. Then the lights were out, and the strange, insane reality of Clara and the drama took hold of him again.

The play went on. But he was obsessed by the desire to kiss the tiny blue vein that nestled in the bend of her arm. He could feel it. His whole life seemed suspended till he had put his lips there. It must be done. And the other people!

At last he bent quickly forward and touched it with his lips. His moustache brushed the sensitive flesh. Clara shivered, drew away her arm.

When all was over, the lights up, the people clapping, he came to himself and looked at his watch. His train was gone.

'I s'll have to walk home!' he said.

Clara looked at him.

'Is it too late?' she asked.

He nodded. Then he helped her on with her coat.

'I love you! You look beautiful in that dress,' he murmured over her shoulder, among the throng of bustling people.

She remained quiet. Together they went out of the theatre. He saw the cabs waiting, the people passing. It seemed he met a pair of brown eyes which hated him. But he did not know. He and Clara turned away, mechanically taking the direction to the station.

The train had gone. He would have to walk the ten miles home.

'It doesn't matter,' he said. 'I shall enjoy it.'

'Won't you,' she said, flushing, 'come home for the night? I can sleep with mother.'

He looked at her. Their eyes met.

'What will your mother say?' he asked.

'She won't mind.'

'You're sure?'

'Quite!'

'Shall I come?'

'If you will.'

'Very well.'

And they turned away. At the first stopping-place they took the car. The wind blew fresh in their faces. The town was dark; the tram tipped in its haste. He sat with her hand fast in his.

'Will your mother be gone to bed?' he asked.

'She may be. I hope not.'

They hurried along the silent, dark little street, the only people out of doors. Clara quickly entered the house. He hesitated.

'Come in,' she said.

He leaped up the step and was in the room. Her mother appeared in the inner doorway, large and hostile.

'Who have you got there?' she asked.

'It's Mr Morel; he has missed his train. I thought we might put him up for the night, and save him a ten-mile walk.'

'H'm!' exclaimed Mrs Radford. 'That's *your* lookout! If you've invited him, he's very welcome as far as I'm concerned. *You* keep the house!'

'If you don't like me, I'll go away again,' he said.

'Nay, nay, you needn't! Come along in! I dunno what you'll think of the supper I'd got her.'

It was a little dish of chip potatoes and a piece of bacon. The table was roughly laid for one.

'You can have some more bacon,' continued Mrs Radford. 'More chips you can't have.'

'It's a shame to bother you,' he said.

'Oh, don't you be apologetic! It doesn't *do* wi' me! You treated her to the theatre, didn't you?' There was a sarcasm in the last question.

'Well?' laughed Paul uncomfortably.

'Well, and what's an inch of bacon! Take your coat off.'

The big, straight-standing woman was trying to estimate the situation. She moved about the cupboard. Clara took his coat. The room was very warm and cosy in the lamplight.

'My sirs!' exclaimed Mrs Radford; 'but you two's a pair of bright beauties, I must say! What's all that get-up for?'

'I believe we don't know,' he said, feeling a victim.

'There isn't room in *this* house for two such bobby-dazzlers, if you fly your kites *that* high!' she rallied them. It was a nasty thrust.

He in his dinner jacket, and Clara in her green dress and bare arms, were confused. They felt they must shelter each other in that little kitchen.

'And look at *that* blossom!' continued Mrs Radford, pointing to Clara. 'What does she reckon she did it for?'

Paul looked at Clara. She was rosy; her neck was warm with blushes. There was a moment of silence.

'You like to see it, don't you?' he asked.

The mother had them in her power. All the time his heart was beating hard, and he was tight with anxiety. But he would fight her.

'Me like to see it!' exclaimed the old woman. 'What should I like to see her make a fool of herself for?'

'I've seen people look bigger fools,' he said. Clara was under his protection now.

'Oh, ay! and when was that?' came the sarcastic rejoinder.

'When they made frights of themselves,' he answered.

Mrs Radford, large and threatening, stood suspended on the hearthrug, holding her fork.

'They're fools either road,' she answered at length, turning to the Dutch oven.

'No,' he said, fighting stoutly. 'Folk ought to look as well as they can.'

'And do you call *that* looking nice!' cried the mother, pointing a scornful fork at Clara. 'That – that looks as if it wasn't properly dressed!'

'I believe you're jealous that you can't swank as well,' he said laughing.

'Me! I could have worn evening dress with anybody, if I'd wanted to!' came the scornful answer.

'And why didn't you want to?' he asked pertinently. 'Or *did* you wear it?'

There was a long pause. Mrs Radford readjusted the bacon in the Dutch oven. His heart beat fast, for fear he had offended her.

'Me!' she exclaimed at last. 'No, I didn't! And when I was in service, I knew as soon as one of the maids came out in bare shoulders what sort *she* was, going to her sixpenny hop!'

'Were you too good to go to a sixpenny hop?' he said.

Clara sat with bowed head. His eyes were dark and glittering. Mrs Radford took the Dutch oven from the fire, and stood near him, putting bits of bacon on his plate.

'*There's* a nice crozzly bit!' she said.

'Don't give me the best!' he said.

'*She's* got what *she* wants,' was the answer.

There was a sort of scornful forbearance in the woman's tone that made Paul know she was mollified.

'But *do* have some!' he said to Clara.

She looked up at him with her grey eyes, humiliated and lonely.

'No thanks!' she said.

'Why won't you?' he answered caressively.

The blood was beating up like fire in his veins. Mrs Radford sat down again, large and impressive and aloof. He left Clara altogether to attend to the mother.

'They say Sarah Bernhardt's fifty,' he said.

'Fifty! She's turned sixty!' came the scornful answer.

'Well,' he said, 'you'd never think it! She made me want to howl even now.'

'I should like to see myself howling at *that* bad old baggage!' said Mrs

Radford. 'It's time she began to think herself a grandmother, not a shrieking catamaran – '

He laughed.

'A catamaran is a boat the Malays use,' he said.

'And it's a word as *I* use,' she retorted.

'My mother does sometimes, and it's no good my telling her,' he said.

'I s'd think she boxes your ears,' said Mrs Radford, good-humouredly.

'She'd like to, and she says she will, so I give her a little stool to stand on.'

'That's the worst of my mother,' said Clara. 'She never wants a stool for anything.'

'But she often can't touch *that* lady with a long prop,' retorted Mrs Radford to Paul.

'I s'd think she doesn't want touching with a prop,' he laughed. '*I* shouldn't.'

'It might do the pair of you good to give you a crack on the head with one,' said the mother, laughing suddenly.

'Why are you so vindictive towards me?' he said. 'I've not stolen anything from you.'

'No; I'll watch that,' laughed the older woman.

Soon the supper was finished. Mrs Radford sat guard in her chair. Paul lit a cigarette. Clara went upstairs, returning with a sleeping-suit, which she spread on the fender to air.

'Why, I'd forgot all about *them*!' said Mrs Radford. 'Where have they sprung from?'

'Out of my drawer.'

'H'm! You bought 'em for Baxter, an' he wouldn't wear 'em, would he?' – laughing. 'Said he reckoned to do wi'out trousers i' bed.' She turned confidentially to Paul, saying: 'He couldn't *bear* 'em, them pyjama things.'

The young man sat making rings of smoke.

'Well, it's everyone to his taste,' he laughed.

Then followed a little discussion of the merits of pyjamas.

'My mother loves me in them,' he said. 'She says I'm a pierrot.'

'I can imagine they'd suit you,' said Mrs Radford.

After a while he glanced at the little clock that was ticking on the mantelpiece. It was half-past twelve.

'It is funny,' he said, 'but it takes hours to settle down to sleep after the theatre.'

'It's about time you did,' said Mrs Radford, clearing the table.

'Are you tired?' he asked of Clara.

'Not the least bit,' she answered, avoiding his eyes.

'Shall we have a game at cribbage?' he said.

'I've forgotten it.'

'Well, I'll teach you again. May we play crib, Mrs Radford?' he asked.

'You'll please yourselves,' she said; 'but it's pretty late.'

'A game or so will make us sleepy,' he answered.

Clara brought the cards, and sat spinning her wedding ring whilst he shuffled them. Mrs Radford was washing up in the scullery. As it grew later Paul felt the situation getting more and more tense.

'Fifteen two, fifteen four, fifteen six, and two's eight!'

The clock struck one. Still the game continued. Mrs Radford had done all the little jobs preparatory to going to bed, had locked the door and filled the kettle. Still Paul went on dealing and counting. He was obsessed by Clara's arms and throat. He believed he could see where the division was just beginning for her breasts. He could not leave her. She watched his hands, and felt her joints melt as they moved quickly. She was so near; it was almost as if he touched her, and yet not quite. His mettle was roused. He hated Mrs Radford. She sat on, nearly dropping asleep, but determined and obstinate in her chair. Paul glanced at her, then at Clara. She met his eyes, that were angry, mocking, and hard as steel. Her own answered him in shame. He knew she, at any rate, was of his mind. He played on.

At last Mrs Radford roused herself stiffly, and said, 'Isn't it nigh on time you two was thinking o' bed?'

Paul played on without answering. He hated her sufficiently to murder her.

'Half a minute,' he said.

The elder woman rose and sailed stubbornly into the scullery, returning with his candle, which she put on the mantelpiece. Then she sat down again. The hatred of her went so hot down his veins, he dropped his cards.

'We'll stop, then,' he said, but his voice was still a challenge.

Clara saw his mouth shut hard. Again he glanced at her. It seemed like an agreement. She bent over the cards, coughing, to clear her throat.

'Well, I'm glad you've finished,' said Mrs Radford. 'Here, take your things' – she thrust the warm suit in his hand – 'and this is your candle. Your room's over this; there's only two, so you can't go far wrong. Well, good-night. I hope you'll rest well.'

'I'm sure I shall; I always do,' he said.

'Yes; and so you ought at your age,' she replied.

He bade good-night to Clara, and went. The twisting stairs of white, scrubbed wood creaked and clanged at every step. He went doggedly. The two doors faced each other. He went in his room, pushed the door to, without fastening the latch.

It was a small room with a large bed. Some of Clara's hairpins were on the dressing-table – her hairbrush. Her clothes and some skirts hung under a cloth in a corner. There was actually a pair of stockings over a chair. He explored the room. Two books of his own were there on the shelf. He undressed, folded his suit, and sat on the bed listening. Then he blew out the candle, lay down, and in two minutes was almost asleep. Then click! – he was wide awake and writhing in torment. It was as if, when he had nearly got to sleep, something had bitten him suddenly and sent him mad. He sat up and looked at the room in the darkness, his feet doubled under him, perfectly motionless, listening. He heard a cat somewhere away outside; then the heavy, poised tread of the mother; then Clara's distinct voice, 'Will you unfasten my dress?'

There was silence for some time. At last the mother said, 'Now then! aren't you coming up?'

'No, not yet,' replied the daughter calmly.

'Oh, very well then! If it's not late enough, stop a bit longer. Only you needn't come waking me up when I've got to sleep.'

'I shan't be long,' said Clara.

Immediately afterwards Paul heard the mother slowly mounting the stairs. The candlelight flashed through the cracks in his door. Her dress brushed the door, and his heart jumped. Then it was dark, and he heard the clatter of her latch. She was very leisurely indeed in her preparations for sleep. After a long time it was quite still. He sat strung up on the bed, shivering slightly. His door was an inch open. As Clara came upstairs, he would intercept her. He waited. All was dead silence. The clock struck two. Then he heard a slight scrape of the fender downstairs. Now he could not help himself. His shivering was uncontrollable. He felt he must go or die.

He stepped off the bed, and stood a moment, shuddering. Then he went straight to the door. He tried to step lightly. The first stair cracked like a shot. He listened. The old woman stirred in her bed. The staircase was dark. There was a slit of light under the stair-foot door, which opened into the kitchen. He stood a moment. Then he went on, mechanically. Every step creaked, and his back was creeping, lest the old woman's door should open behind him up above. He fumbled with the door at the bottom. The latch opened with a loud clack. He went through into the kitchen, and shut the door noisily behind him. The old woman daren't come now.

Then he stood, arrested. Clara was kneeling on a pile of white underclothing on the hearthrug, her back towards him, warming herself. She did not look round, but sat crouching on her heels, and her rounded, beautiful back was towards him, and her face was hidden. She was warming her body at the fire for consolation. The glow was rosy on one side, the shadow was dark and warm on the other. Her arms hung slack.

He shuddered violently, clenching his teeth and fists hard to keep control. Then he went forward to her. He put one hand on her shoulder, the fingers of the other hand under her chin to raise her face. A convulsed shiver ran through her, once, twice, at his touch. She kept her head bent.

'Sorry!' he murmured, realising that his hands were very cold.

Then she looked up at him, frightened, like a thing that is afraid of death.

'My hands are so cold,' he murmured.

'I like it,' she whispered, closing her eyes.

The breath of her words was on his mouth. Her arms clasped his knees. The cord of his sleeping-suit dangled against her and made her shiver. As the warmth went into him, his shuddering became less.

At length, unable to stand so any more, he raised her, and she buried her head on his shoulder. His hands went over her slowly with an infinite tenderness of caress. She clung close to him, trying to hide herself against him. He clasped her very fast. Then at last she looked at him, mute, imploring, looking to see if she must be ashamed.

His eyes were dark, very deep, and very quiet. It was as if her beauty and his taking it hurt him, made him sorrowful. He looked at her with a little pain, and was afraid. He was so humble before her. She kissed him fervently on the eyes, first one, then the other, and she folded herself to him. She gave herself. He held her fast. It was a moment intense almost to agony.

She stood letting him adore her and tremble with joy of her. It healed her hurt pride. It healed her; it made her glad. It made her feel erect and proud again. Her pride had been wounded inside her. She had been cheapened. Now she radiated with joy and pride again. It was her restoration and her recognition.

Then he looked at her, his face radiant. They laughed to each other, and he strained her to his chest. The seconds ticked off, the minutes passed; and still the two stood clasped rigid together, mouth to mouth, like a statue in one block.

But again his fingers went seeking over her, restless, wandering, dissatisfied. The hot blood came up wave upon wave. She laid her head on his shoulder.

'Come you to my room,' he murmured.

She looked at him and shook her head, her mouth pouting disconsolately, her eyes heavy with passion. He watched her fixedly.

'Yes!' he said.

Again she shook her head.

'Why not?' he asked.

She looked at him still heavily, sorrowfully, and again she shook her head. His eyes hardened, and he gave way.

When, later on, he was back in bed, he wondered why she had refused to come to him openly, so that her mother would know. At any rate, then things would have been definite. And she could have stayed with him the night, without having to go, as she was, to her mother's bed. It was strange, and he could not understand it. And then almost immediately he fell asleep.

He awoke in the morning with someone speaking to him. Opening his eyes, he saw Mrs Radford, big and stately, looking down on him. She held a cup of tea in her hand.

'Do you think you're going to sleep till Doomsday?' she said.

He laughed at once.

'It ought only to be about five o'clock,' he said.

'Well,' she answered, 'it's half-past seven, whether or not. Here, I've brought you a cup of tea.'

He rubbed his face, pushed the tumbled hair off his forehead, and roused himself.

'What's it so late for!' he grumbled.

He resented being wakened. It amused her. She saw his neck in the flannel sleeping-jacket, as white and round as a girl's. He rubbed his hair crossly.

'It's no good your scratching your head,' she said. 'It won't make it no earlier. Here, an' how long d'you think I'm going to stand waiting wi' this here cup?'

'Oh, dash tho cup!' he said.

'You should go to bed earlier,' said the woman.

He looked up at her, laughing with impudence.

'I went to bed before *you* did,' he said.

'Yes, my Guyney, you did!' she exclaimed.

'Fancy,' he said, stirring his tea, 'having tea brought to bed to me! My mother'll think I'm ruined for life.'

'Don't she never do it?' asked Mrs Radford.

'She'd as leave think of flying.'

'Ah, I always spoilt my lot! That's why they've turned out such bad 'uns,' said the elderly woman.

'You'd only Clara,' he said. 'And Mr Radford's in heaven. So I suppose there's only you left to be the bad un.'

'I'm not bad; I'm only soft,' she said, as she went out of the bedroom. 'I'm only a fool, I am!'

Clara was very quiet at breakfast, but she had a sort of air of proprietorship over him that pleased him infinitely. Mrs Radford was evidently fond of him. He began to talk of his painting.

'What's the good,' exclaimed the mother, 'of your whittling and worrying and twistin' and too-in' at that painting of yours? What *good* does it do you, I should like to know? You'd better be enjoyin' yourself.'

'Oh, but,' exclaimed Paul, 'I made over thirty guineas last year.'

'Did you! Well, that's a consideration, but it's nothing to the time you put in.'

'And I've got four pounds owing. A man said he'd give me five pounds if I'd paint him and his missis and the dog and the cottage. And I went and put the fowls in instead of the dog, and he was waxy, so I had to knock a quid off. I was sick of it, and I didn't like the dog. I made a picture of it. What shall I do when he pays me the four pounds?'

'Nay! you know your own uses for your money,' said Mrs Radford.

'But I'm going to bust this four pounds. Should we go to the seaside for a day or two?'

'Who?'

'You and Clara and me.'

'What, on your money!' she exclaimed, half wrathful.

'Why not?'

'*You* wouldn't be long in breaking your neck at a hurdle race!' she said.

'So long as I get a good run for my money! Will you?'

'Nay; you may settle that atween you.'

'And you're willing?' he asked, amazed and rejoicing.

'You'll do as you like,' said Mrs Radford, 'whether I'm willing or not.'

CHAPTER 13

Baxter Dawes

Soon after Paul had been to the theatre with Clara, he was drinking in the Punch Bowl with some friends of his when Dawes came in. Clara's husband was growing stout; his eyelids were getting slack over his brown eyes; he was losing his healthy firmness of flesh. He was very evidently on the downward track. Having quarrelled with his sister, he had gone into cheap lodgings. His mistress had left him for a man who would marry her. He had been in prison one night for fighting when he was drunk, and there was a shady betting episode in which he was concerned.

Paul and he were confirmed enemies, and yet there was between them that peculiar feeling of intimacy, as if they were secretly near to each other, which sometimes exists between two people, although they never speak to one another. Paul often thought of Baxter Dawes, often wanted to get at him and be friends with him. He knew that Dawes often thought about him, and that the man was drawn to him by some bond or other. And yet the two never looked at each other save in hostility.

Since he was a superior employee at Jordan's, it was the thing for Paul to offer Dawes a drink.

'What'll you have?' he asked of him.

'Nowt wi' a bleeder like you!' replied the man.

Paul turned away with a slight disdainful movement of the shoulders, very irritating.

'The aristocracy,' he continued, 'is really a military institution. Take Germany, now. She's got thousands of aristocrats whose only means of existence is the army. They're deadly poor, and life's deadly slow. So they hope for a war. They look for war as a chance of getting on. Till there's a war they are idle good-for-nothings. When there's a war, they are leaders and commanders. There you are, then – they *want* war!'

He was not a favourite debater in the public-house, being too quick and overbearing. He irritated the older men by his assertive manner, and his cock-sureness. They listened in silence, and were not sorry when he finished.

Dawes interrupted the young man's flow of eloquence by asking, in a loud sneer, 'Did you learn all that at th' theatre th' other night?'

Paul looked at him; their eyes met. Then he knew Dawes had seen him coming out of the theatre with Clara.

'Why, what about th' theatre?' asked one of Paul's associates, glad to get a dig at the young fellow, and sniffing something tasty.

'Oh, him in a bobtailed evening suit, on the lardy-da!' sneered Dawes, jerking his head contemptuously at Paul.

'That's comin' it strong,' said the mutual friend. 'Tart an' all?'

'Tart, begod!' said Dawes.

'Go on; let's have it!' cried the mutual friend.

'You've got it,' said Dawes, 'an' I reckon Morelly had it an' all.'

'Well, I'll be jiggered!' said the mutual friend. 'An' was it a proper tart?'

'Tart, God blimey – yes!'

'How do you know?'

'Oh,' said Dawes, 'I reckon he spent th' night – '

There was a good deal of laughter at Paul's expense.

'But who *was* she? D'you know her?' asked the mutual friend.

'I should *shay sho,*' said Dawes.

This brought another burst of laughter.

'Then spit it out,' said the mutual friend.

Dawes shook his head, and took a gulp of beer.

'It's a wonder he hasn't let on himself,' he said. 'He'll be braggin' of it in a bit.'

'Come on, Paul,' said the friend; 'it's no good. You might just as well own up.'

'Own up what? That I happened to take a friend to the theatre?'

'Oh well, if it was all right, tell us who she was, lad,' said the friend.

'She *was* all right,' said Dawes.

Paul was furious. Dawes wiped his golden moustache with his fingers, sneering.

'Strike me – ! One o' that sort?' said the mutual friend. 'Paul, boy, I'm surprised at you. And do you know her, Baxter?'

'Just a bit, like!'

He winked at the other men.

'Oh well,' said Paul, 'I'll be going!'

The mutual friend laid a detaining hand on his shoulder.

'Nay,' he said, 'you don't get off as easy as that, my lad. We've got to have a full account of this business.'

'Then get it from Dawes!' he said.

'You shouldn't funk your own deeds, man,' remonstrated the friend.

Then Dawes made a remark which caused Paul to throw half a glass of beer in his face.

'Oh, Mr Morel!' cried the barmaid, and she rang the bell for the 'chucker-out'.

Dawes spat and rushed for the young man. At that minute a brawny fellow with his shirt-sleeves rolled up and his trousers tight over his haunches intervened.

'Now, then!' he said, pushing his chest in front of Dawes.

'Come out!' cried Dawes.

Paul was leaning, white and quivering, against the brass rail of the bar. He hated Dawes, wished something could exterminate him at that minute; and at the same time, seeing the wet hair on the man's forehead, he thought he looked pathetic. He did not move.

'Come out, you,' said Dawes.

'That's enough, Dawes,' cried the barmaid.

'Come on,' said the 'chucker-out', with kindly insistence, 'you'd better be getting on.'

And, by making Dawes edge away from his own close proximity, he worked him to the door.

'*That's* the little sod as started it!' cried Dawes, half cowed, pointing to Paul Morel.

'Why, what a story, Mr Dawes!' said the barmaid. 'You know it was you all the time.'

Still the 'chucker-out' kept thrusting his chest forward at him, still he kept edging back, until he was in the doorway and on the steps outside; then he turned round.

'All right,' he said, nodding straight at his rival.

Paul had a curious sensation of pity, almost of affection mingled with violent hate, for the man. The coloured door swung to; there was silence in the bar.

'Serve him jolly well right!' said the barmaid.

'But it's a nasty thing to get a glass of beer in your eyes,' said the mutual friend.

'I tell you *I* was glad he did,' said the barmaid. 'Will you have another, Mr Morel?'

She held up Paul's glass questioningly. He nodded.

'He's a man as doesn't care for anything, is Baxter Dawes,' said one.

'Pooh! is he?' said the barmaid. 'He's a loud-mouthed one, he is, and they're never much good. Give me a pleasant-spoken chap, if you want a devil!'

'Well, Paul, my lad,' said the friend, 'you'll have to take care of yourself now for a while.'

'You won't have to give him a chance over you, that's all,' said the barmaid.

'Can you box?' asked a friend.

'Not a bit,' he answered, still very white.

'I might give you a turn or two,' said the friend.

'Thanks, I haven't time.'

And presently he took his departure.

'Go along with him, Mr Jenkinson,' whispered the barmaid, tipping Mr Jenkinson the wink.

The man nodded, took his hat, said 'Good-night all!' very heartily, and followed Paul, calling, 'Half a minute, old man. You an' me's going the same road, I believe.'

'Mr Morel doesn't like it,' said the barmaid. 'You'll see, we shan't have him in much more. I'm sorry; he's good company. And Baxter Dawes wants locking up, that's what he wants.'

Paul would have died rather than his mother should get to know of this affair.

He suffered tortures of humiliation and self-consciousness. There was now a good deal of his life of which necessarily he could not speak to his mother. He had a life apart from her – his sexual life. The rest she still kept. But he felt he had to conceal something from her, and it irked him. There was a certain silence between them, and he felt he had, in that silence, to defend himself against her; he felt condemned by her. Then sometimes he hated her, and pulled at her bondage. His life wanted to free itself of her. It was like a circle where life turned back on itself, and got no farther. She bore him, loved him, kept him, and his love turned back into her, so that he could not be free to go forward with his own life, really love another woman. At this period, unknowingly, he resisted his mother's influence. He did not tell her things; there was a distance between them.

Clara was happy, almost sure of him. She felt she had at last got him for herself; and then again came the uncertainty. He told her jestingly of the affair with her husband. Her colour came up, her grey eyes flashed.

'That's him to a "T",' she cried – 'like a navvy! He's not fit for mixing with decent folk.'

'Yet you married him,' he said.

It made her furious that he reminded her.

'I did!' she cried. 'But how was I to know!'

'I think he might have been rather nice,' he said.

'You think *I* made him what he is!' she exclaimed.

'Oh no! he made himself. But there's something about him –'

Clara looked at her lover closely. There was something in him she hated, a sort of detached criticism of herself, a coldness which made her woman's soul harden against him.

'And what are you going to do?' she asked.

'How?'

'About Baxter.'

'There's nothing to do, is there?' he replied.

'You can fight him if you have to, I suppose?' she said.

'No; I haven't the least sense of the "fist". It's funny. With most men there's the instinct to clench the fist and hit. It's not so with me. I should want a knife or a pistol or something to fight with.'

'Then you'd better carry something,' she said.

'Nay,' he laughed; 'I'm not daggeroso.'

'But he'll do something to you. You don't know him.'

'All right,' he said, 'we'll see.'

'And you'll let him?'

'Perhaps, if I can't help it.'

'And if he kills you?' she said.

'I should be sorry, for his sake and mine.'

Clara was silent for a moment.

'You *do* make me angry!' she exclaimed.

'That's nothing afresh,' he laughed.

'But why are you so silly? You don't know him.'

'And don't want.'

'Yes, but you're not going to let a man do as he likes with you?'

'What must I do?' he replied, laughing.

'*I* should carry a revolver,' she said. 'I'm sure he's dangerous.'

'I might blow my fingers off,' he said.

'No; but won't you?' she pleaded.

'No.'

'Not anything?'

'No.'

'And you'll leave him to – ?'

'Yes.'

'You are a fool!'

'Fact!'

She set her teeth with anger. 'I could *shake* you!' she cried, trembling with passion.

'Why?'

'Let a man like *him* do as he likes with you.'

'You can go back to him if he triumphs,' he said.

'Do you want me to hate you?' she asked.

'Well, I only tell you,' he said.

'And *you* say you *love* me!' she exclaimed, low and indignant.

'Ought I to slay him to please you?' he said. 'But if I did, see what a hold he'd have over me.'

'Do you think I'm a fool!' she exclaimed.

'Not at all. But you don't understand me, my dear.'

There was a pause between them.

'But you ought *not* to expose yourself,' she pleaded.

He shrugged his shoulders.

> 'The man in righteousness arrayed,
> The pure and blameless liver,
> Needs not the keen Toledo blade
> Nor venom-freighted quiver,'

he quoted.

She looked at him searchingly.

'I wish I could understand you,' she said.

'There's simply nothing to understand,' he laughed.

She bowed her head, brooding.

He did not see Dawes for several days; then one morning as he ran upstairs from the spiral room he almost collided with the burly metalworker.

'What the – !' cried the smith.

'Sorry!' said Paul, and passed on.

'*Sorry!*' sneered Dawes.

Paul whistled lightly 'Put Me among the Girls'.

'I'll stop your whistle, my jockey!' he said.

The other took no notice.

'You're goin' to answer for that job of the other night.'

Paul went to his desk in his corner, and turned over the leaves of the ledger.

'Go and tell Fanny I want order 097, quick!' he said to his boy.

Dawes stood in the doorway, tall and threatening, looking at the top of the young man's head.

'Six and five's eleven and seven's one-and-six,' Paul added aloud.

'An' you hear, do you!' said Dawes.

'*Five and ninepence!*' He wrote a figure. 'What's that?' he said.

'I'm going to show you what it is,' said the smith.

The other went on adding the figures aloud.

'Yer crawlin' little —, yer daresn't face me proper!'

Paul quickly snatched the heavy ruler. Dawes started. The young man ruled some lines in his ledger. The elder man was infuriated.

'But wait till I light on you, no matter where it is, I'll settle your hash for a bit, yer little swine!'

'All right,' said Paul.

At that the smith started heavily from the doorway. Just then a whistle piped shrilly. Paul went to the speaking tube.

'Yes!' he said, and he listened. 'Er – yes!' He listened, then he laughed. 'I'll come down directly I've got a visitor just now.'

Dawes knew from his tone that he had been speaking to Clara. He stepped forward.

'Yer little devil!' he said. 'I'll visitor you, inside of two minutes! Think I'm goin' ter have *you* whipperty-snappin' round?'

The other clerks in the warehouse looked up. Paul's office-boy appeared, holding some white article.

'Fanny says you could have had it last night if you'd let her know,' he said.

'All right,' answered Paul, looking at the stocking. 'Get it off.'

Dawes stood frustrated, helpless with rage. Morel turned round.

'Excuse me a minute,' he said to Dawes, and he would have run downstairs.

'By God, I'll stop your gallop!' shouted the smith, seizing him by the arm. He turned quickly.

'Hey! Hey!' cried the office-boy, alarmed.

Thomas Jordan started out of his little glass office, and came running down the room.

'What's a-matter, what's a-matter?' he said, in his old man's sharp voice.

'I'm just goin' ter settle this little —, that's all,' said Dawes desperately.

'What do you mean?' snapped Thomas Jordan.

'What I say,' said Dawes, but he hung fire.

Morel was leaning against the counter, ashamed, half grinning.

'What's it all about?' snapped Thomas Jordan.

'Couldn't say,' said Paul, shaking his head and shrugging his shoulders.

'Couldn't yer, couldn't yer!' cried Dawes, thrusting forward his handsome, furious face, and squaring his fist.

'Have you finished?' cried the old man, strutting. 'Get off about your business, and don't come here tipsy in the morning.'

Dawes turned his big frame slowly upon him.

'Tipsy!' he said. 'Who's tipsy? I'm no more tipsy than *you* are!'

'We've heard that song before,' snapped the old man. 'Now you get off, and don't be long about it. Comin' *here* with your rowdying.'

The smith looked down contemptuously on his employer. His hands, large and grimy, and yet well shaped for his labour, worked restlessly. Paul remembered they were the hands of Clara's husband, and a flash of hate went through him.

'Get out before you're turned out!' snapped Thomas Jordan.

'Why, who'll turn me out?' said Dawes, beginning to sneer.

Mr Jordan started, marched up to the smith, waving him off, thrusting his stout little figure at the man, saying, 'Get off my premises – get off!'

He seized and twitched Dawes' arm.

'Come off!' said the smith, and with a jerk of the elbow he sent the little manufacturer staggering backwards.

Before anyone could help him, Thomas Jordan had collided with the flimsy spring-door. It had given way, and let him crash down the half-dozen steps into Fanny's room. There was a second of amazement; then men and girls were running. Dawes stood a moment looking bitterly on the scene, then he took his departure.

Thomas Jordan was shaken and bruised, not otherwise hurt. He was, however, beside himself with rage. He dismissed Dawes from his employment, and summoned him for assault.

At the trial Paul Morel had to give evidence. Asked how the trouble began, he said, 'Dawes took occasion to insult Mrs Dawes and me because I accompanied her to the theatre one evening; then I threw some beer at him, and he wanted his revenge.'

'*Cherchez la femme!*' smiled the magistrate.

The case was dismissed after the magistrate had told Dawes he thought him a skunk.

'You gave the case away,' snapped Mr Jordan to Paul.

'I don't think I did,' replied the latter. 'Besides, you didn't really want a conviction, did you?'

'What do you think I took the case up for?'

'Well,' said Paul, 'I'm sorry if I said the wrong thing.' Clara was also very angry.

'Why need *my* name have been dragged in?' she said.

'Better speak it openly than leave it to be whispered.'

'There was no need for anything at all,' she declared.

'We are none the poorer,' he said indifferently.

'*You* may not be,' she said.

'And you?' he asked.

'I need never have been mentioned.'

'I'm sorry,' he said; but he did not sound sorry.

He told himself easily: 'She will come round.' And she did.

He told his mother about the fall of Mr Jordan and the trial of Dawes. Mrs Morel watched him closely.

'And what do you think of it all?' she asked him.

'I think he's a fool,' he said.

But he was very uncomfortable, nevertheless.

'Have you ever considered where it will end?' his mother said.

'No,' he answered; 'things work out of themselves.'

'They do, in a way one doesn't like, as a rule,' said his mother.

'And then one has to put up with them,' he said.

'You'll find you're not as good at "putting up" as you imagine,' she said.

He went on working rapidly at his design.

'Do you ever ask *her* opinion?' she said at length.

'What of?'

'Of you, and the whole thing.'

'I don't care what her opinion of me is. She's fearfully in love with me, but it's not very deep.'

'But quite as deep as your feeling for her.'

He looked up at his mother curiously.

'Yes,' he said. 'You know, mother, I think there must be something the matter with me, that I *can't* love. When she's there, as a rule, I *do* love her. Sometimes, when I see her just as *the woman*, I love her, mother; but then, when she talks and criticises, I often don't listen to her.'

'Yet she's as much sense as Miriam.'

'Perhaps; and I love her better than Miriam. But *why* don't they hold me?'

The last question was almost a lamentation. His mother turned away her face, sat looking across the room, very quiet, grave, with something of renunciation.

'But you wouldn't want to marry Clara?' she said.

'No; at first perhaps I would. But why – why don't I want to marry her or anybody? I feel sometimes as if I wronged my women, mother.'

'How wronged them, my son?'

'I don't know.'

He went on painting rather despairingly; he had touched the quick of the trouble.

'And as for wanting to marry,' said his mother, 'there's plenty of time yet.'

'But no, mother. I even love Clara, and I did Miriam; but to *give* myself to them in marriage I couldn't. I couldn't belong to them. They seem to want *me*, and I can't ever give it them.'

'You haven't met the right woman.'

'And I never shall meet the right woman while you live,' he said.

She was very quiet. Now she began to feel again tired, as if she were done.

'We'll see, my son,' she answered.

The feeling that things were going in a circle made him mad.

Clara was, indeed, passionately in love with him, and he with her, as far as passion went. In the daytime he forgot her a good deal. She was working in the same building, but he was not aware of it. He was busy, and her existence was of no matter to him. But all the time she was in her spiral room she had a sense that he was upstairs, a physical sense of his person in the same building. Every second she expected him to come through the door, and when he came it was a shock to her. But he was often short and offhand with her. He gave her his directions in an official manner, keeping her at bay. With what wits she had left she listened to him. She dared not misunderstand or fail to remember, but it was a cruelty to her. She wanted to touch his chest. She knew exactly how his breast was shapen under the waistcoat, and she wanted to touch it. It maddened her to hear his mechanical voice giving orders about the work. She wanted to break through the sham of it, smash the trivial coating of business which covered him with hardness, get at the man again, but she was afraid, and before she could feel one touch of his warmth he was gone, and she ached again.

He knew that she was dreary every evening she did not see him, so he gave her a good deal of his time. The days were often a misery to her, but the evenings and the nights were usually a bliss to them both. Then they were silent. For hours they sat together, or walked together in the dark, and talked only a few, almost meaningless words. But he had her hand in his, and her bosom left its warmth in his chest making him feel whole.

One evening they were walking down by the canal, and something was troubling him. She knew she had not got him. All the time he whistled softly and persistently to himself. She listened, feeling she could learn more from his whistling than from his speech. It was a sad dissatisfied tune – a tune that made her feel he would not stay with her. She walked on in silence. When they came to the swing bridge he sat down on the great pole, looking at the stars in the water. He was a long way from her. She had been thinking.

'Will you always stay at Jordan's?' she asked.

'No,' he answered without reflecting. 'No; I s'll leave Nottingham and go abroad – soon.'

'Go abroad! What for?'

'I dunno! I feel restless.'

'But what shall you do?'

'I shall have to get some steady designing work, and some sort of sale for my pictures first,' he said. 'I am gradually making my way. I know I am.'

'And when do you think you'll go?'

'I don't know. I shall hardly go for long, while there's my mother.'

'You couldn't leave her?'

'Not for long.'

She looked at the stars in the black water. They lay very white and staring. It was an agony to know he would leave her, but it was almost an agony to have him near her.

'And if you made a nice lot of money, what would you do?' she asked.

'Go somewhere in a pretty house near London with my mother.'

'I see.'

There was a long pause.

'I could still come and see you,' he said. 'I don't know. Don't ask me what I should do; I don't know.'

There was a silence. The stars shuddered and broke upon the water. There came a breath of wind. He went suddenly to her, and put his hand on her shoulder.

'Don't ask me anything about the future,' he said miserably. 'I don't know anything. Be with me now, will you, no matter what it is?'

And she took him in her arms. After all, she was a married woman, and she had no right even to what he gave her. He needed her badly. She had him in her arms, and he was miserable. With her warmth she folded him over, consoled him, loved him. She would let the moment stand for itself.

After a moment he lifted his head as if he wanted to speak.

'Clara,' he said, struggling.

She caught him passionately to her, pressed his head down on her breast with her hand. She could not bear the suffering in his voice. She was afraid in her soul. He might have anything of her – anything; but she did not want to *know*. She felt she could not bear it. She wanted him to be soothed upon her – soothed. She stood clasping him and caressing him, and he was something unknown to her – something almost uncanny. She wanted to soothe him into forgetfulness.

And soon the struggle went down in his soul, and he forgot. But then Clara was not there for him, only a woman, warm, something he loved and almost worshipped, there in the dark. But it was not Clara, and she submitted to him. The naked hunger and inevitability of his loving her, something strong and blind and ruthless in its primitiveness, made the hour almost terrible to her. She knew how stark and alone he was, and she felt it was great that he came to her; and she took him simply because his need was bigger either than her or him, and her soul was still within her. She did this for him in his need, even if he left her, for she loved him.

All the while the peewits were screaming in the field. When he came to, he wondered what was near his eyes, curving and strong with life in the dark, and what voice it was speaking. Then he realised it was the grass, and the peewit was calling. The warmth was Clara's breathing heaving. He lifted his head, and looked into her eyes. They were dark and shining and strange, life wild at the source staring into his life, stranger to him, yet meeting him; and he put his face down on her throat, afraid. What was she? A strong, strange, wild life, that breathed with his in the darkness through this hour. It was all so much bigger than themselves that he was hushed. They had met, and included in their meeting the thrust of the manifold grass-stems, the cry of the peewit, the wheel of the stars.

When they stood up they saw other lovers stealing down the opposite hedge. It seemed natural they were there; the night contained them.

And after such an evening they both were very still, having known the immensity of passion. They felt small, half afraid, childish, and wondering, like Adam and Eve when they lost their innocence and realised the magnificence of the power which drove them out of Paradise and across the great night and the great day of humanity. It was for each of them an initiation and a satisfaction. To know their own nothingness, to know the tremendous living flood which carried them always, gave them rest within themselves. If so great a magnificent power could overwhelm them, identify them altogether with itself, so that they knew they were only grains in the tremendous heave that lifted every grass-blade its little height, and every tree, and living thing, then why fret about themselves? They could let themselves be carried by life, and they felt a sort of peace each in the other. There was a verification which they had had together. Nothing could nullify it, nothing could take it away; it was almost their belief in life.

But Clara was not satisfied. Something great was there, she knew; something great enveloped her. But it did not keep her. In the morning it was not the same. They had *known*, but she could not keep the moment. She wanted it again; she wanted something permanent. She had not realised fully. She thought it was he whom she wanted. He was not safe to her. This that had been between them might never be again; he might leave her. She had not got him; she was not satisfied. She had been there, but she had not gripped the – the something – she knew not what – which she was mad to have.

In the morning he had considerable peace, and was happy in himself. It seemed almost as if he had known the baptism of fire in passion, and it left him at rest. But it was not Clara. It was something that happened because of her, but it was not her. They were scarcely any nearer each other. It was as if they had been blind agents of a great force.

When she saw him that day at the factory her heart melted like a drop of fire. It was his body, his brows. The drop of fire grew more intense in her breast; she must hold him. But he, very quiet, very subdued this morning, went on giving his instructions. She followed him into the dark, ugly basement, and lifted her arms to him. He kissed her, and the intensity of passion began to burn him again. Somebody was at the door. He ran upstairs; she returned to her room, moving as if in a trance.

After that the fire slowly went down. He felt more and more that his experience had been impersonal, and not Clara. He loved her. There was a big tenderness, as after a strong emotion they had known together; but it was not she who could keep his soul steady. He had wanted her to be something she could not be.

And she was mad with desire of him. She could not see him without touching him. In the factory, as he talked to her about spiral hose, she ran her hand secretly along his side. She followed him out into the basement for a quick kiss;

her eyes, always mute and yearning, full of unrestrained passion, she kept fixed on his. He was afraid of her, lest she should too flagrantly give herself away before the other girls. She invariably waited for him at dinner-time for him to embrace her before she went. He felt as if she were helpless, almost a burden to him, and it irritated him.

'But what do you always want to be kissing and embracing for?' he said. 'Surely there's a time for everything?'

She looked up at him, and the hate came into her eyes.

'*Do* I always want to be kissing you?' she said.

'Always, even if I come to ask you about the work. I don't want anything to do with love when I'm at work. Work's work – '

'And what is love?' she asked. 'Has it to have special hours?'

'Yes; out-of-work hours.'

'And you'll regulate it according to Mr Jordan's closing time?'

'Yes; and according to the freedom from business of any sort.'

'It is only to exist in spare time?'

'That's all, and not always then – not the kissing sort of love.'

'And that's all you think of it?'

'It's quite enough.'

'I'm glad you think so.'

And she was cold to him for some time – she hated him; and while she was cold and contemptuous, he was uneasy till she had forgiven him again. But when they started afresh they were not any nearer. He kept her because he never satisfied her.

In the spring they went together to the seaside. They had rooms at a little cottage near Theddlethorpe, and lived as man and wife. Mrs Radford sometimes went with them.

It was known in Nottingham that Paul Morel and Mrs Dawes were going together, but as nothing was very obvious, and Clara was always a solitary person, and he seemed so simple and innocent, it did not make much difference.

He loved the Lincolnshire coast, and she loved the sea. In the early morning they often went out together to bathe. The grey of the dawn, the far, desolate reaches of the fenland smitten with winter, the sea-meadows rank with herbage, were stark enough to rejoice his soul. As they stepped on to the highroad from their plank bridge, and looked round at the endless monotony of levels, the land a little darker than the sky, the sea sounding small beyond the sand-hills, his heart filled strong with the sweeping relentlessness of life. She loved him then. He was solitary and strong, and his eyes had a beautiful light.

They shuddered with cold; then he raced her down the road to the green turf bridge. She could run well. Her colour soon came, her throat was bare, her eyes shone. He loved her for being so luxuriously heavy, and yet so quick. Himself was light; she went with a beautiful rush. They grew warm, and walked hand in hand.

A flush came into the sky, the wan moon, halfway down the west, sank into insignificance. On the shadowy land things began to take life, plants with great leaves became distinct. They came through a pass in the big, cold sand-hills on to the beach. The long waste of foreshore lay moaning under the dawn and the sea; the ocean was a flat dark strip with a white edge. Over the gloomy sea the sky grew red. Quickly the fire spread among the clouds and scattered them. Crimson burned to orange, orange to dull gold, and in a golden glitter the sun came up, dribbling fierily over the waves in little splashes, as if someone had gone along and the light had spilled from her pail as she walked.

The breakers ran down the shore in long, hoarse strokes. Tiny seagulls, like specks of spray, wheeled above the line of surf. Their crying seemed larger than they. Far away the coast reached out, and melted into the morning, the tussocky sand-hills seeming to sink to a level with the beach. Mablethorpe was tiny on their right. They had alone the space of all this level shore, the sea, and the up-coming sun, the faint noise of the waters, the sharp crying of the gulls.

They had a warm hollow in the sand-hills where the wind did not come. He stood looking out to sea.

'It's very fine,' he said.

'Now don't get sentimental,' she said.

It irritated her to see him standing gazing at the sea, like a solitary and poetic person. He laughed. She quickly undressed.

'There are some fine waves this morning,' she said triumphantly.

She was a better swimmer than he; he stood idly watching her.

'Aren't you coming?' she said.

'In a minute,' he answered.

She was white and velvet skinned, with heavy shoulders. A little wind, coming from the sea, blew across her body and ruffled her hair.

The morning was of a lovely limpid gold colour. Veils of shadow seemed to be drifting away on the north and the south. Clara stood shrinking slightly from the touch of the wind, twisting her hair. The sea-grass rose behind the white stripped woman. She glanced at the sea, then looked at him. He was watching her with dark eyes which she loved and could not understand. She hugged her breasts between her arms, cringing, laughing: 'Oo, it will be so cold!' she said.

He bent forward and kissed her, held her suddenly close, and kissed her again. She stood waiting. He looked into her eyes, then away at the pale sands.

'Go, then!' he said quietly.

She flung her arms round his neck, drew him against her, kissed him passionately, and went, saying, 'But you'll come in?'

'In a minute.'

She went plodding heavily over the sand that was soft as velvet. He, on the sand-hills, watched the great pale coast envelop her. She grew smaller, lost proportion, seemed only like a large white bird toiling forward.

'Not much more than a big white pebble on the beach, not much more than a clot of foam being blown and rolled over the sand,' he said to himself.

She seemed to move very slowly across the vast sounding shore. As he watched, he lost her. She was dazzled out of sight by the sunshine. Again he saw her, the merest white speck moving against the white, muttering sea-edge.

'Look how little she is!' he said to himself. 'She's lost like a grain of sand in the beach – just a concentrated speck blown along, a tiny white foam-bubble, almost nothing among the morning. Why does she absorb me?'

The morning was altogether uninterrupted: she was gone in the water. Far and wide the beach, the sand-hills with their blue marram, the shining water, glowed together in immense, unbroken solitude.

'What is she, after all?' he said to himself. 'Here's the sea-coast morning, big and permanent and beautiful; there is she, fretting, always unsatisfied, and temporary as a bubble of foam. What does she mean to me, after all? She represents something, like a bubble of foam represents the sea. But what is *she*? It's not her I care for.'

Then, startled by his own unconscious thoughts, that seemed to speak so distinctly that all the morning could hear, he undressed and ran quickly down the sands. She was watching for him. Her arm flashed up to him, she heaved on a wave, subsided, her shoulders in a pool of liquid silver. He jumped through the breakers, and in a moment her hand was on his shoulder.

He was a poor swimmer, and could not stay long in the water. She played round him in triumph, sporting with her superiority, which he begrudged her. The sunshine stood deep and fine on the water. They laughed in the sea for a minute or two, then raced each other back to the sand-hills.

When they were drying themselves, panting heavily, he watched her laughing, breathless face, her bright shoulders, her breasts that swayed and made him frightened as she rubbed them, and he thought again, 'But she is magnificent, and even bigger than the morning and the sea. Is she – ? is she – ?'

She, seeing his dark eyes fixed on her, broke off from her drying with a laugh.

'What are you looking at?' she said.

'You,' he answered, laughing.

Her eyes met his, and in a moment he was kissing her white 'goose-fleshed' shoulder, and thinking, 'What is she? What is she?'

She loved him in the morning. There was something detached, hard, and elemental about his kisses then, as if he were only conscious of his own will, not in the least of her and her wanting him.

Later in the day he went out sketching.

'You,' he said to her, 'go with your mother to Sutton. I am so dull.'

She stood and looked at him. He knew she wanted to come with him, but he preferred to be alone. She made him feel imprisoned when she was there, as if he could not get a free deep breath, as if there were something on top of him. She felt his desire to be free of her.

In the evening he came back to her. They walked down the shore in the darkness, then sat for a while in the shelter of the sand-hills.

'It seems,' she said, as they stared over the darkness of the sea, where no light was to be seen – 'it seems as if you only loved me at night – as if you didn't love me in the daytime.'

He ran the cold sand through his fingers, feeling guilty under the accusation. 'The night is free to you,' he replied. 'In the daytime I want to be by myself.'

'But why?' she said. 'Why, even now, when we are on this short holiday?'

'I don't know. Love-making stifles me in the daytime.'

'But it needn't be always love-making,' she said.

'It always is,' he answered, 'when you and I are together.'

She sat feeling very bitter.

'Do you ever want to marry me?' he asked curiously.

'Do you me?' she replied.

'Yes, yes; I should like us to have children,' he answered slowly.

She sat with her head bent, fingering the sand.

'But you don't really want a divorce from Baxter, do you?' he said.

It was some minutes before she replied.

'No,' she said, very deliberately; 'I don't think I do.'

'Why?'

'I don't know.'

'Do you feel as if you belonged to him?'

'No; I don't think so.'

'What, then?'

'I think he belongs to me,' she replied.

He was silent for some minutes, listening to the wind blowing over the hoarse, dark sea.

'And you never really intended to belong to *me*?' he said.

'Yes, I do belong to you,' she answered.

'No,' he said; 'because you don't want to be divorced.'

It was a knot they could not untie, so they left it, took what they could get; and what they could not attain they ignored.

'I consider you treated Baxter rottenly,' he said another time.

He half expected Clara to answer him, as his mother would: 'You consider your own affairs, and don't know so much about other people's.' But she took him seriously, almost to his own surprise.

'Why?' she said.

'I suppose you thought he was a lily of the valley, and so you put him in an appropriate pot, and tended him according. You made up your mind he was a lily of the valley, and it was no good his being a cow-parsnip. You wouldn't have it.'

'I certainly never imagined him a lily of the valley.'

'You imagined him something he wasn't. That's just what a woman is. She thinks she knows what's good for a man, and she's going to see he gets it; and no matter if he's starving, he may sit and whistle for what he needs, while she's got him, and is giving him what's good for him.'

'And what are you doing?' she asked.

'I'm thinking what tune I shall whistle,' he laughed.

And instead of boxing his ears, she considered him in earnest.

'You think I want to give you what's good for you?' she asked.

'I hope so; but love should give a sense of freedom, not of prison. Miriam made me feel tied up like a donkey to a stake. I must feed on her patch, and nowhere else. It's sickening!'

'And would *you* let a *woman* do as she likes?'

'Yes; I'll see that she likes to love me. If she doesn't – well, I don't hold her.'

'If you were as wonderful as you say –' replied Clara.

'I should be the marvel I am,' he laughed.

There was a silence in which they hated each other, though they laughed.

'Love's a dog in the manger,' he said.

'And which of us is the dog?' she asked.

'Oh well, you, of course.'

So there went on a battle between them. She knew she never fully had him. Some part, big and vital in him, she had no hold over; nor did she ever try to get it, or even to realise what it was. And he knew in some way that she held herself still as Mrs Dawes. She did not love Dawes, never had loved him; but she believed he loved her, at least depended on her. She felt a certain surety about him that she never felt with Paul Morel. Her passion for the young man had filled her soul, given her a certain satisfaction, eased her of her self-mistrust, her doubt. Whatever else she was, she was inwardly assured. It was almost as if she had gained *herself*, and stood now distinct and complete. She had received her confirmation; but she never believed that her life belonged to Paul Morel, nor his to her. They would separate in the end, and the rest of her life would be an ache after him. But at any rate, she *knew* now, she was sure of herself. And the same could almost be said of him. Together they had received the baptism of life, each through the other; but now their missions were separate. Where he wanted to go she could not come with him. They would have to part sooner or later. Even if they married, and were faithful to each other, still he would have to leave her, go on alone, and she would only have to attend to him when he came home. But it was not possible. Each wanted a mate to go side by side with.

Clara had gone to live with her mother upon Mapperley Plains. One evening, as Paul and she were walking along Woodborough Road, they met Dawes. Morel knew something about the bearing of the man approaching, but he was absorbed in his thinking at the moment, so that only his artist's eye watched the form of the stranger. Then he suddenly turned to Clara with a laugh, and put his hand on her shoulder, saying, laughing, 'But we walk side by side, and yet I'm in London arguing with an imaginary Orpen; and where are you?'

At that instant Dawes passed, almost touching Morel. The young man glanced, saw the dark brown eyes burning, full of hate and yet tired.

'Who was that?' he asked of Clara.

'It was Baxter,' she replied.

Paul took his hand from her shoulder and glanced round; then he saw again distinctly the man's form as it approached him. Dawes still walked erect, with his fine shoulders flung back, and his face lifted; but there was a furtive look in his eyes that gave one the impression he was trying to get unnoticed past every person he met, glancing suspiciously to see what they thought of him. And his hands seemed to be wanting to hide. He wore old clothes, the trousers were torn at the knee, and the handkerchief tied round his throat was dirty; but his cap was still defiantly over one eye. As she saw him Clara felt guilty. There was a tiredness and despair on his face that made her hate him, because it hurt her.

'He looks shady,' said Paul.

But the note of pity in his voice reproached her, and made her feel hard.

'His true commonness comes out,' she answered.

'Do you hate him?' he asked.

'You talk,' she said, 'about the cruelty of women; I wish you knew the cruelty of men in their brute force. They simply don't know that the woman exists.'

'Don't I?' he said.

'No,' she answered.

'Don't I know you exist?'

'About me you know nothing,' she said bitterly – 'about me!'

'Not more than Baxter knew?' he asked.

'Perhaps not as much.'

He felt puzzled, and helpless, and angry. There she walked unknown to him, though they had been through such experience together.

'But you know me pretty well,' he said.

She did not answer.

'Did you know Baxter as well as you know me?' he asked.

'He wouldn't let me,' she said.

'And I have let you know me?'

'It's what men won't let you do. They won't let you get really near to them,' she said.

'And haven't I let you?'

'Yes,' she answered slowly; 'but you've never come near to me. You can't come out of yourself, you can't. Baxter could do that better than you.'

He walked on pondering. He was angry with her for preferring Baxter to him.

'You begin to value Baxter now you've not got him,' he said.

'No; I can only see where he was different from you.'

But he felt she had a grudge against him.

One evening, as they were coming home over the fields, she startled him by asking, 'Do you think it's worth it – the – the sex part?'

'The act of loving, itself?'

'Yes; is it worth anything to you?'

'But how can you separate it?' he said. 'It's the culmination of everything. All our intimacy culminates then.'

'Not for me,' she said.

He was silent. A flash of hate for her came up. After all she was dissatisfied with him, even there, where he thought they fulfilled each other. But he believed her too implicitly.

'I feel,' she continued slowly, 'as if I hadn't got you, as if all of you weren't there, and as if it weren't *me* you were taking – '

'Who, then?'

'Something just for yourself. It has been fine, so that I daren't think of it. But is it *me* you want, or is it *It*?'

He again felt guilty. Did he leave Clara out of count, and take simply woman? But he thought that was splitting a hair.

'When I had Baxter, actually had him, then I *did* feel as if I had all of him,' she said.

'And it was better?' he asked.

'Yes, yes; it was more whole. I don't say you haven't given me more than he ever gave me.'

'Or could give you.'

'Yes, perhaps; but you've never given me yourself.'

He knitted his brows angrily.

'If I start to make love to you,' he said, 'I just go like a leaf down the wind.'

'And leave me out of count,' she said.

'And then is it nothing to you?' he asked, almost rigid with chagrin.

'It's something; and sometimes you have carried me away – right away – I know – and – I reverence you for it – but – '

'Don't "but" me,' he said, kissing her quickly, as a fire ran through him.

She submitted, and was silent.

It was true as he said. As a rule, when he started love-making, the emotion was strong enough to carry with it everything – reason, soul, blood – in a great sweep, like the Trent carries bodily its back-swirls and intertwinings, noiselessly. Gradually the little criticisms, the little sensations, were lost, thought also went, everything borne along in one flood. He became, not a man with a mind, but a great instinct. His hands were like creatures, living; his limbs, his body, were all life and consciousness, subject to no will of his, but living in themselves. Just as he was, so it seemed the vigorous, wintry stars were strong also with life. He and they struck with the same pulse of fire, and the same joy of strength which held the bracken-frond stiff near his eyes held his own body firm. It was as if he and the stars, and the dark herbage, and Clara were licked up in an immense tongue of flame, which tore onwards and upwards. Everything rushed along in living beside him; everything was still, perfect in itself, along with him. This wonderful stillness in each thing in itself, while it was being borne along in a very ecstasy of living, seemed the highest point of bliss.

And Clara knew this held him to her, so she trusted altogether to the passion. It, however, failed her very often. They did not often reach again the height of that once when the peewits had called. Gradually, some mechanical effort spoilt their loving, or, where they had splendid moments, they had them separately, and not so satisfactorily. So often he seemed merely to be running on alone; often they realised it had been a failure, not what they had wanted. He left her, knowing that evening had only made a little split between them. Their loving grew more mechanical, without the marvellous glamour. Gradually they began to introduce novelties, to get back some of the feeling of satisfaction. They would be very near, almost dangerously near to the river, so that the black water ran not far from his face, and it gave a little thrill; or they loved sometimes in a little hollow below the fence of the path where people were passing occasionally, on the edge of the town, and they heard footsteps coming, almost felt the vibration of the tread, and they heard what the passers-by said – strange little things that were never intended to be heard. And afterwards each of them was rather ashamed, and these things caused a distance between the two of them. He began to despise her a little, as if she had merited it!

One night he left her to go to Daybrook Station over the fields. It was very dark, with an attempt at snow, although the spring was so far advanced. Morel had not much time; he plunged forward. The town ceases almost abruptly on the edge of a steep hollow; there the houses with their yellow lights stand up against the darkness. He went over the stile, and dropped quickly into the hollow of the fields. Under the orchard one warm window shone in Swineshead Farm. Paul glanced round. Behind, the houses stood on the brim of the dip, bleak against the sky, like wild beasts glaring curiously with yellow eyes down into the darkness. It was the town that seemed savage and uncouth, glaring on the clouds at the back of him. Some creature stirred under the willows of the farm pond. It was too dark to distinguish anything.

He was close up to the next stile before he saw a dark shape leaning against it. The man moved aside.

'Good-evening!' he said.

'Good-evening!' Morel answered, not noticing.

'Paul Morel?' said the man.

Then he knew it was Dawes. The man stopped his way.

'I've got yer, have I?' he said awkwardly.

'I shall miss my train,' said Paul.

He could see nothing of Dawes' face. The man's teeth seemed to chatter as he talked.

'You're going to get it from me now,' said Dawes.

Morel attempted to move forward; the other man stepped in front of him.

'Are yer goin' to take that topcoat off,' he said, 'or are you goin' to lie down to it?'

Paul was afraid the man was mad.

'But,' he said, 'I don't know how to fight.'

'All right, then,' answered Dawes, and before the younger man knew where he was he was staggering backwards from a blow across the face.

The whole night went black. He tore off his overcoat and coat, dodging a blow, and flung the garments over Dawes. The latter swore savagely. Morel, in his shirt-sleeves, was now alert and furious. He felt his whole body unsheath itself like a claw. He could not fight, so he would use his wits. The other man became more distinct to him; he could see particularly the shirt-breast. Dawes stumbled over Paul's coats, then came rushing forward. The young man's mouth was bleeding. It was the other man's mouth he was dying to get at, and the desire was anguish in its strength. He stepped quickly through the stile, and as Dawes was coming through after him, like a flash he got a blow in over the other's mouth. He shivered with pleasure. Dawes advanced slowly, spitting. Paul was afraid; he moved round to get to the stile again. Suddenly, from out of nowhere, came a great blow against his ear, that sent him falling helpless backwards. He heard Dawes' heavy panting, like a wild beast's; then came a kick on the knee, giving him such agony that he got up and, quite blind, leapt clean under his enemy's guard. He felt blows and kicks, but they did not hurt. He hung on to the bigger man like a wild-cat, till at last Dawes fell with a crash, losing his presence of mind. Paul went down with him. Pure instinct brought his hands to the man's neck, and before Dawes, in frenzy and agony, could wrench him free, he had got his fists twisted in the scarf and his knuckles dug in the throat of the other man. He was a pure instinct, without reason or feeling. His body, hard and wonderful in itself, cleaved against the struggling body of the other man; not a muscle in him relaxed. He was quite unconscious, only his body had taken upon itself to kill this other man. For himself, he had neither feeling nor reason. He lay pressed hard against his adversary, his body adjusting itself to its one pure purpose of choking the other man, resisting exactly at the right moment, with exactly the right amount of strength, the struggles of the other, silent, intent, unchanging, gradually pressing its knuckles deeper, feeling the struggles of the other body become wilder and more frenzied. Tighter and tighter grew his body, like a screw that is gradually increasing in pressure, till something breaks.

Then suddenly he relaxed, full of wonder and misgiving. Dawes had been yielding. Morel felt his body flame with pain, as he realised what he was doing; he was all bewildered. Dawes' struggles suddenly renewed themselves in a furious spasm. Paul's hands were wrenched, torn out of the scarf in which they were knotted, and he was flung away, helpless. He heard the horrid sound of the other's gasping, but he lay stunned; then, still dazed, he felt the blows of the other's feet, and lost consciousness.

Dawes, grunting with pain like a beast, was kicking the prostrate body of his rival. Suddenly the whistle of the train shrieked two fields away. He turned round and glared suspiciously. What was coming? He saw the lights of the train draw across his vision. It seemed to him people were approaching. He made off across the field into Nottingham, and dimly in his consciousness as he went, he felt on his foot the place where his boot had knocked against one of the lad's bones. The knock seemed to re-echo inside him; he hurried to get away from it.

Morel gradually came to himself. He knew where he was and what had happened, but he did not want to move. He lay still, with tiny bits of snow tickling his face. It was pleasant to lie quite, quite still. The time passed. It was the bits of snow that kept rousing him when he did not want to be roused. At last his will clicked into action.

'I mustn't lie here,' he said: 'it's silly.'

But still he did not move.

'I said I was going to get up,' he repeated. 'Why don't I?'

And still it was some time before he had sufficiently pulled himself together to stir; then gradually he got up. Pain made him sick and dazed, but his brain was clear. Reeling, he groped for his coats and got them on, buttoning his overcoat up to his ears. It was some time before he found his cap. He did not know whether his face was still bleeding. Walking blindly, every step making him sick with pain, he went back to the pond and washed his face and hands. The icy water hurt, but helped to bring him back to himself. He crawled back up the hill to the tram. He wanted to get to his mother – he must get to his mother – that was his blind intention. He covered his face as much as he could, and struggled sickly along. Continually the ground seemed to fall away from him as he walked, and he felt himself dropping with a sickening feeling into space; so, like a nightmare, he got through with the journey home.

Everybody was in bed. He looked at himself. His face was discoloured and smeared with blood, almost like a dead man's face. He washed it, and went to bed. The night went by in delirium. In the morning he found his mother looking at him. Her blue eyes – they were all he wanted to see. She was there; he was in her hands.

'It's not much, mother,' he said. 'It was Baxter Dawes.'

'Tell me where it hurts you,' she said quietly.

'I don't know – my shoulder. Say it was a bicycle accident, mother.'

He could not move his arm. Presently Minnie, the little servant, came upstairs with some tea.

'Your mother's nearly frightened me out of my wits – fainted away,' she said.

He felt he could not bear it. His mother nursed him; he told her about it.

'And now I should have done with them all,' she said quietly.

'I will, mother.'

She covered him up.

'And don't think about it,' she said – 'only try to go to sleep. The doctor won't be here till eleven.'

He had a dislocated shoulder, and the second day acute bronchitis set in. His mother was pale as death now, and very thin. She would sit and look at him, then away into space. There was something between them that neither dared mention. Clara came to see him. Afterwards he said to his mother, 'She makes me tired, mother.'

'Yes; I wish she wouldn't come,' Mrs Morel replied.

Another day Miriam came, but she seemed almost like a stranger to him.

'You know, I don't care about them, mother,' he said.

'I'm afraid you don't, my son,' she replied sadly.

It was given out everywhere that it was a bicycle accident. Soon he was able to go to work again, but now there was a constant sickness and gnawing at his heart. He went to Clara, but there seemed, as it were, nobody there. He could not work. He and his mother seemed almost to avoid each other. There was some secret between them which they could not bear. He was not aware of it. He only knew that his life seemed unbalanced, as if it were going to smash into pieces.

Clara did not know what was the matter with him. She realised that he seemed unaware of her. Even when he came to her he seemed unaware of her; always he was somewhere else. She felt she was clutching for him, and he was somewhere else. It tortured her, and so she tortured him. For a month at a time she kept him at arm's length. He almost hated her, and was driven to her in spite of himself. He went mostly into the company of men, was always at the George or the White Horse. His mother was ill, distant, quiet, shadowy. He was terrified of something; he dared not look at her. Her eyes seemed to grow darker, her face more waxen; still she dragged about at her work.

At Whitsuntide he said he would go to Blackpool for four days with his friend Newton. The latter was a big, jolly fellow, with a touch of the bounder about him. Paul said his mother must go to Sheffield to stay a week with Annie, who lived there. Perhaps the change would do her good. Mrs Morel was attending a woman's doctor in Nottingham. He said her heart and her digestion were wrong. She consented to go to Sheffield, though she did not want to; but now she would do everything her son wished of her. Paul said he would come for her on the fifth day, and stay also in Sheffield till the holiday was up. It was agreed.

The two young men set off gaily for Blackpool. Mrs Morel was quite lively as Paul kissed her and left her. Once at the station, he forgot everything. Four days were clear – not an anxiety, not a thought. The two young men simply enjoyed themselves. Paul was like another man. None of himself remained – no Clara, no Miriam, no mother that fretted him. He wrote to them all, and long letters to his mother; but they were jolly letters that made her laugh. He was having a good time, as young fellows will in a place like Blackpool. And underneath it all was a shadow for her.

Paul was very gay, excited at the thought of staying with his mother in Sheffield. Newton was to spend the day with them. Their train was late. Joking, laughing, with their pipes between their teeth, the young men swung their bags on to the tramcar. Paul had bought his mother a little collar of real lace that he wanted to see her wear, so that he could tease her about it.

Annie lived in a nice house, and had a little maid. Paul ran gaily up the steps. He expected his mother laughing in the hall, but it was Annie who opened to him. She seemed distant to him. He stood a second in dismay. Annie let him kiss her cheek.

'Is my mother ill?' he said.

'Yes; she's not very well. Don't upset her.'

'Is she in bed?'

'Yes.'

And then the queer feeling went over him, as if all the sunshine had gone out of him, and it was all shadow. He dropped the bag and ran upstairs. Hesitating, he opened the door. His mother sat up in bed, wearing a dressing-gown of old-rose colour. She looked at him almost as if she were ashamed of herself, pleading to him, humble. He saw the ashy look about her.

'Mother!' he said.

'I thought you were never coming,' she answered gaily. But he only fell on his knees at the bedside, and buried his face in the bedclothes, crying in agony, and saying, 'Mother – mother – mother!'

She stroked his hair slowly with her thin hand.

'Don't cry,' she said. 'Don't cry – it's nothing.'

But he felt as if his blood was melting into tears, and he cried in terror and pain.

'Don't – don't cry,' his mother faltered.

Slowly she stroked his hair. Shocked out of himself, he cried, and the tears hurt in every fibre of his body. Suddenly he stopped, but he dared not lift his face out of the bedclothes.

'You *are* late. Where have you been?' his mother asked.

'The train was late,' he replied, muffled in the sheet.

'Yes; that miserable Central! Is Newton come?'

'Yes.'

'I'm sure you must be hungry, and they've kept dinner waiting.'

With a wrench he looked up at her.

'What is it, mother?' he asked brutally.

She averted her eyes as she answered, 'Only a bit of a tumour, my boy. You needn't trouble. It's been there – the lump has – a long time.'

Up came the tears again. His mind was clear and hard, but his body was crying.

'Where?' he said.

She put her hand on her side.

'Here. But you know they can sweal a tumour away.'

He stood feeling dazed and helpless, like a child. He thought perhaps it was as she said. Yes; he reassured himself it was so. But all the while his blood and his body knew definitely what it was. He sat down on the bed, and took her hand. She had never had but the one ring – her wedding ring.

'When were you poorly?' he asked.

'It was yesterday it began,' she answered submissively.

'Pains!'

'Yes; but not more than I've often had at home. I believe Dr Ansell is an alarmist.'

'You ought not to have travelled alone,' he said, to himself more than to her.

'As if that had anything to do with it!' she answered quickly.

They were silent for a while.

'Now go and have your dinner,' she said. 'You *must* be hungry.'

'Have you had yours?'

'Yes; a beautiful sole I had. Annie *is* good to me.'

They talked a little while, then he went downstairs. He was very white and strained. Newton sat in miserable sympathy.

After dinner he went into the scullery to help Annie to wash up. The little maid had gone on an errand.

'Is it really a tumour?' he asked.

Annie began to cry again.

'The pain she had yesterday – I never saw anybody suffer like it!' she cried. 'Leonard ran like a madman for Dr Ansell, and when she'd got to bed she said to me: "Annie, look at this lump on my side. I wonder what it is?" And there I looked, and I thought I should have dropped. Paul, as true as I'm here, it's a lump as big as my double fist. I said: "Good gracious, mother, whenever did that come?" "Why, child," she said, "it's been there a long time." I thought I should have died, our Paul, I did. She's been having these pains for months at home, and nobody looking after her.'

The tears came to his eyes, then dried suddenly.

'But she's been attending the doctor in Nottingham – and she never told me,' he said.

'If I'd have been at home,' said Annie, 'I should have seen for myself.'

He felt like a man walking in unrealities. In the afternoon he went to see the doctor. The latter was a shrewd, lovable man.

'But what is it?' he said.

The doctor looked at the young man, then knitted his fingers.

'It may be a large tumour which has formed in the membrane,' he said slowly, 'and which we *may* be able to make go away.'

'Can't you operate?' asked Paul.

'Not there,' replied the doctor.

'Are you sure?'

'*Quite!*'

Paul meditated a while.

'Are you sure it's a tumour?' he asked. 'Why did Dr Jameson in Nottingham never find out anything about it? She's been going to him for weeks, and he's treated her for heart and indigestion.'

'Mrs Morel never told Dr Jameson about the lump,' said the doctor.

'And do you *know* it's a tumour?'

'No, I am not sure.'

'What else *might* it be? You asked my sister if there was cancer in the family. Might it be cancer?'

'I don't know.'

'And what shall you do?'

'I should like an examination, with Dr Jameson.'

'Then have one.'

'You must arrange about that. His fee wouldn't be less than ten guineas to come here from Nottingham.'

'When would you like him to come?'

'I will call in this evening, and we will talk it over.'

Paul went away, biting his lip.

His mother could come downstairs for tea, the doctor said. Her son went upstairs to help her. She wore the old-rose dressing-gown that Leonard had given Annie, and, with a little colour in her face, was quite young again.

'But you look quite pretty in that,' he said.

'Yes; they make me so fine, I hardly know myself,' she answered.

But when she stood up to walk, the colour went. Paul helped her, half carrying her. At the top of the stairs she was gone. He lifted her up and carried her quickly downstairs; laid her on the couch. She was light and frail. Her face looked as if she were dead, with the blue lips shut tight. Her eyes opened – her blue, unfailing eyes – and she looked at him pleadingly, almost wanting him to forgive her. He held brandy to her lips, but her mouth would not open. All the time she watched him lovingly. She was only sorry for him. The tears ran down his face without ceasing, but not a muscle moved. He was intent on getting a little brandy between her lips. Soon she was able to swallow a teaspoonful. She lay back, so tired. The tears continued to run down his face.

'But,' she panted, 'it'll go off. Don't cry!'

'I'm not doing,' he said.

After a while she was better again. He was kneeling beside the couch. They looked into each other's eyes.

'I don't want you to make a trouble of it,' she said.

'No, mother. You'll have to be quite still, and then you'll get better soon.'

But he was white to the lips, and their eyes as they looked at each other understood. Her eyes were so blue – such a wonderful forget-me-not blue! He felt if only they had been of a different colour he could have borne it better. His heart seemed to be ripping slowly in his breast. He kneeled there, holding her hand, and neither said anything. Then Annie came in.

'Are you all right?' she murmured timidly to her mother.

'Of course,' said Mrs Morel.

Paul sat down and told her about Blackpool. She was curious.

A day or two after, he went to see Dr Jameson in Nottingham, to arrange for a consultation. Paul had practically no money in the world. But he could borrow.

His mother had been used to go to the public consultation on Saturday morning, when she could see the doctor for only a nominal sum. Her son went on the same day. The waiting-room was full of poor women, who sat patiently on a bench around the wall. Paul thought of his mother, in her little black costume, sitting waiting likewise. The doctor was late. The women all looked rather frightened. Paul asked the nurse in attendance if he could see the doctor immediately he came. It was arranged so. The women sitting patiently round the walls of the room eyed the young man curiously.

At last the doctor came. He was about forty, good-looking, brown-skinned. His wife had died, and he, who had loved her, had specialised on women's ailments. Paul told his name and his mother's. The doctor did not remember.

'Number forty-six M,' said the nurse; and the doctor looked up the case in his book.

'There is a big lump that may be a tumour,' said Paul. 'But Dr Ansell is going to write you a letter.'

'Ah, yes!' replied the doctor, drawing the letter from his pocket. He was very friendly, affable, busy, kind. He would come to Sheffield the next day.

'What is your father?' he asked.

'He is a coal-miner,' replied Paul.

'Not very well off, I suppose?'

'No, I see after this,' said Paul.

'And you?' smiled the doctor.

'I am a clerk in Jordan's Appliance Factory.'

The doctor smiled at him.

'Er – to go to Sheffield!' he said, putting the tips of his fingers together, and smiling with his eyes. 'Eight guineas?'

'Thank you!' said Paul, flushing and rising. 'And you'll come tomorrow?'

'Tomorrow – Sunday? Yes! Can you tell me about what time there is a train in the afternoon?'

'There is a Central gets in at four-fifteen.'

'And will there be any way of getting up to the house? Shall I have to walk?' The doctor smiled.

'There is the tram,' said Paul; 'the Western Park Tram.'

The doctor made a note of it.

'Thank you!' he said and shook hands.

Then Paul went on home to see his father, who was left in the charge of Minnie. Walter Morel was getting very grey now. Paul found him digging in the garden. He had written him a letter. He shook hands with his father.

'Hello, son! Tha has landed then?' said the father.

'Yes,' replied the son. 'But I'm going back tonight.'

'Are ter, beguy!' exclaimed the collier. 'An' has ter eaten owt?'

'No.'

'That's just like thee,' said Morel. 'Come thy ways in.'

The father was afraid of the mention of his wife. The two went indoors. Paul ate in silence; his father, with earthy hands, and sleeves rolled up, sat in the armchair opposite and looked at him.

'Well, and how is she?' asked the miner at length, in a little voice.

'She can sit up; she can be carried down to tea,' said Paul.

'That's a blessin'!' exclaimed Morel. 'I hope we s'll soon be having her whoam, then. An' what's that Nottingham doctor say?'

'He's going tomorrow to have an examination of her.'

'Is he, beguy! That's a tidy penny, I'm thinkin'!'

'Eight guineas.'

'Eight guineas!' The miner spoke breathlessly. 'Well we mun find it from somewhere.'

'I can pay that,' said Paul.

There was a silence between them for some time.

'She says she hopes you're getting on all right with Minnie,' Paul said.

'Yes, I'm all right, an' I wish she was,' answered Morel. 'But Minnie's a good little wench, bless 'er heart!' He sat looking dismal.

'I s'll have to be going at half-past three,' said Paul.

'It's a traipse for thee, lad! Eight guineas! An' when dost think she'll be able to get as far as this?'

'We must see what the doctors say tomorrow,' Paul said.

Morel sighed deeply. The house seemed strangely empty, and Paul thought his father looked lost, forlorn and old.

'You'll have to go and see her next week, father,' he said.

'I hope she'll be a-whoam by that time,' said Morel.

'If she's not,' said Paul, 'then you must come.'

'I dunno wheer I s'll find th' money,' said Morel.

'And I'll write to you what the doctor says,' said Paul.

'But tha writes i' such a fashion, I canna ma'e it out,' said Morel.

'Well, I'll write plain.'

It was no good asking Morel to answer, for he could scarcely do more than write his own name.

The doctor came. Leonard felt it his duty to meet him with a cab. The examination did not take long. Annie, Arthur, Paul, and Leonard were waiting in the parlour anxiously. The doctors came down. Paul glanced at them. He had never had any hope, except when he had deceived himself.

'It *may* be a tumour; we must wait and see,' said Dr Jameson.

'And if it is,' said Annie, 'can you sweal it away?'

'Probably,' said the doctor.

Paul put eight sovereigns and half a sovereign on the table. The doctor counted them, took a florin out of his purse, and put that down.

'Thank you!' he said. 'I'm sorry Mrs Morel is so ill. But we must see what we can do.'

'There can't be an operation?' said Paul.

The doctor shook his head.

'No,' he said; 'and even if there could, her heart wouldn't stand it.'

'Is her heart risky?' asked Paul.

'Yes; you must be careful with her.'

'Very risky?'

'No – er – no, no! Just take care.'

And the doctor was gone.

Then Paul carried his mother downstairs. She lay simply, like a child. But when he was on the stairs, she put her arms round his neck, clinging.

'I'm so frightened of these beastly stairs,' she said.

And he was frightened, too. He would let Leonard do it another time. He felt he could not carry her.

'He thinks it's only a tumour!' cried Annie to her mother. 'And he can sweal it away.'

'I *knew* he could,' protested Mrs Morel scornfully.

She pretended not to notice that Paul had gone out of the room. He sat in the kitchen, smoking. Then he tried to brush some grey ash off his coat. He looked again. It was one of his mother's grey hairs. It was so long! He held it up, and it drifted into the chimney. He let go. The long grey hair floated and was gone in the blackness of the chimney.

The next day he kissed her before going back to work. It was very early in the morning, and they were alone.

'You won't fret, my boy!' she said.

'No, mother.'

'No; it would be silly. And take care of yourself.'

'Yes,' he answered. Then, after a while: 'And I shall come next Saturday, and shall bring my father?'

'I suppose he wants to come,' she replied. 'At any rate, if he does you'll have to let him.'

He kissed her again, and stroked the hair from her temples, gently, tenderly, as if she were a lover.

'Shan't you be late?' she murmured.

'I'm going,' he said, very low.

Still he sat a few minutes, stroking the brown and grey hair from her temples.

'And you won't be any worse, mother?'

'No, my son.'

'You promise me?'

'Yes; I won't be any worse.'

He kissed her, held her in his arms for a moment, and was gone. In the early sunny morning he ran to the station, crying all the way; he did not know what for. And her blue eyes were wide and staring as she thought of him.

In the afternoon he went a walk with Clara. They sat in the little wood where bluebells were standing. He took her hand.

'You'll see,' he said to Clara, 'she'll never be better.'

'Oh, you don't know!' replied the other.

'I do,' he said.

She caught him impulsively to her breast.

'Try and forget it, dear,' she said; 'try and forget it.'

'I will,' he answered.

Her breast was there, warm for him; her hands were in his hair. It was comforting, and he held his arms round her. But he did not forget. He only talked to Clara of something else. And it was always so. When she felt it coming, the agony, she cried to him, 'Don't think of it, Paul! Don't think of it, my darling!'

And she pressed him to her breast, rocked him, soothed him like a child. So he put the trouble aside for her sake, to take it up again immediately he was alone. All the time, as he went about, he cried mechanically. His mind and hands were busy. He cried, he did not know why. It was his blood weeping. He was just as much alone whether he was with Clara or with the men in the White Horse. Just himself and this pressure inside him, that was all that existed. He read sometimes. He had to keep his mind occupied. And Clara was a way of occupying his mind.

On the Saturday Walter Morel went to Sheffield. He was a forlorn figure, looking rather as if nobody owned him. Paul ran upstairs.

'My father's come,' he said, kissing his mother.

'Has he?' she answered wearily.

The old collier came rather frightened into the bedroom.

'How dun I find thee, lass?' he said, going forward and kissing her in a hasty, timid fashion.

'Well, I'm middlin',' she replied.

'I see tha art,' he said. He stood looking down on her. Then he wiped his eyes with his handkerchief. Helpless, and as if nobody owned him, he looked.

'Have you gone on all right?' asked the wife, rather wearily, as if it were an effort to talk to him.

'Yis,' he answered. 'Er's a bit behint-hand now and again, as yer might expect.'

'Does she have your dinner ready?' asked Mrs Morel.

'Well, I've 'ad to shout at 'er once or twice,' he said.

'And you *must* shout at her if she's not ready. She *will* leave things to the last minute.'

She gave him a few instructions. He sat looking at her as if she were almost a stranger to him, before whom he was awkward and humble, and also as if he had lost his presence of mind, and wanted to run. This feeling that he wanted to run away, that he was on thorns to be gone from so trying a situation, and yet must linger because it looked better, made his presence so trying. He put up his eyebrows for misery and clenched his fists on his knees, feeling so awkward in presence of a big trouble.

Mrs Morel did not change much. She stayed in Sheffield for two months. If anything, at the end she was rather worse. But she wanted to go home. Annie had her children. Mrs Morel wanted to go home. So they got a motor car from Nottingham – for she was too ill to go by train – and she was driven through the sunshine. It was just August, everything was bright and warm. Under the blue sky they could all see she was dying. Yet she was jollier than she had been for weeks. They all laughed and talked.

'Annie,' she exclaimed, 'I saw a lizard dart on that rock!'

Her eyes were so quick; she was still so full of life.

Morel knew she was coming. He had the front-door open. Everybody was on tiptoe. Half the street turned out. They heard the sound of the great motor car. Mrs Morel, smiling, drove home down the street.

'And just look at them all come out to see me!' she said. 'But there, I suppose I should have done the same. How do you do, Mrs Matthews? How are you, Mrs Harrison?'

They none of them could hear, but they saw her smile and nod. And they all saw death on her face, they said. It was a great event in the street.

Morel wanted to carry her indoors, but he was too old. Arthur took her as if she were a child. They had set her a big, deep chair by the hearth where her rocking-chair used to stand. When she was unwrapped and seated, and had drunk a little brandy, she looked round the room.

'Don't think I didn't like your house, Annie,' she said; 'but it's nice to be in my own home again.'

And Morel answered huskily, 'It is, lass, it is.'

And Minnie, the little quaint maid, said, 'An' we glad t' 'ave yer.'

There was a lovely yellow ravel of sunflowers in the garden. She looked out of the window.

'There are my sunflowers!' she said.

CHAPTER 14

The Release

'By the way,' said Dr Ansell one evening when Morel was in Sheffield, 'we've got a man in the fever hospital here who comes from Nottingham – Dawes. He doesn't seem to have many belongings in this world.'

'Baxter Dawes!' Paul exclaimed.

'That's the man – has been a fine fellow, physically, I should think. Been in a bit of a mess lately. You know him?'

'He used to work at the place where I am.'

'Did he? Do you know anything about him? He's just sulking, or he'd be a lot better than he is by now.'

'I don't know anything of his home circumstances, except that he's separated from his wife and has been a bit down, I believe. But tell him about me, will you? Tell him I'll come and see him.'

The next time Morel saw the doctor he said, 'And what about Dawes?'

'I said to him,' answered the other, ' "Do you know a man from Nottingham named Morel?" and he looked at me as if he'd jump at my throat. So I said, "I see you know the name; it's Paul Morel." Then I told him about your saying you would go and see him. "What does he want?" he said, as if you were a policeman.'

'And did he say he would see me?' asked Paul.

'He wouldn't say anything – good, bad, or indifferent,' replied the doctor.

'Why not?'

'That's what I want to know. There he lies and sulks, day in, day out. Can't get a word of information out of him.'

'Do you think I might go?' asked Paul.

'You might.'

There was a feeling of connection between the rival men more than ever since they had fought. In a way Morel felt guilty towards the other, and more or less responsible. And being in such a state of soul himself, he felt an almost painful nearness to Dawes, who was suffering and despairing too. Besides, they had met in a naked extremity of hate and it was a bond. At any rate, the elemental man in each had met.

He went down to the isolation hospital, with Dr Ansell's card. The sister, a healthy young Irishwoman, led him down the ward.

'A visitor to see you, Jim Crow,' she said.

Dawes turned over suddenly with a startled grunt.

'Eh?'

'Caw!' she mocked. 'He can only say "Caw!" I have brought you a gentleman to see you. Now say "Thank you," and show some manners.'

Dawes looked swiftly with his dark, startled eyes beyond the sister at Paul. His look was full of fear, mistrust, hate, and misery. Morel met the swift, dark eyes, and hesitated. The two men were afraid of the naked selves they had been.

'Dr Ansell told me you were here,' said Morel, holding out his hand.

Dawes mechanically shook hands.

'So I thought I'd come in,' continued Paul.

There was no answer. Dawes lay staring at the opposite wall.

'Say "Caw!" ' mocked the nurse. 'Say "Caw!" Jim Crow.'

'He is getting on all right?' said Paul to her.

'Oh yes! He lies and imagines he's going to die,' said the nurse, 'and it frightens every word out of his mouth.'

'And you must have somebody to talk to,' laughed Morel.

'That's it!' laughed the nurse. 'Only two old men and a boy who always cries. It is hard lines! Here am I dying to hear Jim Crow's voice, and nothing but an odd "Caw!" will he give!'

'So rough on you!' said Morel.

'Isn't it?' said the nurse.

'I suppose I am a godsend,' he laughed.

'Oh, dropped straight from heaven!' laughed the nurse.

Presently she left the two men alone. Dawes was thinner, and handsome again, but life seemed low in him. As the doctor said, he was lying sulking, and would not move forward towards convalescence. He seemed to grudge every beat of his heart.

'Have you had a bad time?' asked Paul.

Suddenly again Dawes looked at him.

'What are you doing in Sheffield?' he asked.

'My mother was taken ill at my sister's in Thurston Street. What are you doing here?'

There was no answer.

'How long have you been in?' Morel asked.

'I couldn't say for sure,' Dawes answered grudgingly.

He lay staring across at the wall opposite, as if trying to believe Morel was not there. Paul felt his heart go hard and angry.

'Dr Ansell told me you were here,' he said coldly.

The other man did not answer.

'Typhoid's pretty bad, I know,' Morel persisted.

Suddenly Dawes said, 'What did you come for?'

'Because Dr Ansell said you didn't know anybody here. Do you?'

'I know nobody nowhere,' said Dawes.

'Well,' said Paul, 'it's because you don't choose to, then.'

There was another silence.

'We s'll be taking my mother home as soon as we can,' said Paul.

'What's a-matter with her?' asked Dawes, with a sick man's interest in illness.

'She's got a cancer.'

There was another silence.

'But we want to get her home,' said Paul. 'We s'll have to get a motor car.'

Dawes lay thinking.

'Why don't you ask Thomas Jordan to lend you his?' said Dawes.

'It's not big enough,' Morel answered.

Dawes blinked his dark eyes as he lay thinking.

'Then ask Jack Pilkington; he'd lend it you. You know him.'

'I think I s'll hire one,' said Paul.

'You're a fool if you do,' said Dawes.

The sick man was gaunt and handsome again. Paul was sorry for him because his eyes looked so tired.

'Did you get a job here?' he asked.

'I was only here a day or two before I was taken bad,' Dawes replied.

'You want to get in a convalescent home,' said Paul.

The other's face clouded again.

'I'm goin' in no convalescent home,' he said.

'My father's been in the one at Seathorpe, an' he liked it. Dr Ansell would get you a recommend.'

Dawes lay thinking. It was evident he dared not face the world again.

'The seaside would be all right just now,' Morel said. 'Sun on those sand-hills, and the waves not far out.'

The other did not answer.

'By Gad!' Paul concluded, too miserable to bother much; 'it's all right when you know you're going to walk again, and swim!'

Dawes glanced at him quickly. The man's dark eyes were afraid to meet any other eyes in the world. But the real misery and helplessness in Paul's tone gave him a feeling of relief.

'Is she far gone?' he asked.

'She's going like wax,' Paul answered; 'but cheerful – lively!'

He bit his lip. After a minute he rose.

'Well, I'll be going,' he said. 'I'll leave you this half-crown.'

'I don't want it,' Dawes muttered.

Morel did not answer, but left the coin on the table.

'Well,' he said, 'I'll try and run in when I'm back in Sheffield. Happen you might like to see my brother-in-law. He works in Pyecrofts.'

'I don't know him,' said Dawes.

'He's all right. Should I tell him to come? He might bring you some papers to look at.'

The other man did not answer. Paul went. The strong emotion that Dawes aroused in him, repressed, made him shiver.

He did not tell his mother, but next day he spoke to Clara about this interview. It was in the dinner-hour. The two did not often go out together now, but this day he asked her to go with him to the Castle grounds. There they sat while the scarlet geraniums and the yellow calceolarias blazed in the sunlight. She was now always rather protective, and rather resentful towards him.

'Did you know Baxter was in Sheffield Hospital with typhoid?' he asked.

She looked at him with startled grey eyes, and her face went pale.

'No,' she said, frightened.

'He's getting better. I went to see him yesterday – the doctor told me.'

Clara seemed stricken by the news.

'Is he very bad?' she asked guiltily.

'He has been. He's mending now.'

'What did he say to you?'

'Oh, nothing! He seems to be sulking.'

There was a distance between the two of them. He gave her more information.

She went about shut up and silent. The next time they took a walk together, she disengaged herself from his arm, and walked at a distance from him. He was wanting her comfort badly.

'Won't you be nice with me?' he asked.

She did not answer.

'What's the matter?' he said, putting his arm across her shoulder.

'Don't!' she said, disengaging herself.

He left her alone, and returned to his own brooding.

'Is it Baxter that upsets you?' he asked at length.

'I *have* been *vile* to him!' she said.

'I've said many a time you haven't treated him well,' he replied.

And there was a hostility between them. Each pursued his own train of thought.

'I've treated him – no, I've treated him badly,' she said. 'And now you treat *me* badly. It serves me right.'

'How do I treat you badly?' he said.

'It serves me right,' she repeated. 'I never considered him worth having, and now you don't consider *me*. But it serves me right. He loved me a thousand times better than you ever did.'

'He didn't!' protested Paul.

'He did! At any rate, he did respect me, and that's what you don't do.'

'It looked as if he respected you!' he said.

'He did! And I *made* him horrid – I know I did! You've taught me that. And he loved me a thousand times better than ever you do.'

'All right,' said Paul.

He only wanted to be left alone now. He had his own trouble, which was almost too much to bear. Clara only tormented him and made him tired. He was not sorry when he left her.

She went on the first opportunity to Sheffield to see her husband. The meeting was not a success. But she left him roses and fruit and money. She wanted to make restitution. It was not that she loved him. As she looked at him lying there her heart did not warm with love. Only she wanted to humble herself to him, to kneel before him. She wanted now to be self-sacrificial. After all, she had failed to make Morel really love her. She was morally frightened. She wanted to do penance. So she kneeled to Dawes, and it gave him a subtle pleasure. But the distance between them was still very great – too great. It frightened the man. It almost pleased the woman. She liked to feel she was serving him across an insuperable distance. She was proud now.

Morel went to see Dawes once or twice. There was a sort of friendship between the two men, who were all the while deadly rivals. But they never mentioned the woman who was between them.

Mrs Morel got gradually worse. At first they used to carry her downstairs, sometimes even into the garden. She sat propped in her chair, smiling, and so pretty. The gold wedding ring shone on her white hand; her hair was carefully brushed. And she watched the tangled sunflowers dying, the chrysanthemums coming out, and the dahlias.

Paul and she were afraid of each other. He knew, and she knew, that she was dying. But they kept up a pretence of cheerfulness. Every morning, when he got up, he went into her room in his pyjamas.

'Did you sleep, my dear?' he asked.

'Yes,' she answered.

'Not very well?'

'Well, yes!'

Then he knew she had lain awake. He saw her hand under the bedclothes, pressing the place on her side where the pain was.

'Has it been bad?' he asked.

'No. It hurt a bit, but nothing to mention.'

And she sniffed in her old scornful way. As she lay she looked like a girl. And all the while her blue eyes watched him. But there were the dark pain-circles beneath that made him ache again.

'It's a sunny day,' he said.

'It's a beautiful day.'

'Do you think you'll be carried down?'

'I shall see.'

Then he went away to get her breakfast. All day long he was conscious of nothing but her. It was a long ache that made him feverish. Then, when he got home in the early evening, he glanced through the kitchen window. She was not there; she had not got up.

He ran straight upstairs and kissed her. He was almost afraid to ask, 'Didn't you get up, Pigeon?'

'No,' she said. 'It was that morphia; it made me tired.'

'I think he gives you too much,' he said.

'I think he does,' she answered.

He sat down by the bed, miserably. She had a way of curling and lying on her side, like a child. The grey and brown hair was loose over her ear.

'Doesn't it tickle you?' he said, gently putting it back.

'It does,' she replied.

His face was near hers. Her blue eyes smiled straight into his, like a girl's – warm, laughing with tender love. It made him pant with terror, agony, and love.

'You want your hair doing in a plait,' he said. 'Lie still.'

And going behind her, he carefully loosened her hair, brushed it out. It was like fine long silk of brown and grey. Her head was snuggled between her shoulders. As he lightly brushed and plaited her hair, he bit his lip and felt dazed. It all seemed unreal, he could not understand it.

At night he often worked in her room, looking up from time to time. And so often he found her blue eyes fixed on him. And when their eyes met, she smiled. He worked away again mechanically, producing good stuff without knowing what he was doing.

Sometimes he came in, very pale and still, with watchful, sudden eyes, like a man who is drunk almost to death. They were both afraid of the veils that were ripping between them.

Then she pretended to be better, chattered to him gaily, made a great fuss over some scraps of news. For they had both come to the condition when they had to make much of the trifles, lest they should give in to the big thing, and their human independence would go smash. They were afraid, so they made light of things and were gay.

Sometimes as she lay he knew she was thinking of the past. Her mouth gradually shut hard in a line. She was holding herself rigid, so that she might die without ever uttering the great cry that was tearing from her. He never forgot that hard, utterly lonely and stubborn clenching of her mouth, which persisted for weeks. Sometimes, when it was lighter, she talked about her husband. Now she hated him. She did not forgive him. She could not bear him to be in the room. And a few things, the things that had been most bitter to her, came up again so strongly that they broke from her, and she told her son.

He felt as if his life were being destroyed, piece by piece, within him. Often the tears came suddenly. He ran to the station, the tear-drops falling on the pavement. Often he could not go on with his work. The pen stopped writing. He sat staring, quite unconscious. And when he came round again he felt sick, and trembled in his limbs. He never questioned what it was. His mind did not try to analyse or understand. He merely submitted, and kept his eyes shut; let the thing go over him.

His mother did the same. She thought of the pain, of the morphia, of the next day; hardly ever of the death. That was coming, she knew. She had to submit to it. But she would never entreat it or make friends with it. Blind, with her face shut hard and blind, she was pushed towards the door. The days passed, the weeks, the months.

Sometimes, in the sunny afternoons, she seemed almost happy.

'I try to think of the nice times – when we went to Mablethorpe, and Robin Hood's Bay, and Shanklin,' she said. 'After all, not everybody has seen those beautiful places. And wasn't it beautiful! I try to think of that, not of the other things.'

Then, again, for a whole evening she spoke not a word; neither did he. They were together, rigid, stubborn, silent. He went into his room at last to go to bed, and leaned against the doorway as if paralysed, unable to go any farther. His consciousness went. A furious storm, he knew not what, seemed to ravage inside him. He stood leaning there, submitting, never questioning.

In the morning they were both normal again, though her face was grey with the morphia, and her body felt like ash. But they were bright again, nevertheless. Often, especially if Annie or Arthur were at home, he neglected her. He did not see much of Clara. Usually he was with men. He was quick and active and lively; but when his friends saw him go white to the gills, his eyes dark and glittering, they had a certain mistrust of him. Sometimes he went to Clara, but she was almost cold to him.

'Take me!' he said simply.

Occasionally she would. But she was afraid. When he had her then, there was something in it that made her shrink away from him – something unnatural. She grew to dread him. He was so quiet, yet so strange. She was afraid of the man who was not there with her, whom she could feel behind this make-belief lover; somebody sinister, that filled her with horror. She began to have a kind of horror of him. It was almost as if he were a criminal. He wanted her – he had her – and it made her feel as if death itself had her in its grip. She lay in horror. There was no man there loving her. She almost hated him. Then came little bouts of tenderness. But she dared not pity him.

Dawes had come to Colonel Seely's Home near Nottingham. There Paul visited him sometimes, Clara very occasionally. Between the two men the friendship had developed peculiarly. Dawes, who mended very slowly and seemed very feeble, seemed to leave himself in the hands of Morel.

In the beginning of November Clara reminded Paul that it was her birthday.

'I'd nearly forgotten,' he said.

'I thought quite,' she replied.

'No. Shall we go to the seaside for the weekend?'

They went. It was cold and rather dismal. She waited for him to be warm and tender with her, instead of which he seemed hardly aware of her. He sat in the railway-carriage, looking out, and was startled when she spoke to him. He was not definitely thinking. Things seemed as if they did not exist. She went across to him.

'What is it, dear?' she asked.

'Nothing!' he said. 'Don't those windmill sails look monotonous?'

He sat holding her hand. He could not talk nor think. It was a comfort, however, to sit holding her hand. She was dissatisfied and miserable. He was not with her; she was nothing.

And in the evening they sat among the sand-hills, looking at the black, heavy sea.

'She will never give in,' he said quietly.

Clara's heart sank.

'No,' she replied.

'There are different ways of dying. My father's people are frightened, and have to be hauled out of life into death like cattle into a slaughterhouse, pulled by the neck; but my mother's people are pushed from behind, inch by inch. They are stubborn people, and won't die.'

'Yes,' said Clara.

'And she won't die. She can't. Mr Renshaw, the parson, was in the other day. "Think!" he said to her; "you will have your mother and father, and your sisters, and your son, in the Other Land." And she said: "I have done without them for a long time, and *can* do without them now. It is the living I want, not the dead." She wants to live even now.'

'Oh, how horrible!' said Clara, too frightened to speak.

'And she looks at me, and she wants to stay with me,' he went on monotonously. 'She's got such a will, it seems as if she would never go – never!'

'Don't think of it!' cried Clara.

'And she was religious – she is religious now – but it is no good. She simply won't give in. And do you know, I said to her on Thursday, "Mother, if I had to die, I'd die. I'd *will* to die." And she said to me, sharp: "Do you think I haven't? Do you think you can die when you like?" '

His voice ceased. He did not cry, only went on speaking monotonously. Clara wanted to run. She looked round. There was the black, re-echoing shore, the dark sky down on her. She got up terrified. She wanted to be where there was light, where there were other people. She wanted to be away from him. He sat with his head dropped, not moving a muscle.

'And I don't want her to eat,' he said, 'and she knows it. When I ask her, "Shall you have anything?" she's almost afraid to say "Yes." "I'll have a cup of Benger's," she says. "It'll only keep your strength up," I said to her. "Yes" – and she almost cried – "but there's such a gnawing when I eat nothing, I can't bear it." So I went and made her the food. It's the cancer that gnaws like that at her. I wish she'd die!'

'Come!' said Clara roughly. 'I'm going.'

He followed her down the darkness of the sands. He did not come to her. He seemed scarcely aware of her existence. And she was afraid of him, and disliked him.

In the same acute daze they went back to Nottingham. He was always busy, always doing something, always going from one to the other of his friends.

On the Monday he went to see Baxter Dawes. Listless and pale, the man rose to greet the other, clinging to his chair as he held out his hand.

'You shouldn't get up,' said Paul.

Dawes sat down heavily, eyeing Morel with a sort of suspicion.

'Don't you waste your time on me,' he said, 'if you've owt better to do.'

'I wanted to come,' said Paul. 'Here! I brought you some sweets.'

The invalid put them aside.

'It's not been much of a weekend,' said Morel.

'How's your mother?' asked the other.

'Hardly any different.'

'I thought she was perhaps worse, being as you didn't come on Sunday.'

'I was at Skegness,' said Paul. 'I wanted a change.'

The other looked at him with dark eyes. He seemed to be waiting, not quite daring to ask, trusting to be told.

'I went with Clara,' said Paul.

'I knew as much,' said Dawes quietly.

'It was an old promise,' said Paul.

'You have it your own way,' said Dawes.

This was the first time Clara had been definitely mentioned between them.

'Nay,' said Morel slowly; 'she's tired of me.'

Again Dawes looked at him.

'Since August she's been getting tired of me,' Morel repeated.

The two men were very quiet together. Paul suggested a game of draughts. They played in silence.

'I s'll go abroad when my mother's dead,' said Paul.

'Abroad!' repeated Dawes.

'Yes; I don't care what I do.'

They continued the game. Dawes was winning.

'I s'll have to begin a new start of some sort,' said Paul; 'and you as well, I suppose.'

He took one of Dawes' pieces.

'I dunno where,' said the other.

'Things have to happen,' Morel said. 'It's no good doing anything – at least – no, I don't know. Give me some toffee.'

The two men ate sweets, and began another game of draughts.

'What made that scar on your mouth?' asked Dawes.

Paul put his hand hastily to his lips, and looked over the garden.

'I had a bicycle accident,' he said.

Dawes' hand trembled as he moved the piece.

'You shouldn't ha' laughed at me,' he said very low.

'When?'

'That night on Woodborough Road, when you and her passed me – you with your hand on her shoulder.'

'I never laughed at you,' said Paul.

Dawes kept his fingers on the draught-piece.

'I never knew you were there till the very second when you passed,' said Morel.

'It was that as did me,' he said, very low.

Paul took another sweet.

'I never laughed,' he said, 'except as I'm always laughing.'

They finished the game.

That night Morel walked home from Nottingham, in order to have something to do. The furnaces flared in a red blotch over Bulwell; the black clouds were like a low ceiling. As he went along the ten miles of highroad, he felt as if he were walking out of life, between the black levels of the sky and the earth. But at the end was only the sick-room. If he walked and walked for ever, there was only that place to come to.

He was not tired when he got near home, or he did not know it. Across the field he could see the red firelight leaping in her bedroom window.

'When she's dead,' he said to himself, 'that fire will go out.'

He took off his boots quietly and crept upstairs. His mother's door was wide open, because she slept alone still. The red firelight dashed its glow on the landing. Soft as a shadow, he peeped in her doorway.

'Paul!' she murmured.

His heart seemed to break again. He went in and sat by the bed.

'How late you are!' she murmured.

'Not very,' he said.

'Why, what time is it?' The murmur came plaintive and helpless.

'It's only just gone eleven.'

That was not true; it was nearly one o'clock.

'Oh!' she said; 'I thought it was later.'

And he knew the unutterable misery of her nights that would not go.

'Can't you sleep, my pigeon?' he said.

'No, I can't,' she wailed.

'Never mind, Little!' he said, crooning. 'Never mind, my love. I'll stop with you half an hour, my pigeon; then perhaps it will be better.'

And he sat by the bedside, slowly, rhythmically stroking her brows with his fingertips, stroking her eyes shut, soothing her, holding her fingers in his free hand. They could hear the sleepers' breathing in the other rooms.

'Now go to bed,' she murmured, lying quite still under his fingers and his love.

'Will you sleep?' he asked.

'Yes, I think so.'

'You feel better, my Little, don't you?'

'Yes,' she said, like a fretful, half-soothed child.

Still the days and the weeks went by. He hardly ever went to see Clara now. But he wandered restlessly from one person to another for some help, and there was none anywhere. Miriam had written to him tenderly. He went to see her. Her heart was very sore when she saw him, white, gaunt, with his eyes dark and bewildered. Her pity came up, hurting her till she could not bear it.

'How is she?' she asked.

'The same – the same!' he said. 'The doctor says she can't last, but I know she will. She'll be here at Christmas.'

Miriam shuddered. She drew him to her; she pressed him to her bosom; she kissed him and kissed him. He submitted, but it was torture. She could not kiss his agony. That remained alone and apart. She kissed his face, and roused his blood, while his soul was apart writhing with the agony of death. And she kissed him and fingered his body, till at last, feeling he would go mad, he got away from her. It was not that he wanted just then – not that. And she thought she had soothed him and done him good.

December came, and some snow. He stayed at home all the while now. They could not afford a nurse. Annie came to look after her mother; the parish nurse, whom they loved, came in morning and evening. Paul shared the nursing with Annie. Often, in the evenings, when friends were in the kitchen with them, they all laughed together and shook with laughter. It was reaction. Paul was so comical, Annie was so quaint. The whole party laughed till they cried, trying to subdue the sound. And Mrs Morel, lying alone in the darkness, heard them, and among her bitterness was a feeling of relief.

Then Paul would go upstairs gingerly, guiltily, to see if she had heard.

'Shall I give you some milk?' he asked.

'A little,' she replied plaintively.

And he would put some water with it, so that it should not nourish her. Yet he loved her more than his own life.

She had morphia every night, and her heart got fitful. Annie slept beside her. Paul would go in in the early morning, when his sister got up. His mother was wasted and almost ashen in the morning with the morphia. Darker and darker grew her eyes, all pupil, with the torture. In the mornings the weariness and ache was too much to bear. Yet she could not – would not – weep, or even complain much.

'You slept a bit later this morning, little one,' he would say to her.

'Did I?' she answered, with fretful weariness.

'Yes; it's nearly eight o'clock.'

He stood looking out of the window. The whole country was bleak and pallid under the snow. Then he felt her pulse. There was a strong stroke and a weak one, like a sound and its echo. That was supposed to betoken the end. She let him feel her wrist, knowing what he wanted.

Sometimes they looked in each other's eyes. Then they almost seemed to make an agreement. It was almost as if he were agreeing to die also. But she did not consent to die; she would not. Her body was wasted to a fragment of ash. Her eyes were dark and full of torture.

'Can't you give her something to put an end to it?' he asked the doctor at last.

But the doctor shook his head.

'She can't last many days now, Mr Morel,' he said.

Paul went indoors.

'I can't bear it much longer; we shall all go mad,' said Annie.

The two sat down to breakfast.

'Go and sit with her while we have breakfast, Minnie,' said Annie. But the girl was frightened.

Paul went through the country, through the woods, over the snow. He saw the marks of rabbits and birds in the white snow. He wandered miles and miles. A smoky red sunset came on slowly, painfully, lingering. He thought she would die that day. There was a donkey that came up to him over the snow by the wood's edge, and put its head against him and walked with him alongside. He put his arms round the donkey's neck, and stroked his cheeks against his ears.

His mother, silent, was still alive, with her hard mouth gripped grimly, her eyes of dark torture only living.

It was nearing Christmas; there was more snow. Annie and he felt as if they could go on no more. Still her dark eyes were alive. Morel, silent and frightened, obliterated himself. Sometimes he would go into the sick-room and look at her. Then he backed out, bewildered.

She kept her hold on life still. The miners had been out on strike, and returned a fortnight or so before Christmas. Minnie went upstairs with the feeding-cup. It was two days after the men had been in.

'Have the men been saying their hands are sore, Minnie?' she asked, in the faint, querulous voice that would not give in. Minnie stood surprised.

'Not as I know of, Mrs Morel,' she answered.

'But I'll bet they are sore,' said the dying woman, as she moved her head with a sigh of weariness. 'But, at any rate there'll be something to buy in with this week.'

Not a thing did she let slip.

'Your father's pit-things will want well airing, Annie,' she said, when the men were going back to work.

'Don't you bother about that, my dear,' said Annie.

One night Annie and Paul were alone. Nurse was upstairs.

'She'll live over Christmas,' said Annie. They were both full of horror.

'She won't,' he replied grimly. 'I s'll give her morphia.'

'Which?' said Annie.

'All that came from Sheffield,' said Paul.

'Ay – do!' said Annie.

The next day he was painting in the bedroom. She seemed to be asleep. He stepped softly backwards and forwards at his painting. Suddenly her small voice wailed, 'Don't walk about, Paul.'

He looked round. Her eyes, like dark bubbles in her face, were looking at him.

'No, my dear,' he said gently. Another fibre seemed to snap in his heart.

That evening he got all the morphia pills there were, and took them downstairs. Carefully he crushed them to powder.

'What are you doing?' said Annie.

'I s'll put 'em in her night milk.'

Then they both laughed together like two conspiring children. On top of all their horror flickered this little sanity.

Nurse did not come that night to settle Mrs Morel down. Paul went up with the hot milk in a feeding-cup. It was nine o'clock.

She was reared up in bed, and he put the feeding-cup between her lips that he would have died to save from any hurt. She took a sip, then put the spout of the cup away and looked at him with her dark, wondering eyes. He looked at her.

'Oh, it *is* bitter, Paul!' she said, making a little grimace.

'It's a new sleeping draught the doctor gave me for you,' he said. 'He thought it wouldn't leave you in such a state in the morning.'

'And I hope it won't,' she said, like a child.

She drank some more of the milk.

'But it *is* horrid!' she said.

He saw her frail fingers over the cup, her lips making a little move.

'I know – I tasted it,' he said. 'But I'll give you some clean milk afterwards.'

'I think so,' she said, and she went on with the draught. She was obedient to him like a child. He wondered if she knew. He saw her poor wasted throat moving as she drank with difficulty. Then he ran downstairs for more milk. There were no grains in the bottom of the cup.

'Has she had it?' whispered Annie.

'Yes – and she said it was bitter.'

'Oh!' laughed Annie, putting her under lip between her teeth.

'And I told her it was a new draught. Where's that milk?'

They both went upstairs.

'I wonder why nurse didn't come to settle me down?' complained the mother, like a child, wistfully.

'She said she was going to a concert, my love,' replied Annie.

'Did she?'

They were silent a minute. Mrs Morel gulped the little clean milk.

'Annie, that draught was horrid!' she said plaintively.

'Was it, my love? Well, never mind.'

The mother sighed again with weariness. Her pulse was very irregular.

'Let *us* settle you down,' said Annie. 'Perhaps nurse will be so late.'

'Ay,' said the mother – 'try.'

They turned the clothes back. Paul saw his mother like a girl curled up in her flannel nightdress. Quickly they made one half the bed, moved her, made the other, straightened her nightgown over her small feet, and covered her up.

'There,' said Paul, stroking her softly. 'There! – now you'll sleep.'

'Yes,' she said. 'I didn't think you could do the bed so nicely,' she added, almost gaily. Then she curled up, with her cheek on her hand, her head snugged between her shoulder. Paul put the long thin plait of grey hair over her shoulder and kissed her.

'You'll sleep, my love,' he said.

'Yes,' she answered trustfully. 'Good-night.'

They put out the light, and it was still.

Morel was in bed. Nurse did not come. Annie and Paul came to look at her at about eleven. She seemed to be sleeping as usual after her draught. Her mouth had come a bit open.

'Shall we sit up?' said Paul.

'I s'll lie with her as I always do,' said Annie. 'She might wake up.'

'All right. And call me if you see any difference.'

'Yes.'

They lingered before the bedroom fire, feeling the night big and black and snowy outside, their two selves alone in the world. At last he went into the next room and went to bed.

He slept almost immediately, but kept waking every now and again. Then he went sound asleep. He started awake at Annie's whispered, 'Paul, Paul!' He saw his sister in her white nightdress, with her long plait of hair down her back, standing in the darkness.

'Yes?' he whispered, sitting up.

'Come and look at her.'

He slipped out of bed. A bud of gas was burning in the sick-chamber. His mother lay with her cheek on her hand, curled up as she had gone to sleep. But her mouth had fallen open, and she breathed with great, hoarse breaths, like snoring, and there were long intervals between.

'She's going!' he whispered.

'Yes,' said Annie.

'How long has she been like it?'

'I only just woke up.'

Annie huddled into the dressing-gown, Paul wrapped himself in a brown blanket. It was three o'clock. He mended the fire. Then the two sat waiting. The great, snoring breath was taken – held awhile – then given back. There was a space – a long space. Then they started. The great, snoring breath was taken again. He bent close down and looked at her.

'Isn't it awful!' whispered Annie.

He nodded. They sat down again helplessly. Again came the great, snoring breath. Again they hung suspended. Again it was given back, long and harsh. The sound, so irregular, at such wide intervals, sounded through the house. Morel, in his room, slept on. Paul and Annie sat crouched, huddled, motionless. The great, snoring sound began again – there was a painful pause while the breath was held – back came the rasping breath. Minute after minute passed. Paul looked at her again, bending low over her.

'She may last like this,' he said.

They were both silent. He looked out of the window, and could faintly discern the snow on the garden.

'You go to my bed,' he said to Annie. 'I'll sit up.'

'No,' she said, 'I'll stop with you.'

'I'd rather you didn't,' he said.

At last Annie crept out of the room, and he was alone. He hugged himself in his brown blanket, crouched in front of his mother, watching. She looked dreadful, with the bottom jaw fallen back. He watched. Sometimes he thought the great breath would never begin again. He could not bear it – the waiting. Then suddenly, startling him, came the great harsh sound. He mended the fire again, noiselessly. She must not be disturbed. The minutes went by. The night was going, breath by breath. Each time the sound came he felt it wring him, till at last he could not feel so much.

His father got up. Paul heard the miner drawing his stocking on, yawning. Then Morel, in shirt and stockings, entered.

'Hush!' said Paul.

Morel stood watching. Then he looked at his son, helplessly, and in horror.

'Had I better stop a-whoam?' he whispered.

'No. Go to work. She'll last through tomorrow.'

'I don't think so.'

'Yes. Go to work.'

The miner looked at her again, in fear, and went obediently out of the room. Paul saw the tape of his garters swinging against his legs.

After another half-hour Paul went downstairs and drank a cup of tea, then returned. Morel, dressed for the pit, came upstairs again.

'Am I to go?' he said.

'Yes.'

And in a few minutes Paul heard his father's heavy steps go thudding over the deadening snow. Miners called in the street as they tramped in gangs to work. The terrible, long-drawn breaths continued – heave – heave – heave; then a long pause – then ah–ah–h–h–h–h! as it came back. Far away over the snow sounded the hooters of the ironworks. One after another they crowed and boomed, some small and far away, some near, the blowers of the collieries and the other works. Then there was silence. He mended the fire. The great breaths broke the silence – she looked just the same. He put back the blind and peered out. Still it was dark. Perhaps there was a lighter tinge. Perhaps the snow was bluer. He drew up the blind and got dressed. Then, shuddering, he drank brandy from the bottle on the washstand. The snow *was* growing blue. He heard a cart clanking down the street. Yes, it was seven o'clock, and it was coming a little bit light. He heard some people calling. The world was waking. A grey, deathly dawn crept over the snow. Yes, he could see the houses. He put out the gas. It seemed very dark. The breathing came still, but he was almost used to it. He could see her. She was just the same. He wondered if he piled heavy clothes on top of her it would make it heavier and the horrible breathing would stop. He looked at her. That was not her – not her a bit. If he piled the blanket and heavy coats on her –

Suddenly the door opened, and Annie entered. She looked at him questioningly.

'Just the same,' he said calmly.

They whispered together a minute, then went downstairs to get breakfast. It was twenty to eight. Soon Annie came down.

'Isn't it awful! Doesn't she look awful!' she whispered, dazed with horror.

He nodded.

'If she looks like that!' said Annie.

'Drink some tea,' he said.

They went upstairs again. Soon the neighbours came with their frightened question, 'How is she?'

It went on just the same. She lay with her cheek in her hand, her mouth fallen open, and the great, ghastly snores came and went.

At ten o'clock nurse came. She looked strange and woebegone.

'Nurse,' cried Paul, 'she'll last like this for days?'

'She can't, Mr Morel,' said nurse, 'she can't.'

There was a silence.

'Isn't it dreadful!' wailed the nurse. 'Who would have thought she could stand it? Go down now, Mr Morel, go down.'

At last, at about eleven o'clock, he went downstairs and sat in the neighbour's house. Annie was downstairs also. Nurse and Arthur were upstairs. Paul sat with his head in his hands. Suddenly Annie came flying across the yard crying, half mad, 'Paul – Paul – she's gone!'

In a second he was back in his own house and upstairs. She lay curled up and still, with her face on her hand, and nurse was wiping her mouth. They all stood back. He kneeled down, and put his face to hers and his arms round her: 'My love – my love – oh, my love!' he whispered again and again. 'My love – oh, my love!'

Then he heard the nurse behind him, crying, saying, 'She's better, Mr Morel, she's better.'

When he took his face up from his warm, dead mother he went straight downstairs and began blacking his boots.

There was a good deal to do, letters to write, and so on. The doctor came and glanced at her, and sighed.

'Ay poor thing!' he said, then turned away 'Well, call at the surgery about six for the certificate.'

The father came home from work at about four o'clock. He dragged silently into the house and sat down. Minnie bustled to give him his dinner. Tired, he laid his black arms on the table. There were swede turnips for his dinner, which he liked. Paul wondered if he knew. It was some time, and nobody had spoken. At last the son said, 'You noticed the blinds were down?'

Morel looked up.

'No,' he said. 'Why – has she gone?'

'Yes.'

'When wor that?'

'About twelve this morning.'

'H'm!'

The miner sat still for a moment, then began his dinner. It was as if nothing had happened. He ate his turnips in silence. Afterwards he washed and went upstairs to dress. The door of her room was shut.

'Have you seen her?' Annie asked of him when he came down.

'No,' he said.

In a little while he went out. Annie went away, and Paul called on the undertaker, the clergyman, the doctor, the registrar. It was a long business. He got back at nearly eight o'clock. The undertaker was coming soon to measure for the coffin. The house was empty except for her. He took a candle and went upstairs.

The room was cold that had been warm for so long. Flowers, bottles, plates, all sick-room litter was taken away; everything was harsh and austere. She lay raised on the bed, the sweep of the sheet from the raised feet was like a clean curve of snow, so silent. She lay like a maiden asleep. With his candle in his hand, he bent over her. She lay like a girl asleep and dreaming of her love. The mouth was a little open, as if wondering from the suffering, but her face was young, her brow clear and white as if life had never touched it. He looked again at the eyebrows, at the small, winsome nose a bit on one side. She was young again. Only the hair as it arched so beautifully from her temples was mixed with silver, and the two simple plaits that lay on her shoulders were filigree of silver and brown. She would wake up. She would lift her eyelids. She was with him still. He bent and kissed her passionately. But there was coldness against his mouth. He bit his lip with horror. Looking at her, he felt he could never, never let her go. No! He stroked the hair from her temples. That, too, was cold. He saw the mouth so dumb and wondering at the hurt. Then he crouched on the floor, whispering to her, 'Mother, mother!'

He was still with her when the undertakers came, young men who had been to school with him. They touched her reverently, and in a quiet, businesslike fashion. They did not look at her. He watched jealously. He and Annie guarded her fiercely. They would not let anybody come to see her, and the neighbours were offended.

After a while Paul went out of the house, and played cards at a friend's. It was midnight when he got back. His father rose from the couch as he entered, saying in a plaintive way, 'I thought tha wor niver comin', lad.'

'I didn't think you'd sit up,' said Paul.

His father looked so forlorn. Morel had been a man without fear – simply nothing frightened him. Paul realised with a start that he had been afraid to go to bed, alone in the house with his dead. He was sorry.

'I forgot you'd be alone, father,' he said.

'Dost want owt to eat?' asked Morel.

'No.'

'Sithee – I made thee a drop o' hot milk. Get it down thee; it's cold enough for owt.'

Paul drank it.

'I must go to Nottingham tomorrow,' he said.

After a while Morel went to bed. He hurried past the closed door, and left his own door open. Soon the son came upstairs also. He went in to kiss her good-night, as usual. It was cold and dark. He wished they had kept her fire burning. Still she dreamed her young dream. But she would be cold.

'My dear!' he whispered. 'My dear!'

And he did not kiss her, for fear she should be cold and strange to him. It eased him she slept so beautifully. He shut her door softly, not to wake her, and went to bed.

In the morning Morel summoned his courage, hearing Annie downstairs and Paul coughing in the room across the landing. He opened her door, and went into the darkened room. He saw the white uplifted form in the twilight, but her he dared not see. Bewildered, too frightened to possess any of his faculties, he got out of the room again and left her. He never looked at her again. He had not seen her for months, because he had not dared to look. And she looked like his young wife again.

'Have you seen her?' Annie asked of him sharply after breakfast.

'Yes,' he said.

'And don't you think she looks nice?'

'Yes.'

He went out of the house soon after. And all the time he seemed to be creeping aside to avoid it.

Paul went about from place to place, doing the business of the death. He met Clara in Nottingham, and they had tea together in a café, when they were quite jolly again. She was infinitely relieved to find he did not take it tragically.

Later, when the relatives began to come for the funeral, the affair became public, and the children became social beings. They put themselves aside. They buried her in a furious storm of rain and wind. The wet clay glistened, all the white flowers were soaked. Annie gripped his arm and leaned forward. Down below she saw a dark corner of William's coffin. The oak box sank steadily. She was gone. The rain poured in the grave. The procession of black, with its umbrellas glistening, turned away. The cemetery was deserted under the drenching cold rain.

Paul went home and busied himself supplying the guests with drinks. His father sat in the kitchen with Mrs Morel's relatives, 'superior' people, and wept, and said what a good lass she'd been, and how he'd tried to do everything he could for her – everything. He had striven all his life to do what he could for her, and he'd nothing to reproach himself with. She was gone, but he'd done his best for her. He wiped his eyes with his white handkerchief. He'd nothing to reproach himself for, he repeated. All his life he'd done his best for her.

And that was how he tried to dismiss her. He never thought of her personally. Everything deep in him he denied. Paul hated his father for sitting sentiment-alising over her. He knew he would do it in the public-houses. For the real tragedy went on in Morel in spite of himself. Sometimes, later, he came down from his afternoon sleep, white and cowering.

'I *have* been dreaming of thy mother,' he said in a small voice.

'Have you, father? When I dream of her it's always just as she was when she was well. I dream of her often, but it seems quite nice and natural, as if nothing had altered.'

But Morel crouched in front of the fire in terror.

The weeks passed half real, not much pain, not much of anything, perhaps a little relief, mostly a *nuit blanche*. Paul went restlessly from place to place. For some months, since his mother had been worse, he had not made love to Clara. She was, as it were, dumb to him, rather distant. Dawes saw her very occasionally, but the two could not get an inch across the great distance between them. The three of them were drifting forward.

Dawes mended very slowly. He was in the convalescent home at Skegness at Christmas, nearly well again. Paul went to the seaside for a few days. His father was with Annie in Sheffield. Dawes came to Paul's lodgings. His time in the home was up. The two men, between whom was such a big reserve, seemed faithful to each other. Dawes depended on Morel now. He knew Paul and Clara had practically separated.

Two days after Christmas Paul was to go back to Nottingham. The evening before he sat with Dawes smoking before the fire.

'You know Clara's coming down for the day tomorrow?' he said.

The other man glanced at him.

'Yes, you told me,' he replied.

Paul drank the remainder of his glass of whisky.

'I told the landlady your wife was coming,' he said.

'Did you?' said Dawes, shrinking, but almost leaving himself in the other's hands. He got up rather stiffly, and reached for Morel's glass.

'Let me fill you up,' he said.

Paul jumped up.

'You sit still,' he said.

But Dawes, with rather shaky hand, continued to mix the drink.

'Say when,' he said.

'Thanks!' replied the other. 'But you've no business to get up.'

'It does me good, lad,' replied Dawes. 'I begin to think I'm right again, then.'

'You are about right, you know.'

'I am, certainly I am,' said Dawes, nodding to him.

'And Len says he can get you on in Sheffield.'

Dawes glanced at him again, with dark eyes that agreed with everything the other would say, perhaps a trifle dominated by him.

'It's funny,' said Paul, 'starting again. I feel in a lot bigger mess than you.'

'In what way, lad?'

'I don't know. I don't know. It's as if I was in a tangled sort of hole, rather dark and dreary, and no road anywhere.'

'I know – I understand it,' Dawes said, nodding. 'But you'll find it'll come all right.'

He spoke caressingly.

'I suppose so,' said Paul.

Dawes knocked his pipe in a hopeless fashion.

'You've not done for yourself like I have,' he said.

Morel saw the wrist and the white hand of the other man gripping the stem of the pipe and knocking out the ash, as if he had given up.

'How old are you?' Paul asked.

'Thirty-nine,' replied Dawes, glancing at him.

Those brown eyes, full of the consciousness of failure, almost pleading for reassurance, for someone to re-establish the man in himself, to warm him, to set him up firm again, troubled Paul.

'You'll just be in your prime,' said Morel. 'You don't look as if much life had gone out of you.'

The brown eyes of the other flashed suddenly.

'It hasn't,' he said. 'The go is there.'

Paul looked up and laughed.

'We've both got plenty of life in us yet to make things fly,' he said.

The eyes of the two men met. They exchanged one look. Having recognised the stress of passion each in the other, they both drank their whisky.

'Yes, begod!' said Dawes, breathless.

There was a pause.

'And I don't see,' said Paul, 'why you shouldn't go on where you left off.'

'What – ' said Dawes, suggestively.

'Yes – fit your old home together again.'

Dawes hid his face and shook his head.

'Couldn't be done,' he said, and he looked up with an ironic smile.

'Why? Because you don't want?'

'Perhaps.'

They smoked in silence. Dawes showed his teeth as he bit his pipe stem.

'You mean you don't want her?' asked Paul.

Dawes stared up at the picture with a caustic expression on his face.

'I hardly know,' he said.

The smoke floated softly up.

'I believe she wants you,' said Paul

'Do you?' replied the other, soft, satirical, abstract.

'Yes. She never really hitched on to me – you were always there in the background. That's why she wouldn't get a divorce.'

Dawes continued to stare in a satirical fashion at the picture over the mantelpiece.

'That's how women are with me,' said Paul. 'They want me like mad, but they don't want to belong to me. And she *belonged* to you all the time. I knew.'

The triumphant male came up in Dawes. He showed his teeth more distinctly.

'Perhaps I was a fool,' he said.

'You were a big fool,' said Morel.

'But perhaps even *then* you were a bigger fool,' said Dawes.

There was a touch of triumph and malice in it.

'Do you think so?' said Paul.

They were silent for a time.

'At any rate, I'm clearing out tomorrow,' said Morel.

'I see,' answered Dawes.

Then they did not talk any more. The instinct to murder each other had returned. They almost avoided each other.

They shared the same bedroom. When they retired Dawes seemed abstract, thinking of something. He sat on the side of the bed in his shirt, looking at his legs.

'Aren't you getting cold?' asked Morel.

'I was lookin' at these legs,' replied the other.

'What's up with 'em? They look all right,' replied Paul from his bed.

'They look all right. But there's some water in 'em yet.'

'And what about it?'

'Come and look.'

Paul reluctantly got out of bed and went to look at the rather handsome legs of the other man that were covered with glistening, dark gold hair.

'Look here,' said Dawes, pointing to his shin. 'Look at the water under here.'

'Where?' said Paul.

The man pressed his fingertips. They left little dents that filled up slowly.

'It's nothing,' said Paul.

'You feel,' said Dawes.

Paul tried with his fingers. It made little dents.

'H'm!' he said.

'Rotten, isn't it?' said Dawes.

'Why? It's nothing much.'

'You're not much of a man with water in your legs.'

'I can't see as it makes any difference,' said Morel. 'I've got a weak chest.'

He returned to his own bed.

'I suppose the rest of me's all right,' said Dawes, and he put out the light.

In the morning it was raining. Morel packed his bag. The sea was grey and shaggy and dismal. He seemed to be cutting himself off from life more and more. It gave him a wicked pleasure to do it.

The two men were at the station. Clara stepped out of the train, and came along the platform, very erect and coldly composed. She wore a long coat and tweed hat. Paul shook hands with her at the barrier. Dawes was leaning against the bookstall, watching. His black overcoat was buttoned up to the chin because of the rain. He was pale, with almost a touch of nobility in his quietness. He came forward, limping slightly.

'You ought to look better than this,' she said.

'Oh, I'm all right now.'

The three stood at a loss. She kept the two men hesitating near her.

'Shall we go to the lodging straight off,' said Paul, 'or somewhere else?'

'We may as well go home,' said Dawes.

Paul walked on the outside of the pavement, then Dawes, then Clara. They made polite conversation. The sitting-room faced the sea, whose tide, grey and shaggy, hissed not far off.

Morel swung up the big armchair.

'Sit down, Jack,' he said.

'I don't want that chair,' said Dawes.

'Sit down!' Morel repeated.

Clara took off her things and laid them on the couch. She had a slight air of resentment. Lifting her hair with her fingers, she sat down, rather aloof and composed. Paul ran downstairs to speak to the landlady.

'I should think you're cold,' said Dawes to his wife. 'Come nearer to the fire.'

'Thank you, I'm quite warm,' she answered.

She looked out of the window at the rain and at the sea. 'When are you going back?' she asked.

'Well, the rooms are taken until tomorrow, so he wants me to stop. He's going back tonight.'

'And then you're thinking of going to Sheffield?'

'Yes.'

'Are you fit to start work?'

'I'm going to start.'

'You've really got a place?'

'Yes – begin on Monday.'

'You don't look fit.'

'Why don't I?'

She looked again out of the window instead of answering. 'And have you got lodgings in Sheffield?'

'Yes.'

Again she looked away out of the window. The panes were blurred with streaming rain.

'And can you manage all right?' she asked.

'I s'd think so. I s'll have to!'

They were silent when Morel returned.

'I shall go by the four-twenty,' he said as he entered.

Nobody answered.

'I wish you'd take your boots off,' he said to Clara. 'There's a pair of slippers of mine.'

'Thank you,' she said. 'They aren't wet.'

He put the slippers near her feet. She felt them there.

Morel sat down. Both the men seemed helpless, and each of them had a rather hunted look. But Dawes now carried himself quietly, seemed to yield himself, while Paul seemed to screw himself up. Clara thought she had never seen him look so small and mean. He was as if trying to get himself into the smallest possible compass. And as he went about arranging, and as he sat talking, there seemed something false about him and out of tune. Watching him unknown, she said to herself there was no stability about him. He was fine in his way, passionate, and able to give her drinks of pure life when he was in one mood. And now he looked paltry and insignificant. There was nothing stable about him. Her husband had more manly dignity. At any rate *he* did not waft about with any wind. There was something evanescent about Morel, she thought, something shifting and false. He would never make sure ground for any woman to stand on.

She despised him rather for his shrinking together, getting smaller. Her husband at least was manly, and when he was beaten gave in. But this other would never own to being beaten. He would shift round and round, prowl, get smaller. She despised him. And yet she watched him rather than Dawes, and it seemed as if their three fates lay in his hands. She hated him for it.

She seemed to understand better now about men, and what they could or would do. She was less afraid of them, more sure of herself. That they were not the small egoists she had imagined them made her more comfortable. She had learned a good deal – almost as much as she wanted to learn. Her cup had been full. It was still as full as she could carry. On the whole, she would not be sorry when he was gone.

They had dinner, and sat eating nuts and drinking by the fire. Not a serious word had been spoken. Yet Clara realised that Morel was withdrawing from the circle, leaving her the option to stay with her husband. It angered her. He was a mean fellow, after all, to take what he wanted and then give her back. She did not remember that she herself had had what she wanted, and really, at the bottom of her heart, wished to be given back.

Paul felt crumpled up and lonely. His mother had really supported his life. He had loved her; they two had, in fact, faced the world together. Now she was gone, and for ever behind him was the gap in life, the tear in the veil, through which his life seemed to drift slowly, as if he were drawn towards death. He wanted someone of their own free initiative to help him. The lesser things he began to let go from him, for fear of this big thing, the lapse towards death, following in the wake of his beloved. Clara could not stand for him to hold on to. She wanted him, but not to understand him. He felt she wanted the man on top, not the real him that was in trouble. That would be too much trouble to her; he dared not give it her. She could not cope with him. It made him ashamed. So, secretly ashamed because he was in such a mess, because his own hold on life was so unsure, because nobody held him, feeling unsubstantial, shadowy, as if he did not count for much in this concrete world, he drew himself together smaller and smaller. He did not want to die; he would not give in. But he was not afraid of death. If nobody would help, he would go on alone.

Dawes had been driven to the extremity of life, until he was afraid. He could go to the brink of death, he could lie on the edge and look in. Then, cowed, afraid, he had to crawl back, and like a beggar take what offered. There was a certain nobility in it. As Clara saw, he owned himself beaten, and he wanted to be taken back whether or not. That she could do for him.

It was three o'clock.

'I am going by the four-twenty,' said Paul again to Clara. 'Are you coming then or later?'

'I don't know,' she said.

'I'm meeting my father in Nottingham at seven-fifteen,' he said.

'Then,' she answered, 'I'll come later.'

Dawes jerked suddenly, as if he had been held on a strain. He looked out over the sea, but he saw nothing.

'There are one or two books in the corner,' said Morel. 'I've done with 'em.'

At about four o'clock he went.

'I shall see you both later,' he said, as he shook hands.

'I suppose so,' said Dawes. 'An' perhaps – one day – I s'll be able to pay you back the money as –'

'I shall come for it, you'll see,' laughed Paul. 'I s'll be on the rocks before I'm very much older.'

'Ay – well –' said Dawes.

'Goodbye,' he said to Clara.

'Goodbye,' she said, giving him her hand. Then she glanced at him for the last time, dumb and humble.

He was gone. Dawes and his wife sat down again.

'It's a nasty day for travelling,' said the man.

'Yes,' she answered.

They talked in a desultory fashion until it grew dark. The landlady brought in the tea. Dawes drew up his chair to the table without being invited, like a husband. Then he sat humbly waiting for his cup. She served him as she would, like a wife, not consulting his wish.

After tea, as it drew near to six o'clock, he went to the window. All was dark outside. The sea was roaring.

'It's raining yet,' he said.

'Is it?' she answered.

'You won't go tonight, shall you?' he said, hesitating.

She did not answer. He waited.

'I shouldn't go in this rain,' he said.

'Do you *want* me to stay?' she asked.

His hand as he held the dark curtain trembled.

'Yes,' he said.

He remained with his back to her. She rose and went slowly to him. He let go the curtain, turned, hesitating, towards her. She stood with her hands behind her back, looking up at him in a heavy, inscrutable fashion.

'Do you want me, Baxter?' she asked.

His voice was hoarse as he answered, 'Do you want to come back to me?'

She made a moaning noise, lifted her arms, and put them round his neck, drawing him to her. He hid his face on her shoulder, holding her clasped.

'Take me back!' she whispered, ecstatic. 'Take me back, take me back!' And she put her fingers through his fine, thin dark hair, as if she were only semi-conscious. He tightened his grasp on her.

'Do you want me again?' he murmured, broken.

CHAPTER 15

Derelict

Clara went with her husband to Sheffield, and Paul scarcely saw her again. Walter Morel seemed to have let all the trouble go over him, and there he was, crawling about on the mud of it, just the same. There was scarcely any bond between father and son, save that each felt he must not let the other go in any actual want. As there was no one to keep on the home, and as they could neither of them bear the emptiness of the house, Paul took lodgings in Nottingham, and Morel went to live with a friendly family in Bestwood.

Everything seemed to have gone smash for the young man. He could not paint. The picture he finished on the day of his mother's death – one that satisfied him – was the last thing he did. At work there was no Clara. When he came home he could not take up his brushes again. There was nothing left.

So he was always in the town at one place or another, drinking, knocking about with the men he knew. It really wearied him. He talked to barmaids, to almost any woman, but there was that dark, strained look in his eyes, as if he were hunting something.

Everything seemed so different, so unreal. There seemed no reason why people should go along the street, and houses pile up in the daylight. There seemed no reason why these things should occupy the space, instead of leaving it empty. His friends talked to him: he heard the sounds, and he answered. But why there should be the noise of speech he could not understand.

He was most himself when he was alone, or working hard and mechanically at the factory. In the latter case there was pure forgetfulness, when he lapsed from consciousness. But it had to come to an end. It hurt him so, that things had lost their reality. The first snowdrops came. He saw the tiny drop-pearls among the grey. They would have given him the liveliest emotion at one time. Now they were there, but they did not seem to mean anything. In a few moments they would cease to occupy that place and just the space would be, where they had been. Tall, brilliant tramcars ran along the street at night. It seemed almost a wonder they should trouble to rustle backwards and forwards. 'Why trouble to go tilting down to Trent Bridges?' he asked of the big trams. It seemed they just as well might *not* be as be.

The realest thing was the thick darkness at night. That seemed to him whole and comprehensible and restful. He could leave himself to it. Suddenly a piece of paper started near his feet and blew along down the pavement. He stood still, rigid, with clenched fists, a flame of agony going over him. And he saw again the sick-room, his mother, her eyes. Unconsciously he had been with her, in her company. The swift hop of the paper reminded him she was gone. But he had been with her. He wanted everything to stand still, so that he could be with her again.

The days passed, the weeks. But everything seemed to have fused, gone into a conglomerated mass. He could not tell one day from another, one week from another, hardly one place from another. Nothing was distinct or distinguishable. Often he lost himself for an hour at a time, could not remember what he had done.

One evening he came home late to his lodging. The fire was burning low; everybody was in bed. He threw on some more coal, glanced at the table, and decided he wanted no supper. Then he sat down in the armchair. It was perfectly still. He did not know anything, yet he saw the dim smoke wavering up the chimney. Presently two mice came out, cautiously, nibbling the fallen crumbs. He watched them as it were from a long way off. The church clock struck two. Far away he could hear the sharp clinking of the trucks on the railway. No, it was not they that were far away. They were there in their places. But where was he himself?

The time passed. The two mice, careering wildly, scampered cheekily over his slippers. He had not moved a muscle. He did not want to move. He was not thinking of anything. It was easier so. There was no wrench of knowing anything. Then, from time to time, some other consciousness, working mechanically, flashed into sharp phrases.

'What am I doing?'

And out of the semi-intoxicated trance came the answer, 'Destroying myself.'

Then a dull, live feeling, gone in an instant, told him that it was wrong. After a while, suddenly came the question, 'Why wrong?'

Again there was no answer, but a stroke of hot stubbornness inside his chest resisted his own annihilation.

There was a sound of a heavy cart clanking down the road. Suddenly the electric light went out; there was a bruising thud in the penny-in-the-slot meter. He did not stir, but sat gazing in front of him. Only the mice had scuttled, and the fire glowed red in the dark room.

Then, quite mechanically and more distinctly, the conversation began again inside him.

'She's dead. What was it all for – her struggle?'

That was his despair wanting to go after her.

'You're alive.'

'She's not.'

'She is – in you.'

Suddenly he felt tired with the burden of it.

'You've got to keep alive for her sake,' said his will in him.

Something felt sulky, as if it would not rouse.

'You've got to carry forward her living, and what she had done, go on with it.'

But he did not want to. He wanted to give up.

'But you can go on with your painting,' said the will in him. 'Or else you can beget children. They both carry on her effort.'

'Painting is not living.'

'Then live.'

'Marry whom?' came the sulky question.

'As best you can.'

'Miriam?'

But he did not trust that.

He rose suddenly, went straight to bed. When he got inside his bedroom and closed the door, he stood with clenched fists.

'Mater, my dear – ' he began, with the whole force of his soul. Then he stopped. He would not say it. He would not admit that he wanted to die, to have done. He would not own that life had beaten him, or that death had beaten him.

Going straight to bed, he slept at once, abandoning himself to the sleep.

So the weeks went on. Always alone, his soul oscillated, first on the side of death, then on the side of life, doggedly. The real agony was that he had nowhere to go, nothing to do, nothing to say, and *was* nothing himself. Sometimes he ran down the streets as if he were mad: sometimes he was mad; things weren't there, things were there. It made him pant. Sometimes he stood before the bar of the public-house where he had called for a drink. Everything suddenly stood back away from him. He saw the face of the barmaid, the gabbling drinkers, his own glass on the slopped, mahogany board, in the distance. There was something between him and them. He could not get into touch. He did not want them; he did not want his drink. Turning abruptly, he went out. On the threshold he stood and looked at the lighted street. But he was not of it or in it. Something separated him. Everything went on there below those lamps, shut away from him. He could not get at them. He felt he couldn't touch the lamp-posts, not if he reached. Where could he go? There was nowhere to go, neither back into the inn, or forward anywhere. He felt stifled. There was nowhere for him. The stress grew inside him; he felt he should smash.

'I mustn't,' he said; and, turning blindly, he went in and drank. Sometimes the drink did him good – sometimes it made him worse. He ran down the road. For ever restless, he went here, there, everywhere. He determined to work. But when he had made six strokes, he loathed the pencil violently, got up, and went away, hurried off to a club where he could play cards or billiards, to a place where he could flirt with a barmaid who was no more to him than the brass pump-handle she drew.

He was very thin and lantern-jawed. He dared not meet his own eyes in the mirror; he never looked at himself. He wanted to get away from himself, but there was nothing to get hold of. In despair he thought of Miriam. Perhaps – perhaps – ?

Then, happening to go into the Unitarian Church one Sunday evening, when they stood up to sing the second hymn he saw her before him. The light glistened on her lower lip as she sang. She looked as if she had got something, at any rate: some hope in heaven, if not in earth. Her comfort and her life seemed in the after-world. A warm, strong feeling for her came up. She seemed to yearn, as she sang, for the mystery and comfort. He put his hope in her. He longed for the sermon to be over, to speak to her.

The throng carried her out just before him. He could nearly touch her. She did not know he was there. He saw the brown humble nape of her neck under its black curls. He would leave himself to her. She was better and bigger than he. He would depend on her.

She went wandering, in her blind way, through the little throngs of people outside the church. She always looked so lost and out of place among people. He went forward and put his hand on her arm. She started violently. Her great brown eyes dilated in fear, then went questioning at the sight of him. He shrank slightly from her.

'I didn't know – ' she faltered.

'Nor I,' he said.

He looked away. His sudden, flaring hope sank again.

'What are you doing in town?' he asked.

'I'm staying at Cousin Anne's.'

'Ha! For long?'

'No; only till tomorrow.'

'Must you go straight home?'

She looked at him, then hid her face under her hat brim.

'No,' she said – 'no; it's not necessary.'

He turned away, and she went with him. They threaded through the throng of church-people. The organ was still sounding in St Mary's. Dark figures came through the lighted doors; people were coming down the steps. The large coloured windows glowed up in the night. The church was like a great lantern suspended. They went down Hollow Stone, and he took the car for the Bridges.

'You will just have supper with me,' he said; 'then I'll bring you back.'

'Very well,' she replied, low and husky.

They scarcely spoke while they were on the car. The Trent ran dark and full under the bridge. Away towards Colwich all was black night. He lived down Holme Road, on the naked edge of the town, facing across the river-meadows towards Sneinton Hermitage and the steep scarp of Colwick Wood. The floods were out. The silent water and the darkness spread away on their left. Almost afraid, they hurried along by the houses.

Supper was laid. He swung the curtain over the window. There was a bowl of freesias and scarlet anemones on the table. She bent to them. Still touching them with her fingertips, she looked up at him, saying, 'Aren't they beautiful?'

'Yes,' he said. 'What will you drink – coffee?'

'I should like it,' she said.

'Then excuse me a moment.'

He went out to the kitchen.

Miriam took off her things and looked round. It was a bare, severe room. Her photo, Clara's, Annie's, were on the wall. She looked on the drawing-board to see what he was doing. There were only a few meaningless lines. She looked to see what books he was reading. Evidently just an ordinary novel. The letters in the rack she saw were from Annie, Arthur, and from some man or other she did not know. Everything he had touched, everything that was in the least personal to him, she examined with lingering absorption. He had been gone from her for so long, she wanted to rediscover him, his position, what he was now. But there was not much in the room to help her. It only made her feel rather sad, it was so hard and comfortless.

She was curiously examining a sketchbook when he returned with the coffee.

'There's nothing new in it,' he said, 'and nothing very interesting.'

He put down the tray, and went to look over her shoulder. She turned the pages slowly, intent on examining everything.

'H'm!' he said, as she paused at a sketch. 'I'd forgotten that. It's not bad, is it?'

'No,' she said. 'I don't quite understand it.'

He took the book from her and went through it. Again he made a curious sound of surprise and pleasure.

'There's some not bad stuff in there,' he said.

'Not at all bad,' she answered gravely.

He felt again her interest in his work. Or was it for himself? Why was she always most interested in him as he appeared in his work?

They sat down to supper.

'By the way,' he said, 'didn't I hear something about your earning your own living?'

'Yes,' she replied, bowing her dark head over her cup.

'And what of it?'

'I'm merely going to the farming college at Broughton for three months, and I shall probably be kept on as a teacher there.'

'I say – that sounds all right for you! You always wanted to be independent.'

'Yes.'

'Why didn't you tell me?'

'I only knew last week.'

'But I heard a month ago,' he said.

'Yes; but nothing was settled then.'

'I should have thought,' he said, 'you'd have told me you were trying.'

She ate her food in the deliberate, constrained way, almost as if she recoiled a little from doing anything so publicly, that he knew so well.

'I suppose you're glad,' he said.

'Very glad.'

'Yes – it will be something.'

He was rather disappointed.

'I think it will be a great deal,' she said, almost haughtily, resentfully.

He laughed shortly.

'Why do you think it won't?' she asked.

'Oh, I don't think it won't be a great deal. Only you'll find earning your own living isn't everything.'

'No,' she said, swallowing with difficulty; 'I don't suppose it is.'

'I suppose work *can* be nearly everything to a man,' he said, 'though it isn't to me. But a woman only works with a part of herself. The real and vital part is covered up.'

'But a man can give *all* himself to a work?' she asked.

'Yes, practically.'

'And a woman only the unimportant part of herself?'

'That's it.'

She looked up at him, and her eyes dilated with anger.

'Then,' she said, 'if it's true, it's a great shame.'

'It is. But I don't know everything,' he answered.

After supper they drew up to the fire. He swung her a chair facing him, and they sat down. She was wearing a dress of dark claret colour, that suited her dark complexion and her large features. Still, the curls were fine and free, but her face was much older, the brown throat much thinner. She seemed old to him, older than Clara. Her bloom of youth had quickly gone. A sort of stiffness, almost of woodenness, had come upon her. She meditated a little while, then looked at him.

'And how are things with you?' she asked.

'About all right,' he answered.

She looked at him, waiting.

'Nay,' she said, very low.

Her brown, nervous hands were clasped over her knee. They had still the lack of confidence or repose, the almost hysterical look. He winced as he saw them. Then he laughed mirthlessly. She put her fingers between her lips. His slim, black, tortured body lay quite still in the chair. She suddenly took her finger from her mouth and looked at him.

'And you have broken off with Clara?'

'Yes.'

His body lay like an abandoned thing, strewn in the chair.

'You know,' she said, 'I think we ought to be married.'

He opened his eyes for the first time since many months and attended to her with respect.

'Why?' he said.

'See,' she said, 'how you waste yourself! You might be ill, you might die, and I never know – be no more then than if I had never known you.'

'And if we married?' he asked.

'At any rate, I could prevent you wasting yourself and being a prey to other women – like – like Clara.'

'A prey?' he repeated, smiling.

She bowed her head in silence. He lay feeling his despair come up again.

'I'm not sure,' he said slowly, 'that marriage would be much good.'

'I only think of you,' she replied.

'I know you do. But – you love me so much, you want to put me in your pocket. And I should die there smothered.'

She bent her head, put her finger between her lips, while the bitterness surged up in her heart.

'And what will you do otherwise?' she asked.

'I don't know – go on, I suppose. Perhaps I shall soon go abroad.'

The despairing doggedness in his tone made her go on her knees on the rug before the fire, very near to him. There she crouched as if she were crushed by something, and could not raise her head. His hands lay quite inert on the arms of his chair. She was aware of them. She felt that now he lay at her mercy. If she could rise, take him, put her arms round him, and say, 'You are mine,' then he would leave himself to her. But dare she? She could easily sacrifice herself. But dare she assert herself? She was aware of his dark-clothed, slender body, that seemed one stroke of life, sprawled in the chair close to her. But no; she dared not put her arms round it, take it up, and say, 'It is mine, this body. Leave it to me.' And she wanted to. It called to all her woman's instinct. But she crouched, and dared not. She was afraid he would not let her. She was afraid it was too much. It lay there, his body, abandoned. She knew she ought to take it up and claim it, and claim every right to it. But – could she do it? Her impotence before him, before the strong demand of some unknown thing in him, was her extremity. Her hands fluttered; she half lifted her head. Her eyes, shuddering, appealing, gone almost distracted, pleaded to him suddenly. His heart caught with pity. He took her hands, drew her to him, and comforted her.

'Will you have me, to marry me?' he said very low.

Oh, why did not he take her? Her very soul belonged to him. Why would he not take what was his? She had borne so long the cruelty of belonging to him and not being claimed by him. Now he was straining her again. It was too much for her. She drew back her head, held his face between her hands, and looked him in the eyes. No, he was hard. He wanted something else. She pleaded to him with all her love not to make it *her* choice. She could not cope with it, with him, she knew not with what. But it strained her till she felt she would break.

'Do you want it?' she asked, very gravely.

'Not much,' he replied, with pain.

She turned her face aside; then, raising herself with dignity, she took his head to her bosom, and rocked him softly. She was not to have him, then! So she could comfort him. She put her fingers through his hair. For her, the anguished sweetness of self-sacrifice. For him, the hate and misery of another failure. He could not bear it – that breast which was warm and which cradled him without taking the burden of him. So much he wanted to rest on her that the feint of rest only tortured him. He drew away.

'And without marriage we can do nothing?' he asked.

His mouth was lifted from his teeth with pain. She put her little finger between her lips.

'No,' she said, low and like the toll of a bell. 'No, I think not.'

It was the end then between them. She could not take him and relieve him of the responsibility of himself. She could only sacrifice herself to him – sacrifice herself every day, gladly. And that he did not want. He wanted her to hold him and say, with joy and authority: 'Stop all this restlessness and beating against death. You are mine for a mate.' She had not the strength. Or was it a mate she wanted? or did she want a Christ in him?

He felt, in leaving her, he was defrauding her of life. But he knew that, in staying, stifling the inner, desperate man, he was denying his own life. And he did not hope to give life to her by denying his own.

She sat very quiet. He lit a cigarette. The smoke went up from it, wavering. He was thinking of his mother, and had forgotten Miriam. She suddenly looked at him. Her bitterness came surging up. Her sacrifice, then, was useless. He lay there aloof, careless about her. Suddenly she saw again his lack of religion, his restless instability. He would destroy himself like a perverse child. Well, then, he would!

'I think I must go,' she said softly.

By her tone he knew she was despising him. He rose quietly.

'I'll come along with you,' he answered.

She stood before the mirror pinning on her hat. How bitter, how unutterably bitter, it made her that he rejected her sacrifice! Life ahead looked dead, as if the glow were gone out. She bowed her face over the flowers – the freesias so sweet and springlike, the scarlet anemones flaunting over the table. It was like him to have those flowers.

He moved about the room with a certain sureness of touch, swift and relentless and quiet. She knew she could not cope with him. He would escape like a weasel out of her hands. Yet without him her life would trail on lifeless. Brooding, she touched the flowers.

'Have them!' he said; and he took them out of the jar, dripping as they were, and went quickly into the kitchen. She waited for him, took the flowers, and they went out together, he talking, she feeling dead.

She was going from him now. In her misery she leaned against him as they sat on the car. He was unresponsive. Where would he go? What would be the end of him? She could not bear it, the vacant feeling where he should be. He was so foolish, so wasteful, never at peace with himself. And now where would he go? And what did he care that he wasted her? He had no religion; it was all for the moment's attraction that he cared, nothing else, nothing deeper. Well, she would wait and see how it turned out with him. When he had had enough he would give in and come to her.

He shook hands and left her at the door of her cousin's house. When he turned away he felt the last hold for him had gone. The town, as he sat upon the car, stretched away over the bay of railway, a level fume of lights. Beyond the town the country, little smouldering spots for more towns – the sea – the night – on and on! And he had no place in it! Whatever spot he stood on, there he stood alone. From his breast, from his mouth, sprang the endless space, and it was there behind him, everywhere. The people hurrying along the streets offered no obstruction to the void in which he found himself. They were small shadows whose footsteps and voices could be heard, but in each of them the same night, the same silence. He got off the car. In the country all was dead still. Little stars shone high up; little stars spread far away in the flood-waters, a firmament below. Everywhere the vastness and terror of the immense night which is roused and stirred for a brief while by the day but which returns, and will remain at last eternal, holding everything in its silence and its living gloom. There was no Time, only Space. Who could say his mother had lived and did not live? She had been in one place, and was in another; that was all. And his soul could not leave her, wherever she was. Now she was gone abroad into the night, and he was with her still. They were together. But yet there was his body, his chest, that leaned against the stile, his hands on the wooden bar. They seemed something. Where was he? – one tiny upright speck of flesh, less than an ear of wheat lost in the field. He could not bear it. On every side the immense dark silence seemed pressing him, so tiny a spark, into extinction, and yet, almost nothing, he could not be extinct. Night, in which everything was lost, went reaching out, beyond stars and sun. Stars and sun, a few bright grains, went spinning round for terror, and holding each other in embrace, there in a darkness that outpassed them all, and left them tiny and daunted. So much, and himself, infinitesimal, at the core a nothingness, and yet not nothing.

'Mother!' he whispered – 'mother!'

She was the only thing that held him up, himself, amid all this. And she was gone, intermingled herself. He wanted her to touch him, have him alongside with her.

But no, he would not give in. Turning sharply, he walked towards the city's gold phosphorescence. His fists were shut, his mouth set fast. He would not take that direction, to the darkness, to follow her. He walked towards the faintly humming, glowing town, quickly.

WOMEN IN LOVE

CONTENTS

CHAPTER I

Sisters

URSULA AND GUDRUN BRANGWEN sat one morning in the window-bay of their father's house in Beldover, working and talking. Ursula was stitching a piece of brightly-coloured embroidery, and Gudrun was drawing upon a board which she held on her knee. They were mostly silent, talking as their thoughts strayed through their minds.

'Ursula,' said Gudrun, 'don't you *really want* to get married?' Ursula laid her embroidery in her lap and looked up. Her face was calm and considerate.

'I don't know,' she replied. 'It depends how you mean.'

Gudrun was slightly taken aback. She watched her sister for some moments.

'Well,' she said, ironically, 'it usually means one thing! But don't you think anyhow, you'd be – ' she darkened slightly – 'in a better position than you are in now.'

A shadow came over Ursula's face.

'I might,' she said. 'But I'm not sure.'

Again Gudrun paused, slightly irritated. She wanted to be quite definite.

'You don't think one needs the *experience* of having been married?' she asked.

'Do you think it need *be* an experience?' replied Ursula.

'Bound to be, in some way or other,' said Gudrun, coolly. 'Possibly undesirable, but bound to be an experience of some sort.'

'Not really,' said Ursula. 'More likely to be the end of experience.'

Gudrun sat very still, to attend to this.

'Of course,' she said, 'there's *that* to consider.' This brought the conversation to a close. Gudrun, almost angrily, took up her rubber and began to rub out part of her drawing. Ursula stitched absorbedly.

'You wouldn't consider a good offer?' asked Gudrun.

'I think I've rejected several,' said Ursula.

'*Really!*' Gudrun flushed dark – 'But anything really worthwhile? Have you *really?*'

'A thousand a year, and an awfully nice man. I liked him awfully,' said Ursula.

'Really! But weren't you fearfully tempted?'

'In the abstract but not in the concrete,' said Ursula. 'When it comes to the point, one isn't even tempted – oh, if I were tempted, I'd marry like a shot. I'm only tempted *not* to.' The faces of both sisters suddenly lit up with amusement.

'Isn't it an amazing thing,' cried Gudrun, 'how strong the temptation is, not to!' They both laughed, looking at each other. In their hearts they were frightened.

There was a long pause, whilst Ursula stitched and Gudrun went on with her sketch. The sisters were women, Ursula twenty-six, and Gudrun twenty-five. But both had the remote, virgin look of modern girls, sisters of Artemis rather than of Hebe. Gudrun was very beautiful, passive, soft-skinned, soft-limbed. She wore a dress of dark-blue silky stuff, with ruches of blue and green linen lace in the neck and sleeves; and she had emerald green stockings. Her look of confidence and diffidence contrasted with Ursula's sensitive expectancy. The provincial people, intimidated by Gudrun's perfect *sang-froid* and exclusive bareness of manner, said of her: 'She is a smart woman.' She had just come back from London, where she had spent several years, working at an art-school, as a student, and living a studio life.

'I was hoping now for a man to come along,' Gudrun said, suddenly catching her underlip between her teeth, and making a strange grimace, half sly smiling, half anguish. Ursula was afraid.

'So you have come home, expecting him here?' she laughed.

'Oh my dear,' cried Gudrun, strident, 'I wouldn't go out of my way to look for him. But if there did happen to come along a highly attractive individual of sufficient means – well – ' she tailed off ironically. Then she looked searchingly at Ursula, as if to probe her. 'Don't you find yourself getting bored?' she asked of her sister. 'Don't you find, that things fail to materialise? *Nothing materialises!* Everything withers in the bud.'

'What withers in the bud?' asked Ursula.

'Oh, everything – oneself – things in general.' There was a pause, whilst each sister vaguely considered her fate.

'It does frighten one,' said Ursula, and again there was a pause. 'But do you hope to get anywhere by just marrying?'

'It seems to be the inevitable next step,' said Gudrun. Ursula pondered this, with a little bitterness. She was a class mistress herself, in Willey Green Grammar School, as she had been for some years.

'I know,' she said, 'it seems like that when one thinks in the abstract. But really imagine it: imagine any man one knows, imagine him coming home to one every evening, and saying "Hello", and giving one a kiss – '

There was a blank pause.

'Yes,' said Gudrun, in a narrowed voice. 'It's just impossible. The man makes it impossible.'

'Of course there's children – ' said Ursula doubtfully.

Gudrun's face hardened.

'Do you *really* want children, Ursula?' she asked coldly. A dazzled, baffled look came on Ursula's face.

'One feels it is still beyond one,' she said.

'*Do* you feel like that?' asked Gudrun. 'I get no feeling whatever from the thought of bearing children.'

Gudrun looked at Ursula with a masklike, expressionless face. Ursula knitted her brows.

'Perhaps it isn't genuine,' she faltered. 'Perhaps one doesn't really want them, in one's soul – only superficially.' A hardness came over Gudrun's face. She did not want to be too definite.

'When one thinks of other people's children – ' said Ursula.

Again Gudrun looked at her sister, almost hostile.

'Exactly,' she said, to close the conversation.

The two sisters worked on in silence, Ursula having always that strange brightness of an essential flame that is caught, meshed, contravened. She lived a good deal by herself, to herself, working, passing on from day to day, and always thinking, trying to lay hold on life, to grasp it in her own understanding. Her active living was suspended, but underneath, in the darkness, something was coming to pass. If only she could break through the last integuments! She seemed to try and put her hands out, like an infant in the womb, and she could not, not yet. Still she had a strange prescience, an intimation of something yet to come.

She laid down her work and looked at her sister. She thought Gudrun so *charming*, so infinitely charming, in her softness and her fine, exquisite richness of texture and delicacy of line. There was a certain playfulness about her too, such a piquancy or ironic suggestion, such an untouched reserve. Ursula admired her with all her soul.

'Why did you come home, Prune?' she asked.

Gudrun knew she was being admired. She sat back from her drawing and looked at Ursula, from under her finely-curved lashes.

'Why did I come back, Ursula?' she repeated. 'I have asked myself a thousand times.'

'And don't you know?'

'Yes, I think I do. I think my coming back home was just *reculer pour mieux sauter*.'

And she looked with a long, slow look of knowledge at Ursula.

'I know!' cried Ursula, looking slightly dazzled and falsified, and as if she did *not* know. 'But where can one jump to?'

'Oh, it doesn't matter,' said Gudrun, somewhat superbly. 'If one jumps over the edge, one is bound to land somewhere.'

'But isn't it very risky?' asked Ursula.

A slow mocking smile dawned on Gudrun's face.

'Ah!' she said laughing. 'What is it all but words!' And so again she closed the conversation. But Ursula was still brooding.

'And how do you find home, now you have come back to it?' she asked.

Gudrun paused for some moments, coldly, before answering. Then, in a cold truthful voice, she said, 'I find myself completely out of it.'

'And father?'

Gudrun looked at Ursula, almost with resentment, as if brought to bay.

'I haven't thought about him: I've refrained,' she said coldly.

'Yes,' wavered Ursula; and the conversation was really at an end. The sisters found themselves confronted by a void, a terrifying chasm, as if they had looked over the edge.

They worked on in silence for some time, Gudrun's cheek was flushed with repressed emotion. She resented its having been called into being.

'Shall we go out and look at that wedding?' she asked at length, in a voice that was too casual.

'Yes!' cried Ursula, too eagerly, throwing aside her sewing and leaping up, as if to escape something, thus betraying the tension of the situation and causing a friction of dislike to go over Gudrun's nerves.

As she went upstairs, Ursula was aware of the house, of her home round about her. And she loathed it, the sordid, too-familiar place! She was afraid at the depth of her feeling against the home, the milieu, the whole atmosphere and condition of this obsolete life. Her feeling frightened her.

The two girls were soon walking swiftly down the main road of Beldover, a wide street, part shops, part dwelling-houses, utterly formless and sordid, without poverty. Gudrun, new from her life in Chelsea and Sussex, shrank cruelly from this amorphous ugliness of a small colliery town in the Midlands. Yet forward she went, through the whole sordid gamut of pettiness, the long amorphous, gritty street. She was exposed to every stare, she passed on through a stretch of torment. It was strange that she should have chosen to come back and test the full effect of this shapeless, barren ugliness upon herself. Why had she wanted to submit herself to it, did she still want to submit herself to it, the insufferable torture of these ugly, meaningless people, this defaced countryside? She felt like a beetle toiling in the dust. She was filled with repulsion.

They turned off the main road, past a black patch of common-garden, where sooty cabbage stumps stood shameless. No one thought to be ashamed. No one was ashamed of it all.

'It is like a country in an underworld,' said Gudrun. 'The colliers bring it above-ground with them, shovel it up. Ursula, it's marvellous, it's really marvellous – it's really wonderful, another world. The people are all ghouls, and everything is ghostly. Everything is a ghoulish replica of the real world, a replica, a ghoul, all soiled, everything sordid. It's like being mad, Ursula.'

The sisters were crossing a black path through a dark, soiled field. On the left was a large landscape, a valley with collieries, and opposite hills with cornfields and woods, all blackened with distance, as if seen through a veil of crape. White and black smoke rose up in steady columns, magic within the dark air. Near at hand came the long rows of dwellings, approaching curved up the hill-slope, in straight lines along the brow of the hill. They were of darkened red brick, brittle, with dark slate roofs. The path on which the sisters walked was black, trodden-in by the feet of the recurrent colliers, and bounded from the field by iron fences; the stile that led again into the road was rubbed shiny by the moleskins of the passing miners. Now the two girls were going between some rows of dwellings, of the poorer sort. Women, their arms folded over their coarse aprons, standing gossiping at the end of their block, stared after the Brangwen sisters with that long, unwearying stare of aborigines; children called out names.

Gudrun went on her way half dazed. If this were human life, if these were human beings, living in a complete world, then what was her own world, outside? She was aware of her grass-green stockings, her large grass-green velour hat, her full soft coat, of a strong blue colour. And she felt as if she were treading in the air, quite unstable, her heart was contracted, as if at any minute she might be precipitated to the ground. She was afraid.

She clung to Ursula, who, through long usage, was inured to this violation of a dark, uncreated, hostile world. But all the time her heart was crying, as if in the midst of some ordeal: 'I want to go back, I want to go away, I want not to know it, not to know that this exists.' Yet she must go forward.

Ursula could feel her suffering.

'You hate this, don't you?' she asked.

'It bewilders me,' stammered Gudrun.

'You won't stay long,' replied Ursula.

And Gudrun went along, grasping at release.

They drew away from the colliery region, over the curve of the hill, into the purer country of the other side, towards Willey Green. Still the faint glamour of blackness persisted over the fields and the wooded hills, and seemed darkly to gleam in the air. It was a spring day, chill, with snatches of sunshine. Yellow celandines showed out from the hedge-bottoms, and in the cottage gardens of Willey Green, currant-bushes were breaking into leaf, and little flowers were coming white on the grey alyssum that hung over the stone walls.

Turning, they passed down the highroad, that went between high banks towards the church. There, in the lowest bend of the road, low under the trees, stood a little group of expectant people, waiting to see the wedding. The daughter of the chief mine-owner of the district, Thomas Crich, was getting married to a naval officer.

'Let us go back,' said Gudrun, swerving away. 'There are all those people.'

And she hung wavering in the road.

'Never mind them,' said Ursula, 'they're all right. They all know me, they don't matter.'

'But must we go through them?' asked Gudrun.

'They're quite all right, really,' said Ursula, going forward. And together the two sisters approached the group of uneasy, watchful common people. They were chiefly women, colliers' wives of the more shiftless sort. They had watchful, underworld faces.

The two sisters held themselves tense, and went straight towards the gate. The women made way for them, but barely sufficient, as if grudging to yield ground. The sisters passed in silence through the stone gateway and up the steps, on the red carpet, a policeman estimating their progress.

'What price the stockings!' said a voice at the back of Gudrun. A sudden fierce anger swept over the girl, violent and murderous. She would have liked them all annihilated, cleared away, so that the world was left clear for her. How she hated walking up the churchyard path, along the red carpet, continuing in motion, in their sight.

'I won't go into the church,' she said suddenly, with such final decision that Ursula immediately halted, turned round, and branched off up a small side path which led to the little private gate of the Grammar School, whose grounds adjoined those of the church.

Just inside the gate of the school shrubbery, outside the churchyard, Ursula sat down for a moment on the low stone wall under the laurel bushes, to rest. Behind her, the large red building of the school rose up peacefully, the windows all open for the holiday. Over the shrubs, before her, were the pale roofs and tower of the old church. The sisters were hidden by the foliage.

Gudrun sat down in silence. Her mouth was shut close, her face averted. She was regretting bitterly that she had ever come back. Ursula looked at her, and thought how amazingly beautiful she was, flushed with discomfiture. But she caused a constraint over Ursula's nature, a certain weariness. Ursula wished to be alone, freed from the tightness, the enclosure of Gudrun's presence.

'Are we going to stay here?' asked Gudrun.

'I was only resting a minute,' said Ursula, getting up as if rebuked. 'We will stand in the corner by the fives-court, we shall see everything from there.'

For the moment, the sunshine fell brightly into the churchyard, there was a vague scent of sap and of spring, perhaps of violets from off the graves. Some white daisies were out, bright as angels. In the air, the unfolding leaves of a copper-beech were blood-red.

Punctually at eleven o'clock, the carriages began to arrive. There was a stir in the crowd at the gate, a concentration as a carriage drove up, wedding guests were mounting up the steps and passing along the red carpet to the church. They were all gay and excited because the sun was shining.

Gudrun watched them closely, with objective curiosity. She saw each one as a complete figure, like a character in a book, or a subject in a picture, or a marionette in a theatre, a finished creation. She loved to recognise their various characteristics, to place them in their true light, give them their own sur-roundings, settle them for ever as they passed before her along the path to the church. She knew them, they were finished, sealed and stamped and finished with, for her. There was none that had anything unknown, unresolved, until the Criches themselves began to appear. Then her interest was piqued. Here was something not quite so preconcluded.

There came the mother, Mrs Crich, with her eldest son Gerald. She was a queer unkempt figure, in spite of the attempts that had obviously been made to bring her into line for the day. Her face was pale, yellowish, with a clear, transparent skin, she leaned forward rather, her features were strongly marked, handsome, with a tense, unseeing, predative look. Her colourless hair was untidy, wisps floating down on to her sac coat of dark blue silk, from under her blue silk hat. She looked like a woman with a monomania, furtive almost, but heavily proud.

Her son was of a fair, sun-tanned type, rather above middle height, well-made, and almost exaggeratedly well-dressed. But about him also was the strange, guarded look, the unconscious glisten, as if he did not belong to the same creation as the people about him. Gudrun lighted on him at once. There was something northern about him that magnetised her. In his clear northern flesh and his fair hair was a glisten like sunshine refracted through crystals of ice. And he looked so new, unbroached, pure as an arctic thing. Perhaps he was thirty years old, perhaps more. His gleaming beauty, maleness, like a young, good-humoured, smiling wolf, did not blind her to the significant, sinister stillness in his bearing, the lurking danger of his unsubdued temper. 'His totem is the wolf,' she repeated to herself. 'His mother is an old, unbroken wolf.' And then she experienced a keen paroxysm, a transport, as if she had made some incredible discovery, known to nobody else on earth. A strange transport took possession of her, all her veins were in a paroxysm of violent sensation. 'Good God!' she exclaimed to herself, 'what is this?' And then, a moment after, she was saying assuredly, 'I shall know more of that man.' She was tortured with desire to see him again, a nostalgia, a necessity to see him again, to make sure it was not all a mistake, that she was not deluding herself, that she really felt this strange and overwhelming sensation on his account, this knowledge of him in her essence, this powerful apprehension of him. 'Am I *really* singled out for him in some way, is there really some pale gold, arctic light that envelops only us two?' she asked herself. And she could not believe it, she remained in a muse, scarcely conscious of what was going on around.

The bridesmaids were here, and yet the bridegroom had not come. Ursula wondered if something was amiss, and if the wedding would yet all go wrong. She felt troubled, as if it rested upon her. The chief bridesmaids had arrived. Ursula watched them come up the steps. One of them she knew, a tall, slow, reluctant woman with a weight of fair hair and a pale, long face. This was Hermione Roddice, a friend of the Criches. Now she came along, with her head held up, balancing an enormous flat hat of pale yellow velvet, on which were streaks of ostrich feathers, natural and grey. She drifted forward as if scarcely conscious, her long blanched face lifted up, not to see the world. She was rich. She wore a dress of silky, frail velvet, of pale yellow colour, and she carried a lot of small rose-coloured cyclamens. Her shoes and stockings were of brownish grey, like the feathers on her hat, her hair was heavy, she drifted along with a peculiar fixity of the hips, a strange unwilling motion. She was impressive, in her lovely pale-yellow and brownish-rose, yet macabre, something repulsive. People were silent when she passed, impressed, roused, wanting to jeer, yet for some reason silenced. Her long, pale face, that she carried lifted up, somewhat in the Rossetti fashion, seemed almost drugged, as if a strange mass of thoughts coiled in the darkness within her, and she was never allowed to escape.

Ursula watched her with fascination. She knew her a little. She was the most remarkable woman in the Midlands. Her father was a Derbyshire Baronet of the old school, she was a woman of the new school, full of intellectuality, and heavy, nerve-worn with consciousness. She was passionately interested in reform, her soul was given up to the public cause. But she was a man's woman, it was the manly world that held her.

She had various intimacies of mind and soul with various men of capacity. Ursula knew, among these men, only Rupert Birkin, who was one of the school-inspectors of the county. But Gudrun had met others, in London. Moving with her artist friends in different kinds of society, Gudrun had already come to know a good many people of repute and standing. She had met Hermione twice, but they did not take to each other. It would be queer to meet again down here in the Midlands, where their social standing was so diverse, after they had known each other on terms of equality in the houses of sundry acquaintances in town. For Gudrun had been a social success, and had her friends among the slack aristocracy that keeps touch with the arts.

Hermione knew herself to be well-dressed; she knew herself to be the social equal, if not far the superior, of anyone she was likely to meet in Willey Green. She knew she was accepted in the world of culture and of intellect. She was a *Kulturträger*, a medium for the culture of ideas. With all that was highest, whether in society or in thought or in public action, or even in art, she was at one, she moved among the foremost, at home with them. No one could put her down, no one could make mock of her, because she stood among the first, and those that were against her were below her, either in rank, or in wealth, or in high association of thought and progress and understanding. So, she was invulnerable. All her life, she had sought to make herself invulnerable, unassailable, beyond reach of the world's judgement.

And yet her soul was tortured, exposed. Even walking up the path to the church, confident as she was that in every respect she stood beyond all vulgar judgement, knowing perfectly that her appearance was complete and perfect, according to the first standards, yet she suffered a torture, under her confidence and her pride, feeling herself exposed to wounds and to mockery and to despite. She always felt vulnerable, vulnerable, there was always a secret chink in her armour. She did not know herself what it was. It was a lack of robust self, she had no natural sufficiency, there was a terrible void, a lack, a deficiency of being within her.

And she wanted someone to close up this deficiency, to close it up for ever. She craved for Rupert Birkin. When he was there, she felt complete, she was sufficient, whole. For the rest of time she was established on the sand, built over a chasm, and, in spite of all her vanity and securities, any common maidservant of positive, robust temper could fling her down this bottomless pit of insufficiency, by the slightest movement of jeering or contempt. And all the while the pensive, tortured woman piled up her own defences of aesthetic knowledge, and culture, and world-visions, and disinterestedness. Yet she could never stop up the terrible gap of insufficiency.

If only Birkin would form a close and abiding connection with her, she would be safe during this fretful voyage of life. He could make her sound and triumphant, triumphant over the very angels of heaven. If only he would do it! But she was tortured with fear, with misgiving. She made herself beautiful, she strove so hard to come to that degree of beauty and advantage, when he should be convinced. But always there was a deficiency.

He was perverse too. He fought her off, he always fought her off. The more she strove to bring him to her, the more he battled her back. And they had been lovers now, for years. Oh, it was so wearying, so aching; she was so tired. But still she believed in herself. She knew he was trying to leave her. She knew he was trying to break away from her finally, to be free. But still she believed in her strength to keep him, she believed in her own higher knowledge. His own knowledge was high, she was the central touchstone of truth. She only needed his conjunction with her.

And this, this conjunction with her, which was his highest fulfilment also, with the perverseness of a wilful child he wanted to deny. With the wilfulness of an obstinate child, he wanted to break the holy connection that was between them.

He would be at this wedding; he was to be groom's man. He would be in the church, waiting. He would know when she came. She shuddered with nervous apprehension and desire as she went through the church-door. He would be there, surely he would see how beautiful her dress was, surely he would see how she had made herself beautiful for him. He would understand, he would be able to see how she was made for him, the first, how she was, for him, the highest. Surely at last he would be able to accept his highest fate, he would not deny her.

In a little convulsion of too-tired yearning, she entered the church and looked slowly along her cheeks for him, her slender body convulsed with agitation. As best man, he would be standing beside the altar. She looked slowly, deferring in her certainty.

And then, he was not there. A terrible storm came over her, as if she were drowning. She was possessed by a devastating hopelessness. And she approached mechanically to the altar. Never had she known such a pang of utter and final hopelessness. It was beyond death, so utterly null, desert.

The bridegroom and the groom's man had not yet come. There was a growing consternation outside. Ursula felt almost responsible. She could not bear it that the bride should arrive, and no groom. The wedding must not be a fiasco, it must not.

But here was the bride's carriage, adorned with ribbons and cockades. Gaily the grey horses curvetted to their destination at the church-gate, a laughter in the whole movement. Here was the quick of all laughter and pleasure. The door of the carriage was thrown open, to let out the very blossom of the day. The people on the roadway murmured faintly with the discontented murmuring of a crowd.

The father stepped out first into the air of the morning, like a shadow. He was a tall, thin, careworn man, with a thin black beard that was touched with grey. He waited at the door of the carriage patiently, self-obliterated.

In the opening of the doorway was a shower of fine foliage and flowers, a whiteness of satin and lace, and a sound of a gay voice saying, 'How do I get out?'

A ripple of satisfaction ran through the expectant people. They pressed near to receive her, looking with zest at the stooping blonde head with its flower buds, and at the delicate, white, tentative foot that was reaching down to the step of the carriage. There was a sudden foaming rush, and the bride like a sudden surf-rush, floating all white beside her father in the morning shadow of trees, her veil flowing with laughter.

'That's done it!' she said.

She put her hand on the arm of her careworn, sallow father, and frothing her light draperies, proceeded over the eternal red carpet. Her father, mute and yellowish, his black beard making him look more careworn, mounted the steps stiffly, as if his spirit were absent; but the laughing mist of the bride went along with him undiminished.

And no bridegroom had arrived! It was intolerable for her. Ursula, her heart strained with anxiety, was watching the hill beyond; the white, descending road, that should give sight of him. There was a carriage. It was running. It had just come into sight. Yes, it was he. Ursula turned towards the bride and the people, and, from her place of vantage, gave an inarticulate cry. She wanted to warn them that he was coming. But her cry was inarticulate and inaudible, and she flushed deeply, between her desire and her wincing confusion.

The carriage rattled down the hill, and drew near. There was a shout from the people. The bride, who had just reached the top of the steps, turned round gaily to see what was the commotion. She saw a confusion among the people, a cab pulling up, and her lover dropping out of the carriage, and dodging among the horses and into the crowd.

'Tibs! Tibs!' she cried in her sudden, mocking excitement, standing high on the path in the sunlight and waving her bouquet. He, dodging with his hat in his hand, had not heard.

'Tibs!' she cried again, looking down to him.

He glanced up, unaware, and saw the bride and her father standing on the path above him. A queer, startled look went over his face. He hesitated for a moment. Then he gathered himself together for a leap, to overtake her.

'Ah-h-h!' came her strange, in-taken cry, as, on the reflex, she started, turned and fled, scudding with an unthinkable swift beating of her white feet and fraying of her white garments, towards the church. Like a hound the young man was after her, leaping the steps and swinging past her father, his supple haunches working like those of a hound that bears down on the quarry.

'Ay, after her!' cried the vulgar women below, carried suddenly into the sport.

She, her flowers shaken from her like froth, was steadying herself to turn the angle of the church. She glanced behind, and with a wild cry of laughter and challenge, veered, poised, and was gone beyond the grey stone buttress. In another instant the bridegroom, bent forward as he ran, had caught the angle of the silent stone with his hand, and had swung himself out of sight, his supple, strong loins vanishing in pursuit.

Instantly cries and exclamations of excitement burst from the crowd at the gate. And then Ursula noticed again the dark, rather stooping figure of Mr Crich, waiting suspended on the path, watching with expressionless face the flight to the church. It was over, and he turned round to look behind him, at the figure of Rupert Birkin, who at once came forward and joined him.

'We'll bring up the rear,' said Birkin, a faint smile on his face.

'Ay!' replied the father laconically. And the two men turned together up the path.

Birkin was as thin as Mr Crich, pale and ill-looking. His figure was narrow but nicely made. He went with a slight trail of one foot, which came only from self-consciousness. Although he was dressed correctly for his part, yet there was an innate incongruity which caused a slight ridiculousness in his appearance. His nature was clever and separate, he did not fit at all in the conventional occasion. Yet he subordinated himself to the common idea, travestied himself.

He affected to be quite ordinary, perfectly and marvellously commonplace. And he did it so well, taking the tone of his surroundings, adjusting himself quickly to his interlocutor and his circumstance, that he achieved a verisimilitude of ordinary commonplaceness that usually propitiated his onlookers for the moment, disarmed them from attacking his singleness.

Now he spoke quite easily and pleasantly to Mr Crich, as they walked along the path; he played with situations like a man on a tightrope: but always on a tightrope, pretending nothing but ease.

'I'm sorry we are so late,' he was saying. 'We couldn't find a button-hook, so it took us a long time to button our boots. But you were to the moment.'

'We are usually to time,' said Mr Crich.

'And I'm always late,' said Birkin. 'But today I was *really* punctual, only accidentally not so. I'm sorry.'

The two men were gone, there was nothing more to see, for the time. Ursula was left thinking about Birkin. He piqued her, attracted her, and annoyed her.

She wanted to know him more. She had spoken with him once or twice, but only in his official capacity as inspector. She thought he seemed to acknowledge some kinship between her and him, a natural, tacit understanding, a using of the same language. But there had been no time for the understanding to develop. And something kept her from him, as well as attracted her to him. There was a certain hostility, a hidden ultimate reserve in him, cold and inaccessible.

Yet she wanted to know him.

'What do you think of Rupert Birkin?' she asked, a little reluctantly, of Gudrun. She did not want to discuss him.

'What do I think of Rupert Birkin?' repeated Gudrun. 'I think he's attractive – decidedly attractive. What I can't stand about him is his way with other people –

his way of treating any little fool as if she were his greatest consideration. One feels so awfully sold, oneself.'

'Why does he do it?' said Ursula.

'Because he has no real critical faculty – of people, at all events,' said Gudrun. 'I tell you, he treats any little fool as he treats me or you – and it's such an insult.'

'Oh, it is,' said Ursula. 'One must discriminate.'

'One *must* discriminate,' repeated Gudrun. 'But he's a wonderful chap, in other respects – a marvellous personality. But you can't trust him.'

'Yes,' said Ursula vaguely. She was always forced to assent to Gudrun's pronouncements, even when she was not in accord altogether.

The sisters sat silent, waiting for the wedding party to come out. Gudrun was impatient of talk. She wanted to think about Gerald Crich. She wanted to see if the strong feeling she had got from him was real. She wanted to have herself ready.

Inside the church, the wedding was going on. Hermione Roddice was thinking only of Birkin. He stood near her. She seemed to gravitate physically towards him. She wanted to stand touching him. She could hardly be sure he was near her, if she did not touch him. Yet she stood subjected through the wedding service.

She had suffered so bitterly when he did not come, that still she was dazed. Still she was gnawed as by a neuralgia, tormented by his potential absence from her. She had awaited him in a faint delirium of nervous torture. As she stood bearing herself pensively, the rapt look on her face, that seemed spiritual, like the angels, but which came from torture, gave her a certain poignancy that tore his heart with pity. He saw her bowed head, her rapt face, the face of an almost demoniacal ecstatic. Feeling him looking, she lifted her face and sought his eyes, her own beautiful grey eyes flaring him a great signal. But he avoided her look, she sank her head in torment and shame, the gnawing at her heart going on. And he too was tortured with shame, and ultimate dislike, and with acute pity for her, because he did not want to meet her eyes, he did not want to receive her flare of recognition.

The bride and bridegroom were married, the party went into the vestry. Hermione crowded involuntarily up against Birkin, to touch him. And he endured it.

Outside, Gudrun and Ursula listened for their father's playing on the organ. He would enjoy playing a wedding march. Now the married pair were coming! The bells were ringing, making the air shake. Ursula wondered if the trees and the flowers could feel the vibration, and what they thought of it, this strange motion in the air. The bride was quite demure on the arm of the bridegroom, who stared up into the sky before him, shutting and opening his eyes unconsciously, as if he were neither here nor there. He looked rather comical, blinking and trying to be in the scene, when emotionally he was violated by his exposure to a crowd. He looked a typical naval officer, manly, and up to his duty.

Birkin came with Hermione. She had a rapt, triumphant look, like the fallen angels restored, yet still subtly demoniacal, now she held Birkin by the arm. And he was expressionless, neutralised, possessed by her as if it were his fate, without question.

Gerald Crich came, fair, good-looking, healthy, with a great reserve of energy. He was erect and complete, there was a strange stealth glistening through his amiable, almost happy appearance. Gudrun rose sharply and went away. She could not bear it. She wanted to be alone, to know this strange, sharp inoculation that had changed the whole temper of her blood.

CHAPTER 2

Shortlands

The Brangwens went home to Beldover, the wedding party gathered at Short-lands, the Criches' home. It was a long, low old house, a sort of manor farm, that spread along the top of a slope just beyond the narrow little lake of Willey Water. Shortlands looked across a sloping meadow that might be a park, because of the large, solitary trees that stood here and there, across the water of the narrow lake, at the wooded hill that successfully hid the colliery valley beyond, but did not quite hide the rising smoke. Nevertheless, the scene was rural and picturesque, very peaceful, and the house had a charm of its own.

It was crowded now with the family and the wedding guests. The father, who was not well, withdrew to rest. Gerald was host. He stood in the homely entrance hall, friendly and easy, attending to the men. He seemed to take pleasure in his social functions, he smiled, and was abundant in hospitality.

The women wandered about in a little confusion, chased hither and thither by the three married daughters of the house. All the while there could be heard the characteristic, imperious voice of one Crich woman or another calling, 'Helen, come here a minute,' 'Marjory, I want you – here.' 'Oh, I say, Mrs Witham – .' There was a great rustling of skirts, swift glimpses of smartly-dressed women, a child danced through the hall and back again, a maidservant came and went hurriedly.

Meanwhile the men stood in calm little groups, chatting, smoking, pretending to pay no heed to the rustling animation of the women's world. But they could not really talk, because of the glassy ravel of women's excited, cold laughter and running voices. They waited, uneasy, suspended, rather bored. But Gerald remained as if genial and happy, unaware that he was waiting or unoccupied, knowing himself the very pivot of the occasion.

Suddenly Mrs Crich came noiselessly into the room, peering about with her strong, clear face. She was still wearing her hat, and her sac coat of blue silk.

'What is it, mother?' said Gerald.

'Nothing, nothing!' she answered vaguely. And she went straight towards Birkin, who was talking to a Crich brother-in-law.

'How do you do, Mr Birkin,' she said, in her low voice, that seemed to take no count of her guests. She held out her hand to him.

'Oh Mrs Crich,' replied Birkin, in his readily-changing voice, 'I couldn't come to you before.'

'I don't know half the people here,' she said, in her low voice. Her son-in-law moved uneasily away.

'And you don't like strangers?' laughed Birkin. 'I myself can never see why one should take account of people, just because they happen to be in the room with one: why *should* I know they are there?'

'Why indeed, why indeed!' said Mrs Crich, in her low, tense voice. 'Except that they *are* there. *I* don't know people whom I find in the house. The children introduce them to me – "Mother, this is Mr So-and-so." I am no further. What has Mr So-and-so to do with his own name? – and what have I to do with either him or his name?'

She looked up at Birkin. She startled him. He was flattered too that she came to talk to him, for she took hardly any notice of anybody. He looked down at her tense clear face, with its heavy features, but he was afraid to look into her heavy-seeing blue eyes. He noticed instead how her hair looped in slack, slovenly strands over her rather beautiful ears, which were not quite clean. Neither was her neck perfectly clean. Even in that he seemed to belong to her, rather than to the rest of the company; though, he thought to himself, he was always well washed, at any rate at the neck and ears.

He smiled faintly, thinking these things. Yet he was tense, feeling that he and the elderly, estranged woman were conferring together like traitors, like enemies within the camp of the other people. He resembled a deer, that throws one ear back upon the trail behind, and one ear forward, to know what is ahead.

'People don't really matter,' he said, rather unwilling to continue.

The mother looked up at him with sudden, dark interrogation, as if doubting his sincerity.

'How do you mean, *matter*?' she asked sharply.

'Not many people are anything at all,' he answered, forced to go deeper than he wanted to. 'They jingle and giggle. It would be much better if they were just wiped out. Essentially, they don't exist, they aren't there.'

She watched him steadily while he spoke.

'But we didn't imagine them,' she said sharply.

'There's nothing to imagine, that's why they don't exist.'

'Well,' she said, 'I would hardly go as far as that. There they are, whether they exist or no. It doesn't rest with me to decide on their existence. I only know that I can't be expected to take count of them all. You can't expect me to know them, just because they happen to be there. As far as *I* go they might as well not be there.'

'Exactly,' he replied.

'Mightn't they?' she asked again.

'Just as well,' he repeated. And there was a little pause.

'Except that they *are* there, and that's a nuisance,' she said. 'There are my sons-in-law,' she went on, in a sort of monologue. Now Laura's got married, there's another. And I really don't know John from James yet. They come up to me and call me mother. I know what they will say – "How are you, mother?" I ought to say, "I am not your mother, in any sense." But what is the use? There they are. I have had children of my own. I suppose I know them from another woman's children.'

'One would suppose so,' he said.

She looked at him, somewhat surprised, forgetting perhaps that she was talking to him. And she lost her thread.

She looked round the room, vaguely. Birkin could not guess what she was looking for, nor what she was thinking. Evidently she noticed her sons.

'Are my children all there?' she asked him abruptly.

He laughed, startled, afraid perhaps.

'I scarcely know them, except Gerald,' he replied.

'Gerald!' she exclaimed. 'He's the most wanting of them all. You'd never think it, to look at him now, would you?'

'No,' said Birkin.

The mother looked across at her eldest son, stared at him heavily for some time.

'Ay,' she said, in an incomprehensible monosyllable, that sounded profoundly cynical. Birkin felt afraid, as if he dared not realise. And Mrs Crich moved away, forgetting him. But she returned on her traces.

'I should like him to have a friend,' she said. 'He has never had a friend.'

Birkin looked down into her eyes, which were blue, and watching heavily. He could not understand them. 'Am I my brother's keeper?' he said to himself, almost flippantly.

Then he remembered, with a slight shock, that that was Cain's cry. And Gerald was Cain, if anybody. Not that he was Cain, either, although he had slain his brother. There was such a thing as pure accident, and the consequences did not attach to one, even though one had killed one's brother in such wise. Gerald as a boy had accidentally killed his brother. What then? Why seek to draw a brand and a curse across the life that had caused the accident? A man can live by accident, and die by accident. Or can he not? Is every man's life subject to pure accident, is it only the race, the genus, the species, that has a universal reference? Or is this not true, is there no such thing as pure accident? Has *everything* that happens a universal significance? Has it? Birkin, pondering as he stood there, had forgotten Mrs Crich, as she had forgotten him.

He did not believe that there was any such thing as accident. It all hung together, in the deepest sense.

Just as he had decided this, one of the Crich daughters came up, saying, 'Won't you come and take your hat off, mother dear? We shall be sitting down to eat in a minute, and it's a formal occasion, darling, isn't it?' She drew her arm through her mother's, and they went away. Birkin immediately went to talk to the nearest man.

The gong sounded for the luncheon. The men looked up, but no move was made to the dining-room. The women of the house seemed not to feel that the sound had meaning for them. Five minutes passed by. The elderly manservant, Crowther, appeared in the doorway exasperatedly. He looked with appeal at Gerald. The latter took up a large, curved conch shell, that lay on a shelf, and without reference to anybody, blew a shattering blast. It was a strange rousing noise, that made the heart beat. The summons was almost magical. Everybody came running, as if at a signal. And then the crowd in one impulse moved to the dining-room.

Gerald waited a moment, for his sister to play hostess. He knew his mother would pay no attention to her duties. But his sister merely crowded to her seat. Therefore the young man, slightly too dictatorial, directed the guests to their places.

There was a moment's lull, as everybody looked at the *hors d'oeuvres* that were being handed round. And out of this lull, a girl of thirteen or fourteen, with her long hair down her back, said in a calm, self-possessed voice, 'Gerald, you forget father, when you make that unearthly noise.'

'Do I?' he answered. And then, to the company, 'Father is lying down, he is not quite well.'

'How is he, really?' called one of the married daughters, peeping round the immense wedding cake that towered up in the middle of the table shedding its artificial flowers.

'He has no pain, but he feels tired,' replied Winifred, the girl with the hair down her back.

The wine was filled, and everybody was talking boisterously. At the far end of the table sat the mother, with her loosely-looped hair. She had Birkin for a neighbour. Sometimes she glanced fiercely down the rows of faces, bending forwards and staring unceremoniously. And she would say in a low voice to Birkin, 'Who is that young man?'

'I don't know,' Birkin answered discreetly.

'Have I seen him before?' she asked.

'I don't think so. *I* haven't,' he replied. And she was satisfied. Her eyes closed wearily, a peace came over her face, she looked like a queen in repose. Then she started, a little social smile came on her face, for a moment she looked the pleasant hostess. For a moment she bent graciously, as if everyone were welcome and delightful. And then immediately the shadow came back, a sullen, eagle look was on her face, she glanced from under her brows like a sinister creature at bay, hating them all.

'Mother,' called Diana, a handsome girl a little older than Winifred, 'I may have wine, mayn't I?'

'Yes, you may have wine,' replied the mother automatically, for she was perfectly indifferent to the question.

And Diana beckoned to the footman to fill her glass.

'Gerald shouldn't forbid me,' she said calmly, to the company at large.

'All right, Di,' said her brother amiably. And she glanced challenge at him as she drank from her glass.

There was a strange freedom, that almost amounted to anarchy, in the house. It was rather a resistance to authority, than liberty. Gerald had some command, by mere force of personality, not because of any granted position. There was a quality in his voice, amiable but dominant, that cowed the others, who were all younger than he.

Hermione was having a discussion with the bridegroom about nationality.

'No,' she said, 'I think that the appeal to patriotism is a mistake. It is like one house of business rivalling another house of business.'

'Well you can hardly say that, can you?' exclaimed Gerald, who had a real *passion* for discussion. 'You couldn't call a race a business concern, could you? – and nationality roughly corresponds to race, I think. I think it is *meant* to.'

There was a moment's pause. Gerald and Hermione were always strangely but politely and evenly inimical.

'*Do* you think race corresponds with nationality?' she asked musingly, with expressionless indecision.

Birkin knew she was waiting for him to participate. And dutifully he spoke up.

'I think Gerald is right – race is the essential element in nationality, in Europe at least,' he said.

Again Hermione paused, as if to allow this statement to cool. Then she said with strange assumption of authority, 'Yes, but even so, is the patriotic appeal an appeal to the racial instinct? Is it not rather an appeal to the proprietary instinct, the *commercial* instinct? And isn't this what we mean by nationality?'

'Probably,' said Birkin, who felt that such a discussion was out of place and out of time.

But Gerald was now on the scent of argument.

'A race may have its commercial aspect,' he said. 'In fact it must. It is like a family. You *must* make provision. And to make provision you have got to strive against other families, other nations. I don't see why you shouldn't.'

Again Hermione made a pause, domineering and cold, before she replied: 'Yes, I think it is always wrong to provoke a spirit of rivalry. It makes bad blood. And bad blood accumulates.'

'But you can't do away with the spirit of emulation altogether?' said Gerald. 'It is one of the necessary incentives to production and improvement.'

'Yes,' came Hermione's sauntering response. 'I think you can do away with it.'

'I must say,' said Birkin, 'I detest the spirit of emulation.' Hermione was biting a piece of bread, pulling it from between her teeth with her fingers, in a slow, slightly derisive movement. She turned to Birkin.

'You do hate it, yes,' she said, intimate and gratified.

'Detest it,' he repeated.

'Yes,' she murmured, assured and satisfied.

'But,' Gerald insisted, 'you don't allow one man to take away his neighbour's living, so why should you allow one nation to take away the living from another nation?'

There was a long slow murmur from Hermione before she broke into speech, saying with a laconic indifference, 'It is not always a question of possessions, is it? It is not all a question of goods?'

Gerald was nettled by this implication of vulgar materialism.

'Yes, more or less,' he retorted. 'If I go and take a man's hat from off his head, that hat becomes a symbol of that man's liberty. When he fights me for his hat, he is fighting me for his liberty.'

Hermione was nonplussed.

'Yes,' she said, irritated. 'But that way of arguing by imaginary instances is not supposed to be genuine, is it? A man does *not* come and take my hat from off my head, does he?'

'Only because the law prevents him,' said Gerald.

'Not only,' said Birkin. 'Ninety-nine men out of a hundred don't want my hat.'

'That's a matter of opinion,' said Gerald.

'Or the hat,' laughed the bridegroom.

'And if he does want my hat, such as it is,' said Birkin, 'why, surely it is open to me to decide, which is a greater loss to me, my hat, or my liberty as a free and indifferent man. If I am compelled to offer fight, I lose the latter. It is a question which is worth more to me, my pleasant liberty of conduct, or my hat.'

'Yes,' said Hermione, watching Birkin strangely. 'Yes.'

'But would you let somebody come and snatch your hat off your head?' the bride asked of Hermione.

The face of the tall straight woman turned slowly and as if drugged to this new speaker.

'No,' she replied, in a low inhuman tone, that seemed to contain a chuckle. 'No, I shouldn't let anybody take my hat off my head.'

'How would you prevent it?' asked Gerald.

'I don't know,' replied Hermione slowly. 'Probably I should kill him.'

There was a strange chuckle in her tone, a dangerous and convincing humour in her bearing.

'Of course,' said Gerald, 'I can see Rupert's point. It is a question to him whether his hat or his peace of mind is more important.'

'Peace of body,' said Birkin.

'Well, as you like there,' replied Gerald. 'But how are you going to decide this for a nation?'

'Heaven preserve me,' laughed Birkin.

'Yes, but suppose you have to?' Gerald persisted.

'Then it is the same. If the national crown-piece is an old hat, then the thieving gent may have it.'

'But *can* the national or racial hat be an old hat?' insisted Gerald.

'Pretty well bound to be, I believe,' said Birkin.

'I'm not so sure,' said Gerald.

'I don't agree, Rupert,' said Hermione.

'All right,' said Birkin.

'I'm all for the old national hat,' laughed Gerald.

'And a fool you look in it,' cried Diana, his pert sister who was just in her teens.

'Oh, we're quite out of our depths with these old hats,' cried Laura Crich. 'Dry up now, Gerald. We're going to drink toasts. Let us drink toasts. Toasts – glasses, glasses – now then, toasts! Speech! Speech!'

Birkin, thinking about race or national death, watched his glass being filled with champagne. The bubbles broke at the rim, the man withdrew, and feeling a sudden thirst at the sight of the fresh wine, Birkin drank up his glass. A queer little tension in the room roused him. He felt a sharp constraint.

'Did I do it by accident, or on purpose?' he asked himself. And he decided that, according to the vulgar phrase, he had done it 'accidentally on purpose'. He looked round at the hired footman. And the hired footman came, with a silent step of cold servant-like disapprobation. Birkin decided that he detested toasts, and footmen, and assemblies, and mankind altogether, in most of its aspects. Then he rose to make a speech. But he was somehow disgusted.

At length it was over, the meal. Several men strolled out into the garden. There was a lawn, and flower-beds, and at the boundary an iron fence shutting off the little field or park. The view was pleasant; a highroad curving round the edge of a low lake, under the trees. In the spring air, the water gleamed and the opposite woods were purplish with new life. Charming Jersey cattle came to the fence, breathing hoarsely from their velvet muzzles at the human beings, expecting perhaps a crust.

Birkin leaned on the fence. A cow was breathing wet hotness on his hand.

'Pretty cattle, very pretty,' said Marshall, one of the brothers-in-law. 'They give the best milk you can have.'

'Yes,' said Birkin.

'Eh, my little beauty, eh, my beauty!' said Marshall, in a queer high falsetto voice, that caused the other man to have convulsions of laughter in his stomach.

'Who won the race, Lupton?' he called to the bridegroom, to hide the fact that he was laughing.

The bridegroom took his cigar from his mouth.

'The race?' he exclaimed. Then a rather thin smile came over his face. He did not want to say anything about the flight to the church door. 'We got there together. At least she touched first, but I had my hand on her shoulder.'

'What's this?' asked Gerald.

Birkin told him about the race of the bride and the bridegroom.

'H'm!' said Gerald, in disapproval. 'What made you late then?'

'Lupton would talk about the immortality of the soul,' said Birkin, 'and then he hadn't got a button-hook.'

'Oh God!' cried Marshall. 'The immortality of the soul on your wedding day! Hadn't you got anything better to occupy your mind?'

'What's wrong with it?' asked the bridegroom, a clean-shaven naval man, flushing sensitively.

'Sounds as if you were going to be executed instead of married. *The immortality of the soul!*' repeated the brother-in-law, with most killing emphasis.

But he fell quite flat.

'And what did you decide?' asked Gerald, at once pricking up his ears at the thought of a metaphysical discussion.

'You don't want a soul today, my boy,' said Marshall. 'It'd be in your road.'

'Christ! Marshall, go and talk to somebody else,' cried Gerald, with sudden impatience.

'By God, I'm willing,' said Marshall, in a temper. 'Too much bloody soul and talk altogether – '

He withdrew in a dudgeon, Gerald staring after him with angry eyes, that grew gradually calm and amiable as the stoutly-built form of the other man passed into the distance.

'There's one thing, Lupton,' said Gerald, turning suddenly to the bridegroom. 'Laura won't have brought such a fool into the family as Lottie did.'

'Comfort yourself with that,' laughed Birkin.

'I take no notice of them,' laughed the bridegroom.

'What about this race then – who began it?' Gerald asked.

'We were late. Laura was at the top of the churchyard steps when our cab came up. She saw Lupton bolting towards her. And she fled. But why do you look so cross? Does it hurt your sense of the family dignity?'

'It does, rather,' said Gerald. 'If you're doing a thing, do it properly, and if you're not going to do it properly, leave it alone.'

'Very nice aphorism,' said Birkin.

'Don't you agree?' asked Gerald.

'Quite,' said Birkin. 'Only it bores me rather, when you become aphoristic.'

'Damn you, Rupert, you want all the aphorisms your own way,' said Gerald.

'No. I want them out of the way, and you're always shoving them in it.'

Gerald smiled grimly at this humorism. Then he made a little gesture of dismissal, with his eyebrows.

'You don't believe in having any standard of behaviour at all, do you?' he challenged Birkin, censoriously.

'Standard – no. I hate standards. But they're necessary for the common ruck. Anybody who is anything can just be himself and do as he likes.'

'But what do you mean by being himself?' said Gerald. 'Is that an aphorism or a cliché?'

'I mean just doing what you want to do. I think it was perfect good form in Laura to bolt from Lupton to the church door. It was almost a masterpiece in good form. It's the hardest thing in the world to act spontaneously on one's impulses – and it's the only really gentlemanly thing to do – provided you're fit to do it.'

'You don't expect me to take you seriously, do you?' asked Gerald.

'Yes, Gerald, you're one of the very few people I do expect that of.'

'Then I'm afraid I can't come up to your expectations here, at any rate. You think people should just do as they like.'

'I think they always do. But I should like them to like the purely individual thing in themselves, which makes them act in singleness. And they only like to do the collective thing.'

'And I,' said Gerald grimly, 'shouldn't like to be in a world of people who acted individually and spontaneously, as you call it. We should have everybody cutting everybody else's throat in five minutes.'

'That means *you* would like to be cutting everybody's throat,' said Birkin.

'How does that follow?' asked Gerald crossly.

'No man,' said Birkin, 'cuts another man's throat unless he wants to cut it, and unless the other man wants it cutting. This is a complete truth. It takes two people to make a murder: a murderer and a murderee. And a murderee is a man who is murderable. And a man who is murderable is a man who in a profound if hidden lust desires to be murdered.'

'Sometimes you talk pure nonsense,' said Gerald to Birkin. 'As a matter of fact, none of us wants our throat cut, and most other people would like to cut it for us – some time or other – '

'It's a nasty view of things, Gerald,' said Birkin, 'and no wonder you are afraid of yourself and your own unhappiness.'

'How am I afraid of myself?' said Gerald; 'and I don't think I am unhappy.'

'You seem to have a lurking desire to have your gizzard slit, and imagine every man has his knife up his sleeve for you,' Birkin said.

'How do you make that out?' said Gerald.

'From you,' said Birkin.

There was a pause of strange enmity between the two men, that was very near to love. It was always the same between them; always their talk brought them into a deadly nearness of contact, a strange, perilous intimacy which was either hate or love, or both. They parted with apparent unconcern, as if their going apart were a trivial occurrence. And they really kept it to the level of trivial occurrence. Yet the heart of each burned from the other. They burned with each other, inwardly. This they would never admit. They intended to keep their relationship a casual free-and-easy friendship, they were not going to be so unmanly and unnatural as to allow any heart-burning between them. They had not the faintest belief in deep relationship between men and men, and their disbelief prevented any development of their powerful but suppressed friendliness.

CHAPTER 3

Classroom

A school-day was drawing to a close. In the classroom the last lesson was in progress, peaceful and still. It was elementary botany. The desks were littered with catkins, hazel and willow, which the children had been sketching. But the sky had come over dark, as the end of the afternoon approached: there was scarcely light to draw any more. Ursula stood in front of the class, leading the children by questions to understand the structure and the meaning of the catkins.

A heavy, copper-coloured beam of light came in at the west window, gilding the outlines of the children's heads with red gold, and falling on the wall opposite in a rich, ruddy illumination. Ursula, however, was scarcely conscious of it. She was busy, the end of the day was here, the work went on as a peaceful tide that is at flood, hushed to retire.

This day had gone by like so many more, in an activity that was like a trance. At the end there was a little haste, to finish what was in hand. She was pressing the children with questions, so that they should know all they were to know, by the time the gong went. She stood in shadow in front of the class, with catkins in her hand, and she leaned towards the children, absorbed in the passion of instruction.

She heard, but did not notice the click of the door. Suddenly she started. She saw, in the shaft of ruddy, copper-coloured light near her, the face of a man. It was gleaming like fire, watching her, waiting for her to be aware. It startled her terribly. She thought she was going to faint. All her suppressed, subconscious fear sprang into being, with anguish.

'Did I startle you?' said Birkin, shaking hands with her. 'I thought you had heard me come in.'

'No,' she faltered, scarcely able to speak. He laughed, saying he was sorry. She wondered why it amused him.

'It is so dark,' he said. 'Shall we have the light?'

And moving aside, he switched on the strong electric lights. The classroom was distinct and hard, a strange place after the soft dim magic that filled it before he came. Birkin turned curiously to look at Ursula. Her eyes were round and wondering, bewildered, her mouth quivered slightly. She looked like one who is suddenly wakened. There was a living, tender beauty, like a tender light of dawn shining from her face. He looked at her with a new pleasure, feeling gay in his heart, irresponsible.

'You are doing catkins?' he asked, picking up a piece of hazel from a scholar's desk in front of him. 'Are they as far out as this? I hadn't noticed them this year.'

He looked absorbedly at the tassel of hazel in his hand.

'The red ones too!' he said, looking at the flickers of crimson that came from the female bud.

Then he went in among the desks, to see the scholars' books. Ursula watched his intent progress. There was a stillness in his motion that hushed the activities of her heart. She seemed to be standing aside in arrested silence, watching him move in another, concentrated world. His presence was so quiet, almost like a vacancy in the corporate air.

Suddenly he lifted his face to her, and her heart quickened at the flicker of his voice.

'Give them some crayons, won't you?' he said, 'so that they can make the gynaecious flowers red, and the androgynous yellow. I'd chalk them in plain, chalk in nothing else, merely the red and the yellow. Outline scarcely matters in this case. There is just the one fact to emphasise.'

'I haven't any crayons,' said Ursula.

'There will be some somewhere – red and yellow, that's all you want.'

Ursula sent out a boy on a quest.

'It will make the books untidy,' she said to Birkin, flushing deeply.

'Not very,' he said. 'You must mark in these things obviously. It's the fact you want to emphasise, not the subjective impression to record. What's the fact? – red little spiky stigmas of the female flower, dangling yellow male catkin, yellow pollen flying from one to the other. Make a pictorial record of the fact, as a child does when drawing a face – two eyes, one nose, mouth with teeth – so – ' And he drew a figure on the blackboard.

At that moment another vision was seen through the glass panels of the door. It was Hermione Roddice. Birkin went and opened to her.

'I saw your car,' she said to him. 'Do you mind my coming to find you? I wanted to see you when you were on duty.'

She looked at him for a long time, intimate and playful, then she gave a short little laugh. And then only she turned to Ursula, who, with all the class, had been watching the little scene between the lovers.

'How do you do, Miss Brangwen,' sang Hermione, in her low, odd, singing fashion, that sounded almost as if she were poking fun. 'Do you mind my coming in?'

Her grey, almost sardonic eyes rested all the while on Ursula, as if summing her up.

'Oh no,' said Ursula.

'Are you *sure*?' repeated Hermione, with complete *sang-froid*, and an odd, half-bullying effrontery.

'Oh no, I like it awfully,' laughed Ursula, a little bit excited and bewildered, because Hermione seemed to be compelling her, coming very close to her, as if intimate with her; and yet, how could she be intimate?

This was the answer Hermione wanted. She turned satisfied to Birkin.

'What are you doing?' she sang, in her casual, inquisitive fashion.

'Catkins,' he replied.

'Really!' she said. 'And what do you learn about them?' She spoke all the while in a mocking, half-teasing fashion, as if making game of the whole business. She picked up a twig of the catkin, piqued by Birkin's attention to it.

She was a strange figure in the classroom, wearing a large, old cloak of greenish cloth, on which was a raised pattern of dull gold. The high collar, and the inside of the cloak, was lined with dark fur. Beneath she had a dress of fine lavender-coloured cloth, trimmed with fur, and her hat was close-fitting, made of fur and of the dull, green-and-gold figured stuff. She was tall and strange, she looked as if she had come out of some new, bizarre picture.

'Do you know the little red ovary flowers, that produce the nuts? Have you ever noticed them?' he asked her. And he came close and pointed them out to her, on the sprig she held.

'No,' she replied. 'What are they?'

'Those are the little seed-producing flowers, and the long catkins, they only produce pollen, to fertilise them.'

'Do they, do they!' repeated Hermione, looking closely.

'From those little red bits, the nuts come; if they receive pollen from the long danglers.'

'Little red flames, little red flames,' murmured Hermione to herself. And she remained for some moments looking only at the small buds out of which the red flickers of the stigma issued.

'Aren't they beautiful? I think they're so beautiful,' she said, moving close to Birkin, and pointing to the red filaments with her long, white finger.

'Had you never noticed them before?' he asked.

'No, never before,' she replied.

'And now you will always see them,' he said.

'Now I shall always see them,' she repeated. 'Thank you so much for showing me. I think they're so beautiful – little red flames – '

Her absorption was strange, almost rhapsodic. Both Birkin and Ursula were suspended. The little red pistillate flowers had some strange, almost mystic-passionate attraction for her.

The lesson was finished, the books were put away, at last the class was dismissed. And still Hermione sat at the table, with her chin in her hand, her elbow on the table, her long white face pushed up, not attending to anything. Birkin had gone to the window, and was looking from the brilliantly-lighted room on to the grey, colourless outside, where rain was noiselessly falling. Ursula put away her things in the cupboard.

At length Hermione rose and came near to her.

'Your sister has come home?' she said.

'Yes,' said Ursula.

'And does she like being back in Beldover?'

'No,' said Ursula.

'No, I wonder she can bear it. It takes all my strength, to bear the ugliness of this district, when I stay here. Won't you come and see me? Won't you come with your sister to stay at Breadalby for a few days? – do – '

'Thank you very much,' said Ursula.

'Then I will write to you,' said Hermione. 'You think your sister will come? I should be so glad. I think she is wonderful. I think some of her work is really wonderful. I have two water-wagtails, carved in wood, and painted – perhaps you have seen it?'

'No,' said Ursula.

'I think it is perfectly wonderful – like a flash of instinct.'

'Her little carvings *are* strange,' said Ursula.

'Perfectly beautiful – full of primitive passion – '

'Isn't it queer that she always likes little things? – she must always work small things, that one can put between one's hands, birds and tiny animals. She likes to look through the wrong end of the opera glasses, and see the world that way – why is it, do you think?'

Hermione looked down at Ursula with that long, detached scrutinising gaze that excited the younger woman.

'Yes,' said Hermione at length. 'It is curious. The little things seem to be more subtle to her – '

'But they aren't, are they? A mouse isn't any more subtle than a lion, is it?'

Again Hermione looked down at Ursula with that long scrutiny, as if she were following some train of thought of her own, and barely attending to the other's speech.

'I don't know,' she replied.

'Rupert, Rupert,' she sang mildly, calling him to her. He approached in silence.

'Are little things more subtle than big things?' she asked, with the odd grunt of laughter in her voice, as if she were making game of him in the question.

'Dunno,' he said.

'I hate subtleties,' said Ursula.

Hermione looked at her slowly.

'Do you?' she said.

'I always think they are a sign of weakness,' said Ursula, up in arms, as if her prestige were threatened.

Hermione took no notice. Suddenly her face puckered, her brow was knit with thought, she seemed twisted in troublesome effort for utterance.

'Do you really think, Rupert,' she asked, as if Ursula were not present, 'do you really think it is worth while? Do you really think the children are better for being roused to consciousness?'

A dark flash went over his face, a silent fury. He was hollow-cheeked and pale, almost unearthly. And the woman, with her serious, conscience-harrowing question tortured him on the quick.

'They are not roused to consciousness,' he said. 'Consciousness comes to them, willy-nilly.'

'But do you think they are better for having it quickened, stimulated? Isn't it better that they should remain unconscious of the hazel, isn't it better that they should see as a whole, without all this pulling to pieces, all this knowledge?'

'Would you rather, for yourself, know or not know, that the little red flowers are there, putting out for the pollen?' he asked harshly. His voice was brutal, scornful, cruel.

Hermione remained with her face lifted up, abstracted. He hung silent in irritation.

'I don't know,' she replied, balancing mildly. 'I don't know.'

'But knowing is everything to you, it is all your life,' he broke out. She slowly looked at him.

'Is it?' she said.

'To know, that is your all, that is your life – you have only this, this knowledge,' he cried. 'There is only one tree, there is only one fruit, in your mouth.'

Again she was some time silent.

'Is there?' she said at last, with the same untouched calm. And then in a tone of whimsical inquisitiveness: 'What fruit, Rupert?'

'The eternal apple,' he replied in exasperation, hating his own metaphors.

'Yes,' she said. There was a look of exhaustion about her. For some moments there was silence. Then, pulling herself together with a convulsed movement, Hermione resumed, in a singsong, casual voice, 'But leaving me apart, Rupert; do you think the children are better, richer, happier, for all this knowledge; do you really think they are? Or is it better to leave them untouched, spontaneous. Hadn't they better be animals, simple animals, crude, violent, *anything*, rather than this self-consciousness, this incapacity to be spontaneous.'

They thought she had finished. But with a queer rumbling in her throat she resumed, 'Hadn't they better be anything than grow up crippled, crippled in their souls, crippled in their feelings – so thrown back – so turned back on themselves – incapable – ' Hermione clenched her fist like one in a trance – 'of any spontaneous action, always deliberate, always burdened with choice, never carried away.'

Again they thought she had finished. But just as he was going to reply, she resumed her queer rhapsody – 'never carried away, out of themselves, always conscious, always self-conscious, always aware of themselves. Isn't *anything* better than this? Better be animals, mere animals with no mind at all, than this, this *nothingness* – '

'But do you think it is knowledge that makes us unliving and self-conscious?' he asked irritably.

She opened her eyes and looked at him slowly.

'Yes,' she said. She paused, watching him all the while, her eyes vague. Then she wiped her fingers across her brow, with a vague weariness. It irritated him bitterly. 'It is the mind,' she said, 'and that is death.' She raised her eyes slowly to him: 'Isn't the mind – ' she said, with the convulsed movement of her body, 'isn't it our death? Doesn't it destroy all our spontaneity, all our instincts? Are not the young people growing up today, really dead before they have a chance to live?'

'Not because they have too much mind, but too little,' he said brutally.

'Are you *sure*?' she cried. 'It seems to me the reverse. They are over-conscious, burdened to death with consciousness.'

'Imprisoned within a limited, false set of concepts,' he cried.

But she took no notice of this, only went on with her own rhapsodic interrogation.

'When we have knowledge, don't we lose everything but knowledge?' she asked pathetically. 'If I know about the flower, don't I lose the flower and have only the knowledge? Aren't we exchanging the substance for the shadow, aren't we forfeiting life for this dead quality of knowledge? And what does it mean to me, after all? What does all this knowing mean to me? It means nothing.'

'You are merely making words,' he said; 'knowledge means everything to you. Even your animalism, you want it in your head. You don't want to *be* an animal, you want to observe your own animal functions, to get a mental thrill out of them. It is all purely secondary – and more decadent than the most hidebound intellectualism. What is it but the worst and last form of intellectualism, this love of yours for passion and the animal instincts? Passion and the instincts – you want them hard enough, but through your head, in your consciousness. It all takes place in your head, under that skull of yours. Only you won't be conscious of what *actually* is: you want the lie that will match the rest of your furniture.'

Hermione set hard and poisonous against this attack. Ursula stood covered with wonder and shame. It frightened her, to see how they hated each other.

'It's all that Lady of Shalott business,' he said, in his strong abstract voice. He seemed to be charging her before the unseeing air. 'You've got that mirror, your own fixed will, your immortal understanding, your own tight conscious world, and there is nothing beyond it. There, in the mirror, you must have everything. But now you have come to all your conclusions, you want to go back and be like a savage, without knowledge. You want a life of pure sensation and "passion". '

He quoted the last word satirically against her. She sat convulsed with fury and violation, speechless, like a stricken pythoness of the Greek oracle.

'But your passion is a lie,' he went on violently. 'It isn't passion at all, it is your *will*. It's your bullying will. You want to clutch things and have them in your power. You want to have things in your power. And why? Because you haven't got any real body, any dark sensual body of life. You have no sensuality. You have only your will and your conceit of consciousness, and your lust for power, to *know*.'

He looked at her in mingled hate and contempt, also in pain because she suffered, and in shame because he knew he tortured her. He had an impulse to kneel and plead for forgiveness. But a bitterer red anger burned up to fury in him. He became unconscious of her, he was only a passionate voice speaking.

'Spontaneous!' he cried. 'You and spontaneity! You, the most deliberate thing that ever walked or crawled! You'd be verily deliberately spontaneous – that's you. Because you want to have everything in your own volition, your deliberate voluntary consciousness. You want it all in that loathsome little skull of yours, that ought to be cracked like a nut. For you'll be the same till it is cracked, like an insect in its skin. If one cracked your skull perhaps one might get a spontaneous, passionate woman out of you, with real sensuality. As it is, what you want is pornography – looking at yourself in mirrors, watching your naked animal actions in mirrors, so that you can have it all in your consciousness, make it all mental.'

There was a sense of violation in the air, as if too much was said, the unforgivable. Yet Ursula was concerned now only with solving her own problems, in the light of his words. She was pale and abstracted.

'But do you really *want* sensuality?' she asked, puzzled.

Birkin looked at her, and became intent in his explanation.

'Yes,' he said, 'that and nothing else, at this point. It is a fulfilment – the great dark knowledge you can't have in your head – the dark involuntary being. It is death to one's self – but it is the coming into being of another.'

'But how? How can you have knowledge not in your head?' she asked, quite unable to interpret his phrases.

'In the blood,' he answered; 'when the mind and the known world is drowned in darkness everything must go – there must be the deluge. Then you find yourself a palpable body of darkness, a demon – '

'But why should I be a demon – ?' she asked.

' "*Woman wailing for her demon lover*" – ' he quoted – 'why, I don't know.'

Hermione roused herself as from a death – annihilation.

'He is such a *dreadful* satanist, isn't he?' she drawled to Ursula, in a queer resonant voice, that ended on a shrill little laugh of pure ridicule. The two women were jeering at him, jeering him into nothingness. The laugh of the shrill, triumphant female sounded from Hermione, jeering him as if he were a neuter.

'No,' he said. 'You are the real devil who won't let life exist.'

She looked at him with a long, slow look, malevolent, supercilious.

'You know all about it, don't you?' she said, with slow, cold, cunning mockery.

'Enough,' he replied, his face fixing fine and clear like steel. A horrible despair, and at the same time a sense of release, liberation, came over Hermione. She turned with a pleasant intimacy to Ursula.

'You are sure you will come to Breadalby?' she said, urging.

'Yes, I should like to very much,' replied Ursula.

Hermione looked down at her, gratified, reflecting, and strangely absent, as if possessed, as if not quite there.

'I'm so glad,' she said, pulling herself together. 'Some time in about a fortnight. Yes? I will write to you here, at the school, shall I? Yes. And you'll be sure to come? Yes. I shall be so glad. Goodbye! Goodbye!'

Hermione held out her hand and looked into the eyes of the other woman. She knew Ursula as an immediate rival, and the knowledge strangely exhilarated her. Also she was taking leave. It always gave her a sense of strength, advantage, to be departing and leaving the other behind. Moreover she was taking the man with her, if only in hate.

Birkin stood aside, fixed and unreal. But now, when it was his turn to bid goodbye, he began to speak again.

'There's the whole difference in the world,' he said, 'between the actual sensual being, and the vicious mental deliberate profligacy our lot goes in for. In our night-time, there's always the electricity switched on, we watch ourselves, we get it all in the head, really. You've got to lapse out before you can know what sensual reality is, lapse into unknowingness, and give up your volition. You've got to do it. You've got to learn not-to-be, before you can come into being.

'But we have got such a conceit of ourselves – that's where it is. We are so conceited, and so unproud. We've got no pride, we're all conceit, so conceited in our own papier mâché realised selves. We'd rather die than give up our little self-righteous self-opinionated self-will.'

There was silence in the room. Both women were hostile and resentful. He sounded as if he were addressing a meeting. Hermione merely paid no attention, stood with her shoulders tight in a shrug of dislike.

Ursula was watching him as if furtively, not really aware of what she was seeing. There was a great physical attractiveness in him – a curious hidden richness, that came through his thinness and his pallor like another voice, conveying another knowledge of him. It was in the curves of his brows and his chin, rich, fine, exquisite curves, the powerful beauty of life itself. She could not say what it was. But there was a sense of richness and of liberty.

'But we are sensual enough, without making ourselves so, aren't we?' she asked, turning to him with a certain golden laughter flickering under her greenish eyes, like a challenge. And immediately the queer, careless, terribly attractive smile came over his eyes and brows, though his mouth did not relax.

'No,' he said, 'we aren't. We're too full of ourselves.'

'Surely it isn't a matter of conceit,' she cried.

'That and nothing else.'

She was frankly puzzled.

'Don't you think that people are most conceited of all about their sensual powers?' she asked.

'That's why they aren't sensual – only sensuous – which is another matter. They're *always* aware of themselves – and they're so conceited, that rather than release themselves, and live in another world, from another centre, they'd – '

'You want your tea, don't you,' said Hermione, turning to Ursula with a gracious kindliness. 'You've worked all day – '

Birkin stopped short. A spasm of anger and chagrin went over Ursula. His face set. And he bade goodbye, as if he had ceased to notice her.

They were gone. Ursula stood looking at the door for some moments. Then she put out the lights. And having done so, she sat down again in her chair, absorbed and lost. And then she began to cry, bitterly, bitterly weeping: but whether for misery or joy, she never knew.

CHAPTER 4

Diver

The week passed away. On the Saturday it rained, a soft drizzling rain that held off at times. In one of the intervals Gudrun and Ursula set out for a walk, going towards Willey Water. The atmosphere was grey and translucent, the birds sang sharply on the young twigs, the earth would be quickening and hastening in growth. The two girls walked swiftly, gladly, because of the soft, subtle rush of morning that filled the wet haze. By the road the blackthorn was in blossom, white and wet, its tiny amber grains burning faintly in the white smoke of blossom. Purple twigs were darkly luminous in the grey air, high hedges glowed like living shadows, hovering nearer, coming into creation. The morning was full of a new creation.

When the sisters came to Willey Water, the lake lay all grey and visionary, stretching into the moist, translucent vista of trees and meadow. Fine electric activity in sound came from the dumbles below the road, the birds piping one against the other, and water mysteriously plashing, issuing from the lake.

The two girls drifted swiftly along. In front of them, at the corner of the lake, near the road, was a mossy boat-house under a walnut tree, and a little landing-stage where a boat was moored, wavering like a shadow on the still grey water, below the green, decayed poles. All was shadowy with coming summer.

Suddenly, from the boat-house, a white figure ran out, frightening in its swift sharp transit, across the old landing-stage. It launched in a white arc through the air, there was a bursting of the water, and among the smooth ripples a swimmer was making out to space, in a centre of faintly heaving motion. The whole other-world, wet and remote, he had to himself. He could move into the pure translucency of the grey, uncreated water.

Gudrun stood by the stone wall, watching.

'How I envy him,' she said, in low, desirous tones.

'Ugh!' shivered Ursula. 'So cold!'

'Yes, but how good, how really fine, to swim out there!' The sisters stood watching the swimmer move further into the grey, moist, full space of the water, pulsing with his own small, invading motion, and arched over with mist and dim woods.

'Don't you wish it were you?' asked Gudrun, looking at Ursula.

'I do,' said Ursula. 'But I'm not sure – it's so wet.'

'No,' said Gudrun, reluctantly. She stood watching the motion on the bosom of the water, as if fascinated. He, having swum a certain distance, turned round and was swimming on his back, looking along the water at the two girls by the wall. In the faint wash of motion, they could see his ruddy face, and could feel him watching them.

'It is Gerald Crich,' said Ursula.

'I know,' replied Gudrun.

And she stood motionless gazing over the water at the face which washed up and down on the flood, as he swam steadily. From his separate element he saw them and he exulted to himself because of his own advantage, his possession of a world to himself. He was immune and perfect. He loved his own vigorous, thrusting motion, and the violent impulse of the very cold water against his limbs, buoying him up. He could see the girls watching him a way off, outside, and that pleased him. He lifted his arm from the water, in a sign to them.

'He is waving,' said Ursula.

'Yes,' replied Gudrun. They watched him. He waved again, with a strange movement of recognition across the difference.

'Like a Nibelung,' laughed Ursula. Gudrun said nothing, only stood still looking over the water.

Gerald suddenly turned, and was swimming away swiftly, with a side stroke. He was alone now, alone and immune in the middle of the waters, which he had all to himself. He exulted in his isolation in the new element, unquestioned and unconditioned. He was happy, thrusting with his legs and all his body, without bond or connection anywhere, just himself in the watery world.

Gudrun envied him almost painfully. Even this momentary possession of pure isolation and fluidity seemed to her so terribly desirable that she felt herself as if damned, out there on the highroad.

'God, what it is to be a man!' she cried.

'What?' exclaimed Ursula in surprise.

'The freedom, the liberty, the mobility!' cried Gudrun, strangely flushed and brilliant. 'You're a man, you want to do a thing, you do it. You haven't the *thousand* obstacles a woman has in front of her.'

Ursula wondered what was in Gudrun's mind, to occasion this outburst. She could not understand.

'What do you want to do?' she asked.

'Nothing,' cried Gudrun, in swift refutation. 'But supposing I did. Supposing I want to swim up that water. It is impossible, it is one of the impossibilities of life, for me to take my clothes off now and jump in. But isn't it *ridiculous*, doesn't it simply prevent our living!'

She was so hot, so flushed, so furious, that Ursula was puzzled.

The two sisters went on, up the road. They were passing between the trees just below Shortlands. They looked up at the long, low house, dim and glamorous in the wet morning, its cedar trees slanting before the windows. Gudrun seemed to be studying it closely.

'Don't you think it's attractive, Ursula?' asked Gudrun.

'Very,' said Ursula. 'Very peaceful and charming.'

'It has form, too – it has a period.'

'What period?'

'Oh, eighteenth century, for certain; Dorothy Wordsworth and Jane Austen, don't you think?'

Ursula laughed.

'Don't you think so?' repeated Gudrun.

'Perhaps. But I don't think the Criches fit the period. I know Gerald is putting in a private electric plant, for lighting the house, and is making all kinds of latest improvements.'

Gudrun shrugged her shoulders swiftly.

'Of course,' she said, 'that's quite inevitable.'

'Quite,' laughed Ursula. 'He is several generations of youngness at one go. They hate him for it. He takes them all by the scruff of the neck, and fairly flings them along. He'll have to die soon, when he's made every possible improvement, and there will be nothing more to improve. He's got *go*, anyhow.'

'Certainly, he's got go,' said Gudrun. 'In fact I've never seen a man that showed signs of so much. The unfortunate thing is, where does his *go* go to, what becomes of it?'

'Oh I know,' said Ursula. 'It goes in applying the latest appliances!'

'Exactly,' said Gudrun.

'You know he shot his brother?' said Ursula.

'Shot his brother?' cried Gudrun, frowning as if in disapprobation.

'Didn't you know? Oh yes! – I thought you knew. He and his brother were playing together with a gun. He told his brother to look down the gun, and it was loaded, and blew the top of his head off. Isn't it a horrible story?'

'How fearful!' cried Gudrun. 'But it is long ago?'

'Oh yes, they were quite boys,' said Ursula. 'I think it is one of the most horrible stories I know.'

'And he of course did not know that the gun was loaded?'

'Yes. You see it was an old thing that had been lying in the stable for years. Nobody dreamed it would ever go off, and of course, no one imagined it was loaded. But isn't it dreadful, that it should happen?'

'Frightful!' cried Gudrun. 'And isn't it horrible too to think of such a thing happening to one, when one was a child, and having to carry the responsibility of it all through one's life. Imagine it, two boys playing together – then this comes upon them, for no reason whatever – out of the air. Ursula, it's very frightening! Oh, it's one of the things I can't bear. Murder, that is thinkable, because there's a will behind it. But a thing like that to *happen* to one – '

'Perhaps there *was* an unconscious will behind it,' said Ursula. 'This playing at killing has some primitive *desire* for killing in it, don't you think?'

'Desire!' said Gudrun, coldly, stiffening a little. 'I can't see that they were even playing at killing. I suppose one boy said to the other, "You look down the barrel while I pull the trigger, and see what happens." It seems to me the purest form of accident.'

'No,' said Ursula. 'I couldn't pull the trigger of the emptiest gun in the world, not if someone were looking down the barrel. One instinctively doesn't do it – one can't.'

Gudrun was silent for some moments, in sharp disagreement.

'Of course,' she said coldly. 'If one is a woman, and grown up, one's instinct prevents one. But I cannot see how that applies to a couple of boys playing together.'

Her voice was cold and angry.

'Yes,' persisted Ursula. At that moment they heard a woman's voice a few yards off say loudly, 'Oh damn the thing!' They went forward and saw Laura Crich and Hermione Roddice in the field on the other side of the hedge, and Laura Crich struggling with the gate, to get out. Ursula at once hurried up and helped to lift the gate.

'Thanks so much,' said Laura, looking up flushed and amazon-like, yet rather confused. 'It isn't right on the hinges.'

'No,' said Ursula. 'And they're so heavy.'

'Surprising!' cried Laura.

'How do you do,' sang Hermione, from out of the field, the moment she could make her voice heard. 'It's nice now. Are you going for a walk? Yes. Isn't the young green beautiful? So beautiful – quite burning. Good-morning – good-morning – you'll come and see me? – thank you so much – next week – yes – goodbye, g–o–o–d–b–y–e.'

Gudrun and Ursula stood and watched her slowly waving her head up and down, and waving her hand slowly in dismissal, smiling a strange affected smile, making a tall queer, frightening figure, with her heavy fair hair slipping to her eyes. Then they moved off, as if they had been dismissed like inferiors. The four women parted.

As soon as they had gone far enough, Ursula said, her cheeks burning, 'I do think she's impudent.'

'Who, Hermione Roddice?' asked Gudrun. 'Why?'

'The way she treats one – impudence!'

'Why, Ursula, what did you notice that was so impudent?' asked Gudrun rather coldly.

'Her whole manner. Oh, it's impossible, the way she tries to bully one. Pure bullying. She's an impudent woman. "You'll come and see me," as if we should be falling over ourselves for the privilege.'

'I can't understand, Ursula, what you are so much put out about,' said Gudrun, in some exasperation. 'One knows those women are impudent – these free women who have emancipated themselves from the aristocracy.'

'But it is so *unnecessary* – so vulgar,' cried Ursula.

'No, I don't see it. And if I did – *pour moi, elle n'existe pas*. I don't grant her the power to be impudent to me.'

'Do you think she likes you?' asked Ursula.

'Well, no, I shouldn't think she did.'

'Then why does she ask you to go to Breadalby and stay with her?'

Gudrun lifted her shoulders in a low shrug.

'After all, she's got the sense to know we're not just the ordinary run,' said Gudrun. 'Whatever she is, she's not a fool. And I'd rather have somebody I detested, than the ordinary woman who keeps to her own set. Hermione Roddice does risk herself in some respects.'

Ursula pondered this for a time.

'I doubt it,' she replied. 'Really she risks nothing. I suppose we ought to admire her for knowing she *can* invite us – school teachers – and risk nothing.'

'Precisely!' said Gudrun. 'Think of the myriads of women that daren't do it. She makes the most of her privileges – that's something. I suppose, really, we should do the same, in her place.'

'No,' said Ursula. 'No. It would bore me. I couldn't spend my time playing her games. It's *infra dig.*'

The two sisters were like a pair of scissors, snipping off everything that came athwart them; or like a knife and a whetstone, the one sharpened against the other.

'Of course,' cried Ursula suddenly, 'she ought to thank her stars if we will go and see her. You are perfectly beautiful, a thousand times more beautiful than ever she is or was, and to my thinking, a thousand times more beautifully dressed, for she never looks fresh and natural, like a flower, always old, thought-out; and we *are* more intelligent than most people.'

'Undoubtedly!' said Gudrun.

'And it ought to be admitted, simply,' said Ursula.

'Certainly it ought,' said Gudrun. 'But you'll find that the really chic thing is to be so absolutely ordinary, so perfectly commonplace and like the person in the street, that you really are a masterpiece of humanity, not the person in the street actually, but the artistic creation of her – '

'How awful!' cried Ursula.

'Yes, Ursula, it *is* awful, in most respects. You daren't be anything that isn't amazingly *à terre*, *so* much *à terre* that it is the artistic creation of ordinariness.'

'It's very dull to create oneself into nothing better,' laughed Ursula.

'Very dull!' retorted Gudrun. 'Really Ursula, it is dull, that's just the word. One longs to be high-flown, and make speeches like Corneille, after it.'

Gudrun was becoming flushed and excited over her own cleverness.

'Strut,' said Ursula. 'One wants to strut, to be a swan among geese.'

'Exactly,' cried Gudrun, 'a swan among geese.'

'They are all so busy playing the ugly duckling,' cried Ursula, with mocking laughter. 'And I don't feel a bit like a humble and pathetic ugly duckling. I do feel like a swan among geese – I can't help it. They make one feel so. And I don't care what *they* think of me. *Je m'en fiche.*'

Gudrun looked up at Ursula with a queer, uncertain envy and dislike.

'Of course, the only thing to do is to despise them all — just all,' she said.

The sisters went home again, to read and talk and work, and wait for Monday, for school. Ursula often wondered what else she waited for, besides the beginning and end of the school week, and the beginning and end of the holidays. This was a whole life! Sometimes she had periods of tight horror, when it seemed to her that her life would pass away, and be gone, without having been more than this. But she never really accepted it. Her spirit was active, her life like a shoot that is growing steadily, but which has not yet come above ground.

CHAPTER 5

In the Train

One day at this time Birkin was called to London. He was not very fixed in his abode. He had rooms in Nottingham, because his work lay chiefly in that town. But often he was in London, or in Oxford. He moved about a great deal, his life seemed uncertain, without any definite rhythm, any organic meaning.

On the platform of the railway station he saw Gerald Crich, reading a newspaper, and evidently waiting for the train. Birkin stood some distance off, among the people. It was against his instinct to approach anybody.

From time to time, in a manner characteristic of him, Gerald lifted his head and looked round. Even though he was reading the newspaper closely, he must keep a watchful eye on his external surroundings. There seemed to be a dual consciousness running in him. He was thinking vigorously of something he read in the newspaper, and at the same time his eye ran over the surfaces of the life round him, and he missed nothing. Birkin, who was watching him, was irritated by his duality. He noticed too, that Gerald seemed always to be at bay against everybody, in spite of his queer, genial, social manner when roused.

Now Birkin started violently at seeing this genial look flash on to Gerald's face, at seeing Gerald approaching with hand outstretched.

'Hallo, Rupert, where are you going?'

'London. So are you, I suppose.'

'Yes – '

Gerald's eyes went over Birkin's face in curiosity.

'We'll travel together if you like,' he said.

'Don't you usually go first?' asked Birkin.

'I can't stand the crowd,' replied Gerald. 'But third'll be all right. There's a restaurant car, we can have some tea.'

The two men looked at the station clock, having nothing further to say.

'What were you reading in the paper?' Birkin asked.

Gerald looked at him quickly.

'Isn't it funny, what they *do* put in the newspapers,' he said. 'Here are two leaders – ' he held out his *Daily Telegraph*, 'full of the ordinary newspaper cant – ' he scanned the columns down – 'and then there's this little – I dunno what you'd call it, essay, almost – appearing with the leaders, and saying there must arise a man who will give new values to things, give us new truths, a new attitude to life, or else we shall be a crumbling nothingness in a few years, a country in ruin – '

'I suppose that's a bit of newspaper cant, as well,' said Birkin.

'It sounds as if the man meant it, and quite genuinely,' said Gerald.

'Give it to me,' said Birkin, holding out his hand for the paper.

The train came, and they went on board, sitting on either side a little table, by the window, in the restaurant car. Birkin glanced over his paper, then looked up at Gerald, who was waiting for him.

'I believe the man means it,' he said, 'as far as he means anything.'

'And do you think it's true? Do you think we really want a new gospel?' asked Gerald.

Birkin shrugged his shoulders.

'I think the people who say they want a new religion are the last to accept anything new. They want novelty right enough. But to stare straight at this life that we've brought upon ourselves, and reject it, absolutely smash up the old idols of ourselves, that we sh'll never do. You've got very badly to want to get rid of the old, before anything new will appear – even in the self.'

Gerald watched him closely.

'You think we ought to break up this life, just start and let fly?' he asked.

'This life. Yes I do. We've got to bust it completely, or shrivel inside it, as in a tight skin. For it won't expand any more.'

There was a queer little smile in Gerald's eyes, a look of amusement, calm and curious.

'And how do you propose to begin? I suppose you mean, reform the whole order of society?' he asked.

Birkin had a slight, tense frown between the brows. He too was impatient of the conversation.

'I don't propose at all,' he replied. 'When we really want to go for something better, we shall smash the old. Until then, any sort of proposal, or making proposals, is no more than a tiresome game for self-important people.'

The little smile began to die out of Gerald's eyes, and he said, looking with a cool stare at Birkin, 'So you really think things are very bad?'

'Completely bad.'

The smile appeared again.

'In what way?'

'Every way,' said Birkin. 'We are such dreary liars. Our one idea is to lie to ourselves. We have an ideal of a perfect world, clean and straight and sufficient. So we cover the earth with foulness; life is a blotch of labour, like insects scurrying in filth, so that your collier can have a pianoforte in his parlour, and you can have a butler and a motor car in your up to-date house, and as a nation we can sport the Ritz, or the Empire, Gaby Deslys and the Sunday newspapers. It is very dreary.'

Gerald took a little time to readjust himself after this tirade.

'Would you have us live without houses – return to nature?' he asked.

'I would have nothing at all. People only do what they want to do – and what they are capable of doing. If they were capable of anything else, there would be something else.'

Again Gerald pondered. He was not going to take offence at Birkin.

'Don't you think the collier's *pianoforte*, as you call it, is a symbol for something very real, a real desire for something higher, in the collier's life?'

'Higher!' cried Birkin. 'Yes. Amazing heights of upright grandeur. It makes him so much higher in his neighbouring collier's eyes. He sees himself reflected in the neighbouring opinion, like in a Brocken mist, several feet taller on the strength of the pianoforte, and he is satisfied. He lives for the sake of that Brocken spectre, the reflection of himself in the human opinion. You do the same. If you are of high importance to humanity you are of high importance to yourself. That is why you work so hard at the mines. If you can produce coal to cook five thousand dinners a day, you are five thousand times more important than if you cooked only your own dinner.'

'I suppose I am,' laughed Gerald.

'Can't you see,' said Birkin, 'that to help my neighbour to eat is no more than eating myself. "I eat, thou eatest, he eats, we eat, you eat, they eat" – and what then? Why should every man decline the whole verb. First person singular is enough for me.'

'You've got to start with material things,' said Gerald. Which statement Birkin ignored.

'And we've got to live for *something*, we're not just cattle that can graze and have done with it,' said Gerald.

'Tell me,' said Birkin. 'What do you live for?'

Gerald's face went baffled.

'What do I live for?' he repeated. 'I suppose I live to work, to produce something, in so far as I am a purposive being. Apart from that, I live because I am living.'

'And what's your work? Getting so many more thousands of tons of coal out of the earth every day. And when we've got all the coal we want, and all the plush furniture, and pianofortes, and the rabbits are all stewed and eaten, and we're all warm and our bellies are filled and we're listening to the young lady performing on the pianoforte – what then? What then, when you've made a real fair start with your material things?'

Gerald sat laughing at the words and the mocking humour of the other man. But he was cogitating too.

'We haven't got there yet,' he replied. 'A good many people are still waiting for the rabbit and the fire to cook it.'

'So while you get the coal I must chase the rabbit?' said Birkin, mocking at Gerald.

'Something like that,' said Gerald.

Birkin watched him narrowly. He saw the perfect good-humoured callousness, even strange, glistening malice, in Gerald, glistening through the plausible ethics of productivity.

'Gerald,' he said, 'I rather hate you.'

'I know you do,' said Gerald. 'Why do you?'

Birkin mused inscrutably for some minutes.

'I should like to know if you are conscious of hating me,' he said at last. 'Do you ever consciously detest me – hate me with mystic hate? There are odd moments when I hate you starrily.'

Gerald was rather taken aback, even a little disconcerted. He did not quite know what to say.

'I may, of course, hate you sometimes,' he said. 'But I'm not aware of it – never acutely aware of it, that is.'

'So much the worse,' said Birkin.

Gerald watched him with curious eyes. He could not quite make him out.

'So much the worse, is it?' he repeated.

There was a silence between the two men for some time, as the train ran on. In Birkin's face was a little irritable tension, a sharp knitting of the brows, keen and difficult. Gerald watched him warily, carefully, rather calculatingly, for he could not decide what he was after.

Suddenly Birkin's eyes looked straight and overpowering into those of the other man.

'What do you think is the aim and object of your life, Gerald?' he asked.

Again Gerald was taken aback. He could not think what his friend was getting at. Was he poking fun, or not?

'At this moment, I couldn't say offhand,' he replied, with faintly ironic humour.

'Do you think love is the be-all and the end-all of life?' Birkin asked, with direct, attentive seriousness.

'Of my own life?' said Gerald.

'Yes.'

There was a really puzzled pause.

'I can't say,' said Gerald. 'It hasn't been, so far.'

'What has your life been, so far?'

'Oh – finding out things for myself – and getting experiences – and making things go.'

Birkin knitted his brows like sharply moulded steel.

'I find,' he said, 'that one needs some one *really* pure single activity – I should call love a single pure activity. But I *don't* really love anybody – not now.'

'Have you ever really loved anybody?' asked Gerald.

'Yes and no,' replied Birkin.

'Not finally?' said Gerald.

'Finally – finally – no,' said Birkin.

'Nor I,' said Gerald.

'And do you want to?' said Birkin.

Gerald looked with a long, twinkling, almost sardonic look into the eyes of the other man.

'I don't know,' he said.

'I do – I want to love,' said Birkin.

'You do?'

'Yes. I want the finality of love.'

'The finality of love,' repeated Gerald. And he waited for a moment.

'Just one woman?' he added. The evening light, flooding yellow along the fields, lit up Birkin's face with a tense, abstract steadfastness. Gerald still could not make it out.

'Yes, one woman,' said Birkin.

But to Gerald it sounded as if he were insistent rather than confident.

'I don't believe a woman, and nothing but a woman, will ever make my life,' said Gerald.

'Not the centre and core of it – the love between you and a woman?' asked Birkin.

Gerald's eyes narrowed with a queer dangerous smile as he watched the other man.

'I never quite feel it that way,' he said.

'You don't? Then wherein does life centre, for you?'

'I don't know – that's what I want somebody to tell me. As far as I can make out, it doesn't centre at all. It is artificially held *together* by the social mechanism.'

Birkin pondered as if he would crack something.

'I know,' he said, 'it just doesn't centre. The old ideals are dead as nails – nothing there. It seems to me there remains only this perfect union with a woman – sort of ultimate marriage – and there isn't anything else.'

'And you mean if there isn't the woman, there's nothing?' said Gerald.

'Pretty well that – seeing there's no God.'

'Then we're hard put to it,' said Gerald. And he turned to look out of the window at the flying, golden landscape.

Birkin could not help seeing how beautiful and soldierly his face was, with a certain courage to be indifferent.

'You think it's heavy odds against us?' said Birkin.

'If we've got to make our life up out of a woman, one woman, woman only, yes, I do,' said Gerald. 'I don't believe I shall ever make up *my* life, at that rate.'

Birkin watched him almost angrily.

'You are a born unbeliever,' he said.

'I only feel what I feel,' said Gerald. And he looked again at Birkin almost sardonically, with his blue, manly, sharp-lighted eyes. Birkin's eyes were at the moment full of anger. But swiftly they became troubled, doubtful, then full of a warm, rich affectionateness and laughter.

'It troubles me very much, Gerald,' he said, wrinkling his brows.

'I can see it does,' said Gerald, uncovering his mouth in a manly, quick, soldierly laugh.

Gerald was held unconsciously by the other man. He wanted to be near him, he wanted to be within his sphere of influence. There was something very congenial to him in Birkin. But yet, beyond this, he did not take much notice. He felt that he, himself, Gerald, had harder and more durable truths than any the other man knew. He felt himself older, more knowing. It was the quick-changing warmth and venality and brilliant warm utterance he loved in his friend. It was the rich play of words and quick interchange of feelings he enjoyed. The real content of the words he never really considered: he himself knew better.

Birkin knew this. He knew that Gerald wanted to be *fond* of him without taking him seriously. And this made him go hard and cold. As the train ran on, he sat looking at the land, and Gerald fell away, became as nothing to him.

Birkin looked at the land, at the evening, and was thinking: 'Well, if mankind is destroyed, if our race is destroyed like Sodom, and there is this beautiful evening with the luminous land and trees, I am satisfied. That which informs it all is there, and can never be lost. After all, what is mankind but just one expression of the incomprehensible. And if mankind passes away, it will only mean that this particular expression is completed and done. That which is expressed, and that which is to be expressed, cannot be diminished. There it is, in the shining evening. Let mankind pass away – time it did. The creative utterances will not cease, they will only be there. Humanity doesn't embody the utterance of the incomprehensible any more. Humanity is a dead letter. There will be a new embodiment, in a new way. Let humanity disappear as quick as possible.'

Gerald interrupted him by asking, 'Where are you staying in London?'

Birkin looked up.

'With a man in Soho. I pay part of the rent of a flat, and stop there when I like.'

'Good idea – have a place more or less your own,' said Gerald.

'Yes. But I don't care for it much. I'm tired of the people I am bound to find there.'

'What kind of people?'

'Art – music – London Bohemia – the most pettifogging calculating Bohemia that ever reckoned its pennies. But there are a few decent people, decent in some respects. They are really very thorough rejecters of the world – perhaps they live only in the gesture of rejection and negation – but negatively something, at any rate.'

'What are they? – painters, musicians?'

'Painters, musicians, writers – hangers-on, models, advanced young people, anybody who is openly at outs with the conventions, and belongs to nowhere particularly. They are often young fellows down from the University, and girls who are living their own lives, as they say.'

'All loose?' said Gerald.

Birkin could see his curiosity roused.

'In one way. Most bound, in another. For all their shockingness, all on one note.'

He looked at Gerald, and saw how his blue eyes were lit up with a little flame of curious desire. He saw too how good-looking he was. Gerald was attractive, his blood seemed fluid and electric. His blue eyes burned with a keen, yet cold light, there was a certain beauty, a beautiful passivity in all his body, his moulding.

'We might see something of each other – I am in London for two or three days,' said Gerald.

'Yes,' said Birkin, 'I don't want to go to the theatre, or the music hall – you'd better come round to the flat, and see what you can make of Halliday and his crowd.'

'Thanks – I should like to,' laughed Gerald. 'What are you doing tonight?'

'I promised to meet Halliday at the Pompadour. It's a bad place, but there is nowhere else.'

'Where is it?' asked Gerald.

'Piccadilly Circus.'

'Oh yes – well, shall I come round there?'

'By all means, it might amuse you.'

The evening was falling. They had passed Bedford. Birkin watched the country, and was filled with a sort of hopelessness. He always felt this, on approaching London.

His dislike of mankind, of the mass of mankind, amounted almost to an illness.

> ' "Where the quiet coloured end of evening smiles
> Miles and miles – " '

he was murmuring to himself, like a man condemned to death. Gerald, who was very subtly alert, wary in all his senses, leaned forward and asked smilingly, 'What were you saying?' Birkin glanced at him, laughed, and repeated:

> ' "Where the quiet coloured end of evening smiles,
> Miles and miles,
> Over pastures where the something something sheep
> Half asleep – " '

Gerald also looked now at the country. And Birkin, who, for some reason, was now tired and dispirited, said to him, 'I always feel doomed when the train is running into London. I feel such a despair, so hopeless, as if it were the end of the world.'

'Really!' said Gerald. 'And does the end of the world frighten you?'

Birkin lifted his shoulders in a slow shrug.

'I don't know,' he said. 'It does while it hangs imminent and doesn't fall. But people give me a bad feeling – very bad.'

There was a roused glad smile in Gerald's eyes.

'Do they?' he said. And he watched the other man critically.

In a few minutes the train was running through the disgrace of outspread London. Everybody in the carriage was on the alert, waiting to escape. At last they were under the huge arch of the station, in the tremendous shadow of the town. Birkin shut himself together – he was in now.

The two men went together in a taxi-cab.

'Don't you feel like one of the damned?' asked Birkin, as they sat in a little, swiftly-running enclosure, and watched the hideous great street.

'No,' laughed Gerald.

'It is real death,' said Birkin.

CHAPTER 6

Crème de Menthe

They met again in the café several hours later. Gerald went through the push doors into the large, lofty room where the faces and heads of the drinkers showed dimly through the haze of smoke, reflected more dimly, and repeated *ad infinitum* in the great mirrors on the walls, so that one seemed to enter a vague, dim world of shadowy drinkers humming within an atmosphere of blue tobacco smoke. There was, however, the red plush of the seats to give substance within the bubble of pleasure.

Gerald moved in his slow, observant, glistening-attentive motion down between the tables and the people whose shadowy faces looked up as he passed. He seemed to be entering in some strange element, passing into an illuminated new region, among a host of licentious souls. He was pleased, and entertained. He looked over all the dim, evanescent, strangely illuminated faces that bent across the tables. Then he saw Birkin rise and signal to him.

At Birkin's table was a girl with dark, soft, fluffy hair cut short in the artist fashion, hanging level and full almost like the Egyptian princess's. She was small and delicately made, with warm colouring and large, dark hostile eyes. There was a delicacy, almost a beauty in all her form, and at the same time a certain attractive grossness of spirit, that made a little spark leap instantly alight in Gerald's eyes.

Birkin, who looked muted, unreal, his presence left out, introduced her as Miss Darrington. She gave her hand with a sudden, unwilling movement, looking all the while at Gerald with a dark, exposed stare. A glow came over him as he sat down.

The waiter appeared. Gerald glanced at the glasses of the other two. Birkin was drinking something green, Miss Darrington had a small liqueur glass that was empty save for a tiny drop.

'Won't you have some more – ?'

'Brandy,' she said, sipping her last drop and putting down the glass. The waiter disappeared.

'No,' she said to Birkin. 'He doesn't know I'm back. He'll be terrified when he sees me here.'

She spoke her 'r's like 'w's, lisping with a slightly babyish pronunciation which was at once affected and true to her character. Her voice was dull and toneless.

'Where is he then?' asked Birkin.

'He's doing a private show at Lady Snellgrove's,' said the girl. 'Warens is there too.'

There was a pause.

'Well, then,' said Birkin, in a dispassionate protective manner, 'what do you intend to do?'

The girl paused sullenly. She hated the question.

'I don't intend to do anything,' she replied. 'I shall look for some sittings tomorrow.'

'Who shall you go to?' asked Birkin.

'I shall go to Bentley's first. But I believe he's angwy with me for running away.'

'That is from the Madonna?'

'Yes. And then if he doesn't want me, I know I can get work with Carmarthen.'

'Carmarthen?'

'Lord Carmarthen – he does photographs.'

'Chiffon and shoulders – '

'Yes. But he's awfully decent.' There was a pause.

'And what are you going to do about Julius?' he asked.

'Nothing,' she said. 'I shall just ignore him.'

'You've done with him altogether?' But she turned aside her face sullenly, and did not answer the question.

Another young man came hurrying up to the table.

'Hallo Birkin! Hallo *Pussum*, when did you come back?' he said eagerly.

'Today.'

'Does Halliday know?'

'I don't know. I don't care either.'

'Ha-ha! The wind still sits in that quarter, does it? Do you mind if I come over to this table?'

'I'm talking to Wupert, do you mind?' she replied, coolly and yet appealingly, like a child.

'Open confession – good for the soul, eh?' said the young man. 'Well, so long.'

And giving a sharp look at Birkin and at Gerald, the young man moved off, with a swing of his coat skirts.

All this time Gerald had been completely ignored. And yet he felt that the girl was physically aware of his proximity. He waited, listened, and tried to piece together the conversation.

'Are you staying at the flat?' the girl asked, of Birkin.

'For three days,' replied Birkin. 'And you?'

'I don't know yet. I can always go to Bertha's.' There was a silence.

Suddenly the girl turned to Gerald, and said, in a rather formal, polite voice, with the distant manner of a woman who accepts her position as a social inferior, yet assumes intimate *camaraderie* with the male she addresses, 'Do you know London well?'

'I can hardly say,' he laughed. 'I've been up a good many times, but I was never in this place before.'

'You're not an artist, then?' she said, in a tone that placed him an outsider.

'No,' he replied.

'He's a soldier, and an explorer, and a Napoleon of industry,' said Birkin, giving Gerald his credentials for Bohemia.

'Are you a soldier?' asked the girl, with a cold yet lively curiosity.

'No, I resigned my commission,' said Gerald, 'some years ago.'

'He was in the last war,' said Birkin.

'Were you really?' said the girl.

'And then he explored the Amazon,' said Birkin, 'and now he is ruling over coal-mines.'

The girl looked at Gerald with steady, calm curiosity. He laughed, hearing himself described. He felt proud too, full of male strength. His blue, keen eyes were lit up with laughter, his ruddy face, with its sharp fair hair, was full of satisfaction, and glowing with life. He piqued her.

'How long are you staying?' she asked him.

'A day or two,' he replied. 'But there is no particular hurry.'

Still she stared into his face with that slow, full gaze which was so curious and so exciting to him. He was acutely and delightfully conscious of himself, of his own attractiveness. He felt full of strength, able to give off a sort of electric power. And he was aware of her dark, hot-looking eyes upon him. She had beautiful eyes, dark, fully-opened, hot, naked in their looking at him. And on them there seemed to float a film of disintegration, a sort of misery and sullenness, like oil on water. She wore no hat in the heated café, her loose, simple jumper was strung on a string round her neck. But it was made of rich peach-coloured *crêpe de Chine*, that hung heavily and softly from her young throat and her slender wrists. Her appearance was simple and complete, really beautiful, because of her regularity and form, her soft dark hair falling full and level on either side of her head, her straight, small, softened features, Egyptian in the slight fullness of their curves, her slender neck and the simple, rich-coloured smock hanging on her slender shoulders. She was very still, almost null, in her manner, apart and watchful.

She appealed to Gerald strongly. He felt an awful, enjoyable power over her, an instinctive cherishing very near to cruelty. For she was a victim. He felt that she was in his power, and he was generous. The electricity was turgid and voluptuously rich, in his limbs. He would be able to destroy her utterly in the strength of his discharge. But she was waiting in her separation, given.

They talked banalities for some time. Suddenly Birkin said, 'There's Julius!' and he half rose to his feet, motioning to the newcomer. The girl, with a curious, almost evil motion, looked round over her shoulder without moving her body. Gerald watched her dark, soft hair swing over her ears. He felt her watching intensely the man who was approaching, so he looked too. He saw a pale, full-built young man with rather long, solid fair hair hanging from under his black hat, moving cumbrously down the room, his face lit up with a smile at once naïve and warm, and vapid. He approached towards Birkin, with a haste of welcome.

It was not till he was quite close that he perceived the girl. He recoiled, went pale, and said, in a high squealing voice, 'Pussum, what are *you* doing here?'

The café looked up like animals when they hear a cry. Halliday hung motionless, an almost imbecile smile flickering palely on his face. The girl only stared at him with a black look in which flared an unfathomable hell of knowledge, and a certain impotence. She was limited by him.

'Why have you come back?' repeated Halliday, in the same high, hysterical voice. 'I told you not to come back.'

The girl did not answer, only stared in the same viscous, heavy fashion, straight at him, as he stood recoiled, as if for safety, against the next table.

'You know you wanted her to come back – come and sit down,' said Birkin to him.

'No I didn't want her to come back, and I told her not to come back. What have you come for, Pussum?'

'For nothing from *you*,' she said in a heavy voice of resentment.

'Then why have you come back at *all*?' cried Halliday, his voice rising to a kind of squeal.

'She comes as she likes,' said Birkin. 'Are you going to sit down, or are you not?'

'No, I won't sit down with Pussum,' cried Halliday.

'I won't hurt you, you needn't be afraid,' she said to him, very curtly, and yet with a sort of protectiveness towards him, in her voice.

Halliday came and sat at the table, putting his hand on his heart, and crying, 'Oh, it's given me such a turn! Pussum, I wish you wouldn't do these things. Why did you come back?'

'Not for anything from you,' she repeated.

'You've said that before,' he cried in a high voice.

She turned completely away from him, to Gerald Crich, whose eyes were shining with a subtle amusement.

'Were you ever vewy much afwaid of the savages?' she asked in her calm, dull, childish voice.

'No – never very much afraid. On the whole they're harmless – they're not born yet, you can't feel really afraid of them. You know you can manage them.'

'Do you weally? Aren't they very fierce?'

'Not very. There aren't many fierce things, as a matter of fact. There aren't many things, neither people nor animals, that have it in them to be really dangerous.'

'Except in herds,' interrupted Birkin.

'Aren't there really?' she said. 'Oh, I thought savages were all so dangerous, they'd have your life before you could look round.'

'Did you?' he laughed. 'They are overrated, savages. They're too much like other people, not exciting, after the first acquaintance.'

'Oh, it's not so very wonderfully brave then, to be an explorer?'

'No. It's more a question of hardships than of terrors.'

'Oh! And weren't you ever afraid?'

'In my life? I don't know. Yes, I'm afraid of some things – of being shut up, locked up anywhere – or being fastened. I'm afraid of being bound hand and foot.'

She looked at him steadily with her dark eyes, that rested on him and roused him so deeply, that it left his upper self quite calm. It was rather delicious, to feel her drawing his self-revelations from him, as from the very innermost dark marrow of his body. She wanted to know. And her dark eyes seemed to be looking through into his naked organism. He felt, she was compelled to him, she was fated to come into contact with him, must have the seeing him and knowing him. And this roused a curious exultance. Also he felt, she must relinquish herself into his hands, and be subject to him. She was so profane, slave-like, watching him, absorbed by him. It was not that she was interested in what he said; she was absorbed by his self-revelation, by *him*, she wanted the secret of him, the experience of his male being.

Gerald's face was lit up with an uncanny smile, full of light and rousedness, yet unconscious. He sat with his arms on the table, his sun-browned, rather sinister hands, that were animal and yet very shapely and attractive, pushed forward towards her. And they fascinated her. And she knew, she watched her own fascination.

Other men had come to the table, to talk with Birkin and Halliday. Gerald said in a low voice, apart, to Pussum, 'Where have you come back from?'

'From the country,' replied Pussum, in a very low, yet fully resonant voice. Her face closed hard. Continually she glanced at Halliday, and then a black flare came over her eyes. The heavy, fair young man ignored her completely; he was really afraid of her. For some moments she would be unaware of Gerald. He had not conquered her yet.

'And what has Halliday to do with it?' he asked, his voice still muted.

She would not answer for some seconds. Then she said, unwillingly, 'He made me go and live with him, and now he wants to throw me over. And yet he won't let me go to anybody else. He wants me to live hidden in the country. And then he says I persecute him, that he can't get rid of me.'

'Doesn't know his own mind,' said Gerald.

'He hasn't any mind, so he can't know it,' she said. 'He waits for what somebody tells him to do. He never does anything he wants to do himself – because he doesn't know what he wants. He's a perfect baby.'

Gerald looked at Halliday for some moments, watching the soft, rather degenerate face of the young man. Its very softness was an attraction; it was a soft, warm, corrupt nature, into which one might plunge with gratification.

'But he has no hold over you, has he?' Gerald asked.

'You see he *made* me go and live with him, when I didn't want to,' she replied. 'He came and cried to me, tears, you never saw so many, saying *he couldn't* bear it unless I went back to him. And he wouldn't go away, he would have stayed for ever. He made me go back. Then every time he behaves in this fashion. And now I'm going to have a baby, he wants to give me a hundred pounds and send me into the country, so that he would never see me nor hear of me again. But I'm not going to do it, after – '

A queer look came over Gerald's face.

'Are you going to have a child?' he asked incredulous. It seemed, to look at her, impossible, she was so young and so far in spirit from any child-bearing.

She looked full into his face, and her dark, inchoate eyes had now a furtive look, and a look of a knowledge of evil, dark and indomitable. A flame ran secretly to his heart.

'Yes,' she said. 'Isn't it beastly?'

'Don't you want it?' he asked.

'I don't,' she replied emphatically.

'But – ' he said, 'how long have you known?'

'Ten weeks,' she said.

All the time she kept her dark, inchoate eyes full upon him. He remained silent, thinking. Then, switching off and becoming cold, he asked, in a voice full of considerate kindness, 'Is there anything we can eat here? Is there anything you would like?'

'Yes,' she said, 'I should adore some oysters.'

'All right,' he said. 'We'll have oysters.' And he beckoned to the waiter.

Halliday took no notice, until the little plate was set before her. Then suddenly he cried, 'Pussum, you can't eat oysters when you're drinking brandy.'

'What has it go to do with you?' she asked.

'Nothing, nothing,' he cried. 'But you can't eat oysters when you're drinking brandy.'

'I'm not drinking brandy,' she replied, and she sprinkled the last drops of her liqueur over his face. He gave an odd squeal. She sat looking at him, as if indifferent.

'Pussum, why do you do that?' he cried in panic. He gave Gerald the impression that he was terrified of her, and that he loved his terror. He seemed to relish his own horror and hatred of her, turn it over and extract every flavour from it, in real panic. Gerald thought him a strange fool, and yet piquant.

'But Pussum,' said another man, in a very small, quick Eton voice, 'you promised not to hurt him.'

'I haven't hurt him,' she answered.

'What will you drink?' the young man asked. He was dark, and smooth-skinned, and full of a stealthy vigour.

'I don't like porter, Maxim,' she replied.

'You must ask for champagne,' came the whispering, gentlemanly voice of the other.

Gerald suddenly realised that this was a hint to him.

'Shall we have champagne?' he asked, laughing.

'Yes please, dwy,' she lisped childishly.

Gerald watched her eating the oysters. She was delicate and finicking in her eating, her fingers were fine and seemed very sensitive in the tips, so she put her food apart with fine, small motions, she ate carefully, delicately. It pleased him very much to see her, and it irritated Birkin. They were all drinking champagne. Maxim, the prim young Russian with the smooth, warm-coloured face and black, oiled hair, was the only one who seemed to be perfectly calm and sober. Birkin was white and abstract, unnatural, Gerald was smiling with a constant bright, amused, cold light in his eyes, leaning a little protectively towards the Pussum, who was very handsome, and soft, unfolded like some red lotus in dreadful flowering nakedness, vainglorious now, flushed with wine and with the excitement of men. Halliday looked foolish. One glass of wine was enough to make him drunk and giggling. Yet there was always a pleasant, warm naïveté about him, that made him attractive.

'I'm not afwaid of anything except black-beetles,' said the Pussum, looking up suddenly and staring with her black eyes, on which there seemed an unseeing film of flame, fully upon Gerald. He laughed dangerously, from the blood. Her childish speech caressed his nerves, and her burning, filmed eyes, turned now full upon him, oblivious of all her antecedents, gave him a sort of licence.

'I'm not,' she protested. 'I'm not afraid of other things. But black-beetles – ugh!' she shuddered convulsively, as if the very thought were too much to bear.

'Do you mean,' said Gerald, with the punctiliousness of a man who has been drinking, 'that you are afraid of the sight of a black-beetle, or you are afraid of a black-beetle biting you, or doing you some harm?'

'Do they bite?' cried the girl.

'How perfectly loathsome!' exclaimed Halliday.

'I don't know,' replied Gerald, looking round the table. 'Do black-beetles bite? But that isn't the point. Are you afraid of their biting, or is it a metaphysical antipathy?'

The girl was looking full upon him all the time with inchoate eyes.

'Oh, I think they're beastly, they're horrid,' she cried. 'If I see one, it gives me the creeps all over. If one were to crawl on me, I'm *sure* I should die – I'm sure I should.'

'I hope not,' whispered the young Russian.

'I'm sure I should, Maxim,' she asseverated.

'Then one won't crawl on you,' said Gerald, smiling and knowing. In some strange way he understood her.

'It's metaphysical, as Gerald says,' Birkin stated.

There was a little pause of uneasiness.

'And are you afraid of nothing else, Pussum?' asked the young Russian, in his quick, hushed, elegant manner.

'Not weally,' she said. 'I am afwaid of some things, but not weally the same. I'm not afwaid of *blood*.'

'Not afwaid of blood!' exclaimed a young man with a thick, pale, jeering face, who had just come to the table and was drinking whisky.

The Pussum turned on him a sulky look of dislike, low and ugly.

'Aren't you really afraid of blud?' the other persisted, a sneer all over his face.

'No, I'm not,' she retorted.

'Why, have you ever seen blood, except in a dentist's spittoon?' jeered the young man.

'I wasn't speaking to you,' she replied rather superbly.

'You can answer me, can't you?' he said.

For reply, she suddenly jabbed a knife across his thick, pale hand. He started up with a vulgar curse.

'Shows what you are,' said the Pussum in contempt.

'Curse you,' said the young man, standing by the table and looking down at her with acrid malevolence.

'Stop that,' said Gerald, in quick, instinctive command.

The young man stood looking down at her with sardonic contempt, a cowed, self-conscious look on his thick, pale face. The blood began to flow from his hand.

'Oh, how horrible, take it away!' squealed Halliday, turning green and averting his face.

'D'you feel ill?' asked the sardonic young man, in some concern. 'Do you feel ill, Julius? Garn, it's nothing, man, don't give her the pleasure of letting her think she's performed a feat – don't give her the satisfaction, man – it's just what she wants.'

'Oh!' squealed Halliday.

'He's going to cat, Maxim,' said the Pussum warningly. The suave young Russian rose and took Halliday by the arm, leading him away. Birkin, white and diminished, looked on as if he were displeased. The wounded, sardonic young man moved away, ignoring his bleeding hand in the most conspicuous fashion.

'He's an awful coward, really,' said the Pussum to Gerald. 'He's got such an influence over Julius.'

'Who is he?' asked Gerald.

'He's a Jew, really. I can't bear him.'

'Well, he's quite unimportant. But what's wrong with Halliday?'

'Julius's the most awful coward you've ever seen,' she cried. 'He always faints if I lift a knife – he's tewwified of me.'

'H'm!' said Gerald.

'They're all afwaid of me,' she said. 'Only the Jew thinks he's going to show his courage. But he's the biggest coward of them all, really, because he's afwaid what people will think about him – and Julius doesn't care about that.'

'They've a lot of valour between them,' said Gerald good-humouredly.

The Pussum looked at him with a slow, slow smile. She was very handsome, flushed, and confident in dreadful knowledge. Two little points of light glinted on Gerald's eyes.

'Why do they call you Pussum, because you're like a cat?' he asked her.

'I expect so,' she said.

The smile grew more intense on his face.

'You are, rather; or a young, female panther.'

'Oh God, Gerald!' said Birkin, in some disgust.

They both looked uneasily at Birkin.

'You're silent tonight, Wupert,' she said to him, with a slight insolence, being safe with the other man.

Halliday was coming back, looking forlorn and sick.

'Pussum,' he said, 'I wish you wouldn't do these things – Oh!' He sank in his chair with a groan.

'You'd better go home,' she said to him.

'I *will* go home,' he said. 'But won't you all come along. Won't you come round to the flat?' he said to Gerald. 'I should be so glad if you would. Do – that'll be splendid. I say?' He looked round for a waiter. 'Get me a taxi.' Then he groaned again. 'Oh I do feel – perfectly ghastly! Pussum, you see what you do to me.'

'Then why are you such an idiot?' she said with sullen calm.

'But I'm not an idiot! Oh, how awful! Do come, everybody, it will be so splendid. Pussum, you are coming. What? Oh but you *must* come, yes, you must. What? Oh, my dear girl, don't make a fuss now, I feel perfectly – Oh, it's so ghastly – Ho! – er! Oh!'

'You know you can't drink,' she said to him, coldly.

'I tell you it isn't drink – it's your disgusting behaviour, Pussum, it's nothing else. Oh, how awful! Libidnikov, do let us go.'

'He's only drunk one glass – only one glass,' came the rapid, hushed voice of the young Russian.

They all moved off to the door. The girl kept near to Gerald, and seemed to be at one in her motion with him. He was aware of this, and filled with demon-satisfaction that his motion held good for two. He held her in the hollow of his will, and she was soft, secret, invisible in her stirring there.

They crowded five of them into the taxi-cab. Halliday lurched in first, and dropped into his seat against the other window. Then the Pussum took her place, and Gerald sat next to her. They heard the young Russian giving orders to the driver, then they were all seated in the dark, crowded close together, Halliday groaning and leaning out of the window. They felt the swift, muffled motion of the car.

The Pussum sat near to Gerald, and she seemed to become soft, subtly to infuse herself into his bones, as if she were passing into him in a black, electric flow. Her being suffused into his veins like a magnetic darkness, and concentrated at the base of his spine like a tearful source of power. Meanwhile her voice sounded out reedy and nonchalant, as she talked indifferently with Birkin and with Maxim. Between her and Gerald was this silence and this black, electric comprehension in the darkness. Then she found his hand, and grasped it in her own firm, small clasp. It was so utterly dark, and yet such a naked statement, that rapid vibrations ran through his blood and over his brain, he was no longer responsible. Still her voice rang on like a bell, tinged with a tone of mockery. And as she swung her head, her fine mane of hair just swept his face, and all his nerves were on fire, as with a subtle friction of electricity. But the great centre of his force held steady, a magnificent pride to him, at the base of his spine.

They arrived at a large block of buildings, went up in a lift, and presently a door was being opened for them by a Hindu. Gerald looked in surprise, wondering if he were a gentleman, one of the Hindus down from Oxford, perhaps. But no, he was the manservant.

'Make tea, Hasan,' said Halliday.

'There is a room for me?' said Birkin.

To both of which questions the man grinned, and murmured.

He made Gerald uncertain, because, being tall and slender and reticent, he looked like a gentleman.

'Who is your servant?' he asked of Halliday. 'He looks a swell.'

'Oh yes – that's because he's dressed in another man's clothes. He's anything but a swell, really. We found him in the road, starving. So I took him here, and another man gave him clothes. He's anything but what he seems to be – his only advantage is that he can't speak English and can't understand it, so he's perfectly safe.'

'He's very dirty,' said the young Russian swiftly and silently.

Directly, the man appeared in the doorway.

'What is it?' said Halliday.

The Hindu grinned, and murmured shyly, 'Want to speak to master.'

Gerald watched curiously. The fellow in the doorway was good-looking and clean-limbed, his bearing was calm, he looked elegant, aristocratic. Yet he was half a savage, grinning foolishly. Halliday went out into the corridor to speak with him.

'What?' they heard his voice. 'What? What do you say? Tell me again. What? Want money? Want *more* money? But what do you want money for?' There was the confused sound of the Hindu's talking, then Halliday appeared in the room, smiling also foolishly, and saying, 'He says he wants money to buy underclothing. Can anybody lend me a shilling? Oh thanks, a shilling will do to buy all the underclothes he wants.' He took the money from Gerald and went out into the passage again, where they heard him saying, 'You can't want more money, you had three and six yesterday. You mustn't ask for any more. Bring the tea in quickly.'

Gerald looked round the room. It was an ordinary London sitting-room in a flat, evidently taken furnished, rather common and ugly. But there were several negro statues, wood-carvings from West Africa, strange and disturbing, the carved negroes looked almost like the foetus of a human being. One was a woman sitting naked in a strange posture, and looking tortured, her abdomen stuck out. The young Russian explained that she was sitting in childbirth, clutching the ends of the band that hung from her neck, one in each hand, so that she could bear down, and help labour. The strange, transfixed, rudimentary face of the woman again reminded Gerald of a foetus, it was also rather wonderful, conveying the suggestion of the extreme of physical sensation, beyond the limits of mental consciousness.

'Aren't they rather obscene?' he asked, disapproving.

'I don't know,' murmured the other rapidly. 'I have never defined the obscene. I think they are very good.'

Gerald turned away. There were one or two new pictures in the room, in the Futurist manner; there was a large piano. And these, with some ordinary London lodging-house furniture of the better sort, completed the whole.

The Pussum had taken off her hat and coat, and was seated on the sofa. She was evidently quite at home in the house, but uncertain, suspended. She did not quite know her position. Her alliance for the time being was with Gerald, and she did not know how far this was admitted by any of the men. She was considering how she should carry off the situation. She was determined to have her experience. Now, at this eleventh hour, she was not to be baulked. Her face was flushed as with battle, her eye was brooding but inevitable.

The man came in with tea and a bottle of kümmel. He set the tray on a little table before the couch.

'Pussum,' said Halliday, 'pour out the tea.'

She did not move.

'Won't you do it?' Halliday repeated, in a state of nervous apprehension.

'I've not come back here as it was before,' she said. 'I only came because the others wanted me to, not for your sake.'

'My dear Pussum, you know you are your own mistress. I don't want you to do anything but use the flat for your own convenience – you know it, I've told you so many times.'

She did not reply, but silently, reservedly reached for the teapot. They all sat round and drank tea. Gerald could feel the electric connection between him and her so strongly, as she sat there quiet and withheld, that another set of conditions altogether had come to pass. Her silence and her immutability perplexed him. *How* was he going to come to her? And yet he felt it quite inevitable. He trusted completely to the current that held them. His perplexity was only superficial, new conditions reigned, the old were surpassed; here one did as one was possessed to do, no matter what it was.

Birkin rose. It was nearly one o'clock.

'I'm going to bed,' he said. 'Gerald, I'll ring you up in the morning at your place or you ring me up here.'

'Right,' said Gerald, and Birkin went out.

When he was well gone, Halliday said in a stimulated voice, to Gerald, 'I say, won't you stay here – oh do!'

'You can't put everybody up,' said Gerald.

'Oh but I can, perfectly – there are three more beds besides mine – do stay, won't you. Everything is quite ready – there is always somebody here – I always put people up – I love having the house crowded.'

'But there are only two rooms,' said the Pussum, in a cold, hostile voice, 'now Rupert's here.'

'I know there are only two rooms,' said Halliday, in his odd, high way of speaking. 'But what does that matter?'

He was smiling rather foolishly, and he spoke eagerly, with an insinuating determination.

'Julius and I will share one room,' said the Russian in his discreet, precise voice. Halliday and he were friends since Eton.

'It's very simple,' said Gerald, rising and pressing back his arms, stretching himself. Then he went again to look at one of the pictures. Every one of his limbs was turgid with electric force, and his back was tense like a tiger's, with slumbering fire. He was very proud.

The Pussum rose. She gave a black look at Halliday, black and deadly, which brought the rather foolishly pleased smile to that young man's face. Then she went out of the room, with a cold good-night to them all generally.

There was a brief interval, they heard a door close, then Maxim said, in his refined voice, 'That's all right.'

He looked significantly at Gerald, and said again, with a silent nod, 'That's all right – you're all right.'

Gerald looked at the smooth, ruddy, comely face, and at the strange, significant eyes, and it seemed as if the voice of the young Russian, so small and perfect, sounded in the blood rather than in the air.

'I'm all right then,' said Gerald.

'Yes! Yes! You're all right,' said the Russian.

Halliday continued to smile, and to say nothing.

Suddenly the Pussum appeared again in the door, her small, childish face looking sullen and vindictive.

'I know you want to catch me out,' came her cold, rather resonant voice. 'But I don't care, I don't care how much you catch me out.'

She turned and was gone again. She had been wearing a loose dressing-gown of purple silk, tied round her waist. She looked so small and childish and vulnerable, almost pitiful. And yet the black looks of her eyes made Gerald feel drowned in some potent darkness that almost frightened him.

The men lit another cigarette and talked casually.

CHAPTER 7

Fetish

In the morning Gerald woke late. He had slept heavily. Pussum was still asleep, sleeping childishly and pathetically. There was something small and curled up and defenceless about her, that roused an unsatisfied flame of passion in the young man's blood, a devouring avid pity. He looked at her again. But it would be too cruel to wake her. He subdued himself, and went away.

Hearing voices coming from the sitting-room, Halliday talking to Libidnikov, he went to the door and glanced in. He had on a silk wrap of a beautiful bluish colour, with an amethyst hem.

To his surprise he saw the two young men by the fire, stark naked. Halliday looked up, rather pleased.

'Good-morning,' he said. 'Oh – did you want towels?' And stark naked he went out into the hall, striding a strange, white figure between the unliving furniture. He came back with the towels, and took his former position, crouching seated before the fire on the fender.

'Don't you love to feel the fire on your skin?' he said.

'It *is* rather pleasant,' said Gerald.

'How perfectly splendid it must be to be in a climate where one could do without clothing altogether,' said Halliday.

'Yes,' said Gerald, 'if there weren't so many things that sting and bite.'

'That's a disadvantage,' murmured Maxim.

Gerald looked at him, and with a slight revulsion saw the human animal, golden skinned and bare, somehow humiliating. Halliday was different. He had a rather heavy, slack, broken beauty, white and firm. He was like a Christ in a *pietà*. The animal was not there at all, only the heavy, broken beauty. And Gerald realised how Halliday's eyes were beautiful too, so blue and warm and confused, broken also in their expression. The fire-glow fell on his heavy, rather bowed shoulders, he sat slackly crouched on the fender, his face was uplifted, weak, perhaps slightly disintegrate, and yet with a moving beauty of its own.

'Of course,' said Maxim, 'you've been in hot countries where the people go about naked.'

'Oh really!' exclaimed Halliday. 'Where?'

'South America – Amazon,' said Gerald.

'Oh but how perfectly splendid! It's one of the things I want most to do – to live from day to day without *ever* putting on any sort of clothing whatever. If I could do that, I should feel I had lived.'

'But why?' said Gerald. 'I can't see that it makes so much difference.'

'Oh, I think it would be perfectly splendid. I'm sure life would be entirely another thing – entirely different, and perfectly wonderful.'

'But why?' asked Gerald. 'Why should it?'

'Oh – one would *feel* things instead of merely looking at them. I should feel the air move against me, and feel the things I touched, instead of having only to look at them. I'm sure life is all wrong because it has become much too visual – we can neither hear nor feel nor understand, we can only see. I'm sure that is entirely wrong.'

'Yes, that is true, that is true,' said the Russian.

Gerald glanced at him, and saw him, his suave, golden coloured body with the black hair growing fine and freely, like tendrils, and his limbs like smooth plant-stems. He was so healthy and well-made, why did he make one ashamed, why did one feel repelled? Why should Gerald even dislike it, why did it seem to him to detract from his own dignity. Was that all a human being amounted to? So uninspired! thought Gerald.

Birkin suddenly appeared in the doorway, in white pyjamas and wet hair, and a towel over his arm. He was aloof and white, and somehow evanescent.

'There's the bathroom now, if you want it,' he said generally, and was going away again, when Gerald called, 'I say, Rupert!'

'What?' The single white figure appeared again, a presence in the room.

'What do you think of that figure there? I want to know,' Gerald asked.

Birkin, white and strangely ghostly, went over to the carved figure of the negro woman in labour. Her nude, protuberant body crouched in a strange, clutching posture, her hands gripping the ends of the band, above her breast.

'It is art,' said Birkin.

'Very beautiful, it's very beautiful,' said the Russian.

They all drew near to look. Gerald looked at the group of men, the Russian golden and like a water-plant, Halliday tall and heavily, brokenly beautiful, Birkin very white and indefinite, not to be assigned, as he looked closely at the carven woman. Strangely elated, Gerald also lifted his eyes to the face of the wooden figure. And his heart contracted.

He saw vividly with his spirit the grey, forward-stretching face of the negro woman, African and tense, abstracted in utter physical stress. It was a terrible face, void, peaked, abstracted almost into meaninglessness by the weight of sensation beneath. He saw the Pussum in it. As in a dream, he knew her.

'Why is it art?' Gerald asked, shocked, resentful.

'It conveys a complete truth,' said Birkin. 'It contains the whole truth of that state, whatever you feel about it.'

'But you can't call it *high* art,' said Gerald.

'High! There are centuries and hundreds of centuries of development in a straight line, behind that carving; it is an awful pitch of culture, of a definite sort.'

'What culture?' Gerald asked, in opposition. He hated the sheer African thing.

'Pure culture in sensation, culture in the physical consciousness, really ultimate *physical* consciousness, mindless, utterly sensual. It is so sensual as to be final, supreme.'

But Gerald resented it. He wanted to keep certain illusions, certain ideas like clothing.

'You like the wrong things, Rupert,' he said, 'things against yourself.'

'Oh, I know, this isn't everything,' Birkin replied, moving away.

When Gerald went back to his room from the bath, he also carried his clothes. He was so conventional at home, that when he was really away, and on the loose, as now, he enjoyed nothing so much as full outrageousness. So he strode with his blue silk wrap over his arm and felt defiant.

The Pussum lay in her bed, motionless, her round, dark eyes like black, unhappy pools. He could only see the black, bottomless pools of her eyes. Perhaps she suffered. The sensation of her inchoate suffering roused the old sharp flame in him, a mordant pity, a passion almost of cruelty.

'You are awake now,' he said to her.

'What time is it?' came her muted voice.

She seemed to flow back, almost like liquid, from his approach, to sink helplessly away from him. Her inchoate look of a violated slave, whose fulfilment lies in her further and further violation, made his nerves quiver with acutely desirable sensation. After all, his was the only will, she was the passive substance of his will. He tingled with the subtle, biting sensation. And then he knew, he must go away from her, there must be pure separation between them.

It was a quiet and ordinary breakfast, the four men all looking very clean and bathed. Gerald and the Russian were both correct and *comme il faut* in appearance and manner, Birkin was gaunt and sick, and looked a failure in his attempt to be a properly dressed man, like Gerald and Maxim. Halliday wore tweeds and a green flannel shirt, and a rag of a tie, which was just right for him. The Hindu brought in a great deal of soft toast, and looked exactly the same as he had looked the night before, statically the same.

At the end of the breakfast the Pussum appeared, in a purple silk wrap with a shimmering sash. She had recovered herself somewhat, but was mute and lifeless still. It was a torment to her when anybody spoke to her. Her face was like a small, fine mask, sinister too, masked with unwilling suffering. It was almost midday. Gerald rose and went away to his business, glad to get out. But he had not finished. He was coming back again at evening, they were all dining together, and he had booked seats for the party, excepting Birkin, at a music-hall.

At night they came back to the flat very late again, again flushed with drink. Again the manservant – who invariably disappeared between the hours of ten and twelve at night – came in silently and inscrutably with tea, bending in a slow, strange, leopard-like fashion to put the tray softly on the table. His face was immutable, aristocratic-looking, tinged slightly with grey under the skin; he was young and good-looking. But Birkin felt a slight sickness, looking at him, and feeling the slight greyness as an ash or a corruption, in the aristocratic inscrutability of expression a nauseating, bestial stupidity.

Again they talked cordially and rousedly together. But already a certain friability was coming over the party, Birkin was mad with irritation, Halliday was turning in an insane hatred against Gerald, the Pussum was becoming hard and cold, like a flint knife, and Halliday was laying himself out to her. And her intention, ultimately, was to capture Halliday, to have complete power over him.

In the morning they all stalked and lounged about again. But Gerald could feel a strange hostility to himself in the air. It roused his obstinacy, and he stood up against it. He hung on for two more days. The result was a nasty and insane scene with Halliday on the fourth evening. Halliday turned with absurd animosity upon Gerald, in the café. There was a row. Gerald was on the point of knocking-in Halliday's face; when he was filled with sudden disgust and indifference, and he went away, leaving Halliday in a foolish state of gloating triumph, the Pussum hard and established, and Maxim standing clear. Birkin was absent, he had gone out of town again.

Gerald was piqued because he had left without giving the Pussum money. It was true, she did not care whether he gave her money or not, and he knew it. But she would have been glad of ten pounds, and he would have been *very* glad to give them to her. Now he felt in a false position. He went away chewing his lips to get at the ends of his short clipped moustache. He knew the Pussum was merely glad to be rid of him. She had got her Halliday whom she wanted. She wanted him completely in her power. Then she would marry him. She wanted to marry him. She had set her will on marrying Halliday. She never wanted to hear of Gerald again; unless, perhaps, she were in difficulty; because after all, Gerald was what she called a man, and these others, Halliday, Libidnikov, Birkin, the whole Bohemian set, they were only half men. But it was half men she could deal with. She felt sure of herself with them. The real men, like Gerald, put her in her place too much.

Still, she respected Gerald, she really respected him. She had managed to get his address, so that she could appeal to him in time of distress. She knew he wanted to give her money. She would perhaps write to him on that inevitable rainy day.

CHAPTER 8

Breadalby

Breadalby was a Georgian house with Corinthian pillars, standing among the softer, greener hills of Derbyshire, not far from Cromford. In front, it looked over a lawn, over a few trees, down to a string of fish-ponds in the hollow of the silent park. At the back were trees, among which were to be found the stables, and the big kitchen garden, behind which was a wood.

It was a very quiet place, some miles from the highroad, back from the Derwent Valley, outside the show scenery. Silent and forsaken, the golden stucco showed between the trees, the house-front looked down the park, unchanged and unchanging.

Of late, however, Hermione had lived a good deal at the house. She had turned away from London, away from Oxford, towards the silence of the country. Her father was mostly absent, abroad, she was either alone in the house, with her visitors, of whom there were always several, or she had with her her brother, a bachelor, and a Liberal member of Parliament. He always came down when the House was not sitting, seemed always to be present in Breadalby, although he was most conscientious in his attendance to duty.

The summer was just coming in when Ursula and Gudrun went to stay the second time with Hermione. Coming along in the car, after they had entered the park, they looked across the dip, where the fish-ponds lay in silence, at the pillared front of the house, sunny and small like an English drawing of the old school, on the brow of the green hill, against the trees. There were small figures on the green lawn, women in lavender and yellow moving to the shade of the enormous, beautifully balanced cedar tree.

'Isn't it complete!' said Gudrun. 'It is as final as an old aquatint.' She spoke with some resentment in her voice, as if she were captivated unwillingly, as if she must admire against her will.

'Do you love it?' asked Ursula.

'I don't *love* it, but in its way, I think it is quite complete.'

The motor car ran down the hill and up again in one breath, and they were curving to the side door. A parlourmaid appeared, and then Hermione, coming forward with her pale face lifted, and her hands outstretched, advancing straight to the newcomers, her voice singing, 'Here you are – I'm so glad to see you – ' she kissed Gudrun – 'so glad to see you – ' she kissed Ursula and remained with her arm round her. 'Are you very tired?'

'Not at all tired,' said Ursula.

'Are you tired, Gudrun?'

'Not at all, thanks,' said Gudrun.

'No –' drawled Hermione. And she stood and looked at them. The two girls were embarrassed because she would not move into the house, but must have her little scene of welcome there on the path. The servants waited.

'Come in,' said Hermione at last, having fully taken in the pair of them. Gudrun was the more beautiful and attractive, she had decided again, Ursula was more physical, more womanly. She admired Gudrun's dress more. It was of green poplin, with a loose coat above it, of broad, dark-green and dark-brown stripes. The hat was of a pale, greenish straw, the colour of new hay, and it had a plaited ribbon of black and orange, the stockings were dark green, the shoes black. It was a good get-up, at once fashionable and individual. Ursula, in dark blue, was more ordinary, though she also looked well.

Hermione herself wore a dress of prune-coloured silk, with coral beads and coral-coloured stockings. But her dress was both shabby and soiled, even rather dirty.

'You would like to see your rooms now, wouldn't you! Yes. We will go up now, shall we?'

Ursula was glad when she could be left alone in her room. Hermione lingered so long, made such a stress on one. She stood so near to one, pressing herself near upon one, in a way that was most embarrassing and oppressive. She seemed to hinder one's workings.

Lunch was served on the lawn, under the great tree, whose thick, blackish boughs came down close to the grass. There were present a young Italian woman, slight and fashionable, a young, athletic-looking Miss Bradley, a learned, dry Baronet of fifty, who was always making witticisms and laughing at them heartily in a harsh, horse-laugh, there was Rupert Birkin, and then a woman secretary, a Fräulein März, young and slim and pretty.

The food was very good, that was one thing. Gudrun, critical of everything, gave it her full approval. Ursula loved the situation, the white table by the cedar tree, the scent of new sunshine, the little vision of the leafy park, with far-off deer feeding peacefully. There seemed a magic circle drawn about the place, shutting out the present, enclosing the delightful, precious past, trees and deer and silence, like a dream.

But in spirit she was unhappy. The talk went on like a rattle of small artillery, always slightly sententious, with a sententiousness that was only emphasised by the continual crackling of a witticism, the continual spatter of verbal jest, designed to give a tone of flippancy to a stream of conversation that was all critical and general, a canal of conversation rather than a stream.

The attitude was mental and very wearying. Only the elderly sociologist, whose mental fibre was so tough as to be insentient, seemed to be thoroughly happy. Birkin was down in the mouth. Hermione appeared, with amazing persistence, to wish to ridicule him and make him look ignominious in the eyes of everybody. And it was surprising how she seemed to succeed, how helpless he seemed against her. He looked completely insignificant. Ursula and Gudrun, both very unused, were mostly silent, listening to the slow, rhapsodic singsong of Hermione, or the verbal sallies of Sir Joshua, or the prattle of Fräulein, or the responses of the other two women.

Luncheon was over, coffee was brought out on the grass, the party left the table and sat about in lounge chairs, in the shade or in the sunshine as they wished. Fräulein departed into the house, Hermione took up her embroidery, the little contessa took a book, Miss Bradley was weaving a basket out of fine grass, and there they all were on the lawn in the early summer afternoon, working leisurely and spattering with half-intellectual, deliberate talk.

Suddenly there was the sound of the brakes and the shutting off of a motor car.

'There's Salsie!' sang Hermione, in her slow, amusing singsong. And laying down her work, she rose slowly, and slowly passed over the lawn, round the bushes, out of sight.

'Who is it?' asked Gudrun.

'Mr Roddice – Miss Roddice's brother – at least, I suppose it's he,' said Sir Joshua.

'Salsie, yes, it is her brother,' said the little contessa, lifting her head for a moment from her book, and speaking as if to give information, in her slightly deepened, guttural English.

They all waited. And then round the bushes came the tall form of Alexander Roddice, striding romantically like a Meredith hero who remembers Disraeli. He was cordial with everybody, he was at once a host, with an easy, offhand hospitality that he had learned for Hermione's friends. He had just come down from London, from the House. At once the atmosphere of the House of Commons made itself felt over the lawn: the Home Secretary had said such and such a thing, and he, Roddice, on the other hand, thought such and such a thing, and had said so-and-so to the PM.

Now Hermione came round the bushes with Gerald Crich. He had come along with Alexander. Gerald was presented to everybody, was kept by Hermione for a few moments in full view, then he was led away, still by Hermione. He was evidently her guest of the moment.

There had been a split in the Cabinet; the Minister for Education had resigned owing to adverse criticism. This started a conversation on education.

'Of course,' said Hermione, lifting her face like a rhapsodist, 'there *can* be no reason, no *excuse* for education, except the joy and beauty of knowledge in itself.' She seemed to rumble and ruminate with subterranean thoughts for a minute, then she proceeded: 'Vocational education *isn't* education, it is the close of education.'

Gerald, on the brink of discussion, sniffed the air with delight and prepared for action.

'Not necessarily,' he said. 'But isn't education really like gymnastics, isn't the end of education the production of a well-trained, vigorous, energetic mind?'

'Just as athletics produce a healthy body, ready for anything,' cried Miss Bradley, in hearty accord.

Gudrun looked at her in silent loathing.

'Well – ' rumbled Hermione, 'I don't know. To me the pleasure of knowing is so great, so *wonderful* – nothing has meant so much to me in all life, as certain knowledge – no, I am sure – nothing.'

'What knowledge, for example, Hermione?' asked Alexander.

Hermione lifted her face and rumbled –

'M–m–m – I don't know . . . But one thing was the stars, when I really understood something about the stars. One feels so *uplifted*, so *unbounded* . . . '

Birkin looked at her in a white fury.

'What do you want to feel unbounded for?' he said sarcastically. 'You don't want to *be* unbounded.'

Hermione recoiled in offence.

'Yes, but one does have that limitless feeling,' said Gerald. 'It's like getting on top of the mountain and seeing the Pacific.'

'Silent, upon a peak in Dariayn,' murmured the Italian, lifting her face for a moment from her book.

'Not necessarily in Darien,' said Gerald, while Ursula began to laugh.

Hermione waited for the dust to settle, and then she said, untouched, 'Yes, it is the greatest thing in life – to *know*. It is really to be happy, to be *free*.'

'Knowledge is, of course, liberty,' said Mattheson.

'In compressed tabloids,' said Birkin, looking at the dry, stiff little body of the Baronet. Immediately Gudrun saw the famous sociologist as a flat bottle, containing tabloids of compressed liberty. That pleased her. Sir Joshua was labelled and placed for ever in her mind.

'What does that mean, Rupert?' sang Hermione, in a calm snub.

'You can only have knowledge, strictly,' he replied, 'of things concluded, in the past. It's like bottling the liberty of last summer in the bottled gooseberries.'

'*Can* one have knowledge only of the past?' asked the Baronet, pointedly. 'Could we call our knowledge of the laws of gravitation for instance, knowledge of the past?'

'Yes,' said Birkin.

'There is a most beautiful thing in my book,' suddenly piped the little Italian woman. 'It says the man came to the door and threw his eyes down the street.'

There was a general laugh in the company. Miss Bradley went and looked over the shoulder of the contessa.

'See!' said the contessa.

'Bazarov came to the door and threw his eyes hurriedly down the street,' she read.

Again there was a loud laugh, the most startling of which was the Baronet's, which rattled out like a clatter of falling stones.

'What is the book?' asked Alexander, promptly.

'*Fathers and Sons* by Turgenev,' said the little foreigner, pronouncing every syllable distinctly. She looked at the cover, to verify herself.

'An old American edition,' said Birkin.

'Ha! – of course – translated from the French,' said Alexander, with a fine declamatory voice. '*Bazarov ouvra la porte et jeta les yeux dans la rue.*'

He looked brightly round the company.

'I wonder what the "hurriedly" was,' said Ursula.

They all began to guess.

And then, to the amazement of everybody, the maid came hurrying with a large tea-tray. The afternoon had passed so swiftly.

After tea, they were all gathered for a walk.

'Would you like to come for a walk?' said Hermione to each of them, one by one. And they all said yes, feeling somehow like prisoners marshalled for exercise. Birkin only refused.

'Will you come for a walk, Rupert?'

'No, Hermione.'

'But are you *sure*?'

'Quite sure.' There was a second's hesitation.

'And why not?' sang Hermione's question. It made her blood run sharp, to be thwarted in even so trifling a matter. She intended them all to walk with her in the park.

'Because I don't like trooping off in a gang,' he said.

Her voice rumbled in her throat for a moment. Then she said, with a curious stray calm, 'Then we'll leave a little boy behind, if he's sulky.'

And she looked really gay, while she insulted him. But it merely made him stiff.

She trailed off to the rest of the company, only turning to wave her handkerchief to him, and to chuckle with laughter, singing out, 'Goodbye, goodbye, little boy.'

'Goodbye, impudent hag,' he said to himself.

They all went through the park. Hermione wanted to show them the wild daffodils on a little slope. 'This way, this way,' sang her leisurely voice at intervals. And they had all to come this way. The daffodils were pretty, but who could see them? Ursula was stiff all over with resentment by this time, resentment of the whole atmosphere. Gudrun, mocking and objective, watched and registered everything.

They looked at the shy deer, and Hermione talked to the stag, as if he too were a boy she wanted to wheedle and fondle. He was male, so she must exert some kind of power over him. They trailed home by the fish-ponds, and Hermione told them about the quarrel of two male swans, who had striven for the love of the one lady. She chuckled and laughed as she told how the ousted lover had sat with his head buried under his wing, on the gravel.

When they arrived back at the house, Hermione stood on the lawn and sang out, in a strange, small, high voice that carried very far, 'Rupert! Rupert!' The first syllable was high and slow, the second dropped down. 'Roo–o–opert.'

But there was no answer. A maid appeared.

'Where is Mr Birkin, Alice?' asked the mild straying voice of Hermione. But under the straying voice, what a persistent, almost insane *will*!

'I think he's in his room, madam.'

'Is he?'

Hermione went slowly up the stairs, along the corridor, singing out in her high, small call, 'Ru–oo–pert! Ru–oo–pert!'

She came to his door, and tapped, still crying: 'Roo–pert.'

'Yes,' sounded his voice at last.

'What are you doing?'

The question was mild and curious.

There was no answer. Then he opened the door.

'We've come back,' said Hermione. 'The daffodils are *so* beautiful.'

'Yes,' he said, 'I've seen them.'

She looked at him with her long, slow, impassive look, along her cheeks.

'Have you?' she echoed. And she remained looking at him. She was stimulated above all things by this conflict with him, when he was like a sulky boy, helpless, and she had him safe at Breadalby. But underneath she knew the split was coming, and her hatred of him was subconscious and intense.

'What were you doing?' she reiterated, in her mild, indifferent tone. He did not answer, and she made her way, almost unconsciously, into his room. He had taken a Chinese drawing of geese from the boudoir, and was copying it, with much skill and vividness.

'You are copying the drawing,' she said, standing near the table, and looking down at his work. 'Yes. How beautifully you do it! You like it very much, don't you?'

'It's a marvellous drawing,' he said.

'Is it? I'm so glad you like it, because I've always been fond of it. The Chinese Ambassador gave it me.'

'I know,' he said.

'But why do you copy it?' she asked, casual and singsong. 'Why not do something original?'

'I want to know it,' he replied. 'One gets more of China, copying this picture, than reading all the books.'

'And what do you get?'

She was at once roused, she laid as it were violent hands on him, to extract his secrets from him. She *must* know. It was a dreadful tyranny, an obsession in her, to know all he knew. For some time he was silent, hating to answer her. Then, compelled, he began, 'I know what centres they live from – what they perceive and feel – the hot, stinging centrality of a goose in the flux of cold water and mud – the curious bitter stinging heat of a goose's blood, entering their own blood like an inoculation of corruptive fire – fire of the cold-burning mud – the lotus mystery.'

Hermione looked at him along her narrow, pallid cheeks. Her eyes were strange and drugged, heavy under their heavy, drooping lids. Her thin bosom shrugged convulsively. He stared back at her, devilish and unchanging. With another strange, sick convulsion, she turned away, as if she were sick, could feel dissolution setting in in her body. For with her mind she was unable to attend to his words, he caught her, as it were, beneath all her defences, and destroyed her with some insidious occult potency.

'Yes,' she said, as if she did not know what she were saying. 'Yes,' and she swallowed, and tried to regain her mind. But she could not, she was witless, decentralised. Use all her will as she might, she could not recover. She suffered the ghastliness of dissolution, broken and gone in a horrible corruption. And he stood and looked at her unmoved. She strayed out, pallid and preyed-upon like a ghost, like one attacked by the tomb-influences which dog us. And she was gone like a corpse, that has no presence, no connection. He remained hard and vindictive.

Hermione came down to dinner strange and sepulchral, her eyes heavy and full of sepulchral darkness, strength. She had put on a dress of stiff old greenish brocade, that fitted tight and made her look tall and rather terrible, ghastly. In the gay light of the drawing-room she was uncanny and oppressive. But seated in the half light of the dining-room, sitting stiffly before the shaded candles on the table, she seemed a power, a presence. She listened and attended with a drugged attention.

The party was gay and extravagant in appearance, everybody had put on evening dress except Birkin and Joshua Mattheson. The little Italian contessa wore a dress of tissue, of orange and gold and black velvet in soft wide stripes, Gudrun was emerald green with strange network, Ursula was in yellow with dull silver veiling, Miss Bradley was of grey, crimson and jet, Fräulein März wore pale blue. It gave Hermione a sudden convulsive sensation of pleasure, to see these rich colours under the candlelight. She was aware of the talk going on, ceaselessly, Joshua's voice dominating; of the ceaseless pitter-patter of women's light laughter and responses; of the brilliant colours and the white table and the shadow above and below; and she seemed in a swoon of gratification, convulsed with pleasure and yet sick, like a *revenant*. She took very little part in the conversation, yet she heard it all, it was all hers.

They all went together into the drawing-room, as if they were one family, easily, without any attention to ceremony. Fräulein handed the coffee, everybody smoked cigarettes, or else long warden pipes of white clay, of which a sheaf was provided.

'Will you smoke? – cigarettes or pipe?' asked Fräulein prettily. There was a circle of people, Sir Joshua with his eighteenth-century appearance, Gerald the amused, handsome young Englishman, Alexander tall and the handsome politician, democratic and lucid, Hermione strange like a long Cassandra, and the women lurid with colour, all dutifully smoking their long white pipes, and sitting in a half-moon in the comfortable, soft-lighted drawing-room, round the logs that flickered on the marble hearth.

The talk was very often political or sociological, and interesting, curiously anarchistic. There was an accumulation of powerful force in the room, powerful and destructive. Everything seemed to be thrown into the melting pot, and it seemed to Ursula they were all witches, helping the pot to bubble. There was an elation and a satisfaction in it all, but it was cruelly exhausting for the newcomers, this ruthless mental pressure, this powerful, consuming, destructive mentality that emanated from Joshua and Hermione and Birkin and dominated the rest.

But a sickness, a fearful nausea gathered possession of Hermione. There was a lull in the talk, as it was arrested by her unconscious but all-powerful will.

'Salsie, won't you play something?' said Hermione, breaking off completely. 'Won't somebody dance? Gudrun, you will dance, won't you? I wish you would. *Anche tu, Palestra, ballerai? – sì, per piacere.* You too, Ursula.'

Hermione rose and slowly pulled the gold-embroidered band that hung by the mantel, clinging to it for a moment, then releasing it suddenly. Like a priestess she looked, unconscious, sunk in a heavy half-trance.

A servant came, and soon reappeared with armfuls of silk robes and shawls and scarves, mostly oriental, things that Hermione, with her love for beautiful extravagant dress, had collected gradually.

'The three women will dance together,' she said.

'What shall it be?' asked Alexander, rising briskly.

'*Vergini delle Rocchette*,' said the contessa at once.

'They are so languid,' said Ursula.

'The three witches from Macbeth,' suggested Fräulein usefully. It was finally decided to do Naomi and Ruth and Orpah. Ursula was Naomi, Gudrun was Ruth, the contessa was Orpah. The idea was to make a little ballet, in the style of the Russian Ballet of Pavlova and Nijinsky.

The contessa was ready first, Alexander went to the piano, a space was cleared. Orpah, in beautiful oriental clothes, began slowly to dance the death of her husband. Then Ruth came, and they wept together, and lamented, then Naomi came to comfort them. It was all done in dumb show, the women danced their emotion in gesture and motion. The little drama went on for a quarter of an hour.

Ursula was beautiful as Naomi. All her men were dead, it remained to her only to stand alone in indomitable assertion, demanding nothing. Ruth, woman-loving, loved her. Orpah, a vivid, sensational, subtle widow, would go back to the former life, a repetition. The interplay between the women was real and rather frightening. It was strange to see how Gudrun clung with heavy, desperate passion to Ursula, yet smiled with subtle malevolence against her, how Ursula accepted silently, unable to provide any more either for herself or for the other, but dangerous and indomitable, refuting her grief.

Hermione loved to watch. She could see the contessa's rapid, stoat-like sensationalism, Gudrun's ultimate but treacherous cleaving to the woman in her sister, Ursula's dangerous helplessness, as if she were helplessly weighted, and unreleased.

'That was very beautiful,' everybody cried with one accord. But Hermione writhed in her soul, knowing what she could not know. She cried out for more dancing, and it was her will that set the contessa and Birkin moving mockingly in Malbrouk.

Gerald was excited by the desperate cleaving of Gudrun to Naomi. The essence of that female, subterranean recklessness and mockery penetrated his blood. He could not forget Gudrun's lifted, offered, cleaving, reckless, yet withal mocking weight. And Birkin, watching like a hermit crab from its hole, had seen the brilliant frustration and helplessness of Ursula. She was rich, full of dangerous power. She was like a strange unconscious bud of powerful woman-hood. He was unconsciously drawn to her. She was his future.

Alexander played some Hungarian music, and they all danced, seized by the spirit. Gerald was marvellously exhilarated at finding himself in motion, moving towards Gudrun, dancing with feet that could not yet escape from the waltz and the two-step, but feeling his force stir along his limbs and his body, out of captivity. He did not know yet how to dance their convulsive, ragtime sort of dancing, but he knew how to begin. Birkin, when he could get free from the weight of the people present, whom he disliked, danced rapidly and with a real gaiety. And how Hermione hated him for this irresponsible gaiety.

'Now I see,' cried the contessa excitedly, watching his purely gay motion, which he had all to himself. 'Mr Birkin, he is a changer.'

Hermione looked at her slowly, and shuddered, knowing that only a foreigner could have seen and have said this.

'*Cosa vuol'dire, Palestra*?' she asked, singsong.

'Look,' said the contessa, in Italian. 'He is not a man, he is a chameleon, a creature of change.'

'He is not a man, he is treacherous, not one of us,' said itself over in Hermione's consciousness. And her soul writhed in the black subjugation to him, because of his power to escape, to exist, other than she did, because he was not consistent, not a man, less than a man. She hated him in a despair that shattered her and broke her down, so that she suffered sheer dissolution like a corpse, and was unconscious of everything save the horrible sickness of dissolution that was taking place within her, body and soul.

The house being full, Gerald was given the smaller room, really the dressing-room, communicating with Birkin's bedroom. When they all took their candles and mounted the stairs, where the lamps were burning subduedly, Hermione captured Ursula and brought her into her own bedroom, to talk to her. A sort of constraint came over Ursula in the big, strange bedroom. Hermione seemed to be bearing down on her, awful and inchoate, making some appeal. They were looking at some Indian silk shirts, gorgeous and sensual in themselves, their shape, their almost corrupt gorgeousness. And Hermione came near, and her bosom writhed, and Ursula was for a moment blank with panic. And for a moment Hermione's haggard eyes saw the fear on the face of the other, there was again a sort of crash, a crashing down. And Ursula picked up a shirt of rich red and blue silk, made for a young princess of fourteen, and was crying mechanically, 'Isn't it wonderful – who would dare to put those two strong colours together – '

Then Hermione's maid entered silently and Ursula, overcome with dread, escaped, carried away by powerful impulse.

Birkin went straight to bed. He was feeling happy, and sleepy. Since he had danced he was happy. But Gerald would talk to him. Gerald, in evening dress, sat on Birkin's bed when the other lay down, and must talk.

'Who are those two Brangwens?' Gerald asked.

'They live in Beldover.'

'In Beldover! Who are they then?'

'Teachers in the Grammar School.'

There was a pause.

'They are!' exclaimed Gerald at length. 'I thought I had seen them before.'

'It disappoints you?' said Birkin.

'Disappoints me! No – but how is it Hermione has them here?'

'She knew Gudrun in London – that's the younger one, the one with the darker hair – she's an artist – does sculpture and modelling.'

'She's not a teacher in the Grammar School, then – only the other?'

'Both – Gudrun art mistress, Ursula a class mistress.'

'And what's the father?'

'Handicraft instructor in the schools.'

'Really!'

'Class-barriers are breaking down!'

Gerald was always uneasy under the slightly jeering tone of the other.

'That their father is handicraft instructor in a school! What does it matter to me?'

Birkin laughed. Gerald looked at his face, as it lay there laughing and bitter and indifferent on the pillow, and he could not go away.

'I don't suppose you will see very much more of Gudrun, at least. She is a restless bird, she'll be gone in a week or two,' said Birkin.

'Where will she go?'

'London, Paris, Rome – heaven knows. I always expect her to sheer off to Damascus or San Francisco; she's a bird of paradise. God knows what she's got to do with Beldover. It goes by contraries, like dreams.'

Gerald pondered for a few moments.

'How do you know her so well?' he asked.

'I knew her in London,' he replied, 'in the Algernon Strange set. She'll know about Pussum and Libidnikov and the rest – even if she doesn't know them personally. She was never quite that set – more conventional, in a way. I've known her for two years, I suppose.'

'And she makes money, apart from her teaching?' asked Gerald.

'Some – irregularly. She can sell her models. She has a certain *réclame*.'

'How much for?'

'A guinea, ten guineas.'

'And are they good? What are they?'

'I think sometimes they are marvellously good. That is hers, those two wagtails in Hermione's boudoir – you've seen them – they are carved in wood and painted.'

'I thought it was savage carving again.'

'No, hers. That's what they are – animals and birds, sometimes odd small people in everyday dress, really rather wonderful when they come off. They have a sort of funniness that is quite unconscious and subtle.'

'She might be a well-known artist one day?' mused Gerald.

'She might. But I think she won't. She drops her art if anything else catches her. Her contrariness prevents her taking it seriously – she must never be too serious, she feels she might give herself away. And she won't give herself away – she's always on the defensive. That's what I can't stand about her type. By the way, how did things go off with Pussum after I left you? I haven't heard anything.'

'Oh, rather disgusting. Halliday turned objectionable, and I only just saved myself from jumping in his stomach, in a real old-fashioned row.'

Birkin was silent.

'Of course,' he said, 'Julius is somewhat insane. On the one hand he's had religious mania, and on the other, he is fascinated by obscenity. Either he is a pure servant, washing the feet of Christ, or else he is making obscene drawings of Jesus – action and reaction – and between the two, nothing. He is really insane. He wants a pure lily, another girl, with a baby face, on the one hand, and on the other, he *must* have the Pussum, just to defile himself with her.'

'That's what I can't make out,' said Gerald. 'Does he love her, the Pussum, or doesn't he?'

'He neither does nor doesn't. She is the harlot, the actual harlot of adultery to him. And he's got a craving to throw himself into the filth of her. Then he gets up and calls on the name of the lily of purity, the baby-faced girl, and so enjoys himself all round. It's the old story – action and reaction, and nothing between.'

'I don't know,' said Gerald, after a pause, 'that he does insult the Pussum so very much. She strikes me as being rather foul.'

'But I thought you liked her,' exclaimed Birkin. 'I always felt fond of her. I never had anything to do with her, personally, that's true.'

'I liked her all right, for a couple of days,' said Gerald. 'But a week of her would have turned me over. There's a certain smell about the skin of those women, that in the end is sickening beyond words – even if you like it at first.'

'I know,' said Birkin. Then he added, rather fretfully, 'But go to bed, Gerald. God knows what time it is.'

Gerald looked at his watch, and at length rose off the bed, and went to his room. But he returned in a few minutes, in his shirt.

'One thing,' he said, seating himself on the bed again. 'We finished up rather stormily, and I never had time to give her anything.'

'Money?' said Birkin. 'She'll get what she wants from Halliday or from one of her acquaintances.'

'But then,' said Gerald, 'I'd rather give her her dues and settle the account.'

'She doesn't care.'

'No, perhaps not. But one feels the account is left open, and one would rather it were closed.'

'Would you?' said Birkin. He was looking at the white legs of Gerald, as the latter sat on the side of the bed in his shirt. They were white-skinned, full, muscular legs, handsome and decided. Yet they moved Birkin with a sort of pathos, tenderness, as if they were childish.

'I think I'd rather close the account,' said Gerald, repeating himself vaguely.

'It doesn't matter one way or another,' said Birkin.

'You always say it doesn't matter,' said Gerald, a little puzzled, looking down at the face of the other man affectionately.

'Neither does it,' said Birkin.

'But she was a decent sort, really – '

'Render unto Caesarina the things that are Caesarina's,' said Birkin, turning aside. It seemed to him Gerald was talking for the sake of talking. 'Go away, it wearies me – it's too late at night,' he said.

'I wish you'd tell me something that *did* matter,' said Gerald, looking down all the time at the face of the other man, waiting for something. But Birkin turned his face aside.

'All right then, go to sleep,' said Gerald, and he laid his hand affectionately on the other man's shoulder, and went away.

In the morning when Gerald awoke and heard Birkin move, he called out: 'I still think I ought to give the Pussum ten pounds.'

'Oh God!' said Birkin, 'don't be so matter-of-fact. Close the account in your own soul, if you like. It is there you can't close it.'

'How do you know I can't?'

'Knowing you.'

Gerald meditated for some moments.

'It seems to me the right thing to do, you know, with the Pussums, is to pay them.'

'And the right thing for mistresses: keep them. And the right thing for wives: live under the same roof with them. *Integer vitae scelerisque purus* – ' said Birkin.

'There's no need to be nasty about it,' said Gerald.

'It bores me. I'm not interested in your peccadilloes.'

'And I don't care whether you are or not – I am.'

The morning was again sunny. The maid had been in and brought the water, and had drawn the curtains. Birkin, sitting up in bed, looked lazily and pleasantly out on the park, that was so green and deserted, romantic, belonging to the past. He was thinking how lovely, how sure, how formed, how final all the things of the past were – the lovely accomplished past – this house, so still and golden, the park slumbering its centuries of peace. And then, what a snare and a delusion, this beauty of static things – what a horrible, dead prison Breadalby really was, what an intolerable confinement, the peace! Yet it was better than the sordid scrambling conflict of the present. If only one might create the future after one's own heart – for a little pure truth, a little unflinching application of simple truth to life, the heart cried out ceaselessly.

'I can't see what you will leave me at all, to be interested in,' came Gerald's voice from the lower room. 'Neither the Pussums, nor the mines, nor anything else.'

'You be interested in what you can, Gerald. Only I'm not interested myself,' said Birkin.

'What am I to do at all, then?' came Gerald's voice.

'What you like. What am I to do myself?'

In the silence Birkin could feel Gerald musing this fact.

'I'm blest if I know,' came the good-humoured answer.

'You see,' said Birkin, 'part of you wants the Pussum, and nothing but the Pussum, part of you wants the mines, the business, and nothing but the business – and there you are – all in bits – '

'And part of me wants something else,' said Gerald, in a queer, quiet, real voice.

'What?' said Birkin, rather surprised.

'That's what I hoped you could tell me,' said Gerald.

There was a silence for some time.

'I can't tell you – I can't find my own way, let alone yours. You might marry,' Birkin replied.

'Who – the Pussum?' asked Gerald.

'Perhaps,' said Birkin. And he rose and went to the window.

'That is your panacea,' said Gerald. 'But you haven't even tried it on yourself yet, and you are sick enough.'

'I am,' said Birkin. 'Still, I shall come right.'

'Through marriage?'

'Yes,' Birkin answered obstinately.

'And no,' added Gerald. 'No, no, no, my boy.'

There was a silence between them, and a strange tension of hostility. They always kept a gap, a distance between them, they wanted always to be free each of the other. Yet there was a curious heart-straining towards each other.

'*Salvator femininus*,' said Gerald, satirically.

'Why not?' said Birkin.

'No reason at all,' said Gerald, 'if it really works. But whom will you marry?'

'A woman,' said Birkin.

'Good,' said Gerald.

Birkin and Gerald were the last to come down to breakfast. Hermione liked everybody to be early. She suffered when she felt her day was diminished, she felt she had missed her life. She seemed to grip the hours by the throat, to force her life from them. She was rather pale and ghastly, as if left behind, in the morning. Yet she had her power, her will was strangely pervasive. With the entrance of the two young men a sudden tension was felt.

She lifted her face, and said, in her amused singsong, 'Good-morning! Did you sleep well? I'm so glad.'

And she turned away, ignoring them. Birkin, who knew her well, saw that she intended to discount his existence.

'Will you take what you want from the sideboard?' said Alexander, in a voice slightly suggesting disapprobation. 'I hope the things aren't cold. Oh no! Do you mind putting out the flame under the chafing-dish, Rupert? Thank you.'

Even Alexander was rather authoritative where Hermione was cool. He took his tone from her, inevitably. Birkin sat down and looked at the table. He was so used to this house, to this room, to this atmosphere, through years of intimacy, and now he felt in complete opposition to it all, it had nothing to do with him. How well he knew Hermione, as she sat there, erect and silent and somewhat bemused, and yet so potent, so powerful! He knew her statically, so finally, that it was almost like a madness. It was difficult to believe one was not mad, that one was not a figure in the hall of kings in some Egyptian tomb, where the dead all sat immemorial and tremendous. How utterly he knew Joshua Mattheson, who was talking in his harsh, yet rather mincing voice, endlessly, endlessly, always with a strong mentality working, always interesting, and yet always known, everything he said known beforehand, however novel it was, and clever. Alexander the up-to-date host, so bloodlessly free-and-easy, Fräulein so prettily chiming in just as she should, the little Italian Countess taking notice of everybody, only playing her little game, objective and cold, like a weasel watching everything, and extracting her own amusement, never giving herself in the slightest; then Miss Bradley, heavy and rather subservient, treated with cool, almost amused contempt by Hermione, and therefore slighted by everybody – how known it all was, like a game with the figures set out, the same figures, the Queen of chess, the knights, the pawns, the same now as they were hundreds of years ago, the same figures moving round in one of the innumerable permutations that make up the game. But the game is known, its going on is like a madness, it is so exhausted.

There was Gerald, an amused look on his face; the game pleased him. There was Gudrun, watching with steady, large, hostile eyes; the game fascinated her, and she loathed it. There was Ursula, with a slightly startled look on her face, as if she were hurt, and the pain were just outside her consciousness.

Suddenly Birkin got up and went out.

'That's enough,' he said to himself involuntarily.

Hermione knew his motion, though not in her consciousness. She lifted her heavy eyes and saw him lapse suddenly away, on a sudden, unknown tide, and the waves broke over her. Only her indomitable will remained static and mechanical, she sat at the table making her musing, stray remarks. But the darkness had covered her, she was like a ship that has gone down. It was finished for her too, she was wrecked in the darkness. Yet the unfailing mechanism of her will worked on, she had that activity.

'Shall we bathe this morning?' she said, suddenly looking at them all.

'Splendid,' said Joshua. 'It is a perfect morning.'

'Oh, it is beautiful,' said Fräulein.

'Yes, let us bathe,' said the Italian woman.

'We have no bathing suits,' said Gerald.

'Have mine,' said Alexander. 'I must go to church and read the lessons. They expect me.'

'Are you a Christian?' asked the Italian Countess, with sudden interest.

'No,' said Alexander. 'I'm not. But I believe in keeping up the old institutions.'

'They are so beautiful,' said Fräulein daintily.

'Oh, they are,' cried Miss Bradley.

They all trailed out on to the lawn. It was a sunny, soft morning in early summer, when life ran in the world subtly, like a reminiscence. The church bells were ringing a little way off, not a cloud was in the sky, the swans were like lilies on the water below, the peacocks walked with long, prancing steps across the shadow and into the sunshine of the grass. One wanted to swoon into the bygone perfection of it all.

'Goodbye,' called Alexander, waving his gloves cheerily, and he disappeared behind the bushes, on his way to church.

'Now,' said Hermione, 'shall we all bathe?'

'I won't,' said Ursula.

'You don't want to?' said Hermione, looking at her slowly.

'No. I don't want to,' said Ursula.

'Nor I,' said Gudrun.

'What about my suit?' asked Gerald.

'I don't know,' laughed Hermione, with an odd, amused intonation. 'Will a handkerchief do – a large handkerchief?'

'That will do,' said Gerald.

'Come along then,' sang Hermione.

The first to run across the lawn was the little Italian, small and like a cat, her white legs twinkling as she went, ducking slightly her head, that was tied in a gold silk kerchief. She tripped through the gate and down the grass, and stood, like a tiny figure of ivory and bronze, at the water's edge, having dropped off her towelling, watching the swans, which came up in surprise. Then out ran Miss Bradley, like a large, soft plum in her dark-blue suit. Then Gerald came, a scarlet silk kerchief round his loins, his towels over his arms. He seemed to flaunt himself a little in the sun, lingering and laughing, strolling easily, looking white but natural in his nakedness. Then came Sir Joshua, in an overcoat, and lastly Hermione, striding with stiff grace from out of a great mantle of purple silk, her head tied up in purple and gold. Handsome was her stiff, long body, her straight-stepping white legs, there was a static magnificence about her as she let the cloak float loosely away from her striding. She crossed the lawn like some strange memory, and passed slowly and statelily towards the water.

There were three ponds, in terraces descending the valley, large and smooth and beautiful, lying in the sun. The water ran over a little stone wall, over small rocks, splashing down from one pond to the level below. The swans had gone out on to the opposite bank, the reeds smelled sweet, a faint breeze touched the skin.

Gerald had dived in, after Sir Joshua, and had swum to the end of the pond. There he climbed out and sat on the wall. There was a dive, and the little Countess was swimming like a rat, to join him. They both sat in the sun, laughing and crossing their arms on their breasts. Sir Joshua swam up to them, and stood near them, up to his armpits in the water. Then Hermione and Miss Bradley swam over, and they sat in a row on the embankment.

'Aren't they terrifying? Aren't they really terrifying?' said Gudrun. 'Don't they look saurian? They are just like great lizards. Did you ever see anything like Sir Joshua? But really, Ursula, he belongs to the primeval world, when great lizards crawled about.'

Gudrun looked in dismay on Sir Joshua, who stood up to the breast in the water, his long, greyish hair washed down into his eyes, his neck set into thick, crude shoulders. He was talking to Miss Bradley, who, seated on the bank above, plump and big and wet, looked as if she might roll and slither in the water almost like one of the slithering sea-lions in the Zoo.

Ursula watched in silence. Gerald was laughing happily, between Hermione and the Italian. He reminded her of Dionysos, because his hair was really yellow, his figure so full and laughing. Hermione, in her large, stiff, sinister grace, leaned near him, frightening, as if she were not responsible for what she might do. He knew a certain danger in her, a convulsive madness. But he only laughed the more, turning often to the little Countess, who was flashing up her face at him.

They all dropped into the water, and were swimming together like a shoal of seals. Hermione was powerful and unconscious in the water, large and slow and powerful. Palestra was quick and silent as a water rat, Gerald wavered and flickered, a white natural shadow. Then, one after the other, they waded out, and went up to the house.

But Gerald lingered a moment to speak to Gudrun.

'You don't like the water?' he said.

She looked at him with a long, slow inscrutable look, as he stood before her negligently, the water standing in beads all over his skin.

'I like it very much,' she replied.

He paused, expecting some sort of explanation.

'And you swim?'

'Yes, I swim.'

Still he would not ask her why she would not go in then. He could feel something ironic in her. He walked away, piqued for the first time.

'Why wouldn't you bathe?' he asked her again, later, when he was once more the properly-dressed young Englishman.

She hesitated a moment before answering, opposing his persistence.

'Because I didn't like the crowd,' she replied.

He laughed, her phrase seemed to re-echo in his consciousness. The flavour of her slang was piquant to him. Whether he would or not, she signified the real world to him. He wanted to come up to her standards, fulfil her expectations. He knew that her criterion was the only one that mattered. The others were all outsiders, instinctively, whatever they might be socially. And Gerald could not help it, he was bound to strive to come up to her criterion, fulfil her idea of a man and a human being.

After lunch, when all the others had withdrawn, Hermione and Gerald and Birkin lingered, finishing their talk. There had been some discussion, on the whole quite intellectual and artificial, about a new state, a new world of man. Supposing this old social state *were* broken and destroyed, then, out of the chaos, what then?

The great social idea, said Sir Joshua, was the *social* equality of man. No, said Gerald, the idea was, that every man was fit for his own little bit of a task – let him do that, and then please himself. The unifying principle was the work in hand. Only work, the business of production, held men together. It was mechanical, but then society *was* a mechanism. Apart from work they were isolated, free to do as they liked.

'Oh!' cried Gudrun. 'Then we shan't have names any more – we shall be like the Germans, nothing but Herr Obermeister and Herr Untermeister. I can imagine it – "I am Mrs Colliery-Manager Crich – I am Mrs Member-of-Parliament Roddice. I am Miss Art-Teacher Brangwen." Very pretty that.'

'Things would work very much better, Miss Art-Teacher Brangwen,' said Gerald.

'What things, Mr Colliery-Manager Crich? The relation between you and me, *par exemple*?'

'Yes, for example,' cried the Italian. 'That which is between men and women – !'

'That is non-social,' said Birkin, sarcastically.

'Exactly,' said Gerald. 'Between me and a woman, the social question does not enter. It is my own affair.'

'A ten-pound note on it,' said Birkin.

'You don't admit that a woman is a social being?' asked Ursula of Gerald.

'She is both,' said Gerald. 'She is a social being, as far as society is concerned. But for her own private self, she is a free agent, it is her own affair, what she does.'

'But won't it be rather difficult to arrange the two halves?' asked Ursula.

'Oh no,' replied Gerald. 'They arrange themselves naturally – we see it now, everywhere.'

'Don't you laugh so pleasantly till you're out of the wood,' said Birkin.

Gerald knitted his brows in momentary irritation.

'Was I laughing?' he said.

'*If*,' said Hermione at last, 'we could only realise, that in the *spirit* we are all one, all equal in the spirit, all brothers there – the rest wouldn't matter, there would be no more of this carping and envy and this struggle for power, which destroys, only destroys.'

This speech was received in silence, and almost immediately the party rose from the table. But when the others had gone, Birkin turned round in bitter declamation, saying, 'It is just the opposite, just the contrary, Hermione. We are all different and unequal in spirit – it is only the *social* differences that are based on accidental material conditions. We are all abstractly or mathematically equal, if you like. Every man has hunger and thirst, two eyes, one nose and two legs. We're all the same in point of number. But spiritually, there is pure difference and neither equality nor inequality counts. It is upon these two bits of knowledge that you must found a state. Your democracy is an absolute lie – your brotherhood of man is a pure falsity, if you apply it further than the mathematical abstraction. We all drank milk first, we all eat bread and meat, we all want to ride in motor cars – therein lies the beginning and the end of the brotherhood of man. But no equality.

'But I, myself, who am myself, what have I to do with equality with any other man or woman? In the spirit, I am as separate as one star is from another, as different in quality and quantity. Establish a state on *that*. One man isn't any better than another, not because they are equal, but because they are intrinsically *other*, that there is no term of comparison. The minute you begin to compare, one man is seen to be far better than another, all the inequality you can imagine is there by nature. I want every man to have his share in the world's goods, so that I am rid of his importunity, so that I can tell him: "Now you've got what you want – you've got your fair share of the world's gear. Now, you one-mouthed fool, mind yourself and don't obstruct me." '

Hermione was looking at him with leering eyes, along her cheeks. He could feel violent waves of hatred and loathing of all he said, coming out of her. It was dynamic hatred and loathing, coming strong and black out of the unconsciousness. She heard his words in her unconscious self, *consciously* she was as if deafened, she paid no heed to them.

'It *sounds* like megalomania, Rupert,' said Gerald, genially.

Hermione gave a queer, grunting sound. Birkin stood back.

'Yes, let it,' he said suddenly, the whole tone gone out of his voice, that had been so insistent, bearing everybody down. And he went away.

But he felt, later, a little compunction. He had been violent, cruel with poor Hermione. He wanted to recompense her, to make it up. He had hurt her, he had been vindictive. He wanted to be on good terms with her again.

He went into her boudoir, a remote and very cushiony place. She was sitting at her table writing letters. She lifted her face abstractedly when he entered, watched him go to the sofa, and sit down. Then she looked down at her paper again.

He took up a large volume which he had been reading before, and became minutely attentive to his author. His back was towards Hermione. She could not go on with her writing. Her whole mind was a chaos, darkness breaking in upon it, and herself struggling to gain control with her will, as a swimmer struggles with the swirling water. But in spite of her efforts she was borne down, darkness seemed to break over her, she felt as if her heart was bursting. The terrible tension grew stronger and stronger, it was most fearful agony, like being walled up.

And then she realised that his presence was the wall, his presence was destroying her. Unless she could break out, she must die most fearfully, walled up in horror. And he was the wall. She must break down the wall – she must break him down before her, the awful obstruction of him who obstructed her life to the last. It must be done, or she must perish most horribly.

Terrible shocks ran over her body, like shocks of electricity, as if many volts of electricity suddenly struck her down. She was aware of him sitting silently there, an unthinkable evil obstruction. Only this blotted out her mind, pressed out her very breathing, his silent, stooping back, the back of his head.

A terrible voluptuous thrill ran down her arms – she was going to know her voluptuous consummation. Her arms quivered and were strong, immeasurably and irresistibly strong. What delight, what delight in strength, what delirium of pleasure! She was going to have her consummation of voluptuous ecstasy at last. It was coming! In utmost terror and agony, she knew it was upon her now, in extremity of bliss. Her hand closed on a blue, beautiful ball of lapis lazuli that stood on her desk for a paperweight. She rolled it round in her hand as she rose silently. Her heart was a pure flame in her breast, she was purely unconscious in ecstasy. She moved towards him and stood behind him for a moment in ecstasy. He, closed within the spell, remained motionless and unconscious.

Then swiftly, in a flame that drenched down her body like fluid lightning and gave her a perfect, unutterable consummation, unutterable satisfaction, she brought down the ball of jewel stone with all her force, crash on his head. But her fingers were in the way and deadened the blow. Nevertheless, down went his head on the table on which his book lay, the stone slid aside and over his ear, it was one convulsion of pure bliss for her, lit up by the crushed pain of her fingers. But it was not somehow complete. She lifted her arm high to aim once more, straight down on the head that lay dazed on the table. She must smash it, it must be smashed before her ecstasy was consummated, fulfilled for ever. A thousand lives, a thousand deaths mattered nothing now, only the fulfilment of this perfect ecstasy.

She was not swift, she could only move slowly. A strong spirit in him woke him and made him lift his face and twist to look at her. Her arm was raised, the hand clasping the ball of lapis lazuli. It was her left hand, he realised again with horror that she was left-handed. Hurriedly, with a burrowing motion, he covered his head under the thick volume of Thucydides, and the blow came down, almost breaking his neck, and shattering his heart.

He was shattered, but he was not afraid. Twisting round to face her he pushed the table over and got away from her. He was like a flask that is smashed to atoms, he seemed to himself that he was all fragments, smashed to bits. Yet his movements were perfectly coherent and clear, his soul was entire and unsurprised.

'No you don't, Hermione,' he said in a low voice. 'I don't let you.'

He saw her standing tall and livid and attentive, the stone clenched tense in her hand.

'Stand away and let me go,' he said, drawing near to her.

As if pressed back by some hand, she stood away, watching him all the time without changing, like a neutralised angel confronting him.

'It is no good,' he said, when he had gone past her. 'It isn't I who will die. You hear?'

He kept his face to her as he went out, lest she should strike again. While he was on his guard, she dared not move. And he was on his guard, she was powerless. So he had gone, and left her standing.

She remained perfectly rigid, standing as she was for a long time. Then she staggered to the couch and lay down, and went heavily to sleep. When she awoke, she remembered what she had done, but it seemed to her, she had only hit him, as any woman might do, because he tortured her. She was perfectly right. She knew that, spiritually, she was right. In her own infallible purity, she had done what must be done. She was right, she was pure. A drugged, almost sinister religious expression became permanent on her face.

Birkin, barely conscious, and yet perfectly direct in his motion, went out of the house and straight across the park, to the open country, to the hills. The brilliant day had become overcast, spots of rain were falling. He wandered on to a wild valleyside, where were thickets of hazel, many flowers, tufts of heather, and little clumps of young fir trees, budding with soft paws. It was rather wet everywhere, there was a stream running down at the bottom of the valley, which was gloomy, or seemed gloomy. He was aware that he could not regain his consciousness, that he was moving in a sort of darkness.

Yet he wanted something. He was happy in the wet hillside, that was overgrown and obscure with bushes and flowers. He wanted to touch them all, to saturate himself with the touch of them all. He took off his clothes, and sat down naked among the primroses, moving his feet softly among the primroses, his legs, his knees, his arms right up to the armpits, lying down and letting them touch his belly, his breasts. It was such a fine, cool, subtle touch all over him, he seemed to saturate himself with their contact.

But they were too soft. He went through the long grass to a clump of young fir trees, that were no higher than a man. The soft sharp boughs beat upon him, as he moved in keen pangs against them, threw little cold showers of drops on his belly, and beat his loins with their clusters of soft-sharp needles. There was a thistle which pricked him vividly, but not too much, because all his movements were too discriminate and soft. To lie down and roll in the sticky, cool young hyacinths, to lie on one's belly and cover one's back with handfuls of fine wet grass, soft as a breath, soft and more delicate and more beautiful than the touch of any woman; and then to sting one's thigh against the living dark bristles of the fir-boughs; and then to feel the light whip of the hazel on one's shoulders, stinging, and then to clasp the silvery birch-trunk against one's breast, its smoothness, its hardness, its vital knots and ridges – this was good, this was all very good, very satisfying. Nothing else would do, nothing else would satisfy, except this coolness and subtlety of vegetation travelling into one's blood. How fortunate he was, that there was this lovely, subtle, responsive vegetation, waiting for him, as he waited for it; how fulfilled he was, how happy!

As he dried himself a little with his handkerchief, he thought about Hermione and the blow. He could feel a pain on the side of his head. But after all, what did it matter? What did Hermione matter, what did people matter altogether? There was this perfect cool loneliness, so lovely and fresh and unexplored. Really, what a mistake he had made, thinking he wanted people, thinking he wanted a woman. He did not want a woman – not in the least. The leaves and the primroses and the trees, they were really lovely and cool and desirable, they really came into the blood and were added on to him. He was enrichened now immeasurably, and so glad.

It was quite right of Hermione to want to kill him. What had he to do with her? Why should he pretend to have anything to do with human beings at all? Here was his world, he wanted nobody and nothing but the lovely, subtle, responsive vegetation, and himself, his own living self.

It was necessary to go back into the world. That was true. But that did not matter, so one knew where one belonged. He knew now where he belonged. This was his place, his marriage place. The world was extraneous.

He climbed out of the valley, wondering if he were mad. But if so, he preferred his own madness, to the regular sanity. He rejoiced in his own madness, he was free. He did not want that old sanity of the world, which was become so repulsive. He rejoiced in the new found world of his madness. It was so fresh and delicate and so satisfying.

As for the certain grief he felt at the same time, in his soul, that was only the remains of an old ethic, that bade a human being adhere to humanity. But he was weary of the old ethic, of the human being, and of humanity. He loved now the soft, delicate vegetation, that was so cool and perfect. He would overlook the old grief, he would put away the old ethic, he would be free in his new state.

He was aware of the pain in his head becoming more and more difficult every minute. He was walking now along the road to the nearest station. It was raining and he had no hat. But then plenty of cranks went out nowadays without hats, in the rain.

He wondered again how much of his heaviness of heart, a certain depression, was due to fear, fear lest anybody should have seen him naked lying against the vegetation. What a dread he had of mankind, of other people! It amounted almost to horror, to a sort of dream terror – his horror of being observed by some other people. If he were on an island, like Alexander Selkirk, with only the creatures and the trees, he would be free and glad, there would be none of this heaviness, this misgiving. He could love the vegetation and be quite happy and unquestioned, by himself.

He had better send a note to Hermione: she might trouble about him, and he did not want the onus of this. So at the station, he wrote saying: I will go on to town – I don't want to come back to Breadalby for the present. But it is quite all right – I don't want you to mind having biffed me, in the least. Tell the others it is just one of my moods. You were quite right, to biff me – because I know you wanted to. So there's the end of it.

In the train, however, he felt ill. Every motion was insufferable pain, and he was sick. He dragged himself from the station into a cab, feeling his way step by step, like a blind man, and held up only by a dim will.

For a week or two he was ill, but he did not let Hermione know, and she thought he was sulking; there was a complete estrangement between them. She became rapt, abstracted in her conviction of exclusive righteousness. She lived in and by her own self-esteem, conviction of her own rightness of spirit.

CHAPTER 9

Coaldust

Going home from school in the afternoon, the Brangwen girls descended the hill between the picturesque cottages of Willey Green till they came to the railway crossing. There they found the gate shut, because the colliery train was rumbling nearer. They could hear the small locomotive panting hoarsely as it advanced with caution between the embankments. The one-legged man in the little signal-hut by the road stared out from his security, like a crab from a snail-shell.

Whilst the two girls waited, Gerald Crich trotted up on a red Arab mare. He rode well and softly, pleased with the delicate quivering of the creature between his knees. And he was very picturesque, at least in Gudrun's eyes, sitting soft and close on the slender red mare, whose long tail flowed on the air. He saluted the two girls, and drew up at the crossing to wait for the gate, looking down the railway for the approaching train. In spite of her ironic smile at his picturesqueness, Gudrun liked to look at him. He was well-set and easy, his face with its warm tan showed up his whitish, coarse moustache, and his blue eyes were full of sharp light as he watched the distance.

The locomotive chuffed slowly between the banks, hidden. The mare did not like it. She began to wince away, as if hurt by the unknown noise. But Gerald pulled her back and held her head to the gate. The sharp blasts of the chuffing engine broke with more and more force on her. The repeated sharp blows of unknown, terrifying noise struck through her till she was rocking with terror. She recoiled like a spring let go. But a glistening, half-smiling look came into Gerald's face. He brought her back again, inevitably.

The noise was released, the little locomotive with her clanking steel connecting-rod emerged on the highroad, clanking sharply. The mare rebounded like a drop of water from hot iron. Ursula and Gudrun pressed back into the hedge, in fear. But Gerald was heavy on the mare, and forced her back. It seemed as if he sank into her magnetically, and could thrust her back against herself.

'The fool!' cried Ursula loudly. 'Why doesn't he ride away till it's gone by?'

Gudrun was looking at him with black-dilated, spellbound eyes. But he sat glistening and obstinate, forcing the wheeling mare, which spun and swerved like a wind, and yet could not get out of the grasp of his will, nor escape from the mad clamour of terror that resounded through her, as the trucks thumped slowly, heavily, horrifying, one after the other, one pursuing the other, over the rails of the crossing.

The locomotive, as if wanting to see what could be done, put on the brakes, and back came the trucks rebounding on the iron buffers, striking like horrible cymbals, clashing nearer and nearer in frightful strident concussions. The mare opened her mouth and rose slowly, as if lifted up on a wind of terror. Then suddenly her forefeet struck out, as she convulsed herself utterly away from the horror. Back she went, and the two girls clung to each other, feeling she must fall backwards on top of him. But he leaned forward, his face shining with fixed amusement, and at last he brought her down, sank her down, and was bearing her back to the mark. But as strong as the pressure of his compulsion was the repulsion of her utter terror, throwing her back away from the railway, so that she spun round and round, on two legs, as if she were in the centre of some whirlwind. It made Gudrun faint with poignant dizziness, which seemed to penetrate to her heart.

'No – ! No – ! Let her go! Let her go, you fool, you *fool* – !' cried Ursula at the top of her voice, completely outside herself. And Gudrun hated her bitterly for being outside herself. It was unendurable that Ursula's voice was so powerful and naked.

A sharpened look came on Gerald's face. He bit himself down on the mare like a keen edge biting home, and *forced* her round. She roared as she breathed, her nostrils were two wide, hot holes, her mouth was apart, her eyes frenzied. It was a repulsive sight. But he held on her unrelaxed, with an almost mechanical relentlessness, keen as a sword pressing in to her. Both man and horse were sweating with violence. Yet he seemed calm as a ray of cold sunshine.

Meanwhile the eternal trucks were rumbling on, very slowly, treading one after the other, one after the other, like a disgusting dream that has no end. The connecting chains were grinding and squeaking as the tension varied, the mare pawed and struck away mechanically now, her terror fulfilled in her, for now the man encompassed her; her paws were blind and pathetic as she beat the air, the man closed round her, and brought her down, almost as if she were part of his own physique.

'And she's bleeding! She's bleeding!' cried Ursula, frantic with opposition and hatred of Gerald. She alone understood him perfectly, in pure opposition.

Gudrun looked and saw the trickles of blood on the sides of the mare, and she turned white. And then on the very wound the bright spurs came down, pressing relentlessly. The world reeled and passed into nothingness for Gudrun, she could not know any more.

When she recovered, her soul was calm and cold, without feeling. The trucks were still rumbling by, and the man and the mare were still fighting. But she herself was cold and separate, she had no more feeling for them. She was quite hard and cold and indifferent.

They could see the top of the hooded guard's-van approaching, the sound of the trucks was diminishing, there was hope of relief from the intolerable noise. The heavy panting of the half-stunned mare sounded automatically, the man seemed to be relaxing confidently, his will bright and unstained. The guard's-van came up, and passed slowly, the guard staring out in his transition on the spectacle in the road. And, through the man in the closed wagon, Gudrun could see the whole scene spectacularly, isolated and momentary, like a vision isolated in eternity.

Lovely, grateful silence seemed to trail behind the receding train. How sweet the silence is! Ursula looked with hatred on the buffers of the diminishing wagon. The gatekeeper stood ready at the door of his hut, to proceed to open the gate. But Gudrun sprang suddenly forward, in front of the struggling horse, threw off the latch and flung the gates asunder, throwing one half to the keeper, and running with the other half, forwards. Gerald suddenly let go the horse and leaped forwards, almost on to Gudrun. She was not afraid. As he jerked aside the mare's head, Gudrun cried, in a strange, high voice, like a gull, or like a witch screaming out from the side of the road, 'I should think you're proud.'

The words were distinct and formed. The man, twisting aside on his dancing horse, looked at her in some surprise, some wondering interest. Then the mare's hoofs had danced three times on the drum-like sleepers of the crossing, and man and horse were bounding springily, unequally up the road.

The two girls watched them go. The gatekeeper hobbled thudding over the logs of the crossing, with his wooden leg. He had fastened the gate. Then he also turned, and called to the girls, 'A masterful young jockey, that; he'll have his own road, if ever anybody would.'

'Yes,' cried Ursula, in her hot, overbearing voice. 'Why couldn't he take the horse away, till the trucks had gone by? He's a fool, and a bully. Does he think it's manly, to torture a horse? It's a living thing, why should he bully it and torture it?'

There was a pause, then the gatekeeper shook his head, and replied, 'Yes, it's as nice a little mare as you could set eyes on – beautiful little thing, beautiful. Now you couldn't see his father treat any animal like that – not you. They're as different as they welly can be, Gerald Crich and his father – two different men, different made.'

Then there was a pause.

'But why does he do it?' cried Ursula, 'why does he? Does he think he's grand, when he's bullied a sensitive creature, ten times as sensitive as himself?'

Again there was a cautious pause. Then again the man shook his head, as if he would say nothing, but would think the more.

'I expect he's got to train the mare to stand to anything,' he replied. 'A pure-bred Harab – not the sort of breed as is used to round here – different sort from our sort altogether. They say as he got her from Constantinople.'

'He would!' said Ursula. 'He'd better have left her to the Turks, I'm sure they would have had more decency towards her.'

The man went in to drink his can of tea, the girls went on down the lane, that was deep in soft black dust. Gudrun was as if numbed in her mind by the sense of indomitable soft weight of the man, bearing down into the living body of the horse: the strong, indomitable thighs of the blond man clenching the palpitating body of the mare into pure control; a sort of soft white magnetic domination from the loins and thighs and calves, enclosing and encompassing the mare heavily into unutterable subordination, soft blood-subordination, terrible.

On the left, as the girls walked silently, the coal-mine lifted its great mounds and its patterned head-stocks, the black railway with the trucks at rest looked like a harbour just below, a large bay of railroad with anchored wagons.

Near the second level-crossing, that went over many bright rails, was a farm belonging to the collieries, and a great round globe of iron, a disused boiler, huge and rusty and perfectly round, stood silently in a paddock by the road. The hens were pecking round it, some chickens were balanced on the drinking trough, wagtails flew away in among trucks, from the water.

On the other side of the wide crossing, by the roadside, was a heap of pale-grey stones for mending the roads, and a cart standing, and a middle-aged man with whiskers round his face was leaning on his shovel, talking to a young man in gaiters, who stood by the horse's head. Both men were facing the crossing.

They saw the two girls appear, small, brilliant figures in the near distance, in the strong light of the late afternoon. Both wore light, gay summer dresses, Ursula had an orange-coloured knitted coat, Gudrun a pale yellow, Ursula wore canary yellow stockings, Gudrun bright rose, the figures of the two women seemed to glitter in progress over the wide bay of the railway crossing, white and orange and yellow and rose glittering in motion across a hot world silted with coal-dust.

The two men stood quite still in the heat, watching. The elder was a short, hard-faced energetic man of middle age, the younger a labourer of twenty-three or so. They stood in silence watching the advance of the sisters. They watched whilst the girls drew near, and whilst they passed, and whilst they receded down the dusty road, that had dwellings on one side, and dusty young corn on the other.

Then the elder man, with the whiskers round his face, said in a prurient manner to the young man, 'What price that, eh? She'll do, won't she?'

'Which?' asked the young man, eagerly, with laugh.

'Her with the red stockings. What d'you say? I'd give my week's wages for five minutes; what! – just for five minutes.'

Again the young man laughed.

'Your missis 'ud have summat to say to you,' he replied.

Gudrun had turned round and looked at the two men. They were to her sinister creatures, standing watching after her, by the heap of pale grey slag. She loathed the man with whiskers round his face.

'You're first class, you are,' the man said to her, and to the distance.

'Do you think it would be worth a week's wages?' said the younger man, musing.

'Do I? I'd put 'em bloody-well down this second – '

The younger man looked after Gudrun and Ursula objectively, as if he wished to calculate what there might be, that was worth his week's wages. He shook his head with fatal misgiving.

'No,' he said. 'It's not worth that to me.'

'Isn't?' said the old man. 'By God, if it isn't to me!'

And he went on shovelling his stones.

The girls descended between the houses with slate roofs and blackish brick walls. The heavy gold glamour of approaching sunset lay over all the colliery district, and the ugliness overlaid with beauty was like a narcotic to the senses. On the roads silted with black dust, the rich light fell more warmly, more heavily, over all the amorphous squalor a kind of magic was cast, from the glowing close of day.

'It has a foul kind of beauty, this place,' said Gudrun, evidently suffering from fascination. 'Can't you feel in some way, a thick, hot attraction in it? I can. And it quite stupefies me.'

They were passing between blocks of miners' dwellings. In the back yards of several dwellings, a miner could be seen washing himself in the open on this hot evening, naked down to the loins, his great trousers of moleskin slipping almost away. Miners already cleaned were sitting on their heels, with their backs near the walls, talking and silent in pure physical well-being, tired, and taking physical rest. Their voices sounded out with strong intonation, and the broad dialect was curiously caressing to the blood. It seemed to envelop Gudrun in a labourer's caress, there was in the whole atmosphere a resonance of physical men, a glamorous thickness of labour and maleness, surcharged in the air. But it was universal in the district, and therefore unnoticed by the inhabitants.

To Gudrun, however, it was potent and half-repulsive. She could never tell why Beldover was so utterly different from London and the south, why one's whole feelings were different, why one seemed to live in another sphere. Now she realised that this was the world of powerful, underworld men who spent most of their time in the darkness. In their voices she could hear the voluptuous resonance of darkness, the strong, dangerous underworld, mindless, inhuman. They sounded also like strange machines, heavy, oiled. The voluptuousness was like that of machinery, cold and iron.

It was the same every evening when she came home, she seemed to move through a wave of disruptive force, that was given off from the presence of thousands of vigorous, underworld, half-automatised colliers, and which went to the brain and the heart, awaking a fatal desire, and a fatal callousness.

There came over her a nostalgia for the place. She hated it, she knew how utterly cut off it was, how hideous and how sickeningly mindless. Sometimes she beat her wings like a new Daphne, turning not into a tree but a machine. And yet, she was overcome by the nostalgia. She struggled to get more and more into accord with the atmosphere of the place, she craved to get her satisfaction of it.

She felt herself drawn out at evening into the main street of the town, that was uncreated and ugly, and yet surcharged with this same potent atmosphere of intense, dark callousness. There were always miners about. They moved with their strange, distorted dignity, a certain beauty, and unnatural stillness in their bearing, a look of abstraction and half resignation in their pale, often gaunt faces. They belonged to another world, they had a strange glamour, their voices were full of an intolerable deep resonance, like a machine's burring, a music more maddening than the sirens' long ago.

She found herself, with the rest of the common women, drawn out on Friday evenings to the little market. Friday was pay-day for the colliers, and Friday night was market night. Every woman was abroad, every man was out, shopping with his wife, or gathering with his pals. The pavements were dark for miles around with people coming in; the little market-place on the crown of the hill and the main street of Beldover were black with thickly-crowded men and women.

It was dark, the market-place was hot with kerosene flares, which threw a ruddy light on the grave faces of the purchasing wives, and on the pale abstract faces of the men. The air was full of the sound of criers and of people talking, thick streams of people moved on the pavements towards the solid crowd of the market. The shops were blazing and packed with women, in the streets were men, mostly men, miners of all ages. Money was spent with almost lavish freedom.

The carts that came could not pass through. They had to wait, the driver calling and shouting, till the dense crowd would make way. Everywhere, young fellows from the outlying districts were making conversation with the girls, standing in the road and at the corners. The doors of the public-houses were open and full of light, men passed in and out in a continual stream, everywhere men were calling out to one another, or crossing to meet one another, or standing in little gangs and circles, discussing, endlessly discussing. The sense of talk, buzzing, jarring, half-secret, the endless mining and political wrangling, vibrated in the air like discordant machinery. And it was their voices which affected Gudrun almost to swooning. They aroused a strange, nostalgic ache of desire, something almost demoniacal, never to be fulfilled.

Like any other common girl of the district, Gudrun strolled up and down, up and down the length of the brilliant two-hundred paces of the pavement nearest the market-place. She knew it was a vulgar thing to do; her father and mother could not bear it; but the nostalgia came over her, she must be among the people. Sometimes she sat among the louts in the cinema: rakish-looking, unattractive louts they were. Yet she must be among them.

And, like any other common lass, she found her 'boy'. It was an electrician, one of the electricians introduced according to Gerald's new scheme. He was an earnest, clever man, a scientist with a passion for sociology. He lived alone in a cottage, in lodgings, in Willey Green. He was a gentleman, and sufficiently well-to-do. His landlady spread the reports about him; he *would* have a large wooden tub in his bedroom, and every time he came in from work, he *would* have pails and pails of water brought up, to bathe in, then he put on clean shirt and underclothing *every* day, and clean silk socks; fastidious and exacting he was in these respects, but in every other way, most ordinary and unassuming.

Gudrun knew all these things. The Brangwens' house was one to which the gossip came naturally and inevitably. Palmer was in the first place a friend of Ursula's. But in his pale, elegant, serious face there showed the same nostalgia that Gudrun felt. He too must walk up and down the street on Friday evening. So he walked with Gudrun, and a friendship was struck up between them. But he was not in love with Gudrun; he *really* wanted Ursula, but for some strange reason, nothing could happen between her and him. He liked to have Gudrun about, as a fellow-mind – but that was all. And she had no real feeling for him. He was a scientist, he had to have a woman to back him. But he was really impersonal, he had the fineness of an elegant piece of machinery. He was too cold, too destructive to care really for women, too great an egoist. He was polarised by the men. Individually he detested and despised them. In the mass they fascinated him, as machinery fascinated him. They were a new sort of machinery to him – but incalculable, incalculable.

So Gudrun strolled the streets with Palmer, or went to the cinema with him. And his long, pale, rather elegant face flickered as he made his sarcastic remarks. There they were, the two of them: two elegants in one sense: in the other sense, two units, absolutely adhering to the people, teeming with the distorted colliers. The same secret seemed to be working in the souls of all alike, Gudrun, Palmer, the rakish young bloods, the gaunt, middle-aged men. All had a secret sense of power, and of inexpressible destructiveness, and of fatal half-heartedness, a sort of rottenness in the will.

Sometimes Gudrun would start aside, see it all, see how she was sinking in. And then she was filled with a fury of contempt and anger. She felt she was sinking into one mass with the rest – all so close and intermingled and breathless. It was horrible. She stifled. She prepared for flight, feverishly she flew to her work. But soon she let go. She started off into the country – the darkish, glamorous country. The spell was beginning to work again.

CHAPTER 10

Sketchbook

One morning the sisters were sketching by the side of Willey Water, at the remote end of the lake. Gudrun had waded out to a gravelly shoal, and was seated like a Buddhist, staring fixedly at the water-plants that rose succulent from the mud of the low shores. What she could see was mud, soft, oozy, watery mud, and from its festering chill, water-plants rose up, thick and cool and fleshy, very straight and turgid, thrusting out their leaves at right angles, and having dark lurid colours, dark green and blotches of black-purple and bronze. But she could feel their turgid fleshy structure as in a sensuous vision, she *knew* how they rose out of the mud, she *knew* how they thrust out from themselves, how they stood stiff and succulent against the air.

Ursula was watching the butterflies, of which there were dozens near the water, little blue ones suddenly snapping out of nothingness into a jewel-life, a large black-and-red one standing upon a flower and breathing with his soft wings, intoxicatingly, breathing pure, ethereal sunshine; two white ones wrestling in the low air; there was a halo round them; ah, when they came tumbling nearer they were orange-tips, and it was the orange that had made the halo. Ursula rose and drifted away, unconscious like the butterflies.

Gudrun, absorbed in a stupor of apprehension of surging water-plants, sat crouched on the shoal, drawing, not looking up for a long time, and then staring unconsciously, absorbedly at the rigid, naked, succulent stems. Her feet were bare, her hat lay on the bank opposite.

She started out of her trance, hearing the knocking of oars. She looked round. There was a boat with a gaudy Japanese parasol, and a man in white, rowing. The woman was Hermione, and the man was Gerald. She knew it instantly. And instantly she perished in the keen *frisson* of anticipation, an electric vibration in her veins, intense, much more intense than that which was always humming low in the atmosphere of Beldover.

Gerald was her escape from the heavy slough of the pale, underworld, automatic colliers. He started out of the mud. He was master. She saw his back, the movement of his white loins. But not that – it was the whiteness he seemed to enclose as he bent forwards, rowing. He seemed to stoop to something. His glistening, whitish hair seemed like the electricity of the sky.

'There's Gudrun,' came Hermione's voice floating distinct over the water. 'We will go and speak to her. Do you mind?'

Gerald looked round and saw the girl standing by the water's edge, looking at him. He pulled the boat towards her, magnetically, without thinking of her. In his world, his conscious world, she was still nobody. He knew that Hermione had a curious pleasure in treading down all the social differences, at least apparently, and he left it to her.

'How do you do, Gudrun?' sang Hermione, using the Christian name in the fashionable manner. 'What are you doing?'

'How do you do, Hermione? I *was* sketching.'

'Were you?' The boat drifted nearer, till the keel ground on the bank. 'May we see? I should like to *so* much.'

It was no use resisting Hermione's deliberate intention.

'Well – ' said Gudrun reluctantly, for she always hated to have her unfinished work exposed – 'there's nothing in the least interesting.'

'Isn't there? But let me see, will you?'

Gudrun reached out the sketchbook, Gerald stretched from the boat to take it. And as he did so, he remembered Gudrun's last words to him, and her face lifted up to him as he sat on the swerving horse. An intensification of pride went over his nerves, because he felt, in some way she was compelled by him. The exchange of feeling between them was strong and apart from their consciousness.

And as if in a spell, Gudrun was aware of his body, stretching and surging like the marsh-fire, stretching towards her, his hand coming straight forward like a stem. Her voluptuous, acute apprehension of him made the blood faint in her veins, her mind went dim and unconscious. And he rocked on the water perfectly, like the rocking of phosphorescence. He looked round at the boat. It was drifting off a little. He lifted the oar to bring it back. And the exquisite pleasure of slowly arresting the boat, in the heavy-soft water, was complete as a swoon.

'*That's* what you have done,' said Hermione, looking searchingly at the plants on the shore, and comparing with Gudrun's drawing. Gudrun looked round in the direction of Hermione's long, pointing finger. 'That is it, isn't it?' repeated Hermione, needing confirmation.

'Yes,' said Gudrun automatically, taking no real heed.

'Let me look,' said Gerald, reaching forward for the book. But Hermione ignored him, he must not presume, before she had finished. But he, his will as unthwarted and as unflinching as hers, stretched forward till he touched the book. A little shock, a storm of revulsion against him, shook Hermione unconsciously. She released the book when he had not properly got it, and it tumbled against the side of the boat and bounced into the water.

'There!' sang Hermione, with a strange ring of malevolent victory. 'I'm so sorry, so awfully sorry. Can't you get it, Gerald?'

This last was said in a note of anxious sneering that made Gerald's veins tingle with fine hate for her. He leaned far out of the boat, reaching down into the water. He could feel his position was ridiculous, his loins exposed behind him.

'It is of no importance,' came the strong, clanging voice of Gudrun. She seemed to touch him. But he reached further, the boat swayed violently. Hermione, however, remained unperturbed. He grasped the book, under the water, and brought it up, dripping.

'I'm so dreadfully sorry – dreadfully sorry,' repeated Hermione. 'I'm afraid it was all my fault.'

'It's of no importance – really, I assure you – it doesn't matter in the least,' said Gudrun loudly, with emphasis, her face flushed scarlet. And she held out her hand impatiently for the wet book, to have done with the scene. Gerald gave it to her. He was not quite himself.

'I'm so dreadfully sorry,' repeated Hermione, till both Gerald and Gudrun were exasperated. 'Is there nothing that can be done?'

'In what way?' asked Gudrun, with cool irony.

'Can't we save the drawings?'

There was a moment's pause, wherein Gudrun made evident all her refutation of Hermione's persistence.

'I assure you,' said Gudrun, with cutting distinctness, 'the drawings are quite as good as ever they were, for my purpose. I want them only for reference.'

'But can't I give you a new book? I wish you'd let me do that. I feel so truly sorry. I feel it was all my fault.'

'As far as I saw,' said Gudrun, 'it wasn't your fault at all. If there was any *fault*, it was Mr Crich's. But the whole thing is *entirely* trivial, and it really is ridiculous to take any notice of it.'

Gerald watched Gudrun closely, whilst she repulsed Hermione. There was a body of cold power in her. He watched her with an insight that amounted to clairvoyance. He saw her a dangerous, hostile spirit, that could stand undiminished and unabated. It was so finished, and of such perfect gesture, moreover.

'I'm awfully glad if it doesn't matter,' he said; 'if there's no real harm done.'

She looked back at him, with her fine blue eyes, and signalled full into his spirit, as she said, her voice ringing with intimacy almost caressive now it was addressed to him, 'Of course, it doesn't matter in the *least*.'

The bond was established between them, in that look, in her tone. In her tone, she made the understanding clear – they were of the same kind, he and she, a sort of diabolic freemasonry subsisted between them. Henceforward, she knew, she had her power over him. Wherever they met, they would be secretly associated. And he would be helpless in the association with her. Her soul exulted.

'Goodbye! I'm so glad you forgive me. Goooodbye!'

Hermione sang her farewell, and waved her hand. Gerald automatically took the oar and pushed off. But he was looking all the time, with a glimmering, subtly-smiling admiration in his eyes, at Gudrun, who stood on the shoal shaking the wet book in her hand. She turned away and ignored the receding boat. But Gerald looked back as he rowed, beholding her, forgetting what he was doing.

'Aren't we going too much to the left?' sang Hermione, as she sat ignored under her coloured parasol.

Gerald looked round without replying, the oars balanced and glancing in the sun.

'I think it's all right,' he said good-humouredly, beginning to row again without thinking of what he was doing. And Hermione disliked him extremely for his good-humoured obliviousness, she was nullified, she could not regain ascendancy.

CHAPTER II

An Island

Meanwhile Ursula had wandered on from Willey Water along the course of the bright little stream. The afternoon was full of larks' singing. On the bright hillsides was a subdued smoulder of gorse. A few forget-me-nots flowered by the water. There was a rousedness and a glancing everywhere.

She strayed absorbedly on, over the brooks. She wanted to go to the mill-pond above. The big mill-house was deserted, save for a labourer and his wife who lived in the kitchen. So she passed through the empty farmyard and through the wilderness of a garden, and mounted the bank by the sluice. When she got to the top, to see the old, velvety surface of the pond before her, she noticed a man on the bank, tinkering with a punt. It was Birkin sawing and hammering away.

She stood at the head of the sluice, looking at him. He was unaware of anybody's presence. He looked very busy, like a wild animal, active and intent. She felt she ought to go away, he would not want her. He seemed to be so much occupied. But she did not want to go away. Therefore she moved along the bank till he would look up.

Which he soon did. The moment he saw her, he dropped his tools and came forward, saying, 'How do you do? I'm making the punt watertight. Tell me if you think it is right.'

She went along with him.

'You are your father's daughter, so you can tell me if it will do,' he said.

She bent to look at the patched punt.

'I am sure I am my father's daughter,' she said, fearful of having to judge. 'But I don't know anything about carpentry. It *looks* right, don't you think?'

'Yes, I think. I hope it won't let me to the bottom, that's all. Though even so, it isn't a great matter, I should come up again. Help me to get it into the water, will you?'

With combined efforts they turned over the heavy punt and set it afloat.

'Now,' he said, 'I'll try it and you can watch what happens. Then if it carries, I'll take you over to the island.'

'Do,' she cried, watching anxiously.

The pond was large, and had that perfect stillness and the dark lustre of very deep water. There were two small islands overgrown with bushes and a few trees, towards the middle. Birkin pushed himself off, and veered clumsily in the pond. Luckily the punt drifted so that he could catch hold of a willow bough, and pull it to the island.

'Rather overgrown,' he said, looking into the interior, 'but very nice. I'll come and fetch you. The boat leaks a little.'

In a moment he was with her again, and she stepped into the wet punt.

'It'll float us all right,' he said, and manoeuvred again to the island.

They landed under a willow tree. She shrank from the little jungle of rank plants before her, evil-smelling figwort and hemlock. But he explored into it.

'I shall mow this down,' he said, 'and then it will be romantic – like Paul et Virginie.'

'Yes, one could have lovely Watteau picnics here,' cried Ursula with enthusiasm.

His face darkened.

'I don't want Watteau picnics here,' he said.

'Only your Virginie,' she laughed.

'Virginie enough,' he smiled wryly. 'No, I don't want her either.'

Ursula looked at him closely. She had not seen him since Breadalby. He was very thin and hollow, with a ghastly look in his face.

'You have been ill, haven't you?' she asked, rather repulsed.

'Yes,' he replied coldly.

They had sat down under the willow tree, and were looking at the pond, from their retreat on the island.

'Has it made you frightened?' she asked.

'What of?' he asked, turning his eyes to look at her. Something in him, inhuman and unmitigated, disturbed her, and shook her out of her ordinary self.

'It *is* frightening to be very ill, isn't it?' she said.

'It isn't pleasant,' he said. 'Whether one is really afraid of death, or not, I have never decided. In one mood, not a bit, in another, very much.'

'But doesn't it make you feel ashamed? I think it makes one so ashamed, to be ill – illness is so terribly humiliating, don't you think?'

He considered for some minutes.

'Maybe,' he said. 'Though one knows all the time one's life isn't really right, at the source. That's the humiliation. I don't see that the illness counts so much, after that. One is ill because one doesn't live properly – can't. It's the failure to live that makes one ill, and humiliates one.'

'But do you fail to live?' she asked, almost jeering.

'Why yes – I don't make much of a success of my days. One seems always to be bumping one's nose against the blank wall ahead.'

Ursula laughed. She was frightened, and when she was frightened she always laughed and pretended to be jaunty.

'Your poor nose!' she said, looking at that feature of his face.

'No wonder it's ugly,' he replied.

She was silent for some minutes, struggling with her own self-deception. It was an instinct in her, to deceive herself.

'But *I'm* happy – I think life is *awfully* jolly,' she said.

'Good,' he answered, with a certain cold indifference.

She reached for a bit of paper which had wrapped a small piece of chocolate she had found in her pocket, and began making a boat. He watched her without heeding her. There was something strangely pathetic and tender in her moving, unconscious fingertips, that were agitated and hurt, really.

'I *do* enjoy things – don't you?' she asked.

'Oh yes! But it infuriates me that I can't get right, at the really growing part of me. I feel all tangled and messed up, and I *can't* get straight anyhow. I don't know what really to *do*. One must do something somewhere.'

'Why should you always be *doing*?' she retorted. 'It is so plebeian. I think it is much better to be really patrician, and to do nothing but just be oneself, like a walking flower.'

'I quite agree,' he said, 'if one has burst into blossom. But I can't get my flower to blossom anyhow. Either it is blighted in the bud, or has got the smother-fly, or it isn't nourished. Curse it, it isn't even a bud. It is a contravened knot.'

Again she laughed. He was so very fretful and exasperated. But she was anxious and puzzled. How was one to get out, anyhow. There must be a way out somewhere.

There was a silence, wherein she wanted to cry. She reached for another bit of chocolate paper, and began to fold another boat.

'And why is it,' she asked at length, 'that there is no flowering, no dignity of human life now?'

'The whole idea is dead. Humanity itself is dry-rotten, really. There are myriads of human beings hanging on the bush – and they look very nice and rosy, your healthy young men and women. But they are apples of Sodom, as a matter of fact, Dead Sea Fruit, gall-apples. It isn't true that they have any significance – their insides are full of bitter, corrupt ash.'

'But there *are* good people,' protested Ursula.

'Good enough for the life of today. But mankind is a dead tree, covered with fine brilliant galls of people.'

Ursula could not help stiffening herself against this, it was too picturesque and final. But neither could she help making him go on.

'And if it is so, *why* is it?' she asked, hostile. They were rousing each other to a fine passion of opposition.

'Why, why are people all balls of bitter dust? Because they won't fall off the tree when they're ripe. They hang on to their old positions when the position is over-past, till they become infested with little worms and dry-rot.'

There was a long pause. His voice had become hot and very sarcastic. Ursula was troubled and bewildered, they were both oblivious of everything but their own immersion.

'But even if everybody is wrong – where are you right?' she cried, 'where are you any better?'

'I? – I'm not right,' he cried back. 'At least my only rightness lies in the fact that I know it. I detest what I am, outwardly. I loathe myself as a human being.

Humanity is a huge aggregate lie, and a huge lie is less than a small truth. Humanity is less, far less than the individual, because the individual may sometimes be capable of truth, and humanity is a tree of lies. And they say that love is the greatest thing; they persist in *saying* this, the foul liars, and just look at what they do! Look at all the millions of people who repeat every minute that love is the greatest, and charity is the greatest – and see what they are doing all the time. By their works ye shall know them, for dirty liars and cowards, who daren't stand by their own actions, much less by their own words.'

'But,' said Ursula sadly, 'that doesn't alter the fact that love is the greatest, does it? What they *do* doesn't alter the truth of what they say, does it?'

'Completely, because if what they say *were* true, then they couldn't help fulfilling it. But they maintain a lie, and so they run amok at last. It's a lie to say that love is the greatest. You might as well say that hate is the greatest, since the opposite of everything balances. What people want is hate – hate and nothing but hate. And in the name of righteousness and love, they get it. They distil themselves with nitro-glycerine, all the lot of them, out of very love. It's the lie that kills. If we want hate, let us have it – death, murder, torture, violent destruction – let us have it: but not in the name of love. But I abhor humanity, I wish it was swept away. It could go, and there would be no *absolute* loss, if every human being perished tomorrow. The reality would be untouched. Nay, it would be better. The real tree of life would then be rid of the most ghastly, heavy crop of Dead Sea Fruit, the intolerable burden of myriad simulacra of people, an infinite weight of mortal lies.'

'So you'd like everybody in the world destroyed?' said Ursula.

'I should indeed.'

'And the world empty of people?'

'Yes truly. You yourself, don't you find it a beautiful clean thought, a world empty of people, just uninterrupted grass, and a hare sitting up?'

The pleasant sincerity of his voice made Ursula pause to consider her own proposition. And really it *was* attractive: a clean, lovely, humanless world. It was the *really* desirable. Her heart hesitated, and exulted. But still, she was dissatisfied with *him*.

'But,' she objected, 'you'd be dead yourself, so what good would it do you?'

'I would die like a shot, to know that the earth would really be cleaned of all the people. It is the most beautiful and freeing thought. Then there would *never* be another foul humanity created, for a universal defilement.'

'No,' said Ursula, 'there would be nothing.'

'What! Nothing? Just because humanity was wiped out? You flatter yourself. There'd be everything.'

'But how, if there were no people?'

'Do you think that creation depends on *man*! It merely doesn't. There are the trees and the grass and birds. I much prefer to think of the lark rising up in the morning upon a humanless world. Man is a mistake, he must go. There is the grass, and hares and adders, and the unseen hosts, actual angels that go about freely when a dirty humanity doesn't interrupt them – and good pure-tissued demons: very nice.'

It pleased Ursula, what he said, pleased her very much, as a fantasy. Of course it was only a pleasant fancy. She herself knew too well the actuality of humanity, its hideous actuality. She knew it could not disappear so cleanly and conveniently. It had a long way to go yet, a long and hideous way. Her subtle, feminine, demoniacal soul knew it well.

'If only man was swept off the face of the earth, creation would go on so marvellously, with a new start, non-human. Man is one of the mistakes of creation – like the ichthyosauri. If only he were gone again, think what lovely things would come out of the liberated days; – things straight out of the fire.'

'But man will never be gone,' she said, with insidious, diabolical knowledge of the horrors of persistence. 'The world will go with him.'

'Ah no,' he answered, 'not so. I believe in the proud angels and the demons that are our forerunners. They will destroy us, because we are not proud enough. The ichthyosauri were not proud: they crawled and floundered as we do. And besides, look at elder-flowers and bluebells – they are a sign that pure creation takes place – even the butterfly. But humanity never gets beyond the caterpillar stage – it rots in the chrysalis, it never will have wings. It is anti-creation, like monkeys and baboons.'

Ursula watched him as he talked. There seemed a certain impatient fury in him, all the while, and at the same time a great amusement in everything, and a final tolerance. And it was this tolerance she mistrusted, not the fury. She saw that, all the while, in spite of himself, he would have to be trying to save the world. And this knowledge, whilst it comforted her heart somewhere with a little self-satisfaction, stability, yet filled her with a certain sharp contempt and hate of him. She wanted him to herself, she hated the Salvator Mundi touch. It was something diffuse and generalised about him, which she could not stand. He would behave in the same way, say the same things, give himself as completely to anybody who came along, anybody and everybody who liked to appeal to him. It was despicable, a very insidious form of prostitution.

'But,' she said, 'you believe in individual love, even if you don't believe in loving humanity – ?'

'I don't believe in love at all – that is, any more than I believe in hate, or in grief. Love is one of the emotions like all the others – and so it is all right whilst you feel it. But I can't see how it becomes an absolute. It is just part of human relationships, no more. And it is only part of *any* human relationship. And why one should be required *always* to feel it, any more than one always feels sorrow or distant joy, I cannot conceive. Love isn't a desideratum – it is an emotion you feel or you don't feel, according to circumstance.'

'Then why do you care about people at all?' she asked, 'if you don't believe in love? Why do you bother about humanity?'

'Why do I? Because I can't get away from it.'

'Because you love it,' she persisted.

It irritated him.

'If I do love it,' he said, 'it is my disease.'

'But it is a disease you don't want to be cured of,' she said, with some cold sneering.

He was silent now, feeling she wanted to insult him.

'And if you don't believe in love, what *do* you believe in?' she asked, mocking. 'Simply in the end of the world, and grass?'

He was beginning to feel a fool.

'I believe in the unseen hosts,' he said.

'And nothing else? You believe in nothing visible, except grass and birds? Your world is a poor show.'

'Perhaps it is,' he said, cool and superior now he was offended, assuming a certain insufferable aloof superiority, and withdrawing into his distance.

Ursula disliked him. But also she felt she had lost something. She looked at him as he sat crouched on the bank. There was a certain priggish Sunday-school stiffness over him, priggish and detestable. And yet, at the same time, the moulding of him was so quick and attractive, it gave such a great sense of freedom: the moulding of his brows, his chin, his whole physique, something so alive, somewhere, in spite of the look of sickness.

And it was this duality in feeling which he created in her, that made a fine hate of him quicken in her bowels. There was his wonderful, desirable life-rapidity, the rare quality of an utterly desirable man: and there was at the same time this ridiculous, mean effacement into a Salvator Mundi and a Sunday-school teacher, a prig of the stiffest type.

He looked up at her. He saw her face strangely enkindled, as if suffused from within by a powerful sweet fire. His soul was arrested in wonder. She was enkindled in her own living fire. Arrested in wonder and in pure, perfect attraction, he moved towards her. She sat like a strange queen, almost super-natural in her glowing smiling richness.

'The point about love,' he said, his consciousness quickly adjusting itself, 'is that we hate the word because we have vulgarised it. It ought to be proscribed, tabooed from utterance, for many years, till we get a new, better idea.'

There was a beam of understanding between them.

'But it always means the same thing,' she said.

'Ah God, no, let it not mean that any more,' he cried. 'Let the old meanings go.'

'But still it is love,' she persisted. A strange, wicked yellow light shone at him in her eyes.

He hesitated, baffled, withdrawing.

'No,' he said, 'it isn't. Spoken like that, never in the world. You've no business to utter the word.'

'I must leave it to you, to take it out of the Ark of the Covenant at the right moment,' she mocked.

Again they looked at each other. She suddenly sprang up, turned her back to him, and walked away. He too rose slowly and went to the water's edge, where, crouching, he began to amuse himself unconsciously. Picking a daisy he dropped it on the pond, so that the stem was a keel, the flower floated like a little water lily, staring with its open face up to the sky. It turned slowly round, in a slow, slow Dervish dance, as it veered away.

He watched it, then dropped another daisy into the water, and after that another, and sat watching them with bright, absolved eyes, crouching near on the bank. Ursula turned to look. A strange feeling possessed her, as if something were taking place. But it was all intangible. And some sort of control was being put on her. She could not know. She could only watch the brilliant little discs of the daisies veering slowly in travel on the dark, lustrous water. The little flotilla was drifting into the light, a company of white specks in the distance.

'Do let us go to the shore, to follow them,' she said, afraid of being any longer imprisoned on the island. And they pushed off in the punt.

She was glad to be on the free land again. She went along the bank towards the sluice. The daisies were scattered broadcast on the pond, tiny radiant things, like an exaltation, points of exaltation here and there. Why did they move her so strongly and mystically?

'Look,' he said, 'your boat of purple paper is escorting them, and they are a convoy of rafts.'

Some of the daisies came slowly towards her, hesitating, making a shy bright little cotillion on the dark clear water. Their gay bright candour moved her so much as they came near, that she was almost in tears.

'Why are they so lovely,' she cried. 'Why do I think them so lovely?'

'They are nice flowers,' he said, her emotional tones putting a constraint on him.

'You know that a daisy is a company of florets, a concourse, become individual. Don't the botanists put it highest in the line of development? I believe they do.'

'The compositae, yes, I think so,' said Ursula, who was never very sure of anything. Things she knew perfectly well, at one moment, seemed to become doubtful the next.

'Explain it so, then,' he said. 'The daisy is a perfect little democracy, so it's the highest of flowers, hence its charm.'

'No,' she cried, 'no – never. It isn't democratic.'

'No,' he admitted. 'It's the golden mob of the proletariat, surrounded by a showy white fence of the idle rich.'

'How hateful – your hateful social orders!' she cried.

'Quite! It's a daisy – we'll leave it alone.'

'Do. Let it be a dark horse for once,' she said: 'if anything can be a dark horse to you,' she added satirically.

They stood aside, forgetful. As if a little stunned, they both were motionless, barely conscious. The little conflict into which they had fallen had torn their consciousness and left them like two impersonal forces, there in contact.

He became aware of the lapse. He wanted to say something, to get on to a new more ordinary footing.

'You know,' he said, 'that I am having rooms here at the mill? Don't you think we can have some good times?'

'Oh are you?' she said, ignoring all his implication of admitted intimacy.

He adjusted himself at once, became normally distant.

'If I find I can live sufficiently by myself,' he continued, 'I shall give up my work altogether. It has become dead to me. I don't believe in the humanity I pretend to be part of, I don't care a straw for the social ideals I live by, I hate the dying organic form of social mankind – so it can't be anything but trumpery, to work at education. I shall drop it as soon as I am clear enough – tomorrow perhaps – and be by myself.'

'Have you enough to live on?' asked Ursula.

'Yes – I've about four hundred a year. That makes it easy for me.'

There was a pause.

'And what about Hermione?' asked Ursula.

'That's over, finally – a pure failure, and never could have been anything else.'

'But you still know each other?'

'We could hardly pretend to be strangers, could we?'

There was a stubborn pause.

'But isn't that a half-measure?' asked Ursula at length.

'I don't think so,' he said. 'You'll be able to tell me if it is.'

Again there was a pause of some minutes' duration. He was thinking.

'One must throw everything away, everything – let everything go, to get the one last thing one wants,' he said.

'What thing?' she asked in challenge.

'I don't know – freedom together,' he said.

She had wanted him to say 'love'.

There was heard a loud barking of the dogs below. He seemed disturbed by it. She did not notice. Only she thought he seemed uneasy.

'As a matter of fact,' he said, in rather a small voice, 'I believe that is Hermione come now, with Gerald Crich. She wanted to see the rooms before they are furnished.'

'I know,' said Ursula. 'She will superintend the furnishing for you.'

'Probably. Does it matter?'

'Oh no, I should think not,' said Ursula. 'Though personally, I can't bear her. I think she is a lie, if you like, you who are always talking about lies.' Then she ruminated for a moment, when she broke out: 'Yes, and I do mind if she furnishes your rooms – I do mind. I mind that you keep her hanging on at all.'

He was silent now, frowning.

'Perhaps,' he said. 'I don't *want* her to furnish the rooms here – and I don't keep her hanging on. Only, I needn't be churlish to her, need I? At any rate, I shall have to go down and see them now. You'll come, won't you?'

'I don't think so,' she said coldly and irresolutely.

'Won't you? Yes do. Come and see the rooms as well. Do come.'

CHAPTER 12

Carpeting

He set off down the bank, and she went unwillingly with him. Yet she would not have stayed away, either.

'We know each other well, you and I, already,' he said. She did not answer.

In the large darkish kitchen of the mill, the labourer's wife was talking shrilly to Hermione and Gerald, who stood, he in white and she in a glistening bluish foulard, strangely luminous in the dusk of the room; whilst from the cages on the walls, a dozen or more canaries sang at the top of their voices. The cages were all placed round a small square window at the back, where the sunshine came in, a beautiful beam, filtering through green leaves of a tree. The voice of Mrs Salmon shrilled against the noise of the birds, which rose ever more wild and triumphant, and the woman's voice went up and up against them, and the birds replied with wild animation.

'Here's Rupert!' shouted Gerald in the midst of the din. He was suffering badly, being very sensitive in the ear.

'O–o–h them birds, they won't let you speak – !' shrilled the labourer's wife in disgust. 'I'll cover them up.'

And she darted here and there, throwing a duster, an apron, a towel, a tablecloth over the cages of the birds.

'Now will you stop it, and let a body speak for your row,' she said, still in a voice that was too high.

The party watched her. Soon the cages were covered, they had a strange funereal look. But from under the towels odd defiant trills and bubblings still shook out.

'Oh, they won't go on,' said Mrs Salmon reassuringly. 'They'll go to sleep now.'

'Really,' said Hermione, politely.

'They will,' said Gerald. 'They will go to sleep automatically, now the impression of evening is produced.'

'Are they so easily deceived?' cried Ursula.

'Oh, yes,' replied Gerald. 'Don't you know the story of Fabre, who, when he was a boy, put a hen's head under her wing, and she straight away went to sleep? It's quite true.'

'And did that make him a naturalist?' asked Birkin.

'Probably,' said Gerald.

Meanwhile Ursula was peeping under one of the cloths. There sat the canary in a corner, bunched and fluffed up for sleep.

'How ridiculous!' she cried. 'It really thinks the night has come! How absurd! Really, how can one have any respect for a creature that is so easily taken in!'

'Yes,' sang Hermione, coming also to look. She put her hand on Ursula's arm and chuckled a low laugh. 'Yes, doesn't he look comical?' she chuckled. 'Like a stupid husband.'

Then, with her hand still on Ursula's arm, she drew her away, saying, in her mild singsong, 'How did you come here? We saw Gudrun too.'

'I came to look at the pond,' said Ursula, 'and I found Mr Birkin there.'

'Did you? This is quite a Brangwen land, isn't it!'

'I'm afraid I hoped so,' said Ursula. 'I ran here for refuge, when I saw you down the lake, just putting off.'

'Did you! And now we've run you to earth.'

Hermione's eyelids lifted with an uncanny movement, amused but over-wrought. She had always her strange, rapt look, unnatural and irresponsible.

'I was going on,' said Ursula. 'Mr Birkin wanted me to see the rooms. Isn't it delightful to live here? It is perfect.'

'Yes,' said Hermione, abstractedly. Then she turned right away from Ursula, ceased to know her existence.

'How do you feel, Rupert?' she sang in a new, affectionate tone, to Birkin.

'Very well,' he replied.

'Were you quite comfortable?' The curious, sinister, rapt look was on Hermione's face, she shrugged her bosom in a convulsed movement, and seemed like one half in a trance.

'Quite comfortable,' he replied.

There was a long pause, whilst Hermione looked at him for a long time, from under her heavy, drugged eyelids.

'And you think you'll be happy here?' she said at last.

'I'm sure I shall.'

'I'm sure I shall do anything for him as I can,' said the labourer's wife. 'And I'm sure our master will; so I *hope* he'll find himself comfortable.'

Hermione turned and looked at her slowly.

'Thank you so much,' she said, and then she turned completely away again. She recovered her position, and lifting her face towards him, and addressing him exclusively, she said, 'Have you measured the rooms?'

'No,' he said, 'I've been mending the punt.'

'Shall we do it now?' she said slowly, balanced and dispassionate.

'Have you got a tape measure, Mrs Salmon?' he said, turning to the woman.

'Yes sir, I think I can find one,' replied the woman, bustling immediately to a basket. 'This is the only one I've got, if it will do.'

Hermione took it, though it was offered to him.

'Thank you so much,' she said. 'It will do very nicely. Thank you so much.' Then she turned to Birkin, saying with a little gay movement: 'Shall we do it now, Rupert?'

'What about the others, they'll be bored,' he said reluctantly.

'Do you mind?' said Hermione, turning to Ursula and Gerald vaguely.

'Not in the least,' they replied.

'Which room shall we do first?' she said, turning again to Birkin, with the same gaiety, now she was going to *do* something with him.

'We'll take them as they come,' he said.

'Should I be getting your teas ready, while you do that?' said the labourer's wife, also gay because *she* had something to do.

'Would you?' said Hermione, turning to her with the curious motion of intimacy that seemed to envelop the woman, draw her almost to Hermione's breast, and which left the others standing apart. 'I should be so glad. Where shall we have it?'

'Where would you like it? Shall it be in here, or out on the grass?'

'Where shall we have tea?' sang Hermione to the company at large.

'On the bank by the pond. And *we'll* carry the things up, if you'll just get them ready, Mrs Salmon,' said Birkin.

'All right,' said the pleased woman.

The party moved down the passage into the front room. It was empty, but clean and sunny. There was a window looking on to the tangled front garden.

'This is the dining-room,' said Hermione. 'We'll measure it this way, Rupert – you go down there – '

'Can't I do it for you,' said Gerald, coming to take the end of the tape.

'No, thank you,' cried Hermione, stooping to the ground in her bluish, brilliant foulard. It was a great joy to her to *do* things, and to have the ordering of the job, with Birkin. He obeyed her subduedly. Ursula and Gerald looked on. It was a peculiarity of Hermione's, that at every moment, she had one intimate, and turned all the rest of those present into onlookers. This raised her into a state of triumph.

They measured and discussed in the dining-room, and Hermione decided what the floor coverings must be. It sent her into a strange, convulsed anger, to be thwarted. Birkin always let her have her way, for the moment.

Then they moved across, through the hall, to the other front room, that was a little smaller than the first.

'This is the study,' said Hermione. 'Rupert, I have a rug that I want you to have for here. Will you let me give it to you? Do – I want to give it you.'

'What is it like?' he asked ungraciously.

'You haven't seen it. It is chiefly rose red, then blue, a metallic, mid-blue, and a very soft dark blue. I think you would like it. Do you think you would?'

'It sounds very nice,' he replied. 'What is it? Oriental? With a pile?'

'Yes. Persian! It is made of camel's hair, silky. I think it is called Bergamos – twelve feet by seven – . Do you think it will do?'

'It would *do*,' he said. 'But why should you give me an expensive rug? I can manage perfectly well with my old Oxford Turkish.'

'But may I give it to you? Do let me.'

'How much did it cost?'

She looked at him, and said, 'I don't remember. It was quite cheap.'

He looked at her, his face set.

'I don't want to take it, Hermione,' he said.

'Do let me give it to the rooms,' she said, going up to him and putting her hand on his arm lightly, pleadingly. 'I shall be so disappointed.'

'You know I don't want you to give me things,' he repeated helplessly.

'I don't want to give you *things*,' she said teasingly. 'But will you have this?'

'All right,' he said, defeated, and she triumphed.

They went upstairs. There were two bedrooms to correspond with the rooms downstairs. One of them was half furnished, and Birkin had evidently slept there. Hermione went round the room carefully, taking in every detail, as if absorbing the evidence of his presence, in all the inanimate things. She felt the bed and examined the coverings.

'Are you *sure* you were quite comfortable?' she said, pressing the pillow.

'Perfectly,' he replied coldly.

'And were you warm? There is no down quilt. I am sure you need one. You mustn't have a great pressure of clothes.'

'I've got one,' he said. 'It is coming down.'

They measured the rooms, and lingered over every consideration. Ursula stood at the window and watched the woman carrying the tea up the bank to the pond. She hated the palaver Hermione made, she wanted to drink tea, she wanted anything but this fuss and business.

At last they all mounted the grassy bank, to the picnic. Hermione poured out tea. She ignored now Ursula's presence. And Ursula, recovering from her ill-humour, turned to Gerald saying, 'Oh, I hated you so much the other day, Mr Crich.'

'What for?' said Gerald, wincing slightly away.

'For treating your horse so badly. Oh, I hated you so much!'

'What did he do?' sang Hermione.

'He made his lovely sensitive Arab horse stand with him at the railway-crossing whilst a horrible lot of trucks went by; and the poor thing, she was in a perfect frenzy, a perfect agony. It was the most horrible sight you can imagine.'

'Why did you do it, Gerald?' asked Hermione, calm and interrogative.

'She must learn to stand – what use is she to me in this country, if she shies and goes off every time an engine whistles.'

'But why inflict unnecessary torture?' said Ursula. 'Why make her stand all that time at the crossing? You might just as well have ridden back up the road, and saved all that horror. Her sides were bleeding where you had spurred her. It was too horrible – !'

Gerald stiffened.

'I have to use her,' he replied. 'And if I'm going to be sure of her at *all*, she'll have to learn to stand noises.'

'Why should she?' cried Ursula in a passion. 'She is a living creature, why should she stand anything, just because you choose to make her? She has as much right to her own being, as you have to yours.'

'There I disagree,' said Gerald. 'I consider that mare is there for my use. Not because I bought her, but because that is the natural order. It is more natural for a man to take a horse and use it as he likes, than for him to go down on his knees to it, begging it to do as it wishes, and to fulfil its own marvellous nature.'

Ursula was just breaking out, when Hermione lifted her face and began, in her musing singsong, 'I do think – I do really think we must have the *courage* to use the lower animal life for our needs. I do think there is something wrong, when we look on every living creature as if it were ourselves. I do feel, that it is false to project our own feelings on every animate creature. It is a lack of discrimination, a lack of criticism.'

'Quite,' said Birkin sharply. 'Nothing is so detestable as the maudlin attributing of human feelings and consciousness to animals.'

'Yes,' said Hermione, wearily, 'we must really take a position. Either we are going to use the animals, or they will use us.'

'That's a fact,' said Gerald. 'A horse has got a will like a man, though it has no *mind* strictly. And if your will isn't master, then the horse is master of you. And this is a thing I can't help. I can't help being master of the horse.'

'If only we could learn how to use our will,' said Hermione, 'we could do anything. The will can cure anything, and put anything right. That I am convinced of – if only we use the will properly, intelligibly.'

'What do you mean by using the will properly?' said Birkin.

'A very great doctor taught me,' she said, addressing Ursula and Gerald vaguely. 'He told me, for instance, that to cure oneself of a bad habit, one should *force* oneself to do it, when one would not do it – make oneself do it – and then the habit would disappear.'

'How do you mean?' said Gerald.

'If you bite your nails, for example. Then, when you don't want to bite your nails, bite them, make yourself bite them. And you would find the habit was broken.'

'Is that so?' said Gerald.

'Yes. And in so many things, I have *made* myself well. I was a very queer and nervous girl. And by learning to use my will, simply by using my will, I *made* myself right.'

Ursula looked all the while at Hermione, as she spoke in her slow, dispassionate, and yet strangely tense voice. A curious thrill went over the younger woman. Some strange, dark, convulsive power was in Hermione, fascinating and repelling.

'It is fatal to use the will like that,' cried Birkin harshly, 'disgusting. Such a will is an obscenity.'

Hermione looked at him for a long time, with her shadowed, heavy eyes. Her face was soft and pale and thin, almost phosphorescent, her jaw was lean.

'I'm sure it isn't,' she said at length. There always seemed an interval, a strange split between what she seemed to feel and experience, and what she actually said and thought. She seemed to catch her thoughts at length from off the surface of a maelstrom of chaotic black emotions and reactions, and Birkin was always filled with repulsion, she caught so infallibly, her will never failed her. Her voice was always dispassionate and tense, and perfectly confident. Yet she shuddered with a sense of nausea, a sort of seasickness that always threatened to overwhelm her mind. But her mind remained unbroken, her will was still perfect. It almost sent Birkin mad. But he would never, never dare to break her will, and let loose the maelstrom of her subconsciousness, and see her in her ultimate madness. Yet he was always striking at her.

'And of course,' he said to Gerald, 'horses *haven't* got a complete will, like human beings. A horse has no *one* will. Every horse, strictly, has two wills. With one will, it wants to put itself in the human power completely – and with the other, it wants to be free, wild. The two wills sometimes lock – you know that, if ever you've felt a horse bolt, while you've been driving it.'

'I have felt a horse bolt while I was driving it,' said Gerald, 'but it didn't make me know it had two wills. I only knew it was frightened.'

Hermione had ceased to listen. She simply became oblivious when these subjects were started.

'Why should a horse want to put itself in the human power?' asked Ursula. 'That is quite incomprehensible to me. I don't believe it ever wanted it.'

'Yes it did. It's the last, perhaps highest, love-impulse: resign your will to the higher being,' said Birkin.

'What curious notions you have of love,' jeered Ursula.

'And woman is the same as horses: two wills act in opposition inside her. With one will, she wants to subject herself utterly. With the other she wants to bolt, and pitch her rider to perdition.'

'Then I'm a bolter,' said Ursula, with a burst of laughter.

'It's a dangerous thing to domesticate even horses, let alone women,' said Birkin. 'The dominant principle has some rare antagonists.'

'Good thing too,' said Ursula.

'Quite,' said Gerald, with a faint smile. 'There's more fun.'

Hermione could bear no more. She rose, saying in her easy singsong, 'Isn't the evening beautiful! I get filled sometimes with such a great sense of beauty, that I feel I can hardly bear it.'

Ursula, to whom she had appealed, rose with her, moved to the last impersonal depths. And Birkin seemed to her almost a monster of hateful arrogance. She went with Hermione along the bank of the pond, talking of beautiful, soothing things, picking the gentle cowslips.

'Wouldn't you like a dress,' said Ursula to Hermione, 'of this yellow spotted with orange – a cotton dress?'

'Yes,' said Hermione, stopping and looking at the flower, letting the thought come home to her and soothe her. 'Wouldn't it be pretty? I should *love* it.'

And she turned smiling to Ursula, in a feeling of real affection.

But Gerald remained with Birkin, wanting to probe him to the bottom, to know what he meant by the dual will in horses. A flicker of excitement danced on Gerald's face.

Hermione and Ursula strayed on together, united in a sudden bond of deep affection and closeness.

'I really do not want to be forced into all this criticism and analysis of life. I really *do* want to see things in their entirety, with their beauty left to them, and their wholeness, their natural holiness. Don't you feel it, don't you feel you *can't* be tortured into any more knowledge?' said Hermione, stopping in front of Ursula, and turning to her with clenched fists thrust downwards.

'Yes,' said Ursula. 'I do. I am sick of all this poking and prying.'

'I'm so glad you are. Sometimes,' said Hermione, again stopping arrested in her progress and turning to Ursula, 'sometimes I wonder if I *ought* to submit to all this realisation, if I am not being weak in rejecting it. But I feel I *can't – I can't*. It seems to destroy *everything*. All the beauty and the – and the true holiness is destroyed – and I feel I can't live without them.'

'And it would be simply wrong to live without them,' cried Ursula. 'No, it is so *irreverent* to think that everything must be realised in the head. Really, something must be left to the Lord, there always is and always will be.'

'Yes,' said Hermione, reassured like a child, 'it should, shouldn't it? And Rupert – ' she lifted her face to the sky, in a muse – 'he *can* only tear things to pieces. He really *is* like a boy who must pull everything to pieces to see how it is made. And I can't think it is right – it does seem so irreverent, as you say.'

'Like tearing open a bud to see what the flower will be like,' said Ursula.

'Yes. And that kills everything, doesn't it? It doesn't allow any possibility of flowering.'

'Of course not,' said Ursula. 'It is purely destructive.'

'It is, isn't it!'

Hermione looked long and slow at Ursula, seeming to accept confirmation from her. Then the two women were silent. As soon as they were in accord, they began mutually to mistrust each other. In spite of herself, Ursula felt herself recoiling from Hermione. It was all she could do to restrain her revulsion.

They returned to the men, like two conspirators who have withdrawn to come to an agreement. Birkin looked up at them. Ursula hated him for his cold watchfulness. But he said nothing.

'Shall we be going?' said Hermione. 'Rupert, you are coming to Shortlands to dinner? Will you come at once, will you come now, with us?'

'I'm not dressed,' replied Birkin. 'And you know Gerald stickles for convention.'

'I don't stickle for it,' said Gerald. 'But if you'd got as sick as I have of rowdy go-as-you-please in the house, you'd prefer it if people were peaceful and conventional, at least at meals.'

'All right,' said Birkin.

'But can't we wait for you while you dress?' persisted Hermione.

'If you like.'

He rose to go indoors. Ursula said she would take her leave.

'Only,' she said, turning to Gerald, 'I must say that, however man is lord of the beast and the fowl, I still don't think he has any right to violate the feelings of the inferior creation. I still think it would have been much more sensible and nice of you if you'd trotted back up the road while the train went by, and been considerate.'

'I see,' said Gerald, smiling, but somewhat annoyed. 'I must remember another time.'

'They all think I'm an interfering female,' thought Ursula to herself, as she went away. But she was in arms against them.

She ran home plunged in thought. She had been very much moved by Hermione, she had really come into contact with her, so that there was a sort of league between the two women. And yet she could not bear her. But she put the thought away. 'She's really good,' she said to herself. 'She really wants what is right.' And she tried to feel at one with Hermione, and to shut off from Birkin. She was strictly hostile to him. But she was held to him by some bond, some deep principle. This at once irritated her and saved her.

Only now and again, violent little shudders would come over her, out of her subconsciousness, and she knew it was the fact that she had stated her challenge to Birkin, and he had, consciously or unconsciously, accepted. It was a fight to the death between them – or to new life: though in what the conflict lay, no one could say.

CHAPTER 13

Mino

The days went by, and she received no sign. Was he going to ignore her, was he going to take no further notice of her secret? A dreary weight of anxiety and acrid bitterness settled on her. And yet Ursula knew she was only deceiving herself, and that he would proceed. She said no word to anybody.

Then, sure enough, there came a note from him, asking if she would come to tea with Gudrun, to his rooms in town.

'Why does he ask Gudrun as well?' she asked herself at once. 'Does he want to protect himself, or does he think I would not go alone?'

She was tormented by the thought that he wanted to protect himself. But at the end of all, she only said to herself, 'I don't want Gudrun to be there, because I want him to say something more to me. So I shan't tell Gudrun anything about it, and I shall go alone. Then I shall know.'

She found herself sitting on the tramcar, mounting up the hill going out of the town, to the place where he had his lodging. She seemed to have passed into a kind of dream world, absolved from the conditions of actuality. She watched the sordid streets of the town go by beneath her, as if she were a spirit disconnected from the material universe. What had it all to do with her? She was palpitating and formless within the flux of the ghost life. She could not consider any more, what anybody would say of her or think about her. People had passed out of her range, she was absolved. She had fallen strange and dim, out of the sheath of the material life, as a berry falls from the only world it has ever known, down out of the sheath on to the real unknown.

Birkin was standing in the middle of the room, when she was shown in by the landlady. He too was moved outside himself. She saw him agitated and shaken, a frail, unsubstantial body silent like the node of some violent force, that came out from him and shook her almost into a swoon.

'You are alone?' he said.

'Yes – Gudrun could not come.'

He instantly guessed why.

And they were both seated in silence, in the terrible tension of the room. She was aware that it was a pleasant room, full of light and very restful in its form – aware also of a fuchsia tree, with dangling scarlet and purple flowers.

'How nice the fuchsias are!' she said, to break the silence.

'Aren't they! Did you think I had forgotten what I said?'

A swoon went over Ursula's mind.

'I don't want you to remember it – if you don't want to,' she struggled to say, through the dark mist that covered her.

There was silence for some moments.

'No,' he said. 'It isn't that. Only – if we are going to know each other, we must pledge ourselves for ever. If we are going to make a relationship, even of friendship, there must be something final and infallible about it.'

There was a clang of mistrust and almost anger in his voice. She did not answer. Her heart was too much contracted. She could not have spoken.

Seeing she was not going to reply, he continued, almost bitterly, giving himself away, 'I can't say it is love I have to offer – and it isn't love I want. It is something much more impersonal and harder – and rarer.'

There was a silence, out of which she said, 'You mean you don't love me?'

She suffered furiously, saying that.

'Yes, if you like to put it like that. Though perhaps that isn't true. I don't know. At any rate, I don't feel the emotion of love for you – no, and I don't want to. Because it gives out in the last issues.'

'Love gives out in the last issues?' she asked, feeling numb to the lips.

'Yes, it does. At the very last, one is alone, beyond the influence of love. There is a real impersonal me, that is beyond love, beyond any emotional relationship. So it is with you. But we want to delude ourselves that love is the root. It isn't. It is only the branches. The root is beyond love, a naked kind of isolation, an isolated me, that does *not* meet and mingle, and never can.'

She watched him with wide, troubled eyes. His face was incandescent in its abstract earnestness.

'And you mean you can't love?' she asked, in trepidation.

'Yes, if you like. I have loved. But there is a beyond, where there is not love.'

She could not submit to this. She felt it swooning over her. But she could not submit.

'But how do you know – if you have never *really* loved?' she asked.

'It is true, what I say; there is a beyond, in you, in me, which is further than love, beyond the scope, as stars are beyond the scope of vision, some of them.'

'Then there is no love,' cried Ursula.

'Ultimately, no, there is something else. But, ultimately, there *is* no love.'

Ursula was given over to this statement for some moments. Then she half rose from her chair, saying, in a final, repellent voice, 'Then let me go home – what am I doing here?'

'There is the door,' he said. 'You are a free agent.'

He was suspended finely and perfectly in this extremity. She hung motionless for some seconds, then she sat down again.

'If there is no love, what is there?' she cried, almost jeering.

'Something,' he said, looking at her, battling with his soul, with all his might.

'What?'

He was silent for a long time, unable to be in communication with her while she was in this state of opposition.

'There is,' he said, in a voice of pure abstraction, 'a final me which is stark and impersonal and beyond responsibility. So there is a final you. And it is there I would want to meet you – not in the emotional, loving plane – but there beyond, where there is no speech and no terms of agreement. There we are two stark, unknown beings, two utterly strange creatures, I would want to approach you, and you me. And there could be no obligation, because there is no standard for action there, because no understanding has been reaped from that plane. It is quite inhuman – so there can be no calling to book, in any form whatsoever – because one is outside the pale of all that is accepted, and nothing known applies. One can only follow the impulse, taking that which lies in front, and responsible for nothing, asked for nothing, giving nothing, only each taking according to the primal desire.'

Ursula listened to this speech, her mind dumb and almost senseless, what he said was so unexpected and so untoward.

'It is just purely selfish,' she said.

'If it is pure, yes. But it isn't selfish at all. Because I don't *know* what I want of you. I deliver *myself* over to the unknown, in coming to you, I am without reserves or defences, stripped entirely, into the unknown. Only there needs the pledge between us, that we will both cast off everything, cast off ourselves even, and cease to be, so that that which is perfectly ourselves can take place in us.'

She pondered along her own line of thought.

'But it is because you love me, that you want me?' she persisted.

'No it isn't. It is because I believe in you – if I *do* believe in you.'

'Aren't you sure?' she laughed, suddenly hurt.

He was looking at her steadfastly, scarcely heeding what she said.

'Yes, I must believe in you, or else I shouldn't be here saying this,' he replied.

'But that is all the proof I have. I don't feel any very strong belief at this particular moment.'

She disliked him for this sudden relapse into weariness and faithlessness.

'But don't you think me good-looking?' she persisted, in a mocking voice.

He looked at her, to see if he felt that she was good-looking.

'I don't *feel* that you're good-looking,' he said.

'Not even attractive?' she mocked, bitingly.

He knitted his brows in sudden exasperation.

'Don't you see that it's not a question of visual appreciation in the least,' he cried. 'I don't *want* to see you. I've seen plenty of women, I'm sick and weary of seeing them. I want a woman I don't see.'

'I'm sorry I can't oblige you by being invisible,' she laughed.

'Yes,' he said, 'you are invisible to me, if you don't force me to be visually aware of you. But I don't want to see you or hear you.'

'What did you ask me to tea for, then?' she mocked.

But he would take no notice of her. He was talking to himself.

'I want to find you, where you don't know your own existence, the you that your common self denies utterly. But I don't want your good looks, and I don't want your womanly feelings, and I don't want your thoughts nor opinions nor your ideas – they are all bagatelles to me.'

'You are very conceited, Monsieur,' she mocked. 'How do you know what my womanly feelings are, or my thoughts or my ideas? You don't even know what I think of you now.'

'Nor do I care in the slightest.'

'I think you are very silly. I think you want to tell me you love me, and you go all this way round to do it.'

'All right,' he said, looking up with sudden exasperation. 'Now go away then, and leave me alone. I don't want any more of your meretricious persiflage.'

'Is it really persiflage?' she mocked, her face really relaxing into laughter. She interpreted it, that he had made a deep confession of love to her. But he was so absurd in his words, also.

They were silent for many minutes, she was pleased and elated like a child. His concentration broke, he began to look at her simply and naturally.

'What I want is a strange conjunction with you – ' he said quietly; 'not meeting and mingling – you are quite right – but an equilibrium, a pure balance of two single beings – as the stars balance each other.'

She looked at him. He was very earnest, and earnestness was always rather ridiculous, commonplace, to her. It made her feel unfree and uncomfortable. Yet she liked him so much. But why drag in the stars.

'Isn't this rather sudden?' she mocked.

He began to laugh.

'Best to read the terms of the contract, before we sign,' he said.

A young grey cat that had been sleeping on the sofa jumped down and stretched, rising on its long legs, and arching its slim back. Then it sat considering for a moment, erect and kingly. And then, like a dart, it had shot out of the room, through the open window-doors, and into the garden.

'What's he after?' said Birkin, rising.

The young cat trotted lordly down the path, waving his tail. He was an ordinary tabby with white paws, a slender young gentleman. A crouching, fluffy, brownish-grey cat was stealing up the side of the fence. The Mino walked statelily up to her, with manly nonchalance. She crouched before him and pressed herself on the ground in humility, a fluffy soft outcast, looking up at him with wild eyes that were green and lovely as great jewels. He looked casually down on her. So she crept a few inches further, proceeding on her way to the back door, crouching in a wonderful, soft, self-obliterating manner, and moving like a shadow.

He, going statelily on his slim legs, walked after her, then suddenly, for pure excess, he gave her a light cuff with his paw on the side of her face. She ran off a few steps, like a blown leaf along the ground, then crouched unobtrusively, in submissive, wild patience. The Mino pretended to take no notice of her. He blinked his eyes superbly at the landscape. In a minute she drew herself together and moved softly, a fleecy brown-grey shadow, a few paces forward. She began to quicken her pace, in a moment she would be gone like a dream, when the young grey lord sprang before her, and gave her a light handsome cuff. She subsided at once, submissively.

'She is a wild cat,' said Birkin. 'She has come in from the woods.'

The eyes of the stray cat flared round for a moment, like great green fires staring at Birkin. Then she had rushed in a soft swift rush, halfway down the garden. There she paused to look round. The Mino turned his face in pure superiority to his master, and slowly closed his eyes, standing in statuesque young perfection. The wild cat's round, green, wondering eyes were staring all the while like uncanny fires. Then again, like a shadow, she slid towards the kitchen.

In a lovely springing leap, like a wind, the Mino was upon her, and had boxed her twice, very definitely, with a white, delicate fist. She sank and slid back, unquestioning. He walked after her, and cuffed her once or twice, leisurely, with sudden little blows of his magic white paws.

'Now why does he do that?' cried Ursula in indignation.

'They are on intimate terms,' said Birkin.

'And is that why he hits her?'

'Yes,' laughed Birkin, 'I think he wants to make it quite obvious to her.'

'Isn't it horrid of him!' she cried; and going out into the garden she called to the Mino, 'Stop it, don't bully. Stop hitting her.'

The stray cat vanished like a swift, invisible shadow. The Mino glanced at Ursula, then looked from her disdainfully to his master.

'Are you a bully, Mino?' Birkin asked.

The young slim cat looked at him, and slowly narrowed its eyes. Then it glanced away at the landscape, looking into the distance as if completely oblivious of the two human beings.

'Mino,' said Ursula, 'I don't like you. You are a bully like all males.'

'No,' said Birkin, 'he is justified. He is not a bully. He is only insisting to the poor stray that she shall acknowledge him as a sort of fate, her own fate: because you can see she is fluffy and promiscuous as the wind. I am with him entirely. He wants superfine stability.'

'Yes, I know!' cried Ursula. 'He wants his own way – I know what your fine words work down to – bossiness, I call it, bossiness.'

The young cat again glanced at Birkin in disdain of the noisy woman.

'I quite agree with you, Miciotto,' said Birkin to the cat. 'Keep your male dignity, and your higher understanding.'

Again the Mino narrowed his eyes as if he were looking at the sun. Then, suddenly affecting to have no connection at all with the two people, he went trotting off, with assumed spontaneity and gaiety, his tail erect, his white feet blithe.

'Now he will find the *belle sauvage* once more, and entertain her with his superior wisdom,' laughed Birkin.

Ursula looked at the man who stood in the garden with his hair blowing and his eyes smiling ironically, and she cried, 'Oh it makes me so cross, this assumption of male superiority! And it is such a lie! One wouldn't mind if there were any justification for it.'

'The wild cat,' said Birkin, 'doesn't mind. She perceives that it is justified.'

'Does she!' cried Ursula. 'And tell it to the Horse Marines.'

'To them also.'

'It is just like Gerald Crich with his horse – a lust for bullying – a real *Wille zur Macht* – so base, so petty.'

'I agree that the *Wille zur Macht* is a base and petty thing. But with the Mino, it is the desire to bring this female cat into a pure stable equilibrium, a transcendent and abiding *rapport* with the single male. Whereas without him, as you see, she is a mere stray, a fluffy sporadic bit of chaos. It is a *volonté de pouvoir*, if you like, a will to ability, taking *pouvoir* as a verb.'

'Ah –! Sophistries! It's the old Adam.'

'Oh yes. Adam kept Eve in the indestructible paradise, when he kept her single with himself, like a star in its orbit.'

'Yes – yes –' cried Ursula, pointing her finger at him. 'There you are – a star in its orbit! A satellite – a satellite of Mars – that's what she is to be! There – there – you've given yourself away! You want a satellite, Mars and his satellite! You've said it – you've said it – you've dished yourself!'

He stood smiling in frustration and amusement and irritation and admiration and love. She was so quick, and so lambent, like discernible fire, and so vindictive, and so rich in her dangerous flamy sensitiveness.

'I've not said it at all,' he replied, 'if you will give me a chance to speak.'

'No, no!' she cried. 'I won't let you speak. You've said it, a satellite, you're not going to wriggle out of it. You've said it.'

'You'll never believe now that I *haven't* said it,' he answered. 'I neither implied nor indicated nor mentioned a satellite, nor intended a satellite, never.'

'*You prevaricator!*' she cried, in real indignation.

'Tea is ready, sir,' said the landlady from the doorway.

They both looked at her, very much as the cats had looked at them, a little while before.

'Thank you, Mrs Daykin.'

An interrupted silence fell over the two of them, a moment of breach.

'Come and have tea,' he said.

'Yes, I should love it,' she replied, gathering herself together.

They sat facing each other across the tea table.

'I did not say, nor imply, a satellite. I meant two single equal stars balanced in conjunction –'

'You gave yourself away, you gave away your little game completely,' she cried, beginning at once to eat. He saw that she would take no further heed of his expostulation, so he began to pour the tea.

'What *good* things to eat!' she cried.

'Take your own sugar,' he said.

He handed her her cup. He had everything so nice, such pretty cups and plates, painted with mauve-lustre and green, also shapely bowls and glass plates, and old spoons, on a woven cloth of pale grey and black and purple. It was very rich and fine. But Ursula could see Hermione's influence.

'Your things are so lovely!' she said, almost angrily.

'I like them. It gives me real pleasure to use things that are attractive in themselves – pleasant things. And Mrs Daykin is good. She thinks everything is wonderful, for my sake.'

'Really,' said Ursula, 'landladies are better than wives, nowadays. They certainly *care* a great deal more. It is much more beautiful and complete here now, than if you were married.'

'But think of the emptiness within,' he laughed.

'No,' she said. 'I am jealous that men have such perfect landladies and such beautiful lodgings. There is nothing left them to desire.'

'In the housekeeping way, we'll hope not. It is disgusting, people marrying for a home.'

'Still,' said Ursula, 'a man has very little need for a woman now, has he?'

'In outer things, maybe – except to share his bed and bear his children. But essentially, there is just the same need as there ever was. Only nobody takes the trouble to be essential.'

'How essential?' she said.

'I do think,' he said, 'that the world is only held together by the mystic conjunction, the ultimate unison between people – a bond. And the immediate bond is between man and woman.'

'But it's such old hat,' said Ursula. 'Why should love be a bond? No, I'm not having any.'

'If you are walking westward,' he said, 'you forfeit the northern and eastward and southern direction. If you admit a unison, you forfeit all the possibilities of chaos.'

'But love is freedom,' she declared.

'Don't cant to me,' he replied. 'Love is a direction which excludes all other directions. It's a freedom *together*, if you like.'

'No,' she said, 'love includes everything.'

'Sentimental cant,' he replied. 'You want the state of chaos, that's all. It is ultimate nihilism, this freedom-in-love business, this freedom which is love and love which is freedom. As a matter of fact, if you enter into a pure unison, it is irrevocable, and it is never pure till it is irrevocable. And when it is irrevocable, it is one way, like the path of a star.'

'Ha!' she cried bitterly. 'It is the old dead morality.'

'No,' he said, 'it is the law of creation. One is committed. One must commit oneself to a conjunction with the other – for ever. But it is not selfless – it is a maintaining of the self in mystic balance and integrity – like a star balanced with another star.'

'I don't trust you when you drag in the stars,' she said. 'If you were quite true, it wouldn't be necessary to be so far-fetched.'

'Don't trust me then,' he said, angry. 'It is enough that I trust myself.'

'And that is where you make another mistake,' she replied. 'You *don't* trust yourself. You don't fully believe yourself what you are saying. You don't really want this conjunction, otherwise you wouldn't talk so much about it, you'd get it.'

He was suspended for a moment, arrested.

'How?' he said.

'By just loving,' she retorted in defiance.

He was still a moment, in anger. Then he said, 'I tell you, I don't believe in love like that. I tell you, you want love to administer to your egoism, to subserve you. Love is a process of subservience with you – and with everybody. I hate it.'

'No,' she cried, pressing back her head like a cobra, her eyes flashing. 'It is a process of pride – I want to be proud – '

'Proud and subservient, proud and subservient, I know you,' he retorted dryly. 'Proud and subservient, then subservient to the proud – I know you and your love. It is a tick-tack, tick-tack, a dance of opposites.'

'Are you sure?' she mocked wickedly, 'what my love is?'

'Yes, I am,' he retorted.

'So cocksure!' she said. 'How can anybody ever be right, who is so cocksure? It shows you are wrong.'

He was silent in chagrin.

They had talked and struggled till they were both wearied out.

'Tell me about yourself and your people,' he said.

And she told him about the Brangwens, and about her mother, and about Skrebensky, her first love, and about her later experiences. He sat very still, watching her as she talked. And he seemed to listen with reverence. Her face was beautiful and full of baffled light as she told him all the things that had hurt her or perplexed her so deeply. He seemed to warm and comfort his soul at the beautiful light of her nature.

'If she *really* could pledge herself,' he thought to himself, with passionate insistence but hardly any hope. Yet a curious little irresponsible laughter appeared in his heart.

'We have all suffered so much,' he mocked, ironically.

She looked up at him, and a flash of wild gaiety went over her face, a strange flash of yellow light coming from her eyes.

'Haven't we!' she cried, in a high, reckless cry. 'It is almost absurd, isn't it?'

'Quite absurd,' he said. 'Suffering bores me, any more.'

'So it does me.'

He was almost afraid of the mocking recklessness of her splendid face. Here was one who would go to the whole lengths of heaven or hell, whichever she had to go. And he mistrusted her, he was afraid of a woman capable of such abandon, such dangerous thoroughness of destructivity. Yet he chuckled within himself also.

She came over to him and put her hand on his shoulder, looking down at him with strange golden-lighted eyes, very tender, but with a curious devilish look lurking underneath.

'Say you love me, say "my love" to me,' she pleaded

He looked back into her eyes, and saw. His face flickered with sardonic comprehension.

'I love you right enough,' he said, grimly. 'But I want it to be something else.'

'But why? But why?' she insisted, bending her wonderful luminous face to him. 'Why isn't it enough?'

'Because we can go one better,' he said, putting his arms round her.

'No, we can't,' she said, in a strong, voluptuous voice of yielding. 'We can only love each other. Say "my love" to me, say it, say it.'

She put her arms round his neck. He enfolded her, and kissed her subtly, murmuring in a subtle voice of love, and irony, and submission, 'Yes, – my love, yes, – my love. Let love be enough then. I love you then – I love you. I'm bored by the rest.'

'Yes,' she murmured, nestling very sweet and close to him.

CHAPTER 14

Water-Party

Every year Mr Crich gave a more or less public water-party on the lake. There was a little pleasure-launch on Willey Water and several rowing boats, and guests could take tea either in the marquee that was set up in the grounds of the house, or they could picnic in the shade of the great walnut tree at the boat-house by the lake. This year the staff of the Grammar School was invited, along with the chief officials of the firm. Gerald and the younger Criches did not care for this party, but it had become customary now, and it pleased the father, as being the only occasion when he could gather some people of the district together in festivity with him. For he loved to give pleasures to his dependants and to those poorer than himself. But his children preferred the company of their own equals in wealth. They hated their inferiors' humility or gratitude or awkwardness.

Nevertheless they were willing to attend at this festival, as they had done almost since they were children, the more so, as they all felt a little guilty now, and unwilling to thwart their father any more, since he was so ill in health. Therefore, quite cheerfully Laura prepared to take her mother's place as hostess, and Gerald assumed responsibility for the amusements on the water.

Birkin had written to Ursula saying he expected to see her at the party, and Gudrun, although she scorned the patronage of the Criches, would nevertheless accompany her mother and father if the weather were fine.

The day came blue and full of sunshine, with little wafts of wind. The sisters both wore dresses of white crêpe, and hats of soft grass. But Gudrun had a sash of brilliant black and pink and yellow colour wound broadly round her waist, and she had pink silk stockings, and black and pink and yellow decoration on the brim of her hat, weighing it down a little. She carried also a yellow silk coat over her arm, so that she looked remarkable, like a painting from the Salon. Her appearance was a sore trial to her father, who said angrily, 'Don't you think you might as well get yourself up for a Christmas cracker, an' ha' done with it?'

But Gudrun looked handsome and brilliant, and she wore her clothes in pure defiance. When people stared at her, and giggled after her, she made a point of saying loudly, to Ursula, *'Regarde, regarde ces gens-là! Ne sont-ils pas des hiboux incroyables?'* And with the words of French in her mouth, she would look over her shoulder at the giggling party.

'No, really, it's impossible!' Ursula would reply distinctly. And so the two girls took it out of their universal enemy. But their father became more and more enraged.

Ursula was all snowy white, save that her hat was pink, and entirely without trimming, and her shoes were dark red, and she carried an orange-coloured coat. And in this guise they were walking all the way to Shortlands, their father and mother going in front.

They were laughing at their mother, who, dressed in a summer material of black and purple stripes, and wearing a hat of purple straw, was setting forth with much more of the shyness and trepidation of a young girl than her daughters ever felt, walking demurely beside her husband, who, as usual, looked rather crumpled in his best suit, as if he were the father of a young family and had been holding the baby whilst his wife got dressed.

'Look at the young couple in front,' said Gudrun calmly. Ursula looked at her mother and father, and was suddenly seized with uncontrollable laughter.

The two girls stood in the road and laughed till the tears ran down their faces, as they caught sight again of the shy, unworldly couple of their parents going on ahead.

'We are roaring at you, mother,' called Ursula, helplessly following after her parents.

Mrs Brangwen turned round with a slightly puzzled, exasperated look. 'Oh indeed!' she said. 'What is there so very funny about *me*, I should like to know?'

She could not understand that there could be anything amiss with her appearance. She had a perfect calm sufficiency, an easy indifference to any criticism whatsoever, as if she were beyond it. Her clothes were always rather odd, and as a rule slipshod, yet she wore them with a perfect ease and satisfaction. Whatever she had on, so long as she was barely tidy, she was right, beyond remark; such an aristocrat she was by instinct.

'You look so stately, like a country Baroness,' said Ursula, laughing with a little tenderness at her mother's naïve puzzled air.

'*Just* like a country Baroness!' chimed in Gudrun. Now the mother's natural hauteur became self-conscious, and the girls shrieked again.

'Go home, you pair of idiots, great giggling idiots!' cried the father, inflamed with irritation.

'Mm-m-er!' booed Ursula, pulling a face at his crossness.

The yellow lights danced in his eyes, he leaned forward in real rage.

'Don't be so silly as to take any notice of the great gabies,' said Mrs Brangwen, turning on her way.

'I'll see if I'm going to be followed by a pair of giggling yelling jackanapes – ' he cried vengefully.

The girls stood still, laughing helplessly at his fury, upon the path beside the hedge.

'Why you're as silly as they are, to take any notice,' said Mrs Brangwen, also becoming angry now he was really enraged.

'There are some people coming, father,' cried Ursula, with mocking warning. He glanced round quickly, and went on to join his wife, walking stiff with rage. And the girls followed, weak with laughter.

When the people had passed by, Brangwen cried in a loud, stupid voice, 'I'm going back home if there's any more of this. I'm damned if I'm going to be made a fool of in this fashion, in the public road.'

He was really out of temper. At the sound of his blind, vindictive voice, the laughter suddenly left the girls, and their hearts contracted with contempt. They hated his words 'in the public road'. What did they care for the public road? But Gudrun was conciliatory.

'But we weren't laughing to *hurt* you,' she cried, with an uncouth gentleness which made her parents uncomfortable. 'We were laughing because we're fond of you.'

'We'll walk on in front, if they are *so* touchy,' said Ursula, angry. And in this wise they arrived at Willey Water. The lake was blue and fair, the meadows sloped down in sunshine on one side, the thick dark woods dropped steeply on the other. The little pleasure-launch was fussing out from the shore, twanging its music, crowded with people, flapping its paddles. Near the boat-house was a throng of gaily-dressed persons, small in the distance. And on the highroad, some of the common people were standing along the hedge, looking at the festivity beyond, enviously, like souls not admitted to paradise.

'My eye!' said Gudrun, *sotto voce*, looking at the motley of guests, 'there's a pretty crowd if you like! Imagine yourself in the midst of that, my dear.'

Gudrun's apprehensive horror of people in the mass unnerved Ursula. 'It looks rather awful,' she said anxiously.

'And imagine what they'll be like – *imagine*!' said Gudrun, still in that unnerving, subdued voice. Yet she advanced determinedly.

'I suppose we can get away from them,' said Ursula anxiously.

'We're in a pretty fix if we can't,' said Gudrun. Her extreme ironic loathing and apprehension was very trying to Ursula.

'We needn't stay,' she said.

'I certainly shan't stay five minutes among that little lot,' said Gudrun. They advanced nearer, till they saw policemen at the gates.

'Policemen to keep you in, too!' said Gudrun. 'My word, this is a beautiful affair.'

'We'd better look after father and mother,' said Ursula anxiously.

'Mother's *perfectly* capable of getting through this little celebration,' said Gudrun with some contempt.

But Ursula knew that her father felt uncouth and angry and unhappy, so she was far from her ease. They waited outside the gate till their parents came up. The tall, thin man in his crumpled clothes was unnerved and irritable as a boy, finding himself on the brink of this social function. He did not feel a gentleman, he did not feel anything except pure exasperation.

Ursula took her place at his side, they gave their tickets to the policeman, and passed in on to the grass, four abreast; the tall, hot, ruddy-dark man with his narrow boyish brow drawn with irritation, the fresh-faced, easy woman, perfectly collected though her hair was slipping on one side, then Gudrun, her eyes round and dark and staring, her full soft face impassive, almost sulky, so that she seemed to be backing away in antagonism even whilst she was advancing; and then Ursula, with the odd, brilliant, dazzled look on her face, that always came when she was in some false situation.

Birkin was the good angel. He came smiling to them with his affected social grace, that somehow was never *quite* right. But he took off his hat and smiled at them with a real smile in his eyes, so that Brangwen cried out heartily in relief, 'How do you do? You're better, are you?'

'Yes, I'm better. How do you do, Mrs Brangwen? I know Gudrun and Ursula very well.'

His eyes smiled full of natural warmth. He had a soft, flattering manner with women, particularly with women who were not young.

'Yes,' said Mrs Brangwen, cool but yet gratified. 'I have heard them speak of you often enough.'

He laughed. Gudrun looked aside, feeling she was being belittled. People were standing about in groups, some women were sitting in the shade of the walnut tree, with cups of tea in their hands, a waiter in evening dress was hurrying round, some girls were simpering with parasols, some young men, who had just come in from rowing, were sitting cross-legged on the grass, coatless, their shirt-sleeves rolled up in manly fashion, their hands resting on their white flannel trousers, their gaudy ties floating about, as they laughed and tried to be witty with the young damsels.

'Why,' thought Gudrun churlishly, 'don't they have the manners to put their coats on, and not to assume such intimacy in their appearance.'

She abhorred the ordinary young man, with his hair plastered back, and his easy-going chumminess.

Hermione Roddice came up, in a handsome gown of white lace, trailing an enormous silk shawl blotched with great embroidered flowers, and balancing an enormous plain hat on her head. She looked striking, astonishing, almost macabre, so tall, with the fringe of her great cream-coloured vividly-blotched shawl trailing on the ground after her, her thick hair coming low over her eyes, her face strange and long and pale, and the blotches of brilliant colour drawn round her.

'Doesn't she look *weird*!' Gudrun heard some girls titter behind her. And she could have killed them.

'How do you do!' sang Hermione, coming up very kindly, and glancing slowly over Gudrun's father and mother. It was a trying moment, exasperating for Gudrun. Hermione was really so strongly entrenched in her class superiority, she could come up and know people out of simple curiosity, as if they were creatures on exhibition. Gudrun would do the same herself. But she resented being in the position when somebody might do it to her.

Hermione, very remarkable, and distinguishing the Brangwens very much, led them along to where Laura Crich stood receiving the guests.

'This is Mrs Brangwen,' sang Hermione, and Laura, who wore a stiff embroidered linen dress, shook hands and said she was glad to see her. Then Gerald came up, dressed in white, with a black and brown blazer, and looking handsome. He too was introduced to the Brangwen parents, and immediately he spoke to Mrs Brangwen as if she were a lady, and to Brangwen as if he were *not* a gentleman. Gerald was so obvious in his demeanour. He had to shake hands with his left hand, because he had hurt his right, and carried it, bandaged up, in the pocket of his jacket. Gudrun was *very* thankful that none of her party asked him what was the matter with the hand.

The steam launch was fussing in, all its music jingling, people calling excitedly from on board. Gerald went to see to the debarkation, Birkin was getting tea for Mrs Brangwen, Brangwen had joined a Grammar School group, Hermione was sitting down by their mother, the girls went to the landing-stage to watch the launch come in.

She hooted and tooted gaily, then her paddles were silent, the ropes were thrown ashore, she drifted in with a little bump. Immediately the passengers crowded excitedly to come ashore.

'Wait a minute, wait a minute,' shouted Gerald in sharp command.

They must wait till the boat was tight on the ropes, till the small gangway was put out. Then they streamed ashore, clamouring as if they had come from America.

'Oh it's *so* nice!' the young girls were crying. 'It's quite lovely.'

The waiters from on board ran out to the boat-house with baskets, the captain lounged on the little bridge. Seeing all safe, Gerald came to Gudrun and Ursula.

'You wouldn't care to go on board for the next trip, and have tea there?' he asked.

'No thanks,' said Gudrun coldly.

'You don't care for the water?'

'For the water? Yes, I like it very much.'

He looked at her, his eyes searching.

'You don't care for going on a launch, then?'

She was slow in answering, and then she spoke slowly.

'No,' she said. 'I can't say that I do.' Her colour was high, she seemed angry about something.

'*Un peu trop de monde*,' said Ursula, explaining.

'Eh? *Trop de monde*!' He laughed shortly. 'Yes, there's a fair number of 'em.'

Gudrun turned on him brilliantly.

'Have you ever been from Westminster Bridge to Richmond on one of the Thames steamers?' she cried.

'No,' he said, 'I can't say I have.'

'Well, it's one of the most *vile* experiences I've ever had.' She spoke rapidly and excitedly, the colour high in her cheeks. 'There was absolutely nowhere to sit down, nowhere, a man just above sang "Rocked in the Cradle of the Deep" the *whole* way; he was blind and he had a small organ, one of those portable organs, and he expected money; so you can imagine what *that* was like; there came a constant smell of luncheon from below, and puffs of hot oily machinery; the journey took hours and hours and hours; and for miles, literally for miles, dreadful boys ran with us on the shore, in that *awful* Thames mud, going in *up to the waist* – they had their trousers turned back, and they went up to their hips in that indescribable Thames mud, their faces always turned to us, and screaming, exactly like carrion creatures, screaming " 'Ere y'are sir, 'ere y'are sir, 'ere y'are sir," exactly like some foul carrion objects, perfectly obscene; and paterfamilias on board, laughing when the boys went right down in that awful mud, occasionally throwing them a ha'penny. And if you'd seen the intent look on the faces of these boys, and the way they darted in the filth when a coin was flung – really, no vulture or jackal could dream of approaching them, for foulness. I *never* would go on a pleasure boat again – never.'

Gerald watched her all the time she spoke, his eyes glittering with faint rousedness. It was not so much what she said; it was she herself who roused him, roused him with a small, vivid pricking.

'Of course,' he said, 'every civilised body is bound to have its vermin.'

'Why?' cried Ursula. '*I* don't have vermin.'

'And it's not that – it's the *quality* of the whole thing – paterfamilias laughing and thinking it sport, and throwing the ha'pennies, and materfamilias spreading her fat little knees and eating, continually eating – ' replied Gudrun.

'Yes,' said Ursula. 'It isn't the boys so much who are vermin; it's the people themselves, the whole body politic, as you call it.'

Gerald laughed.

'Never mind,' he said. 'You shan't go on the launch.'

Gudrun flushed quickly at his rebuke.

There were a few moments of silence. Gerald, like a sentinel, was watching the people who were going on to the boat. He was very good-looking and self-contained, but his air of soldierly alertness was rather irritating.

'Will you have tea here then, or go across to the house, where there's a tent on the lawn?' he asked.

'Can't we have a rowing boat, and get out?' asked Ursula, who was always rushing in too fast.

'To get out?' smiled Gerald.

'You see,' cried Gudrun, flushing at Ursula's outspoken rudeness, 'we don't know the people, we are almost *complete* strangers here.'

'Oh, I can soon set you up with a few acquaintances,' he said easily.

Gudrun looked at him, to see if it were ill-meant. Then she smiled at him.

'Ah,' she said, 'you know what we mean. Can't we go up there, and explore that coast?' She pointed to a grove on the hillock of the meadow-side, near the shore halfway down the lake. 'That looks perfectly lovely. We might even bathe. Isn't it beautiful in this light! Really, it's like one of the reaches of the Nile – as one imagines the Nile.'

Gerald smiled at her factitious enthusiasm for the distant spot.

'You're sure it's far enough off?' he asked ironically, adding at once: 'Yes, you might go there, if we could get a boat. They seem to be all out.'

He looked round the lake and counted the rowing boats on its surface.

'How lovely it would be!' cried Ursula wistfully.

'And don't you want tea?' he said.

'Oh,' said Gudrun, 'we could just drink a cup, and be off.'

He looked from one to the other, smiling. He was somewhat offended – yet sporting.

'Can you manage a boat pretty well?' he asked.

'Yes,' replied Gudrun, coldly, 'pretty well.'

'Oh yes,' cried Ursula. 'We can both of us row like water-spiders.'

'You can? There's a light little canoe of mine, that I didn't take out for fear somebody should drown themselves. Do you think you'd be safe in that?'

'Oh perfectly,' said Gudrun.

'What an angel!' cried Ursula.

'Don't, for *my* sake, have an accident – because I'm responsible for the water.'

'Sure,' pledged Gudrun.

'Besides, we can both swim quite well,' said Ursula.

'Well – then I'll get them to put you up a tea-basket, and you can picnic all to yourselves – that's the idea, isn't it?'

'How fearfully good! How frightfully nice if you could!' cried Gudrun warmly, her colour flushing up again. It made the blood stir in his veins, the subtle way she turned to him and infused her gratitude into his body.

'Where's Birkin?' he said, his eyes twinkling. 'He might help me to get it down.'

'But what about your hand? Isn't it hurt?' asked Gudrun, rather muted, as if avoiding the intimacy. This was the first time the hurt had been mentioned. The curious way she skirted round the subject sent a new, subtle caress through his veins. He took his hand out of his pocket. It was bandaged. He looked at it, then put it in his pocket again. Gudrun quivered at the sight of the wrapped-up paw.

'Oh, I can manage with one hand. The canoe is as light as a feather,' he said. 'There's Rupert! – Rupert!'

Birkin turned from his social duties and came towards them.

'What have you done to it?' asked Ursula, who had been aching to put the question for the last half hour.

'To my hand?' said Gerald. 'I trapped it in some machinery.'

'Ugh!' said Ursula. 'And did it hurt much?'

'Yes,' he said. 'It did at the time. It's getting better now. It crushed the fingers.'

'Oh,' cried Ursula, as if in pain, 'I hate people who hurt themselves. I can *feel* it.' And she shook her hand.

'What do you want?' said Birkin.

The two men carried down the slim brown boat, and set it on the water.

'You're quite sure you'll be safe in it?' Gerald asked.

'Quite sure,' said Gudrun. 'I wouldn't be so mean as to take it, if there was the slightest doubt. But I've had a canoe at Arundel, and I assure you I'm perfectly safe.'

So saying, having given her word like a man, she and Ursula entered the frail craft, and pushed gently off. The two men stood watching them. Gudrun was paddling. She knew the men were watching her, and it made her slow and rather clumsy. The colour flew in her face like a flag.

'Thanks awfully,' she called back to him, from the water, as the boat slid away. 'It's lovely – like sitting in a leaf.'

He laughed at the fancy. Her voice was shrill and strange, calling from the distance. He watched her as she paddled away. There was something childlike about her, trustful and deferential, like a child. He watched her all the while, as she rowed. And to Gudrun it was a real delight, in make-belief, to be the childlike, clinging woman to the man who stood there on the quay, so good-looking and efficient in his white clothes, and moreover the most important man she knew at the moment. She did not take any notice of the wavering, indistinct, lambent Birkin, who stood at his side. One figure at a time occupied the field of her attention.

The boat rustled lightly along the water. They passed the bathers whose striped tents stood between the willows of the meadow's edge, and drew along the open shore, past the meadows that sloped golden in the light of the already late afternoon. Other boats were stealing under the wooded shore opposite, they could hear people's laughter and voices. But Gudrun rowed on towards the clump of trees that balanced perfect in the distance, in the golden light.

The sisters found a little place where a tiny stream flowed into the lake, with reeds and flowery marsh of pink willow herb, and a gravelly bank to the side. Here they ran delicately ashore, with their frail boat, the two girls took off their shoes and stockings and went through the water's edge to the grass. The tiny ripples of the lake were warm and clear, they lifted their boat on to the bank, and looked round with joy. They were quite alone in a forsaken little stream-mouth, and on the knoll just behind was the clump of trees.

'We will bathe just for a moment,' said Ursula, 'and then we'll have tea.'

They looked round. Nobody could notice them, or could come up in time to see them. In less than a minute Ursula had thrown off her clothes and had slipped naked into the water, and was swimming out. Quickly, Gudrun joined her. They swam silently and blissfully for a few minutes, circling round their little stream-mouth. Then they slipped ashore and ran into the grove again, like nymphs.

'How lovely it is to be free,' said Ursula, running swiftly here and there between the tree trunks, quite naked, her hair blowing loose. The grove was of beech trees, big and splendid, a steel-grey scaffolding of trunks and boughs, with level sprays of strong green here and there, whilst through the northern side the distance glimmered open as through a window.

When they had run and danced themselves dry, the girls quickly dressed and sat down to the fragrant tea. They sat on the northern side of the grove, in the yellow sunshine facing the slope of the grassy hill, alone in a little wild world of their own. The tea was hot and aromatic, there were delicious little sandwiches of cucumber and of caviare, and winy cakes.

'Are you happy, Prune?' cried Ursula in delight, looking at her sister.

'Ursula, I'm perfectly happy,' replied Gudrun gravely, looking at the westering sun.

'So am I.'

When they were together, doing the things they enjoyed, the two sisters were quite complete in a perfect world of their own. And this was one of the perfect moments of freedom and delight, such as children alone know, when all seems a perfect and blissful adventure.

When they had finished tea, the two girls sat on, silent and serene. Then

Ursula, who had a beautiful strong voice, began to sing to herself, softly: 'Annchen von Tharau'. Gudrun listened, as she sat beneath the trees, and the yearning came into her heart. Ursula seemed so peaceful and sufficient unto herself, sitting there unconsciously crooning her song, strong and unquestioned at the centre of her own universe. And Gudrun felt herself outside. Always this desolating, agonised feeling, that she was outside of life, an onlooker, whilst Ursula was a partaker, caused Gudrun to suffer from a sense of her own negation, and made her, that she must always demand the other to be aware of her, to be in connection with her.

'Do you mind if I do Dalcroze to that tune, Hurtler?' she asked in a curious muted tone, scarce moving her lips.

'What did you say?' asked Ursula, looking up in peaceful surprise.

'Will you sing while I do Dalcroze?' said Gudrun, suffering at having to repeat herself.

Ursula thought a moment, gathering her straying wits together.

'While you do – ?' she asked vaguely.

'Dalcroze movements,' said Gudrun, suffering tortures of self-consciousness, even because of her sister.

'Oh Dalcroze! I couldn't catch the name. *Do* – I should love to see you,' cried Ursula, with childish surprised brightness. 'What shall I sing?'

'Sing anything you like, and I'll take the rhythm from it.'

But Ursula could not for her life think of anything to sing. However, she suddenly began, in a laughing, teasing voice, 'My love is a high-born lady – '

Gudrun, looking as if some invisible chain weighed on her hands and feet, began slowly to dance in the eurhythmic manner, pulsing and fluttering rhythmically with her feet, making slower, regular gestures with her hands and arms, now spreading her arms wide, now raising them above her head, now flinging them softly apart, and lifting her face, her feet all the time beating and running to the measure of the song, as if it were some strange incantation, her white, rapt form drifting here and there in a strange impulsive rhapsody, seeming to be lifted on a breeze of incantation, shuddering with strange little runs. Ursula sat on the grass, her mouth open in her singing, her eyes laughing as if she thought it was a great joke, but a yellow light flashing up in them, as she caught some of the unconscious ritualistic suggestion of the complex shuddering and waving and drifting of her sister's white form, that was clutched in pure, mindless, tossing rhythm, and a will set powerful in a kind of hypnotic influence.

'My love is a high-born lady – She is–s–s – rather dark than shady – ' rang out Ursula's laughing, satiric song, and quicker, fiercer went Gudrun in the dance, stamping as if she were trying to throw off some bond, flinging her hands suddenly and stamping again, then rushing with face uplifted and throat full and beautiful, and eyes half closed, sightless. The sun was low and yellow, sinking down, and in the sky floated a thin, ineffectual moon.

Ursula was quite absorbed in her song, when suddenly Gudrun stopped and said mildly, ironically, 'Ursula!'

'Yes?' said Ursula, opening her eyes out of the trance.

Gudrun was standing still and pointing, a mocking smile on her face, towards the side.

'Ugh!' cried Ursula in sudden panic, starting to her feet.

'They're quite all right,' rang out Gudrun's sardonic voice.

On the left stood a little cluster of Highland cattle, vividly coloured and fleecy in the evening light, their horns branching into the sky, pushing forward their muzzles inquisitively, to know what it was all about. Their eyes glittered through their tangle of hair, their naked nostrils were full of shadow.

'Won't they do anything?' cried Ursula in fear.

Gudrun, who was usually frightened of cattle, now shook her head in a queer, half-doubtful, half-sardonic motion, a faint smile round her mouth.

'Don't they look charming, Ursula?' cried Gudrun, in a high, strident voice, something like the scream of a seagull.

'Charming,' cried Ursula in trepidation. 'But won't they do anything to us?'

Again Gudrun looked back at her sister with an enigmatic smile, and shook her head.

'I'm sure they won't,' she said, as if she had to convince herself also, and yet, as if she were confident of some secret power in herself, and had to put it to the test. 'Sit down and sing again,' she called in her high, strident voice.

'I'm frightened,' cried Ursula, in a pathetic voice, watching the group of sturdy short cattle, that stood with their knees planted, and watched with their dark, wicked eyes, through the matted fringe of their hair. Nevertheless, she sank down again, in her former posture.

'They are quite safe,' came Gudrun's high call. 'Sing something, you've only to sing something.'

It was evident she had a strange passion to dance before the sturdy, handsome cattle.

Ursula began to sing, in a false quavering voice, 'Way down in Tennessee –'

She sounded purely anxious. Nevertheless, Gudrun, with her arms outspread and her face uplifted, went in a strange palpitating dance towards the cattle, lifting her body towards them as if in a spell, her feet pulsing as if in some little frenzy of unconscious sensation, her arms, her wrists, her hands stretching and heaving and falling and reaching and reaching and falling, her breasts lifted and shaken towards the cattle, her throat exposed as in some voluptuous ecstasy towards them, whilst she drifted imperceptibly nearer, an uncanny white figure, towards them, carried away in its own rapt trance, ebbing in strange fluctuations upon the cattle, that waited, and ducked their heads a little in sudden contraction from her, watching all the time as if hypnotised, their bare horns branching in the clear light, as the white figure of the woman ebbed upon them, in the slow, hypnotising convulsion of the dance. She could feel them just in front of her, it was as if she had the electric pulse from their breasts running into her hands. Soon she would touch them, actually touch them. A terrible shiver of fear and pleasure went through her. And all the while, Ursula, spellbound, kept up her high-pitched thin, irrelevant song, which pierced the fading evening like an incantation.

Gudrun could hear the cattle breathing heavily with helpless fear and fascination. Oh, they were brave little beasts, these wild Scotch bullocks, wild and fleecy. Suddenly one of them snorted, ducked its head, and backed.

'Hue! Hi–eee!' came a sudden loud shout from the edge of the grove. The cattle broke and fell back quite spontaneously, went running up the hill, their fleece waving like fire to their motion. Gudrun stood suspended out on the grass, Ursula rose to her feet.

It was Gerald and Birkin come to find them, and Gerald had cried out to frighten off the cattle.

'What do you think you're doing?' he now called, in a high, wondering vexed tone.

'Why have you come?' came back Gudrun's strident cry of anger.

'What do you think you were doing?' Gerald repeated, automatically.

'We were doing eurhythmics,' laughed Ursula, in a shaken voice.

Gudrun stood aloof looking at them with large dark eyes of resentment, suspended for a few moments. Then she walked away up the hill, after the cattle, which had gathered in a little, spellbound cluster higher up.

'Where are you going?' Gerald called after her. And he followed her up the hillside. The sun had gone behind the hill, and shadows were clinging to the earth, the sky above was full of travelling light.

'A poor song for a dance,' said Birkin to Ursula, standing before her with a sardonic, flickering laugh on his face. And in another second, he was singing softly to himself, and dancing a grotesque step-dance in front of her, his limbs and body shaking loose, his face flickering palely, a constant thing, whilst his feet beat a rapid mocking tattoo, and his body seemed to hang all loose and quaking in between, like a shadow.

'I think we've all gone mad,' she said, laughing rather frightened.

'Pity we aren't madder,' he answered, as he kept up the incessant shaking dance. Then suddenly he leaned up to her and kissed her fingers lightly, putting his face to hers and looking into her eyes with a pale grin. She stepped back, affronted.

'Offended – ?' he asked ironically, suddenly going quite still and reserved again. 'I thought you liked the light fantastic.'

'Not like that,' she said, confused and bewildered, almost affronted. Yet somewhere inside her she was fascinated by the sight of his loose, vibrating body, perfectly abandoned to its own dropping and swinging, and by the pallid, sardonic-smiling face above. Yet automatically she stiffened herself away, and disapproved. It seemed almost an obscenity, in a man who talked as a rule so very seriously.

'Why not like that?' he mocked. And immediately he dropped again into the incredibly rapid, slack-waggling dance, watching her malevolently. And moving in the rapid, stationary dance, he came a little nearer, and reached forward with an incredibly mocking, satiric gleam on his face, and would have kissed her again, had she not started back.

'No, don't!' she cried, really afraid.

'Cordelia after all,' he said satirically. She was stung, as if this were an insult. She knew he intended it as such, and it bewildered her.

'And you,' she cried in retort, 'why do you always take your soul in your mouth, so frightfully full?'

'So that I can spit it out the more readily,' he said, pleased by his own retort.

Gerald Crich, his face narrowing to an intent gleam, followed up the hill with quick strides, straight after Gudrun. The cattle stood with their noses together on the brow of a slope, watching the scene below, the men in white hovering about the white forms of the women, watching above all Gudrun, who was advancing slowly towards them. She stood a moment, glancing back at Gerald, and then at the cattle.

Then in a sudden motion, she lifted her arms and rushed sheer upon the long-horned bullocks, in shuddering irregular runs, pausing for a second and looking at them, then lifting her hands and running forward with a flash, till they ceased pawing the ground, and gave way, snorting with terror, lifting their heads from the ground and flinging themselves away, galloping off into the evening, becoming tiny in the distance, and still not stopping.

Gudrun remained staring after them, with a masklike defiant face.

'Why do you want to drive them mad?' asked Gerald, coming up with her.

She took no notice of him, only averted her face from him. 'It's not safe, you know,' he persisted. 'They're nasty, when they do turn.'

'Turn where? Turn away?' she mocked loudly.

'No,' he said, 'turn against you.'

'Turn against *me*?' she mocked.

He could make nothing of this.

'Anyway, they gored one of the farmer's cows to death, the other day,' he said.

'What do I care?' she said.

'*I* cared though,' he replied, 'seeing that they're my cattle.'

'How are they yours! You haven't swallowed them. Give me one of them now,' she said, holding out her hand.

'You know where they are,' he said, pointing over the hill. 'You can have one if you'd like it sent to you later on.'

She looked at him inscrutably.

'You think I'm afraid of you and your cattle, don't you?' she asked.

His eyes narrowed dangerously. There was a faint domineering smile on his face.

'Why should I think that?' he said.

She was watching him all the time with her dark, dilated, inchoate eyes. She leaned forward and swung round her arm, catching him a light blow on the face with the back of her hand.

'That's why,' she said, mocking.

And she felt in her soul an unconquerable desire for deep violence against him. She shut off the fear and dismay that filled her conscious mind. She wanted to do as she did, she was not going to be afraid.

He recoiled from the slight blow on his face. He became deadly pale, and a dangerous flame darkened his eyes. For some seconds he could not speak, his lungs were so suffused with blood, his heart stretched almost to bursting with a great gush of ungovernable emotion. It was as if some reservoir of black emotion had burst within him, and swamped him.

'You have struck the first blow,' he said at last, forcing the words from his lungs, in a voice so soft and low, it sounded like a dream within her, not spoken in the outer air.

'And I shall strike the last,' she retorted involuntarily, with confident assurance. He was silent, he did not contradict her.

She stood negligently, staring away from him, into the distance. On the edge of her consciousness the question was asking itself, automatically, 'Why *are* you behaving in this *impossible* and ridiculous fashion?' But she was sullen, she half shoved the question out of herself. She could not get it clean away, so she felt self-conscious.

Gerald, very pale, was watching her closely. His eyes were lit up with intent lights, absorbed and gleaming. She turned suddenly on him.

'It's you who make me behave like this, you know,' she said, almost suggestive. 'I? How?' he said.

But she turned away, and set off towards the lake. Below, on the water, lanterns were coming alight, faint ghosts of warm flame floating in the pallor of the first twilight. The earth was spread with darkness, like lacquer, overhead was a pale sky, all primrose, and the lake was pale as milk in one part. Away at the landing stage, tiniest points of coloured rays were stringing themselves in the dusk. The launch was being illuminated. All round, shadow was gathering from the trees.

Gerald, white like a presence in his summer clothes, was following down the open grassy slope. Gudrun waited for him to come up. Then she softly put out her hand and touched him, saying softly, 'Don't be angry with me.'

A flame flew over him, and he was unconscious. Yet he stammered, 'I'm not angry with you. I'm in love with you.'

His mind was gone, he grasped for sufficient mechanical control, to save himself. She laughed a silvery little mockery, yet intolerably caressive.

'That's one way of putting it,' she said.

The terrible swooning burden on his mind, the awful swooning, the loss of all his control, was too much for him. He grasped her arm in his one hand, as if his hand were iron.

'It's all right, then, is it?' he said, holding her arrested.

She looked at the face with the fixed eyes, set before her, and her blood ran cold.

'Yes, it's all right,' she said softly, as if drugged, her voice crooning and witchlike.

He walked on beside her, a striding, mindless body. But he recovered a little as he went. He suffered badly. He had killed his brother when a boy, and was set apart, like Cain.

They found Birkin and Ursula sitting together by the boats, talking and laughing. Birkin had been teasing Ursula.

'Do you smell this little marsh?' he said, sniffing the air. He was very sensitive to scents, and quick in understanding them.

'It's rather nice,' she said.

'No,' he replied, 'alarming.'

'Why alarming?' she laughed.

'It seethes and seethes, a river of darkness,' he said, 'putting forth lilies and snakes, and the *ignis fatuus*, and rolling all the time onward. That's what we never take into count – that it rolls onwards.'

'What does?'

'The other river, the black river. We always consider the silver river of life, rolling on and quickening all the world to a brightness, on and on to heaven, flowing into a bright eternal sea, a heaven of angels thronging. But the other is our real reality – '

'But what other? I don't see any other,' said Ursula.

'It is your reality, nevertheless,' he said; 'that dark river of dissolution. You see it rolls in us just as the other rolls – the black river of corruption. And our flowers are of this – our sea-born Aphrodite, all our white phosphorescent flowers of sensuous perfection, all our reality, nowadays.'

'You mean that Aphrodite is really deathly?' asked Ursula.

'I mean she is the flowering mystery of the death-process, yes,' he replied. 'When the stream of synthetic creation lapses, we find ourselves part of the inverse process, the blood of destructive creation. Aphrodite is born in the first spasm of universal dissolution – then the snakes and swans and lotus – marsh-flowers – and Gudrun and Gerald – born in the process of destructive creation.'

'And you and me – ?' she asked.

'Probably,' he replied. 'In part, certainly. Whether we are that, *in toto*, I don't yet know.'

'You mean we are flowers of dissolution – *fleurs du mal*? I don't feel as if I were,' she protested.

He was silent for a time.

'I don't feel as if we were, *altogether*,' he replied. 'Some people are pure flowers of dark corruption – lilies. But there ought to be some roses, warm and flamy. You know Herakleitos says "a dry soul is best". I know so well what that means. Do you?'

'I'm not sure,' Ursula replied. 'But what if people *are* all flowers of dissolution – when they're flowers at all – what difference does it make?'

'No difference – and all the difference. Dissolution rolls on, just as production does,' he said. 'It is a progressive process – and it ends in universal nothing – the end of the world, if you like. But why isn't the end of the world as good as the beginning?'

'I suppose it isn't,' said Ursula, rather angry.

'Oh yes, ultimately,' he said. 'It means a new cycle of creation after – but not for us. If it is the end, then we are of the end – *fleurs du mal* if you like. If we are *fleurs du mal*, we are not roses of happiness, and there you are.'

'But I think I am,' said Ursula. 'I think I am a rose of happiness.'

'Ready-made?' he asked ironically.

'No – real,' she said, hurt.

'If we are the end, we are not the beginning,' he said.

'Yes we are,' she said. 'The beginning comes out of the end.'

'After it, not out of it. After us, not out of us.'

'You are a devil, you know, really,' she said. 'You want to destroy our hope. You *want* us to be deathly.'

'No,' he said, 'I only want us to *know* what we are.'

'Ha!' she cried in anger. 'You only want us to know death.'

'You're quite right,' said the soft voice of Gerald, out of the dusk behind.

Birkin rose. Gerald and Gudrun came up. They all began to smoke, in the moments of silence. One after another, Birkin lighted their cigarettes. The match flickered in the twilight, and they were all smoking peacefully by the waterside. The lake was dim, the light dying from off it, in the midst of the dark land. The air all round was intangible, neither here nor there, and there was an unreal noise of banjoes, or suchlike music.

As the golden swim of light overhead died out, the moon gained brightness, and seemed to begin to smile forth her ascendancy. The dark woods on the opposite shore melted into universal shadow. And amid this universal under-shadow, there was a scattered intrusion of lights. Far down the lake were fantastic pale strings of colour, like beads of wan fire, green and red and yellow. The music came out in a little puff, as the launch, all illuminated, veered into the great shadow, stirring her outlines of half-living lights, puffing out her music in little drifts.

All were lighting up. Here and there, close against the faint water, and at the far end of the lake, where the water lay milky in the last whiteness of the sky, and there was no shadow, solitary, frail flames of lanterns floated from the unseen boats. There was a sound of oars, and a boat passed from the pallor into the darkness under the wood, where her lanterns seemed to kindle into fire, hanging in ruddy lovely globes. And again, in the lake, shadowy red gleams hovered in reflection about the boat. Everywhere were these noiseless ruddy creatures of fire drifting near the surface of the water, caught at by the rarest, scarce visible reflections.

Birkin brought the lanterns from the bigger boat, and the four shadowy white figures gathered round, to light them. Ursula held up the first, Birkin lowered the light from the rosy, glowing cup of his hands, into the depths of the lantern. It was kindled, and they all stood back to look at the great blue moon of light that hung from Ursula's hand, casting a strange gleam on her face. It flickered, and Birkin went bending over the well of light. His face shone out like an apparition, so unconscious, and again, something demoniacal. Ursula was dim and veiled, looming over him.

'That is all right,' said his voice softly.

She held up the lantern. It had a flight of storks streaming through a turquoise sky of light, over a dark earth.

'This is beautiful,' she said.

'Lovely,' echoed Gudrun, who wanted to hold one also, and lift it up full of beauty.

'Light one for me,' she said. Gerald stood by her, incapacitated. Birkin lit the lantern she held up. Her heart beat with anxiety, to see how beautiful it would be. It was primrose yellow, with tall straight flowers growing darkly from their dark leaves, lifting their heads into the primrose day, while butterflies hovered about them, in the pure clear light.

Gudrun gave a little cry of excitement, as if pierced with delight.

'Isn't it beautiful, oh, isn't it beautiful!'

Her soul was really pierced with beauty, she was translated beyond herself. Gerald leaned near to her, into her zone of light, as if to see. He came close to her, and stood touching her, looking with her at the primrose-shining globe. And she turned her face to his, that was faintly bright in the light of the lantern, and they stood together in one luminous union, close together and ringed round with light, all the rest excluded.

Birkin looked away, and went to light Ursula's second lantern. It had a pale ruddy sea-bottom, with black crabs and seaweed moving sinuously under a transparent sea, that passed into flamy ruddiness above.

'You've got the heavens above, and the waters under the earth,' said Birkin to her.

'Anything but the earth itself,' she laughed, watching his live hands that hovered to attend to the light.

'I'm dying to see what my second one is,' cried Gudrun, in a vibrating rather strident voice, that seemed to repel the others from her.

Birkin went and kindled it. It was of a lovely deep blue colour, with a red floor, and a great white cuttlefish flowing in white soft streams all over it. The cuttlefish had a face that stared straight from the heart of the light, very fixed and coldly intent.

'How truly terrifying!' exclaimed Gudrun, in a voice of horror. Gerald, at her side, gave a low laugh.

'But isn't it really fearful!' she cried in dismay.

Again he laughed, and said, 'Change it with Ursula, for the crabs.'

Gudrun was silent for a moment.

'Ursula,' she said, 'could you bear to have this fearful thing?'

'I think the colouring is *lovely*,' said Ursula.

'So do I,' said Gudrun. 'But could you *bear* to have it swinging to your boat? Don't you want to destroy it at *once*?'

'Oh no,' said Ursula. 'I don't want to destroy it.'

'Well do you mind having it instead of the crabs? Are you sure you don't mind?'

Gudrun came forward to exchange lanterns.

'No,' said Ursula, yielding up the crabs and receiving the cuttlefish.

Yet she could not help feeling rather resentful at the way in which Gudrun and Gerald should assume a right over her, a precedence.

'Come then,' said Birkin. 'I'll put them on the boats.'

He and Ursula were moving away to the big boat.

'I suppose you'll row me back, Rupert,' said Gerald, out of the pale shadow of the evening.

'Won't you go with Gudrun in the canoe?' said Birkin. 'It'll be more interesting.'

There was a moment's pause. Birkin and Ursula stood dimly, with their swinging lanterns, by the water's edge. The world was all illusive.

'Is that all right?' said Gudrun to him.

'It'll suit *me* very well,' he said. 'But what about you, and the rowing? I don't see why you should pull me.'

'Why not?' she said. 'I can pull you as well as I could pull Ursula.'

By her tone he could tell she wanted to have him in the boat to herself, and that she was subtly gratified that she should have power over them both. He gave himself, in a strange, electric submission.

She handed him the lanterns, whilst she went to fix the cane at the end of the canoe. He followed after her, and stood with the lanterns dangling against his white-flannelled thighs, emphasising the shadow around.

'Kiss me before we go,' came his voice softly from out of the shadow above.

She stopped her work in real, momentary astonishment.

'But why?' she exclaimed, in pure surprise.

'Why?' he echoed, ironically.

And she looked at him fixedly for some moments. Then she leaned forward and kissed him, with a slow, luxurious kiss, lingering on the mouth. And then she took the lanterns from him, while he stood swooning with the perfect fire that burned in all his joints.

They lifted the canoe into the water, Gudrun took her place, and Gerald pushed off.

'Are you sure you don't hurt your hand, doing that?' she asked, solicitous. 'Because I could have done it *perfectly*.'

'I don't hurt myself,' he said in a low, soft voice, that caressed her with inexpressible beauty.

And she watched him as he sat near her, very near to her, in the stern of the canoe, his legs coming towards hers, his feet touching hers. And she paddled softly, lingeringly, longing for him to say something meaningful to her. But he remained silent.

'You like this, do you?' she said, in a gentle, solicitous voice.

He laughed shortly.

'There is a space between us,' he said, in the same low, unconscious voice, as if something were speaking out of him. And she was as if magically aware of their being balanced in separation, in the boat. She swooned with acute comprehension and pleasure.

'But I'm very near,' she said caressively, gaily.

'Yet distant, distant,' he said.

Again she was silent with pleasure, before she answered, speaking with a reedy, thrilled voice, 'Yet we cannot very well change, whilst we are on the water.' She caressed him subtly and strangely, having him completely at her mercy.

A dozen or more boats on the lake swung their rosy and moon-like lanterns low on the water, that reflected as from a fire. In the distance, the steamer twanged and thrummed and washed with her faintly-splashing paddles, trailing her strings of coloured lights, and occasionally lighting up the whole scene luridly with an effusion of fireworks, Roman candles and sheaves of stars and other simple effects, illuminating the surface of the water, and showing the boats creeping round, low down. Then the lovely darkness fell again, the lanterns and the little threaded lights glimmered softly, there was a muffled knocking of oars and a waving of music.

Gudrun paddled almost imperceptibly. Gerald could see, not far ahead, the rich blue and the rose globes of Ursula's lanterns swaying softly cheek to cheek as Birkin rowed, and iridescent, evanescent gleams chasing in the wake. He was aware, too, of his own delicately coloured lights casting their softness behind him.

Gudrun rested her paddle and looked round. The canoe lifted with the lightest ebbing of the water. Gerald's white knees were very near to her.

'Isn't it beautiful!' she said softly, as if reverently.

She looked at him, as he leaned back against the faint crystal of the lantern-light. She could see his face, although it was a pure shadow. But it was a piece of twilight. And her breast was keen with passion for him, he was so beautiful in his male stillness and mystery. It was a certain pure effluence of maleness, like an aroma from his softly, firmly moulded contours, a certain rich perfection of his presence, that touched her with an ecstasy, a thrill of pure intoxication. She loved to look at him. For the present she did not want to touch him, to know the further, satisfying substance of his living body. He was purely intangible, yet so near. Her hands lay on the paddle like slumber, she only wanted to see him, like a crystal shadow, to feel his essential presence.

'Yes,' he said vaguely. 'It is very beautiful.'

He was listening to the faint near sounds, the dropping of water-drops from the oar-blades, the slight drumming of the lanterns behind him, as they rubbed against one another, the occasional rustling of Gudrun's full skirt, an alien land noise. His mind was almost submerged, he was almost transfused, lapsed out for the first time in his life, into the things about him. For he always kept such a keen attentiveness, concentrated and unyielding in himself. Now he had let go, imperceptibly he was melting into oneness with the whole. It was like pure, perfect sleep, his first great sleep of life. He had been so insistent, so guarded, all his life. But here was sleep, and peace, and perfect lapsing out.

'Shall I row to the landing-stage?' asked Gudrun wistfully.

'Anywhere,' he answered. 'Let it drift.'

'Tell me then, if we are running into anything,' she replied, in that very quiet, toneless voice of sheer intimacy.

'The lights will show,' he said.

So they drifted almost motionless, in silence. He wanted silence, pure and whole. But she was uneasy yet for some word, for some assurance.

'Nobody will miss you?' she asked, anxious for some communication.

'Miss me?' he echoed. 'No! Why?'

'I wondered if anybody would be looking for you.'

'Why should they look for me?' And then he remembered his manners. 'But perhaps you want to get back,' he said, in a changed voice.

'No, I don't want to get back,' she replied. 'No, I assure you.'

'You're quite sure it's all right for you?'

'Perfectly all right.'

And again they were still. The launch twanged and hooted, somebody was singing. Then as if the night smashed, suddenly there was a great shout, a confusion of shouting, warring on the water, then the horrid noise of paddles reversed and churned violently.

Gerald sat up, and Gudrun looked at him in fear.

'Somebody in the water,' he said, angrily, and desperately, looking keenly across the dusk. 'Can you row up?'

'Where, to the launch?' asked Gudrun, in nervous panic.

'Yes.'

'You'll tell me if I don't steer straight,' she said, in nervous apprehension.

'You keep pretty level,' he said, and the canoe hastened forward.

The shouting and the noise continued, sounding horrid through the dusk, over the surface of the water.

'Wasn't this *bound* to happen?' said Gudrun, with heavy hateful irony. But he hardly heard, and she glanced over her shoulder to see her way. The half-dark waters were sprinkled with lovely bubbles of swaying lights, the launch did not look far off. She was rocking her lights in the early night. Gudrun rowed as hard as she could. But now that it was a serious matter, she seemed uncertain and clumsy in her stroke, it was difficult to paddle swiftly. She glanced at his face. He was looking fixedly into the darkness, very keen and alert and single in himself, instrumental. Her heart sank, she seemed to die a death. 'Of course,' she said to herself, 'nobody will be drowned. Of course they won't. It would be too extravagant and sensational.' But her heart was cold, because of his sharp impersonal face. It was as if he belonged naturally to dread and catastrophe, as if he were himself again.

Then there came a child's voice, a girl's high, piercing shriek, 'Di–Di–Di–Di–Oh Di–Oh Di–Oh Di!'

The blood ran cold in Gudrun's veins.

'It's Diana, is it,' muttered Gerald. 'The young monkey, she'd have to be up to some of her tricks.'

And he glanced again at the paddle, the boat was not going quickly enough for him. It made Gudrun almost helpless at the rowing, this nervous stress. She kept up with all her might. Still the voices were calling and answering.

'Where, where? There you are – that's it. Which? No – No-o-o. Damn it all, here, *here* – ' Boats were hurrying from all directions to the scene, coloured lanterns could be seen waving close to the surface of the lake, reflections swaying after them in uneven haste. The steamer hooted again, for some unknown reason. Gudrun's boat was travelling quickly, the lanterns were swinging behind Gerald.

And then again came the child's high, screaming voice, with a note of weeping and impatience in it now, 'Di–Oh Di–Oh Di–Di – !'

It was a terrible sound, coming through the obscure air of the evening.

'You'd be better if you were in bed, Winnie,' Gerald muttered to himself.

He was stooping unlacing his shoes, pushing them off with the foot. Then he threw his soft hat into the bottom of the boat.

'You can't go into the water with your hurt hand,' said Gudrun, panting, in a low voice of horror.

'What? It won't hurt.'

He had struggled out of his jacket, and had dropped it between his feet. He sat bareheaded, all in white now. He felt the belt at his waist. They were nearing the launch, which stood still big above them, her myriad lamps making lovely darts, and sinuous running tongues of ugly red and green and yellow light on the lustrous dark water, under the shadow.

'Oh get her out! Oh Di, *darling*! Oh get her out! Oh Daddy, oh Daddy!' moaned the child's voice, in distraction. Somebody was in the water, with a life belt. Two boats paddled near, their lanterns swinging ineffectually, the boats nosing round.

'Hi there – Rockley! – hi there!'

'Mr Gerald!' came the captain's terrified voice. 'Miss Diana's in the water.'

'Anybody gone in for her?' came Gerald's sharp voice.

'Young Doctor Brindell, sir.'

'Where?'

'Can't see no signs of them, sir. Everybody's looking, but there's nothing so far.'

There was a moment's ominous pause.

'Where did she go in?'

'I think – about where that boat is,' came the uncertain answer, 'that one with red and green lights.'

'Row there,' said Gerald quietly to Gudrun.

'Get her out, Gerald, oh get her out,' the child's voice was crying anxiously He took no heed.

'Lean back that way,' said Gerald to Gudrun, as he stood up in the frail boat. 'She won't upset.'

In another moment, he had dropped clean down, soft and plumb, into the water. Gudrun was swaying violently in her boat, the agitated water shook with transient lights, she realised that it was faintly moonlight, and that he was gone. So it was possible to be gone. A terrible sense of fatality robbed her of all feeling and thought. She knew he was gone out of the world, there was merely the same world, and absence, his absence. The night seemed large and vacuous. Lanterns swayed here and there, people were talking in an undertone on the launch and in the boats. She could hear Winifred moaning: '*Oh do find her, Gerald, do find her,*' and someone trying to comfort the child. Gudrun paddled aimlessly here and there. The terrible, massive, cold, boundless surface of the water terrified her beyond words. Would he never come back? She felt she must jump into the water too, to know the horror also.

She started, hearing someone say: 'There he is.' She saw the movement of his swimming, like a water-rat. And she rowed involuntarily to him. But he was near another boat, a bigger one. Still she rowed towards him. She must be very near. She saw him – he looked like a seal. He looked like a seal as he took hold of the side of the boat. His fair hair was washed down on his round head, his face seemed to glisten suavely. She could hear him panting.

Then he clambered into the boat. Oh, and the beauty of the subjection of his loins, white and dimly luminous as be climbed over the side of the boat, made her want to die, to die. The beauty of his dim and luminous loins as be climbed into the boat, his back rounded and soft – ah, this was too much for her, too final a vision. She knew it, and it was fatal. The terrible hopelessness of fate, and of beauty, such beauty!

He was not like a man to her, he was an incarnation, a great phase of life. She saw him press the water out of his face, and look at the bandage on his hand. And she knew it was all no good, and that she would never go beyond him, he was the final approximation of life to her.

'Put the lights out, we shall see better,' came his voice, sudden and mechanical and belonging to the world of man. She could scarcely believe there was a world of man. She leaned round and blew out her lanterns. They were difficult to blow out. Everywhere the lights were gone save the coloured points on the sides of the launch. The bluey-grey, early night spread level around, the moon was overhead, there were shadows of boats here and there.

Again there was a splash, and he was gone under. Gudrun sat, sick at heart, frightened of the great, level surface of the water, so heavy and deadly. She was so alone, with the level, unliving field of the water stretching beneath her. It was not a good isolation, it was a terrible, cold separation of suspense. She was suspended upon the surface of the insidious reality until such time as she also should disappear beneath it.

Then she knew, by a stirring of voices, that he had climbed out again, into a boat. She sat wanting connection with him. Strenuously she claimed her connection with him, across the invisible space of the water. But round her heart was an isolation unbearable, through which nothing would penetrate.

'Take the launch in. It's no use keeping her there. Get lines for the dragging,' came the decisive, instrumental voice, that was full of the sound of the world.

The launch began gradually to beat the waters.

'Gerald! Gerald!' came the wild crying voice of Winifred. He did not answer. Slowly the launch drifted round in a pathetic, clumsy circle, and slunk away to the land, retreating into the dimness. The wash of her paddles grew duller. Gudrun rocked in her light boat, and dipped the paddle automatically to steady herself.

'Gudrun?' called Ursula's voice.

'Ursula!'

The boats of the two sisters pulled together.

'Where is Gerald?' said Gudrun.

'He's dived again,' said Ursula plaintively. 'And I know he ought not, with his hurt hand and everything.'

'I'll take him in home this time,' said Birkin.

The boats swayed again from the wash of steamer. Gudrun and Ursula kept a look-out for Gerald.

'There he is!' cried Ursula, who had the sharpest eyes. He had not been long under. Birkin pulled towards him, Gudrun following. He swam slowly, and caught hold of the boat with his wounded hand. It slipped, and he sank back.

'Why don't you help him?' cried Ursula sharply.

He came again, and Birkin leaned to help him in to the boat. Gudrun again watched Gerald climb out of the water, but this time slowly, heavily, with the blind clambering motions of an amphibious beast, clumsy. Again the moon shone with faint luminosity on his white wet figure, on the stooping back and the rounded loins. But it looked defeated now, his body, it clambered and fell with slow clumsiness. He was breathing hoarsely too, like an animal that is suffering. He sat slack and motionless in the boat, his head blunt and blind like a seal's, his whole appearance inhuman, unknowing. Gudrun shuddered as she mechanically followed his boat. Birkin rowed without speaking to the landing-stage.

'Where are you going?' Gerald asked suddenly, as if just waking up.

'Home,' said Birkin.

'Oh no!' said Gerald imperiously. 'We can't go home while they're in the water. Turn back again, I'm going to find them.' The women were frightened, his voice was so imperative and dangerous, almost mad, not to be opposed.

'No!' said Birkin. 'You can't.' There was a strange fluid compulsion in his voice. Gerald was silent in a battle of wills. It was as if he would kill the other man. But Birkin rowed evenly and unswerving, with an inhuman inevitability.

'Why should you interfere?' said Gerald, in hate.

Birkin did not answer. He rowed towards the land. And Gerald sat mute, like a dumb beast, panting, his teeth chattering, his arms inert, his head like a seal's head.

They came to the landing-stage. Wet and naked-looking, Gerald climbed up the few steps. There stood his father, in the night.

'Father!' he said.

'Yes my boy? Go home and get those things off.'

'We shan't save them, father,' said Gerald.

'There's hope yet, my boy.'

'I'm afraid not. There's no knowing where they are. You can't find them. And there's a current, as cold as hell.'

'We'll let the water out,' said the father. 'Go home you and look to yourself. See that he's looked after, Rupert,' he added in a neutral voice.

'Well father, I'm sorry. I'm sorry. I'm afraid it's my fault. But it can't be helped; I've done what I could for the moment. I could go on diving, of course – not much, though – and not much use – '

He moved away barefoot, on the planks of the platform. Then he trod on something sharp.

'Of course, you've got no shoes on,' said Birkin.

'His shoes are here!' cried Gudrun from below. She was making fast her boat.

Gerald waited for them to be brought to him. Gudrun came with them. He pulled them on his feet.

'If you once die,' he said, 'then when it's over, it's finished. Why come to life again? There's room under that water there for thousands.'

'Two is enough,' she said, murmuring.

He dragged on his second shoe. He was shivering violently, and his jaw shook as he spoke.

'That's true,' he said, 'maybe. But it's curious how much room there seems, a whole universe under there; and as cold as hell, you're as helpless as if your head was cut off.' He could scarcely speak, he shook so violently. 'There's one thing about our family, you know,' he continued. 'Once anything goes wrong, it can never be put right again – not with us. I've noticed it all my life – you can't put a thing right, once it has gone wrong.'

They were walking across the highroad to the house.

'And do you know, when you are down there, it is so cold, actually, and so endless, so different really from what it is on top, so endless – you wonder how it is so many are alive, why we're up here. Are you going? I shall see you again, shan't I? Good-night, and thank you. Thank you very much!'

The two girls waited a while, to see if there were any hope. The moon shone clearly overhead, with almost impertinent brightness, the small dark boats clustered on the water, there were voices and subdued shouts. But it was all to no purpose. Gudrun went home when Birkin returned.

He was commissioned to open the sluice that let out the water from the lake, which was pierced at one end, near the highroad, thus serving as a reservoir to supply with water the distant mines, in case of necessity. 'Come with me,' he said to Ursula, 'and then I will walk home with you, when I've done this.'

He called at the water-keeper's cottage and took the key of the sluice. They went through a little gate from the highroad, to the head of the water, where was a great stone basin which received the overflow, and a flight of stone steps descended into the depths of the water itself. At the head of the steps was the lock of the sluice-gate.

The night was silver-grey and perfect, save for the scattered restless sound of voices. The grey sheen of the moonlight caught the stretch of water, dark boats plashed and moved. But Ursula's mind ceased to be receptive, everything was unimportant and unreal.

Birkin fixed the iron handle of the sluice, and turned it with a wrench. The cogs began slowly to rise. He turned and turned, like a slave, his white figure became distinct. Ursula looked away. She could not bear to see him winding heavily and laboriously, bending and rising mechanically like a slave, turning the handle.

Then, a real shock to her, there came a loud splashing of water from out of the dark, tree-filled hollow beyond the road, a splashing that deepened rapidly to a harsh roar, and then became a heavy, booming noise of a great body of water falling solidly all the time. It occupied the whole of the night, this great steady booming of water, everything was drowned within it, drowned and lost. Ursula seemed to have to struggle for her life. She put her hands over her ears, and looked at the high bland moon.

'Can't we go now?' she cried to Birkin, who was watching the water on the steps, to see if it would get any lower. It seemed to fascinate him. He looked at her and nodded.

The little dark boats had moved nearer, people were crowding curiously along the hedge by the highroad, to see what was to be seen. Birkin and Ursula went to the cottage with the key, then turned their backs on the lake. She was in great haste. She could not bear the terrible crushing boom of the escaping water.

'Do you think they are dead?' she cried in a high voice, to make herself heard.

'Yes,' he replied.

'Isn't it horrible!'

He paid no heed. They walked up the hill, further and further away from the noise.

'Do you mind very much?' she asked him.

'I don't mind about the dead,' he said, 'once they are dead. The worst of it is, they cling on to the living, and won't let go.'

She pondered for a time.

'Yes,' she said. 'The *fact* of death doesn't really seem to matter much, does it?'

'No,' he said. 'What does it matter if Diana Crich is alive or dead?'

'Doesn't it?' she said, shocked.

'No, why should it? Better she were dead – she'll be much more real. She'll be positive in death. In life she was a fretting, negated thing.'

'You are rather horrible,' murmured Ursula.

'No! I'd rather Diana Crich were dead. Her living somehow, was all wrong. As for the young man, poor devil – he'll find his way out quickly instead of slowly. Death is all right – nothing better.'

'Yet you don't want to die,' she challenged him.

He was silent for a time. Then he said, in a voice that was frightening to her in its change, 'I should like to be through with it – I should like to be through with the death process.'

'And aren't you?' asked Ursula nervously.

They walked on for some way in silence, under the trees. Then he said, slowly, as if afraid, 'There is life which belongs to death, and there is life which isn't death. One is tired of the life that belongs to death – our kind of life. But whether it is finished, God knows. I want love that is like sleep, like being born again, vulnerable as a baby that just comes into the world.'

Ursula listened, half attentive, half avoiding what he said. She seemed to catch the drift of his statement, and then she drew away. She wanted to hear, but she did not want to be implicated. She was reluctant to yield there, where he wanted her, to yield as it were her very identity.

'Why should love be like sleep?' she asked sadly.

'I don't know. So that it is like death – I *do* want to die from this life – and yet it is more than life itself. One is delivered over like a naked infant from the womb, all the old defences and the old body gone, and new air around one, that has never been breathed before.'

She listened, making out what he said. She knew, as well as he knew, that words themselves do not convey meaning, that they are but a gesture we make, a dumb show like any other. And she seemed to feel his gesture through her blood, and she drew back, even though her desire sent her forward.

'But,' she said gravely, 'didn't you say you wanted something that was *not* love – something beyond love?'

He turned in confusion. There was always confusion in speech. Yet it must be spoken. Whichever way one moved, if one were to move forwards, one must break a way through. And to know, to give utterance, was to break a way through the walls of the prison as the infant in labour strives through the walls of the womb. There is no new movement now, without the breaking through of the old body, deliberately, in knowledge, in the struggle to get out.

'I don't want love,' he said. 'I don't want to know you. I want to be gone out of myself, and you to be lost to yourself, so we are found different. One shouldn't talk when one is tired and wretched. One Hamletises, and it seems a lie. Only believe me when I show you a bit of healthy pride and insouciance. I hate myself serious.'

'Why shouldn't you be serious?' she said.

He thought for a minute, then he said, sulkily, 'I don't know.' Then they walked on in silence, at outs. He was vague and lost.

'Isn't it strange,' she said, suddenly putting her hand on his arm, with a loving impulse, 'how we always talk like this! I suppose we do love each other, in some way.'

'Oh yes,' he said; 'too much.'

She laughed almost gaily.

'You'd have to have it your own way, wouldn't you?' she teased. 'You could never take it on trust.'

He changed, laughed softly, and turned and took her in his arms, in the middle of the road.

'Yes,' he said softly.

And he kissed her face and brow, slowly, gently, with a sort of delicate happiness which surprised her extremely, and to which she could not respond. They were soft, blind kisses, perfect in their stillness. Yet she held back from them. It was like strange moths, very soft and silent, settling on her from the darkness of her soul. She was uneasy. She drew away.

'Isn't somebody coming?' she said.

So they looked down the dark road, then set off again walking towards Beldover. Then suddenly, to show him she was no shallow prude, she stopped and held him tight, hard against her, and covered his face with hard, fierce kisses of passion. In spite of his otherness, the old blood beat up in him.

'Not this, not this,' he whimpered to himself, as the first perfect mood of softness and sleep-loveliness ebbed back away from the rushing of passion that came up to his limbs and over his face as she drew him. And soon he was a perfect hard flame of passionate desire for her. Yet in the small core of the flame was an unyielding anguish of another thing. But this also was lost; he only wanted her, with an extreme desire that seemed inevitable as death, beyond question.

Then, satisfied and shattered, fulfilled and destroyed, he went home away from her, drifting vaguely through the darkness, lapsed into the old fire of burning passion. Far away, far away, there seemed to be a small lament in the darkness. But what did it matter? What did it matter, what did anything matter save this ultimate and triumphant experience of physical passion, that had blazed up anew like a new spell of life. 'I was becoming quite dead-alive, nothing but a word-bag,' he said in triumph, scorning his other self. Yet somewhere far off and small, the other hovered.

The men were still dragging the lake when he got back. He stood on the bank and heard Gerald's voice. The water was still booming in the night, the moon was fair, the hills beyond were elusive. The lake was sinking. There came the raw smell of the banks, in the night air.

Up at Shortlands there were lights in the windows, as if nobody had gone to bed. On the landing-stage was the old doctor, the father of the young man who was lost. He stood quite silent, waiting. Birkin also stood and watched, Gerald came up in a boat.

'You still here, Rupert?' he said. 'We can't get them. The bottom slopes, you know, very steep. The water lies between two very sharp slopes, with little branch valleys, and God knows where the drift will take you. It isn't as if it was a level bottom. You never know where you are, with the dragging.'

'Is there any need for you to be working?' said Birkin. 'Wouldn't it be much better if you went to bed?'

'To bed! Good God, do you think I should sleep? We'll find 'em, before I go away from here.'

'But the men would find them just the same without you – why should you insist?'

Gerald looked up at him. Then he put his hand affectionately on Birkin's shoulder, saying, 'Don't you bother about me, Rupert. If there's anybody's health to think about, it's yours, not mine. How do you feel yourself?'

'Very well. But you, you spoil your own chance of life – you waste your best self.'

Gerald was silent for a moment. Then he said, 'Waste it? What else is there to do with it?'

'But leave this, won't you? You force yourself into horrors, and put a millstone of beastly memories round your neck. Come away now.'

'A millstone of beastly memories!' Gerald repeated. Then he put his hand again affectionately on Birkin's shoulder. 'God, you've got such a telling way of putting things, Rupert, you have.'

Birkin's heart sank. He was irritated and weary of having a telling way of putting things.

'Won't you leave it? Come over to my place'– he urged as one urges a drunken man.

'No,' said Gerald coaxingly, his arm across the other man's shoulder. 'Thanks very much, Rupert – I shall be glad to come tomorrow, if that'll do. You understand, don't you? I want to see this job through. But I'll come tomorrow, right enough. Oh, I'd rather come and have a chat with you than – than do anything else, I verily believe. Yes, I would. You mean a lot to me, Rupert, more than you know.'

'What do I mean, more than I know?' asked Birkin irritably. He was acutely aware of Gerald's hand on his shoulder. And he did not want this altercation. He wanted the other man to come out of the ugly misery.

'I'll tell you another time,' said Gerald coaxingly.

'Come along with me now – I want you to come,' said Birkin.

There was a pause, intense and real. Birkin wondered why his own heart beat so heavily. Then Gerald's fingers gripped hard and communicative into Birkin's shoulder, as he said, 'No, I'll see this job through, Rupert. Thank you – I know what you mean. We're all right, you know, you and me.'

'I may be all right, but I'm sure you're not, mucking about here,' said Birkin. And he went away.

The bodies of the dead were not recovered till towards dawn. Diana had her arms tight round the neck of the young man, choking him.

'She killed him,' said Gerald.

The moon sloped down the sky and sank at last. The lake was sunk to quarter size, it had horrible raw banks of clay, that smelled of raw rottenish water. Dawn roused faintly behind the eastern hill. The water still boomed through the sluice.

As the birds were whistling for the first morning, and the hills at the back of the desolate lake stood radiant with the new mists, there was a straggling procession up to Shortlands, men bearing the bodies on a stretcher, Gerald going beside them, the two grey-bearded fathers following in silence. Indoors the family was all sitting up, waiting. Somebody must go to tell the mother, in her room. The doctor in secret struggled to bring back his son, till he himself was exhausted.

Over all the outlying district was a hush of dreadful excitement on that Sunday morning. The colliery people felt as if this catastrophe had happened directly to themselves, indeed they were more shocked and frightened than if their own men had been killed. Such a tragedy in Shortlands, the high home of the district! One of the young mistresses, persisting in dancing on the cabin roof of the launch, wilful young madam, drowned in the midst of the festival, with the young doctor! Everywhere on the Sunday morning, the colliers wandered about, discussing the calamity. At all the Sunday dinners of the people, there seemed a strange presence. It was as if the angel of death were very near, there was a sense of the supernatural in the air. The men had excited, startled faces, the women looked solemn, some of them had been crying. The children enjoyed the excitement at first. There was an intensity in the air, almost magical. Did all enjoy it? Did all enjoy the thrill?

Gudrun had wild ideas of rushing to comfort Gerald. She was thinking all the time of the perfect comforting, reassuring thing to say to him. She was shocked and frightened, but she put that away, thinking of how she should deport herself with Gerald: act her part. That was the real thrill: how she should act her part.

Ursula was deeply and passionately in love with Birkin, and she was capable of nothing. She was perfectly callous about all the talk of the accident, but her estranged air looked like trouble. She merely sat by herself, whenever she could, and longed to see him again. She wanted him to come to the house, – she would not have it otherwise, he must come at once. She was waiting for him. She stayed indoors all day, waiting for him to knock at the door. Every minute, she glanced automatically at the window. He would be there.

CHAPTER 15

Sunday Evening

As the day wore on, the life-blood seemed to ebb away from Ursula, and within the emptiness a heavy despair gathered. Her passion seemed to bleed to death, and there was nothing. She sat suspended in a state of complete nullity, harder to bear than death.

'Unless something happens,' she said to herself, in the perfect lucidity of final suffering, 'I shall die. I am at the end of my line of life.'

She sat crushed and obliterated in a darkness that was the border of death. She realised how all her life she had been drawing nearer and nearer to this brink, where there was no beyond, from which one had to leap like Sappho into the unknown. The knowledge of the imminence of death was like a drug. Darkly, without thinking at all, she knew that she was near to death. She had travelled all her life along the line of fulfilment, and it was nearly concluded. She knew all she had to know, she had experienced all she had to experience, she was fulfilled in a kind of bitter ripeness, there remained only to fall from the tree into death. And one must fulfil one's development to the end, must carry the adventure to its conclusion. And the next step was over the border into death. So it was then! There was a certain peace in the knowledge.

After all, when one was fulfilled, one was happiest in falling into death, as a bitter fruit plunges in its ripeness downwards. Death is a great consummation, a consummating experience. It is a development from life. That we know, while we are yet living. What then need we think for further? One can never see beyond the consummation. It is enough that death is a great and conclusive experience. Why should we ask what comes after the experience, when the experience is still unknown to us? Let us die, since the great experience is the one that follows now upon all the rest, death, which is the next great crisis in front of which we have arrived. If we wait, if we baulk the issue, we do but hang about the gates in undignified uneasiness. There it is, in front of us, as in front of Sappho, the illimitable space. Thereinto goes the journey. Have we not the courage to go on with our journey, must we cry 'I daren't'? On ahead we will go, into death, and whatever death may mean. If a man can see the next step to be taken, why should he fear the next but one? Why ask about the next but one? Of the next step we are certain. It is the step into death.

'I shall die – I shall quickly die,' said Ursula to herself, clear as if in a trance, clear, calm, and certain beyond human certainty. But somewhere behind, in the twilight, there was a bitter weeping and a hopelessness. That must not be attended to. One must go where the unfaltering spirit goes, there must be no baulking the issue, because of fear. No baulking the issue, no listening to the lesser voices. If the deepest desire be now, to go on into the unknown of death, shall one forfeit the deepest truth for one more shallow?

'Then let it end,' she said to herself. It was a decision. It was not a question of taking one's life – she would *never* kill herself, that was repulsive and violent. It was a question of *knowing* the next step. And the next step led into the space of death. Did it? – or was there – ?

Her thoughts drifted into unconsciousness, she sat as if asleep beside the fire. And then the thought came back. The space of death! Could she give herself to it? Ah yes – it was a sleep. She had had enough. So long she had held out; and resisted. Now was the time to relinquish, not to resist any more.

In a kind of spiritual trance, she yielded, she gave way, and all was dark. She could feel, within the darkness, the terrible assertion of her body, the unutterable anguish of dissolution, the only anguish that is too much, the far-off, awful nausea of dissolution set in within the body.

'Does the body correspond so immediately with the spirit?' she asked herself. And she knew, with the clarity of ultimate knowledge, that the body is only one of the manifestations of the spirit, the transmutation of the integral spirit is the transmutation of the physical body as well. Unless I set my will, unless I absolve myself from the rhythm of life, fix myself and remain static, cut off from living, absolved within my own will. But better die than live mechanically a life that is a repetition of repetitions. To die is to move on with the invisible. To die is also a joy, a joy of submitting to that which is greater than the known, namely, the pure unknown. That is a joy. But to live mechanised and cut off within the motion of the will, to live as an entity absolved from the unknown, that is shameful and ignominious. There is no ignominy in death. There is complete ignominy in an unreplenished, mechanised life. Life indeed may be ignominious, shameful to the soul. But death is never a shame. Death itself, like the illimitable space, is beyond our sullying.

Tomorrow was Monday. Monday, the beginning of another school-week! Another shameful, barren school-week, mere routine and mechanical activity. Was not the adventure of death infinitely preferable? Was not death infinitely more lovely and noble than such a life? A life of barren routine, without inner meaning, without any real significance. How sordid life was, how it was a terrible shame to the soul, to live now! How much cleaner and more dignified to be dead! One could not bear any more of this shame of sordid routine and mechanical nullity. One might come to fruit in death. She had had enough. For where was life to be found? No flowers grow upon busy machinery, there is no sky to a routine, there is no space to a rotary motion. And all life was a rotary motion, mechanised, cut off from reality. There was nothing to look for from life – it was the same in all countries and all peoples. The only window was death. One could look out on to the great dark sky of death with elation, as one had looked out of the classroom window as a child, and seen perfect freedom in the outside. Now one was not a child, and one knew that the soul was a prisoner within this sordid vast edifice of life, and there was no escape, save in death.

But what a joy! What a gladness to think that whatever humanity did, it could not seize hold of the kingdom of death, to nullify that. The sea they turned into a murderous alley and a soiled road of commerce, disputed like the dirty land of a city every inch of it. The air they claimed too, shared it up, parcelled it out to certain owners, they trespassed in the air to fight for it. Everything was gone, walled in, with spikes on top of the walls, and one must ignominiously creep between the spiky walls through a labyrinth of life.

But the great, dark, illimitable kingdom of death, there humanity was put to scorn. So much they could do upon earth, the multifarious little gods that they were. But the kingdom of death put them all to scorn, they dwindled into their true vulgar silliness in face of it.

How beautiful, how grand and perfect death was, how good to look forward to. There one would wash off all the lies and ignominy and dirt that had been put upon one here, a perfect bath of cleanness and glad refreshment, and go unknown, unquestioned, unabased. After all, one was rich, if only in the promise of perfect death. It was a gladness above all, that this remained to look forward to, the pure inhuman otherness of death.

Whatever life might be, it could not take away death, the inhuman transcendent death. Oh, let us ask no question of it, what it is or is not. To know is human, and in death we do not know, we are not human. And the joy of this compensates for all the bitterness of knowledge and the sordidness of our humanity. In death we shall not be human, and we shall not know. The promise of this is our heritage, we look forward like heirs to their majority.

Ursula sat quite still and quite forgotten, alone by the fire in the drawing-room. The children were playing in the kitchen, all the others were gone to church. And she was gone into the ultimate darkness of her own soul.

She was startled by hearing the bell ring, away in the kitchen, the children came scudding along the passage in delicious alarm.

'Ursula, there's somebody.'

'I know. Don't be silly,' she replied. She too was startled, almost frightened. She dared hardly go to the door.

Birkin stood on the threshold, his raincoat turned up to his ears. He had come now, now she was gone far away. She was aware of the rainy night behind him.

'Oh, is it you?' she said.

'I am glad you are at home,' he said in a low voice, entering the house.

'They are all gone to church.'

He took off his coat and hung it up. The children were peeping at him round the corner.

'Go and get undressed now, Billy and Dora,' said Ursula. 'Mother will be back soon, and she'll be disappointed if you're not in bed.'

The children, in a sudden angelic mood, retired without a word. Birkin and Ursula went into the drawing-room.

The fire burned low. He looked at her and wondered at the luminous delicacy of her beauty, and the wide shining of her eyes. He watched from a distance, with wonder in his heart, she seemed transfigured with light.

'What have you been doing all day?' he asked her.

'Only sitting about,' she said.

He looked at her. There was a change in her. But she was separate from him. She remained apart, in a kind of brightness. They both sat silent in the soft light of the lamp. He felt he ought to go away again, he ought not to have come. Still he did not gather enough resolution to move. But he was *de trop*, her mood was absent and separate.

Then there came the voices of the two children calling shyly outside the door, softly, with self-excited timidity, 'Ursula! Ursula!'

She rose and opened the door. On the threshold stood the two children in their long nightgowns, with wide-eyed, angelic faces. They were being very good for the moment, playing the role perfectly of two obedient children.

'Shall you take us to bed!' said Billy, in a loud whisper.

'Why you *are* angels tonight,' she said softly. 'Won't you come and say good-night to Mr Birkin?'

The children merged shyly into the room, on bare feet. Billy's face was wide and grinning, but there was a great solemnity of being good in his round blue eyes. Dora, peeping from the floss of her fair hair, hung back like some tiny Dryad, that has no soul.

'Will you say good-night to me?' asked Birkin, in a voice that was strangely soft and smooth. Dora drifted away at once, like a leaf lifted on a breath of wind. But Billy went softly forward, slow and willing, lifting his pinched-up mouth implicitly to be kissed. Ursula watched the full, gathered lips of the man gently touch those of the boy, so gently. Then Birkin lifted his fingers and touched the boy's round, confiding cheek, with a faint touch of love. Neither spoke. Billy seemed angelic like a cherub boy, or like an acolyte, Birkin was a tall, grave angel looking down to him.

'Are you going to be kissed?' Ursula broke in, speaking to the little girl. But Dora edged away like a tiny Dryad that will not be touched.

'Won't you say good-night to Mr Birkin? Go, he's waiting for you,' said Ursula. But the girl-child only made a little motion away from him.

'Silly Dora, silly Dora!' said Ursula.

Birkin felt some mistrust and antagonism in the small child. He could not understand it.

'Come then,' said Ursula. 'Let us go before mother comes.'

'Who'll hear us say our prayers?' asked Billy anxiously.

'Whom you like.'

'Won't you?'

'Yes, I will.'

'Ursula?'

'Well, Billy?'

'Is it *whom* you like?'

'That's it.'

'Well, what is *whom*?'

'It's the accusative of who.'

There was a moment's contemplative silence, then the confiding, 'Is it?'

Birkin smiled to himself as he sat by the fire. When Ursula came down he sat motionless, with his arms on his knees. She saw him, how he was motionless and ageless, like some crouching idol, some image of a deathly religion. He looked round at her, and his face, very pale and unreal, seemed to gleam with a whiteness almost phosphorescent.

'Don't you feel well?' she asked, in indefinable repulsion.

'I hadn't thought about it.'

'But don't you know without thinking about it?'

He looked at her, his eyes dark and swift, and he saw her revulsion. He did not answer her question.

'Don't you know whether you are unwell or not, without thinking about it?' she persisted.

'Not always,' he said coldly.

'But don't you think that's very wicked?'

'Wicked?'

'Yes. I think it's *criminal* to have so little connection with your own body that you don't even know when you are ill.'

He looked at her darkly.

'Yes,' he said.

'Why don't you stay in bed when you are seedy? You look perfectly ghastly.'

'Offensively so?' he asked ironically.

'Yes, quite offensive. Quite repelling.'

'Ah!! Well, that's unfortunate.'

'And it's raining, and it's a horrible night. Really, you shouldn't be forgiven for treating your body like it – you *ought* to suffer, a man who takes as little notice of his body as that.'

' – takes as little notice of his body as that,' he echoed mechanically.

This cut her short, and there was silence.

The others came in from church, and the two had the girls to face, then the mother and Gudrun, and then the father and the boy.

'Good-evening,' said Brangwen, faintly surprised. 'Came to see me, did you?'

'No,' said Birkin, 'not about anything, in particular, that is. The day was dismal, and I thought you wouldn't mind if I called in.'

'It *has* been a depressing day,' said Mrs Brangwen sympathetically. At that moment the voices of the children were heard calling from upstairs: 'Mother! Mother!' She lifted her face and answered mildly into the distance: 'I shall come up to you in a minute, Doysie.' Then to Birkin: 'There is nothing fresh at Shortlands, I suppose? Ah,' she sighed, 'no, poor things, I should think not.'

'You've been over there today, I suppose?' asked the father.

'Gerald came round to tea with me, and I walked back with him. The house is overexcited and unwholesome, I thought.'

'I should think they were people who hadn't much restraint,' said Gudrun.

'Or too much,' Birkin answered.

'Oh yes, I'm sure,' said Gudrun, almost vindictively, 'one or the other.'

'They all feel they ought to behave in some unnatural fashion,' said Birkin. 'When people are in grief, they would do better to cover their faces and keep in retirement, as in the old days.'

'Certainly!' cried Gudrun, flushed and inflammable. 'What can be worse than this public grief – what is more horrible, more false! If *grief* is not private, and hidden, what is?'

'Exactly,' he said. 'I felt ashamed when I was there and they were all going about in a lugubrious false way, feeling they must not be natural or ordinary.'

'Well –' said Mrs Brangwen, offended at this criticism, 'it isn't so easy to bear a trouble like that.'

And she went upstairs to the children.

He remained only a few minutes longer, then took his leave. When he was gone Ursula felt such a poignant hatred of him, that all her brain seemed turned into a sharp crystal of fine hatred. Her whole nature seemed sharpened and intensified into a pure dart of hate. She could not imagine what it was. It merely took hold of her, the most poignant and ultimate hatred, pure and clear and beyond thought. She could not think of it at all, she was translated beyond herself. It was like a possession. She felt she was possessed. And for several days she went about possessed by this exquisite force of hatred against him. It surpassed anything she had ever known before, it seemed to throw her out of the world into some terrible region where nothing of her old life held good. She was quite lost and dazed, really dead to her own life.

It was so completely incomprehensible and irrational. She did not know *why* she hated him, her hate was quite abstract. She had only realised with a shock that stunned her, that she was overcome by this pure transportation. He was the enemy, fine as a diamond, and as hard and jewel-like, the quintessence of all that was inimical.

She thought of his face, white and purely wrought, and of his eyes that had such a dark, constant will of assertion, and she touched her own forehead, to feel if she were mad, she was so transfigured in white flame of essential hate.

It was not temporal, her hatred, she did not hate him for this or for that; she did not want to do anything to him, to have any connection with him. Her relation was ultimate and utterly beyond words, the hate was so pure and gemlike. It was as if he were a beam of essential enmity, a beam of light that did not only destroy her, but denied her altogether, revoked her whole world. She saw him as a clear stroke of uttermost contradiction, a strange gemlike being whose existence defined her own non-existence. When she heard he was ill again, her hatred only intensified itself a few degrees, if that were possible. It stunned her and annihilated her, but she could not escape it. She could not escape this transfiguration of hatred that had come upon her.

CHAPTER 16

Man to Man

He lay sick and unmoved, in pure opposition to everything. He knew how near to breaking was the vessel that held his life. He knew also how strong and durable it was. And he did not care. Better a thousand times take one's chance with death, than accept a life one did not want. But best of all to persist and persist and persist for ever, till one were satisfied in life.

He knew that Ursula was referred back to him. He knew his life rested with her. But he would rather not live than accept the love she proffered. The old way of love seemed a dreadful bondage, a sort of conscription. What it was in him he did not know, but the thought of love, marriage, and children, and a life lived together, in the horrible privacy of domestic and connubial satisfaction, was repulsive. He wanted something clearer, more open, cooler, as it were. The hot narrow intimacy between man and wife was abhorrent. The way they shut their doors, these married people, and shut themselves in to their own exclusive alliance with each other, even in love, disgusted him. It was a whole community of mistrustful couples insulated in private houses or private rooms, always in couples, and no further life, no further immediate, no disinterested relationship admitted: a kaleidoscope of couples, disjoined, separatist, meaningless entities of married couples. True, he hated promiscuity even worse than marriage, and a liaison was only another kind of coupling, reactionary from the legal marriage. Reaction was a greater bore than action.

On the whole, he hated sex, it was such a limitation. It was sex that turned a man into a broken half of a couple, the woman into the other broken half. And he wanted to be single in himself, the woman single in herself. He wanted sex to revert to the level of the other appetites, to be regarded as a functional process, not as a fulfilment. He believed in sex marriage. But beyond this, he wanted a further conjunction, where man had being and woman had being, two pure beings, each constituting the freedom of the other, balancing each other like two poles of one force, like two angels, or two demons.

He wanted so much to be free, not under the compulsion of any need for unification, or tortured by unsatisfied desire. Desire and aspiration should find their object without all this torture, as now, in a world of plenty of water, simple thirst is inconsiderable, satisfied almost unconsciously. And he wanted to be with Ursula as free as with himself, single and clear and cool, yet balanced, polarised with her. The merging, the clutching, the mingling of love was become madly abhorrent to him.

But it seemed to him, woman was always so horrible and clutching, she had such a lust for possession, a greed of self-importance in love. She wanted to have, to own, to control, to be dominant. Everything must be referred back to her, to Woman, the Great Mother of everything, out of whom proceeded everything and to whom everything must finally be rendered up.

It filled him with almost insane fury, this calm assumption of the Magna Mater, that all was hers, because she had borne it. Man was hers because she had borne him. A Mater Dolorosa, she had borne him, a Magna Mater, she now claimed him again, soul and body, sex, meaning, and all. He had a horror of the Magna Mater, she was detestable.

She was on a very high horse again, was woman, the Great Mother. Did he not know it in Hermione. Hermione, the humble, the subservient, what was she all the while but the Mater Dolorosa, in her subservience, claiming with horrible, insidious arrogance and female tyranny, her own again, claiming back the man she had borne in suffering. By her very suffering and humility she bound her son with chains, she held him her everlasting prisoner.

And Ursula, Ursula was the same – or the inverse. She too was the awful, arrogant queen of life, as if she were a queen bee on whom all the rest depended. He saw the yellow flare in her eyes, he knew the unthinkable overweening assumption of primacy in her. She was unconscious of it herself. She was only too ready to knock her head on the ground before a man. But this was only when she was so certain of her man, that she could worship him as a woman worships her own infant, with a worship of perfect possession.

It was intolerable, this possession at the hands of woman. Always a man must be considered as the broken-off fragment of a woman, and the sex was the still aching scar of the laceration. Man must be added on to a woman, before he had any real place or wholeness.

And why? Why should we consider ourselves, men and women, as broken fragments of one whole? It is not true. We are not broken fragments of one whole. Rather we are the singling away into purity and clear being, of things that were mixed. Rather the sex is that which remains in us of the mixed, the unresolved. And passion is the further separating of this mixture, that which is manly being taken into the being of the man, that which is womanly passing to the woman, till the two are clear and whole as angels, the admixture of sex in the highest sense surpassed, leaving two single beings constellated together like two stars.

In the old age, before sex was, we were mixed, each one a mixture. The process of singling into individuality resulted into the great polarisation of sex. The womanly drew to one side, the manly to the other. But the separation was imperfect even them. And so our world-cycle passes. There is now to come the new day, when we are beings each of us, fulfilled in difference. The man is pure man, the woman pure woman, they are perfectly polarised. But there is no longer any of the horrible merging, mingling self-abnegation of love. There is only the pure duality of polarisation, each one free from any contamination of the other. In each, the individual is primal, sex is subordinate, but perfectly polarised. Each has a single, separate being, with its own laws. The man has his pure freedom, the woman hers. Each acknowledges the perfection of the polarised sex-circuit, Each admits the different nature in the other.

So Birkin meditated whilst he was ill. He liked sometimes to be ill enough to take to his bed. For then he got better very quickly, and things came to him clear and sure.

Whilst he was laid up, Gerald came to see him. The two men had a deep, uneasy feeling for each other. Gerald's eyes were quick and restless, his whole manner tense and impatient, he seemed strung up to some activity. According to conventionality, he wore black clothes, he looked formal, handsome and *comme il faut*. His hair was fair almost to whiteness, sharp like splinters of light, his face was keen and ruddy, his body seemed full of northern energy. Gerald really loved Birkin, though he never quite believed in him. Birkin was too unreal; – clever, whimsical, wonderful, but not practical enough. Gerald felt that his own understanding was much sounder and safer. Birkin was delightful, a wonderful spirit, but after all, not to be taken seriously, not quite to be counted as a man among men.

'Why are you laid up again?' he asked kindly, taking the sick man's hand. It was always Gerald who was protective, offering the warm shelter of his physical strength.

'For my sins, I suppose,' Birkin said, smiling a little ironically.

'For your sins? Yes, probably that is so. You should sin less, and keep better in health?'

'You'd better teach me.'

He looked at Gerald with ironic eyes.

'How are things with you?' asked Birkin.

'With me?' Gerald looked at Birkin, saw he was serious, and a warm light came into his eyes.

'I don't know that they're any different. I don't see how they could be. There's nothing to change.'

'I suppose you are conducting the business as successfully as ever, and ignoring the demand of the soul.'

'That's it,' said Gerald. 'At least as far as the business is concerned. I couldn't say about the soul, I'm sure.'

'No.'

'Surely you don't expect me to?' laughed Gerald.

'No. How are the rest of your affairs progressing, apart from the business?'

'The rest of my affairs? What are those? I couldn't say; I don't know what you refer to.'

'Yes, you do,' said Birkin. 'Are you gloomy or cheerful? And what about Gudrun Brangwen?'

'What about her?' A confused look came over Gerald. 'Well,' he added, 'I don't know. I can only tell you she gave me a hit over the face last time I saw her.'

'A hit over the face! What for?'

'That I couldn't tell you, either.'

'Really! But when?'

'The night of the party – when Diana was drowned. She was driving the cattle up the hill, and I went after her – you remember.'

'Yes, I remember. But what made her do that? You didn't definitely ask her for it, I suppose?'

'I? No, not that I know of. I merely said to her, that it was dangerous to drive those Highland bullocks – as it *is*. She turned in such a way, and said – "I suppose you think I'm afraid of you and your cattle, don't you?" So I asked her "why?" and for answer she flung me a backhander across the face.'

Birkin laughed quickly, as if it pleased him. Gerald looked at him, wondering, and began to laugh as well, saying, 'I didn't laugh at the time, I assure you. I was never so taken aback in my life.'

'And weren't you furious?'

'Furious? I should think I was. I'd have murdered her for two pins.'

'H'm!' ejaculated Birkin. 'Poor Gudrun, wouldn't she suffer afterwards for having given herself away!' He was hugely delighted.

'Would she suffer?' asked Gerald, also amused now.

Both men smiled in malice and amusement.

'Badly, I should think; seeing how self-conscious she is.'

'She is self-conscious, is she? Then what made her do it? For I certainly think it was quite uncalled-for, and quite unjustified.'

'I suppose it was a sudden impulse.'

'Yes, but how do you account for her having such an impulse? I'd done her no harm.'

Birkin shook his head.

'The Amazon suddenly came up in her, I suppose,' he said.

'Well,' replied Gerald, 'I'd rather it had been the Orinoco.'

They both laughed at the poor joke. Gerald was thinking how Gudrun had said she would strike the last blow too. But some reserve made him keep this back from Birkin.

'And you resent it?' Birkin asked.

'I don't resent it. I don't care a tinker's curse about it.' He was silent a moment, then he added, laughing, 'No, I'll see it through, that's all. She seemed sorry afterwards.'

'Did she? You've not met since that night?'

Gerald's face clouded.

'No,' he said. 'We've been – you can imagine how it's been, since the accident.'

'Yes. Is it calming down?'

'I don't know. It's a shock, of course. But I don't believe mother minds. I really don't believe she takes any notice. And what's so funny, she used to be all for the children – nothing mattered, nothing whatever mattered but the children. And now, she doesn't take any more notice than if it was one of the servants.'

'No? Did it upset *you* very much?'

'It's a shock. But I don't feel it very much, really. I don't feel any different. We've all got to die, and it doesn't seem to make any great difference, anyhow, whether you die or not. I can't feel any *grief*, you know. It leaves me cold. I can't quite account for it.'

'You don't care if you die or not?' asked Birkin.

Gerald looked at him with eyes blue as the blue-fibred steel of a weapon. He felt awkward, but indifferent. As a matter of fact, he did care terribly, with a great fear.

'Oh,' he said, 'I don't want to die, why should I? But I never trouble. The question doesn't seem to be on the carpet for me at all. It doesn't interest me, you know.'

'*Timor mortis conturbat me*,' quoted Birkin, adding – 'No, death doesn't really seem the point any more. It curiously doesn't concern one. It's like an ordinary tomorrow.'

Gerald looked closely at his friend. The eyes of the two men met, and an unspoken understanding was exchanged.

Gerald narrowed his eyes, his face was cool and unscrupulous as he looked at Birkin, impersonally, with a vision that ended in a point in space, strangely keen-eyed and yet blind.

'If death isn't the point,' he said, in a strangely abstract, cold, fine voice – 'what is?' He sounded as if he had been found out.

'What is?' re-echoed Birkin. And there was a mocking silence.

'There's a long way to go, after the point of intrinsic death, before we disappear,' said Birkin.

'There is,' said Gerald. 'But what sort of way?' He seemed to press the other man for knowledge which he himself knew far better than Birkin did.

'Right down the slopes of degeneration – mystic, universal degeneration. There are many stages of pure degradation to go through: age-long. We live on long after our death, and progressively, in progressive devolution.'

Gerald listened with a faint, fine smile on his face, all the time, as if, some-where, he knew so much better than Birkin, all about this: as if his own knowledge were direct and personal, whereas Birkin's was a matter of observation and inference, not quite hitting the nail on the head: – though aiming near enough at it. But he was not going to give himself away. If Birkin could get at the secrets, let him. Gerald would never help him. Gerald would be a dark horse to the end.

'Of course,' he said, with a startling change of conversation, 'it is father who really feels it. It will finish him. For him the world collapses. All his care now is for Winnie – he must save Winnie. He says she ought to be sent away to school, but she won't hear of it, and he'll never do it. Of course she *is* in rather a queer way. We're all of us curiously bad at living. We can do things – but we can't get on with life at all. It's curious – a family failing.'

'She oughtn't to be sent away to school,' said Birkin, who was considering a new proposition.

'She oughtn't. Why?'

'She's a queer child – a special child, more special even than you. And in my opinion special children should never be sent away to school. Only moderately ordinary children should be sent to school – so it seems to me.'

'I'm inclined to think just the opposite. I think it would probably make her more normal if she went away and mixed with other children.'

'She wouldn't mix, you see. *You* never really mixed, did you? And she wouldn't be willing even to pretend to. She's proud, and solitary, and naturally apart. If she has a single nature, why do you want to make her gregarious?'

'No, I don't want to make her anything. But I think school would be good for her.'

'Was it good for you?'

Gerald's eyes narrowed uglily. School had been torture to him. Yet he had not questioned whether one should go through this torture. He seemed to believe in education through subjection and torment.

'I hated it at the time, but I can see it was necessary,' he said. 'It brought me into line a bit – and you can't live unless you do come into line somewhere.'

'Well,' said Birkin, 'I begin to think that you can't live unless you keep entirely out of the line. It's no good trying to toe the line, when your one impulse is to smash up the line. Winnie is a special nature, and for special natures you must give a special world.'

'Yes, but where's your special world?' said Gerald.

'Make it. Instead of chopping yourself down to fit the world, chop the world down to fit yourself. As a matter of fact, two exceptional people make another world. You and I, we make another, separate world. You don't *want* a world same as your brothers-in-law. It's just the special quality you value. Do you *want* to be normal or ordinary? It's a lie. You want to be free and extraordinary, in an extraordinary world of liberty.'

Gerald looked at Birkin with subtle eyes of knowledge. But he would never openly admit what he felt. He knew more than Birkin, in one direction – much more. And this gave him his gentle love for the other man, as if Birkin were in some way young, innocent, childlike: so amazingly clever, but incurably innocent.

'Yet you are so banal as to consider me chiefly a freak,' said Birkin pointedly.

'A freak!' exclaimed Gerald, startled. And his face opened suddenly, as if lighted with simplicity, as when a flower opens out of the cunning bud. 'No – I never consider you a freak.' And he watched the other man with strange eyes, that Birkin could not understand. 'I feel,' Gerald continued, 'that there is always an element of uncertainty about you – perhaps you are uncertain about yourself. But I'm never sure of you. You can go away and change as easily as if you had no soul.'

He looked at Birkin with penetrating eyes. Birkin was amazed. He thought he had all the soul in the world. He stared in amazement. And Gerald, watching, saw the amazing attractive goodliness of his eyes, a young, spontaneous goodness that attracted the other man infinitely, yet filled him with bitter chagrin, because he mistrusted it so much. He knew Birkin could do without him – could forget, and not suffer. This was always present in Gerald's consciousness, filling him with bitter unbelief: this consciousness of the young, animal-like spontaneity of detachment. It seemed almost like hypocrisy and lying, sometimes, oh, often, on Birkin's part, to talk so deeply and importantly.

Quite other things were going through Birkin's mind. Suddenly he saw himself confronted with another problem – the problem of love and eternal conjunction between two men. Of course this was necessary – it had been a necessity inside himself all his life – to love a man purely and fully. Of course he had been loving Gerald all along, and all along denying it.

He lay in the bed and wondered, whilst his friend sat beside him, lost in brooding. Each man was gone in his own thoughts.

'You know how the old German knights used to swear a *Blutbrüderschaft*,' he said to Gerald, with quite a new happy activity in his eyes.

'Make a little wound in their arms, and rub each other's blood into the cut?' said Gerald.

'Yes – and swear to be true to each other, of one blood, all their lives. That is what we ought to do. No wounds, that is obsolete. But we ought to swear to love each other, you and I, implicitly, and perfectly, finally, without any possibility of going back on it.'

He looked at Gerald with clear, happy eyes of discovery. Gerald looked down at him, attracted, so deeply bondaged in fascinated attraction, that he was mistrustful, resenting the bondage, hating the attraction.

'We will swear to each other, one day, shall we?' pleaded Birkin. 'We will swear to stand by each other – be true to each other – ultimately – infallibly – given to each other, organically – without possibility of taking back.'

Birkin sought hard to express himself. But Gerald hardly listened. His face shone with a certain luminous pleasure. He was pleased. But he kept his reserve. He held himself back.

'Shall we swear to each other, one day?' said Birkin, putting out his hand towards Gerald.

Gerald just touched the extended fine, living hand, as if withheld and afraid.

'We'll leave it till I understand it better,' he said, in a voice of excuse.

Birkin watched him. A little sharp disappointment, perhaps a touch of contempt came into his heart.

'Yes,' he said. 'You must tell me what you think, later. You know what I mean? Not sloppy emotionalism. An impersonal union that leaves one free.'

They lapsed both into silence. Birkin was looking at Gerald all the time. He seemed now to see, not the physical, animal man, which he usually saw in Gerald, and which usually he liked so much, but the man himself, complete, and as if fated, doomed, limited. This strange sense of fatality in Gerald, as if he were limited to one form of existence, one knowledge, one activity, a sort of fatal halfness, which to himself seemed wholeness, always overcame Birkin after their moments of passionate approach, and filled him with a sort of contempt, or boredom. It was the insistence on the limitation which so bored Birkin in Gerald. Gerald could never fly away from himself, in real indifferent gaiety. He had a clog, a sort of monomania.

There was silence for a time. Then Birkin said, in a lighter tone, letting the stress of the contact pass, 'Can't you get a good governess for Winifred? – somebody exceptional?'

'Hermione Roddice suggested we should ask Gudrun to teach her to draw and to model in clay. You know Winnie is astonishingly clever with that plasticine stuff. Hermione declares she is an artist.' Gerald spoke in the usual animated, chatty manner, as if nothing unusual had passed. But Birkin's manner was full of reminder.

'Really! I didn't know that. Oh well then, if Gudrun *would* teach her, it would be perfect – couldn't be anything better – if Winifred is an artist. Because Gudrun somewhere is one. And every true artist is the salvation of every other.'

'I thought they got on so badly, as a rule.'

'Perhaps. But only artists produce for each other the world that is fit to live in. If you can arrange *that* for Winifred, it is perfect.'

'But you think she wouldn't come?'

'I don't know. Gudrun is rather self-opinionated. She won't go cheap anywhere. Or if she does, she'll pretty soon take herself back. So whether she would condescend to do private teaching, particularly here, in Beldover, I don't know. But it would be just the thing. Winifred has got a special nature. And if you can put into her way the means of being self-sufficient, that is the best thing possible. She'll never get on with the ordinary life. You find it difficult enough yourself, and she is several skins thinner than you are. It is awful to think what her life will be like unless she does find a means of expression, some way of fulfilment. You can see what mere leaving it to fate brings. You can see how much marriage is to be trusted to – look at your own mother.'

'Do you think mother is abnormal?'

'No! I think she only wanted something more, or other than the common run of life. And not getting it, she has gone wrong perhaps.'

'After producing a brood of wrong children,' said Gerald gloomily.

'No more wrong than any of the rest of us,' Birkin replied. 'The most normal people have the worst subterranean selves, take them one by one.'

'Sometimes I think it is a curse to be alive,' said Gerald with sudden impotent anger.

'Well,' said Birkin, 'why not! Let it be a curse sometimes to be alive – at other times it is anything but a curse. You've got plenty of zest in it really.'

'Less than you'd think,' said Gerald, revealing a strange poverty in his look at the other man.

There was silence, each thinking his own thoughts.

'I don't see what she has to distinguish between teaching at the Grammar School, and coming to teach Win,' said Gerald.

'The difference between a public servant and a private one. The only nobleman today, king and only aristocrat, is the public, the public. You are quite willing to serve the public – but to be a private tutor – '

'I don't want to serve either – '

'No! And Gudrun will probably feel the same.'

Gerald thought for a few minutes. Then he said, 'At all events, father won't make her feel like a private servant. He will be fussy and grateful enough.'

'So he ought. And so ought all of you. Do you think you can hire a woman like Gudrun Brangwen with money? She is your equal like anything – probably your superior.'

'Is she?' said Gerald.

'Yes, and if you haven't the guts to know it, I hope she'll leave you to your own devices.'

'Nevertheless,' said Gerald, 'if she is my equal, I wish she weren't a teacher, because I don't think teachers as a rule are my equal.'

'Nor do I, damn them. But am I a teacher because I teach, or a parson because I preach?'

Gerald laughed. He was always uneasy on this score. He did not *want* to claim social superiority, yet he *would* not claim intrinsic personal superiority, because he would never base his standard of values on pure being. So he wobbled upon a tacit assumption of social standing. No, Birkin wanted him to accept the fact of intrinsic difference between human beings, which he did not intend to accept. It was against his social honour, his principle. He rose to go.

'I've been neglecting my business all this while,' he said smiling.

'I ought to have reminded you before,' Birkin replied, laughing and mocking.

'I knew you'd say something like that,' laughed Gerald, rather uneasily.

'Did you?'

'Yes, Rupert. It wouldn't do for us all to be like you are – we should soon be in the cart. When I am above the world, I shall ignore all businesses.'

'Of course, we're not in the cart now,' said Birkin, satirically.

'Not as much as you make out. At any rate, we have enough to eat and drink – '

'And be satisfied,' added Birkin.

Gerald came near the bed and stood looking down at Birkin whose throat was exposed, whose tossed hair fell attractively on the warm brow, above the eyes that were so unchallenged and still in the satirical face. Gerald, full-limbed and turgid with energy, stood unwilling to go, he was held by the presence of the other man. He had not the power to go away.

'So,' said Birkin. 'Goodbye.' And he reached out his hand from under the bedclothes, smiling with a glimmering look.

'Goodbye,' said Gerald, taking the warm hand of his friend in a firm grasp. 'I shall come again. I miss you down at the mill.'

'I'll be there in a few days,' said Birkin.

The eyes of the two men met again. Gerald's, that were keen as a hawk's, were suffused now with warm light and with unadmitted love, Birkin looked back as out of a darkness, unsounded and unknown, yet with a kind of warmth, that seemed to flow over Gerald's brain like a fertile sleep.

'Goodbye then. There's nothing I can do for you?'

'Nothing, thanks.'

Birkin watched the black clothed form of the other man move out of the door, the bright head was gone, he turned over to sleep.

CHAPTER 17

The Industrial Magnate

In Beldover, there was both for Ursula and for Gudrun an interval. It seemed to Ursula as if Birkin had gone out of her for the time, he had lost his significance, he scarcely mattered in her world. She had her own friends, her own activities, her own life. She turned back to the old ways with zest, away from him.

And Gudrun, after feeling every moment in all her veins conscious of Gerald Crich, connected even physically with him, was now almost indifferent to the thought of him. She was nursing new schemes for going away and trying a new form of life. All the time, there was something in her urging her to avoid the final establishing of a relationship with Gerald. She felt it would be wiser and better to have no more than a casual acquaintance with him.

She had a scheme for going to St Petersburg, where she had a friend who was a sculptor like herself, and who lived with a wealthy Russian whose hobby was jewel-making. The emotional, rather rootless life of the Russians appealed to her. She did not want to go to Paris. Paris was dry, and essentially boring. She would like to go to Rome, Munich, Vienna, or to St Petersburg or Moscow. She had a friend in St Petersburg and a friend in Munich. To each of these she wrote, asking about rooms.

She had a certain amount of money. She had come home partly to save, and now she had sold several pieces of work, she had been praised in various shows. She knew she could become quite the 'go' if she went to London. But she knew London, she wanted something else. She had seventy pounds, of which nobody knew anything. She would move soon, as soon as she heard from her friends. Her nature, in spite of her apparent placidity and calm, was profoundly restless.

The sisters happened to call in a cottage in Willey Green to buy honey. Mrs Kirk, a stout, pale, sharp-nosed woman, sly, honied, with something shrewish and catlike beneath, asked the girls into her too-cosy, too tidy kitchen. There was a catlike comfort and cleanliness everywhere.

'Yes, Miss Brangwen,' she said, in her slightly whining, insinuating voice, 'and how do you like being back in the old place, then?'

Gudrun, whom she addressed, hated her at once.

'I don't care for it,' she replied abruptly.

'You don't? Ay, well, I suppose you found a difference from London. You like life, and big, grand places. Some of us has to be content with Willey Green and Beldover. And what do you think of our Grammar School, as there's so much talk about?'

'What do I think of it?' Gudrun looked round at her slowly. 'Do you mean, do I think it's a good school?'

'Yes. What is your opinion of it?'

'I *do* think it's a good school.'

Gudrun was very cold and repelling. She knew the common people hated the school.

'Ay, you do, then! I've heard so much, one way and the other. It's nice to know what those that's in it feel. But opinions vary, don't they? Mr Crich up at Highclose is all for it. Ay, poor man, I'm afraid he's not long for this world. He's very poorly.'

'Is he worse?' asked Ursula.

'Eh, yes – since they lost Miss Diana. He's gone off to a shadow. Poor man, he's had a world of trouble.'

'Has he?' asked Gudrun, faintly ironic.

'He has, a world of trouble. And as nice and kind a gentleman as ever you could wish to meet. His children don't take after him.'

'I suppose they take after their mother?' said Ursula.

'In many ways.' Mrs Kirk lowered her voice a little. 'She was a proud haughty lady when she came into these parts – my word, she was that! She mustn't be looked at, and it was worth your life to speak to her.' The woman made a dry, sly face.

'Did you know her when she was first married?'

'Yes, I knew her. I nursed three of her children. And proper little terrors they were, little fiends – that Gerald was a demon if ever there was one, a proper demon, ay, at six months old.' A curious malicious, sly tone came into the woman's voice.

'Really,' said Gudrun.

'That wilful, masterful – he'd mastered one nurse at six months. Kick, and scream, and struggle like a demon. Many's the time I've pinched his little bottom for him, when he was a child in arms. Ay, and he'd have been better if he'd had it pinched oftener. But she wouldn't have them corrected – no-o, wouldn't hear of it. I can remember the rows she had with Mr Crich, my word. When he'd got worked up, properly worked up till he could stand no more, he'd lock the study door and whip them. But she paced up and down all the while like a tiger outside, like a tiger, with very murder in her face. She had a face that could *look* death. And when the door was opened, she'd go in with her hands lifted – "What have you been doing to *my* children, you coward." She was like one out of her mind. I believe he was frightened of her; he had to be driven mad before he'd lift a finger. Didn't the servants have a life of it! And didn't we used to be thankful when one of them caught it. They were the torment of your life.'

'Really!' said Gudrun.

'In every possible way. If you wouldn't let them smash their pots on the table, if you wouldn't let them drag the kitten about with a string round its neck, if you wouldn't give them whatever they asked for, every mortal thing – then there was a shine on, and their mother coming in asking – "What's the matter with him? What have you done to him? What is it, darling?" And then she'd turn on you as if she'd trample you under her feet. But she didn't trample on me. I was the only one that could do anything with her demons – for she wasn't going to be bothered with them herself. No, *she* took no trouble for them. But they must just have their way, they mustn't be spoken to. And Master Gerald was the beauty. I left when he was a year and a half, I could stand no more. But I pinched his little bottom for him when he was in arms, I did, when there was no holding him, and I'm not sorry I did – '

Gudrun went away in fury and loathing. The phrase, 'I pinched his little bottom for him', sent her into a white, stony fury. She could not bear it, she wanted to have the woman taken out at once and strangled. And yet there the phrase was lodged in her mind for ever, beyond escape. She felt, one day, she would *have* to tell him, to see how he took it. And she loathed herself for the thought.

But at Shortlands the lifelong struggle was coming to a close. The father was ill and was going to die. He had bad internal pains, which took away all his attentive life, and left him with only a vestige of his consciousness. More and more a silence came over him, he was less and less acutely aware of his surroundings. The pain seemed to absorb his activity. He knew it was there, he knew it would come again. It was like something lurking in the darkness within him. And he had not the power, or the will, to seek it out and to know it. There it remained in the darkness, the great pain, tearing him at times, and then being silent. And when it tore him he crouched in silent subjection under it, and when it left him alone again, he refused to know of it. It was within the darkness, let it remain unknown. So he never admitted it, except in a secret corner of himself, where all his never-revealed fears and secrets were accumulated. For the rest, he had a pain, it went away, it made no difference. It even stimulated him, excited him.

But it gradually absorbed his life. Gradually it drew away all his potentiality, it bled him into the dark, it weaned him of life and drew him away into the darkness. And in this twilight of his life little remained visible to him. The business, his work, that was gone entirely. His public interests had disappeared as if they had never been. Even his family had become extraneous to him, he could only remember, in some slight non-essential part of himself, that such and such were his children. But it was historical fact, not vital to him. He had to make an effort to know their relation to him. Even his wife barely existed. She indeed was like the darkness, like the pain within him. By some strange association, the darkness that contained the pain and the darkness that contained his wife were identical. All his thoughts and understandings became blurred and fused, and now his wife and the consuming pain were the same dark secret power against him, that he never faced. He never drove the dread out of its lair within him. He only knew that there was a dark place, and something inhabiting this darkness which issued from time to time and rent him. But he dared not penetrate and drive the beast into the open. He had rather ignore its existence. Only, in his vague way, the dread was his wife, the destroyer, and it was the pain, the destruction, a darkness which was one and both.

He very rarely saw his wife. She kept her room. Only occasionally she came forth, with her head stretched forward, and in her low, possessed voice, she asked him how he was. And he answered her, in the habit of more than thirty years: 'Well, I don't think I'm any the worse, dear.' But he was frightened of her, underneath this safeguard of habit, frightened almost to the verge of death.

But all his life, he had been so constant to his lights, he had never broken down. He would die even now without breaking down, without knowing what his feelings were, towards her. All his life, he had said: 'Poor Christiana, she has such a strong temper.' With unbroken will, he had stood by this position with regard to her, he had substituted pity for all his hostility, pity had been his shield and his safeguard, and his infallible weapon. And still, in his consciousness, he was sorry for her, her nature was so violent and so impatient.

But now his pity, with his life, was wearing thin, and the dread almost amounting to horror was rising into being. But before the armour of his pity really broke, he would die, as an insect when its shell is cracked. This was his final resource. Others would live on, and know the living death, the ensuing process of hopeless chaos. He would not. He denied death its victory.

He had been so constant to his lights, so constant to charity, and to his love for his neighbour. Perhaps he had loved his neighbour even better than himself – which is going one further than the commandment. Always, this flame had burned in his heart, sustaining him through everything, the welfare of the people. He was a large employer of labour, he was a great mine-owner. And he had never lost this from his heart, that in Christ he was one with his workmen. Nay, he had felt inferior to them, as if they through poverty and labour were nearer to God than he. He had always the unacknowledged belief, that it was his workmen, the miners, who held in their hands the means of salvation. To move nearer to God, he must move towards his miners, his life must gravitate towards theirs. They were, unconsciously, his idol, his God made manifest. In them he worshipped the highest, the great, sympathetic, mindless Godhead of humanity.

And all the while, his wife had opposed him like one of the great demons of hell. Strange, like a bird of prey, with the fascinating beauty and abstraction of a hawk, she had beat against the bars of his philanthropy, and like a hawk in a cage, she had sunk into silence. By force of circumstance, because all the world combined to make the cage unbreakable, he had been too strong for her, he had kept her prisoner. And because she was his prisoner, his passion for her had always remained keen as death. He had always loved her, loved her with intensity. Within the cage, she was denied nothing, she was given all licence.

But she had gone almost mad. Of wild and over-weening temper, she could not bear the humiliation of her husband's soft, half-appealing kindness to everybody. He was not deceived by the poor. He knew they came and sponged on him, and whined to him, the worse sort; the majority, luckily for him, were much too proud to ask for anything, much too independent to come knocking at his door. But in Beldover, as everywhere else, there were the whining, parasitic, foul human beings who come crawling after charity, and feeding on the living body of the public like lice. A kind of fire would go over Christiana Crich's brain, as she saw two more pale-faced, creeping women in objectionable black clothes, cringing lugubriously up the drive to the door. She wanted to set the dogs on them, 'Hi Rip! Hi Ring! Ranger! At 'em boys, set 'em off.' But Crowther, the butler, with all the rest of the servants, was Mr Crich's man. Nevertheless, when her husband was away, she would come down like a wolf on the crawling supplicants: 'What do you people want? There is nothing for you here. You have no business on the drive at all. Simpson, drive them away and let no more of them through the gate.'

The servants had to obey her. And she would stand watching with an eye like the eagle's, whilst the groom in clumsy confusion drove the lugubrious persons down the drive, as if they were rusty fowls, scuttling before him.

But they learned to know, from the lodge-keeper, when Mrs Crich was away, and they timed their visits. How many times, in the first years, would Crowther knock softly at the door: 'Person to see you, sir.'

'What name?'

'Grocock, sir.'

'What do they want?' The question was half impatient, half gratified. He liked hearing appeals to his charity.

'About a child, sir.'

'Show them into the library, and tell them they shouldn't come after eleven o'clock in the morning.'

'Why do you get up from dinner? – send them off,' his wife would say abruptly.

'Oh, I can't do that. It's no trouble just to hear what they have to say.'

'How many more have been here today? Why don't you establish open house for them? They would soon oust me and the children.'

'You know, dear, it doesn't hurt me to hear what they have to say. And if they really are in trouble – well, it is my duty to help them out of it.'

'It's your duty to invite all the rats in the world to gnaw at your bones.'

'Come, Christiana, it isn't like that. Don't be uncharitable.'

But she suddenly swept out of the room, and out to the study. There sat the meagre charity-seekers, looking as if they were at the doctor's.

'Mr Crich can't see you. He can't see you at this hour. Do you think he is your property, that you can come whenever you like? You must go away, there is nothing for you here.'

The poor people rose in confusion. But Mr Crich, pale and black-bearded and deprecating, came behind her, saying, 'Yes, I don't like you coming as late as this. I'll hear any of you in the morning part of the day, but I can't really do with you after. What's amiss then, Gittens? How is your Missis?'

'Why, she's sunk very low, Mester Crich, she's a'most gone, she is – '

Sometimes, it seemed to Mrs Crich as if her husband were some subtle funeral bird, feeding on the miseries of the people. It seemed to her he was never satisfied unless there was some sordid tale being poured out to him, which he drank in with a sort of mournful, sympathetic satisfaction. He would have no *raison d'être* if there were no lugubrious miseries in the world, as an undertaker would have no meaning if there were no funerals.

Mrs Crich recoiled back upon herself, she recoiled away from this world of creeping democracy. A band of tight, baleful exclusion fastened round her heart, her isolation was fierce and hard, her antagonism was passive but terribly pure, like that of a hawk in a cage. As the years went on, she lost more and more count of the world, she seemed rapt in some glittering abstraction, almost purely unconscious. She would wander about the house and about the surrounding country, staring keenly and seeing nothing. She rarely spoke, she had no con

nection with the world. And she did not even think. She was consumed in a fierce tension of opposition, like the negative pole of a magnet.

And she bore many children. For, as time went on, she never opposed her husband in word or deed. She took no notice of him, externally. She submitted to him, let him take what he wanted and do as he wanted with her. She was like a hawk that sullenly submits to everything. The relation between her and her husband was wordless and unknown, but it was deep, awful, a relation of utter inter-destruction. And he, who triumphed in the world, he became more and more hollow in his vitality, the vitality was bled from within him, as by some haemorrhage. She was hulked like a hawk in a cage, but her heart was fierce and undiminished within her, though her mind was destroyed.

So to the last he would go to her and hold her in his arms sometimes, before his strength was all gone. The terrible white, destructive light that burned in her eyes only excited and roused him. Till he was bled to death, and then he dreaded her more than anything. But he always said to himself, how happy he had been, how he had loved her with a pure and consuming love ever since he had known her. And he thought of her as pure, chaste; the white flame which was known to him alone, the flame of her sex, was a white flower of snow to his mind. She was a wonderful white snow-flower, which he had desired infinitely. And now he was dying with all his ideas and interpretations intact. They would only collapse when the breath left his body. Till then they would be pure truths for him. Only death would show the perfect completeness of the lie. Till death, she was his white snow-flower. He had subdued her, and her subjugation was to him an infinite chastity in her, a virginity which he could never break, and which dominated him as by a spell.

She had let go the outer world, but within herself she was unbroken and unimpaired. She only sat in her room like a moping, dishevelled hawk, motionless, mindless. Her children, for whom she had been so fierce in her youth, now meant scarcely anything to her. She had lost all that, she was quite by herself. Only Gerald, the gleaming, had some existence for her. But of late years, since he had become head of the business, he too was forgotten. Whereas the father, now he was dying, turned for compassion to Gerald. There had always been opposition between the two of them. Gerald had feared and despised his father, and to a great extent had avoided him all through boyhood and young manhood. And the father had felt very often a real dislike of his eldest son, which, never wanting to give way to, he had refused to acknowledge. He had ignored Gerald as much as possible, leaving him alone.

Since, however, Gerald had come home and assumed responsibility in the firm, and had proved such a wonderful director, the father, tired and weary of all outside concerns, had put all his trust of these things in his son, implicitly, leaving everything to him, and assuming a rather touching dependence on the young enemy. This immediately roused a poignant pity and allegiance in Gerald's heart, always shadowed by contempt and by unadmitted enmity. For Gerald was in reaction against Charity; and yet he was dominated by it, it assumed supremacy in the inner life, and he could not confute it. So he was partly subject to that which his father stood for, but he was in reaction against it. Now he could not save himself. A certain pity and grief and tenderness for his father overcame him, in spite of the deeper, more sullen hostility.

The father won shelter from Gerald through compassion. But for love he had Winifred. She was his youngest child, she was the only one of his children whom he had ever closely loved. And her he loved with all the great, overweening, sheltering love of a dying man. He wanted to shelter her infinitely, infinitely, to wrap her in warmth and love and shelter, perfectly. If he could save her she should never know one pain, one grief, one hurt. He had been so right all his life, so constant in his kindness and his goodness. And this was his last passionate righteousness, his love for the child Winifred. Some things troubled him yet. The world had passed away from him, as his strength ebbed. There were no more poor and injured and humble to protect and succour. These were all lost to him. There were no more sons and daughters to trouble him, and to weigh on him as an unnatural responsibility. These too had faded out of reality All these things had fallen out of his hands, and left him free.

There remained the covert fear and horror of his wife, as she sat mindless and strange in her room, or as she came forth with slow, prowling step, her head bent forward. But this he put away. Even his lifelong righteousness, however, would not quite deliver him from the inner horror. Still, he could keep it sufficiently at bay. It would never break forth openly. Death would come first.

Then there was Winifred! If only he could be sure about her, if only he could be sure. Since the death of Diana, and the development of his illness, his craving for surety with regard to Winifred amounted almost to obsession. It was as if, even dying, he must have some anxiety, some responsibility of love, of Charity, upon his heart.

She was an odd, sensitive, inflammable child, having her father's dark hair and quiet bearing, but being quite detached, momentaneous. She was like a changeling indeed, as if her feelings did not matter to her, really. She often seemed to be talking and playing like the gayest and most childish of children, she was full of the warmest, most delightful affection for a few things – for her father, and for her animals in particular. But if she heard that her beloved kitten Leo had been run over by the motor car she put her head on one side, and replied, with a faint contraction like resentment on her face: 'Has he?' Then she took no more notice. She only disliked the servant who would force bad news on her, and wanted her to be sorry. She wished not to know, and that seemed her chief motive. She avoided her mother, and most of the members of her family. She *loved* her Daddy, because he wanted her always to be happy, and because he seemed to become young again, and irresponsible in her presence. She liked Gerald, because he was so self-contained. She loved people who would make life a game for her. She had an amazing instinctive critical faculty, and was a pure anarchist, a pure aristocrat at once. For she accepted her equals wherever she found them, and she ignored with blithe indifference her inferiors, whether they were her brothers and sisters, or whether they were wealthy guests of the house, or whether they were the common people or the servants. She was quite single and by herself, deriving from nobody. It was as if she were cut off from all purpose or continuity, and existed simply moment by moment.

The father, as by some strange final illusion, felt as if all his fate depended on his ensuring to Winifred her happiness. She who could never suffer, because she never formed vital connections, she who could lose the dearest things of her life and be just the same the next day, the whole memory dropped out, as if deliberately, she whose will was so strangely and easily free, anarchistic, almost nihilistic, who like a soulless bird flits on its own will, without attachment or responsibility beyond the moment, who in her every motion snapped the threads of serious relationship with blithe, free hands, really nihilistic, because never troubled, she must be the object of her father's final passionate solicitude.

When Mr Crich heard that Gudrun Brangwen might come to help Winifred with her drawing and modelling he saw a road to salvation for his child. He believed that Winifred had talent, he had seen Gudrun, he knew that she was an exceptional person. He could give Winifred into her hands as into the hands of a right being. Here was a direction and a positive force to be lent to his child, he need not leave her directionless and defenceless. If he could but graft the girl on to some tree of utterance before he died, he would have fulfilled his responsibility. And here it could be done. He did not hesitate to appeal to Gudrun.

Meanwhile, as the father drifted more and more out of life, Gerald experienced more and more a sense of exposure. His father after all had stood for the living world to him. Whilst his father lived Gerald was not responsible for the world. But now his father was passing away, Gerald found himself left exposed and unready before the storm of living, like the mutinous first mate of a ship that has lost his captain, and who sees only a terrible chaos in front of him. He did not inherit an established order and a living idea. The whole unifying idea of mankind seemed to be dying with his father, the centralising force that had held the whole together seemed to collapse with his father, the parts were ready to go asunder in terrible disintegration. Gerald was as if left on board of a ship that was going asunder beneath his feet, he was in charge of a vessel whose timbers were all coming apart.

He knew that all his life he had been wrenching at the frame of life to break it apart. And now, with something of the terror of a destructive child, he saw himself on the point of inheriting his own destruction. And during the last months, under the influence of death, and of Birkin's talk, and of Gudrun's penetrating being, he had lost entirely that mechanical certainty that had been his triumph. Sometimes spasms of hatred came over him, against Birkin and Gudrun and that whole set. He wanted to go back to the dullest conservatism, to the most stupid of conventional people. He wanted to revert to the strictest Toryism. But the desire did not last long enough to carry him into action.

During his childhood and his boyhood he had wanted a sort of savagedom. The days of Homer were his ideal, when a man was chief of an army of heroes, or spent his years in wonderful Odyssey. He hated remorselessly the circumstances of his own life, so much that he never really saw Beldover and the colliery valley. He turned his face entirely away from the blackened mining region that stretched away on the right hand of Shortlands, he turned entirely to the country and the woods beyond Willey Water. It was true that the panting and rattling of the coal-mines could always be heard at Shortlands. But from his earliest childhood, Gerald had paid no heed to this. He had ignored the whole of the industrial sea which surged in coal-blackened tides against the grounds of the house. The world was really a wilderness where one hunted and swam and rode. He rebelled against all authority. Life was a condition of savage freedom.

Then he had been sent away to school, which was so much death to him. He refused to go to Oxford, choosing a German university. He had spent a certain time at Bonn, at Berlin, and at Frankfurt. There, a curiosity had been aroused in his mind. He wanted to see and to know, in a curious objective fashion, as if it were an amusement to him. Then he must try war. Then he must travel into the savage regions that had so attracted him.

The result was, he found humanity very much alike everywhere, and to a mind like his, curious and cold, the savage was duller, less exciting than the European. So he took hold of all kinds of sociological ideas, and ideas of reform. But they never went more than skin-deep, they were never more than a mental amusement. Their interest lay chiefly in the reaction against the positive order, the destructive reaction.

He discovered at last a real adventure in the coal-mines. His father asked him to help in the firm. Gerald had been educated in the science of mining, and it had never interested him. Now, suddenly, with a sort of exultation, he laid hold of the world.

There was impressed photographically on his consciousness the great industry. Suddenly, it was real, he was part of it. Down the valley ran the colliery railway, linking mine with mine. Down the railway ran the trains, short trains of heavily laden trucks, long trains of empty wagons, each one bearing in big white letters the initials, 'C. B. & Co.'

These white letters on all the wagons he had seen since his first childhood, and it was as if he had never seen them, they were so familiar, and so ignored. Now at last he saw his own name written on the wall. Now he had a vision of power.

So many wagons, bearing his initial, running all over the country. He saw them as he entered London in the train, he saw them at Dover. So far his power ramified. He looked at Beldover, at Selby, at Whatmore, at Lethley Bank, the great colliery villages which depended entirely on his mines. They were hideous and sordid, during his childhood they had been sores in his consciousness. And now he saw them with pride. Four raw new towns, and many ugly industrial hamlets were crowded under his dependence. He saw the stream of miners flowing along the causeways from the mines at the end of the afternoon, thousands of blackened, slightly distorted human beings with red mouths, all moving subjugate to his will. He pushed slowly in his motor car through the little market-top on Friday nights in Beldover, through a solid mass of human beings that were making their purchases and doing their weekly spending. They were all subordinate to him. They were ugly and uncouth, but they were his instruments. He was the God of the machine. They made way for his motor car automatically, slowly.

He did not care whether they made way with alacrity, or grudgingly. He did not care what they thought of him. His vision had suddenly crystallised. Suddenly he had conceived the pure instrumentality of mankind. There had been so much humanitarianism, so much talk of sufferings and feelings. It was ridiculous. The sufferings and feelings of individuals did not matter in the least. They were mere conditions, like the weather. What mattered was the pure instrumentality of the individual. As a man as of a knife: does it cut well? Nothing else mattered.

Everything in the world has its function, and is good or not good in so far as it fulfils this function more or less perfectly. Was a miner a good miner? Then he was complete. Was a manager a good manager? That was enough. Gerald himself, who was responsible for all this industry, was he a good director? If he were, he had fulfilled his life. The rest was by-play.

The mines were there, they were old. They were giving out, it did not pay to work the seams. There was talk of closing down two of them. It was at this point that Gerald arrived on the scene.

He looked around. There lay the mines. They were old, obsolete. They were like old lions, no more good. He looked again. Pah! the mines were nothing but the clumsy efforts of impure minds. There they lay, abortions of a half-trained mind. Let the idea of them be swept away. He cleared his brain of them, and thought only of the coal in the under earth. How much was there?

There was plenty of coal. The old workings could not get at it, that was all. Then break the neck of the old workings. The coal lay there in its seams, even though the seams were thin. There it lay, inert matter, as it had always lain, since the beginning of time, subject to the will of man. The will of man was the determining factor. Man was the arch-god of earth. His mind was obedient to serve his will. Man's will was the absolute, the only absolute.

And it was his will to subjugate Matter to his own ends. The subjugation itself was the point, the fight was the be-all, the fruits of victory were mere results. It was not for the sake of money that Gerald took over the mines. He did not care about money, fundamentally. He was neither ostentatious nor luxurious, neither did he care about social position, not finally. What he wanted was the pure fulfilment of his own will in the struggle with the natural conditions. His will was now, to take the coal out of the earth, profitably. The profit was merely the condition of victory, but the victory itself lay in the feat achieved. He vibrated with zest before the challenge. Every day he was in the mines, examining, testing, he consulted experts, he gradually gathered the whole situation into his mind, as a general grasps the plan of his campaign.

Then there was need for a complete break. The mines were run on an old system, an obsolete idea. The initial idea had been, to obtain as much money from the earth as would make the owners comfortably rich, would allow the workmen sufficient wages and good conditions, and would increase the wealth of the country altogether. Gerald's father, following in the second generation, having a sufficient fortune, had thought only of the men. The mines, for him, were primarily great fields to produce bread and plenty for all the hundreds of human beings gathered about them. He had lived and striven with his fellow owners to benefit the men every time. And the men had been benefited in their fashion. There were few poor, and few needy. All was plenty, because the mines were good and easy to work. And the miners, in those days, finding themselves richer than they might have expected, felt glad and triumphant. They thought themselves well off, they congratulated themselves on their good fortune, they remembered how their fathers had starved and suffered, and they felt that better times had come. They were grateful to those others, the pioneers, the new owners, who had opened out the pits, and let forth this stream of plenty.

But man is never satisfied, and so the miners, from gratitude to their owners, passed on to murmuring. Their sufficiency decreased with knowledge, they wanted more. Why should the master be so out-of-all-proportion rich?

There was a crisis when Gerald was a boy, when the Masters' Federation closed down the mines because the men would not accept a reduction. This lock-out had forced home the new conditions to Thomas Crich. Belonging to the Federation, he had been compelled by his honour to close the pits against his men. He, the father, the Patriarch, was forced to deny the means of life to his sons, his people. He, the rich man who would hardly enter heaven because of his possessions, must now turn upon the poor, upon those who were nearer Christ than himself, those who were humble and despised and closer to perfection, those who were manly and noble in their labours, and must say to them: 'Ye shall neither labour nor eat bread.'

It was this recognition of the state of war which really broke his heart. He wanted his industry to be run on love. Oh, he wanted love to be the directing power even of the mines. And now, from under the cloak of love, the sword was cynically drawn, the sword of mechanical necessity.

This really broke his heart. He must have the illusion and now the illusion was destroyed. The men were not against *him*, but they were against the masters. It was war, and willy nilly he found himself on the wrong side, in his own conscience. Seething masses of miners met daily, carried away by a new religious impulse. The idea flew through them: 'All men are equal on earth,' and they would carry the idea to its material fulfilment. After all, is it not the teaching of Christ? And what is an idea, if not the germ of action in the material world. 'All men are equal in spirit, they are all sons of God. Whence then this obvious *disquality*?' It was a religious creed pushed to its material conclusion. Thomas Crich at least had no answer. He could but admit, according to his sincere tenets, that the disquality was wrong. But he could not give up his goods, which were the stuff of disquality. So the men would fight for their rights. The last impulses of the last religious passion left on earth, the passion for equality, inspired them.

Seething mobs of men marched about, their faces lighted up as for holy war, with a smoke of cupidity. How disentangle the passion for equality from the passion of cupidity, when begins the fight for equality of possessions? But the God was the machine. Each man claimed equality in the Godhead of the great productive machine. Every man equally was part of this Godhead. But somehow, somewhere, Thomas Crich knew this was false. When the machine is the Godhead, and production or work is worship, then the most mechanical mind is purest and highest, the representative of God on earth. And the rest are subordinate, each according to his degree.

Riots broke out, Whatmore pit-head was in flames. This was the pit furthest in the country, near the woods. Soldiers came. From the windows of Shortlands, on that fatal day, could be seen the flare of fire in the sky not far off, and now the little colliery train, with the workmen's carriages which were used to convey the miners to the distant Whatmore, was crossing the valley full of soldiers, full of redcoats. Then there was the far-off sound of firing, then the later news that the mob was dispersed, one man was shot dead, the fire was put out.

Gerald, who was a boy, was filled with the wildest excitement and delight. He longed to go with the soldiers to shoot the men. But he was not allowed to go out of the lodge gates. At the gates were stationed sentries with guns. Gerald stood near them in delight, whilst gangs of derisive miners strolled up and down the lanes, calling and jeering, 'Now then, three ha'porth o' coppers, let's see thee shoot thy gun.' Insults were chalked on the walls and the fences, the servants left.

And all this while Thomas Crich was breaking his heart, and giving away hundreds of pounds in charity. Everywhere there was free food, a surfeit of free food. Anybody could have bread for asking, and a loaf cost only three-ha'pence.

Every day there was a free tea somewhere, the children had never had so many treats in their lives. On Friday afternoon great basketfuls of buns and cakes were taken into the schools, and great pitchers of milk, the school children had what they wanted. They were sick with eating too much cake and milk.

And then it came to an end, and the men went back to work. But it was never the same as before. There was a new situation created, a new idea reigned. Even in the machine, there should be equality. No part should be subordinate to any other part: all should be equal. The instinct for chaos had entered. Mystic equality lies in abstraction, not in having or in doing, which are processes. In function and process, one man, one part, must of necessity be subordinate to another. It is a condition of being. But the desire for chaos had risen, and the idea of mechanical equality was the weapon of disruption which should execute the will of man, the will for chaos.

Gerald was a boy at the time of the strike, but he longed to be a man, to fight the colliers. The father however was trapped between two half-truths, and broken. He wanted to be a pure Christian, one and equal with all men. He even wanted to give away all he had, to the poor. Yet he was a great promoter of industry, and he knew perfectly that he must keep his goods and keep his authority. This was as divine a necessity in him, as the need to give away all he possessed – more divine, even, since this was the necessity he acted upon. Yet because he did *not* act on the other ideal, it dominated him, he was dying of chagrin because he must forfeit it. He wanted to be a father of loving kindness and sacrificial benevolence. The colliers shouted to him about his thousands a year. They would not be deceived.

When Gerald grew up in the ways of the world, he shifted the position. He did not care about the equality. The whole Christian attitude of love and self-sacrifice was old hat. He knew that position and authority were the right thing in the world, and it was useless to cant about it. They were the right thing, for the simple reason that they were functionally necessary. They were not the be-all and the end-all. It was like being part of a machine. He himself happened to be a controlling, central part, the masses of men were the parts variously controlled. This was merely as it happened. As well get excited because a central hub drives a hundred outer wheels or because the whole universe wheels round the sun. After all, it would be mere silliness to say that the moon and the earth and Saturn and Jupiter and Venus have just as much right to be the centre of the universe, each of them separately, as the sun. Such an assertion is made merely in the desire of chaos.

Without bothering to *think* to a conclusion, Gerald jumped to a conclusion. He abandoned the whole democratic-equality problem as a problem of silliness. What mattered was the great social productive machine. Let that work perfectly, let it produce a sufficiency of everything, let every man be given a rational portion, greater or less according to his functional degree or magnitude, and then, provision made, let the devil supervene, let every man look after his own amusements and appetites, so long as he interfered with nobody.

So Gerald set himself to work, to put the great industry in order. In his travels, and in his accompanying readings, he had come to the conclusion that the essential secret of life was harmony. He did not define to himself at all clearly what harmony was. The word pleased him, he felt he had come to his own conclusions. And he proceeded to put his philosophy into practice by forcing order into the established world, translating the mystic word harmony into the practical word organisation.

Immediately he *saw* the firm, he realised what he could do. He had a fight to fight with Matter, with the earth and the coal it enclosed. This was the sole idea, to turn upon the inanimate matter of the underground, and reduce it to his will. And for this fight with matter, one must have perfect instruments in perfect organisation, a mechanism so subtle and harmonious in its workings that it represents the single mind of man, and by its relentless repetition of given movement, will accomplish a purpose irresistibly, inhumanly. It was this inhuman principle in the mechanism he wanted to construct that inspired Gerald with an almost religious exaltation. He, the man, could interpose a perfect, changeless, godlike medium between himself and the Matter he had to subjugate. There were two opposites, his will and the resistant Matter of the earth. And between these he could establish the very expression of his will, the incarnation of his power, a great and perfect machine, a system, an activity of pure order, pure mechanical repetition, repetition *ad infinitum*, hence eternal and infinite. He found his eternal and his infinite in the pure machine-principle of perfect co-ordination into one pure, complex, infinitely repeated motion, like the spinning of a wheel; but a productive spinning, as the revolving of the universe may be called a productive spinning, a productive repetition through eternity, to infinity. And this is the God-motion, this productive repetition *ad infinitum*. And Gerald was the God of the machine, *Deus ex machina*. And the whole productive will of man was the Godhead.

He had his life-work now, to extend over the earth a great and perfect system in which the will of man ran smooth and unthwarted, timeless, a Godhead in process. He had to begin with the mines. The terms were given: first the resistant Matter of the underground; then the instruments of its subjugation, instruments human and metallic; and finally his own pure will, his own mind. It would need a marvellous adjustment of myriad instruments, human, animal, metallic, kinetic, dynamic, a marvellous casting of myriad tiny wholes into one great perfect entirety. And then, in this case there was perfection attained, the will of the highest was perfectly fulfilled, the will of mankind was perfectly enacted; for was not mankind mystically contradistinguished against inanimate Matter, was not the history of mankind just the history of the conquest of the one by the other?

The miners were overreached. While they were still in the toils of divine equality of man, Gerald had passed on, granted essentially their case, and proceeded in his quality of human being to fulfil the will of mankind as a whole. He merely represented the miners in a higher sense when he perceived that the only way to fulfil perfectly the will of man was to establish the perfect, inhuman machine. But he represented them very essentially, they were far behind, out of date, squabbling for their material equality. The desire had already transmuted into this new and greater desire, for a perfect intervening mechanism between man and Matter, the desire to translate the Godhead into pure mechanism.

As soon as Gerald entered the firm, the convulsion of death ran through the old system. He had all his life been tortured by a furious and destructive demon, which possessed him sometimes like an insanity. This temper now entered like a virus into the firm, and there were cruel eruptions. Terrible and inhuman were his examinations into every detail; there was no privacy he would spare, no old sentiment but he would turn it over. The old grey managers, the old grey clerks, the doddering old pensioners, he looked at them, and removed them as so much lumber. The whole concern seemed like a hospital of invalid employees. He had no emotional qualms. He arranged what pensions were necessary, he looked for efficient substitutes, and when these were found, he substituted them for the old hands.

'I've a pitiful letter here from Letherington,' his father would say, in a tone of deprecation and appeal. 'Don't you think the poor fellow might keep on a little longer? I always fancied he did very well.'

'I've got a man in his place now, father. He'll be happier out of it, believe me. You think his allowance is plenty, don't you?'

'It is not the allowance that he wants, poor man. He feels it very much, that he is superannuated. Says he thought he had twenty more years of work in him yet.'

'Not of this kind of work I want. He doesn't understand.'

The father sighed. He wanted not to know any more. He believed the pits would have to be overhauled if they were to go on working. And after all, it would be worst in the long run for everybody, if they must close down. So he could make no answer to the appeals of his old and trusty servants, he could only repeat 'Gerald says'.

So the father drew more and more out of the light. The whole frame of the real life was broken for him. He had been right according to his lights. And his lights had been those of the great religion. Yet they seemed to have become obsolete, to be superseded in the world. He could not understand. He only withdrew with his lights into an inner room, into the silence. The beautiful candles of belief, that would not do to light the world any more, they would still burn sweetly and sufficiently in the inner room of his soul, and in the silence of his retirement.

Gerald rushed into the reform of the firm, beginning with the office. It was needful to economise severely, to make possible the great alterations he must introduce.

'What are these widows' coals?' he asked.

'We have always allowed all widows of men who worked for the firm a load of coals every three months.'

'They must pay cost price henceforward. The firm is not a charity institution, as everybody seems to think.'

Widows, these stock figures of sentimental humanitarianism, he felt a dislike at the thought of them. They were almost repulsive. Why were they not immolated on the pyre of the husband, like the sati in India? At any rate, let them pay the cost of their coals.

In a thousand ways he cut down the expenditure, in ways so fine as to be hardly noticeable to the men. The miners must pay for the cartage of their coals, heavy cartage too; they must pay for their tools, for the sharpening, for the care of lamps, for the many trifling things that made the bill of charges against every man mount up to a shilling or so in the week. It was not grasped very definitely by the miners, though they were sore enough. But it saved hundreds of pounds every week for the firm.

Gradually Gerald got hold of everything. And then began the great reform. Expert engineers were introduced in every department. An enormous electric plant was installed, both for lighting and for haulage underground, and for power. The electricity was carried into every mine. New machinery was brought from America, such as the miners had never seen before, great iron men, as the cutting machines were called, and unusual appliances. The working of the pits was thoroughly changed, all the control was taken out of the hands of the miners, the butty system was abolished. Everything was run on the most accurate and delicate scientific method, educated and expert men were in control everywhere, the miners were reduced to mere mechanical instruments. They had to work hard, much harder than before, the work was terrible and heart-breaking in its mechanicalness.

But they submitted to it all. The joy went out of their lives, the hope seemed to perish as they became more and more mechanised. And yet they accepted the new conditions. They even got a further satisfaction out of them. At first they hated Gerald Crich, they swore to do something to him, to murder him. But as time went on, they accepted everything with some fatal satisfaction. Gerald was their high priest, he represented the religion they really felt. His father was forgotten already. There was a new world, a new order, strict, terrible, inhuman, but satisfying in its very destructiveness. The men were satisfied to belong to the great and wonderful machine, even whilst it destroyed them. It was what they wanted. It was the highest that man had produced, the most wonderful and superhuman. They were exalted by belonging to this great and superhuman system which was beyond feeling or reason, something really godlike. Their hearts died within them, but their souls were satisfied. It was what they wanted. Otherwise Gerald could never have done what he did. He was just ahead of them in giving them what they wanted, this participation in a great and perfect system that subjected life to pure mathematical principles. This was a sort of freedom, the sort they really wanted. It was the first great step in undoing, the first great phase of chaos, the substitution of the mechanical principle for the organic, the destruction of the organic purpose, the organic unity, and the subordination of every organic unit to the great mechanical purpose. It was pure organic disintegration and pure mechanical organisation. This is the first and finest state of chaos.

Gerald was satisfied. He knew the colliers said they hated him. But he had long ceased to hate them. When they streamed past him at evening, their heavy boots slurring on the pavement wearily, their shoulders slightly distorted, they took no notice of him, they gave him no greeting whatever, they passed in a grey-black stream of unemotional acceptance. They were not important to him, save as instruments, nor he to them, save as a supreme instrument of control. As miners they had their being, he had his being as director. He admired their qualities. But as men, personalities, they were just accidents, sporadic little unimportant phenomena. And tacitly, the men agreed to this. For Gerald agreed to it in himself.

He had succeeded. He had converted the industry into a new and terrible purity. There was a greater output of coal than ever, the wonderful and delicate system ran almost perfectly. He had a set of really clever engineers, both mining and electrical, and they did not cost much. A highly educated man cost very little more than a workman. His managers, who were all rare men, were no more expensive than the old bungling fools of his father's days, who were merely colliers promoted. His chief manager, who had twelve hundred a year, saved the firm at least five thousand. The whole system was now so perfect that Gerald was hardly necessary any more.

It was so perfect that sometimes a strange fear came over him, and he did not know what to do. He went on for some years in a sort of trance of activity. What he was doing seemed supreme, he was almost like a divinity. He was a pure and exalted activity.

But now he had succeeded – he had finally succeeded. And once or twice lately, when he was alone in the evening and had nothing to do, he had suddenly stood up in terror, not knowing what he was. And he went to the mirror and looked long and closely at his own face, at his own eyes, seeking for something. He was afraid, in mortal dry fear, but he knew not what of. He looked at his own face. There it was, shapely and healthy and the same as ever, yet somehow, it was not real, it was a mask. He dared not touch it, for fear it should prove to be only a composition mask. His eyes were blue and keen as ever, and as firm in their sockets. Yet he was not sure that they were not blue false bubbles that would burst in a moment and leave clear annihilation. He could see the darkness in them, as if they were only bubbles of darkness. He was afraid that one day he would break down and be a purely meaningless babble lapping round a darkness.

But his will yet held good, he was able to go away and read, and think about things. He liked to read books about the primitive man, books of anthropology, and also works of speculative philosophy. His mind was very active. But it was like a bubble floating in the darkness. At any moment it might burst and leave him in chaos. He would not die. He knew that. He would go on living, but the meaning would have collapsed out of him, his divine reason would be gone. In a strangely indifferent, sterile way, he was frightened. But he could not react even to the fear. It was as if his centres of feeling were drying up. He remained calm, calculative and healthy, and quite freely deliberate, even whilst he felt, with faint, small but final sterile horror, that his mystic reason was breaking, giving way now, at this crisis.

And it was a strain. He knew there was no equilibrium. He would have to go in some direction, shortly, to find relief. Only Birkin kept the fear definitely off him, saved him his quick sufficiency in life, by the odd mobility and changeableness which seemed to contain the quintessence of faith. But then Gerald must always come away from Birkin, as from a Church service, back to the outside real world of work and life. There it was, it did not alter, and words were futilities. He had to keep himself in reckoning with the world of work and material life. And it became more and more difficult, such a strange pressure was upon him, as if the very middle of him were a vacuum, and outside were an awful tension.

He had found his most satisfactory relief in women. After a debauch with some desperate woman, he went on quite easy and forgetful. The devil of it was, it was so hard to keep up his interest in women nowadays. He didn't care about them any more. A Pussum was all right in her way, but she was an exceptional case, and even she mattered extremely little. No, women, in that sense, were useless to him any more. He felt that his *mind* needed acute stimulation, before he could be physically roused.

CHAPTER 18

Rabbit

Gudrun knew that it was a critical thing for her to go to Shortlands. She knew it was equivalent to accepting Gerald Crich as a lover. And though she hung back, disliking the condition, yet she knew she would go on. She equivocated. She said to herself, in torment recalling the blow and the kiss, 'After all, what is it? What is a kiss? What even is a blow? It is an instant, vanished at once. I can go to Shortlands just for a time, before I go away, if only to see what it is like.' For she had an insatiable curiosity to see and to know everything.

She also wanted to know what Winifred was really like. Having heard the child calling from the steamer in the night, she felt some mysterious connection with her.

Gudrun talked with the father in the library. Then he sent for his daughter. She came accompanied by Mademoiselle.

'Winnie, this is Miss Brangwen, who will be so kind as to help you with your drawing and making models of your animals,' said the father.

The child looked at Gudrun for a moment with interest, before she came forward and with face averted offered her hand. There was a complete *sang-*

froid and indifference under Winifred's childish reserve, a certain irresponsible callousness.

'How do you do?' said the child, not lifting her face.

'How do you do?' said Gudrun.

Then Winifred stood aside, and Gudrun was introduced to Mademoiselle.

'You have a fine day for your walk,' said Mademoiselle, in a bright manner.

'*Quite* fine,' said Gudrun.

Winifred was watching from her distance. She was as if amused, but rather unsure as yet what this new person was like. She saw so many new persons, and so few who became real to her. Mademoiselle was of no count whatever, the child merely put up with her, calmly and easily, accepting her little authority with faint scorn, compliant out of childish arrogance of indifference.

'Well, Winifred,' said the father, 'aren't you glad Miss Brangwen has come? She makes animals and birds in wood and in clay, that the people in London write about in the papers, praising them to the skies.'

Winifred smiled slightly.

'Who told you, Daddie?' she asked.

'Who told me? Hermione told me, and Rupert Birkin.'

'Do you know them?' Winifred asked of Gudrun, turning to her with faint challenge.

'Yes,' said Gudrun.

Winifred readjusted herself a little. She had been ready to accept Gudrun as a sort of servant. Now she saw it was on terms of friendship they were intended to meet. She was rather glad. She had so many half inferiors, whom she tolerated with perfect good humour.

Gudrun was very calm. She also did not take these things very seriously. A new occasion was mostly spectacular to her. However, Winifred was a detached, ironic child, she would never attach herself. Gudrun liked her and was intrigued by her. The first meetings went off with a certain humiliating clumsiness. Neither Winifred nor her instructress had any social grace.

Soon, however, they met in a kind of make-belief world. Winifred did not notice human beings unless they were like herself, playful and slightly mocking. She would accept nothing but the world of amusement, and the serious people of her life were the animals she had for pets. On those she lavished, almost ironically, her affection and her companionship. To the rest of the human scheme she submitted with a faint bored indifference.

She had a Pekinese dog called Looloo, which she loved.

'Let us draw Looloo,' said Gudrun, 'and see if we can get his Looliness, shall we?'

'Darling!' cried Winifred, rushing to the dog, that sat with contemplative sadness on the hearth, and kissing its bulging brow. 'Darling one, will you be drawn? Shall its mummy draw its portrait?' Then she chuckled gleefully, and turning to Gudrun, said: 'Oh let's!'

They proceeded to get pencils and paper, and were ready.

'Beautifullest,' cried Winifred, hugging the dog, 'sit still while its mummy draws its beautiful portrait.' The dog looked up at her with grievous resignation in its large, prominent eyes. She kissed it fervently, and said: 'I wonder what mine will be like. It's sure to be awful.'

As she sketched she chuckled to herself, and cried out at times, 'Oh darling, you're so beautiful!'

And again chuckling, she rushed to embrace the dog, in penitence, as if she were doing him some subtle injury. He sat all the time with the resignation and fretfulness of ages on his dark velvety face. She drew slowly, with a wicked concentration in her eyes, her head on one side, an intense stillness over her. She was as if working the spell of some enchantment. Suddenly she had finished. She looked at the dog, and then at her drawing, and then cried, with real grief for the dog, and at the same time with a wicked exultation, 'My beautiful, why did they?'

She took her paper to the dog, and held it under his nose. He turned his head aside as in chagrin and mortification, and she impulsively kissed his velvety bulging forehead.

' 's a Loolie, 's a little Loozie! Look at his portrait, darling, look at his portrait, that his mother has done of him.' She looked at her paper and chuckled. Then, kissing the dog once more, she rose and came gravely to Gudrun, offering her the paper.

It was a grotesque little diagram of a grotesque little animal, so wicked and so comical, a slow smile came over Gudrun's face, unconsciously. And at her side Winifred chuckled with glee, and said, 'It isn't like him, is it? He's much lovelier than that. He's *so* beautiful – mmm, Looloo, my sweet darling.' And she flew off to embrace the chagrined little dog. He looked up at her with reproachful, saturnine eyes, vanquished in his extreme agedness of being. Then she flew back to her drawing, and chuckled with satisfaction.

'It isn't like him, is it?' she said to Gudrun.

'Yes, it's very like him,' Gudrun replied.

The child treasured her drawing, carried it about with her, and showed it, with a silent embarrassment, to everybody.

'Look,' she said, thrusting the paper into her father's hand.

'Why that's Looloo!' he exclaimed. And he looked down in surprise, hearing the almost inhuman chuckle of the child at his side.

Gerald was away from home when Gudrun first came to Shortlands. But the first morning he came back he watched for her. It was a sunny, soft morning, and he lingered in the garden paths, looking at the flowers that had come out during his absence. He was clean and fit as ever, shaven, his fair hair scrupulously parted at the side, bright in the sunshine, his short, fair moustache closely clipped, his eyes with their humorous kind twinkle, which was so deceptive. He was dressed in black, his clothes sat well on his well-nourished body. Yet as he lingered before the flower-beds in the morning sunshine, there was a certain isolation, a fear about him, as of something wanting.

Gudrun came up quickly, unseen. She was dressed in blue, with woollen yellow stockings, like the Bluecoat boys. He glanced up in surprise. Her stockings always disconcerted him, the pale-yellow stockings and the heavy, heavy black shoes. Winifred, who had been playing about the garden with Mademoiselle and the dogs, came flitting towards Gudrun. The child wore a dress of black and-white stripes. Her hair was rather short, cut round and hanging level in her neck.

'We're going to do Bismarck, aren't we?' she said, linking her hand through Gudrun's arm.

'Yes, we're going to do Bismarck. Do you want to?'

'Oh yes – oh I do! I want most awfully to do Bismarck. He looks *so* splendid this morning, so *fierce*. He's almost as big as a lion.' And the child chuckled sardonically at her own hyperbole. 'He's a real king, he really is.'

'*Bonjour, mademoiselle,*' said the little French governess, wavering up with a slight bow, a bow of the sort that Gudrun loathed, insolent.

'*Winifred veut tant faire le portrait de Bismarck – ! Oh, mais toute la matinée –* "We will do Bismarck this morning!" *– Bismarck, Bismarck, toujours Bismarck! C'est un lapin, n'est-ce pas, mademoiselle?*'

'*Oui, c'est un grand lapin blanc et noir. Vous ne l'avez pas vu?*' said Gudrun in her good, but rather heavy French.

'*Non, mademoiselle, Winifred n'a jamais voulu me le faire voir. Tant de fois je le lui ai demandé, "Qu'est ce donc que ce Bismarck, Winifred?" Mais elle n'a pas voulu me le dire. Son Bismarck, c'était un mystère.*'

'*Oui, c'est un mystère, vraiment un mystère!* Miss Brangwen, say that Bismarck is a mystery,' cried Winifred.

'Bismarck, is a mystery, *Bismarck, c'est un mystère, der Bismarck, er ist ein Wunder,*' said Gudrun, in mocking incantation.

'*Ja, er ist ein Wunder,*' repeated Winifred, with odd seriousness, under which lay a wicked chuckle.

'*Ist er auch ein Wunder?*' came the slightly insolent sneering of Mademoiselle.

'*Doch!*' said Winifred briefly, indifferent.

'*Doch ist er nicht ein König.* Beesmarck, he was not a king, Winifred, as you have said. He was only – *il n'était que chancelier.*'

'*Qu'est-ce qu'un chancelier?*' said Winifred, with slightly contemptuous in-difference.

'A *chancelier* is a chancellor, and a chancellor is, I believe, a sort of judge,' said Gerald coming up and shaking hands with Gudrun. 'You'll have made a song of Bismarck soon,' said he.

Mademoiselle waited, and discreetly made her inclination, and her greeting.

'So they wouldn't let you see Bismarck, mademoiselle?' he said.

'*Non, monsieur.*'

'Ay, very mean of them. What are you going to do to him, Miss Brangwen? I want him sent to the kitchen and cooked.'

'Oh no,' cried Winifred.

'We're going to draw him,' said Gudrun.

'Draw him and quarter him and dish him up,' he said, being purposely fatuous.

'Oh no,' cried Winifred with emphasis, chuckling.

Gudrun detected the tang of mockery in him, and she looked up and smiled into his face. He felt his nerves caressed. Their eyes met in knowledge.

'How do you like Shortlands?' he asked.

'Oh, very much,' she said, with nonchalance.

'Glad you do. Have you noticed these flowers?'

He led her along the path. She followed intently. Winifred came, and the governess lingered in the rear. They stopped before some veined salpiglossis flowers.

'Aren't they wonderful?' she cried, looking at them absorbedly. Strange how her reverential, almost ecstatic admiration of the flowers caressed his nerves. She stooped down, and touched the trumpets, with infinitely fine and delicate-touching fingertips. It filled him with ease to see her. When she rose, her eyes, hot with the beauty of the flowers, looked into his.

'What are they?' she asked.

'Sort of petunia, I suppose,' he answered. 'I don't really know them.'

'They are quite strangers to me,' she said.

They stood together in a false intimacy, a nervous contact. And he was in love with her.

She was aware of Mademoiselle standing near, like a little French beetle, observant and calculating. She moved away with Winifred, saying they would go to find Bismarck.

Gerald watched them go, looking all the while at the soft, full, still body of Gudrun, in its silky cashmere. How silky and rich and soft her body must be. An excess of appreciation came over his mind, she was the all-desirable, the all-beautiful. He wanted only to come to her, nothing more. He was only this, this being that should come to her, and be given to her.

At the same time he was finely and acutely aware of Mademoiselle's neat, brittle finality of form. She was like some elegant beetle with thin ankles, perched on her high heels, her glossy black dress perfectly correct, her dark hair done high and admirably. How repulsive her completeness and her finality was! He loathed her.

Yet he did admire her. She was perfectly correct. And it did rather annoy him, that Gudrun came dressed in startling colours, like a macaw, when the family was in mourning. Like a macaw she was! He watched the lingering way she took her feet from the ground. And her ankles were pale yellow, and her dress a deep blue. Yet it pleased him. It pleased him very much. He felt the challenge in her very attire – she challenged the whole world. And he smiled as to the note of a trumpet.

Gudrun and Winifred went through the house to the back, where were the stables and the outbuildings. Everywhere was still and deserted. Mr Crich had gone out for a short drive, the stableman had just led round Gerald's horse. The two girls went to the hutch that stood in a corner, and looked at the great black-and-white rabbit.

'Isn't he beautiful! Oh, do look at him listening! Doesn't he look silly!' she laughed quickly, then added 'Oh, do let's do him listening, do let us, he listens with so much of himself; – don't you, darling Bismarck?'

'Can we take him out?' said Gudrun.

'He's very strong. He really is extremely strong.' She looked at Gudrun, her head on one side, in odd calculating mistrust.

'But we'll try, shall we?'

'Yes, if you like. But he's a fearful kicker!'

They took the key to unlock the door. The rabbit exploded in a wild rush round the hutch.

'He scratches most awfully sometimes,' cried Winifred in excitement. 'Oh do look at him, isn't he wonderful!' The rabbit tore round the hutch in a hurry. 'Bismarck!' cried the child, in rousing excitement. 'How *dreadful* you are! You are beastly.' Winifred looked up at Gudrun with some misgiving in her wild excitement. Gudrun smiled sardonically with her mouth. Winifred made a strange crooning noise of unaccountable excitement. 'Now he's still!' she cried, seeing the rabbit settled down in a far corner of the hutch. 'Shall we take him now?' she whispered excitedly, mysteriously, looking up at Gudrun and edging very close. 'Shall we get him now? – ' she chuckled wickedly to herself.

They unlocked the door of the hutch. Gudrun thrust in her arm and seized the great, lusty rabbit as it crouched still, she grasped its long ears. It set its four feet flat, and thrust back. There was a long scraping sound as it was hauled forward, and in another instant it was in midair, lunging wildly, its body flying like a spring coiled and released, as it lashed out, suspended from the ears. Gudrun held the black-and-white tempest at arms' length, averting her face. But the rabbit was magically strong, it was all she could do to keep her grasp. She almost lost her presence of mind.

'Bismarck, Bismarck, you are behaving terribly,' said Winifred in a rather frightened voice, 'Oh, do put him down, he's beastly.'

Gudrun stood for a moment astounded by the thunderstorm that had sprung into being in her grip. Then her colour came up, a heavy rage came over her like a cloud. She stood shaken as a house in a storm, and utterly overcome. Her heart was arrested with fury at the mindlessness and the bestial stupidity of this struggle, her wrists were badly scored by the claws of the beast, a heavy cruelty welled up in her.

Gerald came round as she was trying to capture the flying rabbit under her arm. He saw, with subtle recognition, her sullen passion of cruelty.

'You should let one of the men do that for you,' he said hurrying up.

'Oh, he's *so* horrid!' cried Winifred, almost frantic.

He held out his nervous, sinewy hand and took the rabbit by the ears, from Gudrun.

'It's most *fearfully* strong,' she cried, in a high voice, like the crying of a seagull, strange and vindictive.

The rabbit made itself into a ball in the air, and lashed out, flinging itself into a bow. It really seemed demoniacal. Gudrun saw Gerald's body tighten, saw a sharp blindness come into his eyes.

'I know these beggars of old,' he said.

The long, demon-like beast lashed out again, spread on the air as if it were flying, looking something like a dragon, then closing up again, inconceivably powerful and explosive. The man's body, strung to its efforts, vibrated strongly. Then a sudden sharp, white-edged wrath came up in him. Swift as lightning he drew back and brought his free hand down like a hawk on the neck of the rabbit. Simultaneously, there came the unearthly abhorrent scream of a rabbit in the fear of death. It made one immense writhe, tore his wrists and his sleeves in a final convulsion, all its belly flashed white in a whirlwind of paws, and then he had slung it round and had it under his arm, fast. It cowered and skulked. His face was gleaming with a smile.

'You wouldn't think there was all that force in a rabbit,' he said, looking at Gudrun. And he saw her eyes black as night in her pallid face, she looked almost unearthly. The scream of the rabbit, after the violent tussle, seemed to have torn the veil of her consciousness. He looked at her, and the whitish, electric gleam in his face intensified.

'I don't really like him,' Winifred was crooning. 'I don't care for him as I do for Loozie. He's hateful really.'

A smile twisted Gudrun's face, as she recovered. She knew she was revealed. 'Don't they make the most fearful noise when they scream?' she cried, the high note in her voice, like a seagull's cry.

'Abominable,' he said.

'He shouldn't be so silly when he has to be taken out,' Winifred was saying, putting out her hand and touching the rabbit tentatively, as it skulked under his arm, motionless as if it were dead.

'He's not dead, is he Gerald?' she asked.

'No, he ought to be,' he said.

'Yes, he ought!' cried the child, with a sudden flush of amusement. And she touched the rabbit with more confidence. 'His heart is beating *so* fast. Isn't he funny? He really is.'

'Where do you want him?' asked Gerald.

'In the little green court,' she said.

Gudrun looked at Gerald with strange, darkened eyes, strained with under-world knowledge, almost supplicating, like those of a creature which is at his mercy, yet which is his ultimate victor. He did not know what to say to her. He felt the mutual hellish recognition. And he felt he ought to say something, to cover it. He had the power of lightning in his nerves, she seemed like a soft recipient of his magical, hideous white fire. He was unconfident, he had qualms of fear.

'Did he hurt you?' he asked.

'No,' she said.

'He's an insensible beast,' he said, turning his face away.

They came to the little court, which was shut in by old red walls in whose crevices wallflowers were growing. The grass was soft and fine and old, a level floor carpeting the court, the sky was blue overhead. Gerald tossed the rabbit down. It crouched still and would not move. Gudrun watched it with faint horror.

'Why doesn't it move?' she cried.

'It's skulking,' he said.

She looked up at him, and a slight sinister smile contracted her white face.

'Isn't it a *fool*!' she cried. 'Isn't it a sickening *fool*?' The vindictive mockery in her voice made his brain quiver. Glancing up at him, into his eyes, she revealed again the mocking, white-cruel recognition. There was a league between them, abhorrent to them both. They were implicated with each other in abhorrent mysteries.

'How many scratches have you?' he asked, showing his hard forearm, white and hard and torn in red gashes.

'How really vile!' she cried, flushing with a sinister vision. 'Mine is nothing.'

She lifted her arm and showed a deep red score down the silken white flesh.

'What a devil!' he exclaimed. But it was as if he had had knowledge of her in the long red rent of her forearm, so silken and soft. He did not want to touch her. He would have to make himself touch her, deliberately. The long, shallow red rip seemed torn across his own brain, tearing the surface of his ultimate consciousness, letting through the forever unconscious, unthinkable red ether of the beyond, the obscene beyond.

'It doesn't hurt you very much, does it?' he asked, solicitous.

'Not at all,' she cried.

And suddenly the rabbit, which had been crouching as if it were a flower, so still and soft, suddenly burst into life. Round and round the court it went, as if shot from a gun, round and round like a furry meteorite, in a tense hard circle that seemed to bind their brains. They all stood in amazement, smiling uncannily, as if the rabbit were obeying some unknown incantation. Round and round it flew, on the grass under the old red walls like a storm.

And then quite suddenly it settled down, hobbled among the grass, and sat considering, its nose twitching like a bit of fluff in the wind. After having considered for a few minutes, a soft bunch with a black, open eye, which perhaps was looking at them, perhaps was not, it hobbled calmly forward and began to nibble the grass with that mean motion of a rabbit's quick eating.

'It's mad,' said Gudrun. 'It is most decidedly mad.'

He laughed.

'The question is,' he said, 'what is madness? I don't suppose it is rabbit-mad.'

'Don't you think it is?' she asked.

'No. That's what it is to be a rabbit.'

'There was a queer, faint, obscene smile over his face. She looked at him and saw him, and knew that he was initiate as she was initiate. This thwarted her, and contravened her, for the moment.

'God be praised we aren't rabbits,' she said, in a high, shrill voice.

The smile intensified a little, on his face.

'Not rabbits?' he said, looking at her fixedly.

Slowly her face relaxed into a smile of obscene recognition.

'Ah Gerald,' she said, in a strong, slow, almost manlike way. ' – All that, and more.' Her eyes looked up at him with shocking nonchalance.

He felt again as if she had torn him across the breast, dully, finally. He turned aside.

'Eat, eat my darling!' Winifred was softly conjuring the rabbit, and creeping forward to touch it. It hobbled away from her. 'Let its mother stroke its fur then, darling, because it is so mysterious – '

CHAPTER 19

Moony

After his illness Birkin went to the south of France for a time. He did not write, nobody heard anything of him. Ursula, left alone, felt as if everything were lapsing out. There seemed to be no hope in the world. One was a tiny little rock with the tide of nothingness rising higher and higher. She herself was real, and only herself – just like a rock in a wash of flood water. The rest was all nothingness. She was hard and indifferent, isolated in herself.

There was nothing for it now, but contemptuous, resistant indifference. All the world was lapsing into a grey wish-wash of nothingness, she had no contact and no connection anywhere. She despised and detested the whole show. From the bottom of her heart, from the bottom of her soul, she despised and detested people, adult people. She loved only children and animals: children she loved passionately, but coldly. They made her want to hug them, to protect them, to give them life. But this very love, based on pity and despair, was only a bondage and a pain to her. She loved best of all the animals, that were single and unsocial as she herself was. She loved the horses and cows in the field. Each was single and to itself, magical. It was not referred away to some detestable social principle. It was incapable of soulfulness and tragedy, which she detested so profoundly.

She could be very pleasant and flattering, almost subservient, to people she met. But no one was taken in. Instinctively each felt her contemptuous mockery of the human being in himself, or herself. She had a profound grudge against the human being. That which the word 'human' stood for was despicable and repugnant to her.

Mostly her heart was closed in this hidden, unconscious strain of contemptuous ridicule. She thought she loved, she thought she was full of love. This was her idea of herself. But the strange brightness of her presence, a marvellous radiance of intrinsic vitality, was a luminousness of supreme repudiation, nothing but repudiation.

Yet, at moments, she yielded and softened, she wanted pure love, only pure love. This other, this state of constant unfailing repudiation, was a strain, a suffering also. A terrible desire for pure love overcame her again.

She went out one evening, numbed by this constant essential suffering. Those who are timed for destruction must die now. The knowledge of this reached a finality, a finishing in her. And the finality released her. If fate would carry off in death or downfall all those who were timed to go, why need she trouble, why repudiate any further. She was free of it all, she could seek a new union elsewhere.

Ursula set off to Willey Green, towards the mill. She came to Willey Water. It was almost full again, after its period of emptiness. Then she turned off through the woods. The night had fallen, it was dark. But she forgot to be afraid, she who had such great sources of fear. Among the trees, far from any human beings, there was a sort of magic peace. The more one could find a pure loneliness, with no taint of people, the better one felt. She was in reality terrified, horrified in her apprehension of people.

She started, noticing something on her right hand, between the tree trunks. It was like a great presence, watching her, dodging her. She started violently. It was only the moon, risen through the thin trees. But it seemed so mysterious, with its white and deathly smile. And there was no avoiding it. Night or day, one could not escape the sinister face, triumphant and radiant like this moon, with a high smile. She hurried on, cowering from the white planet. She would just see the pond at the mill before she went home.

Not wanting to go through the yard, because of the dogs, she turned off along the hillside to descend on the pond from above. The moon was transcendent over the bare, open space, she suffered from being exposed to it. There was a glimmer of nightly rabbits across the ground. The night was as clear as crystal, and very still. She could hear a distant coughing of a sheep.

So she swerved down to the steep, tree-hidden bank above the pond, where the alders twisted their roots. She was glad to pass into the shade out of the moon. There she stood, at the top of the fallen-away bank, her hand on the rough trunk of a tree, looking at the water, that was perfect in its stillness, floating the moon upon it. But for some reason she disliked it. It did not give her anything. She listened for the hoarse rustle of the sluice. And she wished for something else out of the night, she wanted another night, not this moon-brilliant hardness. She could feel her soul crying out in her, lamenting desolately.

She saw a shadow moving by the water. It would be Birkin. He had come back then, unawares. She accepted it without remark, nothing mattered to her. She sat down among the roots of the alder tree, dim and veiled, hearing the sound of the sluice like dew distilling audibly into the night. The islands were dark and half revealed, the reeds were dark also, only some of them had a little frail fire of reflection. A fish leaped secretly, revealing the light in the pond. This fire of the chill night, breaking constantly on to the pure darkness, repelled her. She wished it were perfectly dark, perfectly, and noiseless and without motion. Birkin, small and dark also, his hair tinged with moonlight, wandered nearer. He was quite near, and yet he did not exist in her. He did not know she was there. Supposing he did something he would not wish to be seen doing, thinking he was quite private? But there, what did it matter? What did the small privacies matter? How could it matter, what he did? How can there be any secrets, we are all the same organisms? How can there be any secrecy, when everything is known to all of us?

He was touching unconsciously the dead husks of flowers as he passed by, and talking disconnectedly to himself.

'You can't go away,' he was saying. 'There *is* no away. You only withdraw upon yourself.'

He threw a dead flower-husk on to the water.

'An antiphony – they lie, and you sing back to them. There wouldn't have to be any truth, if there weren't any lies. Then one needn't assert anything – '

He stood still, looking at the water, and throwing upon it the husks of the flowers.

'Cybele – curse her! The accursed *Syria Dea*! Does one begrudge it her? What else is there – ?'

Ursula wanted to laugh loudly and hysterically, hearing his isolated voice speaking out. It was so ridiculous.

He stood staring at the water. Then he stooped and picked up a stone, which he threw sharply at the pond. Ursula was aware of the bright moon leaping and swaying, all distorted, in her eyes. It seemed to shoot out arms of fire like a cuttlefish, like a luminous polyp, palpitating strongly before her.

And his shadow on the border of the pond was watching for a few moments, then he stooped and groped on the ground. Then again there was a burst of sound, and a burst of brilliant light, the moon had exploded on the water, and was flying asunder in flakes of white and dangerous fire. Rapidly, like white birds, the fires all broken rose across the pond, fleeing in clamorous confusion, battling with the flock of dark waves that were forcing their way in. The furthest waves of light, fleeing out, seemed to be clamouring against the shore for escape, the waves of darkness came in heavily, running under towards the centre. But at the centre, the heart of all, was still a vivid, incandescent quivering of a white moon not quite destroyed, a white body of fire writhing and striving and not even now broken open, not yet violated. It seemed to be drawing itself together with strange, violent pangs, in blind effort. It was getting stronger, it was reasserting itself, the inviolable moon. And the rays were hastening in in thin lines of light, to return to the strengthened moon, that shook upon the water in triumphant reassumption.

Birkin stood and watched, motionless, till the pond was almost calm, the moon was almost serene. Then, satisfied of so much, he looked for more stones. She felt his invisible tenacity. And in a moment again, the broken lights scattered in explosion over her face, dazzling her; and then, almost immediately, came the second shot. The moon leapt up white and burst through the air. Darts of bright light shot asunder, darkness swept over the centre. There was no moon, only a battlefield of broken lights and shadows, running close together. Shadows, dark and heavy, struck again and again across the place where the heart of the moon had been, obliterating it altogether. The white fragments pulsed up and down, and could not find where to go, apart and brilliant on the water like the petals of a rose that a wind has blown far and wide.

Yet again, they were flickering their way to the centre, finding the path blindly, enviously. And again, all was still, as Birkin and Ursula watched. The waters were loud on the shore. He saw the moon regathering itself insidiously, saw the heart of the rose intertwining vigorously and blindly, calling back the scattered fragments, winning home the fragments, in a pulse and in effort of return.

And he was not satisfied. Like a madness, he must go on. He got large stones, and threw them, one after the other, at the white-burning centre of the moon, till there was nothing but a rocking of hollow noise, and a pond surged up, no moon any more, only a few broken flakes tangled and glittering broadcast in the darkness, without aim or meaning, a darkened confusion, like a black and white kaleidoscope tossed at random. The hollow night was rocking and crashing with noise, and from the sluice came sharp, regular flashes of sound. Flakes of light appeared here and there, glittering tormented among the shadows, far off, in strange places; among the dripping shadow of the willow on the island. Birkin stood and listened and was satisfied.

Ursula was dazed, her mind was all gone. She felt she had fallen to the ground and was spilled out, like water on the earth. Motionless and spent she remained in the gloom. Though even now she was aware, unseeing, that in the darkness was a little tumult of ebbing flakes of light, a cluster dancing secretly in a round, twining and coming steadily together. They were gathering a heart again, they were coming once more into being. Gradually the fragments caught together reunited, heaving, rocking, dancing, falling back as in panic, but working their way home again persistently, making semblance of fleeing away when they had advanced, but always flickering nearer, a little closer to the mark, the cluster growing mysteriously larger and brighter, as gleam after gleam fell in with the whole, until a ragged rose, a distorted, frayed moon was shaking upon the waters again, reasserted, renewed, trying to recover from its convulsion, to get over the disfigurement and the agitation, to be whole and composed, at peace.

Birkin lingered vaguely by the water. Ursula was afraid that he would stone the moon again. She slipped from her seat and went down to him, saying, 'You won't throw stones at it any more, will you?'

'How long have you been there?'

'All the time. You won't throw any more stones, will you?'

'I wanted to see if I could make it be quite gone off the pond,' he said.

'Yes, it was horrible, really. Why should you hate the moon? It hasn't done you any harm, has it?'

'Was it hate?' he said.

And they were silent for a few minutes.

'When did you come back?' she said.

'Today.'

'Why did you never write?'

'I could find nothing to say.'

'Why was there nothing to say?'

'I don't know. Why are there no daffodils now?'

'No.'

Again there was a space of silence. Ursula looked at the moon. It had gathered itself together, and was quivering slightly.

'Was it good for you, to be alone?' she asked.

'Perhaps. Not that I know much. But I got over a good deal. Did you do anything important?'

'No. I looked at England, and thought I'd done with it.'

'Why England?' he asked in surprise.

'I don't know, it came like that.'

'It isn't a question of nations,' he said. 'France is far worse.'

'Yes, I know. I felt I'd done with it all.'

They went and sat down on the roots of the trees, in the shadow. And being silent, he remembered the beauty of her eyes, which were sometimes filled with light, like spring, suffused with wonderful promise. So he said to her, slowly, with difficulty, 'There is a golden light in you, which I wish you would give me.' It was as if he had been thinking of this for some time.

She was startled, she seemed to leap clear of him. Yet also she was pleased.

'What kind of a light?' she asked.

But he was shy, and did not say any more. So the moment passed for this time. And gradually a feeling of sorrow came over her.

'My life is unfulfilled,' she said.

'Yes,' he answered briefly, not wanting to hear this.

'And I feel as if nobody could ever really love me,' she said.

But he did not answer.

'You think, don't you,' she said slowly, 'that I only want physical things? It isn't true. I want you to serve my spirit.'

'I know you do. I know you don't want physical things by themselves. But, I want you to give me – to give your spirit to me – that golden light which is you – which you don't know – give it me – '

After a moment's silence she replied, 'But how can I, you don't love me! You only want your own ends. You don't want to serve *me*, and yet you want me to serve you. It is so one-sided!'

It was a great effort to him to maintain this conversation, and to press for the thing he wanted from her, the surrender of her spirit.

'It is different,' he said. 'The two kinds of service are so different. I serve you in another way – not through *yourself* – somewhere else. But I want us to be together without bothering about ourselves – to be really together because we *are* together, as if it were a phenomenon, not a thing we have to maintain by our own effort.'

'No,' she said, pondering. 'You are just egocentric. You never have any enthusiasm, you never come out with any spark towards me. You want yourself, really, and your own affairs. And you want me just to be there, to serve you.'

But this only made him shut off from her.

'Ah well,' he said, 'words make no matter, anyway. The thing *is* between us, or it isn't.'

'You don't even love me,' she cried.

'I do,' he said angrily. 'But I want – ' His mind saw again the lovely golden light of spring transfused through her eyes, as through some wonderful window. And he wanted her to be with him there, in this world of proud indifference. But what was the good of telling her he wanted this company in proud indifference. What was the good of talking, anyway? It must happen beyond the sound of words. It was merely ruinous to try to work her by conviction. This was a paradisal bird that could never be netted, it must fly by itself to the heart.

'I always think I am going to be loved – and then I am let down. You *don't* love me, you know. You don't want to serve me. You only want yourself.'

A shiver of rage went over his veins, at this repeated: 'You don't want to serve me.' All the paradisal disappeared from him.

'No,' he said, irritated, 'I don't want to serve you, because there is nothing there to serve. What you want me to serve, is nothing, mere nothing. It isn't even you, it is your mere female quality. And I wouldn't give a straw for your female ego – it's a rag doll.'

'Ha!' she laughed in mockery. 'That's all you think of me, is it? And then you have the impudence to say you love me.'

She rose in anger, to go home.

'You want the paradisal unknowing,' she said, turning round on him as he still sat half-visible in the shadow. 'I know what that means, thank you. You want me to be your thing, never to criticise you or to have anything to say for myself. You want me to be a mere *thing* for you! No thank you! *If* you want that, there are plenty of women who will give it to you. There are plenty of women who will lie down for you to walk over them – *go* to them then, if that's what you want – go to them.'

'No,' he said, outspoken with anger. 'I want you to drop your assertive *will*, your frightened apprehensive self-insistence, that is what I want. I want you to trust yourself so implicitly, that you can let yourself go.'

'Let myself go!' she re-echoed in mockery. '*I* can let myself go, easily enough. It is you who can't let yourself go, it is you who hang on to yourself as if it were your only treasure. *You – you* are the Sunday-school teacher. *You –* you preacher.'

The amount of truth that was in this made him stiff and unheeding of her.

'I don't mean let yourself go in the Dionysic ecstatic way,' he said. 'I know you can do that. But I hate ecstasy, Dionysic or any other. It's like going round in a squirrel cage. I want you not to care about yourself, just to be there and not to care about yourself, not to insist – be glad and sure and indifferent.'

'Who insists?' she mocked. 'Who is it that keeps on insisting? It isn't *me*!'

There was a weary, mocking bitterness in her voice. He was silent for some time.

'I know,' he said. 'While ever either of us insists to the other, we are all wrong. But there we are, the accord doesn't come.'

They sat in stillness under the shadow of the trees by the bank. The night was white around them, they were in the darkness, barely conscious.

Gradually, the stillness and peace came over them. She put her hand tentatively on his. Their hands clasped softly and silently, in peace.

'Do you really love me?' she said.

He laughed.

'I call that your war-cry,' he replied, amused.

'Why!' she cried, amused and really wondering.

'Your insistence – Your war-cry – "A Brangwen, A Brangwen" – an old battle-cry. Yours is, "Do you love me? Yield knave, or die." '

'No,' she said, pleading, 'not like that. Not like that. But I must know that you love me, mustn't I?'

'Well then, know it and have done with it.'

'But do you?'

'Yes, I do. I love you, and I know it's final. It is final, so why say any more about it.'

She was silent for some moments, in delight and doubt.

'Are you sure?' she said, nestling happily near to him.

'Quite sure – so now have done – accept it and have done.'

She was nestled quite close to him.

'Have done with what?' she murmured, happily.

'With bothering,' he said.

She clung nearer to him. He held her close, and kissed her softly, gently. It was such peace and heavenly freedom, just to fold her and kiss her gently, and not to have any thoughts or any desires or any will, just to be still with her, to be perfectly still and together, in a peace that was not sleep, but content in bliss. To be content in bliss, without desire or insistence anywhere, this was heaven: to be together in happy stillness.

For a long time she nestled to him, and he kissed her softly, her hair, her face, her ears, gently, softly, like dew falling. But this warm breath on her ears disturbed her again, kindled the old destructive fires. She cleaved to him, and he could feel his blood changing like quicksilver.

'But we'll be still, shall we?' he said.

'Yes,' she said, as if submissively.

And she continued to nestle against him.

But in a little while she drew away and looked at him.

'I must be going home,' she said.

'Must you – how sad,' he replied.

She leaned forward and put up her mouth to be kissed.

'Are you really sad?' she murmured, smiling.

'Yes,' he said, 'I wish we could stay as we were, always.'

'Always! Do you?' she murmured, as he kissed her. And then, out of a full throat, she crooned: 'Kiss me! Kiss me!' And she cleaved close to him. He kissed her many times. But he too had his idea and his will. He wanted only gentle communion, no other, no passion now. So that soon she drew away, put on her hat and went home.

The next day, however, he felt wistful and yearning. He thought he had been wrong, perhaps. Perhaps he had been wrong to go to her with an idea of what he wanted. Was it really only an idea, or was it the interpretation of a profound yearning? If the latter, how was it he was always talking about sensual fulfilment? The two did not agree very well.

Suddenly he found himself face to face with a situation. It was as simple as this: fatally simple. On the one hand, he knew he did not want a further sensual experience – something deeper, darker, than ordinary life could give. He remembered the African fetishes he had seen at Halliday's so often. There came back to him one, a statuette about two feet high, a tall, slim, elegant figure from West Africa, in dark wood, glossy and suave. It was a woman, with hair dressed high, like a melon-shaped dome. He remembered her vividly: she was one of his soul's intimates. Her body was long and elegant, her face was crushed tiny like a beetle's, she had rows of round heavy collars, like a column of quoits, on her neck. He remembered her: her astonishing cultured elegance, her diminished, beetle face, the astounding long elegant body, on short, ugly legs, with such protuberant buttocks, so weighty and unexpected below her slim long loins. She knew what he himself did not know. She had thousands of years of purely sensual, purely unspiritual knowledge behind her. It must have been thousands of years since her race had died, mystically: that is, since the relation between the senses and the outspoken mind had broken, leaving the experience all in one sort, mystically sensual. Thousands of years ago, that which was imminent in himself must have taken place in these Africans: the goodness, the holiness, the desire for creation and productive happiness must have lapsed, leaving the single impulse for knowledge in one sort, mindless progressive knowledge through the senses, knowledge arrested and ending in the senses, mystic knowledge in disintegration and dissolution, knowledge such as the beetles have, which live purely within the world of corruption and cold dissolution. This was why her face looked like a beetle's: this was why the Egyptians worshipped the ball-rolling scarab: because of the principle of knowledge in dissolution and corruption.

There is a long way we can travel, after the death-break: after that point when the soul in intense suffering breaks, breaks away from its organic hold like a leaf that falls. We fall from the connection with life and hope, we lapse from pure integral being, from creation and liberty, and we fall into the long, long African process of purely sensual understanding, knowledge in the mystery of dissolution.

He realised now that this is a long process – thousands of years it takes, after the death of the creative spirit. He realised that there were great mysteries to be unsealed, sensual, mindless, dreadful mysteries, far beyond the phallic cult. How far, in their inverted culture, had these West Africans gone beyond phallic knowledge? Very, very far. Birkin recalled again the female figure: the elongated, long, long body, the curious unexpected heavy buttocks, the long, imprisoned neck, the face with tiny features like a beetle's. This was far beyond any phallic knowledge, sensual subtle realities far beyond the scope of phallic investigation.

There remained this way, this awful African process, to be fulfilled. It would be done differently by the white races. The white races, having the arctic north behind them, the vast abstraction of ice and snow, would fulfil a mystery of ice-destructive knowledge, snow-abstract annihilation. Whereas the West Africans, controlled by the burning death-abstraction of the Sahara, had been fulfilled in sun-destruction, the putrescent mystery of sun-rays.

Was this then all that remained? Was there left now nothing but to break off from the happy creative being, was the time up? Is our day of creative life finished? Does there remain to us only the strange, awful afterwards of the knowledge in dissolution, the African knowledge, but different in us, who are blond and blue-eyed from the north?

Birkin thought of Gerald. He was one of these strange white wonderful demons from the north, fulfilled in the destructive frost mystery. And was he fated to pass away in this knowledge, this one process of frost-knowledge, death by perfect cold? Was he a messenger, an omen of the universal dissolution into whiteness and snow?

Birkin was frightened. He was tired too, when he had reached this length of speculation. Suddenly his strange, strained attention gave way, he could not attend to these mysteries any more. There was another way, the way of freedom. There was the paradisal entry into pure, single being, the individual soul taking precedence over love and desire for union, stronger than any pangs of emotion, a lovely state of free proud singleness, which accepted the obligation of the permanent connection with others, and with the other, submits to the yoke and leash of love, but never forfeits its own proud individual singleness, even while it loves and yields.

There was the other way, the remaining way. And he must run to follow it. He thought of Ursula, how sensitive and delicate she really was, her skin so over-fine, as if one skin were wanting. She was really so marvellously gentle and sensitive. Why did he ever forget it? He must go to her at once. He must ask her to marry him. They must marry at once, and so make a definite pledge, enter into a definite communion. He must set out at once and ask her, this moment. There was no moment to spare.

He drifted on swiftly to Beldover, half-unconscious of his own movement. He saw the town on the slope of the hill, not straggling, but as if walled-in with the straight, final streets of miners' dwellings, making a great square, and it looked like Jerusalem to his fancy. The world was all strange and transcendent.

Rosalind opened the door to him. She started slightly, as a young girl will, and said, 'Oh, I'll tell father.'

With which she disappeared, leaving Birkin in the hall, looking at some reproductions from Picasso, lately introduced by Gudrun. He was admiring the almost wizard, sensuous apprehension of the earth, when Will Brangwen appeared, rolling down his shirt-sleeves.

'Well,' said Brangwen, 'I'll get a coat.' And he too disappeared for a moment. Then he returned, and opened the door of the drawing-room, saying, 'You must excuse me, I was just doing a bit of work in the shed. Come inside, will you.'

Birkin entered and sat down. He looked at the bright, reddish face of the other man, at the narrow brow and the very bright eyes, and at the rather sensual lips that unrolled wide and expansive under the black cropped moustache. How curious it was that this was a human being! What Brangwen thought himself to be, how meaningless it was, confronted with the reality of him. Birkin could see only a strange, inexplicable, almost patternless collection of passions and desires and suppressions and traditions and mechanical ideas, all cast unfused and disunited into this slender, bright-faced man of nearly fifty, who was as unresolved now as he was at twenty, and as uncreated. How could he be the parent of Ursula, when he was not created himself. He was not a parent. A slip of living flesh had been transmitted through him, but the spirit had not come from him. The spirit had not come from any ancestor, it had come out of the unknown. A child is the child of the mystery, or it is uncreated.

'The weather's not so bad as it has been,' said Brangwen, after waiting a moment. There was no connection between the two men.

'No,' said Birkin. 'It was full moon two days ago.'

'Oh! You believe in the moon then, affecting the weather?'

'No, I don't think I do. I don't really know enough about it.'

'You know what they say? The moon and the weather may change together, but the change of the moon won't change the weather.'

'Is that it?' said Birkin. 'I hadn't heard it.'

There was a pause. Then Birkin said, 'Am I hindering you? I called to see Ursula, really. Is she at home?'

'I don't believe she is. I believe she's gone to the library. I'll just see.'

Birkin could hear him enquiring in the dining-room.

'No,' he said, coming back. 'But she won't be long. You wanted to speak to her?'

Birkin looked across at the other man with curious calm, clear eyes.

'As a matter of fact,' he said, 'I wanted to ask her to marry me.'

A point of light came on the golden-brown eyes of the elder man.

'O–oh?' he said, looking at Birkin, then dropping his eyes before the calm, steadily watching look of the other: 'Was she expecting you then?'

'No,' said Birkin.

'No? I didn't know anything of this sort was on foot – ' Brangwen smiled awkwardly.

Birkin looked back at him, and said to himself: 'I wonder why it should be "on foot"!' Aloud he said, 'No, it's perhaps rather sudden.' At which, thinking of his relationship with Ursula, he added – 'but I don't know – '

'Quite sudden, is it? Oh!' said Brangwen, rather baffled and annoyed.

'In one way,' replied Birkin, ' – not in another.'

There was a moment's pause, after which Brangwen said, 'Well, she pleases herself – '

'Oh yes!' said Birkin, calmly.

A vibration came into Brangwen's strong voice, as he replied, 'Though I shouldn't want her to be in too big a hurry, either. It's no good looking round afterwards, when it's too late.'

'Oh, it need never be too late,' said Birkin, 'as far as that goes.'

'How do you mean?' asked the father.

'If one repents being married, the marriage is at an end,' said Birkin.

'You think so?'

'Yes.'

'Ay, well that may be your way of looking at it.'

Birkin, in silence, thought to himself. 'So it may. As for *your* way of looking at it, William Brangwen, it needs a little explaining.'

'I suppose,' said Brangwen, 'you know what sort of people we are? What sort of a bringing-up she's had?'

' "She",' thought Birkin to himself, remembering his childhood's corrections, 'is the cat's mother.'

'Do I know what sort of a bringing-up she's had?' he said aloud.

He seemed to annoy Brangwen intentionally.

'Well,' he said, 'she's had everything that's right for a girl to have – as far as possible, as far as we could give it her.'

'I'm sure she has,' said Birkin, which caused a perilous full-stop. The father was becoming exasperated. There was something naturally irritant to him in Birkin's mere presence.

'And I don't want to see her going back on it all,' he said, in a clanging voice.

'Why?' said Birkin.

This monosyllable exploded in Brangwen's brain like a shot.

'Why! *I* don't believe in your newfangled ways and newfangled ideas – in and out like a frog in a gallipot. It would never do for me.'

Birkin watched him with steady emotionless eyes. The radical antagonism in the two men was rousing.

'Yes, but are my ways and ideas newfangled?' asked Birkin.

'Are they?' Brangwen caught himself up. 'I'm not speaking of you in particular,' he said. 'What I mean is that my children have been brought up to think and do according to the religion I was brought up in myself, and I don't want to see them going away from *that*.'

There was a dangerous pause.

'And beyond that – ?' asked Birkin.

The father hesitated, he was in a nasty position.

'Eh? What do you mean? All I want to say is that my daughter' – he tailed off into silence, overcome by futility. He knew that in some way he was off the track.

'Of course,' said Birkin, 'I don't want to hurt anybody or influence anybody. Ursula does exactly as she pleases.'

There was a complete silence, because of the utter failure in mutual understanding. Birkin felt bored. Her father was not a coherent human being, he was a roomful of old echoes. The eyes of the younger man rested on the face of the elder. Brangwen looked up, and saw Birkin looking at him. His face was covered with inarticulate anger and humiliation and sense of inferiority in strength.

'And as for beliefs, that's one thing,' he said. 'But I'd rather see my daughters dead tomorrow than that they should be at the beck and call of the first man that likes to come and whistle for them.'

A queer painful light came into Birkin's eyes.

'As to that,' he said, 'I only know that it's much more likely that it's I who am at the beck and call of the woman, than she at mine.'

Again there was a pause. The father was somewhat bewildered.

'I know,' he said, 'she'll please herself – she always has done. I've done my best for them, but that doesn't matter. They've got themselves to please, and if they can help it they'll please nobody *but* themselves. But she's a right to consider her mother, and me as well – '

Brangwen was thinking his own thoughts.

'And I tell you this much, I would rather bury them, than see them getting into a lot of loose ways such as you see everywhere nowadays. I'd rather bury them – '

'Yes, but, you see,' said Birkin slowly, rather wearily, bored again by this new turn, 'they won't give either you or me the chance to bury them, because they're not to be buried.'

Brangwen looked at him in a sudden flare of impotent anger.

'Now, Mr Birkin,' he said, 'I don't know what you've come here for, and I don't know what you're asking for. But my daughters are my daughters – and it's my business to look after them while I can.'

Birkin's brows knitted suddenly, his eyes concentrated in mockery. But he remained perfectly stiff and still. There was a pause.

'I've nothing against your marrying Ursula,' Brangwen began at length. 'It's got nothing to do with me, she'll do as she likes, me or no me.'

Birkin turned away, looking out of the window and letting go his consciousness. After all, what good was this? It was hopeless to keep it up. He would sit on till Ursula came home, then speak to her, then go away. He would not accept trouble at the hands of her father. It was all unnecessary, and he himself need not have provoked it.

The two men sat in complete silence, Birkin almost unconscious of his own whereabouts. He had come to ask her to marry him – well then, he would wait on, and ask her. As for what she said, whether she accepted or not, he did not think about it. He would say what he had come to say, and that was all he was conscious of. He accepted the complete insignificance of this household, for him. But everything now was as if fated. He could see one thing ahead, and no more. From the rest, he was absolved entirely for the time being. It had to be left to fate and chance to resolve the issues.

At length they heard the gate. They saw her coming up the steps with a bundle of books under her arm. Her face was bright and abstracted as usual, with the abstraction, that look of being not quite *there*, not quite present to the facts of reality, that galled her father so much. She had a maddening faculty of assuming a light of her own, which excluded the reality, and within which she looked radiant as if in sunshine.

They heard her go into the dining-room, and drop her armful of books on the table.

'Did you bring me that Girl's Own?' cried Rosalind.

'Yes, I brought it. But I forgot which one it was you wanted.'

'You would,' cried Rosalind angrily. 'It's right for a wonder.'

Then they heard her say something in a lowered tone.

'Where?' cried Ursula.

Again her sister's voice was muffled.

Brangwen opened the door, and called, in his strong, brazen voice, 'Ursula.'

She appeared in a moment, wearing her hat.

'Oh how do you do!' she cried, seeing Birkin, and all dazzled as if taken by surprise. He wondered at her, knowing she was aware of his presence. She had her queer, radiant, breathless manner, as if confused by the actual world, unreal to it, having a complete bright world of her self alone.

'Have I interrupted a conversation?' she asked.

'No, only a complete silence,' said Birkin.

'Oh,' said Ursula, vaguely, absent. Their presence was not vital to her, she was withheld, she did not take them in. It was a subtle insult that never failed to exasperate her father.

'Mr Birkin came to speak to *you*, not to me,' said her father.

'Oh, did he!' she exclaimed vaguely, as if it did not concern her. Then, recollecting herself, she turned to him rather radiantly, but still quite superficially, and said: 'Was it anything special?'

'I hope so,' he said, ironically.

' – To propose to you, according to all accounts,' said her father.

'Oh,' said Ursula.

'Oh,' mocked her father, imitating her. 'Have you nothing more to say?'

She winced as if violated.

'Did you really come to propose to me?' she asked of Birkin, as if it were a joke.

'Yes,' he said. 'I suppose I came to propose.' He seemed to fight shy of the last word.

'Did you?' she cried, with her vague radiance. He might have been saying anything whatsoever. She seemed pleased.

'Yes,' he answered. 'I wanted to – I wanted you to agree to marry me.'

She looked at him. His eyes were flickering with mixed lights, wanting something of her, yet not wanting it. She shrank a little, as if she were exposed to his eyes, and as if it were a pain to her. She darkened, her soul clouded over, she turned aside. She had been driven out of her own radiant, single world. And she dreaded contact, it was almost unnatural to her at these times.

'Yes,' she said vaguely, in a doubting, absent voice.

Birkin's heart contracted swiftly, in a sudden fire of bitterness. It all meant nothing to her. He had been mistaken again. She was in some self-satisfied world of her own. He and his hopes were accidentals, violations to her. It drove her father to a pitch of mad exasperation. He had had to put up with this all his life, from her.

'Well, what do you say?' he cried.

She winced. Then she glanced down at her father, half-frightened, and she said, 'I didn't speak, did I?' as if she were afraid she might have committed herself.

'No,' said her father, exasperated. 'But you needn't look like an idiot. You've got your wits, haven't you?'

She ebbed away in silent hostility.

'I've got my wits, what does that mean?' she repeated, in a sullen voice of antagonism.

'You heard what was asked you, didn't you?' cried her father in anger.

'Of course I heard.'

'Well then, can't you answer?' thundered her father.

'Why should I?'

At the impertinence of this retort, he went stiff. But he said nothing.

'No,' said Birkin, to help out the occasion, 'there's no need to answer at once. You can say when you like.'

Her eyes flashed with a powerful light.

'Why should I say anything?' she cried. 'You do this off your *own* bat, it has nothing to do with me. Why do you both want to bully me?'

'Bully you! Bully you!' cried her father, in bitter, rancorous anger. 'Bully you! Why, it's a pity you can't be bullied into some sense and decency. Bully you! *You'll* see to that, you self-willed creature.'

She stood suspended in the middle of the room, her face glimmering and dangerous. She was set in satisfied defiance. Birkin looked up at her. He too was angry.

'But none is bullying you,' he said, in a very soft dangerous voice also.

'Oh yes,' she cried. 'You both want to force me into something.'

'That is an illusion of yours,' he said ironically.

'Illusion!' cried her father. 'A self-opinionated fool, that's what she is.'

Birkin rose, saying, 'However, we'll leave it for the time being.'

And without another word, he walked out of the house.

'You fool! You fool!' her father cried to her, with extreme bitterness. She left the room, and went upstairs, singing to herself. But she was terribly fluttered, as after some dreadful fight. From her window, she could see Birkin going up the road. He went in such a blithe drift of rage, that her mind wondered over him. He was ridiculous, but she was afraid of him. She was as if escaped from some danger.

Her father sat below, powerless in humiliation and chagrin. It was as if he were possessed with all the devils, after one of these unaccountable conflicts with Ursula. He hated her as if his only reality were in hating her to the last degree. He had all hell in his heart. But he went away, to escape himself. He knew he must despair, yield, give in to despair, and have done.

Ursula's face closed, she completed herself against them all. Recoiling upon herself, she became hard and self-completed, like a jewel. She was bright and invulnerable, quite free and happy, perfectly liberated in her self-possession. Her father had to learn not to see her blithe obliviousness, or it would have sent him mad. She was so radiant with all things, in her possession of perfect hostility.

She would go on now for days like this, in this bright frank state of seemingly pure spontaneity, so essentially oblivious of the existence of anything but herself, but so ready and facile in her interest. Ah, it was a bitter thing for a man to be near her, and her father cursed his fatherhood. But he must learn not to see her, not to know.

She was perfectly stable in resistance when she was in this state: so bright and radiant and attractive in her pure opposition, so very pure, and yet mistrusted by everybody, disliked on every hand. It was her voice, curiously clear and repellent, that gave her away. Only Gudrun was in accord with her. It was at these times that the intimacy between the two sisters was most complete, as if their intelligence were one. They felt a strong, bright bond of understanding between them, surpassing everything else. And during all these days of blind bright abstraction and intimacy of his two daughters, the father seemed to breathe an air of death, as if he were destroyed in his very being. He was irritable to madness, he could not rest, his daughters seemed to be destroying him. But he was inarticulate and helpless against them. He was forced to breathe the air of his own death. He cursed them in his soul, and only wanted that they should be removed from him.

They continued radiant in their easy female transcendancy, beautiful to look at. They exchanged confidences, they were intimate in their revelations to the last degree, giving each other at last every secret. They withheld nothing, they told everything, till they were over the border of evil. And they armed each other with knowledge, they extracted the subtlest flavours from the apple of knowledge. It was curious how their knowledge was complementary, that of each to that of the other.

Ursula saw her men as sons, pitied their yearning and admired their courage, and wondered over them as a mother wonders over her child, with a certain delight in their novelty. But to Gudrun, they were the opposite camp. She feared them and despised them, and respected their activities even overmuch.

'Of course,' she said easily, 'there is a quality of life in Birkin which is quite remarkable. There is an extraordinary rich spring of life in him, really amazing, the way he can give himself to things. But there are so many things in life that he simply doesn't know. Either he is not aware of their existence at all, or he dismisses them as merely negligible – things which are vital to the other person. In a way, he is not clever enough, he is too intense in spots.'

'Yes,' cried Ursula, 'too much of a preacher. He is really a priest.'

'Exactly! He can't hear what anybody else has to say – he simply cannot hear. His own voice is so loud.'

'Yes. He cries you down.'

'He cries you down,' repeated Gudrun. 'And by mere force of violence. And of course it is hopeless. Nobody is convinced by violence. It makes talking to him impossible – and living with him I should think would be more than impossible.'

'You don't think one could live with him?' asked Ursula.

'I think it would be too wearing, too exhausting. One would be shouted down every time, and rushed into his way without any choice. He would want to control you entirely. He cannot allow that there is any other mind than his own. And then the real clumsiness of his mind is its lack of self-criticism. No, I think it would be perfectly intolerable.'

'Yes,' assented Ursula vaguely. She only half agreed with Gudrun. 'The nuisance is,' she said, 'that one would find almost any man intolerable after a fortnight.'

'It's perfectly dreadful,' said Gudrun. 'But Birkin – he is too positive. He couldn't bear it if you called your soul your own. Of him that is strictly true.'

'Yes,' said Ursula. 'You must have *his* soul.'

'Exactly! And what can you conceive more deadly?' This was all so true, that Ursula felt jarred to the bottom of her soul with ugly distaste.

She went on, with the discord jarring and jolting through her, in the most barren of misery.

Then there started a revulsion from Gudrun. She finished life off so thoroughly, she made things so ugly and so final. As a matter of fact, even if it were as Gudrun said, about Birkin, other things were true as well. But Gudrun would draw two lines under him and cross him out like an account that is settled. There he was, summed up, paid for, settled, done with. And it was such a lie. This finality of Gudrun's, this dispatching of people and things in a sentence, it was all such a lie. Ursula began to revolt from her sister.

One day as they were walking along the lane, they saw a robin sitting on the top twig of a bush, singing shrilly. The sisters stood to look at him. An ironical smile flickered on Gudrun's face.

'Doesn't he feel important?' smiled Gudrun.

'Doesn't he!' exclaimed Ursula, with a little ironical grimace. 'Isn't he a little Lloyd George of the air!'

'Isn't he! Little Lloyd George of the air! That's just what they are,' cried Gudrun in delight. Then for days, Ursula saw the persistent, obtrusive birds as stout, short politicians lifting up their voices from the platform, little men who must make themselves heard at any cost.

But even from this there came the revulsion. Some yellowhammers suddenly shot along the road in front of her. And they looked to her so uncanny and inhuman, like flaring yellow barbs shooting through the air on some weird, living errand, that she said to herself: 'After all, it is impudence to call them little Lloyd Georges. They are really unknown to us, they are the unknown forces. It is impudence to look at them as if they were the same as human beings. They are of another world. How stupid anthropomorphism is! Gudrun is really impudent, insolent, making herself the measure of everything, making everything come down to human standards. Rupert is quite right, human beings are boring, painting the universe with their own image. The universe is non-human, thank God.' It seemed to her irreverence, destructive of all true life, to make little Lloyd Georges of the birds. It was such a lie towards the robins, and such a defamation. Yet she had done it herself. But under Gudrun's influence: so she exonerated herself.

So she withdrew away from Gudrun and from that which she stood for, she turned in spirit towards Birkin again. She had not seen him since the fiasco of his proposal. She did not want to, because she did not want the question of her acceptance thrust upon her. She knew what Birkin meant when he asked her to marry him; vaguely, without putting it into speech, she knew. She knew what kind of love, what kind of surrender he wanted. And she was not at all sure that this was the kind of love that she herself wanted. She was not at all sure that it was this mutual unison in separateness that she wanted. She wanted unspeakable intimacies. She wanted to have him, utterly, finally to have him as her own, oh, so unspeakably, in intimacy. To drink him down – ah, like a life-draught. She made great professions, to herself, of her willingness to warm his foot-soles between her breasts, after the fashion of the nauseous Meredith poem. But only on condition that he, her lover, loved her absolutely, with complete self-abandon. And subtly enough, she knew he would never abandon himself *finally* to her. He did not believe in final self-abandonment. He said it openly. It was his challenge. She was prepared to fight him for it. For she believed in an absolute surrender to love. She believed that love far surpassed the individual. He said the individual was *more* than love, or than any relationship. For him, the bright, single soul accepted love as one of its conditions, a condition of its own equilibrium. She believed that love was *everything*. Man must render himself up to her. He must be quaffed to the dregs by her. Let him be *her man* utterly, and she in return would be his humble slave – whether she wanted it or not.

CHAPTER 20

Gladiatorial

After the fiasco of the proposal, Birkin had hurried blindly away from Beldover, in a whirl of fury. He felt he had been a complete fool, that the whole scene had been a farce of the first water. But that did not trouble him at all. He was deeply, mockingly angry that Ursula persisted always in this old cry: 'Why do you want to bully me?' and in her bright, insolent abstraction.

He went straight to Shortlands. There he found Gerald standing with his back to the fire, in the library, as motionless as a man is who is completely and emptily restless, utterly hollow. He had done all the work he wanted to do – and now there was nothing. He could go out in the car, he could run to town. But he did not want to go out in the car, he did not want to run to town, he did not want to call on the Thirlbys. He was suspended motionless, in an agony of inertia, like a machine that is without power.

This was very bitter to Gerald, who had never known what boredom was, who had gone from activity to activity, never at a loss. Now, gradually, everything seemed to be stopping in him. He did not want any more to do the things that offered. Something dead within him just refused to respond to any suggestion. He cast over in his mind, what it would be possible to do, to save himself from this misery of nothingness, relieve the stress of this hollowness. And there were only three things left, that would rouse him, make him live. One was to drink or smoke hashish, the other was to be soothed by Birkin, and the third was women. And there was no one for the moment to drink with. Nor was there a woman. And he knew Birkin was out. So there was nothing to do but to bear the stress of his own emptiness.

When he saw Birkin his face lit up in a sudden, wonderful smile.

'By God, Rupert,' he said, 'I'd just come to the conclusion that nothing in the world mattered except somebody to take the edge off one's being alone: the right somebody.'

The smile in his eyes was very astonishing, as he looked at the other man. It was the pure gleam of relief. His face was pallid and even haggard.

'The right woman, I suppose you mean,' said Birkin spitefully.

'Of course, for choice. Failing that, an amusing man.'

He laughed as he said it. Birkin sat down near the fire.

'What were you doing?' he asked.

'I? Nothing. I'm in a bad way just now, everything's on edge, and I can neither work nor play. I don't know whether it's a sign of old age, I'm sure.'

'You mean you are bored?'

'Bored, I don't know. I can't apply myself. And I feel the devil is either very present inside me, or dead.'

Birkin glanced up and looked in his eyes.

'You should try hitting something,' he said.

Gerald smiled.

'Perhaps,' he said. 'So long as it was something worth hitting.'

'Quite!' said Birkin, in his soft voice. There was a long pause during which each could feel the presence of the other.

'One has to wait,' said Birkin.

'Ah God! Waiting! What are we waiting for?'

'Some old Johnny says there are three cures for *ennui*, sleep, drink, and travel,' said Birkin.

'All cold eggs,' said Gerald. 'In sleep, you dream, in drink you curse, and in travel you yell at a porter. No, work and love are the two. When you're not at work you should be in love.'

'Be it then,' said Birkin.

'Give me the object,' said Gerald. 'The possibilities of love exhaust themselves.'

'Do they? And then what?'

'Then you die,' said Gerald.

'So you ought,' said Birkin.

'I don't see it,' replied Gerald. He took his hands out of his trousers pockets, and reached for a cigarette. He was tense and nervous. He lit the cigarette over a lamp, reaching forward and drawing steadily. He was dressed for dinner, as usual in the evening, although he was alone.

'There's a third one even to your two,' said Birkin. 'Work, love, and fighting. You forget the fight.'

'I suppose I do,' said Gerald. 'Did you ever do any boxing – ?'

'No, I don't think I did,' said Birkin.

'Ay – ' Gerald lifted his head and blew the smoke slowly into the air.

'Why?' said Birkin.

'Nothing. I thought we might have a round. It is perhaps true, that I want something to hit. It's a suggestion.'

'So you think you might as well hit me?' said Birkin.

'You? Well ! Perhaps – ! In a friendly kind of way, of course.'

'Quite!' said Birkin, bitingly.

Gerald stood leaning back against the mantelpiece. He looked down at Birkin, and his eyes flashed with a sort of terror like the eyes of a stallion, that are bloodshot and overwrought, turned glancing backwards in a stiff terror.

'I feel that if I don't watch myself, I shall find myself doing something silly,' he said.

'Why not do it?' said Birkin coldly.

Gerald listened with quick impatience. He kept glancing down at Birkin, as if looking for something from the other man.

'I used to do some Japanese wrestling,' said Birkin. 'A Jap lived in the same house with me in Heidelberg, and he taught me a little. But I was never much good at it.'

'You did!' exclaimed Gerald. 'That's one of the things I've never ever seen done. You mean ju-jitsu, I suppose?'

'Yes. But I am no good at those things – they don't interest me.'

'They don't? They do me. What's the start?'

'I'll show you what I can, if you like,' said Birkin.

'You will?' A queer, smiling look tightened Gerald's face for a moment, as he said, 'Well, I'd like it very much.'

'Then we'll try ju-jitsu. Only you can't do much in a starched shirt.'

'Then let us strip, and do it properly. Hold a minute – ' He rang the bell, and waited for the butler.

'Bring a couple of sandwiches and a syphon,' he said to the man, 'and then don't trouble me any more tonight – or let anybody else.'

The man went. Gerald turned to Birkin with his eyes lighted.

'And you used to wrestle with a Jap?' he said. 'Did you strip?'

'Sometimes.'

'You did! What was he like then, as a wrestler?'

'Good, I believe. I am no judge. He was very quick and slippery and full of electric fire. It is a remarkable thing, what a curious sort of fluid force they seem to have in them, those people – not like a human grip – like a polyp – '

Gerald nodded.

'I should imagine so,' he said, 'to look at them. They repel me, rather.'

'Repel and attract, both. They are very repulsive when they are cold, and they look grey. But when they are hot and roused, there is a definite attraction – a curious kind of full electric fluid – like eels.'

'Well – yes – probably.'

The man brought in the tray and set it down.

'Don't come in any more,' said Gerald.

The door closed.

'Well then,' said Gerald; 'shall we strip and begin? Will you have a drink first?'

'No, I don't want one.'

'Neither do I.'

Gerald fastened the door and pushed the furniture aside. The room was large, there was plenty of space, it was thickly carpeted. Then he quickly threw off his clothes, and waited for Birkin. The latter, white and thin, came over to him. Birkin was more a presence than a visible object, Gerald was aware of him completely, but not really visually. Whereas Gerald himself was concrete and noticeable, a piece of pure final substance.

'Now,' said Birkin, 'I will show you what I learned, and what I remember. You let me take you so – ' And his hands closed on the naked body of the other man. In another moment, he had Gerald swung over lightly and balanced against his knee, head downwards. Relaxed, Gerald sprang to his foot with eyes glittering.

'That's smart,' he said. 'Now try again.'

So the two men began to struggle together. They were very dissimilar. Birkin was tall and narrow, his bones were very thin and fine. Gerald was much heavier and more plastic. His bones were strong and round, his limbs were rounded, all his contours were beautifully and fully moulded. He seemed to stand with a proper, rich weight on the face of the earth, whilst Birkin seemed to have the centre of gravitation in his own middle. And Gerald had a rich, frictional kind of strength, rather mechanical, but sudden and invincible, whereas Birkin was abstract as to be almost intangible. He impinged invisibly upon the other man, scarcely seeming to touch him, like a garment, and then suddenly piercing in a tense fine grip that seemed to penetrate into the very quick of Gerald's being.

They stopped, they discussed methods, they practised grips and throws, they became accustomed to each other, to each other's rhythm, they got a kind of mutual physical understanding. And then again they had a real struggle. They seemed to drive their white flesh deeper and deeper against each other, as if they would break into a oneness. Birkin had a great subtle energy, that would press upon the other man with an uncanny force, weigh him like a spell put upon him. Then it would pass, and Gerald would heave free, with white, heaving, dazzling movements.

So the two men entwined and wrestled with each other, working nearer and nearer. Both were white and clear, but Gerald flushed smart red where he was touched, and Birkin remained white and tense. He seemed to penetrate into Gerald's more solid, more diffuse bulk, to interfuse his body through the body of the other, as if to bring it subtly into subjection, always seizing with some rapid necromantic foreknowledge every motion of the other flesh, converting and counteracting it, playing upon the limbs and trunk of Gerald like some hard wind. It was as if Birkin's whole physical intelligence interpenetrated into Gerald's body, as if his fine, sublimated energy entered into the flesh of the fuller man, like some potency, casting a fine net, a prison, through the muscles into the very depths of Gerald's physical being.

So they wrestled swiftly, rapturously, intent and mindless at last, two essential white figures working into a tighter closer oneness of struggle, with a strange, octopus-like knotting and flashing of limbs in the subdued light of the room; a tense white knot of flesh gripped in silence between the walls of old brown books. Now and again came a sharp gasp of breath, or a sound like a sigh, then the rapid thudding of movement on the thickly-carpeted floor, then the strange sound of flesh escaping under flesh. Often, in the white interlaced knot of violent living being that swayed silently, there was no head to be seen, only the swift, tight limbs, the solid white backs, the physical junction of two bodies clinched into oneness. Then would appear the gleaming, ruffled head of Gerald, as the struggle changed, then for a moment the dun-coloured, shadow-like head of the other man would lift up from the conflict, the eyes wide and dreadful and sightless.

At length Gerald lay back inert on the carpet, his breast rising in great slow

544 SELECTED WORKS OF D. H. LAWRENCE

panting, whilst Birkin kneeled over him, almost unconscious. Birkin was much more exhausted. He caught little, short breaths, he could scarcely breathe any more. The earth seemed to tilt and sway, and a complete darkness was coming over his mind. He did not know what happened. He slid forward quite unconscious, over Gerald, and Gerald did not notice. Then he was half-conscious again, aware only of the strange tilting and sliding of the world. The world was sliding, everything was sliding off into the darkness. And he was sliding, endlessly, endlessly away.

He came to consciousness again, hearing an immense knocking outside. What could be happening, what was it, the great hammer-stroke resounding through the house? He did not know. And then it came to him that it was his own heart beating. But that seemed impossible, the noise was outside. No, it was inside himself, it was his own heart. And the beating was painful, so strained, surcharged. He wondered if Gerald heard it. He did not know whether he were standing or lying or falling.

When he realised that he had fallen prostrate upon Gerald's body he wondered, he was surprised. But he sat up, steadying himself with his hand and waiting for his heart to become stiller and less painful. It hurt very much, and took away his consciousness.

Gerald however was still less conscious than Birkin. They waited dimly, in a sort of not-being, for many uncounted, unknown minutes.

'Of course –' panted Gerald, 'I didn't have to be rough – with you – I had to keep back – my force –'

Birkin heard the sound as if his own spirit stood behind him, outside him, and listened to it. His body was in a trance of exhaustion, his spirit heard thinly. His body could not answer. Only he knew his heart was getting quieter. He was divided entirely between his spirit, which stood outside, and knew, and his body, that was a plunging, unconscious stroke of blood.

'I could have thrown you – using violence –' panted Gerald. 'But you beat me right enough.'

'Yes,' said Birkin, hardening his throat and producing the words in the tension there, 'you're much stronger than I – you could beat me – easily.'

Then he relaxed again to the terrible plunging of his heart and his blood.

'It surprised me,' panted Gerald, 'what strength you've got. Almost supernatural.'

'For a moment,' said Birkin.

He still heard as if it were his own disembodied spirit hearing, standing at some distance behind him. It drew nearer, however, his spirit. And the violent striking of blood in his chest was sinking quieter, allowing his mind to come back. He realised that he was leaning with all his weight on the soft body of the other man. It startled him, because he thought he had withdrawn. He recovered himself, and sat up. But he was still vague and unestablished. He put out his hand to steady himself. It touched the hand of Gerald, that was lying out on the floor. And Gerald's hand closed warm and sudden over Birkin's, they remained exhausted and breathless, the one hand clasped closely over the other. It was Birkin whose hand, in swift response, had closed in a strong, warm clasp over the hand of the other. Gerald's clasp had been sudden and momentaneous.

The normal consciousness, however, was returning, ebbing back. Birkin could breathe almost naturally again. Gerald's hand slowly withdrew, Birkin slowly, dazedly rose to his feet and went towards the table. He poured out a whisky and soda. Gerald also came for a drink.

'It was a real set-to, wasn't it?' said Birkin, looking at Gerald with darkened eyes.

'God, yes,' said Gerald. He looked at the delicate body of the other man, and added: 'It wasn't too much for you, was it?'

'No. One ought to wrestle and strive and be physically close. It makes one sane.'

'You do think so?'

'I do. Don't you?'

'Yes,' said Gerald.

There were long spaces of silence between their words. The wrestling had some deep meaning to them – an unfinished meaning.

'We are mentally, spiritually intimate, therefore we should be more or less physically intimate too – it is more whole.'

'Certainly it is,' said Gerald. Then he laughed pleasantly, adding: 'It's rather wonderful to me.' He stretched out his arms handsomely.

'Yes,' said Birkin. 'I don't know why one should have to justify oneself.'

'No.'

The two men began to dress.

'I think also that you are beautiful,' said Birkin to Gerald, 'and that is enjoyable too. One should enjoy what is given.'

'You think I am beautiful – how do you mean, physically?' asked Gerald, his eyes glistening.

'Yes. You have a northern kind of beauty, like light refracted from snow – and a beautiful, plastic form. Yes, that is there to enjoy as well. We should enjoy everything.'

Gerald laughed in his throat, and said, 'That's certainly one way of looking at it. I can say this much, I feel better. It has certainly helped me. Is this the *Brüderschaft* you wanted?'

'Perhaps. Do you think this pledges anything?'

'I don't know,' laughed Gerald.

'At any rate, one feels freer and more open now – and that is what we want.'

'Certainly,' said Gerald.

They drew to the fire, with the decanters and the glasses and the food.

'I always eat a little before I go to bed,' said Gerald. 'I sleep better.'

'I should not sleep so well,' said Birkin.

'No? There you are, we are not alike. I'll put a dressing-gown on.' Birkin remained alone, looking at the fire. His mind had reverted to Ursula. She seemed to return again into his consciousness. Gerald came down wearing a gown of broad-barred, thick black-and-green silk, brilliant and striking.

'You are very fine,' said Birkin, looking at the full robe.

'It was a caftan in Bokhara,' said Gerald. 'I like it.'

'I like it too.'

Birkin was silent, thinking how scrupulous Gerald was in his attire, how expensive too. He wore silk socks, and studs of fine workmanship, and silk underclothing, and silk braces. Curious! This was another of the differences between them. Birkin was careless and unimaginative about his own appearance.

'Of course you,' said Gerald, as if he had been thinking; 'there's something curious about you. You're curiously strong. One doesn't expect it, it is rather surprising.'

Birkin laughed. He was looking at the handsome figure of the other man, blond and comely in the rich robe, and he was half thinking of the difference between it and himself – so different; as far, perhaps, apart as man from woman, yet in another direction. But really it was Ursula, it was the woman who was gaining ascendance over Birkin's being, at this moment. Gerald was becoming dim again, lapsing out of him.

'Do you know,' he said suddenly, 'I went and proposed to Ursula Brangwen tonight, that she should marry me.'

He saw the blank shining wonder come over Gerald's face.

'You did?'

'Yes. Almost formally – speaking first to her father, as it should be, in the world – though that was accident – or mischief.'

Gerald only stared in wonder, as if he did not grasp.

'You don't mean to say that you seriously went and asked her father to let you marry her?'

'Yes,' said Birkin, 'I did.'

'What, had you spoken to her before about it, then?'

'No, not a word. I suddenly thought I would go there and ask her – and her father happened to come instead of her – so I asked him first.'

'If you could have her?' concluded Gerald.

'Ye–es, that.'

'And you didn't speak to her?'

'Yes. She came in afterwards. So it was put to her as well.'

'It was! And what did she say then? You're an engaged man?'

'No – she only said she didn't want to be bullied into answering.'

'She what?'

'Said she didn't want to be bullied into answering.'

'"Said she didn't want to be bullied into answering!" Why, what did she mean by that?'

Birkin raised his shoulders. 'Can't say,' he answered. 'Didn't want to be bothered just then, I suppose.'

'But is this really so? And what did you do then?'

'I walked out of the house and came here.'

'You came straight here?'

'Yes.'

Gerald stared in amazement and amusement. He could not take it in.

'But is this really true, as you say it now?'

'Word for word.'

'It is?'

He leaned back in his chair, filled with delight and amusement.

'Well, that's good,' he said. 'And so you came here to wrestle with your good angel, did you?'

'Did I?' said Birkin.

'Well, it looks like it. Isn't that what you did?'

Now Birkin could not follow Gerald's meaning.

'And what's going to happen?' said Gerald. 'You're going to keep open the proposition, so to speak?'

'I suppose so. I vowed to myself I would see them all to the devil. But I suppose I shall ask her again, in a little while.'

Gerald watched him steadily.

'So you're fond of her then?' he asked.

'I think – I love her,' said Birkin, his face going very still and fixed.

Gerald glistened for a moment with pleasure, as if it were something done specially to please him. Then his face assumed a fitting gravity, and he nodded his head slowly.

'You know,' he said, 'I always believed in love – true love. But where does one find it nowadays?'

'I don't know,' said Birkin.

'Very rarely,' said Gerald. Then, after a pause, 'I've never felt it myself – not what I should call love. I've gone after women – and been keen enough over some of them. But I've never felt *love*. I don't believe I've ever felt as much *love* for a woman, as I have for you – not *love*. You understand what I mean?'

'Yes. I'm sure you've never loved a woman.'

'You feel that, do you? And do you think I ever shall? You understand what I mean?' He put his hand to his breast, closing his fist there, as if he would draw something out. 'I mean that – that I can't express what it is, but I know it.'

'What is it, then?' asked Birkin.

'You see, I can't put it into words. I mean, at any rate, something abiding, something that can't change – '

His eyes were bright and puzzled.

'Now do you think I shall ever feel that for a woman?' he said, anxiously.

Birkin looked at him, and shook his head.

'I don't know,' he said. 'I could not say.'

Gerald had been on the *qui vive*, as awaiting his fate. Now he drew back in his chair.

'No,' he said, 'and neither do I, and neither do I.'

'We are different, you and I,' said Birkin. 'I can't tell your life.'

'No,' said Gerald, 'no more can I. But I tell you – I begin to doubt it!'

'That you will ever love a woman?'

'Well – yes – what you would truly call love – '

'You doubt it?'

'Well – I begin to.'

There was a long pause.

'Life has all kinds of things,' said Birkin. 'There isn't only one road.'

'Yes, I believe that too. I believe it. And mind you, I don't care how it is with me – I don't care how it is – so long as I don't feel – ' he paused, and a blank, barren look passed over his face, to express his feeling – ' so long as I feel I've *lived*, somehow – and I don't care how it is – but I want to feel that – '

'Fulfilled,' said Birkin.

'We–ell, perhaps it is fulfilled; I don't use the same words as you.'

'It is the same.'

CHAPTER 2 I

Threshold

Gudrun was away in London, having a little show of her work, with a friend, and looking round, preparing for flight from Beldover. Come what might she would be on the wing in a very short time. She received a letter from Winifred Crich, ornamented with drawings.

'Father also has been to London, to be examined by the doctors. It made him very tired. They say he must rest a very great deal, so he is mostly in bed. He brought me a lovely tropical parrot in faience, of Dresden ware, also a man ploughing, and two mice climbing up a stalk, also in faience. The mice were Copenhagen ware. They are the best, but mice don't shine so much, otherwise they are very good, their tails are slim and long. They all shine nearly like glass. Of course it is the glaze, but I don't like it. Gerald likes the man ploughing the best, his trousers are torn, he is ploughing with an ox, being I suppose a German peasant. It is all grey and white, white shirt and grey trousers, but very shiny and clean. Mr Birkin likes the girl best, under the hawthorn blossom, with a lamb, and with daffodils painted on her skirts, in the drawing-room. But that is silly, because the lamb is not a real lamb, and she is silly too.

'Dear Miss Brangwen, are you coming back soon, you are very much missed here. I enclose a drawing of father sitting up in bed. He says he hopes you are not going to forsake us. Oh dear Miss Brangwen, I am sure you won't. Do come back and draw the ferrets, they are the most lovely noble darlings in the world. We might carve them in holly-wood, playing against a background of green leaves. Oh do let us, for they are most beautiful.

'Father says we might have a studio. Gerald says we could easily have a beautiful one over the stables, it would only need windows to be put in the slant of the roof, which is a simple matter. Then you could stay here all day and work, and we could live in the studio, like two real artists, like the man in the picture in the hall, with the frying-pan and the walls all covered with drawings. I long to be free, to live the free life of an artist. Even Gerald told father that only an artist is free, because he lives in a creative world of his own – '

Gudrun caught the drift of the family intentions, in this letter. Gerald wanted her to be attached to the household at Shortlands, he was using Winifred as his stalking-horse. The father thought only of his child, he saw a rock of salvation in Gudrun. And Gudrun admired him for his perspicacity. The child, moreover, was really exceptional. Gudrun was quite content. She was quite willing, given a studio, to spend her days at Shortlands. She disliked the Grammar School already thoroughly, she wanted to be free. If a studio were provided, she would be free to go on with her work, she would await the turn of events with complete serenity. And she was really interested in Winifred, she would be quite glad to understand the girl.

So there was quite a little festivity on Winifred's account, the day Gudrun returned to Shortlands.

'You should make a bunch of flowers to give to Miss Brangwen when she arrives,' Gerald said, smiling to his sister.

'Oh no,' cried Winifred, 'it's silly.'

'Not at all. It is a very charming and ordinary attention.'

'Oh, it is silly,' protested Winifred, with all the extreme *mauvaise honte* of her years. Nevertheless, the idea appealed to her. She wanted very much to carry it out. She flitted round the greenhouses and the conservatory looking wistfully at the flowers on their stems. And the more she looked, the more she *longed* to have a bunch of the blossoms she saw, the more fascinated she became with her little vision of ceremony, and the more consumedly shy and self-conscious she grew, till she was almost beside herself. She could not get the idea out of her mind. It was as if some haunting challenge prompted her, and she had not enough courage to take it up. So again she drifted into the greenhouses, looking at the lovely roses in their pots, and at the virginal cyclamen, and at the mystic white clusters of a creeper. The beauty, oh the beauty of them, and oh the paradisal bliss, if she should have a perfect bouquet and could give it to Gudrun the next day. Her passion and her complete indecision almost made her ill.

At last she slid to her father's side.

'Daddie – ' she said.

'What, my precious?'

But she hung back, the tears almost coming to her eyes, in her sensitive confusion. Her father looked at her, and his heart ran hot with tenderness, an anguish of poignant love.

'What do you want to say to me, my love?'

'Daddie – !' her eyes smiled laconically – 'isn't it silly if I give Miss Brangwen some flowers when she comes?'

The sick man looked at the bright, knowing eyes of his child, and his heart burned with love.

'No, darling, that's not silly. It's what they do to queens.'

This was not very reassuring to Winifred. She half suspected that queens in themselves were a silliness. Yet she so wanted her little romantic occasion.

'Shall I then?' she asked.

'Give Miss Brangwen some flowers? Do, Birdie. Tell Wilson I say you are to have what you want.'

The child smiled a small, subtle, unconscious smile to herself, in anticipation of her way.

'But I won't get them till tomorrow,' she said.

'Not till tomorrow, Birdie. Give me a kiss then – '

Winifred silently kissed the sick man, and drifted out of the room. She again went the round of the greenhouses and the conservatory, informing the gardener, in her high, peremptory, simple fashion, of what she wanted, telling him all the blooms she had selected.

'What do you want these for?' Wilson asked.

'I want them,' she said. She wished servants did not ask questions.

'Ay, you've said as much. But what do you want them for, for decoration, or to send away, or what?'

'I want them for a presentation bouquet.'

'A presentation bouquet! Who's coming then? – the Duchess of Portland?'

'No.'

'Oh, not her? Well you'll have a rare poppy-show if you put all the things you've mentioned into your bouquet.'

'Yes, I want a rare poppy-show.'

'You do! Then there's no more to be said.'

The next day Winifred, in a dress of silvery velvet, and holding a gaudy bunch of flowers in her hand, waited with keen impatience in the schoolroom, looking down the drive for Gudrun's arrival. It was a wet morning. Under her nose was the strange fragrance of hothouse flowers, the bunch was like a little fire to her, she seemed to have a strange new fire in her heart. This slight sense of romance stirred her like an intoxicant.

At last she saw Gudrun coming, and she ran downstairs to warn her father and Gerald. They, laughing at her anxiety and gravity, came with her into the hall. The manservant came hastening to the door, and there he was, relieving Gudrun of her umbrella, and then of her raincoat. The welcoming party hung back till their visitor entered the hall.

Gudrun was flushed with the rain, her hair was blown in loose little curls, she was like a flower just opened in the rain, the heart of the blossom just newly visible, seeming to emit a warmth of retained sunshine. Gerald winced in spirit, seeing her so beautiful and unknown. She was wearing a soft blue dress, and her stockings were of dark red.

Winifred advanced with odd, stately formality.

'We are so glad you've come back,' she said. 'These are your flowers.' She presented the bouquet.

'Mine!' cried Gudrun. She was suspended for a moment, then a vivid flush went over her, she was as if blinded for a moment with a flame of pleasure. Then her eyes, strange and flaming, lifted and looked at the father, and at Gerald. And again Gerald shrank in spirit, as if it would be more than he could bear, as her hot, exposed eyes rested on him. There was something so revealed, she was revealed beyond bearing, to his eyes. He turned his face aside. And he felt he would not be able to avert her. And he writhed under the imprisonment.

Gudrun put her face into the flowers.

'But how beautiful they are!' she said, in a muffled voice. Then, with a strange, suddenly revealed passion, she stooped and kissed Winifred.

Mr Crich went forward with his hand held out to her.

'I was afraid you were going to run away from us,' he said, playfully.

Gudrun looked up at him with a luminous, roguish, unknown face.

'Really!' she replied. 'No, I didn't want to stay in London.' Her voice seemed to imply that she was glad to get back to Shortlands, her tone was warm and subtly caressing.

'That is a good thing,' smiled the father. 'You see you are very welcome here among us.'

Gudrun only looked into his face with dark-blue, warm, shy eyes. She was unconsciously carried away by her own power.

'And you look as if you came home in every possible triumph,' Mr Crich continued, holding her hand.

'No,' she said, glowing strangely. 'I haven't had any triumph till I came here.'

'Ah, come, come! We're not going to hear any of those tales. Haven't we read notices in the newspaper, Gerald?'

'You came off pretty well,' said Gerald to her, shaking hands. 'Did you sell anything?'

'No,' she said, 'not much.'

'Just as well,' he said.

She wondered what he meant. But she was all aglow with her reception, carried away by this little flattering ceremonial on her behalf.

'Winifred,' said the father, 'have you a pair of shoes for Miss Brangwen? You had better change at once –'

Gudrun went out with her bouquet in her hand.

'Quite a remarkable young woman,' said the father to Gerald, when she had gone.

'Yes,' replied Gerald briefly, as if he did not like the observation.

Mr Crich liked Gudrun to sit with him for half an hour. Usually he was ashy and wretched, with all the life gnawed out of him. But as soon as he rallied, he liked to make believe that he was just as before, quite well and in the midst of life – not of the outer world, but in the midst of a strong essential life. And to this belief, Gudrun contributed perfectly. With her, he could get by stimulation those precious half-hours of strength and exaltation and pure freedom, when he seemed to live more than he had ever lived.

She came to him as he lay propped up in the library. His face was like yellow wax, his eyes darkened, as it were sightless. His black beard, now streaked with grey, seemed to spring out of the waxy flesh of a corpse. Yet the atmosphere about him was energetic and playful. Gudrun subscribed to this, perfectly. To her fancy, he was just an ordinary man. Only his rather terrible appearance was photographed upon her soul, away beneath her consciousness. She knew that, in spite of his playfulness, his eyes could not change from their darkened vacancy, they were the eyes of a man who is dead.

'Ah, this is Miss Brangwen,' he said, suddenly rousing as she entered, announced by the manservant. 'Thomas, put Miss Brangwen a chair here – that's right.' He looked at her soft, fresh face with pleasure. It gave him the illusion of life. 'Now, you will have a glass of sherry and a little piece of cake. Thomas – '

'No, thank you,' said Gudrun. And as soon as she had said it, her heart sank horribly. The sick man seemed to fall into a gap of death, at her contradiction. She ought to play up to him, not to contravene him. In an instant she was smiling her rather roguish smile.

'I don't like sherry very much,' she said. 'But I like almost anything else.'

The sick man caught at this straw instantly.

'Not sherry! No! Something else! What then? What is there, Thomas?'

'Port wine – curaçao – '

'I would love some curaçao – ' said Gudrun, looking at the sick man confidingly.

'You would. Well then, Thomas, curaçao – and a little cake, or a biscuit?'

'A biscuit,' said Gudrun. She did not want anything, but she was wise.

'Yes.'

He waited till she was settled with her little glass and her biscuit. Then he was satisfied.

'You have heard the plan,' he said with some excitement, 'for a studio for Winifred, over the stables?'

'No!' exclaimed Gudrun, in mock wonder.

'Oh! – I thought Winnie wrote it to you, in her letter!'

'Oh – yes – of course. But I thought perhaps it was only her own little idea – ' Gudrun smiled subtly, indulgently. The sick man smiled also, elated.

'Oh no. It is a real project. There is a good room under the roof of the stables – with sloping rafters. We had thought of converting it into a studio.'

'How *very* nice that would be!' cried Gudrun, with excited warmth. The thought of the rafters stirred her.

'You think it would? Well, it can be done.'

'But how perfectly splendid for Winifred! Of course, it is just what is needed, if she is to work at all seriously. One must have one's workshop, otherwise one never ceases to be an amateur.'

'Is that so? Yes. Of course, I should like you to share it with Winifred.'

'Thank you *so* much.'

Gudrun knew all these things already, but she must look shy and very grateful, as if overcome.

'Of course, what I should like best would be if you could give up your work at the Grammar School, and just avail yourself of the studio, and work there – well, as much or as little as you liked – '

He looked at Gudrun with dark, vacant eyes. She looked back at him as if full of gratitude. These phrases of a dying man were so complete and natural, coming like echoes through his dead mouth.

'And as to your earnings – you don't mind taking from me what you have taken from the Education Committee, do you? I don't want you to be a loser.'

'Oh,' said Gudrun, 'if I can have the studio and work there, I can earn money enough, really I can.'

'Well,' he said, pleased to be the benefactor, 'we can see about all that. You wouldn't mind spending your days here?'

'If there were a studio to work in,' said Gudrun, 'I could ask for nothing better.'

'Is that so?'

He was really very pleased. But already he was getting tired. She could see the grey, awful semi-consciousness of mere pain and dissolution coming over him again, the torture coming into the vacancy of his darkened eyes. It was not over yet, this process of death. She rose softly saying, 'Perhaps you will sleep. I must look for Winifred.'

She went out, telling the nurse that she had left him. Day by day the tissue of the sick man was further and further reduced, nearer and nearer the process came, towards the last knot which held the human being in its unity. But this knot was hard and unrelaxed, the will of the dying man never gave way. He might be dead in nine-tenths, yet the remaining tenth remained unchanged, till it too was torn apart. With his will he held the unit of himself firm, but the circle of his power was ever and ever reduced, it would be reduced to a point at last, then swept away.

To adhere to life, he must adhere to human relationships, and he caught at every straw. Winifred, the butler, the nurse, Gudrun, these were the people who meant all to him, in these last resources. Gerald, in his father's presence, stiffened with repulsion. It was so, to a less degree, with all the other children except Winifred. They could not see anything but the death, when they looked at their father. It was as if some subterranean dislike overcame them. They could not see the familiar face, hear the familiar voice. They were overwhelmed by the antipathy of visible and audible death. Gerald could not breathe in his father's presence. He must get out at once. And so, in the same way, the father could not bear the presence of his son. It sent a final irritation through the soul of the dying man.

The studio was made ready, Gudrun and Winifred moved in. They enjoyed so much the ordering and the appointing of it. And now they need hardly be in the house at all. They had their meals in the studio, they lived there safely. For the house was becoming dreadful. There were two nurses in white, flitting silently about, like heralds of death. The father was confined to his bed, there was a come and go of *sotto-voce* sisters and brothers and children.

Winifred was her father's constant visitor. Every morning, after breakfast, she went into his room when he was washed and propped up in bed, to spend half an hour with him.

'Are you better, Daddie?' she asked him invariably.

And invariably he answered, 'Yes, I think I'm a little better, pet.'

She held his hand in both her own, lovingly and protectively. And this was very dear to him.

She ran in again as a rule at lunchtime, to tell him the course of events, and every evening, when the curtains were drawn, and his room was cosy, she spent a long time with him. Gudrun was gone home, Winifred was alone in the house: she liked best to be with her father. They talked and prattled at random, he always as if he were well, just the same as when he was going about. So that Winifred, with a child's subtle instinct for avoiding the painful things, behaved as if nothing serious was the matter. Instinctively, she withheld her attention, and was happy. Yet in her remoter soul, she knew as well as the adults knew: perhaps better.

Her father was quite well in his make-believe with her. But when she went away, he relapsed under the misery of his dissolution. But still there were these bright moments, though as his strength waned, his faculty for attention grew weaker, and the nurse had to send Winifred away, to save him from exhaustion.

He never admitted that he was going to die. He knew it was so, he knew it was the end. Yet even to himself he did not admit it. He hated the fact, mortally. His will was rigid. He could not bear being overcome by death. For him, there was no death. And yet, at times, he felt a great need to cry out and to wail and complain. He would have liked to cry aloud to Gerald, so that his son should be horrified out of his composure. Gerald was instinctively aware of this, and he recoiled, to avoid any such thing. This uncleanness of death repelled him too much. One should die quickly, like the Romans, one should be master of one's fate in dying as in living. He was convulsed in the clasp of this death of his father's, as in the coils of the great serpent of Laocoön. The great serpent had got the father, and the son was dragged into the embrace of horrifying death along with him. He resisted always. And in some strange way, he was a tower of strength to his father.

The last time the dying man asked to see Gudrun he was grey with near death. Yet he must see someone, he must, in the intervals of consciousness, catch into connection with the living world, lest he should have to accept his own situation. Fortunately he was most of his time dazed and half gone. And he spent many hours dimly thinking of the past, as it were, dimly reliving his old experiences. But there were times even to the end when he was capable of realising what was happening to him in the present, the death that was on him.

And these were the times when he called in outside help, no matter whose. For to realise this death that he was dying was a death beyond death, never to be borne. It was an admission never to be made.

Gudrun was shocked by his appearance, and by the darkened, almost dis-integrated eyes, that still were unconquered and firm.

'Well,' he said in his weakened voice, 'and how are you and Winifred getting on?'

'Oh, very well indeed,' replied Gudrun.

There were slight dead gaps in the conversation, as if the ideas called up were only elusive straws floating on the dark chaos of the sick man's dying.

'The studio answers all right?' he said.

'Splendid. It couldn't be more beautiful and perfect,' said Gudrun.

She waited for what he would say next.

'And you think Winifred has the makings of a sculptor?'

It was strange how hollow the words were, meaningless.

'I'm sure she has. She will do good things one day.'

'Ah! Then her life won't be altogether wasted, you think?'

Gudrun was rather surprised.

'Sure it won't!' she exclaimed softly.

'That's right.'

Again Gudrun waited for what he would say.

'You find life pleasant, it is good to live, isn't it?' he asked, with a pitiful faint smile that was almost too much for Gudrun.

'Yes,' she smiled – she would lie at random – 'I get a pretty good time, I believe.'

'That's right. A happy nature is a great asset.'

Again Gudrun smiled, though her soul was dry with repulsion. Did one have to die like this – having the life extracted forcibly from one, whilst one smiled and made conversation to the end? Was there no other way? Must one go through all the horror of this victory over death, the triumph of the integral will, that would not be broken till it disappeared utterly? One must, it was the only way. She admired the self-possession and the control of the dying man exceedingly. But she loathed the death itself. She was glad the everyday world held good, and she need not recognise anything beyond.

'You are quite all right here? – nothing we can do for you? – nothing you find wrong in your position?'

'Except that you are too good to me,' said Gudrun.

'Ah, well, the fault of that lies with yourself,' he said, and he felt a little exultation, that he had made this speech.

He was still so strong and living! But the nausea of death began to creep back on him, in reaction.

Gudrun went away, back to Winifred. Mademoiselle had left, Gudrun stayed a good deal at Shortlands, and a tutor came in to carry on Winifred's education. But he did not live in the house, he was connected with the Grammar School.

One day, Gudrun was to drive with Winifred and Gerald and Birkin to town, in the car. It was a dark, showery day. Winifred and Gudrun were ready and waiting at the door. Winifred was very quiet, but Gudrun had not noticed. Suddenly the child asked, in a voice of unconcern, 'Do you think my father's going to die, Miss Brangwen?'

Gudrun started.

'I don't know,' she replied.

'Don't you truly?'

'Nobody knows for certain. He *may* die, of course.'

The child pondered a few moments, then she asked, 'But do you *think* he will die?'

It was put almost like a question in geography or science, insistent, as if she would force an admission from the adult. The watchful, slightly triumphant child was almost diabolical.

'Do I think he will die?' repeated Gudrun. 'Yes, I do.'

But Winifred's large eyes were fixed on her, and the girl did not move.

'He is very ill,' said Gudrun.

A small smile came over Winifred's face, subtle and sceptical.

'*I* don't believe he will,' the child asserted, mockingly, and she moved away into the drive. Gudrun watched the isolated figure, and her heart stood still. Winifred was playing with a little rivulet of water, absorbedly as if nothing had been said.

'I've made a proper dam,' she said, out of the moist distance.

Gerald came to the door from out of the hall behind.

'It is just as well she doesn't choose to believe it,' he said.

Gudrun looked at him. Their eyes met; and they exchanged a sardonic understanding.

'Just as well,' said Gudrun.

He looked at her again, and a fire flickered up in his eyes.

'Best to dance while Rome burns, since it must burn, don't you think?' he said.

She was rather taken aback. But, gathering herself together, she replied, 'Oh – better dance than wail, certainly.'

'So I think.'

And they both felt the subterranean desire to let go, to fling away everything, and lapse into a sheer unrestraint, brutal and licentious. A strange black passion surged up pure in Gudrun. She felt strong. She felt her hands so strong, as if she could tear the world asunder with them. She remembered the abandonments of Roman licence, and her heart grew hot. She knew she wanted this herself also – or something, something equivalent. Ah, if that which was unknown and suppressed in her were once let loose, what an orgiastic and satisfying event it would be. And she wanted it, she trembled slightly from the proximity of the man, who stood just behind her, suggestive of the same black licentiousness that rose in herself. She wanted it with him, this unacknowledged frenzy. For a moment the clear perception of this preoccupied her, distinct and perfect in its final reality. Then she shut it off completely, saying, 'We might as well go down to the lodge after Winifred – we can get in the car there.'

'So we can,' he answered, going with her.

They found Winifred at the lodge admiring the litter of pure-bred white puppies. The girl looked up, and there was a rather ugly, unseeing cast in her eyes as she turned to Gerald and Gudrun. She did not want to see them.

'Look!' she cried. 'Three new puppies! Marshall says this one seems perfect. Isn't it a sweetling? But it isn't so nice as its mother.' She turned to caress the fine white bull-terrier bitch that stood uneasily near her.

'My dearest Lady Crich,' she said, 'you are beautiful as an angel on earth. Angel – angel – don't you think she's good enough and beautiful enough to go to heaven, Gudrun? They will be in heaven, won't they – and *especially* my darling Lady Crich! Mrs Marshall, I say!'

'Yes, Miss Winifred?' said the woman, appearing at the door.

'Oh do call this one Lady Winifred, if she turns out perfect, will you? Do tell Marshall to call it Lady Winifred.'

'I'll tell him – but I'm afraid that's a gentleman puppy, Miss Winifred.'

'Oh *no!*' There was the sound of a car. 'There's Rupert!' cried the child, and she ran to the gate.

Birkin, driving his car, pulled up outside the lodge gate.

'We're ready!' cried Winifred. 'I want to sit in front with you, Rupert. May I?'

'I'm afraid you'll fidget about and fall out,' he said.

'No I won't. I do want to sit in front next to you. It makes my feet so lovely and warm, from the engines.'

Birkin helped her up, amused at sending Gerald to sit by Gudrun in the body of the car.

'Have you any news, Rupert?' Gerald called, as they rushed along the lanes.

'News?' exclaimed Birkin.

'Yes.' Gerald looked at Gudrun, who sat by his side, and he said, his eyes narrowly laughing, 'I want to know whether I ought to congratulate him, but I can't get anything definite out of him.'

Gudrun flushed deeply.

'Congratulate him on what?' she asked.

'There was some mention of an engagement – at least, he said something to me about it.'

Gudrun flushed darkly.

'You mean with Ursula?' she said, in challenge.

'Yes. That is so, isn't it?'

'I don't think there's any engagement,' said Gudrun, coldly.

'That so? Still no developments, Rupert?' he called.

'Where? Matrimonial? No.'

'How's that?' called Gudrun.

Birkin glanced quickly round. There was irritation in his eyes also.

'Why?' he replied. 'What do you think of it, Gudrun?'

'Oh,' she cried, determined to fling her stone also into the pool, since they had begun, 'I don't think she wants an engagement. Naturally, she's a bird that prefers the bush.' Gudrun's voice was clear and gong-like. It reminded Rupert of her father's, so strong and vibrant.

'And I,' said Birkin, his face playful but yet determined, 'I want a binding contract, and am not keen on love, particularly free love.'

They were both amused. *Why* this public avowal? Gerald seemed suspended a moment, in amusement.

'Love isn't good enough for you?' he called.

'No!' shouted Birkin.

'Ha, well that's being over-refined,' said Gerald, and the car ran through the mud.

'What's the matter, really?' said Gerald, turning to Gudrun.

This was an assumption of a sort of intimacy that irritated Gudrun almost like an affront. It seemed to her that Gerald was deliberately insulting her, and infringing on the decent privacy of them all.

'What is it?' she said, in her high, repellent voice. 'Don't ask me! – I know nothing about *ultimate* marriage, I assure you: or even penultimate.'

'Only the ordinary unwarrantable brand!' replied Gerald. 'Just so – same here. I am no expert on marriage, and degrees of ultimateness. It seems to be a bee that buzzes loudly in Rupert's bonnet.'

'Exactly! But that is his trouble, exactly! Instead of wanting a woman for herself, he wants his *ideas* fulfilled. Which, when it comes to actual practice, is not good enough.'

'Oh no. Best go slap for what's womanly in woman, like a bull at a gate.' Then he seemed to glimmer in himself. 'You think love is the ticket, do you?' he asked.

'Certainly, while it lasts – you only can't insist on permanency,' came Gudrun's voice, strident above the noise.

'Marriage or no marriage, ultimate or penultimate or just so-so? – take the love as you find it.'

'As you please, or as you don't please,' she echoed. 'Marriage is a social arrangement, I take it, and has nothing to do with the question of love.'

His eyes were flickering on her all the time. She felt as if he were kissing her freely and malevolently. It made the colour burn in her cheeks, but her heart was quite firm and unfailing.

'You think Rupert is off his head a bit?' Gerald asked.

Her eyes flashed with acknowledgement.

'As regards a woman, yes,' she said, 'I do. There *is* such a thing as two people being in love for the whole of their lives – perhaps. But marriage is neither here nor there, even then. If they are in love, well and good. If not – why break eggs about it!'

'Yes,' said Gerald. 'That's how it strikes me. But what about Rupert?'

'I can't make out – neither can he nor anybody. He seems to think that if you marry you can get through marriage into a third heaven, or something – all very vague.'

'Very! And who wants a third heaven? As a matter of fact, Rupert has a great yearning to be *safe* – to tie himself to the mast.'

'Yes. It seems to me he's mistaken there too,' said Gudrun. 'I'm sure a mistress is more likely to be faithful than a wife – just because she is her *own* mistress. No – he says he believes that a man and wife can go further than any other two beings – but *where*, is not explained. They can know each other, heavenly and hellish, but particularly hellish, so perfectly that they go beyond heaven and hell – into – there it all breaks down – into nowhere.'

'Into Paradise, he says,' laughed Gerald.

Gudrun shrugged her shoulders. '*Je m'en fiche* of your Paradise!' she said.

'Not being a Mohammedan,' said Gerald. Birkin sat motionless, driving the car, quite unconscious of what they said. And Gudrun, sitting immediately behind him, felt a sort of ironic pleasure in thus exposing him.

'He says,' she added, with a grimace of irony, 'that you can find an eternal equilibrium in marriage, if you accept the unison, and still leave yourself separate, don't try to fuse.'

'Doesn't inspire me,' said Gerald.

'That's just it,' said Gudrun.

'I believe in love, in a real *abandon*, if you're capable of it,' said Gerald.

'So do I,' said she.

'And so does Rupert, too – though he is always shouting.'

'No,' said Gudrun. 'He won't abandon himself to the other person. You can't be sure of him. That's the trouble I think.'

'Yet he wants marriage! Marriage – *et puis*?'

'*Le paradis!*' mocked Gudrun.

Birkin, as he drove, felt a creeping of the spine, as if somebody was threatening his neck. But he shrugged with indifference. It began to rain. Here was a change. He stopped the car and got down to put up the hood.

CHAPTER 22

Woman to Woman

They came to the town, and left Gerald at the railway station. Gudrun and Winifred were to come to tea with Birkin, who expected Ursula also. In the afternoon, however, the first person to turn up was Hermione. Birkin was out, so she went in the drawing-room, looking at his books and papers, and playing on the piano. Then Ursula arrived. She was surprised, unpleasantly so, to see Hermione, of whom she had heard nothing for some time.

'It is a surprise to see you,' she said.

'Yes,' said Hermione – 'I've been away at Aix – '

'Oh, for your health?'

'Yes.'

The two women looked at each other. Ursula resented Hermione's long, grave, downward-looking face. There was something of the stupidity and the unenlightened self-esteem of a horse in it. 'She's got a horse-face,' Ursula said to herself, 'she runs between blinkers.' It did seem as if Hermione, like the moon, had only one side to her penny. There was no obverse. She stared out all the time on the narrow, but to her, complete world of the extant consciousness. In the darkness, she did not exist. Like the moon, one half of her was lost to life. Her self was all in her head, she did not know what it was spontaneously to run or move, like a fish in the water, or a weasel on the grass. She must always *know*.

But Ursula only suffered from Hermione's one-sidedness. She only felt Hermione's cool evidence, which seemed to put her down as nothing. Hermione, who brooded and brooded till she was exhausted with the ache of her effort at consciousness, spent and ashen in her body, who gained so slowly and with such effort her final and barren conclusions of knowledge, was apt, in the presence of other women, whom she thought simply female, to wear the conclusions of her bitter assurance like jewels which conferred on her an unquestionable distinction, established her in a higher order of life. She was apt, mentally, to condescend to women such as Ursula, whom she regarded as purely emotional. Poor Hermione, it was her one possession, this aching certainty of hers, it was her only justification. She must be confident here, for God knows, she felt rejected and deficient enough elsewhere. In the life of thought, of the spirit, she was one of the elect. And she wanted to be universal. But there was a devastating cynicism at the bottom of her. She did not believe in her own universals – they were sham. She did not believe in the inner life – it was a trick, not a reality. She did not believe in the spiritual world – it was an affectation. In the last resort, she believed in Mammon, the flesh, and the devil – these at least were not sham. She was a priestess without belief, without conviction, suckled in a creed outworn, and condemned to the reiteration of mysteries that were not divine to her. Yet there was no escape. She was a leaf upon a dying tree. What help was there then, but to fight still for the old, withered truths, to die for the old, outworn belief, to be a sacred and inviolate priestess of desecrated mysteries? The old great truths *had* been true. And she was a leaf of the old great tree of knowledge that was withering now. To the old and last truth then she must be faithful even though cynicism and mockery took place at the bottom of her soul.

'I am so glad to see you,' she said to Ursula, in her slow voice, that was like an incantation. 'You and Rupert have become quite friends?'

'Oh yes,' said Ursula. 'He is always somewhere in the background.'

Hermione paused before she answered. She saw perfectly well the other woman's vaunt: it seemed truly vulgar.

'Is he?' she said slowly, and with perfect equanimity. 'And do you think you will marry?'

The question was so calm and mild, so simple and bare and dispassionate that Ursula was somewhat taken aback, rather attracted. It pleased her almost like a wickedness. There was some delightful naked irony in Hermione.

'Well,' replied Ursula, '*He* wants to, awfully, but I'm not so sure.'

Hermione watched her with slow calm eyes. She noted this new expression of vaunting. How she envied Ursula a certain unconscious positivity! even her vulgarity!

'Why aren't you sure?' she asked, in her easy singsong. She was perfectly at her ease, perhaps even rather happy in this conversation. 'You don't really love him?'

Ursula flushed a little at the mild impertinence of this question. And yet she could not definitely take offence. Hermione seemed so calmly and sanely candid. After all, it was rather great to be able to be so sane.

'He says it isn't love he wants,' she replied.

'What is it then?' Hermione was slow and level.

'He wants me really to accept him in marriage.'

Hermione was silent for some time, watching Ursula with slow, pensive eyes.

'Does he?' she said at length, without expression. Then, rousing, 'And what is it you don't want? You don't want marriage?'

'No—I don't—not really. I don't want to give the sort of *submission* he insists on. He wants me to give myself up—and I simply don't feel that I *can* do it.'

Again there was a long pause, before Hermione replied, 'Not if you don't want to.' Then again there was silence. Hermione shuddered with a strange desire. Ah, if only he had asked *her* to subserve him, to be his slave! She shuddered with desire.

'You see I can't—'

'But exactly in what does—'

They had both begun at once, they both stopped. Then, Hermione, assuming priority of speech, resumed as if wearily, 'To what does he want you to submit?'

'He says he wants me to accept him non-emotionally, and finally—I really don't know what he means. He says he wants the demon part of himself to be mated—physically—not the human being. You see he says one thing one day, and another the next—and he always contradicts himself—'

'And always thinks about himself, and his own dissatisfaction,' said Hermione slowly.

'Yes,' cried Ursula. 'As if there were no one but himself concerned. That makes it so impossible.'

But immediately she began to retract.

'He insists on my accepting God knows what in *him*,' she resumed. 'He wants me to accept *him* as—as an absolute—But it seems to me he doesn't want to *give* anything. He doesn't want real warm intimacy—he won't have it—he rejects it. He won't let me think, really, and he won't let me *feel*—he hates feelings.'

There was a long pause, bitter for Hermione. Ah, if only he would have made this demand of her! Her he *drove* into thought, drove inexorably into knowledge – and then execrated her for it.

'He wants me to sink myself,' Ursula resumed, 'not to have any being of my own – '

'Then why doesn't he marry an odalisque?' said Hermione in her mild singsong, 'if it is that he wants.' Her long face looked sardonic and amused.

'Yes,' said Ursula vaguely. After all, the tiresome thing was, he did not want an odalisque, he did not want a slave. Hermione would have been his slave – there was in her a horrible desire to prostrate herself before a man – a man who worshipped her, however, and admitted her as the supreme thing. He did not want an odalisque. He wanted a woman to *take* something from him, to give herself up so much that she could take the last realities of him, the last facts, the last physical facts, physical and unbearable.

And if she did, would he acknowledge her? Would he be able to acknowledge her through everything, or would he use her just as his instrument, use her for his own private satisfaction, not admitting her? That was what the other men had done. They had wanted their own show, and they would not admit her, they turned all she was into nothingness. Just as Hermione now betrayed herself as a woman. Hermione was like a man, she believed only in men's things. She betrayed the woman in herself. And Birkin, would he acknowledge, or would he deny her?

'Yes,' said Hermione, as each woman came out of her own separate reverie. 'It would be a mistake – I think it would be a mistake – '

'To marry him?' asked Ursula.

'Yes,' said Hermione slowly – 'I think you need a man – soldierly, strong-willed – ' Hermione held out her hand and clenched it with rhapsodic intensity. 'You should have a man like the old heroes – you need to stand behind him as he goes into battle, you need to *see* his strength, and to *hear* his shout – . You need a man physically strong, and virile in his will, *not* a sensitive man – ' There was a break, as if the pythoness had uttered the oracle, and now the woman went on, in a rhapsody-wearied voice: 'And you see, Rupert isn't this, he isn't. He is frail in health and body, he needs great, great care. Then he is so changeable and unsure of himself – it requires the greatest patience and understanding to help him. And I don't think you are patient. You would have to be prepared to suffer – dreadfully. I can't *tell* you how much suffering it would take to make him happy. He lives an *intensely* spiritual life, at times – too, too wonderful. And then come the reactions. I can't speak of what I have been through with him. We have been together so long, I really do know him, I *do* know what he is. And I feel I must say it; I feel it would be perfectly *disastrous* for you to marry him – for you even more than for him.' Hermione lapsed into bitter reverie. 'He is so uncertain, so unstable – he wearies, and then reacts. I couldn't *tell* you what his reactions are. I couldn't *tell* you the agony of them. That which he affirms and loves one day – a little later he turns on it in a fury of destruction. He is never constant, always this awful, dreadful reaction. Always the quick change from good to bad, bad to good. And nothing is so devastating, nothing – '

'Yes,' said Ursula humbly, 'you must have suffered.'

An unearthly light came on Hermione's face. She clenched her hand like one inspired.

'And one must be willing to suffer – willing to suffer for him hourly, daily – if you are going to help him, if he is to keep true to anything at all – '

'And I do*n't want* to suffer hourly and daily,' said Ursula. 'I don't, I should be ashamed. I think it is degrading not to be happy.'

Hermione stopped and looked at her a long time.

'Do you?' she said at last. And this utterance seemed to her a mark of Ursula's far distance from herself. For to Hermione suffering was the greatest reality, come what might. Yet she too had a creed of happiness.

'Yes,' she said. 'One *should* be happy – ' But it was a matter of will.

'Yes,' said Hermione, listlessly now, 'I can only feel that it would be disastrous, disastrous – at least, to marry in a hurry. Can't you be together without marriage? Can't you go away and live somewhere without marriage? I do feel that marriage would be fatal, for both of you. I think for you even more than for him – and I think of his health – '

'Of course,' said Ursula, '*I* don't care about marriage – it isn't really important to me – it's he who wants it.'

'It is his idea for the moment,' said Hermione, with that weary finality, and a sort of *si jeunesse savait* infallibility.

There was a pause. Then Ursula broke into faltering challenge.

'You think I'm merely a physical woman, don't you?'

'No, indeed,' said Hermione. 'No, indeed! But I think you are vital and young – it isn't a question of years, or even of experience – it is almost a question of race. Rupert is race-old, he comes of an old race – and you seem to me so young, you come of a young, inexperienced race.'

'Do I!' said Ursula. 'But I think he is awfully young, on one side.'

'Yes, perhaps childish in many respects. Nevertheless – '

They both lapsed into silence. Ursula was filled with deep resentment and a touch of hopelessness. 'It isn't true,' she said to herself, silently addressing her adversary. 'It isn't true. And it is *you* who want a physically strong, bullying man, not I. It is you who want an unsensitive man, not I. You *don't* know anything about Rupert, not really, in spite of the years you have had with him. You don't give him a woman's love, you give him an ideal love, and that is why he reacts away from you. You don't know. You only know the dead things. Any kitchen-maid would know something about him, you don't know. What do you think your knowledge is but dead understanding, that doesn't mean a thing. You are so false, and untrue, how could you know anything? What is the good of your talking about love – you untrue spectre of a woman! How can you know anything, when you don't believe? You don't believe in yourself and your own womanhood, so what good is your conceited, shallow cleverness – !'

The two women sat on in antagonistic silence. Hermione felt injured, that all her good intention, all her offering, only left the other woman in vulgar antagonism. But then, Ursula could not understand, never would understand, could never be more than the usual jealous and unreasonable female, with a good deal of powerful female emotion, female attraction, and a fair amount of female understanding, but no mind. Hermione had decided long ago that where there was no mind, it was useless to appeal for reason – one had merely to ignore the ignorant. And Rupert – he had now reacted towards the strongly female, healthy, selfish woman – it was his reaction for the time being – there was no helping it all. It was all a foolish backward and forward, a violent oscillation that would at length be too violent for his coherency, and he would smash and be dead. There was no saving him. This violent and directionless reaction between animalism and spiritual truth would go on in him till he tore himself in two between the opposite directions, and disappeared meaninglessly out of life. It was no good – he too was without unity, without *mind*, in the ultimate stages of living; not quite man enough to make a destiny for a woman.

They sat on till Birkin came in and found them together. He felt at once the antagonism in the atmosphere, something radical and insuperable, and he bit his lip. But he affected a bluff manner.

'Hello, Hermione, are you back again? How do you feel?'

'Oh, better. And how are you – you don't look well – '

'Oh! – I believe Gudrun and Winnie Crich are coming in to tea. At least they said they were. We shall be a tea-party. What train did you come by, Ursula?'

It was rather annoying to see him trying to placate both women at once. Both women watched him, Hermione with deep resentment and pity for him, Ursula very impatient. He was nervous and apparently in quite good spirits, chattering the conventional commonplaces. Ursula was amazed and indignant at the way he made small-talk; he was adept as any *fat* in Christendom. She became quite stiff, she would not answer. It all seemed to her so false and so belittling. And still Gudrun did not appear.

'I think I shall go to Florence for the winter,' said Hermione at length.

'Will you?' he answered. 'But it is so cold there.'

'Yes, but I shall stay with Palestra. It is quite comfortable.'

'What takes you to Florence?'

'I don't know,' said Hermione slowly. Then she looked at him with her slow, heavy gaze. 'Barnes is starting his school of aesthetics, and Olandese is going to give a set of discourses on the Italian national policy – '

'Both rubbish,' he said.

'No, I don't think so,' said Hermione.

'Which do you admire, then?'

'I admire both. Barnes is a pioneer. And then I am interested in Italy, in her coming to national consciousness.'

'I wish she'd come to something different from national consciousness, then,' said Birkin; 'especially as it only means a sort of commercial-industrial consciousness. I hate Italy and her national rant. And I think Barnes is an amateur.'

Hermione was silent for some moments, in a state of hostility. But yet, she had got Birkin back again into her world! How subtle her influence was, she seemed to start his irritable attention into her direction exclusively, in one minute. He was her creature.

'No,' she said, 'you are wrong.' Then a sort of tension came over her, she raised her face like the pythoness inspired with oracles, and went on, in rhapsodic manner: '*Il Sandro mi scrive che ha accolto il più grande entusiasmo, tutti i giovani, e fanciulle e ragazzi, sono tutti –* ' She went on in Italian, as if in thinking of the Italians she thought in their language.

He listened with a shade of distaste to her rhapsody, then he said, 'For all that, I don't like it. Their nationalism is just industrialism – that and a shallow jealousy I detest so much.'

'I think you are wrong – I think you are wrong – ' said Hermione. 'It seems to me purely spontaneous and beautiful, the modern Italian's *passion*, for it is a passion, for Italy, *l'Italia* – '

'Do you know Italy well?' Ursula asked of Hermione. Hermione hated to be broken in upon in this manner. Yet she answered mildly, 'Yes, pretty well. I spent several years of my girlhood there, with my mother. My mother died in Florence.'

'Oh.'

There was a pause, painful to Ursula and to Birkin. Hermione, however, seemed abstracted and calm. Birkin was white, his eyes glowed as if he were in a fever, he was far too overwrought. How Ursula suffered in this tense atmosphere of strained wills! Her head seemed bound round by iron bands.

Birkin rang the bell for tea. They could not wait for Gudrun any longer. When the door was opened, the cat walked in.

'Micio! Micio!' called Hermione, in her slow, deliberate singsong. The young cat turned to look at her, then, with his slow and stately walk he advanced to her side.

'*Vieni – vieni quá,*' Hermione was saying, in her strange caressive, protective voice, as if she were always the elder, the mother superior. '*Vieni dire Buon' Giorno alla zia. Mi ricordi, mi ricordi bene – non è vero, piccolo? È vero che mi ricordi? È vero?*' And slowly she rubbed his head, slowly and with ironic indifference.

'Does he understand Italian?' said Ursula, who knew nothing of the language.

'Yes,' said Hermione at length. 'His mother was Italian. She was born in my wastepaper basket in Florence, on the morning of Rupert's birthday. She was his birthday present.'

Tea was brought in. Birkin poured out for them. It was strange how inviolable was the intimacy which existed between him and Hermione. Ursula felt that she was an outsider. The very teacups and the old silver was a bond between Hermione and Birkin. It seemed to belong to an old, past world which they had inhabited together, and in which Ursula was a foreigner. She was almost a parvenue in their old cultured milieu. Her convention was not their convention, their standards were not her standards. But theirs were established, they had the sanction and the grace of age. He and she together, Hermione and Birkin, were people of the same old tradition, the same withered deadening culture. And she, Ursula, was an intruder. So they always made her feel.

Hermione poured a little cream into a saucer. The simple way she assumed her rights in Birkin's room maddened and discouraged Ursula. There was a fatality about it, as if it were bound to be. Hermione lifted the cat and put the cream before him. He planted his two paws on the edge of the table and bent his gracious young head to drink.

'*Sicuro che capisce italiano,*' sang Hermione, '*non l'avrà dimenticato, la lingua della Mamma.*'

She lifted the cat's head with her long, slow, white fingers, not letting him drink, holding him in her power. It was always the same, this joy in power she manifested, peculiarly in power over any male being. He blinked forbearingly, with a male, bored expression, licking his whiskers. Hermione laughed in her short, grunting fashion.

'*Ecco, il bravo ragazzo, com' è superbo, questo!*'

She made a vivid picture, so calm and strange with the cat. She had a true static impressiveness, she was a social artist in some ways.

The cat refused to look at her, indifferently avoided her fingers, and began to drink again, his nose down to the cream, perfectly balanced, as he lapped with his odd little click.

'It's bad for him, teaching him to eat at table,' said Birkin.

'Yes,' said Hermione, easily assenting.

Then, looking down at the cat, she resumed her old, mocking, humorous singsong.

'*Ti imparano fare brutte cose, brutte cose –*'

She lifted the Mino's white chin on her forefinger, slowly. The young cat looked round with a supremely forbearing air, avoided seeing anything, withdrew his chin, and began to wash his face with his paw. Hermione grunted her laughter, pleased.

'*Bel giovanetto –*' she said.

The cat reached forward again and put his fine white paw on the edge of the saucer. Hermione lifted it down with delicate slowness. This deliberate, delicate carefulness of movement reminded Ursula of Gudrun.

'*No! Non è permesso di mettere il zampino nel tondinetto. Non piace al babbo. Un signor gatto così selvatico – !*'

And she kept her finger on the softly planted paw of the cat, and her voice had the same whimsical, humorous note of bullying.

Ursula had her nose out of joint. She wanted to go away now. It all seemed no good. Hermione was established for ever, she herself was ephemeral and had not yet even arrived.

'I will go now,' she said suddenly.

Birkin looked at her almost in fear – he so dreaded her anger. 'But there is no need for such hurry,' he said.

'Yes,' she answered. 'I will go.' And turning to Hermione, before there was time to say any more, she held out her hand and said 'Goodbye.'

'Goodbye – ' sang Hermione, detaining the hand. 'Must you really go now?'

'Yes, I think I'll go,' said Ursula, her face set, and averted from Hermione's eyes.

'You think you will – '

But Ursula had got her hand free. She turned to Birkin with a quick, almost jeering: 'Goodbye,' and she was opening the door before he had time to do it for her.

When she got outside the house she ran down the road in fury and agitation. It was strange, the unreasoning rage and violence Hermione roused in her, by her very presence. Ursula knew she gave herself away to the other woman, she knew she looked ill-bred, uncouth, exaggerated. But she did not care. She only ran up the road, lest she should go back and jeer in the faces of the two she had left behind. For they outraged her.

CHAPTER 23

Excurse

Next day Birkin sought Ursula out. It happened to be the half-day at the Grammar School. He appeared towards the end of the morning, and asked her, would she drive with him in the afternoon. She consented. But her face was closed and unresponding, and his heart sank.

The afternoon was fine and dim. He was driving the motor car, and she sat beside him. But still her face was closed against him, unresponding. When she became like this, like a wall against him, his heart contracted.

His life now seemed so reduced, that he hardly cared any more. At moments it seemed to him he did not care a straw whether Ursula or Hermione or anybody else existed or did not exist. Why bother! Why strive for a coherent, satisfied life? Why not drift on in a series of accidents – like a picaresque novel? Why not? Why bother about human relationships? Why take them seriously – male or female? Why form any serious connections at all? Why not be casual, drifting along, taking all for what it was worth?

And yet, still, he was damned and doomed to the old effort at serious living.

'Look,' he said, 'what I bought.' The car was running along a broad white road, between autumn trees.

He gave her a little bit of screwed-up paper. She took it and opened it.

'How lovely,' she cried.

She examined the gift.

568 SELECTED WORKS OF D. H. LAWRENCE

'How perfectly lovely!' she cried again. 'But why do you give them me?' She put the question offensively.

His face flickered with bored irritation. He shrugged his shoulders slightly.

'I wanted to,' he said, coolly.

'But why? Why should you?'

'Am I called on to find reasons?' he asked.

There was a silence, whilst she examined the rings that had been screwed up in the paper.

'I think they are *beautiful*,' she said, 'especially this. This is wonderful – '

It was a round opal, red and fiery, set in a circle of tiny rubies.

'You like that best?' he said.

'I think I do.'

'I like the sapphire,' he said.

'This?'

It was a rose-shaped, beautiful sapphire, with small brilliants.

'Yes,' she said, 'it is lovely.' She held it in the light. 'Yes, perhaps it *is* the best – '

'The blue – ' he said.

'Yes, wonderful – '

He suddenly swung the car out of the way of a farm-cart. It tilted on the bank. He was a careless driver, yet very quick. But Ursula was frightened. There was always that something regardless in him which terrified her. She suddenly felt he might kill her, by making some dreadful accident with the motor car. For a moment she was stony with fear.

'Isn't it rather dangerous, the way you drive?' she asked him.

'No, it isn't dangerous,' he said. And then, after a pause: 'Don't you like the yellow ring at all?'

It was a squarish topaz set in a frame of steel, or some other similar mineral, finely wrought.

'Yes,' she said, 'I do like it. But why did you buy these rings?'

'I wanted them. They are second-hand.'

'You bought them for yourself?'

'No. Rings look wrong on my hands.'

'Why did you buy them then?'

'I bought them to give to you.'

'But why? Surely you ought to give them to Hermione! You belong to her.'

He did not answer. She remained with the jewels shut in her hand. She wanted to try them on her fingers, but something in her would not let her. And moreover, she was afraid her hands were too large, she shrank from the mortification of a failure to put them on any but her little finger. They travelled in silence through the empty lanes.

Driving in a motor car excited her, she forgot his presence even.

'Where are we?' she asked suddenly.

'Not far from Worksop.'

'And where are we going?'

'Anywhere.'

It was the answer she liked.

She opened her hand to look at the rings. They gave her *such* pleasure, as they lay, the three circles, with their knotted jewels, entangled in her palm. She would have to try them on. She did so secretly, unwilling to let him see, so that he should not know her finger was too large for them. But he saw nevertheless. He always saw, if she wanted him not to. It was another of his hateful, watchful characteristics.

Only the opal, with its thin wire loop, would go on her ring finger. And she was superstitious. No, there was ill-portent enough, she would not accept this ring from him in pledge.

'Look,' she said, putting forward her hand, that was half-closed and shrinking. 'The others don't fit me.'

He looked at the red-glinting, soft stone, on her over-sensitive skin.

'Yes,' he said.

'But opals are unlucky, aren't they?' she said wistfully.

'No. I prefer unlucky things. Luck is vulgar. Who wants what *luck* would bring? I don't.'

'But why?' she laughed.

And, consumed with a desire to see how the other rings would look on her hand, she put them on her little finger.

'They can be made a little bigger,' he said.

'Yes,' she replied, doubtfully. And she sighed. She knew that, in accepting the rings, she was accepting a pledge. Yet fate seemed more than herself. She looked again at the jewels. They were very beautiful to her eyes – not as ornament, or wealth, but as tiny fragments of loveliness.

'I'm glad you bought them,' she said, putting her hand, half unwillingly, gently on his arm.

He smiled, slightly. He wanted her to come to him. But he was angry at the bottom of his soul, and indifferent. He knew she had a passion for him, really. But it was not finally interesting. There were depths of passion when one became impersonal and indifferent, unemotional. Whereas Ursula was still at the emotional personal level – always so abominably personal. He had taken her as he had never been taken himself. He had taken her at the roots of her darkness and shame – like a demon, laughing over the fountain of mystic corruption which was one of the sources of her being, laughing, shrugging, accepting, accepting finally. As for her, when would she so much go beyond herself as to accept him at the quick of death?

She now became quite happy. The motor car ran on, the afternoon was soft and dim. She talked with lively interest, analysing people and their motives – Gudrun, Gerald. He answered vaguely. He was not very much interested any more in personalities and in people – people were all different, but they were all enclosed nowadays in a definite limitation, he said; there were only about two great ideas, two great streams of activity remaining, with various forms of reaction therefrom. The reactions were all varied in various people, but they followed a few great laws, and intrinsically there was no difference. They acted and reacted involuntarily according to a few great laws, and once the laws, the great principles, were known, people were no longer mystically interesting. They were all essentially alike, the differences were only variations on a theme. None of them transcended the given terms.

Ursula did not agree – people were still an adventure to her – but – perhaps not as much as she tried to persuade herself. Perhaps there was something mechanical, now, in her interest. Perhaps also her interest was destructive, her analysing was a real tearing to pieces. There was an under-space in her where she did not care for people and their idiosyncrasies, even to destroy them. She seemed to touch for a moment this under-silence in herself, she became still, and she turned for a moment purely to Birkin.

'Won't it be lovely to go home in the dark?' she said. 'We might have tea rather late – shall we? – and have high tea? Wouldn't that be rather nice?'

'I promised to be at Shortlands for dinner,' he said.

'But – it doesn't matter – you can go tomorrow – '

'Hermione is there,' he said, in rather an uneasy voice. 'She is going away in two days. I suppose I ought to say goodbye to her. I shall never see her again.'

Ursula drew away, closed in a violent silence. He knitted his brows, and his eyes began to sparkle again in anger.

'You don't mind, do you?' he asked irritably.

'No, I don't care. Why should I? Why should I mind?' Her tone was jeering and offensive.

'That's what I ask myself,' he said; 'why *should* you mind! But you seem to.' His brows were tense with violent irritation.

'I *assure* you I don't, I don't mind in the least. Go where you belong – it's what I want you to do.'

'Ah you fool!' he cried, 'with your "go where you belong". It's finished between Hermione and me. She means much more to *you*, if it comes to that, than she does to me. For you can only revolt in pure reaction from her – and to be her opposite is to be her counterpart.'

'Ah, opposite!' cried Ursula. 'I know your dodges. I am not taken in by your word-twisting. You belong to Hermione and her dead show. Well, if you do, you do. I don't blame you. But then you've nothing to do with me.'

In his inflamed, overwrought exasperation, he stopped the car, and they sat there, in the middle of the country lane, to have it out. It was a crisis of war between them, so they did not see the ridiculousness of their situation.

'If you weren't a fool, if only you weren't a fool,' he cried in bitter despair, 'you'd see that one could be decent, even when one has been wrong. I *was* wrong to go on all those years with Hermione – it was a deathly process. But after all, one can have a little human decency. But no, you would tear my soul out with your jealousy at the very mention of Hermione's name.'

'I jealous! *I* – jealous! You *are* mistaken if you think that. I'm not jealous in the least of Hermione, she is nothing to me, not *that*!' And Ursula snapped her fingers. 'No, it's you who are a liar. It's you who must return, like a dog to his vomit. It is what Hermione *stands for* that I *hate*. I *hate* it. It is lies, it is false, it is death. But you want it, you can't help it, you can't help yourself. You belong to that old, deathly way of living – then go back to it. But don't come to me, for I've nothing to do with it.'

And in the stress of her violent emotion, she got down from the car and went to the hedgerow, picking unconsciously some flesh-pink spindleberries, some of which were burst, showing their orange seeds.

'Ah, you are a fool,' he cried, bitterly, with some contempt.

'Yes, I am. I *am* a fool. And thank God for it. I'm too big a fool to swallow your cleverness. God be praised. You go to your women – go to them – they are your sort – you've always had a string of them trailing after you – and you always will. Go to your spiritual brides – but don't come to me as well, because I'm not having any, thank you. You're not satisfied, are you? Your spiritual brides can't give you what you want, they aren't common and fleshy enough for you, are they? So you come to me, and keep them in the background! You will marry me for daily use. But you'll keep yourself well provided with spiritual brides in the background. I know your dirty little game.' Suddenly a flame ran over her, and she stamped her foot madly on the road, and he winced, afraid that she would strike him. 'And *I*, *I'm* not spiritual enough, *I'm* not as spiritual as that Hermione – !' Her brows knitted, her eyes blazed like a tiger's. 'Then go to her, that's all I say, *go* to her, *go*. Ha, she spiritual – *spiritual*, she! A dirty materialist as she is. *She* spiritual? What does she care for, what is her spirituality? What *is* it?' Her fury seemed to blaze out and burn his face. He shrank a little. 'I tell you it's *dirt*, *dirt*, and nothing *but* dirt. And it's dirt you want, you crave for it. Spiritual! Is *that* spiritual, her bullying, her conceit, her sordid materialism? She's a fishwife, a fishwife, she is such a materialist. And all so sordid. What does she work out to, in the end, with all her social passion, as you call it. Social passion – what social passion has she? – show it me! – where is it? She wants petty, immediate *power*, she wants the illusion that she is a great woman, that is all. In her soul she's a devilish unbeliever, common as dirt. That's what she is at the bottom. And all the rest is pretence – but you love it. You love the sham spirituality, it's your food. And why? Because of the dirt underneath. Do you think I don't know the foulness of your sex life – and hers? – I do. And it's that foulness you want, you liar. Then have it, have it. You're such a liar.'

She turned away, spasmodically tearing the twigs of spindleberry from the hedge, and fastening them, with vibrating fingers, in the bosom of her coat.

He stood watching in silence. A wonderful tenderness burned in him, at the sight of her quivering, so sensitive fingers: and at the same time he was full of rage and callousness.

'This is a degrading exhibition,' he said coolly.

'Yes, degrading indeed,' she said. 'But more to me than to you.'

'Since you choose to degrade yourself,' he said. Again the flash came over her face, the yellow lights concentrated in her eyes.

'*You!*' she cried. 'You! You truth-lover! You purity-monger! It *stinks*, your truth and your purity. It stinks of the offal you feed on, you scavenger dog, you eater of corpses. You are foul, *foul* and you must know it. Your purity, your candour, your goodness – yes, thank you, we've had some. What you are is a foul, deathly thing, obscene, that's what you are, obscene and perverse. You, and love! You may well say, you don't want love. No, you want *yourself*, and dirt, and death – that's what you want. You are so *perverse*, so death-eating. And then – '

'There's a bicycle coming,' he said, writhing under her loud denunciation.

She glanced down the road.

'I don't care,' she cried.

Nevertheless she was silent. The cyclist, having heard the voices raised in altercation, glanced curiously at the man, and the woman, and at the standing motor car as he passed.

' – Afternoon,' he said, cheerfully.

'Good-afternoon,' replied Birkin coldly.

They were silent as the man passed into the distance.

A clearer look had come over Birkin's face. He knew she was in the main right. He knew he was perverse, so spiritual on the one hand, and in some strange way, degraded on the other. But was she herself any better? Was anybody any better?

'It may all be true, lies and stink and all,' he said. 'But Hermione's spiritual intimacy is no rottener than your emotional-jealous intimacy. One can preserve the decencies, even to one's enemies: for one's own sake. Hermione is my enemy – to her last breath! That's why I must bow her off the field.'

'You! You and your enemies and your bows! A pretty picture you make of yourself. But it takes nobody in but yourself. I *jealous*! *I*! What I say,' her voice sprang into flame, 'I say because it is *true*, do you see, because you are *you*, a foul and false liar, a whited sepulchre. That's why I say it. And *you* hear it.'

'And be grateful,' he added, with a satirical grimace.

'Yes,' she cried, 'and if you have a spark of decency in you, be grateful.'

'Not having a spark of decency, however – ' he retorted.

'No,' she cried, 'you haven't a *spark*. And so you can go your way, and I'll go mine. It's no good, not the slightest. So you can leave me now, I don't want to go any further with you – leave me – '

'You don't even know where you are,' he said.

'Oh, don't bother, I assure you I shall be all right. I've got ten shillings in my purse, and that will take me back from anywhere *you* have brought me to.' She hesitated. The rings were still on her fingers, two on her little finger, one on her ring finger. Still she hesitated.

'Very good,' he said. 'The only hopeless thing is a fool.'

'You are quite right,' she said.

Still she hesitated. Then an ugly, malevolent look came over her face, she pulled the rings from her fingers, and tossed them at him. One touched his face, the others hit his coat, and they scattered into the mud.

'And take your rings,' she said, 'and go and buy yourself a female elsewhere – there are plenty to be had, who will be quite glad to share your spiritual mess – or to have your physical mess, and leave your spiritual mess to Hermione.'

With which she walked away, desultorily, up the road. He stood motionless, watching her sullen, rather ugly walk. She was sullenly picking and pulling at the twigs of the hedge as she passed. She grew smaller, she seemed to pass out of his sight. A darkness came over his mind. Only a small, mechanical speck of consciousness hovered near him.

He felt tired and weak. Yet also he was relieved. He gave up his old position. He went and sat on the bank. No doubt Ursula was right. It was true, really, what she said. He knew that his spirituality was concomitant of a process of depravity, a sort of pleasure in self-destruction. There really *was* a certain stimulant in self-destruction, for him – especially when it was translated spiritually. But then he knew it – he knew it, and had done. And was not Ursula's way of emotional intimacy, emotional and physical, was it not just as dangerous as Hermione's abstract spiritual intimacy? Fusion, fusion, this horrible fusion of two beings, which every woman and most men insisted on, was it not nauseous and horrible anyhow, whether it was a fusion of the spirit or of the emotional body? Hermione saw herself as the perfect Idea, to which all men must come: and Ursula was the perfect Womb, the bath of birth, to which all men must come! And both were horrible. Why could they not remain individuals, limited by their own limits? Why this dreadful all-comprehensiveness, this hateful tyranny? Why not leave the other being free, why try to absorb, or melt, or merge? One might abandon oneself utterly to the *moments*, but not to any other being.

He could not bear to see the rings lying in the pale mud of the road. He picked them up, and wiped them unconsciously on his hands. They were the little tokens of the reality of beauty, the reality of happiness in warm creation. But he had made his hands all dirty and gritty.

There was a darkness over his mind. The terrible knot of consciousness that had persisted there like an obsession was broken, gone, his life was dissolved in darkness over his limbs and his body. But there was a point of anxiety in his heart now. He wanted her to come back. He breathed lightly and regularly like an infant, that breathes innocently, beyond the touch of responsibility.

She was coming back. He saw her drifting desultorily under the high hedge, advancing towards him slowly. He did not move, he did not look again. He was as if asleep, at peace, slumbering and utterly relaxed.

She came up and stood before him, hanging her head.

'See what a flower I found you,' she said, wistfully holding a piece of purple-red bell-heather under his face. He saw the clump of coloured bells, and the treelike, tiny branch: also her hands, with their over-fine, over-sensitive skin.

'Pretty!' he said, looking up at her with a smile, taking the flower. Everything had become simple again, quite simple, the complexity gone into nowhere. But he badly wanted to cry: except that he was weary and bored by emotion.

Then a hot passion of tenderness for her filled his heart. He stood up and looked into her face. It was new and oh, so delicate in its luminous wonder and fear. He put his arms round her, and she hid her face on his shoulder.

It was peace, just simple peace, as he stood folding her quietly there on the open lane. It was peace at last. The old, detestable world of tension had passed away at last, his soul was strong and at ease.

She looked up at him. The wonderful yellow light in her eyes now was soft and yielded, they were at peace with each other. He kissed her, softly, many, many times. A laugh came into her eyes.

'Did I abuse you?' she asked.

He smiled too, and took her hand, that was so soft and given.

'Never mind,' she said, 'it is all for the good.' He kissed her again, softly, many times.

'Isn't it?' she said.

'Certainly,' he replied. 'Wait! I shall have my own back.'

She laughed suddenly, with a wild catch in her voice, and flung her arms around him.

'You are mine, my love, aren't you?' she cried straining him close.

'Yes,' he said, softly.

His voice was so soft and final, she went very still, as if under a fate which had taken her. Yes, she acquiesced – but it was accomplished without her acquiescence. He was kissing her quietly, repeatedly, with a soft, still happiness that almost made her heart stop beating.

'My love!' she cried, lifting her face and looking with frightened, gentle wonder of bliss. Was it all real? But his eyes were beautiful and soft and immune from stress or excitement, beautiful and smiling lightly to her, smiling with her. She hid her face on his shoulder, hiding before him, because he could see her so completely. She knew he loved her, and she was afraid, she was in a strange element, a new heaven round about her. She wished he were passionate, because in passion she was at home. But this was so still and frail, as space is more frightening than force.

Again, quickly, she lifted her head.

'Do you love me?' she said, quickly, impulsively.

'Yes,' he replied, not heeding her motion, only her stillness.

She knew it was true. She broke away.

'So you ought,' she said, turning round to look at the road. 'Did you find the rings?'

'Yes.'

'Where are they?'

'In my pocket.'

She put her hand into his pocket and took them out.

She was restless.

'Shall we go?' she said.

'Yes,' he answered. And they mounted to the car once more, and left behind them this memorable battlefield.

They drifted through the wild, late afternoon, in a beautiful motion that was smiling and transcendent. His mind was sweetly at ease, the life flowed through him as from some new fountain, he was as if born out of the cramp of a womb.

'Are you happy?' she asked him, in her strange, delighted way.

'Yes,' he said.

'So am I,' she cried in sudden ecstasy, putting her arm round him and clutching him violently against her, as he steered the motor car.

'Don't drive much more,' she said. 'I don't want you to be always doing something.'

'No,' he said. 'We'll finish this little trip, and then we'll be free.'

'We will, my love, we will,' she cried in delight, kissing him as he turned to her.

He drove on in a strange new wakefulness, the tension of his consciousness broken. He seemed to be conscious all over, all his body awake with a simple, glimmering awareness, as if he had just come awake, like a thing that is born, like a bird when it comes out of an egg, into a new universe.

They dropped down a long hill in the dusk, and suddenly Ursula recognised on her right hand, below in the hollow, the form of Southwell Minster.

'Are we here!' she cried with pleasure.

The rigid, sombre, ugly cathedral was settling under the gloom of the coming night, as they entered the narrow town, the golden lights showed like slabs of revelation, in the shop-windows.

'Father came here with mother,' she said, 'when they first knew each other. He loves it – he loves the Minster. Do you?'

'Yes. It looks like quartz crystals sticking up out of the dark hollow. We'll have our high tea at the Saracen's Head.'

As they descended, they heard the Minster bells playing a hymn, when the hour had struck six.

> Glory to thee my God this night
> For all the blessings of the light –

So, to Ursula's ear, the tune fell out, drop by drop, from the unseen sky on to the dusky town. It was like dim, bygone centuries sounding. It was all so far off. She stood in the old yard of the inn, smelling of straw and stables and petrol. Above, she could see the first stars. What was it all? This was no actual world, it was the dream-world of one's childhood – a great circumscribed reminiscence. The world had become unreal. She herself was a strange, transcendent reality.

They sat together in a little parlour by the fire.

'Is it true?' she said, wondering.

'What?'

'Everything – is everything true?'

'The best is true,' he said, grimacing at her.

'Is it?' she replied, laughing, but unassured.

She looked at him. He seemed still so separate. New eyes were opened in her soul. She saw a strange creature from another world, in him. It was as if she were enchanted, and everything were metamorphosed. She recalled again the old magic of the Book of Genesis, where the sons of God saw the daughters of men, that they were fair. And he was one of these, one of these strange creatures from the beyond, looking down at her, and seeing she was fair.

He stood on the hearthrug looking at her, at her face that was upturned exactly like a flower, a fresh, luminous flower, glinting faintly golden with the dew of the first light. And he was smiling faintly as if there were no speech in the world, save the silent delight of flowers in each other. Smilingly they delighted in each other's presence, pure presence, not to be thought of, even known. But his eyes had a faintly ironical contraction.

And she was drawn to him strangely, as in a spell. Kneeling on the hearthrug before him, she put her arms round his loins, and put her face against his thigh. Riches! Riches! She was overwhelmed with a sense of a heaven full of riches.

'We love each other,' she said in delight.

'More than that,' he answered, looking down at her with his glimmering, easy face.

Unconsciously, with her sensitive fingertips, she was tracing the back of his thighs, following some mysterious life-flow there. She had discovered some-thing, something more than wonderful, more wonderful than life itself. It was the strange mystery of his life-motion, there, at the back of the thighs, down the flanks. It was a strange reality of his being, the very stuff of being, there in the straight down-flow of the thighs. It was here she discovered him one of the sons of God such as were in the beginning of the world, not a man, something other, something more.

This was release at last. She had had lovers, she had known passion. But this was neither love nor passion. It was the daughters of men coming back to the sons of God, the strange inhuman sons of God who are in the beginning.

Her face was now one dazzle of released, golden light, as she looked up at him, and laid her hands full on his thighs, behind, as he stood before her. He looked down at her with a rich bright brow like a diadem above his eyes. She was beautiful as a new marvellous flower opened at his knees, a paradisal flower she was, beyond womanhood, such a flower of luminousness. Yet something was tight and unfree in him. He did not like this crouching, this radiance – not altogether.

It was all achieved, for her. She had found one of the sons of God from the Beginning, and he had found one of the first most luminous daughters of men.

She traced with her hands the line of his loins and thighs, at the back, and a living fire ran through her, from him, darkly. It was a dark flood of electric passion she released from him, drew into herself. She had established a rich new circuit, a new current of passional electric energy, between the two of them, released from the darkest poles of the body and established in perfect circuit. It was a dark fire of electricity that rushed from him to her, and flooded them both with rich peace, satisfaction.

'My love,' she cried, lifting her face to him, her eyes, her mouth open in transport.

'My love,' he answered, bending and kissing her, always kissing her.

She closed her hands over the full, rounded body of his loins, as he stooped over her, she seemed to touch the quick of the mystery of darkness that was bodily him. She seemed to faint beneath, and he seemed to faint, stooping over her. It was a perfect passing away for both of them, and at the same time the most intolerable accession into being, the marvellous fullness of immediate gratification, overwhelming, out-flooding from the source of the deepest life-force, the darkest, deepest, strangest life-source of the human body, at the back and base of the loins.

After a lapse of stillness, after the rivers of strange dark fluid richness had passed over her, flooding, carrying away her mind and flooding down her spine and down her knees, past her feet, a strange flood, sweeping away everything and leaving her an essential new being, she was left quite free, she was free in complete ease, her complete self. So she rose, stilly and blithe, smiling at him. He stood before her, glimmering, so awfully real, that her heart almost stopped beating. He stood there in his strange, whole body, that had its marvellous fountains, like the bodies of the sons of God who were in the beginning. There were strange fountains of his body, more mysterious and potent than any she had imagined or known, more satisfying, ah, finally, mystically-physically satisfying. She had thought there was no source deeper than the phallic source. And now, behold, from the smitten rock of the man's body, from the strange marvellous flanks and thighs, deeper, further in mystery than the phallic source, came the floods of ineffable darkness and ineffable riches.

They were glad, and they could forget perfectly. They laughed, and went to the meal provided. There was a venison pasty, of all things, a large broad-faced cut ham, eggs and cresses and red beetroot, and medlars and apple-tart, and tea.

'What *good* things!' she cried with pleasure. 'How noble it looks! – shall I pour out the tea? – '

She was usually nervous and uncertain at performing these public duties, such as giving tea. But today she forgot, she was at her ease, entirely forgetting to have misgivings. The teapot poured beautifully from a proud slender spout. Her eyes were warm with smiles as she gave him his tea. She had learned at last to be still and perfect.

'Everything is ours,' she said to him.

'Everything,' he answered.

She gave a queer little crowing sound of triumph.

'I'm so glad!' she cried, with unspeakable relief.

'So am I,' he said. 'But I'm thinking we'd better get out of our responsibilities as quick as we can.'

'What responsibilities?' she asked, wondering.

'We must drop our jobs, like a shot.'

A new understanding dawned into her face.

'Of course,' she said, 'there's that.'

'We must get out,' he said. 'There's nothing for it but to get out, quick.'

She looked at him doubtfully across the table.

'But where?' she said.

'I don't know,' he said. 'We'll just wander about for a bit.'

Again she looked at him quizzically.

'I should be perfectly happy at the Mill,' she said.

'It's very near the old thing,' he said. 'Let us wander a bit.'

His voice could be so soft and happy-go-lucky, it went through her veins like an exhilaration. Nevertheless she dreamed of a valley, and wild gardens, and peace. She had a desire too for splendour – an aristocratic extravagant splendour. Wandering seemed to her like restlessness, dissatisfaction.

'Where will you wander to?' she asked.

'I don't know. I feel as if I would just meet you and we'd set off – just towards the distance.'

'But where can one go?' she asked anxiously. 'After all, there is only the world, and none of it is very distant.'

'Still,' he said, 'I should like to go with you – nowhere. It would be rather wandering just to nowhere. That's the place to get to – nowhere. One wants to wander away from the world's somewheres, into our own nowhere.'

Still she meditated.

'You see, my love,' she said, 'I'm so afraid that while we are only people, we've got to take the world that's given – because there isn't any other.'

'Yes there is,' he said. 'There's somewhere where we can be free – somewhere where one needn't wear much clothes – none even – where one meets a few people who have gone through enough, and can take things for granted – where you can be yourself, without bothering. There is somewhere – there are one or two people – '

'But where – ?' she sighed.

'Somewhere – anywhere. Let's wander off. That's the thing to do – let's wander off.'

'Yes – ' she said, thrilled at the thought of travel. But to her it was only travel.

'To be free,' he said. 'To be free, in a free place, with a few other people!'

'Yes,' she said wistfully. Those 'few other people' depressed her.

'It isn't really a locality, though,' he said. 'It's a perfected relation between you and me, and others – the perfect relation – so that we are free together.'

'It is, my love, isn't it,' she said. 'It's you and me. It's you and me, isn't it?' She stretched out her arms to him. He went across and stooped to kiss her face. Her arms closed round him again, her hands spread upon his shoulders, moving slowly there, moving slowly on his back, down his back slowly, with a strange recurrent, rhythmic motion, yet moving slowly down, pressing mysteriously over his loins, over his flanks. The sense of the awfulness of riches that could never be impaired flooded her mind like a swoon, a death in most marvellous possession, mystic-sure. She possessed him so utterly and intolerably, that she herself lapsed out. And yet she was only sitting still in the chair, with her hands pressed upon him, and lost.

Again he softly kissed her.

'We shall never go apart again,' he murmured quietly And she did not speak, but only pressed her hands firmer down upon the source of darkness in him.

They decided, when they woke again from the pure swoon, to write their resignations from the world of work there and then. She wanted this.

He rang the bell, and ordered notepaper without a printed address. The waiter cleared the table.

'Now then,' he said, 'yours first. Put your home address, and the date – then "Director of Education, Town Hall – Sir – " Now then! – I don't know how one really stands – I suppose one could get out of it in less than a month – Anyhow, "Sir – I beg to resign my post as class-mistress in the Willey Green Grammar School. I should be very grateful if you would liberate me as soon as possible, without waiting for the expiration of the month's notice." That'll do. Have you got it? Let me look. "Ursula Brangwen". Good! Now I'll write mine. I ought to give them three months, but I can plead health. I can arrange it all right.'

He sat and wrote out his formal resignation.

'Now,' he said, when the envelopes were sealed and addressed, 'shall we post them here, both together? I know Jackie will say, "Here's a coincidence!" when he receives them in all their identity. Shall we let him say it, or not?'

'I don't care,' she said.

'No – ?' he said, pondering.

'It doesn't matter, does it?' she said.

'Yes,' he replied. 'Their imaginations shall not work on us. I'll post yours here, mine after. I cannot be implicated in their imaginings.'

He looked at her with his strange, non-human singleness.

'Yes, you are right,' she said.

She lifted her face to him, all shining and open. It was as if he might enter straight into the source of her radiance. His face became a little distracted.

'Shall we go?' he said.

'As you like,' she replied.

They were soon out of the little town, and running through the uneven lanes of the country. Ursula nestled near him, into his constant warmth, and watched the pale-lit revelation racing ahead, the visible night. Sometimes it was a wide old road, with grass-spaces on either side, flying magic and elfin in the greenish illumination, sometimes it was trees looming overhead, sometimes it was bramble bushes, sometimes the walls of a crew-yard and the butt of a barn.

'Are you going to Shortlands to dinner?' Ursula asked him suddenly. He started.

'Good God!' he said. 'Shortlands! Never again. Not that. Besides, we should be too late.'

'Where are we going then – to the Mill?'

'If you like. Pity to go anywhere on this good dark night. Pity to come out of it, really. Pity we can't stop in the good darkness. It is better than anything ever would be – this good immediate darkness.'

She sat wondering. The car lurched and swayed. She knew there was no leaving him, the darkness held them both and contained them, it was not to be surpassed. Besides, she had a full mystic knowledge of his suave loins of darkness, dark-clad and suave, and in this knowledge there was some of the inevitability and the beauty of fate, fate which one asks for, which one accepts in full.

He sat still like an Egyptian Pharaoh, driving the car. He felt as if he were seated in immemorial potency, like the great carven statues of real Egypt, as real and as fulfilled with subtle strength, as these are, with a vague inscrutable smile on the lips. He knew what it was to have the strange and magical current of force in his back and loins, and down his legs, force so perfect that it stayed him immobile, and left his face subtly, mindlessly smiling. He knew what it was to be awake and potent in that other basic mind, the deepest physical mind. And from this source he had a pure and magic control, magical, mystical, a force in darkness, like electricity.

It was very difficult to speak, it was so perfect to sit in this pure living silence, subtle, full of unthinkable knowledge and unthinkable force, upheld immemorially in timeless force, like the immobile, supremely potent Egyptians, seated for ever in their living, subtle silence.

'We need not go home,' he said. 'This car has seats that let down and make a bed, and we can lift the hood.'

She was glad and frightened. She cowered near to him.

'But what about them at home?' she said.

'Send a telegram.'

Nothing more was said. They ran on in silence. But with a sort of second consciousness he steered the car towards a destination. For he had the free intelligence to direct his own ends. His arms and his breast and his head were rounded and living like those of the Greek, he had not the unawakened straight arms of the Egyptian, nor the sealed, slumbering head. A lambent intelligence played secondarily above his pure Egyptian concentration in darkness.

They came to a village that lined along the road. The car crept slowly along, until he saw the post-office. Then he pulled up.

'I will send a telegram to your father,' he said. 'I will merely say "spending the night in town", shall I?'

'Yes,' she answered. She did not want to be disturbed into taking thought.

She watched him move into the post-office. It was also a shop, she saw. Strange, he was. Even as he went into the lighted, public place he remained dark and magic, the living silence seemed the body of reality in him, subtle, potent, indiscoverable. There he was! In a strange uplift of elation she saw him, the being never to be revealed, awful in its potency, mystic and real. This dark, subtle reality of him, never to be translated, liberated her into perfection, her own perfected being. She too was dark and fulfilled in silence.

He came out, throwing some packages into the car.

'There is some bread, and cheese, and raisins, and apples, and hard chocolate,' he said, in his voice that was as if laughing, because of the unblemished stillness and force which was the reality in him. She would have to touch him. To speak, to see, was nothing. It was a travesty to look and to comprehend the man there. Darkness and silence must fall perfectly on her, then she could know mystically, in unrevealed touch. She must lightly, mindlessly connect with him, have the knowledge which is death of knowledge, the reality of surety in not-knowing.

Soon they had run on again into the darkness. She did not ask where they were going, she did not care. She sat in a fullness and a pure potency that was like apathy, mindless and immobile. She was next to him, and hung in a pure rest, as a star is hung, balanced unthinkably. Still there remained a dark lambency of anticipation. She would touch him. With perfect fine fingertips of reality she would touch the reality in him, the suave, pure, untranslatable reality of his loins of darkness. To touch, mindlessly in darkness to come in pure touching upon the living reality of him, his suave perfect loins and thighs of darkness, this was her sustaining anticipation.

And he too waited in the magical steadfastness of suspense, for her to take this knowledge of him as he had taken it of her. He knew her darkly, with the fullness of dark knowledge. Now she would know him, and he too would be liberated. He would be night-free, like an Egyptian, steadfast in perfectly suspended equilibrium, pure mystic nodality of physical being. They would give each other this star-equilibrium which alone is freedom.

She saw that they were running among trees – great old trees with dying bracken undergrowth. The palish, gnarled trunks showed ghostly, and like old priests in the hovering distance, the fern rose magical and mysterious. It was a night all darkness, with low cloud. The motor car advanced slowly.

'Where are we?' she whispered.

'In Sherwood Forest.'

It was evident he knew the place. He drove softly, watching. Then they came to a green road between the trees. They turned cautiously round, and were advancing between the oaks of the forest, down a green lane. The green lane widened into a little circle of grass, where there was a small trickle of water at the bottom of a sloping bank. The car stopped.

'We will stay here,' he said, 'and put out the lights.'

He extinguished the lamps at once, and it was pure night, with shadows of trees like realities of other, nightly being. He threw a rug on to the bracken, and they sat in stillness and mindless silence. There were faint sounds from the wood, but no disturbance, no possible disturbance, the world was under a strange ban, a new mystery had supervened. They threw off their clothes, and he gathered her to him, and found her, found the pure lambent reality of her forever invisible flesh. Quenched, inhuman, his fingers upon her unrevealed nudity were the fingers of silence upon silence, the body of mysterious night upon the body of mysterious night, the night masculine and feminine, never to be seen with the eye, or known with the mind, only known as a palpable revelation of living otherness.

She had her desire of him, she touched, she received the maximum of unspeakable communication in touch, dark, subtle, positively silent, a magnificent gift and give again, a perfect acceptance and yielding, a mystery, the reality of that which can never be known, vital, sensual reality that can never be transmuted into mind content, but remains outside, living body of darkness and silence and subtlety, the mystic body of reality. She had her desire fulfilled. He had his desire fulfilled. For she was to him what he was to her, the immemorial magnificence of mystic, palpable, real otherness.

They slept the chilly night through under the hood of the car, a night of unbroken sleep. It was already high day when he awoke. They looked at each other and laughed, then looked away, filled with darkness and secrecy. Then they kissed and remembered the magnificence of the night. It was so magnificent, such an inheritance of a universe of dark reality, that they were afraid to seem to remember. They hid away the remembrance and the knowledge.

CHAPTER 24

Death and Love

Thomas Crich died slowly, terribly slowly. It seemed impossible to everybody that the thread of life could be drawn out so thin, and yet not break. The sick man lay unutterably weak and spent, kept alive by morphia and by drinks, which he sipped slowly. He was only half conscious – a thin strand of consciousness linking the darkness of death with the light of day. Yet his will was unbroken, he was integral, complete. Only he must have perfect stillness about him.

Any presence but that of the nurses was a strain and an effort to him now. Every morning Gerald went into the room, hoping to find his father passed away at last. Yet always he saw the same transparent face, the same dread dark hair on the waxen forehead, and the awful, inchoate dark eyes, which seemed to be decomposing into formless darkness, having only a tiny grain of vision within them.

And always, as the dark, inchoate eyes turned to him, there passed through Gerald's bowels a burning stroke of revolt, that seemed to resound through his whole being, threatening to break his mind with its clangour, and making him mad.

Every morning, the son stood there, erect and taut with life, gleaming in his blondness. The gleaming blondness of his strange, imminent being put the father into a fever of fretful irritation. He could not bear to meet the uncanny, downward look of Gerald's blue eyes. But it was only for a moment. Each on the brink of departure, the father and son looked at each other, then parted.

For a long time Gerald preserved a perfect *sang-froid*, he remained quite collected. But at last, fear undermined him. He was afraid of some horrible collapse in himself. He had to stay and see this thing through. Some perverse will made him watch his father drawn over the borders of life. And yet, now, every day, the great red-hot stroke of horrified fear through the bowels of the son struck a further inflammation. Gerald went about all day with a tendency to cringe, as if there were the point of a sword of Damocles pricking the nape of his neck.

There was no escape – he was bound up with his father, he had to see him through. And the father's will never relaxed or yielded to death. It would have to snap when death at last snapped it – if it did not persist after a physical death. In the same way, the will of the son never yielded. He stood firm and immune, he was outside this death and this dying.

It was a trial by ordeal. Could he stand and see his father slowly dissolve and disappear in death, without once yielding his will, without once relenting before the omnipotence of death. Like a Red Indian undergoing torture, Gerald would experience the whole process of slow death without wincing or flinching. He even triumphed in it. He somehow *wanted* this death, even forced it. It was as if he himself were dealing the death, even when he most recoiled in horror. Still, he would deal it, he would triumph through death.

But in the stress of this ordeal, Gerald too lost his hold on the outer, daily life. That which was much to him, came to mean nothing. Work, pleasure – it was all left behind. He went on more or less mechanically with his business, but this activity was all extraneous. The real activity was this ghastly wrestling for death in his own soul. And his own will should triumph. Come what might, he would not bow down or submit or acknowledge a master. He had no master in death.

But as the fight went on, and all that he had been and was continued to be destroyed, so that life was a hollow shell all round him, roaring and clattering like the sound of the sea, a noise in which he participated externally, and inside this hollow shell was all the darkness and fearful space of death, he knew he would have to find reinforcements, otherwise he would collapse inwards upon the great dark void which circled at the centre of his soul. His will held his outer life, his outer mind, his outer being unbroken and unchanged. But the pressure was too great. He would have to find something to make good the equilibrium. Something must come with him into the hollow void of death in his soul, fill it up, and so equalise the pressure within to the pressure without. For day by day he felt more and more like a bubble filled with darkness, round which whirled the iridescence of his consciousness, and upon which the pressure of the outer world, the outer life, roared vastly.

In this extremity his instinct led him to Gudrun. He threw away everything now – he only wanted the relation established with her. He would follow her to the studio, to be near her, to talk to her. He would stand about the room, aimlessly picking up the implements, the lumps of clay, the little figures she had cast – they were whimsical and grotesque – looking at them without perceiving them. And she felt him following her, dogging her heels like a doom. She held away from him, and yet she knew he drew always a little nearer, a little nearer.

'I say,' he said to her one evening, in an odd, unthinking, uncertain way, 'won't you stay to dinner tonight? I wish you would.'

She started slightly. He spoke to her like a man making a request of another man.

'They'll be expecting me at home,' she said.

'Oh, they won't mind, will they?' he said. 'I should be awfully glad if you'd stay.'

Her long silence gave consent at last.

'I'll tell Thomas, shall I?' he said.

'I must go almost immediately after dinner,' she said.

It was a dark, cold evening. There was no fire in the drawing-room, they sat in the library. He was mostly silent, absent, and Winifred talked little. But when Gerald did rouse himself, he smiled and was pleasant and ordinary with her. Then there came over him again the long blanks, of which he was not aware.

She was very much attracted by him. He looked so preoccupied, and his strange, blank silences, which she could not read, moved her and made her wonder over him, made her feel reverential towards him.

But he was very kind. He gave her the best things at the table, he had a bottle of slightly sweet, delicious golden wine brought out for dinner, knowing she would prefer it to the burgundy. She felt herself esteemed, needed almost.

As they took coffee in the library, there was a soft, very soft knocking at the door. He started, and called, 'Come in.' The timbre of his voice, like something vibrating at high pitch, unnerved Gudrun. A nurse in white entered, half hovering in the doorway like a shadow. She was very good-looking, but strangely enough, shy and self-mistrusting.

'The doctor would like to speak to you, Mr Crich,' she said, in her low, discreet voice.

'The doctor!' he said, starting up. 'Where is he?'

'He is in the dining-room.'

'Tell him I'm coming.'

He drank up his coffee, and followed the nurse, who had dissolved like a shadow.

'Which nurse was that?' asked Gudrun.

'Miss Inglis – I like her best,' replied Winifred.

After a while Gerald came back, looking absorbed by his own thoughts, and having some of that tension and abstraction which is seen in a slightly drunken man. He did not say what the doctor had wanted him for, but stood before the fire, with his hands behind his back, and his face open and as if rapt. Not that he was really thinking – he was only arrested in pure suspense inside himself, and thoughts wafted through his mind without order.

'I must go now and see Mama,' said Winifred, 'and see Dadda before he goes to sleep.'

She bade them both good-night.

Gudrun also rose to take her leave.

'You needn't go yet, need you?' said Gerald, glancing quickly at the clock. 'It is early yet. I'll walk down with you when you go. Sit down, don't hurry away.'

Gudrun sat down, as if, absent as he was, his will had power over her. She felt almost mesmerised. He was strange to her, something unknown. What was he thinking, what was he feeling, as he stood there so rapt, saying nothing? He kept her – she could feel that. He would not let her go. She watched him in humble submissiveness.

'Had the doctor anything new to tell you?' she asked, softly, at length, with that gentle, timid sympathy which touched a keen fibre in his heart. He lifted his eyebrows with a negligent, indifferent expression.

'No – nothing new,' he replied, as if the question were quite casual, trivial. 'He says the pulse is very weak indeed, very intermittent – but that doesn't necessarily mean much, you know.'

He looked down at her. Her eyes were dark and soft and unfolded, with a stricken look that roused him.

'No,' she murmured at length. 'I don't understand anything about these things.'

'Just as well not,' he said. 'I say, won't you have a cigarette? – do!' He quickly fetched the box, and held her a light. Then he stood before her on the hearth again.

'No,' he said, 'we've never had much illness in the house, either – not till father.' He seemed to meditate a while. Then looking down at her, with strangely communicative blue eyes, that filled her with dread, he continued: 'It's something you don't reckon with, you know, till it is there. And then you realise that it was there all the time – it was always there – you understand what I mean? – the possibility of this incurable illness, this slow death.'

He moved his feet uneasily on the marble hearth, and put his cigarette to his mouth, looking up at the ceiling.

'I know,' murmured Gudrun: 'it is dreadful.'

He smoked without knowing. Then he took the cigarette from his lips, bared his teeth, and putting the tip of his tongue between his teeth, spat off a grain of tobacco, turning slightly aside, like a man who is alone, or who is lost in thought.

'I don't know what the effect actually *is* on one,' he said, and again he looked down at her. Her eyes were dark and stricken with knowledge, looking into his. He saw her submerged, and he turned aside his face. 'But I absolutely am not the same. There's nothing left, if you understand what I mean. You seem to be clutching at the void – and at the same time you are void yourself. And so you don't know what to *do*.'

'No,' she murmured. A heavy thrill ran down her nerves, heavy, almost pleasure, almost pain. 'What can be done?' she added.

He turned, and flipped the ash from his cigarette on to the great marble hearthstones, that lay bare in the room, without fender or bar.

'I don't know, I'm sure,' he replied. 'But I do think you've got to find some way of resolving the situation – not because you want to, but because you've *got* to, otherwise you're done. The whole of everything, and yourself included, is just on the point of caving in, and you are just holding it up with your hands. Well, it's a situation that obviously can't continue. You can't stand holding the roof up with your hands, for ever. You know that sooner or later you'll *have* to let go. Do you understand what I mean? And so something's got to be done, or there's a universal collapse – as far as you yourself are concerned.'

He shifted slightly on the hearth, crunching a cinder under his heel. He looked down at it. Gudrun was aware of the beautiful old marble panels of the fireplace, swelling softly carved, round him and above him. She felt as if she were caught at last by fate, imprisoned in some horrible and fatal trap.

'But what *can* be done?' she murmured humbly. 'You must use me if I can be of any help at all – but how can I? I don't see how I *can* help you.'

He looked down at her critically.

'I don't want you to *help*,' he said, slightly irritated, 'because there's nothing to be *done*. I only want sympathy, do you see: I want somebody I can talk to sympathetically. That eases the strain. And there *is* nobody to talk to sympathetically. That's the curious thing. There *is* nobody. There's Rupert Birkin. But then he *isn't* sympathetic, he wants to *dictate*. And that is no use whatsoever.'

She was caught in a strange snare. She looked down at her hands.

Then there was the sound of the door softly opening. Gerald started. He was chagrined. It was his starting that really startled Gudrun. Then he went forward, with quick, graceful, intentional courtesy.

'Oh, mother!' he said. 'How nice of you to come down. How are you?'

The elderly woman, loosely and bulkily wrapped in a purple gown, came forward silently, slightly hulked, as usual. Her son was at her side. He pushed her up a chair, saying 'You know Miss Brangwen, don't you?'

The mother glanced at Gudrun indifferently.

'Yes,' she said. Then she turned her wonderful, forget-me-not-blue eyes up to her son, as she slowly sat down in the chair he had brought her.

'I came to ask you about your father,' she said, in her rapid, scarcely-audible voice. 'I didn't know you had company.'

'No? Didn't Winifred tell you? Miss Brangwen stayed to dinner, to make us a little more lively – '

Mrs Crich turned slowly round to Gudrun, and looked at her, but with unseeing eyes.

'I'm afraid it would be no treat to her.' Then she turned again to her son. 'Winifred tells me the doctor had something to say about your father. What is it?'

'Only that the pulse is very weak – misses altogether a good many times – so that he might not last the night out,' Gerald replied.

Mrs Crich sat perfectly impassive, as if she had not heard. Her bulk seemed hunched in the chair, her fair hair hung slack over her ears. But her skin was clear and fine, her hands, as she sat with them forgotten and folded, were quite beautiful, full of potential energy. A great mass of energy seemed decaying up in that silent, hulking form.

She looked up at her son, as he stood, keen and soldierly, near to her. Her eyes were most wonderfully blue, bluer than forget-me-nots. She seemed to have a certain confidence in Gerald, and to feel a certain motherly mistrust of him.

'How are *you*?' she muttered, in her strangely quiet voice, as if nobody should hear but him. 'You're not getting into a state, are you? You're not letting it make you hysterical?'

The curious challenge in the last words startled Gudrun.

'I don't think so, mother,' he answered, rather coldly cheery. 'Somebody's got to see it through, you know.'

'Have they? Have they?' answered his mother rapidly. 'Why should *you* take it on yourself? What have you got to do, seeing it through. It will see itself through. You are not needed.'

'No, I don't suppose I can do any good,' he answered. 'It's just how it affects us, you see.'

'You like to be affected – don't you? It's quite nuts for you? You would have to be important. You have no need to stop at home. Why don't you go away!'

These sentences, evidently the ripened grain of many dark hours, took Gerald by surprise.

'I don't think it's any good going away now, mother, at the last minute,' he said, coldly.

'You take care,' replied his mother. 'You mind *yourself* – that's your business. You take too much on yourself. You mind *yourself*, or you'll find yourself in Queer Street, that's what will happen to you. You're hysterical, always were.'

'I'm all right, mother,' he said. 'There's no need to worry about *me*, I assure you.'

'Let the dead bury their dead – don't go and bury yourself along with them – that's what I tell you. I know you well enough.'

He did not answer this, not knowing what to say. The mother sat bunched up in silence, her beautiful white hands, that had no rings whatsoever, clasping the pommels of her armchair.

'You can't do it,' she said, almost bitterly. 'You haven't the nerve. You're as weak as a cat, really – always were. Is this young woman staying here?'

'No,' said Gerald. 'She is going home tonight.'

'Then she'd better have the dog-cart. Does she go far?'

'Only to Beldover.'

'Ah!' The elderly woman never looked at Gudrun, yet she seemed to take knowledge of her presence.

'You are inclined to take too much on yourself, Gerald,' said the mother, pulling herself to her feet, with a little difficulty.

'Will you go, mother?' he asked, politely.

'Yes, I'll go up again,' she replied. Turning to Gudrun, she bade her 'Good-night'. Then she went slowly to the door, as if she were unaccustomed to walking. At the door she lifted her face to him, implicitly. He kissed her.

'Don't come any further with me,' she said, in her barely audible voice. 'I don't want you any further.'

He bade her good-night, watched her cross to the stairs and mount slowly. Then he closed the door and came back to Gudrun. Gudrun rose also, to go.

'A queer being, my mother,' he said.

'Yes,' replied Gudrun.

'She has her own thoughts.'

'Yes,' said Gudrun.

Then they were silent.

'You want to go?' he asked. 'Half a minute, I'll just have a horse put in –'

'No,' said Gudrun. 'I want to walk.'

He had promised to walk with her down the long, lonely mile of drive, and she wanted this.

'You might *just* as well drive,' he said.

'I'd *much rather* walk,' she asserted, with emphasis.

'You would! Then I will come along with you. You know where your things are? I'll put boots on.'

He put on a cap, and an overcoat over his evening dress. They went out into the night.

'Let us light a cigarette,' he said, stopping in a sheltered angle of the porch. 'You have one too.'

So, with the scent of tobacco on the night air, they set off down the dark drive that ran between close-cut hedges through sloping meadows.

He wanted to put his arm round her. If he could put his arm round her, and draw her against him as they walked, he would equilibrate himself. For now he felt like a pair of scales, the half of which tips down and down into an indefinite void. He must recover some sort of balance. And here was the hope and the perfect recovery.

Blind to her, thinking only of himself, he slipped his arm softly round her waist, and drew her to him. Her heart fainted, feeling herself taken. But then, his arm was so strong, she quailed under its powerful close grasp. She died a little death, and was drawn against him as they walked down the stormy darkness. He seemed to balance her perfectly in opposition to himself, in their dual motion of walking. So, suddenly, he was liberated and perfect, strong, heroic.

He put his hand to his mouth and threw his cigarette away, a gleaming point, into the unseen hedge. Then he was quite free to balance her.

'That's better,' he said, with exultancy.

The exultation in his voice was like a sweetish, poisonous drug to her. Did she then mean so much to him! She sipped the poison.

'Are you happier?' she asked, wistfully.

'Much better,' he said, in the same exultant voice, 'and I was rather far gone.'

She nestled against him. He felt her all soft and warm, she was the rich, lovely substance of his being. The warmth and motion of her walk suffused through him wonderfully.

'I'm *so* glad if I help you,' she said.

'Yes,' he answered. 'There's nobody else could do it, if you wouldn't.'

'That is true,' she said to herself, with a thrill of strange, fatal elation.

As they walked, he seemed to lift her nearer and nearer to himself, till she moved upon the firm vehicle of his body. He was so strong, so sustaining, and he could not be opposed. She drifted along in a wonderful interfusion of physical motion, down the dark, blowy hillside. Far across shone the little yellow lights of Beldover, many of them, spread in a thick patch on another dark hill. But he and she were walking in perfect, isolated darkness, outside the world.

'But how much do you care for me!' came her voice, almost querulous. 'You see, I don't know, I don't understand!'

'How much!' His voice rang with a painful elation. 'I don't know either – but everything.' He was startled by his own declaration. It was true. So he stripped himself of every safeguard, in making this admission to her. He cared everything for her – she was everything.

'But I can't believe it,' said her low voice, amazed, trembling. She was trembling with doubt and exultance. This was the thing she wanted to hear, only this. Yet now she heard it, heard the strange clapping vibration of truth in his voice as he said it, she could not believe. She could not believe – she did not believe. Yet she believed, triumphantly, with fatal exultance.

'Why not?' he said. 'Why don't you believe it? It's true. It is true, as we stand at this moment – ' he stood still with her in the wind; 'I care for nothing on earth, or in heaven, outside this spot where we are. And it isn't my own presence I care about, it is all yours. I'd sell my soul a hundred times – but I couldn't bear not to have you here. I couldn't bear to be alone. My brain would burst. It is true.' He drew her closer to him, with definite movement.

'No,' she murmured, afraid. Yet this was what she wanted. Why did she so lose courage?

They resumed their strange walk. They were such strangers – and yet they were so frightfully, unthinkably near. It was like a madness. Yet it was what she wanted, it was what she wanted. They had descended the hill, and now they were coming to the square arch where the road passed under the colliery railway. The arch, Gudrun knew, had walls of squared stone, mossy on one side with water that trickled down, dry on the other side. She had stood under it to hear the train rumble thundering over the logs overhead. And she knew that under this dark and lonely bridge the young colliers stood in the darkness with their sweethearts, in rainy weather. And so she wanted to stand under the bridge with *her* sweetheart, and be kissed under the bridge in the invisible darkness. Her steps dragged as she drew near.

So, under the bridge, they came to a standstill, and he lifted her upon his breast. His body vibrated taut and powerful as he closed upon her and crushed her, breathless and dazed and destroyed, crushed her upon his breast. Ah, it was terrible, and perfect. Under this bridge, the colliers pressed their lovers to their breast. And now, under the bridge, the master of them all pressed her to himself! And how much more powerful and terrible was his embrace than theirs, how much more concentrated and supreme his love was, than theirs in the same sort! She felt she would swoon, die, under the vibrating, inhuman tension of his arms and his body – she would pass away. Then the unthinkable high vibration slackened and became more undulating. He slackened and drew her with him to stand with his back to the wall.

She was almost unconscious. So the colliers' lovers would stand with their backs to the walls, holding their sweethearts and kissing them as she was being kissed. Ah, but would their kisses be fine and powerful as the kisses of the firm-mouthed master? Even the keen, short-cut moustache – the colliers would not have that.

And the colliers' sweethearts would, like herself, hang their heads back limp over their shoulder, and look out from the dark archway, at the close patch of yellow lights on the unseen hill in the distance, or at the vague form of trees, and at the buildings of the colliery wood-yard, in the other direction.

His arms were fast around her, he seemed to be gathering her into himself, her warmth, her softness, her adorable weight, drinking in the suffusion of her physical being, avidly. He lifted her, and seemed to pour her into himself, like wine into a cup.

'This is worth everything,' he said, in a strange, penetrating voice.

So she relaxed, and seemed to melt, to flow into him, as if she were some infinitely warm and precious suffusion filling into his veins, like an intoxicant. Her arms were round his neck, he kissed her and held her perfectly suspended, she was all slack and flowing into him, and he was the firm, strong cup that receives the wine of her life. So she lay cast upon him, stranded, lifted up against him, melting and melting under his kisses, melting into his limbs and bones, as if he were soft iron becoming surcharged with her electric life.

Till she seemed to swoon, gradually her mind went, and she passed away, everything in her was melted down and fluid, and she lay still, become contained by him, sleeping in him as lightning sleeps in a pure, soft stone. So she was passed away and gone in him, and he was perfected.

When she opened her eyes again, and saw the patch of lights in the distance, it seemed to her strange that the world still existed, that she was standing under the bridge resting her head on Gerald's breast. Gerald – who was he? He was the exquisite adventure, the desirable unknown to her.

She looked up, and in the darkness saw his face above her, his shapely, male face. There seemed a faint, white light emitted from him, a white aura, as if he were a visitor from the unseen. She reached up, like Eve reaching to the apples on the tree of knowledge, and she kissed him, though her passion was a transcendent fear of the thing he was, touching his face with her infinitely delicate, encroaching, wondering fingers. Her fingers went over the mould of his face, over his features. How perfect and foreign he was – ah, how dangerous! Her soul thrilled with complete knowledge. This was the glistening, forbidden apple, this face of a man. She kissed him, putting her fingers over his face, his eyes, his nostrils, over his brows and his ears, to his neck, to know him, to gather him in by touch. He was so firm, and shapely, with such satisfying, inconceivable shapeliness, strange, yet unutterably clear. He was such an unutterable enemy, yet glistening with uncanny white fire. She wanted to touch him and touch him and touch him, till she had him all in her hands, till she had strained him into her knowledge. Ah, if she could have the precious *knowledge* of him, she would be filled, and nothing could deprive her of this. For he was so unsure, so risky in the common world of day.

'You are so *beautiful*,' she murmured in her throat.

He wondered, and was suspended. But she felt him quiver, and she came down involuntarily nearer upon him. He could not help himself. Her fingers had him under their power. The fathomless, fathomless desire they could evoke in him was deeper than death, where he had no choice.

But she knew now, and it was enough. For the time, her soul was destroyed with the exquisite shock of his invisible fluid lightning. She knew. And this knowledge was a death from which she must recover. How much more of him was there to know? Ah much, much, many days harvesting for her large, yet perfectly subtle and intelligent hands upon the field of his living, radioactive body. Ah, her hands were eager, greedy for knowledge. But for the present it was enough, enough, as much as her soul could bear. Too much, and she would shatter herself, she would fill the fine vial of her soul too quickly, and it would break. Enough now – enough for the time being. There were all the after days when her hands, like birds, could feed upon the fields of his mystical plastic form – till then enough.

And even he was glad to be checked, rebuked, held back. For to desire is better than to possess, the finality of the end was dreaded as deeply as it was desired.

They walked on towards the town, towards where the lamps threaded singly, at long intervals down the dark highroad of the valley. They came at length to the gate of the drive.

'Don't come any further,' she said.

'You'd rather I didn't?' he asked, relieved. He did not want to go up the public streets with her, his soul all naked and alight as it was.

'Much rather – good-night.' She held out her hand. He grasped it, then touched the perilous, potent fingers with his lips.

'Good-night,' he said. 'Tomorrow.'

And they parted. He went home full of the strength and the power of living desire.

But the next day, she did not come, she sent a note that she was kept indoors by a cold. Here was a torment! But he possessed his soul in some sort of patience, writing a brief answer, telling her how sorry he was not to see her.

The day after this, he stayed at home – it seemed so futile to go down to the office. His father could not live the week out. And he wanted to be at home, suspended.

Gerald sat on a chair by the window in his father's room. The landscape outside was black and winter-sodden. His father lay grey and ashen on the bed, a nurse moved silently in her white dress, neat and elegant, even beautiful. There was a scent of eau-de-cologne in the room. The nurse went out of the room, Gerald was alone with death, facing the winter-black landscape.

'Is there much more water in Denley?' came the faint voice, determined and querulous, from the bed. The dying man was asking about a leakage from Willey Water into one of the pits.

'Some more – we shall have to run off the lake,' said Gerald.

'Will you?' The faint voice filtered to extinction. There was dead stillness. The grey-faced, sick man lay with eyes closed, more dead than death. Gerald looked away. He felt his heart was seared, it would perish if this went on much longer.

Suddenly he heard a strange noise. Turning round, he saw his father's eyes wide open, strained and rolling in a frenzy of inhuman struggling. Gerald started to his feet, and stood transfixed in horror.

'Wha–a–ah–h–h!' came a horrible choking rattle from his father's throat, the fearful, frenzied eye, rolling awfully in its wild fruitless search for help, passed blindly over Gerald, then up came the dark blood and mess pumping over the face of the agonised being. The tense body relaxed, the head fell aside, down the pillow.

Gerald stood transfixed, his soul echoing in horror. He would move, but he could not. He could not move his limbs. His brain seemed to re-echo, like a pulse.

The nurse in white softly entered. She glanced at Gerald, then at the bed.

'Ah!' came her soft whimpering cry, and she hurried forward to the dead man. 'Ah-h!' came the slight sound of her agitated distress, as she stood bending over the bedside. Then she recovered, turned, and came for towel and sponge. She was wiping the dead face carefully, and murmuring, almost whimpering, very softly: 'Poor Mr Crich! – Poor Mr Crich! Poor Mr Crich!'

'Is he dead?' clanged Gerald's sharp voice.

'Oh yes, he's gone,' replied the soft, moaning voice of the nurse, as she looked up at Gerald's face. She was young and beautiful and quivering. A strange sort of grin went over Gerald's face, over the horror. And he walked out of the room.

He was going to tell his mother. On the landing he met his brother Basil.

'He's gone, Basil,' he said, scarcely able to subdue his voice, not to let an unconscious, frightening exultation sound through.

'What?' cried Basil, going pale.

Gerald nodded. Then he went on to his mother's room.

She was sitting in her purple gown, sewing, very slowly sewing, putting in a stitch then another stitch. She looked up at Gerald with her blue undaunted eyes.

'Father's gone,' he said.

'He's dead? Who says so?'

'Oh, you know, mother, if you see him.'

She put her sewing down, and slowly rose.

'Are you going to see him?' he asked.

'Yes,' she said.

By the bedside the children already stood in a weeping group.

'Oh, mother!' cried the daughters, almost in hysterics, weeping loudly.

But the mother went forward. The dead man lay in repose, as if gently asleep, so gently, so peacefully, like a young man sleeping in purity. He was still warm. She stood looking at him in gloomy, heavy silence, for some time.

'Ay,' she said bitterly, at length, speaking as if to the unseen witnesses of the air. 'You're dead.' She stood for some minutes in silence, looking down. 'Beautiful,' she asserted, 'beautiful as if life had never touched you – never touched you. God send I look different. I hope I shall look my years, when I am dead. Beautiful, beautiful,' she crooned over him. 'You can see him in his teens, with his first beard on his face. A beautiful soul, beautiful – ' Then there was a tearing in her voice as she cried: 'None of you look like this, when you are dead! Don't let it happen again.' It was a strange, wild command from out of the unknown. Her children moved unconsciously together, in a nearer group, at the dreadful command in her voice. The colour was flushed bright in her cheek, she looked awful and wonderful. 'Blame me, blame me if you like, that he lies there like a lad in his teens, with his first beard on his face. Blame me if you like. But you none of you know.' She was silent in intense silence.

Then there came, in a low, tense voice: 'If I thought that the children I bore would lie looking like that in death, I'd strangle them when they were infants, yes – '

'No, mother,' came the strange, clarion voice of Gerald from the background, 'we are different, we don't blame you.'

She turned and looked full in his eyes. Then she lifted her hands in a strange half-gesture of mad despair.

'Pray!' she said strongly. 'Pray for yourselves to God, for there's no help for you from your parents.'

'Oh mother!' cried her daughters wildly.

But she had turned and gone, and they all went quickly away from each other.

When Gudrun heard that Mr Crich was dead, she felt rebuked. She had stayed away lest Gerald should think her too easy of winning. And now, he was in the midst of trouble, whilst she was cold.

The following day she went up as usual to Winifred, who was glad to see her, glad to get away into the studio. The girl had wept, and then, too frightened, had turned aside to avoid any more tragic eventuality. She and Gudrun resumed work as usual, in the isolation of the studio, and this seemed an immeasurable happiness, a pure world of freedom, after the aimlessness and misery of the house. Gudrun stayed on till evening. She and Winifred had dinner brought up to the studio, where they ate in freedom, away from all the people in the house.

After dinner Gerald came up. The great high studio was full of shadow and a fragrance of coffee. Gudrun and Winifred had a little table near the fire at the far end, with a white lamp whose light did not travel far. They were a tiny world to themselves, the two girls surrounded by lovely shadows, the beams and rafters shadowy overhead, the benches and implements shadowy down the studio.

'You are cosy enough here,' said Gerald, going up to them.

There was a low brick fireplace, full of fire, an old blue Turkish rug, the little oak table with the lamp and the white-and-blue cloth and the dessert, and Gudrun making coffee in an odd brass coffee-maker, and Winifred scalding a little milk in a tiny saucepan.

'Have you had coffee?' said Gudrun.

'I have, but I'll have some more with you,' he replied.

'Then you must have it in a glass – there are only two cups,' said Winifred.

'It is the same to me,' he said, taking a chair and coming into the charmed circle of the girls. How happy they were, how cosy and glamorous it was with them, in a world of lofty shadows! The outside world, in which he had been transacting funeral business all the day, was completely wiped out. In an instant he snuffed glamour and magic.

They had all their things very dainty, two odd and lovely little cups, scarlet and solid gilt, and a little black jug with scarlet discs, and the curious coffee-machine, whose spirit-flame flowed steadily, almost invisibly. There was the effect of rather sinister richness, in which Gerald at once escaped himself.

They all sat down, and Gudrun carefully poured out the coffee.

'Will you have milk?' she asked calmly, yet nervously poising the little black jug with its big red dots. She was always so completely controlled, yet so bitterly nervous.

'No, I won't,' he replied.

So, with a curious humility, she placed him the little cup of coffee, and herself took the awkward tumbler. She seemed to want to serve him.

'Why don't you give me the glass – it is so clumsy for you,' he said. He would much rather have had it, and seen her daintily served. But she was silent, pleased with the disparity, with her self-abasement.

'You are quite *en ménage*,' he said.

'Yes. We aren't really at home to visitors,' said Winifred.

'You're not? Then I'm an intruder?'

For once he felt his conventional dress was out of place, he was an outsider.

Gudrun was very quiet. She did not feel drawn to talk to him. At this stage, silence was best – or mere light words. It was best to leave serious things aside. So they talked gaily and lightly, till they heard the man below lead out the horse, and call it to 'back-back!' into the dog-cart that was to take Gudrun home. So she put on her things, and shook hands with Gerald, without once meeting his eyes. And she was gone.

The funeral was detestable. Afterwards, at the tea-table, the daughters kept saying – 'He was a good father to us – the best father in the world' – or else – 'We shan't easily find another man as good as father was.'

Gerald acquiesced in all this. It was the right conventional attitude, and, as far as the world went, he believed in the conventions. He took it as a matter of course. But Winifred hated everything, and hid in the studio, and cried her heart out, and wished Gudrun would come.

Luckily everybody was going away. The Criches never stayed long at home. By dinner-time, Gerald was left quite alone. Even Winifred was carried off to London, for a few days with her sister Laura.

But when Gerald was really left alone, he could not bear it. One day passed by, and another. And all the time he was like a man hung in chains over the edge of an abyss. Struggle as he might, he could not turn himself to the solid earth, he could not get footing. He was suspended on the edge of a void, writhing. Whatever he thought of, was the abyss – whether it were friends or strangers, or work or play, it all showed him only the same bottomless void, in which his heart swung perishing. There was no escape, there was nothing to grasp hold of. He must writhe on the edge of the chasm, suspended in chains of invisible physical life.

At first he was quiet, he kept still, expecting the extremity to pass away, expecting to find himself released into the world of the living, after this extremity of penance. But it did not pass, and a crisis gained upon him.

As the evening of the third day came on, his heart rang with fear. He could not bear another night. Another night was coming on, for another night he was to be suspended in chain of physical life, over the bottomless pit of nothingness. And he could not bear it. He could not bear it. He was frightened deeply, and coldly, frightened in his soul. He did not believe in his own strength any more. He could not fall into this infinite void, and rise again. If he fell, he would be gone for ever. He must withdraw, he must seek reinforcements. He did not believe in his own single self, any further than this.

After dinner, faced with the ultimate experience of his own nothingness, he turned aside. He pulled on his boots, put on his coat, and set out to walk in the night.

It was dark and misty. He went through the wood, stumbling and feeling his way to the Mill. Birkin was away. Good – he was half glad. He turned up the hill, and stumbled blindly over the wild slopes, having lost the path in the complete darkness. It was boring. Where was he going? No matter. He stumbled on till he came to a path again. Then he went on through another wood. His mind became dark, he went on automatically. Without thought or sensation, he stumbled unevenly on, out into the open again, fumbling for stiles, losing the path, and going along the hedges of the fields till he came to the outlet.

And at last he came to the highroad. It had distracted him to struggle blindly through the maze of darkness. But now, he must take a direction. And he did not even know where he was. But he must take a direction now. Nothing would be resolved by merely walking, walking away. He had to take a direction.

He stood still on the road, that was high in the utterly dark night, and he did not know where he was. It was a strange sensation, his heart beating, and ringed round with the utterly unknown darkness. So he stood for some time.

Then he heard footsteps, and saw a small, swinging light. He immediately went towards this. It was a miner.

'Can you tell me,' he said, 'where this road goes?'

'Road? Ay, it goes ter Whatmore.'

'Whatmore! Oh thank you, that's right. I thought I was wrong. Good-night.'

'Good-night,' replied the broad voice of the miner.

Gerald guessed where he was. At least, when he came to Whatmore, he would know. He was glad to be on a highroad. He walked forward as in a sleep of decision.

That was Whatmore Village – ? Yes, the King's Head – and there the hall gates. He descended the steep hill almost running. Winding through the hollow, he passed the Grammar School, and came to Willey Green Church. The churchyard! He halted.

Then in another moment he had clambered up the wall and was going among the graves. Even in this darkness he could see the heaped pallor of old white flowers at his feet. This then was the grave. He stooped down. The flowers were cold and clammy. There was a raw scent of chrysanthemums and tube-roses, deadened. He felt the clay beneath, and shrank, it was so horribly cold and sticky. He stood away in revulsion.

Here was one centre then, here in the complete darkness beside the unseen, raw grave. But there was nothing for him here. No, he had nothing to stay here for. He felt as if some of the clay were sticking cold and unclean, on his heart. No, enough of this.

Where then? – home? Never! It was no use going there. That was less than no use. It could not be done. There was somewhere else to go. Where?

A dangerous resolve formed in his heart, like a fixed idea. There was Gudrun – she would be safe in her home. But he could get at her – he would get at her. He would not go back tonight till he had come to her, if it cost him his life. He staked his all on this throw.

He set off walking straight across the fields towards Beldover. It was so dark, nobody could ever see him. His feet were wet and cold, heavy with clay. But he went on persistently, like a wind, straight forward, as if to his fate. There were great gaps in his consciousness. He was conscious that he was at Winthorpe hamlet, but quite unconscious how he had got there. And then, as in a dream, he was in the long street of Beldover, with its street-lamps.

There was a noise of voices, and of a door shutting loudly, and being barred, and of men talking in the night. The 'Lord Nelson' had just closed, and the drinkers were going home. He had better ask one of these where she lived – for he did not know the side streets at all.

'Can you tell me where Somerset Drive is?' he asked of one of the uneven men.

'Where what?' replied the tipsy miner's voice.

'Somerset Drive.'

'Somerset Drive! – I've heard o' such a place, but I couldn't for my life say where it is. Who might you be wanting?'

'Mr Brangwen – William Brangwen.'

'William Brangwen – ?'

'Who teaches at the Grammar School, at Willey Green – his daughter teaches there too.'

'O–o–o–oh, Brangwen! *Now* I've got you. Of *course*, William Brangwen! Yes, yes, he's got two lasses as teachers, aside hisself. Ay, that's him – that's him! Why certainly I know where he lives, back your life I do! Yi – *what* place do they ca' it?'

'Somerset Drive,' repeated Gerald patiently. He knew his own colliers fairly well.

'Somerset Drive, for certain!' said the collier, swinging his arm as if catching something up. 'Somerset Drive – yi! I couldn't for my life lay hold o' the lercality o' the place. Yis, I know the place, to be sure I do – '

He turned unsteadily on his feet, and pointed up the dark, nigh-deserted road.

'You go up theer – an' you ta'e th' first – yi, th' first turnin' on your left – o' that side – past Williamses tuffy shop – '

'*I* know,' said Gerald.

'Ay! You go down a bit, past wheer th' water-man lives – and then Somerset Drive, as they ca' it, branches off on t' right-hand side – an' there's nowt but three houses in it, no more than three, I believe, – an' I'm a'most certain as theirs is th' last – th' last o' th' three – you see – '

'Thank you very much,' said Gerald. 'Good-night.'

And he started off, leaving the tipsy man there standing rooted.

Gerald went past the dark shops and houses, most of them sleeping now, and twisted round to the little blind road that ended on a field of darkness. He slowed down, as he neared his goal, not knowing how he should proceed. What if the house were closed in darkness?

But it was not. He saw a big lighted window, and heard voices, then a gate banged. His quick ears caught the sound of Birkin's voice, his keen eyes made out Birkin, with Ursula standing in a pale dress on the step of the garden path. Then Ursula stepped down, and came along the road, holding Birkin's arm.

Gerald went across into the darkness and they dawdled past him, talking happily, Birkin's voice low, Ursula's high and distinct. Gerald went quickly to the house.

The blinds were drawn before the big, lighted window of the dining-room. Looking up the path at the side he could see the door left open, shedding a soft, coloured light from the hall lamp. He went quickly and silently up the path, and looked up into the hall. There were pictures on the walls, and the antlers of a stag – and the stairs going up on one side – and just near the foot of the stairs the half-opened door of the dining-room.

With heart drawn fine, Gerald stepped into the hall, whose floor was of coloured tiles, went quickly and looked into the large, pleasant room. In a chair by the fire, the father sat asleep, his head tilted back against the side of the big oak chimney-piece, his ruddy face seen foreshortened, the nostrils open, the mouth fallen a little. It would take the merest sound to wake him.

Gerald stood a second suspended. He glanced down the passage behind him. It was all dark. Again he was suspended. Then he went swiftly upstairs. His senses were so finely, almost supernaturally keen, that he seemed to cast his own will over the half-unconscious house.

He came to the first landing. There he stood, scarcely breathing. Again, corresponding to the door below, there was a door again. That would be the mother's room. He could hear her moving about in the candle-light. She would be expecting her husband to come up. He looked along the dark landing.

Then, silently, on infinitely careful feet, he went along the passage, feeling the wall with the extreme tips of his fingers. There was a door. He stood and listened. He could hear two people's breathing. It was not that. He went stealthily forward. There was another door, slightly open. The room was in darkness. Empty. Then there was the bathroom, he could smell the soap and the heat. Then at the end another bedroom – one soft breathing. This was she.

With an almost occult carefulness he turned the door handle, and opened the door an inch. It creaked slightly. Then he opened it another inch – then another. His heart did not beat, he seemed to create a silence about himself, an obliviousness.

He was in the room. Still the sleeper breathed softly. It was very dark. He felt his way forward inch by inch, with his feet and hands. He touched the bed, he could hear the sleeper. He drew nearer, bending close as if his eyes would disclose whatever there was. And then, very near to his face, to his fear, he saw the round, dark head of a boy.

He recovered, turned round, saw the door ajar, a faint light revealed. And he retreated swiftly, drew the door to without fastening it, and passed rapidly down the passage. At the head of the stairs he hesitated. There was still time to flee.

But it was unthinkable. He would maintain his will. He turned past the door of the parental bedroom like a shadow, and was climbing the second flight of stairs. They creaked under his weight – it was exasperating. Ah what disaster, if the mother's door opened just beneath him, and she saw him! It would have to be, if it were so. He held the control still.

He was not quite up these stairs when he heard a quick running of feet below, the outer door was closed and locked, he heard Ursula's voice, then the father's sleepy exclamation. He pressed on swiftly to the upper landing.

Again a door was ajar, a room was empty. Feeling his way forward, with the tips of his fingers, travelling rapidly, like a blind man, anxious lest Ursula should come upstairs, he found another door. There, with his preternaturally fine senses alert, he listened. He heard someone moving in bed. This would be she.

Softly now, like one who has only one sense, the tactile sense, he turned the latch. It clicked. He held still. The bedclothes rustled. His heart did not beat. Then again he drew the latch back, and very gently pushed the door. It made a sticking noise as it gave.

'Ursula?' said Gudrun's voice, frightened. He quickly opened the door and pushed it behind him.

'Is it you, Ursula?' came Gudrun's frightened voice. He heard her sitting up in bed. In another moment she would scream.

'No, it's me,' he said, feeling his way towards her. 'It is I, Gerald.'

She sat motionless in her bed in sheer astonishment. She was too astonished, too much taken by surprise, even to be afraid.

'Gerald!' she echoed, in blank amazement. He had found his way to the bed, and his outstretched hand touched her warm breast blindly. She shrank away.

'Let me make a light,' she said, springing out.

He stood perfectly motionless. He heard her touch the matchbox, he heard her fingers in their movement. Then he saw her in the light of a match, which she held to the candle. The light rose in the room, then sank to a small dimness, as the flame sank down on the candle, before it mounted again.

She looked at him, as he stood near the other side of the bed. His cap was pulled low over his brow, his black overcoat was buttoned close up to his chin. His face was strange and luminous. He was inevitable as a supernatural being. When she had seen him, she knew. She knew there was something fatal in the situation, and she must accept it. Yet she must challenge him.

'How did you come up?' she asked.

'I walked up the stairs – the door was open.'

She looked at him.

'I haven't closed this door, either,' he said. She walked swiftly across the room, and closed her door, softly, and locked it. Then she came back.

She was wonderful, with startled eyes and flushed cheeks, and her plait of hair rather short and thick down her back, and her long, fine white nightdress falling to her feet.

She saw that his boots were all clayey, even his trousers were plastered with clay. And she wondered if he had made footprints all the way up. He was a very strange figure, standing in her bedroom, near the tossed bed.

'Why have you come?' she asked, almost querulous.

'I wanted to,' he replied.

And this she could see from his face. It was fate.

'You are so muddy,' she said, in distaste, but gently.

He looked down at his feet.

'I was walking in the dark,' he replied. But he felt vividly elated. There was a pause. He stood on one side of the tumbled bed, she on the other. He did not even take his cap from his brows.

'And what do you want of me?' she challenged.

He looked aside, and did not answer. Save for the extreme beauty and mystic attractiveness of this distinct, strange face, she would have sent him away. But his face was too wonderful and undiscovered to her. It fascinated her with the fascination of pure beauty, cast a spell on her, like nostalgia, an ache.

'What do you want of me?' she repeated in an estranged voice.

He pulled off his cap, in a movement of dream-liberation, and went across to her. But he could not touch her, because she stood barefoot in her nightdress, and he was muddy and damp. Her eyes, wide and large and wondering, watched him, and asked him the ultimate question.

'I came – because I must,' he said. 'Why do you ask?'

She looked at him in doubt and wonder.

'I must ask,' she said.

He shook his head slightly.

'There is no answer,' he replied, with strange vacancy.

There was about him a curious and almost godlike air of simplicity and naïve directness. He reminded her of an apparition, the young Hermes.

'But why did you come to me?' she persisted.

'Because – it has to be so. If there weren't you in the world, then *I* shouldn't be in the world, either.'

She stood looking at him, with large, wide, wondering, stricken eyes. His eyes were looking steadily into hers all the time, and he seemed fixed in an odd supernatural steadfastness. She sighed. She was lost now. She had no choice.

'Won't you take off your boots?' she said. 'They must be wet.'

He dropped his cap on a chair, unbuttoned his overcoat, lifting up his chin to unfasten the throat buttons. His short, keen hair was ruffled. He was so beautifully blond, like wheat. He pulled off his overcoat.

Quickly he pulled off his jacket, pulled loose his black tie, and was unfastening his studs, which were headed each with a pearl. She listened, watching, hoping no one would hear the starched linen crackle. It seemed to snap like pistol shots.

He had come for vindication. She let him hold her in his arms, clasp her close against him. He found in her an infinite relief. Into her he poured all his pent-up darkness and corrosive death, and he was whole again. It was wonderful, marvellous, it was a miracle. This was the ever-recurrent miracle of his life, at the knowledge of which he was lost in an ecstasy of relief and wonder. And she, subject, received him as a vessel filled with his bitter potion of death. She had no power at this crisis to resist. The terrible frictional violence of death filled her, and she received it in an ecstasy of subjection, in throes of acute, violent sensation.

As he drew nearer to her, he plunged deeper into her enveloping soft warmth, a wonderful creative heat that penetrated his veins and gave him life again. He felt himself dissolving and sinking to rest in the bath of her living strength. It seemed as if her heart in her breast were a second unconquerable sun, into the glow and creative strength of which he plunged further and further. All his veins, that were murdered and lacerated, healed softly as life came pulsing in, stealing invisibly in to him as if it were the all-powerful effluence of the sun. His blood, which seemed to have been drawn back into death, came ebbing on the return, surely, beautifully, powerfully.

He felt his limbs growing fuller and flexible with life, his body gained an unknown strength. He was a man again, strong and rounded. And he was a child, so soothed and restored and full of gratitude.

And she, she was the great bath of life, he worshipped her. Mother and substance of all life she was. And he, child and man, received of her and was made whole. His pure body was almost killed. But the miraculous, soft effluence of her breast suffused over him, over his seared, damaged brain, like a healing lymph, like a soft, soothing flow of life itself, perfect as if he were bathed in the womb again.

His brain was hurt, seared, the tissue was as if destroyed. He had not known how hurt he was, how his tissue, the very tissue of his brain was damaged by the corrosive flood of death. Now, as the healing lymph of her effluence flowed through him, he knew how destroyed he was, like a plant whose tissue is burst from inwards by a frost.

He buried his small, hard head between her breasts, and pressed her breasts against him with his hands. And she with quivering hands pressed his head against her, as he lay suffused out, and she lay fully conscious. The lovely creative warmth flooded through him like a sleep of fecundity within the womb. Ah, if only she would grant him the flow of this living effluence, he would be restored, he would be complete again. He was afraid she would deny him before it was finished. Like a child at the breast, he cleaved intensely to her, and she could not put him away. And his seared, ruined membrane relaxed, softened, that which was seared and stiff and blasted yielded again, became soft and flexible, palpitating with new life. He was infinitely grateful, as to God, or as an infant is at its mother's breast. He was glad and grateful like a delirium, as he felt his own wholeness come over him again, as he felt the full, unutterable sleep coming over him, the sleep of complete exhaustion and restoration.

But Gudrun lay wide awake, destroyed into perfect consciousness. She lay motionless, with wide eyes staring motionless into the darkness, whilst he was sunk away in sleep, his arms round her.

She seemed to be hearing waves break on a hidden shore, long, slow, gloomy waves, breaking with the rhythm of fate, so monotonously that it seemed eternal. This endless breaking of slow, sullen waves of fate held her life a possession, whilst she lay with dark, wide eyes looking into the darkness. She could see so far, as far as eternity – yet she saw nothing. She was suspended in perfect consciousness – and of what was she conscious?

This mood of extremity, when she lay staring into eternity, utterly suspended, and conscious of everything, to the last limits, passed and left her uneasy. She had lain so long motionless. She moved, she became self-conscious. She wanted to look at him, to see him.

But she dared not make a light, because she knew he would wake, and she did not want to break his perfect sleep, that she knew he had got of her.

She disengaged herself, softly, and rose up a little to look at him. There was a faint light, it seemed to her, in the room. She could just distinguish his features, as he slept the perfect sleep. In this darkness, she seemed to see him so distinctly. But he was far off, in another world. Ah, she could shriek with torment, he was so far off, and perfected, in another world. She seemed to look at him as at a pebble far away under clear dark water. And here was she, left with all the anguish of consciousness, whilst he was sunk deep into the other element of mindless, remote, living shadow-gleam. He was beautiful, far-off, and perfected. They would never be together. Ah, this awful, inhuman distance which would always be interposed between her and the other being!

There was nothing to do but to lie still and endure. She felt an overwhelming tenderness for him, and a dark, under-stirring of jealous hatred, that he should lie so perfect and immune, in an other-world, whilst she was tormented with violent wakefulness, cast out in the outer darkness.

She lay in intense and vivid consciousness, an exhausting superconsciousness. The church clock struck the hours, it seemed to her, in quick succession. She heard them distinctly in the tension of her vivid consciousness. And he slept as if time were one moment, unchanging and unmoving.

She was exhausted, wearied. Yet she must continue in this state of violent active superconsciousness. She was conscious of everything – her childhood, her girlhood, all the forgotten incidents, all the unrealised influences and all the happenings she had not understood, pertaining to herself, to her family, to her friends, her lovers, her acquaintances, everybody. It was as if she drew a glittering rope of knowledge out of the sea of darkness, drew and drew and drew it out of the fathomless depths of the past, and still it did not come to an end, there was no end to it, she must haul and haul at the rope of glittering consciousness, pull it out phosphorescent from the endless depths of the unconsciousness, till she was weary, aching, exhausted, and fit to break, and yet she had not done.

Ah, if only she might wake him! She turned uneasily. When could she rouse him and send him away? When could she disturb him? And she relapsed into her activity of automatic consciousness, that would never end.

But the time was drawing near when she could wake him. It was like a release. The clock had struck four, outside in the night. Thank God the night had passed almost away. At five he must go, and she would be released. Then she could relax and fill her own place. Now she was driven up against his perfect sleeping motion like a knife white-hot on a grindstone. There was something monstrous about him, about his juxtaposition against her.

The last hour was the longest. And yet, at last it passed. Her heart leapt with relief – yes, there was the slow, strong stroke of the church clock – at last, after this night of eternity. She waited to catch each slow, fatal reverberation. 'Three – four – five!' There, it was finished. A weight rolled off her.

She raised herself, leaned over him tenderly, and kissed him. She was sad to wake him. After a few moments, she kissed him again. But he did not stir. The darling, he was so deep in sleep! What a shame to take him out of it. She let him lie a little longer. But he must go – he must really go.

With full over-tenderness she took his face between her hands, and kissed his eyes. The eyes opened, he remained motionless, looking at her. Her heart stood still. To hide her face from his dreadful opened eyes, in the darkness, she bent down and kissed him, whispering, 'You must go, my love.'

But she was sick with terror, sick.

He put his arms round her. Her heart sank.

'But you must go, my love. It's late.'

'What time is it?' he said.

Strange, his man's voice. She quivered. It was an intolerable oppression to her.

'Past five o'clock,' she said.

But he only closed his arms round her again. Her heart cried within her in torture. She disengaged herself firmly.

'You really must go,' she said.

'Not for a minute,' he said.

She lay still, nestling against him, but unyielding.

'Not for a minute,' he repeated, clasping her closer.

'Yes,' she said, unyielding, 'I'm afraid if you stay any longer.'

There was a certain coldness in her voice that made him release her, and she broke away, rose and lit the candle. That then was the end.

He got up. He was warm and full of life and desire. Yet he felt a little bit ashamed, humiliated, putting on his clothes before her, in the candlelight. For he felt revealed, exposed to her, at a time when she was in some way against him. It was all very difficult to understand. He dressed himself quickly, without collar or tie. Still he felt full and complete, perfected. She thought it humiliating to see a man dressing: the ridiculous shirt, the ridiculous trousers and braces. But again an idea saved her.

'It is like a workman getting up to go to work,' thought Gudrun. 'And I am like a workman's wife.' But an ache like nausea was upon her: a nausea of him.

He pushed his collar and tie into his overcoat pocket. Then he sat down and pulled on his boots. They were sodden, as were his socks and trouser-bottoms. But he himself was quick and warm.

'Perhaps you ought to have put your boots on downstairs,' she said.

At once, without answering, he pulled them off again, and stood holding them in his hand. She had thrust her feet into slippers, and flung a loose robe round her. She was ready. She looked at him as he stood waiting, his black coat buttoned to the chin, his cap pulled down, his boots in his hand. And the passionate almost hateful fascination revived in her for a moment. It was not exhausted. His face was so warm-looking, wide-eyed and full of newness, so perfect. She felt old, old. She went to him heavily, to be kissed. He kissed her quickly. She wished his warm, expressionless beauty did not so fatally put a spell on her, compel her and subjugate her. It was a burden upon her, that she resented, but could not escape. Yet when she looked at his straight man's brows, and at his rather small, well-shaped nose, and at his blue, indifferent eyes, she knew her passion for him was not yet satisfied, perhaps never could be satisfied. Only now she was weary, with an ache like nausea. She wanted him gone.

They went downstairs quickly. It seemed they made a prodigious noise. He followed her as, wrapped in her vivid green wrap, she preceded him with the light. She suffered badly with fear, lest her people should be roused. He hardly cared. He did not care now who knew. And she hated this in him. One *must* be cautious. One must preserve oneself.

She led the way to the kitchen. It was neat and tidy, as the woman had left it. He looked up at the clock – twenty minutes past five. Then he sat down on a chair to put on his boots. She waited, watching his every movement. She wanted it to be over, it was a great nervous strain on her.

He stood up – she unbolted the back door, and looked out. A cold, raw night, not yet dawn, with a piece of a moon in the vague sky. She was glad she need not go out.

'Goodbye then,' he murmured.

'I'll come to the gate,' she said.

And again she hurried on in front, to warn him of the steps. And at the gate, once more she stood on the step whilst he stood below her.

'Goodbye,' she whispered.

He kissed her dutifully, and turned away.

She suffered torments hearing his firm tread going so distinctly down the road. Ah, the insensitiveness of that firm tread!

She closed the gate, and crept quickly and noiselessly back to bed. When she was in her room, and the door closed, and all safe, she breathed freely, and a great weight fell off her. She nestled down in bed, in the groove his body had made, in the warmth he had left. And excited, worn-out, yet still satisfied, she fell soon into a deep, heavy sleep.

Gerald walked quickly through the raw darkness of the coming dawn. He met nobody. His mind was beautifully still and thoughtless, like a still pool, and his body full and warm and rich. He went quickly along towards Shortlands, in a grateful self-sufficiency.

CHAPTER 25

Marriage or Not

The Brangwen family was going to move from Beldover. It was necessary now for the father to be in town.

Birkin had taken out a marriage licence, yet Ursula deferred from day to day. She would not fix any definite time – she still wavered. Her month's notice to leave the Grammar School was in its third week. Christmas was not far off.

Gerald waited for the Ursula–Birkin marriage. It was something crucial to him.

'Shall we make it a double-barrelled affair?' he said to Birkin one day.

'Who for the second shot?' asked Birkin.

'Gudrun and me,' said Gerald, the venturesome twinkle in his eyes.

Birkin looked at him steadily, as if somewhat taken aback.

'Serious – or joking?' he asked.

'Oh, serious. Shall I? Shall Gudrun and I rush in along with you?'

'Do by all means,' said Birkin. 'I didn't know you'd got that length.'

'What length?' said Gerald, looking at the other man, and laughing.

'Oh yes, we've gone all the lengths.'

'There remains to put it on a broad social basis, and to achieve a high moral purpose,' said Birkin.

'Something like that: the length and breadth and height of it,' replied Gerald, smiling.

'Oh well,' said Birkin, 'it's a very admirable step to take, I should say.'

Gerald looked at him closely.

'Why aren't you enthusiastic?' he asked. 'I thought you were such dead nuts on marriage.'

Birkin lifted his shoulders.

'One might as well be dead nuts on noses. There are all sorts of noses, snub and otherwise – '

Gerald laughed.

'And all sorts of marriage, also snub and otherwise?' he said.

'That's it.'

'And you think if I marry, it will be snub?' asked Gerald quizzically, his head a little on one side.

Birkin laughed quickly.

'How do I know what it will be!' he said. 'Don't lambaste me with my own parallels – '

Gerald pondered a while.

'But I should like to know your opinion, exactly,' he said.

'On your marriage? – or marrying? Why should you want my opinion? I've got no opinions. I'm not interested in legal marriage, one way or another. It's a mere question of convenience.'

Still Gerald watched him closely.

'More than that, I think,' he said seriously. 'However you may be bored by the ethics of marriage, yet really to marry, in one's own personal case, is something critical, final – '

'You mean there is something final in going to the registrar with a woman?'

'If you're coming back with her, I do,' said Gerald. 'It is in some way irrevocable.'

'Yes, I agree,' said Birkin.

'No matter how one regards legal marriage, yet to enter into the married state, in one's own personal instance, is final – '

'I believe it is,' said Birkin, 'somewhere.'

'The question remains then, should one do it,' said Gerald.

Birkin watched him narrowly, with amused eyes.

'You are like Lord Bacon, Gerald,' he said. 'You argue it like a lawyer – or like Hamlet's to-be-or-not-to-be. If I were you I would *not* marry: but ask Gudrun, not me. You're not marrying me, are you?'

Gerald did not heed the latter part of this speech.

'Yes,' he said, 'one must consider it coldly. It is something critical. One comes to the point where one must take a step in one direction or another. And marriage is one direction – '

'And what is the other?' asked Birkin quickly.

Gerald looked up at him with hot, strangely-conscious eyes, that the other man could not understand.

'I can't say,' he replied. 'If I knew *that* – ' He moved uneasily on his feet, and did not finish.

'You mean if you knew the alternative?' asked Birkin. 'And since you don't know it, marriage is a *pis aller*.'

Gerald looked up at Birkin with the same hot, constrained eyes.

'One does have the feeling that marriage is a *pis aller*,' he admitted.

'Then don't do it,' said Birkin. 'I tell you,' he went on, 'the same as I've said before, marriage in the old sense seems to me repulsive. *Égoïsme à deux* is nothing to it. It's a sort of tacit hunting in couples: the world all in couples, each couple in its own little house, watching its own little interests, and stewing in its own little privacy – it's the most repulsive thing on earth.'

'I quite agree,' said Gerald. 'There's something inferior about it. But as I say, what's the alternative.'

'One should avoid this *home* instinct. It's not an instinct, it's a habit of cowardliness. One should never have a *home*.'

'I agree really,' said Gerald. 'But there's no alternative.'

'We've got to find one. I do believe in a permanent union between a man and a woman. Chopping about is merely an exhaustive process. But a permanent relation between a man and a woman isn't the last word – It certainly isn't.'

'Quite,' said Gerald.

'In fact,' said Birkin, 'because the relation between man and woman is made the supreme and exclusive relationship, that's where all the tightness and meanness and insufficiency comes in.'

'Yes, I believe you,' said Gerald.

'You've got to take down the love and-marriage ideal from its pedestal. We want something broader. I believe in the *additional* perfect relationship between man and man – additional to marriage.'

'I can never see how they can be the same,' said Gerald.

'Not the same – but equally important, equally creative, equally sacred, if you like.'

'I know,' said Gerald, 'you believe something like that. Only I can't *feel* it, you see.' He put his hand on Birkin's arm, with a sort of deprecating affection. And he smiled as if triumphantly.

He was ready to be doomed. Marriage was like a doom to him. He was willing to condemn himself in marriage, to become like a convict condemned to the mines of the underworld, living no life in the sun, but having a dreadful subterranean activity. He was willing to accept this. And marriage was the seal of his condemnation. He was willing to be sealed thus in the underworld, like a soul damned but living for ever in damnation. But he would not make any pure relationship with any other soul. He could not. Marriage was not the committing of himself into a relationship with Gudrun. It was a committing of himself in acceptance of the established world, he would accept the established order, in which he did not livingly believe, and then he would retreat to the underworld for his life. This he would do.

The other way was to accept Rupert's offer of alliance, to enter into the bond of pure trust and love with the other man, and then subsequently with the woman. If he pledged himself with the man he would later be able to pledge himself with the woman: not merely in legal marriage, but in absolute, mystic marriage.

Yet he could not accept the offer. There was a numbness upon him, a numbness either of unborn, absent volition, or of atrophy. Perhaps it was the absence of volition. For he was strangely elated at Rupert's offer. Yet he was still more glad to reject it, not to be committed.

CHAPTER 26

A Chair

There was a jumble market every Monday afternoon in the old market-place in town. Ursula and Birkin strayed down there one afternoon. They had been talking of furniture, and they wanted to see if there was any fragment they would like to buy, amid the heaps of rubbish collected on the cobble-stones.

The old market-square was not very large, a mere bare patch of granite setts, usually with a few fruit-stalls under a wall. It was in a poor quarter of the town. Meagre houses stood down one side, there was a hosiery factory, a great blank with myriad oblong windows, at the end, a street of little shops with flagstone pavement down the other side, and, for a crowning monument, the public baths, of new red brick, with a clock-tower. The people who moved about seemed stumpy and sordid, the air seemed to smell rather dirty, there was a sense of many mean streets ramifying off into warrens of meanness. Now and again a great chocolate-and-yellow tramcar ground round a difficult bend under the hosiery factory.

Ursula was superficially thrilled when she found herself out among the common people, in the jumbled place piled with old bedding, heaps of old iron, shabby crockery in pale lots, muffled lots of unthinkable clothing. She and Birkin went unwillingly down the narrow aisle between the rusty wares. He was looking at the goods, she at the people.

She excitedly watched a young woman, who was going to have a baby, and who was turning over a mattress and making a young man, down-at-heel and dejected, feel it also. So secretive and active and anxious the young woman seemed, so reluctant, slinking, the young man. He was going to marry her because she was having a child.

When they had felt the mattress, the young woman asked the old man seated on a stool among his wares, how much it was. He told her, and she turned to the young man. The latter was ashamed, and self-conscious. He turned his face away, though he left his body standing there, and muttered aside. And again the woman anxiously and actively fingered the mattress and added up in her mind and bargained with the old, unclean man. All the while, the young man stood by, shamefaced and down-at-heel, submitting.

'Look,' said Birkin, 'there is a pretty chair.'

'Charming!' cried Ursula. 'Oh, charming.'

It was an armchair of simple wood, probably birch, but of such fine delicacy of grace, standing there on the sordid stones, it almost brought tears to the eyes. It was square in shape, of the purest, slender lines, and four short lines of wood in the back, that reminded Ursula of harp-strings.

'It was once,' said Birkin, 'gilded – and it had a cane seat. Somebody has nailed this wooden seat in. Look, here is a trifle of the red that underlay the gilt. The rest is all black, except where the wood is worn pure and glossy. It is the fine unity of the lines that is so attractive. Look, how they run and meet and counteract. But of course the wooden seat is wrong – it destroys the perfect lightness and unity in tension the cane gave. I like it though – '

'Ah yes,' said Ursula, 'so do I.'

'How much is it?' Birkin asked the man.

'Ten shillings.'

'And you will send it – ?'

It was bought.

'So beautiful, so pure!' Birkin said. 'It almost breaks my heart.' They walked along between the heaps of rubbish. 'My beloved country – it had something to express even when it made that chair.'

'And hasn't it now?' asked Ursula. She was always angry when he took this tone.

'No, it hasn't. When I see that clear, beautiful chair, and I think of England, even Jane Austen's England – it had living thoughts to unfold even then, and pure happiness in unfolding them. And now, we can only fish among the rubbish heaps for the remnants of their old expression. There is no production in us now, only sordid and foul mechanicalness.'

'It isn't true,' cried Ursula. 'Why must you always praise the past, at the expense of the present? *Really*, I don't think so much of Jane Austen's England. It was materialistic enough, if you like – '

'It could afford to be materialistic,' said Birkin, 'because it had the power to be something other – which we haven't. We are materialistic because we haven't the power to be anything else – try as we may, we can't bring off anything but materialism: mechanism, the very soul of materialism.'

Ursula was subdued into angry silence. She did not heed what he said. She was rebelling against something else.

'And I hate your past. I'm sick of it,' she cried. 'I believe I even hate that old chair, though it *is* beautiful. It isn't *my* sort of beauty. I wish it had been smashed up when its day was over, not left to preach the beloved past to us. I'm sick of the beloved past.'

'Not so sick as I am of the accursed present,' he said.

'Yes, just the same. I hate the present – but I don't want the past to take its place – I don't want that old chair.'

He was rather angry for a moment. Then he looked at the sky shining beyond the tower of the public baths, and he seemed to get over it all. He laughed.

'All right,' he said, 'then let us not have it. I'm sick of it all, too. At any rate one can't go on living on the old bones of beauty.'

'One can't,' she cried. 'I *don't* want old things.'

'The truth is, we don't want things at all,' he replied. 'The thought of a house and furniture of my own is hateful to me.'

This startled her for a moment. Then she replied, 'So it is to me. But one must live somewhere.'

'Not somewhere – anywhere,' he said. 'One should just live anywhere – not have a definite place. I don't want a definite place. As soon as you get a room, and it is *complete*, you want to run from it. Now my rooms at the Mill are quire complete, I want them at the bottom of the sea. It is a horrible tyranny of a fixed milieu, where each piece of furniture is a commandment-stone.'

She clung to his arm as they walked away from the market.

'But what are we going to do?' she said. 'We must live somehow. And I do want some beauty in my surroundings. I want a sort of natural *grandeur* even, *splendour*.'

'You'll never get it in houses and furniture – or even clothes. Houses and furniture and clothes, they are all terms of an old base world, a detestable society of man. And if you have a Tudor house and old, beautiful furniture, it is only the past perpetuated on top of you, horrible. And if you have a perfect modern house done for you by Poiret, it is something else perpetuated on top of you. It is all horrible. It is all possessions, possessions, bullying you and turning you into a generalisation. You have to be like Rodin, Michelangelo, and leave a piece of raw rock unfinished to your figure. You must leave your surroundings sketchy, unfinished, so that you are never contained, never confined, never dominated from the outside.'

She stood in the street contemplating.

'And we are never to have a complete place of our own – never a home?' she said.

'Pray God, in this world, no,' he answered.

'But there's only this world,' she objected.

He spread out his hands with a gesture of indifference.

'Meanwhile, then, we'll avoid having things of our own,' he said.

'But you've just bought a chair,' she said.

'I can tell the man I don't want it,' he replied.

She pondered again. Then a queer little movement twitched her face.

'No,' she said, 'we don't want it. I'm sick of old things.'

'New ones as well,' he said.

They retraced their steps.

There – in front of some furniture, stood the young couple, the woman who was going to have a baby, and the narrow-faced youth. She was fair, rather short, stout. He was of medium height, attractively built. His dark hair fell sideways over his brow, from under his cap, he stood strangely aloof, like one of the damned.

'Let us give it to *them*,' whispered Ursula. 'Look, they are getting a home together.'

'*I* won't aid and abet them in it,' he said petulantly, instantly sympathising with the aloof, furtive youth, against the active, procreant female.

'Oh yes,' cried Ursula. 'It's right for them – there's nothing else for them.'

'Very well,' said Birkin, 'you offer it to them. I'll watch.'

Ursula went rather nervously to the young couple, who were discussing an iron washstand – or rather, the man was glancing furtively and wonderingly, like a prisoner, at the abominable article, whilst the woman was arguing.

'We bought a chair,' said Ursula, 'and we don't want it. Would you have it? We should be glad if you would.'

The young couple looked round at her, not believing that she could be addressing them.

'Would you care for it?' repeated Ursula. 'It's really *very* pretty – but – but – ' she smiled rather dazzlingly.

The young couple only stared at her, and looked significantly at each other, to know what to do. And the man curiously obliterated himself, as if he could make himself invisible, as a rat can.

'We wanted to *give* it to you,' explained Ursula, now overcome with confusion and dread of them. She was attracted by the young man. He was a still, mindless creature, hardly a man at all, a creature that the towns have produced, strangely pure-bred and fine in one sense, furtive, quick, subtle. His lashes were dark and long and fine over his eyes, that had no mind in them, only a dreadful kind of subject, inward consciousness, glazed and dark. His dark brows and all his lines were finely drawn. He would be a dreadful, but wonderful lover to a woman, so marvellously contributed. His legs would be marvellously subtle and alive, under the shapeless trousers, he had some of the fineness and stillness and silkiness of a dark-eyed, silent rat.

Ursula had apprehended him with a fine *frisson* of attraction. The full-built woman was staring offensively. Again Ursula forgot him.

'Won't you have the chair?' she said.

The man looked at her with a sideways look of appreciation, yet far-off, almost insolent. The woman drew herself up. There was a certain costermonger richness about her. She did not know what Ursula was after, she was on her guard, hostile. Birkin approached, smiling wickedly at seeing Ursula so non-plussed and frightened.

'What's the matter?' he said, smiling. His eyelids had dropped slightly, there was about him the same suggestive, mocking secrecy that was in the bearing of the two city creatures. The man jerked his head a little on one side, indicating Ursula, and said, with curious amiable, jeering warmth, 'What she warnt? – eh?' An odd smile writhed his lips.

Birkin looked at him from under his slack, ironical eyelids.

'To give you a chair – that – with the label on it,' he said, pointing.

The man looked at the object indicated. There was a curious hostility in male, outlawed understanding between the two men.

'What's she warnt to give it *us* for, guv'nor,' he replied, in a tone of free intimacy that insulted Ursula.

'Thought you'd like it – it's a pretty chair. We bought it and don't want it. No need for you to have it, don't be frightened,' said Birkin, with a wry smile.

The man glanced up at him, half inimical, half recognising.

'Why don't you want it for yourselves, if you've just bought it?' asked the woman coolly. ''Taint good enough for you, now you've had a look at it. Frightened it's got something in it, eh?'

She was looking at Ursula, admiringly, but with some resentment.

'I'd never thought of that,' said Birkin. 'But no, the wood's too thin everywhere.'

'You see,' said Ursula, her face luminous and pleased. '*We* are just going to get married, and we thought we'd buy things. Then we decided, just now, that we wouldn't have furniture, we'd go abroad.'

The full-built, slightly blowsy city girl looked at the fine face of the other woman, with appreciation. They appreciated each other. The youth stood aside, his face expressionless and timeless, the thin line of the black moustache drawn strangely suggestive over his rather wide, closed mouth. He was impassive, abstract, like some dark suggestive presence, a gutter-presence.

'It's all right to be some folks,' said the city girl, turning to her own young man. He did not look at her, but he smiled with the lower part of his face, putting his head aside in an odd gesture of assent. His eyes were unchanging, glazed with darkness.

'Cawsts something to change your mind,' he said, in an incredibly low accent.

'Only ten shillings this time,' said Birkin.

The man looked up at him with a grimace of a smile, furtive, unsure.

'Cheap at 'arf a quid, guv'nor,' he said. 'Not like getting divawced.'

'We're not married yet,' said Birkin.

'No, no more aren't we,' said the young woman loudly. 'But we shall be, a Saturday.'

Again she looked at the young man with a determined, protective look, at once overbearing and very gentle. He grinned sicklily, turning away his head. She had got his manhood, but Lord, what did he care! He had a strange furtive pride and slinking singleness.

'Good luck to you,' said Birkin.

'Same to you,' said the young woman. Then, rather tentatively: 'When's yours coming off, then?'

Birkin looked round at Ursula.

'It's for the lady to say,' he replied. 'We go to the registrar the moment she's ready.'

Ursula laughed, covered with confusion and bewilderment.

'No 'urry,' said the young man, grinning suggestive.

'Oh, don't break your neck to get there,' said the young woman. ' 'Slike when you're dead – you're a long time married.'

The young man turned aside as if this hit him.

'The longer the better, let us hope,' said Birkin.

'That's it, guv'nor,' said the young man admiringly. 'Enjoy it while it larsts – niver whip a dead donkey.'

'Only when he's shamming dead,' said the young woman, looking at her young man with caressive tenderness of authority.

'Aw, there's a difference,' he said satirically.

'What about the chair?' said Birkin.

'Yes, all right,' said the woman.

They trailed off to the dealer, the handsome but abject young fellow hanging a little aside.

'That's it,' said Birkin. 'Will you take it with you, or have the address altered?'

'Oh, Fred can carry it. Make him do what he can for the dear old 'ome.'

'Mike use of 'im,' said Fred, grimly humorous, as he took the chair from the dealer. His movements were graceful, yet curiously abject, slinking.

' 'Ere's mother's cosy chair,' he said. 'Warnts a cushion.' And he stood it down on the market stones.

'Don't you think it's pretty?' laughed Ursula.

'Oh, I do,' said the young woman.

' 'Ave a sit in it, you'll wish you'd kept it,' said the young man.

Ursula promptly sat down in the middle of the market-place.

'Awfully comfortable,' she said. 'But rather hard. You try it.' She invited the young man to a seat. But he turned uncouthly, awkwardly aside, glancing up at her with quick bright eyes, oddly suggestive, like a quick, live rat.

'Don't spoil him,' said the young woman. 'He's not used to armchairs, 'e isn't.'

The young man turned away, and said, with averted grin, 'Only warnts legs on 'is.'

The four parted. The young woman thanked them.

'Thank you for the chair – it'll last till it gives way.'

'Keep it for an ornyment,' said the young man.

'Good-afternoon – good-afternoon,' said Ursula and Birkin.

'Goo'-luck to you,' said the young man, glancing and avoiding Birkin's eyes, as he turned aside his head.

The two couples went asunder, Ursula clinging to Birkin's arm. When they had gone some distance, she glanced back and saw the young man going beside the full, easy young woman. His trousers sank over his heels, he moved with a sort of slinking evasion, more crushed with odd self-consciousness now he had the slim old armchair to carry, his arm over the back, the four fine, square tapering legs swaying perilously near the granite setts of the pavement. And yet he was somewhere indomitable and separate, like a quick, vital rat. He had a queer, subterranean beauty, repulsive too.

'How strange they are!' said Ursula.

'Children of men,' he said. 'They remind me of Jesus: "The meek shall inherit the earth." '

'But they aren't the meek,' said Ursula.

'Yes, I don't know why, but they are,' he replied.

They waited for the tramcar. Ursula sat on top and looked out on the town. The dusk was just dimming the hollows of crowded houses.

'And are they going to inherit the earth?' she said.

'Yes – they.'

'Then what are we going to do?' she asked. 'We're not like them – are we? We're not the meek?'

'No. We've got to live in the chinks they leave us.'

'How horrible!' cried Ursula. 'I don't want to live in chinks.'

'Don't worry,' he said. 'They are the children of men, they like market-places and street-corners best. That leaves plenty of chinks.'

'All the world,' she said.

'Ah no – but some room.'

The tramcar mounted slowly up the hill, where the ugly winter-grey masses of houses looked like a vision of hell that is cold and angular. They sat and looked. Away in the distance was an angry redness of sunset. It was all cold, somehow small, crowded, and like the end of the world.

'I don't mind it even then,' said Ursula, looking at the repulsiveness of it all. 'It doesn't concern me.'

'No more it does,' he replied, holding her hand. 'One needn't see. One goes one's way. In my world it is sunny and spacious – '

'It is, my love, isn't it?' she cried, hugging near to him on the top of the tramcar, so that the other passengers stared at them.

'And we will wander about on the face of the earth,' he said, 'and we'll look at the world beyond just this bit.'

There was a long silence. Her face was radiant like gold, as she sat thinking.

'I don't want to inherit the earth,' she said. 'I don't want to inherit anything.'

He closed his hand over hers.

'Neither do I. I want to be disinherited.'

She clasped his fingers closely.

'We won't care about *anything*,' she said.

He sat still, and laughed.

'And we'll be married, and have done with them,' she added.

Again he laughed.

'It's one way of getting rid of everything,' she said, 'to get married.'

'And one way of accepting the whole world,' he added.

'A whole other world, yes,' she said happily.

'Perhaps there's Gerald – and Gudrun – ' he said.

'If there is there is, you see,' she said. 'It's no good our worrying. We can't really alter them, can we?'

'No,' he said. 'One has no right to try – not with the best intentions in the world.'

'Do you try to force them?' she asked.

'Perhaps,' he said. 'Why should I want him to be free, if it isn't his business?'

She paused for a time.

'We can't *make* him happy, anyhow,' she said. 'He'd have to be it of himself.'

'I know,' he said. 'But we want other people with us, don't we?'

'Why should we?' she asked.

'I don't know,' he said uneasily. 'One has a hankering after a sort of further fellowship.'

'But why?' she insisted. 'Why should you hanker after other people? Why should you need them?'

This hit him right on the quick. His brows knitted.

'Does it end with just our two selves?' he asked, tense.

'Yes – what more do you want? If anybody likes to come along, let them. But why must you run after them?'

His face was tense and unsatisfied.

'You see,' he said, 'I always imagine our being really happy with some few other people – a little freedom with people.'

She pondered for a moment.

'Yes, one does want that. But it must *happen*. You can't do anything for it with your will. You always seem to think you can *force* the flowers to come out. People must love us because they love us – you can't *make* them.'

'I know,' he said. 'But must one take no steps at all? Must one just go as if one were alone in the world – the only creature in the world?'

'You've got me,' she said. 'Why should you *need* others? Why must you force people to agree with you? Why can't you be single by yourself, as you are always saying? You try to bully Gerald – as you tried to bully Hermione. You must learn to be alone. And it's so horrid of you. You've got me. And yet you want to force other people to love you as well. You do try to bully them to love you. And even then, you don't want their love.'

His face was full of real perplexity.

'Don't I?' he said. 'It's the problem I can't solve. I *know* I want a perfect and complete relationship with you: and we've nearly got it – we really have. But beyond that. *Do* I want a real, ultimate relationship with Gerald? Do I want a final, almost extra-human relationship with him – a relationship in the ultimate of me and him – or don't I?'

She looked at him for a long time, with strange bright eyes, but she did not answer.

CHAPTER 27

Flitting

That evening Ursula returned home very bright-eyed and wondrous – which irritated her people. Her father came home at supper-time, tired after the evening class, and the long journey home. Gudrun was reading, the mother sat in silence.

Suddenly Ursula said to the company at large, in a bright voice, 'Rupert and I are going to be married tomorrow.'

Her father turned round, stiffly.

'You what?' he said.

'Tomorrow!' echoed Gudrun.

'Indeed!' said the mother.

But Ursula only smiled wonderfully, and did not reply.

'Married tomorrow!' cried her father harshly. 'What are you talking about?'

'Yes,' said Ursula. 'Why not?' Those two words, from her, always drove him mad. 'Everything is all right – we shall go to the registrar's office – '

There was a second's hush in the room, after Ursula's blithe vagueness.

'*Really*, Ursula!' said Gudrun.

'Might we ask why there has been all this secrecy?' demanded the mother, rather superbly.

'But there hasn't,' said Ursula. 'You knew.'

'Who knew?' now cried the father. 'Who knew? What do you mean by your "you knew"?'

He was in one of his stupid rages, she instantly closed against him.

'Of course you knew,' she said coolly. 'You knew we were going to get married.'

There was a dangerous pause.

'We knew you were going to get married, did we? Knew! Why, does anybody know anything about you, you shifty bitch!'

'Father!' cried Gudrun, flushing deep in violent remonstrance. Then, in a cold, but gentle voice, as if to remind her sister to be tractable: 'But isn't it a *fearfully* sudden decision, Ursula?' she asked.

'No, not really,' replied Ursula, with the same maddening cheerfulness. 'He's been *wanting* me to agree for weeks – he's had the licence ready. Only I – I wasn't ready in myself. Now I am ready – is there anything to be disagreeable about?'

'Certainly not,' said Gudrun, but in a tone of cold reproof. 'You are perfectly free to do as you like.'

' "Ready in yourself" – *yourself*, that's all that matters, isn't it! "I wasn't ready in myself," ' he mimicked her phrase offensively. 'You and *yourself*, you're of some importance, aren't you?'

She drew herself up and set back her throat, her eyes shining yellow and dangerous.

'I am to myself,' she said, wounded and mortified. 'I know I am not to anybody else. You only wanted to *bully* me – you never cared for my happiness.'

He was leaning forward watching her, his face intense like a spark.

'Ursula, what are you saying? Keep your tongue still,' cried her mother

Ursula swung round, and the lights in her eyes flashed.

'No, I won't,' she cried. 'I won't hold my tongue and be bullied. What does it matter which day I get married – what does it *matter*! It doesn't affect anybody but myself.'

Her father was tense and gathered together like a cat about to spring.

'Doesn't it?' he cried, coming nearer to her. She shrank away.

'No, how can it?' she replied, shrinking but stubborn.

'It doesn't matter to *me* then, what you do – what becomes of you?' he cried, in a strange voice like a cry.

The mother and Gudrun stood back as if hypnotised.

'No,' stammered Ursula. Her father was very near to her. 'You only want to –'

She knew it was dangerous, and she stopped. He was gathered together, every muscle ready.

'What?' he challenged.

'Bully me,' she muttered, and even as her lips were moving, his hand had caught her smack at the side of the face and she was sent up against the door.

'Father!' cried Gudrun in a high voice, 'it is impossible!'

He stood unmoving. Ursula recovered, her hand was on the door handle. She slowly drew herself up. He seemed doubtful now.

'It's true,' she declared, with brilliant tears in her eyes, her head lifted up in defiance. 'What has your love meant, what did it ever mean? – bullying, and denial – it did –'

He was advancing again with strange, tense movements, and clenched fist, and the face of a murderer. But swift as lightning she had flashed out of the door, and they heard her running upstairs.

He stood for a moment looking at the door. Then, like a defeated animal, he turned and went back to his seat by the fire.

Gudrun was very white. Out of the intense silence, the mother's voice was heard saying, cold and angry, 'Well, you shouldn't take so much notice of her.'

Again the silence fell, each followed a separate set of emotions and thoughts.

Suddenly the door opened again: Ursula, dressed in hat and furs, with a small valise in her hand: 'Goodbye!' she said, in her maddening, bright, almost mocking tone. 'I'm going.'

And in the next instant the door was closed, they heard the outer door, then her quick steps down the garden path, then the gate banged, and her light footfall was gone. There was a silence like death in the house.

Ursula went straight to the station, hastening heedlessly on winged feet. There was no train, she must walk on to the junction. As she went through the darkness, she began to cry, and she wept bitterly, with a dumb, heart-broken, child's anguish, all the way on the road, and in the train. Time passed unheeded and unknown, she did not know where she was, nor what was taking place. Only she wept from fathomless depths of hopeless, hopeless grief, the terrible grief of a child, that knows no extenuation.

Yet her voice had the same defensive brightness as she spoke to Birkin's landlady at the door.

'Good-evening! Is Mr Birkin in? Can I see him?'

'Yes, he's in. He's in his study.'

Ursula slipped past the woman. His door opened. He had heard her voice.

'Hello!' he exclaimed in surprise, seeing her standing there with the valise in her hand, and marks of tears on her face. She was one who wept without showing many traces, like a child.

'Do I look a sight?' she said, shrinking.

'No – why? Come in,' he took the bag from her hand and they went into the study.

There – immediately, her lips began to tremble like those of a child that remembers again, and the tears came rushing up.

'What's the matter?' he asked, taking her in his arms. She sobbed violently on his shoulder, whilst he held her still, waiting.

'What's the matter?' he said again, when she was quieter. But she only pressed her face further into his shoulder, in pain, like a child that cannot tell.

'What is it, then?' he asked.

Suddenly she broke away, wiped her eyes, regained her composure, and went and sat in a chair.

'Father hit me,' she announced, sitting bunched up, rather like a ruffled bird, her eyes very bright.

'What for?' he said.

She looked away, and would not answer. There was a pitiful redness about her sensitive nostrils, and her quivering lips.

'Why?' he repeated, in his strange, soft, penetrating voice.

She looked round at him, rather defiantly.

'Because I said I was going to be married tomorrow, and he bullied me.'

'Why did he bully you?'

Her mouth dropped again, she remembered the scene once more, the tears came up.

'Because I said he didn't care – and he doesn't, it's only his domineeringness that's hurt – ' she said, her mouth pulled awry by her weeping, all the time she spoke, so that he almost smiled, it seemed so childish. Yet it was not childish, it was a mortal conflict, a deep wound.

'It isn't quite true,' he said. 'And even so, you shouldn't *say* it.'

'It *is* true – it *is* true,' she wept, 'and I won't be bullied by his pretending it's love – when it *isn't* – he doesn't care, how can he – no, he can't – '

He sat in silence. She moved him beyond himself.

'Then you shouldn't rouse him, if he can't,' replied Birkin quietly.

'And I *have* loved him, I have,' she wept. 'I've loved him always, and he's always done this to me, he has – '

'It's been a love of opposition, then,' he said. 'Never mind – it will be all right. It's nothing desperate.'

'Yes,' she wept, 'it is, it is '

'Why?'

'I shall never see him again – '

'Not immediately. Don't cry, you had to break with him, it had to be – don't cry.'

He went over to her and kissed her fine, fragile hair, touching her wet cheeks gently.

'Don't cry,' he repeated, 'don't cry any more.'

He held her head close against him, very close and quiet.

At last she was still. Then she looked up, her eyes wide and frightened.

'Don't you want me?' she asked.

'Want you?' His darkened, steady eyes puzzled her and did not give her play.

'Do you wish I hadn't come?' she asked, anxious now again for fear she might be out of place.

'No,' he said. 'I wish there hadn't been the violence – so much ugliness – but perhaps it was inevitable.'

She watched him in silence. He seemed deadened.

'But where shall I stay?' she asked, feeling humiliated.

He thought for a moment.

'Here, with me,' he said. 'We're married as much today as we shall be tomorrow.'

'But – '

'I'll tell Mrs Varley,' he said. 'Never mind now.'

He sat looking at her. She could feel his darkened steady eyes looking at her all the time. It made her a little bit frightened. She pushed her hair off her forehead nervously.

'Do I look ugly?' she said.

And she blew her nose again.

A small smile came round his eyes.

'No,' he said, 'fortunately.'

And he went across to her, and gathered her like a belonging in his arms. She was so tenderly beautiful, he could not bear to see her, he could only bear to hide her against himself. Now, washed all clean by her tears, she was new and frail like a flower just unfolded, a flower so new, so tender, so made perfect by inner light, that he could not bear to look at her, he must hide her against himself, cover his eyes against her. She had the perfect candour of creation, something translucent and simple, like a radiant, shining flower that moment unfolded in primal blessedness. She was so new, so wonder-clear, so undimmed. And he was so old, so steeped in heavy memories. Her soul was new, undefined and glimmering with the unseen. And his soul was dark and gloomy, it had only one grain of living hope, like a grain of mustard seed. But this one living grain in him matched the perfect youth in her.

'I love you,' he whispered as he kissed her, and trembled with pure hope, like a man who is born again to a wonderful, lively hope far exceeding the bounds of death.

She could not know how much it meant to him, how much he meant by the few words. Almost childish, she wanted proof, and statement, even over-statement, for everything seemed still uncertain, unfixed to her.

But the passion of gratitude with which he received her into his soul, the extreme, unthinkable gladness of knowing himself living and fit to unite with her, he, who was so nearly dead, who was so near to being gone with the rest of his race down the slope of mechanical death, could never be understood by her. He worshipped her as age worships youth, he gloried in her, because, in his one grain of faith, he was young as she, he was her proper mate. This marriage with her was his resurrection and his life.

All this she could not know. She wanted to be made much of, to be adored. There were infinite distances of silence between them. How could he tell her of the immanence of her beauty, that was not form, or weight, or colour, but something like a strange, golden light! How could he know himself what her beauty lay in, for him. He said 'Your nose is beautiful, your chin is adorable.' But it sounded like lies, and she was disappointed, hurt. Even when he said, whispering with truth, 'I love you, I love you,' it was not the real truth. It was something beyond love, such a gladness of having surpassed oneself, of having transcended the old existence. How could he say 'I' when he was something new and unknown, not himself at all? This I, this old formula of the age, was a dead letter.

In the new, superfine bliss, a peace superseding knowledge, there was no I and you, there was only the third, unrealised wonder, the wonder of existing not as oneself, but in a consummation of my being and of her being in a new one, a new, paradisal unit regained from the duality. Nor can I say 'I love you,' when I have ceased to be, and you have ceased to be: we are both caught up and transcended into a new oneness where everything is silent, because there is nothing to answer, all is perfect and at one. Speech travels between the separate parts. But in the perfect One there is perfect silence of bliss.

They were married by law on the next day, and she did as he bade her, she wrote to her father and mother. Her mother replied, not her father.

She did not go back to school. She stayed with Birkin in his rooms, or at the Mill, moving with him as he moved. But she did not see anybody, save Gudrun and Gerald. She was all strange and wondering as yet, but relieved as by dawn.

Gerald sat talking to her one afternoon in the warm study down at the Mill. Rupert had not yet come home.

'You are happy?' Gerald asked her, with a smile.

'Very happy!' she cried, shrinking a little in her brightness.

'Yes, one can see it.'

'Can one?' cried Ursula in surprise.

He looked up at her with a communicative smile.

'Oh yes, plainly.'

She was pleased. She meditated a moment.

'And can you see that Rupert is happy as well?'

He lowered his eyelids, and looked aside.

'Oh yes,' he said.

'Really!'

'Oh yes.'

He was very quiet, as if it were something not to be talked about by him. He seemed sad.

She was very sensitive to suggestion. She asked the question he wanted her to ask.

'Why don't you be happy as well?' she said. 'You could be just the same.'

He paused a moment.

'With Gudrun?' he asked.

'Yes!' she cried, her eyes glowing. But there was a strange tension, an emphasis, as if they were asserting their wishes, against the truth.

'You think Gudrun would have me, and we should be happy?' he said.

'Yes, I'm *sure*!' she cried.

Her eyes were round with delight. Yet underneath she was constrained, she knew her own insistence.

'Oh, I'm *so* glad,' she added.

He smiled.

'What makes you glad?' he said.

'For *her* sake,' she replied. 'I'm sure you'd – you're the right man for her.'

'You are?' he said. 'And do you think she would agree with you?'

'Oh yes!' she exclaimed hastily. Then, upon reconsideration, very uneasy: 'Though Gudrun isn't so very simple, is she? One doesn't know her in five minutes, does one? She's not like me in that.' She laughed at him with her strange, open, dazzled face.

'You think she's not much like you?' Gerald asked.

She knitted her brows.

'Oh, in many ways she is. But I never know what she will do when anything new comes.'

'You don't?' said Gerald. He was silent for some moments. Then he moved tentatively. 'I was going to ask her, in any case, to go away with me at Christmas,' he said, in a very small, cautious voice.

'Go away with you? For a time, you mean?'

'As long as she likes,' he said, with a deprecating movement.

They were both silent for some minutes.

'Of course,' said Ursula at last, 'she *might* just be willing to rush into marriage. You can see.'

'Yes,' smiled Gerald. 'I can see. But in case she won't – do you think she would go abroad with me for a few days – or for a fortnight?'

'Oh yes,' said Ursula. 'I'd ask her.'

'Do you think we might all go together?'

'All of us?' Again Ursula's face lighted up. 'It would be rather fun, don't you think?'

'Great fun,' he said.

'And then you could see,' said Ursula.

'What?'

'How things went. I think it is best to take the honeymoon before the wedding – don't you?'

She was pleased with this *mot*. He laughed.

'In certain cases,' he said. 'I'd rather it were so in my own case.'

'Would you!' exclaimed Ursula. Then doubtingly, 'Yes, perhaps you're right. One should please oneself.'

Birkin came in a little later, and Ursula told him what had been said.

'Gudrun!' exclaimed Birkin. 'She's a born mistress, just as Gerald is a born lover – *amant en titre*. If as somebody says all women are either wives or mistresses, then Gudrun is a mistress.'

'And all men either lovers or husbands,' cried Ursula. 'But why not both?'

'The one excludes the other,' he laughed.

'Then I want a lover,' cried Ursula.

'No you don't,' he said.

'But I do,' she wailed.

He kissed her, and laughed.

It was two days after this that Ursula was to go to fetch her things from the house in Beldover. The removal had taken place, the family had gone. Gudrun had rooms in Willey Green.

Ursula had not seen her parents since her marriage. She wept over the rupture, yet what was the good of making it up! Good or not good, she could not go to them. So her things had been left behind and she and Gudrun were to walk over for them, in the afternoon.

It was a wintry afternoon, with red in the sky, when they arrived at the house. The windows were dark and blank, already the place was frightening. A stark, void entrance-hall struck a chill to the hearts of the girls.

'I don't believe I dare have come in alone,' said Ursula. 'It frightens me.'

'Ursula!' cried Gudrun. 'Isn't it amazing! Can you believe you lived in this place and never felt it? How I lived here a day without dying of terror, I cannot conceive!'

They looked in the big dining-room. It was a good-sized room, but now a cell would have been lovelier. The large bay windows were naked, the floor was stripped, and a border of dark polish went round the tract of pale boarding.

In the faded wallpaper were dark patches where furniture had stood, where pictures had hung. The sense of walls, dry, thin, flimsy-seeming walls, and a flimsy flooring, pale with its artificial black edges, was neutralising to the mind. Everything was null to the senses, there was enclosure without substance, for the walls were dry and papery. Where were they standing, on earth, or suspended in some cardboard box? In the hearth was burnt paper, and scraps of half-burnt paper.

'Imagine that we passed our days here!' said Ursula.

'I know,' cried Gudrun. 'It is too appalling. What must we be like, if we are the contents of *this*!'

'Vile!' said Ursula. 'It really is.'

And she recognised half-burnt covers of *Vogue* half-burnt representations of women in gowns – lying under the grate.

They went to the drawing-room. Another piece of shut-in air; without weight or substance, only a sense of intolerable papery imprisonment in nothingness. The kitchen did look more substantial, because of the red-tiled floor and the stove, but it was cold and horrid.

The two girls tramped hollowly up the bare stairs. Every sound re-echoed under their hearts. They tramped down the bare corridor. Against the wall of Ursula's bedroom were her things – a trunk, a work-basket, some books, loose coats, a hat box, standing desolate in the universal emptiness of the dusk.

'A cheerful sight, aren't they?' said Ursula, looking down at her forsaken possessions.

'Very cheerful,' said Gudrun.

The two girls set to, carrying everything down to the front door. Again and again they made the hollow, re-echoing transit. The whole place seemed to resound about them with a noise of hollow, empty futility. In the distance the empty, invisible rooms sent forth a vibration almost of obscenity. They almost fled with the last articles, into the out-of-door.

But it was cold. They were waiting for Birkin, who was coming with the car. They went indoors again, and upstairs to their parents' front bedroom, whose windows looked down on the road, and across the country at the black-barred sunset, black and red barred, without light.

They sat down in the window-seat, to wait. Both girls were looking over the room. It was void, with a meaninglessness that was almost dreadful.

'Really,' said Ursula, 'this room *couldn't* be sacred, could it?'

Gudrun looked over it with slow eyes.

'Impossible,' she replied.

'When I think of their lives – father's and mother's, their love, and their marriage, and all of us children, and our bringing-up – would you have such a life, Prune?'

'I wouldn't, Ursula.'

'It all seems so *nothing* – their two lives – there's no meaning in it. Really, if they had *not* met, and *not* married, and not lived together – it wouldn't have mattered, would it?'

'Of course – you can't tell,' said Gudrun.

'No. But if I thought my life was going to be like it – Prune,' she caught Gudrun's arm, 'I should run.'

Gudrun was silent for a few moments.

'As a matter of fact, one cannot contemplate the ordinary life – one cannot contemplate it,' replied Gudrun. 'With you, Ursula, it is quite different. You will be out of it all, with Birkin. He's a special case. But with the ordinary man, who has his life fixed in one place, marriage is just impossible. There may be, and there *are*, thousands of women who want it, and could conceive of nothing else. But the very thought of it sends me *mad*. One must be free, above all, one must be free. One may forfeit everything else, but one must be free – one must not become 7, Pinchbeck Street – or Somerset Drive – or Shortlands. No man will be sufficient to make that good – no man! To marry, one must have a free lance, or nothing, a comrade-in-arms, a *Glücksritter*. A man with a position in the social world – well, it is just impossible, impossible!'

'What a lovely word – a *Glücksritter*!' said Ursula. 'So much nicer than a soldier of fortune.'

'Yes, isn't it?' said Gudrun. 'I'd tilt the world with a *Glücksritter*. But a home, an establishment! Ursula, what would it mean? – think!'

'I know,' said Ursula. 'We've had one home – that's enough for me.'

'Quite enough,' said Gudrun.

'The little grey home in the west,' quoted Ursula ironically.

'Doesn't it sound grey, too,' said Gudrun grimly.

They were interrupted by the sound of the car. There was Birkin. Ursula was surprised that she felt so lit up, that she became suddenly so free from the problems of grey homes in the west.

They heard his heels click on the hall pavement below.

'Hello!' he called, his voice echoing alive through the house. Ursula smiled to herself. *He* was frightened of the place too.

'Hello! Here we are,' she called downstairs. And they heard him quickly running up.

'This is a ghostly situation,' he said.

'These houses don't have ghosts – they've never had any personality, and only a place with personality can have a ghost,' said Gudrun.

'I suppose so. Are you both weeping over the past?'

'We are,' said Gudrun, grimly.

Ursula laughed.

'Not weeping that it's gone, but weeping that it ever *was*,' she said.

'Oh,' he replied, relieved.

He sat down for a moment. There was something in his presence, Ursula thought, lambent and alive. It made even the impertinent structure of this null house disappear.

'Gudrun says she could not bear to be married and put into a house,' said Ursula meaningful – they knew this referred to Gerald.

He was silent for some moments.

'Well,' he said, 'if you know beforehand you couldn't stand it, you're safe.'

'Quite!' said Gudrun.

'Why *does* every woman think her aim in life is to have a hubby and a little grey home in the west? Why is this the goal of life? Why should it be?' said Ursula.

'*Il faut avoir le respect de ses bêtises,*' said Birkin

'But you needn't have the respect for the *bêtise* before you've committed it,' laughed Ursula.

'Ah then, *des bêtises du papa?*'

'*Et de la maman,*' added Gudrun satirically.

'*Et des voisins,*' said Ursula.

They all laughed, and rose. It was getting dark. They carried the things to the car. Gudrun locked the door of the empty house. Birkin had lighted the lamps of the automobile. It all seemed very happy, as if they were setting out.

'Do you mind stopping at Coulsons. I have to leave the key there,' said Gudrun.

'Right,' said Birkin, and they moved off.

They stopped in the main street. The shops were just lighted, the last miners were passing home along the causeways, half-visible shadows in their grey pit-dirt, moving through the blue air. But their feet rang harshly in manifold sound, along the pavement.

How pleased Gudrun was to come out of the shop, and enter the car, and be borne swiftly away into the downhill of palpable dusk, with Ursula and Birkin! What an adventure life seemed at this moment! How deeply, how suddenly she envied Ursula! Life for her was so quick, and an open door – so reckless as if not only this world, but the world that was gone and the world to come were nothing to her. Ah, if she could be *just like that*, it would be perfect.

For always, except in her moments of excitement, she felt a want within herself. She was unsure. She had felt that now, at last, in Gerald's strong and violent love, she was living fully and finally. But when she compared herself with Ursula, already her soul was jealous, unsatisfied. She was not satisfied – she was never to be satisfied.

What was she short of now? It was marriage – it was the wonderful stability of marriage. She did want it, let her say what she might. She had been lying. The old idea of marriage was right even now – marriage and the home. Yet her mouth gave a little grimace at the words. She thought of Gerald and Shortlands – marriage and the home! Ah well, let it rest! He meant a great deal to her – but – ! Perhaps it was not in her to marry. She was one of life's outcasts, one of the drifting lives that have no root. No, no it could not be so. She suddenly conjured up a rosy room, with herself in a beautiful gown, and a handsome man in evening dress who held her in his arms in the firelight, and kissed her. This picture she entitled 'Home'. It would have done for the Royal Academy.

'Come with us to tea – *do*,' said Ursula, as they ran nearer to the cottage of Willey Green.

'Thanks awfully – but I *must* go in – ' said Gudrun. She wanted very much to go on with Ursula and Birkin.

That seemed like life indeed to her. Yet a certain perversity would not let her.

'Do come – yes, it would be so nice,' pleaded Ursula.

'I'm awfully sorry – I should love to – but I can't – really – '

She descended from the car in trembling haste.

'Can't you really!' came Ursula's regretful voice.

'No, really I can't,' responded Gudrun's pathetic, chagrined words out of the dusk.

'All right, are you?' called Birkin.

'Quite!' said Gudrun. 'Good-night!'

'Good-night,' they called.

'Come whenever you like, we shall be glad,' called Birkin.

'Thank you very much,' called Gudrun, in the strange, twanging voice of lonely chagrin that was very puzzling to him. She turned away to her cottage gate, and they drove on. But immediately she stood to watch them, as the car ran vague into the distance. And as she went up the path to her strange house, her heart was full of incomprehensible bitterness.

In her parlour was a long-case clock, and inserted into its dial was a ruddy, round, slant-eyed, joyous-painted face, that wagged over with the most ridiculous ogle when the clock ticked, and back again with the same absurd glad-eye at the next tick. All the time the absurd smooth, brown-ruddy face gave her an obtrusive 'glad-eye'. She stood for minutes, watching it, till a sort of maddened disgust overcame her, and she laughed at herself hollowly. And still it rocked, and gave her the glad-eye from one side, then from the other, from one side, then from the other. Ah, how unhappy she was! In the midst of her most active happiness, ah, how unhappy she was! She glanced at the table. Gooseberry jam, and the same home-made cake with too much soda in it! Still, gooseberry jam was good, and one so rarely got it.

All the evening she wanted to go to the Mill. But she coldly refused to allow herself. She went the next afternoon instead. She was happy to find Ursula alone. It was a lovely, intimate secluded atmosphere. They talked endlessly and delightedly. 'Aren't you *fearfully* happy here?' said Gudrun to her sister glancing at her own bright eyes in the mirror. She always envied, almost with resentment, the strange positive fullness that subsisted in the atmosphere around Ursula and Birkin.

'How really beautifully this room is done,' she said aloud. 'This hard plaited matting – what a lovely colour it is, the colour of cool light!'

And it seemed to her perfect.

'Ursula,' she said at length, in a voice of question and detachment, 'did you know that Gerald Crich had suggested our going away all together at Christmas?'

'Yes, he's spoken to Rupert.'

A deep flush dyed Gudrun's cheek. She was silent a moment, as if taken aback, and not knowing what to say.

'But don't you think,' she said at last, 'it is *amazingly cool*!'

Ursula laughed.

'I like him for it,' she said.

Gudrun was silent. It was evident that, whilst she was almost mortified by Gerald's taking the liberty of making such a suggestion to Birkin, yet the idea itself attracted her strongly.

'There's a rather lovely simplicity about Gerald, I think,' said Ursula, 'so defiant, somehow! Oh, I think he's *very* lovable.'

Gudrun did not reply for some moments. She had still to get over the feeling of insult at the liberty taken with her freedom.

'What did Rupert say – do you know?' she asked.

'He said it would be most awfully jolly,' said Ursula.

Again Gudrun looked down, and was silent.

'Don't you think it would?' said Ursula, tentatively. She was never quite sure how many defences Gudrun was having round herself.

Gudrun raised her face with difficulty and held it averted.

'I think it *might* be awfully jolly, as you say,' she replied. 'But don't you think it was an unpardonable liberty to take – to talk of such things to Rupert – who after all – you see what I mean, Ursula – they might have been two men arranging an outing with some little *type* they'd picked up. Oh, I think it's unforgivable, quite!' She used the French word '*type*'.

Her eyes flashed, her soft face was flushed and sullen. Ursula looked on, rather frightened, frightened most of all because she thought Gudrun seemed rather common, really like a little *type*. But she had not the courage quite to think this – not right out.

'Oh no,' she cried, stammering. 'Oh no – not at all like that – oh no! No, I think it's rather beautiful, the friendship between Rupert and Gerald. They just are simple – they say anything to each other, like brothers.'

Gudrun flushed deeper. She could not *bear* it that Gerald gave her away – even to Birkin.

'But do you think even brothers have any right to exchange confidences of that sort?' she asked, with deep anger.

'Oh yes,' said Ursula. 'There's never anything said that isn't perfectly straightforward. No, the thing that's amazed me most in Gerald – how perfectly simple and direct he can be! And you know, it takes rather a big man. Most of them *must* be indirect, they are such cowards.'

But Gudrun was still silent with anger. She wanted the absolute secrecy kept, with regard to her movements.

'Won't you go?' said Ursula. 'Do, we might all be so happy! There is something I *love* about Gerald – he's *much* more lovable than I thought him. He's free, Gudrun, he really is.'

Gudrun's mouth was still closed, sullen and ugly. She opened it at length.

'Do you know where he proposes to go?' she asked.

'Yes – to the Tyrol, where he used to go when he was in Germany – a lovely place where students go, small and rough and lovely, for winter sport!'

Through Gudrun's mind went the angry thought – 'they know everything'.

'Yes,' she said aloud, 'about forty kilometres from Innsbruck, isn't it?'

'I don't know exactly where – but it would be lovely, don't you think, high in the perfect snow – ?'

'Very lovely!' said Gudrun, sarcastically.

Ursula was put out.

'Of course,' she said, 'I think Gerald spoke to Rupert so that it shouldn't seem like an outing with a *type* – '

'I know, of course,' said Gudrun, 'that he quite commonly does take up with that sort.'

'Does he!' said Ursula. 'Why how do you know?'

'I know of a model in Chelsea,' said Gudrun coldly.

Now Ursula was silent.

'Well,' she said at last, with a doubtful laugh, 'I hope he has a good time with her.' At which Gudrun looked more glum.

CHAPTER 28

Gudrun in the Pompadour

Christmas drew near, all four prepared for flight. Birkin and Ursula were busy packing their few personal things, making them ready to be sent off, to whatever country and whatever place they might choose at last. Gudrun was very much excited. She loved to be on the wing.

She and Gerald, being ready first, set off via London and Paris to Innsbruck, where they would meet Ursula and Birkin. In London they stayed one night. They went to the music-hall, and afterwards to the Pompadour Café.

Gudrun hated the Café, yet she always went back to it, as did most of the artists of her acquaintance. She loathed its atmosphere of petty vice and petty jealousy and petty art. Yet she always called in again, when she was in town. It was as if she *had* to return to this small, slow, central whirlpool of disintegration and dissolution: just give it a look.

She sat with Gerald drinking some sweetish liqueur, and staring with black, sullen looks at the various groups of people at the tables. She would greet nobody, but young men nodded to her frequently, with a kind of sneering familiarity. She cut them all. And it gave her pleasure to sit there, cheeks flushed, eyes black and sullen, seeing them all objectively, as put away from her, like creatures in some menagerie of apish degraded souls. God, what a foul crew they were! Her blood beat black and thick in her veins with rage and loathing. Yet she must sit and watch, watch. One or two people came to speak to her. From every side of the Café, eyes turned half furtively, half jeeringly at her, men looking over their shoulders, women under their hats.

The old crowd was there, Carlyon in his corner with his pupils and his girl, Halliday and Libidnikov and the Pussum – they were all there. Gudrun watched Gerald. She watched his eyes linger a moment on Halliday, on Halliday's party. These last were on the look-out – they nodded to him, he nodded again. They giggled and whispered among themselves. Gerald watched them with the steady twinkle in his eyes. They were urging the Pussum to something.

She at last rose. She was wearing a curious dress of dark silk splashed and spattered with different colours, a curious motley effect. She was thinner, her eyes were perhaps hotter, more disintegrated. Otherwise she was just the same. Gerald watched her with the same steady twinkle in his eyes as she came across. She held out her thin brown hand to him.

'How are you?' she said.

He shook hands with her, but remained seated, and let her stand near him, against the table. She nodded blackly to Gudrun, whom she did not know to speak to, but well enough by sight and reputation.

'I am very well,' said Gerald. 'And you?'

'Oh I'm all wight. What about Wupert?'

'Rupert? He's very well, too.'

'Yes, I don't mean that. What about him being married?'

'Oh – yes, he is married.'

The Pussum's eyes had a hot flash.

'Oh, he's weally bwought it off then, has he? When was he married?'

'A week or two ago.'

'Weally! He's never written.'

'No.'

'No. Don't you think it's too bad?'

This last was in a tone of challenge. The Pussum let it be known by her tone, that she was aware of Gudrun's listening.

'I suppose he didn't feel like it,' replied Gerald.

'But why didn't he?' pursued the Pussum.

This was received in silence. There was an ugly, mocking persistence in the small, beautiful figure of the short-haired girl, as she stood near Gerald.

'Are you staying in town long?' she asked.

'Tonight only.'

'Oh, only tonight. Are you coming over to speak to Julius?'

'Not tonight.'

'Oh very well. I'll tell him then.' Then came her touch of diablerie. 'You're looking awf'lly fit.'

'Yes – I feel it.' Gerald was quite calm and easy, a spark of satiric amusement in his eye.

'Are you having a good time?'

This was a direct blow for Gudrun, spoken in a level, toneless voice of callous ease.

'Yes,' he replied, quite colourlessly.

'I'm awf'lly sorry you aren't coming round to the flat. You aren't very faithful to your fwiends.'

'Not very,' he said.

She nodded them both 'Good-night', and went back slowly to her own set. Gudrun watched her curious walk, stiff and jerking at the loins. They heard her level, toneless voice distinctly.

'He won't come over; – he is otherwise engaged,' it said. There was more laughter and lowered voices and mockery at the table.

'Is she a friend of yours?' said Gudrun, looking calmly at Gerald.

'I've stayed at Halliday's flat with Birkin,' he said, meeting her slow, calm eyes. And she knew that the Pussum was one of his mistresses – and he knew she knew.

She looked round, and called for the waiter. She wanted an iced cocktail, of all things. This amused Gerald – he wondered what was up.

The Halliday party was tipsy, and malicious. They were talking out loudly about Birkin, ridiculing him on every point, particularly on his marriage.

'Oh, *don't* make me think of Birkin,' Halliday was squealing. 'He makes me perfectly sick. He is as bad as Jesus. "Lord, *what* must I do to be saved!" '

He giggled to himself tipsily.

'Do you remember,' came the quick voice of the Russian, 'the letters he used to send. "Desire is holy – " '

'Oh yes!' cried Halliday. 'Oh, how perfectly splendid. Why, I've got one in my pocket. I'm sure I have.'

He took out various papers from his pocket book.

'I'm sure I've – *hic! Oh dear!* – got one.'

Gerald and Gudrun were watching absorbedly.

'Oh yes, how perfectly – *hic!* – splendid! Don't make me laugh, Pussum, it gives me the hiccup. *Hic!* – ' They all giggled.

'What did he say in that one?' the Pussum asked, leaning forward, her dark, soft hair falling and swinging against her face. There was something curiously indecent, obscene, about her small, longish, dark skull, particularly when the ears showed.

'Wait – oh do wait! *No-o*, I won't give it to you, I'll read it aloud. I'll read you the choice bits – *hic!* Oh dear! Do you think if I drink water it would take off this hiccup? *Hic!* Oh, I feel perfectly helpless.'

'Isn't that the letter about uniting the dark and the light – and the Flux of Corruption?' asked Maxim, in his precise, quick voice.

'I believe so,' said the Pussum.

'Oh is it? I'd forgotten – *hic!* – it was that one,' Halliday said, opening the letter. '*Hic!* Oh yes. How perfectly splendid! This is one of the best. "There is a phase in every race – " ' he read in the singsong, slow, distinct voice of a clergyman reading the Scriptures, ' "when the desire for destruction overcomes every other desire. In the individual, this desire is ultimately a desire for destruction in the self" – *hic!* – ' he paused and looked up.

'I hope he's going ahead with the destruction of himself,' said the quick voice of the Russian. Halliday giggled, and lolled his head back, vaguely.

'There's not much to destroy in him,' said the Pussum. 'He's so thin already, there's only a fag-end to start on.'

'Oh, isn't it beautiful! I love reading it! I believe it has cured my hiccup!' squealed Halliday. 'Do let me go on. "It is a desire for the reduction process in oneself, a reducing back to the origin, a return along the Flux of Corruption, to the original rudimentary conditions of being – !" Oh, but I *do* think it is wonderful. It almost supersedes the Bible –'

'Yes – Flux of Corruption,' said the Russian, 'I remember that phrase.'

'Oh, he was always talking about Corruption,' said the Pussum. 'He must be corrupt himself, to have it so much on his mind.'

'Exactly!' said the Russian.

'Do let me go on! Oh, this is a perfectly wonderful piece! But do listen to this. "And in the great retrogression, the reducing back of the created body of life, we get knowledge, and beyond knowledge, the phosphorescent ecstasy of acute sensation." Oh, I do think these phrases are too absurdly wonderful. Oh but don't you think they *are* – they're nearly as good as Jesus. "And if, Julius, you want this ecstasy of reduction with the Pussum, you must go on till it is fulfilled. But surely there is in you also, somewhere, the living desire for positive creation, relationships in ultimate faith, when all this process of active corruption, with all its flowers of mud, is transcended, and more or less finished – " I do wonder what the flowers of mud are. Pussum, you are a flower of mud.'

'Thank you – and what are you?'

'Oh, I'm another, surely, according to this letter! We're all flowers of mud – *Fleurs – hic! du mal!* It's perfectly wonderful, Birkin harrowing Hell – harrowing the Pompadour – *Hic!*'

'Go on – go on,' said Maxim. 'What comes next? It's really very interesting.'

'I think it's awful cheek to write like that,' said the Pussum.

'Yes – yes, so do I,' said the Russian. 'He is a megalomaniac, of course, it is a form of religious mania. He thinks he is the Saviour of man – go on reading.'

'Surely,' Halliday intoned, ' "surely goodness and mercy hath followed me all the days of my life – " ' he broke off and giggled. Then he began again, intoning like a clergyman. ' "Surely there will come an end in us to this desire – for the constant going apart – this passion for putting asunder – everything – ourselves, reducing ourselves part from part – reacting in intimacy only for destruction – using sex as a great reducing agent, reducing the two great elements of male and female from their highly complex unity – reducing the old ideas, going back to the savages for our sensations – always seeking to *lose* ourselves in some ultimate black sensation, mindless and infinite – burning only with destructive fires, raging on with the hope of being burnt out utterly – " '

'I want to go,' said Gudrun to Gerald, as she signalled the waiter. Her eyes were flashing, her cheeks were flushed. The strange effect of Birkin's letter read aloud in a perfect clerical singsong, clear and resonant, phrase by phrase, made the blood mount into her head as if she were mad.

She rose, whilst Gerald was paying the bill, and walked over to Halliday's table. They all glanced up at her.

'Excuse me,' she said. 'Is that a genuine letter you are reading?'

'Oh yes,' said Halliday. 'Quite genuine.'

'May I see?'

Smiling foolishly he handed it to her, as if hypnotised.

'Thank you,' she said.

And she turned and walked out of the Café with the letter, all down the brilliant room, between the tables, in her measured fashion. It was some moments before anybody realised what was happening.

From Halliday's table came half articulate cries, then somebody booed, then all the far end of the place began booing after Gudrun's retreating form. She was fashionably dressed in blackish-green and silver, her hat was brilliant green, like the sheen on an insect, but the brim was soft dark green, a falling edge with fine silver, her coat was dark green, lustrous, with a high collar of grey fur, and great fur cuffs, the edge of her dress showed silver and black velvet, her stockings and shoes were silver grey. She moved with slow, fashionable indifference to the door. The porter opened obsequiously for her, and, at her nod, hurried to the edge of the pavement and whistled for a taxi. The two lights of a vehicle almost immediately curved round towards her, like two eyes.

Gerald had followed in wonder, amid all the booing, not having caught her misdeed. He heard the Pussum's voice saying, 'Go and get it back from her. I never heard of such a thing! Go and get it back from her. Tell Gerald Crich – there he goes – go and make him give it up.'

Gudrun stood at the door of the taxi, which the man held open for her.

'To the hotel?' she asked, as Gerald came out, hurriedly.

'Where you like,' he answered.

'Right!' she said. Then to the driver, 'Wagstaff's – Barton Street.'

The driver bowed his head, and put down the flag.

Gudrun entered the taxi, with the deliberate cold movement of a woman who is well-dressed and contemptuous in her soul. Yet she was frozen with overwrought feelings. Gerald followed her.

'You've forgotten the man,' she said coolly, with a slight nod of her hat. Gerald gave the porter a shilling. The man saluted. They were in motion.

'What was all the row about?' asked Gerald, in wondering excitement.

'I walked away with Birkin's letter,' she said, and he saw the crushed paper in her hand.

His eyes glittered with satisfaction.

'Ah!' he said. 'Splendid! A set of jackasses!'

'I could have *killed* them!' she cried in passion. '*Dogs!* – they are dogs! Why is Rupert such a *fool* as to write such letters to them? Why does he give himself away to such *canaille*? It's a thing that *cannot be borne*.'

Gerald wondered over her strange passion.

And she could not rest any longer in London. They must go by the morning train from Charing Cross. As they drew over the bridge, in the train, having glimpses of the river between the great iron girders, she cried, 'I feel I could *never* see this foul town again – I couldn't *bear* to come back to it.'

CHAPTER 29

Continental

Ursula went on in an unreal suspense, the last weeks before going away. She was not herself – she was not anything. She was something that is going to be – soon – soon – very soon. But as yet, she was only imminent.

She went to see her parents. It was a rather stiff, sad meeting, more like a verification of separateness than a reunion. But they were all vague and indefinite with one another, stiffened in the fate that moved them apart.

She did not really come to until she was on the ship crossing from Dover to Ostend. Dimly she had come down to London with Birkin, London had been a vagueness, so had the train-journey to Dover. It was all like a sleep.

And now, at last, as she stood in the stern of the ship, in a pitch-dark, rather blowy night, feeling the motion of the sea, and watching the small, rather desolate little lights that twinkled on the shores of England, as on the shores of nowhere, watched them sinking smaller and smaller on the profound and living darkness, she felt her soul stirring to awake from its anaesthetic sleep.

'Let us go forward, shall we?' said Birkin. He wanted to be at the tip of their projection. So they left off looking at the faint sparks that glimmered out of nowhere, in the far distance, called England, and turned their faces to the unfathomed night in front.

They went right to the bows of the softly plunging vessel. In the complete obscurity, Birkin found a comparatively sheltered nook, where a great rope was coiled up. It was quite near the very point of the ship, near the black, unpierced space ahead. There they sat down, folded together, folded round with the same rug, creeping in nearer and ever nearer to one another, till it seemed they had crept right into each other, and become one substance. It was very cold, and the darkness was palpable.

One of the ship's crew came along the deck, dark as the darkness, not really visible. They then made out the faintest pallor of his face. He felt their presence, and stopped, unsure – then bent forward. When his face was near them, he saw the faint pallor of their faces. Then he withdrew like a phantom. And they watched him without making any sound.

They seemed to fall away into the profound darkness. There was no sky, no earth, only one unbroken darkness, into which, with a soft, sleeping motion, they seemed to fall like one closed seed of life falling through dark, fathomless space.

They had forgotten where they were, forgotten all that was and all that had been, conscious only in their heart, and there conscious only of this pure trajectory through the surpassing darkness. The ship's prow cleaved on, with a faint noise of cleavage, into the complete night, without knowing, without seeing, only surging on.

In Ursula the sense of the unrealised world ahead triumphed over everything. In the midst of this profound darkness, there seemed to glow on her heart the effulgence of a paradise unknown and unrealised. Her heart was full of the most wonderful light, golden like honey of darkness, sweet like the warmth of day, a light which was not shed on the world, only on the unknown paradise towards which she was going, a sweetness of habitation, a delight of living quite unknown, but hers infallibly. In her transport she lifted her face suddenly to him, and he touched it with his lips. So cold, so fresh, so sea-clear her face was, it was like kissing a flower that grows near the surf.

But he did not know the ecstasy of bliss in foreknowledge that she knew. To him, the wonder of this transit was overwhelming. He was falling through a gulf of infinite darkness, like a meteorite plunging across the chasm between the worlds. The world was torn in two, and he was plunging like an unlit star through the ineffable rift. What was beyond was not yet for him. He was overcome by the trajectory.

In a trance he lay enfolding Ursula round about. His face was against her fine, fragile hair, he breathed its fragrance with the sea and the profound night. And his soul was at peace; yielded, as he fell into the unknown. This was the first time that an utter and absolute peace had entered his heart, now, in this final transit out of life.

When there came some stir on the deck, they roused. They stood up. How stiff and cramped they were, in the night-time! And yet the paradisal glow on her heart, and the unutterable peace of darkness in his, this was the all-in-all.

They stood up and looked ahead. Low lights were seen down the darkness. This was the world again. It was not the bliss of her heart, nor the peace of his. It was the superficial unreal world of fact. Yet not quite the old world. For the peace and the bliss in their hearts was enduring.

Strange, and desolate above all things, like disembarking from the Styx into the desolated underworld, was this landing at night. There was the raw, half-lighted, covered-in vastness of the dark place, boarded and hollow underfoot, with only desolation everywhere. Ursula had caught sight of the big, pallid, mystic letters 'OSTEND', standing in the darkness. Everybody was hurrying with a blind, insect-like intentness through the dark grey air, porters were calling in un-English English, then trotting with heavy bags, their colourless blouses looking ghostly as they disappeared; Ursula stood at a long, low, zinc-covered barrier, along with hundreds of other spectral people, and all the way down the vast, raw darkness was this low stretch of open bags and spectral people, whilst, on the other side of the barrier, pallid officials in peaked caps and moustaches were turning the underclothing in the bags, then scrawling a chalk-mark.

It was done. Birkin snapped the hand bags, off they went, the porter coming behind. They were through a great doorway, and in the open night again – ah, a railway platform! Voices were still calling in inhuman agitation through the dark-grey air, spectres were running along the darkness between the train.

'Köln – Berlin – ' Ursula made out on the boards hung on the high train on one side.

'Here we are,' said Birkin. And on her side she saw: 'Elsass – Lothringen – Luxembourg, Metz – Basle.'

'That was it, Basle!'

The porter came up.

'*À Bâle – deuxième classe? – Voilà!*' And he clambered into the high train. They followed. The compartments were already some of them taken. But many were dim and empty. The luggage was stowed, the porter was tipped.

'*Nous avons encore – ?*' said Birkin, looking at his watch and at the porter.

'*Encore une demi-heure.*' With which, in his blue blouse, he disappeared. He was ugly and insolent.

'Come,' said Birkin. 'It is cold. Let us eat.'

There was a coffee-wagon on the platform. They drank hot, watery coffee, and ate the long rolls, split, with ham between, which were such a wide bite that it almost dislocated Ursula's jaw; and they walked beside the high trains. It was all so strange, so extremely desolate, like the underworld, grey, grey, dirt grey, desolate, forlorn, nowhere – grey, dreary nowhere.

At last they were moving through the night. In the darkness Ursula made out the flat fields, the wet flat dreary darkness of the Continent. They pulled up surprisingly soon – Bruges! Then on through the level darkness, with glimpses of sleeping farms and thin poplar trees and deserted highroads. She sat dismayed, hand in hand with Birkin. He pale, immobile like a *revenant* himself, looked sometimes out of the window, sometimes closed his eyes. Then his eyes opened again, dark as the darkness outside.

A flash of a few lights on the darkness – Ghent station! A few more spectres moving outside on the platform – then the bell – then motion again through the level darkness. Ursula saw a man with a lantern come out of a farm by the railway, and cross to the dark farm-buildings. She thought of the Marsh, the old, intimate farm-life at Cossethay. My God, how far was she projected from her childhood, how far was she still to go! In one lifetime one travelled through aeons. The great chasm of memory from her childhood in the intimate country surroundings of Cossethay and the Marsh Farm – she remembered the servant Tilly, who used to give her bread and butter sprinkled with brown sugar, in the old living-room where the grandfather clock had two pink roses in a basket painted above the figures on the face – and now when she was travelling into the unknown with Birkin, an utter stranger – was so great, that it seemed she had no identity, that the child she had been, playing in Cossethay churchyard, was a little creature of history, not really herself.

They were at Brussels – half an hour for breakfast. They got down. On the great station clock it said six o'clock. They had coffee and rolls and honey in the vast desert refreshment room, so dreary, always so dreary, dirty, so spacious, such desolation of space. But she washed her face and hands in hot water, and combed her hair – that was a blessing.

Soon they were in the train again and moving on. The greyness of dawn began. There were several people in the compartment, large florid Belgian businessmen with long brown beards, talking incessantly in an ugly French she was too tired to follow.

It seemed the train ran by degrees out of the darkness into a faint light, then beat after beat into the day. Ah, how weary it was! Faintly, the trees showed, like shadows. Then a house, white, had a curious distinctness. How was it? Then she saw a village – there were always houses passing.

This was an old world she was still journeying through, winter-heavy and dreary. There was plough-land and pasture, and copses of bare trees, copses of bushes, and homesteads naked and work-bare. No new earth had come to pass.

She looked at Birkin's face. It was white and still and eternal, too eternal. She linked her fingers imploringly in his, under the cover of her rug. His fingers responded, his eyes looked back at her. How dark, like a night, his eyes were, like another world beyond! Oh, if he were the world as well, if only the world were he! If only he could call a world into being, that should be their own world!

The Belgians left, the train ran on, through Luxembourg, through Alsace-Lorraine, through Metz. But she was blind, she could see no more. Her soul did not look out.

They came at last to Basle, to the hotel. It was all a drifting trance, from which she never came to. They went out in the morning, before the train departed. She saw the street, the river, she stood on the bridge. But it all meant nothing. She remembered some shops – one full of pictures, one with orange velvet and ermine. But what did these signify? – nothing.

She was not at ease till they were in the train again. Then she was relieved. So long as they were moving onwards, she was satisfied. They came to Zürich, then, before very long, ran under the mountains, that were deep in snow. At last she was drawing near. This was the other world now.

Innsbruck was wonderful, deep in snow, and evening. They drove in an open sledge over the snow: the train had been so hot and stifling. And the hotel, with the golden light glowing under the porch, seemed like a home.

They laughed with pleasure when they were in the hall. The place seemed full and busy.

'Do you know if Mr and Mrs Crich – English – from Paris, have arrived?' Birkin asked in German.

The porter reflected a moment, and was just going to answer, when Ursula caught sight of Gudrun sauntering down the stairs, wearing her dark glossy coat, with grey fur.

'Gudrun! Gudrun!' she called, waving up the well of the staircase. 'Shu–hu!'

Gudrun looked over the rail, and immediately lost her sauntering, diffident air. Her eyes flashed.

'Really – Ursula!' she cried. And she began to move downstairs as Ursula ran up. They met at a turn and kissed with laughter and exclamations inarticulate and stirring.

'But!' cried Gudrun, mortified. 'We thought it was *tomorrow* you were coming! I wanted to come to the station.'

'No, we've come today!' cried Ursula. 'Isn't it lovely here!'

'Adorable!' said Gudrun. 'Gerald's just gone out to get something. Ursula, aren't you *fearfully* tired?'

'No, not so very. But I look a filthy sight, don't I!'

'No, you don't. You look almost perfectly fresh. I like that fur cap *immensely*!' She glanced over Ursula, who wore a big soft coat with a collar of deep, soft, blond fur, and a soft blond cap of fur.

'And you!' cried Ursula. 'What do you think *you* look like!'

Gudrun assumed an unconcerned, expressionless face.

'Do you like it?' she said.

'It's *very* fine!' cried Ursula, perhaps with a touch of satire.

'Go up – or come down,' said Birkin. For there the sisters stood, Gudrun with her hand on Ursula's arm, on the turn of the stairs halfway to the first landing, blocking the way and affording full entertainment to the whole of the hall below, from the door porter to the plump Jew in black clothes.

The two young women slowly mounted, followed by Birkin and the waiter.

'First floor?' asked Gudrun, looking back over her shoulder.

'Second, madam – the lift!' the waiter replied. And he darted to the elevator to forestall the two women. But they ignored him, as, chattering without heed, they set to mount the second flight. Rather chagrined, the waiter followed.

It was curious, the delight of the sisters in each other, at this meeting. It was as if they met in exile, and united their solitary forces against all the world. Birkin looked on with some mistrust and wonder.

When they had bathed and changed, Gerald came in. He looked shining like the sun on frost.

'Go with Gerald and smoke,' said Ursula to Birkin. 'Gudrun and I want to talk.'

Then the sisters sat in Gudrun's bedroom, and talked clothes, and experiences. Gudrun told Ursula the experience of the Birkin letter in the café. Ursula was shocked and frightened.

'Where is the letter?' she asked.

'I kept it,' said Gudrun.

'You'll give it me, won't you?' she said.

But Gudrun was silent for some moments, before she replied, 'Do you really want it, Ursula?'

'I want to read it,' said Ursula.

'Certainly,' said Gudrun.

Even now, she could not admit, to Ursula, that she wanted to keep it, as a memento, or a symbol. But Ursula knew, and was not pleased. So the subject was switched off.

'What did you do in Paris?' asked Ursula.

'Oh,' said Gudrun laconically – 'the usual things. We had a *fine* party one night in Fanny Bath's studio.'

'Did you? And you and Gerald were there! Who else? Tell me about it.'

'Well,' said Gudrun. 'There's nothing particular to tell. You know Fanny is *frightfully* in love with that painter, Billy Macfarlane. He was there – so Fanny spared nothing, she spent *very* freely. It was really remarkable! Of course, everybody got fearfully drunk – but in an interesting way, not like that filthy London crowd. The fact is these were all people that matter, which makes all the difference. There was a Roumanian, a fine chap. He got completely drunk, and climbed to the top of a high studio ladder, and gave the most marvellous address – really, Ursula, it was wonderful! He began in French – *La vie, c'est une affaire d'âmes impériales* – in a most beautiful voice – he was a fine-looking chap – but he had got into Roumanian before he had finished, and not a soul understood. But Donald Gilchrist was worked to a frenzy. He dashed his glass to the ground, and declared, by God, he was glad he had been born, by God, it was a miracle to be alive. And do you know, Ursula, so it was – ' Gudrun laughed rather hollowly.

'But how was Gerald among them all?' asked Ursula.

'Gerald! Oh, my word, he came out like a dandelion in the sun! *He's* a whole saturnalia in himself, once he is roused. I shouldn't like to say whose waist his arm did not go round. Really, Ursula, he seems to reap the women like a harvest. There wasn't one that would have resisted him. It was too amazing! Can you understand it?'

Ursula reflected, and a dancing light came into her eyes.

'Yes,' she said. 'I can. He is such a whole-hogger.'

'Whole-hogger! I should think so!' exclaimed Gudrun. 'But it is true, Ursula, every woman in the room was ready to surrender to him. Chanticleer isn't in it – even Fanny Bath, who is *genuinely* in love with Billy Macfarlane! I never was more amazed in my life! And you know, afterwards – I felt I was a whole *roomful* of women. I was no more myself to him, than I was Queen Victoria. I was a whole roomful of women at once. It was most astounding! But my eye, I'd caught a Sultan that time – '

Gudrun's eyes were flashing, her cheek was hot, she looked strange, exotic, satiric. Ursula was fascinated at once – and yet uneasy.

They had to get ready for dinner. Gudrun came down in a daring gown of vivid green silk and tissue of gold, with green velvet bodice and a strange black-and-white band round her hair. She was really brilliantly beautiful and everybody noticed her. Gerald was in that full-blooded, gleaming state when he was most handsome. Birkin watched them with quick, laughing, half-sinister eyes, Ursula quite lost her head. There seemed a spell, almost a blinding spell, cast round their table, as if they were lighted up more strongly than the rest of the dining-room.

'Don't you love to be in this place?' cried Gudrun. 'Isn't the snow wonderful! Do you notice how it exalts everything? It is simply marvellous. One really does feel *übermenschlich* – more than human.'

'One does,' cried Ursula. 'But isn't that partly the being out of England?'

'Oh, of course,' cried Gudrun. 'One could never feel like this in England, for the simple reason that the damper is *never* lifted off one, there. It is quite impossible really to let go, in England, of that I am assured.'

And she turned again to the food she was eating. She was fluttering with vivid intensity.

'It's quite true,' said Gerald, 'it never is quite the same in England. But perhaps we don't want it to be – perhaps it's like bringing the light a little too near the powder-magazine, to let go altogether, in England. One is afraid what might happen, if *everybody else* let go.'

'My God!' cried Gudrun. 'But wouldn't it be wonderful, if all England did suddenly go off like a display of fireworks.'

'It couldn't,' said Ursula. 'They are all too damp, the powder is damp in them.'

'I'm not so sure of that,' said Gerald.

'Nor I,' said Birkin. 'When the English really begin to go off, *en masse*, it'll be time to shut your ears and run.'

'They never will,' said Ursula.

'We'll see,' he replied.

'Isn't it marvellous,' said Gudrun, 'how thankful one can be, to be out of one's country. I cannot believe myself, I am so transported, the moment I set foot on a foreign shore. I say to myself "Here steps a new creature into life." '

'Don't be too hard on poor old England,' said Gerald. 'Though we curse it, we love it really.'

To Ursula, there seemed a fund of cynicism in these words.

'We may,' said Birkin. 'But it's a damnably uncomfortable love: like a love for an aged parent who suffers horribly from a complication of diseases, for which there is no hope.'

Gudrun looked at him with dilated dark eyes.

'You think there is no hope?' she asked, in her pertinent fashion.

But Birkin backed away. He would not answer such a question.

'Any hope of England's becoming real? God knows. It's a great actual unreality now, an aggregation into unreality. It might be real, if there were no Englishmen.'

'You think the English will have to disappear?' persisted Gudrun. It was strange, her pointed interest in his answer. It might have been her own fate she was enquiring after. Her dark, dilated eyes rested on Birkin, as if she could conjure the truth of the future out of him, as out of some instrument of divination.

He was pale. Then, reluctantly, he answered, 'Well – what else is in front of them, but disappearance? They've got to disappear from their own special brand of Englishness, anyhow.'

Gudrun watched him as if in a hypnotic state, her eyes wide and fixed on him. 'But in what way do you mean, disappear? – ' she persisted.

'Yes, do you mean a change of heart?' put in Gerald.

'I don't mean anything, why should I?' said Birkin. 'I'm an Englishman, and I've paid the price of it. I can't talk about England – I can only speak for myself.'

'Yes,' said Gudrun slowly, 'you love England immensely, *immensely*, Rupert.'

'And leave her,' he replied.

'No, not for good. You'll come back,' said Gerald, nodding sagely.

'They say the lice crawl off a dying body,' said Birkin, with a glare of bitterness. 'So I leave England.'

'Ah, but you'll come back,' said Gudrun, with a sardonic smile.

'*Tant pis pour moi*,' he replied.

'Isn't he angry with his mother country!' laughed Gerald, amused.

'Ah, a patriot!' said Gudrun, with something like a sneer.

Birkin refused to answer any more.

Gudrun watched him still for a few seconds. Then she turned away. It was finished, her spell of divination in him. She felt already purely cynical. She looked at Gerald. He was wonderful like a piece of radium to her. She felt she could consume herself and know *all*, by means of this fatal, living metal. She smiled to herself at her fancy. And what would she do with herself, when she had destroyed herself? For if spirit, if integral being is destructible, Matter is indestructible.

He was looking bright and abstracted, puzzled, for the moment. She stretched out her beautiful arm, with its fluff of green tulle, and touched his chin with her subtle, artist's fingers.

'What are they then?' she asked, with a strange, knowing smile.

'What?' he replied, his eyes suddenly dilating with wonder.

'Your thoughts.'

Gerald looked like a man coming awake.

'I think I had none,' he said.

'Really!' she said, with grave laughter in her voice.

And to Birkin it was as if she killed Gerald, with that touch.

'Ah but,' cried Gudrun, 'let us drink to Britannia – let us drink to Britannia.'

It seemed there was wild despair in her voice. Gerald laughed, and filled the glasses.

'I think Rupert means,' he said, 'that *nationally* all Englishmen must die, so that they can exist individually and – '

'Super-nationally – ' put in Gudrun, with a slight ironic grimace, raising her glass.

The next day, they descended at the tiny railway station of Hohenhausen, at the end of the tiny valley railway. It was snow everywhere, a white, perfect cradle of snow, new and frozen, sweeping up on either side, black crags, and white sweeps of silver towards the blue pale heavens.

As they stepped out on the naked platform, with only snow around and above, Gudrun shrank as if it chilled her heart.

'My God, Jerry,' she said, turning to Gerald with sudden intimacy, 'you've done it now.'

'What?'

She made a faint gesture, indicating the world on either hand.

'Look at it!'

She seemed afraid to go on. He laughed.

They were in the heart of the mountains. From high above, on either side, swept down the white fold of snow, so that one seemed small and tiny in a valley of pure concrete heaven, all strangely radiant and changeless and silent.

'It makes one feel so small and alone,' said Ursula, turning to Birkin and laying her hand on his arm.

'You're not sorry you've come, are you?' said Gerald to Gudrun.

She looked doubtful. They went out of the station between banks of snow.

'Ah,' said Gerald, sniffing the air in elation, 'this is perfect. There's our sledge. We'll walk a bit – we'll run up the road.'

Gudrun, always doubtful, dropped her heavy coat on the sledge, as he did his, and they set off. Suddenly she threw up her head and set off scudding along the road of snow, pulling her cap down over her ears. Her blue, bright dress fluttered in the wind, her thick scarlet stockings were brilliant above the whiteness. Gerald watched her: she seemed to be rushing towards her fate, and leaving him behind. He let her get some distance, then, loosening his limbs, he went after her.

Everywhere was deep and silent snow. Great snow-eaves weighed down the broad-roofed Tyrolese houses, that were sunk to the window-sashes in snow. Peasant-women, full-skirted, wearing each a cross-over shawl, and thick snow-boots, turned in the way to look at the soft, determined girl running with such heavy fleetness from the man, who was overtaking her, but not gaining any power over her.

They passed the inn with its painted shutters and balcony, a few cottages, half buried in the snow; then the snow-buried silent sawmill by the roofed bridge, which crossed the hidden stream, over which they ran into the very depth of the untouched sheets of snow. It was a silence and a sheer whiteness exhilarating to madness. But the perfect silence was most terrifying, isolating the soul, surrounding the heart with frozen air.

'It's a marvellous place, for all that,' said Gudrun, looking into his eyes with a strange, meaning look. His soul leapt.

'Good,' he said.

A fierce electric energy seemed to flow over all his limbs, his muscles were surcharged, his hands felt hard with strength. They walked along rapidly up the snow-road, that was marked by withered branches of trees stuck in at intervals. He and she were separate, like opposite poles of one fierce energy. But they felt powerful enough to leap over the confines of life into the forbidden places, and back again.

Birkin and Ursula were running along also, over the snow. He had disposed of the luggage, and they had a little start of the sledges. Ursula was excited and happy, but she kept turning suddenly to catch hold of Birkin's arm, to make sure of him.

'This is something I never expected,' she said. 'It is a different world, here.'

They went on into a snow meadow. There they were overtaken by the sledge, that came tinkling through the silence. It was another mile before they came upon Gudrun and Gerald on the steep up-climb, beside the pink, half-buried shrine.

Then they passed into a gulley, where were walls of black rock and a river filled with snow, and a still blue sky above. Through a covered bridge they went, drumming roughly over the boards, crossing the snow-bed once more, then slowly up and up, the horses walking swiftly, the driver cracking his long whip as he walked beside, and calling his strange wild *hue-hue!*, the walls of rock passing slowly by, till they emerged again between slopes and masses of snow. Up and up, gradually they went, through the cold shadow-radiance of the afternoon, silenced by the imminence of the mountains, the luminous, dazing sides of snow that rose above them and fell away beneath.

They came forth at last in a little high tableland of snow, where stood the last peaks of snow like the heart petals of an open rose. In the midst of the last deserted valleys of heaven stood a lonely building with brown wooden walls and white heavy roof, deep and deserted in the waste of snow, like a dream. It stood like a rock that had rolled down from the last steep slopes, a rock that had taken the form of a house, and was now half-buried. It was unbelievable that one could live there uncrushed by all this terrible waste of whiteness and silence and clear, upper, ringing cold.

Yet the sledges ran up in fine style, people came to the door laughing and excited, the floor of the hostel rang hollow, the passage was wet with snow, it was a real, warm interior.

The newcomers tramped up the bare wooden stairs, following the serving woman. Gudrun and Gerald took the first bedroom. In a moment they found themselves alone in a bare, smallish, close-shut room that was all of golden-coloured wood, floor, walls, ceiling, door, all of the same warm gold panelling of oiled pine. There was a window opposite the door, but low down, because the roof sloped. Under the slope of the ceiling were the table with wash-hand bowl and jug, and across, another table with mirror. On either side the door were two beds piled high with an enormous blue-checked overbolster, enormous.

This was all – no cupboard, none of the amenities of life. Here they were shut up together in this cell of golden-coloured wood, with two blue checked beds. They looked at each other and laughed, frightened by this naked nearness of isolation.

A man knocked and came in with the luggage. He was a sturdy fellow with flattish cheek-bones, rather pale, and with coarse fair moustache. Gudrun watched him put down the bags, in silence, then tramp heavily out.

'It isn't too rough, is it?' Gerald asked.

The bedroom was not very warm, and she shivered slightly.

'It is wonderful,' she equivocated. 'Look at the colour of this panelling – it's wonderful, like being inside a nut.'

He was standing watching her, feeling his short-cut moustache, leaning back slightly and watching her with his keen, undaunted eyes, dominated by the constant passion, that was like a doom upon him.

She went and crouched down in front of the window, curious.

'Oh, but this – !' she cried involuntarily, almost in pain.

In front was a valley shut in under the sky, the last huge slopes of snow and black rock, and at the end, like the navel of the earth, a white-folded wall, and two peaks glimmering in the late light. Straight in front ran the cradle of silent snow, between the great slopes that were fringed with a little roughness of pine trees, like hair, round the base. But the cradle of snow ran on to the eternal closing-in, where the walls of snow and rock rose impenetrable, and the mountain peaks above were in heaven immediate. This was the centre, the knot, the navel of the world, where the earth belonged to the skies, pure, unapproachable, impassable.

It filled Gudrun with a strange rapture. She crouched in front of the window, clenching her face in her hands, in a sort of trance. At last she had arrived, she had reached her place. Here at last she folded her venture and settled down like a crystal in the navel of snow, and was gone.

Gerald bent above her and was looking out over her shoulder. Already he felt he was alone. She was gone. She was completely gone, and there was icy vapour round his heart. He saw the blind valley, the great cul-de-sac of snow and mountain peaks, under the heaven. And there was no way out. The terrible silence and cold and the glamorous whiteness of the dusk wrapped him round, and she remained crouching before the window, as at a shrine, a shadow.

'Do you like it?' he asked, in a voice that sounded detached and foreign. At least she might acknowledge he was with her. But she only averted her soft, mute face a little from his gaze. And he knew that there were tears in her eyes, her own tears, tears of her strange religion, that put him to nought.

Quite suddenly, he put his hand under her chin and lifted up her face to him. Her dark blue eyes, in their wetness of tears, dilated as if she was startled in her very soul. They looked at him through their tears in terror and a little horror. His light blue eyes were keen, small-pupilled and unnatural in their vision. Her lips parted, as she breathed with difficulty.

The passion came up in him, stroke after stroke, like the ringing of a bronze bell, so strong and unflawed and indomitable. His knees tightened to bronze as he hung above her soft face, whose lips parted and whose eyes dilated in a strange violation. In the grasp of his hand her chin was unutterably soft and silken. He felt strong as winter, his hands were living metal, invincible and not to be turned aside. His heart rang like a bell clanging inside him.

He took her up in his arms. She was soft and inert, motionless. All the while her eyes, in which the tears had not yet dried, were dilated as if in a kind of swoon of fascination and helplessness. He was super-humanly strong, and unflawed, as if invested with supernatural force.

He lifted her close and folded her against him. Her softness, her inert, relaxed weight lay against his own surcharged, bronzelike limbs in a heaviness of desirability that would destroy him, if he were not fulfilled. She moved convulsively, recoiling away from him. His heart went up like a flame of ice, he closed over her like steel. He would destroy her rather than be denied.

But the overweening power of his body was too much for her. She relaxed again, and lay loose and soft, panting in a little delirium. And to him, she was so sweet, she was such bliss of release, that he would have suffered a whole eternity of torture rather than forgo one second of this pang of unsurpassable bliss.

'My God,' he said to her, his face drawn and strange, transfigured, 'what next?'

She lay perfectly still, with a still, childlike face and dark eyes, looking at him. She was lost, fallen right away.

'I shall always love you,' he said, looking at her.

But she did not hear. She lay, looking at him as at something she could never understand, never: as a child looks at a grown-up person, without hope of understanding, only submitting.

He kissed her, kissed her eyes shut, so that she could not look any more. He wanted something now, some recognition, some sign, some admission. But she only lay silent and childlike and remote, like a child that is overcome and cannot understand, only feels lost. He kissed her again, giving up.

'Shall we go down and have coffee and *Kuchen*?' he asked.

The twilight was falling slate-blue at the window. She closed her eyes, closed away the monotonous level of dead wonder, and opened them again to the everyday world.

'Yes,' she said briefly, regaining her will with a click. She went again to the window. Blue evening had fallen over the cradle of snow and over the great pallid slopes. But in the heaven the peaks of snow were rosy, glistening like transcendent, radiant spikes of blossom in the heavenly upper-world, so lovely and beyond.

Gudrun saw all their loveliness, she *knew* how immortally beautiful they were, great pistils of rose-coloured, snow-fed fire in the blue twilight of the heaven. She could *see* it, she knew it, but she was not of it. She was divorced, debarred, a soul shut out.

With a last look of remorse, she turned away, and was doing her hair. He had unstrapped the luggage, and was waiting, watching her. She knew he was watching her. It made her a little hasty and feverish in her precipitation.

They went downstairs, both with a strange other-world look on their faces, and with a glow in their eyes. They saw Birkin and Ursula sitting at the long table in a corner, waiting for them.

'How good and simple they look together,' Gudrun thought, jealously. She envied them some spontaneity, a childish sufficiency to which she herself could never approach. They seemed such children to her.

'Such good *Kranzkuchen*!' cried Ursula greedily. 'So good!'

'Right,' said Gudrun. 'Can we have *Kaffee mit Kranzkuchen*?' she added to the waiter.

And she seated herself on the bench beside Gerald. Birkin, looking at them, felt a pain of tenderness for them.

'I think the place is really wonderful, Gerald,' he said; '*prachtvoll* and *wunderbar* and *wunderschön* and *unbeschreiblich* and all the other German adjectives.'

Gerald broke into a slight smile.

'*I* like it,' he said.

The tables, of white scrubbed wood, were placed round three sides of the room, as in a Gasthaus. Birkin and Ursula sat with their backs to the wall, which was of oiled wood, and Gerald and Gudrun sat in the corner next them, near to the stove. It was a fairly large place, with a tiny bar, just like a country inn, but quite simple and bare, and all of oiled wood, ceilings and walls and floor, the only furniture being the tables and benches going round three sides, the great green stove, and the bar and the doors on the fourth side. The windows were double, and quite uncurtained. It was early evening.

The coffee came – hot and good – and a whole ring of cake.

'A whole *Kuchen*!' cried Ursula. 'They give you more than us! I want some of yours.'

There were other people in the place, ten altogether, so Birkin had found out: two artists, three students, a man and wife, and a Professor and two daughters – all Germans. The four English people, being newcomers, sat in their coign of vantage to watch. The Germans peeped in at the door, called a word to the waiter, and went away again. It was not meal-time, so they did not come into this dining-room, but betook themselves, when their boots were changed, to the *Reunionsaal*.

The English visitors could hear the occasional twanging of a zither, the strumming of a piano, snatches of laughter and shouting and singing, a faint vibration of voices. The whole building being of wood, it seemed to carry every sound, like a drum, but instead of increasing each particular noise, it decreased it, so that the sound of the zither seemed tiny, as if a diminutive zither were playing somewhere, and it seemed the piano must be a small one, like a little spinet.

The host came when the coffee was finished. He was a Tyrolese, broad, rather flat-cheeked, with a pale, pock-marked skin and flourishing moustaches.

'Would you like to go to the *Reunionsaal* to be introduced to the other ladies and gentlemen?' he asked, bending forward and smiling, showing his large, strong teeth. His blue eyes went quickly from one to the other – he was not quite sure of his ground with these English people. He was unhappy too because he spoke no English and he was not sure whether to try his French.

'Shall we go to the *Reunionsaal*, and be introduced to the other people?' repeated Gerald, laughing.

There was a moment's hesitation.

'I suppose we'd better – better break the ice,' said Birkin.

The women rose, rather flushed. And the Wirt's black, beetle-like, broad-shouldered figure went on ignominiously in front, towards the noise. He opened the door and ushered the four strangers into the playroom.

Instantly a silence fell, a slight embarrassment came over the company. The newcomers had a sense of many blond faces looking their way. Then, the host was bowing to a short, energetic-looking man with large moustaches, and saying in a low voice, '*Herr Professor, darf ich vorstellen –* '

The Herr Professor was prompt and energetic. He bowed low to the English people, smiling, and began to be a comrade at once.

'*Nehmen die Herrschaften teil an unserer Unter-haltung?*' he said, with a vigorous suavity, his voice curling up in the question.

The four English people smiled, lounging with an attentive uneasiness in the middle of the room. Gerald, who was spokesman, said that they would willingly take part in the entertainment. Gudrun and Ursula, laughing, excited, felt the eyes of all the men upon them, and they lifted their heads and looked nowhere, and felt royal.

The Professor announced the names of those present, *sans cérémonie*. There was a bowing to the wrong people and to the right people. Everybody was there, except the man and wife. The two tall, clear-skinned, athletic daughters of the Professor, with their plain-cut, dark blue blouses and loden skirts, their rather long, strong necks, their clear blue eyes and carefully banded hair, and their blushes, bowed and stood back; the three students bowed very low, in the humble hope of making an impression of extreme good-breeding; then there was a thin, dark-skinned man with full eyes, an odd creature, like a child, and like a troll, quick, detached; he bowed slightly; his companion, a large fair young man, stylishly dressed, blushed to the eyes and bowed very low.

It was over.

'Herr Loerke was giving us a recitation in the Cologne dialect,' said the Professor.

'He must forgive us for interrupting him,' said Gerald, 'we should like very much to hear it.'

There was instantly a bowing and an offering of seats. Gudrun and Ursula, Gerald and Birkin sat in the deep sofas against the wall. The room was of naked oiled panelling, like the rest of the house. It had a piano, sofas and chairs, and a couple of tables with books and magazines. In its complete absence of decoration, save for the big, blue stove, it was cosy and pleasant.

Herr Loerke was the little man with the boyish figure, and the round, full, sensitive-looking head, and the quick, full eyes, like a mouse's. He glanced swiftly from one to the other of the strangers, and held himself aloof.

'Please go on with the recitation,' said the Professor, suavely, with his slight authority. Loerke, who was sitting hunched on the piano stool, blinked and did not answer.

'It would be a great pleasure,' said Ursula, who had been getting the sentence ready, in German, for some minutes.

Then, suddenly, the small, unresponding man swung aside, towards his previous audience and broke forth, exactly as he had broken off; in a controlled, mocking voice, giving an imitation of a quarrel between an old Cologne woman and a railway guard.

His body was slight and unformed, like a boy's, but his voice was mature, sardonic, its movement had the flexibility of essential energy, and of a mocking penetrating understanding. Gudrun could not understand a word of his monologue, but she was spellbound, watching him. He must be an artist, nobody else could have such fine adjustment and singleness. The Germans were doubled up with laughter, hearing his strange droll words, his droll phrases of dialect. And in the midst of their paroxysms, they glanced with deference at the four English strangers, the elect. Gudrun and Ursula were forced to laugh. The room rang with shouts of laughter. The blue eyes of the Professor's daughters were swimming over with laughter-tears, their clear cheeks were flushed crimson with mirth, their father broke out in the most astonishing peals of hilarity, the students bowed their heads on their knees in excess of joy. Ursula looked round amazed, the laughter was bubbling out of her involuntarily. She looked at Gudrun. Gudrun looked at her, and the two sisters burst out laughing, carried away. Loerke glanced at them swiftly, with his full eyes. Birkin was sniggering involuntarily. Gerald Crich sat erect, with a glistening look of amusement on his face. And the laughter crashed out again, in wild paroxysms, the Professor's daughters were reduced to shaking helplessness, the veins of the Professor's neck were swollen, his face was purple, he was strangled in ultimate, silent spasms of laughter. The students were shouting half-articulated words that tailed off in helpless explosions. Then suddenly the rapid patter of the artist ceased, there were little whoops of subsiding mirth, Ursula and Gudrun were wiping their eyes, and the Professor was crying loudly.

'*Das war ausgezeichnet, das war famos –*'

'*Wirklich famos,*' echoed his exhausted daughters, faintly.

'And we couldn't understand it,' cried Ursula.

'*Oh leider, leider!*' cried the Professor.

'You couldn't understand it?' cried the students, let loose at last in speech with the newcomers. '*Ja, das ist wirklich schade, das ist schade, gnädige Frau. Wissen Sie –*'

The mixture was made, the newcomers were stirred into the party, like new ingredients, the whole room was alive. Gerald was in his element, he talked freely and excitedly, his face glistened with a strange amusement. Perhaps even Birkin, in the end, would break forth. He was shy and withheld, though full of attention.

Ursula was prevailed upon to sing 'Annie Lowrie', as the Professor called it.

There was a hush of *extreme* deference. She had never been so flattered in her life. Gudrun accompanied her on the piano, playing from memory.

Ursula had a beautiful ringing voice, but usually no confidence, she spoiled everything. This evening she felt conceited and untrammelled. Birkin was well in the background, she shone almost in reaction, the Germans made her feel fine and infallible, she was liberated into overweening self-confidence. She felt like a bird flying in the air, as her voice soared out, enjoying herself extremely in the balance and flight of the song, like the motion of a bird's wings that is up in the wind, sliding and playing on the air, she played with sentimentality, supported by rapturous attention. She was very happy, singing that song by herself, full of a conceit of emotion and power, working upon all those people, and upon herself, exerting herself with gratification, giving immeasurable gratification to the Germans.

At the end, the Germans were all touched with admiring, delicious melancholy, they praised her in soft, reverent voices, they could not say too much.

'*Wie schön, wie rührend! Ach, die Schottischen Lieder, sie haben so viel Stimmung! Aber die gnädige Frau hat eine* wunderbare *Stimme; die gnädige Frau ist wirklich eine Künstlerin, aber wirklich!*'

She was dilated and brilliant, like a flower in the morning sun. She felt Birkin looking at her, as if he were jealous of her, and her breasts thrilled, her veins were all golden. She was as happy as the sun that has just opened above clouds. And everybody seemed so admiring and radiant, it was perfect.

After dinner she wanted to go out for a minute, to look at the world. The company tried to dissuade her – it was so terribly cold. But just to look, she said.

They all four wrapped up warmly, and found themselves in a vague, unsubstantial outdoors of dim snow and ghosts of an upper-world, that made strange shadows before the stars. It was indeed cold, bruisingly, frighteningly, unnaturally cold. Ursula could not believe the air in her nostrils. It seemed conscious, malevolent, purposive in its intense murderous coldness.

Yet it was wonderful, an intoxication, a silence of dim, unrealised snow, of the invisible intervening between her and the visible, between her and the flashing stars. She could see Orion sloping up. How wonderful he was, wonderful enough to make one cry aloud.

And all around was this cradle of snow, and there was firm snow underfoot, that struck with heavy cold through her boot-soles. It was night, and silence. She imagined she could hear the stars. She imagined distinctly she could hear the celestial, musical motion of the stars, quite near at hand. She seemed like a bird flying amongst their harmonious motion.

And she clung close to Birkin. Suddenly she realised she did not know what he was thinking. She did not know where he was ranging.

'My love!' she said, stopping to look at him.

His face was pale, his eyes dark, there was a faint spark of starlight on them. And he saw her face soft and upturned to him, very near. He kissed her softly.

'What then?' he asked.

'Do you love me?' she asked.

'Too much,' he answered quietly.

She clung a little closer.

'Not too much,' she pleaded.

'Far too much,' he said, almost sadly.

'And does it make you sad, that I am everything to you?' she asked, wistful. He held her close to him, kissing her, and saying, scarcely audible, 'No, but I feel like a beggar – I feel poor.'

She was silent, looking at the stars now. Then she kissed him.

'Don't be a beggar,' she pleaded, wistfully. 'It isn't ignominious that you love me.'

'It is ignominious to feel poor, isn't it?' he replied.

'Why? Why should it be?' she asked. He only stood still, in the terribly cold air that moved invisibly over the mountain tops, folding her round with his arms.

'I couldn't bear this cold, eternal place without you,' he said. 'I couldn't bear it, it would kill the quick of my life.'

She kissed him again, suddenly.

'Do you hate it?' she asked, puzzled, wondering.

'If I couldn't come near to you, if you weren't here, I should hate it. I couldn't bear it,' he answered.

'But the people are nice,' she said.

'I mean the stillness, the cold, the frozen eternality,' he said.

She wondered. Then her spirit came home to him, nestling unconscious in him.

'Yes, it is good we are warm and together,' she said.

And they turned home again. They saw the golden lights of the hotel glowing out in the night of snow-silence, small in the hollow, like a cluster of yellow berries. It seemed like a bunch of sun-sparks, tiny and orange in the midst of the snow-darkness. Behind, was a high shadow of a peak, blotting out the stars, like a ghost.

They drew near to their home. They saw a man come from the dark building, with a lighted lantern which swung golden, and made that his dark feet walked in a halo of snow. He was a small, dark figure in the darkened snow. He unlatched the door of an outhouse. A smell of cows, hot, animal, almost like beef, came out on the heavily cold air. There was a glimpse of two cattle in their dark stalls, then the door was shut again, and not a chink of light showed. It had reminded Ursula again of home, of the Marsh, of her childhood, and of the journey to Brussels, and, strangely, of Anton Skrebensky.

Oh, God, could one bear it, this past which was gone down the abyss? Could she bear, that it ever had been! She looked round this silent, upper world of snow and stars and powerful cold. There was another world, like views on a magic lantern; the Marsh, Cossethay, Ilkeston, lit up with a common, unreal light. There was a shadowy unreal Ursula, a whole shadow-play of an unreal life. It was as unreal, and circumscribed, as a magic-lantern show. She wished the slides could all be broken. She wished it could be gone for ever, like a lantern-slide which was broken. She wanted to have no past. She wanted to have come down from the slopes of heaven to this place, with Birkin, not to have toiled out of the murk of her childhood and her upbringing, slowly, all soiled. She felt that memory was a dirty trick played upon her. What was this decree, that she should 'remember'! Why not a bath of pure oblivion, a new birth, without any recollections or blemish of a past life. She was with Birkin, she had just come into life, here in the high snow, against the stars. What had she to do with parents and antecedents? She knew herself new and unbegotten, she had no father, no mother, no anterior connections, she was herself, pure and silvery, she belonged only to the oneness with Birkin, a oneness that struck deeper notes, sounding into the heart of the universe, the heart of reality, where she had never existed before.

Even Gudrun was a separate unit, separate, separate, having nothing to do with this self, this Ursula, in her new world of reality. That old shadow-world, the actuality of the past – ah, let it go! She rose free on the wings of her new condition.

Gudrun and Gerald had not come in. They had walked up the valley straight in front of the house, not like Ursula and Birkin, on to the little hill at the right. Gudrun was driven by a strange desire. She wanted to plunge on and on, till she came to the end of the valley of snow. Then she wanted to climb the wall of white finality, climb over, into the peaks that sprang up like sharp petals in the heart of the frozen, mysterious navel of the world. She felt that there, over the strange blind, terrible wall of rocky snow, there in the navel of the mystic world, among the final cluster of peaks, there, in the infolded navel of it all, was her consummation. If she could but come there, alone, and pass into the infolded navel of eternal snow and of uprising, immortal peaks of snow and rock, she would be a oneness with all, she would be herself the eternal, infinite silence, the sleeping, timeless, frozen centre of the All.

They went back to the house, to the *Reunionsaal*. She was curious to see what was going on. The men there made her alert, roused her curiosity. It was a new taste of life for her, they were so prostrate before her, yet so full of life.

The party was boisterous; they were dancing all together, dancing the *Schuhplatteln*, the Tyrolese dance of the clapping hands and tossing the partner in the air at the crisis. The Germans were all proficient – they were from Munich chiefly. Gerald also was quite passable. There were three zithers twanging away in a corner. It was a scene of great animation and confusion. The Professor was initiating Ursula into the dance, stamping, clapping, and swinging her high, with amazing force and zest. When the crisis came even Birkin was behaving manfully with one of the Professor's fresh, strong daughters, who was exceedingly happy. Everybody was dancing, there was the most boisterous turmoil.

Gudrun looked on with delight. The solid wooden floor resounded to the knocking heels of the men, the air quivered with the clapping hands and the zither music, there was a golden dust about the hanging lamps.

Suddenly the dance finished, Loerke and the students rushed out to bring in drinks. There was an excited clamour of voices, a clinking of mug-lids, a great crying of 'Prosit – Prosit!' Loerke was everywhere at once, like a gnome, suggesting drinks for the women, making an obscure, slightly risky joke with the men, confusing and mystifying the waiter.

He wanted very much to dance with Gudrun. From the first moment he had seen her, he wanted to make a connection with her. Instinctively she felt this, and she waited for him to come up. But a kind of sulkiness kept him away from her, so she thought he disliked her.

'Will you schuhplatteln, gnädige Frau?' said the large, fair youth, Loerke's companion. He was too soft, too humble for Gudrun's taste. But she wanted to dance, and the fair youth, who was called Leitner, was handsome enough in his uneasy, slightly abject fashion, a humility that covered a certain fear. She accepted him as a partner.

The zithers sounded out again, the dance began. Gerald led them, laughing, with one of the Professor's daughters. Ursula danced with one of the students, Birkin with the other daughter of the Professor, the Professor with Frau Kramer, and the rest of the men danced together, with quite as much zest as if they had had women partners.

Because Gudrun had danced with the well-built, soft youth, his companion, Loerke, was more pettish and exasperated than ever, and would not even notice her existence in the room. This piqued her, but she made up to herself by dancing with the Professor, who was strong as a mature, well-seasoned bull, and as full of coarse energy. She could not bear him, critically, and yet she enjoyed being rushed through the dance, and tossed up into the air, on his coarse, powerful impetus. The Professor enjoyed it too, he eyed her with strange, large blue eyes, full of galvanic fire. She hated him for the seasoned, semi-paternal animalism with which he regarded her, but she admired his weight of strength.

The room was charged with excitement and strong, animal emotion. Loerke was kept away from Gudrun, to whom he wanted to speak, as by a hedge of thorns, and he felt a sardonic ruthless hatred for this young love-companion, Leitner, who was his penniless dependant. He mocked the youth, with an acid ridicule, that made Leitner red in the face and impotent with resentment.

Gerald, who had now got the dance perfectly, was dancing again with the younger of the Professor's daughters, who was almost dying of virgin excitement, because she thought Gerald so handsome, so superb. He had her in his power, as if she were a palpitating bird, a fluttering, flushing, bewildered creature. And it made him smile, as she shrank convulsively between his hands, violently, when he must throw her into the air. At the end, she was so overcome with prostrate love for him, that she could scarcely speak sensibly at all.

Birkin was dancing with Ursula. There were odd little fires playing in his eyes, he seemed to have turned into something wicked and flickering, mocking, suggestive, quite impossible. Ursula was frightened of him, and fascinated.

Clear, before her eyes, as in a vision, she could see the sardonic, licentious mockery of his eyes, he moved towards her with subtle, animal, indifferent approach. The strangeness of his hands, which came quick and cunning, inevitably to the vital place beneath her breasts, and, lifting with mocking, suggestive impulse, carried her through the air as if without strength, through black-magic, made her swoon with fear. For a moment she revolted, it was horrible. She would break the spell. But before the resolution had formed she had submitted again, yielded to her fear. He knew all the time what he was doing, she could see it in his smiling, concentrated eyes. It was his responsibility, she would leave it to him.

When they were alone in the darkness, she felt the strange licentiousness of him hovering upon her. She was troubled and repelled. Why should he turn like this?

'What is it?' she asked in dread.

But his face only glistened on her, unknown, horrible. And yet she was fascinated. Her impulse was to repel him violently, break from this spell of mocking brutishness. But she was too fascinated, she wanted to submit, she wanted to know. What would he do to her?

He was so attractive, and so repulsive at once. The sardonic suggestivity that flickered over his face and looked from his narrowed eyes, made her want to hide, to hide herself away from him and watch him from somewhere unseen.

'Why are you like this?' she demanded again, rousing against him with sudden force and animosity.

The flickering fires in his eyes concentrated as he looked into her eyes. Then the lids drooped with a faint motion of satiric contempt. Then they rose again to the same remorseless suggestivity. And she gave way, he might do as he would. His licentiousness was repulsively attractive. But he was self-responsible, she would see what it was.

They might do as they liked – this she realised as she went to sleep. How could anything that gave one satisfaction be excluded? What was degrading? Who cared? Degrading things were real, with a different reality. And he was so unabashed and unrestrained. Wasn't it rather horrible, a man who could be so soulful and spiritual, now to be so – she balked at her own thoughts and memories: then she added – so bestial? So bestial, they two! – so degraded! She winced. But after all, why not? She exulted as well. Why not be bestial, and go the whole round of experience? She exulted in it. She was bestial. How good it was to be really shameful! There would be no shameful thing she had not experienced. Yet she was unabashed, she was herself. Why not? She was free, when she knew everything, and no dark shameful things were denied her.

Gudrun, who had been watching Gerald in the *Reunionsaal*, suddenly thought, 'He should have all the women he can – it is his nature. It is absurd to call him monogamous – he is naturally promiscuous. That is his nature.'

The thought came to her involuntarily. It shocked her somewhat. It was as if she had seen some new *Mene! Mene!* upon the wall. Yet it was merely true. A voice seemed to have spoken it to her so clearly, that for the moment she believed in inspiration.

'It is really true,' she said to herself again.

She knew quite well she had believed it all along. She knew it implicitly. But she must keep it dark – almost from herself. She must keep it completely secret. It was knowledge for her alone, and scarcely even to be admitted to herself.

The deep resolve formed in her, to combat him. One of them must triumph over the other. Which should it be? Her soul steeled itself with strength. Almost she laughed within herself, at her confidence. It woke a certain keen, half contemptuous pity, tenderness for him: she was so ruthless.

Everybody retired early. The Professor and Loerke went into a small lounge to drink. They both watched Gudrun go along the landing by the railing upstairs.

'*Ein schönes Frauenzimmer*,' said the Professor.

'*Ja!*' asserted Loerke, shortly.

Gerald walked with his queer, long wolf-steps across the bedroom to the window, stooped and looked out, then rose again, and turned to Gudrun, his eyes sharp with an abstract smile. He seemed very tall to her, she saw the glisten of his whitish eyebrows, that met between his brows.

'How do you like it?' he said.

He seemed to be laughing inside himself, quite unconsciously. She looked at him. He was a phenomenon to her, not a human being: a sort of creature, greedy.

'I like it very much,' she replied.

'Who do you like best downstairs?' he asked, standing tall and glistening above her, with his glistening stiff hair erect.

'Who do I like best?' she repeated, wanting to answer his question, and finding it difficult to collect herself. 'Why I don't know, I don't know enough about them yet, to be able to say. Who do *you* like best?'

'Oh, I don't care – I don't like or dislike any of them. It doesn't matter about me. I wanted to know about you.'

'But why?' she asked, going rather pale. The abstract, unconscious smile in his eyes was intensified.

'I wanted to know,' he said.

She turned aside, breaking the spell. In some strange way, she felt he was getting power over her.

'Well, I can't tell you already,' she said.

She went to the mirror to take out the hairpins from her hair. She stood before the mirror every night for some minutes, brushing her fine dark hair. It was part of the inevitable ritual of her life.

He followed her, and stood behind her. She was busy with bent head, taking out the pins and shaking her warm hair loose. When she looked up, she saw him in the glass standing behind her, watching unconsciously, not consciously seeing her, and yet watching, with fine-pupilled eyes that *seemed* to smile, and which were not really smiling.

She started. It took all her courage for her to continue brushing her hair, as usual, for her to pretend she was at her ease. She was far, far from being at her ease with him. She beat her brains wildly for something to say to him.

'What are your plans for tomorrow?' she asked nonchalantly, whilst her heart was beating so furiously, her eyes were so bright with strange nervousness, she felt he could not but observe. But she knew also that he was completely blind, blind as a wolf looking at her. It was a strange battle between her ordinary consciousness and his uncanny, black-art consciousness.

'I don't know,' he replied, 'what would you like to do?'

He spoke emptily, his mind was sunk away.

'Oh,' she said, with easy protestation, 'I'm ready for anything – anything will be fine for *me*, I'm sure.'

And to herself she was saying: 'God, why am I so nervous – why are you so nervous, you fool. If he sees it I'm done for for ever – you *know* you're done for for ever, if he sees the absurd state you're in.'

And she smiled to herself as if it were all child's play. Meanwhile her heart was plunging, she was almost fainting. She could see him, in the mirror, as he stood there behind her, tall and over-arching – blond and terribly frightening. She glanced at his reflection with furtive eyes, willing to give anything to save him from knowing she could see him. He did not know she could see his reflection. He was looking unconsciously, glisteningly down at her head, from which the hair fell loose, as she brushed it with wild, nervous hand. She held her head aside and brushed and brushed her hair madly. For her life, she could not turn round and face him. For her life, *she could not*. And the knowledge made her almost sink to the ground in a faint, helpless, spent. She was aware of his frightening, impending figure standing close behind her, she was aware of his hard, strong, unyielding chest, close upon her back. And she felt she could not bear it any more, in a few minutes she would fall down at his feet, grovelling at his feet, and letting him destroy her.

The thought pricked up all her sharp intelligence and presence of mind. She dared not turn round to him – and there he stood motionless, unbroken. Summoning all her strength, she said, in a full, resonant, nonchalant voice, that was forced out with all her remaining self-control, 'Oh, would you mind looking in that bag behind there and giving me my – '

Here her power fell inert. 'My what – my what – ?' she screamed in silence to herself.

But he had started round, surprised and startled that she should ask him to look in her bag, which she always kept so *very* private to herself. She turned now, her face white, her dark eyes blazing with uncanny, overwrought excitement. She saw him stooping to the bag, undoing the loosely buckled strap, unattentive.

'Your what?' he asked.

'Oh, a little enamel box – yellow – with a design of a cormorant plucking her breast – '

She went towards him, stooping her beautiful, bare arm, and deftly turned some of her things, disclosing the box, which was exquisitely painted.

'That is it, see,' she said, taking it from under his eyes.

And he was baffled now. He was left to fasten up the bag, whilst she swiftly did up her hair for the night, and sat down to unfasten her shoes. She would not turn her back to him any more.

He was baffled, frustrated, but unconscious. She had the whip hand over him now. She knew he had not realised her terrible panic. Her heart was beating heavily still. Fool, fool that she was, to get into such a state! How she thanked God for Gerald's obtuse blindness. 'I thank God he could see nothing.

She sat slowly unlacing her shoes, and he too commenced to undress. Thank God that crisis was over. She felt almost fond of him now, almost in love with him.

'Ah, Gerald,' she laughed, caressively, teasingly. 'Ah, what a fine game you played with the Professor's daughter – didn't you now?'

'What game?' he asked, looking round.

'*Isn't* she in love with you – oh *dear*, isn't she in love with you!' said Gudrun, in her gayest, most attractive mood.

'I shouldn't think so,' he said.

'Shouldn't think so!' she teased. 'Why the poor girl is lying at this moment overwhelmed, dying with love for you. She thinks you're *wonderful* – oh marvellous, beyond what man has ever been. *Really*, isn't it funny?'

'Why funny, what is funny?' he asked.

'Why to see you working it on her,' she said, with a half reproach that confused the male conceit in him. 'Really Gerald, the poor girl – !'

'I did nothing to her,' he said.

'Oh, it was too shameful, the way you simply swept her off her feet.'

'That was *Schuhplatteln*,' he replied, with a bright grin.

'Ha – ha – ha!' laughed Gudrun.

Her mockery quivered through his muscles with curious re-echoes. When he slept he seemed to crouch down in the bed, lapped up in his own strength, that yet was hollow.

And Gudrun slept strongly, a victorious sleep. Suddenly, she was almost fiercely awake. The small timber room glowed with the dawn, that came upwards from the low window. She could see down the valley when she lifted her head: the snow with a pinkish, half-revealed magic, the fringe of pine trees at the bottom of the slope. And one tiny figure moved over the vaguely-illuminated space.

She glanced at his watch; it was seven o'clock. He was still completely asleep. And she was so hard awake, it was almost frightening – a hard, metallic wakefulness. She lay looking at him.

He slept in the subjection of his own health and defeat. She was overcome by a sincere regard for him. Till now, she was afraid before him. She lay and thought about him, what he was, what he represented in the world. A fine, independent will, he had. She thought of the revolution he had worked in the mines, in so short a time. She knew that, if he were confronted with any problem, any hard actual difficulty, he would overcome it. If he laid hold of any idea, he would carry it through. He had the faculty of making order out of confusion. Only let him grip hold of a situation, and he would bring to pass an inevitable conclusion.

For a few moments she was borne away on the wild wings of ambition. Gerald, with his force of will and his power for comprehending the actual world, should be set to solve the problems of the day, the problem of industrialism in the modern world. She knew he would, in the course of time, effect the changes he desired, he could reorganise the industrial system. She knew he could do it. As an instrument, in these things, he was marvellous, she had never seen any man with his potentiality. He was unaware of it, but she knew.

He only needed to be hitched on, he needed that his hand should be set to the task, because he was so unconscious. And this she could do. She would marry him, he would go into Parliament in the Conservative interest, he would clear up the great muddle of labour and industry. He was so superbly fearless, masterful, he knew that every problem could be worked out, in life as in geometry. And he would care neither about himself nor about anything but the pure working out of the problem. He was very pure, really.

Her heart beat fast, she flew away on wings of elation, imagining a future. He would be a Napoleon of peace, or a Bismarck – and she the woman behind him. She had read Bismarck's letters, and had been deeply moved by them. And Gerald would be freer, more dauntless than Bismarck.

But even as she lay in fictitious transport, bathed in the strange, false sunshine of hope in life, something seemed to snap in her, and a terrible cynicism began to gain upon her, blowing in like a wind. Everything turned to irony with her: the last flavour of everything was ironical. When she felt her pang of undeniable reality, this was when she knew the hard irony of hopes and ideas.

She lay and looked at him, as he slept. He was sheerly beautiful, he was a perfect instrument. To her mind, he was a pure, inhuman, almost superhuman instrument. His instrumentality appealed so strongly to her, she wished she were God, to use him as a tool.

And at the same instant, came the ironical question: 'What for?' She thought of the colliers' wives, with their linoleum and their lace curtains and their little girls in high-laced boots. She thought of the wives and daughters of the pit-managers, their tennis-parties, and their terrible struggles to be superior each to the other, in the social scale. There was Shortlands with its meaningless distinction, the meaningless crowd of the Criches. There was London, the House of Commons, the extant social world. My God!

Young as she was, Gudrun had touched the whole pulse of social England. She had no ideas of rising in the world. She knew, with the perfect cynicism of cruel youth, that to rise in the world meant to have one outside show instead of another, the advance was like having a spurious half-crown instead of a spurious penny. The whole coinage of valuation was spurious. Yet of course, her cynicism knew well enough that, in a world where spurious coin was current, a bad sovereign was better than a bad farthing. But rich and poor, she despised both alike.

Already she mocked at herself for her dreams. They could be fulfilled easily enough. But she recognised too well, in her spirit, the mockery of her own impulses. What did she care, that Gerald had created a richly-paying industry out of an old worn-out concern? What did she care? The worn-out concern and the rapid, splendidly organised industry, they were bad money. Yet of course, she cared a great deal, outwardly – and outwardly was all that mattered, for inwardly was a bad joke.

Everything was intrinsically a piece of irony to her. She leaned over Gerald and said in her heart, with compassion, 'Oh, my dear, my dear, the game isn't worth even you. You are a fine thing really – why should you be used on such a poor show!'

Her heart was breaking with pity and grief for him. And at the same moment, a grimace came over her mouth, of mocking irony at her own unspoken tirade. Ah, what a farce it was! She thought of Parnell and Katherine O'Shea. Parnell! After all, who can take the nationalisation of Ireland seriously? Who can take political Ireland really seriously, whatever it does? And who can take political England seriously? Who can? Who can care a straw, really, how the old patched-up Constitution is tinkered at any more? Who cares a button for our national ideas, any more than for our national bowler hat? Aha, it is all old hat, it is all old bowler hat!

That's all it is, Gerald, my young hero. At any rate we'll spare ourselves the nausea of stirring the old broth any more. You be beautiful, my Gerald, and reckless. There *are* perfect moments. Wake up, Gerald, wake up, convince me of the perfect moments. Oh, convince me, I need it.

He opened his eyes, and looked at her. She greeted him with a mocking, enigmatic smile in which was a poignant gaiety. Over his face went the reflection of the smile, he smiled, too, purely unconsciously.

That filled her with extraordinary delight, to see the smile cross his face, reflected from her face. She remembered that was how a baby smiled. It filled her with extraordinary radiant delight.

'You've done it,' she said.

'What?' he asked, dazed.

'Convinced me.'

And she bent down, kissing him passionately, passionately, so that he was bewildered. He did not ask her of what he had convinced her, though he meant to. He was glad she was kissing him. She seemed to be feeling for his very heart to touch the quick of him. And he wanted her to touch the quick of his being, he wanted that most of all.

Outside, somebody was singing, in a manly, reckless handsome voice:

'*Mach mir auf, mach mir auf, du Stolze,*
Mach mir ein Feuer von Holze.
Vom Regen bin ich nass
Vom Regen bin ich nass – '

Gudrun knew that that song would sound through her eternity, sung in a manly, reckless, mocking voice. It marked one of her supreme moments, the supreme pangs of her nervous gratification. There it was, fixed in eternity for her.

The day came fine and bluish. There was a light wind blowing among the mountain-tops, keen as a rapier where it touched, carrying with it a fine dust of snow-powder. Gerald went out with the fine, blind face of a man who is in his state of fulfilment. Gudrun and he were in perfect static unity this morning, but unseeing and unwitting. They went out with a toboggan, leaving Ursula and Birkin to follow.

Gudrun was all scarlet and royal blue – a scarlet jersey and cap, and a royal blue skirt and stockings. She went gaily over the white snow, with Gerald beside her, in white and grey, pulling the little toboggan. They grew small in the distance of snow, climbing the steep slope.

For Gudrun herself, she seemed to pass altogether into the whiteness of the snow, she became a pure, thoughtless crystal. When she reached the top of the slope, in the wind, she looked round, and saw peak beyond peak of rock and snow, bluish, transcendent in heaven. And it seemed to her like a garden, with the peaks for pure flowers, and her heart gathering them. She had no separate consciousness for Gerald.

She held on to him as they went sheering down over the keen slope. She felt as if her senses were being whetted on some fine grindstone, that was keen as flame. The snow sprinted on either side, like sparks from a blade that is being sharpened, the whiteness round about ran swifter, swifter, in pure flame the white slope flew against her, and she fused like one molten, dancing globule, rushed through a white intensity. Then there was a great swerve at the bottom, when they swung as it were in a fall to earth, in the diminishing motion.

They came to rest. But when she rose to her feet, she could not stand. She gave a strange cry, turned and clung to him, sinking her face on his breast, fainting in him. Utter oblivion came over her, as she lay for a few moments abandoned against him.

'What is it?' he was saying. 'Was it too much for you?'

But she heard nothing.

When she came to, she stood up and looked round, astonished. Her face was white, her eyes brilliant and large.

'What is it?' he repeated. 'Did it upset you?'

She looked at him with her brilliant eyes that seemed to have undergone some transfiguration, and she laughed, with a terrible merriment.

'No,' she cried, with triumphant joy. 'It was the complete moment of my life.'

And she looked at him with her dazzling, over-weening laughter, like one possessed. A fine blade seemed to enter his heart, but he did not care, or take any notice.

But they climbed up the slope again, and they flew down through the white flame again, splendidly, splendidly. Gudrun was laughing and flashing, powdered with snow crystals, Gerald worked perfectly. He felt he could guide the toboggan to a hair-breadth, almost he could make it pierce into the air and right into the very heart of the sky. It seemed to him the flying sledge was but his strength spread out, he had but to move his arms, the motion was his own. They explored the great slopes, to find another slide. He felt there must be something better than they had known. And he found what he desired, a perfect long, fierce sweep, sheering past the foot of a rock and into the trees at the base. It was dangerous, he knew. But then he knew also he would direct the sledge between his fingers.

The first days passed in an ecstasy of physical motion, sleighing, skiing, skating, moving in an intensity of speed and white light that surpassed life itself, and carried the souls of the human beings beyond into an inhuman abstraction of velocity and weight and eternal, frozen snow.

Gerald's eyes became hard and strange, and as he went by on his skis he was more like some powerful, fateful sigh than a man, his muscles elastic in a perfect, soaring trajectory, his body projected in pure flight, mindless, soulless, whirling along one perfect line of force.

Luckily there came a day of snow, when they must all stay indoors: otherwise Birkin said, they would all lose their faculties, and begin to utter themselves in cries and shrieks, like some strange, unknown species of snow-creatures.

It happened in the afternoon that Ursula sat in the *Reunionsaal* talking to Loerke. The latter had seemed unhappy lately. He was lively and full of mischievous humour, as usual.

But Ursula had thought he was sulky about something. His partner, too, the big, fair, good-looking youth, was ill at ease, going about as if he belonged to nowhere, and was kept in some sort of subjection, against which he was rebelling.

Loerke had hardly talked to Gudrun. His associate, on the other hand, had paid her constantly a soft, over-deferential attention. Gudrun wanted to talk to Loerke. He was a sculptor, and she wanted to hear his view of his art. And his figure attracted her. There was the look of a little wastrel about him, that intrigued her, and an old man's look, that interested her, and then, beside this, an uncanny singleness, a quality of being by himself, not in contact with anybody else, that marked out an artist to her. He was a chatterer, a magpie, a maker of mischievous word-jokes, that were sometimes very clever, but which often were not. And she could see in his brown, gnome's eyes, the black look of inorganic misery, which lay behind all his small buffoonery.

His figure interested her – the figure of a boy, almost a street arab. He made no attempt to conceal it. He always wore a simple loden suit, with knee breeches. His legs were thin, and he made no attempt to disguise the fact: which was of itself remarkable, in a German. And he never ingratiated himself anywhere, not in the slightest, but kept to himself, for all his apparent playfulness.

Leitner, his companion, was a great sportsman, very handsome with his big limbs and his blue eyes. Loerke would go tobogganing or skating, in little snatches, but he was indifferent. And his fine, thin nostrils, the nostrils of a pure-bred street arab, would quiver with contempt at Leitner's splothering gymnastic displays. It was evident that the two men who had travelled and lived together, sharing the same bedroom, had now reached the stage of loathing. Leitner hated Loerke with an injured, writhing, impotent hatred, and Loerke treated Leitner with a fine-quivering contempt and sarcasm. Soon the two would have to go apart.

Already they were rarely together. Leitner ran attaching himself to somebody or other, always deferring, Loerke was a good deal alone. Out of doors he wore a Westphalian cap, a close brown-velvet head with big brown velvet flaps down over his ears, so that he looked like a lop-eared rabbit, or a troll. His face was brown-red, with a dry, bright skin, that seemed to crinkle with his mobile expressions. His eyes were arresting – brown, full, like a rabbit's, or like a troll's, or like the eyes of a lost being, having a strange, dumb, depraved look of knowledge, and a quick spark of uncanny fire. Whenever Gudrun had tried to talk to him he had shied away unresponsive, looking at her with his watchful dark eyes, but entering into no relation with her. He had made her feel that her slow French and her slower German were hateful to him. As for his own inadequate English, he was much too awkward to try it at all. But he understood a good deal of what was said, nevertheless. And Gudrun, piqued, left him alone.

This afternoon, however, she came into the lounge as he was talking to Ursula. His fine, black hair somehow reminded her of a bat, thin as it was on his full, sensitive-looking head, and worn away at the temples. He sat hunched up, as if his spirit were batlike. And Gudrun could see he was making some slow confidence to Ursula, unwilling, a slow, grudging, scanty self-revelation. She went and sat by her sister.

He looked at her, then looked away again, as if he took no notice of her. But as a matter of fact, she interested him deeply.

'Isn't it interesting, Prune,' said Ursula, turning to her sister, 'Herr Loerke is doing a great frieze for a factory in Cologne, for the outside, the street.'

She looked at him, at his thin, brown, nervous hands, that were prehensile, and somehow like talons, like 'griffes', inhuman.

'What *in?*' she asked.

'*Aus was?*' repeated Ursula.

'*Granit,*' he replied.

It had become immediately a laconic series of question and answer between fellow craftsmen.

'What is the relief?' asked Gudrun.

'*Alto relievo.*'

'And at what height?'

It was very interesting to Gudrun to think of his making the great granite

frieze for a great granite factory in Cologne. She got from him some notion of
the design. It was a representation of a fair, with peasants and artisans in an orgy
of enjoyment, drunk and absurd in their modern dress, whirling ridiculously in
roundabouts, gaping at shows, kissing and staggering and rolling in knots,
swinging in swing-boats, and firing down shooting galleries, a frenzy of chaotic
motion.

There was a swift discussion of technicalities. Gudrun was very much
impressed.

'But how wonderful, to have such a factory!' cried Ursula. 'Is the whole
building fine?'

'Oh yes,' he replied. 'The frieze is part of the whole architecture. Yes, it is a
colossal thing.'

Then he seemed to stiffen, shrugged his shoulders, and went on, 'Sculpture
and architecture must go together. The day for irrelevant statues, as for wall
pictures, is over. As a matter of fact sculpture is always part of an architectural
conception. And since churches are all museum stuff, since industry is our
business, now, then let us make our places of industry our art – our factory-area
our Parthenon, *ecco*!'

Ursula pondered.

'I suppose,' she said, 'there is no *need* for our great works to be so hideous.'

Instantly he broke into motion.

'There you are!' he cried, 'there you are! There is not only *no need* for our
places of work to be ugly, but their ugliness ruins the work, in the end. Men
will not go on submitting to such intolerable ugliness. In the end it will hurt
too much, and they will wither because of it. And this will wither the *work*
as well. They will think the work itself is ugly: the machines, the very act
of labour. Whereas the machinery and the acts of labour are extremely,
maddeningly beautiful. But this will be the end of our civilisation, when people
will not work because work has become so intolerable to their senses, it
nauseates them too much, they would rather starve. *Then* we shall see the
hammer used only for smashing, then we shall see it. Yet here we are – we have
the opportunity to make beautiful factories, beautiful machine-houses – we
have the opportunity – '

Gudrun could only partly understand. She could have cried with vexation.

'What does he say?' she asked Ursula. And Ursula translated, stammering
and brief. Loerke watched Gudrun's face, to see her judgement.

'And do you think then,' said Gudrun, 'that art should serve industry?'

'Art should *interpret* industry, as art once interpreted religion,' he said.

'But does your fair interpret industry?' she asked him.

'Certainly. What is man doing, when he is at a fair like this? He is fulfilling
the counterpart of labour – the machine works him, instead of he the machine.
He enjoys the mechanical motion, in his own body.'

'But is there nothing but work – mechanical work?' said Gudrun.

'Nothing but work!' he repeated, leaning forward, his eyes two darknesses, with needle-points of light. 'No, it is nothing but this, serving a machine, or enjoying the motion of a machine – motion, that is all. You have never worked for hunger, or you would know what god governs us.'

Gudrun quivered and flushed. For some reason she was almost in tears.

'No, I have not worked for hunger,' she replied, 'but I have worked!'

'*Travaillé – lavorato?*' he asked. '*E che lavoro – che lavoro? Quel travail est-ce que vous avez fait?*'

He broke into a mixture of Italian and French, instinctively using a foreign language when he spoke to her.

'You have never worked as the world works,' he said to her, with sarcasm.

'Yes,' she said. 'I have. And I do – I work now for my daily bread.'

He paused, looked at her steadily, then dropped the subject entirely. She seemed to him to be trifling.

'But have *you* ever worked as the world works?' Ursula asked him.

He looked at her untrustful.

'Yes,' he replied, with a surly bark. 'I have known what it was to lie in bed for three days, because I had nothing to eat.'

Gudrun was looking at him with large, grave eyes, that seemed to draw the confession from him as the marrow from his bones. All his nature held him back from confessing. And yet her large, grave eyes upon him seemed to open some valve in his veins, and involuntarily he was telling.

'My father was a man who did not like work, and we had no mother. We lived in Austria, Polish Austria. How did we live? Ha! – somehow! Mostly in a room with three other families - one set in each corner – and the WC in the middle of the room – a pan with a plank on it – ha! I had two brothers and a sister – and there might be a woman with my father. He was a free being, in his way – would fight with any man in the town – a garrison town – and was a little man too. But he wouldn't work for anybody – set his heart against it, and wouldn't.'

'And how did you live then?' asked Ursula.

He looked at her – then, suddenly, at Gudrun.

'Do you understand?' he asked.

'Enough,' she replied.

Their eyes met for a moment. Then he looked away. He would say no more.

'And how did you become a sculptor?' asked Ursula.

'How did I become a sculptor – ' he paused. '*Dunque* – ' he resumed, in a changed manner, and beginning to speak French – 'I became old enough – I used to steal from the market-place. Later I went to work – imprinted the stamp on clay bottles, before they were baked. It was an earthenware-bottle factory. There I began making models. One day, I had had enough. I lay in the sun and did not go to work. Then I walked to Munich – then I walked to Italy – begging, begging everything.

'The Italians were very good to me – they were good and honourable to me. From Bozen to Rome, almost every night I had a meal and a bed, perhaps of straw, with some peasant. I love the Italian people, with all my heart.

'*Dunque, adesso – maintenant* – I earn a thousand pounds in a year, or I earn two thousand –'

He looked down at the ground, his voice tailing off into silence.

Gudrun looked at his fine, thin, shiny skin, reddish-brown from the sun, drawn tight over his full temples; and at his thin hair – and at the thick, coarse, brushlike moustache, cut short about his mobile, rather shapeless mouth.

'How old are you?' she asked.

He looked up at her with his full, elfin eyes startled.

'*Wie alt?*' he repeated. And he hesitated. It was evidently one of his reticencies.

'How old are *you?*' he replied, without answering.

'I am twenty-six,' she answered.

'Twenty-six,' he repeated, looking into her eyes. He paused. Then he said, '*Und Ihr Herr Gemahl, wie alt is er?*'

'Who?' asked Gudrun.

'Your husband,' said Ursula, with a certain irony.

'I haven't got a husband,' said Gudrun in English. In German she answered, 'He is thirty-one.'

But Loerke was watching closely, with his uncanny, full, suspicious eyes. Something in Gudrun seemed to accord with him. He was really like one of the 'little people' who have no soul, who has found his mate in a human being. But he suffered in his discovery. She too was fascinated by him, fascinated, as if some strange creature, a rabbit or a bat, or a brown seal, had begun to talk to her. But also, she knew what he was unconscious of, his tremendous power of under-standing, of apprehending her living motion. He did not know his own power. He did not know how, with his full, submerged, watchful eyes, he could look into her and see her, what she was, see her secrets. He would only want her to be herself – he knew her verily, with a subconscious, sinister knowledge, devoid of illusions and hopes.

To Gudrun, there was in Loerke the rock-bottom of all life. Everybody else had their illusion, must have their illusion, their before and after. But he, with a perfect stoicism, did without any before and after, dispensed with all illusion. He did not deceive himself in the last issue. In the last issue he cared about nothing, he was troubled about nothing, he made not the slightest attempt to be at one with anything. He existed a pure, unconnected will, stoical and momentaneous. There was only his work.

It was curious too, how his poverty, the degradation of his earlier life, attracted her. There was something insipid and tasteless to her in the idea of a gentleman, a man who had gone the usual course through school and university. A certain violent sympathy, however, came up in her for this mud-child. He seemed to be the very stuff of the underworld of life. There was no going beyond him.

Ursula too was attracted by Loerke. In both sisters he commanded a certain homage. But there were moments when to Ursula he seemed indescribably inferior, false, a vulgarism.

Both Birkin and Gerald disliked him, Gerald ignoring him with some contempt, Birkin exasperated.

'What do the women find so impressive in that little brat?' Gerald asked.

'God alone knows,' replied Birkin, 'unless it's some sort of appeal he makes to them, which flatters them and has such a power over them.'

Gerald looked up in surprise.

'*Does* he make an appeal to them?' he asked.

'Oh yes,' replied Birkin. 'He is the perfectly subjected being, existing almost like a criminal. And the women rush towards that, like a current of air towards a vacuum.'

'Funny they should rush to that,' said Gerald.

'Makes one mad, too,' said Birkin. 'But he has the fascination of pity and repulsion for them, a little obscene monster of the darkness that he is.'

Gerald stood still, suspended in thought.

'What *do* women want, at the bottom?' he asked.

Birkin shrugged his shoulders.

'God knows,' he said. 'Some satisfaction in basic repulsion, it seems to me. They seem to creep down some ghastly tunnel of darkness, and will never be satisfied till they've come to the end.'

Gerald looked out into the mist of fine snow that was blowing by. Everywhere was blind today, horribly blind.

'And what *is* the end?' he asked.

Birkin shook his head.

'I've not got there yet, so I don't know. Ask Loerke, he's pretty near. He is a good many stages further than either you or I can go.'

'Yes, but stages further in what?' cried Gerald, irritated.

Birkin sighed, and gathered his brows into a knot of anger.

'Stages further in social hatred,' he said. 'He lives like a rat, in the river of corruption, just where it falls over into the bottomless pit. He's further on than we are. He hates the ideal more acutely. He *hates* the ideal utterly, yet it still dominates him. I expect he is a Jew – or part Jewish.'

'Probably,' said Gerald.

'He is a gnawing little negation, gnawing at the roots of life.'

'But why does anybody care about him?' cried Gerald.

'Because they hate the ideal also, in their souls. They want to explore the sewers, and he's the wizard rat that swims ahead.'

Still Gerald stood and stared at the blind haze of snow outside.

'I don't understand your terms, really,' he said, in a flat, doomed voice. 'But it sounds a rum sort of desire.'

'I suppose we want the same,' said Birkin. 'Only we want to take a quick jump downwards, in a sort of ecstasy – and he ebbs with the stream, the sewer stream.'

Meanwhile Gudrun and Ursula waited for the next opportunity to talk to Loerke. It was no use beginning when the men were there. Then they could get into no touch with the isolated little sculptor. He had to be alone with them And he preferred Ursula to be there, as a sort of transmitter to Gudrun.

'Do you do nothing but architectural sculpture?' Gudrun asked him one evening.

'Not now,' he replied. 'I have done all sorts – except portraits – I never did portraits. But other things – '

'What kind of things?' asked Gudrun.

He paused a moment, then rose, and went out of the room. He returned almost immediately with a little roll of paper, which he handed to her. She unrolled it. It was a photogravure reproduction of a statuette, signed F. Loerke.

'That is quite an early thing – *not* mechanical,' he said, 'more popular.'

The statuette was of a naked girl, small, finely made, sitting on a great naked horse. The girl was young and tender, a mere bud. She was sitting sideways on the horse, her face in her hands, as if in shame and grief, in a little abandon. Her hair, which was short and must be flaxen, fell forward, divided, half covering her hands.

Her limbs were young and tender. Her legs, scarcely formed yet, the legs of a maiden just passing towards cruel womanhood, dangled childishly over the side of the powerful horse, pathetically, the small feet folded one over the other, as if to hide. But there was no hiding. There she was exposed naked on the naked flank of the horse.

The horse stood stock still, stretched in a kind of start. It was a massive, magnificent stallion, rigid with pent-up power. Its neck was arched and terrible, like a sickle, its flanks were pressed back, rigid with power.

Gudrun went pale, and a darkness came over her eyes, like shame, she looked up with a certain supplication, almost slave-like. He glanced at her, and jerked his head a little.

'How big is it?' she asked, in a toneless voice, persisting in appearing casual and unaffected.

'How big?' he replied, glancing again at her. 'Without pedestal – so high – ' he measured with his hand – 'with pedestal, so – '

He looked at her steadily. There was a little brusque, turgid contempt for her in his swift gesture, and she seemed to cringe a little.

'And what is it done in?' she asked, throwing back her head and looking at him with affected coldness.

He still gazed at her steadily, and his dominance was not shaken.

'Bronze – green bronze.'

'Green bronze!' repeated Gudrun, coldly accepting his challenge. She was thinking of the slender, immature, tender limbs of the girl, smooth and cold in green bronze.

'Yes, beautiful,' she murmured, looking up at him with a certain dark homage.

He closed his eyes and looked aside, triumphant.

'Why,' said Ursula, 'did you make the horse so stiff? It is as stiff as a block.'

'Stiff?' he repeated, in arms at once.

'Yes. *Look* how stock and stupid and brutal it is. Horses are sensitive, quite delicate and sensitive, really.'

He raised his shoulders, spread his hands in a shrug of slow indifference, as much as to inform her she was an amateur and an impertinent nobody.

'*Wissen Sie*,' he said, with an insulting patience and condescension in his voice, 'that horse is a certain *form*, part of a whole form. It is part of a work of art, a piece of form. It is not a picture of a friendly horse to which you give a lump of sugar, do you see – it is part of a work of art, it has no relation to anything outside that work of art.'

Ursula, angry at being treated quite so insultingly *de haut en bas*, from the height of esoteric art to the depth of general exoteric amateurism, replied, hotly, flushing and lifting her face.

'But it *is* a picture of a horse, nevertheless.'

He lifted his shoulders in another shrug.

'As you like – it is not a picture of a cow, certainly.'

Here Gudrun broke in, flushed and brilliant, anxious to avoid any more of this, any more of Ursula's foolish persistence in giving herself away.

'What do you mean by "it is a picture of a horse"?' she cried at her sister. 'What do you mean by a horse? You mean an idea you have in *your* head, and which you want to see represented. There is another idea altogether, quite another idea. Call it a horse if you like, or say it is not a horse. I have just as much right to say that *your* horse isn't a horse, that it is a falsity of your own make-up.'

Ursula wavered, baffled. Then her words came.

'But why does he have this idea of a horse?' she said. 'I know it is his idea. I know it is a picture of himself, really – '

Loerke snorted with rage.

'A picture of myself!' he repeated, in derision. '*Wissen Sie, gnädige Frau*, that is a *Kunstwerk*, a work of art. It is a work of art, it is a picture of nothing, of absolutely nothing. It has nothing to do with anything but itself, it has no relation with the everyday world of this and other, there is no connection between them, absolutely none, they are two different and distinct planes of existence, and to translate one into the other is worse than foolish, it is a darkening of all counsel, a making confusion everywhere. Do you see, you *must not* confuse the relative work of action, with the absolute world of art. That you *must not do*.'

'That is quite true,' cried Gudrun, let loose in a sort of rhapsody. 'The two things are quite and permanently apart, they have *nothing* to do with one another. *I* and my art, they have nothing to do with each other. My art stands in another world, I am in this world.'

Her face was flushed and transfigured. Loerke, who was sitting with his head ducked, like some creature at bay, looked up at her, swiftly, almost furtively, and murmured, '*Ja – so ist es, so ist es.*'

Ursula was silent after this outburst. She was furious. She wanted to poke a hole into them both.

'It isn't a word of it true, of all this harangue you have made me,' she replied flatly. 'The horse is a picture of your own stock, stupid brutality, and the girl was a girl you loved and tortured and then ignored.'

He looked up at her with a small smile of contempt in his eyes. He would not trouble to answer this last charge.

Gudrun too was silent in exasperated contempt. Ursula *was* such an insufferable outsider, rushing in where angels would fear to tread. But then – fools must be suffered, if not gladly.

But Ursula was persistent too.

'As for your world of art and your world of reality,' she replied, 'you have to separate the two, because you can't bear to know what you are. You can't bear to realise what a stock, stiff, hidebound brutality you *are* really, so you say "it's the world of art". The world of art is only the truth about the real world, that's all – but you are too far gone to see it.'

She was white and trembling, intent. Gudrun and Loerke sat in stiff dislike of her. Gerald too, who had come up in the beginning of the speech, stood looking at her in complete disapproval and opposition. He felt she was undignified, she put a sort of vulgarity over the esotericism which gave man his last distinction. He joined his forces with the other two. They all three wanted her to go away. But she sat on in silence, her soul weeping, throbbing violently, her fingers twisting her handkerchief.

The others maintained a dead silence, letting the display of Ursula's obtrusiveness pass by. Then Gudrun asked, in a voice that was quite cool and casual, as if resuming a casual conversation, 'Was the girl a model?'

'*Nein, sie war kein Modell. Sie war eine kleine Malschülerin.*'

'An art-student!' replied Gudrun.

And how the situation revealed itself to her! She saw the girl art-student, unformed and of pernicious recklessness, too young, her straight flaxen hair cut short, hanging just into her neck, curving inwards slightly, because it was rather thick; and Loerke, the well-known master-sculptor, and the girl, probably well-brought-up, and of good family, thinking herself so great to be his mistress. Oh, how well she knew the common callousness of it all. Dresden, Paris, or London, what did it matter? She knew it.

'Where is she now?' Ursula asked.

Loerke raised his shoulders, to convey his complete ignorance and indifference.

'That is already six years ago,' he said; 'she will be twenty-three years old, no more good.'

Gerald had picked up the picture and was looking at it. It attracted him also. He saw on the pedestal that the piece was called 'Lady Godiva'.

'But this isn't Lady Godiva,' he said, smiling good-humouredly. 'She was the middle-aged wife of some Earl or other, who covered herself with her long hair.'

'*À la* Maud Allan,' said Gudrun with a mocking grimace.

'Why Maud Allan?' he replied. 'Isn't it so? I always thought the legend was that.'

'Yes, Gerald dear, I'm quite *sure* you've got the legend perfectly.'

She was laughing at him, with a little, mock-caressive contempt.

'To be sure, I'd rather see the woman than the hair,' he laughed in return.

'Wouldn't you just!' mocked Gudrun.

Ursula rose and went away, leaving the three together.

Gudrun took the picture again from Gerald, and sat looking at it closely.

'Of course,' she said, turning to tease Loerke now, 'you *understood* your little *Malschülerin.*'

He raised his eyebrows and his shoulders in a complacent shrug.

'The little girl?' asked Gerald, pointing to the figure.

Gudrun was sitting with the picture in her lap. She looked up at Gerald, full into his eyes, so that he seemed to be blinded.

'*Didn't* he understand her!' she said to Gerald, in a slightly mocking, humorous playfulness. 'You've only to look at the feet – *aren't* they darling, so pretty and tender – oh, they're really wonderful, they are really –'

She lifted her eyes slowly, with a hot, flaming look into Loerke's eyes. His soul was filled with her burning recognition, he seemed to grow more uppish and lordly.

Gerald looked at the small, sculptured feet. They were turned together, half covering each other in pathetic shyness and fear. He looked at them a long time, fascinated. Then, in some pain, he put the picture away from him. He felt full of barrenness.

'What was her name?' Gudrun asked Loerke.

'Annette von Weck,' Loerke replied, reminiscent. '*Ja, sie war hübsch.* She was pretty – but she was tiresome. She was a nuisance, – not for a minute would she keep still – not until I'd slapped her hard and made her cry – then she'd sit for five minutes.'

He was thinking over the work, his work, the all important to him.

'Did you really slap her?' asked Gudrun, coolly.

He glanced back at her, reading her challenge.

'Yes, I did,' he said, nonchalant, 'harder than I have ever beat anything in my life. I had to, I had to. It was the only way I got the work done.'

Gudrun watched him with large, dark-filled eyes, for some moments. She seemed to be considering his very soul. Then she looked down, in silence.

'Why did you have such a young Godiva then?' asked Gerald. 'She is so small, besides, on the horse – not big enough for it – such a child.'

A queer spasm went over Loerke's face.

'Yes,' he said. 'I don't like them any bigger, any older. Then they are beautiful, at sixteen, seventeen, eighteen – after that, they are no use to me.'

There was a moment's pause.

'Why not?' asked Gerald.

Loerke shrugged his shoulders.

'I don't find them interesting – or beautiful – they are no good to me, for my work.'

'Do you mean to say a woman isn't beautiful after she is twenty?' asked Gerald.

'For me, no. Before twenty, she is small and fresh and tender and slight. After that – let her be what she likes, she has nothing for me. The Venus of Milo is a bourgeoise – so are they all.'

'And you don't care for women at all after twenty?' asked Gerald.

'They are no good to me, they are of no use in my art,' Loerke repeated impatiently. 'I don't find them beautiful.'

'You are an epicure,' said Gerald, with a slight sarcastic laugh.

'And what about men?' asked Gudrun suddenly.

'Yes, they are good at all ages,' replied Loerke. 'A man should be big and powerful – whether he is old or young is of no account, so he has the size, something of massiveness and – and stupid form.'

Ursula went out alone into the world of pure, new snow. But the dazzling whiteness seemed to beat upon her till it hurt her, she felt the cold was slowly strangling her soul. Her head felt dazed and numb.

Suddenly she wanted to go away. It occurred to her, like a miracle, that she might go away into another world. She had felt so doomed up here in the eternal snow, as if there were no beyond.

Now suddenly, as by a miracle she remembered that away beyond, below her, lay the dark fruitful earth, that towards the south there were stretches of land dark with orange trees and cypress, grey with olives, that ilex trees lifted wonderful plumy tufts in shadow against a blue sky. Miracle of miracles! – this utterly silent, frozen world of the mountain-tops was not universal! One might leave it and have done with it. One might go away.

She wanted to realise the miracle at once. She wanted at this instant to have done with the snow-world, the terrible, static ice-built mountain-tops. She wanted to see the dark earth, to smell its earthy fecundity, to see the patient wintry vegetation, to feel the sunshine touch a response in the buds.

She went back gladly to the house, full of hope. Birkin was reading, lying in bed.

'Rupert,' she said, bursting in on him. 'I want to go away.'

He looked up at her slowly.

'Do you?' he replied mildly.

She sat by him and put her arms round his neck. It surprised her that he was so little surprised.

'Don't *you*?' she asked troubled.

'I hadn't thought about it,' he said. 'But I'm sure I do.'

She sat up, suddenly erect.

'I hate it,' she said. 'I hate the snow, and the unnaturalness of it, the unnatural light it throws on everybody, the ghastly glamour, the unnatural feelings it makes everybody have.'

He lay still and laughed, meditating.

'Well,' he said, 'we can go away – we can go tomorrow. We'll go tomorrow to Verona, and find Romeo and Juliet, and sit in the amphitheatre – shall we?'

Suddenly she hid her face against his shoulder with perplexity and shyness. He lay so untrammelled.

'Yes,' she said softly, filled with relief. She felt her soul had new wings, now he was so uncaring. 'I shall love to be Romeo and Juliet,' she said. 'My love!'

'Though a fearfully cold wind blows in Verona,' he said, 'from out of the Alps. We shall have the smell of the snow in our noses.'

She sat up and looked at him.

'Are you glad to go?' she asked, troubled.

His eyes were inscrutable and laughing. She hid her face against his neck, clinging close to him, pleading, 'Don't laugh at me – don't laugh at me.'

'Why how's that?' he laughed, putting his arms round her.

'Because I don't want to be laughed at,' she whispered.

He laughed more, as he kissed her delicate, finely perfumed hair.

'Do you love me?' she whispered, in wild seriousness.

'Yes,' he answered, laughing.

Suddenly she lifted her mouth to be kissed. Her lips were taut and quivering and strenuous, his were soft, deep and delicate. He waited a few moments in the kiss. Then a shade of sadness went over his soul.

'Your mouth is so hard,' he said, in faint reproach.

'And yours is so soft and nice,' she said gladly.

'But why do you always grip your lips?' he asked, regretful.

'Never mind,' she said swiftly. 'It is my way.'

She knew he loved her; she was sure of him. Yet she could not let go a certain hold over herself, she could not bear him to question her. She gave herself up in delight to being loved by him. She knew that, in spite of his joy when she abandoned herself, he was a little bit saddened too. She could give herself up to his activity. But she could not be herself, she *dared* not come forth quite nakedly to his nakedness, abandoning all adjustment, lapsing in pure faith with him. She abandoned herself to *him*, or she took hold of him and gathered her joy of him. And she enjoyed him fully. But they were never *quite* together, at the same moment, one was always a little left out. Nevertheless she was glad in hope, glorious and free, full of life and liberty. And he was still and soft and patient, for the time.

They made their preparations to leave the next day. First they went to Gudrun's room, where she and Gerald were just dressed ready for the evening indoors.

'Prune,' said Ursula, 'I think we shall go away tomorrow. I can't stand the snow any more. It hurts my skin and my soul.'

'Does it really hurt your soul, Ursula?' asked Gudrun, in some surprise. 'I can believe quite it hurts your skin – it is *terrible*. But I thought it was *admirable* for the soul.'

'No, not for mine. It just injures it,' said Ursula.

'Really!' cried Gudrun.

There was a silence in the room. And Ursula and Birkin could feel that Gudrun and Gerald were relieved by their going.

'You will go south?' said Gerald, a little ring of uneasiness in his voice.

'Yes,' said Birkin, turning away. There was a queer, indefinable hostility between the two men, lately. Birkin was on the whole dim and indifferent, drifting along in a dim, easy flow, unnoticing and patient, since he came abroad, whilst Gerald on the other hand, was intense and gripped into white light, agonistes. The two men revoked one another.

Gerald and Gudrun were very kind to the two who were departing, solicitous for their welfare as if they were two children. Gudrun came to Ursula's bedroom with three pairs of the coloured stockings for which she was notorious, and she threw them on the bed. But these were thick silk stockings, vermilion, cornflower blue, and grey, bought in Paris. The grey ones were knitted, seamless and heavy. Ursula was in raptures. She knew Gudrun must be feeling *very* loving, to give away such treasures.

'I can't take them from you, Prune,' she cried. 'I can't possibly deprive you of them – the jewels.'

'*Aren't* they jewels!' cried Gudrun, eyeing her gifts with an envious eye. '*Aren't* they real lambs!'

'Yes, you *must* keep them,' said Ursula.

'I don't *want* them, I've got three more pairs. I *want* you to keep them – I want you to have them. They're yours, there –'

And with trembling, excited hands she put the coveted stockings under Ursula's pillow.

'One gets the greatest joy of all out of really lovely stockings,' said Ursula.

'One does,' replied Gudrun; 'the greatest joy of all.'

And she sat down in the chair. It was evident she had come for a last talk. Ursula, not knowing what she wanted, waited in silence.

'Do you *feel*, Ursula,' Gudrun began, rather sceptically, 'that you are going-away-for-ever, never-to-return, sort of thing?'

'Oh, we shall come back,' said Ursula. 'It isn't a question of train-journeys.'

'Yes, I know. But spiritually, so to speak, you are going away from us all?'

Ursula quivered.

'I don't know a bit what is going to happen,' she said. 'I only know we are going somewhere.'

Gudrun waited.

'And you are glad?' she asked.

Ursula meditated for a moment.

'I believe I am *very* glad,' she replied.

But Gudrun read the unconscious brightness on her sister's face, rather than the uncertain tones of her speech.

'But don't you think you'll *want* the old connection with the world – father and the rest of us, and all that it means, England and the world of thought – don't you think you'll *need* that, really to make a world?'

Ursula was silent, trying to imagine.

'I think,' she said at length, involuntarily, 'that Rupert is right – one wants a new space to be in, and one falls away from the old.'

Gudrun watched her sister with impassive face and steady eyes.

'One wants a new space to be in, I quite agree,' she said. 'But *I* think that a new world is a development from this world, and that to isolate oneself with one other person, isn't to find a new world at all, but only to secure oneself in one's illusions.'

Ursula looked out of the window. In her soul she began to wrestle, and she was frightened. She was always frightened of words, because she knew that mere word-force could always make her believe what she did not believe.

'Perhaps,' she said, full of mistrust, of herself and everybody. 'But,' she added, 'I do think that one can't have anything new whilst one cares for the old – do you know what I mean? – even fighting the old is belonging to it. I know, one is tempted to stop with the world, just to fight it. But then it isn't worth it.'

Gudrun considered herself.

'Yes,' she said. 'In a way, one is of the world if one lives in it. But isn't it really an illusion to think you can get out of it? After all, a cottage in the Abruzzi, or wherever it may be, isn't a new world. No, the only thing to do with the world, is to see it through.'

Ursula looked away. She was so frightened of argument.

'But there *can* be something else, can't there?' she said. 'One can see it through in one's soul, long enough before it sees itself through in actuality. And then, when one has seen one's soul, one is something else.'

'*Can* one see it through in one's soul?' asked Gudrun. 'If you mean that you can see to the end of what will happen, I don't agree. I really can't agree. And anyhow, you can't suddenly fly off on to a new planet, because you think you can see to the end of this.'

Ursula suddenly straightened herself.

'Yes,' she said. 'Yes – one knows. One has no more connections here. One has a sort of other self, that belongs to a new planet, not to this. You've got to hop off.'

Gudrun reflected for a few moments. Then a smile of ridicule, almost of contempt, came over her face.

'And what will happen when you find yourself in space?' she cried in derision. 'After all, the great ideas of the world are the same there. You above everybody can't get away from the fact that love, for instance, is the supreme thing, in space as well as on earth.'

'No,' said Ursula, 'it isn't. Love is too human and little. I believe in something inhuman, of which love is only a little part. I believe what we must fulfil comes out of the unknown to us, and it is something infinitely more than love. It isn't so merely *human.*'

Gudrun looked at Ursula with steady, balancing eyes. She admired and despised her sister so much, both! Then, suddenly she averted her face, saying coldly, uglily, 'Well, I've got no further than love, yet.'

Over Ursula's mind flashed the thought: 'Because you never *have* loved, you can't get beyond it.'

Gudrun rose, came over to Ursula and put her arm round her neck.

'Go and find your new world, dear,' she said, her voice clanging with false benignity. 'After all, the happiest voyage is the quest of Rupert's Blessed Isles.'

Her arm rested round Ursula's neck, her fingers on Ursula's cheek for a few moments. Ursula was supremely uncomfortable meanwhile. There was an insult in Gudrun's protective patronage that was really too hurting. Feeling her sister's resistance, Gudrun drew awkwardly away, turned over the pillow, and disclosed the stockings again.

'Ha – ha!' she laughed, rather hollowly. 'How we do talk indeed – new worlds and old – !'

And they passed to the familiar worldly subjects.

Gerald and Birkin had walked on ahead, waiting for the sledge to overtake them, conveying the departing guests.

'How much longer will you stay here?' asked Birkin, glancing up at Gerald's very red, almost blank face.

'Oh, I can't say,' Gerald replied. 'Till we get tired of it.'

'You're not afraid of the snow melting first?' asked Birkin.

Gerald laughed.

'Does it melt?' he said.

'Things are all right with you then?' said Birkin.

Gerald screwed up his eyes a little.

'All right?' he said. 'I never know what those common words mean. All right and all wrong, don't they become synonymous, somewhere?'

'Yes, I suppose. How about going back?' asked Birkin.

'Oh, I don't know. We may never get back. I don't look before and after,' said Gerald.

'*Nor* pine for what is not,' said Birkin.

Gerald looked into the distance, with the small-pupilled, abstract eyes of a hawk.

'No. There's something final about this. And Gudrun seems like the end, to me. I don't know – but she seems so soft, her skin like silk, her arms heavy and soft. And it withers my consciousness, somehow, it burns the pith of my mind.' He went on a few paces, staring ahead, his eyes fixed, looking like a mask used in ghastly religions of the barbarians. 'It blasts your soul's eye,' he said, 'and leaves you sightless. Yet you *want* to be sightless, you *want* to be blasted, you don't want it any different.'

He was speaking as if in a trance, verbal and blank. Then suddenly he braced himself up with a kind of rhapsody, and looked at Birkin with vindictive, cowed eyes, saying, 'Do you know what it is to suffer when you are with a woman? She's so beautiful, so perfect, you find her *so good*, it tears you like a silk, and every stroke and bit cuts hot – ha, that perfection, when you blast yourself, you blast yourself! And then – ' he stopped on the snow and suddenly opened his clenched hands – 'it's nothing – your brain might have gone charred as rags – and – ' he looked round into the air with a queer histrionic movement – 'it's blasting – you understand what I mean – it is a great experience, something final – and then –

you're shrivelled as if struck by electricity.' He walked on in silence. It seemed like bragging, but like a man in extremity bragging truthfully.

'Of course,' he resumed, 'I wouldn't *not* have had it! It's a complete experience. And she's a wonderful woman. But – how I hate her somewhere! It's curious –'

Birkin looked at him, at his strange, scarcely conscious face. Gerald seemed blank before his own words.

'But you've had enough now?' said Birkin. 'You have had your experience. Why work on an old wound?'

'Oh,' said Gerald, 'I don't know. It's not finished –'

And the two walked on.

'I've loved you, as well as Gudrun, don't forget,' said Birkin bitterly. Gerald looked at him strangely, abstractedly.

'Have you?' he said, with icy scepticism. 'Or do you think you have?' He was hardly responsible for what he said.

The sledge came. Gudrun dismounted and they all made their farewell. They wanted to go apart, all of them. Birkin took his place, and the sledge drove away leaving Gudrun and Gerald standing on the snow, waving. Something froze Birkin's heart, seeing them standing there in the isolation of the snow, growing smaller and more isolated.

CHAPTER 30

Snowed Up

When Ursula and Birkin were gone, Gudrun felt herself free in her contest with Gerald. As they grew more used to each other, he seemed to press upon her more and more. At first she could manage him, so that her own will was always left free. But very soon, he began to ignore her female tactics, he dropped his respect for her whims and her privacies, he began to exert his own will blindly, without submitting to hers.

Already a vital conflict had set in, which frightened them both. But he was alone, whilst already she had begun to cast round for external resource.

When Ursula had gone, Gudrun felt her own existence had become stark and elemental. She went and crouched alone in her bedroom, looking out of the window at the big, flashing stars. In front was the faint shadow of the mountain-knot. That was the pivot. She felt strange and inevitable, as if she were centred upon the pivot of all existence, there was no further reality.

Presently Gerald opened the door. She knew he would not be long before he came. She was rarely alone, he pressed upon her like a frost, deadening her.

'Are you alone in the dark?' he said. And she could tell by his tone he resented it, he resented this isolation she had drawn round herself. Yet, feeling static and inevitable, she was kind towards him.

'Would you like to light the candle?' she asked.

He did not answer, but came and stood behind her, in the darkness.

'Look,' she said, 'at that lovely star up there. Do you know its name?'

He crouched beside her, to look through the low window.

'No,' he said. 'It is very fine.'

'Isn't it beautiful! Do you notice how it darts different coloured fires – it flashes really superbly – '

They remained in silence. With a mute, heavy gesture she put her hand on his knee, and took his hand.

'Are you regretting Ursula?' he asked.

'No, not at all,' she said. Then, in a slow mood, she asked, 'How much do you love me?'

He stiffened himself further against her.

'How much do you think I do?' he asked.

'I don't know,' she replied.

'But what is your opinion?' he asked.

There was a pause. At length, in the darkness, came her voice, hard and indifferent, 'Very little indeed,' she said coldly, almost flippant.

His heart went icy at the sound of her voice.

'Why don't I love you?' he asked, as if admitting the truth of her accusation, yet hating her for it.

'I don't know why you don't – I've been good to you. You were in a *fearful* state when you came to me.'

Her heart was beating to suffocate her, yet she was strong and unrelenting.

'When was I in a fearful state?' he asked.

'When you first came to me. I *had* to take pity on you. But it was never love.'

It was that statement 'it was never love', which sounded in his ears with madness.

'Why must you repeat it so often, that there is no love?' he said in a voice strangled with rage.

'Well you don't *think* you love, do you?' she asked.

He was silent with cold passion of anger.

'You don't think you *can* love me, do you?' she repeated almost with a sneer.

'No,' he said.

'You know you never *have* loved me, don't you?'

'I don't know what you mean by the word "love",' he replied.

'Yes, you do. You know all right that you have never loved me. Have you, do you think?'

'No,' he said, prompted by some barren spirit of truthfulness and obstinacy.

'And you never *will* love me,' she said finally, 'will you?'

There was a diabolic coldness in her, too much to bear.

'No,' he said.

'Then,' she replied, 'what have you against me?'

He was silent in cold, frightened rage and despair. 'If only I could kill her,' his heart was whispering repeatedly. 'If only I could kill her – I should be free.'

It seemed to him that death was the only severing of this Gordian knot.

'Why do you torture me?' he said.

She flung her arms round his neck.

'Ah, I don't want to torture you,' she said pityingly, as if she were comforting a child. The impertinence made his veins go cold, he was insensible. She held her arms round his neck, in a triumph of pity. And her pity for him was as cold as stone, its deepest motive was hate of him, and fear of his power over her, which she must always counterfoil.

'Say you love me,' she pleaded. 'Say you will love me for ever – won't you – won't you?'

But it was her voice only that coaxed him. Her senses were entirely apart from him, cold and destructive of him. It was her overbearing *will* that insisted.

'Won't you say you'll love me always?' she coaxed. 'Say it, even if it isn't true – say it Gerald, do.'

'I will love you always,' he repeated, in real agony, forcing the words out.

She gave him a quick kiss.

'Fancy your actually having said it,' she said with a touch of raillery.

He stood as if he had been beaten.

'Try to love me a little more, and to want me a little less,' she said, in a half contemptuous, half coaxing tone.

The darkness seemed to be swaying in waves across his mind, great waves of darkness plunging across his mind. It seemed to him he was degraded at the very quick, made of no account.

'You mean you don't want me?' he said.

'You are so insistent, and there is so little grace in you, so little fineness. You are so crude. You break me – you only waste me – it is horrible to me.'

'Horrible to you?' he repeated.

'Yes. Don't you think I might have a room to myself, now Ursula has gone? You can say you want a dressing-room.'

'You do as you like – you can leave altogether if you like,' he managed to articulate.

'Yes, I know that,' she replied. 'So can you. You can leave me whenever you like – without notice even.'

The great tides of darkness were swinging across his mind, he could hardly stand upright. A terrible weariness overcame him, he felt he must lie on the floor. Dropping off his clothes, he got into bed, and lay like a man suddenly overcome by drunkenness, the darkness lifting and plunging as if he were lying upon a black, giddy sea. He lay still in this strange, horrific reeling for some time, purely unconscious.

At length she slipped from her own bed and came over to him. He remained rigid, his back to her. He was all but unconscious.

She put her arms round his terrifying, insentient body, and laid her cheek against his hard shoulder.

'Gerald,' she whispered. 'Gerald.'

There was no change in him. She caught him against her. She pressed her breasts against his shoulders, she kissed his shoulder, through the sleeping jacket. Her mind wondered, over his rigid, unliving body. She was bewildered, and insistent, only her will was set for him to speak to her.

'Gerald, my dear!' she whispered, bending over him, kissing his ear.

Her warm breath playing, flying rhythmically over his ear, seemed to relax the tension. She could feel his body gradually relaxing a little, losing its terrifying, unnatural rigidity. Her hands clutched his limbs, his muscles, going over him spasmodically.

The hot blood began to flow again through his veins, his limbs relaxed.

'Turn round to me,' she whispered, forlorn with insistence and triumph.

So at last he was given again, warm and flexible. He turned and gathered her in his arms. And feeling her soft against him, so perfectly and wondrously soft and recipient, his arms tightened on her. She was as if crushed, powerless in him. His brain seemed hard and invincible now like a jewel, there was no resisting him.

His passion was awful to her, tense and ghastly, and impersonal, like a destruction, ultimate. She felt it would kill her. She was being killed.

'My God, my God,' she cried, in anguish, in his embrace, feeling her life being killed within her. And when he was kissing her, soothing her, her breath came slowly, as if she were really spent, dying.

'Shall I die, shall I die?' she repeated to herself.

And in the night, and in him, there was no answer to the question.

And yet, next day, the fragment of her which was not destroyed remained intact and hostile, she did not go away, she remained to finish the holiday, admitting nothing. He scarcely ever left her alone, but followed her like a shadow, he was like a doom upon her, a continual 'thou shalt', 'thou shalt not'. Sometimes it was he who seemed strongest, whilst she was almost gone, creeping near the earth like a spent wind; sometimes it was the reverse. But always it was this eternal see-saw, one destroyed that the other might exist, one ratified because the other was nulled.

'In the end,' she said to herself, 'I shall go away from him.'

'I can be free of her,' he said to himself in his paroxysms of suffering.

And he set himself to be free. He even prepared to go away, to leave her in the lurch. But for the first time there was a flaw in his will.

'Where shall I go?' he asked himself.

'Can't you be self-sufficient?' he replied to himself, putting himself upon his pride.

'Self-sufficient!' he repeated.

It seemed to him that Gudrun was sufficient unto herself, closed round and completed, like a thing in a case. In the calm, static reason of his soul, he recognised this, and admitted it was her right, to be closed round upon herself, self-complete, without desire. He realised it, he admitted it, it only needed one last effort on his own part, to win for himself the same completeness. He knew that it only needed one convulsion of his will for him to be able to turn upon himself also, to close upon himself as a stone fixes upon itself, and is impervious, self-completed, a thing isolated.

This knowledge threw him into a terrible chaos. Because, however much he might mentally *will* to be immune and self-complete, the desire for this state was lacking, and he could not create it. He could see that, to exist at all, he must be perfectly free of Gudrun, leave her if she wanted to be left, demand nothing of her, have no claim upon her.

But then, to have no claim upon her, he must stand by himself, in sheer nothingness. And his brain turned to nought at the idea. It was a state of nothingness. On the other hand, he might give in, and fawn to her. Or, finally, he might kill her. Or he might become just indifferent, purposeless, dissipated, momentaneous. But his nature was too serious, not gay enough or subtle enough for mocking licentiousness.

A strange rent had been torn in him; like a victim that is torn open and given to the heavens, so he had been torn apart and given to Gudrun. How should he close again? This wound, this strange, infinitely-sensitive opening of his soul, where he was exposed, like an open flower, to all the universe, and in which he was given to his complement, the other, the unknown, this wound, this disclosure, this unfolding of his own covering, leaving him incomplete, limited, unfinished, like an open flower under the sky, this was his cruellest joy. Why then should he forgo it? Why should he close up and become impervious, immune, like a partial thing in a sheath, when he had broken forth, like a seed that has germinated, to issue forth in being, embracing the unrealised heavens.

He would keep the unfinished bliss of his own yearning even through the torture she inflicted upon him. A strange obstinacy possessed him. He would not go away from her whatever she said or did. A strange, deathly yearning carried him along with her. She was the determinating influence of his very being, though she treated him with contempt, repeated rebuffs, and denials, still he would never be gone, since in being near her, even, he felt the quickening, the going forth in him, the release, the knowledge of his own limitation and the magic of the promise, as well as the mystery of his own destruction and annihilation.

She tortured the open heart of him even as he turned to her. And she was tortured herself. It may have been her will was stronger. She felt, with horror, as if he tore at the bud of her heart, tore it open, like an irreverent persistent being. Like a boy who pulls off a fly's wings, or tears open a bud to see what is in the flower, he tore at her privacy, at her very life, he would destroy her as an immature bud, torn open, is destroyed.

She might open towards him, a long while hence, in her dreams, when she was a pure spirit. But now she was not to be violated and ruined. She closed against him fiercely.

They climbed together, at evening, up the high slope, to see the sun set. In the finely breathing, keen wind they stood and watched the yellow sun sink in crimson and disappear. Then in the east the peaks and ridges glowed with living rose, incandescent like immortal flowers against a brown-purple sky, a miracle, whilst down below the world was a bluish shadow, and above, like an annunciation, hovered a rosy transport in midair.

To her it was so beautiful, it was a delirium, she wanted to gather the glowing, eternal peaks to her breast, and die. He saw them, saw they were beautiful. But there arose no clamour in his breast, only a bitterness that was visionary in itself. He wished the peaks were grey and unbeautiful, so that she should not get her support from them. Why did she betray the two of them so terribly, in embracing the glow of the evening? Why did she leave him standing there, with the ice-wind blowing through his heart, like death, to gratify herself among the rosy snow-tips?

'What does the twilight matter?' he said. 'Why do you grovel before it? Is it so important to you?'

She winced in violation and in fury.

'Go away,' she cried, 'and leave me to it. It is beautiful, beautiful,' she sang in strange, rhapsodic tones. 'It is the most beautiful thing I have ever seen in my life. Don't try to come between it and me. Take yourself away, you are out of place –'

He stood back a little, and left her standing there, statue-like, transported into the mystic glowing east. Already the rose was fading, large white stars were flashing out. He waited. He would forgo everything but the yearning.

'That was the most perfect thing I have ever seen,' she said in cold, brutal tones, when at last she turned round to him. 'It amazes me that you should want to destroy it. If you can't see it yourself, why try to debar me?' But in reality, he had destroyed it for her, she was straining after a dead effect.

'One day,' he said, softly, looking up at her, 'I shall destroy *you*, as you stand looking at the sunset; because you are such a liar.'

There was a soft, voluptuous promise to himself in the words. She was chilled but arrogant.

'Ha!' she said. 'I am not afraid of your threats!' She denied herself to him, she kept her room rigidly private to herself. But he waited on, in a curious patience, belonging to his yearning for her.

'In the end,' he said to himself with real voluptuous promise, 'when it reaches that point, I shall do away with her.' And he trembled delicately in every limb, in anticipation, as he trembled in his most violent accesses of passionate approach to her, trembling with too much desire.

She had a curious sort of allegiance with Loerke, all the while, now, something insidious and traitorous. Gerald knew of it. But in the unnatural state of patience, and the unwillingness to harden himself against her, in which he found himself, he took no notice, although her soft kindliness to the other man, whom he hated as a noxious insect, made him shiver again with an access of the strange shuddering that came over him repeatedly.

He left her alone only when he went skiing, a sport he loved, and which she did not practise. Then he seemed to sweep out of life, to be a projectile into the beyond. And often, when he went away, she talked to the little German sculptor. They had an invariable topic, in their art.

They were almost of the same ideas. He hated Mestrovic, was not satisfied with the Futurists, he liked the West African wooden figures, the Aztec art, Mexican and Central American. He saw the grotesque, and a curious sort of mechanical motion intoxicated him, a confusion in nature. They had a curious game with each other, Gudrun and Loerke, of infinite suggestivity, strange and leering, as if they had some esoteric understanding of life, that they alone were initiated into the fearful central secrets, that the world dared not know. Their whole correspondence was in a strange, barely comprehensible suggestivity, they kindled themselves at the subtle lust of the Egyptians or the Mexicans. The whole game was one of subtle inter-suggestivity, and they wanted to keep it on the plane of suggestion. From their verbal and physical nuances they got the highest satisfaction in the nerves, from a queer interchange of half-suggested ideas, looks, expressions and gestures, which were quite intolerable, though incomprehensible, to Gerald. He had no terms in which to think of their commerce, his terms were much too gross.

The suggestion of primitive art was their refuge, and the inner mysteries of sensation their object of worship. Art and Life were to them the Reality and the Unreality.

'Of course,' said Gudrun, 'life doesn't *really* matter – it is one's art which is central. What one does in one's life has *peu de rapport*, it doesn't signify much.'

'Yes, that is so, exactly,' replied the sculptor. 'What one does in one's art, that is the breath of one's being. What one does in one's life, that is a bagatelle for the outsiders to fuss about.'

It was curious what a sense of elation and freedom Gudrun found in this communication. She felt established for ever. Of course Gerald was *bagatelle*. Love was one of the temporal things in her life, except in so far as she was an artist. She thought of Cleopatra – Cleopatra must have been an artist; she reaped the essential from a man, she harvested the ultimate sensation, and threw away the husk; and Mary Stuart, and the great Rachel, panting with her lovers after the theatre, these were the exoteric exponents of love. After all, what was the lover but fuel for the transport of this subtle knowledge, for a female art, the art of pure, perfect knowledge in sensuous understanding.

One evening Gerald was arguing with Loerke about Italy and Tripoli. The Englishman was in a strange, inflammable state, the German was excited. It was a contest of words, but it meant a conflict of spirit between the two men. And all the while Gudrun could see in Gerald an arrogant English contempt for a foreigner. Although Gerald was quivering, his eyes flashing, his face flushed, in his argument there was a brusqueness, a savage contempt in his manner, that made Gudrun's blood flare up, and made Loerke keen and mortified. For Gerald came down like a sledge-hammer with his assertions, anything the little German said was merely contemptible rubbish.

At last Loerke turned to Gudrun, raising his hands in helpless irony, a shrug of ironical dismissal, something appealing and childlike.

'*Sehen sie, gnädige Frau –* ' he began.

'*Bitte sagen Sie nicht immer, gnädige Frau,*' cried Gudrun, her eyes flashing, her cheeks burning. She looked like a vivid Medusa. Her voice was loud and clamorous, the other people in the room were startled.

'Please don't call me Mrs Crich,' she cried aloud.

The name, in Loerke's mouth particularly, had been an intolerable humiliation and constraint upon her, these many days.

The two men looked at her in amazement. Gerald went white at the cheek-bones.

'What shall I say, then?' asked Loerke, with soft, mocking insinuation.

'*Sagen Sie nur nicht das,*' she muttered, her cheeks flushed crimson. 'Not that, at least.'

She saw, by the dawning look on Loerke's face, that he had understood. She was *not* Mrs Crich! So–o, that explained a great deal.

'*Soll ich Fräulein sagen?*' he asked, malevolently.

'I am not married,' she said, with some hauteur.

Her heart was fluttering now, beating like a bewildered bird. She knew she had dealt a cruel wound, and she could not bear it.

Gerald sat erect, perfectly still, his face pale and calm, like the face of a statue. He was unaware of her, or of Loerke or anybody. He sat perfectly still, in an unalterable calm. Loerke, meanwhile, was crouching and glancing up from under his ducked head.

Gudrun was tortured for something to say, to relieve the suspense. She twisted her face in a smile, and glanced knowingly, almost sneering, at Gerald.

'Truth is best,' she said to him, with a grimace.

But now again she was under his domination; now, because she had dealt him this blow; because she had destroyed him, and she did not know how he had taken it. She watched him. He was interesting to her. She had lost her interest in Loerke.

Gerald rose at length, and went over in a leisurely still movement, to the Professor. The two began a conversation on Goethe.

She was rather piqued by the simplicity of Gerald's demeanour this evening. He did not seem angry or disgusted, only he looked curiously innocent and pure, really beautiful. Sometimes it came upon him, this look of clear distance, and it always fascinated her.

She waited, troubled, throughout the evening. She thought he would avoid her, or give some sign. But he spoke to her simply and unemotionally, as he would to anyone else in the room. A certain peace, an abstraction possessed his soul.

She went to his room, hotly, violently in love with him. He was so beautiful and inaccessible. He kissed her, he was a lover to her. And she had extreme pleasure of him. But he did not come to, he remained remote and candid, unconscious. She wanted to speak to him. But this innocent, beautiful state of unconsciousness that had come upon him prevented her. She felt tormented and dark.

In the morning, however, he looked at her with a little aversion, some horror and some hatred darkening into his eyes. She withdrew on to her old ground. But still he would not gather himself together, against her.

Loerke was waiting for her now. The little artist, isolated in his own complete envelope, felt that here at last was a woman from whom he could get something. He was uneasy all the while, waiting to talk with her, subtly contriving to be near her. Her presence filled him with keenness and excitement, he gravitated cunningly towards her, as if she had some unseen force of attraction.

He was not in the least doubtful of himself, as regards Gerald. Gerald was one of the outsiders. Loerke only hated him for being rich and proud and of fine appearance. All these things, however, riches, pride of social standing, handsome physique, were externals. When it came to the relation with a woman such as Gudrun, he, Loerke, had an approach and a power that Gerald never dreamed of.

How should Gerald hope to satisfy a woman of Gudrun's calibre? Did he think that pride or masterful will or physical strength would help him? Loerke knew a secret beyond these things. The greatest power is the one that is subtle and adjusts itself, not one which blindly attacks. And he, Loerke, had understanding where Gerald was a calf. He, Loerke, could penetrate into depths far out of Gerald's knowledge. Gerald was left behind like a postulant in the anteroom of this temple of mysteries, this woman. But he Loerke, could he not penetrate into the inner darkness, find the spirit of the woman in its inner recess, and wrestle with it there, the central serpent that is coiled at the core of life?

What was it, after all, that a woman wanted? Was it mere social effect, fulfilment of ambition in the social world, in the community of mankind? Was it even a union in love and goodness? Did she want 'goodness'? Who but a fool would accept this of Gudrun? This was but the street view of her wants. Cross the threshold, and you found her completely, completely cynical about the social world and its advantages. Once inside the house of her soul and there was a pungent atmosphere of corrosion, an inflamed darkness of sensation, and a vivid, subtle, critical consciousness, that saw the world distorted, horrific.

What then, what next? Was it sheer blind force of passion that would satisfy her now? Not this, but the subtle thrills of extreme sensation in reduction. It was an unbroken will reacting against her unbroken will in a myriad subtle thrills of reduction, the last subtle activities of analysis and breaking down, carried out in the darkness of her, whilst the outside form, the individual, was utterly unchanged, even sentimental in its poses.

But between two particular people, any two people on earth, the range of pure sensational experience is limited. The climax of sensual reaction, once reached in any direction, is reached finally, there is no going on. There is only repetition possible, or the going apart of the two protagonists, or the subjugating of the one will to the other, or death.

Gerald had penetrated all the outer places of Gudrun's soul. He was to her the most crucial instance of the existing world, the *ne plus ultra* of the world of man as it existed for her. In him she knew the world, and had done with it. Knowing him finally she was the Alexander seeking new worlds. But there *were* no new worlds, there were no more *men*, there were only creatures, little, ultimate *creatures* like Loerke. The world was finished now, for her. There was only the inner, individual darkness, sensation within the ego, the obscene religious mystery of ultimate reduction, the mystic frictional activities of diabolic reducing down, disintegrating the vital organic body of life.

All this Gudrun knew in her subconsciousness, not in her mind. She knew her next step – she knew what she should move on to, when she left Gerald. She was afraid of Gerald, that he might kill her. But she did not intend to be killed. A fine thread still united her to him. It should not be *her* death which broke it. She had further to go, a further, slow exquisite experience to reap, unthinkable subtleties of sensation to know, before she was finished.

Of the last series of subtleties, Gerald was not capable. He could not touch the quick of her. But where his ruder blows could not penetrate, the fine, insinuating blade of Loerke's insect-like comprehension could. At least, it was time for her now to pass over to the other, the creature, the final craftsman. She knew that Loerke, in his innermost soul, was detached from everything, for him there was neither heaven nor earth nor hell. He admitted no allegiance, he gave no adherence anywhere. He was single and, by abstraction from the rest, absolute in himself.

Whereas in Gerald's soul there still lingered some attachment to the rest, to the whole. And this was his limitation. He was limited, *borné*, subject to his necessity, in the last issue, for goodness, for righteousness, for oneness with the ultimate purpose. That the ultimate purpose might be the perfect and subtle experience of the process of death, the will being kept unimpaired, that was not allowed in him. And this was his limitation.

There was a hovering triumph in Loerke, since Gudrun had denied her marriage with Gerald. The artist seemed to hover like a creature on the wing, waiting to settle. He did not approach Gudrun violently, he was never ill-timed. But carried on by a sure instinct in the complete darkness of his soul, he corresponded mystically with her, imperceptibly, but palpably.

For two days, he talked to her, continued the discussions of art, of life, in which they both found such pleasure. They praised the bygone things, they took a sentimental, childish delight in the achieved perfections of the past. Particularly they liked the late eighteenth century, the period of Goethe and of Shelley, and Mozart.

They played with the past, and with the great figures of the past, a sort of little game of chess, or marionettes, all to please themselves. They had all the great men for their marionettes, and they two were the God of the show, working it all. As for the future, that they never mentioned except one laughed out some mocking dream of the destruction of the world by a ridiculous catastrophe of man's invention: a man invented such a perfect explosive that it blew the earth in two, and the two halves set off in different directions through space, to the dismay of the inhabitants: or else the people of the world divided into two halves, and each half decided *it* was perfect and right, the other half was wrong and must be destroyed; so another end of the world. Or else, Loerke's dream of fear, the world went cold, and snow fell everywhere, and only white creatures, polar-bears, white foxes, and men like awful white snow-birds, persisted in ice cruelty.

Apart from these stories, they never talked of the future. They delighted most either in mocking imaginations of destruction, or in sentimental, fine marionette shows of the past. It was a sentimental delight to reconstruct the world of Goethe at Weimar, or of Schiller and poverty and faithful love, or to see again Jean-Jacques in his quakings, or Voltaire at Ferney, or Frederick the Great reading his own poetry.

They talked together for hours, of literature and sculpture and painting, amusing themselves with Flaxman and Blake and Fuseli, with tenderness, and with Feuerbach and Böcklin. It would take them a lifetime, they felt, to live again, *in petto*, the lives of the great artists. But they preferred to stay in the eighteenth and the nineteenth centuries.

They talked in a mixture of languages. The groundwork was French, in either case. But he ended most of his sentences in a stumble of English and a conclusion of German, she skilfully wove herself to her end in whatever phrase came to her. She took a peculiar delight in this conversation. It was full of odd, fantastic expression, of double meanings, of evasions, of suggestive vagueness. It was a real physical pleasure to her to make this thread of conversation out of the different-coloured strands of three languages.

And all the while they two were hovering, hesitating round the flame of some invisible declaration. He wanted it, but was held back by some inevitable reluctance. She wanted it also, but she wanted to put it off, to put it off indefinitely, she still had some pity for Gerald, some connection with him. And the most fatal of all, she had the reminiscent sentimental compassion for herself in connection with him. Because of what *had* been, she felt herself held to him by immortal, invisible threads – because of what *had* been, because of his coming to her that first night, into her own house, in his extremity, because –

Gerald was gradually overcome with a revulsion of loathing for Loerke. He did not take the man seriously, he despised him merely, except as he felt in Gudrun's veins the influence of the little creature. It was this that drove Gerald wild, the feeling in Gudrun's veins of Loerke's presence, Loerke's being, flowing dominant through her.

'What makes you so smitten with that little vermin?' he asked, really puzzled. For he, manlike, could not see anything attractive or important *at all* in Loerke. Gerald expected to find some handsomeness or nobleness, to account for a woman's subjection. But he saw none here, only an insect-like repulsiveness.

Gudrun flushed deeply. It was these attacks she would never forgive.

'What do you mean?' she replied. 'My God, what a mercy I am *not* married to you!'

Her voice of flouting and contempt scotched him. He was brought up short. But he recovered himself.

'Tell me, only tell me,' he reiterated in a dangerous narrowed voice – 'tell me what it is that fascinates you in him.'

'I am not fascinated,' she said, with cold, repelling innocence.

'Yes, you are. You are fascinated by that little dry snake, like a bird gaping ready to fall down its throat.'

She looked at him with black fury.

'I don't choose to be discussed by you,' she said.

'It doesn't matter whether you choose or not,' he replied, 'that doesn't alter the fact that you are ready to fall down and kiss the feet of that little insect. And I don't want to prevent you – do it, fall down and kiss his feet. But I want to know, what it is that fascinates you – what is it?'

She was silent, suffused with black rage.

'How *dare* you come brow-beating me,' she cried, 'how dare you, you little squire, you bully. What right have you over me, do you think?'

His face was white and gleaming, she knew by the light in his eyes that she was in his power – the wolf. And because she was in his power, she hated him with a power that she wondered did not kill him. In her will she killed him as he stood, effaced him.

'It is not a question of right,' said Gerald, sitting down on a chair. She watched the change in his body. She saw his clenched, mechanical body moving there like an obsession. Her hatred of him was tinged with fatal contempt.

'It's not a question of my right over you – though I *have* some right, remember. I want to know, I only want to know what it is that subjugates you to that little scum of a sculptor downstairs, what it is that brings you down like a humble maggot, in worship of him. I want to know what you creep after.'

She stood over against the window, listening. Then she turned round.

'Do you?' she said, in her most easy, most cutting voice. 'Do you want to know what it is in him? It's because he has some understanding of a woman, because he is not stupid. That's why it is.'

A queer, sinister, animal-like smile came over Gerald's face.

'But what understanding is it?' he said. 'The understanding of a flea, a hopping flea with a proboscis. Why should you crawl abject before the understanding of a flea?'

There passed through Gudrun's mind Blake's representation of the soul of a flea. She wanted to fit it to Loerke. Blake was a clown too. But it was necessary to answer Gerald.

'Don't you think the understanding of a flea is more interesting than the understanding of a fool?' she asked.

'A fool!' he repeated.

'A fool, a conceited fool – a *Dummkopf*,' she replied, adding the German word.

'Do you call me a fool?' he replied. 'Well, wouldn't I rather be the fool I am, than that flea downstairs?'

She looked at him. A certain blunt, blind stupidity in him palled on her soul, limiting her.

'You give yourself away by that last,' she said.

He sat and wondered.

'I shall go away soon,' he said.

She turned on him.

'Remember,' she said, 'I am completely independent of you – completely. You make your arrangements, I make mine.'

He pondered this.

'You mean we are strangers from this minute?' he asked.

She halted and flushed. He was putting her in a trap, forcing her hand. She turned round on him.

'Strangers,' she said, 'we can never be. But if you *want* to make any movement apart from me, then I wish you to know you are perfectly free to do so. Do not consider me in the slightest.'

Even so slight an implication that she needed him and was depending on him still was sufficient to rouse his passion. As he sat a change came over his body, the hot, molten stream mounted involuntarily through his veins. He groaned inwardly, under its bondage, but he loved it. He looked at her with clear eyes, waiting for her.

She knew at once, and was shaken with cold revulsion. *How* could he look at her with those clear, warm, waiting eyes, waiting for her, even now? What had been said between them, was it not enough to put them worlds asunder, to freeze them forever apart! And yet he was all transfused and roused, waiting for her.

It confused her. Turning her head aside, she said, 'I shall always *tell* you, whenever I am going to make any change – '

And with this she moved out of the room.

He sat suspended in a fine recoil of disappointment, that seemed gradually to be destroying his understanding. But the unconscious state of patience persisted in him. He remained motionless, without thought or knowledge, for a long time. Then he rose, and went downstairs, to play at chess with one of the students. His face was open and clear, with a certain innocent *laisser-aller* that troubled Gudrun most, made her almost afraid of him, whilst she disliked him deeply for it.

It was after this that Loerke, who had never yet spoken to her personally, began to ask her of her state.

'You are not married at all, are you?' he asked.

She looked full at him.

'Not in the least,' she replied, in her measured way. Loerke laughed, wrinkling up his face oddly. There was a thin wisp of his hair straying on his forehead, she noticed that his skin was of a clear brown colour, his hands, his wrists. And his hands seemed closely prehensile. He seemed like topaz, so strangely brownish and pellucid.

'Good,' he said.

Still it needed some courage for him to go on.

'Was Mrs Birkin your sister?' he asked.

'Yes.'

'And was *she* married?'

'She was married.'

'Have you parents, then?'

'Yes,' said Gudrun, 'we have parents.'

And she told him, briefly, laconically, her position. He watched her closely, curiously all the while.

'So!' he exclaimed, with some surprise. 'And the Herr Crich, is he rich?'

'Yes, he is rich, a coal owner.'

'How long has your friendship with him lasted?'

'Some months.'

There was a pause.

'Yes, I am surprised,' he said at length. 'The English, I thought they were so – cold. And what do you think to do when you leave here?'

'What do I think to do?' she repeated.

'Yes. You cannot go back to the teaching. No – ' he shrugged his shoulders – 'that is impossible. Leave that to the *canaille* who can do nothing else. You, for your part – you know, you are a remarkable woman, *eine seltsame Frau*. Why deny it – why make any question of it? You are an extraordinary woman, why should you follow the ordinary course, the ordinary life?'

Gudrun sat looking at her hands, flushed. She was pleased that he said, so simply, that she was a remarkable woman. He would not say that to flatter her – he was far too self-opinionated and objective by nature. He said it as he would say a piece of sculpture was remarkable, because he knew it was so.

And it gratified her to hear it from him. Other people had such a passion to make everything of one degree, of one pattern. In England it was chic to be perfectly ordinary. And it was a relief to her to be acknowledged extraordinary. Then she need not fret about the common standards.

'You see,' she said, 'I have no money whatsoever.'

'Ach, money!' he cried, lifting his shoulders. 'When one is grown up, money is lying about at one's service. It is only when one is young that it is rare. Take no thought for money – that always lies to hand.'

'Does it?' she said, laughing.

'Always. The Gerald will give you a sum, if you ask him for it – '

She flushed deeply.

'I will ask anybody else,' she said, with some difficulty – 'but not him.'

Loerke looked closely at her.

'Good,' he said. 'Then let it be somebody else. Only don't go back to that England, that school. No, that is stupid.'

Again there was a pause. He was afraid to ask her outright to go with him, he was not even quite sure he wanted her; and she was afraid to be asked. He begrudged his own isolation, was *very* chary of sharing his life, even for a day.

'The only other place I know is Paris,' she said, 'and I can't stand that.'

She looked with her wide, steady eyes full at Loerke. He lowered his head and averted his face.

'Paris, no!' he said. 'Between the *réligion d'amour*, and the latest 'ism, and the new turning to Jesus, one had better ride on a carousel all day. But come to Dresden. I have a studio there – I can give you work – oh, that would be easy enough. I haven't seen any of your things, but I believe in you. Come to Dresden – that is a fine town to be in, and as good a life as you can expect of a town. You have everything there, without the foolishness of Paris or the beer of Munich.'

He sat and looked at her, coldly. What she liked about him was that he spoke to her simple and flat, as to himself. He was a fellow craftsman, a fellow being to her, first.

'No – Paris,' he resumed, 'it makes me sick. Pah – *l'amour*. I detest it. *L'amour, l'amore, die Liebe* – I detest it in every language. Women and love, there is no greater tedium,' he cried.

She was slightly offended. And yet, this was her own basic feeling. Men, and love – there was no greater tedium.

'I think the same,' she said.

'A bore,' he repeated. 'What does it matter whether I wear this hat or another. So love. I needn't wear a hat at all, only for convenience. Neither need I love except for convenience. I tell you what, *gnädige Frau* – ' and he leaned towards her – then he made a quick, odd gesture, as of striking something aside – '*gnädige Fräulein*, never mind – I tell you what, I would give everything, everything, all your love, for a little companionship in intelligence – ' his eyes flickered darkly, evilly at her. 'You understand?' he asked, with a faint smile. 'It wouldn't matter if she were a hundred years old, a thousand – it would be all the same to me, so that she can *understand*.' He shut his eyes with a little snap.

Again Gudrun was rather offended. Did he not think her good-looking, then? Suddenly she laughed.

'I shall have to wait about eighty years to suit you, at that!' she said. 'I am ugly enough, aren't I?'

He looked at her with an artist's sudden, critical, estimating eye.

'You are beautiful,' he said, 'and I am glad of it. But it isn't that – it isn't that,' he cried, with emphasis that flattered her. 'It is that you have a certain wit, it is the kind of understanding. For me, I am little, *chétif*, insignificant. Good! Do not ask me to be strong and handsome, then. But it is the *me* – ' he put his fingers to his mouth, oddly – 'it is the *me* that is looking for a mistress, and my *me* is waiting for the *thee* of the mistress, for the match to my particular intelligence. You understand?'

'Yes,' she said, 'I understand.'

'As for the other, this *amour*' – he made a gesture, dashing his hand aside, as if to dash away something troublesome – 'it is unimportant, unimportant. Does it matter, whether I drink white wine this evening, or whether I drink nothing? *It does not matter*, it does not matter. So this love, this *amour*, this *baiser*. Yes or no, *soit ou soit pas*, today, tomorrow, or never, it is all the same, it does not matter – no more than the white wine.'

He ended with an odd dropping of the head in a desperate negation. Gudrun watched him steadily. She had gone pale.

Suddenly she stretched over and seized his hand in her own.

'That is true,' she said, in rather a high, vehement voice, 'that is true for me too. It is the understanding that matters.'

He looked up at her almost frightened, furtive. Then he nodded, a little sullenly. She let go his hand: he had made not the lightest response. And they sat in silence.

'Do you know,' he said, suddenly looking at her with dark, self-important, prophetic eyes, 'your fate and mine, they will run together, till – ' and he broke off in a little grimace.

'Till when?' she asked, blanched, her lips going white. She was terribly susceptible to these evil prognostications, but he only shook his head.

'I don't know,' he said, 'I don't know.'

Gerald did not come in from his skiing until nightfall, he missed the coffee and cake that she took at four o'clock. The snow was in perfect condition, he had travelled a long way, by himself, among the snow ridges, on his skis, he had climbed high, so high that he could see over the top of the pass, five miles distant, could see the Marienhütte, the hostel on the crest of the pass, half buried in snow, and over into the deep valley beyond, to the dusk of the pine trees. One could go that way home; but he shuddered with nausea at the thought of home; – one could travel on skis down there, and come to the old imperial road, below the pass. But why come to any road? He revolted at the thought of finding himself in the world again. He must stay up there in the snow for ever. He had been happy by himself, high up there alone, travelling swiftly on skis, taking far flights, and skimming past the dark rocks veined with brilliant snow.

But he felt something icy gathering at his heart. This strange mood of patience and innocence which had persisted in him for some days, was passing away, he would be left again a prey to the horrible passions and tortures.

So he came down reluctantly, snow-burned, snow-estranged, to the house in the hollow, between the knuckles of the mountain-tops. He saw its lights shining yellow, and he held back, wishing he need not go in, to confront those people, to hear the turmoil of voices and to feel the confusion of other presences. He was isolated as if there were a vacuum round his heart, or a sheath of pure ice.

The moment he saw Gudrun something jolted in his soul. She was looking rather lofty and superb, smiling slowly and graciously to the Germans. A sudden desire leapt in his heart, to kill her. He thought, what a perfect voluptuous fulfilment it would be, to kill her. His mind was absent all the evening, estranged by the snow and his passion. But he kept the idea constant within him, what a perfect voluptuous consummation it would be to strangle her, to strangle every spark of life out of her, till she lay completely inert, soft, relaxed for ever, a soft heap lying dead between his hands, utterly dead. Then he would have had her finally and for ever; there would be such a perfect voluptuous finality.

Gudrun was unaware of what he was feeling, he seemed so quiet and amiable, as usual. His amiability even made her feel brutal towards him.

She went into his room when he was partially undressed. She did not notice the curious, glad gleam of pure hatred, with which he looked at her. She stood near the door, with her hand behind her.

'I have been thinking, Gerald,' she said, with an insulting nonchalance, 'that I shall not go back to England.'

'Oh,' he said, 'where will you go then?'

But she ignored his question. She had her own logical statement to make, and it must be made as she had thought it.

'I can't see the use of going back,' she continued. 'It is over between me and you –'

She paused for him to speak. But he said nothing. He was only talking to himself, saying ' Over, is it? I believe it is over. But it isn't finished. Remember, it isn't finished. We must put some sort of a finish on it. There must be a conclusion, there must be finality.'

So he talked to himself, but aloud he said nothing whatever.

'What has been, has been,' she continued. 'There is nothing that I regret. I hope you regret nothing –'

She waited for him to speak.

'Oh, I regret nothing,' he said, accommodatingly.

'Good then,' she answered, 'good then. Then neither of us cherishes any regrets, which is as it should be.'

'Quite as it should be,' he said aimlessly.

She paused to gather up her thread again.

'Our attempt has been a failure,' she said. 'But we can try again, elsewhere.'

A little flicker of rage ran through his blood. It was as if she were rousing him, goading him. Why must she do it?

'Attempt at what?' he asked.

'At being lovers, I suppose,' she said, a little baffled, yet so trivial she made it all seem.

'Our attempt at being lovers has been a failure?' he repeated aloud.

To himself he was saying, 'I ought to kill her here. There is only this left, for me to kill her.' A heavy, overcharged desire to bring about her death possessed him. She was unaware.

'Hasn't it?' she asked. 'Do you think it has been a success?'

Again the insult of the flippant question ran through his blood like a current of fire.

'It had some of the elements of success, our relationship,' he replied. 'It – might have come off.'

But he paused before concluding the last phrase. Even as he began the sentence, he did not believe in what he was going to say. He knew it never could have been a success.

'No,' she replied. 'You cannot love.'

'And you?' he asked.

Her wide, dark-filled eyes were fixed on him, like two moons of darkness.

'I couldn't love *you*,' she said, with stark cold truth.

A blinding flash went over his brain, his body jolted. His heart had burst into flame. His consciousness was gone into his wrists, into his hands. He was one blind, incontinent desire, to kill her. His wrists were bursting, there would be no satisfaction till his hands had closed on her.

But even before his body swerved forward on her, a sudden, cunning comprehension was expressed on her face, and in a flash she was out of the door. She ran in one flash to her room and locked herself in. She was afraid, but confident. She knew her life trembled on the edge of an abyss. But she was curiously sure of her footing. She knew her cunning could outwit him.

She trembled, as she stood in her room, with excitement and awful exhilaration. She knew she could outwit him. She could depend on her presence of mind, and on her wits. But it was a fight to the death, she knew it now. One slip, and she was lost. She had a strange, tense, exhilarated sickness in her body, as one who is in peril of falling from a great height, but who does not look down, does not admit the fear.

'I will go away the day after tomorrow,' she said.

She only did not want Gerald to think that she was afraid of him, that she was running away because she was afraid of him. She was not afraid of him, fundamentally. She knew it was her safeguard to avoid his physical violence. But even physically she was not afraid of him. She wanted to prove it to him. When she had proved it, that, whatever he was, she was not afraid of him; when she had proved *that*, she could leave him for ever. But meanwhile the fight between them, terrible as she knew it to be, was inconclusive. And she wanted to be confident in herself. However many terrors she might have, she would be unafraid, uncowed by him. He could never cow her, nor dominate her, nor have any right over her; this she would maintain until she had proved it. Once it was proved, she was free of him for ever.

But she had not proved it yet, neither to him nor to herself. And this was what still bound her to him. She was bound to him, she could not live beyond him. She sat up in bed, closely wrapped up, for many hours, thinking endlessly to herself. It was as if she would never have done weaving the great provision of her thoughts.

'It isn't as if he really loved me,' she said to herself. 'He doesn't. Every woman he comes across he wants to make her in love with him. He doesn't even know that he is doing it. But there he is, before every woman he unfurls his male attractiveness, displays his great desirability, he tries to make every woman think how wonderful it would be to have him for a lover. His very ignoring of the women is part of the game. He is never *unconscious* of them. He should have been a cockerel, so he could strut before fifty females, all his subjects. But really, his Don Juan does *not* interest me. I could play Dona Juanita a million times better than he plays Juan. He bores me, you know. His maleness bores me. Nothing is so boring, so inherently stupid and stupidly conceited. Really, the fathomless conceit of these men, it is ridiculous – the little strutters.

'They are all alike. Look at Birkin. Built out of the limitation of conceit they are, and nothing else. Really, nothing but their ridiculous limitation and intrinsic insignificance could make them so conceited.

'As for Loerke, there is a thousand times more in him than in Gerald. Gerald is so limited, there is a dead end to him. He would grind on at the old mills for ever. And really, there is no corn between the millstones any more. They grind on and on, when there is nothing to grind – saying the same things, believing the same things, acting the same things. Oh, my God, it would wear out the patience of a stone.

'I don't worship Loerke, but at any rate, he is a free individual. He is not stiff with conceit of his own maleness. He is not grinding dutifully at the old mills. Oh God, when I think of Gerald, and his work – those offices at Beldover, and the mines – it makes my heart sick. What *have* I to do with it – and him thinking he can be a lover to a woman! One might as well ask it of a self-satisfied lamp-post. These men, with their eternal jobs – and their eternal mills of God that keep on grinding at nothing! It is too boring, just boring. However did I come to take him seriously at all!

'At least in Dresden, one will have one's back to it all. And there will be amusing things to do. It will be amusing to go to these eurhythmic displays, and the German opera, the German theatre. It *will* be amusing to take part in German Bohemian life. And Loerke is an artist, he is a free individual. One will escape from so much, that is the chief thing, escape so much hideous boring repetition of vulgar actions, vulgar phrases, vulgar postures. I don't delude myself that I shall find an elixir of life in Dresden. I know I shan't. But I shall get away from people who have their own homes and their own children and their own acquaintances and their own this and their own that. I shall be among people who *don't* own things and who *haven't* got a home and a domestic servant in the background, who haven't got a standing and a status and a degree and a circle of friends of the same. Oh God, the wheels within wheels of people, it makes one's head tick like a clock, with a very madness of dead mechanical monotony and meaninglessness. How I *hate* life, how I hate it. How I hate the Geralds, that they can offer one nothing else.

'Shortlands! – Heavens! Think of living there, one week, then the next, and *then the third* –

'No, I won't think of it – it is too much –'

And she broke off, really terrified, really unable to bear any more.

The thought of the mechanical succession of day following day, day following day, *ad infinitum*, was one of the things that made her heart palpitate with a real approach of madness. The terrible bondage of this tick-tack of time, this twitching of the hands of the clock, this eternal repetition of hours and days – oh God, it was too awful to contemplate. And there was no escape from it, no escape.

She almost wished Gerald were with her to save her from the terror of her own thoughts. Oh, how she suffered, lying there alone, confronted by the terrible clock, with its eternal tick-tack. All life, all life resolved itself into this: tick-tack, tick-tack, tick-tack; then the striking of the hour; then the tick-tack, tick-tack, and the twitching of the clock-fingers.

Gerald could not save her from it. He, his body, his motion, his life – it was the same ticking, the same twitching across the dial, a horrible mechanical twitching forward over the face of the hours. What were his kisses, his embraces. She could hear their tick-tack, tick-tack.

Ha – ha – she laughed to herself, so frightened that she was trying to laugh it off – ha – ha, how maddening it was, to be sure, to be sure!

Then, with a fleeting self-conscious motion, she wondered if she would be very much surprised, on rising in the morning, to realise that her hair had turned white. She had *felt* it turning white so often, under the intolerable burden of her thoughts, and her sensations. Yet there it remained, brown as ever, and there she was herself, looking a picture of health.

Perhaps she was healthy. Perhaps it was only her unabateable health that left her so exposed to the truth. If she were sickly she would have her illusions, imaginations. As it was, there was no escape. She must always see and know and never escape. She could never escape. There she was, placed before the clock-face of life. And if she turned round as in a railway station, to look at the bookstall, still she could see, with her very spine, she could see the clock, always the great white clock-face. In vain she fluttered the leaves of books, or made statuettes in clay. She knew she was not *really* reading. She was not *really* working. She was watching the fingers twitch across the eternal, mechanical, monotonous clock-face of time. She never really lived, she only watched. Indeed, she was like a little, twelve-hour clock, vis-à-vis with the enormous clock of eternity – there she was, like Dignity and Impudence, or Impudence and Dignity.

The picture pleased her. Didn't her face really look like a clock dial – rather roundish and often pale, and impassive. She would have got up to look, in the mirror, but the thought of the sight of her own face, that was like a twelve-hour clock dial, filled her with such deep terror, that she hastened to think of something else.

Oh, why wasn't somebody kind to her? Why wasn't there somebody who would take her in their arms, and hold her to their breast, and give her rest, pure, deep, healing rest. Oh, why wasn't there somebody to take her in their arms and fold her safe and perfect, for sleep. She wanted so much this perfect enfolded sleep. She lay always so unsheathed in sleep. She would lie always unsheathed in sleep, unrelieved, unsaved. Oh, how could she bear it, this endless unrelief, this eternal unrelief.

Gerald! Could he fold her in his arms and sheathe her in sleep? Ha! He needed putting to sleep himself – poor Gerald. That was all he needed. What did he do, he made the burden for her greater, the burden of her sleep was the more intolerable, when he was there. He was an added weariness upon her unripening nights, her unfruitful slumbers. Perhaps he got some repose from her. Perhaps he did. Perhaps this was what he was always dogging her for, like a child that is famished, crying for the breast. Perhaps this was the secret of his passion, his forever unquenched desire for her – that he needed her to put him to sleep, to give him repose.

What then! Was she his mother? Had she asked for a child, whom she must nurse through the nights, for her lover. She despised him, she despised him, she hardened her heart. An infant crying in the night, this Don Juan.

Ooh, but how she hated the infant crying in the night. She would murder it gladly. She would stifle it and bury it, as Hetty Sorrell did. No doubt Hetty Sorrell's infant cried in the night – no doubt Arthur Donnithorne's infant would. Ha – the Arthur Donnithornes, the Geralds of this world. So manly by day, yet all the while, such a crying of infants in the night. Let them turn into mechanisms, let them. Let them become instruments, pure machines, pure wills, that work like clockwork, in perpetual repetition. Let them be this, let them be taken up entirely in their work, let them be perfect parts of a great machine, having a slumber of constant repetition. Let Gerald manage his firm. There he would be satisfied, as satisfied as a wheelbarrow that goes backwards and forwards along a plank all day – she had seen it.

The wheelbarrow – the one humble wheel – the unit of the firm. Then the cart, with two wheels; then the truck, with four; then the donkey-engine, with eight, then the winding-engine, with sixteen, and so on, till it came to the miner, with a thousand wheels, and then the electrician, with three thousand, and the underground manager, with twenty thousand, and the general manager with a hundred thousand little wheels working away to complete his make-up, and then Gerald, with a million wheels and cogs and axles.

Poor Gerald, such a lot of little wheels to his make-up! He was more intricate than a chronometer-watch. But oh heavens, what weariness! What weariness, God above! A chronometer-watch – a beetle – her soul fainted with utter ennui, from the thought. So many wheels to count and consider and calculate! Enough, enough – there was an end to man's capacity for complications, even. Or perhaps there was no end.

Meanwhile Gerald sat in his room, reading. When Gudrun was gone, he was left stupefied with arrested desire. He sat on the side of the bed for an hour, stupefied, little strands of consciousness appearing and reappearing. But he did not move, for a long time he remained inert, his head dropped on his breast.

Then he looked up and realised that he was going to bed. He was cold. Soon he was lying down in the dark.

But what he could not bear was the darkness. The solid darkness confronting him drove him mad. So he rose, and made a light. He remained seated for a while, staring in front. He did not think of Gudrun, he did not think of anything.

Then suddenly he went downstairs for a book. He had all his life been in terror of the nights that should come, when he could not sleep. He knew that this would be too much for him, to have to face nights of sleeplessness and of horrified watching the hours.

So he sat for hours in bed, like a statue, reading. His mind, hard and acute, read on rapidly, his body understood nothing. In a state of rigid unconsciousness, he read on through the night, till morning, when, weary and disgusted in spirit, disgusted most of all with himself, he slept for two hours.

Then he got up, hard and full of energy. Gudrun scarcely spoke to him, except at coffee when she said, 'I shall be leaving tomorrow.'

'We will go together as far as Innsbruck, for appearance's sake?' he asked.

'Perhaps,' she said.

She said 'Perhaps' between the sips of her coffee. And the sound of her taking her breath in the word, was nauseous to him. He rose quickly to be away from her.

He went and made arrangements for the departure on the morrow. Then, taking some food, he set out for the day on the skis. Perhaps, he said to the Wirt, he would go up to the Marienhütte, perhaps to the village below.

To Gudrun this day was full of a promise like spring. She felt an approaching release, a new fountain of life rising up in her. It gave her pleasure to dawdle through her packing, it gave her pleasure to dip into books, to try on her different garments, to look at herself in the glass. She felt a new lease of life was come upon her, and she was happy like a child, very attractive and beautiful to everybody, with her soft, luxuriant figure, and her happiness. Yet underneath was death itself.

In the afternoon she had to go out with Loerke. Her tomorrow was perfectly vague before her. This was what gave her pleasure. She might be going to England with Gerald, she might be going to Dresden with Loerke, she might be going to Munich, to a girlfriend she had there. Anything might come to pass on the morrow. And today was the white, snowy iridescent threshold of all possibility. All possibility – that was the charm to her, the lovely, iridescent, indefinite charm – pure illusion. All possibility – because death was inevitable, and *nothing* was possible but death.

She did not want things to materialise, to take any definite shape. She wanted, suddenly, at one moment of the journey tomorrow, to be wafted into an utterly new course, by some utterly unforeseen event, or motion. So that, although she wanted to go out with Loerke for the last time into the snow, she did not want to be serious or businesslike.

And Loerke was not a serious figure. In his brown velvet cap, that made his head as round as a chestnut, with the brown-velvet flaps loose and wild over his ears, and a wisp of elflike, thin black hair blowing above his full, elflike dark eyes, the shiny, transparent brown skin crinkling up into odd grimaces on his small-featured face, he looked an odd little boy-man, a bat. But in his figure, in the greeny loden suit, he looked *chétif* and puny, still strangely different from the rest.

He had taken a little toboggan, for the two of them, and they trudged between the blinding slopes of snow, that burned their now hardening faces, laughing in an endless sequence of quips and jests and polyglot fancies. The fancies were the reality to both of them, they were both so happy, tossing about the little coloured balls of verbal humour and whimsicality. Their natures seemed to sparkle in full interplay, they were enjoying a pure game. And they wanted to keep it on the level of a game, their relationship: *such* a fine game.

Loerke did not take the tobogganing very seriously. He put no fire and intensity into it, as Gerald did. Which pleased Gudrun. She was weary, oh so weary of Gerald's gripped intensity of physical motion. Loerke let the sledge go wildly, and gaily, like a flying leaf, and when, at a bend, he pitched both her and him out into the snow, he only waited for them both to pick themselves up unhurt off the keen white ground, to be laughing and pert as a pixie. She knew he would be making ironical, playful remarks as he wandered in hell – if he were in the humour. And that pleased her immensely. It seemed like a rising above the dreariness of actuality, the monotony of contingencies.

They played till the sun went down, in pure amusement, careless and timeless. Then, as the little sledge twirled riskily to rest at the bottom of the slope: 'Wait!' he said suddenly, and he produced from somewhere a large thermos flask, a packet of Keks, and a bottle of Schnapps.

'Oh, Loerke,' she cried. 'What an inspiration! What a *comble de joie* indeed! What is the Schnapps?'

He looked at it, and laughed.

'*Heidelbeer!*' he said.

'No! From the bilberries under the snow. Doesn't it look as if it were distilled from snow. Can you – ' she sniffed, and sniffed at the bottle – 'can you smell bilberries? Isn't it wonderful? It is exactly as if one could smell them through the snow.'

She stamped her foot lightly on the ground. He kneeled down and whistled, and put his ear to the snow. As he did so his black eyes twinkled up.

'Ha! Ha!' she laughed, warmed by the whimsical way in which he mocked at her verbal extravagances. He was always teasing her, mocking her ways. But as he in his mockery was even more absurd than she in her extravagances, what could one do but laugh and feel liberated.

She could feel their voices, hers and his, ringing silvery like bells in the frozen, motionless air of the first twilight. How perfect it was, how *very* perfect it was, this silvery isolation and interplay.

She sipped the hot coffee, whose fragrance flew around them like bees murmuring around flowers, in the snowy air, she drank tiny sips of the *Heidel-beerwasser*, she ate the cold, sweet, creamy wafers. How good everything was!

How perfect everything tasted and smelled and sounded, here in this utter stillness of snow and falling twilight.

'You are going away tomorrow?' his voice came at last.

'Yes.'

There was a pause, when the evening seemed to rise in its silent, ringing pallor infinitely high, to the infinite which was near at hand.

'*Wohin?*'

That was the question – *wohin?* Whither? *Wohin?* What a lovely word! She *never* wanted it answered. Let it chime for ever.

'I don't know,' she said, smiling at him.

He caught the smile from her.

'One never does,' he said.

'One never does,' she repeated.

There was a silence, wherein he ate biscuits rapidly, as a rabbit eats leaves.

'But,' he laughed, 'where will you take a ticket to?'

'Oh heaven!' she cried. 'One must take a ticket.'

Here was a blow. She saw herself at the wicket, at the railway station. Then a relieving thought came to her. She breathed freely.

'But one needn't go,' she cried.

'Certainly not,' he said.

'I mean one needn't go where one's ticket says.'

That struck him. One might take a ticket, so as not to travel to the destination it indicated. One might break off, and avoid the destination. A point located. That was an idea!

'Then take a ticket to London,' he said. 'One should never go there.'

'Right,' she answered.

He poured a little coffee into a tin can.

'You won't tell me where you will go?' he asked.

'Really and truly,' she said, 'I don't know. It depends which way the wind blows.'

He looked at her quizzically, then he pursed up his lips, like Zephyrus, blowing across the snow.

'It goes towards Germany,' he said.

'I believe so,' she laughed.

Suddenly, they were aware of a vague white figure near them. It was Gerald. Gudrun's heart leapt in sudden terror, profound terror. She rose to her feet.

'They told me where you were,' came Gerald's voice, like a judgement in the whitish air of twilight.

'*Maria!* You come like a ghost,' exclaimed Loerke.

Gerald did not answer. His presence was unnatural and ghostly to them.

Loerke shook the flask – then he held it inverted over the snow. Only a few brown drops trickled out.

'All gone!' he said.

To Gerald, the smallish, odd figure of the German was distinct and objective, as if seen through field glasses. And he disliked the small figure exceedingly, he wanted it removed.

Then Loerke rattled the box which held the biscuits.

'Biscuits there are still,' he said.

And reaching from his seated posture in the sledge, he handed them to Gudrun. She fumbled, and took one. He would have held them to Gerald, but Gerald so definitely did not want to be offered a biscuit, that Loerke, rather vaguely, put the box aside. Then he took up the small bottle, and held it to the light.

'Also there is some Schnapps,' he said to himself.

Then suddenly, he elevated the bottle gallantly in the air, a strange, grotesque figure leaning towards Gudrun, and said, '*Gnädiges Fräulein*,' he said, '*wohl* – '

There was a crack, the bottle was flying, Loerke had started back, the three stood quivering in violent emotion.

Loerke turned to Gerald, a devilish leer on his bright-skinned face.

'Well done!' he said, in a satirical demoniac frenzy. '*C'est le sport, sans doute*.'

The next instant he was sitting ludicrously in the snow, Gerald's fist having rung against the side of his head. But Loerke pulled himself together, rose, quivering, looking full at Gerald, his body weak and furtive, but his eyes demoniacal with satire.

'*Vive le héros, vive* – '

But he flinched, as, in a black flash, Gerald's fist came upon him, banged into the other side of his head, and sent him aside like a broken straw.

But Gudrun moved forward. She raised her clenched hand high, and brought it down, with a great downward stroke on to the face and on to the breast of Gerald.

A great astonishment burst upon him, as if the air had broken. Wide, wide his soul opened, in wonder, feeling the pain. Then it laughed, turning, with strong hands outstretched, at last to take the apple of his desire. At last he could finish his desire.

He took the throat of Gudrun between his hands, that were hard and indomitably powerful. And her throat was beautifully, so beautifully soft, save that, within, he could feel the slippery cords of her life. And this he crushed, this he could crush. What bliss! Oh what bliss, at last, what satisfaction, at last! The pure zest of satisfaction filled his soul. He was watching the unconsciousness come unto her swollen face, watching the eyes roll back. How ugly she was! What a fulfilment, what a satisfaction! How good this was, oh how good it was, what a God-given gratification, at last! He was unconscious of her fighting and struggling. The struggling was her reciprocal lustful passion in this embrace, the more violent it became, the greater the frenzy of delight, till the zenith was reached, the crisis, the struggle was overborne, her movement became softer, appeased.

Loerke roused himself on the snow, too dazed and hurt to get up. Only his eyes were conscious.

'*Monsieur!*' he said, in his thin, roused voice: '*Quand vous aurez fini* –'

A revulsion of contempt and disgust came over Gerald's soul. The disgust went to the very bottom of him, a nausea. Ah, what was he doing, to what depths was he letting himself go! As if he cared about her enough to kill her, to have her life on his hands!

A weakness ran over his body, a terrible relaxing, a thaw, a decay of strength. Without knowing, he had let go his grip, and Gudrun had fallen to her knees. Must he see, must he know?

A fearful weakness possessed him, his joints were turned to water. He drifted, as on a wind, veered, and went drifting away.

'I didn't want it, really,' was the last confession of disgust in his soul, as he drifted up the slope, weak, finished, only sheering off unconsciously from any further contact. 'I've had enough – I want to go to sleep. I've had enough.' He was sunk under a sense of nausea.

He was weak, but he did not want to rest, he wanted to go on and on, to the end. Never again to stay, till he came to the end, that was all the desire that remained to him. So he drifted on and on, unconscious and weak, not thinking of anything, so long as he could keep in action.

The twilight spread a weird, unearthly light overhead, bluish-rose in colour, the cold blue night sank on the snow. In the valley below, behind, in the great bed of snow, were two small figures: Gudrun dropped on her knees, like one executed, and Loerke sitting propped up near her. That was all.

Gerald stumbled on up the slope of snow, in the bluish darkness, always climbing, always unconsciously climbing, weary though he was. On his left was a steep slope with black rocks and fallen masses of rock and veins of snow slashing in and about the blackness of rock, veins of snow slashing vaguely in and about the blackness of rock. Yet there was no sound, all this made no noise.

To add to his difficulty, a small bright moon shone brilliantly just ahead, on the right, a painful brilliant thing that was always there, unremitting, from which there was no escape. He wanted so to come to the end – he had had enough. Yet he did not sleep.

He surged painfully up, sometimes having to cross a slope of black rock, that was blown bare of snow. Here he was afraid of falling, very much afraid of falling. And high up here, on the crest, moved a wind that almost overpowered him with a sleep-heavy iciness. Only it was not here, the end, and he must still go on. His indefinite nausea would not let him stay.

Having gained one ridge, he saw the vague shadow of something higher in front. Always higher, always higher. He knew he was following the track towards the summit of the slopes, where was the *Marienhütte*, and the descent on the other side. But he was not really conscious. He only wanted to go on, to go on whilst he could, to move, to keep going, that was all, to keep going, until it was finished. He had lost all his sense of place. And yet in the remaining instinct of life, his feet sought the track where the skis had gone.

He slithered down a sheer snow slope. That frightened him. He had no alpenstock, nothing. But having come safely to rest, he began to walk on, in the illuminated darkness. It was as cold as sleep. He was between two ridges, in a hollow. So he swerved. Should he climb the other ridge, or wander along the hollow? How frail the thread of his being was stretched! He would perhaps climb the ridge. The snow was firm and simple. He went along. There was something standing out of the snow. He approached, with dimmest curiosity.

It was a half-buried crucifix, a little Christ under a little sloping hood, at the top of a pole. He sheered away. Somebody was going to murder him. He had a great dread of being murdered. But it was a dread which stood outside him, like his own ghost.

Yet why be afraid? It was bound to happen. To be murdered! He looked round in terror at the snow, the rocking, pale, shadowy slopes of the upper world. He was bound to be murdered, he could see it. This was the moment when the death was uplifted, and there was no escape.

Lord Jesus, was it then bound to be – Lord Jesus! He could feel the blow descending, he knew he was murdered. Vaguely wandering forward, his hands lifted as if to feel what would happen, he was waiting for the moment when he would stop, when it would cease. It was not over yet.

He had come to the hollow basin of snow, surrounded by sheer slopes and precipices, out of which rose a track that brought one to the top of the mountain. But he wandered unconsciously, till he slipped and fell down, and as he fell something broke in his soul, and immediately he went to sleep.

CHAPTER 31

Exeunt

When they brought the body home, the next morning, Gudrun was shut up in her room. From her window she saw men coming along with a burden, over the snow. She sat still and let the minutes go by.

There came a tap at her door. She opened. There stood a woman, saying softly, oh, far too reverently, 'They have found him, madam!'

'*Il est mort?*'

'Yes – hours ago.'

Gudrun did not know what to say. What should she say? What should she feel? What should she do? What did they expect of her? She was coldly at a loss.

'Thank you,' she said, and she shut the door of her room. The woman went away mortified. Not a word, not a tear – ha! Gudrun was cold, a cold woman.

Gudrun sat on in her room, her face pale and impassive. What was she to do? She could not weep and make a scene. She could not alter herself. She sat motionless, hiding from people. Her one motive was to avoid actual contact with events. She only wrote out a long telegram to Ursula and Birkin.

In the afternoon, however, she rose suddenly to look for Loerke. She glanced with apprehension at the door of the room that had been Gerald's. Not for worlds would she enter there.

She found Loerke sitting alone in the lounge. She went straight up to him.

'It isn't true, is it?' she said.

He looked up at her. A small smile of misery twisted his face. He shrugged his shoulders.

'True?' he echoed.

'We haven't killed him?' she asked.

He disliked her coming to him in such a manner. He raised his shoulders wearily.

'It has happened,' he said.

She looked at him. He sat crushed and frustrated for the time being, quite as emotionless and barren as herself. My God! this was a barren tragedy, barren, barren.

She returned to her room to wait for Ursula and Birkin. She wanted to get away, only to get away. She could not think or feel until she had got away, till she was loosed from this position.

The day passed, the next day came. She heard the sledge, saw Ursula and Birkin alight, and she shrank from these also.

Ursula came straight up to her.

'Gudrun!' she cried, the tears running down her cheeks. And she took her sister in her arms. Gudrun hid her face on Ursula's shoulder, but still she could not escape the cold devil of irony that froze her soul.

'Ha, ha!' she thought, 'this is the right behaviour.'

But she could not weep, and the sight of her cold, pale, impassive face soon stopped the fountain of Ursula's tears. In a few moments, the sisters had nothing to say to each other.

'Was it very vile to be dragged back here again?' Gudrun asked at length.

Ursula looked up in some bewilderment.

'I never thought of it,' she said.

'I felt a beast, fetching you,' said Gudrun. 'But I simply couldn't see people. That is too much for me.'

'Yes,' said Ursula, chilled.

Birkin tapped and entered. His face was white and expressionless. She knew he knew. He gave her his hand, saying, 'The end of *this* trip, at any rate.'

Gudrun glanced at him, afraid.

There was silence between the three of them, nothing to be said. At length Ursula asked in a small voice, 'Have you seen him?'

He looked back at Ursula with a hard, cold look, and did not trouble to answer.

'Have you seen him?' she repeated.

'I have,' he said, coldly.

Then he looked at Gudrun.

'Have you done anything?' he said.

'Nothing,' she replied, 'nothing.'

She shrank in cold disgust from making any statement.

'Loerke says that Gerald came to you, when you were sitting on the sledge at the bottom of the Rudelbahn, that you had words, and Gerald walked away. What were the words about? I had better know, so that I can satisfy the authorities, if necessary.'

Gudrun looked up at him, white, childlike, mute with trouble.

'There weren't even any words,' she said. 'He knocked Loerke down and stunned him, he half strangled me, then he went away.'

To herself she was saying, 'A pretty little sample of the eternal triangle!' And she turned ironically away, because she knew that the fight had been between Gerald and herself and that the presence of the third party was a mere contingency – an inevitable contingency perhaps, but a contingency none the less. But let them have it as an example of the eternal triangle, the trinity of hate. It would be simpler for them.

Birkin went away, his manner cold and abstracted. But she knew he would do things for her, nevertheless, he would see her through. She smiled slightly to herself, with contempt. Let him do the work, since he was so extremely *good* at looking after other people.

Birkin went again to Gerald. He had loved him. And yet he felt chiefly disgust at the inert body lying there. It was so inert, so coldly dead, a carcase, Birkin's bowels seemed to turn to ice. He had to stand and look at the frozen dead body that had been Gerald.

It was the frozen carcase of a dead male. Birkin remembered a rabbit which he had once found frozen like a board on the snow. It had been rigid like a dried board when he picked it up. And now this was Gerald, stiff as a board, curled up as if for sleep, yet with the horrible hardness somehow evident. It filled him with horror. The room must be made warm, the body must be thawed. The limbs would break like glass or like wood if they had to be straightened.

He reached and touched the dead face. And the sharp, heavy bruise of ice bruised his living bowels. He wondered if he himself were freezing too, freezing from the inside. In the short blond moustache the life-breath was frozen into a block of ice, beneath the silent nostrils. And this was Gerald!

Again he touched the sharp, almost glittering fair hair of the frozen body. It was icy-cold, hair icy-cold, almost venomous. Birkin's heart began to freeze. He had loved Gerald. Now he looked at the shapely, strange-coloured face, with the small, fine, pinched nose and the manly cheeks, saw it frozen like an ice-pebble – yet he had loved it. What was one to think or feel? His brain was beginning to freeze, his blood was turning to ice-water. So cold, so cold, a heavy, bruising cold pressing on his arms from outside, and a heavier cold congealing within him, in his heart and in his bowels.

He went over the snow slopes to see where the death had been. At last he came to the great shallow among the precipices and slopes, near the summit of the pass. It was a grey day, the third day of greyness and stillness. All was white, icy, pallid, save for the scoring of black rocks that jutted like roots sometimes, and sometimes were in naked faces. In the distance a slope sheered down from a peak, with many black rock-slides.

It was like a shallow pot lying among the stone and snow of the upper world. In this pot Gerald had gone to sleep. At the far end, the guides had driven iron stakes deep into the snow-wall, so that, by means of the great rope attached, they could haul themselves up the massive snow-front, out on to the jagged summit of the pass, naked to heaven, where the *Marienhütte* hid among the naked rocks. Round about, spiked, slashed snow-peaks pricked the heaven.

Gerald might have found this rope. He might have hauled himself up to the crest. He might have heard the dogs in the *Marienhütte*, and found shelter. He might have gone on, down the steep, steep fall of the south side, down into the dark valley with its pines, on to the great Imperial road leading south to Italy.

He might! And what then? The Imperial road! The south? Italy? What then? Was it a way out? It was only a way in again. Birkin stood high in the painful air, looking at the peaks, and the way south. Was it any good going south, to Italy? Down the old, old Imperial road?

He turned away. Either the heart would break, or cease to care. Best cease to care. Whatever the mystery which has brought forth man and the universe, it is a non-human mystery, it has its own great ends, man is not the criterion. Best leave it all to the vast, creative, non-human mystery. Best strive with oneself only, not with the universe.

'God cannot do without man.' It was a saying of some great French religious teacher. But surely this is false. God can do without man. God could do without the ichthyosauri and the mastodon. These monsters failed creatively to develop, so God, the creative mystery, dispensed with them. In the same way the mystery could dispense with man, should he too fail creatively to change and develop. The eternal creative mystery could dispose of man, and replace him with a finer created being. Just as the horse has taken the place of the mastodon.

It was very consoling to Birkin, to think this. If humanity ran into a *cul de sac* and expended itself, the timeless creative mystery would bring forth some other being, finer, more wonderful, some new, more lovely race, to carry on the embodiment of creation. The game was never up. The mystery of creation was fathomless, infallible, inexhaustible, for ever. Races came and went, species passed away, but ever new species arose, more lovely, or equally lovely, always surpassing wonder. The fountain-head was incorruptible and unsearchable. It had no limits. It could bring forth miracles, create utter new races and new species, in its own hour, new forms of consciousness, new forms of body, new units of being. To be man was as nothing compared to the possibilities of the creative mystery. To have one's pulse beating direct from the mystery, this was perfection, unutterable satisfaction. Human or inhuman mattered nothing. The perfect pulse throbbed with indescribable being, miraculous unborn species.

SELECTED WORKS OF D. H. LAWRENCE

Birkin went home again to Gerald. He went into the room, and sat down on the bed. Dead, dead and cold!

> Imperial Caesar dead, and turned to clay
> Would stop a hole to keep the wind away.

There was no response from that which had been Gerald. Strange, congealed, icy substance – no more. No more!

Terribly weary, Birkin went away, about the day's business. He did it all quietly, without bother. To rant, to rave, to be tragic, to make situations – it was all too late. Best be quiet, and bear one's soul in patience and in fullness.

But when he went in again, at evening, to look at Gerald between the candles, because of his heart's hunger, suddenly his heart contracted, his own candle all but fell from his hand, as, with a strange whimpering cry, the tears broke out. He sat down in a chair, shaken by a sudden access. Ursula, who had followed him, recoiled aghast from him, as he sat with sunken head and body convulsively shaken, making a strange, horrible sound of tears.

'I didn't want it to be like this – I didn't want it to be like this,' he cried to himself. Ursula could but think of the Kaiser's: '*Ich habe es nicht gewollt*.' She looked almost with horror on Birkin.

Suddenly he was silent. But he sat with his head dropped, to hide his face. Then furtively he wiped his face with his fingers. Then suddenly he lifted his head, and looked straight at Ursula, with dark, almost vengeful eyes.

'He should have loved me,' he said. 'I offered him.'

She, afraid, white, with mute lips, answered, 'What difference would it have made!'

'It would!' he said. 'It would.'

He forgot her, and turned to look at Gerald. With head oddly lifted, like a man who draws his head back from an insult, half haughtily, he watched the cold, mute, material face. It had a bluish cast. It sent a shaft like ice through the heart of the living man. Cold, mute, material! Birkin remembered how once Gerald had clutched his hand, with a warm, momentaneous grip of final love. For one second – then let go again, let go for ever. If he had kept true to that clasp, death would not have mattered. Those who die, and dying still can love, still believe, do not die. They live still in the beloved. Gerald might still have been living in the spirit with Birkin, even after death. He might have lived with his friend, a further life.

But now he was dead, like clay, like bluish, corruptible ice. Birkin looked at the pale fingers, the inert mass. He remembered a dead stallion he had seen: a dead mass of maleness, repugnant. He remembered also the beautiful face of one whom he had loved, and who had died still having the faith to yield to the mystery. That dead face was beautiful, no one could call it cold, mute, material. No one could remember it without gaining faith in the mystery, without the soul's warming with new, deep life-trust.

And Gerald! The denier! He left the heart cold, frozen, hardly able to beat.

Gerald's father had looked wistful, to break the heart; but not this last terrible look of cold, mute Matter. Birkin watched and watched.

Ursula stood aside watching the living man stare at the frozen face of the dead man. Both faces were unmoved and unmoving. The candle-flames flickered in the frozen air, in the intense silence.

'Haven't you seen enough?' she said.

He got up.

'It's a bitter thing to me,' he said.

'What – that he's dead?' she said.

His eyes just met hers. He did not answer.

'You've got me,' she said.

He smiled and kissed her.

'If I die,' he said, 'you'll know I haven't left you.'

'And me?' she cried.

'And you won't have left me,' he said. 'We shan't have any need to despair, in death.'

She took hold of his hand.

'But need you despair over Gerald?' she said.

'Yes,' he answered.

They went away. Gerald was taken to England, to be buried. Birkin and Ursula accompanied the body, along with one of Gerald's brothers. It was the Crich brothers and sisters who insisted on the burial in England. Birkin wanted to leave the dead man in the Alps, near the snow. But the family was strident, loudly insistent.

Gudrun went to Dresden. She wrote no particulars of herself. Ursula stayed at the Mill with Birkin for a week or two. They were both very quiet.

'Did you need Gerald?' she asked one evening.

'Yes,' he said.

'Aren't I enough for you?' she asked.

'No,' he said. 'You are enough for me, as far as a woman is concerned. You are all women to me. But I wanted a man friend, as eternal as you and I are eternal.'

'Why aren't I enough?' she said. 'You are enough for me. I don't want anybody else but you. Why isn't it the same with you?'

'Having you, I can live all my life without anybody else, any other sheer intimacy. But to make it complete, really happy, I wanted eternal union with a man too: another kind of love,' he said.

'I don't believe it,' she said. 'It's an obstinacy, a theory, a perversity.'

'Well – ' he said.

'You can't have two kinds of love. Why should you!'

'It seems as if I can't,' he said. 'Yet I wanted it.'

'You can't have it, because it's false, impossible,' she said.

'I don't believe that,' he answered.

LADY CHATTERLEY'S LOVER

Chapter 1

OURS IS ESSENTIALLY A TRAGIC AGE, so we refuse to take it tragically. The cataclysm has happened, we are among the ruins, we start to build up new little habitats, to have new little hopes. It is rather hard work: there is now no smooth road into the future: but we go round, or scramble over the obstacles. We've got to live, no matter how many skies have fallen.

This was more or less Constance Chatterley's position. The war had brought the roof down over her head. And she had realised that one must live and learn.

She married Clifford Chatterley in 1917, when he was home for a month on leave. They had a month's honeymoon. Then he went back to Flanders: to be shipped over to England again six months later, more or less in bits. Constance, his wife, was then twenty-three years old, and he was twenty-nine.

His hold on life was marvellous. He didn't die, and the bits seemed to grow together again. For two years he remained in the doctor's hands. Then he was pronounced a cure, and could return to life again, with the lower half of his body, from the hips down, paralysed for ever.

This was in 1920. They returned, Clifford and Constance, to his home, Wragby Hall, the family 'seat'. His father had died, Clifford was now a baronet, Sir Clifford, and Constance was Lady Chatterley. They came to start house-keeping and married life in the rather forlorn home of the Chatterleys on a rather inadequate income. Clifford had a sister, but she had departed. Otherwise there were no near relatives. The elder brother was dead in the war. Crippled for ever, knowing he could never have any children, Clifford came home to the smoky Midlands to keep the Chatterley name alive while he could.

He was not really downcast. He could wheel himself about in a wheeled chair, and he had a bath-chair with a small motor attachment, so he could drive himself slowly round the garden and into the fine melancholy park, of which he was really so proud, though he pretended to be flippant about it.

Having suffered so much, the capacity for suffering had to some extent left him. He remained strange and bright and cheerful, almost, one might say, chirpy, with his ruddy, healthy-looking face, and his pale-blue, challenging bright eyes. His shoulders were broad and strong, his hands were very strong. He was expensively dressed, and wore handsome neckties from Bond Street. Yet still in his face one saw the watchful look, the slight vacancy of a cripple.

He had so very nearly lost his life, that what remained was wonderfully precious to him. It was obvious in the anxious brightness of his eyes, how proud he was, after the great shock, of being alive, but he had been so much hurt that something inside him had perished, some of his feelings had gone. There was a blank of insentience.

Constance, his wife, was a ruddy, country-looking girl with soft brown hair and sturdy body, and slow movements, full of unusual energy. She had big, wondering eyes, and a soft mild voice, and seemed just to have come from her native village. It was not so at all. Her father was the once well-known R.A., old Sir Malcolm Reid. Her mother had been one of the cultivated Fabians in the palmy, rather pre-Raphaelite days. Between artists and cultured socialists, Constance and her sister Hilda had had what might be called an aesthetically unconventional upbringing. They had been taken to Paris and Florence and Rome to breathe in art, and they had been taken also in the other direction, to the Hague and Berlin, to great Socialist conventions, where the speakers spoke in every civilised tongue, and no one was abashed.

The two girls, therefore, were from an early age not the least daunted by either art or ideal politics. It was their natural atmosphere. They were at once cosmopolitan and provincial, with the cosmopolitan provincialism of art that goes with pure social ideals.

They had been sent to Dresden at the age of fifteen, for music among other things. And they had had a good time there. They lived freely among the students, they argued with the men over philosophical, sociological and artistic matters, they were just as good as the men themselves: only better, since they were women. And they tramped off to the forests with sturdy youths bearing guitars, twang-twang! They sang the Wandervogel songs, and they were free. Free! That was the great word. Out in the open world, out in the forests of the morning, with lusty and splendid-throated young fellows, free to do as they liked, and – above all – to say what they liked. It was the talk that mattered supremely: the impassioned interchange of talk. Love was only a minor accompaniment.

Both Hilda and Constance had had their tentative love affairs by the time they were eighteen. The young men with whom they talked so passionately and sang so lustily and camped under the trees in such freedom wanted, of course, the love connection. The girls were doubtful, but then the thing was so much talked about, it was supposed to be so important. And the men were so humble and craving. Why couldn't a girl be queenly, and give the gift of herself?

So they had given the gift of themselves, each to the youth with whom she had the most subtle and intimate arguments. The arguments, the discussions were the great thing: the love-making and connection were only a sort of primitive reversion and a bit of an anticlimax. One was less in love with the boy afterwards, and a little inclined to hate him, as if he had trespassed on one's privacy and inner freedom. For, of course, being a girl, one's whole dignity and meaning in life consisted in the achievement of an absolute, a perfect, a pure and noble freedom. What else did a girl's life mean? To shake off the old and sordid connections and subjections.

And however one might sentimentalise it, this sex business was one of the most ancient, sordid connections and subjections. Poets who glorified it were mostly men. Women had always known there was something better, something higher. And now they knew it more definitely than ever. The beautiful pure freedom of a woman was infinitely more wonderful than any sexual love. The only unfortunate thing was that men lagged so far behind women in the matter. They insisted on the sex thing like dogs.

And a woman had to yield. A man was like a child with his appetites. A woman had to yield him what he wanted, or like a child he would probably turn nasty and flounce away and spoil what was a very pleasant connection. But a woman could yield to a man without yielding her inner, free self. That the poets and talkers about sex did not seem to have taken sufficiently into account. A woman could take a man without really giving herself away. Certainly she could take him without giving herself into his power. Rather she could use this sex thing to have power over him. For she only had to hold herself back in sexual intercourse, and let him finish and expend himself without herself coming to the crisis: and then she could prolong the connection and achieve her orgasm and her crisis while he was merely her tool.

Both sisters had had their love experience by the time the war came, and they were hurried home. Neither was ever in love with a young man unless he and she were verbally very near: that is unless they were profoundly interested, TALKING to one another. The amazing, the profound, the unbelievable thrill there was in passionately talking to some really clever young man by the hour, resuming day after day for months this they had never realised till it happened! The paradisal promise: Thou shalt have men to talk to! – had never been uttered. It was fulfilled before they knew what a promise it was.

And if after the roused intimacy of these vivid and soul-enlightened discussions the sex thing became more or less inevitable, then let it. It marked the end of a chapter . It had a thrill of its own too: a queer vibrating thrill inside the body, a final spasm of self-assertion, like the last word, exciting, and very like the row of asterisks that can be put to show the end of a paragraph, and a break in the theme.

When the girls came home for the summer holidays of 1913, when Hilda was twenty and Connie eighteen, their father could see plainly that they had had the love experience.

L'amour avait passé par là, as somebody puts it. But he was a man of experience himself, and let life take its course. As for the mother, a nervous invalid in the last few months of her life, she only wanted her girls to be 'free', and to 'fulfil themselves'. She herself had never been able to be altogether herself: it had been denied her. Heaven knows why, for she was a woman who had her own income and her own way. She blamed her husband. But as a matter of fact, it was some old impression of authority on her own mind or soul that she could not get rid of. It had nothing to do with Sir Malcolm, who left his nervously hostile, high-spirited wife to rule her own roost, while he went his own way.

So the girls were 'free', and went back to Dresden, and their music, and the university and the young men. They loved their respective young men, and their respective young men loved them with all the passion of mental attraction. All the wonderful things the young men thought and expressed and wrote, they thought and expressed and wrote for the young women. Connie's young man was musical, Hilda's was technical. But they simply lived for their young women. In their minds and their mental excitements, that is. Somewhere else they were a little rebuffed, though they did not know it.

It was obvious in them too that love had gone through them: that is, the physical experience. It is curious what a subtle but unmistakable transmutation it makes, both in the body of men and women: the woman more blooming, more subtly rounded, her young angularities softened, and her expression either anxious or triumphant: the man much quieter, more inward, the very shapes of his shoulders and his buttocks less assertive, more hesitant.

In the actual sex-thrill within the body, the sisters nearly succumbed to the strange male power. But quickly they recovered themselves, took the sex-thrill as a sensation, and remained free. Whereas the men, in gratitude to the woman for the sex experience, let their souls go out to her. And afterwards looked rather as if they had lost a shilling and found sixpence. Connie's man could be a bit sulky, and Hilda's a bit jeering. But that is how men are! Ungrateful and never satisfied. When you don't have them they hate you because you won't; and when you do have them they hate you again, for some other reason. Or for no reason at all, except that they are discontented children, and can't be satisfied whatever they get, let a woman do what she may.

However, came the war. Hilda and Connie were rushed home again after having been home already in May, to their mother's funeral. Before Christmas of 1914 both their German young men were dead: whereupon the sisters wept, and loved the young men passionately, but underneath forgot them. They didn't exist any more.

Both sisters lived in their father's, really their mother's, Kensington house, and mixed with the young Cambridge group, the group that stood for 'freedom' and flannel trousers, and flannel shirts open at the neck, and a well-bred sort of emotional anarchy, and a whispering, murmuring sort of voice, and an ultra-sensitive sort of manner. Hilda, however, suddenly married a man ten years older than herself, an elder member of the same Cambridge group, a man with a fair amount of money, and a comfortable family job in the government: he also wrote philosophical essays. She lived with him in a smallish house in Westminster, and moved in that good sort of society of people in the government who are not tip-toppers, but who are, or would be, the real intelligent power in the nation: people who know what they're talking about, or talk as if they did.

Connie did a mild form of war-work, and consorted with the flannel-trousers Cambridge intransigents, who gently mocked at everything, so far. Her 'friend' was a Clifford Chatterley, a young man of twenty-two, who had hurried home from Bonn, where he was studying the technicalities of coal-mining. He had previously spent two years at Cambridge. Now he had become a first lieutenant in a smart regiment, so he could mock at everything more becomingly in uniform.

Clifford Chatterley was more upper-class than Connie. Connie was well-to-do intelligentsia, but he was aristocracy. Not the big sort, but still *it*. His father was a baronet, and his mother had been a viscount's daughter.

But Clifford, while he was better bred than Connie, and more 'society', was in his own way more provincial and more timid. He was at his ease in the narrow 'great world', that is, landed aristocracy society, but he was shy and nervous of all that other big world which consists of the vast hordes of the middle and lower classes, and foreigners. If the truth must be told, he was just a little bit frightened of middle- and lower-class humanity, and of foreigners not of his own class. He was, in some paralysing way, conscious of his own defencelessness, though he had all the defence of privilege. Which is curious, but a phenomenon of our day.

Therefore the peculiar soft assurance of a girl like Constance Reid fascinated him. She was so much more mistress of herself in that outer world of chaos than he was master of himself.

Nevertheless he too was a rebel: rebelling even against his class. Or perhaps rebel is too strong a word; far too strong. He was only caught in the general, popular recoil of the young against convention and against any sort of real authority. Fathers were ridiculous: his own obstinate one supremely so. And governments were ridiculous: our own wait-and-see sort especially so. And armies were ridiculous, and old buffers of generals altogether, the red-faced Kitchener supremely. Even the war was ridiculous, though it did kill rather a lot of people.

In fact everything was a little ridiculous, or very ridiculous: certainly everything connected with authority, whether it were in the army or the government or the universities, was ridiculous to a degree. And as far as the governing class made any pretensions to govern, they were ridiculous too. Sir Geoffrey, Clifford's father, was intensely ridiculous, chopping down his trees, and weeding men out of his colliery to shove them into the war; and himself being so safe and patriotic; but, also, spending more money on his country than he'd got.

When Miss Chatterley – Emma – came down to London from the Midlands to do some nursing work, she was very witty in a quiet way about Sir Geoffrey and his determined patriotism. Herbert, the elder brother and heir, laughed outright, though it was his trees that were falling for trench props. But Clifford only smiled a little uneasily. Everything was ridiculous, quite true. But when it came too close and oneself became ridiculous too . . . ? At least people of a different class, like Connie, were earnest about something. They believed in something.

They were rather earnest about the Tommies, and the threat of conscription, and the shortage of sugar and toffee for the children. In all these things, of course, the authorities were ridiculously at fault. But Clifford could not take it to heart. To him the authorities were ridiculous *ab ovo*, not because of toffee or Tommies.

And the authorities felt ridiculous, and behaved in a rather ridiculous fashion, and it was all a mad hatter's tea-party for a while. Till things developed over there, and Lloyd George came to save the situation over here. And this surpassed even ridicule, the flippant young laughed no more.

In 1916 Herbert Chatterley was killed, so Clifford became heir. He was terrified even of this. His importance as son of Sir Geoffrey, and child of Wragby, was so ingrained in him, he could never escape it. And yet he knew that this too, in the eyes of the vast seething world, was ridiculous. Now he was heir and responsible for Wragby. Was that not terrible? and also splendid and at the same time, perhaps, purely absurd?

Sir Geoffrey would have none of the absurdity. He was pale and tense, withdrawn into himself, and obstinately determined to save his country and his own position, let it be Lloyd George or who it might. So cut off he was, so divorced from the England that was really England, so utterly incapable, that he even thought well of Horatio Bottomley. Sir Geoffrey stood for England and Lloyd George as his forebears had stood for England and St George: and he never knew there was a difference. So Sir Geoffrey felled timber and stood for Lloyd George and England, England and Lloyd George.

And he wanted Clifford to marry and produce an heir. Clifford felt his father was a hopeless anachronism. But wherein was he himself any further ahead, except in a wincing sense of the ridiculousness of everything and the paramount ridiculousness of his own position? For willy-nilly he took his baronetcy and Wragby with the last seriousness.

The gay excitement had gone out of the war . . . dead. Too much death and horror. A man needed support and comfort. A man needed to have an anchor in the safe world. A man needed a wife.

The Chatterleys, two brothers and a sister, had lived curiously isolated, shut in with one another at Wragby, in spite of all their connections. A sense of isolation intensified the family tie, a sense of the weakness of their position, a sense of defencelessness, in spite of, or because of, the title and the land. They were cut off from those industrial Midlands in which they passed their lives. And they were cut off from their own class by the brooding, obstinate, shut-up nature of Sir Geoffrey, their father, whom they ridiculed, but whom they were so sensitive about.

The three had said they would all live together always. But now Herbert was dead, and Sir Geoffrey wanted Clifford to marry. Sir Geoffrey barely mentioned it: he spoke very little. But his silent, brooding insistence that it should be so was hard for Clifford to bear up against.

But Emma said No! She was ten years older than Clifford, and she felt his marrying would be a desertion and a betrayal of what the young ones of the family had stood for.

Clifford married Connie, nevertheless, and had his month's honeymoon with her. It was the terrible year 1917, and they were intimate as two people who stand together on a sinking ship. He had been virgin when he married: and the sex part did not mean much to him. They were so close, he and she, apart from that. And Connie exulted a little in this intimacy which was beyond sex, and beyond a man's 'satisfaction'. Clifford anyhow was not just keen on his 'satisfaction', as so many men seemed to be. No, the intimacy was deeper, more personal than that. And sex was merely an accident, or an adjunct: one of the curious obsolete, organic processes which persisted in its own clumsiness, but was not really necessary. Though Connie did want children: if only to fortify her against her sister-in-law Emma.

But early in 1918 Clifford was shipped home smashed, and there was no child. And Sir Geoffrey died of chagrin.

Chapter 2

Connie and Clifford came home to Wragby in the autumn of 1920. Miss Chatterley, still disgusted at her brother's defection, had departed and was living in a little flat in London.

Wragby was a long low old house in brown stone, begun about the middle of the eighteenth century, and added on to, till it was a warren of a place without much distinction. It stood on an eminence in a rather fine old park of oak trees, but alas, one could see in the near distance the chimney of Tevershall pit, with its clouds of steam and smoke, and on the damp, hazy distance of the hill the raw straggle of Tevershall village, a village which began almost at the park gates, and trailed in utter hopeless ugliness for a long and gruesome mile: houses, rows of wretched, small, begrimed, brick houses, with black slate roofs for lids, sharp angles and wilful, blank dreariness.

Connie was accustomed to Kensington or the Scotch hills or the Sussex downs: that was her England. With the stoicism of the young she took in the utter, soulless ugliness of the coal-and-iron Midlands at a glance, and left it at what it was: unbelievable and not to be thought about. From the rather dismal rooms at Wragby she heard the rattle-rattle of the screens at the pit, the puff of the winding-engine, the clink-clink of shunting trucks, and the hoarse little whistle of the colliery locomotives. Tevershall pit-bank was burning, had been burning for years, and it would cost thousands to put it out. So it had to burn. And when the wind was that way, which was often, the house was full of the stench of this sulphurous combustion of the earth's excrement. But even on windless days the air always smelt of something under-earth: sulphur, iron, coal, or acid. And even on the Christmas roses the smuts settled persistently, incredible, like black manna from skies of doom.

Well, there it was: fated like the rest of things! It was rather awful, but why kick? You couldn't kick it away. It just went on. Life, like all the rest! On the low dark ceiling of cloud at night red blotches burned and quavered, dappling and swelling and contracting, like burns that give pain. It was the furnaces. At first they fascinated Connie with a sort of horror; she felt she was living underground. Then she got used to them. And in the morning it rained.

Clifford professed to like Wragby better than London. This country had a grim will of its own, and the people had guts. Connie wondered what else they had: certainly neither eyes nor minds. The people were as haggard, shapeless, and dreary as the countryside, and as unfriendly. Only there was something in their deep-mouthed slurring of the dialect, and the thresh-thresh of their hob-nailed pit-boots as they trailed home in gangs on the asphalt from work, that was terrible and a bit mysterious.

There had been no welcome home for the young squire, no festivities, no deputation, not even a single flower. Only a dank ride in a motor car up a dark, damp drive, burrowing through gloomy trees, out to the slope of the park where grey damp sheep were feeding, to the knoll where the house spread its dark brown façade, and the housekeeper and her husband were hovering, like unsure tenants on the face of the earth, ready to stammer a welcome.

There was no communication between Wragby Hall and Tevershall village, none. No caps were touched, no curtseys bobbed. The colliers merely stared; the tradesmen lifted their caps to Connie as to an acquaintance, and nodded awkwardly to Clifford; that was all. Gulf impassable, and a quiet sort of resentment on either side. At first Connie suffered from the steady drizzle of resentment that came from the village. Then she hardened herself to it, and it became a sort of tonic, something to live up to. It was not that she and Clifford were unpopular, they merely belonged to another species altogether from the colliers. Gulf impassable, breach indescribable, such as is perhaps nonexistent south of the Trent. But in the Midlands and the industrial North gulf impassable, across which no communication could take place. You stick to your side, I'll stick to mine! A strange denial of the common pulse of humanity.

Yet the village sympathised with Clifford and Connie in the abstract. In the flesh it was – You leave me alone! – on either side.

The rector was a nice man of about sixty, full of his duty, and reduced, personally, almost to a nonentity by the silent – You leave me alone! – of the village. The miners' wives were nearly all Methodists. The miners were nothing. But even so much official uniform as the clergyman wore was enough to obscure entirely the fact that he was a man like any other man. No, he was Mester Ashby, a sort of automatic preaching and praying concern.

This stubborn, instinctive – We think ourselves as good as you, if you *are* Lady Chatterley! – puzzled and baffled Connie at first extremely. The curious, suspicious, false amiability with which the miners' wives met her overtures; the curiously offensive tinge of – Oh dear me! I *am* somebody now, with Lady Chatterley talking to me! But she needn't think I'm not as good as her for all that! – which she always heard twanging in the women's half-fawning voices, was impossible. There was no getting past it. It was hopelessly and offensively nonconformist.

Clifford left them alone, and she learnt to do the same: she just went by without looking at them, and they stared as if she were a walking wax figure. When he had to deal with them, Clifford was rather haughty and contemptuous; one could no longer afford to be friendly. In fact he was altogether rather supercilious and contemptuous of anyone not in his own class. He stood his ground, without any attempt at conciliation. And he was neither liked nor disliked by the people: he was just part of things, like the pit-bank and Wragby itself.

But Clifford was really extremely shy and self-conscious now he was lamed. He hated seeing anyone except just the personal servants. For he had to sit in a wheeled chair or a sort of bath-chair. Nevertheless he was just as carefully dressed as ever, by his expensive tailors, and he wore the careful Bond Street neckties just as before, and from the top he looked just as smart and impressive as ever. He had never been one of the modern ladylike young men: rather bucolic even, with his ruddy face and broad shoulders. But his very quiet, hesitating voice, and his eyes, at the same time bold and frightened, assured and uncertain, revealed his nature. His manner was often offensively supercilious, and then again modest and self-effacing, almost tremulous.

Connie and he were attached to one another, in the aloof modern way. He was much too hurt in himself, the great shock of his maiming, to be easy and flippant. He was a hurt thing. And as such Connie stuck to him passionately.

But she could not help feeling how little connection he really had with people. The miners were, in a sense, his own men; but he saw them as objects rather than men, parts of the pit rather than parts of life, crude raw phenomena rather than human beings along with him. He was in some way afraid of them, he could not bear to have them look at him now he was lame. And their queer, crude life seemed as unnatural as that of hedgehogs.

He was remotely interested; but like a man looking down a microscope, or up a telescope. He was not in touch. He was not in actual touch with anybody, save, traditionally, with Wragby, and, through the close bond of family defence, with Emma. Beyond this nothing really touched him. Connie felt that she herself didn't really, not really touch him; perhaps there was nothing to get at ultimately; just a negation of human contact.

Yet he was absolutely dependent on her, he needed her every moment. Big and strong as he was, he was helpless. He could wheel himself about in a wheeled chair, and he had a sort of bath-chair with a motor attachment, in which he could puff slowly round the park. But alone he was like a lost thing. He needed Connie to be there, to assure him he existed at all.

Still he was ambitious. He had taken to writing stories; curious, very personal stories about people he had known. Clever, rather spiteful, and yet, in some mysterious way, meaningless. The observation was extraordinary and peculiar. But there was no touch, no actual contact. It was as if the whole thing took place in a vacuum. And since the field of life is largely an artificially-lighted stage today, the stories were curiously true to modern life, to the modern psychology, that is.

Clifford was almost morbidly sensitive about these stories. He wanted everyone to think them good, of the best, *ne plus ultra*. They appeared in the most modern magazines, and were praised and blamed as usual. But to Clifford the blame was torture, like knives goading him. It was as if the whole of his being were in his stories.

Connie helped him as much as she could. At first she was thrilled. He talked everything over with her monotonously, insistently, persistently, and she had to respond with all her might. It was as if her whole soul and body and sex had to rouse up and pass into these stories of his. This thrilled her and absorbed her.

Of physical life they lived very little. She had to superintend the house. But the housekeeper had served Sir Geoffrey for many years, and the dried-up, elderly, superlatively correct female . . . you could hardly call her a parlourmaid, or even a woman . . . who waited at table, had been in the house for forty years. Even the very housemaids were no longer young. It was awful! What could you do with such a place, but leave it alone! All these endless rooms that nobody used, all the Midlands routine, the mechanical cleanliness and the mechanical order! Clifford had insisted on a new cook, an experienced woman who had served him in his rooms in London. For the rest the place seemed run by mechanical anarchy. Everything went on in pretty good order, strict cleanliness, and strict punctuality; even pretty strict honesty. And yet, to Connie, it was a methodical anarchy. No warmth of feeling united it organically. The house seemed as dreary as a disused street.

What could she do but leave it alone . . . ? So she left it alone. Miss Chatterley came sometimes, with her aristocratic thin face, and triumphed, finding nothing altered. She would never forgive Connie for ousting her from her union in consciousness with her brother. It was she, Emma, who should be bringing forth the stories, these books, with him; the Chatterley stories, something new in the world, that *they*, the Chatterleys, had put there. There was no other standard. There was no organic connection with the thought and expression that had gone before. Only something new in the world: the Chatterley books, entirely personal.

Connie's father, when he paid a flying visit to Wragby, said in private to his daughter: As for Clifford's writing, it's smart, but there's nothing in it. It won't last! . . . Connie looked at the burly Scottish knight who had done himself well all his life, and her eyes, her big, still-wondering blue eyes became vague. Nothing in it! What did he mean by *nothing in it*? If the critics praised it, and Clifford's name was almost famous, and it even brought in money . . . what did her father mean by saying there was nothing in Clifford's writing? What else could there be?

For Connie had adopted the standard of the young: what there was in the moment was everything. And moments followed one another without necessarily belonging to one another.

It was in her second winter at Wragby her father said to her: 'I hope, Connie, you won't let circumstances force you into being a demi-vierge.'

'A demi-vierge!' replied Connie vaguely. 'Why? Why not?'

'Unless you like it, of course!' said her father hastily. To Clifford he said the same, when the two men were alone: 'I'm afraid it doesn't quite suit Connie to be a demi-vierge.'

'A half-virgin!' replied Clifford, translating the phrase to be sure of it.

He thought for a moment, then flushed very red. He was angry and offended. 'In what way doesn't it suit her?' he asked stiffly.

'She's getting thin . . . angular. It's not her style. She's not the pilchard sort of little slip of a girl, she's a bonny Scotch trout.'

'Without the spots, of course!' said Clifford.

He wanted to say something later to Connie about the demi-vierge business . . . the half-virgin state of her affairs. But he could not bring himself to do it. He was at once too intimate with her and not intimate enough. He was so very much at one with her, in his mind and hers, but bodily they were nonexistent to one another, and neither could bear to drag in the *corpus delicti*. They were so intimate, and utterly out of touch.

Connie guessed, however, that her father had said something, and that something was in Clifford's mind. She knew that he didn't mind whether she were demi-vierge or demi-monde, so long as he didn't absolutely know, and wasn't made to see. What the eye doesn't see and the mind doesn't know, doesn't exist.

Connie and Clifford had now been nearly two years at Wragby, living their vague life of absorption in Clifford and his work. Their interests had never ceased to flow together over his work. They talked and wrestled in the throes of composition, and felt as if something were happening, really happening, really in the void.

And thus far it was a life: in the void. For the rest it was nonexistence. Wragby was there, the servants . . . but spectral, not really existing. Connie went for walks in the park, and in the woods that joined the park, and enjoyed the solitude and the mystery, kicking the brown leaves of autumn, and picking the primroses of spring. But it was all a dream; or rather it was like the simulacrum of reality. The oak-leaves were to her like oak-leaves seen ruffling in a mirror, she herself was a figure somebody had read about, picking primroses that were only shadows or memories, or words. No substance to her or anything . . . no touch, no contact! Only this life with Clifford, this endless spinning of webs of yarn, of the minutiae of consciousness, these stories Sir Malcolm said there was nothing in, and they wouldn't last. Why should there be anything in them, why should they last? Sufficient unto the day is the evil thereof. Sufficient unto the moment is the *appearance* of reality.

Clifford had quite a number of friends, acquaintances really, and he invited them to Wragby. He invited all sorts of people, critics and writers, people who would help to praise his books. And they were flattered at being asked to Wragby, and they praised. Connie understood it all perfectly. But why not? This was one of the fleeting patterns in the mirror. What was wrong with it?

She was hostess to these people . . . mostly men. She was hostess also to

Clifford's occasional aristocratic relations. Being a soft, ruddy, country-looking girl, inclined to freckles, with big blue eyes, and curling, brown hair, and a soft voice, and rather strong, female loins she was considered a little old-fashioned and 'womanly'. She was not a 'little pilchard sort of fish', like a boy, with a boy's flat breast and little buttocks. She was too feminine to be quite smart.

So the men, especially those no longer young, were very nice to her indeed. But, knowing what torture poor Clifford would feel at the slightest sign of flirting on her part, she gave them no encouragement at all. She was quiet and vague, she had no contact with them and intended to have none. Clifford was extraordinarily proud of himself.

His relatives treated her quite kindly. She knew that the kindliness indicated a lack of fear, and that these people had no respect for you unless you could frighten them a little. But again she had no contact. She let them be kindly and disdainful, she let them feel they had no need to draw their steel in readiness. She had no real connection with them.

Time went on. Whatever happened, nothing happened, because she was so beautifully out of contact. She and Clifford lived in their ideas and his books. She entertained . . . there were always people in the house. Time went on as the clock does, half-past eight instead of half-past seven.

Chapter 3

Connie was aware, however, of a growing restlessness. Out of her discon- nection, a restlessness was taking possession of her like madness. It twitched her limbs when she didn't want to twitch them, it jerked her spine when she didn't want to jerk upright but preferred to rest comfortably. It thrilled inside her body, in her womb, somewhere, till she felt she must jump into water and swim to get away from it; a mad restlessness. It made her heart beat violently for no reason. And she was getting thinner.

It was just restlessness. She would rush off across the park, and abandon Clifford, and lie prone in the bracken. To get away from the house . . . she must get away from the house and everybody. The wood was her one refuge, her sanctuary.

But it was not really a refuge, a sanctuary, because she had no connection with it. It was only a place where she could get away from the rest. She never really touched the spirit of the wood itself . . . if it had any such nonsensical thing.

Vaguely she knew herself that she was going to pieces in some way. Vaguely she knew she was out of connection: she had lost touch with the substantial and vital world. Only Clifford and his books, which did not exist . . . which had nothing in them! Void to void. Vaguely she knew. But it was like beating her head against a stone.

Her father warned her again: 'Why don't you get yourself a beau, Connie? Do you all the good in the world.'

That winter Michaelis came for a few days. He was a young Irishman who had already made a large fortune by his plays in America. He had been taken up quite enthusiastically for a time by smart society in London, for he wrote smart society plays. Then gradually smart society realised that it had been made ridiculous at the hands of a down at heel Dublin street-rat, and revulsion came. Michaelis was the last word in what was caddish and bounderish. He was discovered to be anti-English, and to the class that made this discovery this was worse than the dirtiest crime. He was cut dead, and his corpse thrown into the refuse-can.

Nevertheless Michaelis had his apartment in Mayfair, and walked down Bond Street the image of a gentleman, for you cannot get even the best tailors to cut their low-down customers, when the customers pay.

Clifford was inviting the young man of thirty at an inauspicious moment in the young man's career. Yet Clifford did not hesitate. Michaelis had the ear of a few million people, probably; and, being a hopeless outsider, he would no doubt be grateful to be asked down to Wragby at this juncture, when the rest of the smart world was cutting him. Being grateful, he would no doubt do Clifford 'good' over there in America. Kudos! A man gets a lot of kudos, whatever that may be, by being talked about in the right way, especially 'over there'. Clifford was a coming man; and it was remarkable what a sound publicity instinct he had. In the end Michaelis did him most nobly in a play, and Clifford was a sort of popular hero. Till the reaction, when he found he had been made ridiculous.

Connie wondered a little over Clifford's blind, imperious instinct to become known: known, that is, to the vast amorphous world he did not himself know, and of which he was uneasily afraid; known as a writer, as a first-class modern writer. Connie was aware from successful, old, hearty, bluffing Sir Malcolm, that artists did advertise themselves, and exert themselves to put their goods over. But her father used channels ready-made, used by all the other R.A.s who sold their pictures. Whereas Clifford discovered new channels of publicity, all kinds. He had all kinds of people at Wragby, without exactly lowering himself. But, determined to build himself a monument of a reputation quickly, he used any handy rubble in the making.

Michaelis arrived duly, in a very neat car, with a chauffeur and a manservant. He was absolutely Bond Street! But at sight of him something in Clifford's county soul recoiled. He wasn't exactly . . . not exactly . . . in fact, he wasn't at all, well, what his appearance intended to imply. To Clifford this was final and enough. Yet he was very polite to the man; to the amazing success in him. The bitch-goddess, as she is called, of Success, roamed, snarling and protective, round the half-humble, half-defiant Michaelis' heels, and intimidated Clifford completely: for he wanted to prostitute himself to the bitch-goddess, Success, also, if only she would have him.

Michaelis obviously wasn't an Englishman, in spite of all the tailors, hatters, barbers, booters of the very best quarter of London. No, no, he obviously wasn't an Englishman: the wrong sort of flattish, pale face and bearing; and the wrong sort of grievance. He had a grudge and a grievance: that was obvious to any true-born English gentleman, who would scorn to let such a thing appear blatant in his own demeanour. Poor Michaelis had been much kicked, so that he had a slightly tail-between-the-legs look even now. He had pushed his way by sheer instinct and sheerer effrontery on to the stage and to the front of it, with his plays. He had caught the public. And he had thought the kicking days were over. Alas, they weren't . . . They never would be. For he, in a sense, asked to be kicked. He pined to be where he didn't belong . . . among the English upper classes. And how they enjoyed the various kicks they got at him! And how he hated them!

Nevertheless he travelled with his manservant and his very neat car, this Dublin mongrel.

There was something about him that Connie liked. He didn't put on airs to himself; he had no illusions about himself. He talked to Clifford sensibly, briefly, practically about all the things Clifford wanted to know. He didn't expand or let himself go. He knew he had been asked down to Wragby to be made use of, and like an old, shrewd, almost indifferent business man, or big-business man, he let himself be asked questions, and he answered with as little waste of feeling as possible.

'Money!' he said. 'Money is a sort of instinct. It's a sort of property of nature in a man to make money. It's nothing you do. It's no trick you play. It's a sort of permanent accident of your own nature; once you start, you make money, and you go on; up to a point, I suppose.'

'But you've got to begin,' said Clifford.

'Oh quite! You've got to get *in*. You can do nothing if you are kept outside. You've got to beat your way in. Once you've done that, you can't help it.'

'But could you have made money except by plays?' asked Clifford.

'Oh probably not! I may be a good writer or I may be a bad one, but a writer and a writer of plays is what I am, and I've got to be. There's no question of that.'

'And you think it's a writer of popular plays that you've got to be?' asked Connie.

'There, exactly!' he said, turning to her in a sudden flash. 'There's nothing in it! There's nothing in popularity. There's nothing in the public, if it comes to that. There's nothing really in my plays to *make* them popular. It's not that. They just are, like the weather . . . the sort that will *have* to be . . . for the time being.'

He turned his slow, rather full eyes, that had been drowned in such fathomless disillusion, on Connie, and she trembled a little. He seemed so old . . . endlessly old, built up of layers of disillusion, going down in him generation after generation, like geological strata; and at the same time he was forlorn like a child. An outcast, in a certain sense; but with the desperate bravery of his rat-like existence.

'At least it's wonderful what you've done at your time of life,' said Clifford contemplatively.

'I'm thirty . . . yes, I'm thirty!' said Michaelis, sharply and suddenly, with a curious laugh; hollow, triumphant, and bitter.

'And are you alone?' asked Connie.

'How do you mean? Do I live alone? I've got my servant. He's a Greek, so he says, and quite incompetent. But I keep him. And I'm going to marry. Oh, yes, I must marry.'

'It sounds like going to have your tonsils cut,' laughed Connie. 'Will it be an effort?'

He looked at her admiringly. 'Well, Lady Chatterley, somehow it will! I find . . . excuse me . . . I find I can't marry an Englishwoman, not even an Irishwoman . . .'

'Try an American,' said Clifford.

'Oh, American!' He laughed a hollow laugh. 'No, I've asked my man if he will find me a Turk or something . . . something nearer to the Oriental.'

Connie really wondered at this queer, melancholy specimen of extraordinary success; it was said he had an income of fifty thousand dollars from America alone. Sometimes he was handsome: sometimes as he looked sideways, downwards, and the light fell on him, he had the silent, enduring beauty of a carved ivory Negro mask, with his rather full eyes, and the strong queerly-arched brows, the immobile, compressed mouth; that momentary but revealed immobility, an immobility, a timelessness which the Buddha aims at, and which Negroes express sometimes without ever aiming at it; something old, old, and acquiescent in the race! Aeons of acquiescence in race destiny, instead of our individual resistance. And then a swimming through, like rats in a dark river. Connie felt a sudden, strange leap of sympathy for him, a leap mingled with compassion, and tinged with repulsion, amounting almost to love. The outsider! The outsider! And they called him a bounder! How much more bounderish and assertive Clifford looked! How much stupider!

Michaelis knew at once he had made an impression on her. He turned his full, hazel, slightly prominent eyes on her in a look of pure detachment. He was estimating her, and the extent of the impression he had made. With the English nothing could save him from being the eternal outsider, not even love. Yet women sometimes fell for him . . . Englishwomen too.

He knew just where he was with Clifford. They were two alien dogs which would have liked to snarl at one another, but which smiled instead, perforce. But with the woman he was not quite so sure.

Breakfast was served in the bedrooms; Clifford never appeared before lunch, and the dining-room was a little dreary. After coffee Michaelis, restless and ill-sitting soul, wondered what he should do. It was a fine November day . . . fine for Wragby. He looked over the melancholy park. My God! What a place!

He sent a servant to ask, could he be of any service to Lady Chatterley: he thought of driving into Sheffield. The answer came, would he care to go up to Lady Chatterley's sitting-room.

Connie had a sitting-room on the third floor, the top floor of the central portion of the house. Clifford's rooms were on the ground floor, of course. Michaelis was flattered by being asked up to Lady Chatterley's own parlour. He followed blindly after the servant . . . he never noticed things, or had contact with his surroundings. In her room he did glance vaguely round at the fine German reproductions of Renoir and Cézanne.

'It's very pleasant up here,' he said, with his queer smile, as if it hurt him to smile, showing his teeth. 'You are wise to get up to the top.'

'Yes, I think so,' she said.

Her room was the only gay, modern one in the house, the only spot in Wragby where her personality was at all revealed. Clifford had never seen it, and she asked very few people up.

Now she and Michaelis sat on opposite sides of the fire and talked. She asked him about himself, his mother and father, his brothers . . . other people were always something of a wonder to her, and when her sympathy was awakened she was quite devoid of class feeling. Michaelis talked frankly about himself, quite frankly, without affectation, simply revealing his bitter, indifferent, stray-dog's soul, then showing a gleam of revengeful pride in his success.

'But why are you such a lonely bird?' Connie asked him; and again he looked at her, with his full, searching, hazel look.

'Some birds *are* that way,' he replied. Then, with a touch of familiar irony: 'but, look here, what about yourself? Aren't you by way of being a lonely bird yourself?' Connie, a little startled, thought about it for a few moments, and then she said: 'Only in a way! Not altogether, like you!'

'Am I altogether a lonely bird?' he asked, with his queer grin of a smile, as if he had toothache; it was so wry, and his eyes were so perfectly unchangingly melancholy, or stoical, or disillusioned, or afraid.

'Why?' she said, a little breathless, as she looked at him. 'You are, aren't you?'

She felt a terrible appeal coming to her from him, that made her almost lose her balance.

'Oh, you're quite right!' he said, turning his head away, and looking sideways, downwards, with that strange immobility of an old race that is hardly here in our present day. It was that that really made Connie lose her power to see him detached from herself.

He looked up at her with the full glance that saw everything, registered everything. At the same time, the infant crying in the night was crying out of his breast to her, in a way that affected her very womb.

'It's awfully nice of you to think of me,' he said laconically.

'Why shouldn't I think of you?' she exclaimed, with hardly breath to utter it.

He gave the wry, quick hiss of a laugh.

'Oh, in that way! . . . May I hold your hand for a minute?' he asked suddenly, fixing his eyes on her with almost hypnotic power, and sending out an appeal that affected her direct in the womb.

She stared at him, dazed and transfixed, and he went over and kneeled beside her, and took her two feet close in his two hands, and buried his face in her lap, remaining motionless. She was perfectly dim and dazed, looking down in a sort of amazement at the rather tender nape of his neck, feeling his face pressing her thighs. In all her burning dismay, she could not help putting her hand, with tenderness and compassion, on the defenceless nape of his neck, and he trembled, with a deep shudder.

Then he looked up at her with that awful appeal in his full, glowing eyes, She was utterly incapable of resisting it. From her breast flowed the answering, immense yearning over him; she must give him anything, anything.

He was a curious and very gentle lover, very gentle with the woman, trembling uncontrollably, and yet at the same time detached, aware, aware of every sound outside.

To her it meant nothing except that she gave herself to him. And at length he ceased to quiver any more, and lay quite still, quite still. Then, with dim, compassionate fingers, she stroked his head, that lay on her breast.

When he rose, he kissed both her hands, then both her feet, in their suède slippers, and in silence went away to the end of the room, where he stood with his back to her. There was silence for some minutes. Then he turned and came to her again as she sat in her old place by the fire.

'And now, I suppose you'll hate me!' he said in a quiet, inevitable way. She looked up at him quickly.

'Why should I?' she asked.

'They mostly do,' he said; then he caught himself up. 'I mean . . . a woman is supposed to.'

'This is the last moment when I ought to hate you,' she said resentfully.

'I know! I know! It should be so! You're *frightfully* good to me . . . ' he cried miserably.

She wondered why he should be miserable. 'Won't you sit down again?' she said. He glanced at the door.

'Sir Clifford!' he said, 'won't he . . . won't he be . . . ?' She paused a moment to consider. 'Perhaps!' she said. And she looked up at him. 'I don't want Clifford to know . . . not even to suspect. It would hurt him so much. But I don't think it's wrong, do you?'

'Wrong! Good God, no! You're only too infinitely good to me . . . I can hardly bear it.'

He turned aside, and she saw that in another moment he would be sobbing.

'But we needn't let Clifford know, need we?' she pleaded. 'It *would* hurt him so. And if he never knows, never suspects, it hurts nobody.'

'Me!' he said, almost fiercely; 'he'll know nothing from me! You see if he does. Me give myself away! Ha! Ha!' he laughed hollowly, cynically at such an idea. She watched him in wonder. He said to her: 'May I kiss your hand and go? I'll run into Sheffield I think, and lunch there, if I may, and be back to tea. May I do anything for you? May I be sure you don't hate me? – and that you won't?' – he ended with a desperate note of cynicism.

'No, I don't hate you,' she said. 'I think you're nice.'

'Ah!' he said to her fiercely, 'I'd rather you said that to me than said you love me! It means such a lot more . . . Till afternoon then. I've plenty to think about till then.' He kissed her hands humbly and was gone.

'I don't think I can stand that young man,' said Clifford at lunch.

'Why?' asked Connie.

'He's such a bounder underneath his veneer . . . just waiting to bounce us.'

'I think people have been so unkind to him,' said Connie.

'Do you wonder? And do you think he employs his shining hours doing deeds of kindness?'

'I think he has a certain sort of generosity.'

'Towards whom?'

'I don't quite know.'

'Naturally you don't. I'm afraid you mistake unscrupulousness for generosity.'

Connie paused. Did she? It was just possible. Yet the unscrupulousness of Michaelis had a certain fascination for her. He went whole lengths where Clifford only crept a few timid paces. In his way he had conquered the world, which was what Clifford wanted to do. Ways and means . . . ? Were those of Michaelis more despicable than those of Clifford? Was the way the poor outsider had shoved and bounced himself forward in person, and by the back doors, any worse than Clifford's way of advertising himself into prominence? The bitch-goddess, Success, was trailed by thousands of gasping dogs with lolling tongues. The one that got her first was the real dog among dogs, if you go by success! So Michaelis could keep his tail up.

The queer thing was, he didn't. He came back towards teatime with a large handful of violets and lilies, and the same hangdog expression. Connie wondered sometimes if it were a sort of mask to disarm opposition, because it was almost too fixed. Was he really such a sad dog?

His sad-dog sort of extinguished self persisted all the evening, though through it Clifford felt the inner effrontery. Connie didn't feel it, perhaps because it was not directed against women; only against men, and their presumptions and assumptions. That indestructible, inward effrontery in the meagre fellow was what made men so down on Michaelis. His very presence was an affront to a man of society, cloak it as he might in an assumed good manner.

Connie was in love with him, but she managed to sit with her embroidery and let the men talk, and not give herself away. As for Michaelis, he was perfect; exactly the same melancholic, attentive, aloof young fellow of the previous evening, millions of degrees remote from his hosts, but laconically playing up to them to the required amount, and never coming forth to them for a moment. Connie felt he must have forgotten the morning. He had not forgotten. But he knew where he was . . . in the same old place outside, where the born outsiders are. He didn't take the love-making altogether personally. He knew it would not change him from an ownerless dog, whom everybody begrudges its golden collar, into a comfortable society dog.

The final fact being that at the very bottom of his soul he *was* an outsider, and antisocial, and he accepted the fact inwardly, no matter how Bond-Streety he was on the outside. His isolation was a necessity to him; just as the appearance of conformity and mixing-in with the smart people was also a necessity.

But occasional love, as a comfort and soothing, was also a good thing, and he was not ungrateful. On the contrary, he was burningly, poignantly grateful for a piece of natural, spontaneous kindness· almost to tears. Beneath his pale, immobile, disillusioned face, his child's soul was sobbing with gratitude to the woman, and burning to come to her again; just as his outcast soul was knowing he would keep really clear of her.

He found an opportunity to say to her, as they were lighting the candles in the hall, 'May I come?'

'I'll come to you,' she said.

'Oh, good!'

He waited for her a long time . . . but she came.

He was the trembling excited sort of lover, whose crisis soon came, and was finished. There was something curiously childlike and defenceless about his naked body: as children are naked. His defences were all in his wits and cunning, his very instincts of cunning, and when these were in abeyance he seemed doubly naked and like a child, of unfinished, tender flesh, and somehow struggling helplessly.

He roused in the woman a wild sort of compassion and yearning, and a wild, craving physical desire. The physical desire he did not satisfy in her; he was always come and finished so quickly, then shrinking down on her breast, and recovering somewhat his effrontery while she lay dazed, disappointed, lost.

But then she soon learnt to hold him, to keep him there inside her when his crisis was over. And there he was generous and curiously potent; he stayed firm inside her, giving to her, while she was active . . . wildly, passionately active, coming to her own crisis. And as he felt the frenzy of her achieving her own orgasmic satisfaction from his hard, erect passivity, he had a curious sense of pride and satisfaction.

'Ah, how good!' she whispered tremulously, and she became quite still, clinging to him. And he lay there in his own isolation, but somehow proud.

He stayed that time only the three days, and to Clifford was exactly the same as on the first evening; to Connie also. There was no breaking down his external man.

He wrote to Connie with the same plaintive melancholy note as ever, sometimes witty, and touched with a queer, sexless affection. A kind of hopeless affection he seemed to feel for her, and the essential remoteness remained the same. He was hopeless at the very core of him, and he wanted to be hopeless. He rather hated hope. '*Une immense espérance a traversé la terre*,' he read somewhere, and his comment was: 'and it's darned-well drowned everything worth having.'

Connie never really understood him, but, in her way, she loved him. And all the time she felt the reflection of his hopelessness in her. She couldn't quite, quite love in hopelessness. And he, being hopeless, couldn't ever quite love at all.

So they went on for quite a time, writing, and meeting occasionally in London. She still wanted the physical, sexual thrill she could get with him by her own activity, his little orgasm being over. And he still wanted to give it her. Which was enough to keep them connected.

And enough to give her a subtle sort of self-assurance, something blind and a little arrogant. It was an almost mechanical confidence in her own powers, and went with a great cheerfulness.

She was terrifically cheerful at Wragby. And she used all her aroused cheerfulness and satisfaction to stimulate Clifford, so that he wrote his best at this time, and was almost happy in his strange blind way. He really reaped the fruits of the sensual satisfaction she got out of Michaelis' male passivity erect inside her. But of course he never knew it, and if he had, he wouldn't have said thank-you!

Yet when those days of her grand joyful cheerfulness and stimulus were gone, quite gone, and she was depressed and irritable, how Clifford longed for them again! Perhaps if he'd known he might even have wished to get her and Michaelis together again.

Chapter 4

Connie always had a foreboding of the hopelessness of her affair with Mick, as people called him. Yet other men seemed to mean nothing to her. She was attached to Clifford. He wanted a good deal of her life and she gave it to him. But she wanted a good deal from the life of a man, and this Clifford did not give her; could not. There were occasional spasms of Michaelis. But, as she knew by foreboding, that would come to an end. Mick *couldn't* keep anything up. It was part of his very being that he must break off any connection, and be loose, isolated, absolutely lone dog again. It was his major necessity, even though he always said: She turned me down!

The world is supposed to be full of possibilities, but they narrow down to pretty few in most personal experience. There's lots of good fish in the sea . . . maybe . . . but the vast masses seem to be mackerel or herring, and if you're not mackerel or herring yourself, you are likely to find very few good fish in the sea.

Clifford was making strides into fame, and even money. People came to see him. Connie nearly always had somebody at Wragby. But if they weren't mackerel they were herring, with an occasional catfish, or conger eel.

There were a few regular men, constants; men who had been at Cambridge with Clifford. There was Tommy Dukes, who had remained in the army, and was a Brigadier-General. 'The army leaves me time to think, and saves me from having to face the battle of life,' he said.

There was Charles May, an Irishman, who wrote scientifically about stars. There was Hammond, another writer. All were about the same age as Clifford; the young intellectuals of the day. They all believed in the life of the mind.

What you did apart from that was your private affair, and didn't much matter. No one thinks of enquiring of another person at what hour he retires to the privy. It isn't interesting to anyone but the person concerned.

And so with most of the matters of ordinary life ... how you make your money, or whether you love your wife, or if you have 'affairs'. All these matters concern only the person concerned, and, like going to the privy, have no interest for anyone else.

'The whole point about the sexual problem,' said Hammond, who was a tall thin fellow with a wife and two children, but much more closely connected with a typewriter, 'is that there is no point to it. Strictly there is no problem. We don't want to follow a man into the W.C., so why should we want to follow him into bed with a woman? And therein lies the problem. If we took no more notice of the one thing than the other, there'd be no problem. It's all utterly senseless and pointless; a matter of misplaced curiosity.'

'Quite, Hammond, quite! But if someone starts making love to Julia, you begin to simmer; and if he goes on, you are soon at boiling point.' . . . Julia was Hammond's wife.

'Why, exactly! So I should be if he began to urinate in a corner of my drawing-room. There's a place for all these things.'

'You mean you wouldn't mind if he made love to Julia in some discreet alcove?'

Charlie May was slightly satirical, for he had flirted a very little with Julia, and Hammond had cut up very roughly.

'Of course I should mind. Sex is a private thing between me and Julia; and of course I should mind anyone else trying to mix in.'

'As a matter of fact,' said the lean and freckled Tommy Dukes, who looked much more Irish than May, who was pale and rather fat: 'As a matter of fact, Hammond, you have a strong property instinct, and a strong will to self-assertion, and you want success. Since I've been in the army definitely, I've got out of the way of the world, and now I see how inordinately strong the craving for self-assertion and success is in men. It is enormously overdeveloped. All our individuality has run that way. And of course men like you think you'll get through better with a woman's backing. That's why you're so jealous. That's what sex is to you ... a vital little dynamo between you and Julia, to bring success. If you began to be unsuccessful you'd begin to flirt, like Charlie, who isn't successful. Married people like you and Julia have labels on you, like travellers' trunks. Julia is labelled *Mrs Arnold B. Hammond* ... just like a trunk on the railway that belongs to somebody. And you are labelled *Arnold B. Hammond, c/o Mrs Arnold B. Hammond*. Oh, you're quite right, you're quite right! The life of the mind needs a comfortable house and decent cooking. You're quite right. It even needs posterity. But it all hinges on the instinct for success. That is the pivot on which all things turn.'

Hammond looked rather piqued. He was rather proud of the integrity of his mind, and of his *not* being a time-server. None the less, he did want success.

'It's quite true, you can't live without cash,' said May. 'You've got to have a certain amount of it to be able to live and get along . . . even to be free to *think* you must have a certain amount of money, or your stomach stops you. But it seems to me you might leave the labels off sex. We're free to talk to anybody; so why shouldn't we be free to make love to any woman who inclines us that way?'

'There speaks the lascivious Celt,' said Clifford.

'Lascivious! well, why not – ? I can't see I do a woman any more harm by sleeping with her than by dancing with her . . . or even talking to her about the weather. It's just an interchange of sensations instead of ideas, so why not?'

'Be as promiscuous as the rabbits!' said Hammond.

'Why not? What's wrong with rabbits? Are they any worse than a neurotic, revolutionary humanity, full of nervous hate?'

'But we're not rabbits, even so,' said Hammond.

'Precisely! I have my mind: I have certain calculations to make in certain astronomical matters that concern me almost more than life or death. Sometimes indigestion interferes with me. Hunger would interfere with me disastrously. In the same way starved sex interferes with me. What then?'

'I should have thought sexual indigestion from surfeit would have interfered with you more seriously,' said Hammond satirically.

'Not it! I don't over-eat myself, and I don't over-fuck myself. One has a choice about eating too much. But you would absolutely starve me.'

'Not at all! You can marry.'

'How do you know I can? It may not suit the process of my mind. Marriage might . . . and would . . . stultify my mental processes. I'm not properly pivoted that way . . . and so must I be chained in a kennel like a monk? All rot and funk, my boy. I must live and do my calculations. I need women sometimes. I refuse to make a mountain of it, and I refuse anybody's moral condemnation or prohibition. I'd be ashamed to see a woman walking round with my name-label on her, address and railway station, like a wardrobe trunk.'

These two men had not forgiven each other about the Julia flirtation.

'It's an amusing idea, Charlie,' said Dukes, 'that sex is just another form of talk, where you act the words instead of saying them. I suppose it's quite true. I suppose we might exchange as many sensations and emotions with women as we do ideas about the weather, and so on. Sex might be a sort of normal, physical conversation between a man and a woman. You don't talk to a woman unless you have ideas in common: that is you don't talk with any interest. And in the same way, unless you had some emotion or sympathy in common with a woman you wouldn't sleep with her. But if you had . . . '

'If you *have* the proper sort of emotion or sympathy with a woman, you *ought* to sleep with her,' said May. 'It's the only decent thing, to go to bed with her. Just as, when you are interested talking to someone, the only decent thing is to have the talk out. You don't prudishly put your tongue between your teeth and bite it. You just say out your say. And the same the other way.'

'No,' said Hammond. 'It's wrong. You, for example, May, you squander half your force with women. You'll never really do what you should do, with a fine mind such as yours. Too much of you goes the other way.'

'Maybe it does . . . and too little of you goes that way, Hammond, my boy, married or not. You can keep the purity and integrity of your mind, but it's going damned dry. Your pure mind is going as dry as fiddlesticks, from what I see of it. You're simply talking it down.'

Tommy Dukes burst into a laugh.

'Go it, you two minds!' he said. 'Look at me . . . I don't do any high and pure mental work, nothing but jot down a few ideas. And yet I neither marry nor run after women. I think Charlie's quite right; if he wants to run after the women, he's quite free not to run too often. But I wouldn't prohibit him from running. As for Hammond, he's got a property instinct, so naturally the straight road and the narrow gate are right for him. You'll see he'll be an English Man of Letters before he's done. A.B.C. from top to toe. Then there's me. I'm nothing. Just a squib. And what about you, Clifford? Do you think sex is a dynamo to help a man on to success in the world?'

Clifford rarely talked much at these times. He never held forth; his ideas were really not vital enough for it, he was too confused and emotional. Now he blushed and looked uncomfortable.

'Well!' he said, 'being myself *hors de combat*, I don't see I've anything to say on the matter.'

'Not at all,' said Dukes; 'the top of you's by no means *hors de combat*. You've got the life of the mind sound and intact. So let us hear your ideas.'

'Well,' stammered Clifford, 'even then I don't suppose I have much idea . . . I suppose marry-and-have-done-with-it would pretty well stand for what I think. Though of course between a man and woman who care for one another, it is a great thing.'

'What sort of great thing?' said Tommy.

'Oh . . . it perfects the intimacy,' said Clifford, uneasy as a woman in such talk.

'Well, Charlie and I believe that sex is a sort of communication like speech. Let any woman start a sex conversation with me, and it's natural for me to go to bed with her to finish it, all in due season. Unfortunately no woman makes any particular start with me, so I go to bed by myself; and am none the worse for it . . . I hope so, anyway, for how should I know? Anyhow I've no starry calculations to be interfered with, and no immortal works to write. I'm merely a fellow skulking in the army . . .'

Silence fell. The four men smoked. And Connie sat there and put another stitch in her sewing . . . Yes, she sat there! She had to sit mum. She had to be quiet as a mouse, not to interfere with the immensely important speculations of these highly-mental gentlemen. But she had to be there. They didn't get on so well without her; their ideas didn't flow so freely. Clifford was much more hedgy and nervous, he got cold feet much quicker in Connie's absence, and the talk didn't run. Tommy Dukes came off best; he was a little inspired by her presence. Hammond she didn't really like; he seemed so selfish in a mental way.

And Charles May, though she liked something about him, seemed a little distasteful and messy, in spite of his stars.

How many evenings had Connie sat and listened to the manifestations of these four men! these, and one or two others. That they never seemed to get anywhere didn't trouble her deeply. She liked to hear what they had to say, especially when Tommy was there. It was fun. Instead of men kissing you, and touching you with their bodies, they revealed their minds to you. It was great fun! But what cold minds!

And also it was a little irritating. She had more respect for Michaelis, on whose name they all poured such withering contempt, as a little mongrel arriviste, and uneducated bounder of the worst sort. Mongrel and bounder or not, he jumped to his own conclusions. He didn't merely walk round them with millions of words, in the parade of the life of the mind.

Connie quite liked the life of the mind, and got a great thrill out of it. But she did think it overdid itself a little. She loved being there, amidst the tobacco smoke of those famous evenings of the cronies, as she called them privately to herself. She was infinitely amused, and proud too, that even their talking they could not do, without her silent presence. She had an immense respect for thought . . . and these men, at least, tried to think honestly. But somehow there was a cat, and it wouldn't jump. They all alike talked at something, though what it was, for the life of her she couldn't say. It was something that Mick didn't clear, either.

But then Mick wasn't trying to do anything, but just get through his life, and put as much across other people as they tried to put across him. He was really antisocial, which was what Clifford and his cronies had against him. Clifford and his cronies were not antisocial; they were more or less bent on saving mankind, or on instructing it, to say the least.

There was a gorgeous talk on Sunday evening, when the conversation drifted again to love.

> 'Blest be the tie that binds
> Our hearts in kindred something-or-other' –

said Tommy Dukes. 'I'd like to know what the tie is . . . The tie that binds *us* just now is mental friction on one another. And, apart from that, there's damned little tie between us. We bust apart, and say spiteful things about one another, like all the other damned intellectuals in the world. Damned everybodies, as far as that goes, for they all do it. Else we bust apart, and cover up the spiteful things we feel against one another by saying false sugaries. It's a curious thing that the mental life seems to flourish with its roots in spite, ineffable and fathomless spite. Always has been so! Look at Socrates, in Plato, and his bunch round him! The sheer spite of it all, just sheer joy in pulling somebody else to bits . . . Protagoras, or whoever it was! And Alcibiades, and all the other little disciple dogs joining in the fray! I must say it makes one prefer Buddha, quietly sitting under a bo tree, or Jesus, telling his disciples little Sunday stories, peacefully, and without any mental fireworks. No, there's something wrong with the mental life, radically. It's rooted in spite and envy, envy and spite. Ye shall know the tree by its fruit.'

'I don't think we're altogether so spiteful,' protested Clifford.

'My dear Clifford, think of the way we talk each other over, all of us. I'm rather worse than anybody else, myself. Because I infinitely prefer the spontaneous spite to the concocted sugaries; now they *are* poison; when I begin saying what a fine fellow Clifford is, etc., etc., then poor Clifford is to be pitied. For God's sake, all of you, say spiteful things about me, then I shall know I mean something to you. Don't say sugaries, or I'm done.'

'Oh, but I do think we honestly like one another,' said Hammond.

'I tell you we must . . . we say such spiteful things to one another, about one another, behind our backs! I'm the worst.'

'And I do think you confuse the mental life with the critical activity. I agree with you, Socrates gave the critical activity a grand start, but he did more than that,' said Charlie May, rather magisterially. The cronies had such a curious pomposity under their assumed modesty. It was all so *ex cathedra*, and it all pretended to be so humble.

Dukes refused to be drawn about Socrates.

'That's quite true, criticism and knowledge are not the same thing,' said Hammond.

'They aren't, of course,' chimed in Berry, a brown, shy young man, who had called to see Dukes, and was staying the night.

They all looked at him as if the ass had spoken.

'I wasn't talking about knowledge . . . I was talking about the mental life,' laughed Dukes. 'Real knowledge comes out of the whole corpus of the consciousness; out of your belly and your penis as much as out of your brain and mind. The mind can only analyse and rationalise. Set the mind and the reason to cock it over the rest, and all they can do is to criticise, and make a deadness. I say *all* they can do. It is vastly important. My God, the world needs criticising today . . . criticising to death. Therefore let's live the mental life, and glory in our spite, and strip the rotten old show. But, mind you, it's like this: while you *live* your life, you are in some way an organic whole with all life. But once you start the mental life you pluck the apple. You've severed the connection between the apple and the tree: the organic connection. And if you've got nothing in your life *but* the mental life, then you yourself are a plucked apple . . . you've fallen off the tree. And then it is a logical necessity to be spiteful, just as it's a natural necessity for a plucked apple to go bad.'

Clifford made big eyes: it was all stuff to him. Connie secretly laughed to herself.

'Well then we're all plucked apples,' said Hammond, rather acidly and petulantly.

'So let's make cider of ourselves,' said Charlie.

'But what do you think of Bolshevism?' put in the brown Berry, as if everything had led up to it.

'Bravo!' roared Charlie. 'What do you think of Bolshevism?'

'Come on! Let's make hay of Bolshevism!' said Dukes.

'I'm afraid Bolshevism is a large question,' said Hammond, shaking his head seriously.

'Bolshevism, it seems to me,' said Charlie, 'is just a superlative hatred of the thing they call the bourgeois, and what the bourgeois is, isn't quite defined. It is Capitalism, among other things. Feelings and emotions are also so decidedly bourgeois that you have to invent a man without them.

'Then the individual, especially the *personal* man, is bourgeois: so he must be suppressed. You must submerge yourselves in the greater thing, the Soviet-social thing. Even an organism is bourgeois: so the ideal must be mechanical. The only thing that is a unit, non-organic, composed of many different, yet equally essential parts, is the machine. Each man a machine-part, and the driving power of the machine, hate . . . hate of the bourgeois. That, to me, is Bolshevism.'

'Absolutely!' said Tommy. 'But also, it seems to me a perfect description of the whole of the industrial ideal. It's the factory-owner's ideal in a nutshell; except that he would deny that the driving power was hate. Hate it is, all the same: hate of life itself. Just look at these Midlands, if it isn't plainly written up . . . but it's all part of the life of the mind, it's a logical development.'

'I deny that Bolshevism is logical, it rejects the major part of the premisses,' said Hammond.

'My dear man, it allows the material premiss; so does the pure mind . . . exclusively.'

'At least Bolshevism has got down to rock bottom,' said Charlie.

'Rock bottom! The bottom that has no bottom! The Bolshevists will have the finest army in the world in a very short time, with the finest mechanical equipment.'

'But this thing can't go on . . . this hate business. There must be a reaction . . . ' said Hammond.

'Well, we've been waiting for years . . . we wait longer. Hate's a growing thing like anything else. It's the inevitable outcome of forcing ideas on to life, of forcing one's deepest instincts; our deepest feelings we force according to certain ideas. We drive ourselves with a formula, like a machine. The logical mind pretends to rule the roost, and the roost turns into pure hate. We're all Bolshevists, only we are hypocrites. The Russians are Bolshevists without hypocrisy.'

'But there are many other ways,' said Hammond, 'than the Soviet way. The Bolshevists aren't really intelligent.'

'Of course not. But sometimes it's intelligent to be half-witted: if you want to make your end. Personally, I consider Bolshevism half-witted; but so do I consider our social life in the west half-witted. So I even consider our far-famed mental life half-witted. We're all as cold as cretins, we're all as passionless as idiots. We're all of us Bolshevists, only we give it another name. We think we're gods . . . men like gods! It's just the same as Bolshevism. One has to be human, and have a heart and a penis if one is going to escape being either a god or a Bolshevist . . . for they are the same thing: they're both too good to be true.'

Out of the disapproving silence came Berry's anxious question: 'You do believe in love then, Tommy, don't you?'

'You lovely lad!' said Tommy. 'No, my cherub, nine times out of ten, no! Love's another of those half-witted performances today. Fellows with swaying waists fucking little jazz girls with small boy buttocks, like two collar studs! Do you mean that sort of love? Or the joint-property, make-a-success-of-it, My-husband-my-wife sort of love? No, my fine fellow, I don't believe in it at all!'

'But you do believe in something?'

'Me? Oh, intellectually I believe in having a good heart, a chirpy penis, a lively intelligence, and the courage to say "shit!" in front of a lady.'

'Well, you've got them all,' said Berry.

Tommy Dukes roared with laughter. 'You angel boy! If only I had! If only I had! No; my heart's as numb as a potato, my penis droops and never lifts its head up, I dare rather cut him clean off than say "shit!" in front of my mother or my aunt . . . they are real ladies, mind you; and I'm not really intelligent, I'm only a "mental-lifer". It would be wonderful to be intelligent: then one would be alive in all the parts mentioned and unmentionable. The penis rouses his head and says: How do you do? – to any really intelligent person. Renoir said he painted his pictures with his penis . . . he did too, lovely pictures! I wish I did something with mine. God! when one can only talk! Another torture added to Hades! And Socrates started it.'

'There are nice women in the world,' said Connie, lifting her head up and speaking at last.

The men resented it . . . she should have pretended to hear nothing. They hated her admitting she had attended so closely to such talk.

'My God!

> "If they be not nice to me
> What care I how nice they be?"

'No, it's hopeless! I just simply can't vibrate in unison with a woman. There's no woman I can really want when I'm faced with her, and I'm not going to start forcing myself to it . . . My God, no! I'll remain as I am, and lead the mental life. It's the only honest thing I can do. I can be quite happy *talking* to women; but it's all pure, hopelessly pure. Hopelessly pure! What do you say, Hildebrand, my chicken?'

'It's much less complicated if one stays pure,' said Berry.

'Yes, life is all too simple!'

Chapter 5

On a frosty morning with a little February sun, Clifford and Connie went for a walk across the park to the wood. That is, Clifford chuffed in his motor chair, and Connie walked beside him.

The hard air was still sulphurous, but they were both used to it. Round the near horizon went the haze, opalescent with frost and smoke, and on the top lay the small blue sky; so that it was like being inside an enclosure, always inside. Life always a dream or a frenzy, inside an enclosure.

The sheep coughed in the rough, sere grass of the park, where frost lay bluish in the sockets of the tufts. Across the park ran a path to the wood-gate, a fine ribbon of pink. Clifford had had it newly gravelled with sifted gravel from the pit-bank. When the rock and refuse of the underworld had burned and given off its sulphur, it turned bright pink, shrimp-coloured on dry days, darker, crab-coloured on wet. Now it was pale shrimp-colour, with a bluish-white hoar of frost. It always pleased Connie, this underfoot of sifted, bright pink. It's an ill wind that brings nobody good.

Clifford steered cautiously down the slope of the knoll from the hall, and Connie kept her hand on the chair. In front lay the wood, the hazel thicket nearest, the purplish density of oaks beyond. From the wood's edge rabbits bobbed and nibbled. Rooks suddenly rose in a black train, and went trailing off over the little sky.

Connie opened the wood-gate, and Clifford puffed slowly through into the broad riding that ran up an incline between the clean-whipped thickets of the hazel. The wood was a remnant of the great forest where Robin Hood hunted, and this riding was an old, old thoroughfare coming across country. But now, of course, it was only a riding through the private wood. The road from Mansfield swerved round to the north.

In the wood everything was motionless, the old leaves on the ground keeping the frost on their underside. A jay called harshly, many little birds fluttered. But there was no game; no pheasants. They had been killed off during the war, and the wood had been left unprotected, till now Clifford had got his gamekeeper again.

Clifford loved the wood; he loved the old oak trees. He felt they were his own through generations. He wanted to protect them. He wanted this place inviolate, shut off from the world.

The chair chuffed slowly up the incline, rocking and jolting on the frozen clods. And suddenly, on the left, came a clearing where there was nothing but a ravel of dead bracken, a thin and spindly sapling leaning here and there, big sawn stumps, showing their tops and their grasping roots, lifeless. And patches of blackness where the woodmen had burned the brushwood and rubbish.

This was one of the places that Sir Geoffrey had cut during the war for trench timber. The whole knoll, which rose softly on the right of the riding, was denuded and strangely forlorn. On the crown of the knoll where the oaks had stood, now was bareness; and from there you could look out over the trees to the colliery railway, and the new works at Stacks Gate. Connie had stood and looked, it was a breach in the pure seclusion of the wood. It let in the world. But she didn't tell Clifford.

This denuded place always made Clifford curiously angry. He had been through the war, had seen what it meant. But he didn't get really angry till he saw this bare hill. He was having it replanted. But it made him hate Sir Geoffrey.

Clifford sat with a fixed face as the chair slowly mounted. When they came to the top of the rise he stopped; he would not risk the long and very jolty down-slope. He sat looking at the greenish sweep of the riding downwards, a clear way through the bracken and oaks. It swerved at the bottom of the hill and disappeared; but it had such a lovely easy curve, of knights riding and ladies on palfreys.

'I consider this is really the heart of England,' said Clifford to Connie, as he sat there in the dim February sunshine.

'Do you?' she said, seating herself, in her blue knitted dress, on a stump by the path.

'I do! this is the old England, the heart of it; and I intend to keep it intact.'

'Oh yes!' said Connie. But, as she said it she heard the eleven-o'clock hooters at Stacks Gate colliery. Clifford was too used to the sound to notice.

'I want this wood perfect . . . untouched. I want nobody to trespass in it,' said Clifford.

There was a certain pathos. The wood still had some of the mystery of wild, old England; but Sir Geoffrey's cuttings during the war had given it a blow. How still the trees were, with their crinkly, innumerable twigs against the sky, and their grey, obstinate trunks rising from the brown bracken! How safely the birds flitted among them! And once there had been deer, and archers, and monks padding along on asses. The place remembered, still remembered.

Clifford sat in the pale sun, with the light on his smooth, rather blond hair, his reddish full face inscrutable.

'I mind more, not having a son, when I come here, than any other time,' he said.

'But the wood is older than your family,' said Connie gently.

'Quite!' said Clifford. 'But we've preserved it. Except for us it would go . . . it would be gone already, like the rest of the forest. One must preserve some of the old England!'

'Must one?' said Connie. 'If it has to be preserved, and preserved against the new England? It's sad, I know.'

'If some of the old England isn't preserved, there'll be no England at all,' said Clifford. 'And we who have this kind of property, and the feeling for it, *must* preserve it.'

There was a sad pause.

'Yes, for a little while,' said Connie.

'For a little while! It's all we can do. We can only do our bit. I feel every man of my family has done his bit here, since we've had the place. One may go against convention, but one must keep up tradition.' Again there was a pause.

'What tradition?' asked Connie.

'The tradition of England! of this!'

'Yes,' she said slowly.

'That's why having a son helps; one is only a link in a chain,' he said.

Connie was not keen on chains, but she said nothing. She was thinking of the curious impersonality of his desire for a son.

'I'm sorry we can't have a son,' she said.

He looked at her steadily, with his full, pale-blue eyes.

'It would almost be a good thing if you had a child by another man,' he said. 'If we brought it up at Wragby, it would belong to us and to the place I don't believe very intensely in fatherhood. If we had the child to rear, it would be our own, and it would carry on. Don't you think it's worth considering?'

Connie looked up at him at last. The child, her child, was just an 'it' to him. It . . . it . . . it!

'But what about the other man?' she asked.

'Does it matter very much? Do these things really affect us very deeply? . . . You had that lover in Germany . . . what is it now? Nothing almost. It seems to me that it isn't these little acts and little connections we make in our lives that matter so very much. They pass away, and where are they? Where . . . Where are the snows of yesteryear? . . . It's what endures through one's life that matters; my own life matters to me, in its long continuance and development. But what do the occasional connections matter? And the occasional sexual connections especially! If people don't exaggerate them ridiculously, they pass like the mating of birds. And so they should. What does it matter? It's the life-long companionship that matters. It's the living together from day to day, not the sleeping together once or twice. You and I are married, no matter what happens to us. We have the habit of each other. And habit, to my thinking, is more vital than any occasional excitement. The long, slow, enduring thing . . . that's what we live by . . . not the occasional spasm of any sort. Little by little, living together, two people fall into a sort of unison, they vibrate so intricately to one another. That's the real secret of marriage, not sex; at least not the simple function of sex. You and I are interwoven in a marriage. If we stick to that we ought to be able to arrange this sex thing, as we arrange going to the dentist; since fate has given us a checkmate physically there.'

Connie sat and listened in a sort of wonder, and a sort of fear. She did not know if he was right or not. There was Michaelis, whom she loved; so she said to herself. But her love was somehow only an excursion from her marriage with Clifford; the long, slow habit of intimacy, formed through years of suffering and patience. Perhaps the human soul needs excursions, and must not be

LADY CHATTERLEY'S LOVER

denied them. But the point of an excursion is that you come home again.

'And wouldn't you mind *what* man's child I had?' she asked.

'Why, Connie, I should trust your natural instinct of decency and selection. You just wouldn't let the wrong sort of fellow touch you.'

She thought of Michaelis! He was absolutely Clifford's idea of the wrong sort of fellow.

'But men and women may have different feelings about the wrong sort of fellow,' she said.

'No,' he replied. 'You care for me. I don't believe you would ever care for a man who was purely antipathetic to me. Your rhythm wouldn't let you.'

She was silent. Logic might be unanswerable because it was so absolutely wrong.

'And should you expect me to tell you?' she asked, glancing up at him almost furtively.

'Not at all. I'd better not know . . . But you do agree with me, don't you, that the casual sex thing is nothing, compared to the long life lived together? Don't you think one can just subordinate the sex thing to the necessities of a long life? Just use it, since that's what we're driven to? After all, *do* these temporary excitements matter? Isn't the whole problem of life the slow building up of an integral personality, through the years? living an integrated life? There's no point in a disintegrated life. If lack of sex is going to disintegrate you, then go out and have a love affair. If lack of a child is going to disintegrate you, then have a child if you possibly can. But only do these things so that you have an integrated life, that makes a long harmonious thing. And you and I can do that together . . . don't you think? . . . if we adapt ourselves to the necessities, and at the same time weave the adaptation together into a piece with our steadily-lived life. Don't you agree?'

Connie was a little overwhelmed by his words. She knew he was right theoretically. But when she actually touched her steadily-lived life with him she . . . hesitated. Was it actually her destiny to go on weaving herself into his life all the rest of her life? Nothing else?

Was it just that? She was to be content to weave a steady life with him, all one fabric, but perhaps brocaded with the occasional flower of an adventure. But how could she know what she would feel next year? How could one ever know? How could one say Yes? for years and years? The little yes, gone on a breath! Why should one be pinned down by that butterfly word? Of course it had to flutter away and be gone, to be followed by other yes's and no's! Like the straying of butterflies.

'I think you're right, Clifford. And as far as I can see I agree with you. Only life may turn quite a new face on it all.'

'But until life turns a new face on it all, you do agree?'

'Oh yes! I think I do, really.'

She was watching a brown spaniel that had run out of a side-path, and was looking towards them with lifted nose, making a soft, fluffy bark. A man with a gun strode swiftly, softly out after the dog, facing their way as if about to attack them; then stopped instead, saluted, and was turning downhill. It was only the new gamekeeper, but he had frightened Connie, he seemed to emerge with such a swift menace. That was how she had seen him, like the sudden rush of a threat out of nowhere.

He was a man in dark green velveteens and gaiters . . . the old style, with a red face and red moustache and distant eyes. He was going quickly downhill.

'Mellors!' called Clifford.

The man faced lightly round, and saluted with a quick little gesture, a soldier!

'Will you turn the chair round and get it started? That makes it easier,' said Clifford.

The man at once slung his gun over his shoulder, and came forward with the same curious swift, yet soft movements, as if keeping invisible. He was moderately tall and lean, and was silent. He did not look at Connie at all, only at the chair.

'Connie, this is the new gamekeeper, Mellors. You haven't spoken to her ladyship yet, Mellors?'

'No, Sir!' came the ready, neutral words.

The man lifted his hat as he stood, showing his thick, almost fair hair. He stared straight into Connie's eyes, with a perfect, fearless, impersonal look, as if he wanted to see what she was like. He made her feel shy. She bent her head to him shyly, and he changed his hat to his left hand and made her a slight bow, like a gentleman; but he said nothing at all. He remained for a moment still, with his hat in his hand.

'But you've been here some time, haven't you?' Connie said to him.

'Eight months, Madam . . . your Ladyship!' he corrected himself calmly.

'And do you like it?'

She looked him in the eyes. His eyes narrowed a little, with irony, perhaps with impudence.

'Why, yes, thank you, your Ladyship! I was reared here . . . ' He gave another slight bow, turned, put his hat on, and strode to take hold of the chair. His voice on the last words had fallen into the heavy broad drag of the dialect . . . perhaps also in mockery, because there had been no trace of dialect before. He might almost be a gentleman. Anyhow, he was a curious, quick, separate fellow, alone, but sure of himself.

Clifford started the little engine, the man carefully turned the chair, and set it nose-forwards to the incline that curved gently to the dark hazel thicket.

'Is that all then, Sir Clifford?' asked the man.

'No, you'd better come along in case she sticks. The engine isn't really strong enough for the uphill work.' The man glanced round for his dog . . . a thoughtful glance. The spaniel looked at him and faintly moved its tail. A little smile, mocking or teasing her, yet gentle, came into his eyes for a moment, then faded away, and his face was expressionless. They went fairly quickly down the slope, the man with his hand on the rail of the chair, steadying it. He looked like a free soldier rather than a servant. And something about him reminded Connie of Tommy Dukes.

When they came to the hazel grove, Connie suddenly ran forward, and opened the gate into the park. As she stood holding it, the two men looked at her in passing, Clifford critically, the other man with a curious, cool wonder; impersonally wanting to see what she looked like. And she saw in his blue, impersonal eyes a look of suffering and detachment, yet a certain warmth. But why was he so aloof, apart?

Clifford stopped the chair, once through the gate, and the man came quickly, courteously, to close it.

'Why did you run to open?' asked Clifford in his quiet, calm voice, that showed he was displeased. 'Mellors would have done it.'

'I thought you would go straight ahead,' said Connie.

'And leave you to run after us?' said Clifford.

'Oh, well, I like to run sometimes!'

Mellors took the chair again, looking perfectly unheeding, yet Connie felt he noted everything. As he pushed the chair up the steepish rise of the knoll in the park, he breathed rather quickly, through parted lips. He was rather frail really. Curiously full of vitality, but a little frail and quenched. Her woman's instinct sensed it.

Connie fell back, let the chair go on. The day had greyed over: the small blue sky that had poised low on its circular rims of haze was closed in again, the lid was down, there was a raw coldness. It was going to snow. All grey, all grey! the world looked worn out.

The chair waited at the top of the pink path. Clifford looked round for Connie.

'Not tired, are you?' he asked.

'Oh, no!' she said.

But she was. A strange, weary yearning, a dissatisfaction had started in her. Clifford did not notice: those were not things he was aware of. But the stranger knew. To Connie, everything in her world and life seemed worn out, and her dissatisfaction was older than the hills.

They came to the house, and round to the back, where there were no steps. Clifford managed to swing himself over on to the low, wheeled house-chair; he was very strong and agile with his arms. Then Connie lifted the burden of his dead legs after him.

The keeper, waiting at attention to be dismissed, watched everything narrowly, missing nothing. He went pale, with a sort of fear, when he saw Connie lifting the inert legs of the man in her arms, into the other chair, Clifford pivoting round as she did so. He was frightened.

'Thanks, then, for the help, Mellors,' said Clifford casually, as he began to wheel down the passage to the servants' quarters.

'Nothing else, Sir?' came the neutral voice, like one in a dream.

'Nothing, good-morning!'

'Good-morning, Sir.'

'Good-morning! it was kind of you to push the chair up that hill . . . I hope it wasn't heavy for you,' said Connie, looking back at the keeper outside the door.

His eyes came to hers in an instant, as if wakened up. He was aware of her.

'Oh no, not heavy!' he said quickly. Then his voice dropped again into the broad sound of the vernacular: 'Good mornin' to your Ladyship!'

'Who is your gamekeeper?' Connie asked at lunch.

'Mellors! You saw him,' said Clifford.

'Yes, but where did he come from?'

'Nowhere! He was a Tevershall boy . . . son of a collier, I believe.'

'And was he a collier himself?'

'Blacksmith on the pit-bank, I believe: overhead smith. But he was keeper here for two years before the war . . . before he joined up. My father always had a good opinion of him, so when he came back, and went to the pit for a blacksmith's job, I just took him back here as keeper. I was really very glad to get him . . . it's almost impossible to find a good man round here, for a game-keeper . . . and it needs a man who knows the people.'

'And isn't he married?'

'He was. But his wife went off with . . . with various men . . . but finally with a collier at Stacks Gate, and I believe she's living there still.'

'So this man is alone?'

'More or less! He has a mother in the village . . . and a child, I believe.'

Clifford looked at Connie, with his pale, slightly prominent blue eyes, in which a certain vagueness was coming. He seemed alert in the foreground, but the background was like the Midlands atmosphere, haze, smoky mist. And the haze seemed to be creeping forward. So when he stared at Connie in his peculiar way, giving her his peculiar, precise information, she felt all the background of his mind filling up with mist, with nothingness. And it frightened her. It made him seem impersonal, almost to idiocy.

And dimly she realised one of the great laws of the human soul: that when the emotional soul receives a wounding shock, which does not kill the body, the soul seems to recover as the body recovers. But this is only appearance. It is really only the mechanism of the re-assumed habit. Slowly, slowly the wound to the soul begins to make itself felt, like a bruise, which only slowly deepens its terrible ache, till it fills all the psyche. And when we think we have recovered and forgotten, it is then that the terrible after-effects have to be encountered at their worst.

So it was with Clifford. Once he was 'well', once he was back at Wragby, and writing his stories, and feeling sure of life, in spite of all, he seemed to forget, and to have recovered all his equanimity. But now, as the years went by, slowly, slowly, Connie felt the bruise of fear and horror coming up, and spreading in him. For a time it had been so deep as to be numb, as it were nonexistent. Now slowly it began to assert itself in a spread of fear, almost paralysis. Mentally he still was alert. But the paralysis, the bruise of the too-great shock, was gradually spreading in his affective self.

And as it spread in him, Connie felt it spread in her. An inward dread, an emptiness, an indifference to everything gradually spread in her soul. When Clifford was roused, he could still talk brilliantly, and, as it were, command the future: as when, in the wood, he talked about her having a child, and giving an heir to Wragby. But the day after, all the brilliant words seemed like dead leaves, crumpling up and turning to powder, meaning really nothing, blown away on any gust of wind. They were not the leafy words of an effective life, young with energy and belonging to the tree. They were the hosts of fallen leaves of a life that is ineffectual.

So it seemed to her everywhere. The colliers at Tevershall were talking again of a strike, and it seemed to Connie there again it was not a manifestation of energy, it was the bruise of the war that had been in abeyance, slowly rising to the surface and creating the great ache of unrest, and stupor of discontent. The bruise was deep, deep, deep . . . the bruise of the false inhuman war. It would take many years for the living blood of the generations to dissolve the vast black clot of bruised blood, deep inside their souls and bodies. And it would need a new hope.

Poor Connie! As the years drew on it was the fear of nothingness in her life that affected her. Clifford's mental life and hers gradually began to feel like nothingness. Their marriage, their integrated life based on a habit of intimacy, that he talked about: there were days when it all became utterly blank and nothing. It was words, just so many words. The only reality was nothingness, and over it a hypocrisy of words.

There was Clifford's success: the bitch-goddess! It was true he was almost famous, and his books brought him in a thousand pounds. His photograph appeared everywhere. There was a bust of him in one of the galleries, and a portrait of him in two galleries. He seemed the most modern of modern voices. With his uncanny lame instinct for publicity, he had become in four or five years one of the best known of the young 'intellectuals'. Where the intellect came in, Connie did not quite see. Clifford was really clever at that slightly humorous analysis of people and motives which leaves everything in bits at the end. But it was rather like puppies tearing the sofa cushions to bits; except that it was not young and playful, but curiously old, and rather obstinately conceited. It was weird and it was nothing. This was the feeling that echoed and re-echoed at the bottom of Connie's soul: it was all nothing, a wonderful display of nothingness. At the same time a display. A display! a display! a display!

Michaelis had seized upon Clifford as the central figure for a play; already he had sketched in the plot, and written the first act. For Michaelis was even better than Clifford at making a display of nothingness. It was the last bit of passion left in these men: the passion for making a display. Sexually they were passionless, even dead. And now it was not money that Michaelis was after. Clifford had never been primarily out for money, though he made it where he could, for money is the seal and stamp of success. And success was what they wanted. They wanted, both of them, to make a real display . . . a man's own very display of himself, that should capture for a time the vast populace.

It was strange . . . the prostitution to the bitch-goddess. To Connie, since she was really outside of it, and since she had grown numb to the thrill of it, it was again nothingness. Even the prostitution to the bitch-goddess was nothingness, though the men prostituted themselves innumerable times. Nothingness even that.

Michaelis wrote to Clifford about the play. Of course she knew about it long ago. And Clifford was again thrilled. He was going to be displayed again this time, somebody was going to display him, and to advantage. He invited Michaelis down to Wragby with Act I.

Michaelis came: in summer, in a pale-coloured suit and white suède gloves, with mauve orchids for Connie, very lovely, and Act I was a great success. Even Connie was thrilled . . . thrilled to what bit of marrow she had left. And Michaelis, thrilled by his power to thrill, was really wonderful . . . and quite beautiful, in Connie's eyes. She saw in him that ancient motionlessness of a race that can't be disillusioned any more, an extreme, perhaps, of impurity that is pure. On the far side of his supreme prostitution to the bitch-goddess he seemed pure, pure as an African ivory mask that dreams impurity into purity, in its ivory curves and planes.

His moment of sheer thrill with the two Chatterleys, when he simply carried Connie and Clifford away, was one of the supreme moments of Michaelis' life. He had succeeded: he had carried them away. Even Clifford was temporarily in love with him . . . if that is the way one can put it.

So next morning Mick was more uneasy than ever: restless, devoured, with his hands restless in his trousers pockets. Connie had not visited him in the night . . . and he had not known where to find her. Coquetry! . . . at his moment of triumph.

He went up to her sitting-room in the morning. She knew he would come. And his restlessness was evident. He asked her about his play . . . did she think it good? He *had* to hear it praised: that affected him with the last thin thrill of passion beyond any sexual orgasm. And she praised it rapturously. Yet all the while, at the bottom of her soul, she knew it was nothing.

'Look here!' he said suddenly at last. 'Why don't you and I make a clean thing of it? Why don't we marry?'

'But I am married,' she said, amazed, and yet feeling nothing.

'Oh that! . . . he'll divorce you all right . . . Why don't you and I marry? I want to marry. I know it would be the best thing for me . . . marry and lead a regular life. I lead the deuce of a life, simply tearing myself to pieces. Look here, you and I, we're made for one another . . . hand and glove. Why don't we marry? Do you see any reason why we shouldn't?'

Connie looked at him amazed: and yet she felt nothing. These men, they were all alike, they left everything out. They just went off from the top of their heads as if they were squibs, and expected you to be carried heavenwards along with their own thin sticks.

'But I am married already,' she said. 'I can't leave Clifford, you know.'

'Why not? but why not?' he cried. 'He'll hardly know you've gone, after six months. He doesn't know that anybody exists, except himself. Why the man has no use for you at all, as far as I can see; he's entirely wrapped up in himself.'

Connie felt there was truth in this. But she also felt that Mick was hardly making a display of selflessness.

'Aren't all men wrapped up in themselves?' she asked.

'Oh, more or less, I allow. A man's got to be, to get through. But that's not the point. The point is, what sort of a time can a man give a woman? Can he give her a damn good time, or can't he? If he can't he's no right to the woman . . . ' He paused and gazed at her with his full, hazel eyes, almost hypnotic. 'Now I consider,' he added, 'I can give a woman the darndest good time she can ask for. I think I can guarantee myself.'

'And what sort of a good time?' asked Connie, gazing on him still with a sort of amazement, that looked like thrill; and underneath feeling nothing at all.

'Every sort of a good time, damn it, every sort! Dress, jewels up to a point, any nightclub you like, know anybody you want to know, live the pace . . . travel and be somebody wherever you go . . . Darn it, every sort of good time.'

He spoke it almost in a brilliancy of triumph, and Connie looked at him as if dazzled, and really feeling nothing at all. Hardly even the surface of her mind was tickled at the glowing prospects he offered her. Hardly even her most outside self responded, that at any other time would have been thrilled. She just got no feeling from it all, she couldn't 'go off'. She just sat and stared and looked dazzled, and felt nothing, only somewhere she smelt the extraordinarily unpleasant smell of the bitch-goddess.

Mick sat on tenterhooks, leaning forward in his chair, glaring at her almost hysterically: and whether he was more anxious out of vanity for her to say Yes! or whether he was more panic-stricken for fear she *should* say Yes! – who can tell?

'I should have to think about it,' she said. 'I couldn't say now. It may seem to you Clifford doesn't count, but he does. When you think how disabled he is . . . '

'Oh damn it all! if a fellow's going to trade on his disabilities, I might begin to say how lonely I am, and always have been, and all the rest of the my-eye-Betty-Martin sob-stuff! Damn it all, if a fellow's got nothing but disabilities to recommend him . . . '

He turned aside, working his hands furiously in his trouser pockets. That evening he said to her, 'You're coming round to my room tonight, aren't you? I don't darned know where your room is.'

'All right!' she said.

He was a more excited lover that night, with his strange, small boy's frail nakedness. Connie found it impossible to come to her crisis before he had really finished his. And he roused a certain craving passion in her, with his little boy's nakedness and softness; she had to go on after he had finished, in the wild tumult and heaving of her loins, while he heroically kept himself up, and present in her, with all his will and self-offering, till she brought about her own crisis, with weird little cries.

When at last he drew away from her, he said, in a bitter, almost sneering little voice, 'You couldn't go off at the same time as a man, could you? You'd have to bring yourself off! You'd have to run the show!'

This little speech, at the moment, was one of the shocks of her life. Because that passive sort of giving himself was so obviously his only real mode of intercourse.

'What do you mean?' she said.

'You know what I mean. You keep on for hours after I've gone off . . . and I have to hang on with my teeth till you bring yourself off by your own exertions.'

She was stunned by this unexpected piece of brutality, at the moment when she was glowing with a sort of pleasure beyond words, and a sort of love for him. Because, after all, like so many modern men, he was finished almost before he had begun. And that forced the woman to be active.

'But you want me to go on, to get my own satisfaction?' she said.

He laughed grimly: 'I want it!' he said. 'That's good! I want to hang on with my teeth clenched, while you go for me!'

'But don't you?' she insisted.

He avoided the question. 'All the darned women are like that,' he said. 'Either they don't go off at all, as if they were dead in there . . . or else they wait till a chap's really done, and then they start in to bring themselves off, and a chap's got to hang on. I never had a woman yet who went off just at the same moment as I did.'

Connie only half heard this piece of novel, masculine information. She was only stunned by his feeling against her . . . his incomprehensible brutality. She felt so innocent.

'But you want me to have my satisfaction too, don't you?' she repeated.

'Oh, all right! I'm quite willing. But I'm darned if hanging on waiting for a woman to go off is much of a game for a man . . .'

This speech was one of the crucial blows of Connie's life. It killed something in her. She had not been so very keen on Michaelis; till he started it, she did not want him. It was as if she never positively wanted him. But once he had started her, it seemed only natural for her to come to her own crisis with him. Almost she had loved him for it . . . almost that night she loved him, and wanted to marry him.

Perhaps instinctively he knew it, and that was why he had to bring down the whole show with a smash; the house of cards. Her whole sexual feeling for him, or for any man, collapsed that night. Her life fell apart from his as completely as if he had never existed.

And she went through the days drearily. There was nothing now but this empty treadmill of what Clifford called the integrated life, the long living together of two people, who are in the habit of being in the same house with one another.

Nothingness! To accept the great nothingness of life seemed to be the one end of living. All the many busy and important little things that make up the grand sum-total of nothingness!

Chapter 6

'Why don't men and women really like one another nowadays?' Connie asked Tommy Dukes, who was more or less her oracle.

'Oh, but they do! I don't think since the human species was invented, there has ever been a time when men and women have liked one another as much as they do today. Genuine liking! Take myself . . . I really *like* women better than men; they are braver, one can be more frank with them.'

Connie pondered this.

'Ah, yes, but you never have anything to do with them!' she said.

'I? What am I doing but talking perfectly sincerely to a woman at this moment?'

'Yes, talking . . .'

'And what more could I do if you were a man, than talk perfectly sincerely to you?'

'Nothing perhaps. But a woman . . .'

'A woman wants you to like her and talk to her, and at the same time love her and desire her; and it seems to me the two things are mutually exclusive.'

'But they shouldn't be!'

'No doubt water ought not to be so wet as it is; it over-does it in wetness. But there it is! I like women and talk to them, and therefore I don't love them and desire them. The two things don't happen at the same time in me.'

'I think they ought to.'

'All right. The fact that things ought to be something else than what they are, is not my department.'

Connie considered this. 'It isn't true,' she said. 'Men can love women and talk to them. I don't see how they can love them *without* talking, and being friendly and intimate. How can they?'

'Well,' he said, 'I don't know. What's the use of my generalising? I only know my own case. I like women, but I don't desire them. I like talking to them; but talking to them, though it makes me intimate in one direction, sets me poles apart from them as far as kissing is concerned. So there you are! But don't take me as a general example, probably I'm just a special case: one of the men who like women, but don't love women, and even hate them if they force me into a pretence of love, or an entangled appearance.'

'But doesn't it make you sad?'

'Why should it? Not a bit! I look at Charlie May, and the rest of the men who have affairs . . . No, I don't envy them a bit! If fate sent me a woman I wanted, well and good. Since I don't know any woman I want, and never see one . . . why, I presume I'm cold, and really *like* some women very much.'

'Do you like me?'

'Very much! And you see there's no question of kissing between us, is there?'

'None at all!' said Connie. 'But oughtn't there to be?'

'*Why*, in God's name? I like Clifford, but what would you say if I went and kissed him?'

'But isn't there a difference?'

'Where does it lie, as far as we're concerned? We're all intelligent human beings, and the male and female business is in abeyance. Just in abeyance. How would you like me to start acting up like a continental male at this moment, and parading the sex thing?'

'I should hate it.'

'Well then! I tell you, if I'm really a male thing at all, I never run across the female of my species. And I don't miss her, I just *like* women. Who's going to force me into loving, or pretending to love them, working up the sex game?'

'No, I'm not. But isn't something wrong?'

'You may feel it, I don't.'

'Yes, I feel something is wrong between men and women. A woman has no glamour for a man any more.'

'Has a man for a woman?'

She pondered the other side of the question.

'Not much,' she said truthfully.

'Then let's leave it all alone, and just be decent and simple, like proper human beings with one another. Be damned to the artificial sex-compulsion! I refuse it!'

Connie knew he was right, really. Yet it left her feeling so forlorn, so forlorn and stray. Like a chip on a dreary pond, she felt. What was the point, of her or anything?

It was her youth which rebelled. These men seemed so old and cold. Everything seemed old and cold. And Michaelis let one down so; he was no good. The men didn't want one; they just didn't really want a woman, even Michaelis didn't.

And the bounders who pretended they did, and started working the sex game, they were worse than ever.

It was just dismal, and one had to put up with it. It was quite true, men had no real glamour for a woman: if you could fool yourself into thinking they had, even as she had fooled herself over Michaelis, that was the best you could do. Meanwhile you just lived on and there was nothing to it. She understood perfectly well why people had cocktail parties, and jazzed, and Charlestoned till they were ready to drop. You had to take it out some way or other, your youth, or it ate you up. But what a ghastly thing, this youth! You felt as old as Methuselah, and yet the thing fizzed somehow, and didn't let you be comfortable. A mean sort of life! And no prospect! She almost wished she had gone off with Mick, and made her life one long cocktail party, and jazz evening. Anyhow that was better than just mooning yourself into the grave.

On one of her bad days she went out alone to walk in the wood, ponderously, heeding nothing, not even noticing where she was. The report of a gun not far off startled and angered her.

Then, as she went, she heard voices, and recoiled. People! She didn't want people. But her quick ear caught another sound, and she roused; it was a child sobbing. At once she attended – someone was ill-treating a child. She strode swinging down the wet drive, her sullen resentment uppermost. She felt just prepared to make a scene.

Turning the corner, she saw two figures in the drive beyond her: the keeper, and a little girl in a purple coat and moleskin cap, crying.

'Ah, shut it up, tha false little bitch!' came the man's angry voice, and the child sobbed louder.

Constance strode nearer, with blazing eyes. The man turned and looked at her, saluting coolly, but he was pale with anger.

'What's the matter? Why is she crying?' demanded Constance, peremptory but a little breathless.

A faint smile like a sneer came on the man's face. 'Nay, yo' mun ax 'er,' he replied callously, in broad vernacular.

Connie felt as if he had hit her in the face, and she changed colour. Then she gathered her defiance, and looked at him, her dark blue eyes blazing rather vaguely.

'I asked *you*,' she panted.

He gave a queer little bow, lifting his hat. 'You did, your Ladyship,' he said; then, with a return to the vernacular – 'but I canna tell yer.' And he became a soldier, inscrutable, only pale with annoyance.

Connie turned to the child, a ruddy, black-haired thing of nine or ten. 'What is it, dear? Tell me why you're crying!' she said, with the conventionalised sweetness suitable. More violent sobs, self-conscious. Still more sweetness on Connie's part.

'There, there, don't you cry! Tell me what they've done to you!' . . . an intense tenderness of tone. At the same time she felt in the pocket of her knitted jacket, and luckily found a sixpence.

'Don't you cry then!' she said, bending in front of the child. 'See what I've got for you!'

Sobs, snuffles, a fist taken from a blubbered face, and a black shrewd eye cast for a second on the sixpence. Then more sobs, but subduing. 'There, tell me what's the matter, tell me!' said Connie, putting the coin into the child's chubby hand, which closed over it.

'It's the . . . it's the . . . pussy!'

Shudders of subsiding sobs.

'What pussy, dear?'

After a silence the shy fist, clenching on sixpence, pointed into the bramble brake.

'There!'

Connie looked, and there, sure enough, was a big black cat, stretched out grimly, with a bit of blood on it.

'Oh!' she said in repulsion.

'A poacher, your Ladyship,' said the man satirically.

She glanced at him angrily. 'No wonder the child cried,' she said, 'if you shot it when she was there. No wonder she cried!'

He looked into Connie's eyes, laconic, contemptuous, not hiding his feelings. And again Connie flushed; she felt she had been making a scene, the man did not respect her.

'What is your name?' she said playfully to the child. 'Won't you tell me your name?'

Sniffs; then very affectedly in a piping voice: 'Connie Mellors!'

'Connie Mellors! Well, that's a nice name! And did you come out with your Daddy, and he shot a pussy? But it was a bad pussy!'

The child looked at her, with bold, dark eyes of scrutiny, sizing her up, and her condolence.

'I wanted to stop with my Gran,' said the little girl.

'Did you? But where is your Gran?'

The child lifted an arm, pointing down the drive. 'At th' cottidge.'

'At the cottage! And would you like to go back to her?'

Sudden, shuddering quivers of reminiscent sobs. 'Yes!'

'Come then, shall I take you? Shall I take you to your Gran? Then your Daddy can do what he has to do.' She turned to the man. 'It is your little girl, isn't it?'

He saluted, and made a slight movement of the head in affirmation.

'I suppose I can take her to the cottage?' asked Connie.

'If your Ladyship wishes.'

Again he looked into her eyes, with that calm, searching detached glance. A man very much alone, and on his own.

'Would you like to come with me to the cottage, to your Gran, dear?'

The child peeped up again. 'Yes!' she simpered.

Connie disliked her, the spoilt, false little female. Nevertheless she wiped her face, and took her hand. The keeper saluted in silence.

'Good-morning!' said Connie.

It was nearly a mile to the cottage, and Connie senior was well bored by Connie junior by the time the gamekeeper's picturesque little home was in sight. The child was already as full to the brim with tricks as a little monkey, and so self-assured.

At the cottage the door stood open, and there was a rattling heard inside. Connie lingered, the child slipped her hand, and ran indoors.

'Gran! Gran!'

'Why, are yer back a'ready!'

The grandmother had been blackleading the stove, it was Saturday morning. She came to the door in her sacking apron, a blacklead-brush in her hand, and a black smudge on her nose. She was a little, rather dry woman.

'Why, whatever?' she said, hastily wiping her arm across her face as she saw Connie standing outside.

'Good-morning!' said Connie. 'She was crying, so I just brought her home.'

The grandmother looked round swiftly at the child: 'Why, wheer was yer Dad?'

The little girl clung to her grandmother's skirts and simpered.

'He was there,' said Connie, 'but he'd shot a poaching cat, and the child was upset.'

'Oh, you'd no right t'ave bothered, Lady Chatterley, I'm sure! I'm sure it was very good of you, but you shouldn't 'ave bothered. Why, did ever you see!' – and the old woman turned to the child: 'Fancy Lady Chatterley takin' all that trouble over yer! Why, she shouldn't 'ave bothered!'

'It was no bother, just a walk,' said Connie smiling.

'Why, I'm sure 'twas very kind of you, I must say! So she was crying! I knew there'd be something afore they got far. She's frightened of 'im, that's wheer it is. Seems 'e's almost a stranger to 'er, fair a stranger, and I don't think they're two as'd hit it off very easy. He's got funny ways.'

Connie didn't know what to say.

'Look, Gran!' simpered the child.

The old woman looked down at the sixpence in the little girl's hand.

'An' sixpence an' all! Oh, your Ladyship, you shouldn't, you shouldn't. Why, isn't Lady Chatterley good to yer! My word, you're a lucky girl this morning!'

She pronounced the name, as all the people did: Chat'ley. 'Isn't Lady Chat'ley *good* to you!' Connie couldn't help looking at the old woman's nose, and the latter again vaguely wiped her face with the back of her wrist, but missed the smudge.

Connie was moving away . . . 'Well, thank you ever so much, Lady Chat'ley, I'm sure. Say thank you to Lady Chat'ley!' – this last to the child.

'Thank you,' piped the child.

'There's a dear!' laughed Connie, and she moved away, saying 'Good-morning', heartily relieved to get away from the contact. Curious, she thought, that that thin, proud man should have that little, sharp woman for a mother!

And the old woman, as soon as Connie had gone, rushed to the bit of mirror in the scullery, and looked at her face. Seeing it, she stamped her foot with impatience. 'Of *course* she had to catch me in my coarse apron, and a dirty face! Nice idea she'd get of me!'

Connie went slowly home to Wragby. 'Home!' . . . it was a warm word to use for that great, weary warren. But then it was a word that had had its day. It was somehow cancelled. All the great words, it seemed to Connie, were cancelled for her generation: love, joy, happiness, home, mother, father, husband, all these great, dynamic words were half dead now, and dying from day to day. Home was a place you lived in, love was a thing you didn't fool yourself about, joy was a word you applied to a good Charleston, happiness was a term of hypocrisy used to bluff other people, a father was an individual who enjoyed his own existence, a husband was a man you lived with and kept going in spirits. As for sex, the last of the great words, it was just a cocktail term for an excitement that bucked you up for a while, then left you more raggy than ever. Frayed! It was as if the very material you were made of was cheap stuff, and was fraying out to nothing.

All that really remained was a stubborn stoicism: and in that there was a certain pleasure. In the very experience of the nothingness of life, phase after phase, *étape* after *étape*, there was a certain grisly satisfaction. So that's *that*! Always this was the last utterance: home, love, marriage, Michaelis: So that's *that*! And when one died, the last words to life would be: So that's *that*! –

Money? Perhaps one couldn't say the same there. Money one always wanted. Money, success, the bitch-goddess, as Tommy Dukes persisted in calling it, after Henry James, that was a permanent necessity. You couldn't spend your last sou, and say finally: So that's *that*! No, if you lived even another ten minutes, you wanted a few more sous for something or other. Just to keep the business mechanically going, you needed money. You had to have it. Money you *have* to have. You needn't really have anything else. So that's that! –

Since, of course, it's not your own fault you are alive. Once you are alive, money is a necessity, and the only absolute necessity. All the rest you can get along without, at a pinch. But not money. Emphatically, that's *that*!

She thought of Michaelis, and the money she might have had with him; and even that she didn't want. She preferred the lesser amount which she helped Clifford to make by his writing. That she actually helped to make. 'Clifford and I together, we make twelve hundred a year out of writing'; so she put it to herself. Make money! Make it! Out of nowhere. Wring it out of the thin air! The last feat to be humanly proud of! The rest all-my-eye-Betty-Martin.

So she plodded home to Clifford, to join forces with him again, to make another story out of nothingness: and a story meant money. Clifford seemed to care very much whether his stories were considered first-class literature or not. Strictly, she didn't care. Nothing in it! said her father. Twelve hundred pounds last year! was the retort simple and final.

If you were young, you just set your teeth, and bit on and held on, till the money began to flow from the invisible; it was a question of power. It was a question of will; a subtle, subtle, powerful emanation of will out of yourself brought back to you the mysterious nothingness of money: a word on a bit of paper. It was a sort of magic, certainly it was triumph. The bitch-goddess! Well, if one had to prostitute oneself, let it be to a bitch-goddess! One could always despise her even while one prostituted oneself to her, which was good.

Clifford, of course, had still many childish taboos and fetishes. He wanted to be thought 'really good', which was all cock-a-hoopy nonsense. What was really good was what actually caught on. It was no good being really good and getting left with it. It seemed as if most of the 'really good' men just missed the bus. After all you only lived one life, and if you missed the bus, you were just left on the pavement, along with the rest of the failures.

Connie was contemplating a winter in London with Clifford, next winter. He and she had caught the bus all right, so they might as well ride on top for a bit, and show it.

The worst of it was, Clifford tended to become vague, absent, and to fall into fits of vacant depression. It was the wound to his psyche coming out. But it made Connie want to scream. Oh God, if the mechanism of the consciousness itself was going to go wrong, then what was one to do? Hang it all, one did one's bit! Was one to be let down *absolutely*?

Sometimes she wept bitterly, but even as she wept she was saying to herself: Silly fool, wetting hankies! As if that would get you anywhere!

Since Michaelis, she had made up her mind she wanted nothing. That seemed the simplest solution of the otherwise insoluble. She wanted nothing more than what she'd got; only she wanted to get ahead with what she'd got: Clifford, the stories, Wragby, the Lady-Chatterley business, money, and fame, such as it was . . . she wanted to go ahead with it all. Love, sex, all that sort of stuff, just water-ices! Lick it up and forget it. If you don't hang on to it in your mind, it's nothing. Sex especially . . . nothing! Make up your mind to it, and you've solved the problem. Sex and a cocktail: they both lasted about as long, had the same effect, and amounted to about the same thing.

But a child, a baby! that was still one of the sensations. She would venture very gingerly on that experiment. There was the man to consider, and it was curious, there wasn't a man in the world whose children you wanted. Mick's children! Repulsive thought! As lief have a child to a rabbit! Tommy Dukes? . . . he was very nice, but somehow you couldn't associate him with a baby, another generation. He ended in himself. And out of all the rest of Clifford's pretty wide acquaintance, there was not a man who did not rouse her contempt, when she thought of having a child by him. There were several who would have been quite possible as lovers, even Mick. But to let them breed a child on you! Ugh! Humiliation and abomination.

So that was that!

Nevertheless, Connie had the child at the back of her mind. Wait! wait! She would sift the generations of men through her sieve, and see if she couldn't find one who would do. 'Go ye into the streets and byways of Jerusalem, and see if ye can find a *man*.' It had been impossible to find a man in the Jerusalem of the prophet, though there were thousands of male humans. But a *man*! *C'est une autre chose!*

She had an idea that he would have to be a foreigner: not an Englishman, still less an Irishman. A real foreigner.

But wait! wait! Next winter she would get Clifford to London; the following winter she would get him abroad to the South of France, Italy. Wait! She was in no hurry about the child. That was her own private affair, and the one point on which, in her own queer, female way, she was serious to the bottom of her soul. She was not going to risk any chance comer, not she! One might take a lover almost at any moment, but a man who should beget a child on one . . . wait! wait! it's a very different matter. 'Go ye into the streets and byways of Jerusalem . . . ' It was not a question of love; it was a question of a *man*. Why, one might even rather hate him, personally. Yet if he was the man, what would one's personal hate matter? This business concerned another part of oneself.

It had rained as usual, and the paths were too sodden for Clifford's chair, but Connie would go out. She went out alone every day now, mostly in the wood, where she was really alone. She saw nobody there.

This day, however, Clifford wanted to send a message to the keeper, and as the boy was laid up with influenza – somebody always seemed to have influenza at Wragby – Connie said she would call at the cottage.

The air was soft and dead, as if all the world were slowly dying. Grey and clammy and silent, even from the shuffling of the collieries, for the pits were working short time, and today they were stopped altogether. The end of all things!

In the wood all was utterly inert and motionless, only great drops fell from the bare boughs, with a hollow little crash. For the rest, among the old trees was depth within depth of grey, hopeless inertia, silence, nothingness.

Connie walked dimly on. From the old wood came an ancient melancholy, somehow soothing to her, better than the harsh insentience of the outer world. She liked the *inwardness* of the remnant of forest, the unspeaking reticence of the old trees. They seemed a very power of silence, and yet a vital presence. They, too, were waiting: obstinately, stoically waiting, and giving off a potency of silence. Perhaps they were only waiting for the end; to be cut down, cleared away, the end of the forest, for them the end of all things. But perhaps their strong and aristocratic silence, the silence of strong trees, meant something else.

As she came out of the wood on the north side, the keeper's cottage, a rather dark, brown stone cottage, with gables and a handsome chimney, looked uninhabited, it was so silent and alone. But a thread of smoke rose from the chimney, and the little railed-in garden in the front of the house was dug and kept very tidy. The door was shut.

Now she was here she felt a little shy of the man, with his curious far-seeing eyes. She did not like bringing him orders, and felt like going away again. She knocked softly, no one came. She knocked again, but still not loudly. There was no answer. She peeped through the window, and saw the dark little room, with its almost sinister privacy, not wanting to be invaded.

She stood and listened, and it seemed to her she heard sounds from the back of the cottage. Having failed to make herself heard, her mettle was roused, she would not be defeated.

So she went round the side of the house. At the back of the cottage the land rose steeply, so the back yard was sunken, and enclosed by a low stone wall. She turned the corner of the house and stopped. In the little yard two paces beyond her, the man was washing himself, utterly unaware. He was naked to the hips, his velveteen breeches slipping down over his slender loins. And his white slim back was curved over a big bowl of soapy water, in which he ducked his head, shaking his head with a queer, quick little motion, lifting his slender white arms, and pressing the soapy water from his ears, quick, subtle as a weasel playing with water, and utterly alone. Connie backed away round the corner of the house, and hurried away to the wood. In spite of herself, she had had a shock. After all, merely a man washing himself; commonplace enough, Heaven knows!

Yet in some curious way it was a visionary experience: it had hit her in the middle of the body. She saw the clumsy breeches slipping down over the pure, delicate, white loins, the bones showing a little, and the sense of aloneness, of a creature purely alone, overwhelmed her. Perfect, white, solitary nudity of a creature that lives alone, and inwardly alone. And beyond that, a certain beauty of a pure creature. Not the stuff of beauty, not even the body of beauty, but a lambency, the warm, white flame of a single life, revealing itself in contours that one might touch: a body!

Connie had received the shock of vision in her womb, and she knew it; it lay inside her. But with her mind she was inclined to ridicule. A man washing himself in a back yard! No doubt with evil-smelling yellow soap! She was rather annoyed; why should she be made to stumble on these vulgar privacies?

So she walked away from herself, but after a while she sat down on a stump. She was too confused to think. But in the coil of her confusion, she was determined to deliver her message to the fellow. She would not be balked. She must give him time to dress himself, but not time to go out. He was probably preparing to go out somewhere.

So she sauntered slowly back, listening. As she came near, the cottage looked just the same. A dog barked, and she knocked at the door, her heart beating in spite of herself.

She heard the man coming lightly downstairs. He opened the door quickly, and startled her. He looked uneasy himself, but instantly a laugh came on his face.

'Lady Chatterley!' he said. 'Will you come in?'

His manner was so perfectly easy and good, she stepped over the threshold into the rather dreary little room.

'I only called with a message from Sir Clifford,' she said in her soft, rather breathless voice.

The man was looking at her with those blue, all-seeing eyes of his, which made her turn her face aside a little. He thought her comely, almost beautiful, in her shyness, and he took command of the situation himself at once.

'Would you care to sit down?' he asked, presuming she would not. The door stood open.

'No thanks! Sir Clifford wondered if you would . . . ' and she delivered her message, looking unconsciously into his eyes again. And now his eyes looked warm and kind, particularly to a woman, wonderfully warm, and kind, and at ease.

'Very good, your Ladyship. I will see to it at once.'

Taking an order, his whole self had changed, glazed over with a sort of hardness and distance. Connie hesitated, she ought to go. But she looked round the clean, tidy, rather dreary little sitting-room with something like dismay.

'Do you live here quite alone?' she asked.

'Quite alone, your Ladyship.'

'But your mother . . . ?'

'She lives in her own cottage in the village.'

'With the child?' asked Connie.

'With the child!'

And his plain, rather worn face took on an indefinable look of derision. It was a face that changed all the time, baffling.

'No,' he said, seeing Connie stand at a loss, 'my mother comes and cleans up for me on Saturdays; I do the rest myself.'

Again Connie looked at him. His eyes were smiling again, a little mockingly, but warm and blue, and somehow kind. She wondered at him. He was in trousers and flannel shirt and a grey tie, his hair soft and damp, his face rather pale and worn-looking. When the eyes ceased to laugh they looked as if they had suffered a great deal, still without losing their warmth. But a pallor of isolation came over him, she was not really there for him.

She wanted to say so many things, and she said nothing. Only she looked up at him again, and remarked: 'I hope I didn't disturb you?'

The faint smile of mockery narrowed his eyes.

'Only combing my hair, if you don't mind. I'm sorry I hadn't a coat on, but then I had no idea who was knocking. Nobody knocks here, and the unexpected sounds ominous.'

He went in front of her down the garden path to hold the gate. In his shirt, without the clumsy velveteen coat, she saw again how slender he was, thin, stooping a little. Yet, as she passed him, there was something young and bright in his fair hair, and his quick eyes. He would be a man about thirty-seven or - eight.

She plodded on into the wood, knowing he was looking after her; he upset her so much, in spite of herself.

And he, as he went indoors, was thinking: 'She's nice, she's real! She's nicer than she knows.'

She wondered very much about him; he seemed so unlike a gamekeeper, so unlike a working-man anyhow; although he had something in common with the local people. But also something very uncommon.

'The gamekeeper, Mellors, is a curious kind of person,' she said to Clifford; 'he might almost be a gentleman.'

'Might he?' said Clifford. 'I hadn't noticed.'

'But isn't there something special about him?' Connie insisted.

'I think he's quite a nice fellow, but I know very little about him. He only came out of the army last year, less than a year ago. From India, I rather think. He may have picked up certain tricks out there, perhaps he was an officer's servant, and improved on his position. Some of the men were like that. But it does them no good, they have to fall back into their old place when they get home again.'

Connie gazed at Clifford contemplatively. She saw in him the peculiar tight rebuff against anyone of the lower classes who might be really climbing up, which she knew was characteristic of his breed.

'But don't you think there is something special about him?' she asked.

'Frankly, no! Nothing I had noticed.'

He looked at her curiously, uneasily, half-suspiciously. And she felt he wasn't telling her the real truth; he wasn't telling himself the real truth, that was it. He disliked any suggestion of a really exceptional human being. People must be more or less at his level, or below it.

Connie felt again the tightness, niggardliness of the men of her generation. They were so tight, so scared of life!

Chapter 7

When Connie went up to her bedroom she did what she had not done for a long time: took off all her clothes, and looked at herself naked in the huge mirror. She did not know what she was looking for, or at, very definitely, yet she moved the lamp till it shone full on her.

And she thought, as she had thought so often . . . what a frail, easily hurt, rather pathetic thing a human body is, naked; somehow a little unfinished, incomplete!

She had been supposed to have rather a good figure, but now she was out of fashion: a little too female, not enough like an adolescent boy. She was not very tall, a bit Scottish and short; but she had a certain fluent, down-slipping grace that might have been beauty. Her skin was faintly tawny, her limbs had a certain stillness, her body should have had a full, down-slipping richness; but it lacked something.

Instead of ripening its firm, down-running curves, her body was flattening and going a little harsh. It was as if it had not had enough sun and warmth; it was a little greyish and sapless.

Disappointed of its real womanhood, it had not succeeded in becoming boyish, and unsubstantial, and transparent; instead it had gone opaque.

Her breasts were rather small, and dropping pear-shaped. But they were unripe, a little bitter, without meaning hanging there. And her belly had lost the fresh, round gleam it had had when she was young, in the days of her German boy, who really loved her physically. Then it was young and expectant, with a real look of its own. Now it was going slack, and a little flat, thinner, but with a slack thinness. Her thighs, too, that used to look so quick and glimpsy in their female roundness, somehow they too were going flat, slack, meaningless.

Her body was going meaningless, going dull and opaque, so much insignificant substance. It made her feel immensely depressed and hopeless. What hope was there? She was old, old at twenty-seven, with no gleam and sparkle in the flesh. Old through neglect and denial, yes, denial. Fashionable women kept their bodies bright like delicate porcelain, by external attention. There was nothing inside the porcelain; but she was not even as bright as that. The mental life! Suddenly she hated it with a rushing fury, the swindle!

She looked in the other mirror's reflection at her back, her waist, her loins. She was getting thinner, but to her it was not becoming. The crumple of her waist at the back, as she bent back to look, was a little weary; and it used to be so gay-looking. And the longish slope of her haunches and her buttocks had lost its gleam and its sense of richness. Gone! Only the German boy had loved it, and he was ten years dead, very nearly. How time went by! Ten years dead, and she was only twenty-seven. The healthy boy with his fresh, clumsy sensuality that she had then been so scornful of! Where would she find it now? It was gone out of men. They had their pathetic, two-seconds spasms like Michaelis; but no healthy human sensuality, that warms the blood and freshens the whole being.

Still she thought the most beautiful part of her was the long-sloping fall of the haunches from the socket of the back, and the slumberous, round stillness of the buttocks. Like hillocks of sand the Arabs say, soft and downward-slipping with a long slope. Here the life still lingered hoping. But here too she was thinner, and going unripe, astringent.

But the front of her body made her miserable. It was already beginning to slacken, with a slack sort of thinness, almost withered, going old before it had ever really lived. She thought of the child she might somehow bear. Was she fit, anyhow?

She slipped into her nightdress, and went to bed, where she sobbed bitterly. And in her bitterness burned a cold indignation against Clifford, and his writings and his talk: against all the men of his sort who defrauded a woman even of her own body.

Unjust! Unjust! The sense of deep physical injustice burned to her very soul.

But in the morning, all the same, she was up at seven, and going downstairs to Clifford. She had to help him in all the intimate things, for he had no man, and refused a womanservant. The housekeepers husband, who had known him as a boy, helped him, and did any heavy lifting; but Connie did the personal things, and she did them willingly. It was a demand on her, but she had wanted to do what she could.

So she hardly ever went away from Wragby, and never for more than a day or two; when Mrs Betts, the housekeeper, attended to Clifford. He, as was inevitable in the course of time, took all the service for granted. It was natural he should.

And yet, deep inside herself, a sense of injustice, of being defrauded, began to burn in Connie. The physical sense of injustice is a dangerous feeling, once it is awakened. It must have outlet, or it eats away the one in whom it is aroused. Poor Clifford, he was not to blame. His was the greater misfortune. It was all part of the general catastrophe.

And yet was he not in a way to blame? This lack of warmth, this lack of the simple, warm, physical contact, was he not to blame for that? He was never really warm, nor even kind, only thoughtful, considerate, in a well-bred, cold sort of way! But never warm as a man can be warm to a woman, as even Connie's father could be warm to her, with the warmth of a man who did himself well, and intended to, but who still could comfort a woman with a bit of his masculine glow.

But Clifford was not like that. His whole race was not like that. They were all inwardly hard and separate, and warmth to them was just bad taste. You had to get on without it, and hold your own; which was all very well if you were of the same class and race. Then you could keep yourself cold and be very estimable, and hold your own, and enjoy the satisfaction of holding it. But if you were of another class and another race it wouldn't do; there was no fun merely holding your own, and feeling you belonged to the ruling class. What was the point, when even the smartest aristocrats had really nothing positive of their own to hold, and their rule was really a farce, not rule at all? What was the point? It was all cold nonsense.

A sense of rebellion smouldered in Connie. What was the good of it all? What was the good of her sacrifice, her devoting her life to Clifford? What was she serving, after all? A cold spirit of vanity, that had no warm human contacts, and that was as corrupt as any low-born Jew, in craving for prostitution to the bitch-goddess, Success. Even Clifford's cool and contactless assurance that he belonged to the ruling class didn't prevent his tongue lolling out of his mouth, as he panted after the bitch-goddess. After all, Michaelis was really more dignified in the matter, and far, far more successful. Really, if you looked closely at Clifford, he was a buffoon, and a buffoon is more humiliating than a bounder.

As between the two men, Michaelis really had far more use for her than Clifford had. He had even more need of her. Any good nurse can attend to crippled legs! And as for the heroic effort, Michaelis was a heroic rat, and Clifford was very much of a poodle showing off.

There were people staying in the house, among them Clifford's Aunt Eva, Lady Bennerley. She was a thin woman of sixty, with a red nose, a widow, and still something of a *grande dame*. She belonged to one of the best families, and had the character to carry it off. Connie liked her, she was so perfectly simple and frank, as far as she intended to be frank, and superficially kind. Inside herself she was a past-mistress in holding her own, and holding other people a little lower. She was not at all a snob: far too sure of herself. She was perfect at the social sport of coolly holding her own, and making other people defer to her.

She was kind to Connie, and tried to worm into her woman's soul with the sharp gimlet of her well-born observations.

'You're quite wonderful, in my opinion,' she said to Connie. 'You've done wonders for Clifford. I never saw any budding genius myself, and there he is all the rage.' Aunt Eva was quite complacently proud of Clifford's success. Another feather in the family cap! She didn't care a straw about his books, but why should she?

'Oh, I don't think it's my doing,' said Connie.

'It must be! Can't be anybody else's. And it seems to me you don't get enough out of it.'

'How?'

'Look at the way you are shut up here. I said to Clifford: If that child rebels one day you'll have yourself to thank!'

'But Clifford never denies me anything,' said Connie.

'Look here, my dear child' – and Lady Bennerley laid her thin hand on Connie's arm. 'A woman has to live her life, or live to repent not having lived it. Believe me!' And she took another sip of brandy, which maybe was her form of repentance.

'But I do live my life, don't I?'

'Not in my idea! Clifford should bring you to London, and let you go about. His sort of friends are all right for him, but what are they for you? If I were you I should think it wasn't good enough. You'll let your youth slip by, and you'll spend your old age, and your middle age too, repenting it.'

Her ladyship lapsed into contemplative silence, soothed by the brandy.

But Connie was not keen on going to London, and being steered into the smart world by Lady Bennerley. She didn't feel really smart, it wasn't interesting. And she did feel the peculiar, withering coldness under it all; like the soil of Labrador, which has gay little flowers on its surface, and a foot down is frozen.

Tommy Dukes was at Wragby, and another man, Harry Winterslow, and Jack Strangeways with his wife Olive. The talk was much more desultory than when only the cronies were there, and everybody was a bit bored, for the weather was bad, and there was only billiards, and the pianola to dance to.

Olive was reading a book about the future, when babies would be bred in bottles, and women would be 'immunised'.

'Jolly good thing too!' she said. 'Then a woman can live her own life.' Strangeways wanted children, and she didn't.

'How'd you like to be immunised?' Winterslow asked her, with an ugly smile.

'I hope I am; naturally,' she said. 'Anyhow the future's going to have more sense, and a woman needn't be dragged down by her *functions*.'

'Perhaps she'll float off into space altogether,' said Dukes.

'I do think sufficient civilisation ought to eliminate a lot of the physical disabilities,' said Clifford. 'All the love-business for example, it might just as well go. I suppose it would if we could breed babies in bottles.'

'No!' cried Olive. 'That might leave all the more room for fun.'

'I suppose,' said Lady Bennerley, contemplatively, 'if the love-business went, something else would take its place. Morphia, perhaps. A little morphine in all the air. It would be wonderfully refreshing for everybody.'

'The government releasing ether into the air on Saturdays, for a cheerful weekend!' said Jack. 'Sounds all right, but where should we be by Wednesday?'

'So long as you can forget your body you are happy,' said Lady Bennerley. 'And the moment you begin to be aware of your body, you are wretched. So, if civilisation is any good, it has to help us to forget our bodies, and then time passes happily without our knowing it.'

'Help us to get rid of our bodies altogether,' said Winterslow. 'It's quite time man began to improve on his own nature, especially the physical side of it.'

'Imagine if we floated like tobacco smoke,' said Connie.

'It won't happen,' said Dukes. 'Our old show will come flop; our civilisation is going to fall. It's going down the bottomless pit, down the chasm. And believe me, the only bridge across the chasm will be the phallus!'

'Oh do! *do* be impossible, General!' cried Olive.

'I believe our civilisation is going to collapse,' said Aunt Eva.

'And what will come after it?' asked Clifford.

'I haven't the faintest idea, but something, I suppose,' said the elderly lady.

'Connie says people like wisps of smoke, and Olive says immunised women, and babies in bottles, and Dukes says the phallus is the bridge to what comes next. I wonder what it will really be?' said Clifford.

'Oh, don't bother! let's get on with today,' said Olive. 'Only hurry up with the breeding bottle, and let us poor women off.'

'There might even be real men, in the next phase,' said Tommy. 'Real, intelligent, wholesome men, and wholesome nice women! Wouldn't that be a change, an enormous change from us? *We're* not men, and the women aren't women. We're only celebrating make-shifts, mechanical and intellectual experiments. There may even come a civilisation of genuine men and women, instead of our little lot of clever-jacks, all at the intelligence-age of seven. It would be even more amazing than men of smoke or babies in bottles.'

'Oh, when people begin to talk about real women, I give up,' said Olive.

'Certainly nothing but the spirit in us is worth having,' said Winterslow.

'Spirits!' said Jack, drinking his whisky and soda.

'Think so? Give me the resurrection of the body!' said Dukes. 'But it'll come, in time, when we've shoved the cerebral stone away a bit, the money and the rest. Then we'll get a democracy of touch, instead of a democracy of pocket.'

Something echoed inside Connie: 'Give me the democracy of touch, the resurrection of the body!' She didn't at all know what it meant, but it comforted her, as meaningless things may do.

Anyhow everything was terribly silly, and she was exasperatedly bored by it all, by Clifford, by Aunt Eva, by Olive and Jack, and Winterslow, and even by Dukes. Talk, talk, talk! What hell it was, the continual rattle of it!

Then, when all the people went, it was no better. She continued plodding on, but exasperation and irritation had got hold of her lower body, she couldn't escape. The days seemed to grind by, with curious painfulness, yet nothing happened. Only she was getting thinner; even the housekeeper noticed it, and asked her about herself. Even Tommy Dukes insisted she was not well, though she said she was all right. Only she began to be afraid of the ghastly white tombstones, that peculiar loathsome whiteness of Carrara marble, detestable as false teeth, which stuck up on the hillside, under Tevershall church, and which she saw with such grim painfulness from the park. The bristling of the hideous false teeth of tombstones on the hill affected her with a grisly kind of horror. She felt the time not far off when she would be buried there, added to the ghastly host under the tombstones and the monuments, in these filthy Midlands.

She needed help, and she knew it; so she wrote a little *cri de coeur* to her sister, Hilda. 'I'm not well lately, and I don't know what's the matter with me.'

Down posted Hilda from Scotland, where she had taken up her abode. She came in March, alone, driving herself in a nimble two-seater. Up the drive she came, tooting up the incline, then sweeping round the oval of grass, where the two great wild beech trees stood, on the flat in front of the house.

Connie had run out to the steps. Hilda pulled up her car, got out, and kissed her sister.

'But Connie!' she said. 'Whatever is the matter?'

'Nothing!' said Connie, rather shamefacedly; but she knew how she had suffered in contrast to Hilda. Both sisters had the same rather golden, glowing skin, and soft brown hair, and naturally strong, warm physique. But now Connie was thin and earthy-looking, with a scraggy, yellowish neck, that stuck out of her jumper.

'But you're ill, child!' said Hilda, in the soft, rather breathless voice, that both sisters had alike. Hilda was nearly, but not quite, two years older than Connie.

'No, not ill. Perhaps I'm bored,' said Connie a little pathetically.

The light of battle glowed in Hilda's face: she was a woman, soft and still as she seemed, of the old amazon sort, not made to fit with men.

'This wretched place!' she said softly, looking at poor, old, lumbering Wragby with real hate. She looked soft and warm herself, as a ripe pear, and she was an amazon of the real old breed.

She went quietly in to Clifford. He thought how handsome she looked, but also he shrank from her. His wife's family did not have his sort of manners, or his sort of etiquette. He considered them rather outsiders, but once they got inside they made him jump through the hoop.

He sat square and well-groomed in his chair, his hair sleek and blond, and his face fresh, his blue eyes pale, and a little prominent, his expression inscrutable, but well-bred. Hilda thought it sulky and stupid, and he waited. He had an air of aplomb, but Hilda didn't care what he had an air of; she was up in arms, and if he'd been Pope or Emperor it would have been just the same.

'Connie's looking awfully unwell,' she said in her soft voice, fixing him with her beautiful, glowering grey eyes. She looked so maidenly, so did Connie; but he well knew the stone of Scottish obstinacy underneath.

'She's a little thinner,' he said.

'Haven't you done anything about it?'

'Do you think it necessary?' he asked, with his suavest English stiffness, for the two things often go together.

Hilda only glowered at him without replying; repartee was not her forte, nor

Connie's; so she glowered, and he was much more uncomfortable than if she had said things.

'I'll take her to a doctor,' said Hilda at length. 'Can you suggest a good one round here?'

'I'm afraid I can't.'

'Then I'll take her to London, where we have a doctor we trust.'

Though boiling with rage, Clifford said nothing.

'I suppose I may as well stay the night,' said Hilda, pulling off her gloves, 'and I'll drive her to town tomorrow.'

Clifford was yellow at the gills with anger, and at evening the whites of his eyes were a little yellow too. He ran to liver. But Hilda was consistently modest and maidenly.

'You must have a nurse or somebody, to look after you personally. You should really have a manservant,' said Hilda as they sat, with apparent calmness, at coffee after dinner. She spoke in her soft, seemingly gentle way, but Clifford felt she was hitting him on the head with a bludgeon.

'You think so?' he said coldly.

'I'm sure! It's necessary. Either that, or Father and I must take Connie away for some months. This can't go on.'

'What can't go on?'

'Haven't you looked at the child?' asked Hilda, gazing at him full stare. He looked rather like a huge, boiled crayfish, at the moment; or so she thought.

'Connie and I will discuss it,' he said.

'I've already discussed it with her,' said Hilda.

Clifford had been long enough in the hands of nurses; he hated them, because they left him no real privacy. And a manservant! . . . he couldn't stand a man hanging round him. Almost better any woman. But why not Connie?

The two sisters drove off in the morning, Connie looking rather like an Easter lamb, rather small beside Hilda, who held the wheel. Sir Malcolm was away, but the Kensington house was open.

The doctor examined Connie carefully, and asked her all about her life. 'I see your photograph, and Sir Clifford's, in the illustrated papers sometimes. Almost notorieties, aren't you? That's how the quiet little girls grow up, though you're only a quiet little girl even now, in spite of the illustrated papers. No, no! There's nothing organically wrong, but it won't do! it won't do! Tell Sir Clifford he's got to bring you to town, or take you abroad, and amuse you. You've got to be amused, got to! Your vitality is much too low; no reserves, no reserves. The nerves of the heart a bit queer already: oh, yes! Nothing but nerves; I'd put you right in a month at Cannes or Biarritz. But it mustn't go on, *mustn't*, I tell you, or I won't be answerable for consequences. You're spending your life without renewing it. You've got to be amused, properly, healthily amused. You're spending your vitality without making any. Can't go on, you know. Depression! avoid depression!'

Hilda set her jaw, and that meant something.

Michaelis heard they were in town, and came running with roses. 'Why, whatever's wrong?' he cried. 'You're a shadow of yourself. Why, I never saw such a change! Why ever didn't you let me know? Come to Nice with me! Come down to Sicily! Go on, come to Sicily with me, it's lovely there just now. You want sun! You want life! Why, you're wasting away! Come away with me! Come to Africa! Oh, hang Sir Clifford! Chuck him, and come along with me. I'll marry you the minute he divorces you. Come along and try a life! God's love! That place Wragby would kill anybody. Beastly place! Foul place! Kill anybody! Come away with me into the sun! It's the sun you want, of course, and a bit of normal life.'

But Connie's heart simply stood still at the thought of abandoning Clifford there and then. She couldn't do it. No . . . no! She just couldn't. She had to go back to Wragby.

Michaelis was disgusted. Hilda didn't like Michaelis, but she *almost* preferred him to Clifford. Back went the sisters to the Midlands.

Hilda talked to Clifford, who still had yellow eyeballs when they got back. He, too, in his way, was overwrought; but he had to listen to all Hilda said, to all the doctor had said, not what Michaelis had said, of course, and he sat mum through the ultimatum.

'Here is the address of a good manservant, who was with an invalid patient of the doctor's till he died last month. He is really a good man, and fairly sure to come.'

'But I'm *not* an invalid, and I will *not* have a manservant,' said Clifford, poor devil.

'And here are the addresses of two women; I saw one of them, she would do very well; a woman of about fifty, quiet, strong, kind, and in her way cultured . . .'

Clifford only sulked, and would not answer.

'Very well, Clifford. If we don't settle something by tomorrow, I shall telegraph to Father, and we shall take Connie away.'

'Will Connie go?' asked Clifford.

'She doesn't want to, but she knows she must. Mother died of cancer, brought on by fretting. We're not running any risks.'

So next day Clifford suggested Mrs Bolton, Tevershall parish nurse. Apparently Mrs Betts had thought of her. Mrs Bolton was just retiring from her parish duties to take up private nursing jobs. Clifford had a queer dread of delivering himself into the hands of a stranger, but this Mrs Bolton had once nursed him through scarlet fever, and he knew her.

The two sisters at once called on Mrs Bolton, in a newish house in a row, quite select for Tevershall. They found a rather good-looking woman of forty-odd, in a nurse's uniform, with a white collar and apron, just making herself tea, in a small, crowded sitting-room.

Mrs Bolton was most attentive and polite, seemed quite nice, spoke with a bit of a broad slur, but in heavily correct English, and from having bossed the sick colliers for a good many years, had a very good opinion of herself, and a fair amount of assurance. In short, in her tiny way, one of the governing class in the village, very much respected.

'Yes, Lady Chatterley's not looking at all well! Why, she used to be that bonny, didn't she now? But she's been failing all winter! Oh, it's hard, it is. Poor Sir Clifford! Eh, that war, it's a lot to answer for.'

And Mrs Bolton would come to Wragby at once, if Dr Shardlow would let her off. She had another fortnight's parish nursing to do, by rights, but they might get a substitute, you know.

Hilda posted off to Dr Shardlow, and on the following Sunday Mrs Bolton drove up in Leiver's cab to Wragby, with two trunks. Hilda had talks with her; Mrs Bolton was ready at any moment to talk. And she seemed so young! the way the passion would flush in her rather pale cheek. She was forty-seven.

Her husband, Ted Bolton, had been killed in the pit, twenty-two years ago, twenty-two years last Christmas, just at Christmas time, leaving her with two children, one a baby in arms. Oh the baby was married now, Edith, to a young man in Boots Cash Chemists in Sheffield. The other one was a schoolteacher in Chesterfield; she came home weekends, when she wasn't asked out somewhere. Young folks enjoyed themselves nowadays, not like when she, Ivy Bolton, was young.

Ted Bolton was twenty-eight when he was killed in an explosion down th' pit. The butty in front shouted to them all to lie down quick, there were four of them. And they all lay down in time, only Ted, and it killed him. Then at the inquiry, on the masters' side they said Ted had been frightened, and trying to run away, and not obeying orders, so it was like his fault really. So the compensation was only three hundred pounds, and they made out as if it was more of a gift than legal compensation, because it was really the man's own fault. And they wouldn't let her have the money down; she wanted to have a little shop. But they said she'd no doubt squander it, perhaps in drink! So she had to draw it thirty shillings a week. Yes, she had to go every Monday morning down to the offices, and stand there a couple of hours waiting her turn; yes, for almost four years she went every Monday. And what could she do with two little children on her hands? But Ted's mother was very good to her. When the baby could toddle she'd keep both the children for the day, while she, Ivy Bolton, went to Sheffield, and attended classes in ambulance, and then the fourth year she even took a nursing course and got qualified. She was determined to be independent and keep her children. So she was assistant at Uthwaite hospital, just a little place, for a while. But when the Company, the Tevershall Colliery Company, really Sir Geoffrey, saw that she could get on by herself, they were very good to her, gave her the parish nursing, and stood by her, she would say that for them. And she'd done it ever since, till now it was getting a bit much for her, she needed something a bit lighter, there was such a lot of traipsing round if you were a district nurse.

'Yes, the Company's been very good to *me*, I always say it. But I should never forget what they said about Ted, for he was as steady and fearless a chap as ever set foot on the cage, and it was as good as branding him a coward. But there, he was dead, and could say nothing to none of 'em.'

It was a queer mixture of feelings the woman showed as she talked. She liked the colliers, whom she had nursed for so long; but she felt very superior to them. She felt almost upper class, and at the same time a resentment against the ruling class smouldered in her. The masters! In a dispute between masters and men, she was always for the men. But when there was no question of contest, she was pining to be superior, to be one of the upper classes. The upper classes fascinated her, appealing to her peculiar English passion for superiority. She was thrilled to come to Wragby; thrilled to talk to Lady Chatterley, my word, different from the common colliers' wives! She said so in so many words. Yet one could see a grudge against the Chatterleys peep out in her; the grudge against the masters.

'Why, yes, of course, it would wear Lady Chatterley out! It's a mercy she had a sister to come and help her. Men don't think, high and low alike, they take what a woman does for them for granted. Oh, I've told the colliers off about it many a time. But it's very hard for Sir Clifford, you know, crippled like that. They were always a haughty family, standoffish in a way, as they've a right to be. But then to be brought down like that! And it's very hard on Lady Chatterley, perhaps harder on her. What she misses! I only had Ted three years, but my word, while I had him I had a husband I could never forget. He was one in a thousand, and jolly as the day. Who'd ever have thought he'd get killed? I don't believe it to this day somehow, I've never believed it, though I washed him with my own hands. But he was never dead for me, he never was. I never took it in.'

This was a new voice in Wragby, very new for Connie to hear; it roused a new ear in her.

For the first week or so, Mrs Bolton, however, was very quiet at Wragby; her assured, bossy manner left her, and she was nervous. With Clifford she was shy, almost frightened, and silent. He liked that, and soon recovered his self-possession, letting her do things for him without even noticing her.

'She's a useful nonentity!' he said. Connie opened her eyes in wonder, but did not contradict him. So different are impressions on two different people!

And he soon became rather superb, somewhat lordly with the nurse. She had rather expected it, and he played up without knowing. So susceptible we are to what is expected of us! The colliers had been so like children, talking to her, and telling her what hurt them, while she bandaged them, or nursed them. They had always made her feel so grand, almost superhuman in her administrations. Now Clifford made her feel small, and like a servant, and she accepted it without a word, adjusting herself to the upper classes.

She came very mute, with her long, handsome face, and downcast eyes, to administer to him. And she said very humbly: 'Shall I do this now, Sir Clifford? Shall I do that?'

'No, leave it for a time. I'll have it done later.'

'Very well, Sir Clifford.'

'Come in again in half an hour.'

'Very well, Sir Clifford.'

'And just take those old papers out, will you?'

'Very well, Sir Clifford.'

She went softly, and in half an hour she came softly again. She was bullied, but she didn't mind. She was experiencing the upper classes. She neither resented nor disliked Clifford; he was just part of a phenomenon, the phenomenon of the high-class folks, so far unknown to her, but now to be known. She felt more at home with Lady Chatterley, and after all it's the mistress of the house matters most.

Mrs Bolton helped Clifford to bed at night, and slept across the passage from his room, and came if he rang for her in the night. She also helped him in the morning, and soon valeted him completely, even shaving him, in her soft, tentative woman's way. She was very good and competent, and she soon knew how to have him in her power. He wasn't so very different from the colliers after all, when you lathered his chin, and softly rubbed the bristles. The stand-offishness and the lack of frankness didn't bother her; she was having a new experience.

Clifford, however, inside himself, never quite forgave Connie for giving up her personal care of him to a strange hired woman. It killed, he said to himself, the real flower of the intimacy between him and her. But Connie didn't mind that. The fine flower of their intimacy was to her rather like an orchid, a bulb stuck parasitic on her tree of life, and producing, to her eyes, a rather shabby flower.

Now she had more time to herself she could softly play the piano, up in her room, and sing: 'Touch not the nettle . . . for the bonds of love are ill to loose.' She had not realised till lately how ill to loose they were, these bonds of love. But thank Heaven she had loosened them! She was so glad to be alone, not always to have to talk to him. When he was alone he tapped-tapped-tapped on a typewriter, to infinity. But when he was not 'working', and she was there, he talked, always talked; infinite small analysis of people and motives, and results, characters and personalities, till now she had had enough. For years she had loved it, until she had enough, and then suddenly it was too much. She was thankful to be alone.

It was as if thousands and thousands of little roots and threads of con-sciousness in him and her had grown together into a tangled mass, till they could crowd no more, and the plant was dying. Now quietly, subtly she was unravelling the tangle of his consciousness and hers, breaking the threads gently, one by one, with patience and impatience to get clear. But the bonds of such love are more ill to loose even than most bonds; though Mrs Bolton's coming had been a great help.

But he still wanted the old intimate evenings of talk with Connie: talk or reading aloud. But now she could arrange that Mrs Bolton should come at ten to disturb them. At ten o'clock Connie could go upstairs and be alone. Clifford was in good hands with Mrs Bolton.

Mrs Bolton ate with Mrs Betts in the housekeeper's room, since they were all agreeable. And it was curious how much closer the servants' quarters seemed to have come; right up to the doors of Clifford's study, when before they were so remote. For Mrs Betts would sometimes sit in Mrs Bolton's room, and Connie heard their lowered voices, and felt somehow the strong, other vibration of the working people almost invading the sitting-rooms, when she and Clifford were alone. So changed was Wragby merely by Mrs Bolton's coming.

And Connie felt herself released, in another world, she felt she breathed differently. But still she was afraid of how many of her roots, perhaps mortal ones, were tangled with Clifford's. Yet still, she breathed freer, a new phase was going to begin in her life.

Chapter 8

Mrs Bolton also kept a cherishing eye on Connie, feeling she must extend to her her female and professional protection. She was always urging her ladyship to walk out, to drive to Uthwaite, to be in the air. For Connie had got into the habit of sitting still by the fire, pretending to read, or to sew feebly, and hardly going out at all.

It was a blowy day soon after Hilda had gone, that Mrs Bolton said: 'Now why don't you go for a walk through the wood, and look at the daffs behind the keeper's cottage? They're the prettiest sight you'd see in a day's march. And you could put some in your room; wild daffs are always so cheerful-looking, aren't they?'

Connie took it in good part, even daffs for daffodils. Wild daffodils! After all, one should not stew in one's own juice. The spring came back . . . 'Seasons return, but not to me returns Day, or the sweet approach of Ev'n or Morn.'

And the keeper, his thin, white body, like a lonely pistil of an invisible flower! She had forgotten him in her unspeakable depression. But now something roused . . . 'Pale beyond porch and portal' . . . the thing to do was to pass the porches and the portals.

She was stronger, she could walk better, and in the wood the wind would not be so tiring as it was across the park, flattening against her. She wanted to forget, to forget the world, and all the dreadful, carrion-bodied people. 'Ye must be born again! I believe in the resurrection of the body! Except a grain of wheat fall into the earth and die, it shall by no means bring forth. When the crocus cometh forth I too will emerge and see the sun!' In the wind of March endless phrases swept through her consciousness.

Little gusts of sunshine blew, strangely bright, and lit up the celandines at the wood's edge, under the hazel-rods, they spangled out bright and yellow. And the wood was still, stiller, but yet gusty with crossing sun. The first windflowers were out, and all the wood seemed pale with the pallor of endless little anemones, sprinkling the shaken floor. 'The world has grown pale with thy breath.' But it was the breath of Persephone, this time; she was out of hell on a cold morning. Cold breaths of wind came, and overhead there was an anger of entangled wind caught among the twigs. It, too, was caught and trying to tear itself free, the wind, like Absalom. How cold the anemones looked, bobbing their naked white shoulders over crinoline skirts of green. But they stood it. A few first bleached little primroses too, by the path, and yellow buds unfolding themselves.

The roaring and swaying was overhead, only cold currents came down below. Connie was strangely excited in the wood, and the colour flew in her cheeks, and burned blue in her eyes. She walked ploddingly, picking a few primroses and the first violets, that smelled sweet and cold, sweet and cold. And she drifted on without knowing where she was.

Till she came to the clearing, at the far end of the wood, and saw the green-stained stone cottage, looking almost rosy, like the flesh underneath a mushroom, its stone warmed in a burst of sun. And there was a sparkle of yellow jasmine by the door; the closed door. But no sound; no smoke from the chimney; no dog barking.

She went quietly round to the back, where the bank rose up; she had an excuse, to see the daffodils.

And they were there, the short-stemmed flowers, rustling and fluttering and shivering, so bright and alive, but with nowhere to hide their faces, as they turned them away from the wind.

They shook their bright, sunny little rags in bouts of distress. But perhaps they liked it really; perhaps they really liked the tossing.

Constance sat down with her back to a young pine-tree, that swayed against her with curious life, elastic, and powerful, rising up. The erect, alive thing, with its top in the sun! And she watched the daffodils turn golden, in a burst of sun that was warm on her hands and lap. Even she caught the faint, tarry scent of the flowers. And then, being so still and alone, she seemed to get into the current of her own proper destiny. She had been fastened by a rope, and jagging and snarring like a boat at its moorings; now she was loose and adrift.

The sunshine gave way to chill; the daffodils were in shadow, dipping silently. So they would dip through the day and the long cold night. So strong in their frailty!

She rose, a little stiff, took a few daffodils, and went down. She hated breaking the flowers, but she wanted just one or two to go with her. She would have to go back to Wragby and its walls, and now she hated it, especially its thick walls. Walls! Always walls! Yet one needed them in this wind.

When she got home Clifford asked her, 'Where did you go?'

'Right across the wood! Look, aren't the little daffodils adorable? To think they should come out of the earth!'

'Just as much out of the air and sunshine,' he said.

'But modelled in the earth,' she retorted, with a prompt contradiction, that surprised her a little.

The next afternoon she went to the wood again. She followed the broad riding that swerved round and up through the larches to a spring called John's Well. It was cold on this hillside, and not a flower in the darkness of larches. But the icy little spring softly pressed upwards from its tiny well-bed of pure, reddish-white pebbles. How icy and clear it was! Brilliant! The new keeper had no doubt put in fresh pebbles. She heard the faint tinkle of water, as the tiny overflow trickled over and downhill. Even above the hissing boom of the larchwood, that spread its bristling, leafless, wolfish darkness on the down-slope, she heard the tinkle as of tiny water-bells.

This place was a little sinister, cold, damp. Yet the well must have been a drinking-place for hundreds of years. Now no more. Its tiny cleared space was lush and cold and dismal.

She rose and went slowly towards home. As she went she heard a faint tapping away on the right, and stood still to listen. Was it hammering, or a woodpecker? It was surely hammering.

She walked on, listening. And then she noticed a narrow track between young fir trees, a track that seemed to lead nowhere. But she felt it had been used. She turned down it adventurously, between the thick young firs, which gave way soon to the old oak wood. She followed the track, and the hammering grew nearer, in the silence of the windy wood, for trees make a silence even in their noise of wind.

She saw a secret little clearing, and a secret little hut made of rustic poles. And she had never been here before! She realised it was the quiet place where the growing pheasants were reared; the keeper in his shirt-sleeves was kneeling, hammering. The dog trotted forward with a short, sharp bark, and the keeper lifted his face suddenly and saw her. He had a startled look in his eyes.

He straightened himself and saluted, watching her in silence, as she came forward with weakening limbs. He resented the intrusion, he cherished his solitude as his only and last freedom in life.

'I wondered what the hammering was,' she said, feeling weak and breathless, and a little afraid of him, as he looked so straight at her.

'Ah'm gettin' th' coops ready for th' young bods,' he said, in broad vernacular.

She did not know what to say, and she felt weak.

'I should like to sit down a bit,' she said.

'Come and sit 'ere i' th' 'ut,' he said, going in front of her to the hut, pushing aside some timber and stuff, and drawing out a rustic chair, made of hazel sticks.

'Am Ah t' light yer a little fire?' he asked, with the curious naïveté of the dialect.

'Oh, don't bother,' she replied.

But he looked at her hands: they were rather blue. So he quickly took some larch twigs to the little brick fireplace in the corner, and in a moment the yellow flame was running up the chimney. He made a place by the brick hearth.

'Sit 'ere then a bit, and warm yer,' he said.

She obeyed him. He had that curious kind of protective authority she obeyed at once. So she sat and warmed her hands at the blaze, and dropped logs on the fire, whilst outside he was hammering again. She did not really want to sit, poked in a corner by the fire; she would rather have watched from the door, but she was being looked after, so she had to submit.

The hut was quite cosy, panelled with unvarnished deal, having a little rustic table and stool beside her chair, and a carpenter's bench, then a big box, tools, new boards, nails; and many things hung from pegs: axe, hatchet, traps, things in sacks, his coat. It had no window, the light came in through the open door. It was a jumble, but also it was a sort of little sanctuary.

She listened to the tapping of the man's hammer; it was not so happy. He was oppressed. Here was a trespass on his privacy, and a dangerous one! A woman! He had reached the point where all he wanted on earth was to be alone. And yet he was powerless to preserve his privacy; he was a hired man, and these people were his masters.

Especially he did not want to come into contact with a woman again. He feared it; for he had a big wound from old contacts. He felt if he could not be alone, and if he could not be left alone, he would die. His recoil away from the outer world was complete; his last refuge was this wood; to hide himself there!

Connie grew warm by the fire, which she had made too big: then she grew hot. She went and sat on the stool in the doorway, watching the man at work. He seemed not to notice her, but he knew. Yet he worked on, as if absorbedly, and his brown dog sat on her tail near him, and surveyed the untrustworthy world.

Slender, quiet and quick, the man finished the coop he was making, turned it over, tried the sliding door, then set it aside. Then he rose, went for an old coop, and took it to the chopping-log where he was working. Crouching, he tried the bars; some broke in his hands; he began to draw the nails. Then he turned the coop over and deliberated, and he gave absolutely no sign of awareness of the woman's presence.

So Connie watched him fixedly. And the same solitary aloneness she had seen in him naked, she now saw in him clothed: solitary, and intent, like an animal that works alone, but also brooding, like a soul that recoils away, away from all human contact. Silently, patiently, he was recoiling away from her even now. It was the stillness, and the timeless sort of patience, in a man impatient and passionate, that touched Connie's womb. She saw it in his bent head, the quick, quiet hands, the crouching of his slender, sensitive loins; something patient and withdrawn. She felt his experience had been deeper and wider than her own; much deeper and wider, and perhaps more deadly. And this relieved her of herself; she felt almost irresponsible.

So she sat in the doorway of the hut in a dream, utterly unaware of time and of particular circumstances. She was so drifted away that he glanced up at her quickly, and saw the utterly still, waiting look on her face. To him it was a look of waiting. And a little thin tongue of fire suddenly flickered in his loins, at the root of his back, and he groaned in spirit. He dreaded with a repulsion almost of death, any further close human contact. He wished above all things she would go away, and leave him to his own privacy. He dreaded her will, her female will, and her modern female insistency. And above all he dreaded her cool, upper-class impudence of having her own way. For after all he was only a hired man. He hated her presence there.

Connie came to herself with sudden uneasiness. She rose. The afternoon was turning to evening, yet she could not go away. She went over to the man, who stood up at attention, his worn face stiff and blank, his eyes watching her.

'It is so nice here, so restful,' she said. 'I have never been here before.'

'No?'

'I think I shall come and sit here sometimes.'

'Yes?'

'Do you lock the hut when you're not here?'

'Yes, your Ladyship.'

'Do you think I could have a key too, so that I could sit here sometimes? Are there two keys?'

'Not as Ah know on, ther' isna.'

He had lapsed into the vernacular. Connie hesitated; he was putting up an opposition. Was it his hut, after all?

'Couldn't we get another key?' she asked in her soft voice, that underneath had the ring of a woman determined to get her way.

'Another!' he said, glancing at her with a flash of anger, touched with derision.

'Yes, a duplicate,' she said, flushing.

"Appen Sir Clifford 'ud know,' he said, putting her off.

'Yes!' she said, 'he might have another. Otherwise we could have one made from the one you have. It would only take a day or so, I suppose. You could spare your key for so long.'

'Ah canna tell yer, m' Lady! Ah know nob'dy as ma'es keys round 'ere.'

Connie suddenly flushed with anger.

'Very well!' she said. 'I'll see to it.'

'All right, your Ladyship.'

Their eyes met. His had a cold, ugly look of dislike and contempt, and indifference to what would happen. Hers were hot with rebuff.

But her heart sank, she saw how utterly he disliked her, when she went against him. And she saw him in a sort of desperation.

'Good-afternoon!'

'Afternoon, my Lady!' He saluted and turned abruptly away. She had wakened the sleeping dogs of old voracious anger in him, anger against the self-willed female. And he was powerless, powerless. He knew it!

And she was angry against the self-willed male. A servant too! She walked sullenly home.

She found Mrs Bolton under the great beech-tree on the knoll, looking for her.

'I just wondered if you'd be coming, my Lady,' the woman said brightly.

'Am I late?' asked Connie.

'Oh . . . only Sir Clifford was waiting for his tea.'

'Why didn't *you* make it then?'

'Oh, I don't think it's hardly my place. I don't think Sir Clifford would like it at all, my Lady.'

'I don't see why not,' said Connie.

She went indoors to Clifford's study, where the old brass kettle was simmering on the tray.

'Am I late, Clifford?' she said, putting down the few flowers and taking up the tea-caddy, as she stood before the tray in her hat and scarf. 'I'm sorry! Why didn't you let Mrs Bolton make the tea?'

'I didn't think of it,' he said ironically. 'I don't quite see her presiding at the tea-table.'

'Oh, there's nothing sacrosanct about a silver teapot,' said Connie.

He glanced up at her curiously.

'What did you do all afternoon?' he said.

'Walked and sat in a sheltered place. Do you know there are still berries on the big holly-tree?'

She took off her scarf, but not her hat, and sat down to make tea. The toast would certainly be leathery. She put the tea-cosy over the teapot, and rose to get a little glass for her violets. The poor flowers hung over, limp on their stalks.

'They'll revive again!' she said, putting them before him in their glass for him to smell.

'Sweeter than the lids of Juno's eyes,' he quoted.

'I don't see a bit of connection with the actual violets,' she said. 'The Elizabethans are rather upholstered.'

She poured him his tea.

'Do you think there is a second key to that little hut not far from John's Well, where the pheasants are reared?' she said.

'There may be. Why?'

'I happened to find it today – and I'd never seen it before. I think it's a darling place. I could sit there sometimes, couldn't I?'

'Was Mellors there?'

'Yes! That's how I found it: his hammering. He didn't seem to like my intruding at all. In fact he was almost rude when I asked about a second key.'

'What did he say?'

'Oh nothing: just his manner; and he said he knew nothing about keys.'

'There may be one in Father's study. Betts knows them all; they're all there. I'll get him to look.'

'Oh do!' she said.

'So Mellors was almost rude?'

'Oh, nothing, really! But I don't think he wanted me to have the freedom of the castle, quite.'

'I don't suppose he did.'

'Still, I don't see why he should mind. It's not his home, after all! It's not his private abode. I don't see why I shouldn't sit there if I want to.'

'Quite!' said Clifford. 'He thinks too much of himself, that man.'

'Do you think he does?'

'Oh decidedly! He thinks he's something exceptional. You know he had a wife he didn't get on with, so he joined up in 1915 and was sent out to India, I believe. Anyhow he was blacksmith to the cavalry in Egypt for a time; always was connected with horses, a clever fellow that way. Then some Indian colonel took a fancy to him, and he was made a lieutenant. Yes, they gave him a commission. I believe he went back to India with his colonel, and up to the north-west frontier. He was ill; he has a pension. He didn't come out of the army till last year, I believe, and then, naturally, it isn't easy for a man like that to get back to his own level. He's bound to flounder. But he does his duty all right, as far as I'm concerned. Only I'm not having any of the Lieutenant Mellors touch.'

'How could they make him an officer when he speaks broad Derbyshire?'

'He doesn't . . . except by fits and starts. He can speak perfectly well, for him. I suppose he has an idea if he's come down to the ranks again, he'd better speak as the ranks speak.'

'Why didn't you tell me about him before?'

'Oh, I've no patience with these romances. They're the ruin of all order. It's a thousand pities they ever happened.'

Connie was inclined to agree. What was the good of discontented people who fitted in nowhere?

In the spell of fine weather Clifford, too, decided to go to the wood. The wind was cold, but not so tiresome, and the sunshine was like life itself, warm and full.

'It's amazing,' said Connie, 'how different one feels when there's a really fresh fine day. Usually one feels the very air is half dead. People are killing the very air.'

'Do you think people are doing it?' he asked.

'I do. The steam of so much boredom, and discontent and anger out of all the people, just kills the vitality in the air. I'm sure of it.'

'Perhaps some condition of the atmosphere lowers the vitality of the people?' he said.

'No, it's man that poisons the universe,' she asserted.

'Fouls his own nest,' remarked Clifford.

The chair puffed on. In the hazel copse catkins were hanging pale gold, and in sunny places the wood-anemones were wide open, as if exclaiming with the joy of life, just as good as in past days, when people could exclaim along with them. They had a faint scent of apple-blossom. Connie gathered a few for Clifford.

He took them and looked at them curiously.

'Thou still unravished bride of quietness,' he quoted. 'It seems to fit flowers so much better than Greek vases.'

'Ravished is such a horrid word!' she said. 'It's only people who ravish things.'

'Oh, I don't know . . . snails and things,' he said.

'Even snails only eat them, and bees don't ravish.'

She was angry with him, turning everything into words. Violets were Juno's eyelids, and windflowers were unravished brides. How she hated words, always coming between her and life: they did the ravishing, if anything did: ready-made words and phrases, sucking all the life-sap out of living things.

The walk with Clifford was not quite a success. Between him and Connie there was a tension that each pretended not to notice, but there it was. Suddenly, with all the force of her female instinct, she was shoving him off. She wanted to be clear of him, and especially of his consciousness, his words, his obsession with himself, his endless treadmill obsession with himself, and his own words.

The weather came rainy again. But after a day or two she went out in the rain, and she went to the wood. And once there, she went towards the hut. It was raining, but not so cold, and the wood felt so silent and remote, inaccessible in the dusk of rain.

She came to the clearing. No one there! The hut was locked. But she sat on the log doorstep, under the rustic porch, and snuggled into her own warmth. So she sat, looking at the rain, listening to the many noiseless noises of it, and to the strange soughings of wind in upper branches, when there seemed to be no wind. Old oak trees stood around, grey, powerful trunks, rain-blackened, round and vital, throwing off reckless limbs. The ground was fairly free of undergrowth, the anemones sprinkled, there was a bush or two, elder, or guelder-rose, and a purplish tangle of bramble; the old russet of bracken almost vanished under green anemone ruffs. Perhaps this was one of the unravished places. Unravished! The whole world was ravished.

Some things can't be ravished. You can't ravish a tin of sardines. And so many women are like that; and men. But the earth . . . !

The rain was abating. It was hardly making darkness among the oaks any more. Connie wanted to go; yet she sat on. But she was getting cold; yet the overwhelming inertia of her inner resentment kept her there as if paralysed.

Ravished! How ravished one could be without ever being touched. Ravished by dead words become obscene, and dead ideas become obsessions.

A wet brown dog came running and did not bark, lifting a wet feather of a tail. The man followed in a wet black oilskin jacket, like a chauffeur, and face flushed a little. She felt him recoil in his quick walk, when he saw her. She stood up in the handbreath of dryness under the rustic porch. He saluted without speaking, coming slowly near. She began to withdraw.

'I'm just going,' she said.

'Was yer waitin' to get in?' he asked, looking at the hut, not at her.

'No, I only sat a few minutes in the shelter,' she said, with quiet dignity.

He looked at her. She looked cold.

'Sir Clifford 'adnt got no other key, then?' he asked.

'No, but it doesn't matter. I can sit perfectly dry under this porch. Good-afternoon!' She hated the excess of vernacular in his speech.

He watched her closely, as she was moving away. Then he hitched up his jacket, and put his hand in his breeches pocket, taking out the key of the hut.

''Appen yer'd better 'ave this key, an' Ah mun fend for t' bods some other road.'

She looked at him. ·

'What do you mean?' she asked.

'I mean as 'appen Ah can find anuther pleece as'll du for rearin' th' pheasants. If yer want ter be 'ere, yo'll non want me messin' abaht a' th' time.'

She looked at him, getting his meaning through the fog of the dialect.

'Why don't you speak ordinary English?' she said coldly.

'Me! Ah thowt it *wor* ordinary.'

She was silent for a few moments in anger.

'So if yer want t' key, yer'd better ta'e it. Or 'appen Ah'd better gi'e 't yer termorrer, an' clear all t' stuff aht fust. Would that du for yer?'

She became more angry.

'I didn't want your key,' she said. 'I don't want you to clear anything out at all. I don't in the least want to turn you out of your hut, thank you! I only wanted to be able to sit here sometimes, like today. But I can sit perfectly well under the porch, so please say no more about it.'

He looked at her again, with his wicked blue eyes.

'Why,' he began, in the broad slow dialect. 'Your Ladyship's as welcome as Christmas ter th' hut an' th' key an' iverythink as is. On'y this time o' th' year ther's bods ter set, an' Ah've got ter be potterin' abaht a good bit, seein' after 'em, an' a'. Winter time Ah ned 'ardly come nigh th' pleece. But what wi' spring, an' Sir Clifford wantin' ter start th' pheasants . . . An' your Ladyship'd non want me tinkerin' around an' about when she was 'ere, all th' time.'

She listened with a dim kind of amazement.

'Why should I mind your being here?' she asked.

He looked at her curiously.

'T'nuisance on me!' he said briefly, but significantly. She flushed. 'Very well!' she said finally. 'I won't trouble you. But I don't think I should have minded at all sitting and seeing you look after the birds. I should have liked it. But since you think it interferes with you, I won't disturb you, don't be afraid. You are Sir Clifford's keeper, not mine.'

The phrase sounded queer, she didn't know why. But she let it pass.

'Nay, your Ladyship. It's your Ladyship's own 'ut. It's as your Ladyship likes an' pleases, every time. Yer can turn me off at a wik's notice. It wor only . . . '

'Only what?' she asked, baffled.

He pushed back his hat in an odd comic way.

'On'y as 'appen yo'd like the place ter yersen, when yer did come, an' not me messin' abaht.'

'But why?' she said, angry. 'Aren't you a civilised human being? Do you think I ought to be afraid of you? Why should I take any notice of you and your being here or not? Why is it important?'

He looked at her, all his face glimmering with wicked laughter.

'It's not, your Ladyship. Not in the very least,' he said.

'Well why then?' she asked.

'Shall I get your Ladyship another key then?'

'No thank you! I don't want it.'

'Ah'll get it anyhow. We'd best 'ave two keys ter th' place.'

'And I consider you are insolent,' said Connie, with her colour up, panting a little.

'Nay, nay!' he said quickly. 'Dunna yer say that! Nay, nay! I niver meant nuthink. Ah on'y thought as if yo' come 'ere, Ah s'd 'ave ter clear out, an' it'd mean a lot o' work, settin' up somewheres else. But if your Ladyship isn't going ter take no notice o' me, then . . . it's Sir Clifford's 'ut, an' everythink is as your Ladyship likes, everythink is as your Ladyship likes an' pleases, barrin' yer take no notice o' me, doin' th' bits of jobs as Ah've got ter do.'

Connie went away completely bewildered. She was not sure whether she had been insulted and mortally offended, or not. Perhaps the man really only meant what he said; that he thought she would expect him to keep away. As if she would dream of it! And as if he could possibly be so important, he and his stupid presence.

She went home in confusion, not knowing what she thought or felt.

Chapter 9

Connie was surprised at her own feeling of aversion from Clifford. What is more, she felt she had always really disliked him. Not hate: there was no passion in it. But a profound physical dislike. Almost it seemed to her, she had married him because she disliked him, in a secret, physical sort of way. But of course, she had married him really because in a mental way he attracted her and excited her. He had seemed, in some way, her master, beyond her.

Now the mental excitement had worn itself out and collapsed, and she was aware only of the physical aversion. It rose up in her from her depths: and she realised how it had been eating her life away.

She felt weak and utterly forlorn. She wished some help would come from outside. But in the whole world there was no help. Society was terrible because it was insane. Civilised society is insane. Money and so-called love are its two great manias; money a long way first. The individual asserts himself in his disconnected insanity in these two modes: money and love. Look at Michaelis! His life and activity were just insanity. His love was a sort of insanity.

And Clifford the same. All that talk! All that writing! All that wild struggling to push himself forwards! It was just insanity. And it was getting worse, really maniacal.

Connie felt washed-out with fear. But at least, Clifford was shifting his grip from her on to Mrs Bolton. He did not know it. Like many insane people, his insanity might be measured by the things he was *not* aware of; the great desert tracts in his consciousness.

Mrs Bolton was admirable in many ways. But she had that queer sort of bossiness, endless assertion of her own will, which is one of the signs of insanity in modern woman. She *thought* she was utterly subservient and living for others. Clifford fascinated her because he always, or so often, frustrated her will, as if by a finer instinct. He had a finer, subtler will of self-assertion than herself. This was his charm for her.

Perhaps that had been his charm, too, for Connie.

'It's a lovely day, today!' Mrs Bolton would say in her caressive, persuasive voice. 'I should think you'd enjoy a little run in your chair today, the sun's just lovely.'

'Yes? Will you give me that book – there, that yellow one. And I think I'll have those hyacinths taken out.'

'Why they're so beautiful!' She pronounced it with the 'y' sound: be-yutiful! 'And the scent is simply gorgeous.'

'The scent is what I object to,' he said. 'It's a little funereal.'

'Do you think so!' she exclaimed in surprise, just a little offended, but impressed. And she carried the hyacinths out of the room, impressed by his higher fastidiousness.

'Shall I shave you this morning, or would you rather do it yourself?' Always the same soft, caressive, subservient, yet managing voice.

'I don't know. Do you mind waiting a while. I'll ring when I'm ready.'

'Very good, Sir Clifford!' she replied, so soft and submissive, withdrawing quietly. But every rebuff stored up new energy of will in her.

When he rang, after a time, she would appear at once. And then he would say, 'I think I'd rather you shaved me this morning.'

Her heart gave a little thrill, and she replied with extra softness: 'Very good, Sir Clifford!'

She was very deft, with a soft, lingering touch, a little slow. At first he had resented the infinitely soft touch of her fingers on his face. But now he liked it, with a growing voluptuousness. He let her shave him nearly every day: her face near his, her eyes so very concentrated, watching that she did it right. And gradually her fingertips knew his cheeks and lips, his jaw and chin and throat perfectly. He was well-fed and well-liking, his face and throat were handsome enough, and he was a gentleman.

She was handsome too, pale, her face rather long and absolutely still, her eyes bright, but revealing nothing. Gradually, with infinite softness, almost with love, she was getting him by the throat, and he was yielding to her.

She now did almost everything for him, and he felt more at home with her, less ashamed of accepting her menial offices, than with Connie. She liked handling him. She loved having his body in her charge, absolutely, to the last menial offices. She said to Connie one day: 'All men are babies, when you come to the bottom of them. Why, I've handled some of the toughest customers as ever went down Tevershall pit. But let anything ail them so that you have to do for them, and they're babies, just big babies. Oh, there's not much difference in men!'

At first Mrs Bolton had thought there really was something different in a gentleman, a *real* gentleman, like Sir Clifford. So Clifford had got a good start of her. But gradually, as she came to the bottom of him, to use her own term, she found he was like the rest, a baby grown to man's proportions: but a baby with a queer temper and a fine manner and power in its control, and all sorts of odd knowledge that she had never dreamed of, with which he could still bully her.

Connie was sometimes tempted to say to him, 'For God's sake, don't sink so horribly into the hands of that woman!' But she found she didn't care for him enough to say it, in the long run.

It was still their habit to spend the evening together, till ten o'clock. Then they would talk, or read together, or go over his manuscript. But the thrill had gone out of it. She was bored by his manuscripts. But she still dutifully typed them out for him. But in time Mrs Bolton would do even that.

For Connie had suggested to Mrs Bolton that she should learn to use a typewriter. And Mrs Bolton, always ready, had begun at once, and practised assiduously. So now Clifford would sometimes dictate a letter to her, and she would take it down rather slowly, but correctly. And he was very patient, spelling for her the difficult words, or the occasional phrases in French. She was so thrilled, it was almost a pleasure to instruct her.

Now Connie would sometimes plead a headache as an excuse for going up to her room after dinner.

'Perhaps Mrs Bolton will play piquet with you,' she said to Clifford.

'Oh, I shall be perfectly all right. You go to your own room and rest, darling.'

But no sooner had she gone, than he rang for Mrs Bolton, and asked her to take a hand at piquet or bezique, or even chess. He had taught her all these games. And Connie found it curiously objectionable to see Mrs Bolton, flushed and tremulous like a little girl, touching her queen or her knight with uncertain fingers, then drawing away again. And Clifford, faintly smiling with a half-teasing superiority, saying to her: 'You must say j'adoube!'

She looked up at him with bright, startled eyes, then murmured shyly, obediently, 'J'adoube!'

Yes, he was educating her. And he enjoyed it, it gave him a sense of power. And she was thrilled. She was coming bit by bit into possession of all that the gentry knew, all that made them upper class: apart from the money. That thrilled her. And at the same time, she was making him want to have her there with him. It was a subtle deep flattery to him, her genuine thrill.

To Connie, Clifford seemed to be coming out in his true colours: a little vulgar, a little common, and uninspired; rather fat. Ivy Bolton's tricks and humble bossiness were also only too transparent. But Connie did wonder at the genuine thrill which the woman got out of Clifford. To say she was in love with him would be putting it wrongly. She was thrilled by her contact with a man of the upper class, this titled gentleman, this author who could write books and poems, and whose photograph appeared in the illustrated newspapers. She was thrilled to a weird passion. And his 'educating' her roused in her a passion of excitement and response much deeper than any love affair could have done. In truth, the very fact that there could *be* no love affair left her free to thrill to her very marrow with this other passion, the peculiar passion of *knowing*, knowing as he knew.

There was no mistake that the woman was in some way in love with him: whatever force we give to the word love. She looked so handsome and so young, and her grey eyes were sometimes marvellous. At the same time, there was a lurking soft satisfaction about her, even of triumph, and private satisfaction. Ugh, that private satisfaction! How Connie loathed it!

But no wonder Clifford was caught by the woman! She absolutely adored him, in her persistent fashion, and put herself absolutely at his service, for him to use as he liked. No wonder he was flattered!

Connie heard long conversations going on between the two. Or rather, it was mostly Mrs Bolton talking. She had unloosed to him the stream of gossip about Tevershall village. It was more than gossip. It was Mrs Gaskell and George Eliot and Miss Mitford all rolled in one, with a great deal more, that these women left out. Once started, Mrs Bolton was better than any book, about the lives of the people. She knew them all so intimately, and had such a peculiar, flamey zest in all their affairs, it was wonderful, if just a *trifle* humiliating to listen to her. At first she had not ventured to 'talk Tevershall', as she called it, to Clifford. But once started, it went on. Clifford was listening for 'material', and he found it in plenty. Connie realised that his so-called genius was just this: a perspicuous talent for personal gossip, clever and apparently detached. Mrs Bolton, of course, was very warm when she 'talked Tevershall'. Carried away, in fact. And it was marvellous, the things that happened and that she knew about. She would have run to dozens of volumes.

Connie was fascinated, listening to her. But afterwards always a little ashamed. She ought not to listen with this queer rabid curiosity. After all, one may hear the most private affairs of other people, but only in a spirit of respect for the struggling, battered thing which any human soul is, and in a spirit of fine, discriminative sympathy. For even satire is a form of sympathy. It is the way our sympathy flows and recoils that really determines our lives. And here lies the vast importance of the novel, properly handled. It can inform and lead into new places the flow of our sympathetic consciousness, and it can lead our sympathy away in recoil from things gone dead. Therefore, the novel, properly handled, can reveal the most secret places of life: for it is in the *passional* secret places of life, above all, that the tide of sensitive awareness needs to ebb and flow, cleansing and freshening.

But the novel, like gossip, can also excite spurious sympathies and recoils, mechanical and deadening to the psyche. The novel can glorify the most corrupt feelings, so long as they are *conventionally* 'pure'. Then the novel, like gossip, becomes at last vicious, and, like gossip, all the more vicious because it is always ostensibly on the side of the angels. Mrs Bolton's gossip was always on the side of the angels. 'And he was such a *bad* fellow, and she was such a *nice* woman.' Whereas, as Connie could see even from Mrs Bolton's gossip, the woman had been merely a mealy-mouthed sort, and the man angrily honest. But angry honesty made a 'bad man' of him, and mealy-mouthedness made a 'nice woman' of her, in the vicious, conventional channelling of sympathy by Mrs Bolton.

For this reason, the gossip was humiliating. And for the same reason, most novels, especially popular ones, are humiliating too. The public responds now only to an appeal to its vices.

Nevertheless, one got a new vision of Tevershall village from Mrs Bolton's talk. A terrible, seething welter of ugly life it seemed: not at all the flat drabness it looked from outside. Clifford of course knew by sight most of the people mentioned, Connie knew only one or two. But it sounded really more like a Central African jungle than an English village.

'I suppose you heard as Miss Allsopp was married last week! Would you ever! Miss Allsopp, old James's daughter, the boot-and-shoe Allsopp. You know they built a house up at Pye Croft. The old man died last year from a fall; eighty-three, he was, an' nimble as a lad. An' then he slipped on Bestwood Hill, on a slide as the lads 'ad made last winter, an' broke his thigh, and that finished him, poor old man, it did seem a shame. Well he left all his money to Tattie: didn't leave the boys a penny. And Tattie, I know, is five years – yes, she's fifty-three last autumn. And you know they were such Chapel people, my word! She taught Sunday school for thirty years, till her father died. And then she started carrying on with a fellow from Kinbrook, I don't know if you know him, an oldish fellow with a red nose, rather dandified, Willcock, 'as works in Harrison's woodyard. Well he's sixty-five if he's a day, yet you'd have thought they were a pair of young turtle-doves, to see them, arm in arm, and kissing at the gate: yes, an' she sitting on his knee right in the bay window on Pye Croft Road, for anybody to see. And he's got sons over forty: only lost his wife two years ago. If old James Allsopp hasn't risen from his grave, it's because there is no rising: for he kept her that strict! Now they're married and gone to live down at Kinbrook, and they say she goes round in a dressing-gown from morning to night, a veritable sight. I'm sure it's awful, the way the old ones go on! Why they're a lot worse than the young, and a sight more disgusting. I lay it down to the pictures, myself. But you can't keep them away. I was always saying: go to a good instructive film, but do for goodness' sake keep away from these melodramas and love films. Anyhow keep the children away! But there you are, the grown-ups are worse than the children: and the old ones beat the band. Talk about morality! nobody cares a thing. Folks does as they like, and much better off they are for it, I must say. But they're having to draw their horns in nowadays, now th' pits are working so bad, and they haven't got the money. And the grumbling they do, it's awful, especially the women. The men are so good and patient! What can they do, poor chaps! But the women, oh, they do carry on! They go and show off, giving contributions for a wedding present for Princess Mary, and then when they see all the grand things that's been given, they simply rave: who's she, any better than anybody else! Why doesn't Swan & Edgar give me *one* fur coat, instead of giving her six. I wish I'd kept my ten shillings! What's she going to give *me*, I should like to know? Here I can't get a new spring coat, my dad's working that bad, and she gets van-loads. It's time as poor folks had some money to spend, rich ones 'as 'ad it long enough. I want a new spring coat, I do, an' wheer am I going to get it? – I say to them, be thankful you're well fed and well clothed, without all the new finery you want! – And they fly back at me: "Why isn't Princess Mary thankful to go about in her old rags, then, an' have nothing! Folks like *her* get van-loads, an' I can't have a new spring coat. It's a damned shame. Princess! bloomin' rot about Princess! It's munney as matters, an' cos she's got lots, they give her more! Nobody's givin' me any, an' I've as much right as anybody else. Don't talk to me about education. It's munney as matters. I want a new spring coat, I do, an' I shan't get it, cos there's no munney . . . ' That's all they care about, clothes. They think nothing of giving seven and eight guineas for a winter coat – colliers' daughters, mind you – and two guineas for a child's summer hat. And then they go to the Primitive Chapel in their two-guinea hat, girls as would have been proud of a three-and-sixpenny one in my day. I heard that at the Primitive Methodist anniversary this year, when they have a built-up platform for the Sunday School children, like a grandstand going almost up to th' ceiling, I heard Miss Thompson, who has the first class of girls in the Sunday School, say there'd be over a thousand pounds in new Sunday clothes sitting on that platform! And times are what they are! But you can't stop them. They're mad for clothes. And boys the same. The lads spend every penny on themselves, clothes, smoking, drinking in the Miners' Welfare, jaunting off to Sheffield two or three times a week. Why, it's another world. And they fear nothing, and they respect nothing, the young don't. The older men are that patient and good, really, they let the women take everything. And this is what it leads to. The women are positive demons. But the lads aren't like their dads. They're sacrificing nothing, they aren't: they're all for self. If you tell them they ought to be putting a bit by, for a home, they say: That'll keep, that will, I'm goin' t' enjoy myself while I can. Owt else'll keep! – Oh, they're rough an' selfish, if you like. Everything falls on the older men, an' it's a bad lookout all round.'

Clifford began to get a new idea of his own village. The place had always frightened him, but he had thought it more or less stable. Now – ?

'Is there much Socialism, Bolshevism, among the people?' he asked.

'Oh!' said Mrs Bolton, 'you hear a few loud-mouthed ones. But they're mostly women who've got into debt. The men take no notice. I don't believe you'll ever turn our Tevershall men into reds. They're too decent for that. But the young ones blether sometimes. Not that they care for it really. They only want a bit of money in their pocket, to spend at the Welfare, or go gadding to Sheffield. That's all they care. When they've got no money, they'll listen to the reds spouting. But nobody believes in it, really.'

'So you think there's no danger?'

'Oh no! Not if trade was good, there wouldn't be. But if things were bad for a long spell, the young ones might go funny. I tell you, they're a selfish, spoilt lot. But I don't see how they'd ever do anything. They aren't ever serious about anything, except showing off on motor bikes and dancing at the Palais-de-danse in Sheffield. You can't *make* them serious. The serious ones dress up in evening clothes and go off to the Pally to show off before a lot of girls and dance these new Charlestons and what not. I'm sure sometimes the bus'll be full of young fellows in evening suits, collier lads, off to the Pally: let alone those that have gone with their girls in motors or on motor bikes. They don't give a serious thought to a thing – save Doncaster races, and the Derby: for they all of them bet on every race. And football! But even football's not what it was, not by a long chalk. It's too much like hard work, they say. No, they'd rather be off on motor bikes to Sheffield or Nottingham, Saturday afternoons.'

'But what do they do when they get there?'

'Oh, hang around – and have tea in some fine tea-place like the Mikado – and go to the Pally or the pictures or the Empire, with some girl. The girls are as free as the lads. They do just what they like.'

'And what do they do when they haven't the money for these things?'

'They seem to get it, somehow. And they begin talking nasty then. But I don't see how you're going to get Bolshevism, when all the lads want is just money to enjoy themselves, and the girls the same, with fine clothes: and they don't care about another thing. They haven't the brains to be Socialists. They haven't enough seriousness to take anything really serious, and they never will have.'

Connie thought, how extremely like all the rest of the classes the lower classes sounded. Just the same thing over again, Tevershall or Mayfair or Kensington. There was only one class nowadays: moneyboys. The moneyboy and the moneygirl, the only difference was how much you'd got, and how much you wanted.

Under Mrs Bolton's influence, Clifford began to take a new interest in the mines. He began to feel he belonged. A new sort of self-assertion came into him. After all, he was the real boss in Tevershall, he was really the pits. It was a new sense of power, something he had till now shrunk from with dread.

Tevershall pits were running thin. There were only two collieries: Tevershall itself, and New London. Tevershall had once been a famous mine, and had made famous money. But its best days were over. New London was never very rich, and in ordinary times just got along decently. But now times were bad, and it was pits like New London that got left.

'There's a lot of Tevershall men left and gone to Stacks Gate and White-over,' said Mrs Bolton. 'You've not seen the new works at Stacks Gate, opened after the war, have you, Sir Clifford? Oh, you must go one day, they're something quite new: great big chemical works at the pit-head, doesn't look a bit like a colliery. They say they get more money out of the chemical by-products than out of the coal – I forget what it is. And the grand new houses for the men, fair mansions! Of course it's brought a lot of riff-raff from all over the country. But a lot of Tevershall men got on there, and doin' well, a lot better than our own men. They say Tevershall's done, finished: only a question of a few more years, and it'll have to shut down. And New London'll go first. My word, won't it be funny, when there's no Tevershall pit working. It's bad enough during a strike, but my word, if it closes for good, it'll be like the end of the world. Even when I was a girl it was the best pit in the country, and a man counted himself lucky if he could get on here. Oh, there's been some money made in Tevershall. And now the men say it's a sinking ship, and it's time they all got out. Doesn't it sound awful! But of course there's a lot as'll never go till they have to. They don't like these new fangled mines, such a depth, and all machinery to work them. Some of them simply dreads those iron men, as they call them, those machines for hewing the coal, where men always did it before. And they say it's wasteful as well. But what goes in waste is saved in wages, and a lot more. It seems soon there'll be no use for men on the face of the earth, it'll be all machines. But they say that's what folks said when they had to give up the old stocking frames. I can remember one or two. But my word, the more machines, the more people, that's what it looks like! They say you can't get the same chemicals out of Tevershall coal as you can out of Stacks Gate, and that's funny, they're not three miles apart. But they say so. But everybody says it's a shame something can't be started, to keep the men going a bit better, and employ the girls. All the girls traipsing off to Sheffield every day! My word, it would be something to talk about if Tevershall Collieries took a new lease of life, after everybody saying they're finished, and a sinking ship, and the men ought to leave them like rats leave a sinking ship. But folks talk so much. Of course there was a boom during the war. When Sir Geoffrey made a trust of himself and got the money safe for ever, somehow. So they say! But they say even the masters and the owners don't get much out of it now. You can hardly believe it, can you! Why I always thought the pits would go on for ever and ever. Who'd have thought, when I was a girl! But New England's shut down, so is Colwick Wood: yes, it's fair haunting to go through that coppy and see Colwick Wood standing there deserted among the trees, and bushes growing up all over the pit-head, and the lines red rusty. It's like death itself, a dead colliery. Why whatever we should do if Tevershall shut down – ? it doesn't bear thinking of. Always that throng it's been, except at strikes, and even then the fan-wheels didn't stand, except when they fetched the ponies up. I'm sure it's a funny world, you don't know where you are from year to year, you really don't.'

It was Mrs Bolton's talk that really put a new fight into Clifford. His income, as she pointed out to him, was secure, from his father's trust, even though it was not large. The pits did not really concern him. It was the other world he wanted to capture, the world of literature and fame: the popular world, not the working world.

Now he realised the distinction between popular success and working success: the populace of pleasure and the populace of work. He, as a private individual, had been catering with his stories for the populace of pleasure. And he had caught on. But beneath the populace of pleasure lay the populace of work, grim, grimy, and rather terrible. They too had to have their providers. And it was a much grimmer business, providing for the populace of work, than for the populace of pleasure. While he was doing his stories, and 'getting on' in the world, Tevershall was going to the wall.

He realised now that the bitch-goddess of Success had two main appetites: one for flattery, adulation, stroking and tickling such as writers and artists gave her; but the other a grimmer appetite for meat and bones. And the meat and bones for the bitch-goddess were provided by the men who made money in industry.

Yes, there were two great groups of dogs wrangling for the bitch-goddess: the group of the flatterers, those who offered her amusement, stories, films, plays: and the other, much less showy, much more savage breed, those who gave her meat, the real substance of money. The well-groomed showy dogs of amusement wrangled and snarled among themselves for the favours of the bitch-goddess. But it was nothing to the silent fight-to-the-death that went on among the indispensables, the bone-bringers.

But under Mrs Bolton's influence, Clifford was tempted to enter this other fight, to capture the bitch-goddess by brute means of industrial production. Somehow, he got his pecker up. In one way, Mrs Bolton made a man of him, as Connie never did. Connie kept him apart, and made him sensitive and conscious of himself and his own states. Mrs Bolton made him aware only of outside things. Inwardly he began to go soft as pulp. But outwardly he began to be effective.

He even roused himself to go to the mines once more: and when he was there, he went down in a tub, and in a tub he was hauled out into the workings. Things he had learned before the war, and seemed utterly to have forgotten, now came back to him. He sat there, crippled, in a tub, with the underground manager showing him the seam with a powerful torch. And he said little. But his mind began to work.

He began to read again his technical works on the coal-mining industry, he studied the government reports, and he read with care the latest things on mining and the chemistry of coal and of shale which were written in German. Of course the most valuable discoveries were kept secret as far as possible. But once you started a sort of research in the field of coal-mining, a study of methods and means, a study of by-products and the chemical possibilities of coal, it was astounding, the ingenuity and the almost uncanny cleverness of the modern technical mind, as if really the devil himself had lent fiend's wits to the technical scientists of industry. It was far more interesting than art, than literature, poor emotional half-witted stuff, was this technical science of industry. In this field, men were like gods, or demons, inspired to discoveries, and fighting to carry them out. In this activity, men were beyond any mental age calculable. But Clifford knew that when it did come to the emotional and human life, these self-made men were of a mental age of about thirteen, feeble boys. The discrepancy was enormous and appalling.

But let that be. Let man slide down to general idiocy in the emotional and 'human' mind, Clifford did not care. Let all that go hang. He was interested in the technicalities of modern coal-mining, and in pulling Tevershall out of the hole.

He went down to the pit day after day, he studied, he put the general manager, and the overhead manager, and the underground manager, and the engineers through a mill they had never dreamed of. Power! He felt a new sense of power flowing through him: power over all these men, over the hundreds and hundreds of colliers. He was finding out: and he was getting things into his grip.

And he seemed verily to be reborn. *Now* life came into him! He had been gradually dying, with Connie, in the isolated private life of the artist and the conscious being. Now let all that go. Let it sleep. He simply felt life rush into him out of the coal, out of the pit. The very stale air of the colliery was better than oxygen to him. It gave him a sense of power, power. He was doing something: and he was *going* to do something. He was going to win, to win: not as he had won with his stories, mere publicity, amid a whole sapping of energy and malice. But a man's victory.

At first he thought the solution lay in electricity: convert the coal into electric power. Then a new idea came. The Germans invented a new locomotive engine with a self-feeder, that did not need a fireman. And it was to be fed with a new fuel, that burnt in small quantities at a great heat, under peculiar conditions.

The idea of a new concentrated fuel that burnt with a hard slowness at a fierce heat was what first attracted Clifford. There must be some sort of external stimulus to the burning of such fuel, not merely air supply. He began to experiment, and got a clever young fellow, who had proved brilliant in chemistry, to help him.

And he felt triumphant. He had at last got out of himself. He had fulfilled his life-long secret yearning to get out of himself. Art had not done it for him. Art had only made it worse. But now, now he had done it.

He was not aware how much Mrs Bolton was behind him. He did not know how much he depended on her. But for all that, it was evident that when he was with her his voice dropped to an easy rhythm of intimacy, almost a trifle vulgar.

With Connie, he was a little stiff. He felt he owed her everything, everything, and he showed her the utmost respect and consideration, so long as she gave him mere outward respect. But it was obvious he had a secret dread of her. The new Achilles in him had a heel, and in this heel the woman, the woman like

Connie his wife, could lame him fatally. He went in a certain half subservient dread of her, and was extremely nice to her. But his voice was a little tense when he spoke to her, and he began to be silent whenever she was present.

Only when he was alone with Mrs Bolton did he really feel a lord and a master, and his voice ran on with her almost as easily and garrulously as her own could run. And he let her shave him or sponge all his body as if he were a child, really as if he were a child.

Chapter 10

Connie was a good deal alone now, fewer people came to Wragby. Clifford no longer wanted them. He had turned against even the cronies. He was queer. He preferred the radio, which he had installed at some expense, with a good deal of success at last. He could sometimes get Madrid or Frankfurt, even there in the uneasy Midlands.

And he would sit alone for hours listening to the loudspeaker bellowing forth. It amazed and stunned Connie. But there he would sit, with a blank entranced expression on his face, like a person losing his mind, and listen, or seem to listen, to the unspeakable thing.

Was he really listening? Or was it a sort of soporific he took, whilst something else worked on underneath in him? Connie did not know. She fled up to her room, or out of doors to the wood. A kind of terror filled her sometimes, a terror of the incipient insanity of the whole civilised species.

But now that Clifford was drifting off to this other weirdness of industrial activity, becoming almost a *creature*, with a hard, efficient shell of an exterior and a pulpy interior, one of the amazing crabs and lobsters of the modern, industrial and financial world, invertebrates of the crustacean order, with shells of steel, like machines, and inner bodies of soft pulp, Connie herself was really completely stranded.

She was not even free, for Clifford must have her there. He seemed to have a nervous terror that she should leave him. The curious pulpy part of him, the emotional and humanly-individual part, depended on her with terror, like a child, almost like an idiot. She must be there, there at Wragby, a Lady Chatterley, his wife. Otherwise he would be lost like an idiot on a moor.

This amazing dependence Connie realised with a sort of horror. She heard him with his pit managers, with the members of his Board, with young scientists, and she was amazed at his shrewd insight into things, his power, his uncanny material power over what is called practical men. He had become a practical man himself, and an amazingly astute and powerful one, a master. Connie attributed it to Mrs Bolton's influence upon him, just at the crisis in his life.

But this astute and practical man was almost an idiot when left alone to his own emotional life. He worshipped Connie, she was his wife, a higher being,

788   SELECTED WORKS OF D. H. LAWRENCE

and he worshipped her with a queer, craven idolatry, like a savage, a worship based on enormous fear, and even hate of the power of the idol, the dread idol. All he wanted was for Connie to swear, to swear not to leave him, not to give him away.

'Clifford,' she said to him – but this was after she had the key to the hut – 'would you really like me to have a child one day?'

He looked at her with a furtive apprehension in his rather prominent pale eyes.

'I shouldn't mind, if it made no difference between us,' he said.

'No difference to what?' she asked.

'To you and me; to our love for one another. If it's going to affect that, then I'm all against it. Why, I might even one day have a child of my own!'

She looked at him in amazement.

'I mean, it might come back to me one of these days.'

She still stared in amazement, and he was uncomfortable.

'So you would not like it if I had a child?' she said.

'I tell you,' he replied quickly, like a cornered dog, 'I am quite willing, provided it doesn't touch your love for me. If it would touch that, I am dead against it.'

Connie could only be silent in cold fear and contempt. Such talk was really the gabbling of an idiot. He no longer knew what he was talking about.

'Oh, it wouldn't make any difference to my feeling for you,' she said, with a certain sarcasm.

'There!' he said. 'That is the point! In that case I don't mind in the least. I mean it would be awfully nice to have a child running about the house, and feel one was building up a future for it. I should have something to strive for then, and I should know it was your child, shouldn't I, dear? And it would seem just the same as my own. Because it is you who count in these matters. You know that, don't you, dear? I don't enter, I am a cypher. You are the great I-am! as far as life goes. You know that, don't you? I mean, as far as I am concerned. I mean, but for you I am absolutely nothing. I live for your sake and your future. I am nothing to myself.'

Connie heard it all with deepening dismay and repulsion. It was one of the ghastly half-truths that poison human existence. What man in his senses would say such things to a woman! But men aren't in their senses. What man with a spark of honour would put this ghastly burden of life-responsibility upon a woman, and leave her there, in the void?

Moreover, in half an hour's time, Connie heard Clifford talking to Mrs Bolton, in a hot, impulsive voice, revealing himself in a sort of passionless passion to the woman, as if she were half mistress, half foster-mother to him. And Mrs Bolton was carefully dressing him in evening clothes, for there were important business guests in the house.

Connie really sometimes felt she would die at this time. She felt she was being crushed to death by weird lies, and by the amazing cruelty of idiocy.

Clifford's strange business efficiency in a way overawed her, and his declaration of private worship put her into a panic. There was nothing between them. She never even touched him nowadays, and he never touched her. He never even took her hand and held it kindly. No, and because they were so utterly out of touch, he tortured her with his declaration of idolatry. It was the cruelty of utter impotence. And she felt her reason would give way, or she would die.

She fled as much as possible to the wood. One afternoon, as she sat brooding, watching the water bubbling coldly in John's Well, the keeper had strode up to her.

'I got you a key made, my Lady!' he said, saluting, and he offered her the key.

'Thank you so much!' she said, startled.

'The hut's not very tidy, if you don't mind,' he said. 'I cleared it what I could.'

'But I didn't want you to trouble!' she said.

'Oh, it wasn't any trouble. I am setting the hens in about a week. But they won't be scared of you. I s'll have to see to them morning and night, but I shan't bother you any more than I can help.'

'But you wouldn't bother me,' she pleaded. 'I'd rather not go to the hut at all, if I am going to be in the way.'

He looked at her with his keen blue eyes. He seemed kindly, but distant. But at least he was sane, and wholesome, if even he looked thin and ill. A cough troubled him.

'You have a cough,' she said.

'Nothing – a cold! The last pneumonia left me with a cough, but it's nothing.'

He kept distant from her, and would not come any nearer.

She went fairly often to the hut, in the morning or in the afternoon, but he was never there. No doubt he avoided her on purpose. He wanted to keep his own privacy.

He had made the hut tidy, put the little table and chair near the fireplace, left a little pile of kindling and small logs, and put the tools and traps away as far as possible, effacing himself. Outside, by the clearing, he had built a low little roof of boughs and straw, a shelter for the birds, and under it stood the five coops. And, one day when she came, she found two brown hens sitting alert and fierce in the coops, sitting on pheasants' eggs, and fluffed out so proud and deep in all the heat of the pondering female blood. This almost broke Connie's heart. She, herself, was so forlorn and unused, not a female at all, just a mere thing of terrors.

Then all the five coops were occupied by hens, three brown and a grey and a black. All alike, they clustered themselves down on the eggs in the soft nestling ponderosity of the female urge, the female nature, fluffing out their feathers. And with brilliant eyes they watched Connie, as she crouched before them, and they gave short sharp clucks of anger and alarm, but chiefly of female anger at being approached.

Connie found corn in the corn-bin in the hut. She offered it to the hens in her hand. They would not eat it. Only one hen pecked at her hand with a fierce little jab, so Connie was frightened. But she was pining to give them something, the brooding mothers who neither fed themselves nor drank. She brought water in a little tin, and was delighted when one of the hens drank.

Now she came every day to the hens, they were the only things in the world that warmed her heart. Clifford's protestations made her go cold from head to foot. Mrs Bolton's voice made her go cold, and the sound of the business men who came. An occasional letter from Michaelis affected her with the same sense of chill. She felt she would surely die if it lasted much longer.

Yet it was spring, and the bluebells were coming in the wood, and the leaf-buds on the hazels were opening like the spatter of green rain. How terrible it was that it should be spring, and everything cold-hearted, cold-hearted. Only the hens, fluffed so wonderfully on the eggs, were warm with their hot, brooding female bodies! Connie felt herself living on the brink of fainting all the time.

Then, one day, a lovely sunny day with great tufts of primroses under the hazels, and many violets dotting the paths, she came in the afternoon to the coops and there was one tiny, tiny perky chicken tinily prancing round in front of a coop, and the mother hen clucking in terror. The slim little chick was greyish-brown with dark markings, and it was the most alive little spark of a creature in seven kingdoms at that moment. Connie crouched to watch in a sort of ecstasy. Life, life! Pure, sparky, fearless new life! New life! So tiny and so utterly without fear! Even when it scampered a little scramblingly into the coop again, and disappeared under the hen's feathers in answer to the mother hen's wild alarm-cries, it was not really frightened, it took it as a game, the game of living. For in a moment a tiny sharp head was poking through the gold-brown feathers of the hen, and eyeing the Cosmos.

Connie was fascinated. And at the same time, never had she felt so acutely the agony of her own female forlornness. It was becoming unbearable.

She had only one desire now, to go to the clearing in the wood. The rest was a kind of painful dream. But sometimes she was kept all day at Wragby, by her duties as hostess. And then she felt as if she too were going blank, just blank and insane.

One evening, guests or no guests, she escaped after tea. It was late, and she fled across the park like one who fears to be called back. The sun was setting rosy as she entered the wood, but she pressed on among the flowers. The light would last long overhead.

She arrived at the clearing flushed and semi-conscious. The keeper was there, in his shirt-sleeves, just closing up the coops for the night, so the little occupants would be safe. But still one little trio was pattering about on tiny feet, alert drab mites, under the straw shelter, refusing to be called in by the anxious mother.

'I had to come and see the chickens!' she said, panting, glancing shyly at the keeper, almost unaware of him. 'Are there any more?'

'Thurty-six so far!' he said. 'Not bad!'

He took took a curious pleasure in watching the young things come out.

Connie crouched in front of the last coop. The three chicks had run in. But still their cheeky heads came poking sharply through the yellow feathers, then withdrawing, then only one beady little head eyeing forth from the vast mother-body.

'I'd love to touch them,' she said, putting her fingers gingerly through the bars of the coop. But the mother-hen pecked at her hand fiercely, and Connie drew back startled and frightened.

'How she pecks at me! She hates me!' she said in a wondering voice, 'But I wouldn't hurt them!'

The man standing above her laughed, and crouched down beside her, knees apart, and put his hand with quiet confidence slowly into the coop. The old hen pecked at him, but not so savagely. And slowly, softly, with sure gentle fingers, he felt among the old bird's feathers and drew out a faintly-peeping chick in his closed hand.

'There!' he said, holding out his hand to her. She took the little drab thing between her hands, and there it stood, on its impossible little stalks of legs, its atom of balancing life trembling through its almost weightless feet into Connie's hands. But it lifted its handsome, clean-shaped little head boldly, and looked sharply round, and gave a little 'peep'. 'So adorable! So cheeky!' she said softly.

The keeper, squatting beside her, was also watching with an amused face the bold little bird in her hands. Suddenly he saw a tear fall on to her wrist.

And he stood up, and stood away, moving to the other coop. For suddenly he was aware of the old flame shooting and leaping up in his loins, that he had hoped was quiescent for ever. He fought against it, turning his back to her. But it leapt, and leapt downwards, circling in his knees.

He turned again to look at her. She was kneeling and holding her two hands slowly forward, blindly, so that the chicken should run in to the mother-hen again. And there was something so mute and forlorn in her, compassion flamed in his bowels for her.

Without knowing, he came quickly towards her and crouched beside her again, taking the chick from her hands, because she was afraid of the hen, and putting it back in the coop. At the back of his loins the fire suddenly darted stronger.

He glanced apprehensively at her. Her face was averted, and she was crying blindly, in all the anguish of her generation's forlornness. His heart melted suddenly, like a drop of fire, and he put out his hand and laid his fingers on her knee.

'You shouldn't cry,' he said softly.

But then she put her hands over her face and felt that really her heart was broken and nothing mattered any more.

He laid his hand on her shoulder, and softly, gently, it began to travel down the curve of her back, blindly, with a blind stroking motion, to the curve of her crouching loins. And there his hand softly, softly, stroked the curve of her flank, in the blind instinctive caress.

She had found her scrap of handkerchief and was blindly trying to dry her face.

'Shall you come to the hut?' he said, in a quiet, neutral voice.

And closing his hand softly on her upper arm, he drew her up and led her slowly to the hut, not letting go of her till she was inside. Then he cleared aside the chair and table, and took a brown soldier's blanket from the tool chest, spreading it slowly. She glanced at his face, as she stood motionless.

His face was pale and without expression, like that of a man submitting to fate.

'You lie there,' he said softly, and he shut the door, so that it was dark, quite dark.

With a queer obedience, she lay down on the blanket. Then she felt the soft, groping, helplessly desirous hand touching her body, feeling for her face. The hand stroked her face softly, softly, with infinite soothing and assurance, and at last there was the soft touch of a kiss on her cheek.

She lay quite still, in a sort of sleep, in a sort of dream. Then she quivered as she felt his hand groping softly, yet with queer thwarted clumsiness, among her clothing. Yet the hand knew, too, how to unclothe her where it wanted. He drew down the thin silk sheath, slowly, carefully, right down and over her feet. Then with a quiver of exquisite pleasure he touched the warm soft body, and touched her navel for a moment in a kiss. And he had to come in to her at once, to enter the peace on earth of her soft, quiescent body. It was the moment of pure peace for him, the entry into the body of the woman.

She lay still, in a kind of sleep, always in a kind of sleep. The activity, the orgasm was his, all his; she could strive for herself no more. Even the tightness of his arms round her, even the intense movement of his body, and the springing of his seed in her, was a kind of sleep, from which she did not begin to rouse till he had finished and lay softly panting against her breast.

Then she wondered, just dimly wondered, why? Why was this necessary? Why had it lifted a great cloud from her and given her peace? Was it real? Was it real?

Her tormented modern-woman's brain still had no rest. Was it real? And she knew, if she gave herself to the man, it was real. But if she kept herself for herself, it was nothing. She was old; millions of years old, she felt. And at last, she could bear the burden of herself no more. She was to be had for the taking. To be had for the taking.

The man lay in a mysterious stillness. What was he feeling? What was he thinking? She did not know. He was a strange man to her, she did not know him. She must only wait, for she did not dare to break his mysterious stillness. He lay there with his arms round her, his body on hers, his wet body touching hers, so close. And completely unknown. Yet not unpeaceful. His very stillness was peaceful.

She knew that, when at last he roused and drew away from her. It was like an abandonment. He drew her dress in the darkness down over her knees and stood a few moments, apparently adjusting his own clothing. Then he quietly opened the door and went out.

She saw a very brilliant little moon shining above the afterglow over the oaks. Quickly she got up and arranged herself; she was tidy. Then she went to the door of the hut.

All the lower wood was in shadow, almost darkness. Yet the sky overhead was crystal. But it shed hardly any light. He came through the lower shadow towards her, his face lifted like a pale blotch.

'Shall we go, then?' he said.

'Where?'

'I'll go with you to the gate.'

He arranged things his own way. He locked the door of the hut and came after her.

'You aren't sorry, are you?' he asked, as he went at her side.

'No! No! Are you?' she said.

'For that! No!' he said. Then after a while he added: 'But there's the rest of things.'

'What rest of things?' she said.

'Sir Clifford. Other folks. All the complications.'

'Why complications?' she said, disappointed.

'It's always so. For you as well as for me. There's always complications.' He walked on steadily in the dark.

'And are you sorry?' she said.

'In a way!' he replied, looking up at the sky. 'I thought I'd done with it all. Now I've begun again.'

'Begun what?'

'Life.'

'Life!' she re-echoed, with a queer thrill.

'It's life,' he said. 'There's no keeping clear. And if you do keep clear you might almost as well die. So if I've got to be broken open again, I have.'

She did not quite see it that way, but still . . .

'It's just love,' she said cheerfully.

'Whatever that may be,' he replied.

They went on through the darkening wood in silence, till they were almost at the gate.

'But you don't hate me, do you?' she said wistfully.

'Nay, nay,' he replied. And suddenly he held her fast against his breast again, with the old connecting passion. 'Nay, for me it was good, it was good. Was it for you?'

'Yes, for me too,' she answered, a little untruthfully, for she had not been conscious of much.

He kissed her softly, softly, with the kisses of warmth.

'If only there weren't so many other people in the world,' he said lugubriously.

She laughed. They were at the gate to the park. He opened for her.

'I won't come any further,' he said.

'No!' And she held out her hand, as if to shake hands. But he took it in both his.

'Shall I come again?' she asked wistfully.

'Yes! Yes!'

She left him and went across the park.

He stood back and watched her going into the dark, against the pallor of the horizon. Almost with bitterness he watched her go. She had connected him up again, when he had wanted to be alone. She had cost him that bitter privacy of a man who at last wants only to be alone.

He turned into the dark of the wood. All was still, the moon had set. But he was aware of the noises of the night, the engines at Stacks Gate, the traffic on the main road. Slowly he climbed the denuded knoll. And from the top he could see the country, bright rows of lights at Stacks Gate, smaller lights at Tevershall pit, the yellow lights of Tevershall and lights everywhere, here and there, on the dark country, with the distant blush of furnaces, faint and rosy, since the night was clear, the rosiness of the outpouring of white-hot metal. Sharp, wicked electric lights at Stacks Gate! An undefinable quick of evil in them! And all the unease, the ever-shifting dread of the industrial night in the Midlands. He could hear the winding-engines at Stacks Gate turning down the seven-o'clock miners. The pit worked three shifts.

He went down again into the darkness and seclusion of the wood. But he knew that the seclusion of the wood was illusory. The industrial noises broke the solitude, the sharp lights, though unseen, mocked it. A man could no longer be private and withdrawn. The world allows no hermits. And now he had taken the woman, and brought on himself a new cycle of pain and doom. For he knew by experience what it meant.

It was not woman's fault, nor even love's fault, nor the fault of sex. The fault lay there, out there, in those evil electric lights and diabolical rattlings of engines. There, in the world of the mechanical greedy, greedy mechanism and mechanised greed, sparkling with lights and gushing hot metal and roaring with traffic, there lay the vast evil thing, ready to destroy whatever did not conform. Soon it would destroy the wood, and the bluebells would spring no more. All vulnerable things must perish under the rolling and running of iron.

He thought with infinite tenderness of the woman. Poor forlorn thing, she was nicer than she knew, and oh! so much too nice for the tough lot she was in contact with. Poor thing, she too had some of the vulnerability of the wild hyacinths, she wasn't all tough rubber-goods and platinum, like the modern girl. And they would do her in! As sure as life, they would do her in, as they do in all naturally tender life. Tender! Somewhere she was tender, tender with a tenderness of the growing hyacinths, something that has gone out of the celluloid women of today. But he would protect her with his heart for a little while. For a little while, before the insentient iron world and the Mammon of mechanised greed did them both in, her as well as him.

He went home with his gun and his dog, to the dark cottage, lit the lamp, started the fire, and ate his supper of bread and cheese, young onions and beer. He was alone, in a silence he loved. His room was clean and tidy, but rather stark. Yet the fire was bright, the hearth white, the petroleum lamp hung bright over the table, with its white oil-cloth. He tried to read a book about India, but tonight he could not read. He sat by the fire in his shirt-sleeves, not smoking, but with a mug of beer in reach. And he thought about Connie.

To tell the truth, he was sorry for what had happened, perhaps most for her sake. He had a sense of foreboding. No sense of wrong or sin; he was troubled by no conscience in that respect. He knew that conscience was chiefly fear of society, or fear of oneself. He was not afraid of himself. But he was quite consciously afraid of society, which he knew by instinct to be a malevolent, partly-insane beast.

The woman! If she could be there with him, and there were nobody else in the world! The desire rose again, his penis began to stir like a live bird. At the same time an oppression, a dread of exposing himself and her to that outside Thing that sparkled viciously in the electric lights, weighed down his shoulders. She, poor young thing, was just a young female creature to him; but a young female creature whom he had gone into and whom he desired again.

Stretching with the curious yawn of desire, for he had been alone and apart from man or woman for four years, he rose and took his coat again, and his gun, lowered the lamp and went out into the starry night, with the dog. Driven by desire and by dread of the malevolent Thing outside, he made his round in the wood, slowly, softly. He loved the darkness and folded himself into it. It fitted the turgidity of his desire which, in spite of all, was like a riches; the stirring restlessness of his penis, the stirring fire in his loins! Oh, if only there were other men to be with, to fight that sparkling electric Thing outside there, to preserve the tenderness of life, the tenderness of women, and the natural riches of desire. If only there were men to fight side by side with! But the men were all outside there, glorying in the Thing, triumphing or being trodden down in the rush of mechanised greed or of greedy mechanism.

Constance, for her part, had hurried across the park, home, almost without thinking. As yet she had no afterthought. She would be in time for dinner.

She was annoyed to find the doors fastened, however, so that she had to ring. Mrs Bolton opened.

'Why there you are, your Ladyship! I was beginning to wonder if you'd gone lost!' she said a little roguishly. 'Sir Clifford hasn't asked for you, though; he's got Mr Linley in with him, talking over something. It looks as if he'd stay to dinner, doesn't it, my Lady?'

'It does rather,' said Connie.

'Shall I put dinner back a quarter of an hour? That would give you time to dress in comfort.'

'Perhaps you'd better.'

Mr Linley was the general manager of the collieries, an elderly man from the north, with not quite enough punch to suit Clifford; not up to post-war conditions, nor post-war colliers either, with their 'ca' canny' creed. But Connie liked Mr Linley, though she was glad to be spared the toadying of his wife.

Linley stayed to dinner, and Connie was the hostess men liked so much, so modest, yet so attentive and aware, with big, wide blue eyes and a soft repose that sufficiently hid what she was really thinking. Connie had played this woman so much, it was almost second nature to her; but still, decidedly second. Yet it was curious how everything disappeared from her consciousness while she played it.

She waited patiently till she could go upstairs and think her own thoughts. She was always waiting, it seemed to be her *forte*.

Once in her room, however, she felt still vague and confused. She didn't know what to think. What sort of a man was he, really? Did he really like her? Not much, she felt. Yet he was kind. There was something, a sort of warm naïve kindness, curious and sudden, that almost opened her womb to him. But she felt he might be kind like that to any woman. Though even so, it was curiously soothing, comforting. And he was a passionate man, wholesome and passionate. But perhaps he wasn't quite individual enough; he might be the same with any woman as he had been with her. It really wasn't personal. She was only really a female to him.

But perhaps that was better. And after all, he was kind to the female in her, which no man had ever been. Men were very kind to the *person* she was, but rather cruel to the female, despising her or ignoring her altogether. Men were awfully kind to Constance Reid or to Lady Chatterley; but not to her womb they weren't kind. And he took no notice of Constance or of Lady Chatterley; he just softly stroked her loins or her breasts.

She went to the wood next day. It was a grey, still afternoon, with the dark-green dogs'-mercury spreading under the hazel copse, and all the trees making a silent effort to open their buds. Today she could almost feel it in her own body, the huge heave of the sap in the massive trees, upwards, up, up to the bud-tips, there to push into little flamey oak-leaves, bronze as blood. It was like a ride running turgid upward, and spreading on the sky.

She came to the clearing, but he was not there. She had only half expected him. The pheasant chicks were running lightly abroad, light as insects, from the coops where the yellow hens clucked anxiously. Connie sat and watched them, and waited. She only waited. Even the chicks she hardly saw. She waited.

The time passed with dream-like slowness, and he did not come. She had only half expected him. He never came in the afternoon. She must go home to tea. But she had to force herself to leave.

As she went home, a fine drizzle of rain fell.

'Is it raining again?' said Clifford, seeing her shake her hat.

'Just drizzle.'

She poured tea in silence, absorbed in a sort of obstinacy. She did want to see the keeper today, to see if it were really real. If it were really real.

'Shall I read a little to you afterwards?' said Clifford.

She looked at him. Had he sensed something?

'The spring makes me feel queer – I thought I might rest a little,' she said.

'Just as you like. Not feeling really unwell, are you?'

'No! Only rather tired – with the spring. Will you have Mrs Bolton to play something with you?'

'No! I think I'll listen in.'

She heard the curious satisfaction in his voice. She went upstairs to her bedroom. There she heard the loudspeaker begin to bellow, in an idiotically velveteen-genteel sort of voice, something about a series of street-cries, the very cream of genteel affectation imitating old criers. She pulled on her old violet-coloured mackintosh, and slipped out of the house at the side door.

The drizzle of rain was like a veil over the world, mysterious, hushed, not cold. She got very warm as she hurried across the park. She had to open her light waterproof.

The wood was silent, still and secret in the evening drizzle of rain, full of the mystery of eggs and half-open buds, half-unsheathed flowers. In the dimness of it all trees glistened naked and dark as if they had unclothed themselves, and the green things on earth seemed to hum with greenness.

There was still no one at the clearing. The chicks had nearly all gone under the mother-hens, only one or two lost adventurous ones still dibbed about in the dryness under the straw roof-shelter. And they were doubtful of themselves.

So! He still had not been. He was staying away on purpose. Or perhaps something was wrong. Perhaps she should go to the cottage and see.

But she was born to wait. She opened the hut with her key. It was all tidy, the corn put in the bin, the blankets folded on the shelf, the straw neat in a corner; a new bundle of straw. The hurricane lamp hung on a nail. The table and chair had been put back where she had lain.

She sat down on a stool in the doorway. How still everything was! The fine rain blew very softly, filmily, but the wind made no noise. Nothing made any sound. The trees stood like powerful beings, dim, twilit, silent and alive. How alive everything was!

Night was drawing near again; she would have to go. He was avoiding her.

But suddenly he came striding into the clearing, in his black oilskin jacket like a chauffeur, shining with wet. He glanced quickly at the hut, half-saluted, then veered aside and went on to the coops. There he crouched in silence, looking carefully at everything, then carefully shutting the hens and chicks up safe against the night.

At last he came slowly towards her. She still sat on her stool. He stood before her under the porch.

'You come then,' he said, using the intonation of the dialect.

'Yes,' she said, looking up at him. 'You're late!'

'Ay!' he replied, looking away into the wood.

She rose slowly, drawing aside her stool.

'Did you want to come in?' she asked.

He looked down at her shrewdly.

'Won't folks be thinkin' somethink, you comin' here every night?' he said.

'Why?' She looked up at him, at a loss. 'I said I'd come. Nobody knows.'

'They soon will, though,' he replied. 'An' what then?'

She was at a loss for an answer.

'Why should they know?' she said.

'Folks always does,' he said fatally.

Her lip quivered a little.

'Well I can't help it,' she faltered.

'Nay,' he said. 'You can help it by not comin' – if yer want to,' he added, in a lower tone.

'But I don't want to,' she murmured.

He looked away into the wood, and was silent.

'But what when folks finds out?' he asked at last. 'Think about it! Think how lowered you'll feel, one of your husband's servants.'

She looked up at his averted face.

'Is it,' she stammered, 'is it that you don't want me?'

'Think!' he said. 'Think what if folks find out – Sir Clifford an' a' – an' everybody talkin' – '

'Well, I can go away.'

'Where to?'

'Anywhere! I've got money of my own. My mother left me twenty thousand pounds in trust, and I know Clifford can't touch it. I can go away.'

'But 'appen you don't want to go away.'

'Yes, yes! I don't care what happens to me.'

'Ay, you think that! But you'll care! You'll have to care, everybody has. You've got to remember your Ladyship is carrying on with a gamekeeper. It's not as if I was a gentleman. Yes, you'd care. You'd care.'

'I shouldn't. What do I care about my ladyship! I hate it really. I feel people are jeering every time they say it. And they are, they are! Even you jeer when you say it.'

'Me!'

For the first time he looked straight at her, and into her eyes.

'I don't jeer at you,' he said.

As he looked into her eyes she saw his own eyes go dark, quite dark, the pupils dilating.

'Don't you care about a' the risk?' he asked in a husky voice. 'You should care. Don't care when it's too late!'

There was a curious warning pleading in his voice.

'But I've nothing to lose,' she said fretfully. 'If you knew what it is, you'd think I'd be glad to lose it. But are you afraid for yourself?'

'Ay!' he said briefly. 'I am. I'm afraid. I'm afraid. I'm afraid o' things.'

'What things?' she asked.

He gave a curious backward jerk of his head, indicating the outer world.

'Things! Everybody! The lot of 'em.'

Then he bent down and suddenly kissed her unhappy face.

'Nay, I don't care,' he said. 'Let's have it, an' damn the rest. But if you was to feel sorry you'd ever done it – !'

'Don't put me off,' she pleaded.

He put his fingers to her cheek and kissed her again suddenly.

'Let me come in then,' he said softly. 'An' take off your mackintosh.'

He hung up his gun, slipped out of his wet leather jacket, and reached for the blankets.

'I brought another blanket,' he said, 'so we can put one over us if you like.'

'I can't stay long,' she said. 'Dinner is half-past seven.'

He looked at her swiftly, then at his watch.

'All right,' he said.

He shut the door, and lit a tiny light in the hanging hurricane lamp.

'One time we'll have a long time,' he said.

He put the blankets down carefully, one folded for her head. Then he sat down a moment on the stool, and drew her to him, holding her close with one arm, feeling for her body with his free hand. She heard the catch of his in-taken breath as he found her. Under her frail petticoat she was naked.

'Eh! what it is to touch thee!' he said, as his finger caressed the delicate, warm, secret skin of her waist and hips. He put his face down and rubbed his cheek against her belly and against her thighs again and again. And again she wondered a little over the sort of rapture it was to him. She did not understand the beauty he found in her, through touch upon her living secret body, almost the ecstasy of beauty. For passion alone is awake to it. And when passion is dead, or absent, then the magnificent throb of beauty is incomprehensible and even a little despicable; warm, live beauty of contact, so much deeper than the beauty of vision. She felt the glide of his cheek on her thighs and belly and buttocks, and the close brushing of his moustache and his soft thick hair, and her knees began to quiver. Far down in her she felt a new stirring, a new nakedness emerging. And she was half afraid. Half she wished he would not caress her so. He was encompassing her somehow. Yet she was waiting, waiting.

And when he came into her, with an intensification of relief and con-summation that was pure peace to him, still she was waiting. She felt herself a little left out. And she knew, partly it was her own fault. She willed herself into this separateness. Now perhaps she was condemned to it. She lay still, feeling his motion within her, his deep-sunk intentness, the sudden quiver of him at the springing of his seed, then the slow-subsiding thrust. That thrust of the buttocks, surely it was a little ridiculous. If you were a woman, and apart in all the business, surely that thrusting of the man's buttocks was supremely ridiculous. Surely the man was intensely ridiculous in this posture and this act!

But she lay still, without recoil. Even when he had finished, she did not rouse herself to get a grip on her own satisfaction, as she had done with Michaelis; she lay still, and the tears slowly filled and ran from her eyes.

He lay still, too. But he held her close and tried to cover her poor naked legs with his legs, to keep them warm. He lay on her with a close, undoubting warmth.

800 SELECTED WORKS OF D. H. LAWRENCE

'Are yer cold?' he asked, in a soft, small voice, as if she were close, so close. Whereas she was left out, distant.

'No! But I must go,' she said gently.

He sighed, held her closer, then relaxed to rest again.

He had not guessed her tears. He thought she was there with him.

'I must go,' she repeated.

He lifted himself, kneeled beside her a moment, kissed the inner side of her thighs, then drew down her skirts, buttoning his own clothes unthinking, not even turning aside, in the faint, faint light from the lantern.

'Tha mun come ter th' cottage one time,' he said, looking down at her with a warm, sure, easy face.

But she lay there inert, and was gazing up at him thinking: Stranger! Stranger! She even resented him a little.

He put on his coat and looked for his hat, which had fallen, then he slung on his gun.

'Come then!' he said, looking down at her with those warm, peaceful sort of eyes.

She rose slowly. She didn't want to go. She also rather resented staying. He helped her with her thin waterproof, and saw she was tidy.

Then he opened the door. The outside was quite dark. The faithful dog under the porch stood up with pleasure seeing him. The drizzle of rain drifted greyly past upon the darkness. It was quite dark.

'Ah mun ta'e th' lantern,' he said. 'The'll be nob'dy.'

He walked just before her in the narrow path, swinging the hurricane lamp low, revealing the wet grass, the black shiny tree-roots like snakes, wan flowers. For the rest, all was grey rain-mist and complete darkness.

'Tha mun come to the cottage one time,' he said, 'shall ta? We might as well be hung for a sheep as for a lamb.'

It puzzled her, his queer, persistent wanting her, when there was nothing between them, when he never really spoke to her, and in spite of herself she resented the dialect. His 'tha mun come' seemed not addressed to her, but some common woman. She recognised the foxglove leaves of the riding and knew, more or less, where they were.

'It's quarter past seven,' he said, 'you'll do it.' He had changed his voice, seemed to feel her distance. As they turned the last bend in the riding towards the hazel wall and the gate, he blew out the light. 'We'll see from here,' he said, taking her gently by the arm.

But it was difficult, the earth under their feet was a mystery, but he felt his way by tread: he was used to it. At the gate he gave her his electric torch. 'It's a bit lighter in the park,' he said; 'but take it for fear you get off th' path.'

It was true, there seemed a ghost-glimmer of greyness in the open space of the park. He suddenly drew her to him and whipped his hand under her dress again, feeling her warm body with his wet, chill hand.

'I could die for the touch of a woman like thee,' he said in his throat. 'If tha' would stop another minute.' She felt the sudden force of his wanting her again

'No, I must run,' she said, a little wildly.

'Ay,' he replied, suddenly changed, letting her go.

She turned away, and on the instant she turned back to him saying: 'Kiss me.'

He bent over her indistinguishable and kissed her on the left eye. She held her mouth and he softly kissed it, but at once drew away. He hated mouth kisses.

'I'll come tomorrow,' she said, drawing away, 'if I can,' she added.

'Ay! not so late,' he replied out of the darkness. Already she could not see him at all.

'Good-night,' she said.

'Good-night, your Ladyship,' his voice.

She stopped and looked back into the wet dark. She could just see the bulk of him. 'Why did you say that?' she said.

'Nay,' he replied. 'Good-night then, run!'

She plunged on in the dark-grey tangible night. She found the side door open, and slipped into her room unseen. As she closed the door the gong sounded, but she would take her bath all the same – she must take her bath. 'But I won't be late any more,' she said to herself; 'it's too annoying.'

The next day she did not go to the wood. She went instead with Clifford to Uthwaite. He could occasionally go out now in the car, and had got a strong young man as chauffeur, who could help him out of the car if need be. He particularly wanted to see his godfather, Leslie Winter, who lived at Shipley Hall, not far from Uthwaite. Winter was an elderly gentleman now, wealthy, one of the wealthy coal-owners who had had their heyday in King Edward's time. King Edward had stayed more than once at Shipley, for the shooting. It was a handsome old stucco hall, very elegantly appointed, for Winter was a bachelor and prided himself on his style; but the place was beset by collieries. Leslie Winter was attached to Clifford, but personally did not entertain a great respect for him, because of the photographs in illustrated papers and the literature. The old man was a buck of the King Edward school, who thought life was life and the scribbling fellows were something else. Towards Connie the Squire was always rather gallant; he thought her an attractive demure maiden and rather wasted on Clifford, and it was a thousand pities she stood no chance of bringing forth an heir to Wragby. He himself had no heir.

Connie wondered what he would say if he knew that Clifford's gamekeeper had been having intercourse with her, and saying to her, 'Tha mun come to th' cottage one time.' He would detest and despise her, for he had come almost to hate the shoving forward of the working classes. A man of her own class he would not mind, for Connie was gifted from nature with this appearance of demure, submissive maidenliness, and perhaps it was part of her nature. Winter called her 'dear child' and gave her a rather lovely miniature of an eighteenth-century lady, rather against her will.

But Connie was preoccupied with her affair with the keeper. After all, Mr Winter, who was really a gentleman and a man of the world, treated her as a person and a discriminating individual; he did not lump her together with all the rest of his female womanhood in his 'thee' and 'tha'.

She did not go to the wood that day nor the next, nor the day following. She did not go so long as she felt, or imagined she felt, the man waiting for her, wanting her. But the fourth day she was terribly unsettled and uneasy. She still refused to go to the wood and open her thighs once more to the man. She thought of all the things she might do – drive to Sheffield, pay visits, and the thought of all these things was repellent. At last she decided to take a walk, not towards the wood, but in the opposite direction; she would go to Marehay, through the little iron gate in the other side of the park fence. It was a quiet grey day of spring, almost warm. She walked on unheeding, absorbed in thoughts she was not even conscious of. She was not really aware of anything outside her, till she was startled by the loud barking of the dog at Marehay Farm. Marehay Farm! Its pastures ran up to Wragby park fence, so they were neighbours, but it was some time since Connie had called.

'Bell!' she said to the big white bull-terrier. 'Bell! have you forgotten me? Don't you know me?' She was afraid of dogs, and Bell stood back and bellowed, and she wanted to pass through the farmyard on to the warren path.

Mrs Flint appeared. She was a woman of Constance's own age, had been a schoolteacher, but Connie suspected her of being rather a false little thing.

'Why, it's Lady Chatterley! Why!' And Mrs Flint's eyes glowed again, and she flushed like a young girl. 'Bell, Bell. Why! barking at Lady Chatterley! Bell! Be quiet!' She darted forward and slashed at the dog with a white cloth she held in her hand, then came forward to Connie.

'She used to know me,' said Connie, shaking hands. The Flints were Chatterley tenants.

'Of course she knows your Ladyship! She's just showing off,' said Mrs Flint, glowing and looking up with a sort of flushed confusion, 'but it's so long since she's seen you. I do hope you are better.'

'Yes thanks, I'm all right.'

'We've hardly seen you all winter. Will you come in and look at the baby?'

'Well!' Connie hesitated. 'Just for a minute.'

Mrs Flint flew wildly in to tidy up, and Connie came slowly after her, hesitating in the rather dark kitchen where the kettle was boiling by the fire. Back came Mrs Flint.

'I do hope you'll excuse me,' she said. 'Will you come in here?'

They went into the living-room, where a baby was sitting on the rag hearth-rug, and the table was roughly set for tea. A young servant-girl backed down the passage, shy and awkward.

The baby was a perky little thing of about a year, with red hair like its father, and cheeky pale-blue eyes. It was a girl, and not to be daunted. It sat among cushions and was surrounded with rag dolls and other toys in modern excess.

'Why, what a dear she is!' said Connie, 'and how she's grown! A big girl! A big girl!'

She had given it a shawl when it was born, and celluloid ducks for Christmas.

'There, Josephine! Who's that come to see you? Who's this, Josephine? Lady Chatterley – you know Lady Chatterley, don't you?'

The queer pert little mite gazed cheekily at Connie. Ladyships were still all the same to her.

'Come! Will you come to me?' said Connie to the baby.

The baby didn't care one way or another, so Connie picked her up and held her in her lap. How warm and lovely it was to hold a child in one's lap, and the soft little arms, the unconscious cheeky little legs.

'I was just having a rough cup of tea all by myself. Luke's gone to market, so I can have it when I like. Would you care for a cup, Lady Chatterley? I don't suppose it's what you're used to, but if you would . . . '

Connie would, though she didn't want to be reminded of what she was used to. There was a great re-laying of the table, and the best cups brought and the best teapot.

'If only you wouldn't take any trouble,' said Connie.

But if Mrs Flint took no trouble, where was the fun! So Connie played with the child and was amused by its little female dauntlessness, and got a deep voluptuous pleasure out of its soft young warmth. Young life! And so fearless! So fearless, because so defenceless. All the other people, so narrow with fear!

She had a cup of tea, which was rather strong, and very good bread and butter, and bottled damsons. Mrs Flint flushed and glowed and bridled with excitement, as if Connie were some gallant knight. And they had a real female chat, and both of them enjoyed it.

'It's a poor little tea, though,' said Mrs Flint.

'It's much nicer than at home,' said Connie truthfully.

'Oh-h!' said Mrs Flint, not believing, of course.

But at last Connie rose.

'I must go,' she said. 'My husband has no idea where I am. He'll be wondering all kinds of things.'

'He'll never think you're here,' laughed Mrs Flint excitedly. 'He'll be sending the crier round.'

'Goodbye, Josephine,' said Connie, kissing the baby and ruffling its red, wispy hair.

Mrs Flint insisted on opening the locked and barred front door. Connie emerged in the farm's little front garden, shut in by a privet hedge. There were two rows of auriculas by the path, very velvety and rich.

'Lovely auriculas,' said Connie.

'Recklesses, as Luke calls them,' laughed Mrs Flint. 'Have some.'

And eagerly she picked the velvet and primrose flowers.

'Enough! Enough!' said Connie.

They came to the little garden gate.

'Which way were you going?' asked Mrs Flint.

'By the warren.'

'Let me see! Oh yes, the cows are in the gin close. But they're not up yet. But the gate's locked, you'll have to climb.'

'I can climb,' said Connie.

'Perhaps I can just go down the close with you.'

They went down the poor, rabbit-bitten pasture. Birds were whistling in wild evening triumph in the wood. A man was calling up the last cows, which trailed slowly over the path-worn pasture.

'They're late, milking, tonight,' said Mrs Flint severely. 'They know Luke won't be back till after dark.'

They came to the fence, beyond which the young fir-wood bristled dense. There was a little gate, but it was locked. In the grass on the inside stood a bottle, empty.

'There's the keeper's empty bottle for his milk,' explained Mrs Flint. 'We bring it as far as here for him, and then he fetches it himself.'

'When?' said Connie.

'Oh, any time he's around. Often in the morning. Well, goodbye Lady Chatterley! And do come again. It was so lovely having you.'

Connie climbed the fence into the narrow path between the dense, bristling young firs. Mrs Flint went running back across the pasture, in a sun-bonnet, because she was really a schoolteacher. Constance didn't like this dense new part of the wood; it seemed gruesome and choking. She hurried on with her head down, thinking of the Flints' baby. It was a dear little thing, but it would be a bit bow-legged like its father. It showed already, but perhaps it would grow out of it. How warm and fulfilling somehow to have a baby, and how Mrs Flint had showed it off! She had something anyhow that Connie hadn't got, and apparently couldn't have. Yes, Mrs Flint had flaunted her motherhood. And Connie had been just a bit, just a little bit jealous. She couldn't help it.

She started out of her muse, and gave a little cry of fear. A man was there.

It was the keeper. He stood in the path like Balaam's ass, barring her way.

'How's this?' he said in surprise.

'How did you come?' she panted.

'How did you? Have you been to the hut?'

'No! No! I went to Marehay.'

He looked at her curiously, searchingly, and she hung her head a little guiltily.

'And were you going to the hut now?' he asked rather sternly.

'No! I mustn't. I stayed at Marehay. No one knows where I am. I'm late. I've got to run.'

'Giving me the slip, like?' he said, with a faint ironic smile.

'No! No. Not that. Only –'

'Why, what else?' he said. And he stepped up to her, and put his arms around her. She felt the front of his body terribly near to her, and alive.

'Oh, not now, not now,' she cried, trying to push him away.

'Why not? It's only six o'clock. You've got half an hour. Nay! Nay! I want you.'

He held her fast and she felt his urgency. Her old instinct was to fight for her freedom. But something else in her was strange and inert and heavy. His body was urgent against her, and she hadn't the heart any more to fight.

He looked around.

'Come – come here! Through here,' he said, looking penetratingly into the dense fir trees, that were young and not more than half-grown.

He looked back at her. She saw his eyes, tense and brilliant, fierce, not loving. But her will had left her. A strange weight was on her limbs. She was giving way. She was giving up.

He led her through the wall of prickly trees, that were difficult to come through, to a place where was a little space and a pile of dead boughs. He threw one or two dry ones down, put his coat and waistcoat over them, and she had to lie down there under the boughs of the tree, like an animal, while he waited, standing there in his shirt and breeches, watching her with haunted eyes. But still he was provident – he made her lie properly, properly. Yet he broke the band of her underclothes, for she did not help him, only lay inert.

He too had bared the front part of his body and she felt his naked flesh against her as he came into her. For a moment he was still inside her, turgid there and quivering. Then as he began to move, in the sudden helpless orgasm, there awoke in her new strange thrills rippling inside her. Rippling, rippling, rippling, like a flapping overlapping of soft flames, soft as feathers, running to points of brilliance, exquisite, exquisite and melting her all molten inside. It was like bells rippling up and up to a culmination. She lay unconscious of the wild little cries she uttered at the last. But it was over too soon, too soon, and she could no longer force her own conclusion with her own activity. This was different, different. She could do nothing. She could no longer harden and grip for her own satisfaction upon him. She could only wait, wait and moan in spirit as she felt him withdrawing, withdrawing and contracting, coming to the terrible moment when he would slip out of her and be gone. Whilst all her womb was open and soft, and softly clamouring, like a sea-anemone under the tide, clamouring for him to come in again and make a fulfilment for her. She clung to him unconscious in passion, and he never quite slipped from her, and she felt the soft bud of him within her stirring, and strange rhythms flushing up into her with a strange rhythmic growing motion, swelling and swelling till it filled all her cleaving consciousness, and then began again the unspeakable motion that was not really motion, but pure deepening whirlpools of sensation swirling deeper and deeper through all her tissue and consciousness, till she was one perfect concentric fluid of feeling, and she lay there crying in unconscious inarticulate cries. The voice out of the uttermost night, the life! The man heard it beneath him with a kind of awe, as his life sprang out into her. And as it subsided, he subsided too and lay utterly still, unknowing, while her grip on him slowly relaxed, and she lay inert. And they lay and knew nothing, not even of each other, both lost. Till at last he began to rouse and become aware of his defenceless nakedness, and she was aware that his body was loosening its clasp on her. He was coming apart; but in her breast she felt she could not bear him to leave her uncovered. He must cover her now for ever.

But he drew away at last, and kissed her and covered her over, and began to cover himself. She lay looking up to the boughs of the tree, unable as yet to move. He stood and fastened up his breeches, looking round. All was dense and silent, save for the awed dog that lay with its paws against its nose. He sat down again on the brushwood and took Connie's hand in silence.

She turned and looked at him. 'We came off together that time,' he said.

She did not answer.

'It's good when it's like that. Most folks live their lives through and they never know it,' he said, speaking rather dreamily.

She looked into his brooding face.

'Do they?' she said. 'Are you glad?'

He looked back into her eyes. 'Glad,' he said. 'Ay, but never mind.' He did not want her to talk. And he bent over her and kissed her, and she felt, so he must kiss her for ever.

At last she sat up.

'Don't people often come off together?' she asked with naïve curiosity.

'A good many of them never. You can see by the raw look of them.' He spoke unwittingly, regretting he had begun.

'Have you come off like that with other women?'

He looked at her amused.

'I don't know,' he said, 'I don't know.'

And she knew he would never tell her anything he didn't want to tell her. She watched his face, and the passion for him moved in her bowels. She resisted it as far as she could, for it was the loss of herself to herself.

He put on his waistcoat and his coat, and pushed a way through to the path again.

The last level rays of the sun touched the wood. 'I won't come with you,' he said; 'better not.'

She looked at him wistfully before she turned. His dog was waiting so anxiously for him to go, and he seemed to have nothing whatever to say. Nothing left.

Connie went slowly home, realising the depth of the other thing in her. Another self was alive in her, burning molten and soft in her womb and bowels, and with this self she adored him. She adored him till her knees were weak as she walked. In her womb and bowels she was flowing and alive now and vulnerable, and helpless in adoration of him as the most naïve woman. It feels like a child, she said to herself; it feels like a child in me. And so it did, as if her womb, that had always been shut, had opened and filled with new life, almost a burden, yet lovely.

'If I had a child!' she thought to herself; 'if I had him inside me as a child!' – and her limbs turned molten at the thought, and she realised the immense difference between having a child to oneself, and having a child to a man whom one's bowels yearned towards. The former seemed in a sense ordinary; but to have a child to a man whom one adored in one's bowels and one's womb, it made her feel she was very different from her old self, and as if she was sinking deep, deep to the centre of all womanhood and the sleep of creation.

It was not the passion that was new to her, it was the yearning adoration. She knew she had always feared it, for it left her helpless; she feared it still, lest if she adored him too much, then she would lose herself, become effaced, and she did not want to be effaced, a slave, like a savage woman. She must not become a slave. She feared her adoration, yet she would not at once fight against it. She knew she could fight it. She had a devil of self-will in her breast that could have fought the full soft heaving adoration of her womb and crushed it. She could even now do it, or she thought so, and she could then take up her passion with her own will.

Ah yes, to be passionate like a Bacchante, like a Bacchanal fleeing through the woods, to call on Iacchos, the bright phallos that had no independent personality behind it, but was pure god-servant to the woman! The man, the individual, let him not dare intrude. He was but a temple-servant, the bearer and keeper of the bright phallos, her own.

So, in the flux of new awakening, the old hard passion flamed in her for a time, and the man dwindled to a contemptible object, the mere phallos-bearer, to be torn to pieces when his service was performed. She felt the force of the Bacchae in her limbs and her body, the woman gleaming and rapid, beating down the male; but while she felt this, her heart was heavy. She did not want it, it was known and barren, birthless; the adoration was her treasure. It was so fathomless, so soft, so deep and so unknown. No, no, she would give up her hard bright female power; she was weary of it, stiffened with it; she would sink in the new bath of life, in the depths of her womb and her bowels that sang the voiceless song of adoration. It was early yet to begin to fear the man.

'I walked over by Marehay, and I had tea with Mrs Flint,' she said to Clifford. 'I wanted to see the baby. It's so adorable, with hair like red cobwebs. Such a dear! Mr Flint had gone to market, so she and I and the baby had tea together. Did you wonder where I was?'

'Well, I wondered, but I guessed you had dropped in somewhere to tea,' said Clifford jealously. With a sort of second sight he sensed something new in her, something to him quite incomprehensible, but he ascribed it to the baby. He thought that all that ailed Connie was that she did not have a baby, automatically bring one forth, so to speak.

'I saw you go across the park to the iron gate, my Lady,' said Mrs Bolton; 'so I thought perhaps you'd called at the Rectory.'

'I nearly did, then I turned towards Marehay instead.'

The eyes of the two women met: Mrs Bolton's grey and bright and searching; Connie's blue and veiled and strangely beautiful. Mrs Bolton was almost sure she had a lover, yet how could it be, and who could it be? Where was there a man?

'Oh, it's so good for you, if you go out and see a bit of company sometimes,' said Mrs Bolton. 'I was saying to Sir Clifford, it would do her Ladyship a world of good if she'd go out among people more.'

'Yes, I'm glad I went, and such a quaint dear cheeky baby, Clifford,' said Connie. 'It's got hair just like spider-webs, and bright orange, and the oddest, cheekiest, pale-blue china eyes. Of course it's a girl, or it wouldn't be so bold, bolder than any little Sir Francis Drake.'

'You're right, my Lady – a regular little Flint. They were always a forward sandy-headed family,' said Mrs Bolton.

'Wouldn't you like to see it, Clifford? I've asked them to tea for you to see it.'

'Who?' he asked, looking at Connie in great uneasiness.

'Mrs Flint and the baby, next Monday.'

'You can have them to tea up in your room,' he said.

'Why, don't you want to see the baby?' she cried.

'Oh, I'll see it, but I don't want to sit through a tea-time with them.'

'Oh,' said Connie, looking at him with wide veiled eyes.

She did not really see him, he was somebody else.

'You can have a nice cosy tea up in your room, my Lady, and Mrs Flint will be more comfortable than if Sir Clifford was there,' said Mrs Bolton.

She was sure Connie had a lover, and something in her soul exulted. But who was he? Who was he? Perhaps Mrs Flint would provide a clue.

Connie would not take her bath this evening. The sense of his flesh touching her, his very stickiness upon her, was dear to her, and in a sense holy.

Clifford was very uneasy. He would not let her go after dinner, and she had wanted so much to be alone. She looked at him, but was curiously submissive.

'Shall we play a game, or shall I read to you, or what shall it be?' he asked uneasily.

'You read to me,' said Connie.

'What shall I read – verse or prose? Or drama?'

'Read Racine,' she said.

It had been one of his stunts in the past, to read Racine in the real French grand manner, but he was rusty now, and a little self-conscious; he really preferred the loudspeaker. But Connie was sewing, sewing a little silk frock of primrose silk, cut out of one of her dresses, for Mrs Flint's baby. Between coming home and dinner she had cut it out, and she sat in the soft quiescent rapture of herself, sewing, while the noise of the reading went on.

Inside herself she could feel the humming of passion, like the after-humming of deep bells.

Clifford said something to her about the Racine. She caught the sense after the words had gone.

'Yes! Yes!' she said, looking up at him. 'It *is* splendid.'

Again he was frightened at the deep blue blaze of her eyes, and of her soft stillness, sitting there. She had never been so utterly soft and still. She fascinated him helplessly, as if some perfume about her intoxicated him. So he went on helplessly with his reading, and the throaty sound of the French was like the wind in the chimneys to her. Of the Racine she heard not one syllable.

She was gone in her own soft rapture, like a forest soughing with the dim, glad moan of spring, moving into bud. She could feel in the same world with her the man, the nameless man, moving on beautiful feet, beautiful in the phallic mystery. And in herself, in all her veins, she felt him and his child. His child was in all her veins, like a twilight.

'For hands she hath none, nor eyes, nor feet, nor golden Treasure of hair . . .'

She was like a forest, like the dark interlacing of the oak-wood, humming inaudibly with myriad unfolding buds. Meanwhile the birds of desire were asleep in the vast interlaced intricacy of her body.

But Clifford's voice went on, clapping and gurgling with unusual sounds. How extraordinary it was! How extraordinary he was, bent there over the book, queer and rapacious and civilised, with broad shoulders and no real legs! What a strange creature, with the sharp, cold inflexible will of some bird, and no warmth, no warmth at all! One of those creatures of the afterwards, that have no soul, but an extra-alert will, cold will. She shuddered a little, afraid of him. But then, the soft warm flame of life was stronger than he, and the real things were hidden from him.

The reading finished. She was startled. She looked up, and was more startled still to see Clifford watching her with pale, uncanny eyes, like hate.

'Thank you so much! You do read Racine beautifully!' she said softly.

'Almost as beautifully as you listen to him,' he said cruelly

'What are you making?' he asked.

'I'm making a child's dress, for Mrs Flint's baby.'

He turned away. A child! A child! That was all her obsession.

'After all,' he said, in a declamatory voice, 'one gets all one wants out of Racine. Emotions that are ordered and given shape are more important than disorderly emotions.'

She watched him with wide, vague, veiled eyes.

'Yes, I'm sure they are,' she said.

'The modern world has only vulgarised emotion by letting it loose. What we need is classic control.'

'Yes,' she said slowly, thinking of him listening with vacant face to the emotional idiocy of the radio. 'People pretend to have emotions, and they really feel nothing. I suppose that is being romantic.'

'Exactly!' he said.

As a matter of fact, he was tired. This evening had tired him. He would rather have been with his technical books, or his pit-manager, or listening-in to the radio.

Mrs Bolton came in with two glasses of malted milk: for Clifford, to make him sleep, and for Connie, to fatten her again. It was a regular nightcap she had introduced.

Connie was glad to go, when she had drunk her glass, and thankful she needn't help Clifford to bed. She took his glass and put it on the tray, then took the tray, to leave it outside.

'Good-night Clifford! *Do* sleep well! The Racine gets into one like a dream. Good-night!'

She had drifted to the door. She was going without kissing him good-night. He watched her with sharp, cold eyes. So! She did not even kiss him good-night, after he had spent an evening reading to her. Such depths of callousness in her! Even if the kiss was but a formality, it was on such formalities that life depends. She was a Bolshevik, really. Her instincts were Bolshevistic! He gazed coldly and angrily at the door whence she had gone. Anger!

And again the dread of the night came on him. He was a network of nerves, and when he was not braced up to work, and so full of energy: or when he was not listening-in, and so utterly neuter: then he was haunted by anxiety and a sense of dangerous impending void. He was afraid. And Connie could keep the fear off him, if she would. But it was obvious she wouldn't, she wouldn't. She was callous, cold and callous to all that he did for her. He gave up his life for her, and she was callous to him. She only wanted her own way. 'The lady loves her will.'

Now it was a baby she was obsessed by. Just so that it should be her own, all her own, and not his!

Clifford was so healthy, considering. He looked so well and ruddy in the face, his shoulders were broad and strong, his chest deep, he had put on flesh. And yet, at the same time, he was afraid of death. A terrible hollow seemed to menace him somewhere, somehow, a void, and into this void his energy would collapse. Energyless, he felt at times he was dead, really dead.

So his rather prominent pale eyes had a queer look, furtive, and yet a little cruel, so cold: and at the same time, almost impudent. It was a very odd look, this look of impudence: as if he were triumphing over life in spite of life. 'Who knoweth the mysteries of the will – for it can triumph even against the angels –'

But his dread was the nights when he could not sleep. Then it was awful indeed, when annihilation pressed in on him on every side. Then it was ghastly, to exist without having any life: lifeless, in the night, to exist.

But now he could ring for Mrs Bolton. And she would always come. That was a great comfort. She would come in her dressing-gown, with her hair in a plait down her back, curiously girlish and dim, though the brown plait was streaked with grey. And she would make him coffee or camomile tea, and she would play chess or piquet with him. She had a woman's queer faculty of playing even chess well enough, when she was three parts asleep, well enough to make her worth beating. So, in the silent intimacy of the night, they sat, or she sat and he lay on the bed, with the reading-lamp shedding its solitary light on them, she almost gone in sleep, he almost gone in a sort of fear, and they played, played together – then they had a cup of coffee and a biscuit together, hardly speaking, in the silence of night, but being a reassurance to one another.

And this night she was wondering who Lady Chatterley's lover was. And she was thinking of her own Ted, so long dead, yet for her never quite dead. And when she thought of him, the old, old grudge against the world rose up, but especially against the masters, that they had killed him. They had not really killed him. Yet, to her, emotionally, they had. And somewhere deep in herself, because of it, she was a nihilist, and really anarchic.

In her half-sleep, thoughts of her Ted and thoughts of Lady Chatterley's unknown lover commingled, and then she felt she shared with the other woman a great grudge against Sir Clifford and all he stood for. At the same time she was playing piquet with him, and they were gambling sixpences. And it was a source of satisfaction to be playing piquet with a baronet, and even losing sixpences to him.

When they played cards, they always gambled. It made him forget himself. And he usually won. Tonight too he was winning. So he would not go to sleep till the first dawn appeared. Luckily it began to appear at half-past four or thereabouts.

Connie was in bed, and fast asleep all this time. But the keeper, too, could not rest. He had closed the coops and made his round of the wood, then gone home and eaten supper. But he did not go to bed. Instead he sat by the fire and thought.

He thought of his boyhood in Tevershall, and of his five or six years of married life. He thought of his wife, and always bitterly. She had seemed so brutal. But he had not seen her now since 1915, in the spring when he joined up. Yet there she was, not three miles away, and more brutal than ever. He hoped never to see her again while he lived.

He thought of his life abroad, as a soldier. India, Egypt, then India again: the blind, thoughtless life with the horses: the colonel who had loved him and whom he had loved: the several years that he had been an officer, a lieutenant with a very fair chance of being a captain. Then the death of the colonel from pneumonia, and his own narrow escape from death: his damaged health: his deep restlessness: his leaving the army and coming back to England to be a working man again.

He was temporising with life. He had thought he would be safe, at least for a time, in this wood. There was no shooting as yet: he had to rear the pheasants. He would have no guns to serve. He would be alone, and apart from life, which was all he wanted. He had to have some sort of a background. And this was his native place. There was even his mother, though she had never meant very much to him. And he could go on in life, existing from day to day, without connection and without hope. For he did not know what to do with himself.

He did not know what to do with himself. Since he had been an officer for some years, and had mixed among the other officers and civil servants, with their wives and families, he had lost all ambition to 'get on'. There was a toughness, a curious rubber-necked toughness and unlivingness about the middle and upper classes, as he had known them, which just left him feeling cold and different from them.

So, he had come back to his own class. To find there, what he had forgotten during his absence of years, a pettiness and a vulgarity of manner extremely distasteful. He admitted now at last, how important manner was. He admitted, also, how important it was even *to pretend* not to care about the halfpence and the small things of life. But among the common people there was no pretence. A penny more or less on the bacon was worse than a change in the Gospel. He could not stand it.

And again, there was the wage-squabble. Having lived among the owning classes, he knew the utter futility of expecting any solution of the wage-squabble. There was no solution, short of death. The only thing was not to care, not to care about the wages.

Yet, if you were poor and wretched you *had* to care. Anyhow, it was becoming the only thing they did care about. The *care* about money was like a great cancer, eating away the individuals of all classes. He refused to *care* about money.

And what then? What did life offer apart from the care of money? Nothing.

Yet he could live alone, in the wan satisfaction of being alone, and raise pheasants to be shot ultimately by fat men after breakfast. It was futility, futility to the *n*th power.

But why care, why bother? And he had not cared nor bothered till now, when this woman had come into his life. He was nearly ten years older than she. And he was a thousand years older in experience, starting from the bottom. The connection between them was growing closer. He could see the day when it would clinch up and they would have to make a life together. 'For the bonds of love are ill to loose!'

And what then? What then? Must he start again, with nothing to start on? Must he entangle this woman? Must he have the horrible broil with her lame husband? And also some sort of horrible broil with his own brutal wife, who hated him? Misery! lots of misery! And he was no longer young and merely buoyant. Neither was he the insouciant sort. Every bitterness and every ugliness would hurt him: and the woman!

But even if they got clear of Sir Clifford and of his own wife, even if they got clear, what were they going to do? What was he, himself, going to do? What was he going to do with his life? For he must do something. He couldn't be a mere hanger-on, on her money and his own very small pension.

It was the insoluble. He could only think of going to America, to try a new air. He disbelieved in the dollar utterly. But perhaps, perhaps there was something else.

He could not rest nor even go to bed. After sitting in a stupor of bitter thoughts until midnight, he got suddenly from his chair and reached for his coat and gun.

'Come on, lass,' he said to the dog. 'We're best outside.'

It was a starry night, but moonless. He went on a slow, scrupulous, soft-stepping and stealthy round. The only thing he had to contend with was the colliers setting snares for rabbits, particularly the Stacks Gate colliers, on the Marehay side. But it was breeding season, and even colliers respected it a little. Nevertheless the stealthy beating of the round in search of poachers soothed his nerves and took his mind off his thoughts.

But when he had done his slow, cautious beating of his bounds – it was nearly a five-mile walk – he was tired. He went to the top of the knoll and looked out There was no sound save the noise, the faint shuffling noise from Stacks Gate colliery, that never ceased working: and there were hardly any lights, save the brilliant electric rows at the works. The world lay darkly and fumily sleeping. It was half-past two. But even in its sleep it was an uneasy, cruel world, stirring with the noise of a train or some great lorry on the road, and flashing with some rosy lightning-flash from the furnaces. It was a world of iron and coal, the cruelty of iron and the smoke of coal, and the endless, endless greed that drove it all. Only greed, greed stirring in its sleep.

It was cold, and he was coughing. A fine cold draught blew over the knoll. He thought of the woman. Now he would have given all he had or ever might have to hold her warm in his arms, both of them wrapped in one blanket, and sleep. All hopes of eternity and all gain from the past he would have given to have her there, to be wrapped warm with him in one blanket, and sleep, only sleep. It seemed the sleep with the woman in his arms was the only necessity.

He went to the hut, and wrapped himself in the blanket and lay on the floor to sleep. But he could not, he was cold. And besides, he felt cruelly his own unfinished nature. He felt his own unfinished condition of aloneness cruelly. He wanted her, to touch her, to hold her fast against him in one moment of completeness and sleep.

He got up again and went out, towards the park gates this time: then slowly along the path towards the house. It was nearly four o'clock, still clear and cold, but no sign of dawn. He was used to the dark, he could see well.

Slowly, slowly the great house drew him, as a magnet. He wanted to be near her. It was not desire, not that. It was the cruel sense of unfinished aloneness, that needed a silent woman folded in his arms. Perhaps he could find her. Perhaps he could even call her out to him: or find some way in to her. For the need was imperious.

He slowly, silently climbed the incline to the hall. Then he came round the great trees at the top of the knoll, on to the drive, which made a grand sweep round a lozenge of grass in front of the entrance. He could already see the two magnificent beeches which stood in this big level lozenge in front of the house, detaching themselves darkly in the dark air.

There was the house, low and long and obscure, with one light burning downstairs, in Sir Clifford's room. But which room she was in, the woman who held the other end of the frail thread which drew him so mercilessly, that he did not know.

He went a little nearer, gun in hand, and stood motionless on the drive, watching the house. Perhaps even now he could find her, come at her in some way. The house was not impregnable: he was as clever as burglars are. Why not come to her?

He stood motionless, waiting, while the dawn faintly and imperceptibly paled behind him. He saw the light in the house go out. But he did not see Mrs Bolton come to the window and draw back the old curtain of dark blue silk, and stand herself in the dark room, looking out on the half-dark of the approaching day, looking for the longed-for dawn, waiting, waiting for Clifford to be really reassured that it was daybreak. For when he was sure of daybreak, he would sleep almost at once.

She stood blind with sleep at the window, waiting. And as she stood, she started, and almost cried out. For there was a man out there on the drive, a black figure in the twilight. She woke up greyly, and watched, but without making a sound to disturb Sir Clifford.

The daylight began to rustle into the world, and the dark figure seemed to go smaller and more defined. She made out the gun and gaiters and baggy jacket – it would be Oliver Mellors, the keeper. Yes, for there was the dog nosing around like a shadow, and waiting for him!

And what did the man want? Did he want to rouse the house? What was he standing there for, transfixed, looking up at the house like a lovesick male dog outside the house where the bitch is?

Goodness! The knowledge went through Mrs Bolton like a shot. He was Lady Chatterley's lover! He! He!

To think of it! Why, she, Ivy Bolton, had once been a tiny bit in love with him herself! When he was a lad of sixteen and she a woman of twenty-six. It was when she was studying, and he had helped her a lot with the anatomy and things she had had to learn. He'd been a clever boy, had a scholarship for Sheffield Grammar School, and learned French and things: and then after all had become an overhead blacksmith shoeing horses, because he was fond of horses, he said: but really because he was frightened to go out and face the world, only he'd never admit it.

But he'd been a nice lad, a nice lad, had helped her a lot, so clever at making things clear to you. He was quite as clever as Sir Clifford, and always one for the women. More with women than men, they said.

Till he'd gone and married that Bertha Coutts, as if to spite himself. Some people do marry to spite themselves, because they're disappointed of something. And no wonder it had been a failure. For years he was gone, all the time of the war: and a lieutenant and all: quite the gentleman, really quite the gentleman! Then to come back to Tevershall and go as a gamekeeper! Really, some people can't take their chances when they've got them! And talking broad Derbyshire again like the worst, when she, Ivy Bolton, knew he spoke like any gentleman, *really*.

Well, well! So her Ladyship had fallen for him! Well – her Ladyship wasn't the first: there was something about him. But fancy! A Tevershall lad born and bred, and she her Ladyship in Wragby Hall! My word, that was a slap back at the high-and-mighty Chatterleys!

But he, the keeper, as the day grew, had realised: it's no good! It's no good trying to get rid of your own aloneness. You've got to stick to it all your life. Only at times, at times, the gap will be filled in. At times! But you have to wait for the times. Accept your own aloneness and stick to it, all your life. And then accept the times when the gap is filled in, when they come. But they've got to come. You can't force them.

With a sudden snap the bleeding desire that had drawn him after her broke. He had broken it, because it must be so. There must be a coming together on both sides. And if she wasn't coming to him, he wouldn't track her down. He mustn't. He must go away, till she came.

He turned slowly, ponderingly, accepting again the isolation. He knew it was better so. She must come to him: it was no use his trailing after her. No use!

Mrs Bolton saw him disappear, saw his dog run after him.

'Well, well!' she said. 'He's the one man I never thought of; and the one man I might have thought of. He was nice to me when he was a lad, after I lost Ted. Well, well! Whatever would *he* say if he knew!'

And she glanced triumphantly at the already sleeping Clifford, as she stepped softly from the room.

Chapter 11

Connie was sorting out one of the Wragby lumber rooms. There were several: the house was a warren, and the family never sold anything. Sir Geoffrey's father had liked pictures and Sir Geoffrey's mother had liked *cinquecento* furniture. Sir Geoffrey himself had liked old carved oak chests, vestry chests. So it went on through the generations. Clifford collected very modern pictures, at very moderate prices.

So in the lumber room there were bad Sir Edwin Land-seers and pathetic William Henry Hunt birds' nests: and other Academy stuff, enough to frighten the daughter of an R.A. She determined to look through it one day, and clear it all. And the grotesque furniture interested her.

Wrapped up carefully to preserve it from damage and dry-rot was the old family cradle, of rosewood. She had to unwrap it, to look at it. It had a certain charm: she looked at it a long time.

'It's a thousand pities it won't be called for,' sighed Mrs Bolton, who was helping. 'Though cradles like that are out of date nowadays.'

'It might be called for. I might have a child,' said Connie casually, as if saying she might have a new hat.

'You mean if anything happened to Sir Clifford!' stammered Mrs Bolton.

'No! I mean as things are. It's only muscular paralysis with Sir Clifford – it doesn't affect *him*,' said Connie, lying as naturally as breathing.

Clifford had put the idea into her head. He had said: 'Of course I may have a child yet. I'm not really mutilated at all. The potency may easily come back, even if the muscles of the hips and legs are paralysed. And then the seed may be transferred.'

He really felt, when he had his periods of energy and worked so hard at the question of the mines, as if his sexual potency were returning. Connie had looked at him in terror. But she was quite quick-witted enough to use his suggestion for her own preservation. For she would have a child if she could: but not his.

Mrs Bolton was for a moment breathless, flabbergasted. Then she didn't believe it: she saw in it a ruse. Yet doctors could do such things nowadays. They might sort of graft seed.

'Well, my Lady, I only hope and pray you may. It would be lovely for you: and for everybody. My word, a child in Wragby, what a difference it would make!'

'Wouldn't it!' said Connie.

And she chose three R.A. pictures of sixty years ago, to send to the Duchess of Shortlands for that lady's next charitable bazaar. She was called 'the bazaar duchess', and she always asked all the county to send things for her to sell. She would be delighted with three framed R.A.s. She might even call, on the strength of them. How furious Clifford was when she called!

But oh my dear! Mrs Bolton was thinking to herself. Is it Oliver Mellors's child you're preparing us for? Oh my dear, that *would* be a Tevershall baby in the Wragby cradle, my word! Wouldn't shame it, neither!

Among other monstrosities in this lumber room was a largeish black japanned box, excellently and ingeniously made some sixty or seventy years ago, and fitted with every imaginable object. On top was a concentrated toilet set: brushes, bottles, mirrors, combs, boxes, even three beautiful little razors in safety sheaths, shaving-bowl and all. Underneath came a sort of escritoire outfit: blotters, pens, ink-bottles, paper, envelopes, memorandum books: and then a perfect sewing-outfit, with three different-sized scissors, thimbles, needles, silks and cottons, darning egg, all of the very best quality and perfectly finished. Then there was a little medicine store, with bottles labelled Laudanum, Tincture of Myrrh, Ess. Cloves and so on: but empty. Everything was perfectly new, and the whole thing, when shut up, was as big as a small, but fat weekend bag. And inside, it fitted together like a puzzle. The bottles could not possibly have spilled: there wasn't room.

The thing was wonderfully made and contrived, excellent craftsmanship of the Victorian order. But somehow it was monstrous. Some Chatterley must even have felt it, for the thing had never been used. It had a peculiar soullessness.

Yet Mrs Bolton was thrilled.

'Look what beautiful brushes, so expensive, even the shaving brushes, three perfect ones! No! and those scissors! They're the best that money could buy. Oh, I call it lovely!'

'Do you?' said Connie. 'Then you have it.'

'Oh no, my Lady!'

'Of course! It will only lie here till Doomsday. If you won't have it, I'll send it to the Duchess as well as the pictures, and she doesn't deserve so much. Do have it!'

'Oh your Ladyship! Why, I shall never be able to thank you.'

'You needn't try,' laughed Connie

And Mrs Bolton sailed down with the huge and very black box in her arms, flushing bright pink in her excitement.

Mr Betts drove her in the trap to her house in the village, with the box. And she *had* to have a few friends in, to show it: the schoolmistress, the chemist's wife, Mrs Weedon the under-cashier's wife. They thought it marvellous. And then started the whisper of Lady Chatterley's child.

'Wonders'll never cease!' said Mrs Weedon.

But Mrs Bolton was *convinced*, if it did come, it would be Sir Clifford's child. So there!

Not long after, the rector said gently to Clifford, 'And may we really hope for an heir to Wragby? Ah, that would be the hand of God in mercy, indeed!'

'Well! We may *hope*,' said Clifford, with a faint irony, and at the same time, a certain conviction. He had begun to believe it really possible it might even be *his* child.

Then one afternoon came Leslie Winter, Squire Winter, as everybody called him: lean, immaculate, and seventy: and every inch a gentleman, as Mrs Bolton said to Mrs Betts. Every millimetre indeed! And with his old-fashioned, rather haw-haw! manner of speaking, he seemed more out of date than bag wigs. Time, in her flight, drops these fine old feathers.

They discussed the collieries. Clifford's idea was, that his coal, even the poor sort, could be made into hard concentrated fuel that would burn at great heat if fed with certain damp, acidulated air at a fairly strong pressure. It had long been observed that in a particularly strong, wet wind the pit-bank burned very vivid, gave off hardly any fumes, and left a fine powder of ash, instead of the slow pink gravel.

'But where will you find the proper engines for burning your fuel?' asked Winter.

'I'll make them myself. And I'll use my fuel myself. And I'll sell electric power. I'm certain I could do it.'

'If you can do it, then splendid, splendid, my dear boy. Haw! Splendid! If I can be of any help, I shall be delighted. I'm afraid I am a little out of date, and my collieries are like me. But who knows, when I'm gone, there may be men like you. Splendid! It will employ all the men again, and you won't have to sell your coal, or fail to sell it. A splendid idea, and I hope it will be a success. If I had sons of my own, no doubt they would have up-to-date ideas for Shipley: no doubt! By the way, dear boy, is there any foundation to the rumour that we may entertain hopes of an heir to Wragby?'

'Is there a rumour?' asked Clifford.

'Well, my dear boy, Marshall from Fillingwood asked *me*, that's all I can say about a rumour. Of course I wouldn't repeat it for the world, if there were no foundation.'

'Well, Sir,' said Clifford uneasily, but with strange bright eyes. 'There is a hope. There is a hope.'

Winter came across the room and wrung Clifford's hand.

'My dear boy, my dear lad, can you believe what it means to me, to hear that! And to hear you are working in the hopes of a son: and that you may again employ every man at Tevershall. Ah, my boy! to keep up the level of the race, and to have work waiting for any man who cares to work! – '

The old man was really moved.

Next day Connie was arranging tall yellow tulips in a glass vase.

'Connie,' said Clifford, 'did you know there was a rumour that you are going to supply Wragby with a son and heir?'

Connie felt dim with terror, yet she stood quite still, touching the flowers.

'No!' she said. 'Is it a joke? Or malice?'

He paused before he answered: 'Neither, I hope. I hope it may be a prophecy.'

Connie went on with her flowers.

'I had a letter from Father this morning,' she said. 'He wants to know if I am aware he has accepted Sir Alexander Cooper's invitation for me for July and August, to the Villa Esmeralda in Venice.'

'July *and* August?' said Clifford.

'Oh, I wouldn't stay all that time. Are you sure you wouldn't come?'

'I won't travel abroad,' said Clifford promptly.

She took her flowers to the window.

'Do you mind if I go?' she said. You know it was promised, for this summer.'

'For how long would you go?'

'Perhaps three weeks.'

There was silence for a time.

'Well,' said Clifford slowly, and a little gloomily, 'I suppose I could stand it for three weeks: if I were absolutely sure you'd want to come back.'

'I should want to come back,' she said, with quiet simplicity, heavy with conviction. She was thinking of the other man.

Clifford felt her conviction, and somehow he believed her, he believed it was for him. He felt immensely relieved, joyful at once.

'In that case,' he said, 'I think it would be all right, don't you?'

'I think so,' she said.

'You'd enjoy the change?'

She looked up at him with strange blue eyes.

'I should like to see Venice again,' she said, 'and to bathe from one of the shingle islands across the lagoon. But you know I loathe the Lido! And I don't fancy I shall like Sir Alexander Cooper and Lady Cooper. But if Hilda is there, and we have a gondola of our own: yes, it will be rather lovely. I *do* wish you'd come.'

She said it sincerely. She would so love to make him happy, in those ways
'Ah, but think of me, though, at the Gare du Nord: at Calais quay!'
'But why not? I see other men carried in litter-chairs, who have been wounded in the war. Besides, we'd motor all the way.'
'We should need to take two men.'
'Oh no! We'd manage with Field. There would always be another man there.'
But Clifford shook his head.
'Not this year, dear! Not this year! Next year probably I'll try.'
She went away gloomily. Next year! What would next year bring? She herself did not really want to go to Venice: not now, now there was the other man. But she was going as a sort of discipline: and also because, if she had a child, Clifford could think she had a lover in Venice.

It was already May, and in June they were supposed to start. Always these arrangements! Always one's life arranged for one! Wheels that worked one and drove one, and over which one had no real control!

It was May, but cold and wet again. A cold wet May, good for corn and hay! Much the corn and hay matter nowadays! Connie had to go into Uthwaite, which was their little town, where the Chatterleys were still *the* Chatterleys. She went alone, Field driving her.

In spite of May and a new greenness, the country was dismal. It was rather chilly, and there was smoke on the rain, and a certain sense of exhaust vapour in the air. One just had to live from one's resistance. No wonder these people were ugly and tough.

The car ploughed uphill through the long squalid straggle of Tevershall, the blackened brick dwellings, the black slate roofs glistening their sharp edges, the mud black with coal-dust, the pavements wet and black. It was as if dismalness had soaked through and through everything. The utter negation of natural beauty, the utter negation of the gladness of life, the utter absence of the instinct for shapely beauty which every bird and beast has, the utter death of the human intuitive faculty was appalling. The stacks of soap in the grocers' shops, the rhubarb and lemons in the greengrocers! the awful hats in the milliners! all went by ugly, ugly, ugly, followed by the plaster-and-gilt horror of the cinema with its wet picture announcements, 'A Woman's Love!', and the new big Primitive chapel, primitive enough in its stark brick and big panes of greenish and raspberry glass in the windows. The Wesleyan chapel, higher up, was of blackened brick and stood behind iron railings and blackened shrubs. The Congregational chapel, which thought itself superior, was built of rusticated sandstone and had a steeple, but not a very high one. Just beyond were the new school buildings, expensive pink brick, and gravelled playground inside iron railings, all very imposing, and mixing the suggestion of a chapel and a prison. Standard Five girls were having a singing lesson, just finishing the la-me-doh-la exercises and beginning a 'sweet children's song'. Anything more unlike song, spontaneous song, would be impossible to imagine: a strange bawling yell that followed the outlines of a tune. It was not like savages: savages have subtle rhythms. It was not like animals: animals *mean* something when they yell. It was like nothing on earth, and it was called singing. Connie sat and listened with her heart in her boots, as Field was filling petrol. What could possibly become of such a people, a people in whom the living intuitive faculty was dead as nails, and only queer mechanical yells and uncanny will-power remained?

A coal-cart was coming downhill, clanking in the rain. Field started upwards, past the big but weary-looking drapers and clothing shops, the post-office, into the little market-place of forlorn space, where Sam Black was peering out of the door of the Sun, that called itself an inn, not a pub, and where the commercial travellers stayed, and was bowing to Lady Chatterley's car.

The church was away to the left among black trees. The car slid on downhill, past the Miners' Arms. It had already passed the Wellington, the Nelson, the Three Tunns and the Sun, now it passed the Miners' Arms, then the Mechanics' Hall, then the new and almost gaudy Miners' Welfare and so, past a few new 'villas', out into the blackened road between dark hedges and dark green fields, towards Stacks Gate.

Tevershall! That was Tevershall! Merrie England! Shakespeare's England! No, but the England of today, as Connie had realised since she had come to live in it. It was producing a new race of mankind, over-conscious in the money and social and political side, on the spontaneous, intuitive side dead, but dead. Half-corpses, all of them: but with a terrible insistent consciousness in the other half. There was something uncanny and underground about it all. It was an under-world. And quite incalculable. How shall we understand the reactions in half-corpses? When Connie saw the great lorries full of steel-workers from Sheffield, weird, distorted smallish beings like men, off for an excursion to Matlock, her bowels fainted and she thought: Ah God, what has man done to man? What have the leaders of men been doing to their fellow men? They have reduced them to less than humanness; and now there can be no fellowship any more! It is just a nightmare.

She felt again in a wave of terror the grey, gritty hopelessness of it all. With such creatures for the industrial masses, and the upper classes as she knew them, there was no hope, no hope any more. Yet she was wanting a baby, and an heir to Wragby! An heir to Wragby! She shuddered with dread.

Yet Mellors had come out of all this! Yes, but he was as apart from it all as she was. Even in him there was no fellowship left. It was dead. The fellowship was dead. There was only apartness and hopelessness, as far as all this was concerned. And this was England, the vast bulk of England: as Connie knew, since she had motored from the centre of it.

The car was rising towards Stacks Gate. The rain was holding off, and in the air came a queer pellucid gleam of May. The country rolled away in long undulations, south towards the Peak, east towards Mansfield and Nottingham. Connie was travelling South.

As she rose on to the high country, she could see on her left, on a height above the rolling land, the shadowy, powerful bulk of Warsop Castle, dark grey, with below it the reddish plastering of miners' dwellings, newish, and below those the plumes of dark smoke and white steam from the great colliery which put so many thousand pounds per annum into the pockets of the Duke and the other shareholders. The powerful old castle was a ruin, yet still it hung its bulk on the low skyline, over the black plumes and the white that waved on the damp air below.

A turn, and they ran on the high level to Stacks Gate. Stacks Gate, as seen from the high road, was just a huge and gorgeous new hotel, the Coningsby Arms, standing red and white and gilt in barbarous isolation off the road. But if you looked, you saw on the left rows of handsome 'modern' dwellings, set down like a game of dominoes, with spaces and gardens, a queer game of dominoes that some weird 'masters' were playing on the surprised earth. And beyond these blocks of dwellings, at the back, rose all the astonishing and frightening overhead erections of a really modern mine, chemical works and long galleries, enormous, and of shapes not before known to man. The head-stocks and pit-bank of the mine itself were insignificant among the huge new installations. And in front of this, the game of dominoes stood forever in a sort of surprise, waiting to be played.

This was Stacks Gate, new on the face of the earth, since the war. But as a matter of fact, though even Connie did not know it, downhill half a mile below the 'hotel' was old Stacks Gate, with a little old colliery and blackish old brick dwellings, and a chapel or two and a shop or two and a little pub or two.

But that didn't count any more. The vast plumes of smoke and vapour rose from the new works up above, and this was now Stacks Gate: no chapels, no pubs, even no shops. Only the great 'works', which are the modern Olympia with temples to all the gods; then the model dwellings: then the hotel. The hotel in actuality was nothing but a miners' pub, though it looked first-classy.

Even since Connie's arrival at Wragby this new place had arisen on the face of the earth, and the model dwellings had filled with riff-raff drifting in from anywhere, to poach Clifford's rabbits among other occupations.

The car ran on along the uplands, seeing the rolling county spread out. The county! It had once been a proud and lordly county. In front, looming again and hanging on the brow of the skyline, was the huge and splendid bulk of Chadwick Hall, more window than wall, one of the most famous Elizabethan houses. Noble it stood alone above a great park, but out of date, passed over. It was still kept up, but as a show place. 'Look how our ancestors lorded it!'

That was the past. The present lay below. God alone knows where the future lies. The car was already turning, between little old blackened miners' cottages, to descend to Uthwaite. And Uthwaite, on a damp day, was sending up a whole array of smoke plumes and steam, to whatever gods there be. Uthwaite down in the valley, with all the steel threads of the railways to Sheffield drawn through it, and the coal-mines and the steel-works sending up smoke and glare from long tubes, and the pathetic little corkscrew spire of the church, that is going to tumble down, still pricking the fumes, always affected Connie strangely. It was an old market-town, centre of the dales. One of the chief inns was the Chatterley Arms. There, in Uthwaite, Wragby was known as Wragby, as if it were a whole place, not just a house, as it was to outsiders: Wragby Hall, near Tevershall: Wragby, a 'seat'.

The miners' cottages, blackened, stood flush on the pavement, with that intimacy and smallness of colliers' dwellings over a hundred years old. They lined all the way. The road had become a street, and as you sank, you forgot instantly the open, rolling country where the castles and big houses still dominated, but like ghosts. Now you were just above the tangle of naked railway-lines, and foundries and other 'works' rose about you, so big you were only aware of walls. And iron clanked with a huge reverberating clank, and huge lorries shook the earth, and whistles screamed.

Yet again, once you had got right down and into the twisted and crooked heart of the town, behind the church, you were in the world of two centuries ago, in the crooked streets where the Chatterley Arms stood, and the old pharmacy, streets which used to lead out to the wild open world of the castles and stately couchant houses.

But at the corner a policeman held up his hand as three lorries loaded with iron rolled past, shaking the poor old church. And not till the lorries were past could he salute her Ladyship.

So it was. Upon the old crooked burgess streets hordes of oldish, blackened miners' dwellings crowded, lining the roads out. And immediately after these came the newer, pinker rows of rather larger houses, plastering the valley: the homes of more modern workmen. And beyond that again, in the wide rolling regions of the castles, smoke waved against steam, and patch after patch of raw reddish brick showed the newer mining settlements, sometimes in the hollows, sometimes gruesomely ugly along the skyline of the slopes. And between, in between, were the tattered remnants of the old coaching and cottage England, even the England of Robin Hood, where the miners prowled with the dis- malness of suppressed sporting instincts, when they were not at work.

England my England! But which is *my* England? The stately homes of England make good photographs, and create the illusion of a connection with the Elizabethans. The handsome old halls are there, from the days of Good Queen Anne and Tom Jones. But smuts fall and blacken on the drab stucco, that has long ceased to be golden. And one by one, like the stately homes, they were abandoned. Now they are being pulled down. As for the cottages of England – there they are – great plasterings of brick dwellings on the hopeless countryside.

Now they are pulling down the stately homes, the Georgian halls are going. Fritchley, a perfect old Georgian mansion, was even now, as Connie passed in the car, being demolished. It was in perfect repair: till the war the Weatherleys had lived in style there. But now it was too big, too expensive, and the country had become too uncongenial. The gentry were departing to pleasanter places, where they could spend their money without having to see how it was made.

This is history. One England blots out another. The mines had made the halls wealthy. Now they were blotting them out, as they had already blotted out the cottages. The industrial England blots out the agricultural England. One meaning blots out another. The new England blots out the old England. And the continuity is not organic, but mechanical.

Connie, belonging to the leisured classes, had clung to the remnants of the old England. It had taken her years to realise that it was really blotted out by this terrifying new and gruesome England, and that the blotting out would go on till it was complete. Fritchley was gone, Eastwood was gone, Shipley was going: Squire Winter's beloved Shipley.

Connie called for a moment at Shipley. The park gates, at the back, opened just near the level crossing of the colliery railway; the Shipley colliery itself stood just beyond the trees. The gates stood open, because through the park was a right-of-way that the colliers used. They hung around the park.

The car passed the ornamental ponds, in which the colliers threw their newspapers, and took the private drive to the house. It stood above, aside, a very pleasant stucco building from the middle of the eighteenth century. It had a beautiful alley of yew trees, that had approached an older house, and the hall stood serenely spread out, winking its Georgian panes as if cheerfully. Behind, there were really beautiful gardens.

Connie liked the interior much better than Wragby. It was much lighter, more alive, chapen and elegant. The rooms were panelled with creamy-painted panelling, the ceilings were touched with gilt, and everything was kept in exquisite order, all the appointments were perfect, regardless of expense. Even the corridors managed to be ample and lovely, softly curved and full of life.

But Leslie Winter was alone. He had adored his house. But his park was bordered by three of his own collieries. He had been a generous man in his ideas. He had almost welcomed the colliers in his park. Had the miners not made him rich! So, when he saw the gangs of unshapely men lounging by his ornamental waters – not on the *private* part of the park, no, he drew the line there – he would say: 'The miners are perhaps not so ornamental as deer, but they are far more profitable.'

But that was in the golden – monetarily – latter half of Queen Victoria's reign. Miners were then 'good working men'.

Winter had made this speech, half apologetic, to his guest, the then Prince of Wales. And the Prince had replied, in his rather guttural English, 'You are quite right. If there were coal under Sandringham, I would open a mine on the lawns, and think it first-rate landscape gardening. Oh, I am quite willing to exchange roe-deer for colliers, at the price. Your men are good men too, I hear.'

But then, the Prince had perhaps an exaggerated idea of the beauty of money, and the blessings of industrialism.

However, the Prince had been a King, and the King had died, and now there was another King, whose chief function seemed to be to open soup-kitchens.

And the good working men were somehow hemming Shipley in. New

824 SELECTED WORKS OF D. H. LAWRENCE

mining villages crowded on the park, and the squire felt somehow that the population was alien. He used to feel, in a good-natured but quite grand way, lord of his own domain and of his own colliers. Now, by a subtle pervasion of the new spirit, he had somehow been pushed out. It was he who did not belong any more. There was no mistaking it. The mines, the industry, had a will of its own, and this will was against the gentleman-owner. All the colliers took part in the will, and it was hard to live up against it. It either shoved you out of the place, or out of life altogether.

Squire Winter, a soldier, had stood it out. But he no longer cared to walk in the park after dinner. He almost hid, indoors. Once he had walked, bareheaded, and in his patent-leather shoes and purple silk socks, with Connie down to the gate, talking to her in his well-bred rather haw-haw fashion. But when it came to passing the little gangs of colliers who stood and stared without either salute or anything else, Connie felt how the lean, well-bred old man winced, winced as an elegant antelope stag in a cage winces from the vulgar stare. The colliers were not *personally* hostile: not at all. But their spirit was cold, and shoving him out. And deep down, there was a profound grudge. They 'worked for him'. And in their ugliness, they resented his elegant, well-groomed, well-bred existence. 'Who's he!' It was the *difference* they resented.

And somewhere, in his secret English heart, being a good deal of a soldier, he believed they were right to resent the difference. He felt himself a little in the wrong, for having all the advantages. Nevertheless he represented a system, and he would not be shoved out.

Except by death. Which came on him soon after Connie's call, suddenly. And he remembered Clifford handsomely in his will.

The heirs at once gave out the order for the demolishing of Shipley. It cost too much to keep up. No one would live there. So it was broken up. The avenue of yews was cut down. The park was denuded of its timber, and divided into lots. It was near enough to Uthwaite. In the strange, bald desert of this still-one-more no-man's-land, new little streets of semi-detacheds were run up, very desirable! The Shipley Hall Estate!

Within a year of Connie's last call, it had happened. There stood Shipley Hall Estate, an array of red-brick semi-detached 'villas' in new streets. No one would have dreamed that the stucco hall had stood there twelve months before.

But this is a later stage of King Edward's landscape gardening, the sort that has an ornamental coal-mine on the lawn.

One England blots out another. The England of the Squire Winters and the Wragby Halls was gone, dead. The blotting out was only not yet complete.

What would come after? Connie could not imagine. She could only see the new brick streets spreading into the fields, the new erections rising at the collieries, the new girls in their silk stockings, the new collier lads lounging into the Pally or the Welfare. The younger generation were utterly unconscious of the old England. There was a gap in the continuity of consciousness, almost American: but industrial really. What next?

Connie always felt there was no next. She wanted to hide her head in the sand: or at least, in the bosom of a living man.

The world was so complicated and weird and gruesome! The common people were so many, and really so terrible. So she thought as she was going home, and saw the colliers trailing from the pits, grey-black, distorted, one shoulder higher than the other, slurring their heavy ironshod boots Underground grey faces, whites of eyes rolling, necks cringing from the pit roof, shoulders out of shape. Men! Men! Alas, in some ways patient and good men. In other ways, nonexistent. Something that men *should* have was bred and killed out of them. Yet they were men. They begot children. One might bear a child to them. Terrible, terrible thought! They were good and kindly. But they were only half, only the grey half of a human being. As yet, they were 'good'. But even that was the goodness of their halfness. Supposing the dead in them ever rose up! But no, it was too terrible to think of. Connie was absolutely afraid of the industrial masses. They seemed so *weird* to her. A life with utterly no beauty in it, no intuition, always 'in the pit'.

Children from such men! Oh God, oh God!

Yet Mellors had come from such a father. Not quite. Forty years had made a difference, an appalling difference in manhood. The iron and the coal had eaten deep into the bodies and souls of the men.

Incarnate ugliness, and yet alive! What would become of them all? Perhaps with the passing of the coal they would disappear again, off the face of the earth. They had appeared out of nowhere in their thousands, when the coal had called for them. Perhaps they were only weird fauna of the coal-seams. Creatures of another reality, they were elementals, serving the elements of coal, as the metalworkers were elementals, serving the element of iron. Men not men, but animas of coal and iron and clay. Fauna of the elements, carbon, iron, silicon: elementals. They had perhaps some of the weird, inhuman beauty of minerals, the lustre of coal, the weight and blueness and resistance of iron, the transparency of glass. Elemental creatures, weird and distorted, of the mineral world! They belonged to the coal, the iron, the clay, as fish belong to the sea and worms to dead wood. The anima of mineral disintegration!

Connie was glad to be home, to bury her head in the sand. She was glad even to babble to Clifford. For her fear of the mining and iron Midlands affected her with a queer feeling that went all over her, like influenza.

'Of course I had to have tea in Miss Bentley's shop,' she said.

'Really! Winter would have given you tea.'

'Oh yes, but I daren't disappoint Miss Bentley.'

Miss Bentley was a sallow old maid with a rather large nose and romantic disposition, who served tea with a careful intensity worthy of a sacrament.

'Did she ask after me?' said Clifford.

'Of course! *May* I ask your Ladyship how Sir Clifford is! I believe she ranks you even higher than Nurse Cavell!'

'And I suppose you said I was blooming.'

'Yes! And she looked as rapt as if I had said the heavens had opened to you. I said if she ever came to Tevershall she was to come to see you.'

'Me! Whatever for! See me!'

'Why yes, Clifford. You can't be so adored without making some slight return. Saint George of Cappadocia was nothing to you, in her eyes.'

'And do you think she'll come?'

'Oh, she blushed! and looked quite beautiful for a moment, poor thing! Why don't men marry the women who would really adore them?'

'The women start adoring too late. But did she say she'd come?'

'Oh!' Connie imitated the breathless Miss Bentley, 'your Ladyship, if ever I should dare to presume!'

'Dare to presume! how absurd! But I hope to God she won't turn up. And how was her tea?'

'Oh, Lipton's and *very* strong! But Clifford, do you realise you are the *Roman de la rose* of Miss Bentley and lots like her?'

'I'm not flattered, even then.'

'They treasure up every one of your pictures in the illustrated papers, and probably pray for you every night. It's rather wonderful.'

She went upstairs to change.

That evening he said to her, 'You do think, don't you, that there is something eternal in marriage?'

She looked at him.

'But Clifford, you make eternity sound like a lid or a long, long chain that trailed after one, no matter how far one went.'

He looked at her, annoyed.

'What I mean,' he said, 'is that if you go to Venice, you won't go in the hopes of some love affair that you can take *au grand sérieux*, will you?'

'A love affair in Venice *au grand sérieux*? No, I assure you! No, I'd never take a love affair in Venice more than *au très petit sérieux*.'

She spoke with a queer kind of contempt. He knitted his brows, looking at her.

Coming downstairs in the morning, she found the keeper's dog Flossie sitting in the corridor outside Clifford's room, and whimpering very faintly.

'Why Flossie!' she said softly. 'What are you doing here?'

And she quietly opened Clifford's door. Clifford was sitting up in bed, with the bed-table and typewriter pushed aside, and the keeper was standing at attention at the foot of the bed. Flossie ran in. With a faint gesture of head and eyes, Mellors ordered her to the door again, and she slunk out.

'Oh good-morning, Clifford!' Connie said. 'I didn't know you were busy.' Then she looked at the keeper, saying good-morning to him. He murmured his reply, looking at her as if vaguely. But she felt a whiff of passion touch her, from his mere presence.

'Did I interrupt you, Clifford? I'm sorry.'

'No, it's nothing of any importance.'

She slipped out of the room again, and up to the blue boudoir on the first floor. She sat in the window, and saw him go down the drive, with his curious, silent motion, effaced. He had a natural sort of quiet distinction, an aloof pride, and also a certain look of frailty. A hireling! One of Clifford's hirelings! 'The fault, dear Brutus, is not in our stars, but in ourselves, that we are underlings.'

Was he an underling? Was he? What did he think of *her*?

It was a sunny day, and Connie was working in the garden, and Mrs Bolton was helping her. For some reason, the two women had drawn together, in one of the unaccountable flows and ebbs of sympathy that exist between people. They were pegging down carnations, and putting in small plants for the summer. It was work they both liked. Connie especially felt a delight in putting the soft roots of young plants into a soft black puddle, and cradling them down. On this spring morning she felt a quiver in her womb too, as if the sunshine had touched it and made it happy.

'It is many years since you lost your husband?' she said to Mrs Bolton, as she took up another little plant and laid it in its hole.

'Twenty-three!' said Mrs Bolton, as she carefully separated the young columbines into single plants. 'Twenty-three years since they brought him home.'

Connie's heart gave a lurch, at the terrible finality of it. 'Brought him home!'

'Why did he get killed, do you think?' she asked. 'He was happy with you?'

It was a woman's question to a woman. Mrs Bolton put aside a strand of hair from her face, with the back of her hand.

'I don't know, my Lady! He sort of wouldn't give in to things: he wouldn't really go with the rest. And then he hated ducking his head for anything on earth. A sort of obstinacy, that *gets* itself killed. You see he didn't really care. I lay it down to the pit. He ought never to have been down pit. But his dad made him go down, as a lad; and then, when you're over twenty, it's not very easy to come out.'

'Did he say he hated it?'

'Oh no! Never! He never said he hated anything. He just made a funny face. He was one of those who wouldn't take care: like some of the first lads as went off so blithe to the war and got killed right away. He wasn't really wezzle-brained. But he wouldn't care. I used to say to him: "You care for nought nor nobody!" But he did! The way he sat when my first baby was born, motionless, and the sort of fatal eyes he looked at me with, when it was over! I had a bad time, but I had to comfort *him*. "It's all right, lad, it's all right!" I said to him. And he gave me a look, and that funny sort of smile. He never said anything. But I don't believe he had any right pleasure with me at nights after; he'd never really let himself go. I used to say to him: Oh, let thysen go, lad! I'd talk broad to him sometimes. And he said nothing. But he wouldn't let himself go, or he couldn't. He didn't want me to have any more children. I always blamed his mother, for letting him in th' room. He'd no right t'ave been there. Men makes so much more of things than they should, once they start brooding.'

'Did he mind so much?' said Connie in wonder.

SELECTED WORKS OF D. H. LAWRENCE

'Yes, he sort of couldn't take it for natural, all that pain. And it spoilt his pleasure in his bit of married love. I said to him: "If I don't care, why should you? It's my look-out!" But all he'd ever say was: "It's not right!" '

'Perhaps he was too sensitive,' said Connie.

'That's it! When you come to know men, that's how they are: too sensitive in the wrong place. And I believe, unbeknown to himself, he hated the pit, just hated it. He looked so quiet when he was dead, as if he'd got free. He was such a nice-looking lad. It just broke my heart to see him, so still and pure looking, as if he'd *wanted* to die. Oh, it broke my heart, that did. But it was the pit.'

She wept a few bitter tears, and Connie wept more. It was a warm spring day, with a perfume of earth and of yellow flowers, many things rising to bud, and the garden still with the very sap of sunshine.

'It must have been terrible for you!' said Connie.

'Oh, my Lady! I never realised at first. I could only say: Oh my lad, what did you want to leave me for! That was all my cry. But somehow I felt he'd come back.'

'But he *didn't* want to leave you,' said Connie.

'Oh no, my Lady! That was only my silly cry. And I kept expecting him back. Especially at nights. I kept waking up thinking: Why he's not in bed with me! It was as if my *feelings* wouldn't believe he'd gone. I just felt he'd *have* to come back and lie against me, so I could feel him with me. That was all I wanted, to feel him there with me, warm. And it took me a thousand shocks before I knew he wouldn't come back, it took me years.'

'The touch of him,' said Connie.

'That's it, my Lady, the touch of him! I've never got over it to this day, and never shall. And if there's a heaven above, he'll be there, and will lie up against me so I can sleep.'

Connie glanced at the handsome, brooding face in fear. Another passionate one out of Tevershall! The touch of him! For the bonds of love are ill to loose!

'It's terrible, once you've got a man into your blood!' she said.

'Oh, my Lady! And that's what makes you feel so bitter. You feel folks *wanted* him killed. You feel the pit fair *wanted* to kill him. Oh, I felt, if it hadn't been for the pit, an' them as runs the pit, there'd have been no leaving me. But they all *want* to separate a woman and a man, if they're together.'

'If they're physically together,' said Connie.

'That's right, my Lady! There's a lot of hard-hearted folks in the world. And every morning when he got up and went to th' pit, I felt it was wrong, wrong. But what else could he do? What can a man do?'

A queer hate flared in the woman.

'But can a touch last so long?' Connie asked suddenly. 'That you could feel him so long?'

'Oh my Lady, what else is there to last? Children grows away from you. But the man, well –! But even *that* they'd like to kill in you, the very thought of the touch of him. Even your own children! Ah well! We might have drifted apart, who knows. But the feeling's something different. It's 'appen better never to care. But there, when I look at women who's never really been warmed through by a man, well, they seem to me poor dool-owls after all, no matter how they may dress up and gad. No, I'll abide by my own. I've not much respect for people.'

Chapter 12

Connie went to the wood directly after lunch. It was really a lovely day, the first dandelions making suns, the first daisies so white. The hazel thicket was a lace-work of half-open leaves, and the last dusty perpendicular of the catkins. Yellow celandines now were in crowds, flat open, pressed back in urgency, and the yellow glitter of themselves. It was the yellow, the powerful yellow of early summer. And primroses were broad, and full of pale abandon, thick-clustered primroses no longer shy. The lush, dark green of hyacinths was a sea, with buds rising like pale corn, while in the riding the forget-me-nots were fluffing up, and columbines were unfolding their ink-purple ruches, and there were bits of blue bird's-eggshell under a bush. Everywhere the bud-knots and the leap of life!

The keeper was not at the hut. Everything was serene, brown chickens running lustily. Connie walked on towards the cottage, because she wanted to find him.

The cottage stood in the sun, off the wood's edge. In the little garden the double daffodils rose in tufts, near the wide-open door, and red double daisies made a border to the path. There was the bark of a dog, and Flossie came running.

The wide-open door! so he was at home. And the sunlight falling on the red-brick floor! As she went up the path, she saw him through the window, sitting at the table in his shirt-sleeves, eating. The dog wuffed softly, slowly wagging her tail.

He rose, and came to the door, wiping his mouth with a red handkerchief, still chewing.

'May I come in?' she said.

'Come in!'

The sun shone into the bare room, which still smelled of a mutton chop, done in a dutch oven before the fire, because the dutch oven still stood on the fender, with the black potato-saucepan on a piece of paper, beside it on the white hearth. The fire was red, rather low, the bar dropped, the kettle singing.

On the table was his plate, with potatoes and the remains of the chop; also bread in a basket, salt, and a blue mug with beer. The tablecloth was white oil-cloth, he stood in the shade.

'You are very late,' she said. 'Do go on eating!'

She sat down on a wooden chair, in the sunlight by the door.

'I had to go to Uthwaite,' he said, sitting down at table but not eating.

'Do eat,' she said.

But he did not touch the food.

'Shall y'ave something?' he asked her. 'Shall y'ave a cup of tea? t' kettle's on t' boil.' He half rose again from his chair.

'If you'll let me make it myself,' she said, rising. He seemed sad, and she felt she was bothering him.

'Well, teapot's in there' – he pointed to a little, drab corner cupboard; 'an' cups. An' tea's on t' mantel ower yer 'ead.'

She got the black teapot, and the tin of tea from the mantelshelf. She rinsed the teapot with hot water, and stood a moment wondering where to empty it.

'Throw it out,' he said, aware of her. 'It's clean.'

She went to the door and threw the drop of water down the path. How lovely it was here, so still, so really woodland. The oaks were putting out ochre yellow leaves; in the garden the red daisies were like red plush buttons. She glanced at the big, hollow sandstone slab of the threshold, now crossed by so few feet.

'But it's lovely here,' she said. 'Such a beautiful stillness, everything alive and still.'

He was eating again, rather slowly and unwillingly, and she could feel he was discouraged. She made the tea in silence, and set the teapot on the hob, as she knew the people did. He pushed his plate aside and went to the back place; she heard a latch click, then he came back with cheese on a plate, and butter.

She set the two cups on the table; there were only two.

'Will you have a cup of tea?' she said.

'If you like. Sugar's in th' cupboard, an' there's a little cream-jug. Milk's in a jug in th' pantry.'

'Shall I take your plate away?' she asked him. He looked up at her with a faint ironical smile.

'Why . . . if you like,' he said, slowly eating bread and cheese. She went to the back, into the penthouse scullery, where the pump was. On the left was a door, no doubt the pantry door. She unlatched it, and almost smiled at the place he called a pantry, a long narrow whitewashed slip of a cupboard. But it managed to contain a little barrel of beer, as well as a few dishes and bits of food. She took a little milk from the yellow jug.

'How do you get your milk?' she asked him, when she came back to the table.

'Flints! They leave me a bottle at the warren end. You know, where I met you!' But he was discouraged.

She poured out the tea, poising the cream-jug.

'No milk,' he said; then he seemed to hear a noise, and looked keenly through the doorway.

"Appen we'd better shut,' he said.

'It seems a pity,' she replied. 'Nobody will come, will they?'

'Not unless it's one time in a thousand, but you never know.'

'And even then it's no matter,' she said. 'It's only a cup of tea. Where are the spoons?'

He reached over, and pulled open the table drawer. Connie sat at the table in the sunshine of the doorway.

'Flossie!' he said to the dog, who was lying on a little mat at the stair foot. 'Go an' hark, hark!'

He lifted his finger, and his 'hark!' was very vivid. The dog trotted out to reconnoitre.

'Are you sad today?' she asked him.

He turned his blue eyes quickly, and gazed direct on her.

'Sad! no, bored! I had to go getting summonses for two poachers I caught, and oh well, I don't like people.'

He spoke cold, good English, and there was anger in his voice.

'Do you hate being a gamekeeper?' she asked.

'Being a gamekeeper, no! So long as I'm left alone. But when I have to go messing around at the police-station, and various other places, and waiting for a lot of fools to attend to me . . . oh well, I get mad . . . ' and he smiled, with a certain faint humour.

'Couldn't you be really independent?' she asked.

'Me? I suppose I could, if you mean manage to exist on my pension. I could! But I've got to work, or I should die. That is, I've got to have something that keeps me occupied. And I'm not in a good enough temper to work for myself. It's got to be a sort of job for somebody else, or I should throw it up in a month, out of bad temper. So altogether I'm very well off here, especially lately . . . '

He laughed at her again, with mocking humour.

'But why are you in a bad temper?' she asked. 'Do you mean you are *always* in a bad temper?'

'Pretty well,' he said, laughing. 'I don't quite digest my bile.'

'But what bile?' she said.

'Bile!' he said. 'Don't you know what that is?' She was silent, and disappointed. He was taking no notice of her.

'I'm going away for a while next month,' she said.

'You are! Where to?'

'Venice.'

'Venice! With Sir Clifford? For how long?'

'For a month or so,' she replied. 'Clifford won't go.'

'He'll stay here?' he asked.

'Yes! He hates to travel as he is.'

'Ay, poor devil!' he said, with sympathy.

There was a pause.

'You won't forget me when I'm gone, will you?' she asked. Again he lifted his eyes and looked full at her.

'Forget?' he said. 'You know nobody forgets. It's not a question of memory.'

She wanted to say: 'What then?' but she didn't. Instead, she said in a mute kind of voice: 'I told Clifford I might have a child.'

Now he really looked at her, intense and searching.

'You did?' he said at last. 'And what did he say?'

'Oh, he wouldn't mind. He'd be glad, really, so long as it seemed to be his.' She dared not look up at him.

He was silent a long time, then he gazed again on her face.

'No mention of *me*, of course?' he said.

'No. No mention of you,' she said.

'No, he'd hardly swallow me as a substitute breeder. Then where are you supposed to be getting the child?'

'I might have a love affair in Venice,' she said.

'You might,' he replied slowly. 'So that's why you're going?'

'Not to have the love affair,' she said, looking up at him, pleading.

'Just the appearance of one,' he said.

There was silence. He sat staring out the window, with a faint grin, half mockery, half bitterness, on his face. She hated his grin.

'You've not taken any precautions against having a child then?' he asked her suddenly. 'Because I haven't.'

'No,' she said faintly. 'I should hate that.'

He looked at her, then again with the peculiar subtle grin out of the window. There was a tense silence.

At last he turned to her and said satirically, 'That was why you wanted me then, to get a child?'

She hung her head.

'No. Not really,' she said.

'What then, *really*?' he asked rather bitingly.

She looked up at him reproachfully, saying: 'I don't know.'

He broke into a laugh.

'Then I'm damned if I do,' he said.

There was a long pause of silence, a cold silence.

'Well,' he said at last. 'It's as your Ladyship likes. If you get the baby, Sir Clifford's welcome to it. I shan't have lost anything. On the contrary, I've had a very nice experience, very nice indeed!' – and he stretched in a half suppressed sort of yawn. 'If you've made use of me,' he said, 'it's not the first time I've been made use of; and I don't suppose it's ever been as pleasant as this time, though of course one can't feel tremendously dignified about it.' He stretched again, curiously, his muscles quivering, and his jaw oddly set.

'But I didn't make use of you,' she said, pleading.

'At your Ladyship's service,' he replied.

'No,' she said. 'I liked your body.'

'Did you?' he replied, and he laughed. 'Well then, we're quits, because I liked yours.'

He looked at her with queer darkened eyes.

'Would you like to go upstairs now?' he asked her, in a strangled sort of voice.

'No, not here. Not now!' she said heavily, though if he had used any power over her, she would have gone, for she had no strength against him.

He turned his face away again, and seemed to forget her.

'I want to touch you like you touch me,' she said. 'I've never really touched your body.'

He looked at her, and smiled again. 'Now?' he said.

'No! No! Not here! At the hut, Would you mind?'

'How do I touch you?' he asked.

'When you feel me.'

He looked at her, and met her heavy, anxious eyes.

'And do you like it when I feel you?' he asked, laughing at her still.

'Yes, do you?' she said.

'Oh, me!' Then he changed his tone. 'Yes,' he said. 'You know without asking.' Which was true.

She rose and picked up her hat. 'I must go,' she said.

'Will you go?' he replied politely.

She wanted him to touch her, to say something to her, but he said nothing, only waited politely.

'Thank you for the tea,' she said.

'I haven't thanked your Ladyship for doing me the honours of my teapot,' he said.

She went down the path, and he stood in the doorway, faintly grinning. Flossie came running with her tail lifted. And Connie had to plod dumbly across into the wood, knowing he was standing there watching her, with that incomprehensible grin on his face.

She walked home very much downcast and annoyed. She didn't at all like his saying he had been made use of; because, in a sense, it was true. But he oughtn't to have said it. Therefore, again, she was divided between two feelings: resentment against him, and a desire to make it up with him.

She passed a very uneasy and irritated tea-time, and at once went up to her room. But when she was there it was no good; she could neither sit nor stand. She would have to do something about it. She would have to go back to the hut; if he was not there, well and good.

She slipped out of the side door, and took her way direct and a little sullen. When she came to the clearing she was terribly uneasy. But there he was again, in his shirt-sleeves, stooping, letting the hens out of the coops, among the chicks that were now growing a little gawky, but were much more trim than hen-chickens.

She went straight across to him.

'You see I've come!' she said.

'Ay, I see it!' he said, straightening his back, and looking at her with a faint amusement.

'Do you let the hens out now?' she asked.

'Yes, they've sat themselves to skin and bone,' he said. 'An' now they're not all that anxious to come out an' feed. There's no self in a sitting hen; she's all in the eggs or the chicks.'

The poor mother-hens; such blind devotion! even to eggs not their own! Connie looked at them in compassion. A helpless silence fell between the man and the woman.

'Shall us go i' th' 'ut?' he asked.

'Do you want me?' she asked, in a sort of mistrust.

'Ay, if you want to come.'

She was silent.

'Come then!' he said.

And she went with him to the hut. It was quite dark when he had shut the door, so he made a small light in the lantern, as before.

'Have you left your underthings off?' he asked her.

'Yes!'

'Ay, well, then I'll take my things off too.'

He spread the blankets, putting one at the side for a coverlet. She took off her hat, and shook her hair. He sat down, taking off his shoes and gaiters, and undoing his cord breeches.

'Lie down then!' he said, when he stood in his shirt. She obeyed in silence, and he lay beside her, and pulled the blanket over them both.

'There!' he said.

And he lifted her dress right back, till he came even to her breasts. He kissed them softly, taking the nipples in his lips in tiny caresses.

'Eh, but tha'rt nice, tha'rt nice!' he said, suddenly rubbing his face with a snuggling movement against her warm belly.

And she put her arms round him under his shirt, but she was afraid, afraid of his thin, smooth, naked body, that seemed so powerful, afraid of the violent muscles. She shrank, afraid.

And when he said, with a sort of little sigh: 'Eh, tha'rt nice!' something in her quivered, and something in her spirit stiffened in resistance: stiffened from the terribly physical intimacy, and from the peculiar haste of his possession. And this time the sharp ecstasy of her own passion did not overcome her; she lay with her hands inert on his striving body, and do what she might, her spirit seemed to look on from the top of her head, and the butting of his haunches seemed ridiculous to her, and the sort of anxiety of his penis to come to its little evacuating crisis seemed farcical. Yes, this was love, this ridiculous bouncing of the buttocks, and the wilting of the poor insignificant, moist little penis. This was the divine love! After all, the moderns were right when they felt contempt for the performance; for it was a performance. It was quite true, as some poets said, that the God who created man must have had a sinister sense of humour, creating him a reasonable being, yet forcing him to take this ridiculous posture, and driving him with blind craving for this ridiculous performance. Even a Maupassant found it a humiliating anticlimax. Men despised the intercourse act, and yet did it.

Cold and derisive her queer female mind stood apart, and though she lay perfectly still, her impulse was to heave her loins, and throw the man out, escape his ugly grip, and the butting overriding of his absurd haunches. His body was a foolish, impudent, imperfect thing, a little disgusting in its unfinished clumsiness. For surely a complete evolution would eliminate this performance, this 'function'.

And yet when he had finished, soon over, and lay very very still, receding into silence, and a strange, motionless distance, far, farther than the horizon of her awareness, her heart began to weep. She could feel him ebbing away, ebbing away, leaving her there like a stone on a shore. He was withdrawing, his spirit was leaving her. He knew.

And in real grief, tormented by her own double consciousness and reaction, she began to weep. He took no notice, or did not even know. The storm of weeping swelled and shook her, and shook him.

'Ay!' he said. 'It was no good that time. You wasn't there.' So he knew! Her sobs became violent.

'But what's amiss?' he said. 'It's once in a while that way.'

'I . . . I can't love you,' she sobbed, suddenly feeling her heart breaking.

'Canna ter? Well, dunna fret! There's no law says as tha's got to. Ta'e it for what it is.'

He still lay with his hand on her breast. But she had drawn both her hands from him.

His words were small comfort. She sobbed aloud.

'Nay, nay!' he said. 'Ta'e the thick wi' th' thin. This wor' a bit o' thin for once.'

She wept bitterly, sobbing. 'But I want to love you, and I can't. It only seems horrid.'

He laughed a little, half bitter, half amused.

'It isna horrid,' he said, 'even if tha thinks it is. An' tha canna ma'e it horrid. Dunna fret thysen about lovin' me. Tha'lt niver force thysen to 't. There's sure to be a bad nut in a basketful. Tha mun ta'e th' rough wi' th' smooth.'

He took his hand away from her breast, not touching her. And now she was untouched she took an almost perverse satisfaction in it. She hated the dialect: the *thee* and the *tha* and the *thysen*. He could get up if he liked, and stand there above her buttoning down those absurd corduroy breeches, straight in front of her. After all, Michaelis had had the decency to turn away. This man was so assured in himself, he didn't know what a clown other people found him, a half-bred fellow.

Yet, as he was drawing away, to rise silently and leave her, she clung to him in terror.

'Don't! Don't go! Don't leave me! Don't be cross with me! Hold me! Hold me fast!' she whispered in blind frenzy, not even knowing what she said, and clinging to him with uncanny force. It was from herself she wanted to be saved, from her own inward anger and resistance. Yet how powerful was that inward resistance that possessed her!

He took her in his arms again and drew her to him, and suddenly she became small in his arms, small and nestling. It was gone, the resistance was gone, and she began to melt in a marvellous peace. And as she melted small and wonderful in his arms, she became infinitely desirable to him, all his blood-vessels seemed to scald with intense yet tender desire, for her, for her softness, for the penetrating beauty of her in his arms, passing into his blood. And softly, with that marvellous swoon-like caress of his hand in pure soft desire, softly he stroked the silky slope of her loins, down, down between her soft warm buttocks, coming nearer and nearer to the very quick of her. And she felt him like a flame of desire, yet tender, and she felt herself melting in the flame. She let herself go. She felt his penis risen against her with silent amazing force and assertion, and she let herself go to him. She yielded with a quiver that was like death, she went all open to him. And oh, if he were not tender to her now, how cruel, for she was all open to him and helpless!

She quivered again at the potent inexorable entry inside her, so strange and terrible. It might come with the thrust of a sword in her softly-opened body, and that would be death. She clung in a sudden anguish of terror. But it came with a strange slow thrust of peace, the dark thrust of peace and a ponderous, primordial tenderness, such as made the world in the beginning. And her terror subsided in her breast, her breast dared to be gone in peace, she held nothing. She dared to let go everything, all herself, and be gone in the flood.

And it seemed she was like the sea, nothing but dark waves rising and heaving, heaving with a great swell, so that slowly her whole darkness was in motion, and she was ocean rolling its dark, dumb mass. Oh, and far down inside her the deeps parted and rolled asunder, in long, far-travelling billows, and ever, at the quick of her, the depths parted and rolled asunder, from the centre of soft plunging, as the plunger went deeper and deeper, touching lower, and she was deeper and deeper and deeper disclosed, the heavier the billows of her rolled away to some shore, uncovering her, and closer and closer plunged the palpable unknown, and further and further rolled the waves of herself away from herself, leaving her, till suddenly, in a soft, shuddering convulsion, the quick of all her plasm was touched, she knew herself touched, the consummation was upon her, and she was gone. She was gone, she was not, and she was born: a woman.

Ah, too lovely, too lovely! In the ebbing she realised all the loveliness. Now all her body clung with tender love to the unknown man, and blindly to the wilting penis, as it so tenderly, frailly, unknowingly withdrew, after the fierce thrust of its potency. As it drew out and left her body, the secret, sensitive thing, she gave an unconscious cry of pure loss, and she tried to put it back. It had been so perfect! And she loved it so!

And only now she became aware of the small, bud-like reticence and tenderness of the penis, and a little cry of wonder and poignancy escaped her again, her woman's heart crying out over the tender frailty of that which had been the power.

'It was so lovely!' she moaned. 'It was so lovely!' But he said nothing, only softly kissed her, lying still above her. And she moaned with a sort of bliss, as a sacrifice, and a new-born thing.

And now in her heart the queer wonder of him was awakened. A man! the strange potency of manhood upon her! Her hands strayed over him, still a little afraid. Afraid of that strange, hostile, slightly repulsive thing that he had been to her, a man. And now she touched him, and it was the sons of god with the daughters of men. How beautiful he felt, how pure in tissue! How lovely, how lovely, strong, and yet pure and delicate, such stillness of the sensitive body! Such utter stillness of potency and delicate flesh. How beautiful! How beautiful! Her hands came timorously down his back, to the soft, smallish globes of the buttocks. Beauty! What beauty! a sudden little flame of new awareness went through her. How was it possible, this beauty here, where she had previously only been repelled? The unspeakable beauty to the touch, of the warm, living buttocks! The life within life, the sheer warm, potent loveliness. And the strange weight of the balls between his legs! What a mystery! What a strange heavy weight of mystery, that could lie soft and heavy in one's hand! The roots, root of all that is lovely, the primeval root of all full beauty.

She clung to him, with a hiss of wonder that was almost awe, terror. He held her close, but he said nothing. He would never say anything. She crept nearer to him, nearer, only to be near to the sensual wonder of him. And out of his utter, incomprehensible stillness, she felt again the slow, momentous, surging rise of the phallus again, the other power. And her heart melted out with a kind of awe.

And this time his being within her was all soft and iridescent, purely soft and iridescent, such as no consciousness could seize. Her whole self quivered unconscious and alive, like plasm. She could not know what it was. She could not remember what it had been. Only that it had been more lovely than anything ever could be. Only that. And afterwards she was utterly still, utterly unknowing, she was not aware for how long. And he was still with her, in an unfathomable silence along with her. And of this, they would never speak.

When awareness of the outside began to come back, she clung to his breast, murmuring: 'My love! my love!' And he held her silently. And she curled on his breast, perfect.

But his silence was fathomless. His hands held her like flowers, so still and strange. 'Where are you?' she whispered to him. 'Where are you? Speak to me! Say something to me!'

He kissed her softly, murmuring: 'Ay, my lass!'

But she did not know what he meant, she did not know where he was. In his silence he seemed lost to her.

'You love me, don't you?' she murmured.

'Ay, tha knows!' he said.

'But tell me!' she pleaded.

'Ay! Ay! 'asn't ter felt it?' he said dimly, but softly and surely. And she clung close to him, closer. He was so much more peaceful in love than she was, and she wanted him to reassure her.

'You do love me!' she whispered, assertive. And his hands stroked her softly, as if she were a flower, without the quiver of desire, but with delicate nearness. And still there haunted her a restless necessity to get a grip on love.

'Say you'll always love me!' she pleaded.

'Ay!' he said, abstractedly. And she felt her questions driving him away from her.

'Mustn't we get up?' he said at last.

'No!' she said.

But she could feel his consciousness straying, listening to the noises outside. 'It'll be nearly dark,' he said. And she heard the pressure of circumstance in his voice. She kissed him, with a woman's grief at yielding up her hour.

He rose, and turned up the lantern, then began to pull on his clothes, quickly disappearing inside them. Then he stood there, above her, fastening his breeches and looking down at her with dark, wide eyes, his face a little flushed and his hair ruffled, curiously warm and still and beautiful in the dim light of the lantern, so beautiful, she would never tell him how beautiful. It made her want to cling fast to him, to hold him, for there was a warm, half-sleepy remoteness in his beauty that made her want to cry out and clutch him, to have him. She would never have him. So she lay on the blanket with curved, soft naked haunches, and he had no idea what she was thinking, but to him too she was beautiful, the soft, marvellous thing he could go into, beyond everything.

'I love thee that I can go into thee,' he said.

'Do you like me?' she said, her heart beating.

'It heals it all up, that I can go into thee. I love thee that tha opened to me. I love thee that I came into thee like that.'

He bent down and kissed her soft flank, rubbed his cheek against it, then covered it up.

'And will you never leave me?' she said.

'Dunna ask them things,' he said.

'But you do believe I love you?' she said.

'Tha loved me just now, wider than iver tha thout tha would. But who knows what'll 'appen, once tha starts thinkin' about it!'

'No, don't say those things! And you don't really think that I wanted to make use of you, do you?'

'How?'

'To have a child – ?'

'Now anybody can 'ave any childt i' th' world,' he said, as he sat down fastening on his leggings.

'Ah no!' she cried. 'You don't mean it?'

'Eh well!' he said, looking at her under his brows. 'This wor t' best.'

She lay still. He softly opened the door. The sky was dark blue, with crystalline, turquoise rim. He went out, to shut up the hens, speaking softly to his dog. And she lay and wondered at the wonder of life, and of being.

When he came back she was still lying there, glowing like a gypsy. He sat on the stool by her.

'Tha mun come one naight ter th' cottage, afore tha goos, sholl ter?' he asked, lifting his eyebrows as he looked at her, his hands dangling between his knees.

'Sholl ter?' she echoed, teasing.

He smiled.

'Ay, sholl ter?' he repeated.

'Ay!' she said, imitating the dialect sound.

'Yi!' he said.

'Yi!' she repeated.

'An' slaip wi' me,' he said. 'It needs that. When sholt come?'

'When sholl I?' she said.

'Nay,' he said, 'tha canna do't. When sholt come then?'

''Appen Sunday,' she said.

''Appen a' Sunday! Ay!'

He laughed at her quickly.

'Nay, tha canna,' he protested.

'Why canna I?' she said.

He laughed. Her attempts at the dialect were so ludicrous, somehow.

'Coom then, tha mun goo!' he said.

'Mun I?' she said.

'Maun Ah!' he corrected.

'Why should I say *maun* when you said *mun*,' she protested. 'You're not playing fair.'

'Arena Ah!' he said, leaning forward and softly stroking her face.

'Th'art good cunt, though, aren't ter? Best bit o' cunt left on earth. When ter likes! When tha'rt willin'!'

'What is cunt?' she said.

'An' doesn't ter know? Cunt! It's thee down theer; an' what I get when I'm i'side thee, and what tha gets when I'm i'side thee; it's a' as it is, all on't.'

'All on't,' she teased. 'Cunt! It's like fuck then.'

'Nay nay! Fuck's only what you do. Animals fuck. But cunt's a lot more than that. It's thee, dost see: an' tha'rt a lot besides an animal, aren't ter? – even ter fuck? Cunt! Eh, that's the beauty o' thee, lass!'

She got up and kissed him between the eyes, that looked at her so dark and soft and unspeakably warm, so unbearably beautiful.

'Is it?' she said. 'And do you care for me?'

He kissed her without answering.

'Tha mun goo, let me dust thee,' he said.

His hand passed over the curves of her body, firmly, without desire, but with soft, intimate knowledge.

As she ran home in the twilight the world seemed a dream; the trees in the park seemed bulging and surging at anchor on a tide, and the heave of the slope to the house was alive.

Chapter 13

On Sunday Clifford wanted to go into the wood. It was a lovely morning, the pear blossom and plum had suddenly appeared in the world, in a wonder of white here and there.

It was cruel for Clifford, while the world bloomed, to have to be helped from chair to bath-chair. But he had forgotten, and even seemed to have a certain conceit of himself in his lameness. Connie still suffered, having to lift his inert legs into place. Mrs Bolton did it now, or Field.

She waited for him at the top of the drive, at the edge of the screen of beeches. His chair came puffing along with a sort of valetudinarian slow importance. As he joined his wife he said, 'Sir Clifford on his foaming steed!'

'Snorting, at least!' she laughed.

He stopped and looked round at the façade of the long, low old brown house.

'Wragby doesn't wink an eyelid!' he said. 'But then why should it! I ride upon the achievements of the mind of man, and that beats a horse.'

'I suppose it does. And the souls in Plato riding up to heaven in a two-horse chariot would go in a Ford car now,' she said.

'Or a Rolls-Royce: Plato was an aristocrat!'

'Quite! No more black horse to thrash and maltreat. Plato never thought we'd go one better than his black steed and his white steed, and have no steeds at all, only an engine!'

'Only an engine and gas!' said Clifford.

'I hope I can have some repairs done to the old place next year. I think I shall have about a thousand to spare for that: but work costs so much!' he added.

'Oh good!' said Connie. 'If only there aren't more strikes!'

'What would be the use of their striking again! Merely ruin the industry, what's left of it: and surely the owls are beginning to see it!'

'Perhaps they don't mind ruining the industry,' said Connie.

'Ah, don't talk like a woman! The industry fills their bellies, even if it can't keep their pockets quite so flush,' he said, using turns of speech that oddly had a twang of Mrs Bolton.

'But didn't you say the other day that you were a conservative-anarchist?' she asked innocently.

'And did you understand what I meant?' he retorted. 'All I meant is, people can be what they like and feel what they like and do what they like, strictly privately, so long as they keep the *form* of life intact, and the apparatus.'

Connie walked on in silence a few paces. Then she said, obstinately, 'It sounds like saying an egg may go as addled as it likes, so long as it keeps its shell on whole. But addled eggs do break of themselves.'

'I don't think people are eggs,' he said. 'Not even angels' eggs, my dear little evangelist.'

He was in rather high feather this bright morning. The larks were trilling away over the park, the distant pit in the hollow was fuming silent steam. It was almost like old days, before the war. Connie didn't really want to argue. But then she did not really want to go to the wood with Clifford either. So she walked beside his chair in a certain obstinacy of spirit.

'No,' he said. 'There will be no more strikes, if the thing is properly managed.'

'Why not?'

'Because strikes will be made as good as impossible.'

'But will the men let you?' she asked.

'We shan't ask them. We shall do it while they aren't looking: for their own good, to save the industry.'

'For your own good too,' she said.

'Naturally! For the good of everybody. But for their good even more than mine. I can live without the pits. They can't. They'll starve if there are no pits. I've got other provision.'

They looked up the shallow valley at the mine, and beyond it, at the black-lidded houses of Tevershall crawling like some serpent up the hill. From the old brown church the bells were ringing: Sunday, Sunday, Sunday!

'But will the men let you dictate terms?' she said.

'My dear, they will have to: if one does it gently.'

'But mightn't there be a mutual understanding?'

'Absolutely: when they realise that the industry comes before the individual.'

'But must you own the industry?' she said.

'I don't. But to the extent I do own it, yes, most decidedly. The ownership of property has now become a religious question: as it has been since Jesus and St Francis. The point is *not*: take all thou hast and give to the poor, but use all thou hast to encourage the industry and give work to the poor. It's the only way to feed all the mouths and clothe all the bodies. Giving away all we have to the poor spells starvation for the poor just as much as for us. And universal starvation is no high aim. Even general poverty is no lovely thing. Poverty is ugly.'

'But the disparity?'

'That is fate. Why is the star Jupiter bigger than the star Neptune? You can't start altering the make-up of things!'

'But when this envy and jealousy and discontent has once started – ' she began.

'Do your best to stop it. Somebody's *got* to be boss of the show.'

'But who is boss of the show?' she asked.

'The men who own and run the industries.'

There was a long silence.

'It seems to me they're a bad boss,' she said.

'Then you suggest what they should do.'

'They don't take their boss-ship seriously enough,' she said.

'They take it far more seriously than you take your ladyship,' he said.

'That's thrust upon me. I don't really want it,' she blurted out. He stopped the chair and looked at her.

'Who's shirking their responsibility now!' he said. 'Who is trying to get away *now* from the responsibility of their own boss-ship, as you call it?'

'But I don't want any boss-ship,' she protested.

'Ah! But that is funk. You've got it: fated to it. And you should live up to it. Who has given the colliers all they have that's worth having: all their political liberty, and their education, such as it is, their sanitation, their health-conditions, their books, their music, everything. Who has given it them? Have colliers given it to colliers? No! All the Wragbys and Shipleys in England have given their part, and must go on giving. There's your responsibility.'

Connie listened, and flushed very red.

'I'd like to give something,' she said. 'But I'm not allowed. Everything is to be sold and paid for now; and all the things you mention now, Wragby and Shipley *sells* them to the people, at a good profit. Everything is sold. You don't give one heartbeat of real sympathy. And besides, who has taken away from the people their natural life and manhood, and given them this industrial horror? Who has done that?'

'And what must I do?' he asked, green. 'Ask them to come and pillage me?'

'Why is Tevershall so ugly, so hideous? Why are their lives so hopeless?'

'They built their own Tevershall, that's part of their display of freedom. They built themselves their pretty Tevershall, and they live their own pretty lives. I can't live their lives for them. Every beetle must live its own life.'

'But you make them work for you. They live the life of your coal-mine.'

'Not at all. Every beetle finds its own food. Not one man is forced to work for me.'

'Their lives are industrialised and hopeless, and so are ours,' she cried.

'I don't think they are. That's just a romantic figure of speech, a relic of the swooning and die-away romanticism. You don't look at all a hopeless figure standing there, Connie my dear.'

Which was true. For her dark-blue eyes were flashing, her colour was hot in her cheeks, she looked full of a rebellious passion far from the dejection of hopelessness. She noticed, in the tussocky places of the grass, cottony young cowslips standing up still bleared in their down. And she wondered with rage, why it was she felt Clifford was so *wrong*, yet she couldn't say it to him, she could not say exactly *where* he was wrong.

'No wonder the men hate you,' she said.

'They don't!' he replied. 'And don't fall into errors: in your sense of the word, they are *not* men. They are animals you don't understand, and never could. Don't thrust your illusions on other people. The masses were always the same, and will always be the same. Nero's slaves were extremely little different from our colliers or the Ford motor-car workmen. I mean Nero's mine slaves and his field slaves. It is the masses: they are the unchangeable. An individual may emerge from the masses. But the emergence doesn't alter the mass. The masses are unalterable. It is one of the most momentous facts of social science. *Panem et circenses!* Only today education is one of the bad substitutes for a circus. What is wrong today, is that we've made a profound hash of the circuses part of the programme, and poisoned our masses with a little education.'

When Clifford became really roused in his feelings about the common people, Connie was frightened. There was something devastatingly true in what he said. But it was a truth that killed.

Seeing her pale and silent, Clifford started the chair again, and no more was said till he halted again at the wood gate, which she opened.

'And what we need to take up now,' he said, 'is whips, not swords. The masses have been ruled since time began, and till time ends, ruled they will have to be. It is sheer hypocrisy and farce to say they can rule themselves.'

'But can you rule them?' she asked.

'I? Oh yes! Neither my mind nor my will is crippled, and I don't rule with my legs. I can do my share of ruling: absolutely, my share; and give me a son, and he will be able to rule his portion after me.'

'But he wouldn't be your own son, of your own ruling class; or perhaps not,' she stammered.

'I don't care who his father may be, so long as he is a healthy man not below normal intelligence. Give me the child of any healthy, normally intelligent man, and I will make a perfectly competent Chatterley of him. It is not who begets us, that matters, but where fate places us. Place any child among the ruling classes, and he will grow up, to his own extent, a ruler. Put kings' and dukes' children among the masses, and they'll be little plebeians, mass products. It is the overwhelming pressure of environment.'

'Then the common people aren't a race, and the aristocrats aren't blood,' she said.

'No, my child! All that is romantic illusion. Aristocracy is a function, a part of fate. And the masses are a functioning of another part of fate. The individual hardly matters. It is a question of which function you are brought up to and adapted to. It is not the individuals that make an aristocracy: it is the functioning of the aristocratic whole. And it is the functioning of the whole mass that makes the common man what he is.'

'Then there is no common humanity between us all!'

'Just as you like. We all need to fill our bellies. But when it comes to expressive or executive functioning, I believe there is a gulf and an absolute one, between the ruling and the serving classes. The two functions are opposed. And the function determines the individual.'

Connie looked at him with dazed eyes.

'Won't you come on?' she said.

And he started his chair. He had said his say. Now he lapsed into his peculiar and rather vacant apathy, that Connie found so trying. In the wood, anyhow, she was determined not to argue.

In front of them ran the open cleft of the riding, between the hazel walls and the gay grey trees. The chair puffed slowly on, slowly surging into the forget-me-nots that rose up in the drive like milk froth, beyond the hazel shadows. Clifford steered the middle course, where feet passing had kept a channel through the flowers. But Connie, walking behind, had watched the wheels jolt over the woodruff and the bugle, and squash the little yellow cups of the creeping-jenny. Now they made a wake through the forget-me-nots.

All the flowers were there, the first bluebells in blue pools, like standing water.

'You are quite right about its being beautiful,' said Clifford. 'It is so amazingly. What is *quite* so lovely as an English spring!'

Connie thought it sounded as if even the spring bloomed by act of Parliament. An English spring! Why not an Irish one? or Jewish? The chair moved slowly ahead, past tufts of sturdy bluebells that stood up like wheat, and over grey burdock leaves. When they came to the open place where the trees had been felled, the light flooded in rather stark. And the bluebells made sheets of bright blue colour, here and there, sheering off into lilac and purple. And between, the bracken was lifting its brown curled heads, like legions of young snakes with a new secret to whisper to Eve.

Clifford kept the chair going till he came to the brow of the hill; Connie followed slowly behind. The oak-buds were opening soft and brown. Everything came tenderly out of the old hardness. Even the snaggy craggy oak trees put out the softest young leaves, spreading thin, brown little wings like young bat-wings in the light. Why had men never any newness in them, any freshness to come forth with! Stale men!

Clifford stopped the chair at the top of the rise and looked down. The bluebells washed blue like floodwater over the broad riding, and lit up the downhill with a warm blueness.

'It's a very fine colour in itself,' said Clifford, 'but useless for making a painting.'

'Quite!' said Connie, completely uninterested.

'Shall I venture as far as the spring?' said Clifford.

'Will the chair get up again?' she said.

'We'll try; nothing venture, nothing win!'

And the chair began to advance slowly, joltingly down the beautiful broad riding washed over with blue encroaching hyacinths. Oh last of all ships, through the hyacinthian shallows! Oh pinnace on the last wild waters, sailing in the last voyage of our civilisation! Whither, O weird wheeled ship, your slow course steering. Quiet and complacent, Clifford sat at the wheel of adventure: in his old black hat and tweed jacket, motionless and cautious. Oh Captain, my Captain, our splendid trip is done! Not yet though! Downhill, in the wake, came Constance in her grey dress, watching the chair jolt downwards.

They passed the narrow track to the hut. Thank heaven it was not wide enough for the chair: hardly wide enough for one person. The chair reached the bottom of the slope, and swerved round, to disappear. And Connie heard a low whistle behind her. She glanced sharply round: the keeper was striding downhill towards her, his dog keeping behind him.

'Is Sir Clifford going to the cottage?' he asked, looking into her eyes.

'No, only to the well.'

'Ah! Good! Then I can keep out of sight. But I shall see you tonight, I shall wait for you at the park gate about ten.'

He looked again direct into her eyes.

'Yes,' she faltered.

They heard the Papp! Papp! of Clifford's horn, tooting for Connie. She 'Coo-eed!' in reply. The keeper's face flickered with a little grimace, and with his hand he softly brushed her breast upwards, from underneath. She looked at him, frightened, and started running down the hill, calling Coo-ee! again to Clifford. The man above watched her, then turned, grinning faintly, back into his path.

She found Clifford slowly mounting to the spring, which was halfway up the slope of the dark larch-wood. He was there by the time she caught him up.

'She did that all right,' he said, referring to the chair.

Connie looked at the great grey leaves of burdock that grew out ghostly from the edge of the larch-wood. The people call it Robin Hood's Rhubarb. How silent and gloomy it seemed by the well! Yet the water bubbled so bright, wonderful! And there were bits of eye-bright and strong blue bugle . . . and there, under the bank, the yellow earth was moving. A mole! It emerged, rowing its pink hands, and waving its blind gimlet of a face, with the tiny pink nose-tip uplifted.

'It seems to see with the end of its nose,' said Connie.

'Better than with its eyes!' he said. 'Will you drink?'

'Will you?'

She took an enamel mug from a twig on a tree, and stooped to fill it for him. He drank in sips. Then she stooped again, and drank a little herself.

'So icy!' she said gasping.

'Good, isn't it! Did you wish?'

'Did you?'

'Yes, I wished. But I won't tell.'

She was aware of the rapping of a woodpecker, then of the wind, soft and eerie through the larches. She looked up. White clouds were crossing the blue.

'Clouds!' she said.

'White lambs only,' he replied.

A shadow crossed the little clearing. The mole had swum out on to the soft yellow earth.

'Unpleasant little beast, we ought to kill him,' said Clifford.

'Look! he's like a parson in a pulpit,' said she.

She gathered some sprigs of woodruff and brought them to him.

'New-mown hay!' he said. 'Doesn't it smell like the romantic ladies of the last century, who had their heads screwed on the right way after all!'

She was looking at the white clouds.

'I wonder if it will rain,' she said.

'Rain! Why! Do you want it to?'

They started on the return journey, Clifford jolting cautiously downhill. They came to the dark bottom of the hollow, turned to the right, and after a hundred yards swerved up the foot of the long slope, where bluebells stood in the light.

'Now, old girl!' said Clifford, putting the chair to it.

It was a steep and jolty climb. The chair pugged slowly, in a struggling unwilling fashion. Still, she nosed her way up unevenly, till she came to where the hyacinths were all around her, then she balked, struggled, jerked a little way out of the flowers, then stopped.

'We'd better sound the horn and see if the keeper will come,' said Connie. 'He could push her a bit. For that matter, I will push. It helps.'

'We'll let her breathe,' said Clifford. 'Do you mind putting a scotch under the wheel?'

Connie found a stone, and they waited. After a while Clifford started his motor again, then set the chair in motion. It struggled and faltered like a sick thing, with curious noises.

'Let me push!' said Connie, coming up behind.

'No! Don't push!' he said angrily. 'What's the good of the damned thing, if it has to be pushed! Put the stone under!'

There was another pause, then another start; but more ineffectual than before.

'You *must* let me push,' said she. 'Or sound the horn for the keeper.'

'Wait!'

She waited; and he had another try, doing more harm than good.

'Sound the horn then, if you won't let me push,' she said.

'Hell! Be quiet a moment!'

She was quiet a moment: he made shattering efforts with the little motor.

'You'll only break the thing down altogether, Clifford,' she remonstrated; 'besides wasting your nervous energy.'

'If I could only get out and look at the damned thing!' he said, exasperated. And he sounded the horn stridently. 'Perhaps Mellors can see what's wrong.'

They waited, among the mashed flowers under a sky softly curdling with cloud. In the silence a wood-pigeon began to coo, roo-hoo hoo! roo-hoo hoo! Clifford shut her up with a blast on the horn.

The keeper appeared directly, striding inquiringly round the corner. He saluted.

'Do you know anything about motors?' asked Clifford sharply.

'I am afraid I don't. Has she gone wrong?'

'Apparently!' snapped Clifford.

The man crouched solicitously by the wheel, and peered at the little engine.

'I'm afraid I know nothing at all about these mechanical things, Sir Clifford,' he said calmly. 'If she has enough petrol and oil – '

'Just look carefully and see if you can see anything broken,' snapped Clifford

The man laid his gun against a tree, took off his coat and threw it beside it. The brown dog sat guard. Then he sat down on his heels and peered under the chair, poking with his finger at the greasy little engine, and resenting the grease-marks on his clean Sunday shirt.

'Doesn't seem anything broken,' he said. And he stood up, pushing back his hat from his forehead, rubbing his brow and apparently studying.

'Have you looked at the rods underneath?' asked Clifford. 'See if they are all right!'

The man lay flat on his stomach on the floor, his neck pressed back, wriggling under the engine and poking with his finger. Connie thought what a pathetic sort of thing a man was, feeble and small-looking, when he was lying on his belly on the big earth.

'Seems all right as far as I can see,' came his muffled voice.

'I don't suppose you can do anything,' said Clifford.

'Seems as if I can't!' And he scrambled up and sat on his heels, collier fashion. 'There's certainly nothing obviously broken.'

Clifford started his engine, then put her in gear. She would not move.

'Run her a bit hard, like,' suggested the keeper.

Clifford resented the interference: but he made his engine buzz like a blue-bottle. Then she coughed and snarled and seemed to go better.

'Sounds as if she'd come clear,' said Mellors.

But Clifford had already jerked her into gear. She gave a sick lurch and ebbed weakly forwards.

'If I give her a push, she'll do it,' said the keeper, going behind.

'Keep off!' snapped Clifford. 'She'll do it by herself.'

'But Clifford!' put in Connie from the bank, 'You know it's too much for her. Why are you so obstinate!'

Clifford was pale with anger. He jabbed at his levers. The chair gave a sort of scurry, reeled on a few more yards, and came to her end amid a particularly promising patch of bluebells.

'She's done!' said the keeper. 'Not power enough.'

'She's been up here before,' said Clifford coldly.

'She won't do it this time,' said the keeper.

Clifford did not reply. He began doing things with his engine, running her fast and slow as if to get some sort of tune out of her. The wood re-echoed with weird noises. Then he put her in gear with a jerk, having jerked off his brake.

'You'll rip her inside out,' murmured the keeper.

The chair charged in a sick lurch sideways at the ditch.

'Clifford!' cried Connie, rushing forward.

But the keeper had got the chair by the rail. Clifford, however, putting on all his pressure, managed to steer into the riding, and with a strange noise the chair was fighting the hill. Mellors pushed steadily behind, and up she went, as if to retrieve herself.

'You see, she's doing it!' said Clifford, victorious, glancing over his shoulder. There he saw the keeper's face.

'Are you pushing her?'

'She won't do it without.'

'Leave her alone. I asked you not.'

'She won't do it.'

'*Let her try!*' snarled Clifford, with all his emphasis.

The keeper stood back: then turned to fetch his coat and gun. The chair seemed to strangle immediately. She stood inert. Clifford, seated a prisoner, was white with vexation. He jerked at the levers with his hand, his feet were no good. He got queer noises out of her. In savage impatience he moved little handles and got more noises out of her. But she would not budge. No, she would not budge. He stopped the engine and sat rigid with anger.

Constance sat on the bank and looked at the wretched and trampled bluebells. 'Nothing quite so lovely as an English spring.' 'I can do my share of ruling.' 'What we need to take up now is whips, not swords.' 'The ruling classes!'

The keeper strode up with his coat and gun, Flossie cautiously at his heels. Clifford asked the man to do something or other to the engine. Connie, who understood nothing at all of the technicalities of motors, and who had had experience of breakdowns, sat patiently on the bank as if she were a cipher. The keeper lay on his stomach again. The ruling classes and the serving classes!

He got to his feet and said patiently, 'Try her again, then.'

He spoke in a quiet voice, almost as if to a child.

Clifford tried her, and Mellors stepped quickly behind and began to push. She was going, the engine doing about half the work, the man the rest.

Clifford glanced round, yellow with anger.

'Will you get off there!'

The keeper dropped his hold at once, and Clifford added: 'How shall I know what she is doing!'

The man put his gun down and began to pull on his coat. He'd done.

The chair began slowly to run backwards.

'Clifford, your brake!' cried Connie.

She, Mellors, and Clifford moved at once, Connie and the keeper jostling lightly. The chair stood. There was a moment of dead silence.

'It's obvious I'm at everybody's mercy!' said Clifford. He was yellow with anger.

No one answered. Mellors was slinging his gun over his shoulder, his face queer and expressionless, save for an abstracted look of patience. The dog Flossie, standing on guard almost between her master's legs, moved uneasily, eyeing the chair with great suspicion and dislike, and very much perplexed between the three human beings. The *tableau vivant* remained set among the squashed bluebells, nobody proffering a word.

'I expect she'll have to be pushed,' said Clifford at last, with an affectation of *sang froid*.

No answer. Mellors' abstracted face looked as if he had heard nothing. Connie glanced anxiously at him. Clifford too glanced round.

'Do you mind pushing her home, Mellors!' he said in a cool, superior tone. 'I hope I have said nothing to offend you,' he added, in a tone of dislike.

'Nothing at all, Sir Clifford! Do you want me to push that chair?'

'If you please.'

The man stepped up to it: but this time it was without effect. The brake was jammed. They poked and pulled, and the keeper took off his gun and his coat once more. And now Clifford said never a word. At last the keeper heaved the back of the chair off the ground and, with an instantaneous push of his foot, tried to loosen the wheels. He failed, the chair sank. Clifford was clutching the sides. The man gasped with the weight.

'Don't do it!' cried Connie to him.

'If you'll pull the wheel that way, so!' he said to her, showing her how.

'No! You mustn't lift it! You'll strain yourself,' she said, flushed now with anger.

But he looked into her eyes and nodded. And she had to go and take hold of the wheel, ready. He heaved and she tugged, and the chair reeled.

'For God's sake!' cried Clifford in terror.

But it was all right, and the brake was off. The keeper put a stone under the wheel, and went to sit on the bank, his heart beating and his face white with the effort, semi-conscious. Connie looked at him, and almost cried with anger. There was a pause and a dead silence. She saw his hands trembling on his thighs.

'Have you hurt yourself?' she asked, going to him.

'No. No!' He turned away almost angrily.

There was dead silence. The back of Clifford's fair head did not move. Even the dog stood motionless. The sky had clouded over.

At last he sighed, and blew his nose on his red handkerchief.

'That pneumonia took a lot out of me,' he said.

No one answered. Connie calculated the amount of strength it must have taken to heave up that chair and the bulky Clifford: too much, far too much! If it hadn't killed him!

He rose, and again picked up his coat, slinging it through the handle of the chair.

'Are you ready, then, Sir Clifford?'

'When you are!'

He stooped and took out the scotch, then put his weight against the chair. He was paler than Connie had ever seen him: and more absent. Clifford was a heavy man: and the hill was steep. Connie stepped to the keeper's side.

'I'm going to push too!' she said.

And she began to shove with a woman's turbulent energy of anger. The chair went faster. Clifford looked round.

'Is that necessary?' he said.

'Very! Do you want to kill the man! If you'd let the motor work while it would – '

But she did not finish. She was already panting. She slackened off a little, for it was surprisingly hard work.

'Ay! slower!' said the man at her side, with a faint smile of his eyes.

'Are you sure you've not hurt yourself?' she said fiercely.

He shook his head. She looked at his smallish, short, alive hand, browned by the weather. It was the hand that caressed her. She had never even looked at it before. It seemed so still, like him, with a curious inward stillness that made her want to clutch it, as if she could not reach it. All her soul suddenly swept towards him: he was so silent, and out of reach! And he felt his limbs revive. Shoving with his left hand, he laid his right on her round white wrist, softly enfolding her wrist, with a caress. And the flame of strength went down his back and his loins, reviving him. And she bent suddenly and kissed his hand. Meanwhile the back of Clifford's head was held sleek and motionless, just in front of them.

At the top of the hill they rested, and Connie was glad to let go. She had had fugitive dreams of friendship between these two men: one her husband, the other the father of her child. Now she saw the screaming absurdity of her dreams. The two males were as hostile as fire and water. They mutually exterminated one another. And she realised for the first time, what a queer subtle thing hate is. For the first time, she had consciously and definitely hated Clifford, with vivid hate: as if he ought to be obliterated from the face of the earth. And it was strange, how free and full of life it made her feel, to hate him and to admit it fully to herself. 'Now I've hated him, I shall never be able to go on living with him,' came the thought into her mind.

On the level the keeper could push the chair alone. Clifford made a little conversation with her, to show his complete composure: about Aunt Eva, who was at Dieppe, and about Sir Malcolm, who had written to ask would Connie drive with him in his small car, to Venice, or would she and Hilda go by train.

'I'd much rather go by train,' said Connie. 'I don't like long motor drives, especially when there's dust. But I shall see what Hilda wants.'

'She will want to drive her own car, and take you with her,' he said.

'Probably! I must help up here. You've no idea how heavy this chair is.'

She went to the back of the chair, and plodded side by side with the keeper, shoving up the pink path. She did not care who saw.

'Why not let me wait, and fetch Field. He is strong enough for the job,' said Clifford.

'It's so near,' she panted.

But both she and Mellors wiped the sweat from their faces when they came to the top. It was curious, but this bit of work together had brought them much closer than they had been before.

'Thanks so much, Mellors,' said Clifford, when they were at the house door. 'I must get a different sort of motor, that's all. Won't you go to the kitchen and have a meal? It must be about time.'

'Thank you, Sir Clifford. I was going to my mother for dinner today, Sunday.'

'As you like.'

Mellors slung into his coat, looked at Connie, saluted, and was gone. Connie, furious, went upstairs

At lunch she could not contain her feeling.

'Why are you so abominably inconsiderate, Clifford?' she said to him.

'Of whom?'

'Of the keeper! If that is what you call ruling classes, I'm sorry for you.'

'Why?'

'A man who's been ill, and isn't strong! My word, if I were the serving classes, I'd let you wait for service. I'd let you whistle.'

'I quite believe it.'

'If he'd been sitting in a chair with paralysed legs, and behaved as you behaved, what would you have done for *him*?'

'My dear evangelist, this confusing of persons and personalities is in bad taste.'

'And your nasty, sterile want of common sympathy is in the worst taste imaginable. *Noblesse oblige!* You and your ruling class!'

'And to what should it oblige me? To have a lot of unnecessary emotions about my gamekeeper? I refuse. I leave it all to my evangelist.'

'As if he weren't a man as much as you are, my word!'

'My gamekeeper to boot, and I pay him two pounds a week and give him a house.'

'Pay him! What do you think you pay for, with two pounds a week and a house?'

'His services.'

'Bah! I would tell you to keep your two pounds a week and your house.'

'Probably he would like to: but can't afford the luxury!'

'You, and *rule*!' she said. 'You don't rule, don't flatter yourself. You have only got more than your share of the money, and make people work for you for two pounds a week, or threaten them with starvation. Rule! What do you give forth of rule? Why, you're dried up! You only bully with your money, like any Jew or any Schieber!'

'You are very elegant in your speech, Lady Chatterley!'

'I assure you, you were very elegant altogether out there in the wood. I was utterly ashamed of you. Why, my father is ten times the human being you are: you *gentleman*!'

He reached and rang the bell for Mrs Bolton. But he was yellow at the gills.

She went up to her room, furious, saying to herself, 'Him and buying people! Well, he doesn't buy me, and therefore there's no need for me to stay with him. Dead fish of a gentleman, with his celluloid soul! And how they take one in, with their manners and their mock wistfulness and gentleness. They've got about as much feeling as celluloid has.'

She made her plans for the night, and determined to get Clifford off her mind. She didn't want to hate him. She didn't want to be mixed up very intimately with him in any sort of feeling. She wanted him not to know anything at all about herself: and especially, not to know anything about her feeling for the keeper. This squabble of her attitude to the servants was an old one. He found her too familiar, she found him stupidly insentient, tough and india-rubbery where other people were concerned.

She went downstairs calmly, with her old demure bearing, at dinner-time. He was still yellow at the gills: in for one of his liver bouts, when he was really very queer. He was reading a French book.

'Have you ever read Proust?' he asked her.

'I've tried, but he bores me.'

'He's really very extraordinary.'

'Possibly! But he bores me: all that sophistication! He doesn't have feelings, he only has streams of words about feelings. I'm tired of self-important mentalities.'

'Would you prefer self-important animalities?'

'Perhaps! But one might possibly get something that wasn't self-important.'

'Well, I like Proust's subtlety and his well-bred anarchy.'

'It makes you very dead, really.'

'There speaks my evangelical little wife.'

They were at it again, at it again! But she couldn't help fighting him. He seemed to sit there like a skeleton, sending out a skeleton's cold grizzly *will* against her. Almost she could feel the skeleton clutching her and pressing her to its cage of ribs. He too was really up in arms: and she was a little afraid of him.

She went upstairs as soon as possible, and went to bed quite early. But at half-past nine she got up, and went outside to listen. There was no sound. She slipped on a dressing-gown and went downstairs. Clifford and Mrs Bolton were playing cards, gambling. They would probably go on until midnight.

Connie returned to her room, threw her pyjamas on the tossed bed, put on a thin nightdress and over that a woollen day-dress, put on rubber tennis-shoes, and then a light coat. And she was ready. If she met anybody, she was just going out for a few minutes. And in the morning, when she came in again, she would just have been for a little walk in the dew, as she fairly often did before breakfast. For the rest, the only danger was that someone should go into her room during the night. But that was most unlikely: not one chance in a hundred.

Betts had not yet locked up. He fastened up the house at ten o'clock, and unfastened it again at seven in the morning. She slipped out silently and unseen. There was a half-moon shining, enough to make a little light in the world, not enough to show her up in her dark-grey coat. She walked quickly across the park, not really in the thrill of the assignation, but with a certain anger and rebellion burning in her heart. It was not the right sort of heart to take to a love-meeting. But *à la guerre comme à la guerre*!

Chapter 14

When she got near the park-gate, she heard the click of the latch. He was there, then, in the darkness of the wood, and had seen her!

'You are good and early,' he said out of the dark. 'Was everything all right?'

'Perfectly easy.'

He shut the gate quietly after her, and made a spot of light on the dark ground, showing the pallid flowers still standing there open in the night. They went on apart, in silence.

'Are you sure you didn't hurt yourself this morning with that chair?' she asked.

'No, no!'

'When you had that pneumonia, what did it do to you?'

'Oh nothing! it left my heart not so strong and the lungs not so elastic. But it always does that.'

'And you ought not to make violent physical efforts?'

'Not often.'

She plodded on in an angry silence.

'Did you hate Clifford?' she said at last.

'Hate him, no! I've met too many like him to upset myself hating him. I know beforehand I don't care for his sort, and I let it go at that.'

'What is his sort?'

'Nay, you know better than I do. The sort of youngish gentleman a bit like a lady, and no balls.'

'What balls?'

'Balls! A man's balls!'

She pondered this.

'But is it a question of that?' she said, a little annoyed.

'You say a man's got no brain, when he's a fool: and no heart, when he's mean; and no stomach when he's a funker. And when he's got none of that spunky wild bit of a man in him, you say he's got no balls. When he's sort of tame.'

She pondered this.

'And is Clifford tame?' she asked.

'Tame, and nasty with it: like most such fellows, when you come up against 'em.'

'And do you think you're not tame?'

'Maybe not quite!'

At length she saw in the distance a yellow light.

She stood still.

'There is a light!' she said.

'I always leave a light in the house,' he said.

She went on again at his side, but not touching him, wondering why she was going with him at all.

He unlocked, and they went in, he bolting the door behind them. As if it were a prison, she thought! The kettle was singing by the red fire, there were cups on the table.

She sat in the wooden armchair by the fire. It was warm after the chill outside.

'I'll take off my shoes, they are wet,' she said.

She sat with her stockinged feet on the bright steel fender. He went to the pantry, bringing food: bread and butter and pressed tongue. She was warm: she took off her coat. He hung it on the door.

'Shall you have cocoa or tea or coffee to drink?' he asked.

'I don't think I want anything,' she said, looking at the table. 'But you eat.'

'Nay, I don't care about it. I'll just feed the dog.'

He tramped with a quiet inevitability over the brick floor, putting food for the dog in a brown bowl. The spaniel looked up at him anxiously.

'Ay, this is thy supper, tha nedna look as if tha wouldna get it!' he said.

He set the bowl on the stairfoot mat, and sat himself on a chair by the wall, to take off his leggings and boots. The dog, instead of eating, came to him again, and sat looking up at him, troubled.

He slowly unbuckled his leggings. The dog edged a little nearer.

'What's amiss wi' thee then? Art upset because there's somebody else here? Tha'rt a female, tha art! Go an' eat thy supper.'

He put his hand on her head, and the bitch leaned her head sideways against him. He slowly, softly pulled the long silky ear.

'There!' he said. 'There! Go an' eat thy supper! Go!'

He tilted his chair towards the pot on the mat, and the dog meekly went, and fell to eating.

'Do you like dogs?' Connie asked him.

'No, not really. They're too tame and clinging.'

He had taken off his leggings and was unlacing his heavy boots. Connie had turned from the fire. How bare the little room was! Yet over his head on the wall hung a hideous enlarged photograph of a young married couple, apparently him and a bold-faced young woman, no doubt his wife.

'Is that you?' Connie asked him.

He twisted and looked at the enlargement above his head.

'Ay! Taken just afore we were married, when I was twenty-one.' He looked at it impassively.

'Do you like it?' Connie asked him.

'Like it? No! I never liked the thing. But she fixed it all up to have it done, like.'

He returned to pulling off his boots.

'If you don't like it, why do you keep it hanging there? Perhaps your wife would like to have it,' she said.

He looked up at her with a sudden grin.

'She carted off ivrything as was worth taking from th' 'ousc,' he said. 'But she left *that*!'

'Then why do you keep it? for sentimental reasons?'

'Nay, I niver look at it. I hardly knowed it wor theer. It's bin theer sin we come to this place.'

'Why don't you burn it?' she said.

He twisted round again and looked at the enlarged photograph. It was framed in a brown-and-gilt frame, hideous. It showed a clean-shaven, alert, very young-looking man in a rather high collar, and a somewhat plump, bold young woman with hair fluffed out and crimped, and wearing a dark satin blouse.

'It wouldn't be a bad idea, would it?' he said.

He had pulled off his boots, and put on a pair of slippers. He stood up on the chair, and lifted down the photograph. It left a pale place on the greenish wallpaper.

'No use dusting it now,' he said, setting the thing against the wall.

He went to the scullery, and returned with hammer and pincers. Sitting where he had sat before, he started to tear off the back-paper from the big frame, and to pull out the sprigs that held the backboard in position, working with the immediate quiet absorption that was characteristic of him.

He soon had the nails out: then he pulled out the backboards, then the enlargement itself, in its solid white mount. He looked at the photograph with amusement.

'Shows me for what I was, a young curate, and her for what she was, a bully,' he said. 'The prig and the bully!'

'Let me look!' said Connie.

He did look indeed very clean-shaven and very clean altogether, one of the clean young men of twenty years ago. But even in the photograph his eyes were alert and dauntless. And the woman was not altogether a bully, though her jowl was heavy. There was a touch of appeal in her.

'One never should keep these things,' said Connie.

'That one shouldn't! One should never have them made!'

He broke the cardboard photograph and mount over his knee, and when it was small enough, put it on the fire.

'It'll spoil the fire though,' he said.

The glass and the backboards he carefully took upstairs.

The frame he knocked asunder with a few blows of the hammer, making the stucco fly. Then he took the pieces into the scullery.

'We'll burn that tomorrow,' he said. 'There's too much plaster-moulding on it.'

Having cleared away, he sat down.

'Did you love your wife?' she asked him.

'Love?' he said. 'Did you love Sir Clifford?'

But she was not going to be put off.

'But you cared for her?' she insisted.

'Cared?' He grinned.

'Perhaps you care for her now,' she said.

'Me!' His eyes widened. 'Ah no, I can't think of her,' he said quietly.

'Why?'

But he shook his head.

'Then why don't you get a divorce? She'll come back to you one day,' said Connie.

He looked up at her sharply.

'She wouldn't come within a mile of me. She hates me a lot worse than I hate her.'

'You'll see she'll come back to you.'

'That she never shall. That's done! It would make me sick to see her.'

'You will see her. And you're not even legally separated, are you?'

'No.'

'Ah well, then she'll come back, and you'll have to take her in.'

He gazed at Connie fixedly. Then he gave the queer toss of his head.

'You may be right. I was a fool ever to come back here. But I felt stranded, and had to go somewhere. A man's a poor bit of a wastrel, blown about. But you're right. I'll get a divorce and get clear. I hate those things like death, officials and courts and judges. But I've got to get through with it. I'll get a divorce.'

And she saw his jaw set. Inwardly she exulted.

'I think I will have a cup of tea now,' she said.

He rose to make it. But his face was set.

As they sat at table she asked him, 'Why did you marry her? She was commoner than yourself. Mrs Bolton told me about her. She could never understand why you married her.'

He looked at her fixedly.

'I'll tell you,' he said. 'The first girl I had, I began with when I was sixteen. She was a schoolmaster's daughter over at Ollerton, pretty, beautiful really. I was supposed to be a clever sort of young fellow from Sheffield Grammar School, with a bit of French and German, very much up aloft. She was the romantic sort that hated commonness. She egged me on to poetry and reading: in a way, she made a man of me. I read and I thought like a house on fire, for her. And I was a clerk in Butterley offices, thin, white-faced fellow fuming with all the things I read. And about *everything* I talked to her: but everything. We talked ourselves into Persepolis and Timbuctoo. We were the most literary-cultured couple in ten counties. I held forth with rapture to her, positively with rapture. I simply went up in smoke. And she adored me. The serpent in the grass was sex. She somehow didn't have any; at least, not where it's supposed to be. I got thinner and crazier. Then I said we'd got to be lovers. I talked her into it, as usual. So she let me. I was excited, and she never wanted it. She just didn't want it. She adored me, she loved me to talk to her and kiss her: in that way she had a passion for me. But the other, she just didn't want. And there are lots of women like her. And it was just the other that I *did* want. So there we split. I was cruel, and left her. Then I took on with another girl, a teacher, who had made a scandal by carrying on with a married man and driving him nearly out of his mind. She was a soft, white-skinned, soft sort of a woman, older than me, and played the fiddle. And she was a demon. She loved everything about love, except the sex. Clinging, caressing, creeping into you in every way: but if you forced her to the sex itself, she just ground her teeth and sent out hate. I forced her to it, and she could simply numb me with hate because of it. So I was balked again. I loathed all that. I wanted a woman who wanted me, and wanted *it*.

'Then came Bertha Coutts. They'd lived next door to us when I was a little lad, so I knew 'em all right. And they were common. Well, Bertha went away to some place or other in Birmingham; she said, as a lady's companion; everybody else said, as a waitress or something in a hotel. Anyhow just when I was more than fed up with that other girl, when I was twenty-one, back comes Bertha, with airs and graces and smart clothes and a sort of bloom on her: a sort of sensual bloom that you'd see sometimes on a woman, or on a trolly. Well I was in a state of murder. I chucked up my job at Butterley because I thought I was a weed, clerking there: and I got on as overhead blacksmith at Tevershall: shoeing horses mostly. It had been my dad's job, and I'd always been with him. It was a job I liked: handling horses: and it came natural to me. So I stopped talking "fine", as they call it, talking proper English, and went back to talking broad. I still read books, at home: but I blacksmithed and had a pony-trap of my own, and was My Lord Duckfoot. My dad left me three hundred pounds when he died. So I took on with Bertha, and I was glad she was common. I wanted her to be common. I wanted to be common myself. Well, I married her, and she wasn't bad. Those other "pure" women had nearly taken all the balls out of me, but she was all right that way. She wanted me, and made no bones about it. And I was as pleased as punch. That was what I wanted: a woman who *wanted* me to fuck her. So I fucked her like a good un. And I think she despised me a bit, for being so pleased about it, and bringin' her her breakfast in bed sometimes. She sort of let things go, didn't get me a proper dinner when I came home from work, and if I said anything, flew out at me. And I flew back, hammer and tongues. She flung a cup at me and I took her by the scruff of the neck and squeezed the life out of her. That sort of thing! But she treated me with insolence. And she got so's she'd never have me when I wanted her: never. Always put me off, brutal as you like. And then when she'd put me right off, and I didn't want her, she'd come all lovey-dovey, and get me. And I always went. But when I had her, she'd never come off when I did. Never! She'd just wait. If I kept back for half an hour, she'd keep back longer. And when I'd come and really finished, then she'd start on her own account, and I had to stop inside her till she brought herself off, wriggling and shouting, she'd clutch clutch with herself down there, an' then she'd come off, fair in ecstasy. And then she'd say: That was lovely! Gradually I got sick of it: and she got worse. She sort of got harder and harder to bring off, and she'd sort of tear at me down there, as if it was a beak tearing at me. By God, you think a woman's soft down there, like a fig. But I tell you the old rampers have beaks between their legs, and they tear at you with it till you're sick. Self! Self! Self! all self! tearing and shouting! They talk about men's selfishness, but I doubt if it can ever touch a woman's blind beakishness, once she's gone that way. Like an old trull! And she couldn't help it. I told her about it, I told her how I hated it. And she'd even try. She'd try to lie still and let *me* work the business. She'd try. But it was no good. She got no feeling off it, from my working. She had to work the thing herself, grind her own coffee. And it came back on her like a raving necessity, she had to let herself go, and tear, tear, tear, as if she had no sensation in her except in the top of her beak, the very outside top tip, that rubbed and tore. That's how old whores used to be, so men used to say. It was a low kind of self-will in her, a raving sort of self-will: like in a woman who drinks. Well in the end I couldn't stand it. We slept apart. She herself had started it, in her bouts when she wanted to be clear of me, when she said I bossed her. She had started having a room for herself. But the time came when I wouldn't have her coming to my room. I wouldn't.

'I hated it. And she hated me. My God, how she hated me before that child was born! I often think she conceived it out of hate. Anyhow, after the child was born I left her alone. And then came the war, and I joined up. And I didn't come back till I knew she was with that fellow at Stacks Gate.'

He broke off, pale in the face.

'And what is the man at Stacks Gate like?' asked Connie.

'A big baby sort of fellow, very low-mouthed. She bullies him, and they both drink.'

'My word, if she came back!'

'My God, yes! I should just go, disappear again.'

There was a silence. The pasteboard in the fire had turned to grey ash.

'So when you did get a woman who wanted you,' said Connie, 'you got a bit too much of a good thing.'

'Ay! Seems so! Yet even then I'd rather have her than the never-never ones: the white love of my youth, and that other poison-smelling lily, and the rest.'

'What about the rest?' said Connie.

'The rest? There is no rest. Only to my experience the mass of women are like this: most of them want a man, but don't want the sex, but they put up with it, as part of the bargain. The more old-fashioned sort just lie there like nothing and let you go ahead. They don't mind afterwards: then they like you. But the actual thing itself is nothing to them, a bit distasteful. And most men like it that way. I hate it. But the sly sort of women who are like that pretend they're not. They pretend they're passionate and have thrills. But it's all cockaloopy. They make it up. Then there's the ones that love everything, every kind of feeling and cuddling and going off, every kind except the natural one. They always make you go off when you're *not* in the only place you should be, when you go off. Then there's the hard sort, that are the devil to bring off at all, and bring themselves off, like my wife. They want to be the active party. Then there's the sort that's just dead inside, but dead: and they know it. Then there's the sort that puts you out before you really "come", and go on writhing their loins till they bring themselves off against your thighs. But they're mostly the Lesbian sort. It's astonishing how Lesbian women are, consciously or unconsciously. Seems to me they're nearly all Lesbian.'

'And do you mind?' asked Connie.

'I could kill them. When I'm with a woman who's really Lesbian, I fairly howl in my soul, wanting to kill her.'

'And what do you do?'

'Just get away as fast as I can.'

'But do you think Lesbian women any worse than homosexual men?'

'*I* do! Because I've suffered more from them. In the abstract, I've no idea. When I get with a Lesbian woman, whether she knows she's one or not, I see red. No, no! But I wanted to have nothing to do with any woman any more. I wanted to keep to myself: keep my privacy and my decency.'

He looked pale, and his brows were sombre.

'And were you sorry when I came along?' she asked.

'I was sorry and I was glad.'

'And what are you now?'

'I'm sorry, from the outside: all the complications and the ugliness and recrimination that's bound to come, sooner or later. That's when my blood sinks, and I'm low. But when my blood comes up, I'm glad. I'm even triumphant. I was really getting bitter. I thought there was no real sex left: never a woman who'd really "come" naturally with a man: except black women, and somehow, well, we're white men: and they're a bit like mud.'

'And now, are you glad of me?' she asked.

'Yes! When I can forget the rest. When I can't forget the rest, I want to get under the table and die.'

'Why under the table?'

'Why?' he laughed. 'Hide, I suppose. Baby!'

'You do seem to have had awful experiences of women,' she said.

'You see, I couldn't fool myself. That's where most men manage. They take an attitude, and accept a lie. I could never fool myself. I knew what I wanted with a woman, and I could never say I'd got it when I hadn't.'

'But have you got it now?'

'Looks as if I might have.'

'Then why are you so pale and gloomy?'

'Bellyful of remembering: and perhaps afraid of myself.'

She sat in silence. It was growing late.

'And you do think it's important, a man and a woman?' she asked him.

'For me it is. For me it's the core to my life: if I have a right relation with a woman.'

'And if you didn't get it?'

'Then I'd have to do without.'

Again she pondered, before she asked, 'And do you think you've always been right with women?'

'God, no! I let my wife get to what she was: my fault a good deal. I spoilt her. And I'm very mistrustful. You'll have to expect it. It takes a lot to make me trust anybody, inwardly. So perhaps I'm a fraud too. I mistrust. And tenderness is not to be mistaken.'

She looked at him.

'You don't mistrust with your body, when your blood comes up,' she said. 'You don't mistrust then, do you?'

'No, alas! That's how I've got into all the trouble. And that's why my mind mistrusts so thoroughly.'

'Let your mind mistrust. What does it matter!'

The dog sighed with discomfort on the mat. The ash-clogged fire sank.

'We *are* a couple of battered warriors,' said Connie.

'Are you battered too?' he laughed. 'And here we are returning to the fray!'

'Yes! I feel really frightened.'

'Ay!'

He got up, and put her shoes to dry, and wiped his own and set them near the fire. In the morning he would grease them. He poked the ash of pasteboard as much as possible out of the fire. 'Even burnt, it's filthy,' he said. Then he brought sticks and put them on the hob for the morning. Then he went out awhile with the dog.

When he came back, Connie said, 'I want to go out too, for a minute.'

She went alone into the darkness. There were stars overhead. She could smell flowers on the night air. And she could feel her wet shoes getting wetter again. But she felt like going away, right away from him and everybody.

It was chilly. She shuddered, and returned to the house. He was sitting in front of the low fire.

'Ugh! Cold!' she shuddered.

He put the sticks on the fire, and fetched more, till they had a good crackling chimneyful of blaze. The rippling running yellow flame made them both happy, warmed their faces and their souls.

'Never mind!' she said, taking his hand as he sat silent and remote. 'One does one's best.'

'Ay!' He sighed, with a twist of a smile.

She slipped over to him, and into his arms, as he sat there before the fire.

'Forget then!' she whispered. 'Forget!'

He held her close, in the running warmth of the fire. The flame itself was like a forgetting. And her soft, warm, ripe weight! Slowly his blood turned, and began to ebb back into strength and reckless vigour again.

'And perhaps the women *really* wanted to be there and love you properly, only perhaps they couldn't. Perhaps it wasn't all their fault,' she said.

'I know it. Do you think I don't know what a broken-backed snake that's been trodden on I was myself!'

She clung to him suddenly. She had not wanted to start all this again. Yet some perversity had made her.

'But you're not now,' she said. 'You're not that now: a broken-backed snake that's been trodden on.'

'I don't know what I am. There's black days ahead.'

'No!' she protested, clinging to him. 'Why? Why?'

'There's black days coming for us all and for everybody,' he repeated with a prophetic gloom.

'No! You're not to say it!'

He was silent. But she could feel the black void of despair inside him. That was the death of all desire, the death of all love: this despair that was like the dark cave inside the men, in which their spirit was lost.

'And you talk so coldly about sex,' she said. 'You talk as if you had only wanted your own pleasure and satisfaction.'

She was protesting nervously against him.

'Nay!' he said. 'I wanted to have my pleasure and satisfaction of a woman, and I never got it: because I could never get my pleasure and satisfaction of *her* unless she got hers of me at the same time. And it never happened. It takes two.'

'But you never believed in your women. You don't even believe really in me,' she said.

'I don't know what believing in a woman means.'

'That's it, you see!'

She still was curled on his lap. But his spirit was grey and absent, he was not there for her. And everything she said drove him further.

'But what *do* you believe in?' she insisted.

'I don't know.'

'Nothing, like all the men I've ever known,' she said.

They were both silent. Then he roused himself and said, 'Yes, I do believe in something. I believe in being warm-hearted. I believe especially in being warm-hearted in love, in fucking with a warm heart. I believe if men could fuck with warm hearts, and the women take it warm-heartedly, everything would come all right. It's all this cold-hearted fucking that is death and idiocy.'

'But you don't fuck me cold-heartedly,' she protested.

'I don't want to fuck you at all. My heart's as cold as cold potatoes just now.'

'Oh!' she said, kissing him mockingly. 'Let's have them *sautées*.' He laughed, and sat erect.

'It's a fact!' he said. 'Anything for a bit of warm-heartedness. But the women don't like it. Even you don't really like it. You like good, sharp, piercing cold-hearted fucking, and then pretending it's all sugar. Where's your tenderness for me? You're as suspicious of me as a cat is of a dog. I tell you it takes two even to be tender and warm-hearted. You love fucking all right: but you want it to be called something grand and mysterious, just to flatter your own self-importance. Your own self-importance is more to you, fifty times more, than any man, or being together with a man.'

'But that's what I'd say of you. Your own self-importance is everything to you.'

'Ay! Very well then!' he said, moving as if he wanted to rise. 'Let's keep apart then. I'd rather die than do any more cold-hearted fucking.'

She slid away from him, and he stood up.

'And do you think *I* want it?' she said.

'I hope you don't,' he replied. 'But anyhow, you go to bed an' I'll sleep down here.'

She looked at him. He was pale, his brows were sullen, he was as distant in recoil as the cold pole. Men were all alike.

'I can't go home till morning,' she said.

'No! Go to bed. It's a quarter to one.'

'I certainly won't,' she said.

He went across and picked up his boots.

'Then I'll go out!' he said.

He began to put on his boots. She stared at him.

'Wait!' she faltered. 'Wait! What's come between us?'

He was bent over, lacing his boot, and did not reply. The moments passed. A dimness came over her, like a swoon. All her consciousness died, and she stood there wide-eyed, looking at him from the unknown, knowing nothing any more.

He looked up, because of the silence, and saw her wide-eyed and lost. And as if a wind tossed him he got up and hobbled over to her, one shoe off and one shoe on, and took her in his arms, pressing her against his body, which somehow felt hurt right through. And there he held her, and there she remained.

Till his hands reached blindly down and felt for her, and felt under the clothing to where she was smooth and warm.

'Ma lass!' he murmured. 'Ma little lass! Dunna let's fight! Dunna let's niver fight! I love thee an' th' touch on thee. Dunna argue wi' me! Dunna! Dunna! Dunna! Let's be together.'

She lifted her face and looked at him.

'Don't be upset,' she said steadily. 'It's no good being upset. Do you really want to be together with me?'

She looked with wide, steady eyes into his face. He stopped, and went suddenly still, turning his face aside. All his body went perfectly still, but did not withdraw.

Then he lifted his head and looked into her eyes, with his odd, faintly mocking grin, saying: 'Ay-ay! Let's be together on oath.'

'But really?' she said, her eyes filling with tears.

'Ay really! Heart an' belly an' cock.'

He still smiled faintly down at her, with the flicker of irony in his eyes, and a touch of bitterness.

She was silently weeping, and he lay with her and went into her there on the hearthrug, and so they gained a measure of equanimity. And then they went quickly to bed, for it was growing chill, and they had tired each other out. And she nestled up to him, feeling small and enfolded, and they both went to sleep at once, fast in one sleep. And so they lay and never moved, till the sun rose over the wood and day was beginning.

Then he woke up and looked at the light. The curtains were drawn. He listened to the loud wild calling of blackbirds and thrushes in the wood. It would be a brilliant morning, about half past five, his hour for rising. He had slept so fast! It was such a new day! The woman was still curled asleep and tender. His hand moved on her, and she opened her blue, wondering eyes, smiling unconsciously into his face.

'Are you awake?' she said to him.

He was looking into her eyes. He smiled, and kissed her. And suddenly she roused and sat up.

'Fancy that I am here!' she said.

She looked round the whitewashed little bedroom with its sloping ceiling and gable window where the white curtains were closed. The room was bare save for a little yellow-painted chest of drawers, and a chair: and the smallish white bed in which she lay with him.

'Fancy that we are here!' she said, looking down at him. He was lying watching her, stroking her breasts with his fingers, under the thin nightdress. When he was warm and smoothed out, he looked young and handsome. His eyes could look so warm. And she was fresh and young like a flower.

'I want to take this off!' he said, gathering the thin batiste nightdress and pulling it over her head. She sat there with bare shoulders and longish breasts faintly golden. He loved to make her breasts swing softly, like bells.

'You must take off your pyjamas too,' she said.

'Eh, nay!'

'Yes! Yes!' she commanded.

And he took off his old cotton pyjama-jacket, and pushed down the trousers. Save for his hands and wrists and face and neck he was white as milk, with fine slender muscular flesh. To Connie he was suddenly piercingly beautiful again, as when she had seen him that afternoon washing himself.

Gold of sunshine touched the closed white curtains. She felt it wanted to come in.

'Oh, do let's draw the curtains! The birds are singing so! Do let the sun in,' she said.

He slipped out of bed with his back to her, naked and white and thin, and went to the window, stooping a little, drawing the curtains and looking out for a moment. The back was white and fine, the small buttocks beautiful with an exquisite, delicate manliness, the back of the neck ruddy and delicate and yet strong.

There was an inward, not an outward strength in the delicate fine body.

'But you are beautiful!' she said. 'So pure and fine! Come!' She held her arms out.

He was ashamed to turn to her, because of his aroused nakedness.

He caught his shirt off the floor, and held it to him, coming to her.

'No!' she said, still holding out her beautiful slim arms from her drooping breasts. 'Let me see you!'

He dropped the shirt and stood still, looking towards her. The sun through the low window sent in a beam that lit up his thighs and slim belly, and the erect phallos rising darkish and hot-looking from the little cloud of vivid gold-red hair. She was startled and afraid.

'How strange!' she said slowly. 'How strange he stands there! So big! and so dark and cocksure! Is he like that?'

The man looked down the front of his slender white body, and laughed. Between the slim breasts the hair was dark, almost black. But at the root of the belly, where the phallos rose thick and arching, it was gold-red, vivid in a little cloud.

'So proud!' she murmured, uneasy. 'And so lordly! Now I know why men are so overbearing! But he's lovely, *really*. Like another being! A bit terrifying! But lovely really! And he comes to *me*! – ' She caught her lower lip between her teeth, in fear and excitement.

The man looked down in silence at the tense phallos, that did not change. 'Ay!' he said at last, in a little voice. 'Ay ma lad! tha'rt theer right enough. Yi, tha mun rear thy head! Theer on thy own, eh? an' ta'es no count o' nob'dy! Tha ma'es nowt o' me, John Thomas. Art boss? of me? Eh well, tha'rt more cocky than me, an' tha says less. John Thomas! Dost want *her*? Dost want my lady Jane? Tha's dipped me in again, tha hast. Ay, an' tha comes up smilin.' Ax 'er then! Ax lady Jane! Say: Lift up your heads o' ye gates, that the king of glory may come in. Ay, th' cheek on thee! Cunt, that's what tha'rt after. Tell lady Jane tha wants cunt. John Thomas, an' th' cunt o' lady Jane! – '

'Oh, don't tease him,' said Connie, crawling on her knees on the bed towards him and putting her arms round his white slender loins, and drawing him to her so that her hanging, swinging breasts touched the tip of the stirring, erect phallos, and caught the drop of moisture. She held the man fast.

'Lie down!' he said. 'Lie down! Let me come!'

He was in a hurry now.

And afterwards, when they had been quite still, the woman had to uncover the man again, to look at the mystery of the phallos.

'And now he's tiny, and soft like a little bud of life!' she said, taking the soft small penis in her hand. 'Isn't he somehow lovely! so on his own, so strange! And so innocent! And he comes so far into me! You must *never* insult him, you know. He's mine too. He's not only yours. He's mine! And so lovely and innocent!' And she held the penis soft in her hand.

He laughed.

'Blest be the tie that binds our hearts in kindred love,' he said.

'Of course!' she said. 'Even when he's soft and little I feel my heart simply tied to him. And how lovely your hair is here! quite quite different!'

'That's John Thomas's hair, not mine!' he said.

'John Thomas! John Thomas!' and she quickly kissed the soft penis, that was beginning to stir again.

'Ay!' said the man, stretching his body almost painfully. 'He's got his root in my soul, has that gentleman! An' sometimes I don' know what ter do wi' him. Ay, he's got a will of his own, an' it's hard to suit him. Yet I wouldn't have him killed.'

'No wonder men have always been afraid of him!' she said. 'He's rather terrible.'

The quiver was going through the man's body, as the stream of consciousness again changed its direction, turning downwards. And he was helpless, as the penis in slow soft undulations filled and surged and rose up, and grew hard, standing there hard and overweening, in its curious towering fashion. The woman too trembled a little as she watched.

'There! Take him then! He's thine,' said the man.

And she quivered, and her own mind melted out. Sharp soft waves of unspeakable pleasure washed over her as he entered her, and started the curious molten thrilling that spread and spread till she was carried away with the last, blind flush of extremity.

He heard the distant hooters of Stacks Gate, for seven o'clock. It was Monday morning. He shivered a little, and with his face between her breasts pressed her soft breasts up over his ears, to deafen him.

She had not even heard the hooters. She lay perfectly still, her soul washed transparent.

'You must get up, mustn't you?' he muttered.

'What time?' came her colourless voice.

'Seven-o'clock blowers a bit sin'.'

'I suppose I must.'

She was resenting, as she always did, the compulsion from outside.

He sat up and looked blankly out of the window.

'You do love me, don't you?' she asked calmly.

He looked down at her.

'Tha knows what tha knows. What dost ax for!' he said, a little fretfully.

'I want you to keep me, not to let me go,' she said.

His eyes seemed full of a warm, soft darkness that could not think.

'When? Now?'

'Now in your heart. Then I want to come and live with you always, soon.'

He sat naked on the bed, with his head dropped, unable to think.

'Don't you want it?' she asked.

'Ay!' he said.

Then with the same eyes darkened with another flame of consciousness, almost like sleep, he looked at her.

'Dunna ax me nowt now,' he said. 'Let me be. I like thee. I luv thee when tha lies theer. A woman's a lovely thing when 'er's deep ter fuck, and cunt's good. Ah luv thee, thy legs, an' th' shape on thee, an' th' womanness on thee. Ah luv th' womanness on thee. Ah luv thee wi' my ba's an' wi' my heart. But dunna ax me nowt. Dunna ma'e me say nowt. Let me stop as I am while I can. Tha can ax me ivrything after. Now let me be, let me be!'

And softly, he laid his hand over her mound of Venus, on the soft brown maidenhair, and himself sat still and naked on the bed, his face motionless in physical abstraction, almost like the face of Buddha. Motionless, and in the invisible flame of another consciousness, he sat with his hand on her, and waited for the turn.

After a while, he reached for his shirt and put it on, dressed himself swiftly in silence, looked at her once as she still lay naked and faintly golden like a Gloire de Dijon rose on the bed, and was gone. She heard him downstairs opening the door.

And still she lay musing, musing. It was very hard to go: to go out of his arms. He called from the foot of the stairs: 'Half-past seven!' She sighed, and got out of bed. The bare little room! Nothing in it at all but the small chest of drawers and the smallish bed. But the board floor was scrubbed clean. And in the corner by the window gable was a shelf with some books, and some from a circulating library. She looked. There were books about Bolshevist Russia, books of travel, a volume about the atom and the electron, another about the composition of the earth's core, and the causes of earthquakes: then a few novels: then three books on India. So! He was a reader after all.

The sun fell on her naked limbs through the gable window. Outside she saw the dog Flossie roaming round. The hazel-brake was misted with green, and dark-green dogs-mercury under. It was a clear clean morning, with birds flying and triumphantly singing. If only she could stay! If only there weren't the other ghastly world of smoke and iron! If only *he* would make her a world.

She came downstairs, down the steep, narrow wooden stairs. Still she would be content with this little house, if only it were in a world of its own.

He was washed and fresh, and the fire was burning.

'Will you eat anything?' he said.

'No! Only lend me a comb.'

She followed him into the scullery, and combed her hair before the handbreadth of mirror by the back door. Then she was ready to go.

She stood in the little front garden, looking at the dewy flowers, the grey bed of pinks in bud already.

'I would like to have all the rest of the world disappear,' she said, 'and live with you here.'

'It won't disappear,' he said.

They went almost in silence through the lovely dewy wood. But they were together in a world of their own.

It was bitter to her to go on to Wragby.

'I want soon to come and live with you altogether,' she said as she left him.

He smiled, unanswering.

She got home quietly and unremarked, and went up to her room.

Chapter 15

There was a letter from Hilda on the breakfast-tray. 'Father is going to London this week, and I shall call for you on Thursday week, June 17th. You must be ready so that we can go at once. I don't want to waste time at Wragby, it's an awful place. I shall probably stay the night at Retford with the Colemans, so I should be with you for lunch Thursday. Then we could start at tea time, and sleep perhaps in Grantham. It is no use our spending an evening with Clifford. If he hates your going, it would be no pleasure to him.'

So! She was being pushed round on the chessboard again.

Clifford hated her going, but it was only because he didn't feel *safe* in her absence. Her presence, for some reason, made him feel safe, and free to do the things he was occupied with. He was a great deal at the pits, and wrestling in spirit with the almost hopeless problems of getting out his coal in the most economical fashion and then selling it when he'd got it out. He knew he ought to find some way of *using* it, or converting it, so that he needn't sell it, or needn't have the chagrin of failing to sell it. But if he made electric power, could he sell that or use it? And to convert into oil was as yet too costly and too elaborate. To keep industry alive there must be more industry, like a madness.

It was a madness, and it required a madman to succeed in it. Well, he was a little mad. Connie thought so. His very intensity and acumen in the affairs of the pits seemed like a manifestation of madness to her, his very inspirations were the inspirations of insanity.

He talked to her of all his serious schemes, and she listened in a kind of wonder, and let him talk. Then the flow ceased, and he turned on the loud-speaker, and became a blank, while apparently his schemes coiled on inside him like a kind of dream.

And every night now he played pontoon, that game of the Tommies, with Mrs Bolton, gambling with sixpences. And again, in the gambling he was gone in a kind of unconsciousness, or blank intoxication, or intoxication of blankness, whatever it was. Connie could not bear to see him. But when she had gone to bed, he and Mrs Bolton would gamble on till two and three in the morning, safely, and with strange lust. Mrs Bolton was caught in the lust as much as Clifford: the more so, as she nearly always lost.

She told Connie one day: 'I lost twenty-three shillings to Sir Clifford last night.'

'And did he take the money from you?' asked Connie, aghast.

'Why of course, my Lady! Debt of honour!'

Connie expostulated roundly, and was angry with both of them. The upshot was, Sir Clifford raised Mrs Bolton's wages a hundred a year, and she could gamble on that. Meanwhile, it seemed to Connie, Clifford was really going deader.

She told him at length she was leaving on the seventeenth.

'Seventeenth!' he said. 'And when will you be back?'

'By the twentieth of July at the latest.'

'Yes! the twentieth of July.'

Strangely and blankly he looked at her, with the vagueness of a child, but with the queer blank cunning of an old man.

'You won't let me down, now, will you?' he said.

'How?'

'While you're away. I mean, you're sure to come back?'

'I'm as sure as I can be of anything, that I shall come back.'

'Yes! Well! Twentieth of July!'

He looked at her so strangely.

Yet he really wanted her to go. That was so curious. He wanted her to go, positively, to have her little adventures and perhaps come home pregnant, and all that. At the same time, he was afraid of her going.

She was quivering, watching her real opportunity for leaving him altogether, waiting till the time, herself, himself, should be ripe.

She sat and talked to the keeper of her going abroad.

'And then when I come back,' she said, 'I can tell Clifford I must leave him. And you and I can go away. They never need even know it is you. We can go to another country, shall we? To Africa or Australia. Shall we?'

She was quite thrilled by her plan.

'You've never been to the Colonies, have you?' he asked her.

'No! Have you?'

'I've been in India, and South Africa, and Egypt.'

'Why shouldn't we go to South Africa?'

'We might!' he said slowly.

'Or don't you want to?' she asked.

'I don't care. I don't much care what I do.'

'Doesn't it make you happy? Why not? We shan't be poor. I have about six hundred a year, I wrote and asked. It's not much, but it's enough, isn't it?'

'It's riches to me.'

'Oh, how lovely it will be!'

'But I ought to get divorced, and so ought you, unless we're going to have complications.'

There was plenty to think about.

Another day she asked him about himself. They were in the hut, and there was a thunderstorm.

'And weren't you happy when you were a lieutenant and an officer and a gentleman?'

'Happy? All right. I liked my Colonel.'

'Did you love him?'

'Yes! I loved him.'

'And did he love you?'

'Yes! In a way, he loved me.'

'Tell me about him.'

'What is there to tell? He had risen from the ranks. He loved the army. And he had never married. He was twenty years older than me. He was a very intelligent man: and alone in the army, as such a man is: a passionate man in his way: and a very clever officer. I lived under his spell while I was with him. I sort of let him run my life. And I never regret it.'

'And did you mind very much when he died?'

'I was as near death myself. But when I came to, I knew another part of me was finished. But then I had always known it would finish in death. All things do, as far as that goes.'

She sat and ruminated. The thunder crashed outside. It was like being in a little ark in the Flood.

'You seem to have such a lot *behind* you,' she said.

'Do I? It seems to me I've died once or twice already. Yet here I am, pegging on, and in for more trouble.'

She was thinking hard, yet listening to the storm.

'And weren't you happy as an officer and a gentleman, when your Colonel was dead?'

'No! They were a mingy lot.' He laughed suddenly. 'The Colonel used to say: Lad, the English middle classes have to chew every mouthful thirty times because their guts are so narrow, a bit as big as a pea would give them a stoppage. They're the mingiest set of ladylike snipe ever invented: full of conceit of themselves, frightened even if their bootlaces aren't correct, rotten as high game, and always in the right. That's what finishes me up. Kow-tow, kow-tow, arse-licking till their tongues are tough: yet they're always in the right. Prigs on top of everything. Prigs! A generation of ladylike prigs with half a ball each – '

Connie laughed. The rain was rushing down.

'He hated them!'

'No,' said he. 'He didn't bother. He just disliked them. There's a difference. Because, as he said, the Tommies are getting just as priggish and half-balled and narrow-gutted. It's the fate of mankind, to go that way.'

'The common people too, the working people?'

'All the lot. Their spunk is gone dead. Motor cars and cinemas and aeroplanes suck the last bit out of them. I tell you, every generation breeds a more rabbity generation, with india rubber tubing for guts and tin legs and tin faces. Tin people! It's all a steady sort of Bolshevism just killing off the human thing, and worshipping the mechanical thing. Money, money, money! All the modern lot get their real kick out of killing the old human feeling out of man, making mincemeat of the old Adam and the old Eve. They're all alike. The world is all alike: kill off the human reality, a quid for every foreskin, two quid for each pair of balls. What is cunt but machine-fucking! It's all alike. Pay 'em money to cut off the world's cock. Pay money, money, money to them that will take spunk out of mankind, and leave 'em all little twiddling machines.'

He sat there in the hut, his face pulled to mocking irony. Yet even then, he had one ear set backwards, listening to the storm over the wood. It made him feel so alone.

'But won't it ever come to an end?' she said.

'Ay, it will. It'll achieve its own salvation. When the last real man is killed, and they're *all* tame: white, black, yellow, all colours of tame ones: then they'll *all* be insane. Because the root of sanity is in the balls. Then they'll all be *insane*, and they'll make their grand *auto da fe*. You know *auto da fe* means *act of faith*? Ay well, they'll make their own grand little act of faith. They'll offer one another up.'

'You mean kill one another?'

'I do, duckie! If we go on at our present rate then in a hundred years' time there won't be ten thousand people in this island: there may not be ten. They'll have lovingly wiped each other out.' The thunder was rolling further away.

'How nice!' she said.

'Quite nice! To contemplate the extermination of the human species and the long pause that follows before some other species crops up, it calms you more than anything else. And if we go on in this way, with everybody, intellectuals, artists, government, industrialists and workers all frantically killing off the last human feeling, the last bit of their intuition, the last healthy instinct; if it goes on in algebraical progression, as it is going on: then ta-tah! to the human species! Goodbye! darling! the serpent swallows itself and leaves a void, considerably messed up, but not hopeless. Very nice! When savage wild dogs bark in Wragby, and savage wild pit-ponies stamp on Tevershall pit-bank! *te deum laudamus!*'

Connie laughed, but not very happily.

'Then you ought to be pleased that they are all Bolshevists,' she said. 'You ought to be pleased that they hurry on towards the end.'

'So I am. I don't stop 'em. Because I couldn't if I would.'

'Then why are you so bitter?'

'I'm not! If my cock gives its last crow, I don't mind.'

'But if you have a child?' she said.

He dropped his head.

'Why,' he said at last. 'It seems to me a wrong and bitter thing to do, to bring a child into this world.'

'No! Don't say it! Don't say it!' she pleaded. 'I think I'm going to have one. Say you'll be pleased.' She laid her hand on his.

'I'm pleased for you to be pleased,' he said. 'But for me it seems a ghastly treachery to the unborn creature.'

'Ah no!' she said, shocked. 'Then you *can't* ever really want me! You *can't* want me, if you feel that!'

Again he was silent, his face sullen. Outside there was only the threshing of the rain.

'It's not quite true!' she whispered. 'It's not quite true! There's another truth.' She felt he was bitter now partly because she was leaving him, deliberately going away to Venice. And this half pleased her.

She pulled open his clothing and uncovered his belly, and kissed his navel. Then she laid her cheek on his belly, and pressed her arm round his warm, silent loins. They were alone in the flood.

'Tell me you want a child, in hope!' she murmured, pressing her face against his belly, 'Tell me you do!'

'Why!' he said at last: and she felt the curious quiver of changing consciousness and relaxation going through his body. 'Why I've thought sometimes if one but tried, here among th' colliers even! They're workin' bad now, an' not earnin' much. If a man could say to 'em: Dunna think o' nowt but th' money. When it comes ter *wants*, we want but little. Let's not live for money –'

She softly rubbed her cheek on his belly, and gathered his balls in her hand. The penis stirred softly, with strange life, but did not rise up. The rain beat bruisingly outside.

'Let's live for summat else. Let's not live ter make money, neither for us-selves nor for anybody else. Now we're forced to. We're forced to make a bit for us-selves, an' a fair lot for th' bosses. Let's stop it! Bit by bit, let's stop it. We needn't rant an' rave. Bit by bit, let's drop the whole industrial life, an' go back. The least little bit o' money'll do. For everybody, me an' you, bosses an' masters, even th' king. The least little bit o' money'll really do. Just make up your mind to it, an' you've got out o' th' mess.' He paused, then went on, 'An I'd tell 'em: Look! Look at Joe! He moves lovely! Look how he moves, alive and aware. He's beautiful! An' look at Jonah! He's clumsy, he's ugly, because he's niver willin' to rouse himself. I'd tell 'em: Look! look at yourselves! one shoulder higher than t'other, legs twisted, feet all lumps! What have yer done ter yer-selves, wi' the blasted work? Spoilt yerselves. No need to work that much. Take yer clothes off an' look at yourselves. Yer ought ter be alive an' beautiful, an' yer ugly an' half dead. So I'd tell 'em. An' I'd get my men to wear different clothes: 'appen close red trousers, bright red, an' little short white jackets. Why, if men had red, fine legs, that alone would change them in a month. They'd begin to be men again, to be men! An' the women could dress as they liked. Because if once the men walked with legs close bright scarlet, and buttocks nice and showing scarlet under a little white jacket: then the women 'ud begin to be women. It's because th' men *aren't* men, that th' women have to be. An' in time pull down Tevershall and build a few beautiful buildings, that would hold us all. An' clean the country up again. An' not have many children, because the world is over-crowded.

'But I wouldn't preach to the men: only strip 'em an' say: Look at yourselves! That's workin' for money! Hark at yourselves! That's working for money. You've been working for money! Look at Tevershall! It's horrible. That's because it was built while you were working for money. Look at your girls! They don't care about you, you don't care about them. It's because you've spent your time working an' caring for money. You can't talk nor move nor live, you can't properly be with a woman. You're not alive. Look at yourselves!'

There fell a complete silence. Connie was half listening, and threading in the hair at the root of his belly a few forget-me-nots that she had gathered on the way to the hut. Outside, the world had gone still, and a little icy.

'You've got four kinds of hair,' she said to him. 'On your chest it's nearly black, and your hair isn't dark on your head: but your moustache is hard and dark red, and your hair here, your love-hair, is like a little bush of bright red-gold mistletoe. It's the loveliest of all!'

He looked down and saw the milky bits of forget-me-nots in the hair on his groin.

'Ay! That's where to put forget-me-nots, in the man-hair, or the maidenhair. But don't you care about the future?'

She looked up at him.

'Oh, I do, terribly!' she said.

'Because when I feel the human world is doomed, has doomed itself by its own mingy beastliness, then I feel the Colonies aren't far enough. The moon wouldn't be far enough, because even there you could look back and see the earth, dirty, beastly, unsavoury among all the stars: made foul by men. Then I feel I've swallowed gall, and it's eating my inside out, and nowhere's far enough away to get away. But when I get a turn, I forget it all again. Though it's a shame, what's been done to people these last hundred years: men turned into nothing but labour-insects, and all their manhood taken away, and all their real life. I'd wipe the machines off the face of the earth again, and end the industrial epoch absolutely, like a black mistake. But since I can't, an' nobody can, I'd better hold my peace, an' try an' live my own life: if I've got one to live, which I rather doubt.'

The thunder had ceased outside, but the rain which had abated, suddenly came striking down, with a last blench of lightning and mutter of departing storm. Connie was uneasy. He had talked so long now, and he was really talking to himself, not to her. Despair seemed to come down on him completely, and she was feeling happy, she hated despair. She knew her leaving him, which he had only just realised inside himself, had plunged him back into this mood. And she triumphed a little.

She opened the door and looked at the straight heavy rain, like a steel curtain, and had a sudden desire to rush out into it, to rush away. She got up, and began swiftly pulling off her stockings, then her dress and underclothing, and he held his breath. Her pointed keen animal breasts tipped and stirred as she moved. She was ivory-coloured in the greenish light. She slipped on her rubber shoes again and ran out with a wild little laugh, holding up her breasts to the heavy rain and spreading her arms, and running blurred in the rain with the eurhythmic dance-movements she had learned so long ago in Dresden. It was a strange pallid figure lifting and falling, bending so the rain beat and glistened on the full haunches, swaying up again and coming belly-forward through the rain, then stooping again so that only the full loins and buttocks were offered in a kind of homage towards him, repeating a wild obeisance.

He laughed wryly, and threw off his clothes. It was too much. He jumped out, naked and white, with a little shiver, into the hard slanting rain. Flossie sprang before him with a frantic little bark. Connie, her hair all wet and sticking to her head, turned her hot face and saw him. Her blue eyes blazed with excitement as she turned and ran fast, with a strange charging movement, out of the clearing and down the path, the wet boughs whipping her. She ran, and he saw nothing but the round wet head, the wet back leaning forward in flight, the rounded buttocks twinkling: a wonderful cowering female nakedness in flight.

She was nearly at the wide riding when he came up and flung his naked arm round her soft, naked-wet middle. She gave a shriek and straightened herself, and the heap of her soft, chill flesh came up against his body. He pressed it all up against him, madly, the heap of soft, chilled female flesh that became quickly warm as flame, in contact. The rain streamed on them till they smoked. He gathered her lovely, heavy posteriors one in each hand and pressed them in towards him in a frenzy, quivering motionless in the rain. Then suddenly he tipped her up and fell with her on the path, in the roaring silence of the rain, and short and sharp, he took her, short and sharp and finished, like an animal.

He got up in an instant, wiping the rain from his eyes.

'Come in,' he said, and they started running back to the hut. He ran straight and swift: he didn't like the rain. But she came slower, gathering forget-me-nots and campion and bluebells, running a few steps and watching him fleeing away from her.

When she came with her flowers, panting to the hut, he had already started a fire, and the twigs were crackling. Her sharp breasts rose and fell, her hair was plastered down with rain, her face was flushed ruddy and her body glistened and trickled. Wide-eyed and breathless, with a small wet head and full, trickling, naïve haunches, she looked another creature.

He took the old sheet and rubbed her down, she standing like a child. Then he rubbed himself, having shut the door of the hut. The fire was blazing up. She ducked her head in the other end of the sheet, and rubbed her wet hair.

'We're drying ourselves together on the same towel, we shall quarrel!' he said.

She looked up for a moment, her hair all odds and ends.

'No!' she said, her eyes wide. 'It's not a towel, it's a sheet.'

And she went on busily rubbing her head, while he busily rubbed his.

Still panting with their exertions, each wrapped in an army blanket, but the front of the body open to the fire, they sat on a log side by side before the blaze, to get quiet. Connie hated the feel of the blanket against her skin. But now the sheet was all wet.

She dropped her blanket and kneeled on the clay hearth, holding her head to the fire, and shaking her hair to dry it. He watched the beautiful curving drop of her haunches. That fascinated him today. How it sloped with a rich down-slope to the heavy roundness of her buttocks! And in between, folded in the secret warmth, the secret entrances!

He stroked her tail with his hand, long and subtly taking in the curves and the globe-fullness.

'Tha's got such a nice tail on thee,' he said, in the throaty caressive dialect. 'Tha's got the nicest arse of anybody. It's the nicest, nicest woman's arse as is! An' ivry bit of it is woman, woman sure as nuts. Tha'rt not one o' them button-arsed lasses as should be lads, are ter! Tha's got a real soft sloping bottom on thee, as a man loves in 'is guts. It's a bottom as could hold the world up, it is!'

All the while he spoke he exquisitely stroked the rounded tail, till it seemed as if a slippery sort of fire came from it into his hands. And his fingertips touched the two secret openings to her body, time after time, with a soft little brush of fire.

'An' if tha shits an' if tha pisses, I'm glad. I don't want a woman as couldna shit nor piss.'

Connie could not help a sudden snort of astonished laughter, but he went on unmoved.

'Tha'rt real, tha art! Tha'rt real, even a bit of a bitch. Here tha shits an' here tha pisses: an' I lay my hand on 'em both an' like thee for it. I like thee for it. Tha's got a proper, woman's arse, proud of itself. It's none ashamed of itself, this isna.'

He laid his hand close and firm over her secret places, in a kind of close greeting.

'I like it,' he said. 'I like it! An' if I only lived ten minutes, an' stroked thy arse an' got to know it, I should reckon I'd lived *one* life, see ter! Industrial system or not! Here's one o' my lifetimes.'

She turned round and climbed into his lap, clinging to him. 'Kiss me!' she whispered.

And she knew the thought of their separation was latent in both their minds, and at last she was sad.

She sat on his thighs, her head against his breast, and her ivory-gleaming legs loosely apart, the fire glowing unequally upon them. Sitting with his head dropped, he looked at the folds of her body in the fire-glow, and at the fleece of soft brown hair that hung down to a point between her open thighs. He reached to the table behind, and took up her bunch of flowers, still so wet that drops of rain fell on to her.

'Flowers stops out of doors all weathers,' he said. 'They have no houses.'

'Not even a hut!' she murmured.

With quiet fingers he threaded a few forget-me-not flowers in the fine brown fleece of the mound of Venus.

'There!' he said. 'There's forget-me-nots in the right place!'

She looked down at the milky odd little flowers among the brown maidenhair at the lower tip of her body.

'Doesn't it look pretty!' she said.

'Pretty as life,' he replied.

And he stuck a pink campion-bud among the hair.

'There! That's me where you won't forget me! That's Moses in the bulrushes.'

'You don't mind, do you, that I'm going away?' she asked wistfully, looking up into his face.

But his face was inscrutable, under the heavy brows. He kept it quite blank.

'You do as you wish,' he said.

And he spoke in good English.

'But I won't go if you don't wish it,' she said, clinging to him.

There was silence. He leaned and put another piece of wood on the fire. The flame glowed on his silent, abstracted face. She waited, but he said nothing.

'Only I thought it would be a good way to begin a break with Clifford. I do want a child. And it would give me a chance to, to – ' she resumed.

'To let them think a few lies,' he said.

'Yes, that among other things. Do you want them to think the truth?'

'I don't care what they think.'

'I do! I don't want them handling me with their unpleasant cold minds, not while I'm still at Wragby. They can think what they like when I'm finally gone.'

He was silent.

'But Sir Clifford expects you to come back to him?'

'Oh, I must come back,' she said: and there was silence.

'And would you have a child in Wragby?' he asked.

She closed her arm round his neck.

'If you wouldn't take me away, I should have to,' she said.

'Take you where to?'

'Anywhere! away! But right away from Wragby.'

'When?'

'Why, when I come back.'

'But what's the good of coming back, doing the thing twice, if you're once gone?' he said.

'Oh, I must come back. I've promised! I've promised so faithfully. Besides, I come back to you, really.'

'To your husband's gamekeeper?'

'I don't see that that matters,' she said.

'No?' He mused a while. 'And when would you think of going away again, then; finally? When exactly?'

'Oh, I don't know. I'd come back from Venice. And then we'd prepare everything.'

'How prepare?'

'Oh, I'd tell Clifford. I'd have to tell him.'

'Would you!'

He remained silent. She put her arms fast round his neck.

'Don't make it difficult for me,' she pleaded.

'Make what difficult?'

'For me to go to Venice and arrange things.'

A little smile, half a grin, flickered on his face.

'I don't make it difficult,' he said. 'I only want to find out just what you are after. But you don't really know yourself. You want to take time: get away and look at it. I don't blame you. I think you're wise. You may prefer to stay mistress of Wragby. I don't blame you. I've no Wragbys to offer. In fact, you know what you'll get out of me. No, no, I think you're right! I really do! And I'm not keen on coming to live on you, being kept by you. There's that too.'

She felt somehow as if he were giving her tit for tat.

'But you want me, don't you?' she asked.

'Do you want me?'

'You know I do. *That's* evident.'

'Quite! And *when* do you want me?'

'You know we can arrange it all when I come back. Now I'm out of breath with you. I must get calm and clear.'

'Quite! Get calm and clear!'

She was a little offended.

'But you trust me, don't you?' she said.

'Oh, absolutely!'

She heard the mockery in his tone.

'Tell me then,' she said flatly; 'do you think it would be better if I *don't* go to Venice?'

'I'm sure it's better if you *do* go to Venice,' he replied in the cool, slightly mocking voice.

'You know it's next Thursday?' she said.

'Yes!'

She now began to muse. At last she said, 'And we *shall* know better where we are when I come back, shan't we?'

'Oh surely!'

The curious gulf of silence between them!

'I've been to the lawyer about my divorce,' he said, a little constrainedly.

She gave a slight shudder.

'Have you!' she said. 'And what did he say?'

'He said I ought to have done it before; that may be a difficulty. But since I was in the army, he thinks it will go through all right. If only it doesn't bring *her* down on my head!'

'Will she have to know?'

'Yes! she is served with a notice: so is the man she lives with, the co-respondent.'

'Isn't it hateful, all the performances! I suppose I'd have to go through it with Clifford.'

There was a silence.

'And of course,' he said, 'I have to live an exemplary life for the next six or eight months. So if you go to Venice, there's temptation removed for a week or two, at least.'

'Am I temptation!' she said, stroking his face. 'I'm so glad I'm temptation to you! Don't let's think about it! You frighten me when you start thinking: you roll me out flat. Don't let's think about it. We can think so much when we are apart. That's the whole point! I've been thinking, I *must* come to you for another night before I go. I must come once more to the cottage. Shall I come on Thursday night?'

'Isn't that when your sister will be there?'

'Yes! But she said we would start at tea-time. So we could start at tea-time. But she could sleep somewhere else and I could sleep with you.'

'But then she'd have to know.'

'Oh, I shall tell her. I've more or less told her already. I must talk it all over with Hilda. She's a great help, so sensible.'

He was thinking of her plan.

'So you'd start off from Wragby at tea-time, as if you were going to London? Which way were you going?'

'By Nottingham and Grantham.'

'And then your sister would drop you somewhere and you'd walk or drive back here? Sounds very risky, to me.'

'Does it? well, then, Hilda could bring me back. She could sleep at Mansfield, and bring me back here in the evening, and fetch me again in the morning. It's quite easy.'

'And the people who see you?'

'I'll wear goggles and a veil.'

He pondered for some time.

'Well,' he said. 'You please yourself as usual.'

'But wouldn't it please you?'

'Oh yes! It'd please me all right,' he said a little grimly, 'I might as well smite while the iron's hot.'

'Do you know what I thought?' she said suddenly. 'It suddenly came to me. You are the "Knight of the Burning Pestle"!'

'Ay! And you? Are you the Lady of the Red-Hot Mortar?'

'Yes!' she said. 'Yes! You're Sir Pestle and I'm Lady Mortar.'

'All right, then I'm knighted. John Thomas is Sir John, to your Lady Jane.'

'Yes! John Thomas is knighted! I'm my-lady-maiden-hair, and you must have flowers too. Yes!'

She threaded two pink campions in the bush of red-gold hair above his penis.

'There!' she said. 'Charming! Charming! Sir John!'

And she pushed a bit of forget-me-not in the dark hair of his breast.

'And you won't forget me *there*, will you?' She kissed him on the breast, and made two bits of forget-me-not lodge one over each nipple, kissing him again.

'Make a calendar of me!' he said. He laughed, and the flowers shook from his breast.

'Wait a bit!' he said.

He rose, and opened the door of the hut. Flossie, lying in the porch, got up and looked at him.

'Ay, it's me!' he said.

The rain had ceased. There was a wet, heavy, perfumed stillness. Evening was approaching.

He went out and down the little path in the opposite direction from the riding. Connie watched his thin, white figure, and it looked to her like a ghost, an apparition moving away from her.

When she could see it no more, her heart sank. She stood in the door of the hut, with a blanket round her, looking into the drenched, motionless silence.

But he was coming back, trotting strangely, and carrying flowers. She was a little afraid of him, as if he were not quite human. And when he came near, his eyes looked into hers, but she could not understand the meaning.

He had brought columbines and campions, and new-mown hay, and oak-tufts and honeysuckle in small bud. He fastened fluffy young oak-sprays round her breasts, sticking in tufts of bluebells and campion: and in her navel he poised a pink campion flower, and in her maidenhair were forget-me-nots and woodruff.

'That's you in all your glory!' he said. 'Lady Jane, at her wedding with John Thomas.'

And he stuck flowers in the hair of his own body, and wound a bit of creeping-jenny round his penis, and stuck a single bell of a hyacinth in his navel. She watched him with amusement, his odd intentness. And she pushed a campion flower in his moustache, where it stuck, dangling under his nose.

'This is John Thomas marryin' Lady Jane,' he said. 'An' we mun let Constance an' Oliver go their ways. Maybe – '

He spread out his hand with a gesture, and then he sneezed, sneezing away the flowers from his nose and his navel. He sneezed again.

'Maybe what?' she said, waiting for him to go on.

He looked at her a little bewildered.

'Eh?' he said.

'Maybe what? Go on with what you were going to say,' she insisted.

'Ay, what *was* I going to say?'

He had forgotten. And it was one of the disappointments of her life, that he never finished.

A yellow ray of sun shone over the trees.

'Sun!' he said. 'And time you went. Time, my Lady, time! What's that as flies without wings, your Ladyship? Time! Time!'

He reached for his shirt.

'Say good-night! to John Thomas,' he said, looking down at his penis. 'He's safe in the arms of creeping-jenny! Not much burning pestle about him just now.'

And he put his flannel shirt over his head.

'A man's most dangerous moment,' he said, when his head had emerged, 'is when he's getting into his shirt. Then he puts his head in a bag. That's why I prefer those American shirts, that you put on like a jacket.' She still stood watching him. He stepped into his short drawers, and buttoned them round the waist.

'Look at Jane!' he said. 'In all her blossoms! Who'll put blossoms on you next year, Jinny? Me, or somebody else? "Goodbye, my bluebell, farewell to you!" I hate that song, it's early war days.' He then sat down, and was pulling on his stockings. She still stood unmoving. He laid his hand on the slope of her buttocks. 'Pretty little Lady Jane!' he said. 'Perhaps in Venice you'll find a man who'll put jasmine in your maidenhair, and a pomegranate flower in your navel. Poor little lady Jane!'

'Don't say those things!' she said. 'You only say them to hurt me.'

He dropped his head. Then he said, in dialect, 'Ay, maybe I do, maybe I do! Well then, I'll say nowt, an' ha' done wi't. But tha mun dress thysen, all' go back to thy stately homes of England, how beautiful they stand. Time's up! Time's up for Sir John, an' for little Lady Jane! Put thy shimmy on, Lady Chatterley! Tha might be anybody, standin' there be-out even a shimmy, an' a few rags o' flowers. There then, there then, I'll undress thee, tha bobtailed young throstle.' And he took the leaves from her hair, kissing her damp hair, and the flowers from her breasts, and kissed her breasts, and kissed her navel, and kissed her maidenhair, where he left the flowers threaded. 'They mun stop while they will,' he said. 'So! There tha'rt bare again, nowt but a bare-arsed lass an' a bit of a Lady Jane! Now put thy shimmy on, for tha mun go, or else Lady Chatterley's goin' to be late for dinner, an' where 'ave yer been to my pretty maid!'

She never knew how to answer him when he was in this condition of the vernacular. So she dressed herself and prepared to go a little ignominiously home to Wragby. Or so she felt it: a little ignominiously home.

He would accompany her to the broad riding. His young pheasants were all right under the shelter.

When he and she came out on to the riding, there was Mrs Bolton faltering palely towards them.

'Oh, my Lady, we wondered if anything had happened!'

'No! Nothing has happened.'

Mrs Bolton looked into the man's face, that was smooth and new-looking with love. She met his half-laughing, half-mocking eyes. He always laughed at mischance. But he looked at her kindly.

'Evening, Mrs Bolton! Your Ladyship will be all right now, so I can leave you. Good-night to your Ladyship! Good-night, Mrs Bolton!'

He saluted and turned away.

Connie arrived home to an ordeal of cross-questioning. Clifford had been out at tea-time, had come in just before the storm, and where was her Ladyship? Nobody knew, only Mrs Bolton suggested she had gone for a walk into the wood. Into the wood, in such a storm! – Clifford for once let himself get into a state of nervous frenzy. He started at every flash of lightning, and blenched at every roll of thunder. He looked at the icy thunder-rain as if it were the end of the world. He got more and more worked up.

Mrs Bolton tried to soothe him.

'She'll be sheltering in the hut, till it's over. Don't worry, her Ladyship is all right.'

'I don't like her being in the wood in a storm like this! I don't like her being in the wood at all! She's been gone now more than two hours. When did she go out?'

'A little while before you came in.'

'I didn't see her in the park. God knows where she is and what has happened to her.'

'Oh, nothing's happened to her. You'll see, she'll be home directly after the rain stops. It's just the rain that's keeping her.'

But her Ladyship did not come home directly the rain stopped. In fact time went by, the sun came out for his last yellow glimpse, and there still was no sign of her. The sun was set, it was growing dark, and the first dinner-gong had rung.

'It's no good!' said Clifford in a frenzy. 'I'm going to send out Field and Betts to find her.'

'Oh don't do that!' cried Mrs Bolton. 'They'll think there's a suicide or something. Oh, don't start a lot of talk going. Let me slip over to the hut and see if she's not there. I'll find her all right.'

So, after some persuasion, Clifford allowed her to go.

And so Connie had come upon her in the drive, alone and palely loitering.

'You mustn't mind me coming to look for you, my Lady! But Sir Clifford worked himself up into such a state. He made sure you were struck by lightning, or killed by a falling tree. And he was determined to send Field and Betts to the wood to find the body. So I thought I'd better come, rather than set all the servants agog.'

She spoke nervously. She could still see on Connie's face the smoothness and the half-dream of passion, and she could feel the irritation against herself.

'Quite!' said Connie. And she could say no more.

The two women plodded on through the wet world, in silence, while great drops splashed like explosions in the wood. When they came to the park, Connie strode ahead, and Mrs Bolton panted a little. She was getting plumper.

'How foolish of Clifford to make a fuss!' said Connie at length, angrily, really speaking to herself.

'Oh, you know what men are! They like working themselves up. But he'll be all right as soon as he sees your Ladyship.'

Connie was very angry that Mrs Bolton knew her secret: for certainly she knew it.

Suddenly Constance stood still on the path.

'It's monstrous that I should have to be followed!' she said, her eyes flashing.

'Oh! your Ladyship, don't say that! He'd certainly have sent the two men, and they'd have come straight to the hut. I didn't know where it was, really.'

Connie flushed darker with rage, at the suggestion. Yet, while her passion was on her, she could not lie. She could not even pretend there was nothing between herself and the keeper. She looked at the other woman, who stood so sly, with her head dropped: yet somehow, in her femaleness, an ally.

'Oh well!' she said. 'If it is so it is so. I don't mind!'

'Why you're all right, my Lady! You've only been sheltering in the hut. It's absolutely nothing.'

They went on to the house. Connie marched in to Clifford's room, furious with him, furious with his pale, overwrought face and prominent eyes.

'I must say, I don't think you need send the servants after me!' she burst out.

'My God!' he exploded. 'Where have you been, woman? You've been gone hours, hours, and in a storm like this! What the hell do you go to that bloody wood for? What have you been up to? It's hours even since the rain stopped, hours! Do you know what time it is? You're enough to drive anybody mad. Where have you been? What in the name of hell have you been doing?'

'And what if I don't choose to tell you?' She pulled her hat from her head and shook her hair.

He looked at her with his eyes bulging, and yellow coming into the whites. It was very bad for him to get into these rages: Mrs Bolton had a weary time with him, for days after. Connie felt a sudden qualm.

'But really!' she said, milder. 'Anyone would think I'd been I don't know where! I just sat in the hut during all the storm, and made myself a little fire, and was happy.'

She spoke now easily. After all, why work him up any more! He looked at her suspiciously.

'And look at your hair!' he said; 'look at yourself!'

'Yes!' she replied calmly. 'I ran out in the rain with no clothes on.'

He stared at her speechless.

'You must be mad!' he said.

'Why? To like a shower-bath from the rain?'

'And how did you dry yourself?'

'On an old towel and at the fire.'

He still stared at her in a dumbfounded way.

'And supposing anybody came,' he said.

'Who would come?'

'Who? Why, anybody! And Mellors. Does he come? He must come in the evenings.'

'Yes, he came later, when it had cleared up, to feed the pheasants with corn.'

She spoke with amazing nonchalance. Mrs Bolton, who was listening in the next room, heard in sheer admiration. To think a woman could carry it off so naturally!

'And suppose he'd come while you were running about in the rain with nothing on, like a maniac?'

'I suppose he'd have had the fright of his life, and cleared out as fast as he could.'

Clifford still stared at her transfixed. What he thought in his under-consciousness he would never know. And he was too much taken aback to form one clear thought in his upper consciousness. He just simply accepted what she said, in a sort of blank. And he admired her. He could not help admiring her. She looked so flushed and handsome and smooth: love smooth.

'At least,' he said, subsiding, 'you'll be lucky if you've got off without a severe cold.'

'Oh, I haven't got a cold,' she replied. She was thinking to herself of the other man's words: Tha's got the nicest woman's arse of anybody! She wished, she dearly wished she could tell Clifford that this had been said to her, during the famous thunderstorm. However! She bore herself rather like an offended queen, and went upstairs to change.

That evening, Clifford wanted to be nice to her. He was reading one of the latest scientific-religious books: he had a streak of a spurious sort of religion in him, and was egocentrically concerned with the future of his own ego. It was like his habit to make conversation to Connie about some book, since the conversation between them had to be made, almost chemically. They had almost chemically to concoct it in their heads.

'What do you think of this, by the way?' he said, reaching for his book. 'You'd have no need to cool your ardent body by running out in the rain, if only we had a few more aeons of evolution behind us. Ah, here it is! – "The universe shows us two aspects: on one side it is physically wasting, on the other it is spiritually ascending."'

Connie listened, expecting more. But Clifford was waiting. She looked at him in surprise.

'And if it spiritually ascends,' she said, 'what does it leave down below, in the place where its tail used to be?'

'Ah!' he said. 'Take the man for what he means. *Ascending* is the opposite of his *wasting*, I presume.'

'Spiritually blown out, so to speak!'

'No, but seriously, without joking: do you think there is anything in it?'

She looked at him again.

'Physically wasting?' she said. 'I see you getting fatter, and I'm not wasting myself. Do you think the sun is smaller than he used to be? He's not to me. And I suppose the apple Adam offered Eve wasn't really much bigger, if any, than one of our orange pippins. Do you think it was?'

'Well, hear how he goes on: "It is thus slowly passing, with a slowness inconceivable in our measures of time, to new creative conditions, amid which the physical world, as we at present know it, will be represented by a ripple barely to be distinguished from nonentity." '

She listened with a glisten of amusement. All sorts of improper things suggested themselves. But she only said, 'What silly hocus-pocus! As if his little conceited consciousness could know what was happening as slowly as all that! It only means *he*'s a physical failure on the earth, so he wants to make the whole universe a physical failure. Priggish little impertinence!'

'Oh, but listen! Don't interrupt the great man's solemn words! – "The present type of order in the world has risen from an unimaginable past, and will find its grave in an unimaginable future. There remains the inexhaustive realm of abstract forms, and creativity with its shifting character ever determined afresh by its own creatures, and God, upon whose wisdom all forms of order depend." – There, that's how he winds up!'

Connie sat listening contemptuously.

'He's spiritually blown out,' she said. 'What a lot of stuff! Unimaginables, and types of order in graves, and realms of abstract forms, and creativity with a shifty character, and God mixed up with forms of order! Why, it's idiotic!'

'I must say, it is a little vaguely conglomerate, a mixture of gases, so to speak,' said Clifford. 'Still, I think there is something in the idea that the universe is physically wasting and spiritually ascending.'

'Do you? Then let it ascend, so long as it leaves me safely and solidly physically here below.'

'Do you like your physique?' he asked.

'I love it!' And through her mind went the words: It's the nicest, nicest woman's arse as is!

'But that is really rather extraordinary, because there's no denying it's an encumbrance. But then I suppose a woman doesn't take a supreme pleasure in the life of the mind.'

'Supreme pleasure?' she said, looking up at him. 'Is that sort of idiocy the supreme pleasure of the life of the mind? No thank you! Give me the body. I believe the life of the body is a greater reality than the life of the mind: when the body is really wakened to life. But so many people, like your famous wind-machine, have only got minds tacked on to their physical corpses.'

He looked at her in wonder.

'The life of the body,' he said, 'is just the life of the animals.'

'And that's better than the life of professional corpses. But it's not true! The human body is only just coming to real life. With the Greeks it gave a lovely flicker, then Plato and Aristotle killed it, and Jesus finished it off. But now the body is coming really to life, it is really rising from the tomb. And it will be a lovely, lovely life in the lovely universe, the life of the human body.'

'My dear, you speak as if you were ushering it all in! True, you are going away on a holiday: but don't please be quite so indecently elated about it. Believe me, whatever God there is is slowly eliminating the guts and alimentary system from the human being, to evolve a higher, more spiritual being.'

'Why should I believe you, Clifford, when I feel that whatever God there is has at last wakened up in my guts, as you call them, and is rippling so happily there, like dawn. Why should I believe you, when I feel so very much the contrary?'

'Oh, exactly! And what has caused this extraordinary change in you? running out stark naked in the rain, and playing Bacchante? desire for sensation, or the anticipation of going to Venice?'

'Both! Do you think it is horrid of me to be so thrilled at going off?' she said.

'Rather horrid to show it so plainly.'

'Then I'll hide it.'

'Oh, don't trouble! You almost communicate a thrill to me. I almost feel that it is *I* who am going off.'

'Well, why don't you come?'

'We've gone over all that. And as a matter of fact, I suppose your greatest thrill comes from being able to say a temporary farewell to all this. Nothing so thrilling, for the moment, as Goodbye-to-it-all! – But every parting means a meeting elsewhere. And every meeting is a new bondage.'

'I'm not going to enter any new bondages.'

'Don't boast, while the gods are listening,' he said.

She pulled up short.

'No! I won't boast!' she said.

But she was thrilled, none the less, to be going off: to feel bonds snap. She couldn't help it.

Clifford, who couldn't sleep, gambled all night with Mrs Bolton, till she was too sleepy almost to live.

And the day came round for Hilda to arrive. Connie had arranged with Mellors that if everything promised well for their night together, she would hang a green shawl out of the window. If there were frustration, a red one.

Mrs Bolton helped Connie to pack.

'It will be so good for your Ladyship to have a change.'

'I think it will. You don't mind having Sir Clifford on your hands alone for a time, do you?'

'Oh no! I can manage him quite all right. I mean, I can do all he needs me to do. Don't you think he's better than he used to be?'

'Oh much! You do wonders with him.'

'Do I though! But men are all alike: just babies, and you have to flatter them and wheedle them and let them think they're having their own way. Don't you find it so, my Lady?'

'I'm afraid I haven't much experience.'

Connie paused in her occupation.

'Even your husband, did you have to manage him, and wheedle him like a baby?' she asked, looking at the other woman.

Mrs Bolton paused too.

'Well!' she said. 'I had to do a good bit of coaxing, with him too. But he always knew what I was after, I must say that. But he generally gave in to me.'

'He was never the lord and master thing?'

'No! At least there'd be a look in his eyes sometimes, and then I knew I'd got to give in. But usually he gave in to me. No, he was never lord and master. But neither was I. I knew when I could go no further with him, and then I gave in: though it cost me a good bit, sometimes.'

'And what if you had held out against him?'

'Oh, I don't know. I never did. Even when he was in the wrong, if he was fixed, I gave in. You see I never wanted to break what was between us. And if you really set your will against a man, that finishes it. If you care for a man, you have to give in to him once he's really determined; whether you're in the right or not, you have to give in. Else you break something. But I must say, Ted 'ud give in to me sometimes, when I was set on a thing, and in the wrong. So I suppose it cuts both ways.'

'And that's how you are with all your patients?' asked Connie.

'Oh, that's different. I don't care at all, in the same way. I know what's good for them, or I try to, and then I just contrive to manage them for their own good. It's not like anybody as you're really fond of. It's quite different. Once you've been really fond of a man, you can be affectionate to almost any man, if he needs you at all. But it's not the same thing. You don't really *care*. I doubt, once you've *really* cared, if you can ever really care again.'

These words frightened Connie.

'Do you think one can only care once?' she asked.

'Or never. Most women never care, never begin to. They don't know what it means. Nor men either. But when I see a woman as cares, my heart stands still for her.'

'And do you think men easily take offence?'

'Yes! If you wound them on their pride. But aren't women the same? Only our two prides are a bit different.'

Connie pondered this. She began again to have some misgiving about her going away. After all, was she not giving her man the go-by, if only for a short time? And he knew it. That's why he was so queer and sarcastic.

Still! the human existence is a good deal controlled by the machine of external circumstance. She was in the power of this machine. She couldn't extricate herself all in five minutes. She didn't even want to.

Hilda arrived in good time on Thursday morning, in a nimble two-seater car, with her suitcase strapped firmly behind. She looked as demure and maidenly as ever, but she had the same will of her own. She had the very hell of a will of her own, as her husband had found out. But the husband was now divorcing her.

Yes, she even made it easy for him to do that, though she had no lover. For the time being, she was 'off' men. She was very well content to be quite her own mistress: and mistress of her two children, whom she was going to bring up 'properly', whatever that may mean.

Connie was only allowed a suitcase, also. But she had sent on a trunk to her father, who was going by train. No use taking a car to Venice. And Italy much too hot to motor in, in July. He was going comfortably by train. He had just come down from Scotland.

So, like a demure arcadian field-marshal, Hilda arranged the material part of the journey. She and Connie sat in the upstairs room, chatting.

'But Hilda!' said Connie, a little frightened. 'I want to stay near here tonight. Not here: near here!'

Hilda fixed her sister with grey, inscrutable eyes. She seemed so calm: and she was so often furious.

'Where, near here?' she asked softly.

'Well, you know I love somebody, don't you?'

'I gathered there was something.'

'Well he lives near here, and I want to spend this last night with him. I must! I've promised.'

Connie became insistent.

Hilda bent her Minerva-like head in silence. Then she looked up.

'Do you want to tell me who he is?' she said.

'He's our gamekeeper,' faltered Connie, and she flushed vividly, like a shamed child.

'Connie!' said Hilda, lifting her nose slightly with disgust: a motion she had from her mother.

'I know: but he's lovely really. He really understands tenderness,' said Connie, trying to apologise for him.

Hilda, like a ruddy, rich-coloured Athena, bowed her head and pondered. She was really violently angry. But she dared not show it, because Connie, taking after her father, would straightway become obstreperous and unmanageable.

It was true, Hilda did not like Clifford: his cool assurance that he was somebody! She thought he made use of Connie shamefully and impudently. She had hoped her sister *would* leave him. But, being solid Scotch middle-class, she loathed any 'lowering' of oneself, or the family. She looked up at last.

'You'll regret it,' she said.

'I shan't,' cried Connie, flushed red. 'He's quite the exception. I *really* love him. He's lovely as a lover.'

Hilda still pondered.

'You'll get over him quite soon,' she said, 'and live to be ashamed of yourself because of him.'

'I shan't! I hope I'm going to have a child of his.'

'*Connie!*' said Hilda, hard as a hammer-stroke, and pale with anger.

'I shall if I possibly can. I should be fearfully proud if I had a child by him.'

It was no use talking to her. Hilda pondered.

'And doesn't Clifford suspect?' she said.

'Oh no! Why should he?'

'I've no doubt you've given him plenty of occasion for suspicion,' said Hilda.

'Not at all.'

'And tonight's business seems quite gratuitous folly. Where does the man live?'

'In the cottage at the other end of the wood.'

'Is he a bachelor?'

'No! His wife left him.'

'How old?'

'I don't know. Older than me.'

Hilda became more angry at every reply, angry as her mother used to be, in a kind of paroxysm. But still she hid it.

'I would give up tonight's escapade if I were you,' she advised calmly.

'I can't! I *must* stay with him tonight, or I can't go to Venice at all. I just can't.'

Hilda heard her father over again, and she gave way, out of mere diplomacy. And she consented to drive to Mansfield, both of them, to dinner, to bring Connie back to the lane-end after dark, and to fetch her from the lane-end the next morning, herself sleeping in Mansfield, only half an hour away, good going. But she was furious. She stored it up against her sister, this baulk in her plans.

Connie flung an emerald-green shawl over her window-sill.

On the strength of her anger, Hilda warmed towards Clifford. After all, he had a mind. And if he had no sex, functionally, all the better: so much the less to quarrel about! Hilda wanted no more of that sex business, where men became nasty, selfish little horrors. Connie really had less to put up with than many women, if she did but know it.

And Clifford decided that Hilda, after all, was a decidedly intelligent woman, and would make a man a first-rate helpmeet, if he were going in for politics for example. Yes, she had none of Connie's silliness, Connie was more a child: you had to make excuses for her, because she was not altogether dependable.

There was an early cup of tea in the hall, where doors were open to let in the sun. Everybody seemed to be panting a little.

'Goodbye, Connie girl! Come back to me safely.'

'Goodbye, Clifford! Yes, I shan't be long.' Connie was almost tender.

'Goodbye Hilda! You will keep an eye on her, won't you?'

'I'll even keep two!' said Hilda. 'She shan't go very far astray.'

'It's a promise!'

'Goodbye Mrs Bolton! I know you'll look after Sir Clifford nobly.'

'I'll do what I can, your Ladyship.'

'And write to me if there is any news, and tell me about Sir Clifford, how he is.'

'Very good, your Ladyship, I will. And have a good time, and come back and cheer us up.'

Everybody waved. The car went off. Connie looked back and saw Clifford sitting at the top of the steps in his house-chair. After all, he was her husband: Wragby was her home: circumstance had done it.

Mrs Chambers held the gate and wished her Ladyship a happy holiday. The car slipped out of the dark spinney that masked the park, on to the highroad where the colliers were trailing home. Hilda turned to the Crosshill Road, that was not a main road, but ran to Mansfield. Connie put on goggles. They ran beside the railway, which was in a cutting below them. Then they crossed the cutting on a bridge.

'That's the lane to the cottage!' said Connie.

Hilda glanced at it impatiently.

'It's a frightful pity we can't go straight off!' she said. 'We could have been in Pall Mall by nine o'clock.'

'I'm sorry for your sake,' said Connie, from behind her goggles.

They were soon at Mansfield, that once-romantic, now utterly disheartening colliery town. Hilda stopped at the hotel named in the motor-car book, and took a room. The whole thing was utterly uninteresting, and she was almost too angry to talk. However, Connie *had* to tell her something of the man's history.

'*He! He!* What name do you call him by? You only say *he*,' said Hilda.

'I've never called him by any name: nor he me: which is curious, when you come to think of it. Unless we say Lady Jane and John Thomas. But his name is Oliver Mellors.'

'And how would you like to be Mrs Oliver Mellors, instead of Lady Chatterley?'

'I'd love it.'

There was nothing to be done with Connie. And anyhow, if the man had been a lieutenant in the army in India for four or five years, he must be more or less presentable. Apparently he had character. Hilda began to relent a little.

'But you'll be through with him in a while,' she said, 'and then you'll be ashamed of having been connected with him. One *can't* mix up with the working people.'

'But you are such a socialist! you're always on the side of the working classes.'

'I may be on their side in a political crisis, but being on their side makes me know how impossible it is to mix one's life with theirs. Not out of snobbery, but just because the whole rhythm is different.'

Hilda had lived among the real political intellectuals, so she was disastrously unanswerable.

The nondescript evening in the hotel dragged out, and at last they had a nondescript dinner. Then Connie slipped a few things into a little silk bag, and combed her hair once more.

'After all, Hilda,' she said, 'love can be wonderful: when you feel you *live*, and are in the very middle of creation.' It was almost like bragging on her part.

'I suppose every mosquito feels the same,' said Hilda.

'Do you think it does? How nice for it!'

The evening was wonderfully clear and long-lingering, even in the small town. It would be half-light all night. With a face like a mask, from resentment, Hilda started her car again, and the two sped back on their traces, taking the other road, through Bolsover.

Connie wore her goggles and disguising cap, and she sat in silence. Because of Hilda's opposition, she was fiercely on the side of the man, she would stand by him through thick and thin.

They had their headlights on, by the time they passed Crosshill, and the small lit-up train that chuffed past in the cutting made it seem like real night. Hilda had calculated the turn into the lane at the bridge-end. She slowed up rather suddenly and swerved off the road, the lights glaring white into the grassy, overgrown lane. Connie looked out. She saw a shadowy figure, and she opened the door.

'Here we are!' she said softly.

But Hilda had switched off the lights, and was absorbed backing, making the turn.

'Nothing on the bridge?' she asked shortly.

'You're all right,' said the man's voice.

She backed on to the bridge, reversed, let the car run forwards a few yards along the road, then backed into the lane, under a wych-elm tree, crushing the grass and bracken. Then all the lights went out. Connie stepped down. The man stood under the trees.

'Did you wait long?' Connie asked.

'Not so very,' he replied.

They both waited for Hilda to get out. But Hilda shut the door of the car and sat tight.

'This is my sister Hilda. Won't you come and speak to her? Hilda! This is Mr Mellors.'

The keeper lifted his hat, but went no nearer.

'Do walk down to the cottage with us, Hilda,' Connie pleaded. 'It's not far.'

'What about the car?'

'People do leave them on the lanes. You have the key.'

Hilda was silent, deliberating. Then she looked backwards down the lane.

'Can I back round the bush?' she said.

'Oh yes!' said the keeper.

She backed slowly round the curve, out of sight of the road, locked the car, and got down. It was night, but luminous dark. The hedges rose high and wild, by the unused lane, and very dark seeming. There was a fresh sweet scent on the air. The keeper went ahead, then came Connie, then Hilda, and in silence. He lit up the difficult places with a flashlight torch, and they went on again, while an owl softly hooted over the oaks, and Flossie padded silently around. Nobody could speak. There was nothing to say.

At length Connie saw the yellow light of the house, and her heart beat fast. She was a little frightened. They trailed on, still in Indian file.

He unlocked the door and preceded them into the warm but bare little room.

The fire burned low and red in the grate. The table was set with two plates and two glasses, on a proper white tablecloth for once. Hilda shook her hair and looked round the bare, cheerless room. Then she summoned her courage and looked at the man.

He was moderately tall, and thin, and she thought him good-looking. He kept a quiet distance of his own, and seemed absolutely unwilling to speak.

'Do sit down, Hilda,' said Connie.

'Do!' he said. 'Can I make you tea or anything, or will you drink a glass of beer? It's moderately cool.'

'Beer!' said Connie.

'Beer for me, please!' said Hilda, with a mock sort of shyness. He looked at her and blinked.

He took a blue jug and tramped to the scullery. When he came back with the beer, his face had changed again.

Connie sat down by the door, and Hilda sat in his seat, with the back to the wall, against the window corner.

'That is his chair,' said Connie softly. And Hilda rose as if it had burnt her.

'Sit yer still, sit yer still! Ta'e ony cheer as yo'n a mind to, none of us is th' big bear,' he said, with complete equanimity.

And he brought Hilda a glass, and poured her beer first from the blue jug.

'As for cigarettes,' he said, 'I've got none, but 'appen you've got your own. I dunna smoke, mysen. Shall y' eat summat?' He turned direct to Connie. 'Shall t'eat a smite o' summat, if I bring it thee? Tha can usually do wi' a bite.' He spoke the vernacular with a curious calm assurance, as if he were the landlord of the inn.

'What is there?' asked Connie, flushing.

'Boiled ham, cheese, pickled wa'nuts, if yer like. Nowt much.'

'Yes,' said Connie. 'Won't you, Hilda?'

Hilda looked up at him.

'Why do you speak Yorkshire?' she said softly.

'That! That's non Yorkshire, that's Derby.'

He looked back at her with that faint, distant grin.

'Derby, then! Why do you speak Derby? You spoke natural English at first.'

'Did Ah though? An' canna Ah change if Ah'n a mind to 't? Nay, nay, let me talk Derby if it suits me. If yo'n nowt against it.'

'It sounds a little affected,' said Hilda.

'Ay, 'appen so! An' up i' Tevershall yo'd sound affected.' He looked again at her, with a queer calculating distance, along his cheek-bones: as if to say: Yi, an' who are you?

He tramped away to the pantry for the food.

The sisters sat in silence. He brought another plate, and knife and fork. Then he said, 'An' if it's the same to you, I s'll ta'e my coat off, like I allers do.'

And he took off his coat, and hung it on the peg, then sat down to table in his shirt-sleeves: a shirt of thin, cream-coloured flannel.

' 'Elp yerselves!' he said. ' 'Elp yerselves! Dunna wait f'r axin'!'

He cut the bread, then sat motionless. Hilda felt, as Connie once used to, his power of silence and distance. She saw his smallish, sensitive, loose hand on the table. He was no simple working man, not he: he was acting! acting!

'Still!' she said, as she took a little cheese. 'It would be more natural if you spoke to us in normal English, not in vernacular.'

He looked at her, feeling her devil of a will.

'Would it?' he said in the normal English. 'Would it? Would anything that was said between you and me be quite natural, unless you said you wished me to hell before your sister ever saw me again: and unless I said something almost as unpleasant back again? Would anything else be natural?'

'Oh yes!' said Hilda. 'Just good manners would be quite natural.'

'Second nature, so to speak!' he said: then he began to laugh. 'Nay,' he said. 'I'm weary o' manners. Let me be!'

Hilda was frankly baffled and furiously annoyed. After all, he might show that he realised he was being honoured. Instead of which, with his play-acting and lordly airs, he seemed to think it was he who was conferring the honour. Just impudence! Poor misguided Connie, in the man's clutches!

The three ate in silence. Hilda looked to see what his table-manners were like. She could not help realising that he was instinctively much more delicate and well-bred than herself. She had a certain Scottish clumsiness. And moreover, he had all the quiet self-contained assurance of the English, no loose edges. It would be very difficult to get the better of him.

But neither would he get the better of her.

'And do you really think,' she said, a little more humanly, 'it's worth the risk?'

'Is what worth what risk?'

'This escapade with my sister.'

He flickered his irritating grin.

'Yo' maun ax 'er!'

Then he looked at Connie.

'Tha comes o' thine own accord, lass, doesn't ter? It's non me as forces thee?'

Connie looked at Hilda.

'I wish you wouldn't cavil, Hilda.'

'Naturally I don't want to. But someone has to think about things. You've got to have some sort of continuity in your life. You can't just go making a mess.'

There was a moment's pause.

'Eh, continuity!' he said. 'An' what by that? What continuity 'ave yer got i' *your* life? I thought you was gettin' divorced. What continuity's that? Continuity o' yer own stubbornness. I can see that much. An' what good's it goin' to do yer? You'll be sick o' yer continuity afore yer a fat sight older. A stubborn woman an' 'er own self-will: ay, they make a fast continuity, they do. Thank heaven, it isn't me as 'as got th' andlin' of yer!'

'What right have you to speak like that to me?' said Hilda.

'Right! What right ha' yo' ter start harnessin' other folks i' your continuity? Leave folks to their own continuities.'

'My dear man, do you think I am concerned with you?' said Hilda softly.

'Ay,' he said. 'Yo' are. For it's a force-put. Yo' more or less my sister-in-law.'

'Still far from it, I assure you.'

'Not a' that far, I assure *you*. I've got my own sort o' continuity, back your life! Good as yours, any day. An' if your sister there comes ter me for a bit o' cunt an' tenderness, she knows what she's after. She's been in my bed afore: which you 'aven't, thank the Lord, with your continuity.' There was a dead pause, before he added: ' – Eh, I don't wear me breeches arse-forrards. An' if I get a windfall, I thank my stars. A man gets a lot of enjoyment out o' that lass theer, which is more than anybody gets out o' th' likes o' you. Which is a pity, for you might 'appen a' bin a good apple, 'stead of a handsome crab. Women like you needs proper graftin'.'

He was looking at her with an odd, flickering smile, faintly sensual and appreciative.

'And men like you,' she said, 'ought to be segregated: justifying their own vulgarity and selfish lust.'

'Ay, ma'am! It's a mercy there's a few men left like me. But you deserve what you get: to be left severely alone.'

Hilda had risen and gone to the door. He rose and took his coat from the peg.

'I can find my way quite well alone,' she said.

'I doubt you can't,' he replied easily.

They tramped in ridiculous file down the lane again, in silence. An owl still hooted. He knew he ought to shoot it.

The car stood untouched, a little dewy. Hilda got in and started the engine. The other two waited.

'All I mean,' she said from her entrenchment, 'is that I doubt if you'll find it's been worth it, either of you!'

'One man's meat is another man's poison,' he said, out of the darkness. 'But it's meat an' drink to me.'

The lights flared out.

'Don't make me wait in the morning, Connie.'

'No, I won't. Good-night!'

The car rose slowly on to the highroad, then slid swiftly away, leaving the night silent.

Connie timidly took his arm, and they went down the lane. He did not speak. At length she drew him to a standstill.

'Kiss me!' she murmured.

'Nay, wait a bit! Let me simmer down,' he said.

That amused her. She still kept hold of his arm, and they went quickly down the lane, in silence. She was so glad to be with him, just now. She shivered, knowing that Hilda might have snatched her away. He was inscrutably silent.

When they were in the cottage again, she almost jumped with pleasure, that she should be free of her sister.

'But you were horrid to Hilda,' she said to him.

'She should ha' been slapped in time.'

'But why? and she's *so* nice.'

He didn't answer, went round doing the evening chores, with a quiet, inevitable sort of motion. He was outwardly angry, but not with her. So Connie felt. And his anger gave him a peculiar handsomeness, an inwardness and glisten that thrilled her and made her limbs go molten

Still, he took no notice of her.

Till he sat down and began to unlace his boots. Then he looked up at her from under his brows, on which the anger still sat firm.

'Shan't you go up?' he said. 'There's a candle!'

He jerked his head swiftly to indicate the candle burning on the table. She took it obediently, and he watched the full curve of her hips as she went up the first stairs.

It was a night of sensual passion, in which she was a little startled and almost unwilling: yet pierced again with piercing thrills of sensuality, different, sharper, more terrible than the thrills of tenderness, but, at the moment, more desirable. Though a little frightened, she let him have his way, and the reckless, shameless sensuality shook her to her foundations, stripped her to the very last, and made a different woman of her. It was not really love. It was not voluptuousness. It was sensuality sharp and searing as fire, burning the soul to tinder.

Burning out the shames, the deepest, oldest shames, in the most secret places. It cost her an effort to let him have his way and his will of her. She had to be a passive, consenting thing, like a slave, a physical slave. Yet the passion licked round her, consuming, and when the sensual flame of it pressed through her bowels and breast, she really though she was dying: yet a poignant, marvellous death.

She had often wondered what Abélard meant, when he said that in their year of love he and Heloïse had passed through all the stages and refinements of passion. The same thing, a thousand years ago: ten thousand years ago! The same on the Greek vases, everywhere! The refinements of passion, the extravagances of sensuality! And necessary, forever necessary, to burn out false shames and smelt out the heaviest ore of the body into purity. With the fire of sheer sensuality.

In the short summer night she learnt so much. She would have thought a woman would have died of shame. Instead of which, the shame died. Shame, which is fear: the deep organic shame, the old, old physical fear which crouches in the bodily roots of us, and can only be chased away by the sensual fire, at last it was roused up and routed by the phallic hunt of the man, and she came to the very heart of the jungle of herself. She felt, now, she had come to the real bedrock of her nature, and was essentially shameless. She was her sensual self, naked and unashamed. She felt a triumph, almost a vainglory. So! That was how it was! That was life! That was how oneself really was! There was nothing left to disguise or be ashamed of. She shared her ultimate nakedness with a man, another being.

And what a reckless devil the man was! really like a devil! One had to be strong to bear him. But it took some getting at, the core of the physical jungle, the last and deepest recess of organic shame. The phallos alone could explore it. And how he had pressed in on her!

And how, in fear, she had hated it. But how she had really wanted it! She knew now. At the bottom of her soul, fundamentally, she had needed this phallic hunting out, she had secretly wanted it, and she had believed that she would never get it. Now suddenly there it was, and a man was sharing her last and final nakedness, she was shameless.

What liars poets and everybody were! They made one think one wanted sentiment. When what one supremely wanted was this piercing, consuming, rather awful sensuality. To find a man who dared do it, without shame or sin or final misgiving! If he had been ashamed afterwards, and made one feel ashamed, how awful! What a pity most men are so doggy, a bit shameful, like Clifford! Like Michaelis even! Both sensually a bit doggy and humiliating. The supreme pleasure of the mind! And what is that to a woman? What is it, really, to the man either! He becomes merely messy and doggy, even in his mind. It needs sheer sensuality even to purify and quicken the mind. Sheer fiery sensuality, not messiness.

Ah, God, how rare a thing a man is! They are all dogs that trot and sniff and copulate. To have found a man who was not afraid and not ashamed! She looked at him now, sleeping so like a wild animal asleep, gone, gone in the remoteness of it. She nestled down, not to be away from him.

Till his rousing waked her completely. He was sitting up in bed, looking down at her. She saw her own nakedness in his eyes, immediate knowledge of her. And the fluid, male knowledge of herself seemed to flow to her from his eyes and wrap her voluptuously. Oh, how voluptuous and lovely it was to have limbs and body half-asleep, heavy and suffused with passion!

'Is it time to wake up?' she said.

'Half-past six.'

She had to be at the lane-end at eight. Always, always, always this compulsion on one!

'I might make the breakfast and bring it up here; should I?' he said.

'Oh yes!'

Flossie whimpered gently below. He got up and threw off his pyjamas, and rubbed himself with a towel. When the human being is full of courage and full of life, how beautiful it is! So she thought, as she watched him in silence.

'Draw the curtain, will you?'

The sun was shining already on the tender green leaves of morning, and the wood stood bluey-fresh, in the nearness. She sat up in bed, looking dreamily out through the dormer window, her naked arms pushing her naked breasts together. He was dressing himself. She was half-dreaming of life, a life together with him: just a life.

He was going, fleeing from her dangerous, crouching nakedness.

'Have I lost my nightie altogether?' she said.

He pushed his hand down in the bed, and pulled out the bit of flimsy silk.

'I knowed I felt silk at my ankles,' he said.

But the nightdress was slit almost in two.

'Never mind!' she said. 'It belongs here, really. I'll leave it.'

'Ay, leave it, I can put it between my legs at night, for company. There's no name nor mark on it, is there?'

She slipped on the torn thing, and sat dreamily looking out of the window. The window was open, the air of morning drifted in, and the sound of birds. Birds flew continuously past. Then she saw Flossie roaming out. It was morning.

Downstairs she heard him making the fire, pumping water, going out at the back door. By and by came the smell of bacon, and at length he came upstairs with a huge black tray that would only just go through the door. He set the tray on the bed, and poured out the tea. Connie squatted in her torn nightdress, and fell on her food hungrily. He sat on the one chair, with his plate on his knees.

'How good it is!' she said. 'How nice to have breakfast together.'

He ate in silence, his mind on the time that was quickly passing. That made her remember.

'Oh, how I wish I could stay here with you, and Wragby were a million miles away! It's Wragby I'm going away from really. You know that, don't you?'

'Ay!'

'And you promise we will live together and have a life together, you and me! You promise me, don't you?'

'Ay! When we can.'

'Yes! And we *will*! we *will*, won't we?' She leaned over, making the tea spill, catching his wrist.

'Ay!' he said, tidying up the tea.

'We can't possibly *not* live together now, can we?' she said appealingly.

He looked up at her with his flickering grin.

'No!' he said. 'Only you've got to start in twenty-five minutes.'

'Have I?' she cried. Suddenly he held up a warning finger, and rose to his feet. Flossie had given a short bark, then three loud sharp yaps of warning.

Silent, he put his plate on the tray and went downstairs. Constance heard him go down the garden path. A bicycle bell tinkled outside there.

'Morning, Mr Mellors! Registered letter!'

'Oh ay! Got a pencil?'

'Here y'are!'

There was a pause.

'Canada!' said the stranger's voice.

'Ay! That's a mate o' mine out there in British Columbia. Dunno what he's got to register.'

''Appen sent y'a fortune, like.'

'More like wants summat.'

Pause.

'Well! Lovely day again!'

'Ay!'

'Morning!'

'Morning!'

After a time he came upstairs again, looking a little angry.

'Postman,' he said.

'Very early!' she replied.

'Rural round; he's mostly here by seven, when he does come.'

'Did your mate send you a fortune?'

'No! Only some photographs and papers about a place out there in British Columbia.'

'Would you go there?'

'I thought perhaps we might.'

'Oh yes! I believe it's lovely!'

But he was put out by the postman's coming.

'Them damned bikes, they're on you afore you know where you are. I hope he twigged nothing.'

'After all, what could he twig!'

'You must get up now, and get ready. I'm just goin' ter look round outside.'

She saw him go reconnoitring into the lane, with dog and gun. She went downstairs and washed, and was ready by the time he came back, with the few things in the little silk bag.

He locked up, and they set off, but through the wood, not down the lane. He was being wary.

'Don't you think one lives for times like last night?' she said to him.

'Ay! But there's the rest o' times to think on,' he replied, rather short.

They plodded on down the overgrown path, he in front, in silence.

'And we *will* live together and make a life together, won't we?' she pleaded.

'Ay!' he replied, striding on without looking round. 'When t' time comes! Just now you're off to Venice or somewhere.'

She followed him dumbly, with sinking heart. Oh, now she *was* to go!

At last he stopped.

'I'll just strike across here,' he said, pointing to the right.

But she flung her arms round his neck, and clung to him.

'But you'll keep the tenderness for me, won't you?' she whispered. 'I loved last night. But you'll keep the tenderness for me, won't you?'

He kissed her and held her close for a moment. Then he sighed, and kissed her again.

'I must go an' look if th' car's there.'

He strode over the low brambles and bracken, leaving a trail through the fern. For a minute or two he was gone. Then he came striding back.

'Car's not there yet,' he said. 'But there's the baker's cart on t' road.'

He seemed anxious and troubled.

'Hark!'

They heard a car softly hoot as it came nearer. It slowed up on the bridge.

She plunged with utter mournfulness in his track through the fern, and came to a huge holly hedge. He was just behind her.

'Here! Go through there!' he said, pointing to a gap. 'I shan't come out.'

She looked at him in despair. But he kissed her and made her go. She crept in sheer misery through the holly and through the wooden fence, stumbled down the little ditch and up into the lane, where Hilda was just getting out of the car in vexation.

'Why you're there!' said Hilda. 'Where's *he*?'

'He's not coming.'

Connie's face was running with tears as she got into the car with her little bag. Hilda snatched up the motoring helmet with the disfiguring goggles.

'Put it on!' she said. And Connie pulled on the disguise, then the long motoring coat, and she sat down, a goggling, inhuman, unrecognisable creature. Hilda started the car with a businesslike motion. They heaved out of the lane, and were away down the road. Connie had looked round, but there was no sight of him. Away! Away! She sat in bitter tears. The parting had come so suddenly, so unexpectedly. It was like death.

'Thank goodness you'll be away from him for some time!' said Hilda, turning to avoid Crosshill village.

Chapter 17

'You see, Hilda,' said Connie after lunch, when they were nearing London, 'you have never known either real tenderness or real sensuality: and if you do know them, with the same person, it makes a great difference.'

'For mercy's sake don't brag about your experiences!' said Hilda. 'I've never met the man yet who was capable of intimacy with a woman, giving himself up to her. That was what I wanted. I'm not keen on their self-satisfied tenderness, and their sensuality. I'm not content to be any man's little petsy-wetsy, nor his *chair à plaisir* either. I wanted a complete intimacy, and I didn't get it. That's enough for me.'

Connie pondered this. Complete intimacy! She supposed that meant revealing everything concerning yourself to the other person, and his revealing everything concerning himself. But that was a bore. And all that weary self-consciousness between a man and a woman! a disease!

'I think you're too conscious of yourself all the time, with everybody,' she said to her sister.

'I hope at least I haven't a slave nature,' said Hilda.

'But perhaps you have! Perhaps you are a slave to your own idea of yourself.'

Hilda drove in silence for some time after this piece of unheard-of insolence from that chit Connie.

'At least I'm not a slave to somebody else's idea of me: and the somebody else a servant of my husband's,' she retorted at last, in crude anger.

'You see, it's not so,' said Connie calmly.

She had always let herself be dominated by her elder sister. Now, though somewhere inside herself she was weeping, she was free of the dominion of *other women*. Ah! that in itself was a relief, like being given another life: to be free of the strange dominion and obsession of *other women*. How awful they were, women!

She was glad to be with her father, whose favourite she had always been. She and Hilda stayed in a little hotel off Pall Mall, and Sir Malcolm was in his club. But he took his daughters out in the evening, and they liked going with him.

He was still handsome and robust, though just a little afraid of the new world that had sprung up around him. He had got a second wife in Scotland, younger than himself, and richer. But he had as many holidays away from her as possible: just as with his first wife.

Connie sat next to him at the opera. He was moderately stout, and had stout thighs, but they were still strong and well-knit, the thighs of a healthy man who had taken his pleasure in life. His good-humoured selfishness, his dogged sort of independence, his unrepenting sensuality, it seemed to Connie she could see them all in his well-knit straight thighs. Just a man! And now becoming an old man, which is sad. Because in his strong, thick male legs there was none of the alert sensitiveness and power of tenderness which is the very essence of youth, that which never dies, once it is there.

Connie woke up to the existence of legs. They became more important to her than faces, which are no longer very real. How few people had live, alert legs! She looked at the men in the stalls. Great puddingy thighs in black pudding-cloth, or lean wooden sticks in black funeral stuff, or well-shaped young legs without any meaning whatever, either sensuality or tenderness or sensitiveness, just mere leggy ordinariness that pranced around. Not even any sensuality like her father's. They were all daunted, daunted out of existence.

But the women were not daunted. The awful mill-posts of most females! really shocking, really enough to justify murder! Or the poor thin pegs! or the trim neat things in silk stockings, without the slightest look of life! Awful, the millions of meaningless legs prancing meaninglessly around!

But she was not happy in London. The people seemed so spectral and blank. They had no alive happiness, no matter how brisk and good-looking they were. It was all barren. And Connie had a woman's blind craving for happiness, to be assured of happiness.

In Paris at any rate she felt a bit of sensuality still. But what a weary, tired, worn-out sensuality. Worn-out for lack of tenderness. Oh! Paris was sad. One of the saddest towns: weary of its now-mechanical sensuality, weary of the tension of money, money, money, weary even of resentment and conceit, just weary to death, and still not sufficiently Americanised or Londonised to hide the weariness under a mechanical jig-jig-jig! Ah, these manly he-men, these *flâneurs*, the oglers, these eaters of good dinners! How weary they were! weary, worn-out for lack of a little tenderness, given and taken. The efficient, sometimes charming women knew a thing or two about the sensual realities: they had that pull over their jigging English sisters. But they knew even less of tenderness. Dry, with the endless dry tension of will, they too were wearing out. The human world was just getting worn out. Perhaps it would turn fiercely destructive. A sort of anarchy! Clifford and his conservative anarchy! Perhaps it wouldn't be conservative much longer. Perhaps it would develop into a very radical anarchy.

Connie found herself shrinking and afraid of the world. Sometimes she was happy for a little while in the Boulevards or in the Bois or the Luxembourg Gardens. But already Paris was full of Americans and English, strange Americans in the oddest uniforms, and the usual dreary English that are so hopeless abroad.

She was glad to drive on. It was suddenly hot weather, so Hilda was going through Switzerland and over the Brenner, then through the Dolomites down to Venice. Hilda loved all the managing and the driving and being mistress of the show. Connie was quite content to keep quiet.

And the trip was really quite nice. Only Connie kept saying to herself: Why don't I really care? Why am I never really thrilled? How awful, that I don't really care about the landscape any more! But I don't. It's rather awful. I'm like Saint Bernard, who could sail down the lake of Lucerne without ever noticing that there were even mountain and green water. I just don't care for landscape any more. Why should one stare at it? Why should one? I refuse to.

No, she found nothing vital in France or Switzerland or the Tyrol or Italy. She just was carted through it all. And it was all less real than Wragby. Less real than the awful Wragby! She felt she didn't care if she never saw France or Switzerland or Italy again. They'd keep. Wragby was more real.

As for people! people were all alike, with very little difference. They all wanted to get money out of you: or, if they were travellers, they wanted to get enjoyment, perforce, like squeezing blood out of a stone. Poor mountains! poor landscape! it all had to be squeezed and squeezed and squeezed again, to provide a thrill, to provide enjoyment. What did people mean, with their simply *determined* enjoying of themselves?

No! said Connie to herself. I'd rather be at Wragby, where I can go about and be still, and not stare at anything or do any performing of any sort. This tourist performance of enjoying oneself is too hopelessly humiliating: it's such a failure.

She wanted to go back to Wragby, even to Clifford, even to poor crippled Clifford. He wasn't such a fool as this swarming holidaying lot, anyhow.

But in her inner consciousness she was keeping touch with the other man. She mustn't let her connection with him go: oh, she mustn't let it go, or she was lost, lost utterly in this world of riff-raffy expensive people and joy-hogs. Oh, the joy-hogs! Oh 'enjoying oneself!' Another modern form of sickness.

They left the car in Mestre, in a garage, and took the regular steamer over to Venice. It was a lovely summer afternoon, the shallow lagoon rippled, the full sunshine made Venice, turning its back to them across the water, look dim.

At the station quay they changed to a gondola, giving the man the address. He was a regular gondolier in a white-and-blue blouse, not very good-looking, not at all impressive.

'Yes! The Villa Esmeralda! Yes! I know it! I have been the gondolier for a gentleman there. But a fair distance out!'

He seemed a rather childish, impetuous fellow. He rowed with a certain exaggerated impetuosity, through the dark side-canals with the horrible, slimy green walls, the canals that go through the poorer quarters, where the washing hangs high up on ropes, and there is a slight, or strong odour of sewage.

But at last he came to one of the open canals with pavement on either side, and looping bridges, that run straight, at right-angles to the Grand Canal. The two women sat under the little awning, the man was perched above, behind them.

'Are the signorine staying long at the Villa Esmeralda?' he asked, rowing easy, and wiping his perspiring face with a white-and-blue handkerchief.

'Some twenty days: we are both married ladies,' said Hilda, in her curious hushed voice, that made her Italian sound so foreign.

'Ah! Twenty days!' said the man. There was a pause. After which he asked: 'Do the signore want a gondolier for the twenty days or so that they will stay at the Villa Esmeralda? Or by the day, or by the week?'

Connie and Hilda considered. In Venice, it is always preferable to have one's own gondola, as it is preferable to have one's own car on land.

'What is there at the Villa? what boats?'

'There is a motor launch, also a gondola. But – ' The *but* meant: they won't be your property.

'How much do you charge?'

It was about thirty shillings a day, or ten pounds a week.

'Is that the regular price?' asked Hilda.

'Less, Signora, less. The regular price – '

The sisters considered.

'Well,' said Hilda, 'come tomorrow morning, and we will arrange it. What is your name?'

His name was Giovanni, and he wanted to know at what time he should come, and then, for whom should he say he was waiting. Hilda had no card. Connie gave him one of hers. He glanced at it swiftly, with his hot, southern blue eyes, then glanced again.

'Ah!' he said, lighting up. 'Milady! Milady, isn't it?'

'Milady Costanza!' said Connie.

He nodded, repeating: 'Milady Costanza!' and putting the card carefully away in his blouse.

The Villa Esmeralda was quite a long way out, on the edge of the lagoon looking towards Chioggia. It was not a very old house, and pleasant, with the terraces looking seawards, and below, quite a big garden with dark trees, walled in from the lagoon.

Their host was a heavy, rather coarse Scotchman who had made a good fortune in Italy before the war, and had been knighted for his ultrapatriotism during the war. His wife was a thin, pale, sharp kind of person with no fortune of her own, and the misfortune of having to regulate her husband's rather sordid amorous exploits. He was terribly tiresome with the servants. But having had a slight stroke during the winter, he was now more manageable.

The house was pretty full. Besides Sir Malcolm and his two daughters, there were seven more people, a Scotch couple, again with two daughters; a young Italian Contessa, a widow; a young Georgian prince, and a youngish English clergyman who had had pneumonia and was being chaplain to Sir Alexander for his health's sake. The prince was penniless, good-looking, would make an excellent chauffeur, with the necessary impudence, and basta! The Contessa was a quiet little puss with a game on somewhere. The clergyman was a raw simple fellow from a Bucks vicarage: luckily he had left his wife and two children at home. And the Guthries, the family of four, were good solid Edinburgh middle class, enjoying everything in a solid fashion, and daring everything while risking nothing.

Connie and Hilda ruled out the prince at once. The Guthries were more or less their own sort, substantial, but boring: and the girls wanted husbands. The chaplain was not a bad fellow, but too deferential. Sir Alexander, after his slight stroke, had a terrible heaviness in his joviality, but he was still thrilled at the presence of so many handsome young women. Lady Cooper was a quiet, catty person who had a thin time of it, poor thing, and who watched every other woman with a cold watchfulness that had become her second nature, and who said cold, nasty little things which showed what an utterly low opinion she had of all human nature. She was also quite venomously overbearing with the servants, Connie found: but in a quiet way. And she skilfully behaved so that Sir Alexander should think that *he* was lord and monarch of the whole caboosh, with his stout, would-be-genial paunch, and his utterly boring jokes, his humorosity, as Hilda called it.

Sir Malcolm was painting. Yes, he still would do a Venetian lagoonscape, now and then, in contrast to his Scottish landscapes. So in the morning he was rowed off with a huge canvas, to his 'site'. A little later, Lady Cooper would be rowed off into the heart of the city, with sketching-block and colours. She was an inveterate watercolour painter, and the house was full of rose-coloured palaces, dark canals, swaying bridges, medieval façades, and so on. A little later the Guthries, the prince, the countess, Sir Alexander, and sometimes Mr Lind, the chaplain, would go off to the Lido, where they would bathe; coming home to a late lunch at half-past one.

The house-party, as a house-party, was distinctly boring. But this did not trouble the sisters. They were out all the time. Their father took them to the exhibition, miles and miles of weary paintings. He took them to all the cronies of his in the Villa Lucchese, he sat with them on warm evenings in the piazza, having got a table at Florian's: he took them to the theatre, to the Goldoni plays.

There were illuminated water-fêtes, there were dances. This was a holiday-place of all holiday-places. The Lido, with its acres of sun-pinked or pyjamaed bodies, was like a strand with an endless heap of seals come up for mating. Too many people in the piazza, too many limbs and trunks of humanity on the Lido, too many gondolas, too many motor launches, too many steamers, too many pigeons, too many ices, too many cocktails, too many menservants wanting tips, too many languages rattling, too much, too much sun, too much smell of Venice, too many cargoes of strawberries, too many silk shawls, too many huge, raw-beef slices of watermelon on stalls: too much enjoyment, altogether far too much enjoyment!

Connie and Hilda went around in their sunny frocks. There were dozens of people they knew, dozens of people knew them. Michaelis turned up like a bad penny. 'Hullo! Where you staying? Come and have an ice-cream or something! Come with me somewhere in my gondola.' Even Michaelis *almost* sunburned: though sun-cooked is more appropriate to the look of the mass of human flesh.

It was pleasant in a way. It was *almost* enjoyment. But anyhow, with all the cocktails, all the lying in warmish water and sunbathing on hot sand in hot sun, jazzing with your stomach up against some fellow in the warm nights, cooling off with ices, it was a complete narcotic. And that was what they all wanted, a drug: the slow water, a drug; the sun, a drug; jazz, a drug; cigarettes, cocktails, ices, vermouth. To be drugged! Enjoyment! Enjoyment!

Hilda half liked being drugged. She liked looking at all the women, speculating about them. The women were absorbingly interested in the women. How does she look! what man has she captured? what fun is she getting out of it? – The men were like great dogs in white flannel trousers, waiting to be patted, waiting to wallow, waiting to plaster some woman's stomach against their own, in jazz.

Hilda liked jazz, because she could plaster her stomach against the stomach of some so-called man, and let him control her movements from the visceral centre, here and there across the floor, and then she could break loose and ignore 'the creature'. He had been merely made use of. Poor Connie was rather unhappy. She wouldn't jazz, because she simply couldn't plaster her stomach against some 'creature's' stomach. She hated the conglomerate mass of nearly nude flesh on the Lido: there was hardly enough water to wet them all. She disliked Sir Alexander and Lady Cooper. She did not want Michaelis or anybody else trailing her.

The happiest times were when she got Hilda to go with her away across the lagoon, far across to some lonely shingle-bank, where they could bathe quite alone, the gondola remaining on the inner side of the reef.

Then Giovanni got another gondolier to help him, because it was a long way and he sweated terrifically in the sun. Giovanni was very nice: affectionate, as the Italians are, and quite passionless. The Italians are not passionate: passion has deep reserves. They are easily moved, and often affectionate, but they rarely have any abiding passion of any sort.

So Giovanni was already devoted to his ladies, as he had been devoted to cargoes of ladies in the past. He was perfectly ready to prostitute himself to them, if they wanted him: he secretly hoped they would want him. They would give him a handsome present, and it would come in very handy, as he was just going to be married. He told them about his marriage, and they were suitably interested.

He thought this trip to some lonely bank across the lagoon probably meant business: business being *l'amore*, love. So he got a mate to help him, for it *was* a long way: and after all, they were two ladies. Two ladies, two mackerels! Good arithmetic! Beautiful ladies, too! He was justly proud of them. And though it was the Signora who paid him and gave him orders, he rather hoped it would be the young milady who would select him for *l'amore*. She would give more money too.

The mate he brought was called Daniele. He was not a regular gondolier, so he had none of the cadger and prostitute about him. He was a sandola man, a sandola being a big boat that brings in fruit and produce from the islands.

Daniele was beautiful, tall and well-shapen, with a light round head of little, close-pale-blond curls, and a good-looking man's face, a little like a lion, and long-distance blue eyes. He was not effusive, loquacious, and bibulous like Giovanni. He was silent and he rowed with a strength and ease as if he were alone on the water. The ladies were ladies, remote from him. He did not even look at them. He looked ahead.

He was a real man, a little angry when Giovanni drank too much wine and rowed awkwardly, with effusive shoves of the great oar. He was a man as Mellors was a man, unprostituted. Connie pitied the wife of the easily-overflowing Giovanni. But Daniele's wife would be one of those sweet Venetian women of the people whom one still sees, modest and flower-like in the back of that labyrinth of a town.

Ah, how sad that man first prostitutes woman, then woman prostitutes man. Giovanni was pining to prostitute himself, dribbling like a dog, wanting to give himself to a woman. And for money!

Connie looked at Venice far off, low and rose-coloured upon the water. Built of money, blossomed of money, and dead with money. The money-deadness! Money, money, money, prostitution and deadness.

Yet Daniele was still a man capable of a man's free allegiance. He did not wear the gondolier's blouse: only the knitted blue jersey. He was a little wild, uncouth and proud. So he was hireling to the rather doggy Giovanni, who was hireling again of two women. So it is! When Jesus refused the devil's money, he left the devil like a Jewish banker, master of the whole situation.

Connie would come home from the blazing light of the lagoon in a kind of stupor, to find letters from home. Clifford wrote regularly. He wrote very good letters: they might all have been printed in a book. And for this reason Connie found them not very interesting.

She lived in the stupor of the light of the lagoon, the lapping saltiness of the water, the space, the emptiness, the nothingness: but health, health, complete stupor of health. It was gratifying, and she was lulled away in it, not caring for anything. Besides, she was pregnant. She knew now. So the stupor of sunlight and lagoon salt and sea-bathing and lying on shingle and finding shells and drifting away, away in a gondola was completed by the pregnancy inside her, another fullness of health, satisfying and stupefying.

She had been at Venice a fortnight, and she was to stay another ten days or a fortnight. The sunshine blazed over any count of time, and the fullness of physical health made forgetfulness complete. She was in a sort of stupor of well-being.

From which a letter from Clifford roused her.

We too have had our mild local excitement. It appears the truant wife of Mellors, the keeper, turned up at the cottage, and found herself unwelcome. He packed her off and locked the door. Report has it, however, that when he returned from the wood he found the no longer fair lady firmly established in his bed, in *puris naturalibus*; or one should say, in *impuris naturalibus*. She had broken a window and got in that way. Unable to evict the somewhat manhandled Venus from his couch, he beat a retreat and retired, it is said, to his mother's house in Tevershall. Meanwhile the Venus of Stacks Gate is established in the cottage, which she claims is her home, and Apollo, apparently, is domiciled in Tevershall.

I repeat this from hearsay, as Mellors has not come to me personally. I had this particular bit of local garbage from our garbage bird, our ibis, our scavenging turkey-buzzard, Mrs Bolton. I would not have repeated it had she not exclaimed: her Ladyship will go no more to the wood if *that* woman's going to be about!

I like your picture of Sir Malcolm striding into the sea with white hair blowing and pink flesh glowing. I envy you that sun. Here it rains. But I don't envy Sir Malcolm his inveterate mortal carnality. However, it suits his age. Apparently one grows more carnal and more mortal as one grows older. Only youth has a taste of immortality –

This news affected Connie in her state of semi-stupefied well-being with vexation amounting to exasperation. Now she had got to be bothered by that beast of a woman! Now she must start and fret! She had no letter from Mellors. They had agreed not to write at all, but now she wanted to hear from him personally. After all, he was the father of the child that was coming. Let him write!

But how hateful! Now everything was messed up. How foul those low people were! How nice it was here, in the sunshine and the indolence, compared to that dismal mess of that English Midlands! After all, a clear sky was almost the most important thing in life.

She did not mention the fact of her pregnancy, even to Hilda. She wrote to Mrs Bolton for exact information.

Duncan Forbes, an artist friend of theirs, had arrived at the Villa Esmeralda, coming north from Rome. Now he made a third in the gondola, and he bathed with them across the lagoon, and was their escort: a quiet, almost taciturn young man, very advanced in his art.

She had a letter from Mrs Bolton:

You will be pleased, I am sure, my Lady, when you see Sir Clifford. He's looking quite blooming and working very hard, and very hopeful. Of course he is looking forward to seeing you among us again. It is a dull house without my Lady, and we shall all welcome her presence among us once more.

About Mr Mellors, I don't know how much Sir Clifford told you. It seems his wife came back all of a sudden one afternoon, and he found her sitting on the doorstep when he came in from the wood. She said she was come back to him and wanted to live with him again, as she was his legal wife, and he wasn't going to divorce her. Because it seems Mr Mellors was trying for a divorce. But he wouldn't have anything to do with her, and wouldn't let her in the house, and did not go in himself, he went back into the wood without ever opening the door.

But when he came back after dark, he found the house broken into, so he went upstairs to see what she'd done, and he found her in bed without a rag on her. He offered her money, but she said she was his wife and he must take her back. I don't know what sort of a scene they had. His mother told me about it, she's terribly upset. Well he told her he'd die rather than ever live with her again, so he took his things and went straight to his mother's on Tevershall hill. He stopped the night and went to the wood next day through the park, never going near the cottage. It seems he never saw his wife that day. But the day after she was at her brother Dan's at Beggarlee, swearing and carrying on, saying she was his legal wife, and that he'd been having women at the cottage, because she'd found a scent-bottle in his drawer, and gold-tipped cigarette-ends on the ash-heap, and I don't know what all. Then it seems the postman Fred Kirk says he heard somebody talking in Mr Mellors' bedroom early one morning, and a motor car had been in the lane.

Mr Mellors stayed on with his mother, and went to the wood through the park, and it seems she stayed on at the cottage. Well, there was no end of talk. So at last Mr Mellors and Tom Phillips went to the cottage and fetched away most of the furniture and bedding, and unscrewed the handle of the pump, so she was forced to go. But instead of going back to Stacks Gate she went and lodged with that Mrs Swain at Beggarlee, because her brother Dan's wife wouldn't have her. And she kept going to old Mrs Mellors' house, to catch him, and she began swearing he'd got in bed with her in the cottage, and she went to a lawyer to make him pay her an allowance. She's grown heavy, and more common than ever, and as strong as a bull. And she goes about saying the most awful things about him, how he has women at the cottage, and how he behaved to her when they were married, the low, beastly things he did to her, and I don't know what all. I'm sure it's awful, the mischief a woman can do, once she starts talking. And no matter how low she may be, there'll be some as will believe her, and some of the dirt will stick. I'm sure the way she makes out that Mr Mellors was one of those low, beastly men with women, is simply shocking. And people are only too ready to believe things against anybody, especially things like that. She declares she'll never leave him alone while he lives. Though what I say is, if he was so beastly to her, why is she so anxious to go back to him? But of course she's coming near her change of life, for she's years older than he is. And these common, violent women always go partly insane when the change of life comes upon them –

This was a nasty blow to Connie. Here she was, sure as life, coming in for her share of the lowness and dirt. She felt angry with him for not having got clear of Bertha Coutts: nay, for ever having married her. Perhaps he had a certain hankering after lowness. Connie remembered the last night she had spent with him, and shivered. He had known all that sensuality, even with Bertha Coutts! It was really rather disgusting. It would be well to be rid of him, clear of him altogether. He was perhaps really common, really low.

She had a revulsion against the whole affair, and almost envied the Guthrie girls their gawky inexperience and crude maidenliness. And she now dreaded the thought that anybody would know about herself and the keeper. How unspeakably humiliating! She was weary, afraid, and felt a craving for utter respectability, even for the vulgar and deadening respectability of the Guthrie girls. If Clifford knew about her affair, how unspeakably humiliating! She was afraid, terrified of society and its unclean bite. She almost wished she could get rid of the child again, and be quite clear. In short, she fell into a state of funk.

As for the scent-bottle, that was her own folly. She had not been able to refrain from perfuming his one or two handkerchiefs and his shirts in the drawer, just out of childishness, and she had left a little bottle of Coty's Wood-violet perfume, half empty, among his things. She wanted him to remember her in the perfume. As for the cigarette-ends, they were Hilda's.

She could not help confiding a little in Duncan Forbes. She didn't say she had been the keeper's lover, she only said she liked him, and told Forbes the history of the man.

'Oh,' said Forbes, 'you'll see, they'll never rest till they've pulled the man down and done him in. If he has refused to creep up into the middle classes, when he had a chance; and if he's a man who stands up for his own sex, then they'll do him in. It's the one thing they won't let you be, straight and open in your sex. You can be as dirty as you like. In fact the more dirt you do on sex, the better they like it. But if you believe in your own sex, and won't have it done dirt to: they'll down you. It's the one insane taboo left: sex as a natural and vital thing. They won't have it, and they'll kill you before they'll let you have it. You'll see, they'll hound that man down. And what's he done, after all? If he's made love to his wife all ends on, hasn't he a right to? She ought to be proud of it. But you see, even a low bitch like that turns on him, and uses the hyena instinct of the mob against sex, to pull him down. You have a snivel and feel sinful or awful about your sex, before you're allowed to have any. Oh, they'll hound the poor devil down.'

Connie had a revulsion in the opposite direction now. What had he done, after all? what had he done to herself, Connie, but give her an exquisite pleasure and a sense of freedom and life? He had released her warm, natural sexual flow. And for that they would hound him down.

No no, it should not be. She saw the image of him, naked white with tanned face and hands, looking down and addressing his erect penis as if it were another being, the odd grin flickering on his face. And she heard his voice again: Tha's got the nicest woman's arse of anybody! And she felt his hand warmly and softly closing over her tail again, over her secret places, like a benediction. And the warmth ran through her womb, and the little flames flickered in her knees, and she said: Oh no! I mustn't go back on it! I must not go back on him. I must stick to him and to what I had of him, through everything. I had no warm, flamy life till he gave it me. And I won't go back on it.

She did a rash thing. She sent a letter to Ivy Bolton, enclosing a note to the keeper, and asking Mrs Bolton to give it him. And she wrote to him:

I am very much distressed to hear of all the trouble your wife is making for you, but don't mind it, it is only a sort of hysteria. It will all blow over as suddenly as it came. But I'm awfully sorry about it, and I do hope you are not minding very much. After all, it isn't worth it. She is only a hysterical woman who wants to hurt you. I shall be home in ten days' time, and I do hope everything will be all right.

A few days later came a letter from Clifford. He was evidently upset.

I am delighted to hear you are prepared to leave Venice on the sixteenth. But if you are enjoying it, don't hurry home. We miss you, Wragby misses you. But it is essential that you should get your full amount of sunshine, sunshine and pyjamas, as the advertisements of the Lido say. So please do stay on a little longer, if it is cheering you up and preparing you for our sufficiently awful winter. Even today, it rains.

I am assiduously, admirably looked after by Mrs Bolton. She is a queer specimen. The more I live, the more I realise what strange creatures human beings are. Some of them might just as well have a hundred legs, like a centipede, or six, like a lobster. The human consistency and dignity one has been led to expect from one's fellow-men seem actually nonexistent. One doubts if they exist to any startling degree even in oneself.

The scandal of the keeper continues and gets bigger like a snowball. Mrs Bolton keeps me informed. She reminds me of a fish which, though dumb, seems to be breathing silent gossip through its gills, while ever it lives. All goes through the sieve of her gills, and nothing surprises her. It is as if the events of other people's lives were the necessary oxygen of her own.

She is preoccupied with the Mellors scandal, and if I will let her begin, she takes me down to the depths. Her great indignation, which even then is like the indignation of an actress playing a role, is against the wife of Mellors, whom she persists in calling Bertha Coutts. I have been to the depths of the muddy lives of the Bertha Couttses of this world, and when, released from the current of gossip, I slowly rise to the surface again, I look at the daylight in wonder that it ever should be.

It seems to me absolutely true, that our world, which appears to us the surface of all things, is really the *bottom* of a deep ocean: all our trees are submarine growths, and we are weird, scaly-clad submarine fauna, feeding ourselves on offal like shrimps. Only occasionally the soul rises gasping through the fathomless fathoms under which we live, far up to the surface of the ether, where there is true air. I am convinced that the air we normally breathe is a kind of water, and men and women are a species of fish.

But sometimes the soul does come up, shoots like a kittiwake into the light, with ecstasy, after having preyed on the submarine depths. It is our mortal destiny, I suppose, to prey upon the ghastly subaqueous life of our fellow-men, in the submarine jungle of mankind. But our immortal destiny is to escape, once we have swallowed our swimmy catch, up again into the bright ether, bursting out from the surface of Old Ocean into real light. Then one realises one's eternal nature.

When I hear Mrs Bolton talk, I feel myself plunging down, down, to the depths where the fish of human secrets wriggle and swim. Carnal appetite makes one seize a beakful of prey: then up, up again, out of the dense into the ethereal, from the wet into the dry. To you I can tell the whole process. But with Mrs Bolton I only feel the downward plunge, down, horribly, among the sea-weeds and the pallid monsters of the very bottom.

I am afraid we are going to lose our gamekeeper. The scandal of the truant wife, instead of dying down, has reverberated to greater and greater dimensions. He is accused of all unspeakable things, and curiously enough, the woman has managed to get the bulk of the colliers' wives behind her, gruesome fish, and the village is putrescent with talk.

I hear this Bertha Coutts besieges Mellors in his mother's house, having ransacked the cottage and the hut. She seized one day upon her own daughter, as that chip of the female block was returning from school; but the little one, instead of kissing the loving mother's hand, bit it firmly, and so received from the other hand a smack in the face which sent her reeling into the gutter: whence she was rescued by an indignant and harassed grandmother.

The woman has blown off an amazing quantity of poison-gas. She has aired in detail all those incidents of her conjugal life which are usually buried down in the deepest grave of matrimonial silence, between married couples. Having chosen to exhume them, after ten years of burial, she has a weird array. I hear these details from Linley and the doctor: the latter being amused. Of course there is really nothing in it. Humanity has always had a strange avidity for unusual sexual postures, and if a man likes to use his wife, as Benvenuto Cellini says, 'in the Italian way', well that is a matter of taste. But I had hardly expected our gamekeeper to be up to so many tricks. No doubt Bertha Coutts herself first put him up to them. In any case, it is a matter of their own personal squalor, and nothing to do with anybody else.

However, everybody listens: as I do myself. A dozen years ago, common decency would have hushed the thing. But common decency no longer exists, and the colliers' wives are all up in arms and unabashed in voice. One would think every child in Tevershall, for the last fifty years, had been an immaculate conception, and every one of our nonconformist females was a shining Joan of Arc. That our estimable gamekeeper should have about him a touch of Rabelais seems to make him more monstrous and shocking than a murderer like Crippen. Yet these people in Tevershall are a loose lot, if one is to believe all accounts.

The trouble is, however, the execrable Bertha Coutts has not confined herself to her own experiences and sufferings. She has discovered, at the top of her voice, that her husband has been 'keeping' women down at the cottage, and has made a few random shots at naming the women. This has brought a few decent names trailing through the mud, and the thing has gone quite considerably too far. An injunction has been taken out against the woman.

I have had to interview Mellors about the business, as it was impossible to keep the woman away from the wood. He goes about as usual, with his Miller-of-the-Dee air, I cares for nobody, no not I, if nobody cares for me! Nevertheless, I shrewdly suspect he feels like a dog with a tin can tied to its tail: though he makes a very good show of pretending the tin can isn't there. But I hear that in the village the women call away their children if he is passing, as if he were the Marquis de Sade in person. He goes on with a certain impudence, but I am afraid the tin can is firmly tied to his tail, and that inwardly he repeats, like Don Rodrigo in the Spanish ballad: 'Ah, now it bites me where I most have sinned!'

I asked him if he thought he would be able to attend to his duty in the wood, and he said he did not think he had neglected it. I told him it was a nuisance to have the woman trespassing: to which he replied that he had no power to arrest her. Then I hinted at the scandal and its unpleasant course. 'Ay,' he said. 'Folks should do their own fuckin', then they wouldn't want to listen to a lot of clatfart about another man's.'

He said it with some bitterness, and no doubt it contains the real germ of truth. The mode of putting it, however, is neither delicate nor respectful. I hinted as much, and then I heard the tin can rattle again. 'It's not for a man i' the shape you're in, Sir Clifford, to twit me for havin' a cod atween my legs.'

These things, said indiscriminately to all and sundry, of course do not help him at all, and the rector, and Linley, and Burroughs all think it would be as well if the man left the place.

I asked him if it was true that he entertained ladies down at the cottage, and all he said was: 'Why, what's that to you, Sir Clifford?' I told him I intended to have decency observed on my estate, to which he replied: 'Then you mun button the mouths o' a' th' women.' – When I pressed him about his manner of life at the cottage, he said: 'Surely you might ma'e a scandal out o' me an' my bitch Flossie. You've missed summat there.' As a matter of fact, for an example of impertinence he'd be hard to beat.

I asked him if it would be easy for him to find another job. He said: 'If you're hintin' that you'd like to shunt me out of this job, it'd be easy as wink.' So he made no trouble at all about leaving at the end of next week, and apparently is willing to initiate a young fellow, Joe Chambers, into as many mysteries of the craft as possible. I told him I would give him a month's wages extra, when he left. He said he'd rather I kept my money, as I'd no occasion to ease my conscience. I asked him what he meant, and he said: 'You don't owe me nothing extra, Sir Clifford, so don't pay me nothing extra. If you think you see my shirt hanging out, just tell me.'

Well, there is the end of it for the time being. The woman has gone away: we don't know where to: but she is liable to arrest if she shows her face in Tevershall. And I hear she is mortally afraid of gaol, because she merits it so well. Mellors will depart on Saturday week, and the place will soon become normal again.

Meanwhile, my dear Connie, if you would enjoy to stay in Venice or in Switzerland till the beginning of August, I should be glad to think you were out of all this buzz of nastiness, which will have died quite away by the end of the month.

So you see, we are deep-sea monsters, and when the lobster walks on mud, he stirs it up for everybody. We must perforce take it philosophically.

The irritation, and the lack of any sympathy in any direction, of Clifford's letter, had a bad effect on Connie. But she understood it better when she received the following from Mellors:

The cat is out of the bag, along with various other pussies. You have heard that my wife Bertha came back to my unloving arms, and took up her abode in the cottage: where, to speak disrespectfully, she smelled a rat, in the shape of a little bottle of Coty. Other evidence she did not find, at least for some days, when she began to howl about the burnt photograph. She noticed the glass and the back-board in the square bedroom. Unfortunately, on the back-board somebody had scribbled little sketches, and the initials, several times repeated: C.S.R. This, however, afforded no clue until she broke into the hut, and found one of your books, an autobiography of the actress Judith, with your name, Constance Stewart Reid, on the front page. After this, for some days she went round loudly saying that my paramour was no less a person than Lady Chatterley herself. The news came at last to the rector, Mr Burroughs, and to Sir Clifford. They then proceeded to take legal steps against my liege lady, who for her part disappeared, having always had a mortal fear of the police.

Sir Clifford asked to see me, so I went to him. He talked around things and seemed annoyed with me. Then he asked if I knew that even her Ladyship's name had been mentioned. I said I never listened to scandal, and was surprised to hear this bit from Sir Clifford himself. He said, of course it was a great insult, and I told him there was Queen Mary on a calendar in the scullery, no doubt because Her Majesty formed part of my harem. But he didn't appreciate the sarcasm. He as good as told me I was a disreputable character who walked about with my breeches' buttons undone, and I as good as told him he'd nothing to unbutton anyhow, so he gave me the sack, and I leave on Saturday week, and the place thereof shall know me no more.

I shall go to London, and my old landlady, Mrs Inger, 17 Coburg Square, will either give me a room or will find one for me.

Be sure your sins will find you out, especially if you're married and her name's Bertha –

There was not a word about herself, or to her. Connie resented this. He might have said some few words of consolation or reassurance. But she knew he was leaving her free, free to go back to Wragby and to Clifford. She resented that too. He need not be so falsely chivalrous. She wished he had said to Clifford: 'Yes, she is my lover and my mistress and I am proud of it!' But his courage wouldn't carry him so far.

So her name was coupled with his in Tevershall! It was a mess. But that would soon die down.

She was angry, with the complicated and confused anger that made her inert. She did not know what to do nor what to say, so she said and did nothing. She went on at Venice just the same, rowing out in the gondola with Duncan Forbes, bathing, letting the days slip by. Duncan, who had been rather depressingly in love with her ten years ago, was in love with her again. But she said to him: 'I only want one thing of men, and that is, that they should leave me alone.'

So Duncan left her alone: really quite pleased to be able to. All the same, he offered her a soft stream of a queer, inverted sort of love. He wanted to be *with* her.

'Have you ever thought,' he said to her one day, 'how very little people are connected with one another. Look at Daniele! He is handsome as a son of the sun. But see how alone he looks in his handsomeness. Yet I bet he has a wife and family, and couldn't possibly go away from them.'

'Ask him,' said Connie.

Duncan did so. Daniele said he was married, and had two children, both male, aged seven and nine. But he betrayed no emotion over the fact.

'Perhaps only people who are capable of real togetherness have that look of being alone in the universe,' said Connie. 'The others have a certain stickiness, they stick to the mass, like Giovanni.' 'And,' she thought to herself, 'like you, Duncan.'

Chapter 18

She had to make up her mind what to do. She would leave Venice on the Saturday that he was leaving Wragby: in six days' time. This would bring her to London on the Monday following, and she would then see him. She wrote to him to the London address, asking him to send her a letter to Hartland's hotel, and to call for her on the Monday evening at seven.

Inside herself, she was curiously and complicatedly angry, and all her responses were numb. She refused to confide even in Hilda, and Hilda, offended by her steady silence, had become rather intimate with a Dutch woman. Connie hated these rather stifling intimacies between women, intimacy into which Hilda always entered ponderously.

Sir Malcolm decided to travel with Connie, and Duncan could come on with Hilda. The old artist always did himself well: he took berths on the Orient Express, in spite of Connie's dislike of *trains de luxe*, the atmosphere of vulgar depravity there is aboard them nowadays. However, it would make the journey to Paris shorter.

Sir Malcolm was always uneasy going back to his wife. It was habit carried over from the first wife. But there would be a house-party for the grouse, and he wanted to be well ahead. Connie, sunburnt and handsome, sat in silence, forgetting all about the landscape.

'A little dull for you, going back to Wragby,' said her father, noticing her glumness.

'I'm not sure I shall go back to Wragby,' she said, with startling abruptness, looking into his eyes with her big blue eyes. His big blue eyes took on the frightened look of a man whose social conscience is not quite clear.

'You mean you'll stay on in Paris a while?'

'No! I mean never go back to Wragby.'

He was bothered by his own little problems, and sincerely hoped he was getting none of hers to shoulder.

'How's that, all at once?' he asked.

'I'm going to have a child.'

It was the first time she had uttered the words to any living soul, and it seemed to mark a cleavage in her life.

'How do you know?' said her father.

She smiled.

'How *should* I know?'

'But not Clifford's child, of course?'

'No! Another man's.'

She rather enjoyed tormenting him.

'Do I know the man?' asked Sir Malcolm.

'No! You've never seen him.'

There was a long pause.

'And what are your plans?'

'I don't know. That's the point.'

'No patching it up with Clifford?'

'I suppose Clifford would take it,' said Connie. 'He told me, after last time you talked to him, he wouldn't mind if I had a child: so long as I went about it discreetly.'

'Only sensible thing he could say, under the circumstances. Then I suppose it'll be all right.'

'In what way?' said Connie, looking into her father's eyes. They were big blue eyes rather like her own, but with a certain uneasiness in them, a look sometimes of an uneasy little boy, sometimes a look of sullen selfishness, usually good-humoured and wary.

'You can present Clifford with an heir to all the Chatterleys, and put another baronet in Wragby.'

Sir Malcolm's face smiled with a half-sensual smile.

'But I don't think I want to,' she said.

'Why not? Feeling entangled with the other man? Well! If you want the truth from me, my child, it's this. The world goes on. Wragby stands and will go on standing. The world is more or less a fixed thing, and externally, we have to adapt ourselves to it. Privately, in my private opinion, we can please ourselves. Emotions change. You may like one man this year and another next. But Wragby still stands. Stick by Wragby as far as Wragby sticks by you. Then please yourself. But you'll get very little out of making a break. You can make a break if you wish. You have an independent income, the only thing that never lets you down. But you won't get much out of it. Put a little baronet in Wragby. It's an amusing thing to do.'

And Sir Malcolm sat back and smiled again. Connie did not answer.

'I hope you had a real man at last,' he said to her after a while, sensually alert.

'I did. That's the trouble. There aren't many of them about,' she said.

'No, by God!' he mused. 'There aren't! Well, my dear, to look at you, he was a lucky man. Surely he wouldn't make trouble for you?'

'Oh no! He leaves me my own mistress entirely.'

'Quite! Quite! A genuine man would.'

Sir Malcolm was pleased. Connie was his favourite daughter, he had always liked the female in her. Not so much of her mother in her as in Hilda. And he had always disliked Clifford. So he was pleased, and very tender with his daughter, as if the unborn child were his child.

He drove with her to Hartland's hotel, and saw her installed: then went round to his club. She had refused his company for the evening.

She found a letter from Mellors: 'I won't come round to your hotel, but I'll wait for you outside the Golden Cock in Adam Street at seven.'

There he stood, tall and slender, and so different, in a formal suit of thin dark cloth. He had a natural distinction, but he had not the cut-to-pattern look of her class. Yet, she saw at once, he could go anywhere. He had a native breeding which was really much nicer than the cut-to-pattern class thing.

'Ah, there you are! How well you look!'

'Yes! But not you.'

She looked in his face anxiously. It was thin, and the cheek-bones showed. But his eyes smiled at her, and she felt at home with him. There it was: suddenly, the tension of keeping up her appearances fell from her. Something flowed out of him physically, that made her feel inwardly at ease and happy, at home. With a woman's now alert instinct for happiness, she registered it at once. 'I'm happy when he's there!' Not all the sunshine of Venice had given her this inward expansion and warmth.

'Was it horrid for you?' she asked as she sat opposite him at table. He was too thin; she saw it now. His hand lay as she knew it, with that curious loose forgottenness of a sleeping animal. She wanted so much to take it and kiss it. But she did not quite dare.

'People are always horrid,' he said.

'And did you mind very much?'

'I minded, as I always shall mind. And I knew I was a fool to mind.'

'Did you feel like a dog with a tin can tied to its tail? Clifford said you felt like that.'

He looked at her. It was cruel of her at that moment: for his pride had suffered bitterly.

'I suppose I did,' he said.

She never knew the fierce bitterness with which he resented insult.

There was a long pause.

'And did you miss me?' she asked.

'I was glad you were out of it.'

Again there was a pause.

'But did people *believe* about you and me?' she asked.

'No! I don't think so for a moment.'

'Did Clifford?'

'I should say not. He put it off without thinking about it. But naturally it made him want to see the last of me.'

'I'm going to have a child.'

The expression died utterly out of his face, out of his whole body. He looked at her with darkened eyes, whose look she could not understand at all: like some dark-flamed spirit looking at her.

'Say you're glad!' she pleaded, groping for his hand. And she saw a certain exultance spring up in him. But it was netted down by things she could not understand.

'It's the future,' he said.

'But aren't you glad?' she persisted.

'I have such a terrible mistrust of the future.'

'But you needn't be troubled by any responsibility. Clifford would have it as his own, he'd be glad.'

She saw him go pale, and recoil under this. He did not answer.

'Shall I go back to Clifford, and put a little baronet into Wragby?' she asked.

He looked at her, pale and very remote. The ugly little grin flickered on his face.

'You wouldn't have to tell him who the father was?'

'Oh!' she said; 'he'd take it even then, if I wanted him to.'

He thought for a time.

'Ay!' he said at last, to himself. 'I suppose he would.'

There was silence. A big gulf was between them.

'But you don't want me to go back to Clifford, do you?' she asked him.

'What do you want yourself?' he replied.

'I want to live with you,' she said simply.

In spite of himself, little flames ran over his belly as he heard her say it, and he dropped his head. Then he looked up at her again, with those haunted eyes.

'If it's worth it to you,' he said. 'I've got nothing.'

'You've got more than most men. Come, you know it,' she said.

'In one way, I know it.' He was silent for a time, thinking. Then he resumed: 'They used to say I had too much of the woman in me. But it's not that. I'm not a woman because I don't want to shoot birds, neither because I don't want to make money, or get on. I could have got on in the army, easily, but I didn't like the army. Though I could manage the men all right: they liked me and they had a bit of a holy fear of me when I got mad. No, it was stupid, dead-handed higher authority that made the army dead: absolutely fool-dead. I like men, and men like me. But I can't stand the twaddling bossy impudence of the people who run this world. That's why I can't get on. I hate the impudence of money, and I hate the impudence of class. So in the world as it is, what have I to offer a woman?'

'But why offer anything? It's not a bargain. It's just that we love one another,' she said.

'Nay, nay! It's more than that. Living is moving and moving on. My life won't go down the proper gutters, it just won't. So I'm a bit of a waste ticket by myself. And I've no business to take a woman into my life, unless my life does something and gets somewhere, inwardly at least, to keep us both fresh. A man must offer a woman *some* meaning in his life, if it's going to be an isolated life, and if she's a genuine woman. I can't be just your male concubine.'

'Why not?' she said.

'Why, because I can't. And you would soon hate it.'

'As if you couldn't trust me,' she said.

The grin flickered on his face.

'The money is yours, the position is yours, the decisions will lie with you. I'm not just my Lady's fucker, after all.'

'What else are you?'

'You may well ask. It no doubt is invisible. Yet I'm something to myself at least. I can see the point of my own existence, though I can quite understand nobody else's seeing it.'

'And will your existence have less point, if you live with me?'

He paused a long time before replying: 'It might.'

She too stayed to think about it.

'And what is the point of your existence?'

'I tell you, it's invisible. I don't believe in the world, not in money, nor in advancement, nor in the future of our civilisation. If there's got to be a future for humanity, there'll have to be a very big change from what now is.'

'And what will the real future have to be like?'

'God knows! I can feel something inside me, all mixed up with a lot of rage. But what it really amounts to, I don't know.'

'Shall I tell you?' she said, looking into his face. 'Shall I tell you what you have that other men don't have, and that will make the future? Shall I tell you?'

'Tell me then,' he replied.

'It's the courage of your own tenderness, that's what it is like when you put your hand on my tail and say I've got a pretty tail.'

The grin came flickering on his face.

'That!' he said.

Then he sat thinking.

'Ay!' he said. 'You're right. It's that really. It's that all the way through. I knew it with the men. I had to be in touch with them, physically, and not go back on it. I had to be bodily aware of them and a bit tender to them, even if I put 'em through hell. It's a question of awareness, as Buddha said. But even he fought shy of the bodily awareness, and that natural physical tenderness, which is the best, even between men; in a proper manly way. Makes 'em really manly, not so monkeyish. Ay! it's tenderness, really; it's cunt-awareness. Sex is really only touch, the closest of all touch. And it's touch we're afraid of. We're only half-conscious, and half alive. We've got to come alive and aware. Especially the English have got to get into touch with one another, a bit delicate and a bit tender. It's our crying need.'

She looked at him.

'Then why are you afraid of me?' she said.

He looked at her a long time before he answered.

'It's the money, really, and the position. It's the world in you.'

'But isn't there tenderness in me?' she said wistfully.

He looked down at her, with darkened, abstract eyes.

'Ay! It comes an' goes, like in me.'

'But can't you trust it between you and me?' she asked, gazing anxiously at him.

She saw his face all softening down, losing its armour.

'Maybe!' he said.

They were both silent.

'I want you to hold me in your arms,' she said. 'I want you to tell me you are glad we are having a child.'

She looked so lovely and warm and wistful, his bowels stirred towards her.

'I suppose we can go to my room,' he said. 'Though it's scandalous again.'

But she saw the forgetfulness of the world coming over him again, his face taking the soft, pure look of tender passion.

They walked by the remoter streets to Coburg Square, where he had a room at the top of the house, an attic room where he cooked for himself on a gas ring. It was small, but decent and tidy.

She took off her things, and made him do the same. She was lovely in the soft first flush of her pregnancy.

'I ought to leave you alone,' he said.

'No!' she said. 'Love me! Love me, and say you'll keep me. Say you'll keep me! Say you'll never let me go, to the world nor to anybody.'

She crept close against him, clinging fast to his thin, strong naked body, the only home she had ever known.

'Then I'll keep thee,' he said. 'If tha wants it, then I'll keep thee.'

He held her round and fast.

'And say you're glad about the child,' she repeated. 'Kiss it! Kiss my womb and say you're glad it's there.'

But that was more difficult for him.

'I've a dread of puttin' children i' th' world,' he said. 'I've such a dread o' th' future for 'em.'

'But you've put it into me. Be tender to it, and that will be its future already. Kiss it!'

He quivered, because it was true. 'Be tender to it, and that will be its future.' – At that moment he felt a sheer love for the woman. He kissed her belly and her mound of Venus, to kiss close to the womb and the foetus within the womb.

'Oh, you love me! You love me!' she said, in a little cry like one of her blind, inarticulate love cries. And he went in to her softly, feeling the stream of tenderness flowing in release from his bowels to hers, the bowels of compassion kindled between them.

And he realised as he went into her that this was the thing he had to do, to come into tender touch, without losing his pride or his dignity or his integrity as a man. After all, if she had money and means, and he had none, he should be too proud and honourable to hold back his tenderness from her on that account. 'I stand for the touch of bodily awareness between human beings,' he said to himself, 'and the touch of tenderness. And she is my mate. And it is a battle against the money, and the machine, and the insentient ideal monkeyishness of the world. And she will stand behind me there. Thank God I've got a woman! Thank God I've got a woman who is with me, and tender and aware of me. Thank God she's not a bully, nor a fool. Thank God she's a tender, aware woman.' And as his seed sprang in her, his soul sprang towards her too, in the creative act that is far more than procreative.

She was quite determined now that there should be no parting between him and her. But the ways and means were still to settle.

'Did you hate Bertha Coutts?' she asked him.

'Don't talk to me about her.'

'Yes! You must let me. Because once you liked her. And once you were as intimate with her as you are with me. So you have to tell me. Isn't it rather terrible, when you've been intimate with her, to hate her so? Why is it?'

'I don't know. She sort of kept her will ready against me, always, always: her ghastly female will: her freedom! A woman's ghastly freedom that ends in the most beastly bullying! Oh, she always kept her freedom against me, like vitriol in my face.'

'But she's not free of you even now. Does she still love you?'

'No no! If she's not free of me, it's because she's got that mad rage, she must try to bully me.'

'But she must have loved you.'

'No! Well, in specks she did. She was drawn to me. And I think even that she hated. She loved me in moments. But she always took it back, and started bullying. Her deepest desire was to bully me, and there was no altering her. Her *will* was wrong, from the first.'

'But perhaps she felt you didn't really love her, and she wanted to make you.'

'My God, it was bloody making.'

'But you didn't really love her, did you? You did her that wrong.'

'How could I? I began to. I began to love her. But somehow, she always ripped me up. No, don't let's talk of it. It was a doom, that was. And she was a doomed woman. This last time, I'd have shot her like I shoot a stoat, if I'd but been allowed: a raving, doomed thing in the shape of a woman! If only I could have shot her, and ended the whole misery! It ought to be allowed. When a woman gets absolutely possessed by her own will, her own will set against everything, then it's fearful, and she should be shot at last.'

'And shouldn't men be shot at last, if they get possessed by their own will?'

'Ay! – the same! But I must get free of her, or she'll be at me again. I wanted to tell you. I must get a divorce if I possibly can. So we must be careful. We mustn't really be seen together, you and I. I never, *never* could stand it if she came down on me and you.'

Connie pondered this.

'Then we can't be together?' she said.

'Not for six months or so. But I think my divorce will go through in September; then till March.'

'But the baby will probably be born at the end of February,' she said.

He was silent.

'I could wish the Cliffords and Berthas all dead,' he said.

'It's not being very tender to them,' she said.

'Tender to them? Yea, even then the tenderest thing you could do for them, perhaps, would be to give them death. They can't live! They only frustrate life. Their souls are awful inside them. Death ought to be sweet to them. And I ought to be allowed to shoot them.'

'But you wouldn't do it,' she said.

'I would though! and with less qualms than I shoot a weasel. It anyhow has a prettiness and a loneliness. But they are legion. Oh, I'd shoot them.'

'Then perhaps it is just as well you daren't.'

'Well.'

Connie had now plenty to think of. It was evident he wanted absolutely to be free of Bertha Coutts. And she felt he was right. The last attack had been too grim. – This meant her living alone, till spring. Perhaps she could get divorced from Clifford. But how? If Mellors were named, then there was an end to *his* divorce. How loathsome! Couldn't one go right away, to the far ends of the earth, and be free from it all?

One could not. The far ends of the world are not five minutes from Charing Cross, nowadays. While the wireless is active, there are no far ends of the earth. Kings of Dahomey and Lamas of Tibet listen in to London and New York.

Patience! Patience! The world is a vast and ghastly intricacy of mechanism, and one has to be very wary, not to get mangled by it.

Connie confided in her father.

'You see, Father, he was Clifford's gamekeeper: but he was an officer in the army in India. Only he is like Colonel C. E. Florence, who preferred to become a private soldier again.'

Sir Malcolm, however, had no sympathy with the unsatisfactory mysticism of the famous C. E. Florence. He saw too much advertisement behind all the humility. It looked just like the sort of conceit the knight most loathed, the conceit of self-abasement.

'Where did your gamekeeper spring from?' asked Sir Malcolm irritably.

'He was a collier's son in Tevershall. But he's absolutely presentable.'

The knighted artist became more angry.

'Looks to me like a gold-digger,' he said. 'And you're a pretty easy gold-mine, apparently.'

'No, Father, it's not like that. You'd know if you saw him. He's a man. Clifford always detested him for not being humble.'

'Apparently he had a good instinct, for once.'

What Sir Malcolm could not bear was the scandal of his daughter's having an intrigue with a gamekeeper. He did not mind the intrigue: he minded the scandal.

'I care nothing about the fellow. He's evidently been able to get round you all right. But by God, think of all the talk. Think of your stepmother, how she'll take it!'

'I know,' said Connie. 'Talk is beastly: especially if you live in society. And he wants so much to get his own divorce. I thought we might perhaps say it was another man's child, and not mention Mellors' name at all.'

'Another man's! What other man's?'

'Perhaps Duncan Forbes. He has been our friend all his life. And he's a fairly well-known artist. And he's fond of me.'

'Well I'm damned! Poor Duncan! And what's he going to get out of it?'

'I don't know. But he might rather like it, even.'

'He might, might he? Well, he's a funny man if he does. Why, you've never even had an affair with him, have you?'

'No! But he doesn't really want it. He only loves me to be near him, but not to touch him.'

'My God, what a generation!'

'He would like me most of all to be a model for him to paint from. Only I never wanted to.'

'God help him! But he looks downtrodden enough for anything.'

'Still, you wouldn't mind so much the talk about him?'

'My God, Connie, all the bloody contriving!'

'I know! It's sickening! But what can I do?'

'Contriving, conniving; conniving, contriving! Makes a man think he's lived too long.'

'Come, Father, if you haven't done a good deal of contriving and conniving in your time, you may talk.'

'But it was different, I assure you.'

'It's *always* different.'

Hilda arrived, also furious when she heard of the new developments. And she also simply could not stand the thought of a public scandal about her sister and a gamekeeper. Too, too humiliating!

'Why should we not just disappear, separately, to British Columbia, and have no scandal?' said Connie.

But that was no good. The scandal would come out just the same. And if Connie was going with the man, she'd better be able to marry him. This was Hilda's opinion. Sir Malcolm wasn't sure. The affair might still blow over.

'But will you see him, Father?'

Poor Sir Malcolm! he was by no means keen on it. And poor Mellors, he was still less keen. Yet the meeting took place: a lunch in a private room at the club, the two men alone, looking one another up and down.

Sir Malcolm drank a fair amount of whisky, Mellors also drank. And they talked all the while about India, on which the young man was well informed.

This lasted during the meal. Only when coffee was served, and the waiter had gone, Sir Malcolm lit a cigar and said, heartily, 'Well, young man, and what about my daughter?'

The grin flickered on Mellors' face.

'Well, Sir, and what about her?'

'You've got a baby in her all right.'

'I have that honour!' grinned Mellors.

'Honour, by God!' Sir Malcolm gave a little squirting laugh, and became Scotch and lewd. 'Honour! How was the going, eh!? Good, my boy, what?'

'Good!'

'I'll bet it was! Ha-ha! My daughter, chip of the old block, what! I never went back on a good bit of fucking, myself. Though her mother, oh, holy saints!' He rolled his eyes to heaven. 'But you warmed her up, oh, you warmed her up, I can see that. Ha–ha! My blood in her! You set fire to her haystack all right. Ha-ha-ha! I was jolly glad of it, I can tell you. She needed it. Oh, she's a nice girl, she's a nice girl, and I knew she'd be good going, if only some damned man would set her stack on fire! Ha-ha-ha! A gamekeeper, eh, my boy! Bloody good poacher, if you ask me. Ha-ha! But now, look here, speaking seriously, what are we going to do about it? Speaking seriously, you know!'

Speaking seriously, they didn't get very far. Mellors, though a little tipsy, was much the soberer of the two. He kept the conversation as intelligent as possible: which isn't saying much.

'So you're a gamekeeper! Oh, you're quite right! That sort of game is worth a man's while, eh, what? The test of a woman is when you pinch her bottom. You can tell just by the feel of her bottom if she's going to come up all right. Ha-ha! I envy you, my boy. How old are you?'

'Thirty-nine.'

The knight lifted his eyebrows.

'As much as that! Well, you've another good twenty years, by the look of you. Oh, gamekeeper or not, you're a good cock. I can see that with one eye shut. Not like that blasted Clifford! A lily-livered hound with never a fuck in him, never had. I like you, my boy, I'll bet you've a good cod on you; oh, you're a bantam, I can see that. You're a fighter. Gamekeeper! Ha-ha, by crikey, I wouldn't trust my game to you! But look here, seriously, what are we going to do about it? The world's full of blasted old women.'

Seriously, they didn't do anything about it, except establish the old free-masonry of male sensuality between them.

'And look here, my boy, if ever I can do anything for you, you can rely on me. Gamekeeper! Christ, but it's rich! I like it! Oh, I like it! Shows the girl's got spunk. What? After all, you know, she has her own income, moderate, moderate, but above starvation. And I'll leave her what I've got. By God, I will. She deserves it for showing spunk, in a world of old women. I've been struggling to get myself clear of the skirts of old women for seventy years, and haven't managed it yet. But you're the man, I can see that.'

'I'm glad you think so. They usually tell me, in a sideways fashion, that I'm the monkey.'

'Oh, they would! My dear fellow, what could you be but a monkey, to all the old women?'

They parted most genially, and Mellors laughed inwardly all the time for the rest of the day.

The following day he had lunch with Connie and Hilda, at some discreet place.

'It's a very great pity it's such an ugly situation all round,' said Hilda.

'I had a lot o' fun out of it,' said he.

'I think you might have avoided putting children into the world until you were both free to marry and have children.'

'The Lord blew a bit too soon on the spark,' said he.

'I think the Lord had nothing to do with it. Of course Connie has enough money to keep you both, but the situation is unbearable.'

'But then you don't have to bear more than a small corner of it, do you?' said he.

'If you'd been in her own class.'

'Or if I'd been in a cage at the Zoo.'

There was silence.

'I think,' said Hilda, 'it will be best if she names quite another man as co-respondent, and you stay out of it altogether.'

'But I thought I'd put my foot right in.'

'I mean, in the divorce proceeding.'

He gazed at her in wonder. Connie had not dared mention the Duncan scheme to him.

'I don't follow,' he said.

'We have a friend who would probably agree to be named as co-respondent, so that your name need not appear,' said Hilda.

'You mean a man?'

'Of course!'

'But she's got no other?'

He looked in wonder at Connie.

'No, no!' she said hastily. 'Only that old friendship, quite simple, no love.'

'Then why should the fellow take the blame? If he's had nothing out of you?'

'Some men are chivalrous and don't only count what they get out of a woman,' said Hilda.

'One for me, eh? But who's the johnny?'

'A friend whom we've known since we were children in Scotland, an artist.'

'Duncan Forbes!' he said at once, for Connie had talked of him. 'And how would you shift the blame on to him?'

'They could stay together in some hotel, or she could even stay in his apartment.'

'Seems to me like a lot of fuss for nothing,' he said.

'What else do you suggest?' said Hilda. 'If your name appears, you will get no divorce from your wife, who is apparently quite an impossible person to be mixed up with.'

'All that!' he said grimly.

There was a long silence.

'We could go right away,' he said.

'There is no right away for Connie,' said Hilda. 'Clifford is too well known.'

Again the silence of pure frustration.

'The world is what it is. If you want to live together without being persecuted, you will have to marry. To marry, you both have to be divorced. So how are you both going about it?'

He was silent for a long time.

'How are *you* going about it for us?' he said.

'We will see if Duncan will consent to figure as co-respondent: then we must get Clifford to divorce Connie: and you must go on with your divorce, and you must both keep apart till you are free.'

'Sounds like a lunatic asylum.'

'Possibly! And the world would look on you as lunatics: or worse.'

'What is worse?'

'Criminals, I suppose.'

'Hope I can plunge in the dagger a few more times yet,' he said, grinning. Then he was silent, and angry.

'Well!' he said at last. 'I agree to anything. The world is a raving idiot, and no man can kill it: though I'll do my best. But you're right. We must rescue ourselves as best we can.'

He looked in humiliation, anger, weariness and misery at Connie.

'Ma lass!' he said. 'The world's goin' to put salt on thy tail.'

'Not if we don't let it,' she said.

She minded this conniving against the world less than he did.

Duncan, when approached, also insisted on seeing the delinquent game-keeper, so there was a dinner, this time in his flat: the four of them. Duncan was a rather short, broad, dark-skinned, taciturn Hamlet of a fellow with straight black hair and a weird Celtic conceit of himself. His art was all tubes and valves and spirals and strange colours, ultramodern, yet with a certain power, even a certain purity of form and tone: only Mellors thought it cruel and repellent. He did not venture to say so, for Duncan was almost insane on the point of his art, it was a personal cult, a personal religion with him.

They were looking at the pictures in the studio, and Duncan kept his smallish brown eyes on the other man. He wanted to hear what the gamekeeper would say. He knew already Connie's and Hilda's opinions.

'It is like a pure bit of murder,' said Mellors at last; a speech Duncan by no means expected from a gamekeeper.

'And who is murdered?' asked Hilda, rather coldly and sneeringly.

'Me! It murders all the bowels of compassion in a man.'

A wave of pure hate came out of the artist. He heard the note of dislike in the other man's voice, and the note of contempt. And he himself loathed the mention of bowels of compassion. Sickly sentiment!

Mellors stood rather tall and thin, worn-looking, gazing with flickering detachment, that was something like the dancing of a moth on the wing, at the pictures.

'Perhaps stupidity is murdered; sentimental stupidity,' sneered the artist.

'Do you think so? I think all these tubes and corrugated vibrations are stupid enough for anything, and pretty sentimental. They show a lot of self-pity and an awful lot of nervous self-opinion, seems to me.'

In another wave of hate, the artist's face looked yellow. But with a sort of silent hauteur he turned the pictures to the wall.

'I think we may go to the dining-room,' he said.

And they trailed off, dismally.

After coffee, Duncan said, 'I don't at all mind posing as the father of Connie's child. But only on the condition that she'll come and pose as a model for me. I've wanted her for years, and she's always refused.' He uttered it with the dark finality of an inquisitor announcing an *auto da fe*.

'Ah!' said Mellors. 'You only do it on condition, then?'

'Quite! I only do it on that condition.' The artist tried to put the utmost contempt of the other person into his speech. He put a little too much.

'Better have me as a model at the same time,' said Mellors. 'Better do us in a group, Vulcan and Venus under the net of art. I used to be a blacksmith, before I was a gamekeeper.'

'Thank you,' said the artist. 'I don't think Vulcan has a figure that interests me.'

'Not even if it was tubified and titivated up?'

There was no answer. The artist was too haughty for further words.

It was a dismal party, in which the artist henceforth steadily ignored the presence of the other man, and talked only briefly, as if the words were wrung out of the depths of his gloomy portentousness, to the women.

'You didn't like him, but he's better than that, really. He's really kind,' Connie explained as they left.

'He's a little black pup with a corrugated distemper,' said Mellors.

'No, he wasn't nice today.'

'And will you go and be a model to him?'

'Oh, I don't really mind any more. He won't touch me. And I don't mind anything, if it paves the way to a life together for you and me.'

'But he'll only shit on you on canvas.'

'I don't care. He'll only be painting his own feelings for me, and I don't mind if he does that. I wouldn't have him touch me, not for anything. But if he thinks he can do anything with his owlish arty staring, let him stare. He can make as many empty tubes and corrugations out of me as he likes. It's his funeral. He hated you for what you said: that his tubified art is sentimental and self-important. But of course it's true.'

Chapter 19

DEAR CLIFFORD – I am afraid what you foresaw has happened. I am really in love with another man, and I do hope you will divorce me. I am staying at present with Duncan in his flat. I told you he was at Venice with us. I'm awfully unhappy for your sake: but do try to take it quietly. You don't really need me any more, and I can't bear to come back to Wragby. I'm most awfully sorry. But do try to forgive me, and divorce me and find someone better. I'm not really the right person for you, I am too impatient and selfish,

I suppose. But I can't ever come back to live with you again. And I feel so frightfully sorry about it all, for your sake. But if you don't let yourself get worked up, you'll see you won't mind so frightfully. You didn't really care about me personally. So do forgive me and get rid of me.

Clifford was not *inwardly* surprised to get this letter. Inwardly, he had known for a long time she was leaving him. But he had absolutely refused any outward admission of it. Therefore, outwardly, it came as the most terrible blow and shock to him. He had kept the surface of his confidence in her quite serene.

And that is how we are. By strength of will we cut off our inner intuitive knowledge from admitted consciousness. This causes a state of dread, or apprehension, which makes the blow ten times worse when it does fall.

Clifford was like a hysterical child. He gave Mrs Bolton a terrible shock, sitting up in bed ghastly and blank.

'Why, Sir Clifford, whatever's the matter?'

No answer! She was terrified lest he had had a stroke. She hurried and felt his face, took his pulse.

'Is there a pain? Do try and tell me where it hurts you. Do tell me!'

No answer!

'Oh dear, oh dear! Then I'll telephone to Sheffield for Dr Carrington, and Dr Lecky may as well run round straight away.'

She was moving to the door, when he said in a hollow tone: 'No!'

She stopped and gazed at him. His face was yellow, blank, and like the face of an idiot.

'Do you mean you'd rather I didn't fetch the doctor?'

'Yes! I don't want him,' came the sepulchral voice.

'Oh, but Sir Clifford, you're ill, and I daren't take the responsibility. I *must* send for the doctor, or *I* shall be blamed.'

A pause: then the hollow voice said, 'I'm not ill. My wife isn't coming back.' – It was as if an image spoke.

'Not coming back? you mean her Ladyship?' Mrs Bolton moved a little nearer to the bed. 'Oh, don't you believe it. You can trust her Ladyship to come back.'

The image in the bed did not change, but it pushed a letter over the counterpane.

'Read it!' said the sepulchral voice.

'Why, if it's a letter from her Ladyship, I'm sure her Ladyship wouldn't want me to read her letter to you, Sir Clifford. You can tell me what she says, if you wish.'

But the face with the fixed blue eyes sticking out did not change.

'Read it!' repeated the voice.

'Why, if I must, I do it to obey you, Sir Clifford,' she said.

And she read the letter.

The face in the bed seemed to deepen its expression of wild, but motionless distraction. Mrs Bolton looked at it and was worried. She knew what she was up against: male hysteria. She had not nursed soldiers without learning something about that very unpleasant disease.

She was a little impatient of Sir Clifford. Any man in his senses must have *known* his wife was in love with somebody else, and was going to leave him. Even, she was sure, Sir Clifford was inwardly absolutely aware of it, only he wouldn't admit it to himself. If he would have admitted it, and prepared himself for it; or if he would have admitted it, and actively struggled with his wife against it, that would have been acting like a man. But no! he knew it, and all the time tried to kid himself it wasn't so. He felt the devil twisting his tail, and pretended it was the angels smiling on him. This state of falsity had now brought on that crisis of falsity and dislocation, hysteria, which is a form of insanity. 'It comes,' she thought to herself, hating him a little, 'because he always thinks of himself. He's so wrapped up in his own immortal self, that when he does get a shock he's like a mummy tangled in its own bandages. Look at him!'

But hysteria is dangerous: and she was a nurse, it was her duty to pull him out. Any attempt to rouse his manhood and his pride would only make him worse: for his manhood was dead, temporarily if not finally. He would only squirm softer and softer, like a worm, and become more dislocated.

The only thing was to release his self-pity. Like the lady in Tennyson, he must weep or he must die.

So Mrs Bolton began to weep first. She covered her face with her hand and burst into little wild sobs. 'I would never have believed it of her Ladyship, I wouldn't!' she wept, suddenly summoning up all her old grief and sense of woe, and weeping the tears of her own bitter chagrin. Once she started, her weeping was genuine enough, for she had had something to weep for.

Clifford thought of the way he had been betrayed by the woman Connie, and in a contagion of grief, tears filled his eyes and began to run down his cheeks. He was weeping for himself. Mrs Bolton, as soon as she saw the tears running over his blank face, hastily wiped her own wet cheeks on her little handkerchief, and leaned towards him.

'Now don't you fret, Sir Clifford!' she said, in a luxury of emotion. 'Now don't you fret, don't, you'll only do yourself an injury!'

His body shivered suddenly in an in-drawn breath of silent sobbing, and the tears ran quicker down his face. She laid her hand on his arm, and her own tears fell again. Again the shiver went through him, like a convulsion, and she laid her arm round his shoulder. 'There, there! There, there! Don't you fret, then, don't you! Don't you fret!' she moaned to him, while her own tears fell. And she drew him to her, and held her arms round his great shoulders, while he laid his face on her bosom and sobbed, shaking and hulking his huge shoulders, whilst she softly stroked his dusky-blond hair and said: 'There! There! There! There then! There then! Never you mind! Never you mind, then!'

And he put his arms round her and clung to her like a child, wetting the bib of her starched white apron, and the bosom of her pale-blue cotton dress, with his tears. He had let himself go altogether, at last.

So at length she kissed him, and rocked him on her bosom, and in her heart she said to herself: 'Oh, Sir Clifford! Oh high and mighty Chatterleys! Is this what you've come down to!' And finally he even went to sleep, like a child. And she felt worn out, and went to her own room, where she laughed and cried at once, with a hysteria of her own. It was so ridiculous! It was so awful! Such a come-down! So shameful! And it was so upsetting as well.

After this, Clifford became like a child with Mrs Bolton. He would hold her hand, and rest his head on her breast, and when she once lightly kissed him, he said: 'Yes! Do kiss me! Do kiss me!' And when she sponged his great blond body, he would say the same: 'Do kiss me!' and she would lightly kiss his body, anywhere, half in mockery.

And he lay with a queer, blank face like a child, with a bit of the wonderment of a child. And he would gaze on her with wide, childish eyes, in a relaxation of madonna-worship. It was sheer relaxation on his part, letting go all his manhood, and sinking back to a childish position that was really perverse. And then he would put his hand into her bosom and feel her breasts, and kiss them in exaltation, the exaltation of perversity, of being a child when he was a man.

Mrs Bolton was both thrilled and ashamed, she both loved and hated it. Yet she never rebuffed nor rebuked him. And they drew into a closer physical intimacy, an intimacy of perversity, when he was a child stricken with an apparent candour and an apparent wonderment, that looked almost like a religious exaltation: the perverse and literal rendering of: 'except ye become again as a little child'. – While she was the Magna Mater, full of power and potency, having the great blond child-man under her will and her stroke entirely.

The curious thing was that when this child-man, which Clifford was now and which he had been becoming for years, emerged into the world, it was much sharper and keener than the real man he used to be. This perverted child-man was now a *real* businessman; when it was a question of affairs, he was an absolute he-man, sharp as a needle, and impervious as a bit of steel. When he was out among men, seeking his own ends, and 'making good' his colliery workings, he had an almost uncanny shrewdness, hardness, and a straight sharp punch. It was as if his very passivity and prostitution to the Magna Mater gave him insight into material business affairs, and lent him a certain remarkable inhuman force. The wallowing in private emotion, the utter abasement of his manly self, seemed to lend him a second nature, cold, almost visionary, business-clever. In business he was quite inhuman.

And in this Mrs Bolton triumphed. 'How he's getting on!' she would say to herself in pride. 'And that's my doing! My word, he'd never have got on like this with Lady Chatterley. She was not the one to put a man forward. She wanted too much for herself.'

At the same time, in some corner of her weird female soul, how she despised him and hated him! He was to her the fallen beast, the squirming monster. And while she aided and abetted him all she could, away in the remotest corner of her ancient healthy womanhood she despised him with a savage contempt that knew no bounds. The merest tramp was better than he.

His behaviour with regard to Connie was curious. He insisted on seeing her again. He insisted, moreover, on her coming to Wragby. On this point he was finally and absolutely fixed. Connie had promised to come back to Wragby, faithfully.

'But is it any use?' said Mrs Bolton. 'Can't you let her go, and be rid of her?'

'No! She said she was coming back, and she's got to come.'

Mrs Bolton opposed him no more. She knew what she was dealing with.

I needn't tell you what effect your letter has had on me [he wrote to Connie to London]. Perhaps you can imagine it if you try, though no doubt you won't trouble to use your imagination on my behalf.

I can only say one thing in answer: I must see you personally, here at Wragby, before I can do anything. You promised faithfully to come back to Wragby, and I hold you to the promise. I don't believe anything nor understand anything until I see you personally, here under normal circumstances. I needn't tell you that nobody here suspects anything, so your return would be quite normal. Then if you feel, after we have talked things over, that you still remain in the same mind, no doubt we can come to terms.

Connie showed this letter to Mellors.

'He wants to begin his revenge on you,' said he, handing the letter back.

Connie was silent. She was somewhat surprised to find that she was afraid of Clifford. She was afraid to go near him. She was afraid of him as if he were evil and dangerous.

'What shall I do?' she said.

'Nothing, if you don't want to do anything.'

She replied, trying to put Clifford off. He answered: 'If you don't come back to Wragby now, I shall consider that you are coming back one day, and act accordingly. I shall just go on the same, and wait for you here, if I wait for fifty years.'

She was frightened. This was bullying of an insidious sort. She had no doubt he meant what he said. He would not divorce her, and the child would be his, unless she could find some means of establishing its illegitimacy.

After a time of worry and harassment, she decided to go to Wragby. Hilda would go with her. She wrote this to Clifford. He replied: 'I shall not welcome your sister, but I shall not deny her the door. I have no doubt she has connived at your desertion of your duties and responsibilities, so do not expect me to show pleasure in seeing her.'

They went to Wragby. Clifford was away when they arrived. Mrs Bolton received them.

'Oh, your Ladyship, it isn't the happy home-coming we hoped for, is it!' she said.

'Isn't it?' said Connie.

So this woman knew! How much did the rest of the servants know or suspect?

She entered the house which now she hated with every fibre in her body. The great, rambling mass of a place seemed evil to her, just a menace over her. She was no longer its mistress, she was its victim.

'I can't stay long here,' she whispered to Hilda, terrified.

And she suffered going into her own bedroom, re-entering into possession as if nothing had happened. She hated every minute inside the Wragby walls.

They did not meet Clifford till they went down to dinner. He was dressed, and with a black tie: rather reserved, and very much the superior gentleman. He behaved perfectly politely during the meal, and kept a polite sort of conversation going: but it seemed all touched with insanity.

'How much do the servants know?' asked Connie, when the woman was out of the room.

'Of your intentions? Nothing whatsoever.'

'Mrs Bolton knows.'

He changed colour.

'Mrs Bolton is not exactly one of the servants,' he said.

'Oh, I don't mind.'

There was tension till after coffee, when Hilda said she would go up to her room.

Clifford and Connie sat in silence when she had gone. Neither would begin to speak. Connie was so glad that he wasn't taking the pathetic line, she kept him up to as much haughtiness as possible. She just sat silent and looked down at her hands.

'I suppose you don't at all mind having gone back on your word?' he said at last.

'I can't help it,' she murmured.

'But if you can't, who can?'

'I suppose nobody.'

He looked at her with curious cold rage. He was used to her. She was as it were embedded in his will. How dared she now go back on him, and destroy the fabric of his daily existence? How dared she try to cause this derangement of his personality!

'And for *what* do you want to go back on everything?' he insisted.

'Love!' she said. It was best to be hackneyed.

'Love of Duncan Forbes? But you didn't think that worth having, when you met me. Do you mean to say you now love him better than anything else in life?'

'One changes,' she said.

'Possibly! Possibly you may have whims. But you still have to convince me of the importance of the change. I merely don't believe in your love of Duncan Forbes.'

'But why *should* you believe in it? You have only to divorce me, not to believe in my feelings.'

'And why should I divorce you?'

'Because I don't want to live here any more. And you really don't want me.'

'Pardon me! I don't change. For my part, since you are my wife, I should prefer that you should stay under my roof in dignity and quiet. Leaving aside personal feelings, and I assure you, on my part it is leaving aside a great deal, it is bitter as death to me to have this order of life broken up, here in Wragby, and the decent round of daily life smashed, just for some whim of yours.'

After a time of silence she said: 'I can't help it. I've got to go. I expect I shall have a child.'

He too was silent for a time.

'And is it for the child's sake you must go?' he asked at length.

She nodded.

'And why? Is Duncan Forbes so keen on his spawn?'

'Surely keener than you would be,' she said.

'But really? I want my wife, and I see no reason for letting her go. If she likes to bear a child under my roof, she is welcome, and the child is welcome: provided that the decency and order of life is preserved. Do you mean to tell me that Duncan Forbes has a greater hold over you? I don't believe it.'

There was a pause.

'But don't you see,' said Connie. 'I *must* go away from you, and I must live with the man I love.'

'No, I don't see it! I don't give tuppence for your love, nor for the man you love. I don't believe in that sort of cant.'

'But you see, I do.'

'Do you? My dear Madam, you are too intelligent, I assure you, to believe in your own love for Duncan Forbes. Believe me, even now you really care more for me. So why should I give in to such nonsense!'

She felt he was right there. And she felt she could keep silent no longer.

'Because it isn't Duncan that I *do* love,' she said, looking up at him. 'We only said it was Duncan, to spare your feelings.'

'To spare my feelings?'

'Yes! Because who I really love, and it'll make you hate me, is Mr Mellors, who was our gamekeeper here.'

If he could have sprung out of his chair, he would have done so. His face went yellow, and his eyes bulged with disaster as he glared at her.

Then he dropped back in the chair, gasping and looking up at the ceiling.

At length he sat up.

'Do you mean to say you're telling me the truth?' he asked, looking gruesome.

'Yes! You know I am.'

'And when did you begin with him?'

'In the spring.'

He was silent like some beast in a trap.

'And it *was* you, then, in the bedroom at the cottage?'

So he had really inwardly known all the time.

'Yes!'

He still leaned forward in his chair, gazing at her like a cornered beast.

'My God, you ought to be wiped off the face of the earth!'

'Why?' she ejaculated faintly.

But he seemed not to hear her.

'That scum! That bumptious lout! That miserable cad! And carrying on with him all the time, while you were here and he was one of my servants! My God, my God, is there any end to the beastly lowness of women!'

He was beside himself with rage, as she knew he would be.

'And you mean to say you want to have a child to a cad like that?'

'Yes! I'm going to.'

'You're going to! You mean you're sure! How long have you been sure?'

'Since June.'

He was speechless, and the queer blank look of a child came over him again.

'You'd wonder,' he said at last, 'that such beings were ever allowed to be born.'

'What beings?' she asked.

He looked at her weirdly, without an answer. It was obvious he couldn't even accept the fact of the existence of Mellors, in any connection with his own life. It was sheer, unspeakable, impotent hate.

'And do you mean to say you'd marry him? – and bear his foul name?' he asked at length.

'Yes, that's what I want.'

He was again as if dumbfounded.

'Yes!' he said at last. 'That proves that what I've always thought about you is correct: you're not normal, you're not in your right senses. You're one of those half-insane, perverted women who must run after depravity, the *nostalgie de la boue*.'

Suddenly he had become almost wistfully moral, seeing himself the incarnation of good, and people like Mellors and Connie the incarnation of mud, of evil. He seemed to be growing vague, inside a nimbus.

'So don't you think you'd better divorce me and have done with it?' she said.

'No! You can go where you like, but I shan't divorce you,' he said idiotically.

'Why not?'

He was silent, in the silence of imbecile obstinacy.

'Would you even let the child be legally yours, and your heir?' she said.

'I care nothing about the child.'

'But if it's a boy it will be legally your son, and it will inherit your title, and have Wragby.'

'I care nothing about that,' he said.

'But you *must*! I shall prevent the child from being legally yours, if I can. I'd so much rather it were illegitimate, and mine: if it can't be Mellors'.'

'Do as you like about that.'

He was immovable.

'And won't you divorce me?' she said. 'You can use Duncan as a pretext! There'd be no need to bring in the real name. Duncan doesn't mind.'

'*I* shall never divorce you,' he said, as if a nail had been driven in.

'But why? Because I want you to?'

'Because I follow my own inclination, and I'm not inclined to.'

It was useless. She went upstairs and told Hilda the upshot.

'Better get away tomorrow,' said Hilda, 'and let him come to his senses.'

So Connie spent half the night packing her really private and personal effects. In the morning she had her trunks sent to the station, without telling Clifford. She decided to see him only to say goodbye, before lunch.

But she spoke to Mrs Bolton.

'I must say goodbye to you, Mrs Bolton, you know why. But I can trust you not to talk.'

'Oh, you can trust me, your Ladyship, though it's a sad blow for us here, indeed. But I hope you'll be happy with the other gentleman.'

'The other gentleman! It's Mr Mellors, and I care for him. Sir Clifford knows. But don't say anything to anybody. And if one day you think Sir Clifford may be willing to divorce me, let me know, will you? I should like to be properly married to the man I care for.'

'I'm sure you would, my Lady! Oh, you can trust me. I'll be faithful to Sir Clifford, and I'll be faithful to you, for I can see you're both right in your own ways.'

'Thank you! And look! I want to give you this – may I?'

So Connie left Wragby once more, and went on with Hilda to Scotland. Mellors went into the country and got work on a farm. The idea was, he should get his divorce, if possible, whether Connie got hers or not. And for six months he should work at farming, so that eventually he and Connie could have some small farm of their own, into which he could put his energy. For he would have to have some work, even hard work, to do, and he would have to make his own living, even if her capital started him.

So they would have to wait till spring was in, till the baby was born, till the early summer came round again.

The Grange Farm, Old Heanor, 29 September

I got on here with a bit of contriving, because I knew Richards, the company engineer, in the army. It is a farm belonging to Butler and Smitham Colliery Company, they use it for raising hay and oats for the pit-ponies; not a private concern. But they've got cows and pigs and all the rest of it, and I get thirty shillings a week as labourer. Rowley, the farmer, puts me on to as many jobs as he can, so that I can learn as much as possible between now and next Easter. I've not heard a thing about Bertha. I've no idea why she didn't show up at the divorce, nor where she is nor what she's up to. But if I keep quiet till March I suppose I shall be free. And don't you bother about Sir Clifford. He'll want to get rid of you one of these days. If he leaves you alone, it's a lot.

I've got lodgings in a bit of an old cottage in Engine Row, very decent. The man is engine-driver at High Park, tall, with a beard, and very chapel. The woman is a birdy bit of a thing who loves anything superior, King's English and allow-me! all the time. But they lost their only son in the war, and it's sort of knocked a hole in them. There's a long gawky lass of a daughter training for a schoolteacher, and I help her with her lessons sometimes, so we're quite the family. But they're very decent people, and only too kind to me. I expect I'm more coddled than you are.

I like farming all right. It's not inspiring, but then I don't ask to be inspired. I'm used to horses, and cows, though they are very female, have a soothing effect on me. When I sit with my head in her side, milking, I feel very solaced. They have six rather fine Herefords. Oat-harvest is just over and I enjoyed it, in spite of sore hands and a lot of rain. I don't take much notice of people, but get on with them all right. Most things one just ignores.

The pits are working badly; this is a colliery district like Tevershall, only prettier. I sometimes sit in the Wellington and talk to the men. They grumble a lot, but they're not going to alter anything. As everybody says, the Notts–Derby miners have got their hearts in the right place. But the rest of their anatomy must be in the wrong place, in a world that has no use for them. I like them, but they don't cheer me much: not enough of the old fighting-cock in them. They talk a lot about nationalisation, nationalisation of royalties, nationalisation of the whole industry. But you can't nationalise coal and leave all the other industries as they are. They talk about putting coal to new uses, like Sir Clifford is trying to do. It may work here and there, but not as a general thing, I doubt. Whatever you make you've got to sell it. The men are very apathetic. They feel the whole damned thing is doomed, and I believe it is. And they are doomed along with it. Some of the young ones spout about a Soviet, but there's not much conviction in them. There's no sort of conviction about anything, except that it's all a muddle and a hole. Even under a Soviet you've still got to sell coal: and that's the difficulty.

We've got this great industrial population, and they've got to be fed, so the damn show has to be kept going somehow. The women talk a lot more than the men, nowadays, and they are a sight more cocksure. The men are limp, they feel a doom somewhere, and they go about as if there was nothing to be done. Anyhow nobody knows what should be done, in spite of all the talk. The young ones get mad because they've no money to spend. Their whole life depends on spending money, and now they've got none to spend. That's our civilisation and our education: bring up the masses to depend entirely on spending money, and then the money gives out. The pits are working two days, two and a half days a week, and there's no sign of betterment even for the winter. It means a man bringing up a family on twenty-five and thirty shillings. The women are the maddest of all. But then they're the maddest for spending, nowadays.

If you could only tell them that living and spending isn't the same thing!

But it's no good. If only they were educated to *live* instead of earn and spend, they could manage very happily on twenty-five shillings. If the men wore scarlet trousers as I said, they wouldn't think so much of money: if they could dance and hop and skip, and sing and swagger and be handsome, they could do with very little cash. And amuse the women themselves, and be amused by the women. They ought to learn to be naked and handsome, and to sing in a mass and dance the old group dances, and carve the stools they sit on, and embroider their own emblems. Then they wouldn't need money. And that's the only way to solve the industrial problem: train the people to be able to live and live in handsomeness, without needing to spend. But you can't do it. They're all one-track minds nowadays. Whereas the mass of people oughtn't even to try to think, because they *can't*. They should be alive and frisky, and acknowledge the great god Pan. He's the only god for the masses, forever. The few can go in for higher cults if they like. But let the mass be forever pagan.

But the colliers aren't pagan, far from it. They're a sad lot, a deadened lot of men: dead to their women, dead to life. The young ones scoot about on motor bikes with girls, and jazz when they get a chance. But they're very dead. And it needs money. Money poisons you when you've got it, and starves you when you haven't.

I'm sure you're sick of all this. But I don't want to harp on myself, and I've nothing happening to me. I don't like to think too much about you, in my head, that only makes a mess of us both. But of course what I live for now is for you and me to live together. I'm frightened, really. I feel the devil in the air, and he'll try to get us. Or not the devil, Mammon: which I think, after all, is only the mass-will of people, wanting money and hating life. Anyhow I feel great grasping white hands in the air, wanting to get hold of the throat of anybody who tries to live, to live beyond money, and squeeze the life out. There's a bad time coming. There's a bad time coming, boys, there's a bad time coming! If things go on as they are, there's nothing lies in the future but death and destruction, for these industrial masses. I feel my inside turn to water sometimes, and there you are, going to have a child by me. But never mind. All the bad times that ever have been, haven't been able to blow the crocus out: not even the love of women. So they won't be able to blow out my wanting you, nor the little glow there is between you and me. We'll be together next year. And though I'm frightened, I believe in your being with me. A man has to fend and fettle for the best, and then trust in something beyond himself. You can't insure against the future, except by really believing in the best bit of you, and in the power beyond it. So I believe in the little flame between us. For me now, it's the only thing in the world. I've got no friends, not inward friends. Only you. And now the little flame is all I care about in my life. There's the baby, but that is a side issue. It's my Pentecost, the forked flame between me and you. The old Pentecost isn't quite right. Me and God is a bit uppish, somehow. But the little forked flame between me and you: there you are! That's what I abide by, and will abide by, Cliffords and Berthas, colliery companies and governments and the money-mass of people all notwithstanding.

That's why I don't like to start thinking about you actually. It only tortures me, and does you no good. I don't want you to be away from me. But if I start fretting it wastes something. Patience, always patience. This is my fortieth winter. And I can't help all the winters that have been. But this winter I'll stick to my little Pentecost flame, and have some peace. And I won't let the breath of people blow it out. I believe in a higher mystery, that doesn't let even the crocus be blown out. And if you're in Scotland and I'm in the Midlands, and I can't put my arms round you, and wrap my legs round you, yet I've got something of you. My soul softly flaps in the little Pentecost flame with you, like the peace of fucking. We fucked a flame into being. Even the flowers are fucked into being between the sun and the earth. But it's a delicate thing, and takes patience and the long pause.

So I love chastity now, because it is the peace that comes of fucking. I love being chaste now. I love it as snowdrops love the snow. I love this chastity, which is the pause of peace of our fucking, between us now like a snowdrop of forked white fire. And when the real spring comes, when the drawing to-gether comes, then we can fuck the little flame brilliant and yellow, brilliant. But not now, not yet! Now is the time to be chaste, it is so good to be chaste, like a river of cool water in my soul. I love the chastity now that it flows between us. It is like fresh water and rain. How can men want wearisomely to philander. What a misery to be like Don Juan, and impotent ever to fuck oneself into peace, and the little flame alight, impotent and unable to be chaste in the cool between-whiles, as by a river.

Well, so many words, because I can't touch you. If I could sleep with my arms round you, the ink could stay in the bottle. We could be chaste together just as we can fuck together. But we have to be separate for a while, and I suppose it is really the wiser way. If only one were sure.

Never mind, never mind, we won't get worked up. We really trust in the little flame, and in the unnamed god that shields it from being blown out. There's so much of you here with me, really, that it's a pity you aren't all here.

Never mind about Sir Clifford. If you don't hear anything from him, never mind. He can't really do anything to you. Wait, he will want to get rid of you at last, to cast you out. And if he doesn't, we'll manage to keep clear of him. But he will. In the end he will want to spew you out as the abominable thing.

Now I can't even leave off writing to you.

But a great deal of us is together, and we can but abide by it, and steer our courses to meet soon. John Thomas says good-night to Lady Jane, a little droopingly, but with a hopeful heart.

THE CAPTAIN'S DOLL

'H ANNELE!'
    '*Ja – a.*'
    '*Wo bist du?*'
    '*Hier.*'
 '*Wo dann?*'

Hannele did not lift her head from her work. She sat in a low chair under a reading-lamp, a basket of coloured silk pieces beside her, and in her hands a doll, or mannikin, which she was dressing. She was doing something to the knee of the mannikin, so that the poor little gentleman flourished head downwards with arms wildly tossed out. And it was not at all seemly, because the doll was a Scotch soldier in tight-fitting tartan trews.

There was a tap at the door, and the same voice, a woman's, calling:

'Hannele?'

'*Ja – a!*'

'Are you here? Are you alone?' asked the voice in German.

'Yes – come in.'

Hannele did not sound very encouraging. She turned round her doll as the door opened, and straightened his coat. A dark-eyed young woman peeped in through the door, with a roguish coyness. She was dressed fashionably for the street, in a thick cape-wrap, and a little black hat pulled down to her ears.

'Quite, quite alone!' said the newcomer, in a tone of wonder. 'Where is he, then?'

'That I don't know,' said Hannele.

'And you sit here alone and wait for him? But no! That I call courage! Aren't you afraid?' Mitchka strolled across to her friend.

'Why shall I be afraid?' said Hannele curtly.

'But no! And what are you doing? Another puppet! He is a good one, though! Ha – ha – ha! *Him!* It is him! No – no – that is too beautiful! No – that is too beautiful, Hannele. It is him – exactly him. Only the trousers.'

'He wears those trousers too,' said Hannele, standing her doll on her knee. It was a perfect portrait of an officer of a Scottish regiment, slender, delicately made, with a slight, elegant stoop of the shoulders and close-fitting tartan trousers. The face was beautifully modelled, and a wonderful portrait, dark-skinned, with a little, close-cut, dark moustache, and wide-open dark eyes, and that air of aloofness and perfect diffidence which marks an officer and a gentleman.

Mitchka bent forward, studying the doll. She was a handsome woman with a warm, dark golden skin and clear black eyebrows over her russet-brown eyes.

'No,' she whispered to herself, as if awestruck. 'That is him. That is him. Only not the trousers. Beautiful, though, the trousers. Has he really such beautiful fine legs?'

Hannele did not answer.

'Exactly him. Just as finished as he is. Just as complete. He is just like that: finished off. Has he seen it?'

'No,' said Hannele.

'What will he say, then?' She started. Her quick ear had caught a sound on the stone stairs. A look of fear came to her face. She flew to the door and out of the room, closing the door to behind her.

'Who is it?' her voice was heard calling anxiously down the stairs.

The answer came in German. Mitchka immediately opened the door again and came back to join Hannele.

'Only Martin,' she said.

She stood waiting. A man appeared in the doorway – erect, military.

'Ah! Countess Hannele,' he said in his quick, precise way, as he stood on the threshold in the distance. 'May one come in?'

'Yes, come in,' said Hannele.

The man entered with a quick, military step, bowed, and kissed the hand of the woman who was sewing the doll. Then, much more intimately, he touched Mitchka's hands with his lips.

Mitchka meanwhile was glancing round the room. It was a very large attic, with the ceiling sloping and then bending in two handsome movements towards the walls. The light from the dark-shaded reading-lamp fell softly on the huge whitewashed vaulting of the ceiling, on the various objects round the walls, and made a brilliant pool of colour where Hannele sat in her soft, red dress, with her basket of silks.

She was a fair woman with dark-blond hair and a beautiful fine skin. Her face seemed luminous, a certain quick gleam of life about it as she looked up at the man. He was handsome, clean-shaven, with very blue eyes strained a little too wide. One could see the war in his face.

Mitchka was wandering round the room, looking at everything, and saying: 'Beautiful! But beautiful! Such good taste! A man, and such good taste! No, they don't need a woman. No, look here, Martin, the Captain Hepburn has arranged all this room himself. Here you have the man. Do you see? So simple, yet so elegant. He needs a woman.'

The room was really beautiful, spacious, pale, soft-lighted. It was heated by a large stove of dark-blue tiles, and had very little furniture save large peasant cupboards or presses of painted wood, and a huge writing-table, on which were writing materials and some scientific apparatus and a cactus plant with fine scarlet blossoms. But it was a man's room. Tobacco and pipes were on a little tray, on the pegs in the distance hung military overcoats and belts, and two guns on a bracket. Then there were two telescopes, one mounted on a stand near a window. Various astronomical apparatus lay upon the table.

'And he reads the stars. Only think – he is an astronomer and reads the stars. Queer, queer people, the English!'

'He is Scottish,' said Hannele.

'Yes, Scottish,' said Mitchka. 'But, you know, I am afraid when I am with him. He is at a closed end. I don't know where I can get to with him. Are you afraid of him too, Hannele? Ach, like a closed road!'

'Why should I be?'

'Ah, you! Perhaps you don't know when you should be afraid. But if he were to come and find us here? No, no – let us go. Let us go, Martin. Come, let us go. I don't want the Captain Hepburn to come and find me in his room. Oh no!' Mitchka was busily pushing Martin to the door, and he was laughing with the queer, mad laugh in his strained eyes. 'Oh no! I don't like. I don't like it,' said Mitchka, trying her English now. She spoke a few sentences prettily. 'Oh no, Sir Captain, I don't want that you come. I don't like it, to be here when you come. Oh no. Not at all. I go. I go, Hannele. I go, my Hannele. And you will really stay here and wait for him? But when will he come? You don't know? Oh dear, I don't like it, I don't like it. I do not wait in the man's room. No, no – Never – *jamais* – *jamais*, *voyez-vous*. Ach, you poor Hannele! And he has got wife and children in England? Nevair! No, nevair shall I wait for him.'

She had bustlingly pushed Martin through the door and settled her wrap and taken a mincing, elegant pose, ready for the street, and waved her hand and made wide, scared eyes at Hannele, and was gone. The Countess Hannele picked up the doll again and began to sew its shoe. What living she now had she earned making these puppets.

But she was restless. She pressed her arms into her lap, as if holding them bent had wearied her. Then she looked at the little clock on his writing-table. It was long after dinner-time – why hadn't he come? She sighed, rather exasperated. She was tired of her doll.

Putting aside her basket of silks, she went to one of the windows. Outside the stars seemed white, and very near. Below was the dark agglomeration of the roofs of houses, a fume of light came up from beneath the darkness of roofs, and a faint breakage of noise from the town far below. The room seemed high, remote, in the sky.

She went to the table and looked at his letter-clip with letters in it, and at his sealing-wax and his stamp-box, touching things and moving them a little, just for the sake of the contrast, not really noticing what she touched. Then she took a pencil, and in stiff Gothic characters began to write her name – Johanna zu Rassentlow – time after time her own name – and then once, bitterly, curiously, with a curious sharpening of her nose: Alexander Hepburn.

But she threw the pencil down, having no more interest in her writing. She wandered to where the large telescope stood near a farther window, and stood for some minutes with her fingers on the barrel, where it was a little brighter from his touching it. Then she drifted restlessly back to her chair. She had picked up her puppet when she heard him on the stairs. She lifted her face and watched as he entered.

'Hello, you there!' he said quietly, as he closed the door behind him. She glanced at him swiftly, but did not move or answer.

He took off his overcoat with quick, quiet movements, and went to hang it up on the pegs. She heard his step, and looked again. He was like the doll, a tall, slender, well-bred man in uniform. When he turned, his dark eyes seemed very wide open. His black hair was growing grey at the temples – the first touch.

She was sewing her doll. Without saying anything, he wheeled round the chair from the writing-table, so that he sat with his knees almost touching her. Then he crossed one leg over the other. He wore fine tartan socks. His ankles seemed slender and elegant, his brown shoes fitted as if they were part of him. For some moments he watched her as she sat sewing. The light fell on her soft, delicate hair, that was full of strands of gold and of tarnished gold and shadow. She did not look up.

In silence he held out his small, naked-looking brown hand for the doll. On his forearm were black hairs.

She glanced up at him. Curious how fresh and luminous her face looked in contrast to his.

'Do you want to see it?' she asked, in natural English.

'Yes,' he said.

She broke off her thread of cotton and handed him the puppet. He sat with one leg thrown over the other, holding the doll in one hand and smiling inscrutably with his dark eyes. His hair, parted perfectly on one side, was jet black and glossy.

'You've got me,' he said at last, in his amused, melodious voice.

'What?' she said.

'You've got me,' he repeated.

'I don't care,' she said.

'What – You don't care?' His face broke into a smile. He had an odd way of answering, as if he were only half attending, as if he were thinking of something else.

'You are very late, aren't you?' she ventured.

'Yes. I am rather late.'

'Why are you?'

'Well, as a matter of fact, I was talking with the Colonel.'

'About me?'

'Yes. It was about you.'

She went pale as she sat looking up into his face. But it was impossible to tell whether there was distress on his dark brow or not.

'Anything nasty?' she said.

'Well, yes. It was rather nasty. Not about you, I mean. But rather awkward for me.'

She watched him. But still he said no more.

'What was it?' she said.

'Oh, well – only what I expected. They seem to know rather too much about you – about you and me, I mean. Not that anybody cares one bit, you know, unofficially. The trouble is, they are apparently going to have to take official notice.'

'Why?'

'Oh, well – it appears my wife has been writing letters to the Major-General. He is one of her family acquaintances – known her all his life. And I suppose she's been hearing rumours. In fact, I know she has. She said so in her letter to me.'

'And what do you say to her then?'

'Oh, I tell her I'm all right – not to worry.'

'You don't expect *that* to stop her worrying, do you?' she asked.

'Oh, I don't know. Why should she worry?' he said.

'I think she might have some reason,' said Hannele. 'You've not seen her for a year. And if she adores you – '

'Oh, I don't think she adores me. I think she quite likes me.'

'Do you think you matter as little as that to her?'

'I don't see why not. Of course she likes to feel *safe* about me.'

'But now she doesn't feel safe?'

'No – exactly. Exactly. That's the point. That's where it is. The Colonel advises me to go home on leave.'

He sat gazing with curious, bright, dark, unseeing eyes at the doll which he held by one arm. It was an extraordinary likeness of himself, true even to the smooth parting of his hair and his peculiar way of fixing his dark eyes.

'For how long?' she asked.

'I don't know. For a month,' he replied, first vaguely, then definitely.

'For a month!' She watched him, and seemed to see him fade from her eyes.

'And will you go?' she asked.

'I don't know. I don't know.' His head remained bent, he seemed to muse rather vaguely. 'I don't know,' he repeated. 'I can't make up my mind what I shall do.'

'Would you like to go?' she asked.

He lifted his brows and looked at her. Her heart always melted in her when he looked straight at her with his black eyes and that curious, bright, unseeing look that was more like second sight than direct human vision. She never knew what he saw when he looked at her.

'No,' he said simply. 'I don't *want* to go. I don't think I've any desire at all to go to England.'

'Why not?' she asked.

'I can't say.' Then again he looked at her, and a curious white light seemed to shine on his eyes, as he smiled slowly with his mouth, and said: 'I suppose you ought to know, if anybody does.'

A glad, half-frightened look came on her face.

'You mean you don't want to leave me?' she asked, breathless.

'Yes. I suppose that's what I mean.'

'But you aren't sure?'

'Yes, I am, I'm quite sure,' he said, and the curious smile lingered on his face, and the strange light shone in his eyes.

'That you don't want to leave me?' she stammered, looking aside.

'Yes, I'm quite sure I don't want to leave you,' he repeated. He had a curious, very melodious Scottish voice. But it was the incomprehensible smile on his face that convinced and frightened her. It was almost a gargoyle smile, a strange, lurking, changeless-seeming grin.

She was frightened, and turned aside her face. When she looked at him again, his face was like a mask, with strange, deep-graven lines and a glossy dark skin and a fixed look – as if carved half grotesquely in some glossy stone. His black hair on his smooth, beautifully-shaped head seemed changeless.

'Are you rather tired?' she asked him.

'Yes, I think I am.' He looked at her with black, unseeing eyes and a mask-like face. Then he glanced as if he heard something. Then he rose with his hand on his belt, saying: 'I'll take off my belt and change my coat, if you don't mind.'

He walked across the room, unfastening his broad, brown belt. He was in well-fitting, well-cut khaki. He hung up his belt and came back to her wearing an old, light tunic, which he left unbuttoned. He carried his slippers in one hand. When he sat down to unfasten his shoes, she noticed again how black and hairy his forearm was, how naked his brown hand seemed. His hair was black and smooth and perfect on his head, like some close helmet, as he stooped down.

He put on his slippers, carried his shoes aside, and resumed his chair, stretching luxuriously.

'There,' he said. 'I feel better now.' And he looked at her. 'Well,' he said, 'and how are you?'

'Me?' she said. 'Do I matter?' She was rather bitter.

'Do you matter?' he repeated, without noticing her bitterness. 'Why, what a question! Of course you are of the very highest importance. What? Aren't you?' And smiling his curious smile – it made her for a moment think of the fixed sadness of monkeys, of those Chinese carved soapstone apes. He put his hand under her chin, and gently drew his finger along her cheek. She flushed deeply.

'But I'm not as important as you, am I?' she asked defiantly.

'As important as me! Why, bless you, I'm not important a bit. I'm not important a bit!' – the odd straying sound of his words mystified her. What did he really mean?

'And I'm even less important than that,' she said bitterly.

'Oh no, you're not. Oh no, you're not. You're very important. You're very important indeed, I assure you.'

'And your wife?' – the question came rebelliously. 'Your wife? Isn't she important?'

'My wife? My wife?' He seemed to let the word stray out of him as if he did not quite know what it meant. 'Why, yes, I suppose she is important in her own sphere.'

'What sphere?' blurted Hannele, with a laugh.

'Why, her own sphere, of course. Her own house, her own home, and her two children: that's her sphere.'

'And you? – where do you come in?'

'At present I don't come in,' he said.

'But isn't that just the trouble,' said Hannele. 'If you have a wife and a home, it's your business to belong to it, isn't it?'

'Yes, I suppose it is, if I want to,' he replied.

'And you *do* want to?' she challenged.

'No, I don't,' he replied.

'Well, then?' she said.

'Yes, quite,' he answered. 'I admit it's a dilemma.'

'But what will you *do*?' she insisted.

'Why, I don't know. I don't know yet. I haven't made up my mind what I'm going to do.'

'Then you'd better begin to make it up,' she said.

'Yes, I know that. I know that.'

He rose and began to walk uneasily up and down the room. But the same vacant darkness was on his brow. He had his hands in his pockets. Hannele sat feeling helpless. She couldn't help being in love with the man: with his hands, with his strange, fascinating physique, with his incalculable presence. She loved the way he put his feet down, she loved the way he moved his legs as he walked, she loved the mould of his loins, she loved the way he dropped his head a little, and the strange, dark vacancy of his brow, his not-thinking. But now the restlessness only made her unhappy. Nothing would come of it. Yet she had driven him to it.

He took his hands out of his pockets and returned to her like a piece of iron returning to a magnet. He sat down again in front of her and put his hands out to her, looking into her face.

'Give me your hands,' he said softly, with that strange, mindless, soft, suggestive tone which left her powerless to disobey. 'Give me your hands, and let me feel that we are together. Words mean so little. They mean nothing. And all that one thinks and plans doesn't amount to anything. Let me feel that we are together, and I don't care about all the rest.'

He spoke in his slow, melodious way, and closed her hands in his. She struggled still for voice.

'But you'll *have* to care about it. You'll *have* to make up your mind. You'll just *have* to,' she insisted.

'Yes, I suppose I shall. I suppose I shall. But now that we are together, I won't bother. Now that we are together, let us forget it.'

'But when we *can't* forget it any more?'

'Well – then I don't know. But – tonight – it seems to me – we might just as well forget it.'

The soft, melodious, straying sound of his voice made her feel helpless. She felt that he never answered her. Words of reply seemed to stray out of him, in the need to say *something*. But he himself never spoke. There he was, a continual blank silence in front of her.

She had a battle with herself. When he put his hand again on her cheek, softly, with the most extraordinary soft half-touch, as a kitten's paw sometimes touches one, like a fluff of living air, then, if it had not been for the magic of that almost indiscernible caress of his hand, she would have stiffened herself and drawn away and told him she could have nothing to do with him, while he was so half-hearted and unsatisfactory. She wanted to tell him these things. But when she began he answered invariably in the same soft, straying voice, that seemed to spin gossamer threads all over her, so that she could neither think nor act nor even feel distinctly. Her soul groaned rebelliously in her. And yet, when he put his hand softly under her chin, and lifted her face and smiled down on her with that gargoyle smile of his – she let him kiss her.

'What are you thinking about tonight?' he said. 'What are you thinking about?'

'What did your Colonel say to you, exactly?' she replied, trying to harden her eyes.

'Oh, that!' he answered. 'Never mind that. That is of no significance whatever.'

'But what *is* of any significance?' she insisted. She almost hated him.

'What is of any significance? Well, nothing to me, outside of this room at this minute. Nothing in time or space matters to me.'

'Yes, *this minute*!' she repeated bitterly. 'But then there's the future. *I've* got to live in the future.'

'The future! The future! The future is used up every day. The future to me is like a big tangle of black thread. Every morning you begin to untangle one loose end – and that's your day. And every evening you break off and throw away what you've untangled, and the heap is so much less: just one thread less, one day less. That's all the future matters to me.'

'Then nothing matters to you. And I don't matter to you. As you say, only an end of waste thread,' she resisted him.

'No, there you're wrong. You aren't the future to me.'

'What am I then? – the past?'

'No, not any of those things. You're nothing. As far as all that goes, you're nothing.'

'Thank you,' she said sarcastically, 'if I'm nothing.'

But the very irrelevancy of the man overcame her. He kissed her with half discernible, dim kisses, and touched her throat. And the meaninglessness of him fascinated her and left her powerless. She could ascribe no meaning to him, none whatever. And yet his mouth, so strange in kissing, and his hairy forearms, and his slender, beautiful breast with black hair – it was all like a mystery to her, as if one of the men from Mars were loving her. And she was heavy and spellbound, and she loved the spell that bound her. But also she didn't love it.

2

Countess zu Rassentlow had a studio in one of the main streets. She was really a refugee. And nowadays you can be a grand-duke and a pauper, if you are a refugee. But Hannele was not a pauper, because she and her friend Mitchka had the studio where they made these dolls, and beautiful cushions of embroidered coloured wools, and suchlike objects of feminine art. The dolls were quite famous, so the two women did not starve.

Hannele did not work much in the studio. She preferred to be alone in her own room, which was another fine attic, not quite so large as the captain's, under the same roof. But often she went to the studio in the afternoon, and if purchasers came, then they were offered a cup of tea.

The Alexander doll was never intended for sale. What made Hannele take it to the studio one afternoon, we do not know. But she did so, and stood it on a little bureau. It was a wonderful little portrait of an officer and gentleman, the physique modelled so that it made you hold your breath.

'And *that* – that is genius!' cried Mitchka. 'That is a *chef d'oeuvre*! That is thy masterpiece, Hannele. That is really marvellous. And beautiful! A beautiful man, what! But no, that is *too* real. I don't understand how you *dare*. I always thought you were *good*, Hannele, so much better-natured than I am. But now you frighten me. I am afraid you are wicked, do you know. It frightens me to think that you are wicked. *Aber nein!* But you won't leave him there?'

'Why not?' said Hannele, satiric.

Mitchka made big dark eyes of wonder, reproach, and fear.

'But you *must* not,' she said.

'Why not?'

'No, that you *may* not do. You love the man.'

'What then?'

'You can't leave his puppet standing there.'

'Why can't I?'

'But you are really wicked. *Du bist wirklich bös.* Only think! – and he is an English officer.'

'He isn't sacrosanct even then.'

'They will expel you from the town. They will deport you.'

'Let them, then.'

'But no! What will you do? That would be horrible if we had to go to Berlin or to Munich and begin again. Here everything has happened so well.'

'I don't care,' said Hannele.

Mitchka looked at her friend and said no more. But she was angry. After some time she turned and uttered her ultimatum.

'When you are not there,' she said, 'I shall put the puppet away in a drawer. I shall show it to nobody, nobody. And I must tell you, it makes me afraid to see it there. It makes me afraid. And you have no right to get me into trouble, do you see. It is not I who look at the English officers. I don't like them, they are too cold and finished off for me. I shall never bring trouble on *myself* because of the English officers.'

'Don't be afraid,' said Hannele. 'They won't trouble *you*. They know every-thing we do, well enough. They have their spies everywhere. Nothing will happen to you.'

'But if they make you go away – and I am planted here with the studio –'

It was no good, however; Hannele was obstinate.

So, one sunny afternoon there was a ring at the door: a little lady in white, with a wrinkled face that still had its prettiness.

'Good-afternoon!' – in rather lardy-dardy, middle-class English. 'I wonder if I may see your things in your studio.'

'Oh yes!' said Mitchka. 'Please come in.'

Entered the little lady in her finery and her crumpled prettiness. She would not be very old: perhaps younger than fifty. And it was odd that her face had gone so crumpled, because her figure was very trim, her eyes were bright, and she had pretty teeth when she laughed. She was very fine in her clothes: a dress of thick knitted white silk, a large ermine scarf with the tails only at the ends, and a black hat over which dripped a trail of green feathers of the osprey sort. She wore rather a lot of jewellery, and two bangles tinkled over her white kid gloves as she put up her fingers to touch her hair, whilst she stood complacently and looked round.

'You've got a *charming* studio – *charming* – perfectly delightful! I couldn't imagine anything more delightful.'

Mitchka gave a slight ironic bow, and said in her odd, plangent English: 'Oh yes. We like it very much also.'

Hannele, who had dodged behind a screen, now came quickly forth.

'Oh, how do you do!' smiled the elderly lady. 'I heard there were two of you. Now which is which, if I may be so bold? This' – and she gave a winsome smile and pointed a white kid finger at Mitchka – 'is the – ?'

'Annamaria von Prielau-Carolath,' said Mitchka, slightly bowing.

'Oh!' – and the white kid finger jerked away. 'Then this –'

'Johanna zu Rassentlow,' said Hannele, smiling.

'Ah, yes! Countess von Rassentlow! And this is Baroness von – von – but I shall never remember even if you tell me, for I'm awful at names. Anyhow, I shall call one Countess and the other Baroness. That will do, won't it, for poor me! Now I should like awfully to see your things, if I may. I want to buy a little present to take back to England with me. I suppose I shan't have to pay the world in duty on things like these, shall I?'

'Oh no,' said Mitchka. 'No duty. Toys, you know, they – there is –' Her English stammered to an end, so she turned to Hannele.

'They don't charge duty on toys, and the embroideries they don't notice,' said Hannele.

'Oh, well. Then I'm all right,' said the visitor. 'I hope I can buy something really nice! I see a perfectly lovely jumper over there, perfectly delightful. But a little too gay for me, I'm afraid. I'm not quite so young as I was, alas.' She smiled her winsome little smile, showing her pretty teeth and the old pearls in her ears shook.

'I've heard so much about your dolls. I hear they're perfectly exquisite, quite works of art. May I see some, please?'

'Oh yes,' came Mitchka's invariable answer, this exclamation being the foundation-stone of all her English.

There were never more than three or four dolls in stock. This time there were only two. The famous captain was hidden in his drawer.

'Perfectly beautiful! Perfectly wonderful!' murmured the little lady, in an artistic murmur. 'I think they're perfectly delightful. It's wonderful of you, Countess, to make them. It is you who make them, is it not? Or do you both do them together?'

Hannele explained, and the inspection and the rhapsody went on together. But it was evident that the little lady was a cautious buyer. She went over the things very carefully, and thought more than twice. The dolls attracted her – but she thought them expensive, and hung fire.

'I do wish,' she said wistfully, 'there had been a larger selection of the dolls. I feel, you know, there might have been one which I *just loved*. Of course these are *darlings* – darlings they are: and worth every *penny*, considering the work there is in them. And the art, of course. But I have a feeling, don't you know how it is, that if there had been just one or two more, I should have found one which I *absolutely* couldn't live without. Don't you know how it is? One is so foolish, of course. What does Goethe say – "*Dort wo du nicht bist. . .*"? My German isn't even a beginning, so you must excuse it. But it means you always feel you would be happy somewhere else, and not just where you are. Isn't that it? Ah, well, it's so very often true – so very often. But not always, thank goodness.' She smiled an odd little smile to herself, pursed her lips, and resumed: 'Well now, that's how I feel about the dolls. If only there had been one or two more. Isn't there a single one?'

She looked winsomely at Hannele.

'Yes,' said Hannele, 'there is one. But it is ordered. It isn't for sale.'

'Oh, do you think I might see it? I'm sure it's lovely. Oh, I'm dying to see it. You know what woman's curiosity is, don't you?' – she laughed her tinkling little laugh. 'Well, I'm afraid I'm all woman, unfortunately. One is so much harder if one has a touch of the man in one, don't you think, and more able to bear things. But I'm afraid I'm all woman.' She sighed and became silent.

Hannele went quietly to the drawer and took out the captain. She handed him to the little woman. The latter looked frightened. Her eyes became round and childish, her face went yellowish. Her jewels tinkled nervously as she stammered: 'Now *that* – isn't that – ' and she laughed a little, hysterical laugh.

She turned round, as if to escape.

'Do you mind if I sit down,' she said. 'I think the standing – ' and she subsided into a chair. She kept her face averted. But she held the puppet fast, her small, white fingers with their heavy jewelled rings clasped round his waist.

'You know,' rushed in Mitchka, who was terrified. 'You know, that is a life picture of one of the Englishmen, of a gentleman, you know. A life picture, you know.'

'A portrait,' said Hannele brightly.

'Yes,' murmured the visitor vaguely. 'I'm sure it is. I'm sure it is a very clever portrait indeed.'

She fumbled with a chain, and put up a small gold lorgnette before her eyes, as if to screen herself. And from behind the screen of her lorgnette she peered at the image in her hand.

'But,' she said, 'none of the English officers, or rather Scottish, wear the close-fitting tartan trews any more – except for fancy dress.'

Her voice was vague and distant.

'No, they don't now,' said Hannele. 'But that is the correct dress. I think they are so handsome, don't you?'

'Well. I don't know. It depends' – and the little woman laughed shakily.

'Oh yes,' said Hannele. 'It needs well-shapen legs.'

'Such as the original of your doll must have had – quite,' said the lady.

'Oh yes,' said Hannele. 'I think his legs are very handsome.'

'Quite!' said the lady. 'Judging from his portrait, as you call it. May I ask the name of the gentleman – if it is not too indiscreet?'

'Captain Hepburn,' said Hannele.

'Yes, of course it is. I knew him at once. I've known him for many years.'

'Oh, please,' broke in Mitchka. 'Oh, please, do not tell him you have seen it! Oh, please! Please do not tell anyone!'

The visitor looked up with a grey little smile.

'But why not?' she said. 'Anyhow, I can't tell him at once, because I hear he is away at present. You don't happen to know when he will be back?'

'I believe tomorrow,' said Hannele.

'Tomorrow!'

'And please!' pleaded Mitchka, who looked lovely in her pleading distress, 'please not to tell anybody that you have seen it.'

'Must I promise?' smiled the little lady wanly. 'Very well, then, I won't tell him I've seen it. And now I think I must be going. Yes, I'll just take the cushion-cover, thank you. Tell me again how much it is, please.'

3

That evening Hannele was restless. He had been away on some duty for three days. He was returning that night – should have been back in time for dinner. But he had not arrived, and his room was locked and dark. Hannele had heard the servant light the stove some hours ago. Now the room was locked and blank as it had been for three days.

Hannele was most uneasy because she seemed to have forgotten him in the three days whilst he had been away. He seemed to have quite disappeared out of her. She could hardly even remember him. He had become so insignificant to her she was dazed.

Now she wanted to see him again, to know if it was really so. She felt that he was coming. She felt that he was already putting out some influence towards her. But what? And was he real? Why had she made his doll? Why had his doll been so important, if he was nothing? Why had she shown it to that funny little woman this afternoon? Why was she herself such a fool, getting herself into tangles in this place where it was so unpleasant to be entangled? Why was she entangled, after all? It was all so unreal. And particularly *he* was unreal: as unreal as a person in a dream, whom one has never heard of in actual life. In actual life, her own German friends were real. Martin was real: German men were real to her. But this other, he was simply not there. He didn't really exist. He was a nullus, in reality. A nullus – and she had somehow got herself complicated with him.

Was it possible? Was it possible she had been so closely entangled with an absolute nothing? Now he was absent she couldn't even *imagine* him. He had gone out of her imagination, and even when she looked at his doll she saw nothing but a barren puppet. And yet for this dead puppet she had been compromising herself, now, when it was so risky for her to be compromised.

Her own German friends – her own German men – they were men, they were real beings. But this English officer, he was neither fish, flesh, fowl, nor good red herring, as they say. He was just a hypothetical presence. She felt that if he never came back, she would be just as if she had read a rather peculiar but false story, a *tour de force* which works up one's imagination all falsely.

Nevertheless, she was uneasy. She had a lurking suspicion that there might be something else. So she kept uneasily wandering out to the landing, and listening to hear if he might be coming.

Yes – there was a sound. Yes, there was his slow step on the stairs, and the slow, straying purr of his voice. And instantly she heard his voice she was afraid again. She knew there *was* something there. And instantly she felt the reality of his presence, she felt the unreality of her own German men friends. The moment she heard the peculiar, slow melody of his foreign voice everything seemed to go changed in her, and Martin and Otto and Albrecht, her German friends, seemed to go pale and dim as if one could almost see through them, like unsubstantial things.

This was what she had to reckon with, this recoil from one to the other. When he was present, he seemed so terribly real. When he was absent he was completely vague, and her own men of her own race seemed so absolutely the only reality.

But he was talking. Who was he talking to? She heard the steps echo up the hollows of the stone staircase slowly, as if wearily, and voices slowly, confusedly mingle. The slow, soft trail of his voice – and then the peculiar, quick tones – yes, of a woman. And not one of the maids, because they were speaking English. She listened hard. The quick, and yet slightly hushed, slightly sad-sounding voice of a woman who talks a good deal, as if talking to herself. Hannele's quick ears caught the sound of what she was saying: 'Yes, I thought the Baroness a perfectly beautiful creature, perfectly lovely. But so extraordinarily like a Spaniard. Do you remember, Alec, at Malaga? I always thought they fascinated you then, with their mantillas. Perfectly lovely she would look in a mantilla. Only perhaps she is too open-hearted, too impulsive, poor thing. She lacks the Spanish reserve. Poor thing, I feel sorry for her. For them both, indeed. It must be very hard to have to do these things for a living, after you've been accustomed to be made much of for your own sake, and for your aristocratic title. It's very hard for them, poor things. Baroness, Countess, it sounds just a little ridiculous, when you're buying woollen embroideries from them. But I suppose, poor things, they can't help it. Better drop the titles altogether, I think – '

'Well, they do, if people will let them. Only English and American people find it so much easier to say Baroness or Countess than Fräulein von Prielau-Carolath, or whatever it is.'

'They could say simply Fräulein, as we do to our governesses – or as we used to, when we *had* German governesses,' came the voice of *her*.

'Yes, we *could*,' said his voice.

'After all, what is the good, what is the good of titles if you have to sell dolls and woollen embroideries – not so very beautiful, either.'

'Oh, quite! Oh, quite! I think titles are perhaps a mistake, anyhow. But they've always had them,' came his slow, musical voice, with its singsong note of hopeless indifference. He sounded rather like a man talking out of his sleep.

Hannele caught sight of the tail of blue-green crane feathers veering round a turn in the stairs away below, and she beat a hasty retreat.

4

There was a little platform out on the roof, where he used sometimes to stand his telescope and observe the stars or the moon: the moon when possible. It was not a very safe platform, just a little ledge of the roof, outside the window at the end of the top corridor: or rather, the top landing, for it was only the space between the attics. Hannele had the one attic room at the back, he had the room we have seen, and a little bedroom which was really only a lumber room. Before he came, Hannele had been alone under the roof. His rooms were then lumber room and laundry room, where the clothes were dried. But he had wanted to be high up, because of his stars, and this was the place that pleased him.

Hannele heard him quite late in the night, wandering about. She heard him also on the ledge outside. She could not sleep. He disturbed her. The moon was risen, large and bright in the sky. She heard the bells from the cathedral slowly strike two: two great drops of sound in the livid night. And again, from outside on the roof, she heard him clear his throat. Then a cat howled.

She rose, wrapped herself in a dark wrap, and went down the landing to the window at the end. The sky outside was full of moonlight. He was squatted like a great cat peering up his telescope, sitting on a stool, his knees wide apart. Quite motionless he sat in that attitude, like some leaden figure on the roof. The moonlight glistened with a gleam of plumbago on the great slope of black tiles. She stood still in the window, watching. And he remained fixed and motionless at the end of the telescope.

She tapped softly on the window-pane. He looked round, like some tomcat staring round with wide night eyes. Then he reached down his hand and pulled the window open.

'Hello,' he said quietly. 'You not asleep?'

'Aren't *you* tired?' she replied, rather resentful.

'No, I was as wide awake as I could be. *Isn't* the moon fine tonight! What? Perfectly amazing. Wouldn't you like to come up and have a look at her?'

'No, thank you,' she said hastily, terrified at the thought.

He resumed his posture, peering up the telescope.

'Perfectly amazing,' he said, murmuring. She waited for some time, bewitched likewise by the great October moon and the sky full of resplendent white-green light. It seemed like another sort of daytime. And there he straddled on the roof like some cat! It was exactly like day in some other planet.

At length he turned round to her. His face glistened faintly, and his eyes were dilated like a cat's at night.

'You know I had a visitor?' he said.

'Yes.'

'My wife.'

'Your *wife*!' – she looked up really astonished. She had thought it might be an acquaintance – perhaps his aunt – or even an elder sister. 'But she's years older than you,' she added.

'Eight years,' he said. 'I'm forty-one.'

There was a silence.

'Yes,' he mused. 'She arrived suddenly, by surprise, yesterday, and found me away. She's staying in the hotel, in the Vier Jahreszeiten.'

There was a pause.

'Aren't you going to stay with her?' asked Hannele.

'Yes, I shall probably join her tomorrow.'

There was a still longer pause.

'Why not tonight?' asked Hannele.

'Oh, well – I put it off for tonight. It meant all the bother of my wife changing her room at the hotel – and it was late – and I was all mucky after travelling.'

'But you'll go tomorrow?'

'Yes, I shall go tomorrow. For a week or so. After that I'm not sure what will happen.'

There was quite a long pause. He remained seated on his stool on the roof, looking with dilated, blank, black eyes at nothingness. She stood below in the open window space, pondering.

'Do you want to go to her at the hotel?' asked Hannele.

'Well, I don't, particularly. But I don't mind, really. We're very good friends. Why, we've been friends for eighteen years – we've been married seventeen. Oh, she's a nice little woman. I don't want to hurt her feelings. I wish her no harm, you know. On the contrary, I wish her all the good in the world.'

He had no idea of the blank amazement in which Hannele listened to these stray remarks.

'But – ' she stammered. 'But doesn't she expect you to make *love* to her?'

'Oh yes, she expects that. You bet she does: woman-like.'

'And you?' – the question had a dangerous ring.

'Why, I don't mind, really, you know, if it's only for a short time. I'm used to her. I've always been fond of her, you know – and so if it gives her any pleasure – why, I like her to get what pleasure out of life she can.'

'But you – you *yourself*! Don't *you* feel anything?' Hannele's amazement was reaching the point of incredulity. She began to feel that he was making it up. It was all so different from her own point of view. To sit there so quiet and to make such statements in all good faith: no, it was impossible.

'I don't consider I count,' he said naïvely.

Hannele looked aside. If that wasn't lying, it was imbecility, or worse. She had for the moment nothing to say. She felt he was a sort of psychic phenomenon like a grasshopper or a tadpole or an ammonite. Not to be regarded from a human point of view. No, he just wasn't normal. And she had been fascinated by him! It was only sheer, amazed curiosity that carried her on to her next question.

'But do you *never* count, then?' she asked, and there was a touch of derision, of laughter in her tone. He took no offence.

'Well – very rarely,' he said. 'I count very rarely. That's how life appears to me. One matters so *very* little.'

She felt quite dizzy with astonishment. And he called himself a man!

'But if you matter so very little, what do you do anything at all for?' she asked.

'Oh, one has to. And then, why not? Why not do things, even if oneself hardly matters. Look at the moon. It doesn't matter in the least to the moon whether I exist or whether I don't. So why should it matter to me?'

After a blank pause of incredulity she said: 'I could die with laughter. It seems to me all so ridiculous – no, I can't believe it.'

'Perhaps it is a point of view,' he said.

There was a long and pregnant silence: we should not like to say pregnant with what.

'And so I don't mean anything to you at all?' she said.

'I didn't say that,' he replied.

'Nothing means anything to you,' she challenged.

'I don't say that.'

'Whether it's your wife – or me – or the moon – *toute la même chose*.'

'No – no – that's hardly the way to look at it.'

She gazed at him in such utter amazement that she felt something would really explode in her if she heard another word. Was this a man? – or what was it? It was too much for her, that was all.

'Well, goodbye,' she said. 'I hope you will have a nice time at the Vier Jahreszeiten.'

So she left him still sitting on the roof.

'I suppose,' she said to herself, 'that is love *à l'anglaise*. But it's more than I can swallow.'

5

'Won't you come and have tea with me – do! Come right along now. Don't you find it bitterly cold? Yes – well now come in with me and we'll have a cup of nice, hot tea in our little sitting-room. The weather changes so suddenly, and really one needs a little reinforcement. But perhaps you don't take tea?'

'Oh yes. I got so used to it in England,' said Hannele.

'Did you now! Well now, were you long in England?'

'Oh yes – '

The two women had met in the Domplatz. Mrs Hepburn was looking extraordinarily like one of Hannele's dolls, in a funny little cape of odd striped skins, and a little dark-green skirt, and a rather fuzzy sort of hat. Hannele looked almost huge beside her.

'But now you will come in and have tea, won't you? Oh, please do. Never mind whether it's *de rigueur* or not. I *always* please myself *what* I do. I'm afraid my husband gets some shocks sometimes – but that we can't help. I won't have anybody laying down the law to me.' She laughed her winsome little laugh. 'So now come along in, and we'll see if there aren't hot scones as well. I love a hot scone for tea in cold weather. And I hope you do. That is, if there are any. We don't know yet.' She tinkled her little laugh. 'My husband may or may not be in. But that makes no difference to you and me, does it? There, it's just striking half past four. In England, we always have tea at half past. My husband *adores* his tea. I don't suppose our man is five minutes off the half past, ringing the gong for tea, not once in twelve months. My husband doesn't mind at all if dinner is a little late. But he gets – quite – well, quite "ratty" if tea is late.' She tinkled a laugh. 'Though I shouldn't say that. He is the soul of kindness and patience. I don't think I've ever known him do an unkind thing – or hardly say an unkind word. But I doubt if he will be in today.'

He *was* in, however, standing with his feet apart and his hands in his trouser pockets in the little sitting-room upstairs in the hotel. He raised his eyebrows the smallest degree, seeing Hannele enter.

'Ah, Countess Hannele – my wife has brought you along! Very nice, very nice! Let me take your wrap. Oh yes, certainly . . .'

'Have you rung for tea, dear?' asked Mrs Hepburn.

'Er – yes. I said as soon as you came in they were to bring it.'

'Yes – well. Won't you ring again, dear, and say for *three*.'

'Yes – certainly. Certainly.'

He rang, and stood about with his hands in his pockets waiting for tea.

'Well now,' said Mrs Hepburn, as she lifted the teapot, and her bangles tinkled, and her huge rings of brilliants twinkled, and her big ear-rings of clustered seed-pearls bobbed against her rather withered cheek, 'isn't it charming of Countess zu – Countess zu – '

'Rassentlow,' said he. 'I believe most people say Countess Hannele. I know we always do among ourselves. We say Countess Hannele's shop.'

'Countess Hannele's shop! Now, isn't that perfectly delightful: such a romance in the very sound of it. You take cream?'

'Thank you,' said Hannele.

The tea passed in a cloud of chatter, while Mrs Hepburn manipulated the teapot, and lit the spirit-flame, and blew it out, and peeped into the steam of the teapot, and couldn't see whether there was any more tea or not – and – 'At home I *know* – I was going to say to a teaspoonful – how much tea there is in the pot. But this teapot – I don't know what it's made of – it isn't silver, I know that – it is so heavy in itself that it's deceived me several times already. And my husband is a greedy man, a greedy man – he likes at least three cups – and four if he can get them, or five! Yes, dear, I've plenty of tea today. You shall have even five, if you don't mind the last two weak. Do let me fill your cup, Countess Hannele. I think it's a *charming* name.'

'There's a play called *Hannele*, isn't there?' said he.

When he had had his five cups, and his wife had got her cigarette perched in the end of a long, long, slim, white holder, and was puffing like a little China-woman from the distance, there was a little lull.

'Alec, dear,' said Mrs Hepburn. 'You won't forget to leave that message for me at Mrs Rackham's. I'm so afraid it will be forgotten.'

'No, dear, I won't forget. Er – would you like me to go round now?'

Hannele noticed how often he said 'er' when he was beginning to speak to his wife. But they *were* such good friends, the two of them.

'Why, if you *would*, dear, I should feel perfectly comfortable. But I don't want you to hurry one bit.'

'Oh, I may as well go now.'

And he went. Mrs Hepburn detained her guest.

'He *is* so charming to me,' said the little woman. 'He's really wonderful. And he always has been the same – invariably. So that if he *did* make a little slip – well, you know, I don't have to take it so seriously.'

'No,' said Hannele, feeling as if her ears were stretching with astonishment.

'It's the war. It's just the war. It's had a terribly deteriorating effect on the men.'

'In what way?' said Hannele.

'Why, morally. Really, there's hardly one man left the same as he was before the war. Terribly degenerated.'

'Is that so?' said Hannele.

'It is indeed. Why, isn't it the same with the German men and officers?'

'Yes, I think so,' said Hannele.

'And I'm sure so, from what I hear. But of course it is the women who are to blame in the first place. We poor women! We are a guilty race, I am afraid. But I never throw stones. I know what it is myself to have temptations. I have to flirt a little – and when I was younger – well, the men didn't escape me, I assure you. And I was *so* often scorched. But never *quite* singed. My husband never minded. He knew I was *really* safe. Oh yes, I have always been faithful to him. But still – I have been very near the flame.' And she laughed her winsome little laugh.

Hannele put her fingers to her ears to make sure they were not falling off.

'Of course during the war it was terrible. I know that in a certain hospital it was quite impossible for a girl to stay on if she kept straight. The matrons and sisters just turned her out. They wouldn't have her unless she was one of themselves. And you know what that means. Quite like the convent in Balzac's story – you know which I mean, I'm sure.' And the laugh tinkled gaily.

'But then, what can you expect, when there aren't enough men to go round! Why, I had a friend in Ireland. She and her husband had been an ideal couple, an *ideal* couple. Real playmates. And you can't say more than that, can you? Well, then, he became a major during the war. And she was so looking forward, poor thing, to the perfectly lovely times they would have together when he came home. She is like me, and is lucky enough to have a little income of her own – not a great fortune – but – well – Well now, what was I going to say? Oh yes, she was looking forward to the perfectly lovely times they would have when he came home: building on her dreams, poor thing, as we unfortunate women always do. I suppose we shall never be cured of it.' A little tinkling laugh. 'Well now, not a bit of it. Not a bit of it.' Mrs Hepburn lifted her heavily-jewelled little hand in a motion of protest. It was curious, her hands were pretty and white, and her neck and breast, now she wore a little tea-gown, were also smooth and white and pretty, under the medley of twinkling little chains and coloured jewels. Why should her face have played her this nasty trick of going all crumpled! However, it was so.

'Not one bit of it,' reiterated the little lady. 'He came home quite changed. She said she could hardly recognise him for the same man. Let me tell you one little incident. Just a trifle, but significant. He was coming home – this was some time after he was free from the army – he was coming home from London, and he told her to meet him at the boat: gave her the time and everything. Well, she went to the boat, poor thing, and he didn't come. She waited, and no word of explanation or anything. So she couldn't make up her mind whether to go next day and meet the boat again. However, she decided she wouldn't. So of course, on that boat he arrived. When he got home, he said to her: "Why didn't you meet the boat?" "Well," she said, "I went yesterday, and you didn't come." "Then why didn't you meet it again today?" Imagine it, the sauce! And they had been real playmates. Heart-breaking isn't it? "Well," she said in self-defence, "why didn't you come yesterday?" "Oh," he said, "I met a woman in town whom I liked, and she asked me to spend the night with her, so I did." Now what do you think of that? Can you conceive of such a thing?'

'Oh no,' said Hannele. 'I call that unnecessary brutality.'

'Exactly! So terrible to say such a thing to her! The brutality of it! Well, that's how the world is today. I'm thankful my husband isn't that sort. I don't say he's perfect. But whatever else he did, he'd never be unkind, and he *couldn't* be brutal. He just couldn't. He'd never tell me a lie – I know *that*. But callous brutality, no, thank goodness, he hasn't a spark of it in him. I'm the wicked one, if either of us is wicked.' The little laugh tinkled. 'Oh, but he's been perfect to me, perfect. Hardly a cross word. Why, on our wedding night, he kneeled down in front of me and promised, with God's help, to make my life happy. And I must say, as far as possible, he's kept his word. It has been his one aim in life, to make my life happy.'

The little lady looked away with a bright, musing look towards the window. She was being a heroine in a romance. Hannele could see her being a heroine, playing the chief part in her own life romance. It is such a feminine occupation, that no woman takes offence when she is made audience.

'I'm afraid I've more of the woman than the mother in my composition,' resumed the little heroine. 'I adore my two children. The boy is at Winchester, and my little girl is in a convent in Brittany. Oh, they are perfect darlings, both of them. But the man is first in my mind, I'm afraid. I fear I'm rather old-fashioned. But never mind. I can see the attractions in other men – can't I indeed! There was a perfectly exquisite creature – he was a very clever engineer – but much, much more than *that*. But never mind.' The little heroine sniffed as if there were perfume in the air, folded her jewelled hands, and resumed: 'However – I know what it is myself to flutter round the flame. You know I'm Irish myself, and we Irish can't help it. Oh, I wouldn't be English for anything. Just that little touch of imagination, you know . . .' The little laugh tinkled. 'And that's what makes me able to sympathise with my husband even when, perhaps, I shouldn't. Why, when he was at home with me, he never gave a thought, not a thought to another woman. I must say, he used to make *me* feel a little guilty sometimes. But there! I don't think he ever thought of another woman as being flesh and blood, after he knew me. I could tell. Pleasant, courteous, charming – but other women were not flesh and blood to him, they were just people, callers – that kind of thing. It used to amaze me, when some perfectly lovely creature came, whom I should have been head over heels in love with in a minute – and he, he was charming, delightful; he could see her points, but she was no more to him than, let me say, a pot of carnations or a beautiful old piece of *punto di Milano*. Not flesh and blood. Well, perhaps one can feel too safe. Perhaps one needs a tiny pinch of salt of jealousy. I believe one does. And I have not had one jealous moment for seventeen years. So that, *really*, when I heard a whisper of something going on here, I felt almost pleased. I felt exonerated for my own little peccadilloes, for one thing. And I felt he was perhaps a little more human. Because, after all, it is nothing but human to fall in love, if you are alone for a long time and in the company of a beautiful woman – and if you're an attractive man yourself.'

Hannele sat with her eyes propped open and her ears buttoned back with amazement, expecting the next revelations.

'Why, of course,' she said, knowing she was expected to say something.

'Yes, of course,' said Mrs Hepburn, eyeing her sharply. 'So I thought I'd better come and see how far things had gone. I had nothing but a hint to go on. I knew no name – nothing. I had just a hint that she was German, and a refugee aristocrat – and that he used to call at the studio.' The little lady eyed Hannele sharply, and gave a breathless little laugh, clasping her hands nervously. Hannele sat absolutely blank: really dazed.

'Of course,' resumed Mrs Hepburn, 'that was enough. That was quite a sufficient clue. I'm afraid my intentions when I called at the studio were not as pure as they might have been. I'm afraid I wanted to see something more than the dolls. But when you showed me *his* doll, then I knew. Of course there wasn't a shadow of doubt after that. And I saw at once that she loved him, poor thing. She was *so* agitated. And no idea who I was. And you were so unkind to show me the doll. Of course, you had no idea who you were showing it to. But for her, poor thing, it was such a trial. I could see how she suffered. And I must say she's very lovely – she's very, very lovely, with her golden skin and her reddish amber eyes and her beautiful, beautiful carriage. And such a naïve, impulsive nature. Give everything away in a minute. And then her deep voice – "*Oh yes – Oh, please!*" – such a child. And such an aristocrat, that lovely turn of her head, and her simple, elegant dress. Oh, she's very charming. And she's just the type I always knew would attract him, if he hadn't got me. I've thought about it many a time – many a time. When a woman is older than a man, she does think these things – especially if he has his attractive points too. And when I've dreamed of the woman he would love if he hadn't got me, it has always been a Spanish type. And the Baroness is extraordinarily Spanish in her appearance. She must have had some noble Spanish ancestor. Don't you think so?'

'Oh yes,' said Hannele. 'There were such a lot of Spaniards in Austria, too, with the various emperors.'

'With Charles V, exactly. Exactly. That's how it must have been. And so she has all the Spanish beauty, and all the German feeling. Of course, for myself, I miss the *reserve*, the haughtiness. But she's very, very lovely, and I'm sure I could never *hate* her. I couldn't even if I tried. And I'm not going to try. But I think she's much too dangerous for my husband to see much of her. Don't you agree, now?'

'Oh, but really,' stammered Hannele. 'There's nothing in it, really.'

'Well,' said the little lady, cocking her head shrewdly aside, 'I shouldn't like there to be any *more* in it.'

And there was a moment's dead pause. Each woman was reflecting. Hannele wondered if the little lady was just fooling her.

'Anyhow,' continued Mrs Hepburn, 'the spark is there, and I don't intend the fire to spread. I am going to be very, very careful, myself, not to fan the flames. The last thing I should think of would be to make my husband scenes. I believe it would be fatal.'

'Yes,' said Hannele, during the pause.

'I am going very carefully. You think there isn't much in it – between him and the Baroness?'

'No – no – I'm sure there isn't,' cried Hannele, with a full voice of conviction. She was almost indignant at being slighted so completely herself, in the little lady's suspicions.

'Hm! – mm!' hummed the little woman, sapiently nodding her head slowly up and down. 'I'm not so sure! I'm not so sure that it hasn't gone pretty far.'

'Oh *no*!' cried Hannele, in real irritation of protest.

'Well,' said the other. 'In any case, I don't intend it to go any farther.'

There was dead silence for some time.

'There's more in it than you say. There's more in it than you say,' ruminated the little woman. 'I know *him*, for one thing. I know he's got a cloud on his brow. And I know it hasn't left his brow for a single minute. And when I told him I had been to the studio, and showed him the cushion-cover, I knew he felt guilty. I am not so easily deceived. We Irish all have a touch of second sight, I believe. Of course I haven't challenged him. I haven't even mentioned the doll. By the way, *who* ordered the doll? Do you mind telling me?'

'No, it wasn't ordered,' confessed Hannele.

'Ah – I thought not – I thought not!' said Mrs Hepburn, lifting her finger. 'At least, I knew no outsider had ordered it. Of course I knew.' And she smiled to herself.

'So,' she continued, 'I had too much sense to say anything about it. I don't believe in stripping wounds bare. I believe in gently covering them and letting them heal. But I *did* say I thought her a lovely creature.' The little lady looked brightly at Hannele.

'Yes,' said Hannele.

'And he was very vague in his manner, "Yes, not bad," he said. I thought to myself: Aha, my boy, you don't deceive me with your *not bad*. She's very much more than not bad. I said so, too. I wanted, of course, to let him know I had a suspicion.'

'And do you think he knew?'

'Of course he did. Of course he did. "She's much too dangerous," I said, "to be in a town where there are so many strange men: married and unmarried." And then he turned round to me and gave himself away, oh, so plainly. "Why?" he said. But such a haughty, distant tone. I said to myself: "It's time, my dear boy, you were removed out of the danger zone." But I answered him: Surely somebody is bound to fall in love with her. Not at all, he said, she keeps to her own countrymen. You don't tell *me*, I answered him, with her pretty broken English! It is a wonder the two of them are allowed to stay in the town. And then again he rounded on me. Good gracious! he said. Would you have them turned out just because they're beautiful to look at, when they have nowhere else to go, and they make their bit of a livelihood here? I assure you, he hasn't rounded on me in that overbearing way, not once before, in all our married life. So I just said quietly: I should like to protect *our own men*. And he didn't say anything more. But he looked at me under his brows and went out of the room.'

There was a silence. Hannele waited with her hands in her lap, and Mrs Hepburn mused, with her hands in *her* lap. Her face looked yellow, and *very* wrinkled.

'Well now,' she said, breaking again suddenly into life. 'What are we to do? I mean what is to be done? You are the Baroness's nearest friend. And I wish her *no* harm, none whatever.'

'What can we do?' said Hannele, in the pause.

'I have been urging my husband for some time to get his discharge from the army,' said the little woman. 'I knew he could have it in three months' time. But like so many more men, he has no income of his own, and he doesn't want to feel dependent. Perfect nonsense! So he says he wants to stay on in the army. I have never known him before go against my real wishes.'

'But it *is* better for a man to be independent,' said Hannele.

'I know it is. But it is also better for him to be *at home*. And I could get him a post in one of the observatories. He could do something in meteorological work.'

Hannele refused to answer any more.

'Of course,' said Mrs Hepburn, 'if he *does* stay on here, it would be much better if the Baroness left the town.'

'I'm sure she will never leave of her own choice,' said Hannele.

'I'm sure she won't either. But she might be made to see that it would be very much *wiser* of her to move of her own free will.'

'Why?' said Hannele.

'Why, because she might any time be removed by the British authorities.'

'Why should she?' said Hannele.

'I think the women who are a menace to our men should be removed.'

'But she is *not* a menace to your men.'

'Well, I have my own opinion on that point.'

Which was a decided deadlock.

'I'm sure I've kept you an awful long time with my chatter,' said Mrs

Hepburn. 'But I did want to make everything as simple as possible. As I said before, I can't feel any ill-will against her. Yet I can't let things just go on. Heaven alone knows when they may end. Of course if I can persuade my husband to resign his commission and come back to England – anyhow, we will see. I'm sure I am the last person in the world to bear malice.'

The tone in which she said it conveyed a dire threat.

Hannele rose from her chair.

'Oh, and one other thing,' said her hostess, taking out a tiny lace hand-kerchief and touching her nose delicately with it. 'Do you think' – dab, dab – 'that I might have that *doll* – you know – ?'

'That – ?'

'Yes, of my husband' – the little lady rubbed her nose with her kerchief.

'The price is three guineas,' said Hannele.

'Oh indeed!' – the tone was very cold. 'I thought it was not for sale.'

Hannele put on her wrap.

'You'll send it round – will you? – if you will be so kind.'

'I must ask my friend first.'

'Yes, of course. But I'm sure she will be so kind as to send it me. It is a little – er – indelicate, don't you think!'

'No,' said Hannele. 'No more than a painted portrait.'

'Don't you?' said her hostess coldly. 'Well, even a painted portrait I think I should like in my own possession. This *doll* –'

Hannele waited, but there was no conclusion.

'Anyhow,' she said, 'the price is three guineas: or the equivalent in marks.'

'Very well,' said the little lady, 'you shall have your three guineas when I get the doll.'

6

Hannele went her way pondering. A man never is quite such an abject specimen as his wife makes him look, talking about 'my husband'. Therefore, if any woman wishes to rescue her husband from the clutches of another female, let her only invite this female to tea and talk quite sincerely about 'my husband, you know'. Every man has made a ghastly fool of himself with a woman at some time or other. No woman ever forgets. And most women will give the show away, with real pathos, to another woman. For instance, the picture of Alec at his wife's feet on his wedding night, vowing to devote himself to her life-long happiness – this picture strayed across Hannele's mind time after time, when-ever she thought of her dear captain. With disastrous consequences to the captain. Of course if he had been at her own feet, then Hannele would have thought it almost natural: almost a necessary part of the show of love. But at the feet of that other little woman! And what was that other little woman wearing? Her wedding night! Hannele hoped before heaven it wasn't some awful little nightie of frail flowered silk. Imagine it, that little lady! Perhaps in a chic little boudoir cap of *punto di Milano*, and this slip of frail flowered silk: and the man, perhaps, in his braces! Oh, merciful heaven, save us from other people's indiscretions. No, let us be sure it was in proper evening dress – twenty years ago – very low cut, with a full skirt gathered behind and trailing a little, and a little feather erection in her high-dressed hair, and all those jewels: pearls of course: and he in a dinner-jacket and a white waistcoat: probably in an hotel bedroom in Lugano or Biarritz. And she? Was she standing with one small hand on his shoulder? – or was she seated on the couch in the bedroom? Oh, dreadful thought! And yet it was almost inevitable, that scene. Hannele had never been married, but she had come quite near enough to the realisation of the event to know that such a scene *was* practically inevitable. An indispensable part of any honeymoon. Him on his knees, with his heels up!

And how black and tidy his hair must have been then! and no grey at the temples at all. Such a good-looking bridegroom. Perhaps with a white rose in his buttonhole still. And she could see him kneeling there, in his new black trousers and a wing collar. And she could see his head bowed. And she could hear his plangent, musical voice saying: 'With God's help, I will make your life happy. I will live for that and for nothing else.' And then the little lady must have had tears in her eyes, and she must have said, rather superbly: 'Thank you, dear, I'm perfectly sure of it.'

Ach! Ach! Husbands should be left to their own wives: and wives should be left to their own husbands. And *no* stranger should ever be made a party to these terrible bits of connubial staging. Nay, thought Hannele, that scene was really true. It actually took place. And with the man of that scene I have been in love! With the devoted husband of that little lady. Oh God, oh God, how was it possible! Him on his knees, on his knees, with his heels up!

Am I a perfect fool? she thought to herself. Am I really just an idiot, gaping with love for him? How *could* I? How could I? The very way he says: 'Yes, dear!' to her! The way he does what she tells him! The way he fidgets about the room with his hands in his pockets! The way he goes off when she sends him away because she wants to talk to me. And he knows she wants to talk to me. And he knows what she *might* have to say to me. Yet he goes off on his errand without a question, like a servant. 'I will do whatever you wish, darling.' He must have said those words time after time to the little lady. And fulfilled them, also. Performed all his pledges and his promises.

Ach! Ach! Hannele wrung her hands to think of *herself* being mixed up with him. And he had seemed to her so manly. He seemed to have so much silent male passion in him. And yet – the little lady! 'My husband has *always* been *perfectly sweet* to me.' Think of it! On his knees too. And his 'Yes, dear! Certainly. Certainly.' Not that he was afraid of the little lady. He was just committed to her, as he might have been committed to gaol, or committed to paradise.

Had she been dreaming, to be in love with him? Oh, she wished so much she had never been. She *wished* she had never given herself away. To him! – given herself away to him! – and so abjectly. Hung upon his words and his motions, and looked up to him as if he were Caesar. So he had seemed to her: like a mute Caesar. Like Germanicus. Like – she did not know what.

How had it all happened? What had taken her in? Was it just his good looks? No, not really. Because they were the kind of staring good looks she didn't really care for. He must have had charm. He must have charm. Yes, he *had* charm. When it worked.

His charm had not worked on her now for some time – never since that evening after his wife's arrival. Since then he had seemed to her – rather awful. Rather awful – stupid – an ass – a limited, rather vulgar person. That was what he seemed to her when his charm wouldn't work. A limited, rather inferior person. And in a world of *Schiebers* and profiteers and vulgar, pretentious persons, this was the worst thing possible. A limited, inferior, slightly pretentious individual! The husband of the little lady! And oh heaven, she was so deeply implicated with him! He had not, however, spoken with her in private since his wife's arrival. Probably he would never speak with her in private again. She hoped to heaven, never again. The awful thing was the past, that which had been between him and her. She shuddered when she thought of it. The husband of the little lady!

But surely there was something to account for it! Charm, just charm. He had a charm. And then, oh, heaven, when the charm left off working! It had left off so completely at this moment, in Hannele's case, that her very mouth tasted salt. What *did* it all amount to?

What was his charm, after all? How could it have affected her? She began to think of him again, at his best: his presence, when they were alone high up in that big, lonely attic near the stars. His room! – the big whitewashed walls, the first scent of tobacco, the silence, the sense of the stars being near, the telescopes, the cactus with fine scarlet flowers: and above all, the strange, remote, insidious silence of his presence, that was so congenial to her also. The curious way he had of turning his head to listen – to listen to what? – as if he heard something in the stars. The strange look, like destiny, in his wide-open, almost staring black eyes. The beautiful lines of his brow, that seemed always to have a certain cloud on it. The slow elegance of his straight, beautiful legs as he walked, and the exquisiteness of his dark, slender chest! Ah, she could feel the charm mounting over her again. She could feel the snake biting her heart. She could feel the arrows of desire rankling.

But then – and she turned from her thoughts back to this last little tea-party in the Vier Jahreszeiten. She thought of his voice: 'Yes, dear. Certainly. Certainly I will.' And she thought of the stupid, inferior look on his face. And the something of a servant-like way in which he went out to do his wife's bidding.

And then the charm was gone again, as the glow of sunset goes off a burning city and leaves it a sordid industrial hole. So much for charm!

So much for charm. She had better have stuck to her own sort of men. Martin, for instance, who was a gentleman and a daring soldier, and a queer soul and pleasant to talk to. Only he hadn't any *magic*. Magic? The very word made her writhe. Magic? Swindle. Swindle, that was all it amounted to. Magic!

And yet – let us not be too hasty. If the magic had *really* been there, on those evenings in that great lofty attic. Had it? Yes. Yes, she was bound to admit it. There had been magic. If there had been magic in his presence and in his contact, the husband of the little lady – But the distaste was in her mouth again.

So she started afresh, trying to keep a tight hold on the tail of that all-too-evanescent magic of his. Dear, it slipped so quickly into disillusion. Nevertheless. If it had existed it did exist. And if it did exist, it was worth having. You could call it an illusion if you liked. But an illusion which is a real experience is worth having. Perhaps this disillusion was a greater illusion than the illusion itself. Perhaps all this disillusion of the little lady and the husband of the little lady was falser than the illusion and magic of those few evenings. Perhaps the long disillusion of life was falser than the brief moments of real illusion. After all – the delicate darkness of his breast, the mystery that seemed to come with him as he trod slowly across the floor of his room, after changing his tunic – Nay, nay, if she could keep the illusion of his charm, she would give all disillusion to the devils. Nay, only let her be under the spell of his charm. Only let the spell be upon her. It was all she yearned for. And the thing she had to fight was the vulgarity of disillusion. The vulgarity of the little lady, the vulgarity of the husband of the little lady, the vulgarity of his insincerity, his 'Yes, dear. Certainly! Certainly!' – this was what she had to fight. He *was* vulgar and horrible, then. But also, the queer figure that sat alone on the roof watching the stars! The wonderful red flower of the cactus. The mystery that advanced with him as he came across the room after changing his tunic. The glamour and sadness of him, his silence, as he stooped unfastening his boots. And the strange gargoyle smile, fixed, when he caressed her with his hand under the chin! Life is all a choice. And if she chose the glamour, the magic, the charm, the illusion, the spell! Better death than that other, the husband of the little lady. When all was said and done, was he as much the husband of the little lady as he was that queer, delicate-breasted Caesar of her own knowledge? Which was he?

No, she was *not* going to send her the doll. The little lady should never have the doll.

What a doll she would make herself! Heavens, what a wizened jewel!

7

Captain Hepburn still called occasionally at the house for his post. The maid always put his letters in a certain place in the hall, so that he should not have to climb the stairs.

Among his letters – that is to say, along with another letter, for his correspondence was very meagre – he one day found an envelope with a crest. Inside this envelope two letters.

DEAR CAPTAIN HEPBURN – I had the enclosed letter from Mrs Hepburn. I don't intend her to have the doll which is your portrait, so I shall not answer this note. Also I don't see why she should try to turn us out of the town. She talked to me after tea that day, and it seems she believes that Mitchka is your lover. I didn't say anything at all – except that it wasn't true. But she needn't be afraid of me. I don't want you to trouble yourself. But you may as well *know* how things are.

JOHANNA Z. R.

The other letter was on his wife's well-known heavy paper, and in her well-known large, 'aristocratic' hand.

MY DEAR COUNTESS – I wonder if there has been some mistake, or some misunderstanding. Four days ago you said you would send round that *doll* we spoke of, but I have seen no sign of it yet. I thought of calling at the studio, but did not wish to disturb the Baroness. I should be very much obliged if you could send the doll at once, as I do not feel easy while it is out of my possession. You may rely on having a cheque by return.

Our old family friend, Major-General Barlow, called on me yesterday, and we had a most interesting conversation on our Tommies, and the protection of their morals here. It seems we have full power to send away any person or persons deemed undesirable, with twenty-four hours' notice to leave. But of course all this is done as quietly and with the intention of causing as little scandal as possible.

Please let me have the doll by tomorrow, and perhaps some hint as to your future intentions.

With very best wishes from one who only seeks to be your friend. Yours very sincerely,

EVANGELINE HEPBURN

8

And then a dreadful thing happened: really a very dreadful thing. Hannele read of it in the evening newspaper of the town – the *Abendblatt*. Mitchka came rushing up with the paper at ten o'clock at night, just when Hannele was going to bed.

Mrs Hepburn had fallen out of her bedroom window, from the third floor of the hotel, down on to the pavement below, and was killed. She was dressing for dinner. And apparently she had in the morning washed a certain little camisole, and put it on the window-sill to dry. She must have stood on a chair, reaching for it when she fell out of the window. Her husband, who was in the dressing-room, heard a queer little noise, a sort of choking cry, and came into her room to see what it was. And she wasn't there. The window was open, and the chair by the window. He looked round, and thought she had left the room for a moment, so returned to his shaving. He was half-shaved when one of the maids rushed in When he looked out of the window down into the street he fainted, and would have fallen too if the maid had not pulled him in in time.

9

The very next day the captain came back to his attic. Hannele did not know, until quite late at night when he tapped on her door. She knew his soft tap immediately.

'Won't you come over for a chat?' he said.

She paused for some moments before she answered. And then perhaps surprise made her agree: surprise and curiosity.

'Yes, in a minute,' she said, closing her door in his face.

She found him sitting quite still, not even smoking, in his quiet attic. He did not rise, but just glanced round with a faint smile. And she thought his face seemed different, more flexible. But in the half-light she could not tell. She sat at some little distance from him.

'I suppose you've heard,' he said.

'Yes.'

After a long pause, he resumed: 'Yes. It seems an impossible thing to have happened. Yet it *has* happened.'

Hannele's ears were sharp. But strain them as she might, she could not catch the meaning of his voice.

'A terrible thing. A *very* terrible thing,' she said.

'Yes.'

'Do you think she fell quite accidentally?' she said.

'Must have done. The maid was in just a minute before, and she seemed as happy as possible. I suppose reaching over that broad window-ledge, her brain must suddenly have turned. I can't imagine why she didn't call me. She could never bear even to look out of a high window. Turned her ill instantly if she saw a space below her. She used to say she couldn't really look at the moon, it made her feel as if she would fall down a dreadful height. She never dared to more than glance at it. She always had the feeling, I suppose, of the awful space beneath her, if she were on the moon.'

Hannele was not listening to his words, but to his voice. There was something a little automatic in what he said. But then that is always so when people have had a shock.

'It must have been terrible for you too,' she said.

'Ah, yes. At the time it was awful. Awful. I felt the smash right inside me, you know.'

'Awful!' she repeated.

'But now,' he said, 'I feel very strangely happy about it. I feel happy about it. I feel happy for her sake, if you can understand that. I feel she has got out of some great tension. I feel she's free now for the first time in her life. She was a gentle soul, and an original soul, but she was like a fairy who is condemned to live in houses and sit on furniture and all that, don't you know. It was never her nature.'

'No?' said Hannele, herself sitting in blank amazement.

'I always felt she was born in the wrong period – or on the wrong planet. Like some sort of delicate creature you take out of a tropical forest the moment it is born, and from the first moment teach it to perform tricks. You know what I mean. All her life she performed the tricks of life, clever little monkey she was at it too. Beat me into fits. But her own poor little soul, a sort of fairy soul, those queer Irish creatures, was cooped up inside her all her life, tombed in. There it was, tombed in, while she went through all the tricks of life that you have to go through if you are born today.'

'But,' stammered Hannele, 'what would she have done if she *had* been free?'

'Why, don't you see, there *is* nothing for her to do in the world today. Take her language, for instance. She never ought to have been speaking English. I don't know what language she ought to have spoken. Because if you take the Irish language, they only learn it back from English. They think in English, and just put Irish words on top. But English was never her language. It bubbled off her lips, so to speak. And she had no other language. Like a starling that you've made talk from the very beginning, and so it can only shout these talking noises, don't you know. It can't whistle its own whistling to save its life. Couldn't do it. It's lost it. All its own natural mode of expressing itself has collapsed, and it can only be artificial.'

There was a long pause.

'Would she have been wonderful, then, if she had been able to talk in some unknown language?' said Hannele jealously.

'I don't say she would have been wonderful. As a matter of fact, we think a talking starling is much more wonderful than an ordinary starling. I don't myself, but most people do. And she would have been a sort of starling. And she would have had her own language and her own ways. As it was, poor thing, she was always arranging herself and fluttering and chattering inside a cage. And she never knew she was in the cage, any more than we know we are inside our own skins.'

'But,' said Hannele, with a touch of mockery, 'how do you know you haven't made it all up – just to console yourself?'

'Oh, I've thought it long ago,' he said.

'Still,' she blurted, 'you may have invented it all – as a sort of consolation for – for – for your life.'

'Yes, I may,' he said. 'But I don't think so. It was her eyes. Did you ever notice her eyes? I often used to catch her eyes. And she'd be talking away, all the language bubbling off her lips. And her eyes were so clear and bright and different. Like a child's that is listening to something, and is going to be frightened. She was always listening – and waiting – for something else. I tell you what, she was exactly like that fairy in the Scotch song, who is in love with a mortal, and sits by the high road in terror waiting for him to come, and hearing the plovers and the curlews. Only nowadays motor lorries go along the moor roads and the poor thing is struck unconscious, and carried into our world in a state of unconsciousness, and when she comes round, she tries to talk our language and behave as we behave, and she can't remember anything else, so she goes on and on, till she falls with a crash, back to her own world.'

Hannele was silent, and so was he.

'You loved her then?' she said at length.

'Yes. But in this way. When I was a boy I caught a bird, a blackcap, and I put it in a cage. And I loved that bird. I don't know why, but I loved it. I simply loved that bird. All the gorse, and the heather, and the rock, and the hot smell of yellow gorse blossom, and the sky that seemed to have no end to it, when I was a boy, everything that I almost was *mad* with, as boys are, seemed to me to be in that little, fluttering blackcap. And it would peck its seed as if it didn't quite know what else to do; and look round about, and begin to sing. But in quite a few days it turned its head aside and died. Yes, it died. I never had the feeling again that I got from that blackcap when I was a boy – not until I saw her. And then I felt it all again. I felt it all again. And it was the same feeling. I knew, quite soon I knew, that she would die. She would peck her seed and look round in the cage just the same. But she would die in the end. Only it would last much longer. But she would die in the cage, like the blackcap.'

'But she loved the cage. She loved her clothes and her jewels. She must have loved her house and her furniture and all that with a perfect frenzy.'

'She did. She did. But like a child with playthings. Only they were big, marvellous playthings to her. Oh yes, she was never away from them. She never forgot her things – her trinkets and her furs and her furniture. She never got away from them for a minute. And everything in her mind was mixed up with them.'

'Dreadful!' said Hannele.

'Yes, it was dreadful,' he answered.

'Dreadful,' repeated Hannele.

'Yes, quite. Quite! And it got worse. And her way of talking got worse. As if it bubbled off her lips. But her eyes never lost their brightness, they never lost that faery look. Only I used to see fear in them. Fear of everything – even all the things she surrounded herself with. Just like my blackcap used to look out of his cage – so bright and sharp, and yet as if he didn't know that it was just the cage that was between him and the outside. He thought it was inside himself, the barrier. He thought it was part of his own nature to be shut in. And she thought it was part of her own nature. And so they both died.'

'What I can't see,' said Hannele, 'is what she would have done outside her cage. What other life could she have, except her *bibelots* and her furniture, and her talk?'

'Why, none. There *is* no life outside for human beings.'

'Then there's nothing,' said Hannele.

'That's true. In a great measure, there's nothing.'

'Thank you,' said Hannele.

There was a long pause.

'And perhaps I was to blame. Perhaps I ought to have made some sort of a move. But I didn't know what to do. For my life, I didn't know what to do, except try to make her happy. She had enough money – and I didn't think it mattered if she shared it with me. I always had a garden – and the astronomy. It's been an immense relief to me watching the moon. It's been wonderful. Instead of looking inside the cage, as I did at my bird, or at her – I look right out – into freedom – into freedom.'

'The moon, you mean?' said Hannele.

'Yes, the moon.'

'And that's your freedom?'

'That's where I've found the greatest sense of freedom,' he said.

'Well, I'm not going to be jealous of the moon,' said Hannele at length.

'Why should you? It's not a thing to be jealous of.'

In a little while, she bade him good-night and left him.

10

The chief thing that the captain knew, at this juncture, was that a hatchet had gone through the ligatures and veins that connected him with the people of his affection, and that he was left with the bleeding ends of all his vital human relationships. Why it should be so he did not know. But then one never can know the whys and the wherefores of one's passional changes.

He only knew that it was so. The emotional flow between him and all the people he knew and cared for was broken, and for the time being he was conscious only of the cleavage. The cleavage that had occurred between him and his fellow-men, the cleft that was now between him and them. It was not the fault of anybody or anything. He could neither reproach himself nor them. What had happened had been preparing for a long time. Now suddenly the cleavage. There had been a long, slow weaning away: and now this sudden silent rupture.

What it amounted to principally was that he did not want even to see Hannele. He did not want to think of her even. But neither did he want to see anybody else, or to think of anybody else. He shrank with a feeling almost of disgust from his friends and acquaintances, and their expressions of sympathy. It affected him with instantaneous disgust when anybody wanted to share emotions with him. He did not want to share emotions or feelings of any sort. He wanted to be by himself, essentially, even if he was moving about among other people.

So he went to England to settle his own affairs, and out of duty to see his children. He wished his children all the well in the world – everything except any emotional connection with himself. He decided to take his girl away from the convent at once, and to put her into a jolly English school. His boy was all right where he was.

The captain had now an income sufficient to give him his independence, but not sufficient to keep up his wife's house. So he prepared to sell the house and most of the things in it. He decided also to leave the army as soon as he could be free. And he thought he would wander about for a time, till he came upon something he wanted.

So the winter passed, without his going back to Germany. He was free of the army. He drifted along, settling his affairs. They were of no very great importance. And all the time he never wrote once to Hannele. He could not get over his disgust that people insisted on his sharing their emotions. He could not bear their emotions, neither their activities. Other people might have all the emotions and feelings and earnestness and busy activities they liked. Quite nice even that they had such a multifarious commotion for themselves. But the moment they approached him to spread their feelings over him or to entangle him in their activities a helpless disgust came up in him, and until he could get away he felt sick, even physically.

This was no state of mind for a lover. He could not even think of Hannele. Anybody else he felt he need not think about. He was deeply, profoundly thankful that his wife was dead. It was an end of pity now; because, poor thing, she had escaped and gone her own way into the void, like a flown bird.

I I

Nevertheless, a man hasn't finished his life at forty. He may, however, have finished one great phase of his life.

And Alexander Hepburn was not the man to live alone. All our troubles, says somebody wise, come upon us because we cannot be alone. And that is all very well. We must all be *able* to be alone, otherwise we are just victims. But when we *are* able to be alone, then we realise that the only thing to do is to start a new relationship with another – or even the same – human being. That people should all be stuck up apart, like so many telegraph-poles, is nonsense.

So with our dear captain. He had his convulsion into a sort of telegraph-pole isolation: which was absolutely necessary for him. But then he began to bud with a new yearning for – for what? For love?

It was a question he kept nicely putting to himself. And really, the nice young girls of eighteen or twenty attracted him very much: so fresh, so impulsive, and looking up to him as if he were something wonderful. If only he could have married two or three of them, instead of just one!

Love! When a man has no particular ambition, his mind turns back perpetually, as a needle towards the pole. That tiresome word Love. It means so many things. It meant the feeling he had had for his wife. He had loved her. But he shuddered at the thought of having to go through such love again. It meant also the feeling he had for the awfully nice young things he met here and there: fresh, impulsive girls ready to give all their hearts away. Oh yes, he could fall in love with half a dozen of them. But he knew he'd better not.

At last he wrote to Hannele: and got no answer. So he wrote to Mitchka and still got no answer. So he wrote for information – and there was none forthcoming, except that the two women had gone to Munich.

For the time being he left it at that. To him, Hannele did not exactly represent rosy love. Rather a hard destiny. He did not adore her. He did not feel one bit of adoration for her. As a matter of fact, not all the beauties and virtues of woman put together with all the gold in the Indies would have tempted him into the business of adoration any more. He had gone on his knees once, vowing with faltering tones to try and make the adored one happy. And now – never again. Never.

The temptation this time was to be adored. One of those fresh young things would have adored him as if he were a god. And there was something *very* alluring about the thought. Very – very alluring. To be god-almighty in your own house, with a lovely young thing adoring you, and you giving off beams of bright effulgence like a Gloria! Who wouldn't be tempted: at the age of forty? And this was why he dallied.

But in the end he suddenly took the train to Munich. And when he got there he found the town beastly uncomfortable, the Bavarians rude and disagreeable, and no sign of the missing females, not even in the Café Stéphanie. He wandered round and round.

And then one day, oh heaven, he saw his doll in a shop window: a little art shop. He stood and stared quite spellbound.

'Well, if that isn't the devil,' he said. 'Seeing yourself in a shop window!'

He was so disgusted that he would not go into the shop.

Then, every day for a week did he walk down that little street and look at himself in the shop window. Yes, there he stood, with one hand in his pocket. And the figure had one hand in its pocket. There he stood, with his cap pulled rather low over his brow. And the figure had its cap pulled low over its brow. But, thank goodness, his own cap now was a civilian tweed. But there he stood, his head rather forward, gazing with fixed dark eyes. And himself in little, that wretched figure, stood there with its head rather forward, staring with fixed dark eyes. It was such a real little *man* that it fairly staggered him. The oftener he saw it, the more it staggered him. And the more he hated it. Yet it fascinated him, and he came again to look.

And it was always there. A lonely little individual lounging there with one hand in its pocket, and nothing to do, among the bric-à-brac and the *bibelots*. Poor devil, stuck so incongruously in the world. And yet losing none of his masculinity.

A male little devil, for all his forlornness. But such an air of isolation, or not-belonging. Yet taut and male, in his tartan trews. And what a situation to be in! –

lounging with his back against a little Japanese lacquer cabinet, with a few old pots on his right hand and a tiresome brass ink-tray on his left, while pieces of not-very-nice filet lace hung their length up and down the background. Poor little devil: it was like a deliberate satire.

And then one day it was gone. There was the cabinet and the filet lace and the tiresome inkstand tray: and the little gentleman wasn't there. The captain at once walked into the shop.

'Have you sold that doll? – that unknown soldier?' he added, without knowing quite what he was saying.

The doll was sold.

'Do you know who bought it?'

The girl looked at him very coldly, and did not know.

'I once knew the lady who made it. In fact, the doll was *me*,' he said.

The girl now looked at him with sudden interest.

'Don't you think it was like me?' he said.

'Perhaps' – she began to smile.

'It was me. And the lady who made it was a friend of mine. Do you know her name?'

'Yes.'

'Gräfin zu Rassentlow,' he cried, his eyes shining.

'Oh yes. But her dolls are famous.'

'Do you know where she is? Is she in Munich?'

'That I don't know.'

'Could you find out?'

'I don't know. I can ask.'

'Or the Baroness von Prielau-Carolath.'

'The Baroness is dead.'

'Dead!'

'She was shot in a riot in Salzburg. They say a lover – '

'How do you know?'

'From the newspapers.'

'Dead! Is it possible. Poor Hannele.'

There was a pause.

'Well,' he said, 'if you would enquire about the address – I'll call again.'

Then he turned back from the door.

'By the way, do you mind telling me how much you sold the doll for?'

The girl hesitated. She was by no means anxious to give away any of her trade details. But at length she answered reluctantly: 'Five hundred marks.'

'So cheap,' he said. 'Good-day. Then I will call again.'

12

Then again he got a trace. It was in the Chit-Chat column of the *Münchener Neue Zeitung*: under Studio-Comments. 'Theodor Worpswede's latest picture is a still-life, containing an entertaining group of a doll, two sunflowers in a glass jar, and a poached egg on toast. The contrast between the three substances is highly diverting and instructive, and this is perhaps one of the most interesting of Worpswede's works. The doll, by the way, is one of the creations of our fertile Countess Hannele. It is the figure of an English, or rather Scottish, officer in the famous tartan trousers which, clinging closely to the legs of the lively Gaul, so shocked the eminent Julius Caesar and his cohorts. We, of course, are no longer shocked, but full of admiration for the creative genius of our dear Countess. The doll itself is a masterpiece, and has begotten another masterpiece in Theodor Worpswede's Still-life. We have heard, by the way, a rumour of Countess zu Rassentlow's engagement. Apparently the Herr Regierungsrat von Poldi, of that most beautiful of summer resorts, Kaprun, in the Tyrol, is the fortunate man –'

13

The captain bought the Still-life. This new version of himself along with the poached egg and the sunflowers was rather frightening. So he packed up for Austria, for Kaprun, with his picture, and had a fight to get the beastly thing out of Germany, and another fight to get it into Austria. Fatigued and furious he arrived in Salzburg, seeing no beauty in anything. Next day he was in Kaprun.

It was an elegant and fashionable watering-place before the war: a lovely little lake in the midst of the Alps, an old Tyrolese town on the waterside, green slopes sheering up opposite, and away beyond a glacier. It was still crowded and still elegant. But alas, with a broken, bankrupt, desperate elegance, and almost empty shops.

The captain felt rather dazed. He found himself in an hotel full of Jews of the wrong, rich sort, and wondered what next. The place was beautiful, but the life wasn't.

14

The Herr Regierungsrat was not at first sight prepossessing. He was approaching fifty, and had gone stout and rather loose, as so many men of his class and race do. Then he wore one of those dreadful full-bottom coats, a kind of poor relation to our full-skirted frock-coat: it would best be described as a family coat. It flapped about him as he walked, and he looked at first glance lower middle class.

But he wasn't. Of course, being in office in the collapsed Austria, he was a republican. But by nature he was a monarchist, nay, an imperialist, as every true Austrian is. And he was a true Austrian. And as such he was much finer and subtler than he looked. As one got used to him, his rather fat face, with its fine nose and slightly bitter, pursed mouth, came to have a resemblance to the busts of some of the late Roman emperors. And as one was with him, one came gradually to realise that out of all his baggy bourgeois appearance came something of a *grand geste*. He could not help it. There was something sweeping and careless about his soul: big, rather assertive, and ill-bred-seeming; but, in fact, not ill-bred at all, only a little bitter and a good deal indifferent to his surroundings. He looked at first sight so common and *parvenu*. And then one had to realise that he was a member of a big, old empire, fallen into a sort of epicureanism, and a little bitter. There was no littleness, no meanness, and no real coarseness. But he was a great talker, and relentless towards his audience.

Hannele was attracted to him by his talk. He began as soon as dinner appeared: and he went on, carrying the decanter and the wine glass with him out on to the balcony of the villa, over the lake, on and on until midnight. The summer night was still and warm: the lake lay deep and full, and the old town twinkled away across. There was the faintest tang of snow in the air, from the great glacier-peaks that were hidden in the night opposite. Sometimes a boat with a lantern twanged a guitar. The clematis flowers were quite black, like leaves, dangling from the terrace.

It was so beautiful, there in the very heart of the Tyrol. The hotels glittered with lights: electric light was still cheap. There seemed a fullness and a loveliness in the night. And yet for some reason it was all terrible and devastating: the life-spirit seemed to be squirming, bleeding all the time.

And on and on talked the Herr Regierungsrat, with all the witty volubility of the more versatile Austrian. He was really very witty, very human, and with a touch of salty cynicism that reminded one of a real old Roman of the Empire. That subtle stoicism, that unsentimental epicureanism, that kind of reckless hopelessness, of course, fascinated the women. And particularly Hannele. He talked on and on – about his work before the war, when he held an important post and was one of the governing class – then about the war – then about the hopelessness of the present: and in it all there seemed a bigness, a carelessness based on indifference and hopelessness that laughed at its very self. The real old Austria had always fascinated Hannele. As represented in the witty, bitter-indifferent Herr Regierungsrat it carried her away.

And he, of course, turned instinctively to her, talking in his rapid, ceaseless fashion, with a laugh and a pause to drink and a new start taken. She liked the sound of his Austrian speech: its racy carelessness, its salty indifference to standards of correctness. Oh yes, here was the *grand geste* still lingering.

He turned his large breast towards her, and made a quick gesture with his fat, well-shapen hand, blurted out another subtle, rough-seeming romance, pursed his mouth, and emptied his glass once more. Then he looked at his half-forgotten cigar and started again.

There was something almost boyish and impulsive about him: the way he turned to her, and the odd way he seemed to open his big breast to her. And again he seemed almost eternal, sitting there in his chair with knees planted apart. It was as if he would never rise again, but would remain sitting for ever, and talking. He seemed as if he had no legs, save to sit with. As if to stand on his feet and walk would not be natural to him.

Yet he rose at last, and kissed her hand with the grand gesture that France or Germany have never acquired: carelessness, profound indifference to other people's standards, and then such a sudden stillness, as he bent and kissed her hand. Of course she felt a queen in exile.

And perhaps it is more dangerous to feel yourself a queen in exile than a queen in situ. She fell in love with him, with this large, stout, loose widower of fifty, with two children. He had no money except some Austrian money that was worth nothing outside Austria. He could not even go to Germany. There he was, fixed in this hollow in the middle of the Tyrol.

But he had an ambition still, old Roman of the decadence that he was. He had year by year and without making any fuss collected the material for a very minute and thorough history of his own district: the Chiemgau and the Pinzgau. Hannele found that his fund of information on this subject was inexhaustible, and his intelligence was so delicate, so human, and his scope seemed so wide, that she felt a touch of reverence for him. He wanted to write this history. And she wanted to help him.

For, of course, as things were he would never write it. He was Regierungsrat: that is, he was the petty local governor of his town and immediate district. The Amthaus was a great old building, and there young ladies in high heels flirted among masses of papers with bare-kneed young gentlemen in Tyrolese costume, and occasionally they parted to take a pleasant, interesting attitude and write a word or two, after which they fluttered together for a little more interesting diversion. It was extraordinary how many finely built, handsome young people of an age fitted for nothing but love-affairs ran the governmental business of this department. And the Herr Regierungsrat sailed in and out of the big, old room, his wide coat flying like wings and making the papers flutter, his rather wine-reddened, old-Roman face smiling with its bitter look. And of course it was a witticism he uttered first, even if Hungary was invading the frontier or cholera was in Vienna.

When he was on his legs, he walked nimbly, briskly, and his coat-bottoms always flew. So he waved through the town, greeting somebody at every few strides and grinning, and yet with a certain haughty reserve. Oh yes, there was a certain salty hauteur about him which made the people trust him. And he spoke the vernacular so racily.

Hannele felt she would like to marry him. She would like to be near him. She would like him to write his history. She would like him to make her feel a queen in exile. No one had ever quite kissed her hand as he kissed it: with that sudden stillness and strange, chivalric abandon of himself. How he would abandon himself to her! – terribly – wonderfully – perhaps a little horribly. His wife, whom he had married late, had died after seven years of marriage. Hannele could understand that too. One or the other must die.

She became engaged. But something made her hesitate before marriage. Being in Austria was like being on a wrecked ship that *must* sink after a certain short length of time. And marrying the Herr Regierungsrat was like marrying the doomed captain of the doomed ship. The sense of fatality was part of the attraction.

And yet she hesitated. The summer weeks passed. The strangers flooded in and crowded the town, and ate up the food like locusts. People no longer counted the paper money, they weighed it by the kilogram. Peasants stored it in a corner of the meal-bin, and mice came and chewed holes in it. Nobody knew where the next lot of food was going to come from: yet it always came. And the lake teemed with bathers. When the captain arrived he looked with amazement on the crowds of strapping, powerful fellows who bathed all day long, magnificent blond flesh of men and women. No wonder the old Romans stood in astonishment before the huge blond limbs of the savage Germana.

Well, the life was like a madness. The hotels charged fifteen hundred kronen a day: the women, old and young, paraded in the peasant costume, in flowery cotton dresses with gaudy, expensive silk aprons: the men wore the Tyrolese costume, bare knees and little short jackets. And for the men, the correct thing was to have the leathern hose and the blue linen jacket as old as possible. If you had a hole in your leathern seat, so much the better.

Everything so physical. Such magnificent naked limbs and naked bodies, and in the streets, in the hotels, everywhere, bare, white arms of women and bare, brown, powerful knees and thighs of men. The sense of flesh everywhere, and the endless ache of flesh. Even in the peasants who rowed across the lake, standing and rowing with a slow, heavy, gondolier motion at the one curved oar, there was the same endless ache of physical yearning.

15

It was August when Alexander met Hannele. She was walking under a chintz parasol, wearing a dress of blue cotton with little red roses, and a red silk apron. She had no hat, her arms were bare and soft, and she had white stockings under her short dress. The Herr Regierungsrat was at her side, large, nimble, and laughing with a new witticism.

Alexander, in a light summer suit and Panama hat, was just coming out of the bank, shoving twenty thousand kronen into his pocket. He saw her coming across from the Amtsgericht, with the Herr Regierungsrat at her side, across the space of sunshine. She was laughing, and did not notice him.

She did not notice till he had taken off his hat and was saluting her. Then what she saw was the black, smooth, shining head, and she went pale. His black, smooth, close head – and all the blue Austrian day seemed to shrivel before her eyes.

'How do you do, Countess! I hoped I should meet you.'

She heard his slow, sad-clanging, straying voice again, and she pressed her hand with the umbrella stick against her breast. She had forgotten it – forgotten his peculiar, slow voice. And now it seemed like a noise that sounds in the silence of night. Ah, how difficult it was, that suddenly the world could split under her eyes, and show this darkness inside. She wished he had not come.

She presented him to the Herr Regierungsrat, who was stiff and cold. She asked where the captain was staying. And then, not knowing what else to say, she said: 'Won't you come to tea?'

She was staying in a villa across the lake. Yes, he would come to tea.

He went. He hired a boat and a man to row him across. It was not far. There stood the villa, with its brown balconies one above the other, the bright red geraniums and white geraniums twinkling all round, the trees of purple clematis tumbling at one corner. All the green window doors were open: but nobody about. In the little garden by the water's edge the rose trees were tall and lank, drawn up by the dark green trees of the background. A white table with chairs and garden seats stood under the shadow of a big willow tree, and a hammock with cushions swung just behind. But no one in sight. There was a little landing bridge on to the garden: and a fairly large boat-house at the garden end.

The captain was not sure that the boat-house belonged to the villa. Voices were shouting and laughing from the water's surface, bathers swimming. A tall, naked youth with a little red cap on his head and a tiny red loincloth round his slender young hips was standing on the steps of the boat-house calling to the three women who were swimming near. The dark-haired woman with the white cap swam up to the steps and caught the boy by the ankle. He cried and laughed and remonstrated, and poked her in the breast with his foot.

'*Nein, nein, Hardu!*' she cried as he tickled her with his toe. '*Hardu! Hardu! Hör' auf!* – Leave off!' – and she fell with a crash back into the water. The youth laughed a loud, deep laugh of a lad whose voice is newly broken.

'*Was macht er dann?*' cried a voice from the waters. 'What is he doing?' It was a dark-skinned girl swimming swiftly, her big dark eyes watching amused from the water surface.

'*Jetzt Hardu hör' auf. Nein. Jetzt ruhig!* Now leave off! Now be quiet.' And the dark-skinned woman was climbing out in the sunshine on to the pale, raw-wood steps of the boat-house, the water glistening on her dark-blue, stockinette, soft-moulded back and loins: while the boy, with his foot stretched out, was trying to push her back into the water. She clambered out, however, and sat on the steps in the sun, panting slightly. She was dark and attractive-looking, with a mature beautiful figure, and handsome, strong woman's legs.

In the garden appeared a black-and-white maidservant with a tray.

'*Kaffee, gnädige Frau!*'

The voice came so distinct over the water.

'*Hannele! Hannele! Kaffee!*' called the woman on the steps of the bathing-house.

'*Tante Hannele! Kaffee!*' called the dark-eyed girl, turning round in the water, then swimming for home.

'*Kaffee! Kaffee!*' roared the youth, in anticipation.

'*Ja–a! Ich kom–m,*' sang Hannele's voice from the water.

The dark-eyed girl, her hair tied up in a silk bandana, had reached the steps and was climbing out, a slim young fish in her close dark suit. The three stood clustered on the steps, the elder woman with one arm over the naked shoulders of the youth, the other arm over the shoulders of the girl. And all in chorus sang:

'*Hannele! Hannele! Hannele! Wir warten auf dich.*'

The boatman had left off rowing, and the boat was drifting slowly in. The family became quiet, because of the intrusion. The attractive-looking woman turned and picked up her blue bathrobe, of a mid-blue colour that became her. She swung it round her as if it were an opera cloak. The youth stared at the boat.

The captain was watching Hannele. With a white kerchief tied round her silky, brownish hair, she was swimming home. He saw her white shoulders and her white, wavering legs below in the clear water. Round the boat fishes were suddenly jumping.

The three on the steps beyond stood silent, watching the intruding boat with resentment. The boatman twisted his head round and watched them. The captain, who was facing them, watched Hannele. She swam slowly and easily up, caught the rail of the steps, and stooping forward, climbed slowly out of the water. Her legs were large and flashing white and looked rich, the rich, white thighs with the blue veins behind, and the full, rich softness of her sloping loins.

'*Ach! Schön! 'S war schön! Das Wasser ist gut,*' her voice was heard, half singing as she took her breath. 'It was lovely.'

'*Heiss,*' said the woman above. '*Zu warm.* Too warm.'

The youth made way for Hannele, who drew herself erect at the top of the steps, looking round, panting a little and putting up her hands to the knot of her kerchief on her head. Her legs were magnificent and white.

'*Kuck de Leut, die da bleiben,*' said the woman in the blue wrap, in a low voice. 'Look at the people stopping there.'

'*Ja!*' said Hannele negligently. Then she looked. She started as if in fear, looked round, as if to run away, looked back again, and met the eyes of the captain, who took off his hat.

She cried in a loud, frightened voice: 'Oh, but – I thought it was *tomorrow*!'

'No – today,' came the quiet voice of the captain over the water.

'*Today!* Are you sure?' she cried, calling to the boat.

'Quite sure. But we'll make it tomorrow if you like,' he said.

'Today! Today!' she repeated in bewilderment. 'No! Wait a minute.' And she ran into the boat-house.

'*Was ist es?*' asked the dark woman, following her. 'What is it?'

'A friend – a visitor – Captain Hepburn,' came Hannele's voice.

The boatman now rowed slowly to the landing-stage. The dark woman, huddled in her blue wrap as in an opera-cloak, walked proudly and unconcernedly across the background of the garden and up the steps to the first balcony. Hannele, her feet slip-slopping in loose slippers, clutching an old yellow wrap round her, came to the landing-stage and shook hands.

'I am so sorry. It is so stupid of me. I was sure it was tomorrow,' she said.

'No, it was today. But I wish for your sake it had been tomorrow,' he replied.

'No. No. It doesn't matter. You won't mind waiting a minute, will you? You mustn't be angry with me for being so stupid.'

So she went away, the heelless slippers flipping up to her naked heels. Then the big-eyed, dusky girl stole into the house: and then the naked youth, who went with *sang-froid*. He would make a fine, handsome man: and he knew it.

16

Hepburn and Hannele were to make a small excursion to the glacier which stood there always in sight, coldly grinning in the sky. The weather had been very hot, but this morning there were loose clouds in the sky. The captain rowed over the lake soon after dawn. Hannele stepped into the little craft, and they pulled back to the town. There was a wind ruffling the water, so that the boat leaped and chuckled. The glacier, in a recess among the folded mountains, looked cold and angry. But morning was very sweet in the sky, and blowing very sweet with a faint scent of the second hay from the low lands at the head of the lake. Beyond stood naked grey rock like a wall of mountains, pure rock, with faint, thin slashes of snow. Yesterday it had rained on the lake. The sun was going to appear from behind the Breitsteinhorn, the sky with its clouds floating in blue light and yellow radiance was lovely and cheering again. But dark clouds seemed to spout up from the Pinzgau valley. And once across the lake, all was shadow, when the water no longer gave back the sky-morning.

The day was a feast day, a holiday. Already so early three young men from the mountains were bathing near the steps of the Badeanstalt. Handsome, physical fellows, with good limbs rolling and swaying in the early morning water. They seemed to enjoy it too. But to Hepburn it was always as if a dark wing were stretched in the sky, over these mountains, like a doom. And these three young, lusty, naked men swimming and rolling in the shadow.

Hepburn's was the first boat stirring. He made fast in the hotel boat-house, and he and Hannele went into the little town. It was deep in shadow, though the light of the sky, curdled with cloud, was bright overhead. But dark and chill and heavy lay the shadow in the black-and-white town, like a sediment.

The shops were all shut, but peasants from the hills were already strolling about in their holiday dress: the men in their short leather trousers, like football drawers, and bare brown knees and great boots: their little grey jackets faced with green, and their green hats with the proud chamois-brush behind. They seemed to stray about like lost souls, and the proud chamois-brush behind their hats, this proud, cocky, perking-up tail, like a mountain-buck with his tail up, was belied by the lost-soul look of the men, as they loitered about with their hands shoved in the front pockets of their trousers. Some women also were creeping about: peasant women, in the funny little black hats that had thick gold under the brim and long black streamers of ribbon, broad, black, water-wave ribbon starting from a bow under the brim behind and streaming right to the bottom of the skirt. These women, in their thick, dark dresses with tight bodices and massive, heavy, full skirts, and bright or dark aprons, strode about with the heavy stride of the mountain women, the heavy, quick, forward-leaning motion. They were waiting for the town-day to begin.

Hepburn had a knapsack on his back, with food for the day. But bread was wanting. They found the door of the bakery open, and got a loaf: a long, hot loaf of pure white bread, beautifully sweet bread. It cost seventy kronen. To Hepburn it was always a mystery where this exquisite bread came from, in a lost land.

In the little square where the clock stood were bunches of people, and a big motor omnibus, and a motor car that would hold about eight people. Hepburn had paid his seven hundred kronen for the two tickets. Hannele tied up her head in a thin scarf and put on her thick coat. She and Hepburn sat in front by the peaked driver. And at seven o'clock away went the car, swooping out of the town, past the handsome old Tyrolese Schloss, or manor, black-and-white, with its little black spires pricking up, past the station, and under the trees by the lakeside. The road was not good, but they ran at a great speed, out past the end of the lake, where the reeds grew, out into the open valley mouth, where the mountains opened in two clefts. It was cold in the car. Hepburn buttoned himself up to the throat and pulled his hat down on his ears. Hannele's scarf fluttered. She sat without saying anything, erect, her face fine and keen, watching ahead. From the deep Pinzgau Valley came the river roaring and raging, a glacier river of pale, seething ice-water. Over went the car, over the log bridge, darting towards the great slopes opposite. And then a sudden immense turn, a swerve under the height of the mountain-side, and again a darting lurch forward, under the pear trees of the high road, past the big old ruined castle that so magnificently watched the valley mouth, and the foaming river; on, rushing under the huge roofs of the balconied peasant houses of a village, then swinging again to take another valley mouth, there where a little village clustered all black and white on a knoll, with a white church that had a black steeple, and a white castle with black spires, and clustering, ample black-and-white houses of the Tyrol. There is a grandeur even in the peasant houses, with their great wide passage halls where the swallows build, and where one could build a whole English cottage.

So the motor car darted up this new, narrow, wilder, more sinister valley. A herd of almost wild young horses, handsome reddish things, burst around the car, and one great mare with full flanks went crashing up the road ahead, her heels flashing to the car, while her foal whinneyed and screamed from behind.

But no, she could not turn from the road. On and on she crashed, forging ahead, the car behind her. And then at last she did swerve aside, among the thin alder trees by the wild river-bed.

'If it isn't a cow, it's a horse,' said the driver, who was thin and weaselish and silent, with his ear-flaps over his ears.

But the great mare had shaken herself in a wild swerve, and screaming and whinneying was plunging back to her foal. Hannele had been frightened.

The car rushed on, through water-meadows, along a naked, white bit of mountain road. Ahead was a darkness of mountain front and pine trees. To the right was the stony, furious, lion-like river, tawny-coloured here, and the slope up beyond. But the road for the moment was swinging fairly level through the stunned water-meadows of the savage valley. There were gates to open, and Hepburn jumped down to open them, as if he were the footboy. The heavy Jews of the wrong sort, seated behind, of course did not stir.

At a house on a knoll the driver sounded his horn, and out rushed children crying Papa! Papa! – then a woman with a basket. A few brief words from the weaselish man, who smiled with warm, manly blue eyes at his children, then the car leaped forward. The whole bearing of the man was so different when he was looking at his own family. He could not even say thank you when Hepburn opened the gates. He hated and even despised his human cargo of middle-class people. Deep, deep is class hatred, and it begins to swallow all human feeling in its abyss. So, stiff, silent, thin, capable, and neuter towards his fares, sat the little driver with the flaps over his ears, and his thin nose cold.

The car swept round, suddenly, into the trees: and into the ravine. The river shouted at the bottom of a gulf. Bristling pine trees stood around. The air was black and cold and forever sunless. The motor car rushed on, in this blackness under the rock-walls and the fir trees.

Then it suddenly stopped. There was a huge motor omnibus ahead, drab and enormous-looking. Tourists and trippers of last night coming back from the glacier. It stood like a great rock. And the smaller motor car edged past, tilting into the rock gutter under the face of stone.

So, after a while of this valley of the shadow of death, lurching in steep loops upwards, the motor car scrambling wonderfully, struggling past trees and rock upwards, at last they came to the end. It was a huge inn or tourist hotel of brown wood: and here the road ended in a little wide bay surrounded and overhung by trees. Beyond was a garage and a bridge over a roaring river: and always the overhung darkness of trees and the intolerable steep slopes immediately above.

Hannele left her big coat. The sky looked blue above the gloom. They set out across the hollow-sounding bridge, over the everlasting mad rush of ice-water, to the immediate upslope of the path, under dark trees. But a little old man in a sort of sentry-box wanted fifty or sixty kronen: apparently for the upkeep of the road, a sort of toll.

The other tourists were coming – some stopping to have a drink first. The second omnibus had not yet arrived. Hannele and Hepburn were the first two, treading slowly up that dark path, under the trees. The grasses hanging on the rock face were still dewy. There were a few wild raspberries, and a tiny tuft of bilberries with black berries here and there, and a few tufts of unripe cranberries. The many hundreds of tourists who passed up and down did not leave much to pick. Some mountain harebells, like bells of blue water, hung coldly glistening in their darkness. Sometimes the hairy mountain-bell, pale-blue and bristling, stood alone, curving his head right down, stiff and taut. There was an occasional big, moist, lolling daisy.

So the two climbed slowly up the steep ledge of a road. This valley was just a mountain cleft, cleft sheer in the hard, living rock, with black trees like hair flourishing in this secret, naked place of the earth. At the bottom of the open wedge for ever roared the rampant, insatiable water. The sky from above was like a sharp wedge forcing its way into the earth's cleavage, and that eternal ferocious water was like the steel edge of the wedge, the terrible tip biting in into the rocks' intensity. Who could have thought that the soft sky of light, and the soft foam of water could thrust and penetrate into the dark, strong earth? But so it was. Hannele and Hepburn, toiling up the steep little ledge of a road that hung halfway down the gulf, looked back, time after time, back down upon the brown timbers and shingle roofs of the hotel, that now, away below, looked damp and wedged in like boulders. Then back at the next tourists struggling up. Then down at the water, that rushed like a beast of prey. And then, as they rose higher, they looked up also at the livid great sides of rock, livid, bare rock that sloped from the sky ridge in a hideous sheer swerve downwards.

In his heart of hearts Hepburn hated it. He hated it, he loathed it, it seemed almost obscene, this livid, naked slide of rock, unthinkably huge and massive, sliding down to this gulf where bushes grew like hair in the darkness and water roared. Above, there were thin slashes of snow.

So the two climbed slowly on, up the eternal side of that valley, sweating with the exertion. Sometimes the sun, now risen high, shone full on their side of the gulley. Tourists were trickling downhill too: two maidens with bare arms and bare heads and huge boots: men tourists with great knapsacks and edelweiss in their hats: giving *Bergheil* for a greeting. But the captain said Good-day. He refused this *Bergheil* business. People swarming touristy on these horrible mountains made him feel almost sick.

He and Hannele also were not in good company together. There was a sort of silent hostility between them. She hated the effort of climbing; but the high air, the cold in the air, the savage cat-howling sound of the water, those awful flanks of livid rock, all this thrilled and excited her to another sort of savageness. And he, dark, rather slender and feline, with something of the physical suavity of a delicate-footed race, he hated beating his way up the rock, he hated the sound of the water, it frightened him, and the high air hit him in the chest, like a viper.

'Wonderful! Wonderful!' she cried, taking great breaths in her splendid chest.

'Yes. And horrible. Detestable,' he said.

She turned with a flash, and the high strident sound of the mountain in her voice.

'If you don't like it,' she said, rather jeering, 'why ever did you come?'

'I had to try,' he said.

'And if you don't like it,' she said, 'why should you try to spoil it for me?'

'I hate it,' he answered.

They were climbing more into the height, more into the light, into the open, in the full sun. The valley cleft was sinking below them. Opposite was only the sheer, livid slide of the naked rock, tipping from the pure sky. At a certain angle they could see away beyond the lake lying far off and small, the wall of those other rocks like a curtain of stone, dim and diminished to the horizon. And the sky with curdling clouds and blue sunshine intermittent.

'Wonderful, wonderful, to be high up,' she said, breathing great breaths.

'Yes,' he said. 'It *is* wonderful. But very detestable. I want to live near the sea-level. I am no mountain-topper.'

'Evidently not,' she said.

'*Bergheil!*' cried a youth with bare arms and bare chest, bare head, terrific fanged boots, a knapsack and an alpenstock, and all the bronzed wind and sun of the mountain snow in his skin and his faintly bleached hair. With his great heavy knapsack, his rumpled thick stockings, his ghastly fanged boots, Hepburn found him repulsive.

'*Guten Tag,*' he answered coldly.

'*Grüss Gott,*' said Hannele.

And the young Tannhäuser, the young Siegfried, this young Balder beautiful strode climbing down the rocks, marching and swinging with his alpenstock. And immediately after the youth came a maiden, with hair on the wind and her shirt-breast open, striding in corduroy breeches, rumpled worsted stockings, thick boots, a knapsack and an alpenstock. She passed without greeting. And our pair stopped in angry silence and watched her dropping down the mountain-side.

17

Ah, well, everything comes to an end, even the longest up-climb. So, after much sweat and effort and crossness, Hepburn and Hannele emerged on to the rounded bluff where the road wound out of that hideous great valley cleft into upper regions. So they emerged more on the level, out of the trees as out of something horrible, on to a naked, great bank of rock and grass.

'Thank the Lord!' said Hannele.

So they trudged on round the bluff, and then in front of them saw what is always, always wonderful, one of those shallow, upper valleys, naked, where the first waters are rocked. A flat, shallow, utterly desolate valley, wide as a wide bowl under the sky, with rock slopes and grey stone-slides and precipices all round, and the zig-zag of snow-stripes and ice-roots descending, and then rivers, streams and rivers rushing from many points downwards, down out of the ice-roots and the snow-dagger-points, waters rushing in newly-liberated frenzy downwards, down in waterfalls and cascades and threads, down into the wide, shallow bed of the valley, strewn with rocks and stones innumerable, and not a tree, not a visible bush.

Only, of course, two hotels or restaurant places. But these no more than low, sprawling, peasant-looking places lost among the stones, with stones on their roofs so that they seemed just a part of the valley bed. There was the valley, dotted with rock and rolled-down stone, and these two house-places, and woven with innumerable new waters, and one hoarse stone-tracked river in the desert, and the thin road-track winding along the desolate flat, past first one house, then the other, over one stream, then another, on to the far rock face above which the glacier seemed to loll like some awful great tongue put out.

'Ah, it is wonderful!' he said, as if to himself.

And she looked quickly at his face, saw the queer, blank, sphinx-look with which he gazed out beyond himself. His eyes were black and set, and he seemed so motionless, as if he were eternal facing these upper facts.

She thrilled with triumph. She felt he was overcome.

'It *is* wonderful,' she said.

'Wonderful. And forever wonderful,' he said.

'Ah, in *winter* – ' she cried.

His face changed, and he looked at her.

'In winter you couldn't get up here,' he said.

They went on. Up the slopes cattle were feeding: came that isolated tong-tong-tong of cow-bells, dropping like the slow clink of ice on the arrested air. The sound always woke in him a primeval, almost hopeless melancholy. Always made him feel *navré*. He looked round. There was no tree, no bush, only great grey rocks and pale boulders scattered in place of trees and bushes. But yes, clinging on one side like a dark, close beard were the alpenrose shrubs.

'In May,' he said, 'that side there must be all pink with alpenroses.'

'I *must* come. I *must* come!' she cried.

There were tourists dotted along the road: and two tiny low carts drawn by silky, long-eared mules. These carts went right down to meet the motor cars, and to bring up provisions for the Glacier Hotel: for there was still another big hotel ahead. Hepburn was happy in that upper valley, that first rocking cradle of early water. He liked to see the great fangs and slashes of ice and snow thrust down into the rock, as if the ice had bitten into the flesh of the earth. And from the fang-tips the hoarse water crying its birth-cry, rushing down.

By the turfy road and under the rocks were many flowers: wonderful hare-bells, big and cold and dark, almost black, and seeming like purple-dark ice: then little tufts of tiny pale-blue bells, as if some fairy frog had been blowing spume-bubbles out of the ice: then the bishops-crosier of the stiff, bigger, hairy mountain-bell: then many stars of pale-lavender gentian, touched with earth colour: and then monkshood, yellow, primrose yellow monkshood and sudden places full of dark monkshood. That dark-blue, black-blue, terrible colour of the strange rich monkshood made Hepburn look and look and look again. How did the ice come by that lustrous blue-purple intense darkness? – and by that royal poison? – that laughing-snake gorgeousness of much monkshood.

18

By one of the loud streams, under a rock in the sun, with scented minty or thyme flowers near, they sat down to eat some lunch. It was about eleven o'clock. A thin bee went in and out the scented flowers and the eyebright. The water poured with all the lust and greed of unloosed water over the stones. He took a cupful for Hannele, bright and icy, and she mixed it with the red Hungarian wine.

Down the road strayed the tourists like pilgrims, and at the closed end of the valley they could be seen, quite tiny, climbing the cut-out road that went up like a stairway. Just by their movements you perceived them. But on the valley-bed they went like rolling stones, little as stones. A very elegant mule came stepping by, following a middle-aged woman in tweeds and a tall, high-browed man in knickerbockers. The mule was drawing a very amusing little cart, a chair, rather like a round office-chair upholstered in red velvet, and mounted on two wheels. The red velvet had gone gold and orange and like fruit-juice, being old: really a lovely colour. And the muleteer, a little shabby creature, waddled beside excitedly.

'*Ach*,' cried Hannele, 'that looks almost like before the war: almost as peaceful.'

'Except that the chair is too shabby, and that they all feel exceptional,' he remarked.

There in that upper valley there was no sense of peace. The rush of the waters seemed like weapons, and the tourists all seemed in a sort of frenzy, in a frenzy to be happy, or to be thrilled. It was a feeling that desolated the heart.

The two sat in the changing sunshine under their rock, with the mountain flowers scenting the snow-bitter air, and they ate their eggs and sausage and cheese, and drank the bright-red Hungarian wine. It seemed lovely: almost like before the war: almost the same feeling of eternal holiday, as if the world was made for man's everlasting holiday. But not quite. Never again quite the same. The world is not made for man's everlasting holiday.

As Alexander was putting the bread back into his shoulder-sack, he exclaimed: 'Oh, look here!'

She looked, and saw him drawing out a flat package wrapped in paper: evidently a picture.

'A picture!' she cried.

He unwrapped the thing and handed it to her. It was Theodor Worpswede's *Stilleben*: not very large, painted on a board.

Hannele looked at it and went pale.

'It's *good*,' she cried, in an equivocal tone.

'Quite good,' he said.

'Especially the poached egg,' she said.

'Yes, the poached egg is almost living.'

'But where did you find it?'

'Oh, I found it in the artist's studio.' And he told her how he had traced her.

'How extraordinary!' she cried. 'But why did you buy it?'

'I don't quite know.'

'Did you *like* it?'

'No, not quite that.'

'You could *never* hang it up.'

'No, never,' he said.

'But do you think it is good as a work of art?'

'I think it is quite clever as a painting. I don't like the spirit of it, of course. I'm too catholic for that.'

'No. No,' she faltered. 'It's rather horrid really. That's why I wonder why you bought it.'

'Perhaps to prevent anyone else's buying it,' he said.

'Do you mind very much, then?' she asked.

'No, I don't mind very much. I didn't quite like it that you sold the doll,' he said.

'I needed the money,' she said quietly.

'Oh, quite.'

There was a pause for some moments.

'I felt you'd sold *me*,' she said, quiet and savage.

'When?'

'When your wife appeared. And when you *disappeared*.'

Again there was a pause: his pause this time.

'I did write to you,' he said.

'When?'

'Oh – March, I believe.'

'Oh yes. I had that letter.' Her voice was just as quiet, and even savager.

So there was a pause that belonged to both of them. Then she rose.

'I want to be going,' she said. 'We shall never get to the glacier at this rate.'

He packed up the picture, slung on his knapsack, and they set off. She stooped now and then to pick the starry, earth-lavender gentians from the roadside. As they passed the second of the valley hotels, they saw the man and wife sitting at a little table outside eating bread and cheese, while the mule-chair with its red velvet waited aside on the grass. They passed a whole grove of black-purple nightshade on the left, and some long, low cattle-huts which, with the stones on their roofs, looked as if they had grown up as stones grow in such places through the grass. In the wild, desert place some black pigs were snouting.

So they wound into the head of the valley, and saw the steep face ahead, and

988 SELECTED WORKS OF D. H. LAWRENCE

high up, like vapour or foam dripping from the fangs of a beast, waterfalls vapouring down from the deep fangs of ice. And there was one end of the glacier, like a great bluey-white fur just slipping over the slope of the rock.

As the valley closed in again the flowers were very lovely, especially the big, dark, icy bells, like harebells, that would sway so easily, but which hung dark and with that terrible motionlessness of upper mountain flowers. And the road turned to get on to the long slant in the cliff face, where it climbed like a stair. Slowly, slowly the two climbed up. Now again they saw the valley below, behind. The mule-chair was coming, hastening, the lady seated tight facing backwards, as the chair faced, and wrapped in rugs. The tall, fair, middle-aged husband in knickerbockers strode just behind, bare-headed.

Alexander and Hannele climbed slowly, slowly up the slant, under the dripping rock-face where the white and veined flowers of the grass of Parnassus still rose straight and chilly in the shadow, like water which had taken on itself white flower-flesh. Above they saw the slipping edge of the glacier, like a terrible great paw, bluey. And from the skyline dark grey clouds were fuming up, fuming up as if breathed black and icily out from some ice-cauldron.

'It is going to rain,' said Alexander.

'Not much,' said Hannele shortly.

'I hope not,' said he.

And still she would not hurry up that steep slant, but insisted on standing to look. So the dark, ice-black clouds fumed solid, and the rain began to fly on a cold wind. The mule-chair hastened past, the lady sitting comfortably with her back to the mule, a little pheasant-trimming in her tweed hat, while her Tann-häuser husband reached for his dark, cape-frilled mantle.

Alexander had his dust-coat, but Hannele had nothing but a light knitted jersey-coat, such as women wear indoors. Over the hollow crest above came the cold, steel rain. They pushed on up the slope. From behind came another mule, and a little old man hurrying, and a little cart like a hand barrow, on which were hampers with cabbage and carrots and peas and joints of meat, for the hotel above.

'*Wird es viel sein?*' asked Alexander of the little gnome. 'Will it be much?'

'*Was meint der Herr?*' replied the other. 'What does the gentleman say?'

'*Der Regen, wir des lang dauern?* Will the rain last long?'

'*Nein. Nein. Dies ist kein langer Regen.*'

So, with his mule, which had to stand exactly at that spot to make droppings, the little man resumed his way, and Hannele and Alexander were the last on the slope. The air smelt steel-cold of rain, and of hot droppings. Alexander watched the rain beat on the shoulders and on the blue skirt of Hannele.

'It is a pity you left your big coat down below,' he said.

'What good is it saying so now!' she replied, pale at the nose with anger.

'Quite,' he said, as his eyes glowed and his brow blackened. 'What good suggesting anything at any time, apparently?'

She turned round on him in the rain, as they stood perched nearly at the summit of that slanting cliff-climb, with a glacier-paw hung almost invisible above, and waters gloating aloud in the gulf below. She faced him, and he faced her.

'What have you ever suggested to me?' she said, her face naked as the rain itself with an ice bitter fury, 'What have you ever suggested to me?'

'When have you ever been open to suggestion?' he said, his face dark and his eyes curiously glowing.

'I? I? Ha! Haven't I waited for you to suggest something? And all you can do is to come here with a picture to reproach me for having sold your doll. Ha! I'm glad I sold it. A foolish barren effigy it was too, a foolish staring thing. What should I do but sell it. Why should I keep it, do you imagine?'

'Why do you come here with me today, then?'

'Why do I come here with you today?' she replied. 'I come to see the mountains, which are wonderful, and give me strength. And I come to see the glacier. Do you think I come here to see *you*? Why should I? You are always in some hotel or other away below.'

'You came to see the glacier and the mountains *with* me,' he replied.

'Did I? Then I made a mistake. You can do nothing but find fault even with God's mountains.'

A dark flame suddenly went over his face.

'Yes,' he said, 'I hate them, I hate them. I hate their snow and their affectations.'

'*Affectation!*' she laughed. 'Oh! Even the mountains are affected for you, are they?'

'Yes,' he said. 'Their loftiness and their uplift. I hate their uplift. I hate people prancing on mountain-tops and feeling exalted. I'd like to make them all stop up there, on their mountain-tops, and chew ice to fill their stomachs. I wouldn't let them down again, I wouldn't. I hate it all, I tell you; I hate it.'

She looked in wonder on his dark, glowing, ineffectual face. It seemed to her like a dark flame burning in the daylight and in the ice-rains: very ineffectual and unnecessary.

'You must be a little mad,' she said superbly, 'to talk like that about the mountains. They are so much bigger than you.'

'No,' he said. 'No! They are not.'

'What!' she laughed aloud. 'The mountains are not bigger than you? But you are extraordinary.'

'They are not bigger than me,' he cried. 'Any more than you are bigger than me if you stand on a ladder. They are not bigger than me. They are less than me.'

'Oh! Oh!' she cried in wonder and ridicule. 'The mountains are less than you.'

'Yes,' he cried, 'they are less.'

He seemed suddenly to go silent and remote as she watched him. The speech had gone out of his face again, he seemed to be standing a long way off from her, beyond some border-line. And in the midst of her indignant amazement she watched him with wonder and a touch of fascination. To what country did he belong then? – to what dark, different atmosphere?

'You must suffer from megalomania,' she said. And she said what she felt.

But he only looked at her out of dark, dangerous, haughty eyes.

They went on their way in the rain in silence. He was filled with a passionate silence and imperiousness, a curious, dark, masterful force that supplanted thought in him. And she, who always pondered, went pondering: 'Is he mad? What does he mean? Is he a madman? He wants to bully me. He wants to bully me into something. What does he want to bully me into? Does he want me to love him?'

At this final question she rested. She decided that what he wanted was that she should love him. And this thought flattered her vanity and her pride and appeased her wrath against him. She felt quite mollified towards him.

But what a way he went about it! He wanted her to love him. Of this she was sure. He had always wanted her to love him, even from the first. Only he had not made up his *mind* about it. He had not made up his mind. After his wife had died he had gone away to make up his mind. Now he had made it up. He wanted her to love him. And he was offended, mortally offended because she had sold his doll.

So, this was the conclusion to which Hannele came. And it pleased her, and it flattered her. And it made her feel quite warm towards him, as they walked in the rain. The rain, by the way, was abating. The spume over the hollow crest to which they were approaching was thinning considerably. They could again see the glacier paw hanging out a little beyond. The rain was going to pass. And they were not far now from the hotel, and the third level of Lammerboden.

He wanted her to love him. She felt again quite glowing and triumphant inside herself, and did not care a bit about the rain on her shoulders. He wanted her to love him. Yes, that was how she had to put it. He didn't want to *love* her. No. He wanted *her* to love *him*.

But then, of course, woman-like, she took his love for granted. So many men had been so very ready to love her. And this one – to her amazement, to her indignation, and rather to her secret satisfaction – just blackly insisted that *she* must love *him* . Very well – she would give him a run for his money. That was it: he blackly insisted that *she* must love *him*. What he felt was not to be considered. *She* must love *him*. And be bullied into it. That was what it amounted to. In his silent, black, overbearing soul, he wanted to compel her, he wanted to have power over her. He wanted to make her love him so that he had power over her. He wanted to bully her, physically, sexually, and from the inside.

And she! Well, she was just as confident that she was not going to be bullied. She would love him: probably she would: most probably she did already. But she was not going to be bullied by him in any way whatsoever. No, he must go down on his knees to her if he wanted her love. And then she would love him. Because she *did* love him. But a dark-eyed little master and bully she would never have.

And this was her triumphant conclusion. Meanwhile the rain had almost ceased, they had almost reached the rim of the upper level, towards which they were climbing, and he was walking in that silent diffidence which made her watch him because she was not sure what he was feeling, what he was thinking, or even what he was. He was a puzzle to her: eternally incomprehensible in his feelings and even his sayings. There seemed to her no logic and no reason in what he felt and said. She could never tell what his next mood would come out of. And this made her uneasy, made her watch him. And at the same time it piqued her attention. He had some of the fascination of the incomprehensible. And his curious inscrutable face – it wasn't really only a meaningless mask, because she had seen it half an hour ago melt with a quite incomprehensible and rather, to her mind, foolish passion. Strange, black, inconsequential passion. Asserting with that curious dark ferocity that he was bigger than the mountains. Madness! Madness! Megalomania.

But because he gave himself away, she forgave him and even liked him. And the strange passion of his, that gave out incomprehensible flashes, *was* rather fascinating to her. She felt just a tiny bit sorry for him. But she wasn't going to be bullied by him. She wasn't going to give in to him and his black passion. No, never. It must be love on equal terms or nothing. For love on equal terms she was quite ready. She only waited for him to offer it.

19

In the hotel was a buzz of tourists. Alexander and Hannele sat in the restaurant drinking hot coffee and milk, and watching the maidens in cotton frocks and aprons and bare arms, and the fair youths with maidenly necks and huge voracious boots, and the many Jews of the wrong sort and the wrong shape. These Jews were all being very Austrian, in Tyrol costume that didn't sit on them, assuming the whole gesture and intonation of aristocratic Austria, so that you might think they *were* Austrian aristocrats, if you weren't properly listening, or if you didn't look twice. Certainly they were lords of the Alps, or at least lords of the Alpine hotels this summer, let prejudice be what it might. Jews of the wrong sort. And yet even they imparted a wholesome breath of sanity, disillusion, unsentimentality to the excited '*Bergheil*' atmosphere. Their dark-eyed, sardonic presence seemed to say to the maidenly-necked mountain youths: 'Don't sprout wings of the spirit too much, my dears.'

The rain had ceased. There was a wisp of sunshine from a grey sky. Alexander left the knapsack, and the two went out into the air. Before them lay the last level of the up-climb, the Lammerboden. It was a rather gruesome hollow between the peaks, a last shallow valley about a mile long. At the end the enormous static stream of the glacier poured in from the blunt mountain-top of ice. The ice was dull, sullen-coloured, melted on the surface by the very hot summer: and so it seemed a huge, arrested, sodden flood, ending in a wave-wall of stone-speckled ice upon the valley bed of rocky débris. A gruesome descent of stone and blocks of rock, the little valley bed, with a river raving through. On the left rose the grey rock, but the glacier was there, sending down great paws of ice. It was like some great, deep-furred ice-bear lying spread upon the top heights, and reaching down terrible paws of ice into the valley: like some immense sky-bear fishing in the earth's solid hollows from above. Hepburn it just filled with terror. Hannele too it scared, but it gave her a sense of ecstasy. Some of the immense, furrowed paws of ice held down between the rock were vivid blue in colour, but of a frightening, poisonous blue, like crystal copper sulphate. Most of the ice was a sullen, semi-translucent greeny grey.

The two set off to walk through the massy, desolate stone-bed, under rocks and over waters, to the main glacier. The flowers were even more beautiful on this last reach. Particularly the dark harebells were large and almost black and ice-metallic: one could imagine they gave a dull ice-chink. And the grass of Parnassus stood erect, white-veined big cups held terribly naked and open to their ice air.

From behind the great blunt summit of ice that blocked the distance at the end of the valley, a pale-grey, woolly mist or cloud was fusing up, exhaling huge, like some grey-dead aura into the sky, and covering the top of the glacier. All the way along the valley people were threading, strangely insignificant, among the grey dishevel of stone and rock, like insects. Hannele and Alexander went ahead quickly, along the tiring track.

'Are you glad now that you came?' she said, looking at him triumphant.

'Very glad I came,' he said. His eyes were dilated with excitement that was ordeal or mystic battle rather than the *Bergheil* ecstasy. The curious vibration of his excitement made the scene strange, rather horrible to her. She too shuddered. But it still seemed to her to hold the key to all glamour and ecstasy, the great silent, living glacier. It seemed to her like a grand beast.

As they came near they saw the wall of ice: the glacier end, thick crusted and speckled with stone and dirt débris. From underneath, secret in stones, water rushed out. When they came quite near, they saw the great monster was sweating all over, trickles and rivulets of sweat running down his sides of pure, slush-translucent ice. There it was, the glacier, ending abruptly in the wall of ice under which they stood. Near to, the ice was pure, but waterlogged, all the surface rather rotten from the hot summer. It was sullenly translucent, and of a watery, darkish bluey-green colour. But near the earth it became again bright coloured, gleams of green like jade, gleams of blue like thin, pale sapphire, in little caverns above the wet stones where the walls trickled for ever.

Alexander wanted to climb on to the glacier. It was his one desire – to stand upon it. So under the pellucid wet wall they toiled among rock upwards, to where the guide-track mounted the ice. Several other people were before them – mere day tourists – and all uncertain about venturing any farther. For the ice-slope rose steep and slithery, pure, sun-locked, sweating ice. Still, it was like a curved back. One could scramble on to it, and on up to the first level, like the flat on top of some huge paw.

There stood the little cluster of people, facing the uphill of sullen, pure, sodden-looking ice. They were all afraid: naturally. But being human, they all wanted to go beyond their fear. It was strange that the ice looked so pure, like flesh. Not bright, because the surface was soft like a soft, deep epidermis. But pure ice away down to immense depths.

Alexander, after some hesitation, began gingerly to try the ice. He was frightened of it. And he had no stick, and only smooth-soled boots. But he had a great desire to stand on the glacier. So, gingerly and shakily, he began to struggle a few steps up the pure slope. The ice was soft on the surface, he could kick his heel in it and get a little sideways grip. So, staggering and going sideways he got up a few yards, and was on the naked ice-slope.

Immediately the youths and the fat man below began to tackle it too: also two maidens. For some time, however, Alexander gingerly and scramblingly led the way. The slope of ice was steeper, and rounded, so that it was difficult to stand up in any way. Sometimes he slipped, and was clinging with burnt finger-ends to the soft ice mass. Then he tried throwing his coat down, and getting a foothold on that. Then he went quite quickly by bending down and getting a little grip with his fingers, and going ridiculously as on four legs.

Hannele watched from below, and saw the ridiculous exhibition, and was frightened and amused, but more frightened. And she kept calling, to the great joy of the Austrians down below: 'Come back. Do come back.'

But when he got on to his feet again he only waved his hand at her, half crossly, as she stood away down there in her blue frock. The other fellows with sticks and nail-boots had now taken heart and were scrambling like crabs past our hero, doing better than he.

He had come to a rift in the ice. He sat near the edge and looked down. Clean, pure ice, fused with pale colour, and fused into intense copper-sulphate blue away down in the crack. It was not like crystal, but fused as one fuses a borax bead under a blow-flame. And keenly, wickedly blue in the depths of the crack.

He looked upwards. He had not half mounted the slope. So on he went, upon the huge body of the soft-fleshed ice, slanting his way sometimes on all fours, sometimes using his coat, usually hitting-in with the side of his heel. Hannele down below was crying him to come back. But two other youths were now almost level with him.

So he struggled on till he was more or less over the brim. There he stood and looked at the ice. It came down from above in a great hollow world of ice. A world, a terrible place of hills and valleys and slopes, all motionless, all of ice. Away above the grey mist-cloud was looming bigger. And near at hand were long, huge cracks, side by side, like gills in the ice. It would seem as if the ice breathed through these great ridged gills. One could look down into the series of gulfs, fearful depths, and the colour burning that acid, intense blue, intenser as the crack went deeper. And the crests of the open gills ridged and grouped pale blue above the crevices. It seemed as if the ice breathed there.

The wonder, the terror, and the bitterness of it. Never a warm leaf to unfold, never a gesture of life to give off. A world sufficient unto itself in lifelessness, all this ice.

He turned to go down, though the youths were passing beyond him. And seeing the naked translucent ice heaving downwards in a vicious curve, always the same dark translucency underfoot, he was afraid. If he slipped, he would certainly slither the whole way down, and break some of his bones. Even when he sat down he had to cling with his fingernails in the ice, because if he had started to slide he would have slid the whole way down on his trouser-seat, precipitously, and have landed heaven knows how.

Hannele was watching from below. And he was frightened, perched, seated on the shoulder of ice and not knowing how to get off. Above he saw the great blue gills of ice ridging the air. Down below were two blue cracks – then the last wet level claws of ice upon the stones. And there stood Hannele and the three or four people who had got so far.

However, he found that by striking in his heels sideways with sufficient sharpness he could keep his footing, no matter how steep the slope. So he started to jerk his way zig-zag downwards.

As he descended, arrived a guide with a black beard and all the paraphernalia of ropes and pole and bristling boots. He and his gentlemen began to strike their way up the ice. With those bristling nails like teeth in one's boots, it was quite easy: and a pole to press on to.

Hannele, who had got sick of waiting, and who was also frightened, had gone scuttling on the return journey. He hurried after her, thankful to be off the ice, but excited and gratified. Looking round, he saw the guide and the men on the ice watching the ice-world and the weather. Then they too turned to come down. The day wasn't safe.

20

Pondering, rather thrilled, they threaded their way through the desert of rock and rushing water back to the hotel. The sun was shining warmly for a moment, and he felt happy, though his finger-ends were bleeding a little from the ice.

'But one day,' said Hannele, 'I should love to go with a guide right up, high, right into the glacier.'

'No,' said he. 'I've been far enough. I prefer the world where cabbages will grow on the soil. Nothing grows on glaciers.'

'They say there are glacier fleas, which only live on glaciers,' she said.

'Well, to me the ice didn't look good to eat, even for a flea.'

'You never know,' she laughed. 'But you're glad you've been, aren't you?'

'Very glad. Now I need never go again.'

'But you *did* think it wonderful?'

'Marvellous. And awful, to my mind.'

21

They ate venison and spinach in the hotel, then set off down again. Both felt happier. She gathered some flowers and put them in her handkerchief so they should not die. And again they sat by the stream, to drink a little wine.

But the fume of cloud was blowing up again, thick from behind the glacier. Hannele was uneasy. She wanted to get down. So they went fairly quickly. Many other tourists were hurrying downwards also. The rain began – a sharp handful of drops flung from beyond the glacier. So Hannele and he did not stay to rest, but dropped easily down the steep, dark valley towards the motor-car terminus.

There they had tea, rather tired, but comfortably so. The big hotel restaurant was hideous, and seemed sordid. So in the gloom of a grey, early twilight they went out again and sat on a seat, watching the tourists and the trippers and the motor-car men. There were three Jews from Vienna: and the girl had a huge white woolly dog, as big as a calf, and white and woolly and silky and amiable as a toy. The men, of course, came patting it and admiring it, just as men always do, in life and in novels. And the girl, holding the leash, posed and leaned backwards in the attitude of heroines on novel-covers. She said the white cool monster was a Siberian steppe-dog. Alexander wondered what the steppes made of such a wuffer. And the three Jews pretended they were elegant Austrians out of popular romances.

'Do you think,' said Alexander, 'you will marry the Herr Regierungsrat?'

She looked round, making wide eyes.

'It looks like it, doesn't it!' she said.

'Quite,' he said.

Hannele watched the woolly white dog. So of course it came wagging its ever-amiable hindquarters towards her. She looked at it still, but did not touch it.

'What makes you ask such a question?' she said.

'I can't say. But even so, you haven't really answered. Do you really fully intend to marry the Herr Regierungsrat? Is that your final intention at this moment?'

She looked at him again.

'But before I answer,' she said, 'oughtn't I to know why you ask?'

'Probably you know already,' he said.

'I assure you I don't.'

He was silent for some moments. The huge, woolly dog stood in front of him and breathed enticingly, with its tongue out. He only looked at it blankly.

'Well,' he said, 'if you were not going to marry the Herr Regierungsrat, I should suggest that you marry me.'

She stared away at the auto-garage, a very faint look of amusement, or pleasure, or ridicule on her face: or all three. And a certain shyness.

'But why?' she said.

'Why what?' he returned.

'Why should you suggest that I should marry you?'

'*Why?*' he replied, in his lingering tones. '*Why?* Well, for what purpose does a man usually ask a woman to marry him?'

'For what *purpose!*' she repeated, rather haughtily.

'For what reason, then!' he corrected.

She was silent for some moments. Her face was closed and a little numb-looking, her hands lay very still in her lap. She looked away from him, across the road.

'There is usually only one reason,' she replied, in a rather small voice.

'Yes?' he replied curiously. 'What would you say that was?'

She hesitated. Then she said, rather stiffly: 'Because he really loved her, I suppose. That seems to me the only excuse for a man asking a woman to marry him.'

Followed a dead silence, which she did not intend to break. He knew he would have to answer, and for some reason he didn't want to say what was obviously the thing to say.

'Leaving aside the question of whether you love me or I love you – ' he began.

'I certainly *won't* leave it aside,' she said.

'And I certainly won't consider it,' he said, just as obstinately.

She turned now and looked full at him, with amazement, ridicule, and anger in her face.

'I really think you must be mad,' she said.

'I doubt if you do think that,' he replied. 'It is only a method of retaliation, that is. I think you understand my point very clearly.'

'Your point!' she cried. 'Your point! Oh, so you have a point in all this palavering?'

'Quite!' said he.

She was silent with indignation for some time. Then she said angrily: 'I assure you I do *not* see your point. I don't see any point at all. I see only impertinence.'

'Very good,' he replied. 'The point is whether we marry on a basis of love.'

'Indeed! Marry! We, marry! I don't think that is by any means the point.'

He took his knapsack from under the seat between his feet. And from the knapsack he took the famous picture.

'When,' he said, 'we were supposed to be in love with one another, you made that doll of me, didn't you?' And he sat looking at the odious picture.

'I never for one moment deluded myself that you *really* loved me,' she said bitterly.

'Take the other point, whether *you* loved *me* or not,' said he.

'How could I love you when I couldn't believe in your love for me?' she cried.

He put the picture down between his knees again.

'All this about love,' he said, 'is very confusing and very complicated.'

'Very! In *your* case. Love to me is simple enough,' she said.

'Is it? Is it? And was it simple love which made you make that doll of me?'

'Why shouldn't I make a doll of you? Does it do you any harm? And *weren't* you a doll, good heavens! You *were* nothing but a doll. So what hurt does it do you?'

'Yes, it does. It does me the greatest possible damage,' he replied.

She turned on him with wide-open eyes of amazement and rage.

'Why? Pray why? Can you tell me why?'

'Not quite, I can't,' he replied, taking up the picture and holding it in front of him. She turned her face from it as a cat turns its nose away from a lighted cigarette. 'But when I look at it – when I look at this – then I *know* that there is no love between you and me.'

'Then why are you talking at me in this shameful way?' she flashed at him, tears of anger and mortification rising to her eyes. 'You want your little revenge on me, I suppose, because I made that doll of you.'

'That may be so, in a small measure,' he said.

'That is *all*. That is all and everything,' she cried. 'And that is all you came back to me for – for this petty revenge. Well, you've had it now. But please don't speak to me any more. I shall see if I can go home in the big omnibus.'

She rose and walked away. He saw her hunting for the motor-bus conductor. He saw her penetrate into the yard of the garage. And he saw her emerge again, after a time, and take the path to the river. He sat on in front of the hotel. There was nothing else to do.

The tourists who had arrived in the big bus now began to collect. And soon the huge, drab vehicle itself rolled up and stood big as a house before the hotel door. The passengers began to scramble into their seats. The two men of the white dog were going: but the woman of the white dog, and the dog, were staying behind. Hepburn wondered if Hannele had managed to get herself transferred. He doubted it, because he knew the omnibus was crowded.

Moreover, he had her ticket.

The passengers were packed in. The conductor was collecting the tickets. And at last the great bus rolled away. The bay of the road-end seemed very empty. Even the woman with the white dog had gone. Soon the other car, the Luxus, so-called, must appear. Hepburn sat and waited. The evening was falling chilly, the trees looked gruesome.

At last Hannele sauntered up again, unwillingly.

'I think,' she said, 'you have my ticket.'

'Yes, I have,' he replied.

'Will you give it me, please?'

He gave it to her. She lingered a moment. Then she walked away.

There was the sound of a motor car. With a triumphant purr the Luxus came steering out of the garage yard and drew up at the hotel door. Hannele came hastening also. She went straight to one of the hinder doors – she and Hepburn had their seats in front, beside the driver. She had her foot on the step of the back seat. And then she was afraid. The little sharp-faced driver – there was no conductor – came round looking at the car. He looked at her with his sharp, metallic eye of a mechanic.

'Are all the people going back who came?' she asked, shrinking.

'*Jawohl.*'

'It is full – this car?'

'*Jawohl.*'

'There's no other place?'

'*Nein.*'

Hannele shrank away. The driver was absolutely laconic.

Six of the passengers were here: four were already seated. Hepburn sat still by the hotel door, Hannele lingered in the road by the car, and the little driver, with a huge woollen muffler round his throat, was running round and in and out looking for the two missing passengers. Of course there were two missing passengers. No, he could not find them. And off he trotted again, silently, like a weasel after two rabbits. And at last, when everybody was getting cross, he unearthed them and brought them scuttling to the car.

Now Hannele took her seat, and Hepburn beside her. The driver snapped up the tickets and climbed in past them. With a vindictive screech the car glided away down the ravine. Another beastly trip was over, another infernal joyful holiday done with.

'I think,' said Hepburn, 'I may as well finish what I had to say.'

'What?' cried Hannele, fluttering in the wind of the rushing car.

'I may as well finish what I had to say,' shouted he, his breath blown away.

'Finish then,' she screamed, the ends of her scarf flickering behind her.

'When my wife died,' he said loudly, 'I knew I couldn't love any more.'

'Oh–h!' she screamed ironically.

'In fact,' he shouted, 'I realised that, as far as I was concerned, love was a mistake.'

'*What* was a mistake?' she screamed.

'Love,' he bawled.

'Love!' she screamed. 'A mistake?' Her tone was derisive.

'For me personally,' he said, shouting.

'Oh, only for you personally,' she cried, with a pouf of laughter.

The car gave a great swerve, and she fell on the driver. Then she righted herself. It gave another swerve, and she fell on Alexander. She righted herself angrily. And now they ran straight on: and it seemed a little quieter.

'I realised,' he said, 'that I had always made a mistake, undertaking to love.'

'It must have been an undertaking for you,' she cried.

'Yes, I'm afraid it was. I never really wanted it. But I thought I did. And that's where I made my mistake.'

'Whom have you ever loved? – even as an undertaking?' she asked.

'To begin with, my mother: and that was a mistake. Then my sister: and that was a mistake. Then a girl I had known all my life: and that was a mistake. Then my wife: and that was my most terrible mistake. And then I began the mistake of loving you.'

'Undertaking to love me, you mean,' she said. 'But then you never did properly undertake it. You never really *undertook* to love me.'

'Not quite, did I?' said he.

And she sat feeling angry that he had never made the undertaking.

'No,' he continued. 'Not quite. That is why I came back to you. I don't want to love you. I don't want marriage on a basis of love.'

'On a basis of what, then?'

'I think you know without my putting it into words,' he said.

'Indeed, I assure you I don't. You are much too mysterious,' she replied.

Talking in a swiftly-running motor car is a nerve-racking business. They both had a pause, to rest, and to wait for a quieter stretch of road.

'It isn't very easy to put it into words,' he said. 'But I tried marriage once on a basis of love, and I must say it was a ghastly affair in the long run. And I believe it would be so, for me, *whatever* woman I had.'

'There must be something wrong with you, then,' said she.

'As far as love goes. And yet I want marriage. I want marriage. I want a woman to honour and obey me.'

'If you are quite reasonable and *very* sparing with your commands,' said Hannele. 'And very careful how you give your orders.'

'In fact, I want a sort of patient Griselda. I want to be honoured and obeyed. I don't want love.'

'How Griselda managed to honour that fool of a husband of hers, even if she obeyed him, is more than I can say,' said Hannele. 'I'd like to know what she *really* thought of him. Just what any woman thinks of a bullying fool of a husband.'

'Well,' said he, 'that's no good to me.'

They were silent now until the car stopped at the station. There they descended and walked on under the trees by the lake.

'Sit on a seat,' he said, 'and let us finish.'

Hannele, who was really anxious to hear what he should say, and who, woman-like, was fascinated by a man when he began to give away his own inmost thoughts – no matter how much she might jeer afterwards – sat down by his side. It was a grey evening, just falling dark. Lights twinkled across the lake, the hotel over there threaded its strings of light. Some little boats came rowing quietly to shore. It was a grey, heavy evening, with that special sense of dreariness with which a public holiday usually winds up.

'Honour and obedience: and the proper physical feelings,' he said. 'To me that is marriage. Nothing else.'

'But what are the proper physical feelings but love?' asked Hannele.

'No,' he said. 'A woman wants you to adore her, and be in love with her – and I shan't. I will not do it again, if I live a monk for the rest of my days. I will neither adore you nor be in love with you.'

'You won't get a chance, thank you. And what do you call the proper physical feelings, if you are not in love? I think you want something vile.'

'If a woman honours me – absolutely from the bottom of her nature honours me – and obeys me because of that, I take it, my desire for her goes very much deeper than if I was in love with her, or if I adored her.'

'It's the same thing. If you love, then everything is there – all the lot: your honour and obedience and everything. And if love isn't there, nothing is there,' she said.

'That isn't true,' he replied. 'A woman may love you, she may adore you, but she'll never honour you nor obey you. The most loving and adoring woman today could any minute start and make a doll of her husband – as you made of me.'

'Oh, that eternal doll. What makes it stick so in your mind?'

'I don't know. But there it is. It wasn't malicious. It was flattering, if you like. But it just sticks in me like a thorn: like a thorn. And there it is, in the world, in Germany somewhere. And you can say what you like, but *any* woman, today, no matter *how* much she loves her man – she could start any minute and make a doll of him. And the doll would be her hero: and her hero would be no more than her doll. My wife might have done it. She did do it, in her mind. She had her doll of me right enough. Why, I heard her talk about me to other women. And her doll was a great deal sillier than the one you made. But it's all the same. If a woman loves you, she'll make a doll out of you. She'll never be satisfied till she's made your doll. And when she's got your doll, that's all she wants. And that's what love means. And so, I won't be loved. And I won't love. I won't have anybody loving me. It is an insult. I feel I've been insulted for forty years: by love, and the women who've loved me. I won't be loved. And I won't love. I'll be honoured and I'll be obeyed: or nothing.'

'Then it'll most probably be nothing,' said Hannele sarcastically. 'For I assure you I've nothing but love to offer.'

'Then keep your love,' said he.

She laughed shortly.

'And you?' she cried. 'You! Even suppose you *were* honoured and obeyed. I suppose all you've got to do is to sit there like a sultan and sup it up.'

'Oh no. I have many things to do. And woman or no woman, I'm going to start to do them.'

'What, pray?'

'Why, nothing very exciting. I'm going to East Africa to join a man who's breaking his neck to get his three thousand acres of land under control. And when I've done a few more experiments and observations, and got all the necessary facts, I'm going to do a book on the moon. Woman or no woman, I'm going to do that.'

'And the woman? – supposing you get the poor thing.'

'Why, she'll come along with me, and we'll set ourselves up out there.'

'And she'll do all the honouring and obeying and housekeeping incidentally, while you ride about in the day and stare at the moon in the night.'

He did not answer. He was staring away across the lake.

'What will you do for the woman, poor thing, while she's racking herself to pieces honouring you and obeying you and doing frightful housekeeping in Africa: because I know it can be *awful*: awful.'

'Well,' he said slowly, 'she'll be my wife, and I shall treat her as such. If the marriage service says love and cherish – well, in that sense I shall do so.'

'Oh!' cried Hannele. 'What, *love* her? Actually love the poor thing?'

'Not in that sense of the word, no. I shan't adore her or be in love with her. But she'll be my wife, and I shall love and cherish her as such.'

'Just because she's your wife. Not because she's herself. Ghastly fate for any miserable woman,' said Hannele.

'I don't think so. I think it's her highest fate.'

'To be your wife?'

'To be a wife – and to be loved and shielded as a wife – not as a flirting woman.'

'To be loved and cherished just because you're his wife! No, thank you. All I can admire is the conceit and impudence of it.'

'Very well, then – there it is,' he said, rising.

She rose too, and they went on towards where the boat was tied.

As they were rowing in silence over the lake, he said: 'I shall leave tomorrow.'

She made no answer. She sat and watched the lights of the villa draw near. And then she said: 'I'll come to Africa with you. But I won't promise to honour and obey you.'

'I don't want you otherwise,' he said, very quietly.

The boat was drifting to the little landing-stage. Hannele's friends were hallooing to her from the balcony.

'Hallo!' she cried. '*Ja. Da bin ich. Ja, 's war wunderschön.*'

Then to him she said: 'You'll come in?'

'No,' he said, 'I'll row straight back.'

From the villa they were running down the steps to meet Hannele.

'But won't you have me even if I love you?' she asked him.

'You must promise the other,' he said. 'It comes in the marriage service.'

'*Hat's geregnet? Wiewar das Wetter? Warst du auf dem Gletscher?*' cried the voices from the garden.

'*Nein – kein Regen. Wunderschön! Ja, er war ganz auf dem Gletscher,*' cried Hannele in reply. And to him, *sotto voce*: 'Don't be a solemn ass. Do come in.'

'No,' he said, 'I don't want to come in.'

'Do you want to go away tomorrow? Go if you *do*. But, anyway, I won't say it *before* the marriage service. I needn't, need I?'

She stepped from the boat on to the plank.

'Oh,' she said, turning round, 'give me that picture, please, will you? I want to burn it.'

He handed it to her.

'And come tomorrow, will you?' she said.

'Yes, in the morning.'

He pulled back quickly into the darkness.

THE FOX

THE TWO GIRLS were usually known by their surnames, Banford and March. They had taken the farm together, intending to work it all by themselves: that is, they were going to rear chickens, make a living by poultry, and add to this by keeping a cow, and raising one or two young beasts. Unfortunately, things did not turn out well.

Banford was a small, thin, delicate thing with spectacles. She, however, was the principal investor, for March had little or no money. Banford's father, who was a tradesman in Islington, gave his daughter the start, for her health's sake, and because he loved her, and because it did not look as if she would marry. March was more robust. She had learned carpentry and joinery at the evening classes in Islington. She would be the man about the place. They had, moreover, Banford's old grandfather living with them at the start. He had been a farmer. But unfortunately the old man died after he had been at Bailey Farm for a year. Then the two girls were left alone.

They were neither of them young: that is, they were near thirty. But they certainly were not old. They set out quite gallantly with their enterprise. They had numbers of chickens, black Leghorns and white Leghorns, Plymouths and Wyandottes; also some ducks, also two heifers in the fields. One heifer, unfortunately, refused absolutely to stay in the Bailey Farm closes. No matter how March made up the fences, the heifer was out, wild in the woods, or trespassing on the neighbouring pasture, and March and Banford were away, flying after her, with more haste than success. So this heifer they sold in despair. Then, just before the other beast was expecting her first calf, the old man died, and the girls, afraid of the coming event, sold her in a panic, and limited their attentions to fowls and ducks.

In spite of a little chagrin, it was a relief to have no more cattle on hand. Life was not made merely to be slaved away. Both girls agreed in this. The fowls were quite enough trouble. March had set up her carpenter's bench at the end of the open shed. Here she worked, making coops and doors and other appurtenances. The fowls were housed in the bigger building, which had served as barn and cowshed in old days. They had a beautiful home, and should have been perfectly content. Indeed, they looked well enough. But the girls were disgusted at their tendency to strange illnesses, at their exacting way of life, and at their refusal, obstinate refusal to lay eggs.

March did most of the outdoor work. When she was out and about, in her puttees and breeches, her belted coat and her loose cap, she looked almost like some graceful, loose-balanced young man, for her shoulders were straight, and her movements easy and confident, even tinged with a little indifference or irony. But her face was not a man's face, ever. The wisps of her crisp dark hair blew about her as she stooped, her eyes were big and wide and dark, when she looked up again, strange, startled, shy and sardonic at once. Her mouth, too, was almost pinched as if in pain and irony. There was something odd and unexplained about her. She would stand balanced on one hip, looking at the fowls pattering about in the obnoxious fine mud of the sloping yard, and calling to her favourite white hen, which came in answer to her name. But there was an almost satirical flicker in March's big, dark eyes as she looked at her three-toed flock pottering about under her gaze, and the same slight dangerous satire in her voice as she spoke to the favoured Patty, who pecked at March's boot by way of friendly demonstration.

Fowls did not flourish at Bailey Farm, in spite of all that March did for them. When she provided hot food for them in the morning, according to rule, she noticed that it made them heavy and dozy for hours. She expected to see them lean against the pillars of the shed in their languid processes of digestion. And she knew quite well that they ought to be busily scratching and foraging about, if they were to come to any good. So she decided to give them their hot food at night, and let them sleep on it. Which she did. But it made no difference.

War conditions, again, were very unfavourable to poultry-keeping. Food was scarce and bad. And when the Daylight Saving Bill was passed, the fowls obstinately refused to go to bed as usual, about nine o'clock in the summertime. That was late enough, indeed, for there was no peace till they were shut up and asleep. Now they cheerfully walked around, without so much as glancing at the barn, until ten o'clock or later. Both Banford and March disbelieved in living for work alone. They wanted to read or take a cycle-ride in the evening, or perhaps March wished to paint curvilinear swans on porcelain, with green background, or else make a marvellous fire-screen by processes of elaborate cabinet work. For she was a creature of odd whims and unsatisfied tendencies. But from all these things she was prevented by the stupid fowls.

One evil there was greater than any other. Bailey Farm was a little homestead, with ancient wooden barn and low-gabled farmhouse, lying just one field removed from the edge of the wood. Since the war the fox was a demon. He carried off the hens under the very noses of March and Banford. Banford would start and stare through her big spectacles with all her eyes, as another squawk and flutter took place at her heels. Too late! Another white Leghorn gone. It was disheartening.

They did what they could to remedy it. When it became permitted to shoot foxes, they stood sentinel with their guns, the two of them, at the favoured hours. But it was no good. The fox was too quick for them. So another year passed, and another, and they were living on their losses, as Banford said. They let their farmhouse one summer, and retired to live in a railway-carriage that was deposited as a sort of out-house in a corner of the field. This amused them, and helped their finances. None the less, things looked dark.

Although they were usually the best of friends, because Banford, though nervous and delicate, was a warm, generous soul, and March, though so odd and absent in herself, had a strange magnanimity, yet, in the long solitude, they were apt to become a little irritable with one another, tired of one another. March had four-fifths of the work to do, and though she did not mind, there seemed no relief, and it made her eyes flash curiously sometimes. Then Banford, feeling more nerve-worn than ever, would become despondent, and March would speak sharply to her. They seemed to be losing ground, somehow, losing hope as the months went by. There alone in the fields by the wood, with the wide country stretching hollow and dim to the round hills of the White Horse, in the far distance, they seemed to have to live too much off themselves. There was nothing to keep them up – and no hope.

The fox really exasperated them both. As soon as they had let the fowls out, in the early summer mornings, they had to take their guns and keep guard: and then again as soon as evening began to mellow, they must go once more. And he was so sly. He slid along in the deep grass; he was difficult as a serpent to see. And he seemed to circumvent the girls deliberately. Once or twice March had caught sight of the white tip of his brush, or the ruddy shadow of him in the deep grass, and she had let fire at him. But he made no account of this.

One evening March was standing with her back to the sunset, her gun under her arm, her hair pushed under her cap. She was half watching, half musing. It was her constant state. Her eyes were keen and observant, but her inner mind took no notice of what she saw. She was always lapsing into this odd, rapt state, her mouth rather screwed up. It was a question whether she was there, actually consciously present, or not.

The trees on the wood-edge were a darkish, brownish green in the full light – for it was the end of August. Beyond, the naked, copper-like shafts and limbs of the pine trees shone in the air. Nearer the rough grass, with its long, brownish stalks all agleam, was full of light. The fowls were round about – the ducks were still swimming on the pond under the pine trees. March looked at it all, saw it all, and did not see it. She heard Banford speaking to the fowls in the distance – and she did not hear. What was she thinking about? Heaven knows. Her consciousness was, as it were, held back.

She lowered her eyes, and suddenly saw the fox. He was looking up at her. Her chin was pressed down, and his eyes were looking up. They met her eyes. And he knew her. She was spellbound – she knew he knew her. So he looked into her eyes, and her soul failed her. He knew her, he was not daunted.

She struggled, confusedly she came to herself, and saw him making off, with slow leaps over some fallen boughs, slow, impudent jumps. Then he glanced over his shoulder, and ran smoothly away. She saw his brush held smooth like a feather, she saw his white buttocks twinkle. And he was gone, softly, soft as the wind.

She put her gun to her shoulder, but even then pursed her mouth, knowing it was nonsense to pretend to fire. So she began to walk slowly after him, in the direction he had gone, slowly, pertinaciously. She expected to find him. In her heart she was determined to find him. What she would do when she saw him again she did not consider. But she was determined to find him. So she walked abstractedly about on the edge of the wood, with wide, vivid dark eyes, and a faint flush in her cheeks. She did not think. In strange mindlessness she walked hither and thither.

At last she became aware that Banford was calling her. She made an effort of attention, turned, and gave some sort of screaming call in answer. Then again she was striding off towards the homestead. The red sun was setting, the fowls were retiring towards their roost. She watched them, white creatures, black creatures, gathering to the barn. She watched them spellbound, without seeing them. But her automatic intelligence told her when it was time to shut the door.

She went indoors to supper, which Banford had set on the table. Banford chatted easily. March seemed to listen, in her distant, manly way. She answered a brief word now and then. But all the time she was as if spellbound. And as soon as supper was over, she rose again to go out, without saying why.

She took her gun again and went to look for the fox. For he had lifted his eyes upon her, and his knowing look seemed to have entered her brain. She did not so much think of him: she was possessed by him. She saw his dark, shrewd, unabashed eye looking into her, knowing her. She felt him invisibly master her spirit. She knew the way he lowered his chin as he looked up, she knew his muzzle, the golden brown, and the greyish white. And again she saw him glance over his shoulder at her, half inviting, half contemptuous and cunning. So she went, with her great startled eyes glowing, her gun under her arm, along the wood-edge. Meanwhile the night fell, and a great moon rose above the pine trees. And again Banford was calling.

So she went indoors. She was silent and busy. She examined her gun, and cleaned it, musing abstractedly by the lamplight. Then she went out again, under the great moon, to see if everything was right. When she saw the dark crests of the pine trees against the blood-red sky, again her heart beat to the fox, the fox. She wanted to follow him, with her gun.

It was some days before she mentioned the affair to Banford. Then suddenly one evening she said, 'The fox was right at my feet on Saturday night.'

'Where?' said Banford, her eyes opening behind her spectacles.

'When I stood just above the pond.'

'Did you fire?' cried Banford.

'No, I didn't.'

'Why not?'

'Why, I was too much surprised, I suppose.'

It was the same old, slow, laconic way of speech March always had. Banford stared at her friend for a few moments.

'You saw him?' she cried.

'Oh yes! He was looking up at me, cool as anything.'

'I tell you,' cried Banford – 'the cheek! They're not afraid of us, Nellie.'

'Oh, no,' said March.

'Pity you didn't get a shot at him,' said Banford.

'Isn't it a pity! I've been looking for him ever since. But I don't suppose he'll come so near again.'

'I don't suppose he will,' said Banford.

And she proceeded to forget about it, except that she was more indignant than ever at the impudence of the beggar. March also was not conscious that she thought of the fox. But whenever she fell into her half-musing, when she was half rapt and half intelligently aware of what passed under her vision, then it was the fox which somehow dominated her unconsciousness, possessed the blank half of her musing. And so it was for weeks, and months. No matter whether she had been climbing the trees for the apples, or beating down the last of the damsons, or whether she had been digging out the ditch from the duck-pond, or clearing out the barn, when she had finished, or when she straightened herself, and pushed the wisps of her hair away again from her forehead, and pursed up her mouth again in an odd, screwed fashion, much too old for her years, there was sure to come over her mind the old spell of the fox, as it came when he was looking at her. It was as if she could smell him at these times. And it always recurred, at unexpected moments, just as she was going to sleep at night, or just as she was pouring the water into the teapot to make tea – it was the fox, it came over her like a spell.

So the months passed. She still looked for him unconsciously when she went towards the wood. He had become a settled effect in her spirit, a state permanently established, not continuous, but always recurring. She did not know what she felt or thought: only the state came over her, as when he looked at her.

The months passed, the dark evenings came, heavy, dark November, when March went about in high boots, ankle deep in mud, when the night began to fall at four o'clock, and the day never properly dawned. Both girls dreaded these times. They dreaded the almost continuous darkness that enveloped them on their desolate little farm near the wood. Banford was physically afraid. She was afraid of tramps, afraid lest someone should come prowling around. March was not so much afraid as uncomfortable, and disturbed. She felt discomfort and gloom in all her physique.

Usually the two girls had tea in the sitting-room. March lighted a fire at dusk, and put on the wood she had chopped and sawed during the day. Then the long evening was in front, dark, sodden, black outside, lonely and rather oppressive inside, a little dismal. March was content not to talk, but Banford could not keep still. Merely listening to the wind in the pines outside, or the drip of water, was too much for her.

One evening the girls had washed up the tea-things in the kitchen, and March had put on her house-shoes, and taken up a roll of crochet-work, which she worked at slowly from time to time. So she lapsed into silence. Banford stared at the red fire, which, being of wood, needed constant attention. She was afraid to begin to read too early, because her eyes would not bear any strain. So she sat staring at the fire, listening to the distant sounds, sound of cattle lowing, of a dull, heavy moist wind, of the rattle of the evening train on the little railway not far off. She was almost fascinated by the red glow of the fire.

Suddenly both girls started, and lifted their heads. They heard a footstep – distinctly a footstep. Banford recoiled in fear. March stood listening. Then rapidly she approached the door that led into the kitchen. At the same time they heard the footsteps approach the back door. They waited a second. The back door opened softly. Banford gave a loud cry. A man's voice said softly, 'Hello!'

March recoiled, and took a gun from a corner.

'What do you want?' she cried, in a sharp voice.

Again the soft, softly-vibrating man's voice said, 'Hello! What's wrong?'

'I shall shoot!' cried March. 'What do you want?'

'Why, what's wrong? What's wrong?' came the soft, wondering, rather scared voice: and a young soldier, with his heavy kit on his back, advanced into the dim light.

'Why,' he said, 'who lives here then?'

'We live here,' said March. 'What do you want?'

'Oh!' came the long, melodious, wonder-note from the young soldier. 'Doesn't William Grenfel live here then?'

'No – you know he doesn't.'

'Do I? Do I? I don't, you see. He *did* live here, because he was my grandfather, and I lived here myself five years ago. What's become of him then?'

The young man – or youth, for he would not be more than twenty – now advanced and stood in the inner doorway. March, already under the influence of his strange, soft, modulated voice, stared at him spellbound. He had a ruddy, roundish face, with fairish hair, rather long, flattened to his forehead with sweat. His eyes were blue, and very bright and sharp. On his cheeks, on the fresh ruddy skin were fine, fair hairs, like a down, but sharper. It gave him a slightly glistening look. Having his heavy sack on his shoulders, he stooped, thrusting his head forward. His hat was loose in one hand. He stared brightly, very keenly from girl to girl, particularly at March, who stood pale, with great dilated eyes, in her belted coat and puttees, her hair knotted in a big crisp knot behind. She still had the gun in her hand. Behind her, Banford, clinging to the sofa-arm, was shrinking away, with half-averted head.

'I thought my grandfather still lived here? I wonder if he's dead.'

'We've been here for three years,' said Banford, who was beginning to recover her wits, seeing something boyish in the round head with its rather long, sweaty hair.

'Three years! You don't say so! And you don't know who was here before you?'

'I know it was an old man, who lived by himself.'

'Ay! Yes, that's him! And what became of him then?'

'He died. I know he died.'

'Ay! He's dead then!'

The youth stared at them without changing colour or expression. If he had any expression, besides a slight baffled look of wonder, it was one of sharp curiosity concerning the two girls; sharp, impersonal curiosity, the curiosity of that round young head.

But to March he was the fox. Whether it was the thrusting forward of his head, or the glisten of fine whitish hairs on the ruddy cheekbones, or the bright, keen eyes, that can never be said: but the boy was to her the fox, and she could not see him otherwise.

'How is it you didn't know if your grandfather was alive or dead?' asked Banford, recovering her natural sharpness.

'Ay, that's it,' replied the softly-breathing youth. 'You see, I joined up in Canada, and I hadn't heard for three or four years. I ran away to Canada.'

'And now have you just come from France?'

'Well – from Salonika really.'

There was a pause, nobody knowing quite what to say.

'So you've nowhere to go now?' said Banford rather lamely.

'Oh, I know some people in the village. Anyhow, I can go to the Swan.'

'You came on the train, I suppose. Would you like to sit down a bit?'

'Well – I don't mind.'

He gave an odd little groan as he swung off his kit. Banford looked at March.

'Put the gun down,' she said. 'We'll make a cup of tea.'

'Ay,' said the youth. 'We've seen enough of rifles.'

He sat down rather tired on the sofa, leaning forward.

March recovered her presence of mind, and went into the kitchen. There she heard the soft young voice musing, 'Well, to think I should come back and find it like this!' He did not seem sad, not at all – only rather interestedly surprised.

'And what a difference in the place, eh?' he continued, looking round the room.

'You see a difference, do you?' said Banford.

'Yes – don't I!'

His eyes were unnaturally clear and bright, though it was the brightness of abundant health.

March was busy in the kitchen preparing another meal. It was about seven o'clock. All the time, while she was active, she was attending to the youth in the sitting-room, not so much listening to what he said as feeling the soft run of his voice. She primmed up her mouth tighter and tighter, puckering it as if it were sewed, in her effort to keep her will uppermost. Yet her large eyes dilated and glowed in spite of her; she lost herself. Rapidly and carelessly she prepared the meal, cutting large chunks of bread and margarine – for there was no butter. She racked her brain to think of something else to put on the tray – she had only bread, margarine, and jam, and the larder was bare. Unable to conjure anything up, she went into the sitting-room with her tray.

She did not want to be noticed. Above all, she did not want him to look at her. But when she came in, and was busy setting the table just behind him, he pulled himself up from his sprawling, and turned and looked over his shoulder. She became pale and wan.

The youth watched her as she bent over the table, looked at her slim, well-shapen legs, at the belted coat dropping around her thighs, at the knot of dark hair, and his curiosity, vivid and widely alert, was again arrested by her.

The lamp was shaded with a dark-green shade, so that the light was thrown downwards and the upper half of the room was dim. His face moved bright under the light, but March loomed shadowy in the distance.

She turned round, but kept her eyes sideways, dropping and lifting her dark lashes. Her mouth unpuckered as she said to Banford, 'Will you pour out?'

Then she went into the kitchen again.

'Have your tea where you are, will you?' said Banford to the youth – 'unless you'd rather come to the table.'

'Well,' said he, 'I'm nice and comfortable here, aren't I? I will have it here, if you don't mind.'

'There's nothing but bread and jam,' she said. And she put his plate on a stool by him. She was very happy now, waiting on him. For she loved company. And now she was no more afraid of him than if he were her own younger brother. He was such a boy.

'Nellie,' she called. 'I've poured you a cup out.'

March appeared in the doorway, took her cup, and sat down in a corner, as far from the light as possible. She was very sensitive in her knees. Having no skirts to cover them, and being forced to sit with them boldly exposed, she suffered. She shrank and shrank, trying not to be seen. And the youth, sprawling low on the couch, glanced up at her, with long, steady, penetrating looks, till she was almost ready to disappear. Yet she held her cup balanced, she drank her tea, screwed up her mouth and held her head averted. Her desire to be invisible was so strong that it quite baffled the youth. He felt he could not see her distinctly. She seemed like a shadow within the shadow. And ever his eyes came back to her, searching, unremitting, with unconscious fixed attention.

Meanwhile he was talking softly and smoothly to Banford, who loved nothing so much as gossip, and who was full of perky interest, like a bird. Also he ate largely and quickly and voraciously, so that March had to cut more chunks of bread and margarine, for the roughness of which Banford apologised.

'Oh, well,' said March, suddenly speaking, 'if there's no butter to put on it, it's no good trying to make dainty pieces.'

Again the youth watched her, and he laughed, with a sudden, quick laugh, showing his teeth and wrinkling his nose.

'It isn't, is it,' he answered in his soft, near voice.

It appeared he was Cornish by birth and upbringing. When he was twelve years old he had come to Bailey Farm with his grandfather, with whom he had never agreed very well. So he had run away to Canada, and worked far away in the West. Now he was here – and that was the end of it.

He was very curious about the girls, to find out exactly what they were doing. His questions were those of a farm youth; acute, practical, a little mocking. He was very much amused by their attitude to their losses: for they were amusing on the score of heifers and fowls.

'Oh, well,' broke in March, 'we don't believe in living for nothing but work.'

'Don't you?' he answered. And again the quick young laugh came over his face. He kept his eyes steadily on the obscure woman in the corner.

'But what will you do when you've used up all your capital?' he said.

'Oh, I don't know,' answered March laconically. 'Hire ourselves out for land-workers, I suppose.'

'Yes, but there won't be any demand for women land-workers now the war's over,' said the youth.

'Oh, we'll see. We shall hold on a bit longer yet,' said March, with a plangent, half-sad, half-ironical indifference.

'There wants a man about the place,' said the youth softly.

Banford burst out laughing. 'Take care what you say,' she interrupted. 'We consider ourselves quite efficient.'

'Oh,' came March's slow, plangent voice, 'it isn't a case of efficiency, I'm afraid. If you're going to do farming you must be at it from morning till night, and you might as well be a beast yourself.'

'Yes, that's it,' said the youth. 'You aren't willing to put yourselves into it.'

'We aren't,' said March, 'and we know it.'

'We want some of our time for ourselves,' said Banford.

The youth threw himself back on the sofa, his face tight with laughter, and laughed silently but thoroughly. The calm scorn of the girls tickled him tremendously.

'Yes,' he said, 'but why did you begin then?'

'Oh,' said March, 'we had a better opinion of the nature of fowls then than we have now.'

'Of Nature altogether, I'm afraid,' said Banford. 'Don't talk to me about Nature.'

Again the face of the youth tightened with delighted laughter.

'You haven't a very high opinion of fowls and cattle, have you?' he said.

'Oh no – quite a low one,' said March.

He laughed out.

'Neither fowls nor heifers,' said Banford, 'nor goats nor the weather.'

The youth broke into a sharp yap of laughter, delighted. The girls began to laugh too, March turning aside her face and wrinkling her mouth in amusement.

'Oh, well,' said Banford, 'we don't mind, do we, Nellie?'

'No,' said March, 'we don't mind.'

The youth was very pleased. He had eaten and drunk his fill. Banford began to question him. His name was Henry Grenfel – no, he was not called Harry, always Henry. He continued to answer with courteous simplicity, grave and charming. March, who was not included, cast long, slow glances at him from her recess, as he sat there on the sofa, his hands clasping his knees, his face under the lamp bright and alert, turned to Banford. She became almost peaceful at last. He was identified with the fox – and he was here in full presence. She need not go after him any more. There in the shadow of her corner she gave herself up to a warm, relaxed peace, almost like sleep, accepting the spell that was on her. But she wished to remain hidden. She was only fully at peace whilst he forgot her, talking to Banford. Hidden in the shadow of the corner, she need not any more be divided in herself, trying to keep up two planes of consciousness. She could at last lapse into the odour of the fox.

For the youth, sitting before the fire in his uniform, sent a faint but distinct odour into the room, indefinable, but something like a wild creature. March no longer tried to reserve herself from it. She was still and soft in her corner like a passive creature in its cave.

At last the talk dwindled. The youth relaxed his clasp of his knees, pulled himself together a little, and looked round. Again he became aware of the silent, half-invisible woman in the corner.

'Well,' he said unwillingly, 'I suppose I'd better be going, or they'll be in bed at the Swan.'

'I'm afraid they're in bed anyhow,' said Banford. 'They've all got this influenza.'

'Have they!' he exclaimed. And he pondered. 'Well,' he continued, 'I shall find a place somewhere.'

'I'd say you could stay here, only – ' Banford began.

He turned and watched her, holding his head forward.

'What?' he asked.

'Oh, well,' she said, 'propriety, I suppose.' She was rather confused.

'It wouldn't be improper, would it?' he said, gently surprised.

'Not as far as we're concerned,' said Banford.

'And not as far as *I'm* concerned,' he said, with grave naïveté. 'After all, it's my own home, in a way.'

Banford smiled at this.

'It's what the village will have to say,' she said.

There was a moment's blank pause.

'What do you say, Nellie?' asked Banford.

'I don't mind,' said March, in her distinct tone. 'The village doesn't matter to me, anyhow.'

'No,' said the youth, quick and soft. 'Why should it? I mean, what should they say?'

'Oh, well,' came March's plangent, laconic voice, 'they'll easily find something to say. But it makes no difference what they say. We can look after ourselves.'

'Of course you can,' said the youth.

'Well then, stop if you like,' said Banford. 'The spare room is quite ready.'

His face shone with pleasure.

'If you're quite sure it isn't troubling you too much,' he said, with that soft courtesy which distinguished him.

'Oh, it's no trouble,' they both said.

He looked, smiling with delight, from one to another.

'It's awfully nice not to have to turn out again, isn't it?' he said gratefully.

'I suppose it is,' said Banford.

March disappeared to attend the room. Banford was as pleased and thoughtful as if she had her own young brother home from France. It gave her just the same kind of gratification to attend on him, to get out the bath for him, and everything. Her natural warmth and kindliness had now an outlet. And the youth luxuriated in her sisterly attention. But it puzzled him slightly to know that March was silently working for him too. She was so curiously silent and obliterated. It seemed to him he had not really seen her. He felt he should not know her if he met her in the road.

That night March dreamed vividly. She dreamed she heard a singing outside which she could not understand, a singing that roamed round the house, in the fields, and in the darkness. It moved her so that she felt she must weep. She went out, and suddenly she knew it was the fox singing. He was very yellow and bright, like corn. She went nearer to him, but he ran away and ceased singing. He seemed near, and she wanted to touch him. She stretched out her hand, but suddenly he bit her wrist, and at the same instant, as she drew back, the fox, turning round to bound away, whisked his brush across her face, and it seemed his brush was on fire, for it seared and burned her mouth with a great pain. She awoke with the pain of it, and lay trembling as if she were really seared.

In the morning, however, she only remembered it as a distant memory. She arose and was busy preparing the house and attending to the fowls. Banford flew into the village on her bicycle to try and buy food. She was a hospitable soul. But alas, in the year 1918 there was not much food to buy. The youth came downstairs in his shirtsleeves. He was young and fresh, but he walked with his head thrust forward, so that his shoulders seemed raised and rounded, as if he had a slight curvature of the spine. It must have been only a manner of bearing himself, for he was young and vigorous. He washed himself and went outside, whilst the women were preparing breakfast.

He saw everything, and examined everything. His curiosity was quick and insatiable. He compared the state of things with that which he remembered before, and cast over in his mind the effect of the changes. He watched the fowls and the ducks, to see their condition; he noticed the flight of wood-pigeons overhead: they were very numerous; he saw the few apples high up, which March had not been able to reach; he remarked that they had borrowed a draw-pump, presumably to empty the big soft-water cistern which was on the north side of the house.

'It's a funny, dilapidated old place,' he said to the girls, as he sat at breakfast.

His eyes were wise and childish, with thinking about things. He did not say much, but ate largely. March kept her face averted. She, too, in the early morning, could not be aware of him, though something about the glint of his khaki reminded her of the brilliance of her dream-fox.

During the day the girls went about their business. In the morning he

SELECTED WORKS OF D. H. LAWRENCE

attended to the guns, shot a rabbit and a wild duck that was flying high towards the wood. That was a great addition to the empty larder. The girls felt that already he had earned his keep. He said nothing about leaving, however. In the afternoon he went to the village. He came back at teatime. He had the same alert, forward-reaching look on his roundish face. He hung his hat on a peg with a little swinging gesture. He was thinking about something.

'Well,' he said to the girls, as he sat at table. 'What am I going to do?'

'How do you mean – what are you going to do?' said Banford.

'Where am I going to find a place in the village to stay?' he said.

'I don't know,' said Banford. 'Where do you think of staying?'

'Well' – he hesitated – 'at the Swan they've got this flu, and at the "Plough and Harrow" they've got the soldiers who are collecting the hay for the army: besides, in the private houses, there's ten men and a corporal altogether billeted in the village, they tell me. I'm not sure where I could get a bed.'

He left the matter to them. He was rather calm about it. March sat with her elbows on the table, her two hands supporting her chin, looking at him unconsciously. Suddenly he lifted his clouded blue eyes, and unthinking looked straight into March's eyes. He was startled as well as she. He, too, recoiled a little. March felt the same sly, taunting, knowing spark leap out of his eyes, as he turned his head aside, and fall into her soul, as it had fallen from the dark eyes of the fox. She pursed her mouth as if in pain, as if asleep too.

'Well, I don't know,' Banford was saying. She seemed reluctant, as if she were afraid of being imposed upon. She looked at March. But, with her weak, troubled sight, she only saw the usual semi-abstraction on her friend's face. 'Why don't you speak, Nellie?' she said.

But March was wide-eyed and silent, and the youth, as if fascinated, was watching her without moving his eyes.

'Go on – answer something,' said Banford. And March turned her head slightly aside, as if coming to consciousness, or trying to come to consciousness.

'What do you expect me to say?' she asked automatically.

'Say what you think,' said Banford.

'It's all the same to me,' said March.

And again there was silence. A pointed light seemed to be on the boy's eyes, penetrating like a needle.

'So it is to me,' said Banford. 'You can stop on here if you like.'

A smile like a cunning little flame came over his face, suddenly and involuntarily. He dropped his head quickly to hide it, and remained with his head dropped, his face hidden.

'You can stop on here if you like. You can please yourself, Henry,' Banford concluded.

Still he did not reply, but remained with his head dropped. Then he lifted his face. It was bright with a curious light, as if exultant, and his eyes were strangely clear as he watched March. She turned her face aside, her mouth suffering as if wounded, and her consciousness dim.

Banford became a little puzzled. She watched the steady, pellucid gaze of the youth's eyes as he looked at March, with the invisible smile gleaming on his face. She did not know how he was smiling, for no feature moved. It seemed only in the gleam, almost the glitter of the fine hairs on his cheeks. Then he looked with quite a changed look at Banford.

'I'm sure,' he said in his soft, courteous voice, 'you're awfully good. You're too good. You don't want to be bothered with me, I'm sure.'

'Cut a bit of bread, Nellie,' said Banford uneasily, adding: 'It's no bother, if you like to stay. It's like having my own brother here for a few days. He's a boy like you are.'

'That's awfully kind of you,' the lad repeated. 'I should like to stay ever so much, if you're sure I'm not a trouble to you.'

'No, of course you're no trouble. I tell you, it's a pleasure to have somebody in the house beside ourselves,' said warm-hearted Banford.

'But Miss March?' he said in his soft voice, looking at her.

'Oh, it's quite all right as far as I'm concerned,' said March vaguely.

His face beamed, and he almost rubbed his hands with pleasure.

'Well then,' he said, 'I should love it, if you'd let me pay my board and help with the work.'

'You've no need to talk about board,' said Banford.

One or two days went by, and the youth stayed on at the farm. Banford was quite charmed by him. He was so soft and courteous in speech, not wanting to say much himself, preferring to hear what she had to say, and to laugh in his quick, half-mocking way. He helped readily with the work – but not too much. He loved to be out alone with the gun in his hands, to watch, to see. For his sharp-eyed, impersonal curiosity was insatiable, and he was most free when he was quite alone, half-hidden, watching.

Particularly he watched March. She was a strange character to him. Her figure, like a graceful young man's, piqued him. Her dark eyes made something rise in his soul, with a curious elate excitement, when he looked into them, an excitement he was afraid to let be seen, it was so keen and secret. And then her odd, shrewd speech made him laugh outright. He felt he must go further, he was inevitably impelled. But he put away the thought of her and went off towards the wood's edge with the gun.

The dusk was falling as he came home, and with the dusk, a fine, late November rain. He saw the firelight leaping in the window of the sitting-room, a leaping light in the little cluster of the dark buildings. And he thought to himself it would be a good thing to have this place for his own. And then the thought entered him shrewdly: why not marry March? He stood still in the middle of the field for some moments, the dead rabbit hanging still in his hand, arrested by this thought. His mind waited in amazement – it seemed to calculate – and then he smiled curiously to himself in acquiescence. Why not? Why not, indeed? It was a good idea. What if it was rather ridiculous? What did it matter? What if she was older than he? It didn't matter. When he thought of her dark, startled, vulnerable eyes he smiled subtly to himself. He was older than she, really. He was master of her.

He scarcely admitted his intention even to himself. He kept it as a secret even from himself. It was all too uncertain as yet. He would have to see how things went. Yes, he would have to see how things went. If he wasn't careful, she would just simply mock at the idea. He knew, sly and subtle as he was, that if he went to her plainly and said: 'Miss March, I love you and want you to marry me,' her inevitable answer would be: 'Get out. I don't want any of that tomfoolery.' This was her attitude to men and their 'tomfoolery'. If he was not careful, she would turn round on him with her savage, sardonic ridicule, and dismiss him from the farm and from her own mind for ever. He would have to go gently. He would have to catch her as you catch a deer or a woodcock when you go out shooting. It's no good walking out into the forest and saying to the deer: 'Please fall to my gun.' No, it is a slow, subtle battle. When you really go out to get a deer, you gather yourself together, you coil yourself inside yourself, and you advance secretly, before dawn, into the mountains. It is not so much what you do, when you go out hunting, as how you feel. You have to be subtle and cunning and absolutely fatally ready. It becomes like a fate. Your own fate overtakes and determines the fate of the deer you are hunting. First of all, even before you come in sight of your quarry, there is a strange battle, like mesmerism. Your own soul, as a hunter, has gone out to fasten on the soul of the deer, even before you see any deer. And the soul of the deer fights to escape. Even before the deer has any wind of you, it is so. It is a subtle, profound battle of wills which takes place in the invisible. And it is a battle never finished till your bullet goes home. When you are *really* worked up to the true pitch, and you come at last into range, you don't then aim as you do when you are firing at a bottle. It is your own *will* which carries the bullet into the heart of your quarry. The bullet's flight home is a sheer projection of your own fate into the fate of the deer. It happens like a supreme wish, a supreme act of volition, not as a dodge of cleverness.

He was a huntsman in spirit, not a farmer, and not a soldier stuck in a regiment. And it was as a young hunter that he wanted to bring down March as his quarry, to make her his wife. So he gathered himself subtly together, seemed to withdraw into a kind of invisibility. He was not quite sure how he would go on. And March was suspicious as a hare. So he remained in appearance just the nice, odd stranger-youth, staying for a fortnight on the place.

He had been sawing logs for the fire in the afternoon. Darkness came very early. It was still a cold, raw mist. It was getting almost too dark to see. A pile of short sawed logs lay beside the trestle. March came to carry them indoors, or into the shed, as he was busy sawing the last log. He was working in his shirtsleeves, and did not notice her approach; she came unwillingly, as if shy. He saw her stooping to the bright-ended logs, and he stopped sawing. A fire like lightning flew down his legs in the nerves.

'March?' he said in his quiet, young voice.

She looked up from the logs she was piling.

'Yes!' she said.

He looked down on her in the dusk. He could see her not too distinctly.

'I wanted to ask you something,' he said.

'Did you? What was it?' she said. Already the fright was in her voice. But she was too much mistress of herself.

'Why' – his voice seemed to draw out soft and subtle, it penetrated her nerves – 'why, what do you think it is?'

She stood up, placed her hands on her hips, and stood looking at him transfixed, without answering. Again he burned with a sudden power.

'Well,' he said, and his voice was so soft it seemed rather like a subtle touch, like the merest touch of a cat's paw, a feeling rather than a sound. 'Well – I wanted to ask you to marry me.'

March felt rather than heard him. She was trying in vain to turn aside her face. A great relaxation seemed to have come over her. She stood silent, her head slightly on one side. He seemed to be bending towards her, invisibly smiling. It seemed to her fine sparks came out of him.

Then very suddenly she said, 'Don't try any of your tomfoolery on me.'

A quiver went over his nerves. He had missed. He waited a moment to collect himself again. Then he said, putting all the strange softness into his voice, as if he were imperceptibly stroking her, 'Why, it's not tomfoolery. It's not tom-foolery. I mean it. I mean it. What makes you disbelieve me?'

He sounded hurt. And his voice had such a curious power over her; making her feel loose and relaxed. She struggled somewhere for her own power. She felt for a moment that she was lost – lost – lost. The word seemed to rock in her as if she were dying. Suddenly again she spoke.

'You don't know what you are talking about,' she said, in a brief and transient stroke of scorn. 'What nonsense! I'm old enough to be your mother.'

'Yes, I do know what I'm talking about. Yes, I do,' he persisted softly, as if he were producing his voice in her blood. 'I know quite well what I'm talking about. You're not old enough to be my mother. That isn't true. And what does it matter even if it was. You can marry me whatever age we are. What is age to me? And what is age to you! Age is nothing.'

A swoon went over her as he concluded. He spoke rapidly – in the rapid Cornish fashion – and his voice seemed to sound in her somewhere where she was helpless against it. 'Age is nothing!' The soft, heavy insistence of it made her sway dimly out there in the darkness. She could not answer.

A great exultance leaped like fire over his limbs. He felt he had won.

'I want to marry you, you see. Why shouldn't I?' he proceeded, soft and rapid. He waited for her to answer. In the dusk he saw her almost phosphorescent. Her eyelids were dropped, her face half-averted and unconscious. She seemed to be in his power. But he waited, watchful. He dared not yet touch her.

'Say then,' he said, 'say then you'll marry me. Say – say!' He was softly insistent.

'What?' she asked, faint, from a distance, like one in pain. His voice was now unthinkably near and soft. He drew very near to her.

'Say yes.'

'Oh, I can't,' she wailed helplessly, half-articulate, as if semiconscious, and as if in pain, like one who dies. 'How can I?'

'You can,' he said softly, laying his hand gently on her shoulder as she stood with her head averted and dropped, dazed. 'You can. Yes, you can. What makes you say you can't? You can. You can.' And with awful softness he bent forward and just touched her neck with his mouth and his chin.

'Don't!' she cried, with a faint mad cry like hysteria, starting away and facing round on him. 'What do you mean?' But she had no breath to speak with. It was as if she was killed.

'I mean what I say,' he persisted softly and cruelly. 'I want you to marry me. I want you to marry me. You know that, now, don't you? You know that, now? Don't you? Don't you?'

'What?' she said.

'Know,' he replied.

'Yes,' she said. 'I know you say so.'

'And you know I mean it, don't you?'

'I know you say so.'

'You believe me?' he said.

She was silent for some time. Then she pursed her lips.

'I don't know what I believe,' she said.

'Are you out there?' came Banford's voice, calling from the house.

'Yes, we're bringing in the logs,' he answered.

'I thought you'd gone lost,' said Banford disconsolately. 'Hurry up, do, and come and let's have tea. The kettle's boiling.'

He stooped at once to take an armful of little logs and carry them into the kitchen, where they were piled in a corner. March also helped, filling her arms and carrying the logs on her breast as if they were some heavy child. The night had fallen cold.

When the logs were all in, the two cleaned their boots noisily on the scraper outside, then rubbed them on the mat. March shut the door and took off her old felt hat – her farm-girl hat. Her thick, crisp, black hair was loose, her face was pale and strained. She pushed back her hair vaguely and washed her hands. Banford came hurrying into the dimly-lighted kitchen, to take from the oven the scones she was keeping hot.

'Whatever have you been doing all this time?' she asked fretfully. 'I thought you were never coming in. And it's ages since you stopped sawing. What were you doing out there?'

'Well,' said Henry, 'we had to stop that hole in the barn to keep the rats out.'

'Why, I could see you standing there in the shed. I could see your shirt-sleeves,' challenged Banford.

'Yes, I was just putting the saw away.'

They went in to tea. March was quite mute. Her face was pale and strained and vague. The youth, who always had the same ruddy, self-contained look on his face, as though he were keeping himself to himself, had come to tea in his shirtsleeves as if he were at home. He bent over his plate as he ate his food.

'Aren't you cold?' said Banford spitefully. 'In your shirtsleeves.'

He looked up at her, with his chin near his plate, and his eyes very clear, pellucid, and unwavering as he watched her.

'No, I'm not cold,' he said with his usual soft courtesy. 'It's much warmer in here than it is outside, you see.'

'I hope it is,' said Banford, feeling nettled by him. He had a strange, suave assurance and a wide-eyed bright look that got on her nerves this evening.

'But perhaps,' he said softly and courteously, 'you don't like me coming to tea without my coat. I forgot that.'

'Oh, I don't mind,' said Banford: although she *did*.

'I'll go and get it, shall I?' he said.

March's dark eyes turned slowly down to him.

'No, don't you bother,' she said in her queer, twanging tone. 'If you feel all right as you are, stop as you are.' She spoke with a crude authority.

'Yes,' said he, 'I *feel* all right, if I'm not rude.'

'It's usually considered rude,' said Banford. 'But we don't mind.'

'Go along, "considered rude",' ejaculated March. 'Who considers it rude?'

'Why, you do, Nellie, in anybody else,' said Banford, bridling a little behind her spectacles, and feeling her food stick in her throat.

But March had again gone vague and unheeding, chewing her food as if she did not know she was eating at all. And the youth looked from one to another, with bright, watching eyes.

Banford was offended. For all his suave courtesy and soft voice, the youth seemed to her impudent. She did not like to look at him. She did not like to meet his clear, watchful eyes, she did not like to see the strange glow in his face, his cheeks with their delicate fine hair, and his ruddy skin that was quite dull and yet which seemed to burn with a curious heat of life. It made her feel a little ill to look at him: the quality of his physical presence was too penetrating, too hot.

After tea the evening was very quiet. The youth rarely went into the village. As a rule, he read: he was a great reader, in his own hours. That is, when he did begin, he read absorbedly. But he was not very eager to begin. Often he walked about the fields and along the hedges alone in the dark at night, prowling with a queer instinct for the night, and listening to the wild sounds.

Tonight, however, he took a Captain Mayne Reid book from Banford's shelf and sat down with knees wide apart and immersed himself in his story. His brownish fair hair was long, and lay on his head like a thick cap, combed sideways. He was still in his shirtsleeves, and bending forward under the lamp-light, with his knees stuck wide apart and the book in his hand and his whole figure absorbed in the rather strenuous business of reading, he gave Banford's sitting-room the look of a lumber-camp. She resented this. For on her sitting-room floor she had a red Turkey rug and dark stain round, the fireplace had fashionable green tiles, the piano stood open with the latest dance music: she played quite well: and on the walls were March's hand-painted swans and water-lilies. Moreover, with the logs nicely, tremulously burning in the grate, the thick curtains drawn, the doors all shut, and the pine trees hissing and shuddering in the wind outside, it was cosy, it was refined and nice. She resented the big, raw, long-legged youth sticking his khaki knees out and sitting there with his soldier's shirt-cuffs buttoned on his thick red wrists. From time to time he turned a page, and from time to time he gave a sharp look at the fire, settling the logs. Then he immersed himself again in the intense and isolated business of reading.

March, on the far side of the table, was spasmodically crocheting. Her mouth was pursed in an odd way, as when she had dreamed the fox's brush burned it, her beautiful, crisp black hair strayed in wisps. But her whole figure was absorbed in its bearing, as if she herself was miles away. In a sort of semi-dream she seemed to be hearing the fox singing round the house in the wind, singing wildly and sweetly and like a madness. With red but well-shaped hands she slowly crocheted the white cotton, very slowly, awkwardly.

Banford was also trying to read, sitting in her low chair. But between those two she felt fidgety. She kept moving and looking round and listening to the wind, and glancing secretly from one to the other of her companions. March, seated on a straight chair, with her knees in their close breeches crossed, and slowly, laboriously crocheting, was also a trial.

'Oh dear!' said Banford, 'My eyes are bad tonight.' And she pressed her fingers on her eyes.

The youth looked up at her with his clear, bright look, but did not speak.

'Are they, Jill?' said March absently.

Then the youth began to read again, and Banford perforce returned to her book. But she could not keep still. After a while she looked up at March, and a queer, almost malignant little smile was on her thin face.

'A penny for them, Nell,' she said suddenly.

March looked round with big, startled black eyes, and went pale as if with terror. She had been listening to the fox singing so tenderly, so tenderly, as he wandered round the house.

'What?' she said vaguely.

'A penny for them,' said Banford sarcastically. 'Or twopence, if they're as deep as all that.'

The youth was watching with bright, clear eyes from beneath the lamp.

'Why,' came March's vague voice, 'what do you want to waste your money for?'

'I thought it would be well spent,' said Banford.

'I wasn't thinking of anything except the way the wind was blowing,' said March.

'Oh dear,' replied Banford, 'I could have had as original thoughts as that myself. I'm afraid I *have* wasted my money this time.'

'Well, you needn't pay,' said March.

The youth suddenly laughed. Both women looked at him: March rather surprised-looking, as if she had hardly known he was there.

'Why, do you ever pay up on these occasions?' he asked.

'Oh yes,' said Banford. 'We always do. I've sometimes had to pass a shilling a week to Nellie, in the winter-time. It costs much less in summer.'

'What, paying for each other's thoughts?' he laughed.

'Yes, when we've absolutely come to the end of everything else.'

He laughed quickly, wrinkling his nose sharply like a puppy and laughing with quick pleasure, his eyes shining.

'It's the first time I ever heard of that,' he said.

'I guess you'd hear of it often enough if you stayed a winter on Bailey Farm,' said Banford lamentably.

'Do you get so tired, then?' he asked.

'So bored,' said Banford.

'Oh!' he said gravely. 'But why should you be bored?'

'Who wouldn't be bored?' said Banford.

'I'm sorry to hear that,' he said gravely.

'You must be, if you were hoping to have a lively time here,' said Banford.

He looked at her long and gravely.

'Well,' he said, with his odd, young seriousness, 'it's quite lively enough for me.'

'I'm glad to hear it,' said Banford.

And she returned to her book. In her thin, frail hair were already many threads of grey, though she was not yet thirty. The boy did not look down, but turned his eyes to March, who was sitting with pursed mouth laboriously crocheting, her eyes wide and absent. She had a warm, pale, fine skin and a delicate nose. Her pursed mouth looked shrewish. But the shrewish look was contradicted by the curious lifted arch of her dark brows, and the wideness of her eyes; a look of startled wonder and vagueness. She was listening again for the fox, who seemed to have wandered farther off into the night.

From under the edge of the lamplight the boy sat with his face looking up, watching her silently, his eyes round and very clear and intent. Banford, biting her fingers irritably, was glancing at him under her hair. He sat there perfectly still, his ruddy face tilted up from the low level under the light, on the edge of the dimness, and watching with perfect abstract intentness. March suddenly lifted her great dark eyes from her crocheting and saw him. She started, giving a little exclamation.

'There he *is*!' she cried involuntarily, as if terribly startled.

Banford looked round in amazement, sitting up straight.

'Whatever has got you, Nellie?' she cried.

But March, her face flushed a delicate rose colour, was looking away to the door.

'Nothing! Nothing!' she said crossly. 'Can't one speak?'

'Yes, if you speak sensibly,' said Banford. 'Whatever did you mean?'

'I don't know what I meant,' cried March testily

'Oh, Nellie, I hope you aren't going jumpy and nervy. I feel I can't stand another *thing*! Whoever did you mean? Did you mean Henry?' cried poor, frightened Banford.

'Yes. I suppose so,' said March laconically. She would never confess to the fox.

'Oh dear, my nerves are all gone for tonight,' wailed Banford.

At nine o'clock March brought in a tray with bread and cheese and tea – Henry had confessed that he liked a cup of tea. Banford drank a glass of milk and ate a little bread. And soon she said, 'I'm going to bed, Nellie, I'm all nerves tonight. Are you coming?'

'Yes, I'm coming the minute I've taken the tray away,' said March.

'Don't be long then,' said Banford fretfully. 'Good-night, Henry. You'll see the fire is safe, if you come up last, won't you?'

'Yes, Miss Banford, I'll see it's safe,' he replied in his reassuring way.

March was lighting the candle to go to the kitchen. Banford took her candle and went upstairs. When March came back to the fire, she said to him, 'I suppose we can trust you to put out the fire and everything?' She stood there with her hand on her hip, and one knee loose, her head averted shyly, as if she could not look at him. He had his face lifted, watching her.

'Come and sit down a minute,' he said softly.

'No, I'll be going. Jill will be waiting, and she'll get upset, if I don't come.'

'What made you jump like that this evening?' he asked.

'When did I jump?' she retorted, looking at him.

'Why, just now you did,' he said. 'When you cried out.'

'Oh!' she said. 'Then! – Why, I thought you were the fox!' And her face screwed into a queer smile, half-ironic.

'The fox! Why the fox?' he asked softly.

'Why, one evening last summer when I was out with the gun I saw the fox in the grass nearly at my feet, looking straight up at me. I don't know – I suppose he made an impression on me.' She turned aside her head again and let one foot stray loose, self-consciously.

'And did you shoot him?' asked the boy.

'No, he gave me such a start, staring straight at me as he did, and then stopping to look back at me over his shoulder with a laugh on his face.'

'A laugh on his face!' repeated Henry, also laughing. 'He frightened you, did he?'

'No, he didn't frighten me. He made an impression on me, that's all.'

'And you thought I was the fox, did you?' he laughed, with the same queer, quick little laugh, like a puppy wrinkling its nose.

'Yes, I did, for the moment,' she said. 'Perhaps he'd been in my mind without my knowing.'

'Perhaps you think I've come to steal your chickens or something,' he said, with the same young laugh.

But she only looked at him with a wide, dark, vacant eye.

'It's the first time,' he said, 'that I've ever been taken for a fox. Won't you sit down for a minute?' His voice was very soft and cajoling.

'No,' she said. 'Jill will be waiting.' But still she did not go, but stood with one foot loose and her face turned aside, just outside the circle of light.

'But won't you answer my question?' he said, lowering his voice still more.

'I don't know what question you mean.'

'Yes, you do. Of course you do. I mean the question of you marrying me.'

'No, I shan't answer that question,' she said flatly.

'Won't you?' The queer, young laugh came on his nose again. 'Is it because I'm like the fox? Is that why?' And still he laughed.

She turned and looked at him with a long, slow look.

'I wouldn't let that put you against me,' he said. 'Let me turn the lamp low, and come and sit down a minute.'

He put his red hand under the glow of the lamp and suddenly made the light very dim. March stood there in the dimness quite shadowy, but unmoving. He rose silently to his feet, on his long legs. And now his voice was extraordinarily soft and suggestive, hardly audible.

'You'll stay a moment,' he said. 'Just a moment.' And he put his hand on her shoulder. She turned her face from him. 'I'm sure you don't really think I'm like the fox,' he said, with the same softness and with a suggestion of laughter in his tone, a subtle mockery. 'Do you now?' And he drew her gently towards him and kissed her neck, softly. She winced and trembled and hung away. But his strong, young arm held her, and he kissed her softly again, still on the neck, for her face was averted.

'Won't you answer my question? Won't you now?' came his soft, lingering voice. He was trying to draw her near to kiss her face. And he kissed her cheek softly, near the ear.

At that moment Banford's voice was heard calling fretfully, crossly from upstairs.

'There's Jill!' cried March, starting and drawing erect.

And as she did so, quick as lightning he kissed her on the mouth, with a quick, brushing kiss. It seemed to burn through her every fibre. She gave a queer little cry.

'You will, won't you? You will?' he insisted softly.

'Nellie! *Nellie!* Whatever are you so long for?' came Banford's faint cry from the outer darkness.

But he held her fast, and was murmuring with that intolerable softness and insistency, 'You will, won't you? Say yes! Say yes!'

March, who felt as if the fire had gone through her and scathed her, and as if she could do no more, murmured, 'Yes! Yes! Anything you like! Anything you like! Only let me go! Only let me go! Jill's calling.'

'You know you've promised,' he said insidiously.

'Yes! Yes! I do!' Her voice suddenly rose into a shrill cry. 'All right, Jill, I'm coming.'

Startled, he let her go, and she went straight upstairs.

In the morning at breakfast, after he had looked round the place and attended to the stock and thought to himself that one could live easily enough here, he said to Banford, 'Do you know what, Miss Banford?'

'Well, what?' said the good-natured, nervy Banford.

He looked at March, who was spreading jam on her bread.

'Shall I tell?' he said to her.

She looked up at him, and a deep pink colour flushed over her face.

'Yes, if you mean Jill,' she said. 'I hope you won't go talking all over the village, that's all.' And she swallowed her dry bread with difficulty.

'Whatever's coming?' said Banford, looking up with wide, tired, slightly reddened eyes. She was a thin, frail little thing, and her hair, which was delicate and thin, was bobbed, so it hung softly by her worn face in its faded brown and grey.

'Why, what do you think?' he said, smiling like one who has a secret.

'How do I know!' said Banford.

'Can't you guess?' he said, making bright eyes and smiling, pleased with himself.

'I'm sure I can't. What's more, I'm not going to try.'

'Nellie and I are going to be married.'

Banford put down her knife out of her thin, delicate fingers, as if she would never take it up to eat any more. She stared with blank, reddened eyes.

'You what?' she exclaimed.

'We're going to get married. Aren't we, Nellie?' and he turned to March.

'You say so, anyway,' said March laconically. But again she flushed with an agonised flush. She, too, could swallow no more.

Banford looked at her like a bird that has been shot: a poor little sick bird. She gazed at her with all her wounded soul in her face, at the deep-flushed March.

'Never!' she exclaimed, helpless.

'It's quite right,' said the bright and gloating youth.

Banford turned aside her face, as if the sight of the food on the table made her sick. She sat like this for some moments, as if she were sick. Then, with one hand on the edge of the table, she rose to her feet.

'I'll *never* believe it, Nellie,' she cried. 'It's absolutely impossible!'

Her plaintive, fretful voice had a thread of hot anger and despair.

'Why? Why shouldn't you believe it?' asked the youth, with all his soft, velvety impertinence in his voice.

Banford looked at him from her wide, vague eyes, as if he were some creature in a museum.

'Oh,' she said languidly, 'because she can never be such a fool. She can't lose her self-respect to such an extent.' Her voice was cold and plaintive, drifting.

'In what way will she lose her self-respect?' asked the boy.

Banford looked at him with vague fixity from behind her spectacles.

'If she hasn't lost it already,' she said.

He became very red, vermilion, under the slow, vague stare from behind the spectacles.

'I don't see it at all,' he said.

'Probably you don't. I shouldn't expect you would,' said Banford, with that straying, mild tone of remoteness which made her words even more insulting.

He sat stiff in his chair, staring with hot, blue eyes from his scarlet face. An ugly look had come on his brow.

'My word, she doesn't know what she's letting herself in for,' said Banford, in her plaintive, drifting, insulting voice.

'What has it got to do with you, anyway?' said the youth, in a temper.

'More than it has to do with you, probably,' she replied, plaintive and venomous.

'Oh, has it! I don't see that at all,' he jerked out.

'No, you wouldn't,' she answered, drifting.

'Anyhow,' said March, pushing back her hair and rising uncouthly, 'it's no good arguing about it.' And she seized the bread and the teapot and strode away to the kitchen.

Banford let her fingers stray across her brow and along her hair, like one bemused. Then she turned and went away upstairs.

Henry sat stiff and sulky in his chair, with his face and his eyes on fire. March came and went, clearing the table. But Henry sat on, stiff with temper. He took no notice of her. She had regained her composure and her soft, even, creamy complexion. But her mouth was pursed up. She glanced at him each time as she came to take things from the table, glanced from her large, curious eyes, more in curiosity than anything. Such a long, red-faced, sulky boy! That was all he was. He seemed as remote from her as if his red face were a red chimney-pot on a cottage across the fields, and she looked at him just as objectively, as remotely.

At length he got up and stalked out into the fields with the gun. He came in only at dinner-time, with the devil still in his face, but his manners quite polite. Nobody said anything particular; they sat each one at the sharp corner of a triangle, in obstinate remoteness. In the afternoon he went out again at once with the gun. He came in at nightfall with a rabbit and a pigeon. He stayed in all the evening, but hardly opened his mouth. He was in the devil of a temper, feeling he had been insulted.

Banford's eyes were red, she had evidently been crying. But her manner was more remote and supercilious than ever; the way she turned her head if he spoke at all, as if he were some tramp or inferior intruder of that sort, made his blue eyes go almost black with rage. His face looked sulkier. But he never forgot his polite intonation, if he opened his mouth to speak.

March seemed to flourish in this atmosphere. She seemed to sit between the two antagonists with a little wicked smile on her face, enjoying herself. There was even a sort of complacency in the way she laboriously crocheted this evening.

When he was in bed, the youth could hear the two women talking and arguing in their room. He sat up in bed and strained his ears to hear what they said. But he could hear nothing, it was too far off. Yet he could hear the soft, plaintive drip of Banford's voice, and March's deeper note.

The night was quiet, frosty. Big stars were snapping outside, beyond the ridge-tops of the pine trees. He listened and listened. In the distance he heard a fox yelping: and the dogs from the farms barking in answer. But it was not that he wanted to hear. It was what the two women were saying.

He got stealthily out of bed and stood by his door. He could hear no more than before. Very, very carefully he began to lift the door latch. After quite a time he had his door open. Then he stepped stealthily out into the passage. The old oak planks were cold under his feet, and they creaked preposterously. He crept very, very gently up the one step, and along by the wall, till he stood outside their door. And there he held his breath and listened. Banford's voice: 'No, I simply couldn't stand it. I should be dead in a month. Which is just what he would be aiming at, of course. That would just be his game, to see me in the churchyard. No, Nellie, if you were to do such a thing as to marry him, you could never stop here. I couldn't, I couldn't live in the same house with him. Oh! – oh! I feel quite sick with the smell of his clothes. And his red face simply turns me over. I can't eat my food when he's at the table. What a fool I was ever to let him stop. One ought *never* to try to do a kind action. It always flies back in your face like a boomerang.'

'Well, he's only got two more days,' said March.

'Yes, thank heaven. And when he's gone he'll never come in this house again. I feel so bad while he's here. And I know, I know he's only counting what he can get out of you. I *know* that's all it is. He's just a good-for-nothing, who doesn't want to work, and who thinks he'll live on us. But he won't live on me. If you're such a fool, then it's your own lookout. Mrs Burgess knew him all the time he was here. And the old man could never get him to do any steady work. He was off with the gun on every occasion, just as he is now. Nothing but the gun! Oh, I do hate it. You don't know what you're doing, Nellie, you don't. If you marry him he'll just make a fool of you. He'll go off and leave you stranded. I know he will, if he can't get Bailey Farm out of us – and he's not going to, while I live. While I live he's never going to set foot here. I know what it would be. He'd soon think he was master of both of us, as he thinks he's master of you already.'

'But he isn't,' said Nellie.

'He thinks he is, anyway. And that's what he wants: to come and be master here. Yes, imagine it! That's what we've got the place together for, is it, to be bossed and bullied by a hateful, red-faced boy, a beastly labourer. Oh, we *did* make a mistake when we let him stop. We ought never to have lowered ourselves. And I've had such a fight with all the people here, not to be pulled down to their level. No, he's not coming here. And then you see – if he can't have the place, he'll run off to Canada or somewhere again, as if he'd never known you. And here you'll be, absolutely ruined and made a fool of. I know I shall never have any peace of mind again.'

'We'll tell him he can't come here. We'll tell him that,' said March.

'Oh, don't you bother; I'm going to tell him that, and other things as well, before he goes. He's not going to have all his own way while I've got the strength left to speak. Oh, Nellie, he'll despise you, he'll despise you, like the awful little beast he is, if you give way to him. I'd no more trust him than I'd trust a cat not to steal. He's deep, he's deep, and he's bossy, and he's selfish through and through, as cold as ice. All he wants is to make use of you. And when you're no more use to him, then I pity you.'

'I don't think he's as bad as all that,' said March.

'No, because he's been playing up to you. But you'll find out, if you see much more of him. Oh, Nellie, I can't bear to think of it.'

'Well, it won't hurt you, Jill darling.'

'Won't it! Won't it! I shall never know a moment's peace again while I live, nor a moment's happiness. No, Nellie – ' and Banford began to weep bitterly.

The boy outside could hear the stifled sound of the woman's sobbing, and could hear March's soft, deep, tender voice comforting, with wonderful gentleness and tenderness, the weeping woman.

His eyes were so round and wide that he seemed to see the whole night, and his ears were almost jumping off his head. He was frozen stiff. He crept back to bed, but felt as if the top of his head were coming off. He could not sleep. He could not keep still. He rose, quietly dressed himself, and crept out on to the landing once more. The women were silent. He went softly downstairs and out to the kitchen.

Then he put on his boots and his overcoat and took the gun. He did not think to go away from the farm. No, he only took the gun. As softly as possible he unfastened the door and went out into the frosty December night. The air was still, the stars bright, the pine trees seemed to bristle audibly in the sky. He went stealthily away down a fence-side, looking for something to shoot. At the same time he remembered that he ought not to shoot and frighten the women.

So he prowled round the edge of the gorse cover, and through the grove of tall old hollies, to the woodside. There he skirted the fence, peering through the darkness with dilated eyes that seemed to be able to grow black and full of sight in the dark, like a cat's. An owl was slowly and mournfully whooing round a great oak tree. He stepped stealthily with his gun, listening, listening, watching.

As he stood under the oaks of the wood-edge he heard the dogs from the neighbouring cottage up the hill yelling suddenly and startlingly, and the wakened dogs from the farms around barking answer. And suddenly it seemed to him England was little and tight, he felt the landscape was constricted even in the dark, and that there were too many dogs in the night, making a noise like a fence of sound, like the network of English hedges netting the view. He felt the fox didn't have a chance. For it must be the fox that had started all this hullabaloo.

Why not watch for him, anyhow! He would, no doubt, be coming sniffing round. The lad walked downhill to where the farmstead with its few pine trees crouched blackly. In the angle of the long shed, in the black dark, he crouched down. He knew the fox would be coming. It seemed to him it would be the last of the foxes in this loudly-barking, thick-voiced England, tight with innumerable little houses.

He sat a long time with his eyes fixed unchanging upon the open gateway, where a little light seemed to fall from the stars or from the horizon, who knows. He was sitting on a log in a dark corner with the gun across his knees. The pine trees snapped. Once a chicken fell off its perch in the barn with a loud crawk and cackle and commotion that startled him, and he stood up, watching with all his eyes, thinking it might be a rat. But he *felt* it was nothing. So he sat down again with the gun on his knees and his hands tucked in to keep them warm, and his eyes fixed unblinking on the pale reach of the open gateway. He felt he could smell the hot, sickly, rich smell of live chickens on the cold air.

And then – a shadow. A sliding shadow in the gateway. He gathered all his vision into a concentrated spark, and saw the shadow of the fox, the fox creeping on his belly through the gate. There he went, on his belly like a snake. The boy smiled to himself and brought the gun to his shoulder. He knew quite well what would happen. He knew the fox would go to where the fowl door was boarded up and sniff there. He knew he would lie there for a minute, sniffing the fowls within. And then he would start again prowling under the edge of the old barn, waiting to get in.

The fowl door was at the top of a slight incline. Soft, soft as a shadow the fox slid up this incline, and crouched with his nose to the boards. And at the same moment there was the awful crash of a gun reverberating between the old buildings, as if all the night had gone smash. But the boy watched keenly. He saw even the white belly of the fox as the beast beat his paws in death. So he went forward.

There was a commotion everywhere. The fowls were scuffling and crawking, the ducks were quark-quarking, the pony had stamped wildly to his feet. But the fox was on his side, struggling in his last tremors. The boy bent over him and smelt his foxy smell.

There was a sound of a window opening upstairs, then March's voice calling, 'Who is it?'

'It's me,' said Henry; 'I've shot the fox.'

'Oh, goodness! You nearly frightened us to death.'

'Did I? I'm awfully sorry.'

'Whatever made you get up?'

'I heard him about.'

'And have you shot him?'

'Yes, he's here,' and the boy stood in the yard holding up the warm, dead brute. 'You can't see, can you? Wait a minute.' And he took his flashlight from his pocket and flashed it on to the dead animal. He was holding it by the brush. March saw, in the middle of the darkness, just the reddish fleece and the white belly and the white underneath of the pointed chin, and the queer, dangling paws. She did not know what to say.

'He's a beauty,' he said. 'He will make you a lovely fur.'

'You don't catch me wearing a fox fur,' she replied.

'Oh!' he said. And he switched off the light.

'Well, I should think you'll come in and go to bed again now,' she said.

'Probably I shall. What time is it?'

'What time is it, Jill?' called March's voice. It was a quarter to one.

That night March had another dream. She dreamed that Banford was dead, and that she, March, was sobbing her heart out. Then she had to put Banford into her coffin. And the coffin was the rough wood-box in which the bits of chopped wood were kept in the kitchen, by the fire. This was the coffin, and there was no other, and March was in agony and dazed bewilderment, looking for something to line the box with, something to make it soft with, something to cover up the poor, dead darling. Because she couldn't lay her in there just in her white, thin nightdress, in the horrible wood-box. So she hunted and hunted, and picked up thing after thing, and threw it aside in the agony of dream-frustration. And in her dream-despair all she could find that would do was a fox-skin. She knew that it wasn't right, that this was not what she should have. But it was all she could find. And so she folded the brush of the fox, and laid her darling Jill's head on this, and she brought round the skin of the fox and laid it on the top of the body, so that it seemed to make a whole ruddy, fiery coverlet, and she cried and cried, and woke to find the tears streaming down her face.

The first thing that both she and Banford did in the morning was to go out to see the fox. Henry had hung it up by the heels in the shed, with its poor brush falling backwards. It was a lovely dog-fox in its prime, with a handsome, thick, winter coat: a lovely golden-red colour, with grey as it passed to the belly, and belly all white, and a great full brush with a delicate black and grey and pure white tip.

'Poor brute!' said Banford. 'If it wasn't such a thieving wretch, you'd feel sorry for it.'

March said nothing, but stood with her foot trailing aside, one hip out; her face was pale and her eyes big and black, watching the dead animal that was suspended upside down. White and soft as snow his belly: white and soft as snow. She passed her hand softly down it. And his wonderful black-glinted brush was full and frictional, wonderful. She passed her hand down this also, and quivered. Time after time she took the full fur of that thick tail between her fingers, and passed her hand slowly downwards. Wonderful, sharp, thick, splendour of a tail. And he was dead! She pursed her lips, and her eyes went black and vacant. Then she took the head in her hand.

Henry was sauntering up, so Banford walked rather pointedly away. March stood there bemused, with the head of the fox in her hand. She was wondering, wondering, wondering over his long, fine muzzle. For some reason it reminded her of a spoon or a spatula. She felt she could not understand it. The beast was a strange beast to her, incomprehensible, out of her range. Wonderful silver whiskers he had, like ice-threads. And pricked ears with hair inside. But that long, long, slender spoon of a nose! – and the marvellous white teeth beneath! It was to thrust forward and bite with, deep, deep, deep into the living prey, to bite and bite the blood.

'He's a beauty, isn't he?' said Henry, standing by.

'Oh yes, he's a fine big fox. I wonder how many chickens he's responsible for,' she replied.

'A good many. Do you think he's the same one you saw in the summer?'

'I should think very likely he is,' she replied.

He watched her, but he could make nothing of her. Partly she was so shy and virgin, and partly she was so grim, matter-of-fact, shrewish. What she said seemed to him so different from the look of her big, queer, dark eyes.

'Are you going to skin him?' she asked.

'Yes, when I've had breakfast, and got a board to peg him on.'

'My word, what a strong smell he's got! Pooo! It'll take some washing off one's hands. I don't know why I was so silly as to handle him.' And she looked at her right hand, that had passed down his belly and along his tail, and had even got a tiny streak of blood from one dark place in his fur.

'Have you seen the chickens when they smell him, how frightened they are?' he said.

'Yes, aren't they!'

'You must mind you don't get some of his fleas.'

'Oh, fleas!' she replied, nonchalant.

Later in the day she saw the fox's skin nailed flat on a board, as if crucified. It gave her an uneasy feeling.

The boy was angry. He went about with his mouth shut, as if he had swallowed part of his chin. But in behaviour he was polite and affable. He did not say anything about his intention. And he left March alone.

That evening they sat in the dining-room. Banford wouldn't have him in her sitting-room any more. There was a very big log on the fire. And everybody was busy. Banford had letters to write. March was sewing a dress, and he was mending some little contrivance.

Banford stopped her letter-writing from time to time to look round and rest her eyes. The boy had his head down, his face hidden over his job.

'Let's see,' said Banford. 'What train do you go by, Henry?'

He looked up straight at her.

'The morning train. In the morning,' he said.

'What, the eight-ten or the eleven-twenty?'

'The eleven-twenty, I suppose,' he said.

'That is the day after tomorrow?' said Banford.

'Yes, the day after tomorrow.'

'Mmm!' murmured Banford, and she returned to her writing. But as she was licking her envelope, she asked, 'And what plans have you made for the future, if I may ask?'

'Plans?' he said, his face very bright and angry.

'I mean about you and Nellie, if you are going on with this business. When do you expect the wedding to come off?' She spoke in a jeering tone.

'Oh, the wedding!' he replied. 'I don't know.'

'Don't you know anything?' said Banford. 'Are you going to clear out on Friday and leave things no more settled than they are?'

'Well, why shouldn't I? We can always write letters.'

'Yes, of course you can. But I wanted to know because of this place. If Nellie is going to get married all of a sudden, I shall have to be looking round for a new partner.'

'Couldn't she stay on here if she were married?' he said. He knew quite well what was coming.

'Oh,' said Banford, 'this is no place for a married couple. There's not enough work to keep a man going, for one thing. And there's no money to be made. It's quite useless your thinking of staying on here if you marry. Absolutely!'

'Yes, but I wasn't thinking of staying on here,' he said.

'Well, that's what I want to know. And what about Nellie, then? How long is *she* going to be here with me, in that case?'

The two antagonists looked at one another.

'That I can't say,' he answered.

'Oh, go along,' she cried petulantly. 'You must have some idea what you are going to do, if you ask a woman to marry you. Unless it's all a hoax.'

'Why should it be a hoax? I am going back to Canada.'

'And taking her with you?'

'Yes, certainly.'

'You hear that, Nellie?' said Banford.

March, who had had her head bent over her sewing, now looked up with a sharp, pink blush on her face, and a queer, sardonic laugh in her eyes and on her twisted mouth.

'That's the first time I've heard that I was going to Canada,' she said.

'Well, you have to hear it for the first time, haven't you?' said the boy.

'Yes, I suppose I have,' she said nonchalantly. And she went back to her sewing.

'You're quite ready, are you, to go to Canada? Are you, Nellie?' asked Banford.

March looked up again. She let her shoulders go slack, and let her hand that held the needle lie loose in her lap.

'It depends on *how* I'm going,' she said. 'I don't think I want to go jammed up in the steerage, as a soldier's wife. I'm afraid I'm not used to that way.'

The boy watched her with bright eyes.

'Would you rather stay over here while I go first?' he asked.

'I would, if that's the only alternative,' she replied.

'That's much the wisest. Don't make it any fixed engagement,' said Banford. 'Leave yourself free to go or not after he's got back and found you a place, Nellie. Anything else is madness, madness.'

'Don't you think,' said the youth, 'we ought to get married before I go – and then go together, or separate, according to how it happens?'

'I think it's a *terrible* idea,' cried Banford.

But the boy was watching March.

'What do you think?' he asked her.

She let her eyes stray vaguely into space.

'Well, I don't know,' she said. 'I shall have to think about it.'

'Why?' he asked pertinently.

'Why?' She repeated his question in a mocking way and looked at him laughing, though her face was pink again. 'I should think there's plenty of reasons why.'

He watched her in silence. She seemed to have escaped him. She had got into league with Banford against him. There was again the queer, sardonic look about her; she would mock stoically at everything he said or which life offered.

'Of course,' he said, 'I don't want to press you to do anything you don't wish to do.'

'I should think not, indeed,' cried Banford indignantly.

At bedtime Banford said plaintively to March, 'You take my hot bottle up for me, Nellie, will you?'

'Yes, I'll do it,' said March, with the kind of willing unwillingness she so often showed towards her beloved but uncertain Jill.

The two women went upstairs. After a time March called from the top of the stairs: 'Good-night, Henry. I shan't be coming down. You'll see to the lamp and the fire, won't you?'

The next day Henry went about with the cloud on his brow and his young cub's face shut up tight. He was cogitating all the time. He had wanted March to marry him and go back to Canada with him. And he had been sure she would do it. Why he wanted her he didn't know. But he did want her. He had set his mind on her. And he was convulsed with a youth's fury at being thwarted. To be thwarted, to be thwarted! It made him so furious inside that he did not know what to do with himself. But he kept himself in hand. Because even now things might turn out differently. She might come over to him. Of course she might. It was her business to do so.

Things drew to a tension again towards evening. He and Banford had avoided each other all day. In fact, Banford went in to the little town by the 11.20 train. It was market day. She arrived back on the 4.25. Just as the night was falling Henry saw her little figure in a dark-blue coat and a dark-blue tam-o'-shanter hat crossing the first meadow from the station. He stood under one of the wild pear trees, with the old dead leaves round his feet. And he watched the little blue figure advancing persistently over the rough winter-ragged meadow. She had her arms full of parcels, and advanced slowly, frail thing she was, but with that devilish little certainty which he so detested in her. He stood invisible under the pear tree, watching her every step. And if looks could have affected her, she would have felt a log of iron on each of her ankles as she made her way forward.

'You're a nasty little thing, you are,' he was saying softly, across the distance. 'You're a nasty little thing. I hope you'll be paid back for all the harm you've done me for nothing. I hope you will – you nasty little thing. I hope you'll have to pay for it. You will, if wishes are anything. You nasty little creature that you are.'

She was toiling slowly up the slope. But if she had been slipping back at every step towards the Bottomless Pit, he would not have gone to help her with her parcels. Aha, there went March, striding with her long land stride in her breeches and her short tunic! Striding downhill at a great pace, and even running a few steps now and then, in her great solicitude and desire to come to the rescue of the little Banford. The boy watched her with rage in his heart. See her leap a ditch, and run, run as if a house was on fire, just to get to that creeping, dark little object down there! So, the Banford just stood still and waited. And March strode up and took *all* the parcels except a bunch of yellow chrysanthemums. These the Banford still carried – yellow chrysanthemums!

'Yes, you look well, don't you?' he said softly into the dusk air. 'You look well, pottering up there with a bunch of flowers, you do. I'd make you eat them for your tea if you hug them so tight. And I'd give them you for breakfast again, I would. I'd give you flowers. Nothing but flowers.'

He watched the progress of the two women. He could hear their voices: March always outspoken and rather scolding in her tenderness, Banford murmuring rather vaguely. They were evidently good friends. He could not hear what they said till they came to the fence of the home meadow, which they must climb. Then he saw March manfully climbing over the bars with all her packages in her arms, and on the still air he heard Banford's fretful, 'Why don't you let me help you with the parcels?' She had a queer, plaintive hitch in her voice. Then came March's robust and reckless, 'Oh, I can manage. Don't you bother about me. You've all you can do to get yourself over.'

'Yes, that's all very well,' said Banford fretfully. 'You say, *Don't you bother about me*, and then all the while you feel injured because nobody thinks of you.'

'When do I feel injured?' said March.

'Always. You always feel injured. Now you're feeling injured because I won't have that boy to come and live on the farm.'

'I'm not feeling injured at all,' said March.

'I know you are. When he's gone you'll sulk over it. I know you will.'

'Shall I?' said March. 'We'll see.'

'Yes, we *shall* see, unfortunately. I can't think how you can make yourself so cheap. I can't *imagine* how you can lower yourself like it.'

'I haven't lowered myself,' said March.

'I don't know what you call it, then. Letting a boy like that come so cheeky and impudent and make a mug of you. I don't know what you think of yourself. How much respect do you think he's going to have for you afterwards? My word, I wouldn't be in your shoes, if you married him.'

'Of course you wouldn't. My boots are a good bit too big for you, and not half dainty enough,' said March, with rather a misfire sarcasm.

'I thought you had too much pride, really I did. A woman's got to hold herself high, especially with a youth like that. Why, he's impudent. Even the way he forced himself on us at the start.'

'We asked him to stay,' said March.

'Not till he'd almost forced us to. And then he's so cocky and self-assured. My word, he puts my back up. I simply can't imagine how you can let him treat you so cheaply.'

'I don't let him treat me cheaply,' said March. 'Don't you worry yourself, nobody's going to treat me cheaply. And even you aren't, either.' She had a tender defiance and a certain fire in her voice.

'Yes, it's sure to come back to me,' said Banford bitterly. 'That's always the end of it. I believe you only do it to spite me.'

They went now in silence up the steep, grassy slope and over the brow, through the gorse bushes. On the other side of the hedge the boy followed in the dusk, at some little distance. Now and then, through the huge ancient hedge of hawthorn, risen into trees, he saw the two dark figures creeping up the hill. As he came to the top of the slope he saw the homestead dark in the twilight, with a huge old pear tree leaning from the near gable, and a little yellow light twinkling in the small side windows of the kitchen. He heard the clink of the latch and saw the kitchen door open into light as the two women went indoors. So they were at home.

And so! – this was what they thought of him. It was rather in his nature to be a listener, so he was not at all surprised whatever he heard. The things people said about him always missed him personally. He was only rather surprised at the women's way with one another. And he disliked the Banford with an acid dislike. And he felt drawn to the March again. He felt again irresistibly drawn to her. He felt there was a secret bond, a secret thread between him and her, something very exclusive, which shut out everybody else and made him and her possess each other in secret.

He hoped again that she would have him. He hoped with his blood suddenly firing up that she would agree to marry him quite quickly: at Christmas, very likely. Christmas was not far off. He wanted, whatever else happened, to snatch her into a hasty marriage and a consummation with him. Then for the future, they could arrange later. But he hoped it would happen as he wanted it. He hoped that tonight she would stay a little while with him, after Banford had gone upstairs. He hoped he could touch her soft, creamy cheek, her strange, frightened face. He hoped he could look into her dilated, frightened dark eyes, quite near. He hoped he might even put his hand on her bosom and feel her soft breasts under her tunic. His heart beat deep and powerful as he thought of that. He wanted very much to do so. He wanted to make sure of her soft woman's breasts under her tunic. She always kept the brown linen coat buttoned so close up to her throat. It seemed to him like some perilous secret, that her soft woman's breasts must be buttoned up in that uniform. It seemed to him, moreover, that they were so much softer, tenderer, more lovely and lovable, shut up in that tunic, than were the Banford's breasts, under her soft blouses and chiffon dresses. The Banford would have little iron breasts, he said to himself. For all her frailty and fretfulness and delicacy, she would have tiny iron breasts. But March, under her crude, fast, workman's tunic, would have soft, white breasts, white and unseen. So he told himself, and his blood burned.

When he went in to tea, he had a surprise. He appeared at the inner door, his face very ruddy and vivid and his blue eyes shining, dropping his head forward as he came in, in his usual way, and hesitating in the doorway to watch the inside of the room, keenly and cautiously, before he entered. He was wearing a long-sleeved waistcoat. His face seemed extraordinarily like a piece of the out-of-doors come indoors: as holly-berries do. In his second of pause in the doorway he took in the two women sitting at table, at opposite ends, saw them sharply. And to his amazement March was dressed in a dress of dull, green silk crape. His mouth came open in surprise. If she had suddenly grown a moustache he could not have been more surprised.

'Why,' he said, 'do you wear a dress, then?'

She looked up, flushing a deep rose colour, and twisting her mouth with a smile, said, 'Of course I do. What else do you expect me to wear but a dress?'

'A land girl's uniform, of course,' said he.

'Oh,' she cried, nonchalant, 'that's only for this dirty, mucky work about here.'

'Isn't it your proper dress, then?' he said.

'No, not indoors it isn't,' she said. But she was blushing all the time as she poured out his tea. He sat down in his chair at table, unable to take his eyes off her. Her dress was a perfectly simple slip of bluey-green crape, with a line of gold stitching round the top and round the sleeves, which came to the elbow. It was cut just plain and round at the top, and showed her white, soft throat. Her arms he knew, strong and firm muscled, for he had often seen her with her sleeves rolled up. But he looked her up and down, up and down.

Banford, at the other end of the table, said not a word, but piggled with the sardine on her plate. He had forgotten her existence. He just simply stared at March while he ate his bread and margarine in huge mouthfuls, forgetting even his tea.

'Well, I never knew anything make such a difference!' he murmured, across his mouthfuls.

'Oh, goodness!' cried March, blushing still more. 'I might be a pink monkey!'

And she rose quickly to her feet and took the teapot to the fire, to the kettle. And as she crouched on the hearth with her green slip about her, the boy stared more wide-eyed than ever. Through the crape her woman's form seemed soft and womanly. And when she stood up and walked he saw her legs move soft within her moderately short skirt. She had on black silk stockings, and small patent shoes with little gold buckles.

No, she was another being. She was something quite different. Seeing her always in the hard-cloth breeches, wide on the hips, buttoned on the knee, strong as armour, and in the brown puttees and thick boots, it had never occurred to him that she had a woman's legs and feet. Now it came upon him. She had a woman's soft, skirted legs, and she was accessible. He blushed to the roots of his hair, shoved his nose in his teacup and drank his tea with a little noise that made Banford simply squirm: and strangely, suddenly he felt a man, no longer a youth. He felt a man, with all a man's grave weight of responsibility. A curious quietness and gravity came over his soul. He felt a man, quiet, with a little of the heaviness of male destiny upon him.

She was soft and accessible in her dress. The thought went home in him like an everlasting responsibility.

'Oh, for goodness' sake, say something, somebody,' cried Banford fretfully. 'It might be a funeral.' The boy looked at her, and she could not bear his face.

'A funeral!' said March, with a twisted smile. 'Why, that breaks my dream.' Suddenly she had thought of Banford in the wood-box for a coffin.

'What, have you been dreaming of a wedding?' said Banford sarcastically.

'Must have been,' said March.

'Whose wedding?' asked the boy.

'I can't remember,' said March.

She was shy and rather awkward that evening, in spite of the fact that, wearing a dress, her bearing was much more subdued than in her uniform. She felt unpeeled and rather exposed. She felt almost improper.

They talked desultorily about Henry's departure next morning, and made the trivial arrangement. But of the matter on their minds, none of them spoke. They were rather quiet and friendly this evening; Banford had practically nothing to say. But inside herself she seemed still, perhaps kindly.

At nine o'clock March brought in the tray with the everlasting tea and a little cold meat which Banford had managed to procure. It was the last supper, so Banford did not want to be disagreeable. She felt a bit sorry for the boy, and felt she must be as nice as she could.

He wanted her to go to bed. She was usually the first. But she sat on in her chair under the lamp, glancing at her book now and then, and staring into the fire. A deep silence had come into the room. It was broken by March asking, in a rather small tone, 'What time is it, Jill?'

'Five past ten,' said Banford, looking at her wrist.

And then not a sound. The boy had looked up from the book he was holding between his knees. His rather wide, cat-shaped face had its obstinate look, his eyes were watchful.

'What about bed?' said March at last.

'I'm ready when you are,' said Banford.

'Oh, very well,' said March. 'I'll fill your bottle.'

She was as good as her word. When the hot-water bottle was ready, she lit a candle and went upstairs with it. Banford remained in her chair, listening acutely. March came downstairs again.

'There you are, then,' she said. 'Are you going up?'

'Yes, in a minute,' said Banford. But the minute passed, and she sat on in her chair under the lamp.

Henry, whose eyes were shining like a cat's as he watched from under his brows, and whose face seemed wider, more chubbed and catlike with unalterable obstinacy, now rose to his feet to try his throw.

'I think I'll go and look if I can see the she-fox,' he said. 'She may be creeping round. Won't you come as well for a minute, Nellie, and see if we see anything?'

'Me!' cried March, looking up with her startled, wondering face.

'Yes. Come on,' he said. It was wonderful how soft and warm and coaxing his voice could be, how near. The very sound of it made Banford's blood boil. 'Come on for a minute,' he said, looking down into her uplifted, unsure face.

And she rose to her feet as if drawn up by his young, ruddy face that was looking down on her.

'I should think you're never going out at this time of night, Nellie!' cried Banford.

'Yes, just for a minute,' said the boy, looking round on her, and speaking with an odd, sharp yelp in his voice.

March looked from one to the other, as if confused, vague. Banford rose to her feet for battle.

'Why, it's ridiculous. It's bitter cold. You'll catch your death in that thin frock. And in those slippers. You're not going to do any such thing.'

There was a moment's pause. Banford turtled up like a little fighting cock, facing March and the boy.

'Oh, I don't think you need worry yourself,' he replied. 'A moment under the stars won't do anybody any damage. I'll get the rug off the sofa in the dining-room. You're coming, Nellie.'

His voice had so much anger and contempt and fury in it as he spoke to Banford: and so much tenderness and proud authority as he spoke to March, that the latter answered, 'Yes, I'm coming.'

And she turned with him to the door.

Banford, standing there in the middle of the room, suddenly burst into a long wail and a spasm of sobs. She covered her face with her poor, thin hands, and her thin shoulders shook in an agony of weeping. March looked back from the door.

'Jill!' she cried in a frantic tone, like someone just coming awake. And she seemed to start towards her darling.

But the boy had March's arm in his grip, and she could not move. She did not know why she could not move. It was as in a dream when the heart strains and the body cannot stir.

'Never mind,' said the boy softly. 'Let her cry. Let her cry. She will have to cry sooner or later. And the tears will relieve her feelings. They will do her good.'

So he drew March slowly through the doorway. But her last look was back to the poor little figure which stood in the middle of the room with covered face and thin shoulders shaken with bitter weeping.

In the dining-room he picked up the rug and said, 'Wrap yourself up in this.'

She obeyed – and they reached the kitchen door, he holding her soft and firm by the arm, though she did not know it. When she saw the night outside she started back.

'I must go back to Jill,' she said. 'I *must*! Oh yes, I must.'

Her tone sounded final. The boy let go of her and she turned indoors. But he seized her again and arrested her.

'Wait a minute,' he said. 'Wait a minute. Even if you go, you're not going yet.'

'Leave go! Leave go!' she cried. 'My place is at Jill's side. Poor little thing, she's sobbing her heart out.'

'Yes,' said the boy bitterly. 'And your heart too, and mine as well.'

'Your heart?' said March. He still gripped her and detained her.

'Isn't it as good as her heart?' he said. 'Or do you think it's not?'

'Your heart?' she said again, incredulous.

'Yes, mine! Mine! Do you think I haven't *got* a heart?' And with his hot grasp he took her hand and pressed it under his left breast. 'There's my heart,' he said, 'if you don't believe in it.'

It was wonder which made her attend. And then she felt the deep, heavy, powerful stroke of his heart, terrible, like something from beyond. It was like something from beyond, something awful from outside, signalling to her. And the signal paralysed her. It beat upon her very soul, and made her helpless. She forgot Jill. She could not think of Jill any more. She could not think of her. That terrible signalling from outside!

The boy put his arm round her waist.

'Come with me,' he said gently. 'Come and let us say what we've got to say.'

And he drew her outside, closed the door. And she went with him darkly down the garden path. That he should have a beating heart! And that he should have his arm round her, outside the blanket! She was too confused to think who he was or what he was.

He took her to a dark corner of the shed, where there was a tool-box with a lid, long and low.

'We'll sit here a minute,' he said.

And obediently she sat down by his side.

'Give me your hand,' he said.

She gave him both her hands, and he held them between his own. He was young, and it made him tremble.

'You'll marry me. You'll marry me before I go back, won't you?' he pleaded.

'Why, aren't we both a pair of fools?' she said.

He had put her in the corner, so that she should not look out and see the lighted window of the house across the dark garden. He tried to keep her all there inside the shed with him.

'In what way a pair of fools?' he said. 'If you go back to Canada with me, I've got a job and a good wage waiting for me, and it's a nice place, near the mountains. Why shouldn't you marry me? Why shouldn't we marry? I should like to have you there with me. I should like to feel I'd got somebody there, at the back of me, all my life.'

'You'd easily find somebody else who'd suit you better,' she said.

'Yes, I might easily find another girl. I know I could. But not one I really wanted. I've never met one I really wanted for good. You see, I'm thinking of all my life. If I marry, I want to feel it's for all my life. Other girls: well, they're just girls, nice enough to go a walk with now and then. Nice enough for a bit of play. But when I think of my life, then I should be very sorry to have to marry one of them, I should indeed.'

'You mean they wouldn't make you a good wife.'

'Yes, I mean that. But I don't mean they wouldn't do their duty by me. I mean – I don't know what I mean. Only when I think of my life, and of you, then the two things go together.'

'And what if they didn't?' she said, with her odd, sardonic touch.

'Well, I think they would.'

They sat for some time silent. He held her hands in his, but he did not make love to her. Since he had realised that she was a woman, and vulnerable, accessible, a certain heaviness had possessed his soul. He did not want to make love to her. He shrank from any such performance, almost with fear. She was a woman, and vulnerable, accessible to him finally, and he held back from that which was ahead, almost with dread. It was a kind of darkness he knew he would enter finally, but of which he did not want as yet even to think. She was the woman, and he was responsible for the strange vulnerability he had suddenly realised in her.

'No,' she said at last, 'I'm a fool. I know I'm a fool.'

'What for?' he asked.

'To go on with this business.'

'Do you mean me?' he asked.

'No, I mean myself. I'm making a fool of myself, and a big one.'

'Why, because you don't want to marry me, really?'

'Oh, I don't know whether I'm against it, as a matter of fact. That's just it. I don't know.'

He looked at her in the darkness, puzzled. He did not in the least know what she meant.

'And don't you know whether you like to sit here with me this minute or not?' he asked.

'No, I don't really. I don't know whether I wish I was somewhere else, or whether I like being here. I don't know, really.'

'Do you wish you were with Miss Banford? Do you wish you'd gone to bed with her?' he asked, as a challenge.

She waited a long time before she answered: 'No,' she said at last. 'I don't wish that.'

'And do you think you would spend all your life with her – when your hair goes white, and you are old?' he said.

'No,' she said, without much hesitation. 'I don't see Jill and me two old women together.'

'And don't you think, when I'm an old man and you're an old woman, we might be together still, as we are now?' he said.

'Well, not as we are now,' she replied. 'But I could imagine – no, I can't. I can't imagine you an old man. Besides, it's dreadful!'

'What, to be an old man?'

'Yes, of course.'

'Not when the time comes,' he said. 'But it hasn't come. Only it will. And when it does, I should like to think you'd be there as well.'

'Sort of old age pensions,' she said dryly.

Her kind of witless humour always startled him. He never knew what she meant. Probably she didn't quite know herself.

'No,' he said, hurt.

'I don't know why you harp on old age,' she said. 'I'm not ninety.'

'Did anybody ever say you were?' he asked, offended.

They were silent for some time, pulling different ways in the silence.

'I don't want you to make fun of me,' he said.

'Don't you?' she replied, enigmatic.

'No, because just this minute I'm serious. And when I'm serious, I believe in not making fun of it.'

'You mean nobody else must make fun of you,' she replied.

'Yes, I mean that. And I mean I don't believe in making fun of it myself. When it comes over me so that I'm serious, then – there it is, I don't want it to be laughed at.'

She was silent for some time. Then she said, in a vague, almost pained voice, 'No, I'm not laughing at you.'

A hot wave rose in his heart.

'You believe me, do you?' he asked.

'Yes, I believe you,' she replied, with a twang of her old, tired nonchalance, as if she gave in because she was tired. But he didn't care. His heart was hot and clamorous.

'So you agree to marry me before I go? – perhaps at Christmas?'

'Yes, I agree.'

'There!' he exclaimed. 'That's settled it.'

And he sat silent, unconscious, with all the blood burning in all his veins, like fire in all the branches and twigs of him. He only pressed her two hands to his chest, without knowing. When the curious passion began to die down, he seemed to come awake to the world.

'We'll go in, shall we?' he said: as if he realised it was cold.

She rose without answering.

'Kiss me before we go, now you've said it,' he said.

And he kissed her gently on the mouth, with a young, frightened kiss. It made her feel so young, too, and frightened, and wondering: and tired, tired, as

If she were going to sleep.

They went indoors. And in the sitting-room, there, crouched by the fire like a queer little witch, was Banford. She looked round with reddened eyes as they entered, but did not rise. He thought she looked frightening, unnatural, crouching there and looking round at them. Evil he thought her look was, and he crossed his fingers.

Banford saw the ruddy, elate face on the youth: he seemed strangely tall and bright and looming. And March had a delicate look on her face; she wanted to hide her face, to screen it, to let it not be seen.

'You've come at last,' said Banford uglily.

'Yes, we've come,' said he.

'You've been long enough for anything,' she said.

'Yes, we have. We've settled it. We shall marry as soon as possible,' he replied.

'Oh, you've settled it, have you! Well, I hope you won't live to repent it,' said Banford.

'I hope so too,' he replied.

'Are you going to bed *now*, Nellie?' said Banford.

'Yes, I'm going now.'

'Then for goodness' sake come along.'

March looked at the boy. He was glancing with his very bright eyes at her and at Banford. March looked at him wistfully. She wished she could stay with him. She wished she had married him already, and it was all over. For oh, she felt suddenly so safe with him. She felt so strangely safe and peaceful in his presence. If only she could sleep in his shelter, and not with Jill. She felt afraid of Jill. In her dim, tender state, it was agony to have to go with Jill and sleep with her. She wanted the boy to save her. She looked again at him.

And he, watching with bright eyes, divined something of what she felt. It puzzled and distressed him that she must go with Jill.

'I shan't forget what you've promised,' he said, looking clear into her eyes, right into her eyes, so that he seemed to occupy all herself with his queer, bright look.

She smiled to him faintly, gently. She felt safe again – safe with him.

But in spite of all the boy's precautions, he had a setback. The morning he was leaving the farm he got March to accompany him to the market-town, about six miles away, where they went to the registrar and had their names stuck up as two people who were going to marry. He was to come at Christmas, and the wedding was to take place then. He hoped in the spring to be able to take March back to Canada with him, now the war was really over. Though he was so young, he had saved some money.

'You never have to be without *some* money at the back of you, if you can help it,' he said.

So she saw him off in the train that was going West: his camp was on Salisbury Plain. And with big, dark eyes she watched him go, and it seemed as if everything real in life was retreating as the train retreated with his queer, chubby, ruddy face, that seemed so broad across the cheeks, and which never seemed to change its expression, save when a cloud of sulky anger hung on the brow, or the bright eyes fixed themselves in their stare. This was what happened now. He leaned there out of the carriage window as the train drew off, saying goodbye and staring back at her, but his face quite unchanged. There was no emotion on his face. Only his eyes tightened and became fixed and intent in their watching like a cat's when suddenly she sees something and stares. So the boy's eyes stared fixedly as the train drew away, and she was left feeling intensely forlorn. Failing his physical presence, she seemed to have nothing of him. And she had nothing of anything. Only his face was fixed in her mind: the full, ruddy, unchanging cheeks, and the straight snout of a nose and the two eyes staring above. All she could remember was how he suddenly wrinkled his nose when he laughed, as a puppy does when he is playfully growling. But him, himself, and what he was – she knew nothing, she had nothing of him when he left her.

On the ninth day after he had left her he received this letter.

DEAR HENRY – I have been over it all again in my mind, this business of me and you, and it seems to me impossible. When you aren't there I see what a fool I am. When you are there you seem to blind me to things as they actually are. You make me see things all unreal, and I don't know what. Then when I am alone again with Jill I seem to come to my own senses and realise what a fool I am making of myself, and how I am treating you unfairly. Because it must be unfair to you for me to go on with this affair when I can't feel in my heart that I really love you. I know people talk a lot of stuff and nonsense about love, and I don't want to do that. I want to keep to plain facts and act in a sensible way. And that seems to me what I'm not doing. I don't see on what grounds I am going to marry you. I know I am not head over heels in love with you, as I have fancied myself to be with fellows when I was a young fool of a girl. You are an absolute stranger to me, and it seems to me you will always be one. So on what grounds am I going to marry you? When I think of Jill, she is ten times more real to me. I know her and I'm awfully fond of her, and I hate myself for a beast if I ever hurt her little finger. We have a life together. And even if it can't last for ever, it is a life while it does last. And it might last as long as either of us lives. Who knows how long we've got to live? She is a delicate little thing, perhaps nobody but me knows how delicate. And as for me, I feel I might fall down the well any day. What I don't seem to see at all is you. When I think of what I've been and what I've done with you, I'm afraid I am a few screws loose. I should be sorry to think that softening of the brain is setting in so soon, but that is what it seems like. You are such an absolute stranger, and so different from what I'm used to, and we don't seem to have a thing in common. As for love, the very word seems impossible. I know what love means even in Jill's case, and I know that in this affair with you it's an absolute impossibility. And then going to Canada. I'm sure I must have been clean off my chump when I promised such a thing. It makes me feel fairly frightened of myself. I feel I might do something really silly that I wasn't responsible for – and end my days in a lunatic asylum. You may think that's all I'm fit for after the way I've gone on, but it isn't a very nice thought for me. Thank goodness Jill is here, and her being here makes me feel sane again, else I don't know what I might do; I might have an accident with the gun one evening. I love Jill, and she makes me feel safe and sane, with her loving anger against me for being such a fool. Well, what I want to say is, won't you let us cry the whole thing off? I can't marry you, and really, I won't do such a thing if it seems to me wrong. It is all a great mistake. I've made a complete fool of myself, and all I can do is to apologise to you and ask you please to forget it, and please to take no further notice of me. Your fox-skin is nearly ready, and seems all right, I will post it to you if you will let me know if this address is still right, and if you will accept my apology for the awful and lunatic way I have behaved with you, and then let the matter rest.

Jill sends her kindest regards. Her mother and father are staying with us over Christmas,

Yours very sincerely,

ELLEN MARCH

The boy read this letter in camp as he was cleaning his kit. He set his teeth, and for a moment went almost pale, yellow round the eyes with fury. He said nothing and saw nothing and felt nothing but a livid rage that was quite unreasoning. Balked! Balked again! Balked! He wanted the woman, he had fixed like doom upon having her. He felt that was his doom, his destiny, and his reward, to have this woman. She was his heaven and hell on earth, and he would have none elsewhere. Sightless with rage and thwarted madness he got through the morning. Save that in his mind he was lurking and scheming towards an issue, he would have committed some insane act. Deep in himself he felt like roaring and howling and gnashing his teeth and breaking things. But he was too intelligent. He knew society was on top of him, and he must scheme. So with his teeth bitten together, and his nose curiously slightly lifted, like some creature that is vicious, and his eyes fixed and staring, he went through the morning's affairs drunk with anger and suppression. In his mind was one thing – Banford. He took no heed of all March's outpouring: none. One thorn rankled, stuck in his mind. Banford. In his mind, in his soul, in his whole being, one thorn rankling to insanity. And he would have to get it out. He would have to get the thorn of Banford out of his life, if he died for it.

With this one fixed idea in his mind, he went to ask for twenty-four hours' leave of absence. He knew it was not due to him. His consciousness was supernaturally keen. He knew where he must go – he must go to the captain. But how could he get at the captain? In that great camp of wooden huts and tents he had no idea where his captain was.

But he went to the officers' canteen. There was his captain standing talking with three other officers. Henry stood in the doorway at attention.

'May I speak to Captain Berryman?' The captain was Cornish like himself.

'What do you want?' called the captain.

'May I speak to you, Captain?'

'What do you want?' replied the captain, not stirring from among his group of fellow officers.

Henry watched his superior for a minute without speaking.

'You won't refuse me, sir, will you?' he asked gravely.

'It depends what it is.'

'Can I have twenty-four hours' leave?'

'No, you've no business to ask.'

'I know I haven't. But I must ask you.'

'You've had your answer.'

'Don't send me away, Captain.'

There was something strange about the boy as he stood there so everlasting in the doorway. The Cornish captain felt the strangeness at once, and eyed him shrewdly.

'Why, what's afoot?' he said, curious.

'I'm in trouble about something. I must go to Blewbury,' said the boy.

'Blewbury, eh? After the girls?'

'Yes, it is a woman, Captain.' And the boy, as he stood there with his head reaching forward a little, went suddenly terribly pale, or yellow, and his lips seemed to give off pain. The captain saw and paled a little also. He turned aside.

'Go on, then,' he said. 'But for God's sake don't cause any trouble of any sort.'

'I won't, Captain, thank you.'

He was gone. The captain, upset, took a gin and bitters. Henry managed to hire a bicycle. It was twelve o'clock when he left the camp. He had sixty miles of wet and muddy cross roads to ride. But he was in the saddle and down the road without a thought of food.

At the farm, March was busy with a work she had had some time in hand. A bunch of Scotch fir trees stood at the end of the open shed, on a little bank where ran the fence between two of the gorse-shaggy meadows. The farthest of these trees was dead – it had died in the summer, and stood with all its needles brown and sere in the air. It was not a very big tree. And it was absolutely dead. So March determined to have it, although they were not allowed to cut any of the timber. But it would make such splendid firing, in these days of scarce fuel.

She had been giving a few stealthy chops at the trunk for a week or more, every now and then hacking away for five minutes, low down, near the ground, so no one should notice. She had not tried the saw, it was such hard work, alone. Now the tree stood with a great yawning gap in his base, perched, as it were, on one sinew, and ready to fall. But he did not fall.

It was late in the damp December afternoon, with cold mists creeping out of the woods and up the hollows, and darkness waiting to sink in from above. There was a bit of yellowness where the sun was fading away beyond the low woods of the distance. March took her axe and went to the tree. The small thud-thud of her blows resounded rather ineffectual about the wintry homestead. Banford came out wearing her thick coat, but with no hat on her head, so that her thin, bobbed hair blew on the uneasy wind that sounded in the pines and in the wood.

'What I'm afraid of,' said Banford, 'is that it will fall on the shed and we shall have another job repairing that.'

'Oh, I don't think so,' said March, straightening herself and wiping her arm over her hot brow. She was flushed red, her eyes were very wide open and queer, her upper lip lifted away from her two white front teeth with a curious, almost rabbit look.

A little stout man in a black overcoat and a bowler hat came pottering across the yard. He had a pink face and a white beard and smallish, pale-blue eyes. He was not very old, but nervy, and he walked with little short steps.

'What do you think, father?' said Banford. 'Don't you think it might hit the shed in falling?'

'Shed, no!' said the old man. 'Can't hit the shed. Might as well say the fence.'

'The fence doesn't matter,' said March, in her high voice.

'Wrong as usual, am I!' said Banford, wiping her straying hair from her eyes.

The tree stood as it were on one spelch of itself, leaning, and creaking in the wind. It grew on the bank of a little dry ditch between the two meadows. On the top of the bank straggled one fence, running to the bushes uphill. Several trees clustered there in the corner of the field near the shed and near the gate which led into the yard. Towards this gate, horizontal across the weary meadows, came the grassy, rutted approach from the high road. There trailed another rickety fence, long split poles joining the short, thick, wide-apart uprights.

The three people stood at the back of the tree, in the corner of the shed meadow, just above the yard gate. The house, with its two gables and its porch, stood tidy in a little grassed garden across the yard. A little, stout, rosy-faced woman in a little red woollen shoulder shawl had come and taken her stand in the porch.

'Isn't it down yet?' she cried, in a high little voice.

'Just thinking about it,' called her husband. His tone towards the two girls was always rather mocking and satirical. March did not want to go on with her hitting while he was there. As for him, he wouldn't lift a stick from the ground if he could help it, complaining, like his daughter, of rheumatics in his shoulder. So the three stood there a moment silent in the cold afternoon, in the bottom corner near the yard.

They heard the far-off taps of a gate, and craned to look. Away across, on the green horizontal approach, a figure was just swinging on to a bicycle again, and lurching up and down over the grass, approaching.

'Why, it's one of our boys – it's Jack,' said the old man.

'Can't be,' said Banford.

March craned her head to look. She alone recognised the khaki figure. She flushed, but said nothing.

'No, it isn't Jack, I don't think,' said the old man, staring with little round blue eyes under his white lashes.

In another moment the bicycle lurched into sight, and the rider dropped off at the gate. It was Henry, his face wet and red and spotted with mud. He was altogether a muddy sight.

'Oh!' cried Banford, as if afraid. 'Why, it's Henry!'

'What?' muttered the old man. He had a thick, rapid, muttering way of speaking, and was slightly deaf. 'What? What? Who is it? Who is it, do you say? That young fellow? That young fellow of Nellie's? Oh! Oh!' And the satiric smile came on his pink face and white eyelashes.

Henry, pushing the wet hair off his steaming brow, had caught sight of them and heard what the old man said. His hot young face seemed to flame in the cold light.

'Oh, are you all there!' he said, giving his sudden, puppy's little laugh. He was so hot and dazed with cycling he hardly knew where he was. He leaned the bicycle against the fence and climbed over into the corner on to the bank, without going into the yard.

'Well, I must say, we weren't expecting *you*,' said Banford laconically.

'No, I suppose not,' said he, looking at March.

She stood aside, slack, with one knee drooped and the axe resting its head loosely on the ground. Her eyes were wide and vacant, and her upper lip lifted from her teeth in that helpless, fascinated rabbit look. The moment she saw his glowing, red face it was all over with her. She was as helpless as if she had been bound. The moment she saw the way his head seemed to reach forward.

'Well, who is it? Who is it, anyway?' asked the smiling, satiric old man in his muttering voice.

'Why, Mr Grenfel, whom you've heard us tell about, father,' said Banford coldly.

'Heard you tell about, I should think so. Heard of nothing else practically,' muttered the elderly man, with his queer little jeering smile on his face. 'How do you do,' he added, suddenly reaching out his hand to Henry.

The boy shook hands just as startled. Then the two men fell apart.

'Cycled over from Salisbury Plain, have you?' asked the old man.

'Yes.'

'Hm! Longish ride. How long d'it take you, eh? Some time, eh? Several hours, I suppose.'

'About four.'

'Eh? Four! Yes, I should have thought so. When are you going back, then?'

'I've got till tomorrow evening.'

'Till tomorrow evening, eh? Yes. Hm! Girls weren't expecting you, were they?'

And the old man turned his pale-blue, round little eyes under their white lashes mockingly towards the girls. Henry also looked round. He had become a little awkward. He looked at March, who was still staring away into the distance as if to see where the cattle were. Her hand was on the pommel of the axe, whose head rested loosely on the ground.

'What were you doing there?' he asked in his soft, courteous voice. 'Cutting a tree down?'

March seemed not to hear, as if in a trance.

'Yes,' said Banford. 'We've been at it for over a week.'

'Oh! And have you done it all by yourselves then?'

'Nellie's done it all, I've done nothing,' said Banford.

'Really! You must have worked quite hard,' he said, addressing himself in a curious gentle tone direct to March. She did not answer, but remained half averted staring away towards the woods above as if in a trance.

'*Nellie!*' cried Banford sharply. 'Can't you answer?'

'What – me?' cried March, starting round and looking from one to the other. 'Did anyone speak to me?'

'Dreaming!' muttered the old man, turning aside to smile. 'Must be in love, eh, dreaming in the daytime!'

'Did you say anything to me?' said March, looking at the boy as from a strange distance, her eyes wide and doubtful, her face delicately flushed.

'I said you must have worked hard at the tree,' he replied courteously.

'Oh, that! Bit by bit. I thought it would have come down by now.'

'I'm thankful it hasn't come down in the night, to frighten us to death,' said Banford.

'Let me just finish it for you, shall I?' said the boy.

March slanted the axe-shaft in his direction.

'Would you like to?' she said.

'Yes, if you wish it,' he said.

'Oh, I'm thankful when the thing's down, that's all,' she replied, nonchalant.

'Which way is it going to fall?' said Banford. 'Will it hit the shed?'

'No, it won't hit the shed,' he said. 'I should think it will fall there – quite clear. Though it might give a twist and catch the fence.'

'Catch the fence!' cried the old man. 'What, catch the fence! When it's leaning at that angle? Why, it's farther off than the shed. It won't catch the fence.'

'No,' said Henry, 'I don't suppose it will. It has plenty of room to fall quite clear, and I suppose it will fall clear.'

'Won't tumble backwards on top of *us*, will it?' asked the old man, sarcastic.

'No, it won't do that,' said Henry, taking off his short overcoat and his tunic. 'Ducks! Ducks! Go back!'

A line of four brown-speckled ducks led by a brown-and-green drake were stemming away downhill from the upper meadow, coming like boats running on a ruffled sea, cackling their way top speed downwards towards the fence and towards the little group of people, and cackling as excitedly as if they brought news of the Spanish Armada.

'Silly things! Silly things!' cried Banford, going forward to turn them off. But they came eagerly towards her, opening their yellow-green beaks and quacking as if they were so excited to say something.

'There's no food. There's nothing here. You must wait a bit,' said Banford to them. 'Go away. Go away. Go round to the yard.'

They didn't go, so she climbed the fence to swerve them round under the gate and into the yard. So off they waggled in an excited string once more, wagging their rumps like the stems of little gondolas, ducking under the bar of the gate. Banford stood on the top of the bank, just over the fence, looking down on the other three.

Henry looked up at her, and met her queer, round-pupilled, weak eyes staring behind her spectacles. He was perfectly still. He looked away, up at the weak, leaning tree. And as he looked into the sky, like a huntsman who is watching a flying bird, he thought to himself: 'If the tree falls in just such a way, and spins just so much as it falls, then the branch there will strike her exactly as she stands on top of that bank.'

He looked at her again. She was wiping the hair from her brow again, with that perpetual gesture. In his heart he had decided her death. A terrible still force seemed in him, and a power that was just his. If he turned even a hair's breadth in the wrong direction, he would lose the power.

'Mind yourself, Miss Banford,' he said. And his heart held perfectly still, in the terrible pure will that she should not move.

'Who, me, mind myself?' she cried, her father's jeering tone in her voice. 'Why, do you think you might hit me with the axe?'

'No, it's just possible the tree might, though,' he answered soberly. But the tone of his voice seemed to her to imply that he was only being falsely solicitous, and trying to make her move because it was his will to move her.

'Absolutely impossible,' she said.

He heard her. But he held himself icy still, lest he should lose his power.

'No, it's just possible. You'd better come down this way.'

'Oh, all right. Let us see some crack Canadian tree-felling,' she retorted.

'Ready, then,' he said, taking the axe, looking round to see he was clear.

There was a moment of pure, motionless suspense, when the world seemed to stand still. Then suddenly his form seemed to flash up enormously tall and fearful, he gave two swift, flashing blows, in immediate succession, the tree was severed, turning slowly, spinning strangely in the air and coming down like a sudden darkness on the earth. No one saw what was happening except himself. No one heard the strange little cry which the Banford gave as the dark end of the bough swooped down, down on her. No one saw her crouch a little and receive the blow on the back of the neck. No one saw her flung outwards and laid, a little twitching heap, at the foot of the fence. No one except the boy. And he watched with intense bright eyes, as he would watch a wild goose he had shot. Was it winged or dead? Dead!

Immediately he gave a loud cry. Immediately March gave a wild shriek that went far, far down the afternoon. And the father started a strange bellowing sound.

The boy leapt the fence and ran to the fringe. The back of the neck and head was a mass of blood, of horror. He turned it over. The body was quivering with little convulsions. But she was dead really. He knew it, that it was so. He knew it in his soul and his blood. The inner necessity of his life was fulfilling itself, it was he who was to live. The thorn was drawn out of his bowels. So he put her down gently. She was dead.

He stood up. March was standing there petrified and absolutely motionless. Her face was dead white, her eyes big black pools. The old man was scrambling horribly over the fence.

'I'm afraid it's killed her,' said the boy.

The old man was making curious, blubbering noises as he huddled over the fence.

'What!' cried March, starting electric.

'Yes, I'm afraid,' repeated the boy.

March was coming forward. The boy was over the fence before she reached it.

'What do you say killed her?' she asked in a sharp voice.

'I'm afraid so,' he answered softly.

She went still whiter, fearful. The two stood facing one another. Her black eyes gazed on him with the last look of resistance. And then in a last agonised failure she began to grizzle, to cry in a shivery little fashion of a child that doesn't want to cry, but which is beaten from within, and gives that little first shudder of sobbing which is not yet weeping, dry and fearful.

He had won. She stood there absolutely helpless, shuddering her dry sobs and her mouth trembling rapidly. And then, as in a child, with a little crash came the tears and the blind agony of sightless weeping. She sank down on the grass, and sat there with her hands on her breast and her face lifted in sightless, convulsed weeping. He stood above her, looking down on her, mute, pale, and everlasting seeming. He never moved, but looked down on her. And among all the torture of the scene, the torture of his own heart and bowels, he was glad, he had won.

After a long time he stooped to her and took her hands.

'Don't cry,' he said softly. 'Don't cry.'

She looked up at him with tears running from her eyes, a senseless look of helplessness and submission. So she gazed on him as if sightless, yet looking up to him. She would never leave him again. He had won her. And he knew it and was glad, because he wanted her for his life. His life must have her. And now he had won her. It was what his life must have.

But if he had won her, he had not yet got her. They were married at Christmas as he had planned, and he got again ten days' leave. They went to Cornwall, to his own village, on the sea. He realised that it was awful for her to be at the farm any more.

But though she belonged to him, though she lived in his shadow, as if she could not be away from him, she was not happy. She did not want to leave him: and yet she did not feel free with him. Everything round her seemed to watch her, seemed to press on her. He had won her, he had her with him, she was his wife. And she – she belonged to him, she knew it. But she was not glad. And he was still foiled. He realised that though he was married to her and possessed her in every possible way, apparently, and though she *wanted* him to possess her, she wanted it, she wanted nothing else, now, still he did not quite succeed.

Something was missing. Instead of her soul swaying with new life, it seemed to droop, to bleed, as if it were wounded. She would sit for a long time with her hand in his, looking away at the sea. And in her dark, vacant eyes was a sort of wound, and her face looked a little peaked. If he spoke to her, she would turn to him with a faint new smile, the strange, quivering little smile of a woman who has died in the old way of love, and can't quite rise to the new way. She still felt she ought to *do* something, to strain herself in some direction. And there was nothing to do, and no direction in which to strain herself. And she could not quite accept the submergence which his new love put upon her. If she was in love, she ought to *exert* herself, in some way, loving. She felt the weary need of our day to *exert* herself in love. But she knew that in fact she must no more exert herself in love. He would not have the love which exerted itself towards him. It made his brow go black. No, he wouldn't let her exert her love towards him. No, she had to be passive, to acquiesce, and to be submerged under the surface of love. She had to be like the seaweeds she saw as she peered down from the boat, swaying forever delicately under water, with all their delicate fibrils put tenderly out upon the flood, sensitive, utterly sensitive and receptive within the shadowy sea, and never, never rising and looking forth above water while they lived. Never. Never looking forth from the water until they died, only then washing, corpses, upon the surface. But while they lived, always submerged, always beneath the wave. Beneath the wave they might have powerful roots, stronger than iron; they might be tenacious and dangerous in their soft waving within the flood. Beneath the water they might be stronger, more indestructible than resistant oak trees are on land. But it was always underwater, always underwater. And she, being a woman, must be like that.

And she had been so used to the very opposite. She had had to take all the thought for love and for life, and all the responsibility. Day after day she had been responsible for the coming day, for the coming year: for her dear Jill's health and happiness and well-being. Verily, in her own small way, she had felt herself responsible for the well-being of the world. And this had been her great stimulant, this grand feeling that, in her own small sphere, she was responsible for the well-being of the world.

And she had failed. She knew that, even in her small way, she had failed. She had failed to satisfy her own feeling of responsibility. It was so difficult. It seemed so grand and easy at first. And the more you tried, the more difficult it became. It had seemed so easy to make one beloved creature happy. And the more you tried, the worse the failure. It was terrible. She had been all her life reaching, reaching, and what she reached for seemed so near, until she had stretched to her utmost limit. And then it was always beyond her.

Always beyond her, vaguely, unrealisably beyond her, and she was left with nothingness at last. The life she reached for, the happiness she reached for, the well-being she reached for all slipped back, became unreal, the farther she stretched her hand. She wanted some goal, some finality – and there was none. Always this ghastly reaching, reaching, striving for something that might be just beyond. Even to make Jill happy. She was glad Jill was dead. For she had realised that she could never make her happy. Jill would always be fretting herself thinner and thinner, weaker and weaker. Her pains grew worse instead of less. It would be so for ever. She was glad she was dead.

And if Jill had married a man it would have been just the same. The woman striving, striving to make the man happy, striving within her own limits for the well-being of her world. And always achieving failure. Little, foolish successes in money or in ambition. But at the very point where she most wanted success, in the anguished effort to make some one beloved human being happy and perfect, there the failure was almost catastrophic. You wanted to make your beloved happy, and his happiness seemed always achievable. If only you did just this, that, and the other. And you did this, that, and the other, in all good faith, and every time the failure became a little more ghastly. You could love yourself to ribbons and strive and strain yourself to the bone, and things would go from bad to worse, bad to worse, as far as happiness went. The awful mistake of happiness.

Poor March, in her good-will and her responsibility, she had strained herself till it seemed to her that the whole of life and everything was only a horrible abyss of nothingness. The more you reached after the fatal flower of happiness, which trembles so blue and lovely in a crevice just beyond your grasp, the more fearfully you became aware of the ghastly and awful gulf of the precipice below you, into which you will inevitably plunge, as into the bottomless pit, if you reach any farther. You pluck flower after flower – it is never *the* flower. The flower itself – its calyx is a horrible gulf, it is the bottomless pit.

That is the whole history of the search for happiness, whether it be your own or somebody else's that you want to win. It ends, and it always ends, in the ghastly sense of the bottomless nothingness into which you will inevitably fall if you strain any farther.

And women? – what goal can any woman conceive, except happiness? Just happiness for herself and the whole world. That, and nothing else. And so, she assumes the responsibility and sets off towards her goal. She can see it there, at the foot of the rainbow. Or she can see it a little way beyond, in the blue distance. Not far, not far.

But the end of the rainbow is a bottomless gulf down which you can fall for ever without arriving, and the blue distance is a void pit which can swallow you and all your efforts into its emptiness, and still be no emptier. You and all your efforts. So, the illusion of attainable happiness!

Poor March, she had set off so wonderfully towards the blue goal. And the farther and farther she had gone, the more fearful had become the realisation of emptiness. An agony, an insanity at last.

She was glad it was over. She was glad to sit on the shore and look westwards over the sea, and know the great strain had ended. She would never strain for love and happiness any more. And Jill was safely dead. Poor Jill, poor Jill. It must be sweet to be dead.

For her own part, death was not her destiny. She would have to leave her destiny to the boy. But then, the boy. He wanted more than that. He wanted her to give herself without defences, to sink and become submerged in him. And she – she wanted to sit still, like a woman on the last milestone, and watch. She wanted to see, to know, to understand. She wanted to be alone: with him at her side.

And he! He did not want her to watch any more, to see any more, to understand any more. He wanted to veil her woman's spirit, as Orientals veil the woman's face. He wanted her to commit herself to him, and to put her independent spirit to sleep. He wanted to take away from her all her effort, all that seemed her very *raison d'être*. He wanted to make her submit, yield, blindly pass away out of all her strenuous consciousness. He wanted to take away her consciousness, and make her just his woman. Just his woman.

And she was so tired, so tired, like a child that wants to go to sleep, but which fights against sleep as if sleep were death. She seemed to stretch her eyes wider in the obstinate effort and tension of keeping awake. She *would* keep awake. She *would* know. She *would* consider and judge and decide. She *would* have the reins of her own life between her own hands. She *would* be an independent woman to the last. But she was so tired, so tired of everything. And sleep seemed near. And there was such rest in the boy.

Yet there, sitting in a niche of the high wild cliffs of West Cornwall, looking over the westward sea, she stretched her eyes wider and wider. Away to the West, Canada, America. She *would* know and she *would* see what was ahead. And the boy, sitting beside her, staring down at the gulls, had a cloud between his brows and the strain of discontent in his eyes. He wanted her asleep, at peace in him. He wanted her at peace asleep in him. And *there* she was, dying with the strain of her own wakefulness. Yet she would not sleep: no, never. Sometimes he thought bitterly that he ought to have left her. He ought never to have killed Banford. He should have left Banford and March to kill one another.

But that was only impatience: and he knew it. He was waiting, waiting to go West. He was aching almost in torment to leave England, to go West, to take March away. To leave this shore! He believed that as they crossed the seas, as they left this England which he so hated, because in some way it seemed to have stung him with poison, she would go to sleep. She would close her eyes at last and give in to him.

And then he would have her, and he would have his own life at last. He chafed, feeling he hadn't got his own life. He would never have it till she yielded and slept in him. Then he would have all his own life as a young man and a male, and she would have all her own life as a woman and a female. There would be no more of this awful straining. She would not be a man any more, an independent woman with a man's responsibility. Nay, even the responsibility for her own soul she would have to commit to him. He knew it was so, and obstinately held out against her, waiting for the surrender.

'You'll feel better when once we get over the seas to Canada over there,' he said to her as they sat among the rocks on the cliff.

She looked away to the sea's horizon, as if it were not real. Then she looked round at him, with the strained, strange look of a child that is struggling against sleep.

'Shall I?' she said.

'Yes,' he answered quietly.

And her eyelids dropped with the slow motion, sleep weighing them unconscious. But she pulled them open again to say, 'Yes, I may. I can't tell. I can't tell what it will be like over there.'

'If only we could go soon!' he said, with pain in his voice.

THE LADYBIRD

HOW MANY SWORDS had Lady Beveridge in her pierced heart! Yet there always seemed room for another. Since she had determined that her heart of pity and kindness should never die. If it had not been for this determination she herself might have died of sheer agony, in the years 1916 and 1917, when her boys were killed, and her brother, and death seemed to be mowing with wide swathes through her family. But let us forget.

Lady Beveridge loved humanity, and come what might, she would continue to love it. Nay, in the human sense, she would love her enemies. Not the criminals among the enemy, the men who committed atrocities. But the men who were enemies through no choice of their own. She would be swept into no general hate.

Somebody had called her the soul of England. It was not ill said, though she was half Irish. But of an old, aristocratic, loyal family famous for its brilliant men. And she, Lady Beveridge, had for years as much influence on the tone of English politics as any individual alive. The close friend of the real leaders in the House of Lords and in the Cabinet, she was content that the men should act, so long as they breathed from her as from the rose of life the pure fragrance of truth and genuine love. She had no misgiving regarding her own spirit.

She, she would never lower her delicate silken flag. For instance, throughout all the agony of the war she never forgot the enemy prisoners; she was determined to do her best for them. During the first years she still had influence. But during the last years of the war power slipped out of the hands of her and her sort, and she found she could do nothing any more: almost nothing. Then it seemed as if the many swords had gone home into the heart of this little, unyielding Mater Dolorosa. The new generation jeered at her. She was a shabby, old-fashioned little aristocrat, and her drawing-room was out of date.

But we anticipate. The years 1916 and 1917 were the years when the old spirit died for ever in England. But Lady Beveridge struggled on. She was being beaten.

It was in the winter of 1917 – or in the late autumn. She had been for a fortnight sick, stricken, paralysed by the fearful death of her youngest boy. She felt she *must* give in, and just die. And then she remembered how many others were lying in agony.

So she rose, trembling, frail, to pay a visit to the hospital where lay the enemy sick and wounded, near London. Countess Beveridge was still a privileged woman. Society was beginning to jeer at this little, worn bird of an out-of-date righteousness and aesthetic. But they dared not think ill of her.

She ordered the car and went alone. The Earl, her husband, had taken his gloom to Scotland. So, on a sunny, wan November morning Lady Beveridge descended at the hospital, Hurst Place. The guard knew her, and saluted as she passed. Ah, she was used to such deep respect! It was strange that she felt it so bitterly, when the respect became shallower. But she did. It was the beginning of the end to her.

The matron went with her into the ward. Alas, the beds were all full, and men were even lying on pallets on the floor. There was a desperate, crowded dreariness and helplessness in the place: as if nobody wanted to make a sound or utter a word. Many of the men were haggard and unshaven, one was delirious, and talking fitfully in the Saxon dialect. It went to Lady Beveridge's heart. She had been educated in Dresden, and had had many dear friendships in the city. Her children also had been educated there. She heard the Saxon dialect with pain.

She was a little, frail, birdlike woman, elegant, but with that touch of the blue-stocking of the nineties which was unmistakable. She fluttered delicately from bed to bed, speaking in perfect German, but with a thin, English intonation: and always asking if there was anything she could do. The men were mostly officers and gentlemen. They made little requests which she wrote down in a book. Her long, pale, rather worn face, and her nervous little gestures somehow inspired confidence.

One man lay quite still, with his eyes shut. He had a black beard. His face was rather small and sallow. He might be dead. Lady Beveridge looked at him earnestly, and fear came into her face.

'Why, Count Dionys!' she said, fluttered. 'Are you asleep?'

It was Count Johann Dionys Psanek, a Bohemian. She had known him when he was a boy, and only in the spring of 1914 he and his wife had stayed with Lady Beveridge in her country house in Leicestershire.

His black eyes opened: large, black, unseeing eyes, with curved black lashes. He was a small man, small as a boy, and his face too was rather small. But all the lines were fine, as if they had been fired with a keen male energy. Now the yellowish swarthy paste of his flesh seemed dead, and the fine black brows seemed drawn on the face of one dead. The eyes, however, were alive: but only just alive, unseeing and unknowing.

'You know me, Count Dionys? You know me, don't you?' said Lady Beveridge, bending forward over the bed.

There was no reply for some time. Then the black eyes gathered a look of recognition, and there came the ghost of a polite smile.

'Lady Beveridge.' The lips formed the words. There was practically no sound.

'I am so glad you can recognise me. And I am so sorry you are hurt. I am so sorry.'

The black eyes watched her from that terrible remoteness of death, without changing.

'There is nothing I can do for you? Nothing at all?' she said, always speaking German.

And after a time, and from a distance, came the answer from his eyes, a look of weariness, of refusal, and a wish to be left alone; he was unable to strain himself into consciousness. His eyelids dropped.

'I am so sorry,' she said. 'If ever there is anything I can do – '

The eyes opened again, looking at her. He seemed at last to hear, and it was as if his eyes made the last weary gesture of a polite bow. Then slowly his eyelids closed again.

Poor Lady Beveridge felt another sword-thrust of sorrow in her heart, as she stood looking down at the motionless face, and at the black fine beard. The black hairs came out of his skin thin and fine, not very close together. A queer, dark, aboriginal little face he had, with a fine little nose: not an Aryan, surely. And he was going to die.

He had a bullet through the upper part of his chest, and another bullet had broken one of his ribs. He had been in hospital five days.

Lady Beveridge asked the matron to ring her up if anything happened. Then she drove away, saddened. Instead of going to Beveridge House, she went to her daughter's flat near the park – near Hyde Park. Lady Daphne was poor. She had married a commoner, son of one of the most famous politicians in England, but a man with no money. And Earl Beveridge had wasted most of the large fortune that had come to him, so that the daughter had very little, comparatively.

Lady Beveridge suffered, going in the narrow doorway into the rather ugly flat. Lady Daphne was sitting by the electric fire in the small yellow drawing-room, talking to a visitor. She rose at once, seeing her little mother.

'Why, mother, ought you to be out? I'm sure not.'

'Yes, Daphne darling. Of course I ought to be out.'

'How are you?' The daughter's voice was slow and sonorous, protective, sad. Lady Daphne was tall, only twenty-five years old. She had been one of the beauties, when the war broke out, and her father had hoped she would make a splendid match. Truly, she had married fame: but without money. Now, sorrow, pain, thwarted passion had done her great damage. Her husband was missing in the East. Her baby had been born dead. Her two darling brothers were dead. And she was ill, always ill.

A tall, beautifully-built girl, she had the fine stature of her father. Her shoulders were still straight. But how thin her white throat! She wore a simple black frock stitched with coloured wool round the top, and held in a loose coloured girdle: otherwise no ornaments. And her face was lovely, fair, with a soft exotic white complexion and delicate pink cheeks. Her hair was soft and heavy, of a lovely pallid gold colour, ash-blonde. Her hair, her complexion were so perfectly cared for as to be almost artificial, like a hot-house flower.

But alas, her beauty was a failure. She was threatened with phthisis, and was far too thin. Her eyes were the saddest part of her. They had slightly reddened rims, nerve-worn, with heavy, veined lids that seemed as if they did not want to keep up. The eyes themselves were large and of a beautiful green-blue colour. But they were full, languid, almost glaucous.

Standing as she was, a tall, finely-built girl, looking down with affectionate care on her mother, she filled the heart with ashes. The little pathetic mother, so wonderful in her way, was not really to be pitied for all her sorrow. Her life was in her sorrows, and her efforts on behalf of the sorrows of others. But Daphne was not born for grief and philanthropy. With her splendid frame, and her lovely, long, strong legs, she was Artemis or Atalanta rather than Daphne. There was a certain width of brow and even of chin that spoke a strong, reckless nature, and the curious, distraught slant of her eyes told of a wild energy dammed up inside her.

That was what ailed her: her own wild energy. She had it from her father, and from her father's desperate race. The earldom had begun with a riotous, daredevil border soldier, and this was the blood that flowed on. And alas, what was to be done with it?

Daphne had married an adorable husband: truly an adorable husband. Whereas she needed a daredevil. But in her *mind* she hated all daredevils: she had been brought up by her mother to admire only the good.

So, her reckless, anti-philanthropic passion could find no outlet – and should find no outlet, she thought. So her own blood turned against her, beat on her own nerves, and destroyed her. It was nothing but frustration and anger which made her ill, and made the doctors fear consumption. There it was, drawn on her rather wide mouth: frustration, anger, bitterness. There it was the same in the roll of her green-blue eyes, a slanting, averted look: the same anger furtively turning back on itself. This anger reddened her eyes and shattered her nerves. And yet her whole will was fixed in her adoption of her mother's creed, and in condemnation of her handsome, proud, brutal father, who had made so much misery in the family. Yes, her will was fixed in the determination that life should be gentle and good and benevolent. Whereas her blood was reckless, the blood of daredevils. Her will was the stronger of the two. But her blood had its revenge on her. So it is with strong natures today: shattered from the inside.

'You have no news, darling?' asked the mother.

'No. My father-in-law had information that British prisoners had been brought into Hasrun, and that details would be forwarded by the Turks. And there was a rumour from some Arab prisoners that Basil was one of the British brought in wounded.'

'When did you hear this?'

'Primrose came in this morning.'

'Then we can hope, dear.'

'Yes.'

Never was anything more dull and bitter than Daphne's affirmative of hope. Hope had become almost a curse to her. She wished there need be no such thing. Ha, the torment of hoping, and the *insult* to one's soul. Like the importunate widow dunning for her deserts. Why could it not all be just clean disaster, and have done with it? This dilly-dallying with despair was worse than despair. She had hoped so much: ah, for her darling brothers she had hoped with such anguish. And the two she loved best were dead. So were most others she had hoped for, dead. Only this uncertainty about her husband still rankling.

'You feel better, dear?' said the little, unquenched mother.

'Rather better,' came the resentful answer.

'And your night?'

'No better.'

There was a pause.

'You are coming to lunch with me, Daphne darling?'

'No, mother dear. I promised to lunch at the Howards' with Primrose. But I needn't go for a quarter of an hour. Do sit down.'

Both women seated themselves near the electric fire. There was that bitter pause, neither knowing what to say. Then Daphne roused herself to look at her mother.

'Are you sure you were fit to go out?' she said. 'What took you out so suddenly?'

'I went to Hurst Place, dear. I had the men on my mind, after the way the newspapers had been talking.'

'Why ever do you read the newspapers!' blurted Daphne, with a certain burning, acid anger. 'Well,' she said, more composed. 'And do you feel better now you've been?'

'So many people suffer besides ourselves, darling.'

'I know they do. Makes it all the worse. It wouldn't matter if it were only just us. At least, it would matter, but one could bear it more easily. To be just one of a crowd all in the same state.'

'And some even worse, dear.'

'Oh, quite! And the worse it is for all, the worse it is for one.'

'Is that so, darling? Try not to see too darkly. I feel if I can give just a little bit of myself to help the others – you know – it alleviates me. I feel that what I can give to the men lying there, Daphne, I give to my own boys. I can only help them now through helping others. But I can still do that, Daphne, my girl.'

And the mother put her little white hand into the long, white cold hand of her daughter. Tears came to Daphne's eyes, and a fearful stony grimace to her mouth.

'It's so wonderful of you that you can feel like that,' she said.

'But you feel the same, my love. I know you do.'

'No, I don't. Everyone I see suffering these same awful things, it makes me wish more for the end of the world. And I quite see that the world won't end – '

'But it will get better, dear. This time it's like a great sickness – like a terrible pneumonia tearing the breast of the world.'

'Do you believe it will get better? I don't.'

'It will get better. Of course it will get better. It is perverse to think otherwise, Daphne. Remember what *has* been before, even in Europe. Ah, Daphne, we must take a bigger view.'

'Yes, I suppose we must.'

The daughter spoke rapidly, from the lips, in a resonant, monotonous tone. The mother spoke from the heart.

'And Daphne, I found an old friend among the men at Hurst Place.'

'Who?'

'Little Count Dionys. You remember him?'

'Quite. What's wrong?'

'Wounded rather badly – through the chest. So ill.'

'Did you speak to him?'

'Yes. I recognised him in spite of his beard.'

'Beard!'

'Yes – a black beard. I suppose he could not be shaven. It seems strange that he is still alive, poor man.'

'Why strange? He isn't old. How old is he?'

'Between thirty and forty. But so ill, so wounded, Daphne. And so small. So small, so sallow – *smorto*, you know the Italian word. The way dark people look. There is something so distressing in it.'

'Does he look *very* small now – uncanny?' asked the daughter.

'No, not uncanny. Something of the terrible far-awayness of a child that is very ill and can't tell you what hurts it. Poor Count Dionys, Daphne. I didn't know, dear, that his eyes were so black, and his lashes so curved and long. I had never thought of him as beautiful.'

'Nor I. Only a little comical. Such a dapper little man.'

'Yes. And yet now, Daphne, there is something remote and in a sad way heroic in his dark face. Something primitive.'

'What did he say to you?'

'He couldn't speak to me. Only with his lips, just my name.'

'So bad as that?'

'Oh yes. They are afraid he will die.'

'Poor Count Dionys. I liked him. He was a bit like a monkey, but he had his points. He gave me a thimble on my seventeenth birthday. Such an amusing thimble.'

'I remember, dear.'

'Unpleasant wife, though. Wonder if he minds dying far away from her. Wonder if she knows.'

'I think not. They didn't even know his name properly. Only that he was a colonel of such and such a regiment.'

'Fourth Cavalry,' said Daphne. 'Poor Count Dionys. Such a lovely name, I always thought: Count Johann Dionys Psanek. Extraordinary dandy he was. And an amazingly good dancer, small, yet electric. Wonder if he minds dying.'

'He was so full of life, in his own little animal way. They say small people are always conceited. But he doesn't look conceited now, dear. Something ages old in his face – and, yes, a certain beauty, Daphne.'

'You mean long lashes.'

'No. So still, so solitary – and ages old, in his race. I suppose he must belong to one of those curious little aboriginal races of Central Europe. I felt quite new beside him.'

'How nice of you,' said Daphne.

Nevertheless, next day Daphne telephoned to Hurst Place to ask for news of him. He was about the same. She telephoned every day. Then she was told he was a little stronger. The day she received the message that her husband was wounded and a prisoner in Turkey, and that his wounds were healing, she forgot to telephone for news of the little enemy Count. And the following day she telephoned that she was coming to the hospital to see him.

He was awake, more restless, more in physical excitement. They could see the nausea of pain round his nose. His face seemed to Daphne curiously hidden behind the black beard, which nevertheless was thin, each hair coming thin and fine, singly, from the sallow, slightly translucent skin. In the same way his moustache made a thin black line round his mouth. His eyes were wide open, very black, and of no legible expression. He watched the two women coming down the crowded, dreary room, as if he did not see them. His eyes seemed too wide.

It was a cold day, and Daphne was huddled in a black sealskin coat with a skunk collar pulled up to her ears, and a dull gold cap with wings pulled down on her brow. Lady Beveridge wore her sable coat, and had that odd, untidy elegance which was natural to her, rather like a ruffled chicken.

Daphne was upset by the hospital. She looked from right to left in spite of herself, and everything gave her a dull feeling of horror: the terror of these sick, wounded enemy men. She loomed tall and obtrusive in her furs by the bed, her little mother at her side.

'I hope you don't mind my coming!' she said in German to the sick man. Her tongue felt rusty, speaking the language.

'Who is it then?' he asked.

'It is my daughter, Lady Daphne. You remembered *me*, Lady Beveridge. This is my daughter, whom you knew in Saxony. She was so sorry to hear you were wounded.'

The black eyes rested on the little lady. Then they returned to the looming figure of Daphne. And a certain fear grew on the low, sick brow. It was evident the presence loomed and frightened him. He turned his face aside. Daphne noticed how his fine black hair grew uncut over his small, animal ears.

'You don't remember me, Count Dionys?' she said dully.

'Yes,' he said. But he kept his face averted.

She stood there feeling confused and miserable, as if she had made a *faux pas* in coming.

'Would you rather be left alone?' she said. 'I'm sorry.'

Her voice was monotonous. She felt suddenly stifled in her closed furs, and threw her coat open, showing her thin white throat and plain black slip dress on her flat breast. He turned again unwillingly to look at her. He looked at her as if she were some strange creature standing near him.

1066 SELECTED WORKS OF D. H. LAWRENCE

'Goodbye,' she said. 'Do get better.'

She was looking at him with a queer, slanting, downward look of her heavy eyes as she turned away. She was still a little red round the eyes, with nervous exhaustion.

'You are so tall,' he said, still frightened.

'I was always tall,' she replied, turning half to him again.

'And I, small,' he said.

'I am so glad you are getting better,' she said.

'I am not glad,' he said.

'Why? I'm sure you are. Just as we are glad because we want you to get better.'

'Thank you,' he said. 'I have wished to die.'

'Don't do that, Count Dionys. Do get better,' she said, in the rather deep, laconic manner of her girlhood. He looked at her with a farther look of recognition. But his short, rather pointed nose was lifted with the disgust and weariness of pain, his brows were tense. He watched her with that curious flame of suffering which is forced to give a little outside attention, but which speaks only to itself.

'Why did they not let me die?' he said. 'I wanted death now.'

'No,' she said. 'You mustn't. You must live. If we *can* live we must.'

'I wanted death,' he said.

'Ah, well,' she said, 'even death we can't have when we want it, or when we think we want it.'

'That is true,' he said, watching her with the same wide black eyes. 'Please to sit down. You are too tall as you stand.'

It was evident he was a little frightened still by her looming, overhanging figure.

'I am sorry I am too tall,' she said, smiling, taking a chair which a man-nurse had brought her. Lady Beveridge had gone away to speak with the men. Daphne sat down, not knowing what to say further. The pitch-black look in the Count's wide eyes puzzled her.

'Why do you come here? Why does your lady mother come?' he said.

'To see if we can do anything,' she answered.

'When I am well, I will thank your ladyship.'

'All right,' she replied. 'When you are well I will let my lord the Count thank me. Please do get well.'

'We are enemies,' he said.

'Who? You and I and my mother?'

'Are we not? The most difficult thing is to be sure of anything. If they had let me die!'

'That is at least ungrateful, Count Dionys.'

'*Lady Daphne!* Yes. *Lady Daphne!* Beautiful, the name is. You are always called Lady Daphne? I remember you were so bright a maiden.'

'More or less,' she said, answering his question.

'Ach! We should all have new names now. I thought of a name for myself, but I have forgotten it. No longer Johann Dionys. That is shot away. I am Karl or Wilhelm or Ernst or Georg. Those are names I hate. Do you hate them?'

'I don't like them – but I don't hate them. And you mustn't leave off being Count Johann Dionys. If you do I shall have to leave off being Daphne. I like your name so much.'

'Lady Daphne! Lady Daphne!' he repeated. 'Yes, it rings well, it sounds beautiful to me. I think I talk foolishly. I hear myself talking foolishly to you.' He looked at her anxiously.

'Not at all,' she said.

'Ach! I have a head on my shoulders that is like a child's windmill, and I can't prevent its making foolish words. Please to go away, not to hear me. I can hear myself.'

'Can't I do anything for you?' she asked.

'No, no! No, no! If I could be buried deep, very deep down, where everything is forgotten! But they draw me up, back to the surface. I would not mind if they buried me alive, if it were very deep, and dark, and the earth heavy above.'

'Don't say that,' she replied, rising.

'No, I am saying it when I don't wish to say it. Why am I here? Why am I here? Why have I survived into this? Why can I not stop talking?'

He turned his face aside. The black, fine, elvish hair was so long, and pushed up in tufts from the smooth brown nape of his neck. Daphne looked at him in sorrow. He could not turn his body. He could only move his head. And he lay with his face hard averted, the fine hair of his beard coming up strange from under his chin and from his throat, up to the socket of his ear. He lay quite still in this position. And she turned away, looking for her mother. She had suddenly realised that the bonds, the connections between him and his life in the world had broken, and he lay there, a bit of loose, palpitating humanity, shot away from the body of humanity.

It was ten days before she went to the hospital again. She had wanted never to go again, to forget him, as one tries to forget incurable things. But she could not forget him. He came again and again into her mind. She had to go back. She had heard that he was recovering very slowly.

He looked really better. His eyes were not so wide open, they had lost that black, inky exposure which had given him such an unnatural look, unpleasant. He watched her guardedly. She had taken off her furs, and wore only her dress and a dark, soft feather toque.

'How are you?' she said, keeping her face averted, unwilling to meet his eyes.

'Thank you, I am better. The nights are not so long.'

She shuddered, knowing what long nights meant. He saw the worn look in her face too, the reddened rims of her eyes.

'Are you not well? Have you some trouble?' he asked her.

'No, no,' she answered.

She had brought a handful of pinky, daisy-shaped flowers.

'Do you care for flowers?' she asked.

He looked at them. Then he slowly shook his head.

'No,' he said. 'If I am on horseback, riding through the marshes or through the hills, I like to see them below me. But not here. Not now. Please do not bring flowers into this grave. Even in gardens, I do not like them. When they are upholstery to human life.'

'I will take them away again,' she said.

'Please do. Please give them to the nurse.'

Daphne paused.

'Perhaps,' she said, 'you wish I would not come to disturb you.'

He looked into her face.

'No,' he said. 'You are like a flower behind a rock, near an icy water. No, you do not live too much. I am afraid I cannot talk sensibly. I wish to hold my mouth shut. If I open it, I talk this absurdity. It escapes from my mouth.'

'It is not so very absurd,' she said.

But he was silent – looking away from her.

'I want you to tell me if there is really nothing I can do for you,' she said.

'Nothing,' he answered.

'If I can write any letter for you.'

'None,' he answered.

'But your wife and your two children. Do they know where you are?'

'I should think not.'

'And where are they?'

'I do not know. Probably they are in Hungary.'

'Not at your home?'

'My castle was burnt down in a riot. My wife went to Hungary with the children. She has her relatives there. She went away from me. I wished it too. Alas for her, I wished to be dead. Pardon me the personal tone.'

Daphne looked down at him – the queer, obstinate little fellow.

'But you have somebody you wish to tell – somebody you want to hear from?'

'Nobody. Nobody. I wish the bullet had gone through my heart. I wish to be dead. It is only I have a devil in my body that will not die.'

She looked at him as he lay with closed, averted face.

'Surely it is not a devil which keeps you alive,' she said. 'It is something good.'

'No, a devil,' he said.

She sat looking at him with a long, slow, wondering look.

'Must one hate a devil that makes one live?' she asked.

He turned his eyes to her with a touch of a satiric smile.

'If one lives, no,' he said.

She looked away from him the moment he looked at her. For her life she could not have met his dark eyes direct.

She left him, and he lay still. He neither read nor talked throughout the long winter nights and the short winter days. He only lay for hours with black, open eyes, seeing everything around with a touch of disgust, and heeding nothing.

Daphne went to see him now and then. She never forgot him for long. He seemed to come into her mind suddenly, as if by sorcery.

One day he said to her, 'I see you are married. May I ask you who is your husband?'

She told him. She had had a letter also from Basil. The Count smiled slowly.

'You can look forward,' he said, 'to a happy reunion and new, lovely children, Lady Daphne. Is it not so?'

'Yes, of course,' she said.

'But you are ill,' he said to her.

'Yes – rather ill.'

'Of what?'

'Oh!' she answered fretfully, turning her face aside. 'They talk about lungs.' She hated speaking of it. 'Why, how do you know I am ill?' she added quickly.

Again he smiled slowly.

'I see it in your face, and hear it in your voice. One would say the Evil One had cast a spell on you.'

'Oh no,' she said hastily. 'But do I look ill?'

'Yes. You look as if something had struck you across the face, and you could not forget it.'

'Nothing has,' she said. 'Unless it's the war.'

'The war!' he repeated.

'Oh, well, don't let us talk of it,' she said.

Another time he said to her, 'The year has turned – the sun must shine at last, even in England. I am afraid of getting well too soon. I am a prisoner, am I not? But I wish the sun would shine. I wish the sun would shine on my face.'

'You won't always be a prisoner. The war will end. And the sun *does* shine even in the winter in England,' she said.

'I wish it would shine on my face,' he said.

So that when in February there came a blue, bright morning, the morning that suggests yellow crocuses and the smell of a mezereon tree and the smell of damp, warm earth, Daphne hastily got a taxi and drove out to the hospital.

'You have come to put me in the sun,' he said the moment he saw her.

'Yes, that's what I came for,' she said.

She spoke to the matron, and had his bed carried out where there was a big window that came low. There he was put full in the sun. Turning, he could see the blue sky and the twinkling tops of purplish, bare trees.

'The world! The world!' he murmured.

He lay with his eyes shut, and the sun on his swarthy, transparent, immobile face. The breath came and went through his nostrils invisibly. Daphne wondered how he could lie so still, how he could look so immobile. It was true as her mother had said: he looked as if he had been cast in the mould when the metal was white hot, all his lines were so clean. So small, he was, and in his way perfect.

Suddenly his dark eyes opened and caught her looking.

'The sun makes even anger open like a flower,' he said.

'Whose anger?' she said.

'I don't know. But I can make flowers, looking through my eyelashes. Do you know how?'

'You mean rainbows?'

'Yes, flowers.'

And she saw him, with a curious smile on his lips, looking through his almost closed eyelids at the sun.

'The sun is neither English nor German nor Bohemian,' he said. 'I am a subject of the sun. I belong to the fire-worshippers.'

'Do you?' she replied.

'Yes, truly, by tradition.' He looked at her smiling. 'You stand there like a flower that will melt,' he added.

She smiled slowly at him, with a slow, cautious look of her eyes, as if she feared something.

'I am much more solid than you imagine,' she said.

Still he watched her.

'One day,' he said, 'before I go, let me wrap your hair round my hands, will you?' He lifted his thin, short, dark hands. 'Let me wrap your hair round my hands, like a bandage. They hurt me. I don't know what it is. I think it is all the gun explosions. But if you let me wrap your hair round my hands. You know, it is the hermetic gold – but so much of water in it, of the moon. That will soothe my hands. One day, will you?'

'Let us wait till the day comes,' she said.

'Yes,' he answered, and was still again.

'It troubles me,' he said after a while, 'that I complain like a child, and ask for things. I feel I have lost my manhood for the time being. The continual explosions of guns and shells! It seems to have driven my soul out of me like a bird frightened away at last. But it will come back, you know. And I am so grateful to you; you are good to me when I am soulless, and you don't take advantage of me. Your soul is quiet and heroic.'

'Don't,' she said. 'Don't talk!'

The expression of shame and anguish and disgust crossed his face.

'It is because I can't help it,' he said. 'I have lost my soul, and I can't stop talking to you. I can't stop. But I don't talk to anyone else. I try not to talk, but I can't prevent it. Do you draw the words out of me?'

Her wide, green-blue eyes seemed like the heart of some curious, full-open flower, some Christmas rose with its petals of snow and flush. Her hair glinted heavy, like water-gold. She stood there passive and indomitable with the wide-eyed persistence of her wintry, blond nature.

Another day when she came to see him, he watched her for a time, then he said, 'Do they all tell you you are lovely, you are beautiful?'

'Not quite all,' she replied.

'But your husband?'

'He has said so.'

'Is he gentle? Is he tender? Is he a dear lover?'

She turned her face aside, displeased.

'Yes,' she replied curtly.

He did not answer. And when she looked again he was lying with his eyes shut, a faint smile seeming to curl round his short, transparent nose. She could faintly see the flesh through his beard, as water through reeds. His black hair was brushed smooth as glass, his black eyebrows glinted like a curve of black glass on the swarthy opalescence of his brow.

Suddenly he spoke, without opening his eyes.

'You have been very kind to me,' he said.

'Have I? Nothing to speak of.'

He opened his eyes and looked at her.

'Everything finds its mate,' he said. 'The ermine and the polecat and the buzzard. One thinks so often that only the dove and the nightingale and the stag with his antlers have gentle mates. But the polecat and the ice-bears of the north have their mates. And a white she-bear lies with her cubs under a rock as a snake lies hidden, and the male bear slowly swims back from the sea, like a clot of snow or a shadow of a white cloud passing on the speckled sea. I have seen her too, and I did not shoot her, nor him when he landed with fish in his mouth, wading wet and slow and yellow-white over the black stones.'

'You have been in the North Sea?'

'Yes. And with the Eskimo in Siberia, and across the Tundras. And a white sea-hawk makes a nest on a high stone, and sometimes looks out with her white head over the edge of the rocks. It is not only a world of men, Lady Daphne.'

'Not by any means,' said she.

'Else it were a sorry place.'

'It is bad enough,' said she.

'Foxes have their holes. They have even their mates, Lady Daphne, that they bark to and are answered. And an adder finds his female. Psanek means an outlaw; did you know?'

'I did not.'

'Outlaws, and brigands, have often the finest woman-mates.'

'They do,' she said.

'I will be Psanek, Lady Daphne. I will not be Johann Dionys any more, I will be Psanek. The law has shot me through.'

'You might be Psanek and Johann and Dionys as well,' she said.

'With the sun on my face? Maybe,' he said, looking to the sun.

There were some lovely days in the spring of 1918. In March the Count was able to get up. They dressed him in a simple, dark-blue uniform. He was not very thin, only swarthy-transparent, now his beard was shaven and his hair was cut. His smallness made him noticeable, but he was masculine, perfect in his small stature. All the smiling dapperness that had made him seem like a monkey to Daphne when she was a girl had gone now. His eyes were dark and haughty;

he seemed to keep inside his own reserves, speaking to nobody if he could help it, neither to the nurses nor the visitors nor to his fellow-prisoners, fellow-officers. He seemed to put a shadow between himself and them, and from across this shadow he looked with his dark, beautifully-fringed eyes, as a proud little beast from the shadow of its lair. Only to Daphne he laughed and chatted.

She sat with him one day in March on the terrace of the hospital, on a morning when white clouds went endlessly and magnificently about a blue sky, and the sunshine felt warm after the blots of shadow.

'When you had a birthday, and you were seventeen, didn't I give you a thimble?' he asked her.

'Yes. I have it still.'

'With a gold snake at the bottom, and a Mary-beetle of green stone at the top, to push the needle with.'

'Yes.'

'Do you ever use it?'

'No. I sew so rarely.'

'Would it displease you to sew something for me?'

'You won't admire my stitches. What would you wish me to sew?'

'Sew me a shirt that I can wear. I have never before worn shirts from a shop, with a maker's name inside. It is very distasteful to me.'

She looked at him – his haughty little brows.

'Shall I ask my maid to do it?' she said.

'Oh, please, no! Oh, please, no, do not trouble. No, please, I would not want it unless you sewed it yourself, with the Psanek thimble.'

She paused before she answered. Then came her slow, 'Why?'

He turned and looked at her with dark, searching eyes.

'I have no reason,' he said, rather haughtily.

She left the matter there. For two weeks she did not go to see him. Then suddenly one day she took the bus down Oxford Street and bought some fine white flannel. She decided he must wear flannel.

That afternoon she drove out to Hurst Place. She found him sitting on the terrace, looking across the garden at the red suburb of London smoking fumily in the near distance, interrupted by patches of uncovered ground and a flat, tin-roofed laundry.

'Will you give me measurements for your shirt?' she said.

'The number of the neck-band of this English shirt is fifteen. If you ask the matron she will give you the measurement. It is a little too large, too long in the sleeves, you see,' and he shook his shirt cuff over his wrist. 'Also too long altogether.'

'Mine will probably be unwearable when I've made them,' said she.

'Oh no. Let your maid direct you. But please do not let her sew them.'

'Will you tell me why you want me to do it?'

'Because I am a prisoner, in other people's clothes, and I have nothing of my own. All the things I touch are distasteful to me. If your maid sews for me, it will still be the same. Only you might give me what I want, something that buttons round my throat and on my wrists.'

'And in Germany – or in Austria?'

'My mother sewed for me. And after her, my mother's sister, who was the head of my house.'

'Not your wife?'

'Naturally not. She would have been insulted. She was never more than a guest in my house. In my family there are old traditions – but with me they have come to an end. I had best try to revive them.'

'Beginning with traditions of shirts?'

'Yes. In our family the shirt should be made and washed by a woman of our own blood: but when we marry, by the wife. So when I married I had sixty shirts, and many other things – sewn by my mother and my aunt, all with my initial, and the ladybird, which is our crest.'

'And where did they put the initial?'

'Here!' He put his finger on the back of his neck, on the swarthy, transparent skin. 'I fancy I can feel the embroidered ladybird still. On our linen we had no crown: only the ladybird.'

She was silent, thinking.

'You will forgive what I ask you?' he said, 'since I am a prisoner and can do no other, and since fate has made you so that you understand the world as I understand it. It is not really indelicate, what I ask you. There will be a ladybird on your finger when you sew, and those who wear the ladybird understand.'

'I suppose,' she mused, 'it is as bad to have your bee in your shirt as in your bonnet.'

He looked at her with round eyes.

'Don't you know what it is to have a bee in your bonnet?' she said.

'No.'

'To have a bee buzzing among your hair! To be out of your wits,' she smiled at him.

'So!' he said. 'Ah, the Psaneks have had a ladybird in their bonnets for many hundred years.'

'Quite, quite mad,' she said.

'It may be,' he answered. 'But with my wife I was quite sane for ten years. Now give me the madness of the ladybird. The world I was sane about has gone raving. The ladybird I was mad with is wise still.'

'At least, when I sew the shirts, if I sew them,' she said, 'I shall have the ladybird at my finger's end.'

'You want to laugh at me.'

'But surely you know you are funny, with your family insect.'

'My family insect? Now you want to be rude to me.'

'How many spots must it have?'

'Seven.'

'Three on each wing. And what do I do with the odd one?'

'You put that one between its teeth, like the cake for Cerebus.'

'I'll remember that.'

When she brought the first shirt, she gave it to the matron. Then she found Count Dionys sitting on the terrace. It was a beautiful spring day. Near at hand were tall elm trees and some rooks cawing.

'What a lovely day!' she said. 'Are you liking the world any better?'

'The world?' he said, looking up at her with the same old discontent and disgust on his fine, transparent nose.

'Yes,' she replied, a shadow coming over her face.

'Is this the world – all those little red-brick boxes in rows, where couples of little people live, who decree my destiny?'

'You don't like England?'

'Ah, England! Little houses like little boxes, each with its domestic Englishman and his domestic wife, each ruling the world because all are alike, so alike.'

'But England isn't all houses.'

'Fields then! Little fields with innumerable hedges. Like a net with an irregular mesh, pinned down over this island and everything under the net. Ah, Lady Daphne, forgive me. I am ungrateful. I am so full of bile, of spleen, you say. My only wisdom is to keep my mouth shut.'

'Why do you hate everything?' she said, her own face going bitter.

'Not everything. If I were free! If I were outside the law. Ah, Lady Daphne, how does one get outside the law?'

'By going inside oneself,' she said. 'Not outside.'

His face took on a greater expression of disgust.

'No, no. I am a man, I am a man, even if I am little. I am not a spirit, that coils itself inside a shell. In my soul is anger, anger, anger. Give me room for my anger. Give me room for that.'

His black eyes looked keenly into hers. She rolled her eyes as if in a half-trance. And in a monotonous, tranced voice she said, 'Much better get over your anger. And *why* are you angry?'

'There is no why. If it were love, you would not ask me, *why do you love?* But it is anger, anger, anger. What else can I call it? And there is no why.'

Again he looked at her with his dark, sharp, questioning, tormented eyes.

'Can't you get rid of it?' she said, looking aside.

'If a shell exploded and blew me into a thousand fragments,' he said, 'it would not destroy the anger that is in me. I know that. No, it will never dissipate. And to die is no release. The anger goes on gnashing and whimpering in death. Lady Daphne, Lady Daphne, we have used up all the love, and this is what is left.'

'Perhaps *you* have used up all your love,' she replied. 'You are not everybody.'

'I know it. I speak for me and you.'

'Not for me,' she said rapidly.

He did not answer, and they remained silent.

At length she turned her eyes slowly to him.

'Why do you say you speak for me?' she said, in an accusing tone.

'Pardon me. I was hasty.'

But a faint touch of superciliousness in his tone showed he meant what he had said. She mused, her brow cold and stony.

'And why do you tell *me* about your anger?' she said. 'Will that make it better?'

'Even the adder finds his mate. And she has as much poison in her mouth as he.'

She gave a little sudden squirt of laughter.

'Awfully poetic thing to say about me,' she said.

He smiled, but with the same corrosive quality.

'Ah,' he said, 'you are not a dove. You are a wildcat with open eyes, half dreaming on a bough, in a lonely place, as I have seen her. And I ask myself – What are her memories, then?'

'I wish I were a wildcat,' she said suddenly.

He eyed her shrewdly, and did not answer.

'You want more war?' she said to him bitterly.

'More trenches? More Big Berthas, more shells and poison-gas, more machine-drilled science-manoeuvred so-called armies? Never. Never. I would rather work in a factory that makes boots and shoes. And I would rather deliberately starve to death than work in a factory that makes boots and shoes.'

'Then what do you want?'

'I want my anger to have room to grow.'

'How?'

'I do not know. That is why I sit here, day after day. I wait.'

'For your anger to have room to grow?'

'For that.'

'Goodbye, Count Dionys.'

'Goodbye, Lady Daphne.'

She had determined never to go and see him again. She had no sign from him. Since she had begun the second shirt, she went on with it. And then she hurried to finish it, because she was starting a round of visits that would end in the summer sojourn in Scotland. She intended to post the shirt. But after all, she took it herself.

She found Count Dionys had been removed from Hurst Place to Voynich Hall, where other enemy officers were interned. The being thwarted made her more determined. She took the train next day to go to Voynich Hall.

When he came into the ante-room where he was to receive her, she felt at once the old influence of his silence and his subtle power. His face had still that swarthy-transparent look of one who is unhappy, but his bearing was proud and reserved. He kissed her hand politely, leaving her to speak.

'How are you?' she said. 'I didn't know you were here. I am going away for the summer.'

'I wish you a pleasant time,' he said. They were speaking English.

'I brought the other shirt,' she said. 'It is finished at last.'

'That is a greater honour than I dared expect,' he said.

'I'm afraid it may be more honourable than useful. The other didn't fit, did it?'

'Almost,' he said. 'It fitted the spirit, if not the flesh,' he smiled.

'I'd rather it had been the reverse, for once,' she said. 'Sorry.'

'I would not have it one stitch different.'

'Can we sit in the garden?'

'I think we may.'

They sat on a bench. Other prisoners were playing croquet not far off. But these two were left comparatively alone.

'Do you like it better here?' she said.

'I have nothing to complain of,' he said.

'And the anger?'

'It is doing well, I thank you,' he smiled.

'You mean getting better?'

'Making strong roots,' he said, laughing.

'Ah, so long as it only makes roots!' she said.

'And your ladyship, how is she?'

'My ladyship is rather better,' she replied.

'Much better, indeed,' he said, looking into her face.

'Do you mean I *look* much better?' she asked quickly.

'Very much. It is your beauty you think of. Well, your beauty is almost itself again.'

'Thanks.'

'You brood on your beauty as I on my anger. Ah, your ladyship, be wise, and make friends with your anger. That is the way to let your beauty blossom.'

'I was not unfriendly with you, was I?' she said.

'With me?' His face flickered with a laugh. 'Am I your anger? Your wrath incarnate? So then, be friends with the angry me, your ladyship. I ask nothing better.'

'What is the use,' she said, 'being friends with the *angry* you? I would much rather be friends with the happy you.'

'That little animal is extinct,' he laughed. 'And I am glad of it.'

'But what remains? Only the angry you? Then it is no use my trying to be friends.'

'You remember, dear Lady Daphne, that the adder does not suck his poison all alone, and the polecat knows where to find his she-polecat. You remember that each one has his own dear mate,' he laughed. 'Dear, deadly mate.'

'And what if I do remember those bits of natural history, Count Dionys?'

'The she-adder is dainty, delicate, and carries her poison lightly. The wildcat has wonderful green eyes that she closes with memory like a screen. The ice-bear hides like a snake with her cubs, and her snarl is the strangest thing in the world.'

'Have you ever heard me snarl?' she asked suddenly.

He only laughed, and looked away.

They were silent. And immediately the strange thrill of secrecy was between them. Something had gone beyond sadness into another, secret, thrilling communion which she would never admit.

'What do you do all day here?' she asked.

'Play chess, play this foolish croquet, play billiards, and read, and wait, and remember.'

'What do you wait for?'

'I don't know.'

'And what do you remember?'

'Ah, that. Shall I tell you what amuses me? Shall I tell you a secret?'

'Please don't, if it's anything that matters.'

'It matters to nobody but me. Will you hear it?'

'If it does not implicate me in any way.'

'It does not. Well, I am a member of a certain old secret society – no, don't look at me, nothing frightening – only a society like the free-masons.'

'And?'

'And – well, as you know, one is initiated into certain so-called secrets and rites. My family has always been initiated. So I am an initiate too. Does it interest you?'

'Why, of course.'

'Well. I was always rather thrilled by these secrets. Or some of them. Some seemed to me far-fetched. The ones that thrilled me even never had any relation to actual life. When you knew me in Dresden and Prague, you would not have thought me a man invested with awful secret knowledge, now would you?'

'Never.'

'No. It was just a little exciting sideshow. And I was a grimacing little society man. But now they become true. It becomes true.'

'The secret knowledge?'

'Yes.'

'What, for instance?'

'Take actual fire. It will bore you. Do you want to hear?'

'Go on.'

'This is what I was taught. The true fire is invisible. Flame, and the red fire we see burning, has its back to us. It is running away from us. Does that mean anything to you?'

'Yes.'

'Well then, the yellowness of sunshine – light itself – that is only the glancing aside of the real original fire. You know that is true. There would be no light if there was no refraction, no bits of dust and stuff to turn the dark fire into visibility. You know that's a fact. And that being so, even the sun is dark. It is only his jacket of dust that makes him visible. You know that too. And the true sunbeams coming towards us flow darkly, a moving darkness of the genuine fire. The sun is dark, the sunshine flowing to us is dark. And light is only the inside-out of it all, the living, and the yellow beams are only the turning away of the sun's directness that was coming to us. Does that interest you at all?'

'Yes,' she said dubiously.

'Well, we've got the world inside out. The true living world of fire is dark, throbbing, darker than blood. Our luminous world that we go by is only the white lining of this.'

'Yes, I like that,' she said.

'Well! Now listen. The same with love. This white love that we have is the same. It is only the reverse, the whited sepulchre of the true love. True love is dark, a throbbing together in darkness, like the wildcat in the night, when the green screen opens and her eyes are on the darkness.'

'No, I don't see that,' she said in a slow, clanging voice.

'You, and your beauty – that is only the inside-out of you. The real you is the wildcat invisible in the night, with red fire perhaps coming out of its wide, dark eyes. Your beauty is your whited sepulchre.'

'You mean cosmetics,' she said. 'I've got none on today – not even powder.'

He laughed.

'Very good,' he said. 'Consider me. I used to think myself small but handsome, and the ladies used to admire me moderately, never very much. A trim little fellow, you know. Well, that was just the inside-out of me. I am a black tom-cat howling in the night, and it is then that fire comes out of me. This me you look at is my whited sepulchre. What do you say?'

She was looking into his eyes. She could see the darkness swaying in the depths. She perceived the invisible, catlike fire stirring deep inside them, felt it coming towards her. She turned her face aside. Then he laughed, showing his strong white teeth, that seemed a little too large, rather dreadful.

She rose to go.

'Well,' she said. 'I shall have the summer in which to think about the world inside-out. Do write if there is anything to say. Write to Thoresway. Goodbye!'

'Ah, your eyes!' he said. 'They are like jewels of stone.'

Being away from the Count, she put him out of her mind. Only she was sorry for him a prisoner in that sickening Voynich Hall. But she did not write. Nor did he.

As a matter of fact, her mind was now much more occupied with her husband. All arrangements were being made to effect his exchange. From month to month she looked for his return. And so she thought of him.

Whatever happened to her, she thought about it, thought and thought a great deal. The consciousness of her mind was like tablets of stone weighing her down. And whoever would make a new entry into her must break these tablets of stone piece by piece. So it was that in her own way she thought often enough of the Count's world inside-out. A curious latency stirred in her consciousness that was not yet an idea.

He said her eyes were like jewels of stone. What a horrid thing to say! What did he want her eyes to be like? He wanted them to dilate and become all black pupil, like a cat's at night. She shrank convulsively from the thought, and tightened her breast.

He said her beauty was her whited sepulchre. Even that, she knew what he meant. The invisibility of her he wanted to love. But ah, her pearl-like beauty was so dear to her, and it was so famous in the world.

He said her white love was like moonshine, harmful, the reverse of love. He meant Basil, of course. Basil always said she was the moon. But then Basil loved her for that. The ecstasy of it! She shivered, thinking of her husband. But it had also made her nerve-worn, her husband's love. Ah, nerve-worn.

What then would the Count's love be like? Something so secret and different. She would not be lovely and a queen to him. He hated her loveliness. The wildcat has its mate. The little wildcat that he was. Ah!

She caught her breath, determined not to think. When she thought of Count Dionys she felt the world slipping away from her. She would sit in front of a mirror, looking at her wonderful cared-for face that had appeared in so many society magazines. She loved it so, it made her feel so vain. And she looked at her blue-green eyes – the eyes of the wildcat on a bough. Yes, the lovely blue-green iris drawn tight like a screen. Supposing it should relax. Supposing it should unfold, and open out the dark depths, the dark, dilated pupil! Supposing it should?

Never! She always caught herself back. She felt she might be killed before she could give way to that relaxation that the Count wanted of her. She could not. She just could not. At the very thought of it some hypersensitive nerve started with a great twinge in her breast; she drew back, forced to keep her guard. Ah no, Monsieur le Comte, you shall never take her ladyship off her guard.

She disliked the thought of the Count. An impudent little fellow. An impertinent little fellow! A little madman, really. A little outsider. No, no. She would think of her husband: an adorable, tall, well-bred Englishman, so easy and simple, and with the amused look in his blue eyes. She thought of the cultured, casual trail of his voice. It set her nerves on fire. She thought of his strong, easy body – beautiful, white-fleshed, with the fine springing of warm-brown hair like tiny flames. He was the Dionysos, full of sap, milk and honey, and northern golden wine: he, her husband. Not that little unreal Count. Ah, she dreamed of her husband, of the love-days, and the honeymoon, the lovely, simple intimacy. Ah, the marvellous revelation of that intimacy, when he left himself to her so generously. Ah, she was his wife for this reason, that he had given himself to her so greatly, so generously. Like an ear of corn he was there for her gathering – her husband, her own, lovely, English husband. Ah, when would he come again, when would he come again!

She had letters from him – and how he loved her. Far away, his life was all hers. All hers, flowing to her as the beam flows from a white star right down to us, to our heart. Her lover, her husband.

He was now expecting to come home soon. It had all been arranged. 'I hope you won't be disappointed in me when I do get back,' he wrote. 'I am afraid I am no longer the plump and well-looking young man I was. I've got a big scar at the side of my mouth, and I'm as thin as a starved rabbit, and my hair's going grey.

Doesn't sound attractive, does it? And it isn't attractive. But once I can get out of this infernal place, and once I can be with you again, I shall come in for my second blooming. The very thought of being quietly in the same house with you, quiet and in peace, makes me realise that if I've been through hell, I have known heaven on earth and can hope to know it again. I am a miserable brute to look at now. But I have faith in you. You will forgive my appearance, and that alone will make me feel handsome.'

She read this letter many times. She was not afraid of his scar or his looks. She would love him all the more.

Since she had started making shirts – those two for the Count had been an enormous labour, even though her maid had come to her assistance forty times: but since she had started making shirts, she thought she might continue. She had some good suitable silk: her husband liked silk underwear.

But she still used the Count's thimble. It was gold outside and silver inside, and was too heavy. A snake was coiled round the base, and at the top, for pressing the needle, was inlet a semi-translucent apple-green stone, perhaps jade, carved like a scarab, with little dots. It was too heavy. But then she sewed so slowly. And she liked to feel her hand heavy, weighted. And as she sewed she thought about her husband, and she felt herself in love with him. She thought of him, how beautiful he was, and how she would love him now he was thin: she would love him all the more. She would love to trace his bones, as if to trace his living skeleton. The thought made her rest her hands in her lap and drift into a muse. Then she felt the weight of the thimble on her finger, and took it off, and sat looking at the green stone. The ladybird. The ladybird. And if only her husband would come soon, soon. It was wanting him that made her so ill. Nothing but that. She had wanted him so badly. She wanted him now. Ah, if she could go to him now, and find him, wherever he was, and see him and touch him and take all his love.

As she mused, she put the thimble down in front of her, took up a little silver pencil from her work-basket, and on a bit of blue paper that had been the band of a small skein of silk she wrote the lines of the silly little song

> *Wenn ich ein Vöglein wär'*
> *Und auch zwei Flüglein hätt',*
> *Flög' ich zu dir –*

That was all she could get on her bit of pale-blue paper.

> If I were a little bird
> And had two little wings,
> I'd fly to thee –

Silly enough, in all conscience. But she did not translate it, so it did not seem quite so silly.

At that moment her maid announced Lady Bingham – her husband's sister. Daphne crumpled up the bit of paper in a flurry, and in another minute

Primrose, his sister, came in. The newcomer was not a bit like a primrose, being long-faced and clever, smart, but not a bit elegant, in her new clothes.

'Daphne dear, what a domestic scene! I suppose it's rehearsal. Well, you may as well rehearse, he's with Admiral Burns on the *Ariadne*. Father just heard from the Admiralty; quite fit. He'll be here in a day or two. Splendid, isn't it? And the war is going to end. At least it seems like it. You'll be safe of your man now, dear. Thank heaven when it's all over. What are you sewing?'

'A shirt,' said Daphne.

'A shirt! Why, how clever of you. I should never know which end to begin. Who showed you?'

'Millicent.'

'And how did *she* know? She's no business to know how to sew shirts: nor cushions nor sheets either. Do let me look. Why, how perfectly marvellous you are! – every bit by hand too. Basil isn't worth it, dear, really he isn't. Let him order his shirts in Oxford Street. Your business is to be beautiful, not to sew shirts. What a dear little pin-poppet, or rather needle-woman! I say, a satire on us, that is. But what a darling, with mother-of-pearl wings to her skirts! And darling little gold-eyed needles inside her. You screw her head off, and you find she's full of pins and needles. Woman for you! Mother says won't you come to lunch tomorrow. And won't you come to Brassey's to tea with me at this minute. Do, there's a dear. I've got a taxi.'

Daphne bundled her sewing loosely together.

When she tried to do a bit more, two days later, she could not find her thimble. She asked her maid, whom she could absolutely trust. The girl had not seen it. She searched everywhere. She asked her nurse – who was now her housekeeper – and footman. No, nobody had seen it. Daphne even asked her sister-in-law.

'Thimble, darling? No, I don't remember a thimble. I remember a dear little needle-lady, whom I thought such a precious satire on us women. I didn't notice a thimble.'

Poor Daphne wandered about in a muse. She did not want to believe it lost. It had been like a talisman to her. She tried to forget it. Her husband was coming, quite soon, quite soon. But she could not raise herself to joy. She had lost her thimble. It was as if Count Dionys accused her in her sleep of something, she did not quite know what.

And though she did not really want to go to Voynich Hall, yet like a fatality she went, like one doomed. It was already late autumn, and some lovely days. This was the last of the lovely days. She was told that Count Dionys was in the small park, finding chestnuts. She went to look for him. Yes, there he was in his blue uniform stooping over the brilliant yellow leaves of the sweet chestnut tree, that lay around him like a fallen nimbus of glowing yellow, under his feet, as he kicked and rustled, looking for the chestnut burrs. And with his short, brown hands he was pulling out the small chestnuts and putting them in his pockets. But as she approached he peeled a nut to eat it. His teeth were white and powerful.

'You remind me of a squirrel laying in a winter store,' said she.

'Ah, Lady Daphne – I was thinking and did not hear you.'

'I thought you were gathering chestnuts – even eating them.'

'Also!' he laughed. He had a dark, sudden charm when he laughed, showing his rather large white teeth. She was not quite sure whether she found him a little repulsive.

'Were you *really* thinking?' she said, in her slow, resonant way.

'Very truly.'

'And weren't you enjoying the chestnut a bit?'

'Very much. Like sweet milk. Excellent, excellent.' He had the fragments of the nut between his teeth, and bit them freely. 'Will you take one too.' He held out the little, pointed brown nuts on the palm of his hand.

She looked at them doubtfully.

'Are they as tough as they always were?' she said.

'No, they are fresh and good. Wait, I will peel one for you.'

They strayed about through the thin clump of trees.

'You have had a pleasant summer; you are strong?'

'Almost *quite* strong,' said she. 'Lovely summer, thanks. I suppose it's no good asking you if you have been happy?'

'Happy?' He looked at her direct. His eyes were black, and seemed to examine her. She always felt he had a little contempt of her. 'Oh yes,' he said, smiling. 'I have been very happy.'

'So glad.'

They drifted a little farther, and he picked up an apple-green chestnut burr out of the yellow-brown leaves, handling it with sensitive fingers that still suggested paws to her.

'How did you succeed in being happy?' she said.

'How shall I tell you? I felt that the same power which put up the mountains could pull them down again – no matter how long it took.'

'And was that all?'

'Was it not enough?'

'I should say decidedly too little.'

He laughed broadly, showing the strong, negroid teeth.

'You do not know all it means,' he said.

'The thought that the mountains were going to be pulled down?' she said. 'It will be so long after my day.'

'Ah, you are bored,' he said. 'But I – I found the God who pulls things down: especially the things that men have put up. Do they not say that life is a search after God, Lady Daphne? I have found my God.'

'The god of destruction,' she said, blanching.

'Yes – not the devil of destruction, but the god of destruction. The blessed god of destruction. It is strange' – he stood before her, looking up at her – 'but I have found my God. The god of anger, who throws down the steeples and the factory chimneys. Ah, Lady Daphne, he is a man's God, he is a man's God. I have found my God, Lady Daphne.'

'Apparently. And how are you going to serve him?'

A naïve glow transfigured his face.

'Oh, I will help. With my heart I will help while I can do nothing with my hands. I say to my heart: Beat, hammer, beat with little strokes. Beat, hammer of God, beat them down. Beat it all down.'

Her brows knitted, her face took on a look of discontent.

'Beat what down?' she asked harshly.

'The world, the world of man. Not the trees – these chestnuts, for example' – he looked up at them, at the tufts and loose pinions of yellow – 'not these – nor the chattering sorcerers, the squirrels – nor the hawk that comes. Not those.'

'You mean beat England?' she said.

'Ah, no. Ah, no. Not England any more than Germany – perhaps not as much. Not Europe any more than Asia.'

'Just the end of the world?'

'No, no. No, no. What grudge have I against a world where little chestnuts are so sweet as these! Do you like yours? Will you take another?'

'No, thanks.'

'What grudge have I against a world where even the hedges are full of berries, bunches of black berries that hang down, and red berries that thrust up. Never would I hate the world. But the world of man. Lady Daphne' – his voice sank to a whisper – '*I hate it.* Zzz!' he hissed. '*Strike, little heart! Strike, strike, hit, smite!* Oh, Lady Daphne!' – his eyes dilated with a ring of fire.

'What?' she said, scared.

'I believe in the power of my red, dark heart. God has put the hammer in my breast – the little eternal hammer. Hit – hit – hit! It hits on the world of man. It hits, it hits! And it hears the thin sound of cracking. The thin sound of cracking. Hark!'

He stood still and made her listen. It was late afternoon. The strange laugh of his face made the air seem dark to her. And she could easily have believed that she heard a faint, fine shivering, cracking, through the air, a delicate crackling noise.

'You hear it? Yes? Oh, may I live long! May I live long, so that my hammer may strike and strike, and the cracks go deeper, deeper! Ah, the world of man! Ah, the joy, the passion in every heartbeat! Strike home, strike true, strike sure. Strike to destroy it. Strike! Strike! To destroy the world of man. Ah, God. Ah, God, prisoner of peace. Do I not know you, Lady Daphne? Do I not? Do I not?'

She was silent for some moments, looking away at the twinkling lights of a station beyond.

'Not the white plucked lily of your body. I have gathered no flower for my ostentatious life. But in the cold dark, your lily root, Lady Daphne. Ah, yes, you will know it all your life, that I know where your root lies buried, with its sad, sad quick of life. What does it matter!'

They had walked slowly towards the house. She was silent. Then at last she said, in a peculiar voice, 'And you would never want to kiss me?'

'Ah, no!' he answered sharply.

She held out her hand.

'Goodbye, Count Dionys,' she drawled, fashionably. He bowed over her hand, but did not kiss it.

'Goodbye, Lady Daphne.'

She went away, with her brow set hard. And henceforth she thought only of her husband, of Basil. She made the Count die out of her. Basil was coming, he was near. He was coming back from the East, from war and death. Ah, he had been through awful fire of experience. He would be something new, something she did not know. He was something new, a stronger lover who had been through terrible fire, and had come out strange and new, like a god. Ah, new and terrible his love would be, pure and intensified by the awful fire of suffering. A new lover – a new bridegroom – a new, supernatural wedding-night. She shivered in anticipation, waiting for her husband. She hardly noticed the wild excitement of the Armistice. She was waiting for something more wonderful to her.

And yet the moment she heard his voice on the telephone, her heart contracted with fear. It was his well-known voice, deliberate, diffident, almost drawling, with the same subtle suggestion of deference, and the rather exaggerated Cambridge intonation, up and down. But there was a difference, a new icy note that went through her veins like death.

'Is that you, Daphne? I shall be with you in half an hour. Is that all right for you? Yes, I've just landed, and shall come straight to you. Yes, a taxi. Shall I be too sudden for you, darling? No? Good, oh good! Half an hour, then! I say, Daphne? There won't be anyone else there, will there? Quite alone! Good! I can ring up Dad afterwards. Yes, splendid, splendid. Sure you're all right, my darling? I'm at death's door till I see you. Yes. Goodbye – half an hour. Goodbye.'

When Daphne had hung up the receiver she sat down almost in a faint. What was it that so frightened her? His terrible, terrible altered voice, like cold, blue steel. She had no time to think. She rang for her maid.

'Oh, my lady, it isn't bad news?' cried Millicent, when she caught sight of her mistress white as death.

'No, good news. Major Apsley will be here in half an hour. Help me to dress. Ring to Murry's first to send in some roses, red ones, and some lilac-coloured iris – two dozen of each, at once.'

Daphne went to her room. She didn't know what to wear, she didn't know how she wanted her hair dressed. She spoke hastily to her maid. She chose a violet-coloured dress. She did not know what she was doing. In the middle of dressing the flowers came, and she left off to put them in the bowls. So that when she heard his voice in the hall, she was still standing in front of the mirror reddening her lips and wiping it away again.

'Major Apsley, my lady!' murmured the maid, in excitement.

'Yes, I can hear. Go and tell him I shall be *one* minute.'

Daphne's voice had become slow and sonorous, like bronze, as it always did when she was upset. Her face looked almost haggard, and in vain she dabbed with the rouge.

'How does he look?' she asked curtly, when her maid came back.

'A long scar here,' said the maid, and she drew her finger from the left-hand corner of her mouth into her cheek, slanting downwards.

'Make him look very different?' asked Daphne.

'Not so *very* different, my lady,' said Millicent gently. 'His eyes are the same, I think.' The girl also was distressed.

'All right,' said Daphne. She looked at herself a long, last look as she turned away from the mirror. The sight of her own face made her feel almost sick. She had seen so much of herself. And yet even now she was fascinated by the heavy droop of her lilac-veined lids over her slow, strange, large, green-blue eyes. They *were* mysterious-looking. And she gave herself a long, sideways glance, curious and Chinese. How was it possible there was a touch of the Chinese in her face? – she so purely an English blonde, an Aphrodite of the foam, as Basil had called her in poetry. Ah well! She left off her thoughts and went through the hall to the drawing-room.

He was standing nervously in the middle of the room in his uniform. She hardly glanced at his face – and saw only the scar.

'Hullo, Daphne,' he said, in a voice full of the expected emotion. He stepped forward and took her in his arms, and kissed her forehead.

'So glad! So glad it's happened at last,' she said, hiding her tears.

'So glad what has happened, darling?' he asked, in his deliberate manner.

'That you're back.' Her voice had the bronze resonance, she spoke rather fast.

'Yes, I'm back, Daphne darling – as much of me as there is to bring back.'

'Why?' she said. 'You've come back whole, surely?' She was frightened.

'Yes, apparently I have. Apparently. But don't let's talk of that. Let's talk of you, darling. How are you? Let me look at you. You are thinner, you are older. But you are more wonderful than ever. Far more wonderful.'

'How?' said she.

'I can't exactly say how. You were only a girl. Now you are a woman. I suppose it's all that's happened. But you are wonderful as a woman, Daphne darling – more wonderful than all that's happened. I couldn't have believed you'd be so wonderful. I'd forgotten – or else I'd never known. I say, I'm a lucky chap really. Here I am, alive and well, and I've got you for a wife. It's brought you out like a flower. I say, darling, there is more now than Venus of the foam – grander. How beautiful you are! But you look like the beauty of all life – as if you were moon-mother of the world – Aphrodite. God is good to me after all, darling. I ought never to utter a single complaint. How lovely you are – how lovely you are, my darling! I'd forgotten you – and I thought I knew you so well. Is it true that you belong to me? Are you really mine?'

They were seated on the yellow sofa. He was holding her hand, and his eyes were going up and down, from her face to her throat and her breast. The sound of his words, and the strong, cold desire in his voice excited her, pleased her, and made her heart freeze. She turned and looked into his light blue eyes. They had no longer the amused light, nor the young look. They burned with a hard, focused light, whitish.

'It's all right. You are mine, aren't you, Daphne darling?' came his cultured, musical voice, that had always the well-bred twang of diffidence.

She looked back into his eyes.

'Yes, I am yours,' she said, from the lips.

'Darling! Darling!' he murmured, kissing her hand.

Her heart beat suddenly so terribly, as if her breast would be ruptured, and she rose in one movement and went across the room. She leaned her hand on the mantelpiece and looked down at the electric fire. She could hear the faint, faint noise of it. There was silence for a few moments.

Then she turned and looked at him. He was watching her intently. His face was gaunt, and there was a curious deathly sub-pallor, though his cheeks were not white. The scar ran livid from the side of his mouth. It was not so very big. But it seemed like a scar in him himself, in his brain, as it were. In his eyes was that hard, white, focused light that fascinated her and was terrible to her. He was different. He was like death; like risen death. She felt she dared not touch him. White death was still upon him. She could tell that he shrank with a kind of agony from contact. 'Touch me not, I am not yet ascended unto the Father.' Yet for contact he had come. Something, someone seemed to be looking over his shoulder. His own young ghost looking over his shoulder. Oh, God! She closed her eyes, seeming to swoon. He remained leaning forward on the sofa, watching her.

'Aren't you well, darling?' he asked. There was a strange, incomprehensible coldness in his very fire. He did not move to come near her.

'Yes, I'm well. It is only that after all it is so sudden. Let me get used to you,' she said, turning aside her face from him. She felt utterly like a victim of his white, awful face.

'I suppose I must be a bit of a shock to you,' he said. 'I hope you won't leave off loving me. It won't be that, will it?'

The strange coldness in his voice! And yet the white, uncanny fire.

'No, I shan't leave off loving you,' she admitted, in a low tone, as if almost ashamed. She *dared* not have said otherwise. And the saying it made it true.

'Ah, if you're sure of that,' he said. 'I'm a pretty unlovely sight to behold, I know, with this wound-scar. But if you can forgive it me, darling. Do you think you can?' There was something like compulsion in his tone.

She looked at him, and shivered slightly.

'I love you – more than before,' she said hurriedly.

'Even the scar?' came his terrible voice, enquiring.

She glanced again, with that slow, Chinese side-look, and felt she would die.

'Yes,' she said, looking away at nothingness. It was an awful moment to her. A little, slightly imbecile smile widened on his face.

He suddenly knelt at her feet, and kissed the toe of her slipper, and kissed the instep, and kissed the ankle in the thin black stocking.

'I knew,' he said in a muffled voice. 'I knew you would make good. I knew if I had to kneel, it was before you. I knew you were divine, you were the one – Cybele – Isis. I knew I was your slave. I knew. It has all been just a long initiation. I had to learn how to worship you.'

He kissed her feet again and again, without the slightest self-consciousness, or the slightest misgiving. Then he went back to the sofa, and sat there looking at her, saying, 'It isn't love, it is worship. Love between me and you will be a sacrament, Daphne. That's what I had to learn. You are beyond me. A mystery to me. My God, how great it all is. How marvellous!'

She stood with her hand on the mantelpiece, looking down and not answering. She was frightened – almost horrified: but she was thrilled deep down to her soul. She really felt she could glow white and fill the universe like the moon, like Astarte, like Isis, like Venus. The grandeur of her own pale power. The man religiously worshipped her, not merely amorously. She was ready for him – for the sacrament of his supreme worship.

He sat on the sofa with his hands spread on the yellow brocade and pushing downwards behind him, down between the deep upholstery of the back and the seat. He had long, white hands with pale freckles. And his fingers touched something. With his long white fingers he groped and brought it out. It was the lost thimble. And inside it was the bit of screwed-up blue paper.

'I say, is that *your* thimble?' he asked.

She started, and went hurriedly forward for it.

'Where was it?' she said, agitated.

But he did not give it to her. He turned it round and pulled out the bit of blue paper. He saw the faint pencil marks on the screwed-up ball, and unrolled the band of paper, and slowly deciphered the verse.

> 'Wenn ich ein Vöglein wär'
> Und auch zwei Flüglein hätt',
> Flög' ich zu dir – '

How awfully touching that is,' he said. 'A *Vöglein* with two little *Flüglein*! But what a precious darling child you are! Whom did you want to fly to, if you were a *Vöglein*?' He looked up at her with a curious smile.

'I can't remember,' she said, turning aside her head.

'I hope it was to me,' he said. 'Anyhow, I shall consider it was, and shall love you all the more for it. What a darling child! A *Vöglein* if you please, with two little wings! Why, how beautifully absurd of you, darling!'

He folded the scrap of paper carefully, and put it in his pocketbook, keeping the thimble all the time between his knees.

'Tell me when you lost it, Daphne,' he said, examining the bauble.

'About a month ago – or two months.'

'About a month ago – or two months. And what were you sewing? Do you mind if I ask? I like to think of you then. I was still in that beastly El Hasrun. What were you sewing, darling, two months ago, when you lost your thimble?'

'A shirt.'

'I say, a shirt! Whose shirt?'

'Yours.'

'There. Now we've run it to earth. Were you really sewing a shirt for me! Is it finished? Can I put it on at this minute?'

'That one isn't finished, but the first one is.'

'I say, darling, let me go and put it on. To think I should have it next my skin! I shall feel you all round me, all over me. I say, how marvellous that will be! Won't you come?'

'Won't you give me the thimble?' she said.

'Yes, of course. What a noble thimble too! Who gave it you?'

'Count Dionys Psanek.'

'Who was he?'

'A Bohemian Count, in Dresden. He once stayed with us in Thoresway – with a tall wife. Didn't you meet them?'

'I don't think I did. I don't think I did. I don't remember. What was he like?'

'A little man with black hair and a rather low, dark forehead – rather dressy.'

'No, I don't remember him at all. So he gave it you. Well, I wonder where he is now? Probably rotted, poor devil.'

'No, he's interned in Voynich Hall. Mother and I have been to see him several times. He was awfully badly wounded.'

'Poor little beggar! In Voynich Hall! I'll look at him before he goes. Odd thing, to give you a thimble. Odd gift! You were a girl then, though. Do you think he had it made, or do you think he found it in a shop?'

'I think it belonged to the family. The ladybird at the top is part of their crest – and the snake as well, I think.'

'A ladybird! Funny thing for a crest. Americans would call it a bug. I must look at him before he goes. And you were sewing a shirt for me! And then you posted me this little letter into the sofa. Well, I'm awfully glad I received it, and that it didn't go astray in the post, like so many things. *Wenn ich ein Vöglein wär* – you perfect child! But that is the beauty of a woman like you: you are so superb and beyond worship, and then such an exquisite naïve child. Who could help worshipping you and loving you: immortal and mortal together. What, you want the thimble? Here! Wonderful, wonderful, white fingers. Ah, darling, you are more goddess than child, you long, limber Isis with sacred hands. White, white, and immortal! Don't tell me your hands could die, darling: your wonderful Proserpine fingers. They are immortal as February and snowdrops. If you lift your hands the spring comes. I *can't* help kneeling before you, darling. I am no more than a sacrifice to you, an offering. I *wish* I could die in giving myself to you, give you all my blood on your altar, for ever.'

She looked at him with a long, slow look, as he turned his face to her. His face was white with ecstasy. And she was not afraid. Somewhere, saturnine, she knew it was absurd. But she chose not to know. A certain swoon-sleep was on her. With her slow, green-blue eyes she looked down on his ecstasised face, almost benign. But in her right hand unconsciously she held the thimble fast, she only gave him her left hand. He took her hand and rose to his feet in that curious priestly ecstasy which made him more than a man or a soldier, far, far more than a lover to her.

Nevertheless, his homecoming made her begin to be ill again. Afterwards, after his love, she had to bear herself in torment. To her shame and her heaviness, she knew she was not strong enough, or pure enough, to bear this awful outpouring adoration-lust. It was not her fault she felt weak and fretful afterwards, as if she wanted to cry and be fretful and petulant, wanted someone to save her. She could not turn to Basil, her husband. After his ecstasy of adoration-lust for her, she recoiled from him. Alas, she was not the goddess, the superb person he named her. She was flawed with the fatal humility of her age. She could not harden her heart and burn her soul pure of this humility, this misgiving. She could not finally believe in her own woman-godhead – only in her own female mortality.

That fierce power of being alone, even with your lover, the fierce power of the woman *in excelsis* – alas, she could not keep it. She could rise to the height for the time, the incandescent, transcendent, moon-fierce womanhood. But alas, she could not stay intensified and resplendent in her white, womanly powers, her female mystery. She relaxed, she lost her glory, and became fretful. Fretful and ill and never to be soothed. And then naturally her man became ashy and somewhat acrid, while she ached with nerves, and could not eat.

Of course she began to dream about Count Dionys: to yearn wistfully for him. And it was absolutely a fatal thought to her that he was going away. When she thought that – that he was leaving England soon – going away into the dark for ever – then the last spark seemed to die in her. She felt her soul perish, whilst she herself was worn and soulless like a prostitute. A prostitute goddess. And her husband, the gaunt, white, intensified priest of her, who never ceased from being before her like a lust.

'Tomorrow,' she said to him, gathering her last courage and looking at him with a side look, 'I want to go to Voynich Hall.'

'What, to see Count Psanek? Oh, good! Yes, very good! I'll come along as well. I should like very much to see him. I suppose he'll be getting sent back before long.'

It was a fortnight before Christmas, very dark weather. Her husband was in khaki. She wore her black furs and a black lace veil over her face, so that she seemed mysterious. But she lifted the veil and looped it behind, so that it made a frame for her face. She looked very lovely like that – her face pure like the most white hellebore flower, touched with winter pink, amid the blackness of her drapery and furs. Only she was rather too much like the picture of a modern beauty: too much the actual thing. She had half an idea that Dionys would hate her for her effective loveliness. He would see it and hate it. The thought was like a bitter balm to her. For herself, she loved her loveliness almost with obsession.

The Count came cautiously forward, glancing from the lovely figure of Lady Daphne to the gaunt well-bred Major at her side. Daphne was so beautiful in her dark furs, the black lace of her veil thrown back over her close-fitting, dull-gold-threaded hat, and her face fair like a winter flower in a cranny of darkness. But on her face, that was smiling with a slow self-satisfaction of beauty and of knowledge that she was dangling the two men, and setting all the imprisoned officers wildly on the alert, the Count could read that acridity of dissatisfaction and of inefficiency. And he looked away to the livid scar on the Major's cheek.

'Count Dionys, I wanted to bring my husband to see you. May I introduce him to you? Major Apsley – Count Dionys Psanek.'

The two men shook hands rather stiffly.

'I can sympathise with you being fastened up in this place,' said Basil in his slow, easy fashion. 'I hated it, I assure you, out there in the East.'

'But your conditions were much worse than mine,' smiled the Count.

'Well, perhaps they were. But prison is prison, even if it were heaven itself.'

'Lady Apsley has been the one angel of my heaven,' smiled the Count.

'I'm afraid I was as inefficient as most angels,' said she.

The small smile never left the Count's dark face. It was true as she said, he was low-browed, the black hair growing low on his brow, and his eyebrows making a thick bow above his dark eyes, which had again long black lashes. So that the upper part of his face seemed very dusky-black. His nose was small and somewhat translucent. There was a touch of mockery about him, which was intensified even by his small, energetic stature. He was still carefully dressed in the dark-blue uniform, whose shabbiness could not hinder the dark flame of life which seemed to glow through the cloth from his body. He was not thin – but still had a curious swarthy translucency of skin in his low-browed face.

'What would you have been more?' he laughed, making equivocal dark eyes at her.

'Oh, of course, a delivering angel – a cinema heroine,' she replied, closing her eyes and turning her face aside.

All the while the white-faced, tall Major watched the little man with a fixed, half-smiling scrutiny. The Count seemed to notice. He turned to the Englishman.

'I am glad that I can congratulate you, Major Apsley, on your safe and happy return to your home.'

'Thanks. I hope I may be able to congratulate you in the same way before long.'

'Oh yes,' said the Count. 'Before long I shall be shipped back.'

'Have you any news of your family?' interrupted Daphne.

'No news,' he replied briefly, with sudden gravity.

'It seems you'll find a fairish mess out in Austria,' said Basil.

'Yes, probably. It is what we had to expect,' replied the Count.

'Well, I don't know. Sometimes things do turn out for the best. I feel that's as good as true in my case,' said the Major.

'Things have turned out for the best?' said the Count, with an intonation of polite enquiry.

'Yes. Just for me personally, I mean – to put it quite selfishly. After all, what we've learned is that a man can only speak for himself. And I feel it's been dreadful, but it's not been lost. It was like an ordeal one had to go through,' said Basil.

'You mean the war?'

'The war and everything that went with it.'

'And when you've been through the ordeal?' politely enquired the Count.

'Why, you arrive at a higher state of consciousness, and therefore of life. And so, of course, at a higher plane of love. A surprisingly higher plane of love, that you had never suspected the existence of before.'

The Count looked from Basil to Daphne, who was posing her head a little self-consciously.

'Then indeed the war has been a valuable thing,' he said.

'Exactly!' cried Basil. 'I am another man.'

'And Lady Apsley?' queried the Count.

'Oh' – her husband faced round to her – 'she is *absolutely* another woman – and *much* more wonderful, more marvellous.'

The Count smiled and bowed slightly.

'When we knew her ten years ago, we should have said then that it was impossible,' said he, 'for her to be more wonderful.'

'Oh, quite!' returned the husband. 'It always seems impossible. And the impossible is always happening. As a matter of fact, I think the war has opened another circle of life to us – a wider ring.'

'It may be so,' said the Count.

'You don't feel it so yourself?' The Major looked with his keen, white attention into the dark, low-browed face of the other man. The Count looked smiling at Daphne.

'I am only a prisoner still, Major, therefore I feel my ring quite small.'

'Yes, of course you do. Of course. Well, I do hope you won't be a prisoner much longer. You must be dying to get back into your own country.'

'Yes, I shall be glad to be free. Also,' he smiled, 'I shall miss my prison and my visits from the angels.'

Even Daphne could not be sure he was mocking her. It was evident the visit was unpleasant to him. She could see he did not like Basil. Nay, more, she could feel that the presence of her tall, gaunt, idealistic husband was hateful to the little swarthy man. But he passed it all off in smiles and polite speeches.

On the other hand, Basil was as if fascinated by the Count. He watched him absorbedly all the time, quite forgetting Daphne. She knew this. She knew that she was quite gone out of her husband's consciousness, like a lamp that has been carried away into another room. There he stood completely in the dark, as far as she was concerned, and all his attention focused on the other man. On his pale, gaunt face was a fixed smile of amused attention.

'But don't you get awfully bored,' he said, 'between the visits?'

The Count looked up with an affectation of frankness.

'No, I do not,' he said. 'I can brood, you see, on the things that come to pass.'

'I think that's where the harm comes in,' replied the Major. 'One sits and broods, and is cut off from everything, and one loses one's contact with reality. That's the effect it had on me, being a prisoner.'

'Contact with reality – what is that?'

'Well – contact with anybody, really – or anything.'

'Why must one have contact?'

'Well, because one must,' said Basil.

The Count smiled slowly.

'But I can sit and watch fate flowing, like black water, deep down in my own soul,' he said. 'I feel that there, in the dark of my own soul, things are happening.'

'That may be. But whatever happens, it is only one thing, really. It is a contact between your own soul and the soul of one other being, or of many other beings. Nothing else can happen to man. That's how I figured it out for myself. I may be wrong. But that's how I figured it out when I was wounded and a prisoner.'

The Count's face had gone dark and serious.

'But is this contact an aim in itself?' he asked.

'Well,' said the Major – he had taken his degree in philosophy – 'it seems to me it is. It results inevitably in some form of activity. But the cause and the origin and the life-impetus of all action, activity, whether constructive or destructive, seems to me to be in the dynamic contact between human beings. You bring to pass a certain dynamic contact between men, and you get war. Another sort of dynamic contact, and you get them all building a cathedral, as they did in the Middle Ages.'

'But was not the war, or the cathedral, the real aim, and the emotional contact just the means?' said the Count.

'I don't think so,' said the Major, his curious white passion beginning to glow through his face. The three were seated in a little card-room, left alone by courtesy by the other men. Daphne was still draped in her dark, too-becoming drapery. But alas, she sat now ignored by both men. She might just as well have been an ugly little nobody, for all the notice that was taken of her. She sat in the window-seat of the dreary small room with a look of discontent on her exotic, rare face, that was like a delicate white and pink hot-house flower. From time to time she glanced with long, slow looks from man to man: from her husband, whose pallid, intense, white glowing face was pressed forward across the table to the Count, who sat back in his chair, as if in opposition, and whose dark face seemed clubbed together in a dark, unwilling stare. Her husband was *quite* unaware of anything but his own white identity. But the Count still had a grain of secondary consciousness which hovered round and remained aware of the woman in the window-seat. The whole of his face, and his forward-looking attention was concentrated on Basil. But somewhere at the back of him he kept track of Daphne. She sat uneasy, in discontent, as women always do sit when men are locked together in a combustion of words. At the same time, she followed the argument. It was curious that, while her sympathy at this moment was with the Count, it was her husband whose words she believed to be true. The contact, the emotional contact was the real thing, the so-called 'aim' was only a by-product. Even wars and cathedrals, in her mind, were only by-products. The real thing was what the warriors and cathedral-builders had had in common, as a great uniting feeling: the thing they felt for one another, and for their women in particular, of course.

'There are a great many kinds of contact, nevertheless,' said Dionys.

'Well, do you know,' said the Major, 'it seems to me there is really only one supreme contact, the contact of love. Mind you, the love may take on an infinite variety of forms. And in my opinion, no form of love is wrong, so long as it *is* love, and you yourself *honour* what you are doing. Love has an extraordinary variety of forms! And that is all that there is in life, it seems to me. But I grant you, if you deny the *variety* of love you deny love altogether. If you try to specialise love into one set of accepted feelings, you wound the very soul of love. Love *must* be multiform, else it is just tyranny, just death.'

'But why call it all *love?*' said the Count.

'Because it seems to me it *is* love: the great power that draws human beings together, no matter what the result of the contact may be. Of course there is hate, but hate is only the recoil of love.'

'Do you think the old Egypt was established on love?' asked Dionys.

'Why, of course! And perhaps the most multiform, the most comprehensive love that the world has seen. All that we suffer from now is that our way of love is narrow, exclusive, and therefore not love at all; more like death and tyranny.'

The Count slowly shook his head, smiling slowly and as if sadly.

'No,' he said. 'No. It is no good. You must use another word than love.'

'I don't agree at all,' said Basil.

'What word then?' blurted Daphne.

The Count looked at her.

'Obedience, submission, faith, belief, responsibility, power,' he said slowly, picking out the words slowly, as if searching for what he wanted, and never quite finding it. He looked with his quiet dark eyes into her eyes. It was curious, she disliked his words intensely, but she liked him. On the other hand, she believed absolutely what her husband said, yet her physical sympathy was against him.

'Do you agree, Daphne?' asked Basil.

'Not a bit,' she replied, with a heavy look at her husband.

'Nor I,' said Basil. 'It seems to me, if you love, there is no obedience nor submission, except to the soul of love. If you mean obedience, submission, and all the rest, to the soul of love itself, I quite agree. But if you mean obedience, submission of one person to another, and one man having power over others – I don't agree, and never shall. It seems to me just there where we have gone wrong. Kaiser Wilhelm II wanted power – '

'No, no,' said the Count. 'He was a mountebank. He had no conception of the sacredness of power.'

'He proved himself very dangerous.'

'Oh yes. But peace can be even more dangerous still.'

'Tell me, then. Do you believe that you, as an aristocrat, should have feudal power over a few hundreds of other men, who happen to be born serfs, or not aristocrats?'

'Not as a hereditary aristocrat, but as a *man* who is by nature an aristocrat,' said the Count, 'it is my sacred duty to hold the lives of other men in my hands, and to shape the issue. But I can never fulfil my destiny till men will willingly put their lives in my hands.'

'You don't expect them to, do you?' smiled Basil.

'At this moment, no.'

'Or at any moment!' The Major was sarcastic.

'At a certain moment the men who are really living will come beseeching to put their lives into the hands of the greater men among them, beseeching the greater men to take the sacred responsibility of power.'

'Do you think so? Perhaps you mean men will at last begin to choose leaders whom they will *love*,' said Basil. 'I wish they would.'

'No, I mean that they will at last yield themselves before men who are greater than they: become vassals by choice.'

'Vassals!' exclaimed Basil, smiling. 'You are still in the feudal ages, Count.'

'Vassals. Not to any hereditary aristocrat – Hohenzollern or Hapsburg or Psanek,' smiled the Count. 'But to the man whose soul is born single, able to be alone, to choose and to command. At last the masses will come to such men and say: "You are greater than we. Be our lords. Take our life and our death in your hands, and dispose of us according to your will. Because we see a light in your face, and burning on your mouth." '

The Major smiled for many moments, really piqued and amused, watching the Count, who did not turn a hair.

'I say, you must be awfully naïve, Count, if you believe the modern masses are ever going to behave like that. I assure you, they never will.'

'If they did,' said the Count, 'would you call it a new reign of love, or something else?'

'Well, of course, it would contain an element of love. There would have to be an element of love in their feeling for their leaders.'

'Do you think so? I thought that love assumed an equality in difference. I thought that love gave to every man the right to judge the acts of other men – "This was not an act of love, therefore it was wrong." Does not democracy, and love, give to every man this right?'

'Certainly,' said Basil.

'Ah, but my chosen aristocrat would say to those who chose him: "If you choose me, you give up forever your right to judge me. If you have truly chosen to follow me, you have thereby rejected all your right to criticise me. You can no longer either approve or disapprove of me. You have performed the sacred act of choice. Henceforth you can only obey." '

'They wouldn't be able to help criticising, for all that,' said Daphne, blurting in her say.

He looked at her slowly, and for the first time in her life she was doubtful of what she was saying.

'The day of Judas,' he said, 'ends with the day of love.'

Basil woke up from a sort of trance.

'I think, of course, Count,' he said, 'that it's an awfully amusing idea. A retrogression slap back to the Dark Ages.'

'Not so,' said the Count. 'Men – the mass of men – were never before free to perform the sacred act of choice. Today – soon – they may be free.'

'Oh, I don't know. Many tribes chose their kings and chiefs.'

'Men have never before been quite free to choose: and to know what they are doing.'

'You mean they've only made themselves free in order voluntarily to saddle themselves with new lords and masters?'

'I do mean that.'

'In short, life is just a vicious circle?'

'Not at all. An ever-widening circle, as you say. Always more wonderful.'

'Well, it's all frightfully interesting and amusing – don't you think so, Daphne? By the way, Count, where would women be? Would they be allowed to criticise their husbands?'

'Only before marriage,' smiled the Count. 'Not after.'

'Splendid!' said Basil. 'I'm all for that bit of your scheme, Count. I hope you're listening, Daphne.'

'Oh yes. But then I've only married *you*. I've got my right to criticise all the other men,' she said in a dull, angry voice.

'Exactly. Clever of you! So the Count won't get off! Well now, what do you think of the Count's aristocratic scheme for the future, Daphne? Do you approve?'

'Not at all. But then little men have always wanted power,' she said cruelly.

'Oh, big men as well, for that matter,' said Basil, conciliatory.

'I have been told before,' smiled the Count, 'little men are always bossy. I am afraid I have offended Lady Daphne?'

'No,' she said. 'Not really. I'm amused, really. But I always dislike any suggestion of bullying.'

'Indeed, so do I,' said he.

'The Count didn't mean bullying, Daphne,' said Basil. 'Come, there is really an allowable distinction between responsible power and bullying.'

'When men put their heads together about it,' said she.

She was haughty and angry, as if she were afraid of losing something. The Count smiled mischievously at her.

'You are offended, Lady Daphne? But why? You are safe from any spark of my dangerous and extensive authority.'

Basil burst into a roar of laughter.

'It *is* rather funny, you to be talking of power and of not being criticised,' he said. 'But I should like to hear more: I would like to hear more.'

As they drove home, he said to his wife, 'You know I like that little man. He's a quaint little bantam. And he sets one thinking.'

Lady Daphne froze to four degrees below zero, under the north wind of this statement, and not another word was to be thawed out of her.

Curiously enough, it was now Basil who was attracted by the Count, and Daphne who was repelled. Not that she was so bound up in her husband. Not at all. She was feeling rather sore against men altogether. But as so often happens, in this life based on the wicked triangle, Basil could only follow his enthusiasm for the Count in his wife's presence. When the two men were alone together, they were awkward, resistant, they could hardly get out a dozen words to one another. When Daphne was there, however, to complete the circuit of the opposing currents, things went like a house on fire.

This, however, was not much consolation to Lady Daphne. Merely to sit as a passive medium between two men who are squibbing philosophical nonsense to one another: no, it was not good enough! She almost hated the Count: low-browed little fellow, belonging to the race of prehistoric slaves. But her grudge against her white-faced, spiritually intense husband was sharp as vinegar. Let down: she was let down between the pair of them.

What next? Well, what followed was entirely Basil's fault. The winter was passing: it was obvious the war was really over, that Germany was finished. The Hohenzollern had fizzled out like a very poor squib, the Hapsburg was popping feebly in obscurity, the Romanov was smudged out without a sputter. So much for imperial royalty. Henceforth democratic peace.

The Count, of course, would be shipped back now like returned goods that had no market any more. There was a world peace ahead. A week or two, and Voynich Hall would be empty.

Basil, however, could not let matters follow their simple course. He was awfully intrigued by the Count. He wanted to entertain him as a guest before he went. And Major Apsley could get anything in reason, at this moment. So he obtained permission for the poor little Count to stay a fortnight at Thoresway, before being shipped back to Austria. Earl Beveridge, whose soul was black as ink since the war, would never have allowed the little alien enemy to enter his house, had it not been for the hatred which had been aroused in him, during the last two years, by the degrading spectacle of the so-called patriots who had been howling their mongrel indecency in the public face. These mongrels had held the Press and the British public in abeyance for almost two years. Their one aim was to degrade and humiliate anything that was proud or dignified remaining in England. It was almost the worst nightmare of all, this coming to the top of a lot of public filth which was determined to suffocate the souls of all dignified men.

Hence, the Earl, who never intended to be swamped by unclean scum, whatever else happened to him, stamped his heels in the ground and stood on his own feet. When Basil said to him, would he allow the Count to have a fortnight's decent peace in Thoresway before all was finished, Lord Beveridge gave a slow consent, scandal or no scandal. Indeed, it was really to defy scandal that he took such a step. For the thought of his dead boys was bitter to him: and the thought of England fallen under the paws of smelly mongrels was bitterer still.

Lord Beveridge was at Thoresway to receive the Count, who arrived escorted by Basil. The English Earl was a big, handsome man, rather heavy, with a dark, sombre face that would have been haughty if haughtiness had not been made so ridiculous. He was a passionate man, with a passionate man's sensitiveness, generosity, and instinctive overbearing. But *his* dark passionate nature, and his violent sensitiveness had been subjected now to fifty-five years' subtle repression, condemnation, repudiation, till he had almost come to believe in his own wrongness. His little, frail wife, all love for humanity, she was the genuine article. Himself, he was labelled selfish, sensual, cruel, etc., etc. So by now he always seemed to be standing aside, in the shadow, letting himself be obliterated by the pallid rabble of the democratic hurry. That was the impression he gave of a man standing back, half-ashamed, half-haughty, semi-hidden in the dark background.

He was a little on the defensive as Basil came in with the Count.

'Ah – how do you do, Count Psanek?' he said, striding largely forward and holding out his hand. Because he was the father of Daphne the Count felt a certain tenderness for the taciturn Englishman.

'You do me too much honour, my lord, receiving me in your house,' said the small Count proudly.

The Earl looked at him slowly, without speaking: seemed to look down on him, in every sense of the words.

'We are still men, Count. We are not beasts altogether.'

'You wish to say that my countrymen are so very nearly beasts, Lord Beveridge?' smiled the Count, curling his fine nose.

Again the Earl was slow in replying.

'You have a low opinion of my manners, Count Psanek.'

'But perhaps a just appreciation of your meaning, Lord Beveridge,' smiled the Count, with the same reckless little look of contempt on his nose.

Lord Beveridge flushed dark, with all his native anger offended.

'I am glad Count Psanek makes my own meaning clear to me,' he said.

'I beg your pardon a thousand times, my lord, if I give offence in doing so,' replied the Count.

The Earl went black, and felt a fool. He turned his back on the Count. And then he turned round again, offering his cigar-case.

'Will you smoke?' he said. There was kindness in his tone.

'Thank you,' said the Count, taking a cigar.

'I dare say,' said Lord Beveridge, 'that all men are beasts in some way. I am afraid I have fallen into the common habit of speaking by rote, and not what I really mean. Won't you take a seat?'

'It is only as a prisoner that I have learned that I am *not* truly a beast. No, I am myself. I am not a beast,' said the Count, seating himself.

The Earl eyed him curiously.

'Well,' he said, smiling, 'I suppose it is best to come to a decision about it.'

'It is necessary, if one is to be safe from vulgarity.'

The Earl felt a twinge of accusation. With his agate-brown, hard-looking eyes he watched the black-browed little Count.

'You are probably right,' he said.

But he turned his face aside.

They were five people at dinner – Lady Beveridge was there as hostess.

'Ah, Count Dionys,' she said with a sigh, 'do you really feel that the war is over?'

'Oh yes,' he replied quickly. 'This war is over. The armies will go home. *Their* cannon will not sound any more. Never again like this.'

'Ah, I hope so,' she sighed.

'I am sure,' he said.

'You think there'll be no more war?' said Daphne.

For some reason she had made herself very fine, in her newest dress of silver and black and pink-chenille, with bare shoulders, and her hair fashionably done. The Count in his shabby uniform turned to her. She was nervous, hurried. Her slim white arm was near him, with the bit of silver at the shoulder. Her skin was white like a hot-house flower. Her lips moved hurriedly.

'Such a war as this there will never be again,' he said.

'What makes you so sure?' she replied, glancing into his eyes.

'The machine of war has got out of our control. We shall never start it again, till it has fallen to pieces. We shall be afraid.'

'Will everybody be afraid?' said she, looking down and pressing back her chin.

'I think so.'

'We will hope so,' said Lady Beveridge.

'Do you mind if I ask you, Count,' said Basil, 'what you feel about the way the war has ended? The way it has ended for *you*, I mean.'

'You mean that Germany and Austria have lost the war? It was bound to be. We have all lost the war. All Europe.'

'I agree there,' said Lord Beveridge.

'We've all lost the war?' said Daphne, turning to look at him.

There was pain on his dark, low-browed face. He suffered having the sensitive woman beside him. Her skin had a hot-house delicacy that made his head go round. Her shoulders were broad, rather thin, but the skin was white and so sensitive, so hot-house delicate. It affected him like the perfume of some white, exotic flower. And she seemed to be sending her heart towards him. It was as if she wanted to press her breast to his. From the breast she loved him, and sent out love to him. And it made him unhappy; he wanted to be quiet, and to keep his honour before these hosts.

He looked into her eyes, his own eyes dark with knowledge and pain. She, in her silence and her brief words seemed to be holding them all under her spell. She seemed to have cast a certain muteness on the table, in the midst of which she remained silently master, leaning forward to her plate, and silently mastering them all.

'Don't I think we've all lost the war?' he replied, in answer to her question. 'It was a war of suicide. Nobody could win it. It was suicide for all of us.'

'Oh, I don't know,' she replied. 'What about America and Japan?'

'They don't count. They only helped *us* to commit suicide. They did not enter vitally.'

There was such a look of pain on his face, and such a sound of pain in his voice, that the other three closed their ears, shut off from attending. Only Daphne was making him speak. It was she who was drawing the soul out of him, trying to read the future in him as the augurs read the future in the quivering entrails of the sacrificed beast. She looked direct into his face, searching his soul.

'You think Europe has committed suicide?' she said.

'Morally.'

'Only morally?' came her slow, bronze-like words, so fatal.

'That is enough,' he smiled.

'Quite,' she said, with a slow droop of her eyelids. Then she turned away her face. But he felt the heart strangling inside his breast. What was she doing now? What was she thinking? She filled him with uncertainty and with uncanny fear.

'At least,' said Basil, 'those infernal guns are quiet.'

'For ever,' said Dionys.

'I wish I could believe you, Count,' said the Major.

The talk became more general – or more personal. Lady Beveridge asked Dionys about his wife and family. He knew nothing save that they had gone to Hungary in 1916, when his own house was burnt down. His wife might even have gone to Bulgaria with Prince Bogorik. He did not know.

'But your children, Count!' cried Lady Beveridge.

'I do not know. Probably in Hungary, with their grandmother. I will go when I get back.'

'But have you never *written*? – never enquired?'

'I could not write. I shall know soon enough – everything.'

'You have no son?'

'No. Two girls.'

'Poor things!'

'Yes.'

'I say, isn't it an odd thing to have a ladybird on your crest?' asked Basil, to cheer up the conversation.

'Why queer? Charlemagne had bees. And it is a *Marienkäfer* – a Mary-beetle. The beetle of Our Lady. I think it is quite a heraldic insect, Major,' smiled the Count.

'You're proud of it?' said Daphne, suddenly turning to look at him again, with her slow, pregnant look.

'I am, you know. It has such a long genealogy – our spotted beetle. Much longer than the Psaneks. I think, you know, it is a descendant of the Egyptian scarabeus, which is a very mysterious emblem. So I connect myself with the Pharaohs: just through my ladybird.'

'You feel your ladybird has crept through so many ages,' she said.

'Imagine it!' he laughed.

'The scarab *is* a piquant insect,' said Basil.

'Do you know Fabre?' put in Lord Beveridge. 'He suggests that the beetle rolling a little ball of dung before him, in a dry old field, must have suggested to the Egyptians the First Principle that set the globe rolling. And so the scarab became the symbol of the creative principle – or something like that.'

'That the earth is a tiny ball of dry dung is good,' said Basil.

'Between the claws of a ladybird,' added Daphne.

'That is what it is, to go back to one's origin,' said Lady Beveridge.

'Perhaps they meant that it was the principle of decomposition which first set the ball rolling,' said the Count.

'The ball would have to be *there* first,' said Basil.

'Certainly. But it hadn't started to roll. Then the principle of decomposition started it.' The Count smiled as if it were a joke.

'I am no Egyptologist,' said Lady Beveridge, 'so I can't judge.'

The Earl and Countess Beveridge left next day. Count Dionys was left with the two young people in the house. It was a beautiful Elizabethan mansion, not very large, but with those magical rooms that are all a twinkle of small-paned windows, looking out from the dark panelled interior. The interior was cosy, panelled to the ceiling, and the ceiling moulded and touched with gold. And then the great square bow of the window with its little panes intervening like magic between oneself and the world outside, the crest in stained glass crowning its colour, the broad window-seat cushioned in faded green. Dionys wandered round the house like a little ghost, through the succession of small and large twinkling sitting-rooms and lounge rooms in front, down the long, wide corridor with the wide stairhead at each end, and up the narrow stairs to the bedrooms above, and on to the roof.

It was early spring, and he loved to sit on the leaded, pale-grey roof that had its queer seats and slopes, a little pale world in itself. Then to look down over the garden and the sloping lawn to the ponds massed round with trees, and away to the elms and furrows and hedges of the shires. On the left of the house was the farmstead, with ricks and great-roofed barns and dark-red cattle. Away to the right, beyond the park, was a village among trees, and the spark of a grey church spire.

He liked to be alone, feeling his soul heavy with its own fate. He would sit for hours watching the elm trees standing in rows like giants, like warriors across the country. The Earl had told him that the Romans had brought these elms to Britain. And he seemed to see the spirit of the Romans in them still. Sitting there alone in the spring sunshine, in the solitude of the roof, he saw the glamour of this England of hedgerows and elm trees, and the labourers with slow horses slowly drilling the sod, crossing the brown furrow: and the roofs of the village, with the church steeple rising beside a big black yew tree: and the chequer of fields away to the distance.

And the charm of the old manor around him, the garden with its grey stone walls and yew hedges – broad, broad yew hedges and a peacock pausing to glitter and scream in the busy silence of an English spring, when celandines open their yellow under the hedges, and violets are in the secret, and by the broad paths of the garden polyanthus and crocuses vary the velvet and flame, and bits of yellow wallflower shake raggedly, with a wonderful triumphance, out of the cracks of the wall. There was a fold somewhere near, and he could hear the treble bleat of the growing lambs, and the deeper, contented baa-ing of the ewes.

This was Daphne's home, where she had been born. She loved it with an ache of affection. But now it was hard to forget her dead brothers. She wandered about in the sun, with two old dogs padding after her. She talked with everybody – gardener, groom, stableman, with the farm-hands. That filled a large part of her life – straying round talking with the work-people. They were, of course, respectful to her – but not at all afraid of her. They knew she was poor, that she could not afford a car, nor anything. So they talked to her very freely: perhaps a little too freely. Yet she let it be. It was her one passion at Thoresway to hear the dependants talk and talk – about everything. The curious feeling of intimacy across a breach fascinated her. Their lives fascinated her: what they thought, what they *felt* These, what they felt. That fascinated her. There was a gamekeeper she could have loved – an impudent, ruddy-faced, laughing, ingratiating fellow; she could have loved him, if he had not been isolated beyond the breach of his birth, her culture, her consciousness. Her *consciousness* seemed to make a great gulf between her and the lower classes, the unconscious classes. She accepted it as her doom. She could never meet in real contact anyone but a super-conscious, finished being like herself: or like her husband. Her father had some of the unconscious blood-warmth of the lower classes. But he was like a man who is damned. And the Count, of course. The Count had something that was hot and invisible, a dark flame of life that might warm the cold white fire of her own blood. But –

They avoided each other. All three, they avoided one another. Basil, too, went off alone. Or he immersed himself in poetry. Sometimes he and the Count played billiards. Sometimes all three walked in the park. Often Basil and Daphne walked to the village, to post. But truly, they avoided one another, all three. The days slipped by.

At evening they sat together in the small west room that had books and a piano and comfortable shabby furniture of faded rose-coloured tapestry: a shabby room. Sometimes Basil read aloud: sometimes the Count played the piano. And they talked. And Daphne stitch by stitch went on with a big embroidered bedspread, which she might finish if she lived long enough. But they always went to bed early. They were nearly always avoiding one another.

Dionys had a bedroom in the east bay – a long way from the rooms of the others. He had a habit, when he was quite alone, of singing, or rather crooning, to himself the old songs of his childhood. It was only when he felt he was quite alone: when other people seemed to fade out of him, and all the world seemed to dissolve into darkness, and there was nothing but himself, his own soul, alive in the middle of his own small night, isolate for ever. Then, half unconscious, he would croon in a small, high-pitched, squeezed voice, a sort of high dream-voice, the songs of his childhood dialect. It was a curious noise: the sound of a man who is alone in his own blood: almost the sound of a man who is going to be executed.

Daphne heard the sound one night when she was going downstairs again with the corridor lantern to find a book. She was a bad sleeper, and her nights were a torture to her. She, too, like a neurotic, was nailed inside her own fretful self-consciousness. But she had a very keen ear. So she started as she heard the small, bat-like sound of the Count's singing to himself. She stood in the midst of the wide corridor, that was wide as a room, carpeted with a faded lavender-coloured carpet, with a piece of massive dark furniture at intervals by the wall, and an oak armchair and sometimes a faded, reddish Oriental rug. The big horn lantern which stood at nights at the end of the corridor she held in her hand. The intense 'peeping' sound of the Count, like a witchcraft, made her forget everything. She could not understand a word, of course. She could not understand the noise even. After listening for a long time, she went on downstairs. When she came back again he was still, and the light was gone from under his door.

After this, it became almost an obsession to her to listen for him. She waited with fretful impatience for ten o'clock, when she could retire. She waited more fretfully still for the maid to leave her, and for her husband to come and say good-night. Basil had the room across the corridor. And then in resentful impatience she waited for the sounds of the house to become still. Then she opened her door to listen.

And far away, as if from far, far away in the unseen, like a ventriloquist sound or a bat's uncanny peeping, came the frail, almost inaudible sound of the Count's singing to himself before he went to bed. It *was* inaudible to anyone but herself. But she, by concentration, seemed to hear supernaturally. She had a low armchair by the door, and there, wrapped in a huge old black silk shawl, she sat and listened. At first she could not hear. That is, she could hear the sound. But it was only a sound. And then, gradually, gradually she began to follow the thread of it. It was like a thread which she followed out of the world: out of the world. And as she went, slowly, by degrees, far, far away, down the thin thread of his singing, she knew peace – she knew forgetfulness. She could pass beyond the world, away beyond where her soul balanced like a bird on wings, and was perfected.

So it was, in her upper spirit. But underneath was a wild, wild yearning, actually to go, actually to be given. Actually to go, actually to die the death, actually to cross the border and be gone, to be gone. To be gone from this herself, from this Daphne, to be gone from father and mother, brothers and husband, and home and land and world: to be gone. To be gone to the call from the beyond: the call. It was the Count calling. He was calling her. She was sure he was calling her. Out of herself, out of her world, he was calling her.

Two nights she sat just inside her room, by the open door, and listened. Then when he finished she went to sleep, a queer, light, bewitched sleep. In the day she was bewitched. She felt strange and light, as if pressure had been removed from around her. Some pressure had been clamped round her all her life. She had never realised it till now; now it was removed, and her feet felt so light, and her breathing delicate and exquisite. There had always been a pressure against her breathing. Now she breathed delicate and exquisite, so that it was a delight to breathe. Life came in exquisite breaths, quickly, as if it delighted to come to her.

The third night he was silent – though she waited and waited till the small hours of the morning. He was silent, he did not sing. And then she knew the terror and blackness of the feeling that he might never sing any more. She waited like one doomed, throughout the day. And when the night came she trembled. It was her greatest nervous terror, lest her spell should be broken, and she should be thrown back to what she was before.

Night came, and the kind of swoon upon her. Yes, and the call from the night. The call! She rose helplessly and hurried down the corridor. The light was under his door. She sat down in the big oak armchair that stood near his door, and huddled herself tight in her black shawl. The corridor was dim with the big, star-studded, yellow lantern-light. Away down she could see the lamp-light in her doorway; she had left her door ajar.

But she saw nothing. Only she wrapped herself close in the black shawl, and listened to the sound from the room. It called. Oh, it called her! Why could she not go? Why could she not cross through the closed door.

Then the noise ceased. And then the light went out, under the door of his room. Must she go back? Must she go back? Oh, impossible. As impossible as that the moon should go back on her tracks, once she has risen. Daphne sat on, wrapped in her black shawl. If it must be so, she would sit on through eternity. Return she never could.

And then began the most terrible song of all. It began with a rather dreary, slow, horrible sound, like death. And then suddenly came a real call – fluty, and a kind of whistling and a strange whirr at the changes, most imperative, and utterly inhuman. Daphne rose to her feet. And at the same moment up rose the whistling throb of a summons out of the death moan.

Daphne tapped low and rapidly at the door. 'Count! Count!' she whispered. The sound inside ceased. The door suddenly opened. The pale, obscure figure of Dionys.

'Lady Daphne!' he said in astonishment, automatically standing aside.

'You called,' she murmured rapidly, and she passed intent into his room.

'No, I did not call,' he said gently, his hand on the door still.

'Shut the door,' she said abruptly.

He did as he was bid. The room was in complete darkness. There was no moon outside. She could not see him.

'Where can I sit down?' she said abruptly.

'I will take you to the couch,' he said, putting out his hand and touching her in the dark. She shuddered.

She found the couch and sat down. It was quite dark.

'What are you singing?' she said rapidly.

'I am so sorry. I did not think anyone could hear.'

'What was it you were singing?'

'A song of my country.'

'Had it any words?'

'Yes, it is a woman who was a swan, and who loved a hunter by the marsh. So she became a woman and married him and had three children. Then in the night one night the king of the swans called to her to come back, or else he would die. So slowly she turned into a swan again, and slowly she opened her wide, wide wings, and left her husband and her children.'

There was silence in the dark room. The Count had been really startled, startled out of his mood of the song into the day-mood of human convention. He was distressed and embarrassed by Daphne's presence in his dark room. She, however, sat on and did not make a sound. He, too, sat down in a chair by the window. It was everywhere dark. A wind was blowing in gusts outside. He could see nothing inside his room: only the faint, faint strip of light under the door. But he could feel her presence in the darkness. It was uncanny, to feel her near in the dark, and not to see any sign of her, nor to hear any sound.

She had been wounded in her bewitched state by the contact with the everyday human being in him. But now she began to relapse into her spell, as she sat there in the dark. And he, too, in the silence, felt the world sinking away from him once more, leaving him once more alone on a darkened earth, with nothing between him and the infinite dark space. Except now her presence. Darkness answering to darkness, and deep answering to deep. An answer, near to him, and invisible.

But he did not know what to do. He sat still and silent as she was still and silent. The darkness inside the room seemed alive like blood. He had no power to move. The distance between them seemed absolute.

Then suddenly, without knowing, he went across in the dark, feeling for the end of the couch. And he sat beside her on the couch. But he did not touch her. Neither did she move. The darkness flowed about them thick like blood, and time seemed dissolved in it. They sat with the small, invisible distance between them, motionless, speechless, thoughtless.

Then suddenly he felt her fingertips touch his arm, and a flame went over him that left him no more a man. He was something seated in flame, in flame unconscious, seated erect, like an Egyptian King-god in the statues. Her fingertips slid down him, and she herself slid down in a strange, silent rush, and he felt her face against his closed feet and ankles, her hands pressing his ankles. He felt her brow and hair against his ankles, her face against his feet, and there she clung in the dark, as if in space below him. He still sat erect and motionless. Then he bent forward and put his hand on her hair.

'Do you come to me?' he murmured. 'Do you come to me?'

The flame that enveloped him seemed to sway him silently.

'Do you really come to me?' he repeated. 'But we have nowhere to go.'

He felt his bare feet wet with her tears. Two things were struggling in him, the sense of eternal solitude, like space, and the rush of dark flame that would throw him out of his solitude towards her.

He was thinking too. He was thinking of the future. He had no future in the world: of that he was conscious. He had no future in this life. Even if he lived on, it would only be a kind of enduring. But he felt that in the afterlife the inheritance was his. He felt the afterlife belonged to him.

Future in the world he could not give her. Life in the world he had not to offer her. Better go on alone. Surely better go on alone.

But then the tears on his feet: and her face that would face him as he left her! No, no. The next life was his. He was master of the afterlife. Why fear for this life? Why not take the soul she offered him? Now and for ever, for the life that would come when they both were dead. Take her into the underworld. Take her into the dark Hades with him, like Francesca and Paolo. And in hell hold her fast, queen of the underworld, himself master of the underworld. Master of the life to come. Father of the soul that would come after.

'Listen,' he said to her softly. 'Now you are mine. In the dark you are mine. And when you die you are mine. But in the day you are not mine, because I have no power in the day. In the night, in the dark, and in death, you are mine. And that is for ever. No matter if I must leave you. I shall come again from time to time. In the dark you are mine. But in the day I cannot claim you. I have no power in the day, and no place. So remember. When the darkness comes, I shall always be in the darkness of you. And as long as I live, from time to time I shall come to find you, when I am able to, when I am not a prisoner. But I shall have to go away soon. So don't forget – you are the night wife of the ladybird, while you live and even when you die.'

Later, when he took her back to her room, he saw the door still ajar.

'You shouldn't leave a light in your room,' he murmured.

In the morning there was a curious remote look about him. He was quieter than ever, and seemed very far away. Daphne slept late. She had a strange feeling as if she had slipped off all her cares. She did not care, she did not grieve, she did not fret any more. All that had left her. She felt she could sleep, sleep, sleep – for ever. Her face, too, was very still, with a delicate look of virginity that she had never had before. She had always been Aphrodite, the self-conscious one. And her eyes, the green-blue, had been like slow, living jewels, resistant. Now they had unfolded from the hard flower-bud, and had the wonder, and the stillness of a quiet night.

Basil noticed it at once.

'You're different, Daphne,' he said. 'What are you thinking about?'

'I wasn't thinking,' she said, looking at him with candour.

'What were you doing then?'

'What does one do when one doesn't think? Don't make me puzzle it out, Basil.'

'Not a bit of it, if you don't want to.'

But he was puzzled by her. The sting of his ecstatic love for her seemed to have left him. Yet he did not know what else to do but to make love to her. She went very pale. She submitted to him, bowing her head because she was his wife. But she looked at him with fear, with sorrow, with real suffering. He could feel the heaving of her breast, and knew she was weeping. But there were no tears on her face, she was only death pale. Her eyes were shut.

'Are you in pain?' he asked her.

'No! no!' She opened her eyes, afraid lest she had disturbed him. She did not want to disturb him.

He was puzzled. His own ecstatic, deadly love for her had received a check. He was out of the reckoning.

He watched her when she was with the Count. Then she seemed so meek – so maidenly – so different from what he had known of her. She was so still, like a virgin girl. And it was this quiet, intact quality of Virginity in her which puzzled him most, puzzled his emotions and his ideas. He became suddenly ashamed to make love to her. And because he was ashamed, he said to her as he stood in her room that night, 'Daphne, are you in love with the Count?'

He was standing by the dressing-table, uneasy. She was seated in a low chair by the tiny dying wood fire. She looked up at him with wide, slow eyes. Without a word, with wide, soft, dilated eyes she watched him. What was it that made him feel all confused? He turned his face aside, away from her wide, soft eyes.

'Pardon me, dear. I didn't intend to ask such a question. Don't take any notice of it,' he said. And he strode away and picked up a book. She lowered her head and gazed abstractedly into the fire, without a sound. Then he looked at her again, at her bright hair that the maid had plaited for the night. Her plait hung down over her soft pinkish wrap. His heart softened to her as he saw her sitting there. She seemed like his sister. The excitement of desire had left him, and now he seemed to see clear and feel true for the first time in his life. She was like a dear, dear sister to him. He felt that she was his blood-sister, nearer to him than he had imagined any woman could be. So near – so dear – and all the sex and the desire gone. He didn't want it – he hadn't wanted it. This new pure feeling was so much more wonderful.

He went to her side.

'Forgive me, darling,' he said, 'for having questioned you.'

She looked up at him with the wide eyes, without a word. His face was good and beautiful. Tears came to her eyes.

'You have the right to question me,' she said sadly.

'No,' he said. 'No, darling. I have no right to question you. Daphne! Daphne, darling! It shall be as *you* wish, between us. Shall it? Shall it be as you wish?'

'You are the husband, Basil,' she said sadly.

'Yes, darling. But' – he went on his knees beside her – 'perhaps, darling, something has changed in us. I feel as if I ought never to touch you again – as if I never wanted to touch you – in that way. I feel it was wrong, darling. Tell me what you think.'

'Basil, don't be angry with me.'

'It isn't anger; it's pure love, darling – it is.'

'Let us not come any nearer to one another than this, Basil – physically – shall we?' she said. 'And don't be angry with me, will you?'

'Why,' he said. 'I think myself the sexual part has been a mistake. I had rather love you – as I love now. I *know* that this is true love. The other was always a bit whipped up. I *know* I love you now, darling: now I'm free from that other. But what if it comes upon me, that other, Daphne?'

'I am always your wife,' she said quietly. 'I am always your wife. I want always to obey you, Basil: what you wish.'

'Give me your hand, dear.'

She gave him her hand. But the look in her eyes at the same time warned him and frightened him. He kissed her hand and left her.

It was to the Count she belonged. This had decided itself in her down to the depths of her soul. If she could not marry him and be his wife in the world, it had nevertheless happened to her for ever. She could no more question it. Question had gone out of her.

Strange how different she had become – a strange new quiescence. The last days were slipping past. He would be going away – Dionys: he with the still remote face, the man she belonged to in the dark and in the light, for ever. He would be going away. He said it must be so. And she acquiesced. The grief was deep, deep inside her. He must go away. Their lives could not be one life, in this world's day. Even in her anguish she knew it was so. She knew he was right. He was for her infallible. He spoke the deepest soul in her.

She never *saw* him as a lover. When she saw him, he was the little officer, a prisoner, quiet, claiming nothing in all the world. And when she went to him as his lover, his wife, it was always dark. She only knew his voice and his contact in darkness. 'My wife in darkness,' he said to her. And in this too she believed him. She would not have contradicted him, no, not for anything on earth: lest contradicting him she should lose the dark treasures of stillness and bliss which she kept in her breast even when her heart was wrung with the agony of knowing he must go.

No, she had found this wonderful thing after she had heard him singing: she had suddenly collapsed away from her old self into this darkness, this peace, this quiescence that was like a full dark river flowing eternally in her soul. She had gone to sleep from the *nuit blanche* of her days. And Basil, wonderful, had changed almost at once. She feared him, lest he might change back again. She would always have him to fear. But deep inside her she only feared for this love of hers for the Count: this dark, everlasting love that was like a full river flowing for ever inside her. Ah, let that not be broken.

She was so still inside her. She could sit so still, and feel the day slowly, richly changing to night. And she wanted nothing, she was short of nothing. If only Dionys need not go away! If only he need not go away!

But he said to her, the last morning, 'Don't forget me. Always remember me. I leave my soul in your hands and your womb. Nothing can ever separate us, unless we betray one another. If you have to give yourself to your husband, do so, and obey him. If you are true to me, innerly, innerly true, he will not hurt us. He is generous, be generous to him. And never fail to believe in me. Because even on the other side of death I shall be watching for you. I shall be king in Hades when I am dead. And you will be at my side. You will never leave me any more, in the after-death. So don't be afraid in life. Don't be afraid. If you have to cry tears, cry them. But in your heart of hearts know that I shall come again, and that I have taken you for ever. And so, in your heart of hearts be still, be still, since you are the wife of the ladybird.' He laughed as he left her, with his own beautiful, fearless laugh. But they were strange eyes that looked after him.

He went in the car with Basil back to Voynich Hall.

'I believe Daphne will miss you,' said Basil.

The Count did not reply for some moments.

'Well, if she does,' he said, 'there will be no bitterness in it.'

'Are you sure?' smiled Basil.

'Why – if we are sure of anything,' smiled the Count.

'She's changed, isn't she?'

'Is she?'

'Yes, she's quite changed since you came, Count.'

'She does not seem to me so very different from the girl of seventeen whom I knew.'

'No – perhaps not. I didn't know her then. But she's very different from the wife I have known.'

'A regrettable difference?'

'Well – no, not as far as she goes. She is much quieter inside herself. You know, Count, something of me died in the war. I feel it will take me an eternity to sit and think about it all.'

'I hope you may think it out to your satisfaction, Major.'

'Yes, I hope so too. But that is how it has left me – feeling as if I needed eternity now to brood about it all, you know. Without the need to act – or even to love, really. I suppose love is action.'

'Intense action,' said the Count.

'Quite so. I know really how I feel. I only ask of life to spare me from further effort of action of any sort – even love. And then to fulfil myself, brooding through eternity. Of course, I don't mind *work*, mechanical action. That in itself is a form of inaction.'

'A man can only be happy following his own inmost need,' said the Count.

'Exactly!' said Basil. 'I will lay down the law for nobody, not even for myself. And live my day – '

'Then you will be happy in your own way. I find it so difficult to keep from laying the law down for myself,' said the Count. 'Only the thought of death and the afterlife saves me from doing it any more.'

'As the thought of eternity helps me,' said Basil. 'I suppose it amounts to the same thing.'

ST MAWR

LOU WITT HAD HAD HER OWN WAY so long, that by the age of twenty-five she didn't know where she was. Having one's own way landed one completely at sea.

To be sure for a while she had failed in her grand love affair with Rico. And then she had had something really to despair about. But even that had worked out as she wanted. Rico had come back to her, and was dutifully married to her. And now, when she was twenty-five and he was three months older, they were a charming married couple. He flirted with other women still, to be sure. He wouldn't be the handsome Rico if he didn't. But she had 'got' him. Oh yes! You had only to see the uneasy backward glance at her, from his big blue eyes: just like a horse that is edging away from its master: to know how completely he was mastered.

She, with her odd little *museau*, not exactly pretty, but very attractive; and her quaint air of playing at being well-bred, in a sort of charade game; and her queer familiarity with foreign cities and foreign languages; and the lurking sense of being an outsider everywhere, like a sort of gipsy, who is at home anywhere and nowhere: all this made up her charm and her failure. She didn't quite belong.

Of course she was American: Louisiana family, moved down to Texas. And she was moderately rich, with no close relation except her mother. But she had been sent to school in France when she was twelve, and since she had finished school, she had drifted from Paris to Palermo, Biarritz to Vienna and back via Munich to London, then down again to Rome. Only fleeting trips to her America.

So what sort of American was she, after all?

And what sort of European was she either? She didn't 'belong' anywhere. Perhaps most of all in Rome, among the artists and the Embassy people.

It was in Rome she had met Rico. He was an Australian, son of a government official in Melbourne, who had been made a baronet. So one day Rico would be Sir Henry, as he was the only son. Meanwhile he floated round Europe on a very small allowance – his father wasn't rich in capital – and was being an artist.

They met in Rome when they were twenty-two, and had a love affair in Capri. Rico was handsome, elegant, but mostly he had spots of paint on his trousers and he ruined a necktie pulling it off. He behaved in a most floridly elegant fashion, fascinating to the Italians. But at the same time he was canny and shrewd and sensible as any young poser could be and, on principle, good-hearted, anxious. He was anxious for his future, and anxious for his place in the world, he was poor, and suddenly wasteful in spite of all his tension of economy, and suddenly spiteful in spite of all his ingratiating efforts, and suddenly ungrateful in spite of all his burden of gratitude, and suddenly rude in spite of all his good manners, and suddenly detestable in spite of all his suave, courtier-like amiability.

He was fascinated by Lou's quaint aplomb, her experiences, her 'knowledge', her *gamine* knowingness, her aloneness, her pretty clothes that were sometimes an utter failure, and her southern 'drawl' that was sometimes so irritating. That sing-song which was so American. Yet she used no Americanisms at all, except when she lapsed into her odd spasms of acid irony, when she was very American indeed!

And she was fascinated by Rico. They played to each other like two butter-flies at one flower. They pretended to be very poor in Rome – he *was* poor: and very rich in Naples. Everybody stared their eyes out at them. And they had that love affair in Capri.

But they reacted badly on each other's nerves. She became ill. Her mother appeared. He couldn't stand Mrs Witt, and Mrs Witt couldn't stand him. There was a terrible fortnight. Then Lou was popped into a convent nursing-home in Umbria, and Rico dashed off to Paris. Nothing would stop him. He must go back to Australia.

He went to Melbourne, and while there his father died, leaving him a baronet's title and an income still very moderate. Lou visited America once more, as the strangest of strange lands to her. She came away disheartened, panting for Europe, and of course, doomed to meet Rico again.

They couldn't get away from one another, even though in the course of their rather restrained correspondence he informed her that he was 'probably' marrying a very dear girl, friend of his childhood, only daughter of one of the oldest families in Victoria. Not saying much.

He didn't commit the probability, but reappeared in Paris, wanting to paint his head off, terribly inspired by Cézanne and by old Renoir. He dined at the Rotonde with Lou and Mrs Witt, who, with her queer democratic New Orleans sort of conceit looked round the drinking-hall with savage contempt, and at Rico as part of the show. 'Certainly,' she said, 'when these people here have got any money, they fall in love on a full stomach. And when they've got no money, they fall in love with a full pocket. I never was in a more disgusting place. They take their love like some people take after-dinner pills.'

She would watch with her arching, full, strong grey eyes, sitting there erect and silent in her well-bought American clothes. And then she would deliver some such charge of grape-shot. Rico always writhed.

Mrs Witt hated Paris: 'this sordid, unlucky city', she called it. 'Something unlucky is bound to happen to me in this sinister, unclean town,' she said. 'I feel *contagion* in the air of this place. For heaven's sake, Louise, let us go to Morocco or somewhere.'

'No, mother dear, I can't now. Rico has proposed to me, and I have accepted him. Let us think about a wedding, shall we?'

'There!' said Mrs Witt. 'I said it was an unlucky city!'

And the peculiar look of extreme New Orleans annoyance came round her sharp nose. But Lou and Rico were both twenty-four years old, and beyond management. And anyhow, Lou would be Lady Carrington. But Mrs Witt was exasperated beyond exasperation. She would almost rather have preferred Lou to elope with one of the great, evil porters at Les Halles. Mrs Witt was at the age when the malevolent male in man, the old Adam, begins to loom above all the social tailoring. And yet – and yet – it was better to have Lady Carrington for a daughter, seeing Lou was that sort.

There was a marriage, after which Mrs Witt departed to America, Lou and Rico leased a little old house in Westminster, and began to settle into a certain layer of English society. Rico was becoming an almost fashionable portrait painter. At least, *he* was almost fashionable, whether his portraits were or not. And Lou too was almost fashionable: almost a hit. There was some flaw somewhere. In spite of their appearances, both Rico and she would never quite go down in any society. They were the drifting artist sort. Yet neither of them was content to be of the drifting artist sort. They wanted to fit in, to make good.

Hence the little house in Westminster, the portraits, the dinners, the friends, and the visits. Mrs Witt came and sardonically established herself in a suite in a quiet but good-class hotel not far off. Being on the spot. And her terrible grey eyes with the touch of a leer looked on at the hollow mockery of things. As if *she* knew of anything better!

Lou and Rico had a curious exhausting effect on one another: neither knew why. They were fond of one another. Some inscrutable bond held them together. But it was a strange vibration of nerves, rather than of the blood. A nervous attachment, rather than a sexual love. A curious tension of will, rather than a spontaneous passion. Each was curiously under the domination of the other. They were a pair – they had to be together. Yet quite soon they shrank from one another. This attachment of the will and the nerves was destructive. As soon as one felt strong, the other felt ill. As soon as the ill one recovered strength, down went the one who had been well.

And soon, tacitly, the marriage became more like a friendship, Platonic. It was a marriage, but without sex. Sex was shattering and exhausting, they shrank from it, and became like brother and sister. But still they were husband and wife. And the lack of physical relation was a secret source of uneasiness and chagrin to both of them. They would neither of them accept it. Rico looked with contemplative, anxious eyes at other women.

Mrs Witt kept track of everything, watching as it were from outside the fence, like a potent well-dressed demon, full of uncanny energy and a shattering sort of sense. She said little: but her small, occasionally biting remarks revealed her attitude of contempt for the *ménage*.

Rico entertained clever and well-known people. Mrs Witt would appear, in her New York gowns and few good jewels. She was handsome, with her vigorous grey hair. And her heavy-lidded grey eyes were the despair of any hostess. They looked too many shattering things. And it was but too obvious that these clever, well-known English people got on her nerves terribly, with their finickiness and their fine-drawn discriminations. She wanted to put her foot through all these fine-drawn distinctions. She thought continually of the house of her girlhood, the plantation, the negroes, the planters: the sardonic grimness that underlay all the big, shiftless life. And she wanted to cleave with some of this grimness of the big, dangerous America, into the safe, finicky drawing-rooms of London. So naturally she was not popular

But being a woman of energy, she had to do *something*. During the latter part of the war she had worked in the American Red Cross in France, nursing. She loved men – real men. But, on close contact, it was difficult to define what she meant by 'real' men. She never met any.

Out of the *débâcle* of the war she had emerged with an odd piece of *débris*, in the shape of Gerónimo Trujillo. He was an American, son of a Mexican father and a Navajo Indian mother, from Arizona. When you knew him well, you recognised the real half-breed, though at a glance he might pass as a sunburnt citizen of any nation, particularly of France. He looked like a certain sort of Frenchman, with his curiously-set dark eyes, his straight black hair, his thin black moustache, his rather long cheeks, and his almost slouching, diffident, sardonic bearing. Only when you knew him, and looked right into his eyes, you saw that unforgettable glint of the Indian.

He had been badly shell-shocked, and was for a time a wreck. Mrs Witt, having nursed him into convalescence, asked him where he was going next. He didn't know. His father and mother were dead, and he had nothing to take him back to Phoenix, Arizona. Having had an education in one of the Indian high schools, the unhappy fellow had now no place in life at all. Another of the many misfits.

There was something of the Paris *Apache* in his appearance: but he was all the time withheld, and nervously shut inside himself. Mrs Witt was intrigued by him.

'Very well, Phoenix,' she said, refusing to adopt his Spanish name, 'I'll see what I can do.'

What she did was to get him a place on a sort of manor farm, with some acquaintances of hers. He was very good with horses, and had a curious success with turkeys and geese and fowls.

Some time after Lou's marriage, Mrs Witt reappeared in London, from the country, with Phoenix in tow, and a couple of horses. She had decided that she would ride in the Park in the morning, and see the world that way. Phoenix was to be her groom.

So, to the great misgiving of Rico, behold Mrs Witt in splendidly tailored habit and perfect boots, a smart black hat on her smart grey hair, riding a grey gelding as smart as she was, and looking down her conceited, inquisitive, scornful, aristocratic-democratic Louisiana nose at the people in Piccadilly, as she crossed to the Row, followed by the taciturn shadow of Phoenix, who sat on a chestnut with three white feet as if he had grown there.

Mrs Witt, like many other people, always expected to find the real *beau monde* and the real *grand monde* somewhere or other. She didn't quite give in to what she saw in the Bois de Boulogne, or in Monte Carlo, or on the Pincio; all a bit shoddy, and not very *beau* and not at all *grand*. There she was, with her grey eagle eye, her splendid complexion and her weapon-like health of a woman of fifty, dropping her eyelids a little, very slightly nervous, but completely prepared to despise the *monde* she was entering in Rotten Row.

In she sailed, and up and down that regatta-canal of horsemen and horse-women under the trees of the Park. And yes, there were lovely girls with fair hair down their backs, on happy ponies. And awfully well-groomed papas, and tight mamas who looked as if they were going to pour tea between the ears of their horses, and converse with banal skill, one eye on the teapot, one on the visitor with whom she was talking, and all the rest of her hostess's argus-eyes upon everybody in sight. The alert argus capability of the English matron was startling and a bit horrifying. Mrs Witt would at once think of the old negro mammies, away in Louisiana. And her eyes became dagger-like as she watched the clipped, shorn, mincing young Englishmen. She refused to look at the prosperous Jews.

It was still the days before motor cars were allowed in the Park, but Rico and Lou, sliding round Hyde Park Corner and up Park Lane in their car would watch the steely horsewoman and the saturnine groom with a sort of dismay. Mrs Witt seemed to be pointing a pistol at the bosom of every other horseman or horsewoman, and announcing: *Your virility or your life! Your femininity or your life!* She didn't know herself what she really wanted them to be: but it was something as democratic as Abraham Lincoln and as aristocratic as a Russian Czar, as highbrow as Arthur Balfour, and as taciturn and unideal as Phoenix. Everything at once.

There was nothing for it: Lou had to buy herself a horse and ride at her mother's side, for very decency's sake. Mrs Witt was *so* like a smooth, levelled, gunmetal pistol, Lou had to be a sort of sheath. And she really looked pretty, with her clusters of dark, curly, New Orleans hair, like grapes, and her quaint brown eyes that didn't quite match, and that looked a bit sleepy and vague, and at the same time quick as a squirrel's. She was slight and elegant, and a tiny bit rakish, and somebody suggested she might be on the movies.

Nevertheless, they were in the society columns next morning – *two new and striking figures in the Row this morning were Lady Henry Carrington and her mother Mrs Witt*, etc. And Mrs Witt liked it, let her say what she might. So did Lou. Lou liked it immensely. She simply luxuriated in the sun of publicity.

'Rico dear, you must get a horse.'

The tone was soft and southern and drawling, but the overtone had a decisive finality. In vain Rico squirmed – he had a way of writhing and squirming which perhaps he had caught at Oxford. In vain he protested that he couldn't ride, and that he didn't care for riding. He got quite angry, and his handsome arched nose tilted and his upper lip lifted from his teeth, like a dog that is going to bite. Yet daren't quite bite.

And that was Rico. He daren't quite bite. Not that he was really afraid of the others. He was afraid of himself, once he let himself go. He might rip up in an eruption of life-long anger all this pretty-pretty picture of a charming young wife and a delightful little home and a fascinating success as a painter of fashionable, and at the same time 'great' portraits: with colour, wonderful colour, and at the same time, form, marvellous form. He had composed this little *tableau vivant* with great effort. He didn't want to erupt like some suddenly wicked horse – Rico was really more like a horse than a dog, a horse that might go nasty any moment. For the time, he was good, very good, dangerously good.

'Why, Rico dear, I thought you used to ride so much, in Australia, when you were young? Didn't you tell me all about it, hm?' – and as she ended on that slow, singing *hm?*, which acted on him like an irritant and a drug, he knew he was beaten.

Lou kept the sorrel mare in a mews just behind the house in Westminster, and she was always slipping round to the stables. She had a funny little nostalgia for the place: something that really surprised her. She had never had the faintest notion that she cared for horses and stables and grooms. But she did. She was fascinated. Perhaps it was her childhood's Texas associations come back. What-ever it was, her life with Rico in the elegant little house, and all her social engagements seemed like a dream, the substantial reality of which was those mews in Westminster, her sorrel mare, the owner of the mews, Mr Saintsbury, and the grooms he employed. Mr Saintsbury was a horsey elderly man like an old maid, and he loved the sound of titles.

'Lady Carrington! – well I never! You've come to us for a bit of company again, I see. I don't know whatever we shall do if you go away, we shall be that lonely!' and he flashed his old-maid's smile at her. 'No matter how grey the morning, your Ladyship would make a beam of sunshine. Poppy is all right, I think . . .'

Poppy was the sorrel mare with the no white feet and the startled eye, and she was all right. And Mr Saintsbury was smiling with his old-maid's mouth, and showing all his teeth.

'Come across with me, Lady Carrington, and look at a new horse just up from the country. I think he's worth a look, and I believe you have a moment to spare, your Ladyship.'

Her Ladyship had too many moments to spare. She followed the sprightly, elderly, clean-shaven man across the yard to a loose box, and waited while he opened the door.

In the inner dark she saw a handsome bay horse with his clean ears pricked like daggers from his naked head as he swung handsomely round to stare at the open doorway. He had big, black, brilliant eyes, with a sharp questioning glint, and that air of tense, alert quietness which betrays an animal that can be dangerous.

'Is he quiet?' Lou asked.

'Why – yes – my Lady! He's quiet, with those that know how to handle him. *Cup! my boy! Cup, my beauty! Cup then! St Mawr!*'

Loquacious even with the animals, he went softly forward and laid his hand on the horse's shoulder, soft and quiet as a fly settling. Lou saw the brilliant skin of the horse crinkle a little in apprehensive anticipation, like the shadow of the descending hand on a bright red-gold liquid. But then the animal relaxed again.

'Quiet with those that know how to handle him, and a bit of a ruffian with those that don't. Isn't that the ticket, eh, St Mawr?'

'What is his name?' Lou asked.

The man repeated it, with a slight Welsh twist – 'He's from the Welsh borders, belonging to a Welsh gentleman, Mr Griffith Edwards. But they're wanting to sell him.'

'How old is he?' asked Lou.

'About seven years – seven years and five months,' said Mr Saintsbury, dropping his voice as if it were a secret.

'Could one ride him in the Park?'

'Well – yes! I should say a gentleman who knew how to handle him could ride him very well and make a very handsome figure in the Park.'

Lou at once decided that this handsome figure should be Rico's. For she was already half in love with St Mawr. He was of such a lovely red-gold colour, and a dark, invisible fire seemed to come out of him. But in his big black eyes there was a lurking afterthought. Something told her that the horse was not quite happy: that somewhere deep in his animal consciousness lived a dangerous, half-revealed resentment, a diffused sense of hostility. She realised that he was sensitive, in spite of his flaming, healthy strength, and nervous with a touchy uneasiness that might make him vindictive.

'Has he got any tricks?' she asked.

'Not that I know of, my Lady: not tricks exactly. But he's one of these temperamental creatures, as they say. Though I say, every horse is temperamental, when you come down to it. But this one, it is as if he was a trifle raw somewhere. Touch this raw spot, and there's no answering for him.'

'Where is he raw?' asked Lou, somewhat mystified. She thought he might really have some physical sore.

'Why, that's hard to say, my Lady. If he was a human being, you'd say something had gone wrong in his life. But with a horse it's not that, exactly. A high-bred animal like St Mawr needs understanding, and I don't know as anybody has quite got the hang of him. I confess I haven't myself. But I do realise that he is a special animal and needs a special sort of touch, and I'm willing he should have it, did I but know exactly what it is.'

She looked at the glowing bay horse that stood there with his ears back, his face averted, but attending as if he were some lightning conductor. He was a stallion. When she realised this, she became more afraid of him.

'Why does Mr Griffith Edwards want to sell him?' she asked.

'Well – my Lady – they raised him for stud purposes – but he didn't answer. There are horses like that: don't seem to fancy the mares, for some reason. Well anyway, they couldn't keep him for the stud. And as you see, he's a powerful, beautiful hackney, clean as a whistle, and eaten up with his own power. But there's no putting him between the shafts. He won't stand it. He's a fine saddle-horse, beautiful action, and lovely to ride. But he's got to be handled, and there you are.'

Lou felt there was something behind the man's reticence.

'Has he ever made a break?' she asked, apprehensive.

'Made a break?' replied the man. 'Well, if I must admit it, he's had two accidents. Mr Griffith Edwards's son rode him a bit wild, away there in the Forest of Dean, and the young fellow had his skull smashed in, against a low oak bough. Last autumn, that was. And some time back, he crushed a groom against the side of the stall – injured him fatally. But they were both accidents, my Lady. Things will happen.'

The man spoke in a melancholy, fatalistic way. The horse, with his ears laid back, seemed to be listening tensely, his face averted. He looked like something finely bred and passionate, that has been judged and condemned.

'May I say *how do you do*?' she said to the horse, drawing a little nearer in her white, summery dress, and lifting her hand that glittered with emeralds and diamonds.

He drifted away from her, as if some wind blew him. Then he ducked his head, and looked sideways at her, from his black, full eye.

'I think I'm all right,' she said, edging nearer, while he watched her.

She laid her hand on his side, and gently stroked him. Then she stroked his shoulder, and then the hard, tense arch of his neck. And she was startled to feel the vivid heat of his life come through to her, through the lacquer of red-gold gloss. So slippery with vivid, hot life!

She paused, as if thinking, while her hand rested on the horse's sun-arched neck. Dimly, in her weary young-woman's soul, an ancient understanding seemed to flood in.

She wanted to buy St Mawr.

'I think,' she said to Saintsbury, 'if I can, I will buy him.'

The man looked at her long and shrewdly.

'Well, my Lady,' he said at last, 'there shall be nothing kept from you. But what would your Ladyship do with him, if I may make so bold?'

'I don't know,' she replied, vaguely. 'I might take him to America.'

The man paused once more, then said, 'They say it's been the making of some horses, to take them over the water, to Australia or such places. It might repay you – you never know.'

She wanted to buy St Mawr. She wanted him to belong to her. For some reason the sight of him, his power, his alive, alert intensity, his unyieldingness, made her want to cry.

She never did cry: except sometimes with vexation, or to get her own way. As far as weeping went, her heart felt as dry as a Christmas walnut. What was the good of tears, anyhow? You had to keep on holding on, in this life, never give way, and never give in. Tears only left one weakened and ragged.

But now, as if that mysterious fire of the horse's body had split some rock in her, she went home and hid herself in her room, and just cried. The wild, brilliant, alert head of St Mawr seemed to look at her out of another world. It was as if she had had a vision, as if the walls of her own world had suddenly melted away, leaving her in a great darkness, in the midst of which the large, brilliant eyes of that horse looked at her with demonish question, while his naked ears stood up like daggers from the naked lines of his inhuman head, and his great body glowed red with power.

What was it? Almost like a god looking at her terribly out of the everlasting dark, she had felt the eyes of that horse; great, glowing, fearsome eyes, arched with a question, and containing a white blade of light like a threat. What was his non-human question, and his uncanny threat? She didn't know. He was some splendid demon, and she must worship him.

She hid herself away from Rico. She could not bear the triviality and superficiality of her human relationships. Looming like some god out of the darkness was the head of that horse, with the wide, terrible, questioning eyes. And she felt that it forbade her to be her ordinary, commonplace self. It forbade her to be just Rico's wife, young Lady Carrington, and all that.

It haunted her, the horse. It had looked at her as she had never been looked at before: terrible, gleaming, questioning eyes arching out of darkness, and backed by all the fire of that great ruddy body. What did it mean, and what ban did it put upon her? She felt it put a ban on her heart: wielded some uncanny authority over her, that she dared not, could not understand.

No matter where she was, what she was doing, at the back of her consciousness loomed a great, over aweing figure out of a dark background: St Mawr, looking at her without really seeing her, yet gleaming a question at her, from his wide terrible eyes, and gleaming a sort of menace, doom. Master of doom, he seemed to be!

'You are thinking about something, Lou dear!' Rico said to her that evening.

He was so quick and sensitive to detect her moods – so exciting in this respect. And his big, slightly prominent blue eyes, with the whites a little bloodshot, glanced at her quickly, with searching, and anxiety, and a touch of fear, as if his conscience were always uneasy. He, too, was rather like a horse – but for ever quivering with a sort of cold, dangerous mistrust, which he covered with anxious love.

At the middle of his eyes was a central powerlessness, that left him anxious. It used to touch her to pity, that central look of powerlessness in him. But now, since she had seen the full, dark, passionate blaze of power and of different life in the eyes of the thwarted horse, the anxious powerlessness of the man drove her mad. Rico was so handsome, and he was so self-controlled, he had a gallant sort of kindness and a real worldly shrewdness. One had to admire him: at least *she* had to.

But after all, and after all, it was a bluff, an attitude. He kept it all working in himself, deliberately. It was an attitude. She read psychologists who said that everything was an attitude. Even the best of everything. But now she realised that, with men and women, everything is an attitude only when something else is lacking. Something is lacking and they are thrown back on their own devices. That black fiery flow in the eyes of the horse was not 'attitude'. It was something much more terrifying, and real, the only thing that was real. Gushing from the darkness in menace and question, and blazing out in the splendid body of the horse.

'Was I thinking about something?' she replied, in her slow, amused, casual fashion. As if everything was so casual and easy to her. And so it was, from the hard, polished side of herself. But that wasn't the whole story.

'I think you were, Loulina. May we offer the penny?'

'Don't trouble,' she said. 'I was thinking, if I was thinking of anything, about a bay horse called St Mawr.' – Her secret *almost* crept into her eyes.

'The name is awfully attractive,' he said with a laugh.

'Not so attractive as the creature himself. I'm going to buy him.'

'Not really!' he said. 'But why?'

'He *is* so attractive. I'm going to buy him for you.'

'For *me!*?*Darling!* how you do take me for granted. He may not be in the least attractive to me. As you know, I have hardly any feeling for horses at all. – Besides, how much does he cost?'

'That I don't know, Rico dear. But I'm sure you'll love him, for my sake.' – She felt, now, she was merely playing for her own ends.

'Lou dearest, *don't* spend a fortune on a horse for me, which I *don't* want. Honestly, I prefer a car.'

'Won't you ride with me in the Park, Rico?'

'Honestly, dear Lou, I don't want to.'

'Why not, dear boy? You'd look so beautiful. I wish you would. – And anyhow, come with me to look at St Mawr.'

Rico was divided. He had a certain uneasy feeling about horses. At the same time, he *would* like to cut a handsome figure in the Park.

They went across to the mews. A little Welsh groom was watering the brilliant horse.

'Yes dear, he certainly *is* beautiful: such a marvellous colour! Almost orange! But rather large, I should say, to ride in the Park.'

'No, for you he's perfect. You are so tall.'

'He'd be marvellous in a Composition. That colour!'

And all Rico could do was to gaze with the artist's eye at the horse, with a glance at the groom.

'Don't you think the man is rather fascinating too?' he said, nursing his chin artistically and penetratingly.

The groom, Lewis, was a little, quick, rather bow-legged, loosely-built fellow of indeterminate age, with a mop of black hair and a little black beard. He was grooming the brilliant St Mawr, out in the open. The horse was really glorious: like a marigold, with a pure golden sheen, a shimmer of green-gold lacquer, upon a burning red-orange. There on the shoulder you saw the yellow lacquer glisten. Lewis, a little scrub of a fellow, worked absorbedly, unheedingly at the horse, with an absorption that was almost ritualistic. He seemed the attendant shadow of the ruddy animal.

'He goes with the horse,' said Lou. 'If we buy St Mawr we get the man thrown in.'

'They'd be *so* amusing to paint: such an extraordinary contrast! But darling, I *hope* you won't insist on buying the horse. It's so frightfully expensive.'

'Mother will help me. – You'd look so well on him, Rico.'

'If ever I dared take the liberty of getting on his back – !'

'Why not?' She went quickly across the cobbled yard.

'Good-morning, Lewis. How is St Mawr?'

Lewis straightened himself and looked at her from under the falling mop of his black hair.

'All right,' he said.

He peered straight at her from under his overhanging black hair. He had pale grey eyes, that looked phosphorescent, and suggested the eyes of a wild cat peering intent from under the darkness of some bush where it lies unseen. Lou, with her brown, unmatched, oddly perplexed eyes, felt herself found out. – 'He's a common little fellow,' she thought to herself. 'But he knows a woman and a horse, at sight.' – Aloud she said, in her southern drawl, 'How do you think he'd be with Sir Henry?'

Lewis turned his remote, coldly watchful eyes on the young baronet. Rico was tall and handsome and balanced on his hips. His face was long and well-defined, and with the hair taken straight back from the brow. It seemed as well-made as his clothing, and as perpetually presentable. You could not imagine his face dirty, or scrubby and unshaven, or bearded, or even moustached. It was perfectly prepared for social purposes. If his head had been cut off, like John the Baptist's, it would have been a thing complete in itself, would not have missed the body in the least. The body was perfectly tailored. The head was one of the famous 'talking heads' of modern youth, with eyebrows a trifle Mephistophelian, large blue eyes a trifle bold, and curved mouth thrilling to death to kiss.

Lewis, the groom, staring from between his bush of hair and his beard, watched like an animal from the underbrush. And Rico was still sufficiently a colonial to be uneasily aware of the underbrush, uneasy under the watchfulness of the pale grey eyes, and uneasy in that man-to-man exposure which is characteristic of the democratic colonies and of America. He knew he must ultimately be judged on his merits as a man, alone without a background: an ungarnished colonial.

This lack of background, this defenceless man-to-man business which left him at the mercy of every servant, was bad for his nerves. For he was *also* an artist. He bore up against it in a kind of desperation, and was easily moved to rancorous resentment. At the same time he was free of the Englishman's water-tight *suffisance*. He really was aware that he would have to hold his own all alone, thrown alone on his own defences in the universe. The extreme democracy of the Colonies had taught him this.

And this, the little aboriginal Lewis recognised in him. He recognised also Rico's curious hollow misgiving, fear of some deficiency in himself, beneath all his handsome, young-hero appearance.

'He'd be all right with anybody as would meet him half-way,' said Lewis, in the quick Welsh manner of speech, impersonal.

'You hear, Rico!' said Lou in her sing song, turning to her husband.

'Perfectly, darling!'

'Would you be willing to meet St Mawr half-way, hm?'

'All the way, darling! Mahomet would go *all* the way to that mountain. Who would dare do otherwise?'

He spoke with a laughing, yet piqued sarcasm.

'Why, I think St Mawr would understand perfectly,' she said in the soft voice of a woman haunted by love. And she went and laid her hand on the slippery, life-smooth shoulder of the horse. He, with his strange equine head lowered, its exquisite fine lines reaching a little snake-like forward, and his ears a little back, was watching her sideways, from the corner of his eye. He was in a state of absolute mistrust, like a cat crouching to spring.

'St Mawr!' she said. 'St Mawr! What is the matter? Surely you and I are all right!'

And she spoke softly, dreamily stroked the animal's neck. She could feel a response gradually coming from him. But he would not lift up his head. And when Rico suddenly moved nearer, he sprang with a sudden jerk backwards, as if lightning exploded in his four hoofs.

The groom spoke a few low words in Welsh. Lou, frightened, stood with lifted hand arrested. She had been going to stroke him.

'Why did he do that?' she said.

'They gave him a beating once or twice,' said the groom in a neutral voice, 'and he doesn't forget.'

She could hear a neutral sort of judgement in Lewis's voice. And she thought of the 'raw spot'.

Not any raw spot at all. A battle between two worlds. She realised that St Mawr drew his hot breaths in another world from Rico's, from our world. Perhaps the old Greek horses had lived in St Mawr's world. And the old Greek heroes, even Hippolytus, had known it.

With their strangely naked equine heads, and something of a snake in their way of looking round, and lifting their sensitive, dangerous muzzles, they moved in a prehistoric twilight where all things loomed phantasmagoric, all on one plane, sudden presences suddenly jutting out of the matrix. It was another world, an older, heavily potent world. And in this world the horse was swift and fierce and supreme, undominated and unsurpassed. – 'Meet him half-way,' Lewis said. But half-way across from our human world to that terrific equine twilight was not a small step. It was a step, she knew, that Rico would never take. She knew it. But she was prepared to sacrifice Rico.

St Mawr was bought, and Lewis was hired along with him. At first, Lewis rode him behind Lou, in the Row, to get him going. He behaved perfectly.

Phoenix, the half Indian, was very jealous when he saw the black-bearded Welsh groom on St Mawr.

'What horse you got there?' he asked, looking at the other man with the curious unseeing stare in his hard, Navajo eyes, in which the Indian glint moved like a spark upon a dark chaos. In Phoenix's high-boned face there was all the race-misery of the dispossessed Indian, with an added blankness left by shell-shock. But at the same time, there was that unyielding, save to death, which is characteristic of his tribe; his mother's tribe. Difficult to say what subtle thread bound him to the Navajo, and made his destiny a Red Man's destiny still.

They were a curious pair of grooms, following the correct, and yet extra-ordinary, pair of American mistresses. Mrs Witt and Phoenix both rode with long stirrups and straight leg, sitting close to the saddle, without posting. Phoenix looked as if he and the horse were all one piece, he never seemed to rise in the saddle at all, neither trotting nor galloping, but sat like a man riding bareback. And all the time he stared round, at the riders in the Row, at the people grouped outside the rail, chatting, at the children walking with their nurses, as if he were looking at a mirage, in whose actuality he never believed for a moment. London was all a sort of dark mirage to him. His wide, nervous-looking brown eyes with a smallish brown pupil, that showed the white all round, seemed to be focused on the far distance, as if he could not see things too near. He was watching the pale deserts of Arizona shimmer with moving light, the long mirage of a shallow lake ripple, the great pallid concave of earth and sky expanding with interchanged light. And a horse-shape loom large and portentous in the mirage, like some prehistoric beast.

That was real to him: the phantasm of Arizona. But this London was some-thing his eye passed over, as a false mirage.

He looked too smart in his well-tailored groom's clothes, so smart, he might have been one of the satirised new-rich. Perhaps it was a sort of half-breed physical assertion that came through his clothing, the savage's physical assertion of himself. Anyhow, he looked 'common', rather horsey and loud.

Except his face. In the golden suavity of his high-boned Indian face, that was hairless, with hardly any eyebrows, there was a blank, lost look that was almost touching. The same startled blank look was in his eyes. But in the smallish dark pupils the dagger-point of light still gleamed unbroken.

He was a good groom, watchful, quick, and on the spot in an instant if anything went wrong. He had a curious quiet power over the horses, un-emotional, unsympathetic, but silently potent. In the same way, watching the traffic of Piccadilly with his blank, glinting eye, he would calculate everything instinctively, as if it were an enemy, and pilot Mrs Witt by the strength of his silent will. He threw around her the tense watchfulness of her own America, and made her feel at home.

'Phoenix,' she said, turning abruptly in her saddle as they walked the horses past the sheltering policeman at Hyde Park Corner, 'I can't tell you how glad I am to have something a hundred per cent American at the back of me, when I go through these gates.'

She looked at him from dangerous grey eyes as if she meant it indeed, in vindictive earnest. A ghost of a smile went up to his high cheek-bones, but he did not answer.

'Why, mother?' said Lou, sing-song. 'It feels to me so friendly – !'

'Yes, Louise, it does. *So* friendly! That's why I mistrust it so entirely – '

And she set off at a canter up the Row, under the green trees, her face like the face of Medusa at fifty, a weapon in itself. She stared at everything and every-body, with that stare of cold dynamite waiting to explode them all. Lou posted trotting at her side, graceful and elegant, and faintly amused. Behind came Phoenix, like a shadow, with his yellowish, high-boned face still looking sick. And at his side, on the big brilliant bay horse, the smallish, black-bearded Welshman.

Between Phoenix and Lewis there was a latent, but unspoken and wary sympathy. Phoenix was terribly impressed by St Mawr, he could not leave off staring at him. And Lewis rode the brilliant, handsome-moving stallion so very quietly, like an insinuation.

Of the two men, Lewis looked the darker, with his black beard coming up to his thick black eyebrows. He was swarthy, with a rather short nose, and the uncanny pale-grey eyes that watched everything and cared about nothing. He cared about nothing in the world, except, at the present, St Mawr. People did not matter to him. He rode his horse and watched the world from the vantage ground of St Mawr, with a final indifference.

'You have been with that horse long?' asked Phoenix.

'Since he was born.'

Phoenix watched the action of St Mawr as they went. The bay moved proud and springy, but with perfect good sense, among the stream of riders. It was a beautiful June morning, the leaves overhead were thick and green; there came the first whiff of lime tree scent. To Phoenix, however, the city was a sort of nightmare mirage, and to Lewis, it was a sort of prison. The presence of people he felt as a prison around him.

Mrs Witt and Lou were turning, at the end of the Row, bowing to some acquaintances. The grooms pulled aside. Mrs Witt looked at Lewis with a cold eye.

'It seems an extraordinary thing to me, Louise,' she said, 'to see a groom with a beard.'

'It isn't usual, mother,' said Lou. 'Do you mind?'

'Not at all. At least, I think I don't. I get very tired of modern bare-faced young men, *very!* The clean, pure boy, don't you know! Doesn't it make you tired? – No, I think a groom with a beard is quite attractive.'

She gazed into the crowd defiantly, perching her finely shod toe with warlike firmness on the stirrup-iron. Then suddenly she reined in, and turned her horse towards the grooms.

'Lewis!' she said. 'I want to ask you a question. Supposing, now, that Lady Carrington wanted you to shave off that beard, what should you say?'

Lewis instinctively put up his hand to the said beard.

'They've wanted me to shave it off, Mam,' he said. 'But I've never done it.'

'But why? Tell me why?'

'It's part of me, Mam.'

Mrs Witt pulled on again.

'Isn't that extraordinary, Louise?' she said. 'Don't you like the way he says *Mam*? It sounds so impossible to me. Could any woman think of herself as Mam? Never! – Since Queen Victoria. But, do you know it hadn't occurred to me that a man's beard was really part of him. It always seemed to me that men wore their beards, like they wear their neckties, for show. I shall always remember Lewis for saying his beard was part of him. Isn't it curious, the way he rides? He seems to sink himself in the horse. When I speak to him, I'm not sure whether I'm speaking to a man or to a horse.'

A few days later, Rico himself appeared on St Mawr, for the morning ride. He rode self-consciously, as he did everything, and he was just a little nervous. But his mother-in-law was benevolent. She made him ride between her and Lou, like three ships slowly sailing abreast.

And that very day, who should come driving in an open carriage through the Park but the Queen Mother! Dear old Queen Alexandra, there was a flutter everywhere. And she bowed expressly to Rico, mistaking him, no doubt, for somebody else.

'Do you know,' said Rico, as they sat at lunch, he and Lou and Mrs Witt, in Mrs Witt's sitting-room in the dark, quiet hotel in Mayfair; 'I really like riding St Mawr *so* much. He really is a noble animal. – If ever I am made a Lord – which heaven forbid! – I shall be Lord St Mawr.'

'You mean,' said Mrs Witt, 'his real lordship would be the horse?'

'Very possible, I admit,' said Rico, with a curl of his long upper lip.

'Don't you think, mother,' said Lou, 'there *is* something quite noble about St Mawr? He strikes me as the first noble thing I have ever seen.'

'Certainly I've not seen any *man* that could compare with him. Because these English noblemen – well! I'd rather look at a Negro Pullman-boy, if I was looking for what *I* call nobility.'

Poor Rico was getting crosser and crosser. There was a devil in Mrs Witt. She had a hard, bright devil inside her, that she seemed to be able to let loose at will.

She let it loose the next day, when Rico and Lou joined her in the Row. She was silent but deadly with the horses, balking them in every way. She suddenly crowded over against the rail, in front of St Mawr, so that the stallion had to rear to pull himself up. Then, having a clear track, she suddenly set off at a gallop, like an explosion, and the stallion, all on edge, set off after her.

It seemed as if the whole Park, that morning, were in a state of nervous tension. Perhaps there was thunder in the air. But St Mawr kept on dancing and pulling at the bit, and wheeling sideways up against the railing, to the terror of the children and the onlookers, who squealed and jumped back suddenly, sending the nerves of the stallion into a rush like rockets. He reared and fought as Rico pulled him round.

Then he went on: dancing, pulling, springily progressing sideways, possessed with all the demons of perversity. Poor Rico's face grew longer and angrier. A fury rose in him, which he could hardly control. He hated his horse, and viciously tried to force him to a quiet, straight trot. Up went St Mawr on his hind legs, to the terror of the Row. He got the bit in his teeth, and began to fight.

But Phoenix, cleverly, was in front of him.

'You get off, Rico!' called Mrs Witt's voice, with all the calm of her wicked exultance.

And almost before he knew what he was doing, Rico had sprung lightly to the ground, and was hanging on to the bridle of the rearing stallion.

Phoenix also lightly jumped down, and ran to St Mawr, handing his bridle to Rico. Then began a dancing and a splashing, a rearing and a plunging. St Mawr was being wicked. But Phoenix, the indifference of conflict in his face, sat tight and immovable, without any emotion, only the heaviness of his impersonal will settling down like a weight, all the time, on the horse. There was, perhaps, a curious barbaric exultance in bare, dark will devoid of emotion or personal feeling.

So they had a little display in the Row for almost five minutes, the brilliant horse rearing and fighting. Rico, with a stiff long face, scrambled on to Phoenix's horse, and withdrew to a safe distance. Policemen came, and an officious mounted policeman rode up to save the situation. But it was obvious that Phoenix, detached and apparently unconcerned, but barbarically potent in his will, would bring the horse to order.

Which he did, and rode the creature home. Rico was requested not to ride St Mawr in the Row any more, as the stallion was dangerous to public safety. The authorities knew all about him.

Where ended the first fiasco of St Mawr.

'We didn't get on very well with his lordship this morning,' said Mrs Witt triumphantly.

'No, he didn't like his company *at all*!' Rico snarled back.

He wanted Lou to sell the horse again.

'I doubt if anyone would buy him, dear,' she said. 'He's a known character.'

'Then make a gift of him – to your mother,' said Rico with venom.

'Why to mother?' asked Lou innocently.

'She might be able to cope with him – or he with her!' The last phrase was deadly. Having delivered it, Rico departed.

Lou remained at a loss. She felt almost always a little bit dazed, as if she could not see clear nor feel clear. A curious deadness upon her, like the first touch of death. And through this cloud of numbness, or deadness, came all her muted experiences.

Why was it? She did not know. But she felt that in some way it came from a battle of wills. Her mother, Rico, herself, it was always an unspoken, unconscious battle of wills, which was gradually numbing and paralysing her. She knew Rico meant nothing but kindness by her. She knew her mother only wanted to watch over her. Yet always there was this tension of will, that was so numbing. As if at the depths of him, Rico were always angry, though he seemed so 'happy' on top. And Mrs Witt was organically angry. So they were like a couple of bombs, timed to explode some day, but ticking on like two ordinary timepieces, in the meanwhile.

She had come definitely to realise this: that Rico's anger was wound up tight at the bottom of him, like a steel spring that kept his works going, while he himself was 'charming', like a bomb-clock with Sèvres paintings or Dresden figures on the outside. But his very charm was a sort of anger, and his love was a destruction in itself. He just couldn't help it.

And she? Perhaps she was a good deal the same herself. Wound up tight inside, and enjoying herself being 'lovely'. But wound up tight on some tension that, she realised now with wonder, was really a sort of anger. This, the mainspring that drove her on the round of 'joys'.

She used really to enjoy the tension, and the *élan* it gave her. While she knew nothing about it. So long as she felt it really was life and happiness, this *élan*, this tension and excitement of 'enjoying oneself'.

Now suddenly she doubted the whole show. She attributed to it the curious numbness that was overcoming her, as if she couldn't feel any more.

She wanted to come unwound. She wanted to escape this battle of wills.

Only St Mawr gave her some hint of the possibility. He was so powerful, and so dangerous. But in his dark eye, that looked, with its cloudy brown pupil, a cloud within a dark fire, like a world beyond our world, there was a dark vitality glowing, and within the fire, another sort of wisdom. She felt sure of it: even when he put his ears back, and bared his teeth, and his great eyes came bolting out of his naked horse's head, and she saw demons upon demons in the chaos of his horrid eyes.

Why did he seem to her like some living background, into which she wanted to retreat? When he reared his head and neighed from his deep chest, like deep wind-bells resounding, she seemed to hear the echoes of another darker, more spacious, more dangerous, more splendid world than ours, that was beyond her. And there she wanted to go.

She kept it utterly a secret, to herself. Because Rico would just have lifted his long upper lip, in his bare face, in a condescending sort of 'understanding'. And her mother would, as usual, have suspected her of side-stepping. People, all the people she knew, seemed so entirely contained within their cardboard let's-be-happy world. Their wills were fixed like machines on happiness, or fun, or the-best-ever. This ghastly cheery-o! touch, that made all her blood go numb.

Since she had really seen St Mawr looming fiery and terrible in an outer darkness, she could not believe the world she lived in. She could not believe it was actually happening, when she was dancing in the afternoon at Claridge's, or in the evening at the Carlton, sliding about with some suave young man who wasn't like a man at all to her. Or down in Sussex for the weekend with the Enderleys: the talk, the eating and drinking, the flirtation, the endless dancing: it all seemed far more bodiless and, in a strange way, wraith-like, than any fairy story. She seemed to be eating Barmecide food, that had been conjured up out of thin air, by the power of words. She seemed to be talking to handsome young bare-faced unrealities, not men at all: as she slid about with them, in the perpetual dance, they too seemed to have been conjured up out of air, merely for this soaring, slithering dance-business. And she could not believe that, when the lights went out, they wouldn't melt back into thin air again, and complete nonentity. The strange nonentity of it all! Everything just conjured up, and nothing real. '*Isn't this the best ever!*' they would beamingly assert, like the wraiths of enjoyment, without any genuine substance. And she would beam back: '*Lots of fun!*'

She was thankful the season was over, and everybody was leaving London. She and Rico were due to go to Scotland, but not till August. In the meantime they would go to her mother.

Mrs Witt had taken a cottage in Shropshire, on the Welsh border, and had moved down there with Phoenix and her horses. The open, heather-and-bilberry-covered hills were splendid for riding.

Rico consented to spend the month in Shropshire, because for near neighbours Mrs Witt had the Manbys, at Corrabach Hall. The Manbys were rich Australians returned to the old country and set up as Squires, all in full blow. Rico had known them in Victoria: they were of good family: and the girls made a great fuss of him.

So down went Lou and Rico, Lewis, Poppy and St Mawr, to Shrewsbury, then out into the country. Mrs Witt's 'cottage' was a tall red-brick Georgian house looking straight on to the churchyard, and the dark, looming big church.

'I never knew what a comfort it would be,' said Mrs Witt, 'to have grave-stones under my drawing-room windows, and funerals for lunch.'

She really did take a strange pleasure in sitting in her panelled room, that was painted grey, and watching the Dean or one of the curates officiating at the graveside, among a group of black country mourners with black-bordered handkerchiefs luxuriantly in use.

'Mother!' said Lou. 'I think it's gruesome!'

She had a room at the back, looking over the walled garden and the stables. Nevertheless there was the *boom! boom!* of the passing-bell, and the chiming and pealing on Sundays. The shadow of the Church, indeed! A very audible shadow, making itself heard insistently.

The Dean was a big, burly, fat man with a pleasant manner. He was a gentleman, and a man of learning in his own line. But he let Mrs Witt know that he looked down on her just a trifle – as a parvenu American, a Yankee – though she never was a Yankee: and at the same time he had a sincere respect for her, as a rich woman. Yes, a sincere respect for her, as a rich woman.

Lou knew that every Englishman, especially of the upper classes, has a wholesome respect for riches. But then, who hasn't?

The Dean was more *impressed* by Mrs Witt than by little Lou. But to Lady Carrington he was charming: she was *almost* 'one of us', you know. And he was very gracious to Rico: 'your father's splendid colonial service'.

Mrs Witt had now a new pantomime to amuse her: the Georgian house, her own pew in Church – it went with the old house: a village of thatched cottages – some of them with corrugated iron over the thatch: the cottage people, farm labourers and their families, with a few, very few, outsiders: the wicked little group of cottagers down at Mile End, famous for ill-living. The Mile-Enders were all Allisons and Jephsons, and in-bred, the Dean said: result of working through the centuries at the Quarry, and living isolated there at Mile End.

Isolated! Imagine it! A mile and a half from the railway station, ten miles from Shrewsbury. Mrs Witt thought of Texas, and said, 'Yes, they are *very* isolated, away down there!'

And the Dean never for a moment suspected sarcasm.

But there she had the whole thing staged complete for her: English village life. Even miners breaking in to shatter the rather stuffy, unwholesome harmony. All the men touched their caps to her, all the women did a bit of reverence, the children stood aside for her, if she appeared in the street.

They were all poor again: the labourers could no longer afford even a glass of beer in the evenings, since the Glorious War.

'Now I think that *is* terrible,' said Mrs Witt. 'Not to be able to get away from those stuffy, squalid, picturesque cottages for an hour in the evening, to drink a glass of beer.'

'It's a pity, I do agree with you, Mrs Witt. But Mr Watson has organised a men's reading-room, where the men can smoke and play dominoes, and read if they wish.'

'But that,' said Mrs Witt, 'is not the same as that cosy parlour in the Moon and Stars.'

'I quite agree,' said the Dean. 'It isn't.'

Mrs Witt marched to the landlord of the 'Moon and Stars', and asked for a glass of cider.

'I want', she said, in her American accent, 'these poor labourers to have their glass of beer in the evenings.'

'They want it themselves,' said Harvey.

'Then they must have it – '

The upshot was, she decided to supply one large barrel of beer per week and the landlord was to sell it to the labourers at a penny a glass.

'My own country has gone dry,' she asserted. 'But not because we can't *afford* it.'

By the time Lou and Rico appeared, she was deep in. She actually interfered very little: the barrel of beer was her one public act. But she *did* know everybody by sight, already, and she *did* know everybody's circumstances. And she had

SELECTED WORKS OF D. H. LAWRENCE

attended one prayer-meeting, one mother's meeting, one sewing-bee, one 'social', one Sunday School meeting, one Band of Hope meeting, and one Sunday School treat. She ignored the poky little Wesleyan and Baptist chapels, and was true-blue Episcopalian.

'How strange these picturesque old villages are, Louise!' she said, with a duskiness around her sharp, well-bred nose. 'How easy it all seems, all on a definite pattern. And how false! And underneath, how corrupt!'

She gave that queer, triumphant leer from her grey eyes, and queer demonish wrinkles seemed to twitter on her face.

Lou shrank away. She was beginning to be afraid of her mother's insatiable curiosity, that always looked for the snake under the flowers. Or rather, for the maggots.

Always this same morbid interest in other people and their doings, their privacies, their dirty linen. Always this air of alertness for personal happenings, personalities, personalities, personalities. Always this subtle criticism and appraisal of other people, this analysis of other people's motives. If anatomy presupposes a corpse, then psychology presupposes a world of corpses. Personalities, which means personal criticism and analysis, presupposes a whole world-laboratory of human psyches waiting to be vivisected. If you cut a thing up, of course it will smell. Hence, nothing raises such an infernal stink, at last, as human psychology.

Mrs Witt was a pure psychologist, a fiendish psychologist. And Rico, in his way, was a psychologist too. But he had a formula. 'Let's *know* the worst, dear! But let's look on the bright side, and believe the best.'

'Isn't the Dean a priceless old darling!' said Rico at breakfast.

And it had begun. Work had started in the psychic vivisection laboratory.

'Isn't he wonderful!' said Lou vaguely.

'So delightfully worldly! – *Some of us are not born to make money, dear boy. Luckily for us, we can marry it.*' – Rico made a priceless face.

'Is Mrs Vyner so rich?' asked Lou.

'She is, quite a wealthy woman – in coal,' replied Mrs Witt. 'But the Dean is surely worth his weight even in gold. And he's a massive figure. I can imagine there would be great satisfaction in having him for a husband.'

'Why, mother?' asked Lou.

'Oh, such a presence! One of these old Englishmen, that nobody can put in their pocket. You can't imagine his wife asking him to thread her needle. Something after all so *robust*! So different from *young* Englishmen, who all seem to me like ladies, perfect ladies.'

'*Somebody* has to keep up the tradition of the perfect lady,' said Rico.

'I know it,' said Mrs Witt. 'And if the women won't do it, the young gentlemen take on the burden. They bear it very well.'

It was in full swing, the cut and thrust. And poor Lou, who had reached the point of stupefaction in the game, felt she did not know what to do with herself.

Rico and Mrs Witt were deadly enemies, yet neither could keep clear of the other. It might have been they who were married to one another, their duet and their duet were so relentless.

But Rico immediately started the social round: first the Manbys: then motor twenty miles to luncheon at Lady Tewkesbury's: then young Mr Burns came flying down in his aeroplane from Chester: then they must motor to the sea, to Sir Edward Edwards's place, where there was a moonlight bathing party. Everything intensely thrilling, and so innerly wearisome, Lou felt.

But back of it all was St Mawr, looming like a bonfire in the dark. He really was a tiresome horse to own. He worried the mares, if they were in the same paddock with him, always driving them round. And with any other horse he just fought with definite intent to kill. So he had to stay alone.

'That St Mawr, he's a bad horse,' said Phoenix.

'Maybe!' said Lewis.

'You don't like quiet horses?' said Phoenix.

'Most horses *is* quiet,' said Lewis. 'St Mawr, he's different.'

'Why don't he never get any foals?'

'Doesn't want to, I should think. Same as me.'

'What good is a horse like that? Better shoot him, before he kill somebody.'

'What good'll they get, shooting St Mawr?' said Lewis.

'If he kills somebody!' said Phoenix.

But there was no answer.

The two grooms both lived over the stables, and Lou, from her window, saw a good deal of them. They were two quiet men, yet she was very much aware of their presence, aware of Phoenix's rather high square shoulders and his fine, straight, vigorous black hair that tended to stand up assertively on his head, as he went quietly drifting about his various jobs. He was not lazy, but he did everything with a sort of diffidence, as if from a distance, and handled his horses carefully, cautiously, and cleverly, but without sympathy. He seemed to be holding something back, all the time, unconsciously, as if in his very being there was some secret. But it was a secret of *will*. His quiet, reluctant movements, as if he never really wanted to do anything; his long flat-stepping stride; the permanent challenge in his high cheek-bones, the Indian glint in his eyes, and his peculiar stare, watchful and yet unseeing, made him unpopular with the women servants.

Nevertheless, women had a certain fascination for him: he would stare at the pretty young maids with an intent blank stare, when they were not looking. Yet he was rather overbearing, domineering with them, and they resented him. It was evident to Lou that he looked upon himself as belonging to the master, not to the servant class. When he flirted with the maids, as he very often did, for he had a certain crude ostentatiousness, he seemed to let them feel that he despised them as inferiors, servants, while he admired their pretty charms, as fresh, country maids.

'I'm fair nervous of that Phoenix,' said Fanny, the fair-haired maid. 'He makes you feel what he'd do to you if he could.'

'He'd better not try with me,' said Mabel. 'I'd scratch his cheeky eyes out. Cheek! – for it's nothing else! He's nobody – common as they're made!'

'He makes you feel you was there for him to trample on,' said Fanny.

'Mercy, you *are* soft! If anybody's that it's him. Oh my, Fanny, you've no right to let a fellow make you feel like *that*! Make *them* feel that *they're* dirt, for you to trample on: which they are!'

Fanny, however, being a shy little blonde thing, wasn't good at assuming the trampling rôle. She was definitely nervous of Phoenix. And he enjoyed it. An invisible smile seemed to creep up his cheek-bones, and the glint moved in his eyes as he teased her. He tormented her by his very presence, as he knew.

He would come silently up when she was busy, and stand behind her perfectly still, so that she was unaware of his presence. Then, silently, he would *make* her aware. Till she glanced nervously round, and with a scream, saw him.

One day Lou watched this little play. Fanny had been picking over a bowl of black currants, sitting on the bench under the maple tree in a corner of the yard. She didn't look round till she had picked up her bowl to go to the kitchen. Then there was a scream and a crash.

When Lou came out, Phoenix was crouching down silently gathering up the currants, which the little maid, scarlet and trembling, was collecting into another bowl. Phoenix seemed to be smiling down his back.

'Phoenix!' said Lou. 'I wish you wouldn't startle Fanny!'

He looked up, and she saw the glint of ridicule in his eyes.

'Who, me?' he said.

'Yes, you. You go up behind Fanny, to startle her. You're not to do it.'

He slowly stood erect, and lapsed into his peculiar invisible silence. Only for a second his eyes glanced at Lou's, and then she saw the cold anger, the gleam of malevolence and contempt. He could not bear being commanded, or reprimanded, by a woman.

Yet it was even worse with a man.

'What's that, Lou?' said Rico, appearing all handsome and in the picture, in white flannels with an apricot silk shirt.

'I'm telling Phoenix he's not to torment Fanny!'

'Oh!' – and Rico's voice immediately became his father's, the important government official. 'Certainly *not*! Most certainly *not*!' He looked at the scattered currants and the broken bowl. Fanny melted into tears. 'This, I suppose, is some of the results! Now look here, Phoenix, you're to leave the maids strictly alone. I shall ask them to report to me whenever, or *if* ever, you interfere with them. But I hope you *won't* interfere with them – in any way. You understand?'

As Rico became more and more Sir Henry and the government official, Lou's bones melted more and more into discomfort. Phoenix stood in his peculiar silence, the invisible smile on his cheek-bones.

'You understand what I'm saying to you?' Rico demanded, in intensified acid tones.

But Phoenix only stood there, as it were behind a cover of his own will, and looked back at Rico with a faint smile on his face and the glint moving in his eyes.

'Do you intend to answer?' Rico's upper lip lifted nastily.

'Mrs Witt is my boss,' came from Phoenix.

The scarlet flew up Rico's throat and flushed his face, his eyes went glaucous. Then quickly his face turned yellow.

Lou looked at the two men: her husband, whose rages, over-controlled, were organically terrible: the half-breed, whose dark-coloured lips were widened in a faint smile of derision, but in whose eyes caution and hate were playing against one another. She realised that Phoenix would accept *her* reprimand, or her mother's, because he could despise the two of them as mere women. But Rico's bossiness aroused murder pure and simple.

She took her husband's arm.

'Come dear!' she said, in her half plaintive way. 'I'm sure Phoenix understands. We all understand. Go to the kitchen, Fanny, never mind the currants. There are plenty more in the garden.'

Rico was always thankful to be drawn quickly, submissively away from his own rage. He was afraid of it. He was afraid lest he should fly at the groom in some horrible fashion. The very thought horrified him. But in actuality he came very near to it.

He walked stiffly, feeling paralysed by his own fury. And those words, *Mrs Witt is my boss*, were like hot acid in his brain. An insult!

'By the way, Belle-Mère!' he said when they joined Mrs Witt – she hated being called Belle-Mère, and once said: 'If I'm the bell-mare, are you one of the colts?' – She also hated his voice of smothered fury – 'I had to speak to Phoenix about persecuting the maids. He took the liberty of informing me that you were his boss, so perhaps you had better speak to him.'

'I certainly will. I believe they're my maids, and nobody else's, so it's my duty to look after them. Who was he persecuting?'

'I'm the responsible one, mother,' said Lou –

Rico disappeared in a moment. He must get out: get away from the house. How? Something was wrong with the car. Yet he must get away, away. He would go over to Corrabach. He would ride St Mawr. He had been talking about the horse, and Flora Manby was dying to see him. She had said: 'Oh, I can't *wait* to see that marvellous horse of yours.'

He would ride him over. It was only seven miles. He found Lou's maid Elena, and sent her to tell Lewis. Meanwhile, to soothe himself, he dressed himself most carefully in white riding breeches and a shirt of purple silk crêpe, with a flowing black tie spotted red like a ladybird, and black riding boots. Then he took a *chic* little white hat with a black band.

St Mawr was saddled and waiting, and Lewis had saddled a second horse.

'Thanks, Lewis, I'm going alone!' said Rico.

This was the first time he had ridden St Mawr in the country, and he was nervous. But he was also in the hell of a smothered fury. All his careful dressing had not really soothed him. So his fury consumed his nervousness.

He mounted with a swing, blind and rough. St Mawr reared.

'Stop that!' snarled Rico, and put him to the gate.

Once out in the village street, the horse went dancing sideways. He insisted on dancing at the sidewalk, to the exaggerated terror of the children. Rico, exasperated, pulled him across. But no, he wouldn't go down the centre of the village street. He began dancing and edging on to the other sidewalk, so the foot-passengers fled into the shops in terror.

The devil was in him. He would turn down every turning where he was not meant to go. He reared with panic at a furniture van. He *insisted* on going down the wrong side of the road. Rico was riding him with a martingale, and he could see the rolling, bloodshot eye.

'Damn you, *go!*' said Rico, giving him a dig with the spurs.

And away they went, down the high road, in a thunderbolt. It was a hot day, with thunder threatening, so Rico was soon in a flame of heat. He held on tight, with fixed eyes, trying all the time to rein in the horse. What he really was afraid of was that the brute would shy suddenly, as he galloped. Watching for this, he didn't care when they sailed past the turning to Corrabach.

St Mawr flew on, in a sort of *élan*. Marvellous the power and life in the creature. There was really a great joy in the motion. If only he wouldn't take the corners at a gallop, nearly swerving Rico off! Luckily the road was clear. To ride, to ride at this terrific gallop, on into eternity!

After several miles, the horse slowed down, and Rico managed to pull him into a lane that might lead to Corrabach. When all was said and done, it was a wonderful ride. St Mawr could go like the wind, but with that luxurious heavy ripple of life which is like nothing else on earth. It seemed to carry one at once into another world, away from the life of the nerves.

So Rico arrived after all something of a conqueror at Corrabach. To be sure, he was perspiring, and so was his horse. But he was a hero from another, heroic world.

'Oh, such a hot ride!' he said, as he walked on to the lawn at Corrabach Hall. 'Between the sun and the horse, really! – between two fires!'

'Don't you trouble, you're looking dandy, a bit hot and flushed like,' said Flora Manby. 'Let's go and see your horse.'

And her exclamation was: 'Oh, he's *lovely*! He's *fine*! I'd love to try him once – '

Rico decided to accept the invitation to stay overnight at Corrabach. Usually he was very careful, and refused to stay, unless Lou was with him. But they telephoned to the post-office at Chomesbury, would Mr Jones please send a message to Lady Carrington that Sir Henry was staying the night at Corrabach Hall, but would be home next day. Mr Jones received the request with unction, and said he would go over himself to give the message to Lady Carrington.

Lady Carrington was in the walled garden. The peculiarity of Mrs Witt's house was that, for grounds proper, it had the churchyard.

'I never thought, Louise, that one day I should have an old English church-yard for my lawns and shrubbery and park, and funeral mourners for my herds of deer. It's curious. For the first time in my life a funeral has become a real thing to me. I feel I could write a book on them.'

But Louise only felt intimidated.

At the back of the house was a flagged courtyard, with stables and a maple tree in a corner, and big doors opening on to the village street. But at the side was a walled garden, with fruit trees and currant bushes and a great bed of rhubarb, and some tufts of flowers, peonies, pink roses, sweet williams. Phoenix, who had a certain taste for gardening, would be out there thinning the carrots or tying up the lettuce. He was not lazy. Only he would not take work seriously, as a job. He would be quite amused tying up lettuces, and would tie up head after head, quite prettily. Then, becoming bored, he would abandon his task, light a cigarette, and go and stand on the threshold of the big doors, in full view of the street, watching, and yet completely indifferent.

After Rico's departure on St Mawr, Lou went into the garden. And there she saw Phoenix working in the onion bed. He was bending over, in his own silence, busy with nimble, amused fingers among the grassy young onions. She thought he had not seen her, so she went down another path to where a swing bed hung under the apple trees. There she sat with a book and a bundle of magazines. But she did not read.

She was musing vaguely. Vaguely, she was glad that Rico was away for a while. Vaguely, she felt a sense of bitterness, of complete futility: the complete futility of her living. This left her drifting in a sea of utter chagrin. And Rico seemed to her the symbol of the futility. Vaguely, she was aware that something else existed, but she didn't know where it was or what it was.

In the distance she could see Phoenix's dark, rather tall-built head, with its black, fine, intensely-living hair tending to stand on end, like a brush with long, very fine black bristles. His hair, she thought, betrayed him as an animal of a different species. He was growing a little bored by weeding onions: that also she could tell. Soon he would want some other amusement.

Presently Lewis appeared. He was small, energetic, a little bit bow-legged, and he walked with a slight strut. He wore khaki riding-breeches, leather gaiters, and a blue shirt. And, like Phoenix, he rarely had any cap or hat on his head. His thick black hair was parted at the side and brushed over heavily sideways, dropping on his forehead at the right. It was very long, a real mop, under which his eyebrows were dark and steady.

'Seen Lady Carrington?' he asked of Phoenix.

'Yes, she's sitting on that swing over there – she's been there quite a while.'

The wretch – he had seen her from the very first!

Lewis came striding over, looking towards her with his pale-grey eyes, from under his mop of hair.

'Mr Jones from the post office wants to see you, my Lady, with a message from Sir Henry.'

Instantly alarm took possession of Lou's soul.

'Oh! – Does he want to see me personally? – What message? Is anything wrong?' – And her voice trailed out over the last word, with a sort of anxious nonchalance.

'I don't think it's anything amiss,' said Lewis reassuringly.

'Oh! You don't,' the relief came into her voice. Then she looked at Lewis with a slight, winning smile in her unmatched eyes. 'I'm so afraid of St Mawr, you know.' Her voice was soft and cajoling. Phoenix was listening in the distance.

'St Mawr's all right, if you don't do nothing to him,' Lewis replied.

'I'm sure he is! – But how is one to know when one is doing something to him? – Tell Mr Jones to come here, please,' she concluded, on a changed tone.

Mr Jones, a man of forty-five, thick-set, with a fresh complexion and rather foolish brown eyes, and a big brown moustache, came prancing down the path, smiling rather fatuously, and doffing his straw hat with a gorgeous bow the moment he saw Lou sitting in her slim white frock on the coloured swing bed under the trees with their hard green apples.

'Good-morning, Mr Jones!'

'Good-morning, Lady Carrington. – If I may say so, what a picture you make – a beautiful picture – '

He beamed under his big brown moustache like the greatest lady-killer.

'Do I! – Did Sir Henry say he was all right?'

'He didn't *say* exactly, but I should expect he is all right – ' and Mr Jones delivered his message, in the mayonnaise of his own unction.

'Thank you so much, Mr Jones. It's awfully good of you to come and tell me. Now I shan't worry about Sir Henry *at all*.'

'It's a great pleasure to come and deliver a satisfactory message to Lady Carrington. But it won't be kind to Sir Henry if you don't worry about him *at all* in his absence. We all enjoy being worried about by those we love – so long as there is nothing to worry about, of course!'

'Quite!' said Lou. 'Now won't you take a glass of port and a biscuit, or a whisky and soda? And thank you ever so much.'

'Thank *you*, my Lady. I might drink a whisky and soda, since you are so good.' And he beamed fatuously.

'Let Mr Jones mix himself a whisky and soda, Lewis,' said Lou.

'Heavens!' she thought, as the postmaster retreated a little uncomfortably down the garden path, his bald spot passing in and out of the sun, under the trees: 'How ridiculous everything is, how ridiculous, ridiculous!' Yet she didn't really dislike Mr Jones and his interlude.

Phoenix was melting away out of the garden. He had to follow the fun.

'Phoenix!' Lou called. 'Bring me a glass of water, will you? Or send somebody with it.'

He stood in the path looking round at her.

'All right!' he said.

And he turned away again.

She did not like being alone in the garden. She liked to have the men working somewhere near. Curious how pleasant it was to sit there in the garden when Phoenix was about, or Lewis. It made her feel she could never be lonely or jumpy. But when Rico was there, she was all aching nerve.

Phoenix came back with a glass of water, lemon juice, sugar, and a small bottle of brandy. He knew Lou liked a spoonful of brandy in her iced lemonade.

'How thoughtful of you, Phoenix!' she said. 'Did Mr Jones get his whisky?'

'He was just getting it.'

'That's right. – By the way, Phoenix, I wish you wouldn't get mad if Sir Henry speaks to you. He is *really* so kind.'

She looked up at the man. He stood there watching her in silence, the invisible smile on his face, and the inscrutable Indian glint moving in his eyes. What was he thinking? There was something passive and almost submissive about him, but underneath this, an unyielding resistance and cruelty: yes, even cruelty. She felt that, on top, he was submissive and attentive, bringing her her lemonade as she liked it, without being told: thinking for her quite subtly. But underneath there was an unchanging hatred. He submitted circumstantially, he worked for a wage. And even circumstantially, he *liked* his mistress – *la patrona* – and her daughter. But much deeper than any circumstance or any circumstantial liking, was the categorical hatred upon which he was founded, and with which he was powerless. His liking for Lou and for Mrs Witt, his serving them and working for a wage, was all side-tracking his own nature, which was grounded on hatred of their very existence. But what was he to do? He had to live. Therefore he had to serve, to work for a wage, and even to be faithful.

And yet *their* existence made his own existence negative. If he was to exist, positively, they would have to cease to exist. At the same time, a fatal sort of tolerance made him serve these women, and go on serving.

'Sir Henry is *so* kind to everybody,' Lou insisted.

The half-breed met her eyes, and smiled uncomfortably.

'Yes, he's a kind man,' he replied, as if sincerely.

'Then why do you mind if he speaks to you?'

'I don't mind,' said Phoenix glibly.

'But you do. Or else you wouldn't make him so angry.'

'Was he angry? I don't know,' said Phoenix.

'He was very angry. And you *do* know.'

'No, I don't know if he's angry. I don't know,' the fellow persisted. And there was a glib sort of satisfaction in his tone.

'That's awfully unkind of you, Phoenix,' she said, growing offended in her turn.

'No, I don't know if he's angry. I don't want to make him angry. I don't know – '

He had taken on a tone of naïve ignorance, which at once gratified her pride as a woman, and deceived her.

'Well, you believe me when I tell you you *did* make him angry, don't you?'

'Yes, I believe when you tell me.'

'And you promise me, won't you, not to do it again? It's *so* bad for him – so bad for his nerves, and for his eyes. It makes them inflamed, and injures his eyesight. And you know, as an artist, it's terrible if anything happens to his eyesight – '

Phoenix was watching her closely, to take it in. He still was not good at understanding continuous, logical statement. Logical connectgion in speech seemed to stupefy him, make him stupid. He understood in disconnected assertions of fact. But he had gathered what she said. 'He gets mad at you. When he gets mad, it hurts his eyes. His eyes hurt him. He wants to paint a picture, he can't. He can't paint a picture, he can't see clear – '

Yes, he had understood. She saw he had understood. The bright glint of satisfaction moved in his eyes.

'So now promise me, won't you, you won't make him mad again: you won't make him angry?'

'No, I won't make him angry. I don't do anything to make him angry,' Phoenix answered, rather glibly.

'And you do understand, don't you? You do know how kind he is: how he'd do a good turn to anybody?'

'Yes, he's a kind man,' said Phoenix.

'I'm so glad you realise. There, that's luncheon! How nice it is to sit here in the garden, when everybody is nice to you! No, I can carry the tray, don't you bother.'

But he took the tray from her hand, and followed her to the house. And as he walked behind her, he watched the slim white nape of her neck, beneath the clustering of her bobbed hair, something as a stoat watches a rabbit he is following.

In the afternoon Lou retreated once more to her place in the garden. There she lay, sitting with a bunch of pillows behind her, neither reading nor working, just musing. She had learned the new joy: to do absolutely nothing, but to lie and let the sunshine filter through the leaves, to see the bunch of red-hot-poker flowers pierce scarlet into the afternoon, beside the comparative neutrality of some foxgloves. The mere colour of hard red, like the big oriental poppies that had fallen, and these poker flowers, lingered in her consciousness like a communication.

Into this peaceful indolence, when even the big, dark-grey tower of the church beyond the wall and the yew trees was keeping its bells in silence, advanced Mrs Witt, in a broad panama hat and a white dress.

'Don't you want to ride, or do something, Louise?' she asked ominously.

'Don't you want to be peaceful, mother?' retorted Louise.

'Yes – an *active* peace. – I can't *believe* that my daughter can be content to lie on a hammock and do *nothing*, not even read or improve her mind, the greater part of the day.'

'Well, your daughter *is* content to do that. It's her greatest pleasure.'

'I know it. I can see it. And it surprises me *very* much. When I was your age, I was never still. I had so much *go* –'

> ' "Those maids, thank God,
>   Are 'neath the sod,
>   And all their generation."

'No, but, mother, I only take life differently. Perhaps you used up that sort of *go*. I'm the harem type, mother: only I never want the men inside the lattice.'

'Are you really my daughter? – Well! A woman never knows what will happen to her. I'm an *American* woman, and I suppose I've got to remain one, no matter where I am. – What did you want, Lewis?'

The groom had approached down the path.

'If I am to saddle Poppy?' said Lewis.

'No, apparently *not*!' replied Mrs Witt. 'Your mistress prefers the hammock to the saddle.'

'Thank you, Lewis. What mother says is true this afternoon, at least.' And she gave him a peculiar little cross-eyed smile.

'Who,' said Mrs Witt to the man, 'has been cutting at your hair?'

There was a moment of silent resentment.

'I did it myself, Mam! Sir Henry said it was too long.'

'He certainly spoke the truth. But I believe there's a barber in the village on Saturdays – or you could ride over to Shrewsbury. Just turn round, and let me look at the back. Is it the money?'

'No, Mam. I don't like these fellows touching my head.'

He spoke coldly, with a certain hostile reserve that at once piqued Mrs Witt.

'Don't you really!' she said. 'But it's quite *impossible* for you to go about as you are. It gives you a half-witted appearance. Go now into the yard, and get a chair and a dust-sheet. I'll cut your hair.'

The man hesitated, hostile.

'Don't be afraid, I know how it's done. I've cut the hair of many a poor wounded boy in hospital: and shaved them too. *You've got such a touch, nurse!* Poor fellow, he was dying, though none of us knew it. – Those are the compliments I value, Louise. – Get that chair now, and a dust-sheet. I'll borrow your hair-scissors from Elena, Louise.'

Mrs Witt, happily on the war-path, was herself again. She didn't care for work, actual work. But she loved trimming. She loved arranging unnatural and pretty salads, devising new and piquant-looking ice-creams, having a turkey stuffed exactly as she knew a stuffed turkey in Louisiana, with chestnuts and butter and stuff, or showing a servant how to turn waffles on a waffle-iron, or to bake a ham with brown sugar and cloves and a moistening of rum. She liked pruning rose trees, or beginning to cut a yew hedge into shape. She liked ordering her own and Louise's shoes, with an exactitude and a knowledge of shoemaking that sent the salesman crazy. She was a demon in shoes. Reappearing from America, she would pounce on her daughter. 'Louise, throw those shoes away. Give them to one of the maids.' – 'But, mother, they are some of the best French shoes. I like them.' – 'Throw them away. A shoe has only two excuses for existing: perfect comfort or perfect appearance. Those have neither. I have brought you some shoes.' – Yes, she had brought ten pairs of shoes from New York. She knew her daughter's foot as she knew her own.

So now she was in her element, looming behind Lewis as he sat in the middle of the yard swathed in a dust-sheet. She had on an overall and a pair of wash-leather gloves, and she poised a pair of long scissors like one of the Fates. In her big hat she looked curiously young, but with the youth of a bygone generation. Her heavy-lidded, laconic grey eyes were alert, studying the groom's black mop of hair. Her eyebrows made thin, uptilting black arches on her brow. Her fresh skin was slightly powdered, and she was really handsome, in a bold, bygone, eighteenth-century style. Some of the curious, adventurous stoicism of the eighteenth century: and then a certain blatant American efficiency.

Lou, who had strayed into the yard to see, looked so much younger and so many thousands of years older than her mother, as she stood in her wisp-like diffidence, the clusters of grape-like bobbed hair hanging beside her face, with its fresh colouring and its ancient weariness, her slightly squinting eyes, that were so disillusioned they were becoming faun-like.

'Not too short, mother, not too short!' she remonstrated, as Mrs Witt, with a terrific flourish of efficiency, darted at the man's black hair, and the thick flakes fell like black snow.

'Now, Louise, I'm right in this job, please don't interfere. Two things I hate to see: a man with his wool in his neck and ears: and a bare-faced young man who looks as if he'd bought his face as well as his hair from a men's beauty specialist.'

And efficiently she bent down, clip – clip – clipping! while Lewis sat utterly immobile, with sunken head, in a sort of despair.

Phoenix stood against the stable door, with his restless, eternal cigarette. And in the kitchen doorway the maids appeared and fled, appeared and fled in delight. The old gardener, a fixture who went with the house, creaked in and stood with his legs apart, silent in intense condemnation.

'First time I ever see such a thing!' he muttered to himself, as he creaked on into the garden. He was a bad-tempered old soul, who thoroughly disapproved of the household, and would have given notice, but that he knew which side his bread was buttered: and there was butter unstinted on his bread, in Mrs Witt's kitchen.

Mrs Witt stood back to survey her handiwork, holding those terrifying shears with their beak erect. Lewis lifted his head and looked stealthily round, like a creature in a trap.

'Keep still!' she said. 'I haven't finished.'

And she went for his front hair, with vigour, lifting up long layers and snipping off the ends artistically: till at last he sat with a black aureole upon the floor, and his ears standing out with curious new alertness from the sides of his clean-clipped head.

'Stand up,' she said, 'and let me look.'

He stood up, looking absurdly young, with the hair all cut away from his neck and ears, left thick only on top. She surveyed her work with satisfaction.

'You look so much younger,' she said; 'you would be surprised. Sit down again.'

She clipped the back of his neck with the shears, and then, with a very slight hesitation, she said, 'Now about the beard!'

But the man rose suddenly from the chair, pulling the dust-cloth from his neck with desperation.

'No, I'll do that myself,' he said, looking her in the eyes with a cold light in his pale-grey, uncanny eyes.

She hesitated in a kind of wonder at his queer male rebellion.

'Now, listen, I shall do it much better than you – and besides,' she added hurriedly, snatching at the dust-cloth he was flinging on the chair – 'I haven't quite finished round the ears.'

'I think I shall do,' he said, again looking her in the eyes, with a cold, white gleam of finality. 'Thank you for what you've done.'

And he walked away to the stable.

'You'd better sweep up here,' Mrs Witt called.

'Yes, Mam,' he replied, looking round at her again with an odd resentment, but continuing to walk away.

'However!' said Mrs Witt. 'I suppose he'll do.'

And she divested herself of gloves and overall, and walked indoors to wash and to change. Lou went indoors too.

'It is extraordinary what hair that man has!' said Mrs Witt. 'Did I tell you when I was in Paris, I saw a woman's face in the hotel that I thought I knew? I couldn't place her, till she was coming towards me. *Aren't you Rachel Fannière?* she said. *Aren't you Janette Leroy?* We hadn't seen each other since we were girls of twelve and thirteen, at school in New Orleans. *Oh!* she said to me. *Is every illusion doomed to perish? You had such wonderful golden curls! All my life I've said, Oh, if only I had such lovely hair as Rachel Fannière! I've seen those beautiful golden curls of yours all my life. And now I meet you, you're grey!* Wasn't that terrible, Louise? Well, that man's hair made me think of it – so thick and curious. It's strange, what a difference there is in hair; I suppose it's because he's just an animal – no mind! There's nothing I admire in a man like a good *mind*. Your father was a very clever man, and all the men I've admired have been clever. But isn't it curious now, I've never cared much to touch their hair. How strange life is! If it gives one thing, it takes away another. – And even those poor boys in hospital: I have shaved them, or cut their hair, like a mother, never thinking anything of it. Lovely, intelligent, clean boys, most of them were. Yet it never did anything to me. I never knew before that something could happen to one from a person's *hair*! Like to Janette Leroy from my curls when I was a child.

And now I'm grey, as she says. – I wonder how old a man Lewis is, Louise! Didn't he look absurdly young, with his ears pricking up?'

'I think Rico said he was forty or forty-one.'

'And never been married?'

'No – not as far as I know.'

'Isn't that curious now! – just an animal! no mind! A man with no mind! I've always thought that the *most* despicable thing. Yet such wonderful hair to touch. Your Henry has quite a good mind, yet I would simply shrink from touching his hair. I suppose one likes stroking a cat's fur, just the same. Just the animal in man. Curious that I never seem to have met it, Louise. Now I come to think of it, he has the eyes of a human cat: a human tom-cat. Would you call him stupid? Yes, he's very stupid.'

'No, mother, he's not stupid. He only doesn't care about most things.'

'Like an animal! But what a strange look he has in his eyes! a strange sort of intelligence! and a confidence in himself. Isn't that curious, Louise, in a man with as little mind as he has? Do you know, I should say he could see through a woman pretty well.'

'Why, mother!' said Lou impatiently. 'I think one gets so tired of your men with mind, as you call it. There are so many of that sort of clever men. And there are lots of men who aren't very clever, but are rather nice: and lots are stupid. It seems to me there's something else besides mind and cleverness, or niceness or cleanness. Perhaps it is the animal. Just think of St Mawr! I've thought so much about him. We call him an animal, but we never know what it means. He seems a far greater mystery to me than a clever man. He's a horse. Why can't one say in the same way, of a man: *He's a man?* There seems no mystery in being a man. But there's a terrible mystery in St Mawr.'

Mrs Witt watched her daughter quizzically.

'Louise,' she said, 'you won't tell me that the mere animal is all that counts in a man. I will never believe it. Man is wonderful because he is able to *think*.'

'But is he?' cried Lou, with sudden exasperation. 'Their thinking seems to me all so childish: like stringing the same beads over and over again. Ah, men! They and their thinking are all so *paltry*. How can you be impressed?'

Mrs Witt raised her eyebrows sardonically.

'Perhaps I'm not – any more,' she said with a grim smile.

'But,' she added, 'I still can't see that I am to be impressed by the mere animal in man. The animals are the same as we are. It seems to me they have the same feelings and wants as we do in a commonplace way. The only difference is that they have no minds: no human minds, at least. And no matter what you say, Louise, lack of mind makes the commonplace.'

Lou knitted her brows nervously.

'I suppose it does, mother. – But men's minds *are* so commonplace: look at Dean Vyner and his mind! Or look at Arthur Balfour, as a shining example. Isn't *that* commonplace, that cleverness? I would hate St Mawr to be spoilt by such a mind.'

'Yes, Louise, so would I. Because the men you mention are really old women, knitting the same pattern over and over again. Nevertheless, I shall never alter my belief that real mind is all that matters in a man, and it's *that* that we women love.'

'Yes, mother! But what *is* real mind? The old woman who knits the most complicated pattern? Oh, I can hear all their needles clicking, the clever men! As a matter of fact, mother, I believe Lewis has far more real mind than Dean Vyner or any of the clever ones. He has a good intuitive mind, he knows things without thinking them.'

'That may be, Louise! But he is a servant. He is *under*. A real man should never be under. And then you could never be intimate with a man like Lewis.'

'I don't want intimacy, mother. I'm too tired of it all. I love St Mawr because he isn't intimate. He stands where one can't get at him. And he burns with life. And where does his life come from, to him? That's the mystery. That great burning life in him, which never is dead. Most men have a deadness in them, that frightens me so, because of my own deadness. Why can't men get their life straight, like St Mawr, and then think? Why can't they think quick, mother: quick as a woman: only farther than we do? Why isn't men's thinking quick like fire, mother? Why is it so slow, so dead, so deadly dull?'

'I can't tell you, Louise. My own opinion of the men of today has grown very small. But I can live in spite of it.'

'No, mother. We seem to be living off old fuel, like the camel when he lives off his hump. Life doesn't rush into us, as it does even into St Mawr, and he's a dependent animal. I can't live, mother. I just can't.'

'I don't see why not! *I'm* full of life.'

'I know you are, mother. But I'm not, and I'm your daughter. – And don't misunderstand me, mother. I don't want to be an animal like a horse or a cat or a lioness, though they all fascinate me, the way they get their life *straight*, not from a lot of old tanks, as we do. I don't admire the cave man, and that sort of thing. But think, mother, if we could get our lives straight from the source, as the animals do, and still be ourselves. You don't like men yourself. But you've no idea how men just tire me out: even the very thought of them. You say they are too animal. But they're not, mother. It's the animal in them has gone perverse, or cringing, or humble, or domesticated, like dogs. I don't know one single man who is a proud living animal. I know they've left off really thinking. But then men always do leave off really thinking, when the last bit of wild animal dies in them.'

'Because we have minds – '

'We have no minds once we are tame, mother. Men are all women, knitting and crocheting words together.'

'I can't altogether agree, you know, Louise.'

'I know you don't. – You like clever men. But clever men are mostly such unpleasant *animals*. As animals, so very unpleasant. And in men like Rico, the animal has gone queer and wrong. And in those nice clean boys you liked so much in the war, there is no wild animal left in them. They're all tame dogs, even when they're brave and well-bred. They're all tame dogs, mother, with human masters. There's no mystery in them.'

'What do you want, Louise? You *do* want the cave man, who'll knock you on the head with a club.'

'Don't be silly, mother. That's much more your subconscious line, you admirer of Mind. – I don't consider the cave man is a real human animal at all. He's a brute, a degenerate. A pure animal man would be as lovely as a deer or a leopard, burning like a flame fed straight from underneath. And he'd be part of the unseen, like a mouse is, even. And he'd never cease to wonder, he'd breathe silence and unseen wonder, as the partridges do, running in the stubble. He'd be all the animals in turn, instead of one, fixed, automatic thing, which he is now, grinding on the nerves. – Ah no, mother, I want the wonder back again, or I shall die. I don't want to be like you, just criticising and annihilating these dreary people, and enjoying it.'

'My dear daughter, whatever else the human animal might be, he'd be a dangerous commodity.'

'I wish he would, mother. I'm dying of these empty dangerless men, who are only sentimental and spiteful.'

'Nonsense, you're not dying.'

'I am, mother. And I should be dead if there weren't St Mawr and Phoenix and Lewis in the world.'

'St Mawr and Phoenix and Lewis! I thought you said they were servants.'

'That's the worst of it. If only they were masters! If only there were some men with as much natural life as they have, and their brave, quick minds that commanded instead of serving!'

'There are no such men,' said Mrs Witt, with a certain grim satisfaction.

'I know it. But I'm young, and I've got to live. And the thing that is offered me as life just starves me, starves me to death, mother. What am I to do? You enjoy shattering people like Dean Vyner. But I am young, I can't live that way.'

'That may be.'

It had long ago struck Lou how much more her mother realised and understood than ever Rico did. Rico was afraid, always afraid of realising. Rico, with his good manners and his habitual kindness, and that peculiar imprisoned sneer of his.

He arrived home next morning on St Mawr, rather flushed and gaudy, and over-kind, with an *empressé* anxiety about Lou's welfare which spoke too many volumes. Especially as he was accompanied by Flora Manby, and by Flora's sister Elsie, and Elsie's husband, Frederick Edwards. They all came on horseback.

'Such awful ages since I saw you!' said Flora to Lou. 'Sorry if we burst in on you. We're only just saying *How do you do!* and going on to the inn. They've got rooms all ready for us there. We thought we'd stay just one night over here, and ride tomorrow to the Devil's Chair. Won't you come? Lots of fun! Isn't Mrs Witt at home?'

Mrs Witt was out for the moment. When she returned she had on her curious stiff face, yet she greeted the newcomers with a certain cordiality: she felt it would be diplomatic, no doubt.

'There *are* two rooms here,' she said, 'and if you care to poke into them, why we shall be *delighted* to have you. But I'll show them to you first, because they are poor, inconvenient rooms, with no running water and *miles* from the baths.'

Flora and Elsie declared that they were 'perfectly darling sweet rooms – not overcrowded'.

'Well,' said Mrs Witt, 'the conveniences certainly don't fill up much space. But if you like to take them for what they are – '

'Why we feel absolutely overwhelmed, don't we, Elsie! – But we've no clothes – !'

Suddenly the silence had turned into a house-party. The Manby girls appeared to lunch in fine muslin dresses, bought in Paris, fresh as daisies. Women's clothing takes up so little space, especially in summer! Fred Edwards was one of those blond Englishmen with a little brush moustache and those strong blue eyes which were always attempting the sentimental, but which Lou, in her prejudice, considered cruel: upon what grounds she never analysed. However, he took a gallant tone with her at once, and she had to seem to simper. Rico, watching her, was so relieved when he saw the simper coming.

It had begun again, the whole clockwork of 'lots of fun'!

'Isn't Fred flirting perfectly outrageously with Lady Carrington! – She looks so *sweet*!' cried Flora, over her coffee-cup 'Don't you mind, Harry!'

They called Rico 'Harry'! His boy-name.

'Only a very little,' said Harry. '*L'uomo è cacciatore.*'

'Oh now, what does that mean?' cried Flora, who always thrilled to Rico's bits of affectation.

'It means,' said Mrs Witt, leaning forward and speaking in her most suave voice, 'that man is a hunter.'

Even Flora shrank under the smooth acid of the irony.

'Oh, well now!' she cried. 'If he is, then what is woman?'

'The hunted,' said Mrs Witt, in a still smoother acid.

'At least,' said Rico, 'she is always *game*!'

'Ah, is she though!' came Fred's manly, well-bred tones. 'I'm not so sure.'

Mrs Witt looked from one man to the other, as if she were dropping them down the bottomless pit.

Lou escaped to look at St Mawr. He was still moist where the saddle had been. And he seemed a little bit extinguished, as if virtue had gone out of him.

But when he lifted his lovely naked head, like a bunch of flames, to see who it was had entered, she saw he was still himself. For ever sensitive and alert, his head lifted like the summit of a fountain. And within him the clean bones striking to the earth, his hoofs intervening between him and the ground like lesser jewels.

He knew her and did not resent her. But he took no notice of her. He would never 'respond'. At first she had resented it. Now she was glad. He would never be intimate, thank heaven.

She hid herself away till tea-time, but she could not hide from the sound of voices. Dinner was early, at seven. Dean Vyner came – Mrs Vyner was an invalid – and also an artist who had a studio in the village and did etchings. He was a man of about thirty eight, and poor, just beginning to accept himself as a failure, as far as making money goes. But he worked at his etchings and studied esoteric matters like astrology and alchemy. Rico patronised him, and was a little afraid of him. Lou could not quite make him out. After knocking about Paris and London and Munich, he was trying to become staid, and to persuade himself that English village life, with squire and dean in the background, humble artist in the middle and labourer in the common foreground, was genuine life. His self-persuasion was only moderately successful. This was betrayed by the curious arrest in his body: he seemed to have to force himself into movement: and by the curious duplicity in his yellow-grey, twinkling eyes, that twinkled and expanded like a goat's; with mockery, irony, and frustration.

'Your face is curiously like Pan's,' said Lou to him at dinner.

It was true, in a commonplace sense. He had the tilted eyebrows, the twinkling goaty look, and the pointed ears of a goat-Pan.

'People have said so,' he replied. 'But I'm afraid it's not the face of the Great God Pan. Isn't it rather the Great Goat Pan!'

'I say, that's good!' cried Rico. 'The Great Goat Pan!'

'I have always found it difficult,' said the Dean, 'to see the Great God Pan in that goat-legged old father of satyrs. He may have a good deal of influence – the world will always be full of goaty old satyrs. But we find them somewhat vulgar. Even our late King Edward. The goaty old satyrs are too comprehensible to me to be venerable, and I fail to see a Great God in the father of them all.'

'Your ears should be getting red,' said Lou to Cartwright. She, too, had an odd squinting smile that suggested nymphs, so irresponsible and unbelieving.

'Oh no, nothing personal!' cried the Dean.

'I am not sure,' said Cartwright, with a small smile. 'But don't you imagine Pan once *was* a great god, before the anthropomorphic Greeks turned him into half a man?'

'Ah! – maybe. That is very possible. But – I have noticed the limitation in myself – my mind has no grasp whatsoever of Europe before the Greeks arose. Mr Wells's *Outline* does not help me there, either,' the Dean added with a smile.

'But what was Pan before he was a man with goat legs?' asked Lou.

'Before he looked like me?' said Cartwright, with a faint grin. 'I should say he was the god that is hidden in everything. In those days you saw the thing, you never saw the god in it: I mean in the tree or the fountain or the animal. If you ever saw the God instead of the thing, you died. If you saw it with the naked eye, that is. But in the night you might see the God. And you knew it was there.'

'The modern pantheist not only sees the God in everything, he takes photographs of it,' said the Dean.

'Oh, and the divine pictures he paints!' cried Rico.

'Quite!' said Cartwright.

'But if they never *saw* the God in the thing, the old ones, how did they know he was there? How did they have any Pan at all?' said Lou.

'Pan was the hidden mystery – the hidden cause. That's how it was a Great God. Pan wasn't *he* at all: not even a great God. He was Pan. All. What you see when you see in full. In the daytime you see the thing. But if your third eye is open, which sees only the things that can't be seen, you may see Pan within the thing, hidden: you may see with your third eye, which is darkness.'

'Do you think I might see Pan in a horse, for example?'

'Easily. In St Mawr!' – Cartwright gave her a knowing look.

'But,' said Mrs Witt, 'it would be difficult, I should say, to open the third eye and see Pan in a man.'

'Probably,' said Cartwright, smiling. 'In man he is over-visible: the old satyr: the fallen Pan.'

'Exactly!' said Mrs Witt. And she fell into a muse. 'The fallen Pan!' she re-echoed. 'Wouldn't a man be wonderful in whom Pan hadn't fallen!'

Over the coffee in the grey drawing-room she suddenly asked, 'Supposing, Mr Cartwright, one *did* open the third eye and see Pan in an actual man – I wonder what it would be like?'

She half lowered her eyelids and tilted her face in a strange way, as if she were tasting something, and not quite sure.

'I wonder!' he said, smiling his enigmatic smile. But she could see he did not understand.

'Louise!' said Mrs Witt at bedtime. 'Come into my room for a moment, I want to ask you something.'

'What is it, mother?'

'You, you *get* something from what Mr Cartwright said about seeing Pan with the third eye? Seeing Pan in something?'

Mrs Witt came rather close, and tilted her face with strange insinuating question at her daughter.

'I think I do, mother.'

'In what?' – The question came as a pistol-shot.

'I think, mother,' said Lou reluctantly, 'in St Mawr.'

'In a horse!' – Mrs Witt contracted her eyes slightly. 'Yes, I can see that. I know what you mean. It *is* in St Mawr. It *is*! But in St Mawr it makes me *afraid* – ' she dragged out the word. Then she came a step closer. 'But, Louise, did you ever see it in a man?'

'What, mother?'

'Pan. Did you ever see Pan in a man, as you see Pan in St Mawr?'

Louise hesitated.

'No, mother, I don't think I did. When I look at men with my third eye, as you call it – I think I see – mostly – a sort of – pan-cake.' She uttered the last word with a despairing grin, not knowing quite what to say.

'Oh, Louise, isn't that it! Doesn't one always see a pancake! Now listen, Louise. Have you ever been in love?'

'Yes, as far as I understand it.'

'Listen, now. Did you ever see Pan in the man you loved? Tell me if you did.'

'As I see Pan in St Mawr? – no, mother.' And suddenly her lips began to tremble and the tears came to her eyes.

'Listen, Louise. I've been in love innumerable times – and *really* in love twice. Twice! – yet for fifteen years I've left off wanting to have anything to do with a man, really. For fifteen years! And why? Do you know? Because I couldn't see that peculiar hidden Pan in any of them. And I became that I needed to. I needed it. But it wasn't there. Not in any man. Even when I was in love with a man, it was for other things: because I *understood* him so well, or he understood me, or we had such sympathy. Never the hidden Pan. Do you understand what I mean? Unfallen Pan!'

'More or less, mother.'

'But now my third eye is coming open, I believe. I am tired of all these men like breakfast cakes, with a teaspoonful of mind or a teaspoonful of spirit in them, for baking powder. Isn't it extraordinary: that young man Cartwright talks about Pan, but he knows nothing of it all. He knows nothing of the unfallen Pan: only the fallen Pan with goat legs and a leer – and that sort of power, don't you know.'

'But what do you know of the unfallen Pan, mother?'

'Don't ask me, Louise! I feel all of a tremble, as if I was just on the verge.'

She flashed a little look of incipient triumph, and said goodnight.

An excursion on horseback had been arranged for the next day, to two old groups of rocks, called the Angel's Chair and the Devil's Chair, which crowned the moor-like hills looking into Wales, ten miles away. Everybody was going – they were to start early in the morning, and Lewis would be the guide, since no one exactly knew the way.

Lou got up soon after sunrise. There was a summer scent in the trees of early morning, and monkshood flowers stood up dark and tall, with shadows. She dressed in the green linen riding-skirt her maid had put ready for her, with a close bluish smock.

'Are you going out already, dear?' called Rico from his room.

'Just to smell the roses before we start, Rico.'

He appeared in the doorway in his yellow silk pyjamas. His large blue eyes had that rolling irritable look and the slightly bloodshot whites which made her want to escape.

'Booted and spurred! – the *energy*!' he cried.

'It's a lovely day to ride,' she said.

'A lovely day to do anything *except* ride!' he said. 'Why spoil the day riding!' – A curious bitter-acid escaped into his tone. It was evident he hated the excursion.

'Why, we needn't go if you don't want to, Rico.'

'Oh, I'm sure I shall love it, once I get started. It's all this business of *starting*, with horses and paraphernalia – '

Lou went into the yard. The horses were drinking at the trough under the pump, their colours strong and rich in the shadow of the tree.

'You're not coming with us, Phoenix?' she said.

'Lewis, he's riding my horse.'

She could tell Phoenix did not like being left behind.

By half-past seven everybody was ready. The sun was in the yard, the horses were saddled. They came swishing their tails. Lewis brought out St Mawr from his separate box, speaking to him very quietly in Welsh: a murmuring, soothing little speech. Lou, alert, could see that he was uneasy.

'How is St Mawr this morning?' she asked.

'He's all right. He doesn't like so many people. He'll be all right once he's started.'

The strangers were in the saddle: they moved out to the deep shade of the village road outside. Rico came to his horse to mount. St Mawr jumped away as if he had seen the devil.

'Steady, fool!' cried Rico.

The bay stood with his four feet spread, his neck arched, his big dark eye glancing sideways with that watchful, frightening look.

'You shouldn't be irritable with him, Rico!' said Lou. 'Steady then, St Mawr! Be steady.'

But a certain anger rose also in her. The creature was so big, so brilliant, and so stupid, standing there with his hind legs spread, ready to jump aside or to rear terrifically, and his great eye glancing with a sort of suspicious frenzy. What was there to be suspicious of, after all? – Rico would do him no harm.

'No one will harm you, St Mawr,' she reasoned, a bit exasperated.

The groom was talking quietly, murmuringly, in Welsh. Rico was slowly advancing again, to put his foot in the stirrup. The stallion was watching from the corner of his eye, a strange glare of suspicious frenzy burning stupidly. Any moment his immense physical force might be let loose in a frenzy of panic – or malice. He was really very irritating.

'Probably he doesn't like that apricot shirt,' said Mrs Witt, 'although it tones into him wonderfully well.'

She pronounced it *ap*–ricot, and it irritated Rico terribly.

'Ought we to have *asked* him before we put it on?' he flashed, his upper lip lifting venomously.

'I should say you should,' replied Mrs Witt coolly.

Rico turned with a sudden rush to the horse. Back went the great animal, with a sudden splashing crash of hoofs on the cobble-stones, and Lewis hanging on like a shadow. Up went the forefeet, showing the belly.

'The thing is accursed,' said Rico, who had dropped the reins in sudden shock, and stood marooned. His rage overwhelmed him like a black flood.

'Nothing in the world is so irritating as a horse that is acting up,' thought Lou.

'Say, Harry!' called Flora from the road. 'Come out here into the road to mount him.'

Lewis looked at Rico and nodded. Then soothing the big, quivering animal, he led him springily out to the road under the trees, where the three friends were waiting. Lou and her mother got quickly into the saddle to follow. And in another moment Rico was mounted and bouncing down the road in the wrong direction, Lewis following on the chestnut. It was some time before Rico could get St Mawr round. Watching him from behind, those waiting could judge how the young baronet hated it.

But at last they set off – Rico ahead, unevenly but quietly, with the two Manby girls, Lou following with the fair young man who had been in a cavalry regiment and who kept looking round for Mrs Witt.

'Don't look round for me,' she called. 'I'm riding behind, out of the dust.'

Just behind Mrs Witt came Lewis. It was a whole cavalcade trotting in the morning sun past the cottages and the cottage gardens, round the field that was the recreation ground, into the deep hedges of the lane.

'Why is St Mawr so bad at starting? Can't you get him into better shape?' she asked over her shoulder.

'Beg your pardon, Mam!'

Lewis trotted a little nearer. She glanced over her shoulder at him, at his dark, unmoved face, his cool little figure.

'I think *Mam* is so ugly. Why not leave it out!' she said. Then she repeated her question.

'St Mawr doesn't trust anybody,' Lewis replied.

'Not you?'

'Yes, he trusts me – mostly.'

'Then why not other people?'

'They're different.'

'All of them?'

'About all of them.'

'How are they different?'

He looked at her with his remote, uncanny grey eyes.

'Different,' he said, not knowing how else to put it.

They rode on slowly, up the steep rise of the wood, then down into a glade where ran a little railway built for hauling some mysterious mineral out of the hill, in war-time, and now already abandoned. Even on this countryside the dead hand of the war lay like a corpse decomposing.

They rode up again, past the foxgloves under the trees. Ahead the brilliant St Mawr and the sorrel and grey horses were swimming like butterflies through the sea of bracken, glittering from sun to shade, shade to sun. Then once more they were on a crest, and through the thinning trees could see the slopes of the moors beyond the next dip.

Soon they were in the open, rolling hills, golden in the morning and empty save for a couple of distant bilberry-pickers, whitish figures pick – pick – picking with curious, rather disgusting assiduity. The horses were on an old trail, which climbed through the pinky tips of heather and ling, across patches of green bilberry. Here and there were tufts of harebells blue as bubbles.

They were out, high on the hills. And there to west lay Wales, folded in crumpled folds, goldish in the morning light, with its moor-like slopes and patches of corn uncannily distinct. Between was a hollow, wide valley of summer haze, showing white farms among trees, and grey slate roofs.

'Ride beside me,' she said to Lewis. 'Nothing makes me want to go back to America like the old look of these little villages. – You have never been to America?'

'No, Mam.'

'Don't you ever want to go?'

'I wouldn't mind going.'

'But you're not just crazy to go?'

'No, Mam.'

'Quite content as you are?'

He looked at her, and his pale, remote eyes met hers.

'I don't fret myself,' he replied.

'Not about anything at all – ever?'

His eyes glanced ahead, at the other riders.

'No, Mam!' he replied, without looking at her.

She rode a few moments in silence.

'What is that over there?' she asked, pointing across the valley. 'What is it called?'

'Yon's Montgomery.'

'Montgomery! And is that *Wales* – ?' she trailed the ending curiously.

'Yes, Mam.'

'Where you come from?'

'No, Mam! I come from Merioneth.'

'Not from Wales? I thought you were Welsh?'

'Yes, Mam. Merioneth *is* Wales.'

'And you are Welsh?'

'Yes, Mam.'

'I had a Welsh grandmother. But I come from Louisiana, and when I go back home, the Negroes still call me Miss Rachel. *Oh, my, it's little Miss Rachel come back home! Why, ain't I mighty glad to see you – u, Miss Rachel!* That gives me such a strange feeling, you know.'

The man glanced at her curiously, especially when she imitated the Negroes.

'Do you feel strange when you go home?' she asked.

'I was brought up by an aunt and uncle,' he said. 'I never want to see them.'

'And you don't have any home?'

'No, Mam.'

'No wife nor anything?'

'No, Mam.'

'But what do you do with your life?'

'I keep to myself.'

'And care about nothing?'

'I mind St Mawr.'

'But you've not always had St Mawr – and you won't always have him. – Were you in the war?'

'Yes, Mam.'

'At the front?'

'Yes, Mam – but I was a groom.'

'And you came out all right?'

'I lost my little finger from a bullet.'

He held up his small, dark left hand, from which the little finger was missing.

'And did you like the war – or didn't you?'

'I didn't like it.'

Again his pale grey eyes met hers, and they looked so non-human and uncommunicative, so without connection, and inaccessible, she was troubled.

'Tell me,' she said. 'Did you never want a wife and a home and children, like other men?'

'No, Mam. I never wanted a home of my own.'

'Nor a wife of your own?'

'No, Mam.'

'Nor children of your own?'

'No, Mam.'

She reined in her horse.

'Now wait a minute,' she said. 'Now tell me why.'

His horse came to standstill, and the two riders faced one another.

'Tell me why – I must know why you never wanted a wife and children and a home. I must know why you're not like other men.'

'I never felt like it,' he said. 'I made my life with horses.'

'Did you hate people very much? Did you have a very unhappy time as a child?'

'My aunt and uncle didn't like me, and I didn't like them.'

'So you've never liked anybody?'

'Maybe not,' he said. 'Not to get as far as marrying them.'

She touched her horse and moved on.

'Isn't that curious!' she said. 'I've loved people, at various times. But I don't believe *I've* ever liked anybody, except a few of our Negroes. I don't like Louise, though she's my daughter and I love her. But I don't really *like* her. – I think you're the first person I've ever liked since I was on our plantation, and we had some *very fine* Negroes. – And I think that's very curious. – Now I want to know if you like *me*.'

She looked at him searchingly, but he did not answer.

'Tell me,' she said. 'I don't mind if you say no. But tell me if you like me. I feel I must know.'

The flicker of a smile went over his face – a very rare thing with him.

'Maybe I do,' he said. He was thinking that she put him on a level with a Negro slave on a plantation: in his idea, Negroes were still slaves. But he did not care where she put him.

'Well, I'm glad – I'm glad if you like me. Because you *don't* like most people, I know that.'

They had passed the hollow where the old Aldecar Chapel hid in damp isolation, beside the ruined mill, over the stream that came down from the moors. Climbing the sharp slope, they saw the folded hills like great shut fingers, with steep, deep clefts between. On the near skyline was a bunch of rocks: and away to the right another bunch.

'Yon's the Angel's Chair,' said Lewis, pointing to the nearer rocks. 'And yon's the Devil's Chair, where we're going.'

'Oh!' said Mrs Witt. 'And aren't we going to the Angel's Chair?'

'No, Mam!'

'Why not?'

'There's nothing to see there. The other's higher, and bigger, and that's where folks mostly go.'

'Is that so! – They give the Devil the higher seat in this country, do they? I think they're right.' And as she got no answer, she added: 'You believe in the Devil, don't you?'

'I never met him,' he answered, evasively.

Ahead, they could see the other horses twinkling in a cavalcade up the slope, the black, the bay, the two greys and the sorrel, sometimes bunching, sometimes straggling. At a gate all waited for Mrs Witt. The fair young man fell in beside her, and talked hunting at her. He had hunted the fox over these hills, and was vigorously excited locating the spot where the hounds first gave cry, etc.

'Really!' said Mrs Witt. '*Really!* Is that so!'

If irony could have been condensed to prussic acid, the fair young man would have ended his life's history with his reminiscences.

They came at last, trotting in file along a narrow track between heather, along the saddle of a hill, to where the knot of pale granite suddenly cropped out. It was one of those places where the spirit of aboriginal England still lingers, the old savage England, whose last blood flows still in a few Englishmen, Welshmen, Cornishmen. The rocks, whitish with weather of all the ages, jutted against the blue August sky, heavy with age-moulded roundnesses.

Lewis stayed below with the horses, the party scrambled rather awkwardly, in their riding-boots, up the foot-worn boulders. At length they stood in the place called the Chair, looking west, west towards Wales, that rolled in golden folds upwards. It was neither impressive nor a very picturesque landscape: the hollow valley with farms, and then the rather bare upheaval of hills, slopes with corn and moor and pasture, rising like a barricade, seemingly high, slantingly. Yet it had a strange effect on the imagination.

'Oh mother,' said Lou, 'doesn't it make you feel old, old, older than anything ever was?'

'It certainly does seem aged,' said Mrs Witt.

'It makes me want to die,' said Lou. 'I feel we've lasted almost too long.'

'Don't say that, Lady Carrington. Why, you're a spring chicken yet: or shall I say an unopened rosebud,' remarked the fair young man.

'No,' said Lou. 'All these millions of ancestors have used all the life up. We're not really alive, in the sense that they were alive.'

'But who?' said Rico. 'Who are *they*?'

'The people who lived on these hills, in the days gone by.'

'But the same people still live on the hills, darling. It's just the same stock.'

'No, Rico. That old fighting stock that worshipped devils among these stones – I'm sure they did – '

'But look here, do you mean they were any better than we are?' asked the fair young man.

Lou looked at him quizzically.

'We don't exist,' she said, squinting at him oddly.

'I jolly well know *I* do,' said the fair young man.

'I consider these days are the best ever, especially for girls,' said Flora Manby. 'And anyhow they're our own days, so I don't jolly well see the use of crying them down.'

They were all silent, with the last echoes of emphatic *joie de vivre* trumpeting on the air, across the hills of Wales.

'Spoken like a brick, Flora,' said Rico. 'Say it again, we may not have the Devil's Chair for a pulpit next time.'

'I do,' reiterated Flora. 'I think this is the best age there ever was for a girl to have a good time in. I read all through H. G. Wells's history, and I shut it up and thanked my stars I live in nineteen-twenty odd, not in some other beastly date when a woman had to cringe before mouldy domineering men.'

After this they turned to scramble to another part of the rocks, to the famous Needle's Eye.

'Thank you so much, I am really better without help,' said Mrs Witt to the fair young man, as she slid downwards till a piece of grey silk stocking showed above her tall boot. But she got her toe in a safe place, and in a moment stood beside him, while he caught her arm protectingly. He might as well have caught the paw of a mountain lion protectingly.

'I should like *so* much to know,' she said suavely, looking into his eyes with a demonish straight look, 'what makes you so certain that you exist?'

He looked back at her, and his jaunty blue eyes went baffled. Then a slow, hot, salmon-coloured flush stole over his face, and he turned abruptly round.

The Needle's Eye was a hole in the ancient grey rock, like a window, looking to England; England at the moment in shadow. A stream wound and glinted in the flat shadow, and beyond that the flat, insignificant hills heaped in mounds of shade. Cloud was coming – the English side was in shadow. Wales was still in the sun, but the shadow was spreading. The day was going to disappoint them. Lou was a tiny bit chilled, already.

Luncheon was still several miles away. The party hastened down to the horses. Lou picked a few sprigs of ling, and some hare-bells, and some straggling yellow flowers: not because she wanted them, but to distract herself. The atmosphere of 'enjoying ourselves' was becoming cruel to her: it sapped all the life out of her. 'Oh, if only I needn't enjoy myself,' she moaned inwardly. But the Manby girls were enjoying themselves so much. 'I think it's frantically lovely up here,' said the other one – not Flora – Elsie.

'It *is* beautiful, isn't it! I'm *so* glad you like it,' replied Rico. And he was really relieved and gratified, because the other one said she was enjoying it so frightfully. He dared not say to Lou, as he wanted to: 'I'm afraid, Lou darling, you don't love it as much as we do.' – He was afraid of her answer: 'No dear, I don't love it at all! I want to be away from these people.'

Slightly piqued, he rode on with the Manby group, and Lou came behind with her mother. Cloud was covering the sky with grey. There was a cold wind. Everybody was anxious to get to the farm for luncheon, and be safely home before rain came.

They were riding along one of the narrow little foot-tracks, mere grooves of grass between heather and bright green bilberry. The blond young man was ahead, then his wife, then Flora, then Rico. Lou, from a little distance, watched the glossy, powerful haunches of St Mawr swaying with life, always too much life, like a menace. The fair young man was whistling a new dance tune.

'That's an awfully attractive tune,' Rico called. 'Do whistle it again, Fred, I should like to memorise it.'

Fred began to whistle it again.

At that moment St Mawr exploded again, shied sideways as if a bomb had gone off, and kept backing through the heather.

'Fool!' cried Rico, thoroughly unnerved: he had been terribly sideways in the saddle, Lou had feared he was going to fall. But he got his seat, and pulled the reins viciously, to bring the horse to order, and put him on the track again. St Mawr began to rear: his favourite trick. Rico got him forward a few yards, when up he went again.

'Fool!' yelled Rico, hanging in the air.

He pulled the horse over backwards on top of him.

Lou gave a loud, unnatural, horrible scream: she heard it herself, at the same time as she heard the crash of the falling horse. Then she saw a pale gold belly, and hoofs that worked and flashed in the air, and St Mawr writhing, straining his head terrifically upwards, his great eyes starting from the naked lines of his nose. With a great neck arching cruelly from the ground, he was pulling frantically at the reins, which Rico still held tight. – Yes, Rico, lying strangely sideways, his eyes also starting from his yellow-white face, among the heather, still clutched the reins.

Young Edwards was rushing forward, and circling round the writhing, immense horse, whose pale-gold, inverted bulk seemed to fill the universe.

'Let him get up, Carrington! Let him get up!' he was yelling, darting warily near, to get the reins. – Another spasmodic convulsion of the horse.

Horror! The young man reeled backwards with his face in his hands. He had got a kick in the face. Red blood running down his chin!

Lewis was there, on the ground, getting the reins out of Rico's hands. St Mawr gave a great curve like a fish, spread his forefeet on the earth and reared his head, looking round in a ghastly fashion. His eyes were arched, his nostrils wide, his face ghastly in a sort of panic. He rested thus, seated with his forefeet planted and his face in panic, almost like some terrible lizard, for several moments. Then he heaved sickeningly to his feet, and stood convulsed, trembling.

There lay Rico, crumpled and rather sideways, staring at the heavens from a yellow, dead-looking face. Lewis, glancing round in a sort of horror, looked in dread at St Mawr again. Flora had been hovering. – She now rushed screeching to the prostrate Rico: 'Harry! Harry! you're not dead! Oh, Harry! Harry! Harry!' Lou had dismounted. – She didn't know when. She stood a little way off, as if spellbound, while Flora cried *Harry! Harry! Harry!*

Suddenly Rico sat up.

'Where is the horse?' he said.

At the same time an added whiteness came on his face, and he bit his lip with pain, and he fell prostrate again in a faint. Flora rushed to put her arm round him.

Where was the horse? He had backed slowly away, in an agony of suspicion, while Lewis murmured to him in vain. His head was raised again, the eyes still starting from their sockets, and a terrible guilty, ghost-like look on his face. When Lewis drew a little nearer he twitched and shrank like a shaken steel spring, away – not to be touched. He seemed to be seeing legions of ghosts, down the dark avenues of all the centuries that have lapsed since the horse became subject to man.

And the other young man? He was still standing, at a little distance, with his face in his hands, motionless, the blood falling on his white shirt, and his wife at his side, pleading, distracted.

Mrs Witt too was there, as if cast in steel, watching. She made no sound and did not move, only, from a fixed, impassive face, watched each thing.

'Do tell me what you think is the matter,' Lou pleaded, distracted, to Flora, who was supporting Rico and weeping torrents of unknown tears.

Then Mrs Witt came forward and began in a very practical manner to unclose the shirt-neck and feel the young man's heart. Rico opened his eyes again, said '*Really!*' and closed his eyes once more.

'It's fainting!' said Mrs Witt. 'We have no brandy.'

Lou, too weary to be able to feel anything, said, 'I'll go and get some.'

She went to her alarmed horse, who stood among the others with her head down, in suspense. Almost unconsciously Lou mounted, set her face ahead, and was riding away.

Then Poppy shied too, with a sudden start, and Lou pulled up. 'Why?' she said to her horse. 'Why did you do that?'

She looked round, and saw in the heather a glimpse of yellow and black.

'A snake!' she said wonderingly.

And she looked closer.

It was a dead adder that had been drinking at a reedy pool in a little depression just off the road, and had been killed with stones. There it lay, also crumpled, its head crushed, its gold-and-yellow back still glittering dully, and a bit of pale-blue belly showing, killed that morning.

Lou rode on, her face set towards the farm. An unspeakable weariness had overcome her. She could not even suffer. Weariness of spirit left her in a sort of apathy.

And she had a vision, a vision of evil. Or not strictly a vision. She became aware of evil, evil, evil, rolling in great waves over the earth. Always she had thought there was no such thing – only a mere negation of good. Now, like an ocean to whose surface she had risen, she saw the dark-grey waves of evil rearing in a great tide.

And it had swept mankind away without mankind's knowing. It had caught up the nations as the rising ocean might lift the fishes, and was sweeping them on in a great tide of evil. They did not know. The people did not know. They did not even wish it. They wanted to be good and to have everything joyful and enjoyable. Everything joyful and enjoyable: for everybody. This was what they wanted, if you asked them.

But at the same time, they had fallen under the spell of evil. It was a soft, subtle thing, soft as water, and its motion was soft and imperceptible, as the running of a tide is invisible to one who is out on the ocean. And they were all out on the ocean, being borne along in the current of the mysterious evil, creatures of the evil principle, as fishes are creatures of the sea.

There was no relief. The whole world was enveloped in one great flood. All the nations, the white, the brown, the black, the yellow, all were immersed in the strange tide of evil that was subtly, irresistibly rising. No one, perhaps, deliberately wished it. Nearly every individual wanted peace and a good time all round: everybody to have a good time.

But some strange thing had happened, and the vast, mysterious force of positive evil was let loose. She felt that from the core of Asia the evil welled up, as from some strange pole, and slowly was drowning earth.

It was something horrifying, something you could not escape from. It had come to her as in a vision, when she saw the pale gold belly of the stallion upturned, the hoofs working wildly, the wicked curved hams of the horse, and then the evil straining of that arched, fish-like neck, with the dilated eyes of the head. Thrown backwards, and working its hoofs in the air. Reversed, and purely evil.

She saw the same in people. They were thrown backwards, and writhing with evil. And the rider, crushed, was still reining them down.

What did it mean? Evil, evil, and a rapid return to the sordid chaos. Which was wrong, the horse or the rider? Or both?

She thought with horror of St Mawr, and of the look on his face. But she thought with horror, a colder horror, of Rico's face as he snarled *Fool!* His fear, his impotence as a master, as a rider, his presumption. And she thought with horror of those other people, so glib, so glibly evil.

What did they want to do, those Manby girls? Undermine, undermine, undermine. They wanted to undermine Rico, just as that fair young man would have liked to undermine her. Believe in nothing, care about nothing: but keep the surface easy, and have a good time. *Let us undermine one another. There is nothing to believe in, so let us undermine everything. But look out! No scenes, no spoiling the game. Stick to the rules of the game. Be sporting, and don't do anything that would make a commotion. Keep the game going smooth and jolly, and bear your bit like a sport. Never, by any chance, injure your fellow man openly. But always injure him secretly. Make a fool of him, and undermine his nature. Break him up by undermining him, if you can. It's good sport.*

The evil! The mysterious potency of evil. She could see it all the time, in individuals, in society, in the press. There it was in socialism and bolshevism: the same evil. But bolshevism made a mess of the outside of life, so turn it down. Try fascism. Fascism would keep the surface of life intact, and carry on the undermining business all the better. All the better sport. Never draw blood. Keep the haemorrhage internal, invisible.

And as soon as fascism makes a break – which it is bound to, because all evil works up to a break – then turn it down. With gusto, turn it down.

Mankind, like a horse, ridden by a stranger, smooth-faced, evil rider. Evil himself, smooth-faced and pseudo-handsome, riding mankind past the dead snake, to the last break.

Mankind no longer its own master. Ridden by this pseudo-handsome ghoul of outward loyalty, inward treachery, in a game of betrayal, betrayal, betrayal. The last of the gods of our era, Judas supreme!

People performing outward acts of loyalty, piety, self-sacrifice. But inwardly bent on undermining, betraying. Directing all their subtle evil will against any positive living thing. Masquerading as the ideal, in order to poison the real.

Creation destroys as it goes, throws down one tree for the rise of another. But ideal mankind would abolish death, multiply itself million upon million, rear up city upon city, save every parasite alive, until the accumulation of mere existence is swollen to a horror. But go on saving life, the ghastly salvation army of ideal mankind. At the same time secretly, viciously, potently undermine the natural creation, betray it with kiss after kiss, destroy it from the inside, till you have the swollen rottenness of our teeming existences. – But keep the game going. Nobody's going to make another bad break, such as Germany and Russia made.

Two bad breaks the secret evil has made: in Germany and in Russia. Watch it! Let evil keep a policeman's eyes on evil! The surface of life must remain unruptured. Production must be heaped upon production. And the natural creation must be betrayed by many more kisses, yet. Judas is the last God, and, by heaven, the most potent.

But even Judas made a break: hanged himself, and his bowels gushed out. Not long after his triumph.

Man must destroy as he goes, as trees fall for trees to rise. The accumulation of life and things means rottenness. Life must destroy life, in the unfolding of creation. We save up life at the expense of the unfolding, till all is full of rottenness. Then at last, we make a break.

What's to be done? Generally speaking, nothing. The dead will have to bury their dead, while the earth stinks of corpses. The individual can but depart from the mass, and try to cleanse himself. Try to hold fast to the living thing, which destroys as it goes, but remains sweet. And in his soul fight, fight, fight to preserve that which is life in him from the ghastly kisses and poison-bites of the myriad evil ones. Retreat to the desert, and fight. But in his soul adhere to that which is life itself, creatively destroying as it goes: destroying the stiff old thing to let the new bud come through. The one passionate principle of creative being, which recognises the natural good, and has a sword for the swarms of evil. Fights, fights, fights to protect itself. But with itself, is strong and at peace.

Lou came to the farm, and got brandy, and asked the men to come out to carry in the injured.

It turned out that the kick in the face had knocked a couple of young Edwards's teeth out, and would disfigure him a little.

'To go through the war, and then get this!' he mumbled, with a vindictive glance at St Mawr.

And it turned out that Rico had two broken ribs and a crushed ankle. Poor Rico, he would limp for life.

'I want St Mawr *shot*!' was almost his first word, when he was in bed at the farm and Lou was sitting beside him.

'What good would that do, dear?' she said.

'The brute is evil. I want him *shot*!'

Rico could make the last word sound like the spitting of a bullet.

'Do you want to shoot him yourself?'

'No. But I want to have him shot. I shall never be easy till I know he has a bullet through him. He's got a wicked character. I don't feel you are safe, with him down there. I shall get one of the Manbys' gamekeepers to shoot him. You might tell Flora – or I'll tell her myself, when she comes.'

'Don't talk about it now, dear. You've got a temperature.'

Was it true St Mawr was evil? She would never forget him writhing and lunging on the ground, nor his awful face when he reared up. But then that noble look of his: surely he was not mean? Whereas all evil had an inner meanness, mean! Was he mean? Was he meanly treacherous? Did he know he could kill, and meanly wait his opportunity?

She was afraid. And if this were true, then he *should* be shot. Perhaps he ought to be shot.

This thought haunted her. Was there something mean and treacherous in St Mawr's spirit, the vulgar evil? If so, then have him shot. At moments, an anger would rise in her, as she thought of his frenzied rearing, and his mad, hideous writhing on the ground, and in the heat of her anger she would want to hurry down to her mother's house and have the creature shot at once. It would be a satisfaction, and a vindication of human rights. Because after all, Rico was so considerate of the brutal horse. But not a spark of consideration did the stallion have for Rico. No, it was the slavish malevolence of a domesticated creature that kept cropping up in St Mawr. The slave, taking his slavish vengeance, then dropping back into subservience.

All the slaves of this world, accumulating their preparations for slavish vengeance, and then, when they have taken it, ready to drop back into servility. Freedom! Most slaves can't be freed, no matter how you let them loose. Like domestic animals, they are, in the long run, more afraid of freedom than of masters: and freed by some generous master, they will at last crawl back to some mean boss, who will have no scruples about kicking them. Because, for them, far better kicks and servility than the hard, lonely responsibility of real freedom.

The wild animal is at every moment intensely self-disciplined, poised in the tension of self-defence, self-preservation, and self-assertion. The moments of relaxation are rare and most carefully chosen. Even sleep is watchful, guarded, unrelaxing, the wild courage pitched one degree higher than the wild fear. Courage, the wild thing's courage to maintain itself alone and living in the midst of a diverse universe.

Did St Mawr have this courage?

And did Rico?

Ah, Rico! He was one of mankind's myriad conspirators, who conspire to live in absolute physical safety, whilst willing the minor disintegration of all positive living.

But St Mawr? Was it the natural wild thing in him which caused these disasters? Or was it the slave, asserting himself for vengeance?

If the latter, let him be shot. It would be a great satisfaction to see him dead.

But if the former –

When she could leave Rico with the nurse, she motored down to her mother for a couple of days. Rico lay in bed at the farm.

Everything seemed curiously changed. There was a new silence about the place, a new coolness. Summer had passed with several thunderstorms, and the blue, cool touch of autumn was about the house. Dahlias and perennial yellow sunflowers were out, the yellow of ending summer, the red coals of early autumn. First mauve tips of Michaelmas daisies were showing. Something suddenly carried her away to the great bare spaces of Texas, the blue sky, the flat, burnt earth, the miles of sunflowers. Another sky, another silence, towards the setting sun.

And suddenly, she craved again for the more absolute silence of America. English stillness was so soft, like an inaudible murmur of voices, of presences. But the silence in the empty spaces of America was still unutterable, almost cruel.

St Mawr was in a small field by himself: she could not bear that he should be always in stable. Slowly she went through the gate towards him. And he stood there looking at her, the bright bay creature.

She could tell he was feeling somewhat subdued, after his late escapade. He was aware of the general human condemnation: the human damning. But something obstinate and uncanny in him made him not relent.

'Hello! St Mawr!' she said, as she drew near, and he stood watching her, his ears pricked, his big eyes glancing sideways at her.

But he moved away when she wanted to touch him.

'Don't trouble,' she said. 'I don't want to catch you or do anything to you.'

He stood still, listening to the sound of her voice, and giving quick, small glances at her. His underlip trembled. But he did not blink. His eyes remained wide and unrelenting. There was a curious malicious obstinacy in him which roused her anger.

'I don't want to touch you,' she said. 'I only want to look at you, and even you can't prevent that.'

She stood gazing hard at him, wanting to know, to settle the question of his meanness or his spirit. A thing with a brave spirit is not mean.

He was uneasy as she watched him. He pretended to hear something, the mares two fields away, and he lifted his head and neighed. She knew the powerful, splendid sound so well: like bells made of living membrane. And he looked so noble again, with his head tilted up, listening, and his male eyes looking proudly over the distance, eagerly.

But it was all a bluff.

He knew, and became silent again. And as he stood there a few yards away from her, his head lifted and wary, his body full of power and tension, his face slightly averted from her, she felt a great animal sadness come from him. A strange animal atmosphere of sadness, that was vague and disseminated through the air, and made her feel as though she breathed grief. She breathed it into her breast, as if it were a great sigh down the ages, that passed into her breast. And she felt a great woe: the woe of human unworthiness. The race of men judged in the consciousness of the animals they have subdued, and there found unworthy, ignoble.

Ignoble men, unworthy of the animals they have subjugated, bred the woe in the spirit of their creatures. St Mawr, that bright horse, one of the kings of creation in the order below man, it had been a fulfilment for him to serve the brave, reckless, perhaps cruel men of the past, who had a flickering, rising flame of nobility in them. To serve that flame of mysterious further nobility. Nothing matters, but that strange flame, of inborn nobility that obliges men to be brave, and onward plunging. And the horse will bear him on.

But now where is the flame of dangerous, forward-pressing nobility in men? Dead, dead, guttering out in a stink of self-sacrifice whose feeble light is a light of exhaustion and *laissez-faire*.

And the horse, is he to go on carrying man forward into this? – this gutter?

No! Man wisely invents motor cars and other machines, automobile and locomotive. The horse is superannuated, for man.

But alas, man is even more superannuated, for the horse.

Dimly in a woman's muse, Lou realised this, as she breathed the horse's sadness, his accumulated vague woe from the generations of latter-day ignobility. And a grief and a sympathy flooded her, for the horse. She realised now how his sadness recoiled into these frenzies of obstinacy and malevolence. Underneath it all was grief, an unconscious, vague, pervading animal grief, which perhaps only Lewis understood, because he felt the same. The grief of the generous creature which sees all ends turning to the morass of ignoble living.

She did not want to say any more to the horse: she did not want to look at him any more. The grief flooded her soul, that made her want to be alone. She knew now what it all amounted to. She knew that the horse, born to serve nobly, had waited in vain for some one noble to serve. His spirit knew that nobility had gone out of men. And this left him high and dry, in a sort of despair.

As she walked away from him, towards the gate, slowly he began to walk after her.

Phoenix came striding through the gate towards her.

'You not afraid of that horse?' he asked sardonically, in his quiet, subtle voice.

'Not at the present moment,' she replied, even more quietly, looking direct at him. She was not in any mood to be jeered at.

And instantly the sardonic grimace left his face, followed by the sudden blankness, and the look of race-misery in the keen eyes.

'Do you want me to be afraid?' she said, continuing to the gate.

'No, I don't want it,' he replied, dejected.

'Are you afraid of him yourself?' she said, glancing round. St Mawr had stopped, seeing Phoenix, and had turned away again.

'I'm not afraid of no horses,' said Phoenix.

Lou went on quietly. At the gate, she asked him, 'Don't you like St Mawr, Phoenix?'

'I like him. He's a very good horse.'

'Even after what he's done to Sir Henry?'

'That don't make no difference to him being a good horse.'

'But suppose he'd done it to you?'

'I don't care. I say it my own fault.'

'Don't you think he is wicked?'

'I don't think so. He don't kick anybody. He don't bite anybody. He don't pitch, he don't buck, he don't do nothing.'

'He rears,' said Lou.

'Well, what is rearing!' said the man, with a slow, contemptuous smile.

'A good deal, when a horse falls back on you.'

'That horse don't want to fall back on you, if you don't make him. If you know how to ride him. That horse want his own way sometime. If you don't let him, you got to fight him. Then look out!'

'Look out he doesn't kill you, you mean!'

'Look out you don't let him,' said Phoenix, with his slow, grim, sardonic smile.

Lou watched the smooth, golden face with its thin line of moustache and its sad eyes with the glint in them. Cruel – there was something cruel in him, right down in the abyss of him. But at the same time, there was an aloneness, and a grim little satisfaction in a fight, and the peculiar courage of an inherited despair. People who inherit despair may at last turn it into greater heroism. It was almost so with Phoenix. Three-quarters of his blood was probably Indian and the remaining quarter, that came through the Mexican father, had the Spanish-American despair to add to the Indian. It was almost complete enough to leave him free to be heroic.

'What are we going to do with him, though?' she asked.

'Why don't you and Mrs Witt go back to America – you never been west. You go west.'

'Where, to California?'

'No. To Arizona or New Mexico or Colorado or Wyoming, anywhere. Not to California.'

Phoenix looked at her keenly, and she saw the desire dark in him. He wanted to go back. But he was afraid to go back alone, empty-handed, as it were. He had suffered too much, and in that country his sufferings would overcome him, unless he had some other background. He had been too much in contact with the white world, and his own world was too dejected, in a sense, too hopeless for his own hopelessness. He needed an alien contact to give him relief.

But he wanted to go back. His necessity to go back was becoming too strong for him.

'What is it like in Arizona?' she asked. 'Isn't it all pale-coloured sand and alkali, and a few cactuses, and terribly hot and deathly?'

'No!' he cried. 'I don't take you there. I take you to the mountains – trees – ' he lifted up his hand and looked at the sky – 'big trees – pine! *Pino-real* and *pinovetes*, smell good. And then you come down, *piñon*, not very tall, and *cedro*, cedar, smell good in the fire. And then you see the desert, away below, go miles and miles, and where the canyon go, the crack where it look red! I know, I been there, working a cattle ranch.'

He looked at her with a haunted glow in his dark eyes. The poor fellow was suffering from nostalgia. And as he glowed at her in that queer mystical way, she too seemed to see that country, with its dark, heavy mountains holding in their lap the great stretches of pale, creased, silent desert that still is virgin of idea, its word unspoken.

Phoenix was watching her closely and subtly. He wanted something of her. He wanted it intensely, heavily, and he watched her as if he could force her to give it him. He wanted her to take him back to America, because, rudderless, he was afraid to go back alone. He wanted her to take him back: avidly he wanted it. She was to be the means to his end.

Why shouldn't he go back by himself? Why should he crave for her to go too? Why should he want her there?

There was no answer, except that he did.

'Why, Phoenix,' she said. 'I might possibly go back to America. But you know, Sir Henry would never go there. He doesn't like America, though he's never been. But I'm sure he'd never go there to live.'

'Let him stay here,' said Phoenix abruptly, the sardonic look on his face as he watched her face. 'You come, and let him stay here.'

'Ah, that's a whole story!' she said, and moved away.

As she went, he looked after her, standing silent and arrested and watching as an Indian watches. It was not love. Personal love counts so little when the greater griefs, the greater hopes, the great despairs and the great resolutions come upon us.

She found Mrs Witt rather more silent, more firmly closed within herself, than usual. Her mouth was shut tight, her brows were arched rather more imperiously than ever, she was revolving some inward problem about which Lou was far too wise to enquire.

In the afternoon Dean Vyner and Mrs Vyner came to call on Lady Carrington.

'What bad luck this is, Lady Carrington!' said the Dean. 'Knocks Scotland on the head for you this year, I'm afraid. How did you leave your husband?'

'He seems to be doing as well as he could do!' said Lou.

'But how *very* unfortunate!' murmured the invalid Mrs Vyner. 'Such a handsome young man, in the bloom of youth! Does he suffer much pain?'

'Chiefly his foot,' said Lou.

'Oh, I *do* so hope they'll be able to restore the ankle. Oh, how dreadful, to be lamed at his age!'

'The doctor doesn't know. There *may* be a limp,' said Lou.

'That horse has certainly left his mark on two good-looking young fellows,' said the Dean. 'If you don't mind my saying so, Lady Carrington, I think he's a bad egg.'

'Who, St Mawr?' said Lou, in her American sing-song.

'Yes, Lady Carrington,' murmured Mrs Vyner, in her invalid's low tone. 'Don't you think he ought to be put away? He seems to me the incarnation of cruelty. His neigh. It goes through me like knives. Cruel! Cruel! Oh, I think he should be put away.'

'How put away?' murmured Lou, taking on an invalid's low tone herself.

'Shot, I suppose,' said the Dean.

'It is quite painless. He'll know nothing,' murmured Mrs Vyner hastily. 'And think of the harm he has done already! Horrible! Horrible!' she shuddered. 'Poor Sir Henry lame for life, and Eddy Edwards disfigured. Besides all that has gone before. Ah no, such a creature ought not to live!'

'To live, and have a groom to look after him and feed him,' said the Dean. 'It's a bit thick, while he's smashing up the very people that give him bread – or oats, since he's a horse. But I suppose you'll be wanting to get rid of him?'

'Rico does,' murmured Lou.

'Very naturally. So should I. A vicious horse is worse than a vicious man – except that you are free to put him six feet underground, and end his vice finally, by your own act.'

'Do you think St Mawr is vicious?' said Lou.

'Well, of course – if we're driven to definitions! – I *know* he's dangerous.'

'And do you think we ought to shoot everything that is dangerous?' asked Lou, her colour rising.

'But Lady Carrington, have you consulted your husband? Surely his wish should be law, in a matter of this sort! And on such an occasion! For *you*, who are a woman, it is enough that the horse is cruel, cruel, evil! I felt it long before anything happened. That evil male cruelty! Ah!' and she clasped her hands convulsively.

'I suppose,' said Lou slowly, 'that St Mawr is really Rico's horse: I gave him to him, I suppose. But I don't believe I could let him shoot him, for all that.'

'Ah, Lady Carrington,' said the Dean breezily, 'you can shift the responsibility. The horse is a public menace, put it at that. We can get an order to have him done away with, at the public expense. And among ourselves we can find some suitable compensation for you, as a mark of sympathy. Which, believe me, is very sincere! One hates to have to destroy a fine-looking animal. But I would sacrifice a dozen rather than have our Rico limping.'

'Yes, indeed,' murmured Mrs Vyner.

'Will you excuse me one moment, while I see about tea,' said Lou, rising and leaving the room. Her colour was high, and there was a glint in her eye. These people almost roused her to hatred. Oh, these awful, house-bred, house-inbred human beings, how repulsive they were!

She hurried to her mother's dressing-room. Mrs Witt was very carefully putting a touch of red on her lips.

'Mother, they want to shoot St Mawr,' she said.

'I know,' said Mrs Witt, as calmly as if Lou had said tea was ready.

'Well – ' stammered Lou, rather put out. 'Don't you think it cheek?'

'It depends, I suppose, on the point of view,' said Mrs Witt dispassionately, looking closely at her lips. 'I don't think the English climate agrees with me. I need something to stand up against, no matter whether it's great heat or great cold. This climate, like the food and the people, is most always lukewarm or tepid, one or the other. And the tepid and the lukewarm are not really my line.' She spoke with a slow drawl.

'But they're in the drawing-room, mother, trying to force me to have St Mawr killed.'

'What about tea?' said Mrs Witt.

'I don't care,' said Lou.

Mrs Witt worked the bell-handle.

'I suppose, Louise,' she said, in her most beaming eighteenth-century manner, 'that these are your guests, so you will preside over the ceremony of pouring out.'

'No, mother, you do it. I can't smile today.'

'I can,' said Mrs Witt.

And she bowed her head slowly, with a faint, ceremoniously-effusive smile, as if handing a cup of tea.

Lou's face flickered to a smile.

'Then you pour out for them. You can stand them better than I can.'

'Yes,' said Mrs Witt. 'I saw Mrs Vyner's hat coming across the churchyard. It looks so like a crumpled cup and saucer, that I have been saying to myself ever since: *Dear Mrs Vyner, can't I fill your cup!* – and then pouring tea into that hat. And I hear the Dean responding: *My head is covered with cream, my cup runneth over.* – That is the way they make *me* feel.'

They marched downstairs, and Mrs Witt poured tea with that devastating correctness which made Mrs Vyner, who was utterly impervious to sarcasm, pronounce her 'indecipherably vulgar'.

But the Dean was the old bull-dog, and he had set his teeth in a subject.

'I was talking to Lady Carrington about that stallion, Mrs Witt.'

'Did you say stallion?' asked Mrs Witt, with perfect neutrality.

'Why, yes, I presume that's what he is.'

'I presume so,' said Mrs Witt colourlessly.

'I'm afraid Lady Carrington is a little sensitive on the wrong score,' said the Dean.

'I beg your pardon,' said Mrs Witt, leaning forward in her most colourless polite manner. 'You mean the stallion's score?'

'Yes,' said the Dean testily. 'The horse St Mawr.'

'The stallion St Mawr,' echoed Mrs Witt, with utmost mild vagueness. She completely ignored Mrs Vyner, who felt plunged like a specimen into methylated spirit. There was a moment's full-stop.

'Yes?' said Mrs Witt naïvely.

'You agree that we can't have any more of these accidents to your young men?' said the Dean rather hastily.

'I certainly do!' Mrs Witt spoke very slowly, and the Dean's lady began to look up. She might find a loop-hole through which to wriggle into the contest. 'You know, Dean, that my son-in-law calls me, for preference, *belle-mère*! It sounds so awfully English when he says it; I always see myself as an old grey mare with a bell round her neck, leading a bunch of horses.' She smiled a prim little smile, *very* conversationally. 'Well!' and she pulled herself up from the aside. 'Now as the bell-mare of the bunch of horses, I shall see to it that my son-in-law doesn't go too near that stallion again. That stallion won't stand mischief.'

She spoke so earnestly that the Dean looked at her with round wide eyes, completely taken aback.

'We all know, Mrs Witt, that the author of the mischief is St Mawr himself,' he said, in a loud tone.

'Really! you think *that*?' Her voice went up in American surprise. 'Why, how *strange* – !' and she lingered over the last word.

'Strange, eh? – After what's just happened?' said the Dean, with a deadly little smile.

'Why, yes! Most strange! I saw with my own eyes my son-in-law pull that stallion over backwards, and hold him down with the reins as tight as he could hold them; pull St Mawr's head backwards on to the ground, till the groom had to crawl up and force the reins out of my son-in-law's hands. Don't you think that was mischievous on Sir Henry's part?'

The Dean was growing purple. He made an apoplectic movement with his hand. Mrs Vyner was turned to a seated pillar of salt, strangely dressed up.

'Mrs Witt, you are playing on words.'

'No, Dean Vyner, I am not. My son-in-law pulled that horse over backwards and pinned him down with the reins.'

'I am sorry for the horse,' said the Dean, with heavy sarcasm.

'I am *very*,' said Mrs Witt, 'sorry for that stallion: *very*!'

Here Mrs Vyner rose as if a chair-spring had suddenly propelled her to her feet. She was streaky pink in the face.

'Mrs Witt,' she panted, 'you misdirect your sympathies. That poor young man – in the beauty of youth.'

'Isn't he *beautiful* – ' murmured Mrs Witt, extravagantly in sympathy. 'He's my daughter's husband!' And she looked at the petrified Lou.

'Certainly!' panted the Dean's wife. 'And you can defend that – that – '

'That stallion,' said Mrs Witt. 'But you see, Mrs Vyner,' she added, leaning forward female and confidential, 'if the old grey mare doesn't defend the stallion, who will? All the blooming young ladies will defend my beautiful son-in-law. You feel so *warmly* for him yourself! I'm an American woman, and I always have to stand up for the accused. And I stand up for that stallion. I say it is not right. He was pulled over backwards and then pinned down by my son-in-law – who may have meant to do it, or may not. And now people abuse him. – Just tell everybody, Mrs Vyner and Dean Vyner' – she looked round at the Dean – 'that the *belle-mère*'s sympathies are with the stallion.'

She looked from one to the other with a faint and gracious little bow, her black eyebrows arching in her eighteenth-century face like black rainbows, and her full, bold grey eyes absolutely incomprehensible.

'Well, it's a peculiar message to have to hand round, Mrs Witt,' the Dean began to boom, when she interrupted him by laying her hand on his arm and leaning forward, looking up into his face like a clinging, pleading female, 'Oh, but *do* hand it, Dean, *do* hand it,' she pleaded, gazing intently into his face.

He backed uncomfortably from that gaze.

'Since you wish it,' he said, in a chest voice.

'I most certainly *do* – ' she said, as if she were wishing the sweetest wish on earth. Then turning to Mrs Vyner, 'Goodbye, Mrs Vyner. We *do* appreciate your coming, my daughter and I.'

'I came out of kindness – ' said Mrs Vyner.

'Oh, I know it, I know it,' said Mrs Witt. 'Thank you *so* much. Goodbye! Goodbye, Dean! Who is taking the morning service on Sunday? I hope it is you, because I want to come.'

'It *is* me,' said the Dean. 'Goodbye! Well, goodbye, Lady Carrington. I shall be going over to see our young man tomorrow, and will gladly take you or anything you have to send.'

'Perhaps mother would like to go,' said Lou, softly, plaintively.

'Well, we shall see,' said the Dean. 'Goodbye for the present!'

Mother and daughter stood at the window watching the two cross the churchyard. Dean and wife knew it, but daren't look round, and daren't admit the fact to one another.

Lou was grinning with a complete grin that gave her an odd, dryad or faun look, intensified.

'It was almost as good as pouring tea into her hat,' said Mrs Witt serenely. 'People like that tire me out. I shall take a glass of sherry.'

'So will I, mother. – It was even better than pouring tea in her hat. – You meant, didn't you, if you poured tea in her hat, to put cream and sugar in first?'

'I did,' said Mrs Witt.

But after the excitement of the encounter had passed away, Lou felt as if her life had passed away too. She went to bed, feeling she could stand no more.

In the morning she found her mother sitting at a window watching a funeral. It was raining heavily, so that some of the mourners even wore mackintosh coats. The funeral was in the poorer corner of the churchyard, where another new grave was covered with wreaths of sodden, shrivelling flowers. The yellowish coffin stood on the wet earth, in the rain: the curate held his hat, in a sort of permanent salute, above his head, like a little umbrella, as he hastened on with the service. The people seemed too wet to weep more wet.

It was a long coffin.

'Mother, do you really *like* watching?' asked Lou irritably, as Mrs Witt sat in complete absorption.

'I do, Louise, I really enjoy it.'

'Enjoy, mother!' – Lou was almost disgusted.

'I'll tell you why. I imagine I'm the one in the coffin – this is a girl of eighteen, who died of consumption – and those are my relatives, and I'm watching them put me away. And you know, Louise, I've come to the conclusion that hardly anybody in the world really lives, and so hardly anybody really dies. They may well say *Oh Death where is thy sting-a-ling-a-ling?* Even Death can't sting those that have never really lived. – I always used to want that – to die without death stinging me. – And I'm sure the girl in the coffin is saying to herself: *Fancy Aunt Emma putting on a drab slicker, and wearing it while they bury me. Doesn't show much respect. But then my mother's family always were common!* I feel there should be a solemn burial of a roll of newspapers containing the account of the death and funeral, next week. It would be just as serious: the grave of all the world's remarks – '

'I don't want to think about it, mother. One ought to be able to laugh at it. I want to laugh at it.'

'Well, Louise, I think it's just as great a mistake to laugh at everything as to cry at everything. Laughter's not the one panacea, either. I should *really* like, before I do come to be buried in a box, to know where I am. That young girl in that coffin never was anywhere – any more than the newspaper remarks on her death and burial. And I begin to wonder if I've ever been anywhere. I seem to have been a daily sequence of newspaper remarks, myself. I'm sure I never really conceived you and gave you birth. It all happened in newspaper notices. It's a newspaper fact that you are my child, and that's about all there is to it.'

Lou smiled as she listened.

'I always knew you were philosophic, mother. But I never dreamed it would come to elegies in a country churchyard, written to your motherhood.'

'*Exactly*, Louise! Here I sit and sing the elegy to my own motherhood I never had any motherhood, except in newspaper fact. I never was a wife, except in newspaper notices. I never was a young girl, except in newspaper remarks. Bury everything I ever said or that was said about me, and you've buried *me*. But since Kind Words Can Never Die, I can't be buried, and death has no sting-a-ling-a-ling for *me!* – Now listen to me, Louise: I want death to be real to me – not as it was to that young girl. I *want* it to hurt me, Louise. If it hurts me enough, I shall know I was alive.'

She set her face and gazed under half-dropped lids at the funeral, stoic, fate-like, and yet, for the first time, with a certain pure wistfulness of a young, virgin girl. This frightened Lou very much. She was so used to the matchless Amazon in her mother, that when she saw her sit there, still, wistful, virginal, tender as a girl who has never taken armour, wistful at the window that only looked on graves, a serious terror took hold of the young woman The terror of *too late*!

Lou felt years, centuries older than her mother, at that moment, with the tiresome responsibility of youth to protect and guide their elders.

'What can we do about it, mother?' she asked protectively.

'Do nothing, Louise. I'm not going to have anybody wisely steering my canoe, now I feel the rapids are near. I shall go with the river. Don't you pretend to do anything for me. I've done enough mischief myself, that way. I'm going down the stream, at last.'

There was a pause.

'But in actuality, what?' asked Lou, a little ironically.

'I don't quite know. Wait a while.'

'Go back to America?'

'That is possible.'

'I may come too.'

'I've always waited for you to go back of your own will.'

Lou went away, wandering round the house. She was so unutterably tired of everything – weary of the house, the graveyard, weary of the thought of Rico. She would have to go back to him tomorrow, to nurse him. Poor old Rico, going on like an amiable machine from day to day. It wasn't his fault. But his life was a rattling nullity, and her life rattled in null correspondence. She had hardly strength enough to stop rattling and be still. Perhaps she had not strength enough.

She did not know. She felt so weak, that unless something carried her away she would go on rattling her bit in the great machine of human life, till she collapsed, and her rattle rattled itself out, and there was a sort of barren silence where the sound of her had been.

She wandered out in the rain, to the coach-house where Lewis and Phoenix were sitting facing one another, one on a bin, the other on the inner doorstep.

'Well,' she said, smiling oddly. 'What's to be done?'

The two men stood up. Outside the rain fell steadily on the flagstones of the yard, past the leaves of trees. Lou sat down on the little iron step of the dogcart.

'That's cold,' said Phoenix. 'You sit here.' And he threw a yellow horse-blanket on the box where he had been sitting.

'I don't want to take your seat,' she said.

'All right, you take it.'

He moved across and sat gingerly on the shaft of the dogcart. Lou seated herself, and loosened her soft tartan shawl. Her face was pink and fresh, and her dark hair curled almost merrily in the damp. But under her eyes were the finger-prints of deadly weariness.

She looked up at the two men, again smiling in her odd fashion.

'What are we going to do?' she asked.

They looked at her closely, seeking her meaning.

'What about?' said Phoenix, a faint smile reflecting on his face, merely because she smiled.

'Oh, everything,' she said, hugging her shawl again. 'You know what they want? They want to shoot St Mawr.'

The two men exchanged glances.

'Who want it?' said Phoenix.

'Why – all our *friends*!' she made a little *moue*. 'Dean Vyner does.'

Again the men exchanged glances. There was a pause. Then Phoenix said, looking aside, 'The boss is selling him.'

'Who?'

'Sir Henry.' – The half-breed always spoke the title with difficulty, and with a sort of sneer. 'He sell him to Miss Manby.'

'How do you know?'

'The man from Corrabach told me last night. Flora, she say it.'

Lou's eyes met the sardonic, empty-seeing eyes of Phoenix direct. There was too much sarcastic understanding. She looked aside.

'What else did he say?' she asked.

'I don't know,' said Phoenix, evasively. 'He say they cut him – else shoot him. Think they cut him – and if he die, he die.'

Lou understood. He meant they would geld St Mawr – at his age.

She looked at Lewis. He sat with his head down, so she could not see his face.

'Do you think it is true?' she asked. 'Lewis? Do you think they would try to geld St Mawr – to make him a gelding?'

Lewis looked up at her. There was a faint deadly glimmer of contempt on his face.

'Very likely, Mam,' he said.

She was afraid of his cold, uncanny pale eyes, with their uneasy grey dawn of contempt. These two men, with their silent, deadly inner purpose, were not like other men. They seemed like two silent enemies of all the other men she knew, Enemies in the great white camp, disguised as servants, waiting the incalculable opportunity. What the opportunity might be, none knew.

'Sir Henry hasn't mentioned anything to me about selling St Mawr to Miss Manby,' she said.

The derisive flicker of a smile came on Phoenix's face.

'He sell him first, and tell you then,' he said, with his deadly impassive manner.

'But do you really think so?' she asked.

It was extraordinary how much corrosive contempt Phoenix could convey, saying nothing. She felt it almost as an insult. Yet it was a relief to her.

'You know, I can't believe it. I can't believe Sir Henry would want to have St Mawr mutilated. I believe he'd rather shoot him.'

'You think so?' said Phoenix, with a faint grin.

Lou turned to Lewis.

'Lewis, will you tell me what you truly think?'

Lewis looked at her with a hard, straight, fearless British stare.

'That man Philips was in the Moon and Stars last night. He said Miss Manby told him she was buying St Mawr, and she asked him, if he thought it would be safe to cut him, and make a horse of him. He said it would be better, take some of the nonsense out of him. He's no good for a sire, anyhow – '

Lewis dropped his head again, and tapped a tattoo with the toe of his rather small foot.

'And what do you think?' said Lou. It occurred to her how sensible and practical Miss Manby was, so much more so than the Dean.

Lewis looked up at her with his pale eyes.

'It won't have anything to do with me,' he said. 'I shan't go to Corrabach Hall.'

'What will you do, then?'

Lewis did not answer. He looked at Phoenix.

'Maybe him and me go to America,' said Phoenix, looking at the void.

'Can he get in?' said Lou.

'Yes, he can. I know how,' said Phoenix.

'And the money?' she said.

'We got money.'

There was a silence, after which she asked of Lewis, 'You'd leave St Mawr to his fate?'

'I can't help his fate,' said Lewis. 'There's too many people in the world for me to help anything.'

'Poor St Mawr!'

She went indoors again, and up to her room: then higher, to the top rooms of the tall Georgian house. From one window she could see the fields in the rain. She could see St Mawr himself, alone as usual, standing with his head up, looking across the fences. He was streaked dark with rain. Beautiful, with his poised head and massive neck, and his supple hindquarters. He was neighing to Poppy. Clear on the wet wind came the sound of his bell-like, stallion's calling, that Mrs Vyner called cruel. It was a strange noise, with a splendour that belonged to another world-age. The mean cruelty of Mrs Vyner's humanitarianism, the barren cruelty of Flora Manby, the eunuch cruelty of Rico. Our whole eunuch civilisation, nasty-minded as eunuchs are, with their kind of sneaking, sterilising cruelty.

Yet even she herself, seeing St Mawr's conceited march along the fence, could not help addressing him, 'Yes, my boy! If you knew what Miss Flora Manby was preparing for you! *She'll* sharpen a knife that will settle you.'

And Lou called her mother.

The two American women stood high at the window, overlooking the wet, close, hedged-and-fenced English landscape. Everything enclosed, enclosed, to stifling. The very apples on the trees looked so shut in, it was impossible to imagine any speck of 'Knowledge' lurking inside them. Good to eat, good to cook, good even for show. But the wild sap of untameable and inexhaustible knowledge – no! Bred out of them. Geldings, even the apples.

Mrs Witt listened to Lou's half-humorous statements.

'You must admit, mother, Flora is a sensible girl,' she said.

'I admit it, Louise.'

'She goes straight to the root of the matter.'

'And eradicates the root. Wise girl! And what is your answer?'

'I don't know, mother. What would you say?'

'I know what *I* should say.'

'Tell me.'

'I should say: *Miss Manby, you may have my husband, but not my horse. My husband won't need emasculating, and my horse I won't have you meddle with. I'll preserve one last male thing in the museum of this world, if I can.*'

Lou listened, smiling faintly.

'That's what I will say,' she replied at length. 'The funny thing is, mother, they think all their men with their bare faces or their little quotation-mark moustaches *are* so tremendously male. That fox-hunting one!'

'I know it. Like little male motor cars. Give him a little gas, and start him on the low gear, and away he goes: all his male gear rattling, like a cheap motor car.'

'I'm afraid I dislike men altogether, mother.'

'You may, Louise. Think of Flora Manby, and how you love the fair sex.'

'After all, St Mawr is better. And I'm glad if he gives them a kick in the face.'

'Ah, Louise!' Mrs Witt suddenly clasped her hands with wicked passion. '*Ay, qué gozo!* as our Juan used to say, on your father's ranch in Texas.' She gazed in a sort of wicked ecstasy out of the window.

They heard Lou's maid softly calling Lady Carrington from below. Lou went to the stairs.

'What is it?'

'Lewis wants to speak to you, my Lady.'

'Send him into the sitting-room.'

The two women went down.

'What is it, Lewis?' asked Lou.

'Am I to bring in St Mawr, in case they send for him from Corrabach?'

'No,' said Lou swiftly.

'Wait a minute,' put in Mrs Witt. 'What makes you think they will send for St Mawr from Corrabach, Lewis?' she asked, suave as a grey leopard cat.

'Miss Manby went up to Flints Farm with Dean Vyner this morning, and they've just come back. They stopped the car, and Miss Manby got out at the field gate, to look at St Mawr. I'm thinking, if she made the bargain with Sir Henry, she'll be sending a man over this afternoon, and if I'd better brush St Mawr down a bit, in case.'

The man stood strangely still, and the words came like shadows of his real meaning. It was a challenge.

'I see,' said Mrs Witt slowly.

Lou's face darkened. She too saw.

'So that is her game,' she said. 'That is why they got me down here.'

'Never mind, Louise,' said Mrs Witt. Then to Lewis: 'Yes, please bring in St Mawr. You wish it, don't you, Louise?'

'Yes,' hesitated Lou. She saw by Mrs Witt's closed face that a counter-move was prepared.

'And Lewis,' said Mrs Witt, 'my daughter may wish you to ride St Mawr this afternoon – not to Corrabach Hall.'

'Very good, Mam.'

Mrs Witt sat silent for some time, after Lewis had gone, gathering inspiration from the wet, grisly gravestones.

'Don't you think it's time we made a move, daughter?' she asked.

'Any move,' said Lou desperately.

'Very well then. My dearest friends, and my *only* friends, in this country, are in Oxfordshire. I will set off to *ride* to Merriton this afternoon, and Lewis will ride with me on St Mawr.'

'But you can't ride to Merriton in an afternoon,' said Lou.

'I know it. I shall ride across country. I shall *enjoy* it, Louise. – Yes. – I shall consider I am on my way back to America. I am most deadly tired of this country. From Merriton I shall make my arrangements to go to America, and take Lewis and Phoenix and St Mawr along with me. I think they want to go. – You will decide for yourself.'

'Yes, I'll come too,' said Lou casually.

'Very well. I'll start immediately after lunch, for I can't *breathe* in this place any longer. Where are Henry's automobile maps?'

Afternoon saw Mrs Witt, in a large waterproof cape, mounted on her horse, Lewis, in another cape, mounted on St Mawr, trotting through the rain, splashing in the puddles, moving slowly southwards. They took the open country, and would pass quite near to Flints Farm. But Mrs Witt did not care. With great difficulty she had managed to fasten a small waterproof roll behind her, containing her night things. She seemed to breathe the first breath of freedom.

And sure enough, an hour or so after Mrs Witt's departure, arrived Flora Manby in a splashed-up motor car, accompanied by her sister, and bringing a groom and a saddle.

'Do you know, Harry sold me St Mawr,' she said. 'I'm just wild to get that horse in hand.'

'How?' said Lou.

'Oh, I don't know. There are ways. Do you mind if Philips rides him over now, to Corrabach? – Oh, I forgot, Harry sent you a note.'

DEAREST LOULINA – Have you been gone from here two days or two years? It seems the latter. You are terribly missed. Flora wanted so much to buy St Mawr, to save us further trouble, that I have sold him to her. She is giving me what we paid: rather, what you paid; so of course the money is yours. I am thankful we are rid of the animal, and that he falls into competent hands – I asked her please to remove him from your charge today. And I can't tell how much easier I am in my mind, to think of him gone. You are coming back to me tomorrow, aren't you? I shall think of nothing else but you, till I see you.

    Arrivederci, darling dear!

R.

'I'm so sorry,' said Lou. 'Mother went on horseback to see some friends, and Lewis went with her on St Mawr. He knows the road.'

'She'll be back this evening?' said Flora.

'I don't know. Mother is so uncertain. She may be away a day or two.'

'Well, here's the cheque for St Mawr.'

'No, I won't take it now – no, thank you – not till mother comes back with the goods.'

Flora was chagrined. The two women knew they hated one another. The visit was a brief one.

Mrs Witt rode on in the rain, which abated as the afternoon wore down, and the evening came without rain, and with a suffusion of pale yellow light. All the time she had trotted in silence, with Lewis just behind her. And she scarcely saw the heather-covered hills with the deep clefts between them, nor the oak-woods, nor the lingering foxgloves, nor the earth at all. Inside herself she felt a profound repugnance for the English country: she preferred even the crudeness of Central Park in New York.

And she felt an almost savage desire to get away from Europe, from every-thing European. Now she was really *en route*, she cared not a straw for St Mawr or for Lewis or anything. Something just writhed inside her, all the time, against Europe. That closeness, that sense of cohesion, that sense of being fused into a lump with all the rest – no matter how much distance you kept – this drove her mad. In America the cohesion was a matter of choice and will. But in Europe it was organic, like the helpless particles of one sprawling body. And the great body in a state of incipient decay.

She was a woman of fifty-one: and she seemed hardly to have lived a day. She looked behind her – the thin trees and swamps of Louisiana, the sultry, sub-tropical excitement of decaying New Orleans, the vast bare dryness of Texas, with mobs of cattle in an illumined dust! The half-European thrills of New York! The false stability of Boston! A clever husband, who was a brilliant lawyer, but who was far more thrilled by his cattle ranch than by his law: and who drank heavily and died. The years of first widowhood in Boston, consoled by a self-satisfied sort of intellectual courtship from clever men. – For curiously enough, while she wanted it, she had always been able to compel men to pay court to her. All kinds of men. – Then a rather dashing time in New York – when she was in her early forties. Then the long *visual* philandering in Europe. She left off 'loving', save through the eye, when she came to Europe. And when she made her trips to America, she found it was finished there also, her 'loving'.

What was the matter? Examining herself, she had long ago decided that her nature was a destructive force. But then, she justified herself, she had only destroyed that which was destructible. If she could have found something indestructible, especially in men, though she would have fought against it, she would have been glad at last to be defeated by it.

That was the point. She really wanted to be defeated, in her own eyes. And nobody had ever defeated her. Men were never really her match. A woman of terrible strong health, she felt even that in her strong limbs there was far more electric power than in the limbs of any man she had met. That curious fluid electric force, that could make any man kiss her hand, if she so willed it. A queen, as far as she wished. And not having been very clever at school, she always had the greatest respect for the mental powers. Her own were not mental powers. Rather electric, as of some strange physical dynamo within her. So she had been ready to bow before Mind.

But alas! After a brief time, she had found Mind, at least the man who was supposed to have the mind, bowing before her. Her own peculiar dynamic force was stronger than the force of Mind. She could make Mind kiss her hand.

And not by any sensual tricks. She did not really care about sensualities, especially as a younger woman. Sex was a mere adjunct. She cared about the mysterious, intense, dynamic sympathy that could flow between her and some 'live' man – a man who was highly conscious, a real live wire. That she cared about.

But she had never rested until she had made the man she admired – and admiration was the root of her attraction to any man – made him kiss her hand. In both senses, actual and metaphorical. Physical and metaphysical. Conquered his country.

She had always succeeded. And she believed that, if she cared, she always *would* succeed. In the world of living men. Because of the power that was in her, in her arms, in her strong, shapely, but terrible hands, in all the great dynamo of her body.

For this reason she had been so terribly contemptuous of Rico, and of Lou's infatuation. Ye gods! what was Rico in the scale of men!

Perhaps she despised the younger generation too easily. Because she did not see its sources of power, she concluded it was powerless. Whereas perhaps the power of accommodating oneself to any circumstances and committing oneself to no circumstance is the last triumph of mankind.

Her generation had had its day. She had had her day. The world of her men had sunk into a sort of insignificance. And with a great contempt she despised the world that had come into place instead: the world of Rico and Flora Manby, the world represented, to her, by the Prince of Wales.

In such a world there was nothing even to conquer. It gave everything and gave nothing to everybody and anybody all the time. *Dio benedetto!* as Rico would say. A great complicated tangle of nonentities ravelled in nothingness. So it seemed to her.

Great God! This was the generation she had helped to bring into the world.

She had had her day. And, as far as the mysterious battle of life went, she had won all the way. Just as Cleopatra, in the mysterious business of a woman's life, won all the way.

Though that bald tough Caesar had drawn his iron from the fire without losing much of its temper. And he had gone his way. And Antony surely was splendid to die with.

In her life there had been no tough Caesar to go his way in cold blood, away from her. Her men had gone from her like dogs on three legs, into the crowd. And certainly there was no gorgeous Antony to die for and with.

Almost she was tempted in her heart to cry: 'Conquer me, oh God, before I die!' – But then she had a terrible contempt for the God that was supposed to rule this universe. She felt she could make *Him* kiss her hand. Here she was a woman of fifty-one, past the change of life. And her great dread was to die an empty, barren death. Oh, if only Death might open dark wings of mystery and consolation. To die an easy, barren death. To pass out as she had passed in, without mystery or the rustling of darkness! That was her last, final, ashy dread.

'Old!' she said to herself. 'I am not *old*! I have lived many years, that is all. But I am as timeless as an hour-glass that turns morning and night, and spills the hours of sleep one way, the hours of consciousness the other way, without itself being affected. Nothing in all my life has ever truly affected me. – I believe Cleopatra only tried the asp, as she tried her pearls in wine, to see if it would really, really have any effect on her. Nothing had ever really had any effect on her, neither Caesar nor Antony nor any of them. Never once had she really been lost, lost to herself. Then try death, see if that trick would work. If she would lose herself that way. – Ah death – !'

But Mrs Witt mistrusted death too. She felt she might pass out as a bed of asters passes out in autumn, to mere nothingness. – And something in her longed to die, at least, *positively*: to be folded then at last into throbbing wings of mystery, like a hawk that goes to sleep. Not like a thing made into a parcel and put into the last rubbish-heap.

So she rode trotting across the hills, mile after mile, in silence. Avoiding the roads, avoiding everything, avoiding everybody, just trotting forwards, towards night.

And by nightfall they had travelled twenty-five miles. She had motored around this country, and knew the little towns and the inns. She knew where she would sleep.

The morning came beautiful and sunny. A woman so strong in health, why should she ride with the fact of death before her eyes? But she did.

Yet in sunny morning she must do something about it.

'Lewis!' she said. 'Come here and tell me something, please! Tell me,' she said, 'do you believe in God?'

'In God!' he said, wondering. 'I never think about it.'

'But do you say your prayers?'

'No, Mam!'

'Why don't you?'

He thought about it for some minutes.

'I don't like religion. My aunt and uncle were religious.'

'You don't like religion,' she repeated. 'And you don't believe in God. – Well, then – '

'Nay!' he hesitated. 'I never said I didn't believe in God. – Only I'm sure I'm not a Methodist. And I feel a fool in a proper church. – And I feel a fool saying my prayers. – And I feel a fool when ministers and parsons come getting at me. – I never think about God, if folks don't try to make me.' He had a small, sly smile, almost gay.

'And you don't like feeling a fool?' She smiled rather patronisingly.

'No, Mam.'

'Do I make you feel a fool?' she asked, drily.

He looked at her without answering.

'Why don't you answer?' she said, pressing.

'I think you'd like to make a fool of me sometimes,' he said.

'Now?' she pressed.

He looked at her with that slow, distant look.

'Maybe!' he said, rather unconcernedly.

Curiously, she couldn't touch him. He always seemed to be watching her from a distance, as if from another country. Even if she made a fool of him, something in him would all the time be far away from her, not implicated.

She caught herself up in the personal game, and returned to her own isolated questions. A vicious habit made her start the personal tricks. She didn't want to, really.

There was something about this little man – sometimes, to herself, she called him *Little Jack Horner, Sat in a corner* – that irritated her and made her want to taunt him. His peculiar little inaccessibility, that was so tight and easy.

Then again, there was something, his way of looking at her as if he looked from out of another country, a country of which he was an inhabitant, and where she had never been: this touched her strangely. Perhaps behind this little man was the mystery. In spite of the fact that in actual life, in her world, he was only a groom, almost chétif, with his legs a little bit horsey and bowed; and of no education, saying *Yes Mam!* and *No Mam!* and accomplishing nothing, simply nothing at all on the face of the earth. Strictly a nonentity.

And yet, what made him perhaps the only real entity to her, his seeming to inhabit another world than hers. A world dark and still, where language never ruffled the growing leaves, and seared their edges like a bad wind.

Was it an illusion, however? Sometimes she thought it was. Just bunkum, which she had faked up, in order to have something to mystify about.

But then, when she saw Phoenix and Lewis silently together, she knew there *was* another communion, silent, excluding her. And sometimes when Lewis was alone with St Mawr: and once, when she saw him pick up a bird that had stunned itself against a wire: she had realised another world, silent, where each creature is alone in its own aura of silence, the mystery of power: as Lewis had power with St Mawr, and even with Phoenix.

The visible world, and the invisible. Or rather, the audible and the inaudible. She had lived so long, and so completely, in the visible, audible world. She would not easily admit that other, inaudible. She always wanted to jeer, as she approached the brink of it.

Even now, she wanted to jeer at the little fellow, because of his holding himself inaccessible within the inaudible, silent world. And she knew he knew it.

'Did you never want to be rich, and be a gentleman, like Sir Henry?' she asked.

'I would many times have liked to be rich. But I never exactly wanted to be a gentleman,' he said.

'Why not?'

'I can't exactly say. I should be uncomfortable if I was like they are.'

'And are you comfortable now?'

'When I'm let alone.'

'And do they let you alone? Does the world let you alone?'

'No, they don't.'

'Well then – !'

'I keep to myself all I can.'

'And are you comfortable, as you call it, when you keep to yourself?'

'Yes, I am.'

'But when you keep to yourself, what do you keep to? What precious treasure have you to keep to?'

He looked, and saw she was jeering.

'None,' he said. 'I've got nothing of that sort.'

She rode impatiently on ahead.

And the moment she had done so, she regretted it. She might put the little fellow, with contempt, out of her reckoning. But no, she would not do it.

She had put so much out of her reckoning: soon she would be left in an empty circle, with her empty self at the centre.

She reined in again.

'Lewis!' she said. 'I don't want you to take offence at anything I say.'

'No, Mam.'

'I don't want you to say just *No Mam!* all the time!' she cried impulsively. 'Promise me.'

'Yes, Mam!'

'But really! Promise me you won't be offended at whatever I say.'

'Yes, Mam!'

She looked at him searchingly. To her surprise, she was almost in tears. A woman of her years! And with a servant!

But his face was blank and stony, with a stony, distant look of pride that made him inaccessible to her emotions. He met her eyes again: with that cold distant look, looking straight into her hot, confused, pained self. So cold and as if merely refuting her. He didn't believe her, nor trust her, nor like her even. She was an attacking enemy to him. Only he stayed really far away from her, looking down at her from a sort of distant hill where her weapons could not reach: not quite.

And at the same time, it hurt him in a dumb, living way, that she made these attacks on him. She could see the cloud of hurt in his eyes, no matter how distantly he looked at her.

They bought food in a village shop, and sat under a tree near a field where men were already cutting oats, in a warm valley. Lewis had stabled the horses for a couple of hours, to feed and rest. But he came to join her under the tree, to eat. – He sat at a little distance from her, with the bread and cheese in his small brown hands, eating silently, and watching the harvesters. She was cross with him, and therefore she was stingy, would give him nothing to eat but dry bread and cheese. Herself, she was not hungry. – So all the time he kept his face a little averted from her. As a matter of fact, he kept his whole being averted from her, away from her. He did not want to touch her, nor to be touched by her. He kept his spirit there, alert, on its guard, but out of contact. It was as if he had unconsciously accepted the battle, the old battle. He was her target, the old object of her deadly weapons. But he refused to shoot back. It was as if he caught all her missiles in full flight, before they touched him, and silently threw them on the ground behind him. And in some essential part of himself he ignored her, staying in another world.

That other world! Mere male armour of artificial imperviousness! It angered her.

Yet she knew, by the way he watched the harvesters, and the grasshoppers popping into notice, that it was another world. And when a girl went by, carrying food to the field, it was at him she glanced. And he gave that quick, animal little smile that came from him unawares. Another world!

Yet also, there was a sort of meanness about him: a *suffisance*! A keep-yourself-for-yourself, and don't give yourself away.

Well! – she rose impatiently.

It was hot in the afternoon, and she was rather tired. She went to the inn and slept, and did not start again till tea-time.

Then they had to ride rather late. The sun sank, among a smell of cornfields, clear and yellow-red behind motionless dark trees. Pale smoke rose from cottage chimneys. Not a cloud was in the sky, which held the upward-floating light like a bowl inverted on purpose. A new moon sparkled and was gone. It was beginning of night.

Away in the distance, they saw a curious pinkish glare of fire, probably furnaces. And Mrs Witt thought she could detect the scent of furnace smoke, or factory smoke. But then she always said that of the English air: it was never quite free of the smell of smoke, coal-smoke.

They were riding slowly on a path through fields, down a long slope. Away below was a puther of lights. All the darkness seemed full of half-spent crossing lights, a curious uneasiness. High in the sky a star seemed to be walking. It was an aeroplane with a light. Its buzz rattled above. Not a space, not a speck of this country that wasn't humanised, occupied by the human claim. Not even the sky.

They descended slowly through a dark wood, which they had entered through a gate. Lewis was all the time dismounting and opening gates, letting her pass, shutting the gate and mounting again.

So, in a while she came to the edge of the wood's darkness, and saw the open pale concave of the world beyond. The darkness was never dark. It shook with the concussion of many invisible lights, lights of towns, villages, mines, factories, furnaces, squatting in the valleys and behind all the hills.

Yet, as Rachel Witt drew rein at the gate emerging from the wood, a very big, soft star fell in heaven, cleaving the hubbub of this human night with a gleam from the greater world.

'See! a star falling!' said Lewis, as he opened the gate.

'I saw it,' said Mrs Witt, walking her horse past him.

There was a curious excitement of wonder, or magic, in the little man's voice. Even in this night something strange had stirred awake in him.

'You ask me about God,' he said to her, walking his horse alongside in the shadow of the wood's-edge, the darkness of the old Pan, that kept our artificially-lit world at bay. 'I don't know about God. But when I see a star fall like that out of long-distance places in the sky: and the moon sinking saying *Goodbye! Goodbye!*

Goodbye! and nobody listening: I think I hear something, though I wouldn't call it God.'

'What then?' said Rachel Witt.

'And you smell the smell of oak-leaves now,' he said, 'now the air is cold. They smell to me more alive than people. The trees hold their bodies hard and still, but they watch and listen with their leaves. And I think they say to me: *Is that you passing there, Morgan Lewis? All right, you pass quickly, we shan't do anything to you. You are like a holly-bush.*'

'Yes,' said Rachel Witt, drily. *'Why?'*

'All the time, the trees grow, and listen. And if you cut a tree down without asking pardon, trees will hurt you some time in your life, in the night time.'

'I suppose,' said Rachel Witt, 'that's an old superstition.'

'They say that ash trees don't like people. When the other people were most in the country – I mean like what they call fairies, that have all gone now – they liked ash trees best. And you know the little green things with little small nuts in them, that come flying down from ash trees – *pigeons*, we call them – they're the seeds – the other people used to catch them and eat them before they fell to the ground. And that made the people so they could hear trees living and feeling things. – But when all these people that there are now came to England, they liked the oak trees best, because their pigs ate the acorns. So now you can tell the ash trees are mad, they want to kill all these people. But the oak trees are many more than the ash trees.'

'And do you eat the ash tree seeds?' she asked.

'I always ate them, when I was little. Then I wasn't frightened of ash trees, like most of the others. And I wasn't frightened of the moon. If you didn't go near the fire all day, and if you didn't eat any cooked food nor anything that had been in the sun, but only things like turnips or radishes or pig-nuts, and then went without any clothes on, in the full moon, then you could see the people in the moon, and go with them. They never have fire, and they never speak, and their bodies are clear almost like jelly. They die in a minute if there's a bit of fire near them. But they know more than we. Because unless fire touches them, they never die. They see people live and they see people perish, and they say, people are only like twigs on a tree, you break them off the tree, and kindle fire with them. You made a fire of them, and they are gone, the fire is gone, everything is gone. But the people of the moon don't die, and fire is nothing to them. They look at it from the distance of the sky, and see it burning things up, people all appearing and disappearing like twigs that come in spring and you cut them in autumn and make a fire of them and they are gone. And they say: what do people matter? If you want to matter, you must become a moon-boy. Then all your life, fire can't blind you and people can't hurt you. Because at full moon you can join the moon people, and go through the air and pass any cool places, pass through rocks and through the trunks of trees, and when you come to people lying warm in bed, you punish them.'

'How?'

'You sit on the pillow where they breathe, and you put a web across their mouth, so they can't breathe the fresh air that comes from the moon. So they go on breathing the same air again and again, and that makes them more and more stupefied. The sun gives out heat, but the moon gives out fresh air. That's what the moon people do: they wash the air clean with moonlight.'

He was talking with a strange eager naiveté that amused Rachel Witt, and made her a little uncomfortable in her skin. Was he after all no more than a sort of imbecile?

'Who told you all this stuff?' she asked abruptly.

And, as abruptly, he pulled himself up.

'We used to say it, when we were children.'

'But you don't believe it? It *is* only childishness, after all.'

He paused a moment or two.

'No,' he said, in his ironical little day-voice. 'I know I shan't make anything but a fool of myself, with that talk. But all sorts of things go through our heads, and some seem to linger, and some don't. But you asking me about God put it into my mind, I suppose. I don't know what sort of things I believe in: only I know it's not what the chapel-folks believe in. We none of us believe in them when it comes to earning a living, or, with you people, when it comes to spending your fortune. Then we know that bread costs money, and even your sleep you have to pay for. – That's work. Or, with you people, it's just owning property and seeing you get your value for your money. – But a man's mind is always full of things. And some people's minds, like my aunt and uncle, are full of religion and hell for everybody except themselves. And some people's minds are all money, money, money, and how to get hold of something they haven't got hold of yet. And some people, like you, are always curious about what everybody else in the world is after. And some people are all for enjoying themselves and being thought much of, and some, like Lady Carrington, don't know what to do with themselves. Myself, I don't want to have in my mind the things other people have in their minds. I'm one that likes my own things best. And if, when I see a bright star fall, like tonight, I think to myself: *There's movement in the sky. The world is going to change again. They're throwing something to us from the distance, and we've got to have it, whether we want it or no*t. Tomorrow *there will be a difference for everybody, thrown out of the sky upon us, whether we want it or not:* then that's how I want to think, so let me please myself.'

'You know what a shooting star actually is, I suppose? – and that there are always many in August, because we pass through a region of them?'

'Yes, Mam, I've been told. But stones don't come at us from the sky for nothing. Either it's like when a man tosses an apple to you out of his orchard, as you go by. Or it's like when somebody shies a stone at you, to cut your head open. You'll never make me believe the sky is like an empty house with a slate falling from the roof. The world has its own life, the sky has a life of its own, and never is it like stones rolling down a rubbish heap and falling into a pond. Many things twitch and twitter within the sky, and many things happen beyond us. My own way of thinking is my own way.'

'I never knew you talk so much.'

'No, Mam. It's your asking me that about God. Or else it's the night-time. I don't believe in God and being good and going to Heaven. Neither do I worship idols, so I'm not a heathen as my aunt called me. Never from a boy did I want to believe the things they kept grinding in their guts at home, and at Sunday school, and at school. A man's mind has to be full of something, so I keep to what we used to think as lads. It's childish nonsense, I know it. But it suits me. Better than other people's stuff. Your man Phoenix is about the same, when he lets on. – Anyhow, it's my own stuff, that we believed as lads, and I like it better than other people's stuff. – You asking about God made me let on. But I would never belong to any club, or trades union, and God's the same to my mind.'

With this he gave a little kick to his horse, and St Mawr went dancing excitedly along the highway they now entered, leaving Mrs Witt to trot after as rapidly as she could.

When she came to the hotel, to which she had telegraphed for rooms, Lewis disappeared, and she was left thinking hard.

It was not till they were twenty miles from Merriton, riding through a slow morning mist, and she had a rather far-away, wistful look on her face, unusual for her, that she turned to him in the saddle and said, 'Now don't be surprised, Lewis, at what I am going to say. I am going to ask you, now, supposing I wanted to marry you, what should you say?'

He looked at her quickly, and was at once on his guard.

'That you didn't mean it,' he replied hastily.

'Yes' – she hesitated, and her face looked wistful and tired. – 'Supposing I *did* mean it. Supposing I did *really*, from my heart, want to marry you and be a wife to you – ' she looked away across the fields – 'then what should you say?'

Her voice sounded sad, a little broken.

'Why, Mam!' he replied, knitting his brow and shaking his head a little. 'I should say you didn't mean it, you know. Something would have come over you.'

'But supposing I *wanted* something to come over me?'

He shook his head.

'It would never do, Mam! Some people's flesh and blood is kneaded like bread: and that's me. And some are rolled like fine pastry, like Lady Carrington. And some are mixed with gunpowder. They're like a cartridge you put in a gun, Mam.'

She listened impatiently.

'Don't talk,' she said, 'about bread and cakes and pastry, it all means nothing. You used to answer short enough, *Yes, Mam! No, Mam!* That will do now. Do you mean *Yes!* or *No!*?'

His eyes met hers. She was again hectoring.

'No, Mam!' he said, quite neutral.

'Why?'

As she waited for his answer, she saw the foundations of his loquacity dry up, his face go distant and mute again, as it always used to be, till these last two days, when it had had a funny touch of inconsequential merriness.

He looked steadily into her eyes, and his look was neutral, sombre, and hurt. He looked at her as if infinite seas, infinite spaces divided him and her. And his eyes seemed to put her away beyond some sort of fence. An anger congealed cold like lava, set impassive against her and all her sort.

'No, Mam. I couldn't give my body to any woman who didn't respect it.'

'But I do respect it, I do!' – she flushed hot like a girl.

'No, Mam. Not as *I* mean it,' he replied.

There was a touch of anger against her in his voice, and a distance of distaste.

'And how do *you* mean it?' she replied, the full sarcasm coming back into her tones. She could see that, as a woman to touch and fondle he saw her as repellent: only repellent.

'I have to be a servant to women now,' he said, 'even to earn my wage. I could never touch with my body a woman whose servant I was.'

'You're not my servant: my daughter pays your wages. – And all that is beside the point, between a man and a woman.'

'No woman who I touched with my body should ever speak to me as you speak to me, or think of me as you think of me,' he said.

'But! –' she stammered. 'I think of you – with love. And can you be so unkind as to notice the way I speak? You know it's only my way.'

'You, as a woman,' he said, 'you have no respect for a man.'

'Respect! Respect!' she cried. 'I'm likely to lose what respect I have left. I know I can *love* a man. But whether a man can love a woman –'

'No,' said Lewis. 'I never could, and I think I never shall. Because I don't want to. The thought of it makes me feel shame.'

'What do you mean?' she cried.

'Nothing in the world,' he said, 'would make me feel such shame as to have a woman shouting at me, or mocking at me, as I see women mocking and despising the men they marry. No woman shall touch my body, and mock me or despise me. No woman.'

'But men must be mocked, or despised even, sometimes.'

'No. Not this man. Not by the woman I touch with my body.'

'Are you perfect?'

'I don't know. But if I touch a woman with my body, it must put a lock on her, to respect what I will never have despised: never!'

'What will you never have despised?'

'My body! And my touch upon the woman.'

'Why insist so on your body?' – And she looked at him with a touch of contemptuous mockery, raillery.

He looked her in the eyes, steadily, and coldly, putting her away from him, and himself far away from her.

'Do you expect that any woman will stay your humble slave, today?' she asked cuttingly.

But he only watched her, coldly, distant, refusing any connection.

'Between men and women, it's a question of give and take. A man can't expect *always* to be humbly adored.'

He watched her still, cold, rather pale, putting her far from him. Then he turned his horse and set off rapidly along the road, leaving her to follow.

She walked her horse and let him go, thinking to herself: 'There's a little bantam cock. And a groom! Imagine it! Thinking he can dictate to a woman!'

She was in love with him. And he, in an odd way, was in love with her. She had known it by the odd, uncanny merriment in him, and his unexpected loquacity. But he would not have her come physically near him. Unapproachable there as a cactus, guarding his 'body' from her contact. As if contact with her would be mortal insult and fatal injury to his marvellous 'body'.

What a little cock-sparrow!

Let him ride ahead. He would have to wait for her somewhere.

She found him at the entrance to the next village. His face was pallid and set. She could tell he felt he had been insulted, so he had congealed into stiff insentience.

'At the bottom of all men is the same,' she said to herself: 'an empty, male conceit of themselves.'

She too rode up with a face like a mask, and straight on to the hotel.

'Can you serve dinner to myself and my servant?' she asked at the inn: which, fortunately for her, accommodated motorists, otherwise they would have said *No!*

'I think,' said Lewis as they came in sight of Merriton, 'I'd better give Lady Carrington a week's notice.'

A complete little stranger! And an impudent one.

'Exactly as you please,' she said.

She found several letters from her daughter at Marshal Place.

DEAR MOTHER – No sooner had you gone off than Flora appeared, not at all in the bud, but rather in full blow. She demanded her victim; Shylock demanding the pound of flesh: and wanted to hand over the shekels.

Joyfully I refused them. She said 'Harry' was much better, and invited him and me to stay at Corrabach Hall till he was quite well: it would be less strain on your household, while he was still in bed and helpless. So the plan is, that he shall be brought down on Friday, if he is really fit for the journey, and we drive straight to Corrabach. I am packing his bags and mine, clearing up our traces: his trunks to go to Corrabach, mine to stay here and make up their minds. – I am going to Flints Farm again tomorrow, dutifully, though I am no flower for the bedside. – I do so want to know if Rico has already called her Fiorita: or perhaps Florecita. It reminds me of old William's joke: *Now yuh tell me, little Missy: which is the best posey that grow?* And the hushed whisper in which he said the answer: *The Collyposy!* Oh dear, I am so tired of feeling spiteful, but how else is one to feel?

You looked most prosaically romantic, setting off in a rubber cape, followed by Lewis. Hope the roads were not very slippery, and that you had a good time, *à la Mademoiselle de Maupin*. Do remember, dear, not to devour little Lewis before you have got half way –

DEAR MOTHER – I half expected word from you before I left, but nothing came. Forrester drove me up here just before lunch. Rico seems much better, almost himself, and a little more than that. He broached our staying at Corrabach very tactfully. I told him Flora had asked me, and it seemed a good plan. Then I told him about St Mawr. He was a little piqued, and there was a pause of very disapproving silence. Then he said: *Very well, darling. If you wish to keep the animal, do so by all means. I make a present of him again.* Me: *That's so good of you, Rico. Because I know revenge is sweet.* Rico: *Revenge, Loulina! I don't think I was selling him for vengeance! Merely to get rid of him to Flora, who can keep better hold over him.* Me: *But you know, dear, she was going to geld him!* Rico: *I don't think anybody knew it. We only wondered if it were possible, to make him more amenable. Did she tell you?* Me: *No – Phoenix did. He had it from a groom.* Rico: *Dear me! A concatenation of grooms! So your mother rode off with Lewis, and carried St Mawr out of danger! I understand! Let us hope worse won't befall.* Me: *Whom?* Rico: *Never mind, dear! It's so lovely to see you. You are looking rested. I thought those Countess of Wilton roses the most marvellous things in the world, till you came, now they're quite in the background.* He had some very lovely red roses, in a crystal bowl: the room smelled of roses. Me: *Where did they come from?* Rico: *Oh, Flora brought them!* Me: *Bowl and all?* Rico: *Bowl and all! Wasn't it dear of her?* Me: *Why yes! But then she's the goddess of flowers, isn't she?* Poor darling, he was offended that I should twit him while he is ill, so I relented. He has had a couple of marvellous invalid's bed-jackets sent from London: one a pinkish yellow, with rose-arabesque facings: this one in fine cloth. But unfortunately he has already dropped soup on it. The other is a lovely silvery and blue and green soft brocade. He had that one on to receive me, and I at once complimented him on it. He has got a new ring too: sent by Aspasia Weingartner, a rather lovely intaglio of Priapus under an apple bough, at least, so he says it is. He made a naughty face, and said: *The Priapus stage is rather advanced for poor me.* I asked what the Priapus stage was, but he said *Oh, nothing!* Then nurse said: *There's a big classical dictionary that Miss Manby brought up, if you wish to see it.* So I have been studying the Classical Gods. The world always was a queer place. It's a very queer one when Rico is the god Priapus. He would go round the orchard painting life-like apples on the trees, and inviting nymphs to come and eat them. And the nymphs would pretend they were real: *Why, Sir Prippy, what stunningly naughty apples!* There's nothing so artificial as sinning nowadays. I suppose it once was real.

I'm bored here: wish I had my horse.

DEAR MOTHER – I'm so glad you are enjoying your ride. I'm sure it is like riding into history, like the Yankee at the Court of King Arthur, in those old bye-lanes and Roman roads. They still fascinate me: at least, more before I get there than when I am actually there. I begin to feel real American and to resent the past. Why doesn't the past decently bury itself, instead of sitting waiting to be admired by the present?

Phoenix brought Poppy. I am so fond of her: rode for five hours yesterday. I was glad to get away from this farm. The doctor came, and said Rico would be able to go down to Corrabach tomorrow. Flora came to hear the bulletin, and sailed back full of zest. Apparently Rico is going to do a portrait of her, sitting up in bed. What a mercy the bedclothes won't be mine, when Priapus wields his palette from the pillow.

Phoenix thinks you intend to go to America with St Mawr, and that I am coming too, leaving Rico this side. – I wonder. I feel so unreal, nowadays, as if I too were nothing more than a painting by Rico on a millboard. I feel almost too unreal even to make up my mind to anything. It is terrible when the life-flow dies out of one, and everything is like cardboard, and oneself is like cardboard. I'm sure it is worse than being dead. I realised it yesterday when Phoenix and I had a picnic lunch by a stream. You see I must imitate you in all things. He found me some watercresses, and they tasted so damp and *alive*, I knew how deadened I was. Phoenix wants us to go and have a ranch in Arizona, and raise horses, with St Mawr, if willing, for Father Abraham. I wonder if it matters what one does: if it isn't all the same thing over again? Only Phoenix, his funny blank face, makes my heart melt and go sad. But I believe he'd be cruel too. I saw it in his face when he didn't know I was looking. Anything though, rather than this deadness and this paint-Priapus business. *Au revoir*, mother dear! Keep on having a good time –

DEAR MOTHER – I had your letter from Merriton: am so glad you arrived safe and sound in body and temper. There was such a funny letter from Lewis, too: I enclose it. What makes him take this extraordinary line? But I'm writing to tell him to take St Mawr to London, and wait for me there. I have telegraphed Mrs Squire to get the house ready for me. I shall go straight there.

Things developed here, as they were bound to. I just couldn't bear it. No sooner was Rico put in the automobile than a self-conscious importance came over him, like when the wounded hero is carried into the middle of the stage. *Why so solemn, Rico dear?* I asked him, trying to laugh him out of it. *Not solemn, dear, only feeling a little transient.* I don't think he knew himself what he meant. Flora was on the steps as the car drew up, dressed in severe white. She only needed an apron, to become a nurse: or a veil, to become a bride. Between the two, she had an unbearable air of a woman in seduced circum-stances, as *The Times* said. She ordered two menservants about in subdued, you would have said hushed, but competent tones. And then I saw there was a touch of the priestess about her as well: Cassandra preparing for her viola-tion: Iphigenia, with Rico for Orestes, on a stretcher: he looking like Adonis, fully prepared to be an unconscionable time in dying. They had given him a lovely room, downstairs, with doors opening on to a little garden all of its own. I believe it was Flora's boudoir. I left nurse and the men to put him to bed. Flora was hovering anxiously in the passage outside. *Oh what a marvellous room! Oh how colourful, how beautiful!* came Rico's tones, the hero behind the scenes. I must say, it was like a harvest festival, with roses and gaillardias in the shadow, and cornflowers in the light, and a bowl of grapes, and nectarines among leaves. *I'm so anxious that he should be happy*, Flora said to me in the passage. *You know him best. Is there anything else I could do for him?* Me: *Why, if you went to the piano and sang, I'm sure he'd love it. Couldn't you sing: Oh, my love is like a rred, rred rrose!* – You know how Rico imitates Scotch!

Thank goodness I have a bedroom upstairs: nurse sleeps in a little antechamber to Rico's room. The Edwards are still here, the blonde young man with some very futuristic plaster on his face. *Awfully good of you to come!* he said to me, looking at me out of one eye, and holding my hand fervently. How's that for cheek: *It's awfully good of Miss Manby to let me come*, said I. He: *Ah, but Flora is always a sport, a topping good sport!*

I don't know what's the matter, but it just all put me into a fiendish temper. I felt I couldn't sit there at luncheon with that bright, youthful company, and hear about their tennis and their polo and their hunting and have their flirtatiousness making me sick. So I asked for a tray in my room. Do as I might, I couldn't help being horrid.

Oh, and Rico! He really is too awful. Lying there in bed with every ear open, like Adonis waiting to be persuaded not to die. Seizing a hushed moment to take Flora's hand and press it to his lips, murmuring: *How awfully good you are to me, dear Flora!* And Flora: *I'd be better, if I knew how, Harry!* So cheerful with it all! No, it's too much. My sense of humour is leaving me: which means, I'm getting into too bad a temper to be able to ridicule it all. I suppose I feel in the minority. It's an awful thought, to think that most all the young people in the world are like this: so bright and cheerful, and *sporting*, and so brimming with libido. How awful!

I said to Rico: *You're very comfortable here, aren't you?* He: *Comfortable! It's comparative heaven*. Me: *Would you mind if I went away?* A deadly pause. He is deadly afraid of being left alone with Flora. He feels safe so long as I am about, and he can take refuge in his marriage ties. He: *Where do you want to go, dear?* Me: *To mother. To London. Mother is planning to go to America, and she wants me to go.* Rico: *But you don't want to go t–he–e–re–e!* You know, mother, how Rico can put a venomous emphasis on a word, till it suggests pure poison. It nettled me. *I'm not sure*, I said. Rico: *Oh, but you can't stand that awful America*. Me: *I want to try again*. Rico: *But Lou dear, it will be winter before you get there. And this is absolutely the wrong moment for me to go over there. I am only just making headway over here. When I am absolutely sure of a position in England, then we nip across the Atlantic and scoop in a few dollars, if you like. Just now, even when I am well, would be fatal. I've only just sketched in the outline of my success in London, and one ought to arrive in New York ready-made as a famous and important Artist.* Me: *But mother and I didn't think of going to New York. We thought we'd sail straight to New Orleans – if we could: or to Havana. And then go west to Arizona.* The poor boy looked at me in such distress. *But Loulina darling, do you mean you want to leave me in the lurch for the winter season? You can't mean it. We're just getting on so splendidly, really!* – I was surprised at the depth of feeling in his voice: how tremendously his career as an artist – a popular artist – matters to him. I can never believe it. – You know, mother, you and I feel alike about daubing paint on canvas: every possible daub that can be daubed has already been done, so people ought to leave off. Rico is so shrewd. I always think he's got his tongue in his cheek, and I'm always staggered once more to find that he takes it absolutely seriously. His career! The Modern British Society of Painters: perhaps even the Royal Academy! Those people we see in London, and those portraits Rico does! He may even be a second Laszlo, or a thirteenth Orpen, and die happy! Oh! mother! How can it really matter to *anybody*!

But I was really rather upset, when I realised how his heart was fixed on his career, and that I might be spoiling everything for him. So I went away to think about it. And then I realised how unpopular you are, and how unpopular I shall be myself, in a little while. A sort of hatred for people has come over me. I hate their ways and their bunk, and I feel like kicking them in the face, as St Mawr did that young man. Not that I should ever do it. And I don't think I should ever have made my final announcement to Rico, if he hadn't been such a beautiful pig in clover, here at Corrabach Hall. He has known the Manbys all his life; they and he are sections of one engine. He would be far happier with Flora: or I won't say happier, because there is something in him which rebels: but he would on the whole fit much better. I myself am at the end of my limit, and beyond it. I can't "mix" any more, and I refuse to. I feel like a bit of eggshell in the mayonnaise: the only thing is to take it out, you can't beat it in. I *know* I shall cause a fiasco, even in Rico's career, if I stay. I shall go on being rude and hateful to people as I am at Corrabach, and Rico will lose all his nerve.

So I have told him. I said this evening, when no one was about: *Rico dear, listen to me seriously. I can't stand these people. If you ask me to endure another week of them, I shall either become ill, or insult them, as mother does. And I don't want to do either.* Rico: *But darling, isn't everybody perfect to you?* Me: *I tell you, I shall just make a break, like St Mawr, if I don't get out. I simply can't stand people.* – The poor darling, his face goes so blank and anxious. He knows what I mean, because, except that they tickle his vanity all the time, he hates them as much as I do. But his vanity is the chief thing to him. He: *Lou darling, can't you wait till I get up, and we can go away to the Tyrol or somewhere for a spell?* Me: *Won't you come with me to America, to the South-West? I believe it's marvellous country.* – I saw his face switch into hostility; quite vicious. He: *Are you so keen on spoiling everything for me? Is that what I married you for? Do you do it deliberately?* Me: *Everything is already spoilt for me. I tell you I can't stand people, your Floras and your Aspasias, and your forthcoming young Englishmen. After all, I am an Ameri-can, like mother, and I've got to go back.* He: *Really! And am I to come along as part of the luggage? Labelled cabin!* Me: *You do as you wish, Rico.* He: *I wish to God you did as you wished, Lou dear. I'm afraid you do as Mrs Witt wishes. I always heard that the holiest thing in the world was a mother.* Me: *No dear, it's just that I can't stand people.* He (with a snarl): *And I suppose I'm lumped in as* PEOPLE! And when he'd said it, it was true. We neither of us said anything for a time. Then he said, calculating: *Very well, dear! You take a trip to the land of stars and stripes, and I'll stay here and go on with my work. And when you've seen enough of their stars and tasted enough of their stripes, you can come back and take your place again with me.* – We left it at that.

You and I are supposed to have important business connected with our estates in Texas – it sounds so well – so we are making a hurried trip to the States, as they call them. I shall leave for London early next week –

Mrs Witt read this long letter with satisfaction. She herself had one strange craving: to get back to America. It was not that she idealised her native country: she was a tartar of restlessness there, quite as much as in Europe. It was not that she expected to arrive at any blessed abiding place. No, in America she would go on fuming and chafing the same. But at least she would be in America, in her own country. And that was what she wanted.

She picked up the sheet of poor paper, that had been folded in Lou's letter. It was the letter from Lewis, quite nicely written. 'Lady Carrington, I write to tell you and Sir Henry that I think I had better quit your service, as it would be more comfortable all round. If you will write and tell me what you want me to do with St Mawr, I will do whatever you tell me. With kind regards to Lady Carrington and Sir Henry, I remain, Your obedient servant, Morgan Lewis.'

Mrs Witt put the letter aside, and sat looking out of the window. She felt, strangely, as if already her soul had gone away from her actual surroundings. She was there, in Oxfordshire, in the body, but her spirit had departed else-where. A listlessness was upon her. It was with an effort she roused herself, to write to her lawyer in London, to get her release from her English obligations. Then she wrote to the London hotel.

For the first time in her life she wished she had a maid, to do little things for her. All her life, she had had too much energy to endure anyone hanging round her, personally. Now she gave up. Her wrists seemed numb, as if the power in her were switched off.

When she went down they said Lewis had asked to speak to her. She had hardly seen him since they arrived at Merriton.

'I've had a letter from Lady Carrington, Mam. She says will I take St Mawr to London and wait for her there. But she says I am to come to you, Mam, for definite orders.'

'Very well, Lewis. I shall be going to London in a few days' time. You arrange for St Mawr to go up one day this week, and you will take him to the Mews.

Come to me for anything you want. And don't talk of leaving my daughter. We want you to go with St Mawr to America, with us and Phoenix.'

'And your horse, Mam?'

'I shall leave him here at Merriton. I shall give him to Miss Atherton.'

'Very good, Mam!'

'Dear Daughter: I shall be in my old quarters in Mayfair next Saturday, calling the same day at your house to see if everything is ready for you. Lewis has fixed up with the railway: he goes to town tomorrow. The reason of his letter was that I had asked him if he would care to marry me, and he turned me down with emphasis. But I will tell you about it. You and I are the scribe and the Pharisee; I never could write a letter, and you could never leave off – '

'Dearest Mother: I smelt something rash, but I know it's no use saying: how *could* you? I only wonder, though, that you should think of marriage. You know, dear, I ache in every fibre to be left alone, from all that sort of thing. I feel all bruises, like one who has been assassinated. I do so understand why Jesus said: *Noli me tangere*. Touch me not, I am not yet ascended unto the Father. Everything had hurt him so much, wearied him so beyond endurance, he felt he could not bear one little human touch on his body. I am like that. I can hardly bear even Elena to hand me a dress. As for a man – and marriage – ah no! *Noli me tangere, homine!* I am not yet ascended unto the Father. Oh, leave me alone, leave me alone! That is all my cry to all the world.

'Curiously, I feel that Phoenix understands what I feel. He leaves me so understandingly alone, he almost gives me my sheath of aloneness: or at least, he protects me in my sheath. I am grateful for him.

'Whereas Rico feels my aloneness as a sort of shame to himself. He wants at least a blinding *pretence* of intimacy. Ah, intimacy! The thought of it fills me with aches, and the pretence of it exhausts me beyond myself.

'Yes, I long to go away to the west, to be away from the world like one dead and in another life, in a valley that life has not yet entered.

'Rico asked me: What are you doing with St Mawr? When I said we were taking him with us, he said: *Oh, the Corpus delicti!* Whether that means anything I don't know. But he has grown sarcastic beyond my depth.

'I shall see you tomorrow – '

Lou arrived in town, at the dead end of August, with her maid and Phoenix. How wonderful it seemed to have London empty of all her set: her own little house to herself, with just the housekeeper and her own maid. The fact of being alone in those surroundings was so wonderful. It made the surroundings themselves seem all the more ghastly. Everything that had been actual to her was turning ghostly: even her little drawing-room was the ghost of a room, belonging to the dead people who had known it, or to all the dead generations that had brought such a room into being, evolved it out of their quaint domestic desires. And now, in herself, those desires were suddenly spent: gone out like a lamp that suddenly dies. And then she saw her pale, delicate room with its little green agate bowl and its two little porcelain birds and its soft, roundish chairs, turned into something ghostly, like a room set out in a museum. She felt like fastening little labels on the furniture: *Lady Louise Carrington Lounge Chair, Last used August 1923.* Not for the benefit of posterity: but to remove her own self into another world, another realm of existence.

'My house, my house, my house, how can I ever have taken so much pains about it!' she kept saying to herself. It was like one of her old hats, suddenly discovered neatly put away in an old hatbox. And what a horror: an old 'fashionable' hat.

Lewis came to see her, and he sat there in one of her delicate mauve chairs, with his feet on a delicate old carpet from Turkestan, and she just wondered. He wore his leather gaiters and khaki breeches as usual, and a faded blue shirt. But his beard and hair were trimmed, he was tidy. There was a certain fineness of contour about him, a certain subtle gleam, which made him seem, apart from his rough boots, not at all gross, or coarse, in that setting of rather silky, oriental furnishings. Rather he made the Asiatic, sensuous exquisiteness of her old rugs and her old white Chinese figures seem a weariness. Beauty! What was beauty, she asked herself? The Oriental exquisiteness seemed to her all like dead flowers whose hour had come, to be thrown away.

Lou could understand her mother's wanting, for a moment, to marry him. His detachedness and his acceptance of something in destiny which people cannot accept. Right in the middle of him he accepted something from destiny, that gave him a quality of eternity. He did not care about persons, people, even events. In his own odd way he was an aristocrat, inaccessible in his aristocracy. But it was the aristocracy of the invisible powers, the greater influences, nothing to do with human society.

'You don't really want to leave St Mawr, do you?' Lou asked him. 'You don't really want to quit, as you said?'

He looked at her steadily, from his pale grey eyes, without answering, not knowing what to say.

'Mother told me what she said to you. – But she doesn't mind, she says you are entirely within your rights. She has a real regard for you. But we mustn't let our regards run us into actions which are beyond our scope, must we? That makes everything unreal. But you will come with us to America with St Mawr, won't you? We depend on you.'

'I don't want to be uncomfortable,' he said.

'Don't be,' she smiled. 'I myself hate unreal situations – I feel I can't stand them any more. And most marriages are unreal situations. But apart from anything exaggerated, you like being with mother and me, don't you?'

'Yes, I do. I like Mrs Witt as well. But not – '

'I know. There won't be any more of that – '

'You see, Lady Carrington,' he said, with a little heat, 'I'm not by nature a marrying man. And I'd feel I was selling myself.'

'Quite! – Why do you think you are not a marrying man, though?'

'Me! I don't feel myself after I've been with women.' He spoke in a low tone, looking down at his hands. 'I feel messed up. I'm better to keep to myself – Because – ' and here he looked up with a flare in his eyes: 'women – they only want to make you give in to them, so that they feel almighty, and you feel small.'

'Don't you like feeling small?' Lou smiled. 'And don't you want to make them give in to you?'

'Not me,' he said. 'I don't want nothing. Nothing, I want.'

'Poor mother!' said Lou. 'She thinks if she feels moved by a man, it must result in marriage – or that kind of thing. Surely she makes a mistake. I think you and Phoenix and mother and I might live somewhere in a far-away wild place, and make a good life: so long as we didn't begin to mix up marriage, or love or that sort of thing into it. It seems to me men and women have really hurt one another so much, nowadays, that they had better stay apart till they have learned to be gentle with one another again. Not all this forced passion and destructive philandering. Men and women should stay apart, till their hearts grow gentle towards one another again. Now, it's only each one fighting for his own – or her own – underneath the cover of tenderness.'

'*Dear! – darling! – Yes, my love!*' mocked Lewis, with a faint smile of amused contempt.

'Exactly. People always say *dearest!* when they hate each other most.'

Lewis nodded, looking at her with a sudden sombre gloom in his eyes. A queer bitterness showed on his mouth. But even then he was so still and remote.

The housekeeper came and announced The Honourable Laura Ridley. This was like a blow in the face to Lou. She rose hurriedly – and Lewis rose, moving to the door.

'Don't go please, Lewis,' said Lou – and then Laura Ridley appeared in the doorway. She was a woman a few years older than Lou, but she looked younger. She might have been a shy girl of twenty-two, with her fresh complexion, her hesitant manner, her round, startled brown eyes, her bobbed hair.

'Hello!' said the newcomer. 'Imagine your being back! I saw you in Paddington.' Those sharp eyes would see everything.

'I thought everyone was out of town,' said Lou. 'This is Mr Lewis.'

Laura gave him a little nod, then sat on the edge of her chair.

'No,' she said. 'I did go to Ireland to my people, but I came back. I prefer London when I can be more or less alone in it. I thought I'd just run in for a moment, before you're gone again. – Scotland, isn't it?'

'No, mother and I are going to America.'

'America! Oh, I thought it was Scotland.'

'It was. But we have suddenly to go to America.'

'I see! – And what about Rico?'

'He is staying on in Shropshire. Didn't you hear of his accident?'

Lou told about it briefly.

'But how awful!' said Laura. 'But there! I knew it! I had a premonition when I saw that horse. We had a horse that killed a man. Then my father got rid of it. But ours was a mare, that one. Yours is a boy.'

'A full grown man, I'm afraid.'

'Yes, of course, I remember – But how awful! I suppose you won't ride in the Row. The awful people that ride there nowadays, anyhow! Oh, aren't they awful! Aren't people monstrous, really! My word, when I see the horses crossing Hyde Park Corner, on a wet day, and coming down smash on those slippery stones, giving their riders a fractured skull! – No joke!'

She enquired details of Rico.

'Oh, I suppose I shall see him when he gets back,' she said. 'But I'm sorry you are going. I shall miss you, I'm afraid. Though you won't be staying long in America. No one stays there longer than they can help.'

'I think the winter through, at least,' said Lou.

'Oh, all the winter! So long? I'm sorry to hear *that*. You're one of the few, very few people one can talk *really* simply with. Extraordinary, isn't it, how few really simple people there are! And they get fewer and fewer. I stayed a fortnight with my people, and a week of that I was in bed. It was really horrible. They really try to take the life out of one, *really!* Just because one won't be as they are, and play their game. I simply refused, and came away.'

'But you can't cut yourself off altogether,' said Lou.

'No, I suppose not. One has to see somebody. Luckily one has a few artists for friends. They're the only real people, anyhow – ' She glanced round inquisitively at Lewis, and said, with a slight, impertinent elvish smile on her virgin face, 'Are you an artist?'

'No, Mam!' he said. 'I'm a groom.'

'Oh, I see!' She looked him up and down.

'Lewis is St Mawr's master,' said Lou.

'Oh, the horse! the terrible horse!' She paused a moment. Then again she turned to Lewis with that faint smile, slightly condescending, slightly impertinent, slightly flirtatious.

'Aren't you afraid of him?' she asked.

'No, Mam.'

'Aren't you, *really!* – And can you always master him?'

'Mostly. He knows me.'

'Yes! I suppose that's it.' – She looked him up and down again, then turned away to Lou.

'What have you been painting lately?' said Lou. Laura was not a bad painter.

'Oh, hardly anything. I haven't been able to get on at all. This is one of my bad intervals.'

Here Lewis rose, and looked at Lou.

'All right,' she said. 'Come in after lunch, and we'll finish those arrangements.'

Laura gazed after the man, as he dived out of the room, as if her eyes were gimlets that could bore into his secret.

In the course of the conversation she said, 'What a curious little man that was!'

'Which?'

'The groom who was here just now. *Very* curious! Such peculiar eyes. I shouldn't wonder if he had psychic powers.'

'What sort of psychic powers?' said Lou.

'Could *see* things. – And hypnotic too. He might have hypnotic powers.'

'What makes you think so?'

'He gives me that sort of feeling. Very curious! Probably he hypnotises the horse – Are you leaving the horse here, by the way, in stable?'

'No, taking him to America.'

'Taking him to America! How extraordinary!'

'It's mother's idea. She thinks he might be valuable as a stock horse on a ranch. You know we still have interest in a ranch in Texas.'

'Oh, I see! Yes, probably he'd be very valuable, to improve the breed of the horses over there. – My father has some very lovely hunters. Isn't it disgraceful, he would never let me ride!'

'Why?'

'Because we girls weren't important, in his opinion. – So you're taking the horse to America! With the little man?'

'Yes, St Mawr will hardly behave without him.'

'I see! – I see–ee–ee! Just you and Mrs Witt and the little man. I'm sure you'll find he has psychic powers.'

'I'm afraid I'm not so good at finding things out,' said Lou.

'Aren't you? No, I suppose not. I am. I have a flair. I sort of *smell* things. – Then the horse is already here, is he? When do you think you'll sail?'

'Mother is finding a merchant boat that will go to Galveston, Texas, and take us along with the horse. She knows people who will find the right thing. But it takes time.'

'What a much nicer way to travel, than on one of those great liners! Oh, how awful they are! So vulgar! Floating palaces they call them! My word, the people inside the palaces! – Yes, I should say that would be a much pleasanter way of travelling: on a cargo boat.'

Laura wanted to go down to the Mews to see St Mawr. The two women went together.

St Mawr stood in his box, bright and tense as usual.

'Yes!' said Laura Ridley, with a slight hiss. 'Yes! Isn't he beautiful. Such very perfect legs!' – She eyed him round with those gimlet, sharp eyes of hers. 'Almost a pity to let him go out of England. We need some of his perfect *bone*, I feel – But his eye! Hasn't he got a look in it, my word!'

'I can never see that he looks wicked,' said Lou.

'Can't you!' – Laura had a slight hiss in her speech, a sort of aristocratic decision in her enunciation, that got on Lou's nerves. – 'He looks wicked to me!'

'He's not *mean*,' said Lou. 'He'd never do anything mean to you.'

'Oh, mean! I daresay not. No! I'll grant him that, he gives fair warning. His eye says *Beware!* – But isn't he a beauty, *isn't* he!' Lou could feel the peculiar reverence for St Mawr's breeding, his show qualities. Herself, all she cared about was the horse himself, his real nature. 'Isn't it extraordinary,' Laura continued, 'that you never get a *really* perfectly satisfactory animal! There's always something wrong. And in men too. Isn't it curious? there's always something – something wrong – or something missing. Why is it?'

'I don't know,' said Lou. She felt unable to cope with any more. And she was glad when Laura left her.

The days passed slowly, quietly, London almost empty of Lou's acquaintances. Mrs Witt was busy getting all sorts of papers and permits: such a fuss! The battle light was still in her eye. But about her nose was a dusky, pinched look that made Lou wonder.

Both women wanted to be gone: they felt they had already flown in spirit, and it was weary, having the body left behind.

At last all was ready: they only awaited the telegram to say when their cargo boat would sail. Trunks stood there packed, like great stones locked for ever. The Westminster house seemed already a shell. Rico wrote and telegraphed, tenderly, but there was a sense of relentless effort in it all, rather than of any real tenderness. He had taken his position.

Then the telegram came, the boat was ready to sail.

'There, now!' said Mrs Witt, as if it had been a sentence of death.

'Why do you look like that, mother?'

'I feel I haven't an ounce of energy left in my body.'

'But how queer, for you, mother. Do you think you are ill?'

'No, Louise. I just feel that way: as if I hadn't an ounce of energy left in my body.'

'You'll feel yourself again, once you are away.'

'Maybe I shall.'

After all, it was only a matter of telephoning. The hotel and the railway porters and taxi-men would do the rest.

It was a grey, cloudy day, cold even. Mother and daughter sat in a cold first-class carriage and watched the little Hampshire countryside go past: little, old, unreal it seemed to them both, and passing away like a dream whose edges only are in consciousness. Autumn! Was this autumn? Were these trees, fields, villages? It seemed but the dim, dissolving edges of a dream, without inward substance.

At Southampton it was raining: and just a chaos, till they stepped on to a clean boat, and were received by a clean young captain, quite sympathetic, and quite a gentleman. Mrs Witt, however, hardly looked at him, but went down to her cabin and lay down in her bunk.

There, lying concealed, she felt the engines start, she knew the voyage had begun. But she lay still. She saw the clouds and the rain, and refused to be disturbed.

Lou had lunch with the young captain, and she felt she ought to be flirty. The young man was so polite and attentive. And she wished so much she were alone.

Afterwards, she sat on deck and saw the Isle of Wight pass shadowy, in a misty rain. She didn't know it was the Isle of Wight. To her, it was just the lowest bit of the British Isles. She saw it fading away: and with it, her life, going like a clot of shadow in a mist of nothingness. She had no feelings about it, none: neither about Rico, nor her London house, nor anything. All passing in a grey curtain of rainy drizzle, like a death, and she, with not a feeling left.

They entered the Channel, and felt the slow heave of the sea. And soon, the clouds broke in a little wind. The sky began to clear. By mid-afternoon it was blue summer, on the blue, running waters of the Channel. And soon, the ship steering for Santander, there was the coast of France, the rocks twinkling like some magic world.

The magic world! And back of it, that post-war Paris, which Lou knew only too well, and which depressed her so thoroughly. Or that post-war Monte Carlo, the Riviera still more depressing even than Paris. No, no one must land, even on magic coasts. Else you found yourself in a railway station and a 'centre of civilisation' in five minutes.

Mrs Witt hated the sea, and stayed, as a rule, practically the whole time of the crossing, in her bunk. There she was now, silent, shut up like a steel trap, as in her tomb. She did not even read. Just lay and stared at the passing sky. And the only thing to do was to leave her alone.

Lewis and Phoenix hung on the rail, and watched everything. Or they went down to see St Mawr. Or they stood talking in the doorway of the wireless operator's cabin. Lou begged the Captain to give them jobs to do.

The queer, transitory, unreal feeling, as the ship crossed the great, heavy Atlantic. It was rather bad weather. And Lou felt, as she had felt before, that this grey, wolf-like, cold-blooded Ocean hated men and their ships and their smoky passage. Heavy grey waves, a low-sagging sky: rain: yellow, weird evenings with snatches of sun: so it went on. Till they got way South, into the westward-running stream. Then they began to get blue weather and blue water.

To go South! Always to go South, away from the arctic horror as far as possible! That was Lou's instinct. To go out of the clutch of greyness and low skies, of sweeping rain, and of slow, blanketing snow. Never again to see the mud and rain and snow of a northern winter, nor to feel the idealistic, Christianised tension of the now irreligious North.

As they neared Havana, and the water sparkled at night with phosphorus, and the flying-fishes came like drops of bright water, sailing out of the massive-slippery waves, Mrs Witt emerged once more. She still had that shut-up, deathly look on her face. But she prowled round the deck, and manifested at least a little interest in affairs not her own. Here at sea, she hardly remembered the existence of St Mawr or Lewis or Phoenix. She was not very deeply aware even of Lou's existence. – But of course, it would all come back, once they were on land.

They sailed in hot sunshine out of a blue, blue sea, past the castle into the harbour at Havana. There was a lot of shipping: and this was already America. Mrs Witt had herself and Lou put ashore immediately. They took a motor car and drove at once to the great boulevard that is the centre of Havana. Here they saw a long rank of motor cars, all drawn up ready to take a couple of hundred American tourists for one more tour. There were the tourists, all with badges in their coats, lest they should get lost.

'They get so drunk by night,' said the driver in Spanish, 'that the policemen find them lying in the road – turn them over, see the badge – and, hup! – carry them to their hotel.' He grinned sardonically.

Lou and her mother lunched at the Hotel d'Angleterre, and Mrs Witt watched transfixed while a couple of her countrymen, a stout successful man and his wife, lunched abroad. They had cocktails – then lobster – and a bottle of hock – then a bottle of champagne – then a half-bottle of port. – And Mrs Witt rose in haste as the liqueurs came. For that successful man and his wife had gone on imbibing with a sort of fixed and deliberate will, apparently tasting nothing, but saying to themselves: Now we're drinking Rhine wine! Now we're drinking 1912 champagne. Yah, Prohibition! Thou canst not put it over me. – Their complexions became more and more lurid. Mrs Witt fled, fearing a Havana débâcle. But she said nothing.

In the afternoon, they motored into the country, to see the great brewery gardens, the new villa suburb, and through the lanes past the old, decaying plantations with palm trees. In one lane they met the fifty motor cars with the two hundred tourists all with badges on their chests and self-satisfaction on their faces. Mrs Witt watched in grim silence.

'*Plus ça change, plus c'est la même chose*,' said Lou, with a wicked little smile. '*On n'est pas mieux ici*, mother.'

'I know it,' said Mrs Witt.

The hotels by the sea were all shut up: it was not yet the 'season'. Not till November. And then! – Why, then Havana would be an American city, in full leaf of green dollar bills. The green leaf of American prosperity shedding itself recklessly, from every roaming sprig of a tourist, over this city of sunshine and alcohol. Green leaves unfolded in Pittsburg, and Chicago, showering in winter downfall in Havana.

Mother and daughter drank tea in a corner of the Hotel d'Angleterre once more, and returned to the ferry.

The Gulf of Mexico was blue and rippling, with the phantom of islands on the south. Great porpoises rolled and leaped, running in front of the ship in the clear water, diving, travelling in perfect motion, straight, with the tip of the ship touching the tip of their tails, then rolling over, cork-screwing, and showing their bellies as they went. Marvellous! The marvellous beauty and fascination of natural wild things! The horror of man's unnatural life, his heaped-up civilisation!

The flying-fishes burst out of the sea in clouds of silvery, transparent motion. Blue above and below, the Gulf seemed a silent, empty, timeless place where man did not really reach. And Lou was again fascinated by the glamour of the universe.

But bump! She and her mother were in a first-class hotel again, calling down the telephone for the bell-boy and iced water. And soon they were in a Pullman, off to San Antonio.

It was America, it was Texas. They were at their ranch, on the great level of yellow autumn, with the vast sky above. And after all, from the hot wide sky, and the hot, wide, red earth, there *did* come something new, something not used-up. Lou *did* feel exhilarated.

The Texans were there, tall blonde people, ingenuously cheerful, ingenuously, childishly intimate, as if the fact that you had never seen them before was as nothing compared to the fact that you'd all been living in one room together all your lives, so that nothing was hidden from either of you. The one room being the mere shanty of the world in which we all live. Strange, uninspired cheerfulness, filling, as it were, the blank of complete incomprehension.

And off they set in their motor cars, chiefly high-legged Fords, rattling away down the red trails between yellow sunflowers or sere grass or dry cotton, away, away into great distances, cheerfully raising the dust of haste. It left Lou in a sort of blank amazement. But it left her amused, not depressed. The old screws of emotion and intimacy that had been screwed down so tightly upon her fell out of their holes, here. The Texan intimacy weighed no more on her than a postage stamp, even if, for the moment, it stuck as close. And there was a certain underneath recklessness, even a stoicism in all the apparently childish people, which left one free. They might appear childish: but they stoically depended on themselves alone, in reality. Not as in England, where every man waited to pour the burden of himself upon you.

St Mawr arrived safely, a bit bewildered. The Texans eyed him closely, struck silent, as ever, by anything pure-bred and beautiful. He was somehow too beautiful, too perfected, in this great open country. The long-legged Texan horses, with their elaborate saddles, seemed somehow more natural.

Even St Mawr felt himself strange, as it were naked and singled out, in this rough place. Like a jewel among stones, a pearl before swine, maybe. But the swine were no fools. They knew a pearl from a grain of maize, and a grain of maize from a pearl. And they knew what they wanted. When it was pearls, it was pearls; though chiefly, it was maize. Which shows good sense. They could see St Mawr's points. Only he needn't draw the point too fine, or it would just not pierce the tough skin of this country.

The ranch-man mounted him – just threw a soft skin over his back, jumped on, and away down the red trail, raising the dust among the tall wild yellow of sunflowers, in the hot wild sun. Then back again in a fume, and the man s lipped off.

'He's got the stuff in him, he sure has,' said the man.

And the horse seemed pleased with this rough handling. Lewis looked on in wonder, and a little envy.

Lou and her mother stayed a fortnight on the ranch. It was all so queer: so crude, so rough, so easy, so artificially civilised, and so meaningless. Lou could not get over the feeling that it all meant nothing. There were no roots of reality at all. No consciousness below the surface, no meaning in anything save the obvious, the blatantly obvious. It was like life enacted in a mirror. Visually, it was wildly vital. But there was nothing behind it. Or like a cinematograph: flat shapes, exactly like men, but without any substance of reality, rapidly, rattling away with talk, emotions, activity, all in the flat, nothing behind it. No deeper consciousness at all. So it seemed to her.

One moved from dream to dream, from phantasm to phantasm.

But at least, this Texan life, if it had no bowels, no vitals, at least it could not prey on one's own vitals. It was this much better than Europe.

Lewis was silent, and rather piqued. St Mawr had already made advances to the boss's long-legged, arch-necked, glossy-maned Texan mare. And the boss was pleased.

What a world!

Mrs Witt eyed it all shrewdly. But she failed to participate. Lou was a bit scared at the emptiness of it all, and the queer, phantasmal self-consciousness. Cowboys just as self-conscious as Rico, far more sentimental, inwardly vague and unreal. Cowboys that went after their cows in black Ford motor cars: and who self-consciously saw Lady Carrington falling to them, as elegant young ladies from the East fall to the noble cowboy of the films, or in Zane Grey. It was all film-psychology.

And at the same time, these boys led a hard, hard life, often dangerous and gruesome. Nevertheless, inwardly they were self-conscious film-heroes. The boss himself, a man over forty, long and lean and with a great deal of stringy energy, showed off before her in a strong silent manner, existing for the time being purely in his imagination of the sort of picture he made to her, the sort of impression he made on her.

So they all were, coloured up like a Zane Grey book-jacket, all of them living in the mirror. The kind of picture they made to somebody else.

And at the same time, with energy, courage, and a stoical grit getting their work done, and putting through what they had to put through.

It left Lou blank with wonder. And in the face of this strange cheerful living in the mirror – a rather cheap mirror at that – England began to seem real to her again.

Then she had to remember herself back in England. And no, oh God, England was not real either, except poisonously.

What was real? What under heaven was real?

Her mother had gone dumb and, as it were, out of range. Phoenix was a bit assured and bouncy, back more or less in his own conditions. Lewis was a bit impressed by the emptiness of everything, the *lack* of concentration. And St Mawr followed at the heels of the boss's long-legged black Texan mare, almost slavishly.

What, in heaven's name, was one to make of it all?

Soon, she could not stand this sort of living in a film-setting, with the mechanical energy of 'making good', that is, making money, to keep the show going. The mystic duty to 'make good', meaning to make the ranch pay a laudable interest on the 'owners' investment. Lou herself being one of the owners. And the interest that came to her, from her father's will, being the money she spent to buy St Mawr and to fit up that house in Westminster. Then also the mystic duty to 'feel good'. Everybody had to *feel good, fine!* 'How are you this morning, Mr Latham?' – '*Fine!* Eh! Don't you feel good out here, eh? Lady Carrington?' – '*Fine!*' – Lou pronounced it with the same ringing conviction. It was Coué all the time!

'Shall we stay here long, mother?' she asked.

'Not a day longer than you want to, Louise. I stay entirely for your sake.'

'Then let us go, mother.'

They left St Mawr and Lewis. But Phoenix wanted to come along. So they motored to San Antonio, got into the Pullman, and travelled as far as El Paso. Then they changed to go North. Santa Fé would be at least 'easy'. And Mrs Witt had acquaintances there.

They found the fiesta over in Santa Fé: Indians, Mexicans, artists had finished their great effort to amuse and attract the tourists. *Welcome Mr Tourist* said a great board on one side of the high-road. And on the other side, a little nearer to town: *Thank You, Mr Tourist*.

'*Plus ça change –*' Lou began.

'*Ça ne change jamais –* except for the worse!' said Mrs Witt, like a pistol going off. And Lou held her peace, after she had sighed to herself, and said in her own mind: '*Welcome Also Mrs and Miss Tourist!*'

There was no getting a word out of Mrs Witt, these days. Whereas Phoenix was becoming almost loquacious.

They stayed a while in Santa Fé, in the clean, comfortable, 'homely' hotel, where 'every room had its bath': a spotless white bath, with very hot water night and day. The tourists and commercial travellers sat in the big hall down below, everybody living in the mirror! And of course, they knew Lady Carrington down to her shoe-soles. And they all expected her to know them down to their shoe-soles. For the only object of the mirror is to reflect images.

For two days mother and daughter ate in the mayonnaise intimacy of the dining-room. Then Mrs Witt struck, and telephoned down every meal-time for her meal in her room. She got to staying in bed later and later, as on the ship. Lou became uneasy. This was worse than Europe.

Phoenix was still there, as a sort of half-friend, half-servant retainer. He was perfectly happy, roving round among the Mexicans and Indians, talking Spanish all day, and telling about England and his two mistresses, rolling the ball of his own importance.

'I'm afraid we've got Phoenix for life,' said Lou.

'Not unless we wish,' said Mrs Witt indifferently. And she picked up a novel which she didn't want to read, but which she was going to read.

'What shall we do next, mother?' Lou asked.

'As far as I am concerned, there is no next,' said Mrs Witt.

'Come, mother! Let's go back to Italy or somewhere, if it's as bad as that.'

'Never again, Louise, shall I cross that water. I have come home to die.'

'I don't see much home about it – the Gonsalez Hotel in Santa Fé.'

'Indeed not! But as good as anywhere else, to die in.'

'Oh mother, don't be silly! Shall we look for somewhere where we can be by ourselves?'

'I leave it to you, Louise. I have made my last decision.'

'What is that, mother?'

'Never, never to make another decision.'

'Not even to decide to die?'

'No, not even that.'

'Or *not* to die?'

'Not that either.'

Mrs Witt shut up like a trap. She refused to rise from her bed that day.

Lou went to consult Phoenix. The result was, the two set out to look at a little ranch that was for sale.

It was autumn, and the loveliest time in the south-west, where there is no spring, snow blowing into the hot lap of summer; and no real summer, hail falling in thick ice, from the thunderstorms: and even no very definite winter, hot sun melting the snow and giving an impression of spring at any time. But autumn there is, when the winds of the desert are almost still, and the mountains fume no clouds. But morning comes cold and delicate, upon the wild sunflowers and the puffing, yellow-flowered greasewood. For the desert blooms in autumn. In spring it is grey ash all the time, and only the strong breath of the summer sun, and the heavy splashing of thunder rain succeeds at last, by September, in blowing it into soft, puffy yellow fire.

It was such a delicate morning when Lou drove out with Phoenix towards the mountains, to look at this ranch that a Mexican wanted to sell. For the brief moment the high mountains had lost their snow: it would be back again in a fortnight: and stood dim and delicate with autumn haze. The desert stretched away pale, as pale as the sky, but silvery and sere, with hummock-mounds of shadow, and long wings of shadow, like the reflection of some great bird. The same eagle-shadows came like rude paintings of the outstretched bird, upon the mountains, where the aspens were turning yellow. For the moment, the brief moment, the great desert-and-mountain landscape had lost its certain cruelty, and looked tender, dreamy. And many, many birds were flickering around.

Lou and Phoenix bumped and hesitated over a long trail: then wound down into a deep canyon: and then the car began to climb, climb, climb, in steep rushes, and in long heart-breaking, uneven pulls. The road was bad, and driving was no joke. But it was the sort of road Phoenix was used to. He sat impassive and watchful, and kept on, till his engine boiled. He was *himself* in this country: impassive, detached, self-satisfied, and silently assertive. Guarding himself at every moment, but, on his guard, sure of himself. Seeing no difference at all between Lou or Mrs Witt and himself, except that they had money and he had none, while he had a native importance which they lacked. He depended on them for money, they on him for the power to live out here in the West Intimately, he was as good as they. Money was their only advantage.

As Lou sat beside him in the front seat of the car, where it bumped less than behind, she felt this. She felt a peculiar tough-necked arrogance in him, as if he were asserting himself to put something over her. He wanted her to allow him to make advances to her, to allow him to suggest that he should be her lover. And then, finally, she would marry him, and he would be on the same footing as she and her mother.

In return, he would look after her, and give her his support and countenance, as a man, and stand between her and the world. In this sense, he would be faithful to her, and loyal. But as far as other women went, Mexican women or Indian women: why, that was none of her business. His marrying her would be a pact between two aliens, on behalf of one another, and he would keep his part of it all right. But himself, as a private man and a predative alien-blooded male, this had nothing to do with her. It didn't enter into her scope and count. She was one of these nervous white women with lots of money. She was very nice too. But as a *squaw* – as a real woman in a shawl whom a man went after for the pleasure of the night – why, she hardly counted. One of these white women who talk clever and know things like a man. She could hardly expect a half-savage male to acknowledge her as his female counterpart. – No! She had the bucks! And she had all the paraphernalia of the white man's civilisation, which a savage can play with and so escape his own hollow boredom. But his own real female counterpart? – Phoenix would just have shrugged his shoulders, and thought the question not worth answering. How could there be any answer in *her*, to the phallic male in him? Couldn't! Yet it would flatter his vanity and his self-esteem immensely, to possess her. That would be possessing the very clue to the white man's overwhelming world. And if she would let him possess her, he would be absolutely loyal to her, as far as affairs and appearances went. Only, the aboriginal phallic male in him simply couldn't recognise her as a woman at all. In this respect, she didn't exist. It needed the shawled Indian or Mexican women, with their squeaky, plaintive voices, their shuffling, watery humility, and the dark glances of their big, knowing eyes. When an Indian woman looked at him from under her black fringe, with dark, half-secretive suggestion in her big eyes: and when she stood before him hugged in her shawl, in such apparently complete quiescent humility: and when she spoke to him in her mousey squeak of a high, plaintive voice, as if it were difficult for her female bashfulness even to emit so much sound: and when she shuffled away with her legs wide apart, because of her wide-topped, white, high buckskin boots with tiny white feet, and her dark-knotted hair so full of hard, yet subtle lure: and when he remembered the almost watery softness of the Indian woman's dark, warm flesh: then he was a male, an old, secretive, rat-like male. But before Lou's straightforwardness and utter sexual incompetence, he just stood in contempt. And to him, even a French cocotte was utterly devoid of the right sort of sex. She couldn't really move him. She couldn't satisfy the furtiveness in him. He needed this plaintive, squeaky, dark-fringed Indian quality, something furtive and soft and rat-like, really to rouse him.

Nevertheless he was ready to trade his sex, which, in his opinion, every white woman was secretly pining for, for the white woman's money and social privileges. In the daytime, all the thrill and excitement of the white man's motor cars and moving pictures and ice-cream sodas and so forth. In the night, the soft, watery-soft warmth of an Indian or half-Indian woman. This was Phoenix's idea of life for himself.

Meanwhile, if a white woman gave him the privileges of the white man's world, he would do his duty by her as far as all that went.

Lou, sitting very, very still beside him as he drove the car – he was not a very good driver, not quick and marvellous as some white men are, particularly some French chauffeurs she had known, but usually a little behindhand in his movements – she knew more or less all that he felt. More or less she divined as a woman does. Even from a certain rather assured stupidity of his shoulders, and a certain rather stupid assertiveness of his knees, she knew him.

But she did not judge him too harshly. Somewhere deep, deep in herself she knew she too was at fault. And this made her sometimes inclined to humble herself, as a woman, before the furtive assertiveness of this underground, 'knowing' savage. He was so different from Rico.

Yet, after all, *was* he? In his rootlessness, his drifting, his real meaninglessness, was he different from Rico? And his childish, spellbound absorption in the motor car, or in the moving-pictures, or in an ice-cream soda – was it very different from Rico? Anyhow, was it really any better? Pleasanter, perhaps, to a woman, because of the childishness of it.

The same with his opinion of himself as a sexual male! So childish, really, it was almost thrilling to a woman. But then, so stupid also, with that furtive lurking in holes and imagining it could not be detected. He imagined he kept himself dark, in his sexual rat holes. He imagined he was not detected!

No, no, Lou was not such a fool as she looked, in his eyes anyhow. She knew what she wanted. She wanted relief from the nervous tension and irritation of her life, she wanted to escape from the friction which is the whole stimulus in modern social life. She wanted to be still: only that, to be very, very still, and recover her own soul.

When Phoenix presumed she was looking for some secretly sexual male such as himself, he was ridiculously mistaken. Even the illusion of the beautiful St Mawr was gone. And Phoenix, roaming round like a sexual rat in promiscuous back yards! – *Merci, mon cher!* For that was all he was: a sexual rat in the great barn-yard of man's habitat, looking for female rats!

Merci, mon cher! You are had.

Nevertheless, in his very mistakenness, he was a relief to her. His mistake was amusing rather than impressive. And the fact that one half of his intelligence was a complete dark blank, that too was a relief.

Strictly, and perhaps in the best sense, he was a servant. His very unconsciousness and his very limitation served as a shelter, as one shelters within the limitations of four walls. The very decided limits to his intelligence were a shelter to her. They made her feel safe.

But that feeling of safety did not deceive her. It was the feeling one derived from having a *true* servant attached to one, a man whose psychic limitations left him incapable of anything but service, and whose strong flow of natural life, at the same time, made him need to serve.

And Lou, sitting there so very still and frail, yet self-contained, had not lived for nothing. She no longer wanted to fool herself. She had no desire at all to fool herself into thinking that a Phoenix might be a husband and a mate. No desire that way at all. His obtuseness was a servant's obtuseness. She was grateful to him for serving, and she paid him a wage. Moreover, she provided him with something to do, to occupy his life. In a sense, she gave him his life, and rescued him from his own boredom. It was a balance.

He did not know what she was thinking. There was a certain physical sympathy between them. His obtuseness made him think it was also a sexual sympathy.

'It's a nice trip, you and me,' he said suddenly, turning and looking her in the eyes with an excited look, and ending on a foolish little laugh.

She realised that she should have sat in the back seat.

'But it's a bad road,' she said. 'Hadn't you better stop and put the sides of the hood up? your engine is boiling.'

He looked away with a quick switch of interest to the red thermometer in front of his machine.

'She's boiling,' he said, stopping, and getting out with a quick alacrity to go to look at the engine.

Lou got out also, and went to the back seat, shutting the door decisively.

'I think I'll ride at the back,' she said, 'it gets so frightfully hot in front, when the engine heats up. – Do you think she needs some water? Have you got some in the canteen?'

'She's full,' he said, peering into the steaming valve.

'You can run a bit out, if you think there's any need. I wonder if it's much farther!'

'*Quién sabe!*' said he, slightly impertinent.

She relapsed into her own stillness. She realised how careful, how very careful she must be of relaxing into sympathy, and reposing, as it were, on Phoenix. He would read it as a sexual appeal. Perhaps he couldn't help it. She had only herself to blame. He was obtuse, as a man and a savage. He had only one interpretation, sex, for any woman's approach to him.

And she knew, with the last clear knowledge of weary disillusion, that she did not want to be mixed up in Phoenix's sexual promiscuities. The very thought was an insult to her. The crude, clumsy servant-male: no, no, not that. He was a good fellow, a very good fellow, as far as he went. But he fell far short of physical intimacy.

'No, no,' she said to herself, 'I was wrong to ride in the front seat with him. I must sit alone, just alone. Because sex, mere sex, is repellent to me. I will never prostitute myself again. Unless something touches my very spirit, the very quick of me, I will stay alone, just alone. Alone, and give myself only to the unseen presences, serve only the other, unseen presences.'

She understood now the meaning of the Vestal Virgins, the Virgins of the holy fire in the old temples. They were symbolic of herself, of woman weary of the embrace of incompetent men, weary, weary, weary of all that, turning to the unseen gods, the unseen spirits, the hidden fire, and devoting herself to that, and that alone. Receiving thence her pacification and her fulfilment.

Not these little, incompetent, childish self-opinionated men! Not these to touch her. She watched Phoenix's rather stupid shoulders, as he drove the car on between the *piñon* trees and the cedars of the narrow mesa ridge, to the mountain foot. He was a good fellow. But let him run among women of his own sort. Something was beyond him. And this something must remain beyond him, never allow itself to come within his reach. Otherwise he would paw it and mess it up, and be as miserable as a child that has broken its father's watch.

No, no! She had loved an American, and lived with him for a fortnight. She had had a long, intimate friendship with an Italian. Perhaps it was love on his part. And she had yielded to him. Then her love and marriage to Rico.

And what of it all? Nothing. It was almost nothing. It was as if only the outside of herself, her top layers, were human. This inveigled her into intimacies. As soon as the intimacy penetrated, or attempted to penetrate inside her, it was a disaster. Just a humiliation and a breaking down.

Within these outer layers of herself lay the successive inner sanctuaries of herself. And these were inviolable. She accepted it.

'I am not a marrying woman,' she said to herself. 'I am not a lover nor a mistress nor a wife. It is no good. Love can't really come into me from the outside, and I can never, never mate with any man, since the mystic new man will never come to me. No, no, let me know myself and my role. I am one of the eternal Virgins, serving the eternal fire. My dealings with men have only broken my stillness and messed up my doorways. It has been my own fault. I ought to stay virgin, and still, very, very still, and serve the most perfect service. I want my temple and my loneliness and my Apollo mystery of the inner fire. And with men, only the delicate, subtler, more remote relations. No coming near. A coming near only breaks the delicate veils, and broken veils, like broken flowers, only lead to rottenness.'

She felt a great peace inside herself as she made this realisation. And a thankfulness. Because, after all, it seemed to her that the hidden fire was alive and burning in this sky, over the desert, in the mountains. She felt a certain latent holiness in the very atmosphere, a young, spring-fire of latent holiness, such as she had never felt in Europe, or in the East. 'For me,' she said, as she looked away at the mountains in shadow and the pale-warm desert beneath, with wings of shadow upon it: 'For me, this place is sacred. It is blessed.'

But as she watched Phoenix as she remembered the motor cars and tourists, and the rather dreary Mexicans of Santa Fé, and the lurking, invidious Indians, with something of a rat-like secretiveness and defeatedness in their bearing, she realised that the latent fire of the vast landscape struggled under a great weight of dirt-like inertia. She had to mind the dirt, most carefully and vividly avoid it and keep it away from her, here in this place that at last seemed sacred to her.

The motor car climbed up, past the tall pine trees, to the foot of the mountains, and came at last to a wire gate, where nothing was to be expected. Phoenix opened the gate, and they drove on, through more trees, into a clearing where dried up bean-plants were yellow.

'This man got no water for his beans,' said Phoenix. 'Not got much beans this year.'

They climbed slowly up the incline, through more pine trees, and out into another clearing, where a couple of horses were grazing. And there they saw the ranch itself, little low cabins with patched roofs, under a few pine trees, and facing the long twelve-acre clearing, or field, where the michaelmas daisies were purple mist, and spangled with clumps of yellow flowers.

'Not got no alfalfa here neither!' said Phoenix, as the car waded past the flowers. 'Must be a dry place up here. Got no water, sure they haven't.'

Yet it was the place Lou wanted. In an instant, her heart sprang to it. The instant the car stopped, and she saw the two cabins inside the rickety fence, the rather broken corral beyond, and behind all, tall, blue balsam pines, the round hills, the solid uprise of the mountain flank: and getting down, she looked across the purple and gold of the clearing, downwards at the ring of pine trees standing so still, so crude and untameable, the motionless desert beyond the bristles of the pine crests, a thousand feet below: and beyond the desert, blue mountains, and far, far-off blue mountains in Arizona: '*This is the place*,' she said to herself.

This little tumble-down ranch, only a homestead of a hundred-and-sixty acres, was, as it were, man's last effort towards the wild heart of the Rockies, at this point. Sixty years before, a restless schoolmaster had wandered out from the East, looking for gold among the mountains. He found a very little, then no more. But the mountains had got hold of him, he could not go back.

There was a little trickling spring of pure water, a thread of treasure perhaps better than gold. So the schoolmaster took up a homestead on the lot where this little spring arose. He struggled, and got himself his log cabin erected, his fence put up, sloping at the mountain-side through the pine trees and dropping into the hollows where the ghost-white mariposa lilies stood leafless and naked in flower, in spring, on tall invisible stems. He made the long clearing for alfalfa.

And fell so into debt, that he had to trade his homestead away, to clear his debt. Then he made a tiny living teaching the children of the few American prospectors who had squatted in the valleys, beside the Mexicans.

The trader who got the ranch tackled it with a will. He built another log cabin, and a big corral, and brought water from the canyon two miles and more across the mountain slope, in a little runnel ditch, and more water, piped a mile or more down the little canyon immediately above the cabins. He got a flow of water for his houses: for being a true American, he felt he could not *really* say he had conquered his environment till he had got running water, taps, and wash-hand basins inside his house.

Taps, running water and wash-hand basins he accomplished. And, undaunted through the years, he prepared the basin for a fountain in the little fenced-in enclosure, and he built a little bath-house. After a number of years, he sent up the enamelled bath-tub to be put in the little log bath-house on the little wild ranch hung right against the savage Rockies, above the desert.

But here the mountains finished him. He was a trader down below, in the Mexican village. This little ranch was, as it were, his hobby, his ideal. He and his New England wife spent their summers there: and turned on the taps in the cabins and turned them off again, and felt really that civilisation had conquered.

All this plumbing from the savage ravines of the canyons – one of them nameless to this day – cost, however, money. In fact, the ranch cost a great deal of money. But it was all to be got back. The big clearing was to be irrigated for alfalfa, the little clearing for beans, and the third clearing, under the corral, for potatoes. All these things the trader could trade to the Mexicans, very advantageously.

And moreover, since somebody had started a praise of the famous goats' cheese made by Mexican peasants in New Mexico, goats there should be.

Goats there were: five hundred of them, eventually. And they fed chiefly in the wild mountain hollows, the no-man's-land. The Mexicans call them fire-mouths, because everything they nibble dies. Not because of their flaming mouths, really, but because they nibble a live plant down, down to the quick, till it can put forth no more.

So, the energetic trader, in the course of five or six years, had got the ranch ready. The long three-roomed cabin was for him and his New England wife. In the two-roomed cabin lived the Mexican family who really had charge of the ranch. For the trader was mostly fixed to his store, seventeen miles away, down in the Mexican village.

The ranch lay over eight thousand feet up, the snows of winter came deep and the white goats, looking dirty yellow, swam in snow with their poor curved horns poking out like dead sticks. But the corral had a long, cosy, shut-in goat-shed all down one side, and into this crowded the five hundred, their acrid goat-smell rising like hot acid over the snow. And the thin, pockmarked Mexican threw them alfalfa out of the log barn. Until the hot sun sank the snow again, and froze the surface, when patter-patter went the two thousand little goat-hoofs, over the silver-frozen snow, up at the mountain. Nibble, nibble, nibble, the fire-mouths, at every tender twig. And the goat-bell climbed, and the baa-ing came from among the dense and shaggy pine trees. And sometimes, in a soft drift under the trees, a goat, or several goats, went through, into the white depths, and some were lost thus, to reappear dead and frozen at the thaw.

By evening, they were driven down again, like a dirty yellowish-white stream carrying dark sticks on its yeasty surface, tripping and bleating over the frozen snow, past the bustling dark green pine trees, down to the trampled mess of the corral. And everywhere, everywhere over the snow, yellow stains and dark pills of goat-droppings melting into the surface crystal. On still, glittering nights, when the frost was hard, the smell of goats came up like some uncanny acid fire, and great stars sitting on the mountain's edge seemed to be watching like the eyes of a mountain lion, brought by the scent. Then the coyotes in the near canyon howled and sobbed, and ran like shadows over the snow. But the goat corral had been built tight.

In the course of years the goat-herd had grown from fifty to five hundred, and surely that was increase. The goat-milk cheeses sat drying on their little racks. In spring, there was a great flowing and skipping of kids. In summer and early autumn, there was a pest of flies, rising from all that goat-smell and that cast-out whey of goats'-milk, after the cheese making. The rats came, and the pack-rats, swarming.

And after all, it was difficult to sell or trade the cheeses, and little profit to be made. And in dry summers, no water came down in the narrow ditch-channel, that straddled in wooden runnels over the deep clefts in the mountain side. No water meant no alfalfa. In winter the goats scarcely drank at all. In summer they could be watered at the little spring. But the thirsty land was not so easy to accommodate.

Five hundred fine white Angora goats, with their massive handsome padres! They were beautiful enough. And the trader made all he could of them. Come summer, they were run down into the narrow tank filled with the fiery dipping fluid. Then their lovely white wool was clipped. It was beautiful, and valuable, but comparatively little of it.

And it all cost, cost, cost. And a man was always let down. At one time no water. At another a poison-weed. Then a sickness. Always, some mysterious malevolence fighting, fighting against the will of man. A strange invisible influence coming out of the livid rock-fastnesses in the bowels of those uncreated Rocky Mountains, preying upon the will of man, and slowly wearing down his resistance, his onward-pushing spirit. The curious, subtle thing, like a mountain fever, got into the blood, so that the men at the ranch, and the animals with them, had bursts of queer, violent, half-frenzied energy, in which, however, they were wont to lose their wariness. And then, damage of some sort. The horses ripped and cut themselves, or they were struck by lightning, the men had great hurts, or sickness. A curious disintegration working all the time, a sort of malevolent breath, like a stupefying, irritant gas, coming out of the unfathomed mountains.

The pack-rats with their bushy tails and big ears came down out of the hills, and were jumping and bouncing about: symbols of the curious debasing malevolence that was in the spirit of the place. The Mexicans in charge, good honest men, worked all they could. But they were like most of the Mexicans in the south-west, as if they had been pithed, to use one of Kipling's words. As if the invidious malevolence of the country itself had slowly taken all the pith of manhood from them, leaving a hopeless sort of corpus of a man.

And the same happened to the white men, exposed to the open country. Slowly, they were pithed. The energy went out of them. And more than that, the interest. An inertia of indifference invading the soul, leaving the body healthy and active, but wasting the soul, the living interest, quite away.

It was the New England wife of the trader who put most energy into the ranch. She looked on it as her home. She had a little white fence put all round the two cabins: the bright brass water-taps she kept shining in the two kitchens: outside the kitchen door she had a little kitchen garden and nasturtiums, after a great fight with invading animals, that nibbled everything away. And she got so far as the preparation of the round concrete basin which was to be a little pool, under the few enclosed pine trees between the two cabins, a pool with a tiny fountain jet.

But this, with the bath-tub, was her limit, as the five hundred goats were her man's limit. Out of the mountains came two breaths of influence: the breath of the curious, frenzied energy, that took away one's intelligence as alcohol or any other stimulus does: and then the most strange invidiousness that ate away the soul. The woman loved her ranch, almost with passion. It was she who felt the stimulus, more than the men. It seemed to enter her like a sort of sex passion, intensifying her ego, making her full of violence and of blind female energy. The energy, and the blindness of it! A strange blind frenzy, like an intoxication while it lasted. And the sense of beauty that thrilled her New England woman's soul.

Her cabin faced the slow downslope of the clearing, the alfalfa field: her long, low cabin, crouching under the great pine tree that threw up its trunk sheer in front of the house, in the yard. That pine tree was the guardian of the place. But a bristling, almost demonish guardian, from the far-off crude ages of the world. Its great pillar of pale, flakey-ribbed copper rose there in strange callous in-difference, and the grim permanence, which is in pine trees. A passionless, non-phallic column, rising in the shadows of the pre-sexual world, before the hot-blooded ithyphallic column ever erected itself. A cold, blossomless, resinous sap surging and oozing gum, from that pallid brownish bark. And the wind hissing in the needles, like a vast nest of serpents. And the pine cones falling plump as the hail hit them. Then lying all over the yard, open in the sun like wooden roses, but hard, sexless, rigid with a blind will.

Past the column of that pine tree, the alfalfa field sloped gently down, to the circling guard of pine trees, from which silent, living barrier isolated pines rose to ragged heights at intervals, in blind assertiveness. Strange, those pine trees! In some lights all their needles glistened like polished steel, all subtly glittering with a whitish glitter among darkness, like real needles. Then again, at evening, the trunks would flare up orange red, and the tufts would be dark, alert tufts like a wolf's tail touching the air. Again, in the morning sunlight they would be soft and still, hardly noticeable. But all the same, present, and watchful. Never sympathetic, always watchfully on their guard, and resistant, they hedged one in with the aroma and the power and the slight horror of the pre-sexual primeval world. The world where each creature was crudely limited to its own ego, crude and bristling and cold, and then crowding in packs like pine trees and wolves.

But beyond the pine trees, ah, there beyond, there was beauty for the spirit to soar in. The circle of pines, with the loose trees rising high and ragged at intervals, this was the barrier, the fence to the foreground. Beyond was only distance, the desert a thousand feet below, and beyond.

The desert swept its great fawn-coloured circle around, away beyond and below like a beach, with a long mountainside of pure blue shadow closing in the near corner, and strange bluish hummocks of mountains rising like wet rock from a vast strand, away in the middle distance, and beyond, in the farthest distance, pale blue crests of mountains looking over the horizon, from the west, as if peering in from another world altogether.

Ah, that was beauty! – perhaps the most beautiful thing in the world. It was pure beauty, *absolute* beauty! There! That was it. To the little woman from New England, with her tense, fierce soul and her egoistic passion of service, this beauty was absolute, a *ne plus ultra*. From her doorway, from her porch, she could watch the vast, eagle-like wheeling of the daylight, that turned as the eagles which lived in the near rocks overhead in the blue, turning their luminous, dark-edged-patterned bellies and under-wings upon the pure air, like winged orbs. So the daylight made the vast turn upon the desert, brushing the farthest outwatching mountains. And sometimes, the vast strand of the desert would float with curious undulations and exhalations amid the blue fragility of mountains, whose upper edges were harder than the floating bases. And sometimes she would see the little brown adobe houses of the village Mexicans, twenty miles away, like little cube crystals of insect-houses dotting upon the desert, very distinct, with a cottonwood tree or two rising near. And sometimes she would see the far-off rocks, thirty miles away, where the canyon made a gateway between the mountains. Quite clear, like an open gateway out of a vast yard, she would see the cutout bit of the canyon-passage. And on the desert itself, curious puckered folds of mesa-sides. And a blackish crack which in places revealed the otherwise invisible canyon of the Rio Grande. And beyond everything, the mountains like icebergs showing up from an outer sea. Then later, the sun would go down blazing above the shallow cauldron of simmering darkness, and the round mountains of Colorado would lump up into uncanny significance, northwards. That was always rather frightening. But morning came again, with the sun peeping over the mountain slopes and lighting the desert away in the distance long, long before it lighted on her yard. And then she would see another valley, like magic and very lovely, with green fields and long tufts of cottonwood trees, and a few long-cubical adobe houses, lying floating in shallow light below, like a vision.

Ah! it was beauty, beauty absolute, at any hour of the day: whether the perfect clarity of morning, or the mountains beyond the simmering desert at noon, or the purple lumping of northern mounds under a red sun at night. Or whether the dust whirled in tall columns, travelling across the desert far away, like pillars of cloud by day, tall, leaning pillars of dust hastening with ghostly haste: or whether, in the early part of the year, suddenly in the morning a whole sea of solid white would rise rolling below, a solid mist from melted snow, ghost-white under the mountain sun, the world below blotted out: or whether the black rain and cloud streaked down, far across the desert, and lightning stung down with sharp white stings on the horizon: or the cloud travelled and burst overhead, with rivers of fluid blue fire running out of heaven and exploding on earth, and hail coming down like a world of ice shattered above: or the hot sun rode in again: or snow fell in heavy silence: or the world was blinding white under a blue sky, and one must hurry under the pine trees for shelter against that vast, white, back-beating light which rushed up at one and made one almost unconscious, amid the snow.

It was always beauty, *always*! It was always great, and splendid, and, for some reason, natural. It was never grandiose or theatrical. Always, for some reason, perfect. And quite simple, in spite of it all.

So it was, when you watched the vast and living landscape. The landscape lived, and lived as the world of the gods, unsullied and unconcerned. The great circling landscape lived its own life, sumptuous and uncaring. Man did not exist for it.

And if it had been a question simply of living through the eyes, into the *distance*, then this would have been Paradise, and the little New England woman on her ranch would have found what she was always looking for, the earthly paradise of the spirit.

But even a woman cannot live only into the distance, the beyond. Willy-nilly she finds herself juxtaposed to the near things, the thing in itself. And willy-nilly she is caught up into the fight with the immediate object.

The New England woman had fought to make the nearness as perfect as the distance: for the distance was absolute beauty. She had been confident of success. She had felt quite assured, when the water came running out of her bright brass taps, the wild water of the hills caught, tricked into the narrow iron pipes, and led tamely to her kitchen, to jump out over her sink, into her wash-basin, at her service. *There!* she said. I have tamed the waters of the mountain to my service.

So she had, for the moment.

At the same time, the invisible attack was being made upon her. While she revelled in the beauty of the luminous world that wheeled around and below her, the grey, rat-like spirit of the inner mountains was attacking her from behind. She could not keep her attention. And, curiously, she could not keep even her speech. When she was saying something, suddenly the next word would be gone out of her, as if a pack-rat had carried it off. And she sat blank, stuttering, staring in the empty cupboard of her mind, like Mother Hubbard, and seeing the cupboard bare. And this irritated her husband intensely.

Her chickens, of which she was so proud, were carried away. Or they strayed. Or they fell sick. At first she could cope with their circumstances. But after a while, she couldn't. She couldn't care. A drug like numbness possessed her spirit, and at the very middle of her, she couldn't care what happened to her chickens.

The same when a couple of horses were struck by lightning. It frightened her. The rivers of fluid fire that suddenly fell out of the sky and exploded on the earth near by, as if the whole earth had burst like a bomb, frightened her from the very core of her, and made her know, secretly and with cynical certainty, *that there was no merciful God in the heavens*. A very tall, elegant pine tree just above her cabin took the lightning, and stood tall and elegant as before, but with a white seam spiralling from its crest, all down its tall trunk, to earth. The perfect scar, white and long as lightning itself. And every time she looked at it, she said to herself, in spite of herself: *There is no Almighty loving God. The God there is shaggy as the pine trees, and horrible as the lightning*. Outwardly, she never confessed this. Openly, she thought of her dear New England Church as usual. But in the violent undercurrent of her woman's soul, after the storms, she would look at that living seamed tree, and the voice would say in her, almost savagely: *What nonsense about Jesus and a God of Love, in a place like this! This is more awful and more splendid. I like it better.* The very chipmunks, in their jerky helter-skelter, the blue jays wrangling in the pine tree in the dawn, the grey squirrel undulating to the tree-trunk, then pausing to chatter at her and scold her, with a shrewd fearlessness, as if she were the alien, the outsider, the creature that should not be permitted among the trees, all destroyed the illusion she cherished, of love, universal love. There was no love on this ranch. There was life, intense, bristling life, full of energy, but also, with an undertone of savage sordidness.

The black ants in her cupboard, the pack-rats bouncing on her ceiling like hippopotamuses in the night, the two sick goats: there was a peculiar under-current of squalor, flowing under the curious *tussle* of wild life. That was it. The wild life, even the life of the trees and flowers, seemed one bristling, hair-raising tussle. The very flowers came up bristly, and many of them were fang-mouthed, like the dead-nettle: and none had any real scent. But they were very fascinating, too, in their very fierceness. In May, the curious columbines of the stream-beds, columbines scarlet outside and yellow in, like the red and yellow of a herald's uniform – farther from the dove nothing could be: then the beautiful rosy-blue of the great tufts of the flower they called bluebell, but which was really a flower of the snap-dragon family: these grew in powerful beauty in the little clearing of the pine trees, followed by the flower the settlers had mysteriously called herb honeysuckle: a tangle of long drops of pure fire-red, hanging from slim invisible stalks of smoke colour. The purest, most perfect vermilion scarlet, cleanest fire colour, hanging in long drops like a shower of fire-rain that is just going to strike the earth. A little later, more in the open, there came another sheer fire-red flower, sparking, fierce red stars running up a bristly grey ladder, as if the earth's fire-centre had blown out some red sparks, white-speckled and deadly inside, puffing for a moment in the day air.

So it was! The alfalfa field was one raging, seething conflict of plants trying to get hold. One dry year, and the bristly wild things had got hold: the spiky, blueleaved thistle-poppy with its moon-white flowers, the low clumps of blue nettle-flower, the later rush, after the sereneness of June and July, the rush of red sparks and michaelmas daisies, and the tough wild sunflowers, strangling and choking the dark, tender green of the clover-like alfalfa! A battle, a battle, with banners of bright scarlet and yellow.

When a really defenceless flower did issue, like the moth-still, ghost-centred mariposa lily, with its inner moth-dust of yellow, it came invisible. There was nothing to be seen, but a hair of greyish grass near the oak-scrub. Behold, this invisible long stalk was balancing a white, ghostly, three-petalled flower, naked out of nothingness. A mariposa lily!

Only the pink wild roses smelled sweet, like the old world. They were sweet-briar roses. And the dark blue hare-bells among the oak-scrub, like the ice-dark bubbles of the mountain flowers in the Alps, the Alpenglocken.

The roses of the desert are the cactus flowers, crystal of translucent yellow or of rose-colour. But set among spines the devil himself must have conceived in a moment of sheer ecstasy.

Nay, it was a world before and after the God of Love. Even the very humming-birds hanging about the flowering squawberry bushes, when the snow had gone, in May, they were before and after the God of Love. And the blue jays were crested dark with challenge, and the yellow-and-dark wood-pecker was fearless like a warrior in war-paint, as he struck the wood. While on the fence hawks sat motionless, like dark fists clenched under heaven, ignoring man and his ways.

Summer, it was true, unfolded the tender cottonwood leaves, and the tender aspen. But what a tangle and a ghostly aloofness in the aspen thickets high up on the mountains, the coldness that is in the eyes and the long cornelian talons of the bear.

Summer brought the little wild strawberries, with their savage aroma, and the late summer brought the rose-jewel raspberries in the valley cleft. But how lonely, how harsh-lonely and menacing it was, to be alone in that shadowy, steep cleft of a canyon just above the cabins, picking raspberries, while the thunder gathered thick and blue-purple at the mountain tops. The many wild raspberries hanging rose-red in the thickets. But the stream bed below all silent, waterless. And the trees all bristling in silence, and waiting like warriors at an outpost. And the berries waiting for the sharp-eyed, cold, long-snouted bear to come rambling and shaking his heavy sharp fur. The berries grew for the bears, and the little New England woman, with her uncanny sensitiveness to under-lying influences, felt all the time she was stealing. Stealing the wild raspberries in the secret little canyon behind her home. And when she had made them into jam, she could almost taste the theft in her preserves.

She confessed nothing of this. She tried even to confess nothing of her dread. But she was afraid. Especially she was conscious of the prowling, intense aerial electricity all the summer, after June. The air was thick with wandering currents of fierce electric fluid, waiting to discharge themselves. And almost every day there was the rage and battle of thunder. But the air was never cleared. There was no relief. However the thunder raged, and spent itself, yet, afterwards, among the sunshine was the strange lurking and wandering of the electric currents, moving invisible, with strange menace, between the atoms of the air. She knew. Oh, she knew!

And her love for her ranch turned sometimes into a certain repulsion. The underlying rat-dirt, the everlasting bristling tussle of the wild life, with the tangle and the bones strewing. Bones of horses struck by lightning, bones of dead cattle, skulls of goats with little horns: bleached, unburied bones. Then the cruel electricity of the mountains. And then, most mysterious but worst of all, the animosity of the spirit of place: the crude, half-created spirit of place, like some serpent-bird for ever attacking man, in a hatred of man's onward-struggle towards further creation.

The seething cauldron of lower life, seething on the very tissue of the higher life, seething the soul away, seething at the marrow. The vast and unrelenting will of the swarming lower life, working for ever against man's attempt at a higher life, a further created being.

At last, after many years, the little woman admitted to herself that she was glad to go down from the ranch, when November came with snows. She was glad to come to a more human home, her house in the village. And as winter passed by, and spring came again, she knew she did not want to go up to the ranch again. It had broken something in her. It had hurt her terribly. It had maimed her for ever in her hope, her belief in paradise on earth. Now, she hid from herself her own corpse, the corpse of her New England belief in a world ultimately all for love. The belief, and herself with it, was a corpse. The gods of those inner mountains were grim and invidious and relentless, huger than man, and lower than man. Yet man could never master them.

The little woman in her flower-garden away below, by the stream-irrigated village, hid away from the thought of it all. She would not go to the ranch any more.

The Mexicans stayed in charge, looking after the goats. But the place didn't pay. It didn't pay, not quite. It had paid. It might pay. But the effort, the effort! And as the marrow is eaten out of a man's bones and the soul out of his belly, contending with the strange rapacity of savage life, the lower stage of creation, he cannot make the effort any more.

Then also, the war came, making many men give up their enterprises at civilisation.

Every new stroke of civilisation has cost the lives of countless brave men, who have fallen defeated by the 'dragon', in their efforts to win the apples of the Hesperides, or the fleece of gold. Fallen in their efforts to overcome the old, half-sordid savagery of the lower stages of creation, and win to the next stage.

For all savagery is half-sordid. And man is only himself when he is fighting on and on, to overcome the sordidness.

And every civilisation, when it loses its inward vision and its cleaner energy, falls into a new sort of sordidness, more vast and more stupendous than the old savage sort. An Augean stables of metallic filth.

And all the time, man has to rouse himself afresh, to cleanse the new accumulations of refuse. To win from the crude wild nature the victory and the power to make another start, and to cleanse behind him the century-deep deposits of layer upon layer of refuse: even of tin cans.

The ranch dwindled. The flock of goats declined. The water ceased to flow. And at length the trader gave it up.

He rented the place to a Mexican, who lived on the handful of beans he raised, and who was being slowly driven out by the vermin.

And now arrived Lou, new blood to the attack. She went back to Santa Fé, saw the trader and a lawyer, and bought the ranch for twelve hundred dollars. She was so pleased with herself.

She went upstairs to tell her mother.

'Mother, I've bought a ranch.'

'It is just as well, for I can't stand the noise of automobiles outside here another week.'

'It is quiet on my ranch, mother: the stillness simply speaks.'

'I had rather it held its tongue. I am simply drugged with all the bad novels I have read. I feel as if the sky was a big cracked bell and a million clappers were hammering human speech out of it.'

'Aren't you interested in my ranch, mother?'

'I hope I may be, by and by.'

Mrs Witt actually got up the next morning, and accompanied her daughter in the hired motor car driven by Phoenix, to the ranch: which was called Las Chivas. She sat like a pillar of salt, her face looking what the Indians call a False Face, meaning a mask. She seemed to have crystallised into neutrality. She watched the desert with its tufts of yellow greasewood go lurching past: she saw the fallen apples on the ground in the orchards near the adobe cottages: she looked down into the deep arroyo, and at the stream they forded in the car, and at the mountains blocking up the sky ahead, all with indifference. High on the mountains was snow: lower, blue-grey livid rock: and below the livid rock the aspens were expiring their daffodil yellow, this year, and the oak-scrub was dark and reddish, like gore. She saw it all with a sort of stony indifference.

'Don't you think it's lovely?' said Lou.

'I can see it is lovely,' replied her mother.

The michaelmas daisies in the clearing as they drove up to the ranch were sharp-rayed with purple, like a coming night.

Mrs Witt eyed the two log cabins, one of which was dilapidated and practically abandoned. She looked at the rather rickety corral, whose long planks had silvered and warped in the fierce sun. On one of the roof-planks a pack-rat was sitting erect like an old Indian keeping watch on a pueblo roof. He showed his white belly, and folded his hands and lifted his big ears, for all the world like an old immobile Indian.

'Isn't it for all the world as if *he* were the real boss of the place, Louise?' she said cynically.

And turning to the Mexican, who was a rag of a man but a pleasant, courteous fellow, she asked him why he didn't shoot the rat.

'Not worth a shell!' said the Mexican, with a faint hopeless smile.

Mrs Witt paced round and saw everything: it did not take long. She gazed in silence at the water of the spring, trickling out of an iron pipe into a barrel, under the cotton wood tree in an arroyo.

'Well, Louise,' she said. 'I am glad you feel competent to cope with so much hopelessness and so many rats.'

'But, mother, you must admit it is beautiful.'

'Yes, I suppose it is. But to use one of your Henry's phrases, beauty is a cold egg, as far as I am concerned.'

'Rico never would have said that beauty was a cold egg to him.'

'No, he wouldn't. He sits on it like a broody old hen on a china imitation. – Are you going to bring him here?'

'*Bring* him! – No. But he can come if he likes,' stammered Lou.

'*Oh – h!* won't it be beau – ti – ful!' cried Mrs Witt, rolling her head and lifting her shoulders in savage imitation of her son-in-law.

'Perhaps he won't come, mother,' said Lou, hurt.

'He will most certainly come, Louise, to see what's doing: unless you tell him you don't want him.'

'Anyhow, I needn't think about it till spring,' said Lou, anxiously pushing the matter aside.

Mrs Witt climbed the steep slope above the cabins, to the mouth of the little canyon. There she sat on a fallen tree, and surveyed the world beyond: a world not of men. She could not fail to be roused.

'What is your idea in coming here, daughter?' she asked.

'I love it here, mother.'

'But what do you expect to achieve by it?'

'I was rather hoping, mother, to escape achievement. I'll tell you – and you mustn't get cross if it sounds silly. As far as people go, my heart is quite broken. As far as people go, I don't want any more. I can't stand any more. What heart I ever had for it – for life with people – is quite broken. I want to be alone, mother: with you here, and Phoenix perhaps to look after horses and drive a car. But I want to be by myself, really.'

'With Phoenix in the background! Are you sure he won't be coming into the foreground before long?'

'No, mother, no more of that. If I've got to say it, Phoenix is a servant: he's really placed, as far as I can see. Always the same, playing about in the old back-yard. I can't take those men seriously. I can't fool round with them, or fool myself about them. I can't and I won't fool myself any more, mother, especially about men. They don't count. So why should you want them to pay me out?'

For the moment, this silenced Mrs Witt. Then she said, 'Why, *I* don't want it. Why should I! But after all you've got to live. You've never *lived* yet: not in my opinion.'

'Neither, mother, in my opinion, have you,' said Lou drily.

And this silenced Mrs Witt altogether. She had to be silent, or angrily on the defensive. And the latter she wouldn't be. She couldn't, really, in honesty.

'What do you call life?' Lou continued. 'Wriggling half-naked at a public show, and going off in a taxi to sleep with some half-drunken fool who thinks he's a man because – Oh, mother, I don't even want to think of it. I know you have a lurking idea that *that is life*. Let it be so then. But leave me out. Men in that aspect simply nauseate me: so grovelling and ratty. Life in that aspect simply drains all my life away. I tell you, for all that sort of thing, I'm broken, absolutely broken: if I wasn't broken to start with.'

'Well, Louise,' said Mrs Witt after a pause, 'I'm convinced that ever since men and women were men and women, people who took things seriously, and had time for it, got their hearts broken. Haven't I had mine broken! It's as sure as having your virginity broken: and it amounts to about as much. It's a beginning rather than an end.'

'So it is, mother. It's the beginning of something else, and the end of something that's done with. I *know*, and there's no altering it, that I've got to live differently. It sounds silly, but I don't know how else to put it. I've got to live for something that matters, way, way down in me. And I think sex would matter, to my very soul, if it was really sacred. But cheap sex kills me.'

'You have had a fancy for rather cheap men, perhaps.'

'Perhaps I have. Perhaps I should always be a fool, where people are concerned. Now I want to leave off that kind of foolery. There's something else, mother, that I want to give myself to. I know it. I know it absolutely. Why should I let myself be shouted down any more?'

Mrs Witt sat staring at the distance, her face a cynical mask.

'What is the something bigger? And *pray*, what is it bigger than?' she asked, in that tone of honied suavity which was her deadliest poison. 'I want to learn. I am out to know. I'm terribly intrigued by it. Something bigger! Girls in my generation occasionally entered convents, for *something bigger*. I always wondered if they found it. They seemed to me inclined in the imbecile direction, but perhaps that was because I was *something less* – '

There was a definite pause between the mother and daughter, a silence that was a pure breach. Then Lou said, 'You know quite well I'm not conventy, mother, whatever else I am – even a bit of an imbecile. But that kind of religion seems to me the other half of men. Instead of running after them you run away from them, and get the thrill that way. I don't hate men *because* they're men, as nuns do. I dislike them because they're not men enough: babies, and playboys, and poor things showing off all the time, even to themselves. I don't say I'm any better. I only wish, with all my soul, that some men *were* bigger and stronger and *deeper* than I am . . . '

'How do you know they're not? – ' asked Mrs Witt.

'How do I know?' said Lou mockingly.

And the pause that was a breach resumed itself. Mrs Witt was teasing with a little stick the bewildered black ants among the fir needles.

'And no doubt you are right about men,' she said at length. 'But at your age, the only sensible thing is to try and keep up the illusion. After all, as you say, you may be no better.'

'I may be no better. But keeping up the illusion means fooling myself. And I won't do it. When I see a man who is even a bit attractive to me – even as much as Phoenix – I say to myself: *Would you care for him afterwards? Does he really mean anything to you, except just a sensation?* – And I know he doesn't. No, mother, of this I am convinced: either my taking a man shall have a meaning and a mystery that penetrates my very soul, or I will keep to myself. – And what I *know* is, that the time has come for me to keep to myself. No more messing about.'

'Very well, daughter. You will probably spend your life keeping to yourself.'

'Do you think I mind! There's something else for me, mother. There's something else even that loves me and wants me. I can't tell you what it is. It's a spirit. And it's here, on this ranch. It's here, in this landscape. It's something more real to me than men are, and it soothes me, and it holds me up. I don't know what it is, definitely. It's something wild, that will hurt me sometimes and will wear me down sometimes. I know it. But it's something big, bigger than men, bigger than people, bigger than religion. It's something to do with wild America. And it's something to do with me. It's a mission, if you like. I am imbecile enough for that! – But it's my mission to keep myself for the spirit that is wild, and has waited so long here: even waited for such as me. Now I've come! Now I'm here. Now I am where I want to be: with the spirit that wants me. – And that's how it is. And neither Rico nor Phoenix nor anybody else really matters to me. They are in the world's back-yard. And I am here, right deep in America, where there's a wild spirit wants me, a wild spirit more than men. And it doesn't want to save me either. It needs me. It craves for me. And to it, my sex is deep and sacred, deeper than I am, with a deep nature aware deep down of my sex. It saves me from cheapness, mother. And even you could never do that for me.'

Mrs Witt rose to her feet, and stood looking far, far away, at the turquoise ridge of mountains half sunk under the horizon.

'How much did you say you paid for Las Chivas?' she asked.

'Twelve hundred dollars,' said Lou, surprised.

'Then I call it cheap, considering all there is to it: even the name.'

THE PRINCESS

TO HER FATHER, she was The Princess. To her Boston aunts and uncles she was just *Dollie Urquhart, poor little thing.*

Colin Urquhart was just a bit mad. He was of an old Scottish family, and he claimed royal blood. The blood of Scottish kings flowed in his veins. On this point, his American relatives said, he was just a bit 'off'. They could not bear any more to be told *which* royal blood of Scotland blued his veins. The whole thing was rather ridiculous, and a sore point. The only fact they remembered was that it was not Stuart.

He was a handsome man, with a wide-open blue eye that seemed sometimes to be looking at nothing, soft black hair brushed rather low on his low, broad brow, and a very attractive body. Add to this a most beautiful speaking voice, usually rather hushed and diffident, but sometimes resonant and powerful like bronze, and you have the sum of his charms. He looked like some old Celtic hero. He looked as if he should have worn a greyish kilt and a sporran, and shown his knees. His voice came direct out of the hushed Ossianic past.

For the rest, he was one of those gentlemen of sufficient but not excessive means who fifty years ago wandered vaguely about, never arriving anywhere, never doing anything, and never definitely being anything, yet well received and familiar in the good society of more than one country.

He did not marry till he was nearly forty, and then it was a wealthy Miss Prescott, from New England. Hannah Prescott at twenty-two was fascinated by the man with the soft black hair not yet touched by grey, and the wide, rather vague blue eyes. Many women had been fascinated before her. But Colin Urquhart, by his very vagueness, had avoided any decisive connection.

Mrs Urquhart lived three years in the mist and glamour of her husband's presence. And then it broke her. It was like living with a fascinating spectre. About most things he was completely, even ghostlily oblivious. He was always charming, courteous, perfectly gracious in that hushed, musical voice of his. But absent. When all came to all, he just wasn't there. 'Not all there,' as the vulgar say.

He was the father of the little girl she bore at the end of the first year. But this did not substantiate him the more. His very beauty and his haunting musical quality became dreadful to her after the first few months. The strange echo: he was like a living echo! His very flesh, when you touched it, did not seem quite the flesh of a real man.

Perhaps it was that he was a little bit mad. She thought it definitely the night her baby was born.

'Ah, so my little princess has come at last!' he said, in his throaty, singing Celtic voice, like a glad chant, swaying absorbed.

It was a tiny, frail baby, with wide, amazed blue eyes. They christened it Mary Henrietta. She called the little thing *My Dollie*. He called it always *My Princess*.

It was useless to fly at him. He just opened his wide blue eyes wider, and took a childlike, silent dignity there was no getting past.

Hannah Prescott had never been robust. She had no great desire to live. So when the baby was two years old she suddenly died.

The Prescotts felt a deep but unadmitted resentment against Colin Urquhart. They said he was selfish. Therefore they discontinued Hannah's income, a month after her burial in Florence, after they had urged the father to give the child over to them, and he had courteously, musically, but quite finally refused. He treated the Prescotts as if they were not of his world, not realities to him: just casual phenomena, or gramophones, talking-machines that had to be answered. He answered them. But of their actual existence he was never once aware.

They debated having him certified unsuitable to be guardian of his own child. But that would have created a scandal. So they did the simplest thing, after all – washed their hands of him. But they wrote scrupulously to the child, and sent her modest presents of money at Christmas, and on the anniversary of the death of her mother.

To The Princess her Boston relatives were for many years just a nominal reality. She lived with her father, and he travelled continually, though in a modest way, living on his moderate income. And never going to America. The child changed nurses all the time. In Italy it was a contadina; in India she had an ayah; in Germany she had a yellow-haired peasant girl.

Father and child were inseparable. He was not a recluse. Wherever he went he was to be seen paying formal calls, going out to luncheon or to tea, rarely to dinner. And always with the child. People called her Princess Urquhart, as if that were her christened name.

She was a quick, dainty little thing with dark gold hair that went a soft brown, and wide, slightly prominent blue eyes that were at once so candid and so knowing. She was always grown up; she never really grew up. Always strangely wise, and always childish.

It was her father's fault.

'My little Princess must never take too much notice of people and the things they say and do,' he repeated to her. 'People don't know what they are doing and saying. They chatter-chatter, and they hurt one another, and they hurt themselves very often, till they cry. But don't take any notice, my little Princess. Because it is all nothing. Inside everybody there is another creature, a demon which doesn't care at all. You peel away all the things they say and do and feel, as cook peels away the outside of the onions. And in the middle of everybody there is a green demon which you can't peel away. And this green demon never changes, and it doesn't care at all about all the things that happen to the outside leaves of the person, all the chatter-chatter, and all the husbands and wives and children, and troubles and fusses. You peel everything away from people, and there is a green, upright demon in every man and woman; and this demon is a man's real self, and a woman's real self. It doesn't really care about anybody, it belongs to the demons and the primitive fairies, who never care. But, even so, there are big demons and mean demons, and splendid demonish fairies, and vulgar ones. But there are no royal fairy women left. Only you, my little Princess. You are the last of the royal race of the old people; the last, my Princess. There are no others. You and I are the last. When I am dead there will only be you. And that is why, darling, you will never care for any of the people in the world very much. Because their demons are all dwindled and vulgar. They are not royal. Only you are royal, after me. Always remember that. And always remember, it is a *great secret*. If you tell people, they will try to kill you, because they will envy you for being a princess. It is our great secret, darling. I am a prince, and you a princess, of the old, old blood. And we keep our secret between us, all alone. And so, darling, you must treat all people very politely, because *noblesse oblige*. But you must never forget that you alone are the last of Princesses, and that all others are less than you are, less noble, more vulgar. Treat them politely and gently and kindly, darling. But you are the Princess, and they are commoners. Never try to think of them as if they were like you. They are not. You will find, always, that they are lacking, lacking in the royal touch, which only you have – '

The Princess learned her lesson early – the first lesson, of absolute reticence, the impossibility of intimacy with any other than her father; the second lesson, of naïve, slightly benevolent politeness. As a small child, something crystallised in her character, making her clear and finished, and as impervious as crystal.

'Dear child!' her hostess said of her. 'She is so quaint and old-fashioned; such a lady, poor little mite!'

She was erect, and very dainty. Always small, nearly tiny in physique, she seemed like a changeling beside her big, handsome, slightly mad father. She dressed very simply, usually in blue or delicate greys, with little collars of old Milan point, or very finely-worked linen. She had exquisite hands that made the piano sound like a spinet when she played. She was rather given to wearing cloaks and capes, instead of coats, out of doors, and little eighteenth-century sort of hats. Her complexion was pure apple-blossom.

She looked as if she had stepped out of a picture. But no one, to her dying day, ever knew exactly the strange picture her father had framed her in and from which she never stepped.

Her grandfather and grandmother and her Aunt Maud demanded twice to see her, once in Rome and once in Paris. Each time they were charmed, piqued, and annoyed. She was so exquisite and such a little virgin. At the same time so knowing and so oddly assured. That odd, assured touch of condescension, and the inward coldness, infuriated her American relations.

Only she really fascinated her grandfather. He was spellbound; in a way, in love with the little faultless thing. His wife would catch him brooding, musing over his grandchild, long months after the meeting, and craving to see her again. He cherished to the end the fond hope that she might come to live with him and her grandmother.

'Thank you so much, grandfather. You are so very kind. But Papa and I are such an old couple, you see, such a crotchety old couple, living in a world of our own.'

Her father let her see the world – from the outside. And he let her read. When she was in her teens she read Zola and Maupassant, and with the eyes of Zola and Maupassant she looked on Paris. A little later she read Tolstoy and Dostoevsky. The latter confused her. The others, she seemed to understand with a very shrewd, canny understanding, just as she understood the Decameron stories as she read them in their old Italian, or the Nibelung poems. Strange and *uncanny*, she seemed to understand things in a cold light perfectly, with all the flush of fire absent. She was something like a changeling, not quite human.

This earned her, also, strange antipathies. Cabmen and railway porters, especially in Paris and Rome, would suddenly treat her with brutal rudeness, when she was alone. They seemed to look on her with sudden violent antipathy. They sensed in her curious impertinence, an easy, sterile impertinence towards the things *they* felt most. She was so assured, and her flower of maidenhood was so scentless. She could look at a lusty, sensual Roman cabman as if he were a sort of grotesque, to make her smile. She knew all about him, in Zola. And the peculiar condescension with which she would give him her order, as if she, frail, beautiful thing, were the only reality, and he, coarse monster, were a sort of Caliban floundering in the mud on the margin of the pool of the perfect lotus, would suddenly enrage the fellow, the real Mediterranean who prided himself on his *beauté mâle*, and to whom the phallic mystery was still the only mystery. And he would turn a terrible face on her, bully her in a brutal, coarse fashion – hideous. For to him she had only the blasphemous impertinence of her own sterility.

Encounters like these made her tremble, and made her know she must have support from the outside. The power of her spirit did not extend to these low people, and they had all the physical power. She realised an implacability of hatred in their turning on her. But she did not lose her head. She quietly paid out money and turned away.

Those were dangerous moments, though, and she learned to be prepared for them. The Princess she was, and the fairy from the north, she could never understand the volcanic phallic rage with which coarse people could turn on her in a paroxysm of hatred. They never turned on her father like that. And quite early she decided it was the New England mother in her whom they hated. Never for one minute could she see with the old Roman eyes, see herself as sterility, the barren flower taking on airs and an intolerable impertinence. This was what the Roman cabman saw in her. And he longed to crush the barren blossom. Its sexless beauty and its authority put him in a passion of brutal revolt.

When she was nineteen her grandfather died, leaving her a considerable fortune in the safe hands of responsible trustees. They would deliver her her income, but only on condition that she resided for six months in the year in the United States.

'Why should they make me conditions?' she said to her father. 'I refuse to be imprisoned for six months in the year in the United States. We will tell them to keep their money.'

'Let us be wise, my little Princess, let us be wise. No, we are almost poor, and we are never safe from rudeness. I cannot allow anybody to be rude to me. I hate it, I hate it!' His eyes flamed as he said it. 'I could kill any man or woman who is rude to me. But we are in exile in the world. We are powerless. If we were really poor, we should be quite powerless, and then I should die. No, my Princess. Let us take their money, then they will not dare to be rude to us. Let us take it, as we put on clothes, to cover ourselves from their aggressions.'

There began a new phase, when the father and daughter spent their summers on the Great Lakes, or in California, or in the South-West. The father was something of a poet, the daughter something of a painter. He wrote poems about the lakes or the redwood trees, and she made dainty drawings. He was physically a strong man, and he loved the out-of-doors. He would go off with her for days, paddling in a canoe and sleeping by a campfire. Frail little Princess, she was always undaunted. She would ride with him on horseback over the mountain trails till she was so tired she was nothing but a bodiless consciousness sitting astride her pony. But she never gave in. And at night he folded her in her blankets on a bed of balsam pine twigs, and she lay and looked at the stars unmurmuring. She was fulfilling her role.

People said to her as the years passed, and she was a woman of twenty-five, then a woman of thirty, and always the same virgin dainty Princess, 'knowing' in a dispassionate way, like an old woman, and utterly intact, 'Don't you ever think what you will do when your father is no longer with you?'

She looked at her interlocutor with that cold, elfin detachment of hers: 'No, I never think of it,' she said.

She had a tiny, but exquisite little house in London, and another small, perfect house in Connecticut, each with a faithful housekeeper. Two homes, if she chose. And she knew many interesting literary and artistic people. What more?

So the years passed imperceptibly. And she had that quality of the sexless fairies, she did not change. At thirty-three she looked twenty-three.

Her father, however, was ageing, and becoming more and more queer. It was now her task to be his guardian in his private madness. He spent the last three years of life in the house in Connecticut. He was very much estranged, sometimes had fits of violence which almost killed the little Princess. Physical violence was horrible to her; it seemed to shatter her heart. But she found a woman a few years younger than herself, well educated and sensitive, to be a sort of nurse-companion to the mad old man. So the fact of madness was never openly admitted. Miss Cummins, the companion, had a passionate loyalty to the Princess, and a curious affection, tinged with love, for the handsome, white-haired, courteous old man, who was never at all aware of his fits of violence once they had passed.

The Princess was thirty-eight years old when her father died. And quite unchanged. She was still tiny, and like a dignified, scentless flower. Her soft brownish hair, almost the colour of beaver fur, was bobbed, and fluffed softly round her apple-blossom face, that was modelled with an arched nose like a proud old Florentine portrait. In her voice, manner and bearing she was exceedingly still, like a flower that has blossomed in a shadowy place. And from her blue eyes looked out the Princess's eternal laconic challenge, that grew almost sardonic as the years passed. She was the Princess, and sardonically she looked out on a princeless world.

She was relieved when her father died, and at the same time, it was as if everything had evaporated around her. She had lived in a sort of hot-house, in the aura of her father's madness. Suddenly the hot-house had been removed from around her, and she was in the raw, vast, vulgar open air.

Quoi faire? What was she to do? She seemed faced with absolute nothingness. Only she had Miss Cummins, who shared with her the secret, and almost the passion for her father. In fact, the Princess felt that her passion for her mad father had in some curious way transferred itself largely to Charlotte Cummins during the last years. And now Miss Cummins was the vessel that held the passion for the dead man. She herself, the Princess, was an empty vessel.

An empty vessel in the enormous warehouse of the world.

Quoi faire? What was she to do? She felt that, since she could not evaporate into nothingness, like alcohol from an unstoppered bottle, she must *do* something. Never before in her life had she felt the incumbency. Never, never had she felt she must *do* anything. That was left to the vulgar.

Now her father was dead, she found herself on the *fringe* of the vulgar crowd, sharing their necessity to *do* something. It was a little humiliating. She felt herself becoming vulgarised. At the same time she found herself looking at men with a shrewder eye: an eye to marriage. Not that she felt any sudden interest in men, or attraction towards them. No. She was still neither interested nor attracted towards men vitally. But *marriage*, that peculiar abstraction, had imposed a sort of spell on her. She thought that *marriage*, in the blank abstract, was the thing she ought to *do*. That *marriage* implied a man she also knew. She knew all the facts. But the man seemed a property of her own mind rather than a thing in himself, another being.

Her father died in the summer, the month after her thirty-eighth birthday. When all was over, the obvious thing to do, of course, was to travel. With Miss Cummins. The two women knew each other intimately, but they were always Miss Urquhart and Miss Cummins to one another, and a certain distance was instinctively maintained. Miss Cummins, from Philadelphia, of scholastic stock, and intelligent but untravelled, four years younger than the Princess, felt herself immensely the junior of her 'lady'. She had a sort of passionate veneration for the Princess, who seemed to her ageless, timeless. She could not see the rows of tiny, dainty, exquisite shoes in the Princess's cupboard without feeling a stab at the heart, a stab of tenderness and reverence, almost of awe.

Miss Cummins also was virginal, but with a look of puzzled surprise in her brown eyes. Her skin was pale and clear, her features well modelled, but there was a certain blankness in her expression, where the Princess had an odd touch of Renaissance grandeur. Miss Cummins's voice was also hushed almost to a whisper; it was the inevitable effect of Colin Urquhart's room. But the hushedness had a hoarse quality.

The Princess did not want to go to Europe. Her face seemed turned west. Now her father was gone, she felt she would go west, westwards, as if for ever. Following, no doubt, the March of Empire, which is brought up rather short on the Pacific coast, among swarms of wallowing bathers.

No, not the Pacific coast. She would stop short of that. The South-West was less vulgar. She would go to New Mexico.

She and Miss Cummins arrived at the Rancho del Cerro Gordo towards the end of August, when the crowd was beginning to drift back east. The ranch lay by a stream on the desert some four miles from the foot of the mountains, a mile away from the Indian pueblo of San Cristobal. It was a ranch for the rich; the Princess paid thirty dollars a day for herself and Miss Cummins. But then she had a little cottage to herself, among the apple trees of the orchard, with an excellent cook. She and Miss Cummins, however, took dinner at evening in the large guesthouse. For the Princess still entertained the idea of *marriage*.

The guests at the Rancho del Cerro Gordo were of all sorts, except the poor sort. They were practically all rich, and many were romantic. Some were charming, others were vulgar, some were movie people, quite quaint and not unattractive in their vulgarity, and many were Jews. The Princess did not care for Jews, though they were usually the most interesting to *talk* to. So she talked a good deal with the Jews, and painted with the artists, and rode with the young men from college, and had altogether quite a good time. And yet she felt something of a fish out of water, or a bird in the wrong forest. And *marriage* remained still completely in the abstract. No connecting it with any of these young men, even the nice ones.

The Princess looked just about twenty-five. The freshness of her mouth, the hushed, delicate-complexioned virginity of her face gave her not a day more. Only a certain laconic look in her eyes was disconcerting. When she was *forced* to write her age, she put twenty-eight, making the figure *two* rather badly, so that it just avoided being a three.

Men hinted marriage at her. Especially boys from college suggested it from a distance. But they all failed before the look of sardonic ridicule in the Princess's eyes. It always seemed to her rather preposterous, quite ridiculous, and a tiny bit impertinent on their part.

The only man that intrigued her at all was one of the guides, a man called Romero – Domingo Romero. It was he who had sold the ranch itself to the Wilkiesons, ten years before, for two thousand dollars. He had gone away, then reappeared at the old place. For he was the son of the old Romero, the last of the Spanish family that had owned miles of land around San Cristobal. But the coming of the white man and the failure of the vast flocks of sheep, and the fatal inertia which overcomes all men, at last, on the desert near the mountains, had finished the Romero family. The last descendants were just Mexican peasants.

Domingo, the heir, had spent his two thousand dollars, and was working for white people. He was now about thirty years old, a tall, silent fellow, with a heavy closed mouth and black eyes that looked across at one almost sullenly. From behind he was handsome, with a strong, natural body, and the back of his neck very dark and well-shapen, strong with life. But his dark face was long and heavy, almost sinister, with that peculiar heavy meaninglessness in it, characteristic of the Mexicans of his own locality. They are strong, they seem healthy. They laugh and joke with one another. But their physique and their natures seem static, as if there were nowhere, nowhere at all for their energies to go, and their faces, degenerating to misshapen heaviness, seem to have no *raison d'être*, no radical meaning. Waiting either to die or to be aroused into passion and hope. In some of the black eyes a queer, haunting mystic quality, sombre and a bit gruesome, the skull-and-crossbones look of the Penitentes. They had found their *raison d'être* in self-torture and death-worship. Unable to wrest *positive* significance for themselves from the vast, beautiful, but vindictive landscape they were born into, they turned on their own selves, and worshipped death through self-torture. The mystic gloom of this showed in their eyes.

But as a rule the dark eyes of the Mexicans were heavy and half-alive, sometimes hostile, sometimes kindly, often with the fatal Indian glaze on them, or the fatal Indian glint.

Domingo Romero was *almost* a typical Mexican to look at, with the typical heavy, dark, long face, clean-shaven, with an almost brutally heavy mouth. His eyes were black and Indian-looking. Only, at the centre of their hopelessness was a spark of pride, of self-confidence, of dauntlessness. Just a spark in the midst of the blackness of static despair.

But this spark was the difference between him and the mass of men. It gave a certain alert sensitiveness to his bearing and a certain beauty to his appearance. He wore a low-crowned black hat, instead of the ponderous headgear of the usual Mexican, and his clothes were thinnish and graceful. Silent, aloof, almost imperceptible in the landscape, he was an admirable guide, with a startling quick intelligence that anticipated difficulties about to rise. He could cook, too, crouching over the camp-fire and moving his lean deft brown hands. The only fault he had was that he was not forthcoming, he wasn't chatty and cosy.

'Oh, don't send Romero with us,' the Jews would say. 'One can't get any response from him.'

Tourists come and go, but they rarely *see* anything, inwardly. None of them ever saw the spark at the middle of Romero's eye; they were not alive enough to see it.

The Princess caught it one day, when she had him for a guide. She was fishing for trout in the canyon, Miss Cummins was reading a book, the horses were tied under the trees, Romero was fixing a proper fly on her line. He fixed the fly and handed her the line, looking up at her. And at that moment she caught the spark in his eye. And instantly she knew that he was a gentleman, that his 'demon', as her father would have said, was a fine demon. And instantly her manner towards him changed.

He had perched her on a rock over a quiet pool, beyond the cottonwood trees. It was early September, and the canyon already cool, but the leaves of the cottonwoods were still green. The Princess stood on her rock, a small but perfectly-formed figure, wearing a soft, close grey sweater and neatly-cut grey riding-breeches, with tall black boots, her fluffy brown hair straggling from under a little grey felt hat. A woman? Not quite. A changeling of some sort, perched in outline there on the rock, in the bristling wild canyon. She knew perfectly well how to handle a line. Her father had made a fisherman of her.

Romero, in a black shirt and with loose black trousers pushed into wide black riding-boots, was fishing a little farther down. He had put his hat on a rock behind him; his dark head was bent a little forward, watching the water. He had caught three trout. From time to time he glanced up-stream at the Princess, perched there so daintily. He saw she had caught nothing.

Soon he quietly drew in his line and came up to her. His keen eye watched her line, watched her position. Then, quietly, he suggested certain changes to her, putting his sensitive brown hand before her. And he withdrew a little, and stood in silence, leaning against a tree, watching her. He was helping her across the distance. She knew it, and thrilled. And in a moment she had a bite. In two minutes she had landed a good trout. She looked round at him quickly, her eyes sparkling, the colour heightened in her cheeks. And as she met his eyes a smile of greeting went over his dark face, very sudden, with an odd sweetness.

She knew he was helping her. And she felt in his presence a subtle, insidious male *kindliness* she had never known before waiting upon her. Her cheek flushed, and her blue eyes darkened.

After this, she always looked for him, and for that curious dark beam of a man's kindliness which he could give her, as it were, from his chest, from his heart. It was something she had never known before.

A vague, unspoken intimacy grew up between them. She liked his voice, his appearance, his presence. His natural language was Spanish; he spoke English like a foreign language, rather slow, with a slight hesitation, but with a sad, plangent sonority lingering over from his Spanish. There was a certain subtle correctness in his appearance; he was always perfectly shaved; his hair was thick and rather long on top, but always carefully groomed behind. And his fine black cashmere shirt, his wide leather belt, his well-cut, wide black trousers going into the embroidered cowboy boots had a certain inextinguishable elegance. He wore no silver rings or buckles. Only his boots were embroidered and decorated at the top with an inlay of white suède. He seemed elegant, slender, yet he was very strong.

And at the same time, curiously, he gave her the feeling that death was not far from him. Perhaps he too was half in love with death. However that may be, the sense she had that death was not far from him made him 'possible' to her.

Small as she was, she was quite a good horsewoman. They gave her at the ranch a sorrel mare, very lovely in colour, and well-made, with a powerful broad neck and the hollow back that betokens a swift runner. Tansy, she was called. Her only fault was the usual mare's failing, she was inclined to be hysterical.

So that every day the Princess set off with Miss Cummins and Romero, on horseback, riding into the mountains. Once they went camping for several days, with two more friends in the party.

'I think I like it better,' the Princess said to Romero, 'when we three go alone.' And he gave her one of his quick, transfiguring smiles.

It was curious no white man had ever showed her this capacity for subtle gentleness, this power to *help* her in silence across a distance, if she were fishing without success, or tired of her horse, or if Tansy suddenly got scared. It was as if Romero could send her *from his heart* a dark beam of succour and sustaining. She had never known this before, and it was very thrilling.

Then the smile that suddenly creased his dark face, showing the strong white teeth. It creased his face almost into a savage grotesque. And at the same time there was in it something so warm, such a dark flame of kindliness for her, she was elated into her true Princess self.

Then that vivid, latent spark, in his eye, which she had seen, and which she knew he was aware she had seen. It made an inter-recognition between them, silent and delicate. Here he was delicate as a woman in this subtle inter-recognition.

And yet his presence only put to flight in her the *idée fixe* of 'marriage'. For some reason, in her strange little brain, the idea of *marrying* him could not enter. Not for any definite reason. He was in himself a gentleman, and she had plenty of money for two. There was no actual obstacle. Nor was she conventional.

No, now she came down to it, it was as if their two 'demons' could marry, were perhaps married. Only their two *selves*, Miss Urquhart and Señor Domingo Romero, were for some reason incompatible. There was a peculiar subtle intimacy of inter-recognition between them. But she did not see in the least how it would lead to marriage. Almost she could more easily marry one of the nice boys from Harvard or Yale.

The time passed, and she let it pass. The end of September came, with aspens going yellow on the mountain heights, and oak-scrub going red. But as yet the cottonwoods in the valley and canyons had not changed.

'When will you go away?' Romero asked her, looking at her fixedly, with a blank black eye.

'By the end of October,' she said. 'I have promised to be in Santa Barbara at the beginning of November.'

He was hiding the spark in his eye from her. But she saw the peculiar sullen thickening of his heavy mouth.

She had complained to him many times that one never saw any wild animals, except chipmunks and squirrels, and perhaps a skunk and a porcupine. Never a deer, or a bear, or a mountain lion.

'Are there no bigger animals in these mountains?' she asked, dissatisfied.

'Yes,' he said. 'There are deer – I see their tracks. And I saw the tracks of a bear.'

'But why can one never see the animals themselves?' She looked dissatisfied and wistful like a child.

'Why, it's pretty hard for you to see them. They won't let you come close. You have to keep still, in a place where they come. Or else you have to follow their tracks a long way.'

'I can't bear to go away till I've seen them: a bear, or a deer –'

The smile came suddenly on his face, indulgent.

'Well, what do you want? Do you want to go up into the mountains to some place, to wait till they come?'

'Yes,' she said, looking up at him with a sudden naïve impulse of recklessness.

And immediately his face became sombre again, responsible.

'Well,' he said, with slight irony, a touch of mockery of her. 'You will have to find a house. It's very cold at night now. You would have to stay all night in a house.'

'And there are no houses up there?' she said.

'Yes,' he replied. 'There is a little shack that belongs to me, that a miner built a long time ago, looking for gold. You can go there and stay one night, and maybe you see something. Maybe! I don't know. Maybe nothing come.'

'How much chance is there?'

'Well, I don't know. Last time when I was there I see three deer come down to drink at the water, and I shot two raccoons. But maybe this time we don't see anything.'

'Is there water there?' she asked.

'Yes, there is a little round pond, you know, below the spruce trees. And the water from the snow runs into it.'

'Is it far away?' she asked.

'Yes, pretty far. You see that ridge there' – and turning to the mountains he lifted his arm in the gesture which is somehow so moving, out in the West, pointing to the distance – 'that ridge where there are no trees, only rock' – his black eyes were focused on the distance, his face impassive, but as if in pain – 'you go round that ridge, and along, then you come down through the spruce trees to where that cabin is. My father bought that placer claim from a miner who was broke, but nobody ever found any gold or anything, and nobody ever goes there. Too lonesome!'

The Princess watched the massive, heavy-sitting, beautiful bulk of the Rocky Mountains. It was early in October, and the aspens were already losing their gold leaves; high up, the spruce and pine seemed to be growing darker; the great flat patches of oak scrub on the heights were red like gore.

'Can I go over there?' she asked, turning to him and meeting the spark in his eye.

His face was heavy with responsibility.

1236   SELECTED WORKS OF D. H. LAWRENCE

'Yes,' he said, 'you can go. But there'll be snow over the ridge, and it's awful cold, and awful lonesome.'

'I should like to go,' she said, persistent.

'All right,' he said. 'You can go if you want to.'

She doubted, though, if the Wilkiesons would let her go; at least alone with Romero and Miss Cummins.

Yet an obstinacy characteristic of her nature, an obstinacy tinged perhaps with madness, had taken hold of her. She wanted to look over the mountains into their secret heart. She wanted to descend to the cabin below the spruce trees, near the tarn of bright green water. She wanted to see the wild animals move about in their wild unconsciousness.

'Let us say to the Wilkiesons that we want to make the trip round the Frijoles canyon,' she said.

The trip round the Frijoles canyon was a usual thing. It would not be strenuous, nor cold, nor lonely: they could sleep in the log house that was called an hotel.

Romero looked at her quickly.

'If you want to say that,' he replied, 'you can tell Mrs Wilkieson. Only I know she'll be mad with me if I take you up in the mountains to that place. And I've got to go there first with a pack-horse, to take lots of blankets and some bread. Maybe Miss Cummins can't stand it. Maybe not. It's a hard trip.'

He was speaking, and thinking, in the heavy, disconnected Mexican fashion.

'Never mind!' The Princess was suddenly very decisive and stiff with authority. 'I want to do it. I will arrange with Mrs Wilkieson. And we'll go on Saturday.'

He shook his head slowly.

'I've got to go up on Sunday with a pack-horse and blankets,' he said. 'Can't do it before.'

'Very well!' she said, rather piqued. 'Then we'll start on Monday.'

She hated being thwarted even the tiniest bit.

He knew that if he started with the pack on Sunday at dawn he would not be back until late at night. But he consented that they should start on Monday morning at seven. The obedient Miss Cummins was told to prepare for the Frijoles trip. On Sunday Romero had his day off. He had not put in an appearance when the Princess retired on Sunday night, but on Monday morning, as she was dressing, she saw him bringing in the three horses from the corral. She was in high spirits.

The night had been cold. There was ice at the edges of the irrigation ditch, and the chipmunks crawled into the sun and lay with wide, dumb, anxious eyes, almost too numb to run.

'We may be away two or three days,' said the Princess.

'Very well. We won't begin to be anxious about you before Thursday, then,' said Mrs Wilkieson, who was young and capable: from Chicago. 'Anyway,' she added, 'Romero will see you through. He's so trustworthy.'

The sun was already on the desert as they set off towards the mountains,

making the greasewood and the sage pale as pale grey oando, luminous the great
level around them. To the right glinted the shadows of the adobe pueblo, flat
and almost invisible on the plain, earth of its earth. Behind lay the ranch and the
tufts of tall, plumy cottonwoods, whose summits were yellowing under the
perfect blue sky.

Autumn breaking into colour in the great spaces of the South-West.

But the three trotted gently along the trail, towards the sun that sparkled
yellow just above the dark bulk of the ponderous mountains. Side-slopes were
already gleaming yellow, flaming with a second light, under the coldish blue of
the pale sky. The front slopes were in shadow, with submerged lustre of red oak
scrub and dull-gold aspens, blue-black pines and grey-blue rock. While the
canyon was full of deep blueness.

They rode single file, Romero first, on a black horse. Himself in black, made
a flickering black spot in the delicate pallor of the great landscape, where even
pine trees at a distance take a film of blue paler than their green. Romero rode
on in silence past the tufts of furry greasewood. The Princess came next, on her
sorrel mare. And Miss Cummins, who was not quite happy on horseback, came
last, in the pale dust that the others had kicked up. Sometimes her horse
sneezed, and she started.

But on they went at a gentle trot. Romero never looked round. He could hear
the sound of the hoofs following, and that was all he wanted.

For the rest, he held ahead. And the Princess, with that black, unheeding
figure always travelling away from her, felt strangely helpless, withal elated.

They neared the pale, round foot-hills, dotted with the round dark piñon and
cedar shrubs. The horses clinked and clattered among stones. Occasionally a big
round greasewood held out fleecy tufts of flowers, pure gold. They wound into
blue shadow, then up a steep stony slope, with the world lying pallid away
behind and below. Then they dropped into the shadow of the San Cristobal
canyon.

The stream was running full and swift. Occasionally the horses snatched at a
tuft of grass. The trail narrowed and became rocky; the rocks closed in; it was
dark and cool as the horses climbed and climbed upwards, and the tree trunks
crowded in the shadowy, silent tightness of the canyon. They were among
cottonwood trees that ran up straight and smooth and round to an extraordinary
height. Above, the tips were gold, and it was sun. But away below, where the
horses struggled up the rocks and wound among the trunks, there was still blue
shadow by the sound of waters and an occasional grey festoon of old man's
beard, and here and there a pale, dipping cranesbill flower among the tangle and
the débris of the virgin place. And again the chill entered the Princess's heart as
she realised what a tangle of decay and despair lay in the virgin forests.

They scrambled downwards, splashed across stream, up rocks and along the
trail of the other side. Romero's black horse stopped, looked down quizzically
at the fallen trees, then stepped over lightly. The Princess's sorrel followed,
carefully. But Miss Cummins's buckskin made a fuss, and had to be got round.

In the same silence, save for the clinking of the horses and the splashing as the trail crossed stream, they worked their way upwards in the tight, tangled shadow of the canyon. Sometimes, crossing stream, the Princess would glance upwards, and then always her heart caught in her breast. For high up, away in heaven, the mountain heights shone yellow, dappled with dark spruce firs, clear almost as speckled daffodils against the pale turquoise blue lying high and serene above the dark-blue shadow where the Princess was. And she would snatch at the blood-red leaves of the oak as her horse crossed a more open slope, not knowing what she felt.

They were getting fairly high, occasionally lifted above the canyon itself, in the low groove below the speckled, gold-sparkling heights which towered beyond. Then again they dipped and crossed stream, the horses stepping gingerly across a tangle of fallen, frail aspen stems, then suddenly floundering in a mass of rocks. The black emerged ahead, his black tail waving. The Princess let her mare find her own footing; then she too emerged from the clatter. She rode on after the black. Then came a great frantic rattle of the buckskin behind. The Princess was aware of Romero's dark face looking round, with a strange, demon-like watchfulness, before she herself looked round, to see the buckskin scrambling rather lamely beyond the rocks, with one of his pale buff knees already red with blood.

'He almost went down!' called Miss Cummins.

But Romero was already out of the saddle and hastening down the path. He made quiet little noises to the buckskin, and began examining the cut knee.

'Is he hurt?' cried Miss Cummins anxiously, and she climbed hastily down.

'Oh, my goodness!' she cried, as she saw the blood running down the slender buff leg of the horse in a thin trickle. 'Isn't that *awful*?' She spoke in a stricken voice, and her face was white.

Romero was still carefully feeling the knee of the buckskin. Then he made him walk a few paces. And at last he stood up straight and shook his head.

'Not very bad!' he said. 'Nothing broken.'

Again he bent and worked at the knees. Then he looked up at the Princess.

'He can go on,' he said. 'It's not bad.'

The Princess looked down at the dark face in silence.

'What, go on right up here?' cried Miss Cummins. 'How many hours?'

'About five!' said Romero simply.

'Five hours!' cried Miss Cummins. 'A horse with a lame knee! And a steep mountain! Why–y!'

'Yes, it's pretty steep up there,' said Romero, pushing back his hat and staring fixedly at the bleeding knee. The buckskin stood in a stricken sort of dejection. 'But I think he'll make it all right,' the man added.

'Oh!' cried Miss Cummins, her eyes bright with sudden passion of unshed tears. 'I wouldn't think of it. I wouldn't ride him up there, not for any money.'

'Why wouldn't you?' asked Romero.

'It *hurts* him.'

Romero bent down again to the horse's knee.

'Maybe it hurts him a little,' he said. 'But he can make it all right, and his leg won't get stiff.'

'What! Ride him five hours up the steep mountains?' cried Miss Cummins. 'I couldn't. I just couldn't do it. I'll lead him a little way and see if he can go. But I *couldn't* ride him again. I couldn't. Let me walk.'

'But Miss Cummins, dear, if Romero says he'll be all right?' said the Princess.

'I know it hurts him. Oh, I just couldn't bear it.'

There was no doing anything with Miss Cummins. The thought of a hurt animal always put her into a sort of hysterics.

They walked forward a little, leading the buckskin. He limped rather badly. Miss Cummins sat on a rock.

'Why, it's agony to see him!' she cried. 'It's *cruel*!'

'He won't limp after a bit, if you take no notice of him,' said Romero. 'Now he plays up, and limps very much, because he wants to make you see.'

'I don't think there can be much playing up,' said Miss Cummins bitterly. 'We can *see* how it must hurt him.'

'It don't hurt much,' said Romero.

But now Miss Cummins was silent with antipathy.

It was a deadlock. The party remained motionless on the trail, the Princess in the saddle, Miss Cummins seated on a rock, Romero standing black and remote near the drooping buckskin.

'Well!' said the man suddenly at last. 'I guess we go back, then.'

And he looked up swiftly at his horse, which was cropping at the mountain herbage and treading on the trailing reins.

'No!' cried the Princess. 'Oh no!' Her voice rang with a great wail of disappointment and anger. Then she checked herself.

Miss Cummins rose with energy.

'Let me lead the buckskin home,' she said, with cold dignity, 'and you two go on.'

This was received in silence. The Princess was looking down at her with a sardonic, almost cruel gaze.

'We've only come about two hours,' said Miss Cummins. 'I don't mind a bit leading him home. But I *couldn't* ride him. I *couldn't* have him ridden with that knee.'

This again was received in dead silence. Romero remained impassive, almost inert.

'Very well, then,' said the Princess. 'You lead him home. You'll be quite all right. Nothing can happen to you, possibly. And say to them that we have gone on and shall be home tomorrow – or the day after.'

She spoke coldly and distinctly. For she could not bear to be thwarted.

'Better all go back, and come again another day,' said Romero – non-committal.

'There will never *be* another day,' cried the Princess. 'I want to go on.'

She looked at him square in the eyes, and met the spark in his eye.

He raised his shoulders slightly.

'If you want it,' he said. 'I'll go on with you. But Miss Cummins can ride my horse to the end of the canyon, and I lead the buckskin. Then I come back to you.'

It was arranged so. Miss Cummins had her saddle put on Romero's black horse, Romero took the buckskin's bridle, and they started back. The Princess rode very slowly on, upwards, alone. She was at first so angry with Miss Cummins that she was blind to everything else. She just let her mare follow her own inclinations.

The peculiar spell of anger carried the Princess on, almost unconscious, for an hour or so. And by this time she was beginning to climb pretty high. Her horse walked steadily all the time. They emerged on a bare slope, and the trail wound through frail aspen stems. Here a wind swept, and some of the aspens were already bare. Others were fluttering their discs of pure, solid yellow leaves, so *nearly* like petals, while the slope ahead was one soft, glowing fleece of daffodil yellow; fleecy like a golden fox-skin, and yellow as daffodils alive in the wind and the high mountain sun.

She paused and looked back. The near great slopes were mottled with gold and the dark hue of spruce, like some unsinged eagle, and the light lay gleaming upon them. Away through the gap of the canyon she could see the pale blue of the egg-like desert, with the crumpled dark crack of the Rio Grande Canyon. And far, far off, the blue mountains like a fence of angels on the horizon.

And she thought of her adventure. She was going on alone with Romero. But then she was very sure of herself, and Romero was not the kind of man to do anything to her against her will. This was her first thought. And she just had a fixed desire to go over the brim of the mountains, to look into the inner chaos of the Rockies. And she wanted to go with Romero, because he had some peculiar kinship with her; there was some peculiar link between the two of them. Miss Cummins anyhow would have been only a discordant note.

She rode on, and emerged at length in the lap of the summit. Beyond her was a great concave of stone and stark, dead-grey trees, where the mountain ended against the sky. But nearer was the dense black, bristling spruce, and at her feet was the lap of the summit, a flat little valley of sere grass and quiet-standing yellow aspens, the stream trickling like a thread across.

It was a little valley or shell from which the stream was gently poured into the lower rocks and trees of the canyon. Around her was a fairy-like gentleness, the delicate sere grass, the groves of delicate-stemmed aspens dropping their flakes of bright yellow. And the delicate, quick little stream threading through the wild, sere grass.

Here one might expect deer and fawns and wild things, as in a little paradise. Here she was to wait for Romero, and they were to have lunch.

She unfastened her saddle and pulled it to the ground with a crash, letting her horse wander with a long rope. How beautiful Tansy looked, sorrel, among the yellow leaves that lay like a patina on the sere ground. The Princess herself wore a fleecy sweater of a pale, sere buff, like the grass, and riding breeches of a pure orange-tawny colour. She felt quite in the picture.

From her saddle-pouches she took the packages of lunch, spread a little cloth, and sat to wait for Romero. Then she made a little fire. Then she ate a devilled egg. Then she ran after Tansy, who was straying across-stream. Then she sat in the sun, in the stillness near the aspens, and waited.

The sky was blue. Her little alp was soft and delicate as fairy-land. But beyond and up jutted the great slopes, dark with the pointed feathers of spruce, bristling with grey dead trees among grey rock, or dappled with dark and gold. The beautiful, but fierce, heavy cruel mountains, with their moments of tenderness.

She saw Tansy start, and begin to run. Two ghost-like figures on horseback emerged from the black of the spruce across the stream. It was two Indians on horseback, swathed like seated mummies in their pale-grey cotton blankets. Their guns jutted beyond the saddles. They rode straight towards her, to her thread of smoke.

As they came near, they unswathed themselves and greeted her, looking at her curiously from their dark eyes. Their black hair was somewhat untidy, the long rolled plaits on their shoulders were soiled. They looked tired.

They got down from their horses near her little fire – a camp was a camp – swathed their blankets round their hips, pulled the saddles from their ponies and turned them loose, then sat down. One was a young Indian whom she had met before, the other was an older man.

'You all alone?' said the younger man.

'Romero will be here in a minute,' she said glancing back along the trail.

'Ah, Romero! You with him? Where are you going?'

'Round the ridge,' she said. 'Where are you going?'

'We going down to Pueblo.'

'Been out hunting? How long have you been out?'

'Yes. Been out five days.' The young Indian gave a little meaningless laugh.

'Got anything?'

'No. We see tracks of two deer – but not got nothing.'

The Princess noticed a suspicious-looking bulk under one of the saddles – surely a folded-up deer. But she said nothing.

'You must have been cold,' she said.

'Yes, very cold in the night. And hungry. Got nothing to eat since yesterday. Eat it all up.' And again he laughed his little meaningless laugh. Under their dark skins, the two men looked peaked and hungry. The Princess rummaged for food among the saddle-bags. There was a lump of bacon – the regular stand-back – and some bread. She gave them this, and they began toasting slices of it on long sticks at the fire. Such was the little camp Romero saw as he rode down the slope: the Princess in her orange breeches, her head tied in a blue-and-brown silk kerchief, sitting opposite the two dark-headed Indians across the camp-fire, while one of the Indians was leaning forward toasting bacon, his two plaits of braid-swathed hair dangling as if wearily.

Romero rode up, his face expressionless. The Indians greeted him in Spanish. He unsaddled his horse, took food from the bags, and sat down at the camp to eat. The Princess went to the stream for water, and to wash her hands.

'Got coffee?' asked the Indians.

'No coffee this outfit,' said Romero.

They lingered an hour or more in the warm midday sun. Then Romero saddled the horses. The Indians still squatted by the fire. Romero and the Princess rode away, calling *Adios!* to the Indians, over the stream and into the dense spruce whence the two strange figures had emerged.

When they were alone, Romero turned and looked at her curiously, in a way she could not understand, with such a hard glint in his eyes. And for the first time she wondered if she was rash.

'I hope you don't mind going alone with me,' she said.

'If you want it,' he replied.

They emerged at the foot of the great bare slope of rocky summit, where dead spruce trees stood sparse and bristling like bristles on a grey dead hog. Romero said the Mexicans, twenty years back, had fired the mountains, to drive out the whites. This grey concave slope of summit was corpse-like.

The trail was almost invisible. Romero watched for the trees which the Forest Service had blazed. And they climbed the stark corpse slope, among dead spruce, fallen and ash-grey, into the wind. The wind came rushing from the west, up the funnel of the canyon, from the desert. And there was the desert, like a vast mirage tilting slowly upwards towards the west, immense and pallid, away beyond the funnel of the canyon. The Princess could hardly look.

For an hour their horses rushed the slope, hastening with a great working of the haunches upwards, and halting to breathe, scrambling again, and rowing their way up length by length, on the livid, slanting wall. While the wind blew like some vast machine.

After an hour they were working their way on the incline, no longer forcing straight up. All was grey and dead around them; the horses picked their way over the silver-grey corpses of the spruce. But they were near the top, near the ridge.

Even the horses made a rush for the last bit. They had worked round to a scrap of spruce forest near the very top. They hurried in, out of the huge, monstrous, mechanical wind, that whistled inhumanly and was palely cold. So stepping through the dark screen of trees, they emerged over the crest.

In front now was nothing but mountains, ponderous, massive, down-sitting mountains, in a huge and intricate knot, empty of life or soul. Under the bristling black feathers of spruce near by lay patches of white snow. The lifeless valleys were concaves of rock and spruce, the rounded summits and the hog-backed summits of grey rock crowded one behind the other like some monstrous herd in arrest.

It frightened the Princess, it was *so* inhuman. She had not thought it could be so inhuman, so, as it were, anti-life. And yet now one of her desires was fulfilled.

She had seen it, the massive, gruesome, repellant core of the Rockies. She saw it there beneath her eyes, in its gigantic, heavy gruesomeness.

And she wanted to go back. At this moment she wanted to turn back. She had looked down into the intestinal knot of these mountains. She was frightened. She wanted to go back.

But Romero was riding on, on the lee side of the spruce forest, above the concaves of the inner mountains. He turned round to her and pointed at the slope with a dark hand.

'Here a miner has been trying for gold,' he said. It was a grey scratched-out heap near a hole – like a great badger hole. And it looked quite fresh.

'Quite lately?' said the Princess.

'No, long ago – twenty, thirty years.' He had reined in his horse and was looking at the mountains. 'Look!' he said. 'There goes the Forest Service trail – along those ridges, on the top, way over there till it comes to Lucytown, where is the Government road. We go down there – no trail – see behind that mountain – you see the top, no trees, and some grass?'

His arm was lifted, his brown hand pointing, his dark eyes piercing into the distance, as he sat on his black horse twisting round to her. Strange and ominous, only the demon of himself, he seemed to her. She was dazed and a little sick, at that height, and she could not see any more. Only she saw an eagle turning in the air beyond, and the light from the west showed the pattern on him underneath.

'Shall I ever be able to go so far?' asked the Princess faintly, petulantly.

'Oh yes! All easy now. No more hard places.'

They worked along the ridge, up and down, keeping on the lee side, the inner side, in the dark shadow. It was cold. Then the trail laddered up again, and they emerged on a narrow ridge-track, with the mountain slipping away enormously on either side. The Princess was afraid. For one moment she looked out, and saw the desert, the desert ridges, more desert, more blue ridges, shining pale and very vast, far below, vastly palely tilting to the western horizon. It was ethereal and terrifying in its gleaming, pale, half-burnished immensity, tilted at the west. She could not bear it. To the left was the ponderous, involved mass of mountains all kneeling heavily.

She closed her eyes and let her consciousness evaporate away. The mare followed the trail. So on and on, in the wind again.

They turned their backs to the wind, facing inwards to the mountains. She thought they had left the trail; it was quite invisible.

'No,' he said, lifting his hand and pointing. 'Don't you see the blazed trees?'

And making an effort of consciousness, she was able to perceive on a pale-grey dead spruce stem the old marks where an axe had chipped a piece away. But with the height, the cold, the wind, her brain was numb.

They turned again and began to descend; he told her they had left the trail. The horses slithered in the loose stones, picking their way downward. It was afternoon, the sun stood obtrusive and gleaming in the lower heavens – about four o'clock. The horses went steadily, slowly, but obstinately onwards. The air was getting colder. They were in among the lumpish peaks and steep concave valleys. She was barely conscious at all of Romero.

He dismounted and came to help her from her saddle. She tottered, but would not betray her feebleness.

'We must slide down here,' he said. 'I can lead the horses.'

They were on a ridge, and facing a steep bare slope of pallid, tawny mountain grass on which the western sun shone full. It was steep and concave. The Princess felt she might start slipping, and go down like a toboggan into the great hollow.

But she pulled herself together. Her eye blazed up again with excitement and determination. A wind rushed past her; she could hear the shriek of spruce trees far below. Bright spots came on her cheeks as her hair blew across. She looked a wild, fairy-like little thing.

'No,' she said. 'I will take my horse.'

'Then mind she doesn't slip down on top of you,' said Romero. And away he went, nimbly dropping down the pale, steep incline, making from rock to rock, down the grass, and following any little slanting groove. His horse hopped and slithered after him, and sometimes stopped dead, with forefeet pressed back, refusing to go farther. He, below his horse, looked up and pulled the reins gently, and encouraged the creature. Then the horse once more dropped his forefeet with a jerk, and the descent continued.

The Princess set off in blind, reckless pursuit, tottering and yet nimble. And Romero, looking constantly back to see how she was faring, saw her fluttering down like some queer little bird, her orange breeches twinkling like the legs of some duck, and her head, tied in the blue and buff kerchief, bound round and round like the head of some blue-topped bird. The sorrel mare rocked and slipped behind her. But down came the Princess in a reckless intensity, a tiny, vivid spot on the great hollow flank of the tawny mountain. So tiny! Tiny as a frail bird's egg. It made Romero's mind go blank with wonder.

But they had to get down, out of that cold and dragging wind. The spruce trees stood below, where a tiny stream emerged in stones. Away plunged Romero, zigzagging down. And away behind, up the slope, fluttered the tiny, bright-coloured Princess, holding the end of the long reins, and leading the lumbering, four-footed, sliding mare.

At last they were down. Romero sat in the sun, below the wind, beside some squaw-berry bushes. The Princess came near, the colour flaming in her cheeks, her eyes dark blue, much darker than the kerchief on her head, and glowing unnaturally.

'We made it,' said Romero.

'Yes,' said the Princess, dropping the reins and subsiding on to the grass, unable to speak, unable to think.

But, thank heaven, they were out of the wind and in the sun.

In a few minutes her consciousness and her control began to come back. She drank a little water. Romero was attending to the saddles. Then they set off again, leading the horses still a little farther down the tiny stream-bed. Then they could mount.

They rode down a bank and into a valley grove dense with aspens. Winding through the thin, crowding, pale-smooth stems, the sun shone flickering beyond them, and the disc-like aspen leaves, waving queer mechanical signals, seemed to be splashing the gold light before her eyes. She rode on in a splashing dazzle of gold.

Then they entered shadow and the dark, resinous spruce trees. The fierce boughs always wanted to sweep her off her horse. She had to twist and squirm past.

But there was a semblance of an old trail. And all at once they emerged in the sun on the edge of a spruce grove, and there was a little cabin, and the bottom of a small, naked valley with a grey rock and heaps of stones, and a round pool of intense green water, dark green. The sun was just about to leave it.

Indeed, as she stood, the shadow came over the cabin and over herself; they were in the lower gloom, a twilight. Above, the heights still blazed.

It was a little hole of a cabin, near the spruce trees, with an earthen floor and an unhinged door. There was a wooden bed-bunk, three old sawn-off log-lengths to sit on as stools, and a sort of fireplace; no room for anything else. The little hole would hardly contain two people. The roof had gone but Romero had laid on thick spruce boughs.

The strange squalor of the primitive forest pervaded the place, the squalor of animals and their droppings, the squalor of the wild. The Princess knew the peculiar repulsiveness of it. She was tired and faint.

Romero hastily got a handful of twigs, set a little fire going in the stove grate, and went out to attend to the horses. The Princess vaguely, mechanically, put sticks on the fire, in a sort of stupor, watching the blaze, stupefied and fascinated. She could not make much fire – it would set the whole cabin alight. And smoke oozed out of the dilapidated mud-and-stone chimney.

When Romero came in with the saddle-pouches and saddles, hanging the saddles on the wall, there sat the little Princess on her stump of wood in front of the dilapidated fire-grate, warming her tiny hands at the blaze, while her orange breeches glowed almost like another fire. She was in a sort of stupor.

'You have some whisky now, or some tea? Or wait for some soup?' he asked.

She rose and looked at him with bright, dazed eyes, half comprehending; the colour glowing hectic in her cheeks.

'Some tea,' she said, 'with a little whisky in it. Where's the kettle?'

'Wait,' he said. 'I'll bring the things.' She took her cloak from the back of her saddle, and followed him into the open. It was a deep cup of shadow. But above the sky was still shining, and the heights of the mountains were blazing with aspen like fire blazing.

Their horses were cropping the grass among the stones. Romero clambered up a heap of grey stones and began lifting away logs and rocks, till he had opened the mouth of one of the miner's little old workings. This was his cache. He brought out bundles of blankets, pans for cooking, a little petrol camp-stove, an axe, the regular camp outfit. He seemed so quick and energetic and full of force. This quick force dismayed the Princess a little.

She took a saucepan and went down the stones to the water. It was very still and mysterious, and of a deep green colour, yet pure, transparent as glass. How cold the place was! How mysterious and fearful.

She crouched in her dark cloak by the water, rinsing the saucepan, feeling the cold heavy above her, the shadow like a vast weight upon her, bowing her down. The sun was leaving the mountain-tops, departing, leaving her under profound shadow. Soon it would crush her down completely.

Sparks? – or eyes looking at her across the water? She gazed, hypnotised. And with her sharp eyes she made out in the dusk the pale form of a bob-cat crouching by the water's edge, pale as the stones among which it crouched, opposite. And it was watching her with cold, electric eyes of strange intentness, a sort of cold, icy wonder and fearlessness. She saw its *museau* pushed forward, its tufted ears pricking intensely up. It was watching her with cold animal curiosity, something demonish and conscienceless.

She made a swift movement, spilling her water. And in a flash the creature was gone, leaping like a cat that is escaping; but strange and soft in its motion, with its little bob-tail. Rather fascinating. Yet that cold, intent, demonish watching! She shivered with cold and fear. She knew well enough the dread and repulsiveness of the wild.

Romero carried in the bundles of bedding and the camp outfit. The window-less cabin was already dark inside. He lit a lantern, and then went out again with the axe. She heard him chopping wood as she fed sticks to the fire under her water. When he came in with an armful of oak-scrub faggots, she had just thrown the tea into the water.

'Sit down,' she said, 'and drink tea.'

He poured a little bootleg whisky into the enamel cups, and in the silence the two sat on the log-ends, sipping the hot liquid and coughing occasionally from the smoke.

'We burn these oak sticks,' he said. 'They don't make hardly any smoke.'

Curious and remote he was, saying nothing except what had to be said. And she, for her part, was as remote from him. They seemed far, far apart, worlds apart, now they were so near.

He unwrapped one bundle of bedding, and spread the blankets and the sheepskin in the wooden bunk.

'You lie down and rest,' he said, 'and I make the supper.'

She decided to do so. Wrapping her cloak round her, she lay down in the bunk, turning her face to the wall. She could hear him preparing supper over the little petrol stove. Soon she could smell the soup he was heating; and soon she heard the hissing of fried chicken in a pan.

'You eat your supper now?' he said.

With a jerky, despairing movement, she sat up in the bunk, tossing back her hair. She felt cornered.

'Give it me here,' she said.

He handed her first the cupful of soup. She sat among the blankets, eating it slowly. She was hungry. Then he gave her an enamel plate with pieces of fried chicken and currant jelly, butter and bread. It was very good. As they ate the chicken he made the coffee. She said never a word. A certain resentment filled her. She was cornered.

When supper was over he washed the dishes, dried them, and put everything away carefully, else there would have been no room to move in the hole of a cabin. The oak-wood gave out a good bright heat.

He stood for a few moments at a loss. Then he asked her, 'You want to go to bed soon?'

'Soon,' she said. 'Where are you going to sleep?'

'I make my bed here – ' he pointed to the floor along the wall. 'Too cold out of doors.'

'Yes,' she said. 'I suppose it is.'

She sat immobile, her cheeks hot, full of conflicting thoughts. And she watched him while he folded the blankets on the floor, a sheepskin underneath. Then she went out into the night.

The stars were big. Mars sat on the edge of a mountain, for all the world like the blazing eye of a crouching mountain lion. But she herself was deep, deep below in a pit of shadow. In the intense silence she seemed to hear the spruce forest crackling with electricity and cold. Strange, foreign stars floated on that unmoving water. The night was going to freeze. Over the hills came the far sobbing-singing howling of coyotes. She wondered how the horses would be.

Shuddering a little, she turned to the cabin. Warm light showed through its chinks. She pushed at the rickety, half-opened door.

'What about the horses?' she said.

'My black, he won't go away. And your mare will stay with him. You want to go to bed now?'

'I think I do.'

'All right. I feed the horses some oats.'

And he went out into the night.

He did not come back for some time. She was lying wrapped up tight in the bunk.

He blew out the lantern, and sat down on his bedding to take off his clothes. She lay with her back turned. And soon, in the silence, she was asleep.

She dreamed it was snowing, and the snow was falling on her through the roof, softly, softly, helplessly, and she was going to be buried alive. She was growing colder and colder, the snow was weighing down on her. The snow was going to absorb her.

She awoke with a sudden convulsion, like pain. She was really very cold; perhaps the heavy blankets had numbed her. Her heart seemed unable to beat, she felt she could not move.

With another convulsion she sat up. It was intensely dark. There was not even a spark of fire, the light wood had burned right away. She sat in thick oblivious darkness. Only through a chink she could see a star.

What did she want? Oh, what did she want? She sat in bed and rocked herself woefully. She could hear the steady breathing of the sleeping man. She was shivering with cold; her heart seemed as if it could not beat. She wanted warmth, protection, she wanted to be taken away from herself. And at the same time, perhaps more deeply than anything, she wanted to keep herself intact, intact, untouched, that no one should have any power over her, or rights to her. It was a wild necessity in her that no one, particularly no man, should have any rights or power over her, that no one and nothing should possess her.

Yet that other thing! And she was so cold, so shivering, and her heart could not beat. Oh, would not someone help her heart to beat?

She tried to speak, and could not. Then she cleared her throat.

'Romero,' she said strangely, 'it is so cold.'

Where did her voice come from, and whose voice was it, in the dark?

She heard him at once sit up, and his voice, startled, with a resonance that seemed to vibrate against her, saying, 'You want me to make you warm?'

'Yes.'

As soon as he had lifted her in his arms, she wanted to scream to him not to touch her. She stiffened herself. Yet she was dumb.

And he was warm, but with a terrible animal warmth that seemed to annihilate her. He panted like an animal with desire. And she was given over to this thing.

She had never, never wanted to be given over to this. But had *willed* that it should happen to her. And according to her will, she lay and let it happen. But she never wanted it. She never wanted to be thus assailed and handled, and mauled. She wanted to keep herself to herself.

However, she had willed it to happen, and it had happened. She panted with relief when it was over.

Yet even now she had to lie within the hard, powerful clasp of this other creature, this man. She dreaded to struggle to go away. She dreaded almost too much the icy cold of that other bunk.

'Do you want to go away from me?' asked his strange voice. Oh, if it could only have been a thousand miles away from her! Yet she had willed to have it thus close.

'No,' she said.

And she could feel a curious joy and pride surging up again in him: at her expense. Because he had got her. She felt like a victim there. And he was exulting in his power over her, his possession, his pleasure.

When dawn came, he was fast asleep. She sat up suddenly.

'I want a fire,' she said.

He opened his brown eyes wide, and smiled with a curious tender luxuriousness.

'I want you to make a fire,' she said.

He glanced at the chinks of light. His brown face hardened to the day.

'All right,' he said. 'I'll make it.'

She did her face while he dressed. She could not bear to look at him. He was so suffused with pride and luxury. She hid her face almost in despair. But feeling the cold blast of air as he opened the door, she wriggled down into the warm place where he had been. How soon the warmth ebbed, when he had gone!

He made a fire and went out, returning after a while with water.

'You stay in bed till the sun comes,' he said. 'It's very cold.'

'Hand me my cloak.'

She wrapped the cloak fast round her, and sat up among the blankets. The warmth was already spreading from the fire.

'I suppose we will start back as soon as we've had breakfast?'

He was crouching at his camp-stove making scrambled eggs. He looked up suddenly, transfixed, and his brown eyes, so soft and luxuriously widened, looked straight at her.

'You want to?' he said.

'We'd better get back as soon as possible,' she said, turning aside from his eyes.

'You want to get away from me?' he asked, repeating the question of the night in a sort of dread.

'I want to get away from here,' she said decisively. And it was true. She wanted supremely to get away, back to the world of people.

He rose slowly to his feet, holding the aluminium frying-pan.

'Don't you like last night?' he asked.

'Not really,' she said. 'Why? Do you?'

He put down the frying-pan and stood staring at the wall. She could see she had given him a cruel blow. But she did not relent. She was getting her own back. She wanted to regain possession of all herself, and in some mysterious way she felt that he possessed some part of her still.

He looked round at her slowly, his face greyish and heavy.

'You Americans,' he said, 'you always want to do a man down.'

'I am not American,' she said. 'I am British. And I don't want to do any man down. I only want to go back, now.'

'And what will you say about me, down there?'

'That you were very kind to me, and very good.'

He crouched down again, and went on turning the eggs. He gave her her plate, and her coffee, and sat down to his own food.

But again he seemed not to be able to swallow. He looked up at her.

'You don't like last night?' he asked.

'Not really,' she said, though with some difficulty. 'I don't care for that kind of thing.'

A blank sort of wonder spread over his face at these words, followed immediately by a black look of anger, and then a stony, sinister despair.

'You don't?' he said, looking her in the eyes.

'Not really,' she replied, looking back with steady hostility into his eyes.

Then a dark flame seemed to come from his face.

'I make you,' he said, as if to himself.

He rose and reached her clothes, that hung on a peg: the fine linen under-wear, the orange breeches, the fleecy jumper, the blue-and-buff kerchief; then he took up her riding-boots and her bead moccasins. Crushing everything in his arms, he opened the door. Sitting up, she saw him stride down to the dark-green pool in the frozen shadow of that deep cup of a valley. He tossed the clothing and the boots out on the pool. Ice had formed. And on the pure, dark green mirror, in the slaty shadow, the Princess saw her things lying, the white linen, the orange breeches, the black boots, the blue moccasins, a tangled heap of colour. Romero picked up rocks and heaved them out at the ice till the surface broke and the fluttering clothing disappeared in the rattling water, while the valley echoed and shouted again with the sound.

She sat in despair among the blankets, hugging tight her pale-blue cloak. Romero strode straight back to the cabin.

'Now you stay here with me,' he said.

She was furious. Her blue eyes met his. They were like two demons watching one another. In his face, beyond a sort of unrelieved gloom, was a demonish desire for death.

He saw her looking round the cabin, scheming. He saw her eyes on his rifle. He took the gun and went out with it. Returning, he pulled out her saddle, carried it to the tarn, and threw it in. Then he fetched his own saddle, and did the same.

'Now will you go away?' he said, looking at her with a smile.

She debated within herself whether to coax him and wheedle him. But she knew he was already beyond it. She sat among her blankets in a frozen sort of despair, hard as hard ice with anger.

He did the chores, and disappeared with the gun. She got up in her blue pyjamas, huddled in her cloak, and stood in the doorway. The dark-green pool was motionless again, the stony slopes were pallid and frozen. Shadow still lay, like an after-death, deep in this valley. Always in the distance she saw the horses feeding. If she could catch one! The brilliant yellow sun was half-way down the mountain. It was nine o'clock.

All day she was alone, and she was frightened. What she was frightened of she didn't know. Perhaps the crackling in the dark spruce wood. Perhaps just the savage, heartless wildness of the mountains. But all day she sat in the sun in the doorway of the cabin, watching, watching for hope. And all the time her bowels were cramped with fear.

She saw a dark spot that probably was a bear, roving across the pale grassy slope in the far distance, in the sun.

When, in the afternoon, she saw Romero approaching, with silent suddenness, carrying his gun and a dead deer, the cramp in her bowels relaxed, then became colder. She dreaded him with a cold dread.

'There is deer-meat,' he said, throwing the dead doe at her feet.

'You don't want to go away from here,' he said. 'This is a nice place.'

She shrank into the cabin.

'Come into the sun,' he said, following her. She looked up at him with hostile, frightened eyes.

'Come into the sun,' he repeated, taking her gently by the arm, in a powerful grasp.

She knew it was useless to rebel. Quietly he led her out, and seated himself in the doorway, holding her still by the arm.

'In the sun it is warm,' he said. 'Look, this is a nice place. You are such a pretty white woman, why do you want to act mean to me? Isn't this a nice place! Come! Come here! It is sure warm here.'

He drew her to him, and in spite of her stony resistance, he took her cloak from her, holding her in her thin blue pyjamas.

'You sure are a pretty little white woman, small and pretty,' he said. 'You sure won't act mean to me – you don't want to, I know you don't.'

She, stony and powerless, had to submit to him. The sun shone on her white, delicate skin.

'I sure don't mind hell fire,' he said. 'After this.'

A queer, luxurious good humour seemed to possess him again. But though outwardly she was powerless, inwardly she resisted him, absolutely and stonily.

When later he was leaving her again, she said to him suddenly, 'You think you can conquer me this way. But you can't. You can never conquer me.'

He stood arrested, looking back at her, with many emotions conflicting in his face – wonder, surprise, a touch of horror, and an unconscious pain that crumpled his face till it was like a mask. Then he went out without saying a word, hung the dead deer on a bough, and started to flay it. While he was at this butcher's work, the sun sank and cold night came on again.

'You see,' he said to her as he crouched, cooking the supper, 'I ain't going to let you go. I reckon you called to me in the night, and I've some right. If you want to fix it up right now with me, and say you want to be with me, we'll fix it up now and go down to the ranch tomorrow and get married or whatever you want. But you've got to say you want to be with me. Else I shall stay right here, till something happens.'

She waited a while before she answered, 'I don't want to be with anybody against my will. I don't dislike you; at least, I didn't, till you tried to put your will over mine. I won't have anybody's will put over me. You can't succeed. Nobody could. You can never get me under your will. And you won't have long to try, because soon they will send someone to look for me.'

He pondered this last, and she regretted having said it. Then, sombre, he bent to the cooking again.

He could not conquer her, however much he violated her. Because her spirit was hard and flawless as a diamond. But he could shatter her. This she knew. Much more, and she would be shattered.

In a sombre, violent excess he tried to expend his desire for her. And she was racked with an agony, and felt each time she would die. Because, in some peculiar way, he had got hold of her, some unrealised part of her which she never wished to realise. Racked with a burning, tearing anguish, she felt that the thread of her being would break, and she would die. The burning heat that racked her inwardly.

If only, only she could be alone again, cool and intact! If only she could recover herself again, cool and intact! Would she ever, ever, ever be able to bear herself again?

Even now she did not hate him. It was beyond that. Like some racking, hot doom. Personally he hardly existed.

The next day he would not let her have any fire, because of attracting attention with the smoke. It was a grey day, and she was cold. He stayed round, and heated soup on the petrol stove. She lay motionless in the blankets.

And in the afternoon she pulled the clothes over her head and broke into tears. She had never really cried in her life. He dragged the blankets away and looked to see what was shaking her. She sobbed in helpless hysterics. He covered her over again and went outside, looking at the mountains, where clouds were dragging and leaving a little snow. It was a violent, windy, horrible day, the evil of winter rushing down.

She cried for hours. And after this a great silence came between them. They were two people who had died. He did not touch her any more. In the night she lay and shivered like a dying dog. She felt that her very shivering would rupture something in her body, and she would die.

At last she had to speak.

'Could you make a fire? I am so cold,' she said, with chattering teeth.

'Want to come over here?' came his voice.

'I would rather you made me a fire,' she said, her teeth knocking together and chopping the words in two.

He got up and kindled a fire. At last the warmth spread, and she could sleep.

The next day was still chilly, with some wind. But the sun shone. He went about in silence, with a dead-looking face. It was now so dreary and so like death she wished he would do anything rather than continue in this negation. If now he asked her to go down with him to the world and marry him, she would do it. What did it matter? Nothing mattered any more.

But he would not ask her. His desire was dead and heavy like ice within him. He kept watch around the house.

On the fourth day as she sat huddled in the doorway in the sun, hugged in a blanket, she saw two horsemen come over the crest of the grassy slope – small figures. She gave a cry. He looked up quickly and saw the figures. The men had dismounted. They were looking for the trail.

'They are looking for me,' she said.

'*Muy bien*,' he answered in Spanish.

He went and fetched his gun, and sat with it across his knees.

'Oh!' she said. 'Don't shoot!'

He looked across at her.

'Why?' he said. 'You like staying with me?'

'No,' she said. 'But don't shoot.'

'I ain't going to Pen,' he said.

'You won't have to go to Pen,' she said. 'Don't shoot!'

'I'm going to shoot,' he muttered.

And straightway he kneeled and took very careful aim. The Princess sat on in an agony of helplessness and hopelessness.

The shot rang out. In an instant she saw one of the horses on the pale grassy slope rear and go rolling down. The man had dropped in the grass, and was invisible. The second man clambered on his horse, and on that precipitous place went at a gallop in a long swerve towards the nearest spruce-tree cover. Bang! Bang! went Romero's shots. But each time he missed, and the running horse leaped like a kangaroo towards cover.

It was hidden. Romero now got behind a rock; tense silence, in the brilliant sunshine. The Princess sat on the bunk inside the cabin, crouching, paralysed. For hours, it seemed, Romero knelt behind this rock, in his black shirt, bareheaded, watching. He had a beautiful, alert figure. The Princess wondered why she did not feel sorry for him. But her spirit was hard and cold, her heart could not melt. Though now she would have called him to her, with love.

But no, she did not love him. She would never love any man. Never! It was fixed and sealed in her, almost vindictively.

Suddenly she was so startled she almost fell from the bunk. A shot rang out quite close from behind the cabin. Romero leaped straight into the air, his arms fell outstretched, turning as he leaped. And even while he was in the air, a second shot rang out, and he fell with a crash, squirming, his hands clutching the earth towards the cabin door.

The Princess sat absolutely motionless, transfixed, staring at the prostrate figure. In a few moments the figure of a man in the Forest Service appeared close to the house; a young man in a broad-brimmed Stetson hat, dark flannel shirt, and riding-boots, carrying a gun. He strode over to the prostrate figure.

'Got you, Romero!' he said aloud. And he turned the dead man over. There was already a little pool of blood where Romero's breast had been.

'H'm!' said the Forest Service man. 'Guess I got you nearer than I thought.'

And he squatted there, staring at the dead man.

The distant calling of his comrade aroused him. He stood up.

'Hullo, Bill!' he shouted. 'Yep! Got him! Yep! Done him in, apparently.'

The second man rode out of the forest on a grey horse. He had a ruddy, kind face, and round brown eyes, dilated with dismay.

'He's not passed out?' he asked anxiously.

'Looks like it,' said the first young man coolly.

The second dismounted and bent over the body. Then he stood up again, and nodded.

'Yea–a!' he said. 'He's done in all right. It's him all right, boy! It's Domingo Romero.'

'Yep! I know it!' replied the other.

Then in perplexity he turned and looked into the cabin, where the Princess squatted, staring with big owl eyes from her red blanket.

'Hello!' he said, coming towards the hut. And he took his hat off. Oh, the sense of ridicule she felt! Though he did not mean any.

But she could not speak, no matter what she felt.

'What'd this man start firing for?' he asked.

She fumbled for words, with numb lips.

'He had gone out of his mind!' she said, with solemn, stammering conviction.

'Good Lord! You mean to say he'd gone out of his mind? Whew! That's pretty awful! That explains it then. H'm!'

He accepted the explanation without more ado.

With some difficulty they succeeded in getting the Princess down to the ranch. But she, too, was not a little mad.

'I'm not quite sure where I am,' she said to Mrs Wilkieson, as she lay in bed. 'Do you mind explaining?'

Mrs Wilkieson explained tactfully.

'Oh yes!' said the Princess. 'I remember. And I had an accident in the mountains, didn't I? Didn't we meet a man who'd gone mad, and who shot my horse from under me?'

'Yes, you met a man who had gone out of his mind.'

The real affair was hushed up. The Princess departed east in a fortnight's time, in Miss Cummins's care. Apparently she had recovered herself entirely. She was the Princess, and a virgin intact.

But her bobbed hair was grey at the temples, and her eyes were a little mad. She was slightly crazy.

'Since my accident in the mountains, when a man went mad and shot my horse from under me, and my guide had to shoot him dead, I have never felt quite myself.'

So she put it.

Later, she married an elderly man, and seemed pleased.

THE VIRGIN AND THE GIPSY

W HEN THE VICAR'S WIFE went off with a young and penniless man the scandal knew no bounds. Her two little girls were only seven and nine years old respectively. And the vicar was such a good husband. True, his hair was grey. But his moustache was dark, he was handsome, and still full of furtive passion for his unrestrained and beautiful wife.

Why did she go? Why did she burst away with such an *éclat* of revulsion, like a touch of madness?

Nobody gave any answer. Only the pious said she was a bad woman. While some of the good women kept silent. They knew.

The two little girls never knew. Wounded, they decided that it was because their mother found them negligible.

The ill wind that blows nobody any good swept away the vicarage family on its blast. Then lo and behold! the vicar, who was somewhat distinguished as an essayist and a controversialist, and whose case had aroused sympathy among the bookish men, received the living of Papplewick. The Lord had tempered the wind of misfortune with a rectorate in the north country.

The rectory was a rather ugly stone house down by the river Papple, before you come into the village. Further on, beyond where the road crosses the stream, were the big old stone cotton-mills, once driven by water. The road curved up-hill, into the bleak stone streets of the village.

The vicarage family received decided modification, upon its transference into the rectory. The vicar, now the rector, fetched up his old mother and his sister, and a brother from the city. The two little girls had a very different milieu from the old home.

The rector was now forty-seven years old; he had displayed an intense and not very dignified grief after the flight of his wife. Sympathetic ladies had stayed him from suicide. His hair was almost white, and he had a wide-eyed, tragic look. You had only to look at him, to know how dreadful it all was, and how he had been wronged.

Yet somewhere there was a false note. And some of the ladies who had sympathised most profoundly with the vicar, secretly rather disliked the rector. There was a certain furtive self-righteousness about him, when all was said and done.

The little girls, of course, in the vague way of children, accepted the family verdict. Granny, who was over seventy and whose sight was failing, became the central figure in the house. Aunt Cissie, who was over forty, pale, pious, and gnawed by an inward worm, kept house. Uncle Fred, a stingy and grey-faced man of forty, who just lived dingily for himself, went into town every day. And the rector, of course, was the most important person, after Granny.

They called her the Mater. She was one of those physically vulgar, clever old bodies who had got her own way all her life by buttering the weaknesses of her men-folk. Very quickly she took her cue. The rector still 'loved' his delinquent wife, and would 'love her' till he died. Therefore hush! The rector's feeling was sacred. In his heart was enshrined the pure girl he had wedded and worshipped.

Out in the evil world, at the same time, there wandered a disreputable woman who had betrayed the rector and abandoned his little children. She was now yoked to a young and despicable man, who no doubt would bring her the degradation she deserved. Let this be clearly understood, and then hush! For in the pure loftiness of the rector's heart still bloomed the pure white snow-flower of his young bride. This white snow-flower did not wither. That other creature, who had gone off with that despicable young man, was none of his affair.

The Mater, who had been somewhat diminished and insignificant as a widow in a small house, now climbed into the chief armchair in the rectory, and planted her old bulk firmly again. She was not going to be dethroned. Astutely she gave a sigh of homage to the rector's fidelity to the pure white snow-flower, while she pretended to disapprove. In sly reverence for her son's great love, she spoke no word against that nettle which flourished in the evil world, and which had once been called Mrs Arthur Saywell. Now, thank heaven, having married again, she was no more Mrs Arthur Saywell. No woman bore the rector's name. The pure white snow-flower bloomed *in perpetuum*, without nomenclature. The family even thought of her as She-who-was-Cynthia.

All this was water on the Mater's mill. It secured her against Arthur's ever marrying again. She had him by his feeblest weakness, his skulking self-love. He had married an imperishable white snow-flower. Lucky man! He had been injured. Unhappy man! He had suffered. Ah, what a heart of love! And he had – forgiven! Yes, the white snow-flower was forgiven. He even had made provision in his will for her, when that other scoundrel – But hush! Don't even *think* too near to that horrid nettle in the rank outer world! She-who-was-Cynthia. Let the white snow-flower bloom inaccessible on the heights of the past. The present is another story.

The children were brought up in this atmosphere of cunning self-sanctification and of unmentionability. They, too, saw the snow-flower on inaccessible heights. They too knew that it was throned in lone splendour aloft their lives, never to be touched.

At the same time, out of the squalid world sometimes would come a rank, evil smell of selfishness and degraded lust, the smell of that awful nettle, She-who-was-Cynthia. This nettle actually contrived, at intervals, to get a little note through to the girls, her children. And at this the silver-haired Mater shook inwardly with hate. For if she-who-was-Cynthia ever came back, there wouldn't be much left of the Mater. A secret gust of hate went from the old granny to the girls, children of that foul nettle of just, that Cynthia who had had such an affectionate contempt for the Mater.

Mingled with all this was the children's perfectly distinct recollection of their real home, the vicarage in the south, and their glamorous but not very dependable mother, Cynthia. She had made a great glow, a flow of life, like a swift and dangerous sun in the home, forever coming and going. They always associated her presence with brightness, but also with danger; with glamour, but with fearful selfishness.

Now the glamour was gone, and the white snow-flower, like a porcelain wreath, froze on its grave. The danger of instability, the peculiarly *dangerous* sort of selfishness, like lions and tigers, was also gone. There was now a complete stability, in which one could perish safely.

But they were growing up. And as they grew, they became more definitely confused, more actively puzzled. The Mater, as she grew older, grew blinder. Somebody had to lead her about. She did not get up till towards midday. Yet blind or bed-ridden, she held the house.

Besides, she wasn't bed-ridden. Whenever the *men* were present, the Mater was in her throne. She was too cunning to court neglect. Especially as she had rivals.

Her great rival was the younger girl, Yvette. Yvette had some of the vague, careless blitheness of She-who-was-Cynthia. But this one was more docile. Granny perhaps had caught her in time. Perhaps!

The rector adored Yvette, and spoiled her with a doting fondness; as much as to say: am I not a soft-hearted, indulgent old boy! He liked to have this opinion of himself, and the Mater knew his weaknesses to a hair's breadth. She knew them, and she traded on them by turning them into decorations for him, for his character. He wanted, in his own eyes, to have a fascinating character, as women want to have fascinating dresses. And the Mater cunningly put beauty-spots over his defects and deficiencies. Her mother-love gave her the clue to his weaknesses, and she hid them for him with decorations. Whereas She-who-was-Cynthia – ! But don't mention *her*, in this connection. In her eyes, the rector was almost hump-backed and an idiot.

The funny thing was, Granny secretly hated Lucille, the elder girl, more than the pampered Yvette. Lucille, the uneasy and irritable, was more conscious of being under Granny's power, than was the spoilt and vague Yvette.

On the other hand, Aunt Cissie hated Yvette. She hated her very name. Aunt Cissie's life had been sacrificed to the Mater, and Aunt Cissie knew it, and the Mater knew she knew it. Yet as the years went on, it became a convention. The convention of Aunt Cissie's sacrifice was accepted by everybody, including the self-same Cissie. She prayed a good deal about it. Which also showed that she had her own private feelings somewhere, poor thing. She had ceased to be Cissie, she had lost her life and her sex. And now, she was creeping towards fifty, strange green flares of rage would come up in her, and at such times, she was insane.

But Granny held her in her power. And Aunt Cissie's one object in life was to look after the Mater.

Aunt Cissie's green flares of hellish hate would go up against all young things, sometimes. Poor thing, she prayed and tried to obtain forgiveness from heaven. But what had been done to her, *she* could not forgive, and the vitriol would spurt in her veins sometimes.

It was not as if the Mater were a warm, kindly soul. She wasn't. She only seemed it, cunningly. And the fact dawned gradually on the girls. Under her old-fashioned lace cap, under her silver hair, under the black silk of her stout, short, forward-bulging body, this old woman had a cunning heart, seeking for ever her own female power. And through the weakness of the unfresh, stagnant men she had bred, she kept her power, as her years rolled on, from seventy to eighty, and from eighty on the new lap, towards ninety.

For in the family there was a whole tradition of 'loyalty': loyalty to one another, and especially to the Mater. The Mater, of course, was the pivot of the family. The family was her own extended ego. Naturally she covered it with her power. And her sons and daughters, being weak and disintegrated, naturally were loyal. Outside the family, what was there for them but danger and insult and ignominy? Had not the rector experienced it, in his marriage? So now, caution! Caution and loyalty, fronting the world! Let there be as much hate and friction *inside* the family, as you like. To the outer world, a stubborn fence of unison.

2

But it was not until the girls finally came home from school that they felt the full weight of Granny's dead old hand on their lives. Lucille was now nearly twenty-one, and Yvette nineteen. They had been to a good girls' school, and had had a finishing year in Lausanne, and were quite the usual thing, tall young creatures with fresh, sensitive faces and bobbed hair and young-manly, deuce-take-it manners.

'What's so awfully *boring* about Papplewick,' said Yvette, as they stood on the Channel boat watching the grey, grey cliffs of Dover draw near, 'is that there are no *men* about. Why doesn't Daddy have some good old sports for friends? As for Uncle Fred, he's the limit!'

'Oh, you never know what will turn up,' said Lucille, more philosophic.

'You jolly well know what to expect,' said Yvette. 'Choir on Sundays, and I hate mixed choirs. Boys' voices are *lovely*, when there are no women. And Sunday School and Girls' Friendly, and socials, all the dear old souls that enquire after Granny! Not a decent young fellow for miles.'

'Oh, I don't know!' said Lucille. 'There's always the Framleys. And you know Gerry Somercotes *adores* you.'

'Oh but I *hate* fellows who adore me!' cried Yvette, turning up her sensitive nose. 'They *bore* me. They hang on like lead.'

'Well what *do* you want, if you can't stand being adored? I think it's perfectly all right to be adored. You know you'll never marry them, so why not let them go on adoring, if it amuses them.'

'Oh but I *want* to get married,' cried Yvette.

'Well in that case, let them go on adoring you till you find one that you can *possibly* marry.'

'I never should, that way. Nothing puts me off like an adoring fellow. They *bore* me so! They make me feel beastly.'

'Oh, so they do me, if they get pressing. But at a distance, I think they're rather nice.'

'I should like to fall *violently* in love.'

'Oh, very likely! I shouldn't! I should hate it. Probably so would you, if it actually happened. After all, we've got to settle down a bit, before we know what we want.'

'But don't you *hate* going back to Papplewick?' cried Yvette, turning up her young, sensitive nose.

'No, not particularly. I suppose we shall be rather bored. I wish Daddy would get a car. I suppose we shall have to drag the old bikes out. Wouldn't you like to get up to Tansy Moor?'

'Oh, *love* it! Though it's an awful *strain*, shoving an old push bike up those hills.'

The ship was nearing the grey cliffs. It was summer, but a grey day. The two girls wore their coats with fur collars turned up, and little *chic* hats pulled down over their ears. Tall, slender, fresh-faced, naïve, yet confident, too confident, in their school-girlish arrogance, they were so terribly English. They seemed so free, and were as a matter of fact so tangled and tied up, inside themselves. They seemed so dashing and unconventional, and were really so conventional, so, as it were, shut up indoors inside themselves. They looked like bold, tall young sloops, just slipping from the harbour, into the wide seas of life. And they were, as a matter of fact, two poor young rudderless lives, moving from one chain anchorage to another.

The rectory struck a chill into their hearts as they entered. It seemed ugly, and almost sordid, with the dank air of that middle-class, degenerated comfort which has ceased to be comfortable and has turned stuffy, unclean. The hard, stone house struck the girls as being unclean, they could not have said why. The shabby furniture seemed somehow sordid, nothing was fresh. Even the food at meals had that awful dreary sordidness which is so repulsive to a young thing coming from abroad. Roast beef and wet cabbage, cold mutton and mashed potatoes, sour pickles, inexcusable puddings.

Granny, who 'loved a bit of pork', also had special dishes, beef-tea and rusks, or a small savoury custard. The grey-faced Aunt Cissie ate nothing at all. She would sit at table, and take a single lonely and naked boiled potato on to her plate. She never ate meat. So she sat in sordid durance, while the meal went on, and Granny quickly slobbered her portion – lucky if she spilled nothing on her protuberant stomach. The food was not appetising in itself: how could it be, when Aunt Cissie hated food herself, hated the fact of eating, and never could keep a maidservant for three months? The girls ate with repulsion, Lucille bravely bearing up, Yvette's tender nose showing her disgust. Only the rector, white-haired, wiped his long grey moustache with his serviette, and cracked jokes. He too was getting heavy and inert, sitting in his study all day, never taking exercise. But he cracked sarcastic little jokes all the time, sitting there under the shelter of the Mater.

The country, with its steep hills and its deep, narrow valleys, was dark and gloomy, yet had a certain powerful strength of its own. Twenty miles away was the black industrialism of the north. Yet the village of Papplewick was comparatively lonely, almost lost, the life in it stony and dour. Everything was stone, with a hardness that was almost poetic, it was so unrelenting.

It was as the girls had known: they went back into the choir, they helped in the parish. But Yvette struck absolutely against Sunday School, the Band of Hope, the Girls' Friendlies – indeed against all those functions that were conducted by determined old maids and obstinate, stupid elderly men. She avoided church duties as much as possible, and got away from the rectory whenever she could. The Framleys, a big, untidy, jolly family up at the Grange, were an enormous stand-by. And if anybody asked her out to a meal, even if a woman in one of the workmen's houses asked her to stay to tea, she accepted at once. In fact, she was rather thrilled. She liked talking to the working men, they had often such fine, hard heads. But of course they were in another world.

So the months went by. Gerry Somercotes was still an adorer. There were others, too, sons of farmers or mill-owners. Yvette really ought to have had a good time. She was always out to parties and dances, friends came for her in their motor cars, and off she went to the city, to the afternoon dance in the chief hotel, or in the gorgeous new Palais de Danse, called the Pally.

Yet she always seemed like a creature mesmerised. She was never free to be quite jolly. Deep inside her worked an intolerable irritation, which she thought she *ought* not to feel, and which she hated feeling, thereby making it worse. She never understood at all whence it arose.

At home, she truly was irritable, and outrageously rude to Aunt Cissie. In fact Yvette's awful temper became one of the family by-words.

Lucille, always more practical, got a job in the city as private secretary to a man who needed somebody with fluent French and shorthand. She went back and forth every day, by the same train as Uncle Fred. But she never travelled with him, and wet or fine, bicycled to the station, while he went on foot.

The two girls were both determined that what they wanted was a really jolly social life. And they resented with fury that the rectory was, for their friends, impossible. There were only four rooms downstairs: the kitchen, where lived the two discontented maidservants; the dark dining-room; the rector's study; and the big, 'homely', dreary living-room or drawing-room. In the dining-room there was a gas fire. Only in the living-room was a good hot fire kept going. Because, of course, here Granny reigned.

In this room the family was assembled. At evening, after dinner, Uncle Fred and the rector invariably played crossword puzzles with Granny.

'Now, Mater, are you ready? N blank blank blank blank W: a Siamese functionary.'

'Eh? Eh? M blank blank blank blank W?'

Granny was hard of hearing.

'No, Mater. Not M! N blank blank blank blank W: a Siamese functionary.'

'N blank blank blank blank W: a Chinese functionary.'

'SIAMESE.'

'Eh?'

'SIAMESE! SIAM!'

'A Siamese functionary! Now what can that be?' said the old lady profoundly, folding her hands on her round stomach. Her two sons proceeded to make suggestions, at which she said Ah! Ah! The rector was amazingly clever at crossword puzzles. But Fred had a certain technical vocabulary.

'This certainly is a hard nut to crack,' said the old lady, when they were all stuck.

Meanwhile Lucille sat in a corner with her hands over her ears, pretending to read, and Yvette irritably made drawings, or hummed loud and exasperating tunes, to add to the family concert. Aunt Cissie continually reached for a chocolate, and her jaws worked ceaselessly. She literally lived on chocolates. Sitting in the distance, she put another into her mouth, then looked again at the parish magazine. Then she lifted her head, and saw it was time to fetch Granny's cup of Horlicks.

While she was gone, in nervous exasperation Yvette would open the window. The room was never fresh, she imagined it smelt: smelt of Granny. And Granny, who was hard of hearing, heard like a weasel when she wasn't wanted to.

'Did you open the window, Yvette? I think you might remember there are older people than yourself in the room,' she said.

'It's stifling! It's unbearable! No wonder we've all of us always got colds.'

'I'm sure the room is large enough, and a good fire burning.' The old lady gave a little shudder. 'A draught to give us all our death.'

'Not a draught at all,' roared Yvette. 'A breath of fresh air.'

The old lady shuddered again, and said: 'Indeed!'

The rector, in silence, marched to the window and firmly closed it. He did not look at his daughter meanwhile. He hated thwarting her. But she must know what's what!

The crossword puzzles, invented by Satan himself, continued till Granny had had her Horlicks, and was to go to bed. Then came the ceremony of Goodnight! Everybody stood up. The girls went to be kissed by the blind old woman. The rector gave his arm, and Aunt Cissie followed with a candle.

But this was already nine o'clock, although Granny was really getting old, and should have been in bed sooner. But when she was in bed, she could not sleep, till Aunt Cissie came.

'You see,' said Granny, 'I have *never* slept alone. For fifty-four years I never slept a night without the Pater's arm round me. And when he was gone, I tried to sleep alone. But as sure as my eyes closed to sleep, my heart nearly jumped out of my body, and I lay in a palpitation. Oh, you may think what you will, but it was a fearful experience, after fifty-four years of perfect married life! I would have prayed to be taken first, but the Pater, well, no I don't think he would have been able to bear up.'

So Aunt Cissie slept with Granny. And she hated it. She said *she* could never sleep. And she grew greyer and greyer, and the food in the house got worse, and Aunt Cissie had to have an operation.

But the Mater rose as ever, towards noon, and at the midday meal, she presided from her armchair, with her stomach protruding; her reddish, pendulous face, that had a sort of horrible majesty, dropping soft under the wall of her high brow, and her blue eyes peering unseeing. Her white hair was getting scanty, it was altogether a little indecent. But the rector jovially cracked his jokes to her, and she pretended to disapprove. But she was perfectly complacent, sitting in her ancient obesity, and after meals, getting the wind from her stomach, pressing her bosom with her hand as she 'rifted' in gross physical complacency.

What the girls minded most was that, when they brought their young friends to the house, Granny always was there, like some awful idol of old flesh, consuming all the attention. There was only the one room for everybody. And there sat the old lady, with Aunt Cissie keeping an acrid guard over her. Everybody must be presented first to Granny: she was ready to be genial, she liked company. She had to know who everybody was, where they came from, every circumstance of their lives. And then, when she was *au fait*, she could get hold of the conversation.

Nothing could be more exasperating to the girls. 'Isn't old Mrs Saywell wonderful! She takes *such* an interest in life, at nearly ninety!'

'She does take an interest in people's affairs, if that's life,' said Yvette.

Then she would immediately feel guilty. After all, it *was* wonderful to be nearly ninety, and have such a clear mind! And Granny never *actually* did anybody any harm. It was more that she was in the way. And perhaps it was rather awful to hate somebody because they were old and in the way.

Yvette immediately repented, and was nice. Granny blossomed forth into reminiscences of when she was a girl, in the little town in Buckinghamshire. She talked and talked away, and was *so* entertaining. She really *was* rather wonderful.

Then in the afternoon Lottie and Ella and Bob Framley came, with Leo Wetherell.

'Oh, come in!' – and in they all trooped to the sitting-room, where Granny, in her white cap, sat by the fire.

'Granny, this is Mr Wetherell.'

'Mr what-did-you-say? You must excuse me, I'm a little deaf!'

Granny gave her hand to the uncomfortable young man, and gazed silently at him, sightlessly.

'You are not from our parish?' she asked him.

'Dinnington!' he shouted.

'We want to go a picnic tomorrow, to Bonsall Head, in Leo's car. We can all squeeze in,' said Ella, in a low voice.

'Did you say Bonsall Head?' asked Granny.

'Yes!'

There was a blank silence.

'Did you say you were going in a car?'

'Yes! In Mr Wetherell's.'

'I hope he's a good driver. It's a very dangerous road.'

'He's a *very* good driver.'

'Not a very good driver?'

'Yes! He *is* a very good driver.'

'If you go to Bonsall Head, I think I must send a message to Lady Louth.'

Granny always dragged in this miserable Lady Louth, when there was company.

'Oh, we shan't go that way,' cried Yvette.

'Which way?' said Granny. 'You must go by Heanor.'

The whole party sat, as Bob expressed it, like stuffed ducks, fidgeting on their chairs.

Aunt Cissie came in – and then the maid with the tea. There was the eternal and everlasting piece of bought cake. Then appeared a plate of little fresh cakes. Aunt Cissie had actually sent to the baker's.

'Tea, Mater!'

The old lady gripped the arms on her chair. Everybody rose and stood, while she waded slowly across, on Aunt Cissie's arm, to her place at table.

During tea Lucille came in from town, from her job. She was simply worn out, with black marks under her eyes. She gave a cry, seeing all the company.

As soon as the noise had subsided, and the awkwardness was resumed, Granny said, 'You have never mentioned Mr Wetherell to me, have you, Lucille?'

'I don't remember,' said Lucille.

'You can't have done. The name is strange to me.'

Yvette absently grabbed another cake, from the now almost empty plate. Aunt Cissie, who was driven almost crazy by Yvette's vague and inconsiderate ways, felt the green rage fuse in her heart. She picked up her own plate, on which was the one cake she allowed herself, and said with vitriolic politeness, offering it to Yvette, 'Won't you have mine?'

'Oh thanks!' said Yvette, starting in her angry vagueness. And with an appearance of the same insouciance, she helped herself to Aunt Cissie's cake also, adding as an afterthought: 'If you're sure you don't want it.'

She now had two cakes on her plate. Lucille had gone white as a ghost, bending to her tea. Aunt Cissie sat with a green look of poisonous resignation. The awkwardness was an agony.

But Granny, bulkily enthroned and unaware, only said, in the centre of the cyclone, 'If you are motoring to Bonsall Head tomorrow, Lucille, I wish you would take a message from me to Lady Louth.'

'Oh!' said Lucille, giving a queer look across the table at the sightless old woman. Lady Louth was the King Charles's Head of the family, invariably produced by Granny for the benefit of visitors. 'Very well!'

'She was so very kind last week. She sent her chauffeur over with a Cross-word Puzzle book for me.'

'But you thanked her then,' cried Yvette.

'I should like to send her a note.'

'We can post it,' cried Lucille.

'Oh no! I should like you to take it. When Lady Louth called last time . . . '

The young ones sat like a shoal of young fishes dumbly mouthing at the surface of the water, while Granny went on about Lady Louth. Aunt Cissie, the two girls knew, was still helpless, almost unconscious in a paroxysm of rage about the cake. Perhaps, poor thing, she was praying.

It was a mercy when the friends departed. But by that time the two girls were both haggard-eyed. And it was then that Yvette, looking round, suddenly saw the stony, implacable will-to-power in the old and motherly-seeming Granny. She sat there bulging backwards in her chair, impassive, her reddish, pendulous old face rather mottled, almost unconscious, but implacable, her face like a mask that hid something stony, relentless. It was the static inertia of her unsavoury power. Yet in a minute she would open her ancient mouth to find out every detail about Leo Wetherell. For the moment she was hibernating in her oldness, her agedness. But in a minute her mouth would open, her mind would flicker awake, and with her insatiable greed for life, other people's life, she would start on her quest for every detail. She was like the old toad which Yvette had watched, fascinated, as it sat on the ledge of the bee-hive, immediately in front of the little entrance by which the bees emerged, and which, with a demonish lightning-like snap of its pursed jaws, caught every bee as it came out to launch into the air, swallowed them one after the other, as if it could consume the whole hive-full, into its aged, bulging, purse-like wrinkledness. It had been swallowing bees as they launched into the air of spring, year after year, year after year, for generations.

But the gardener, called by Yvette, was in a rage, and killed the creature with a stone.

''Appen tha *art* good for th' snails,' he said, as he came down with the stone. 'But tha 'rt none goin' ter emp'y th' bee-'ive into thy guts.'

3

The next day was dull and low, and the roads were awful, for it had been raining for weeks, yet the young ones set off on their trip, without taking Granny's message either. They just slipped out while she was making her slow trip upstairs after lunch. Not for anything would they have called at Lady Louth's house. That widow of a knighted doctor, a harmless person indeed, had become an obnoxity in their lives.

Six young rebels, they sat very perkily in the car as they swished through the mud. Yet they had a peaked look too. After all, they had nothing really to rebel against, any of them. They were left so very free in their movements. Their parents let them do almost entirely as they liked. There wasn't really a fetter to break, nor a prison-bar to file through, nor a bolt to shatter. The keys of their lives were in their own hands. And there they dangled inert.

It is very much easier to shatter prison-bars than to open undiscovered doors to life. As the younger generation finds out, somewhat to its chagrin. True, there was Granny. But poor old Granny, you couldn't actually say to her: 'Lie down and die, you old woman!' She might be an old nuisance, but she never really *did* anything. It wasn't fair to hate her.

So the young people set off on their jaunt, trying to be very full of beans. They could really do as they liked. And so, of course, there was nothing to do but sit in the car and talk a lot of criticism of other people, and silly flirty gallantry that was really rather a bore. If there had only been a few 'strict orders' to be disobeyed! But nothing: beyond the refusal to carry the message to Lady Louth, of which the rector would approve, because he didn't encourage King Charles's Head either.

They sang, rather scrappily, the latest would-be comic songs, as they went through the grim villages. In the great park the deer were in groups near the road, roe deer and fallow, nestling in the gloom of the afternoon under the oaks by the road, as if for the stimulus of human company.

Yvette insisted on stopping and getting out to talk to them. The girls, in their Russian boots, tramped through the damp grass, while the deer watched them with big, unfrightened eyes. The hart trotted away mildly, holding back his head, because of the weight of the horns. But the doe, balancing her big ears, did not rise from under the tree, with her half-grown young ones, till the girls were almost in touch. Then she walked light-foot away, lifting her tail from her spotted flanks, while the young ones nimbly trotted.

'Aren't they awfully dainty and nice!' cried Yvette. 'You'd wonder they could lie so cosily in this horrid wet grass.'

'Well I suppose they've got to lie down *sometime*,' said Lucille. 'And it's *fairly* dry under the tree.' She looked at the crushed grass, where the deer had lain.

Yvette went and put her hand down, to feel how it felt.

'Yes!' she said, doubtfully, 'I believe it's a bit warm.'

The deer had bunched again a few yards away, and were standing motionless in the gloom of the afternoon. Away below the slopes of grass and trees, beyond the swift river with its balustraded bridge, sat the huge ducal house, one or two chimneys smoking bluely. Behind it rose purplish woods.

The girls, pushing their fur collars up to their ears, dangling one long arm, stood watching in silence, their wide Russian boots protecting them from the wet grass. The great house squatted square and creamy-grey below. The deer, in little groups, were scattered under the old trees close by. It all seemed so still, so unpretentious, and so sad.

'I wonder where the Duke is now,' said Ella.

'Not here, wherever he is,' said Lucille. 'I expect he's abroad where the sun shines.'

The motor-horn called from the road, and they heard Leo's voice, 'Come on, boys! If we're going to get to the Head and down to Amberdale for tea, we'd better move.'

They crowded into the car again, with chilled feet, and set off through the park, past the silent spire of the church, out through the great gates and over the bridge, on into the wide, damp, stony village of Woodlinkin, where the river ran. And thence, for a long time, they stayed in the mud and dark and dampness of the valley, often with sheer rock above them; the water brawling on one hand, the steep rock or dark trees on the other.

Till, through the darkness of overhanging trees, they began to climb, and Leo changed the gear. Slowly the car toiled up through the whitey-grey mud, into the stony village of Bolehill, that hung on the slope, round the old cross, with its steps, that stood where the road branched, on past the cottages whence came a wonderful smell of hot tea-cakes, and beyond, still upwards, under dripping trees and past broken slopes of bracken, always climbing. Until the cleft became shallower, and the trees finished, and the slopes on either side were bare, gloomy grass, with low dry-stone walls. They were emerging on to the Head.

The party had been silent for some time. On either side the road was grass, then a low stone fence, and the swelling curve of the hill-summit, traced with the low, dry-stone walls. Above this, the low sky.

The car ran out, under the low, grey sky, on the naked tops.

'Shall we stay a moment?' called Leo.

'Oh yes!' cried the girls.

And they scrambled out once more, to look around. They knew the place quite well. But still, if one came to the Head, one got out to look.

The hills were like the knuckles of a hand, the dales were below, between the fingers, narrow, steep, and dark. In the deeps a train was steaming, slowly pulling north: a small thing of the underworld. The noise of the engine re-echoed curiously upwards. Then came the dull, familiar sound of blasting in a quarry.

Leo, always on the go, moved quickly.

'Shall we be going?' he said. 'Do we want to get down to Amberdale for tea? Or shall we try somewhere nearer?'

They all voted for Amberdale, for the Marquis of Grantham.

'Well, which way shall we go back? Shall we go by Codnor and over Crosshill, or shall we go by Ashbourne?'

There was the usual dilemma. Then they finally decided on the Codnor top road. Off went the car, gallantly.

They were on the top of the world, now, on the back of the fist. It was naked, too, as the back of your fist, high under heaven, and dull, heavy green. Only it was veined with a network of old stone walls, dividing the fields, and broken here and there with ruins of old lead-mines and works. A sparse stone farm bristled with six naked sharp trees. In the distance was a patch of smoky grey stone, a hamlet. In some fields grey, dark sheep fed silently, sombrely. But there was not a sound nor a movement. It was the roof of England, stony and arid as any roof. Beyond, below, were the shires.

' "And see the coloured counties – " ' said Yvette to herself. Here anyhow they were not coloured. A stream of rooks trailed out from nowhere. They had been walking, pecking, on a naked field that had been manured. The car ran on between the grass and the stone walls of the upland lane, and the young people were silent, looking out over the far network of stone fences, under the sky, looking for the curves downward that indicated a drop to one of the underneath, hidden dales.

Ahead was a light cart, driven by a man, and trudging along at the side was a woman, sturdy and elderly, with a pack on her back. The man in the cart had caught her up, and now was keeping pace.

The road was narrow. Leo sounded the horn sharply. The man on the cart looked round, but the woman on foot only trudged steadily, rapidly forward, without turning her head.

Yvette's heart gave a jump. The man on the cart was a gipsy, one of the black, loose-bodied, handsome sort. He remained seated on his cart, turning round and gazing at the occupants of the motor car, from under the brim of his cap. And his pose was loose, his gaze insolent in its indifference. He had a thin black moustache under his thin, straight nose, and a big silk handkerchief of red and yellow tied round his neck. He spoke a word to the woman. She stood a second, solid, to turn round and look at the occupants of the car, which had now drawn quite close. Leo honked the horn again, imperiously. The woman, who had a grey-and-white kerchief tied round her head, turned sharply, to keep pace with the cart, whose driver also had settled back, and was lifting the reins, moving his loose, light shoulders. But still he did not pull aside.

Leo made the horn scream, as he put the brakes on and the car slowed up near the back of the cart. The gipsy turned round at the din, laughing in his dark face under his dark-green cap, and said something which they did not hear, showing white teeth under the line of black moustache, and making a gesture with his dark, loose hand.

'Get out o' the way then!' yelled Leo.

For answer, the man delicately pulled the horse to a standstill, as it curved to the side of the road. It was a good roan horse, and a good, natty, dark-green cart.

Leo, in a rage, had to jam on the brake and pull up too.

'Don't the pretty young ladies want to hear their fortunes?' said the gipsy on the cart, laughing except for his dark, watchful eyes, which went from face to face, and lingered on Yvette's young, tender face.

She met his dark eyes for a second, their level search, their insolence, their complete indifference to people like Bob and Leo, and something took fire in her breast. She thought: 'He is stronger than I am! He doesn't care!'

'Oh yes! let's!' cried Lucille at once.

'Oh yes!' chorused the girls.

'I say! What about the time?' cried Leo.

'Oh bother the old time! Somebody's always dragging in time by the fore-lock,' cried Lucille.

'Well, if you don't mind *when* we get back, *I* don't!' said Leo heroically.

The gipsy man had been sitting loosely on the side of his cart, watching the faces. He now jumped softly down from the shaft, his knees a bit stiff. He was apparently a man something over thirty, and a beau in his way. He wore a sort of shooting-jacket, double-breasted, coming only to the hips, of dark green-and-black frieze; rather tight black trousers, black boots, and a dark-green cap; with the big yellow-and-red bandanna handkerchief round his neck. His appearance was curiously elegant, and quite expensive in its gipsy style. He was handsome, too, pressing in his chin with the old, gipsy conceit, and now apparently not heeding the strangers any more, as he led his good roan horse off the road, preparing to back his cart.

The girls saw for the first time a deep recess in the side of the road, and two caravans smoking. Yvette got quickly down. They had suddenly come upon a disused quarry, cut into the slope of the road-side, and in this sudden lair, almost like a cave, were three caravans, dismantled for the winter. There was also, deep at the back, a shelter built of boughs, as a stable for the horse. The grey, crude rock rose high above the caravans, and curved round towards the road. The floor was heaped chips of stone, with grasses growing among. It was a hidden, snug winter camp.

The elderly woman with the pack had gone into one of the caravans, leaving the door open. Two children were peeping out, showing black heads. The gipsy man gave a little call, as he backed his cart into the quarry, and an elderly man came out to help him untackle.

The gipsy himself went up the steps into the newest caravan, that had its door closed. Underneath, a tied-up dog ranged forth. It was a white hound spotted liver-coloured. It gave a low growl as Leo and Bob approached.

At the same moment, a dark-faced gipsy-woman with a pink shawl or kerchief round her head and big gold ear-rings in her ears, came down the steps of the newest caravan, swinging her flounced, voluminous green skirt. She was handsome in a bold, dark, long-faced way, just a bit wolfish. She looked like one of the bold, loping Spanish gipsies.

'Good-morning, my ladies and gentlemen,' she said, eyeing the girls from her bold, predative eyes. She spoke with a certain foreign stiffness.

'Good-afternoon!' said the girls.

'Which beautiful little lady like to hear her fortune? Give me her little hand?'

She was a tall woman, with a frightening way of reaching forward her neck like a menace. Her eyes went from face to face, very active, heartlessly searching out what she wanted. Meanwhile the man, apparently her husband, appeared at the top of the caravan steps smoking a pipe, and with a small, black-haired child in his arms. He stood on his limber legs, casually looking down on the group, as if from a distance, his long black lashes lifted from his full, conceited, impudent black eyes. There was something peculiarly transfusing in his stare. Yvette felt it, felt it in her knees. She pretended to be interested in the white-and-liver-coloured hound.

'How much do you want, if we all have our fortunes told?' asked Lottie Framley, as the six fresh-faced young Christians hung back rather reluctantly from this pagan pariah woman.

'All of you? ladies and gentlemen, all?' said the woman shrewdly.

'I don't want mine told! You go ahead!' cried Leo.

'Neither do I,' said Bob. 'You four girls.'

'The four ladies?' said the gipsy-woman, eyeing them shrewdly, after having looked at the boys. And she fixed her price. 'Each one give me a sheeling, and a little bit more for luck? a little bit!' She smiled in a way that was more wolfish than cajoling, and the force of her will was felt, heavy as iron beneath the velvet of her words.

'All right,' said Leo. 'Make it a shilling a head. Don't spin it out too long.'

'Oh, *you*!' cried Lucille at him. 'We want to hear it *all*.'

The woman took two wooden stools, from under a caravan, and placed them near the wheel. Then she took the tall, dark Lottie Framley by the hand, and bade her sit down.

'You don't care if everybody hear?' she said, looking up curiously into Lottie's face.

Lottie blushed dark with nervousness, as the gipsy-woman held her hand, and stroked her palm with hard, cruel-seeming fingers.

'Oh, I don't mind,' she said.

The gipsy-woman peered into the palm, tracing the lines of the hand with a hard, dark forefinger. But she seemed clean.

And slowly she told the fortune, while the others, standing listening, kept on crying out: 'Oh, that's Jim Baggaley! Oh, I don't believe it! Oh, that's not true! A fair woman who lives beneath a tree! Why, whoever's that?' until Leo stopped them with a manly warning, 'Oh, hold on, girls! You give everything away.'

Lottie retired blushing and confused, and it was Ella's turn. She was much more calm and shrewd, trying to read the oracular words. Lucille kept breaking out with: 'Oh, I say.' The gipsy-man at the top of the steps stood imperturbable, without any expression at all. But his bold eyes kept staring at Yvette, she could feel them on her cheek, on her neck, and she dared not look up. But Framley would sometimes look up at him, and got a level stare back, from the handsome face of the male gipsy, from the dark conceited proud eyes. It was a peculiar look, in the eyes that belonged to the tribe of the humble: the pride of the pariah, the half-sneering challenge of the outcast, who sneered at law-abiding men, and went his own way. All the time, the gipsy-man stood there, holding his child in his arms, looking on without being concerned.

Lucille was having her hand read – 'You have been across the sea, and there you met a man – a brown-haired man – but he was too old – '

'Oh, I *say*!' cried Lucille, looking round at Yvette.

But Yvette was abstracted, agitated, hardly heeding: in one of her mesmerised states.

'You will marry in a few years – not now, but a few years – perhaps four – and you will not be rich, but you will have plenty – enough – and you will go away, a long journey.'

'With my husband, or without?' cried Lucille.

'With him – '

When it came to Yvette's turn, and the woman looked up boldly, cruelly, searching for a long time in her face, Yvette said nervously, 'I don't think I want mine told. No, I won't have mine told! No I won't, really!'

'You are afraid of something?' said the gipsy-woman cruelly.

'No, it's not that – ' Yvette fidgeted.

'You have some secret. You are afraid I shall say it. Come, would you like to go in the caravan, where nobody hears?'

The woman was curiously insinuating; while Yvette was always wayward, perverse. The look of perversity was on her soft, frail young face now, giving her a queer hardness.

'Yes!' she said suddenly. 'Yes! I might do that!'

'Oh, I say!' cried the others. 'Be a sport!'

'I don't think you'd *better*!' cried Lucille.

'Yes!' said Yvette, with that hard little way of hers. 'I'll do that. I'll go in the caravan.'

The gipsy-woman called something to the man on the steps. He went into the caravan for a moment or two, then reappeared, and came down the steps, setting the small child on its uncertain feet, and holding it by the hand. A dandy, in his polished black boots, tight black trousers and tight dark-green jersey, he walked slowly across, with the toddling child, to where the elderly gipsy was giving the roan horse a feed of oats, in the bough shelter between pits of grey rock, with dry bracken upon the stone-chip floor. He looked at Yvette as he passed, staring her full in the eyes, with his pariah's bold yet dishonest stare. Something hard inside her met his stare. But the surface of her body seemed to turn to water. Nevertheless, something hard in her registered the peculiar pure lines of his face, of his straight, pure nose, of his cheeks and temples. The curious dark, suave purity of all his body, outlined in the green jersey: a purity like a living sneer.

And as he loped slowly past her, on his flexible hips, it seemed to her still that he was stronger than she was. Of all the men she had ever seen, this one was the only one who was stronger than she was, in her own kind of strength, her own kind of understanding.

So, with curiosity, she followed the woman up the steps of the caravan, the skirts of her well-cut tan coat swinging and almost showing her knees, under the pale-green cloth dress. She had long, long-striding, fine legs, too slim rather than too thick, and she wore curiously-patterned pale-and-fawn stockings of fine wool, suggesting the legs of some delicate animal.

At the top of the steps she paused and turned, debonair, to the others, saying in her naïve, lordly way, so off-hand, 'I won't let her be long.'

Her grey fur collar was open, showing her soft throat and pale green dress, her little plaited tan-coloured hat came down to her ears, round her soft, fresh face. There was something soft and yet overbearing, unscrupulous, about her. She knew the gipsy-man had turned to look at her. She was aware of the pure dark nape of his neck, the black hair groomed away. He watched as she entered his house.

What the gipsy told her, no one ever knew. It was a long time to wait, the others felt. Twilight was deepening on the gloom, and it was turning raw and cold. From the chimney of the second caravan came smoke and a smell of rich food. The horse was fed, a yellow blanket strapped round him, and two gipsy-men talked together in the distance, in low tones. There was a peculiar feeling of silence and secrecy in that lonely, hidden quarry.

At last the caravan door opened, and Yvette emerged, bending forward and stepping with long, witch-like slim legs down the steps. There was a stooping, witch-like silence about her as she emerged on the twilight.

'Did it seem long?' she said vaguely, not looking at anybody and keeping her own counsel hard within her soft, vague waywardness. 'I hope you weren't bored! Wouldn't tea be nice! Shall we go?'

'You get in!' said Bob. 'I'll pay.'

The gipsy-woman's full, metallic skirts of jade-green alpaca came swinging down the steps. She rose to her height, a big, triumphant-looking woman with a dark-wolf face. The pink cashmere kerchief, stamped with red roses, was slipping to one side over her black and crimped hair. She gazed at the young people in the twilight with bold arrogance.

Bob put two half-crowns in her hand.

'A little bit more, for luck, for your young lady's luck,' she wheedled, like a wheedling wolf. 'Another bit of silver, to bring you luck.'

'You've got a shilling for luck, that's enough,' said Bob calmly and quietly, as they moved away to the car.

'A little bit of silver! Just a little bit, for your luck in love!'

Yvette, with the sudden long, startling gestures of her long limbs, swung round as she was entering the car, and with long arm outstretched, strode and put something into the gipsy's hand, then stepped, bending her height, into the car.

'Prosperity to the beautiful young lady, and the gipsy's blessing on her,' came the suggestive, half-sneering voice of the woman.

The engine *birred!* then *birred!* again more fiercely, and started. Leo switched on the lights, and immediately the quarry with the gipsies fell back into the blackness of night.

'Good-night!' called Yvette's voice, as the car started. But hers was the only voice that piped up, chirpy and impudent in its nonchalance. The headlights glared down the stone lane.

'Yvette, you've got to tell us what she said to you,' cried Lucille, in the teeth of Yvette's silent will *not* to be asked.

'Oh, nothing at *all* thrilling,' said Yvette, with false warmth. 'Just the usual old thing: a dark man who means good luck, and a fair one who means bad: and a death in the family, which if it means Granny, won't be so *very* awful: and I shall marry when I'm twenty-three, and have heaps of money and heaps of love, and two children. All sounds very nice, but it's a bit too much of a good thing, you know.'

'Oh, but why did you give her more money?'

'Oh well, I wanted to! You *have* to be a bit lordly with people like that –'

4

There was a terrific rumpus down at the rectory, on account of Yvette and the Window Fund. After the war, Aunt Cissie had set her heart on a stained-glass window in the church, as a memorial for the men of the parish who had fallen. But the bulk of the fallen had been non-conformists, so the memorial took the form of an ugly little monument in front of the Wesleyan chapel.

This did not vanquish Aunt Cissie. She canvassed, she had bazaars, she made the girls get up amateur theatrical shows, for her precious window. Yvette, who quite liked the acting and showing-off part of it, took charge of the farce called *Mary in the Mirror*, and gathered in the proceeds, which were to be paid to the Window Fund when accounts were settled. Each of the girls was supposed to have a money-box for the Fund.

Aunt Cissie, feeling that the united sums must now almost suffice, suddenly called in Yvette's box. It contained fifteen shillings. There was a moment of green horror.

'Where is all the rest?'

'Oh!' said Yvette casually. 'I just borrowed it. It wasn't so awfully much.'

'What about the three pounds thirteen for *Mary in the Mirror?*' asked Aunt Cissie, as if the jaws of Hell were yawning.

'Oh quite! I just borrowed it. I can pay it back.'

Poor Aunt Cissie! The green tumour of hate burst inside her, and there was a ghastly, abnormal scene, which left Yvette shivering with fear and nervous loathing.

Even the rector was rather severe.

'If you needed money, why didn't you tell me?' he said coldly. 'Have you ever been refused anything in reason?'

'I – I thought it didn't matter,' stammered Yvette.

'And what have you done with the money?'

'I suppose I've spent it,' said Yvette, with wide, distraught eyes and a peaked face.

'Spent it, on what?'

'I can't remember everything: stockings and things, and I gave some of it away.'

Poor Yvette! Her lordly airs and ways were already hitting back at her, on the reflex. The rector was angry: his face had a snarling, doggish look, a sort of sneer. He was afraid his daughter was developing some of the rank, tainted qualities of She-who-was-Cynthia.

'You *would* do the large with somebody else's money, wouldn't you?' he said, with a cold, mongrel sort of sneer, which showed what an utter unbeliever he was, at the heart. The inferiority of a heart which has no core of warm belief in it, no pride in life. He had utterly no belief in her.

Yvette went pale, and very distant. Her pride, that frail, precious flame which everybody tried to quench, recoiled like a flame blown far away, on a cold wind, as if blown out, and her face, white now and still like a snowdrop, the white snow-flower of his conceit, seemed to have no life in it, only this pure, strange abstraction.

'He has no belief in me!' she thought in her soul. 'I am really nothing to him. I am nothing, only a shameful thing. Everything is shameful, everything is shameful!'

A flame of passion or rage, while it might have overwhelmed or infuriated her, would not have degraded her as did her father's unbelief, his final attitude of a sneer against her.

He became a little afraid, in the silence of sterile thought. After all, he needed the *appearance* of love and belief and bright life, he would never dare to face the fat worm of his own unbelief, that stirred in his heart.

'What have you to say for yourself?' he asked.

She only looked at him from that senseless snowdrop face which haunted him with fear, and gave him a helpless sense of guilt. That other one, She-who-was-Cynthia, she had looked back at him with the same numb, white fear, the fear of his degrading unbelief, the worm which was his heart's core. He *knew* his heart's core was a fat, awful worm. His dread was lest anyone else should know. His anguish of hate was against anyone who knew, and recoiled.

He saw Yvette recoiling, and immediately his manner changed to the worldly old good-humoured cynic which he affected.

'Ah well!' he said. 'You have to pay it back, my girl, that's all. I will advance you the money out of your allowance. But I shall charge you four per cent a month interest. Even the devil himself must pay a percentage on his debts. Another time, if you can't trust yourself, don't handle money which isn't your own. Dishonesty isn't pretty.'

Yvette remained crushed, and deflowered and humiliated. She crept about, trailing the rays of her pride. She had a revulsion even from herself. Oh, why had she ever touched the leprous money! Her whole flesh shrank as if it were defiled. Why was that? Why, why was that?

She admitted herself wrong in having spent the money. 'Of course I shouldn't have done it. They are quite right to be angry,' she said to herself.

But where did the horrible wincing of her flesh come from? Why did she feel she had caught some physical contagion?

'Where you're so *silly*, Yvette,' Lucille lectured her: poor Lucille was in great distress – 'is that you give yourself away to them all. You might *know* they'd find out. I could have raised the money for you, and saved all this bother. It's perfectly awful! But you never will think beforehand where your actions are going to land you! Fancy Aunt Cissie saying all those things to you! How *awful*! Whatever would Mamma have said, if she'd heard it?'

When things went very wrong, they thought of their mother, and despised their father and all the low brood of the Saywells. Their mother, of course, had belonged to a higher, if more dangerous and 'immoral' world. More selfish, decidedly. But with a showier gesture. More unscrupulous and more easily moved to contempt: but not so humiliating.

Yvette always considered that she got her fine, delicate flesh from her mother. The Saywells were all a bit leathery, and grubby somewhere inside. But then the Saywells never let you down. Whereas the fine She-who-was-Cynthia had let the rector down with a bang, and his little children along with him. Her little children! They could not quite forgive her.

Only dimly, after the row, Yvette began to realise the other sanctity of herself, the sanctity of her sensitive, clean flesh and blood, which the Saywells with their so-called morality succeeded in defiling. They always wanted to defile it. They were the life unbelievers. Whereas, perhaps She-who-was-Cynthia had only been a moral unbeliever.

Yvette went about dazed and peaked and confused. The rector paid in the money to Aunt Cissie, much to that lady's rage. The helpless tumour of her rage was still running. She would have liked to announce her niece's delinquency in the parish magazine. It was anguish to the destroyed woman that she could not publish the news to all the world. The selfishness! The selfishness! The selfishness!

Then the rector handed his daughter a little account with himself: her debt to him, interest thereon, the amount deducted from her small allowance. But to her credit he had placed a guinea, which was the fee he had to pay for complicity.

'As father of the culprit,' he said humorously, 'I am fined one guinea. And with that I wash the ashes out of my hair.'

He was always generous about money. But somehow, he seemed to think that by being free about money he could absolutely call himself a generous man. Whereas he used money, even generosity, as a hold over her.

But he let the affair drop entirely. He was by this time more amused than anything, to judge from appearances. He thought still he was safe.

Aunt Cissie, however, could not get over her convulsion. One night when Yvette had gone rather early, miserably, to bed, when Lucille was away at a party, and she was lying with soft, peaked limbs aching with a sort of numbness and defilement, the door softly opened, and there stood Aunt Cissie, pushing her grey green face through the opening of the door. Yvette started up in terror.

'Liar! Thief! Selfish little beast!' hissed the maniacal face of Aunt Cissie. 'You little hypocrite! You liar! You selfish beast! You greedy little beast!'

There was such extraordinary impersonal hatred in that grey-green mask, and those frantic words, that Yvette opened her mouth to scream with hysterics. But Aunt Cissie shut the door as suddenly as she had opened it, and disappeared. Yvette leaped from her bed and turned the key. Then she crept back, half demented with fear of the squalid abnormal, half numbed with paralysis of damaged pride. And amid it all, up came a bubble of distracted laughter. It *was* so filthily ridiculous!

Aunt Cissie's behaviour did not hurt the girl so very much. It was after all somewhat fantastic. Yet hurt she was: in her limbs, in her body, in her sex, hurt. Hurt, numbed, and half destroyed, with only her nerves vibrating and jangled. And still so young, she could not conceive what was happening.

Only she lay and wished she were a gipsy. To live in a camp, in a caravan, and never set foot in a house, not know the existence of a parish, never look at a church. Her heart was hard with repugnance against the rectory. She loathed these houses with their indoor sanitation and their bathrooms, and their extraordinary repulsiveness. She hated the rectory, and everything it implied. The whole stagnant, sewerage sort of life, where sewerage is never mentioned, but where it seems to smell from the centre to every two-legged inmate, from Granny to the servants, was foul. If gipsies had no bathrooms, at least they had no sewerage. There was fresh air. In the rectory there was *never* fresh air. And in the souls of the people, the air was stale till it stank.

Hate kindled her heart, as she lay with numbed limbs. And she thought of the words of the gipsy woman: 'There is a dark man who never lived in a house. He loves you. The other people are treading on your heart. They will tread on your heart till you think it is dead. But the dark man will blow the one spark up into fire again, good fire. You will see what good fire.'

Even as the woman was saying it, Yvette felt there was some duplicity somewhere. But she didn't mind. She hated with the cold, acrid hatred of a child the rectory interior, the sort of putridity in the life. She liked that big, swarthy, wolf-like gipsy-woman, with the big gold rings in her ears, the pink scarf over her wavy black hair, the tight bodice of brown velvet, the green, fan-like skirt.

She liked her dusky, strong, relentless hands, that had pressed so firm, like wolf's paws, in Yvette's own soft palm. She liked her. She liked the danger and the covert fearlessness of her. She liked her covert, unyielding sex, that was immoral, but with a hard, defiant pride of its own. Nothing would ever get that woman under. She would despise the rectory and the rectory morality, utterly! She would strangle Granny with one hand. And she would have the same contempt for Daddy and for Uncle Fred, as men, as she would have for fat old slobbery Rover, the Newfoundland dog. A great, sardonic female contempt, for such domesticated dogs, calling themselves men.

And the gipsy-man himself! Yvette quivered suddenly, as if she had seen his big, bold eyes upon her, with the naked insinuation of desire in them. The absolutely naked insinuation of desire made her lie prone and powerless in the bed, as if a drug had cast her in a new, molten mould.

She never confessed to anybody that two of the ill-starred Window Fund pounds had gone to the gipsy-woman. What if Daddy and Aunt Cissie knew *that*! Yvette stirred luxuriously in the bed. The thought of the gipsy had released the life of her limbs, and crystallised in her heart the hate of the rectory: so that now she felt potent, instead of impotent.

When, later, Yvette told Lucille about Aunt Cissie's dramatic interlude in the bedroom doorway, Lucille was indignant.

'Oh, hang it all!' cried she. 'She might let it drop now. I should think we've heard enough about it by now! Good heavens, you'd think Aunt Cissie was a perfect bird of paradise! Daddy's dropped it, and after all, it's his business if it's anybody's. Let Aunt Cissie shut up!'

It was the very fact that the rector had dropped it, and that he again treated the vague and inconsiderate Yvette as if she were some specially-licensed being, that kept Aunt Cissie's bile flowing. The fact that Yvette really was most of the time unaware of other people's feelings, and being unaware, couldn't care about them, nearly sent Aunt Cissie mad. Why should that young creature, with a delinquent mother, go through life as a privileged being, even unaware of other people's existence, though they were under her nose?

Lucille at this time was very irritable. She seemed as if she simply went a little unbalanced, when she entered the rectory. Poor Lucille, she was so thoughtful and responsible. She did all the extra troubling, thought about doctors, medicines, servants, and all that sort of thing. She slaved conscientiously at her job all day in town, working in a room with artificial light from ten till five. And she came home to have her nerves rubbed almost to frenzy by Granny's horrible and persistent inquisitiveness and parasitic agedness.

The affair of the Window Fund had apparently blown over, but there remained a stuffy tension in the atmosphere. The weather continued bad. Lucille stayed at home on the afternoon of her half holiday, and did herself no good by it. The rector was in his study, she and Yvette were making a dress for the latter young woman, Granny was resting on the couch.

The dress was of blue silk velours, French material, and was going to be very becoming. Lucille made Yvette try it on again; she was nervously uneasy about the hang, under the arms.

'Oh bother!' cried Yvette, stretching her long, tender, childish arms, that tended to go bluish with the cold. 'Don't be so frightfully *fussy*, Lucille! It's quite all right.'

'If that's all the thanks I get, slaving my half day away making dresses for you, I might as well do something for myself!'

'Well, Lucille! You know I never *asked* you! You know you can't bear it unless you *do* supervise,' said Yvette, with that irritating blandness of hers, as she raised her naked elbows and peered over her shoulder into the long mirror.

'Oh yes! you never *asked* me!' cried Lucille. 'As if I didn't know what you meant, when you started sighing and flouncing about.'

'I!' said Yvette, with vague surprise. 'Why, when did I start sighing and flouncing about?'

'Of course you know you did.'

'Did I? No, I didn't know! When was it?' Yvette could put a peculiar annoyance into her mild, straying questions.

'I shan't do another thing to this frock, if you don't stand still and *stop* it,' said Lucille, in her rather sonorous, burning voice.

'You know you are most awfully nagging and irritable, Lucille,' said Yvette, standing as if on hot bricks.

'Now, Yvette!' cried Lucille, her eyes suddenly flashing in her sister's face, with wild flashes. 'Stop it at once! Why should everybody put up with your abominable and overbearing temper!'

'Well, I don't know about *my* temper,' said Yvette, writhing slowly out of the half-made frock, and slipping into her dress again.

Then, with an obstinate little look on her face, she sat down again at the table, in the gloomy afternoon, and began to sew at the blue stuff. The room was littered with blue clippings, the scissors were lying on the floor, the work-basket was spilled in chaos all over the table, and a second mirror was perched perilously on the piano.

Granny, who had been in a semi-coma, called a doze, roused herself on the big, soft couch and put her cap straight.

'I don't get much peace for my nap,' she said, slowly feeling her thin white hair, to see that it was in order. She had heard vague noises.

Aunt Cissie came in, fumbling in a bag for a chocolate.

'I never saw such a mess!' she said. 'You'd better clear some of that litter away, Yvette.'

'All right,' said Yvette. 'I will in a minute.'

'Which means never!' sneered Aunt Cissie, suddenly darting and picking up the scissors.

There was silence for a few moments, and Lucille slowly pushed her hands in her hair, as she read a book.

'You'd better clear away, Yvette,' persisted Aunt Cissie.

'I will, before tea,' replied Yvette, rising once more and pulling the blue dress over her head, flourishing her long, naked arms through the sleeveless armholes. Then she went between the mirrors, to look at herself once more.

As she did so, she sent the second mirror, that she had perched carelessly on the piano, sliding with a rattle to the floor. Luckily it did not break. But everybody started badly.

'She's smashed the mirror!' cried Aunt Cissie.

'Smashed a mirror! Which mirror! Who smashed it?' came Granny's sharp voice.

'I haven't smashed anything,' came the calm voice of Yvette. 'It's quite all right.'

'You'd better not perch it up there again,' said Lucille.

Yvette, with a little impatient shrug at all the fuss, tried making the mirror stand in another place. She was not successful.

'If one had a fire in one's own room,' she said crossly, 'one needn't have a lot of people fussing when one wants to sew.'

'Which mirror are you moving about?' asked Granny.

'One of our own, that came from the vicarage,' said Yvette rudely.

'Don't break it in *this* house, wherever it came from,' said Granny.

There was a sort of family dislike for the furniture that had belonged to She-who-was-Cynthia. It was most of it shoved into the kitchen, and the servants' bedrooms.

'Oh, *I'm* not superstitious,' said Yvette, 'about mirrors or any of that sort of thing.'

'Perhaps you're not,' said Granny. 'People who never take the responsibility for their own actions usually don't care what happens.'

'After all,' said Yvette, 'I may say it's my own looking-glass, even if I did break it.'

'And I say,' said Granny, 'that there shall be no mirrors broken in *this* house, if we can help it; no matter who they belong to, or did belong to. Cissie, have I got my cap straight?'

Aunt Cissie went over and straightened the old lady. Yvette loudly and irritatingly trilled a tuneless tune.

'And now, Yvette, will you please clear away,' said Aunt Cissie.

'Oh bother!' cried Yvette angrily. 'It's simply *awful* to live with a lot of people who are always nagging and fussing over trifles.'

'What people, may I ask?' said Aunt Cissie ominously.

Another row was imminent. Lucille looked up with a queer cast in her eyes. In the two girls, the blood of She-who-was-Cynthia was roused.

'Of course you may ask! You know quite well I mean the people in this beastly house,' said the outrageous Yvette.

'At least,' said Granny, 'we don't come of half-depraved stock.'

There was a second's electric pause. Then Lucille sprang from her low seat, with sparks flying from her.

'You shut up!' she shouted, in a blast full upon the mottled majesty of the old lady.

The old woman's breast began to heave with heaven knows what emotions. The pause this time, as after the thunderbolt, was icy.

Then Aunt Cissie, livid, sprang upon Lucille, pushing her like a fury.

'Go to your room!' she cried hoarsely. 'Go to your room!'

And she proceeded to push the white but fiery-eyed Lucille from the room. Lucille let herself be pushed, while Aunt Cissie vociferated, 'Stay in your room till you've apologised for this! – till you've apologised to the Mater for this!'

'I shan't apologise!' came the clear voice of Lucille, from the passage, while Aunt Cissie shoved her.

Aunt Cissie drove her more wildly upstairs.

Yvette stood tall and bemused in the sitting-room, with the air of offended dignity, at the same time bemused, which was so odd on her. She still was bare-armed, in the half-made blue dress. And even *she* was half-aghast at Lucille's attack on the majesty of age. But also, she was coldly indignant against Granny's aspersion of the maternal blood in their veins.

'Of course I meant no offence,' said Granny.

'Didn't you!' said Yvette coolly.

'Of course not. I only said we're not depraved, just because we happen to be superstitious about breaking mirrors.'

Yvette could hardly believe her ears. Had she heard right? Was it possible! Or was Granny, at her age, just telling a barefaced lie?

Yvette knew that the old woman was telling a cool, barefaced lie. But already, so quickly, Granny believed her own statement.

The rector appeared, having left time for a lull.

'What's wrong?' he asked cautiously, genially.

'Oh nothing!' drawled Yvette. 'Lucille told Granny to shut up, when she was saying something. And Aunt Cissie drove her up to her room. *Tant de bruit pour une omelette!* Though Lucille *was* a bit over the mark, that time.'

The old lady couldn't quite catch what Yvette said.

'Lucille really will have to learn to control her nerves,' said the old woman. 'The mirror fell down, and it worried me. I said so to Yvette, and she said something about superstitions and the people in the beastly house. I told her the people in the house were not depraved, if they happened to mind when a mirror was broken. And at that Lucille flew at me and told me to shut up. It really is disgraceful how these children give way to their nerves. I know it's nothing but nerves.'

Aunt Cissie had come in during this speech. At first even she was dumb. Then it seemed to her, it was as Granny had said.

'I have forbidden her to come down until she comes to apologise to the Mater,' she said.

'I doubt if she'll apologise,' said the calm, queenly Yvette, holding her bare arms.

'And I don't want any apology,' said the old lady. 'It is merely nerves. I don't know what they'll come to, if they have nerves like that, at their age! She must take Vibrofat. – I am sure Arthur would like his tea, Cissie.'

Yvette swept her sewing together, to go upstairs. And again she trilled her tune, rather shrill and tuneless. She was trembling inwardly.

'More glad rags!' said her father to her, genially.

'More glad rags!' she reiterated sagely, as she sauntered upstairs, with her day dress over one arm. She wanted to console Lucille, and ask her how the blue stuff hung now.

At the first landing, she stood as she nearly always did, to gaze through the window that looked to the road and the bridge. Like the Lady of Shalott, she seemed always to imagine that someone would come along singing *Tirra-lirra!* or something equally intelligent, by the river.

5

It was nearly tea-time. The snowdrops were out by the short drive going to the gate from the side of the house, and the gardener was pottering at the round, damp flower-beds, on the wet grass that sloped to the stream. Past the gate went the whitish muddy road, crossing the stone bridge almost immediately, and winding in a curve up to the steep, clustering, stony, smoking northern village, that perched over the grim stone mills which Yvette could see ahead down the narrow valley, their tall chimneys long and erect.

The rectory was on one side the Papple, in the rather steep valley, the village was beyond and above, further down, on the other side the swift stream. At the back of the rectory the hill went up steep, with a grove of dark, bare larches, through which the road disappeared. And immediately across stream from the rectory, facing the house, the river-bank rose steep and bushy, up to the sloping, dreary meadows, that sloped up again to dark hillsides of trees, with grey rock cropping out.

But from the end of the house, Yvette could only see the road curving round past the wall with its laurel hedge, down to the bridge, then up again round the shoulder to that first hard cluster of houses in Papplewick village, beyond the dry-stone walls of the steep fields.

She always expected *something* to come down the slant of the road from Papplewick, and she always lingered at the landing window. Often a cart came, or a motor car, or a lorry with stone, or a labourer, or one of the servants. But never anybody who sang *Tirra-lirra!* by the river. The tirralirraing days seem to have gone by.

This day, however, round the corner on the white-grey road, between the grass and the low stone walls, a roan horse came stepping bravely and briskly down-hill, driven by a man in a cap, perched on the front of his light cart. The man swayed loosely to the swing of the cart, as the horse stepped downhill, in the silent sombreness of the afternoon. At the back of the cart, long duster-brooms of reed and feather stuck out, nodding on their stalks of cane.

Yvette stood close to the window, and put the casement-cloth curtains behind her, clutching her bare upper arms with her hands.

At the foot of the slope the horse started into a brisk trot to the bridge. The cart rattled on the stone bridge, the brooms bobbed and flustered, the driver sat as if in a kind of dream, swinging along. It was like something seen in a sleep.

But as he crossed the end of the bridge, and was passing along the rectory wall, he looked up at the grim stone house that seemed to have backed away from the gate, under the hill. Yvette moved her hands quickly on her arms. And as quickly, from under the peak of his cap, he had seen her, his swarthy predative face was alert.

He pulled up suddenly at the white gate, still gazing upwards at the landing window; while Yvette, always clasping her cold and mottled arms, still gazed abstractedly down at him, from the window.

His head gave a little, quick jerk of signal, and he led his horse well aside, on to the grass. Then, limber and alert, he turned back the tarpaulin of the cart, fetched out various articles, pulled forth two or three of the long brooms of reed or turkey-feathers, covered the cart, and turned towards the house, looking up at Yvette as he opened the white gate.

She nodded to him, and flew to the bathroom to put on her dress, hoping she had disguised her nod so that he wouldn't be sure she had nodded. Meanwhile she heard the hoarse deep roaring of that old fool, Rover, punctuated by the yapping of that young idiot, Trixie.

She and the housemaid arrived at the same moment at the sitting-room door. 'Was it the man selling brooms?' said Yvette to the maid. 'All right!' and she opened the door. 'Aunt Cissie, there's a man selling brooms. Shall I go?'

'What sort of a man?' said Aunt Cissie, who was sitting at tea with the rector and the Mater: the girls having been excluded for once from the meal.

'A man with a cart,' said Yvette.

'A gipsy,' said the maid.

Of course Aunt Cissie rose at once. She had to look at him.

The gipsy stood at the back door, under the steep dark bank where the larches grew. The long brooms flourished from one hand, and from the other hung various objects of shining copper and brass: a saucepan, a candlestick, plates of beaten copper. The man himself was neat and dapper, almost rakish, in his dark-green cap and double-breasted green check coat. But his manner was subdued, very quiet: and at the same time proud, with a touch of condescension and aloofness.

'Anything today, lady?' he said, looking at Aunt Cissie with dark, shrewd, searching eyes, but putting a very quiet tenderness into his voice.

Aunt Cissie saw how handsome he was, saw the flexible curve of his lips under the line of black moustache, and she was fluttered. The merest hint of roughness or aggression on the man's part would have made her shut the door contemptuously in his face. But he managed to insinuate such a subtle suggestion of submission into his male bearing, that she began to hesitate.

'The candlestick is lovely!' said Yvette. 'Did you make it?'

And she looked up at the man with her naïve, childlike eyes, that were as capable of double meanings as his own.

'Yes, lady!' He looked back into her eyes for a second, with that naked suggestion of desire which acted on her like a spell, and robbed her of her will. Her tender face seemed to go into a sleep.

'It's awfully nice!' she murmured vaguely.

Aunt Cissie began to bargain for the candlestick: which was a low, thick stem of copper, rising from a double bowl. With patient aloofness the man attended to her, without ever looking at Yvette, who leaned against the doorway and watched in a muse.

'How is your wife?' she asked him suddenly, when Aunt Cissie had gone indoors to show the candlestick to the rector, and ask him if he thought it was worth it.

The man looked fully at Yvette, and a scarcely discernible smile curled his lips. His eyes did not smile: the insinuation in them only hardened to a glare.

'She's all right. When are you coming that way again?' he murmured, in a low, caressive, intimate voice.

'Oh, I don't know,' said Yvette vaguely.

'You come Fridays, when I'm there,' he said.

Yvette gazed over his shoulder as if she had not heard him. Aunt Cissie returned, with the candlestick and the money to pay for it. Yvette turned nonchalant away, trilling one of her broken tunes, abandoning the whole affair with a certain rudeness.

Nevertheless, hiding this time at the landing window, she stood to watch the man go. What she wanted to know, was whether he really had any power over her. She did not intend him to see her this time.

She saw him go down to the gate, with his brooms and pans, and out to the cart. He carefully stowed away his pans and his brooms, and fixed down the tarpaulin over the cart. Then with a slow, effortless spring of his flexible loins, he was on the cart again, and touching the horse with the reins. The roan horse was away at once, the cart-wheels grinding uphill, and soon the man was gone, without looking round. Gone like a dream which was only a dream, yet which she could not shake off.

'No, he hasn't any power over me!' she said to herself: rather disappointed really, because she wanted somebody, or something, to have power over her.

She went up to reason with the pale and overwrought Lucille, scolding her for getting into a state over nothing.

'What does it *matter*,' she expostulated, 'if you told Granny to shut up! Why, everybody ought to be told to shut up, when they're being beastly. But she didn't mean it, you know. No, she didn't mean it. And she's quite sorry she said it. There's absolutely no reason to make a fuss. Come on, let's dress ourselves up and sail down to dinner like duchesses. Let's have our own back that way. Come on, Lucille!'

There was something strange and mazy, like having cobwebs over one's face, about Yvette's vague blitheness; her queer, misty side-stepping from an unpleasantness. It was cheering too. But it was like walking in one of those autumn mists, when gossamer strands blow over your face. You don't quite know where you are.

She succeeded, however, in persuading Lucille, and the girls got out their best party frocks: Lucille in green and silver, Yvette in a pale lilac colour with turquoise chenille threading. A little rouge and powder, and their best slippers, and the gardens of paradise began to blossom. Yvette hummed and looked at herself, and put on her most *dégagé* airs of one of the young marchionesses. She had an odd way of slanting her eyebrows and pursing her lips, and to all appearances detaching herself from every earthly consideration, and floating through the cloud of her own pearl-coloured reserves. It was amusing, and not quite convincing.

'Of course I am beautiful, Lucille,' she said blandly. 'And you're perfectly lovely, now you look a bit reproachful. Of course you're the most aristocratic of the two of us, with your nose! And now your eyes look reproachful, that adds an appealing look, and you're perfect, perfectly lovely. But I'm more *winning*, in a way. – Don't you agree?' She turned with arch, complicated simplicity to Lucille.

She was truly simple in what she said. It was just what she thought. But it gave no hint of the very different *feeling* that also preoccupied her: the feeling that she had been looked upon, not from the outside, but from the inside, from her secret female self. She was dressing herself up and looking her most dazzling, just to counteract the effect that the gipsy had had on her, when he had looked at her, and seen none of her pretty face and her pretty ways, but just the dark, tremulous, potent secret of her virginity.

The two girls started downstairs in state when the dinner-gong rang: but they waited till they heard the voices of the men. Then they sailed down and into the sitting-room, Yvette preening herself in her vague, debonair way, always a little bit absent; and Lucille shy, ready to burst into tears.

'My goodness gracious!' exclaimed Aunt Cissie, who was still wearing her dark-brown knitted sports coat. 'What an apparition! Wherever do you think you're going?'

'We're dining with the family,' said Yvette naïvely, 'and we've put on our best gewgaws in honour of the occasion.'

The rector laughed aloud, and Uncle Fred said, 'The family feels itself highly honoured.'

Both the elderly men were quite gallant, which was what Yvette wanted.

'Come and let me feel your dresses, do!' said Granny. 'Are they your best? It is a shame I can't see them.'

'Tonight, Mater,' said Uncle Fred, 'we shall have to take the young ladies in to dinner, and live up to the honour. Will you go with Cissie?'

'I certainly will,' said Granny. 'Youth and beauty must come first.'

'Well, tonight, Mater!' said the rector, pleased.

And he offered his arm to Lucille, while Uncle Fred escorted Yvette.

But it was a draggled, dull meal, all the same. Lucille tried to be bright and sociable, and Yvette really was most amiable, in her vague, cobwebby way. Dimly, at the back of her mind, she was thinking. Why are we all only like mortal pieces of furniture? Why is nothing *important*?

That was her constant refrain to herself: Why is nothing important? Whether she was in church, or at a party of young people, or dancing in the hotel in the city, the same little bubble of a question rose repeatedly on her consciousness: Why is nothing important?

There were plenty of young men to make love to her: even devotedly. But with impatience she had to shake them off. Why were they so unimportant? – so irritating!

She never even thought of the gipsy. He was a perfectly negligible incident. Yet the approach of Friday loomed strangely significant. 'What are we doing on Friday?' she said to Lucille. To which Lucille replied that they were doing nothing. And Yvette was vexed.

Friday came, and in spite of herself she thought all day of the quarry off the road up high Bonsall Head. She wanted to be there. That was all she was conscious of. She wanted to be there. She had not even a dawning idea of going there. Besides, it was raining again. But as she sewed the blue dress, finishing it for the party up at Lambley Close, tomorrow, she just felt that her soul was up there, at the quarry, among the caravans, with the gipsies. Like one lost, or whose soul was stolen, she was not present in her body, the shell of her body. Her intrinsic body was away at the quarry, among the caravans.

The next day, at the party, she had no idea that she was being sweet to Leo. She had no idea that she was snatching him away from the tortured Ella Framley. Not until, when she was eating her pistachio ice, he said to her, 'Why don't you and me get engaged, Yvette? I'm absolutely sure it's the right thing for us both.'

Leo was a bit common, but good-natured, and well-off. Yvette quite liked him. But engaged! How perfectly silly! She felt like offering him a set of her silk underwear, to get engaged to.

'But, I thought it was Ella!' she said, in wonder.

'Well! It might ha' been, but for you. It's your doings, you know! Ever since those gipsies told your fortune, I felt it was me or nobody, for you, and you or nobody, for me.'

'Really!' said Yvette, simply lost in amazement. 'Really!'

'Didn't you feel a bit the same?' he asked.

'Really!' Yvette kept on gasping softly, like a fish.

'You felt a bit the same, didn't you?' he said.

'What? About what?' she asked, coming to.

'About me, as I feel about you.'

'Why? What? Getting engaged, you mean? I? No! Why how *could* I? I could never have dreamed of such an impossible thing.'

She spoke with her usual heedless candour, utterly unoccupied with his feelings.

'What was to prevent you?' he said, a bit nettled. 'I thought you did.'

'Did you *really now*?' she breathed in amazement, with that soft, virgin, heedless candour which made her her admirers and her enemies.

She was so completely amazed, there was nothing for him to do but twiddle his thumbs in annoyance.

The music began, and he looked at her.

'No! I won't dance any more,' she said, drawing herself up and gazing away rather loftily over the assembly, as if he did not exist. There was a touch of puzzled wonder on her brow, and her soft, dim virgin face did indeed suggest the snowdrop of her father's pathetic imagery.

'But of course *you* will dance,' she said, turning to him with young condescension. 'Do ask somebody to have this with you.'

He rose, angry, and went down the room.

She remained soft and remote in her amazement. Expect Leo to propose to her! She might as well have expected old Rover the Newfoundland dog to propose to her. Get engaged, to any man on earth? No, good heavens, nothing more ridiculous could be imagined!

It was then, in a fleeting side-thought, that she realised that the gipsy existed. Instantly, she was indignant. Him, of all things! Him! Never!

'Now why?' she asked herself, again in hushed amazement. 'Why? It's *absolutely* impossible: absolutely! So why is it?'

This was a nut to crack. She looked at the young men dancing, elbows out, hips prominent, waists elegantly in. They gave her no clue to her problem. Yet she did particularly dislike the forced elegance of the waists and the prominent hips, over which the well-tailored coats hung with such effeminate discretion.

'There is something about me which they don't see and never would see,' she said angrily to herself. And at the same time, she was relieved that they didn't and couldn't. It made life so very much simpler.

And again, since she was one of the people who are conscious in visual images, she saw the dark-green jersey rolled on the black trousers of the gipsy, his fine, quick hips, alert as eyes. They were elegant. The elegance of these dancers seemed so stuffed, hips merely wadded with flesh. Leo the same, thinking himself such a fine dancer! and a fine figure of a fellow!

Then she saw the gipsy's face; the straight nose, the slender mobile lips, and the level, significant stare of the black eyes, which seemed to shoot her in some vital, undiscovered place, unerring.

She drew herself up angrily. How dared he look at her like that? So she gazed glaringly at the insipid beaux on the dancing floor. And she despised them. Just as the raggle-taggle gipsy-women despise men who are not gipsies, despise their dog-like walk down the streets, she found herself despising this crowd. Where among them was the subtle, lonely, insinuating challenge that could reach her?

She did not want to mate with a house-dog.

Her sensitive nose turned up, her soft brown hair fell like a soft sheath round her tender, flower-like face, as she sat musing. She seemed so virginal. At the same time, there was a touch of the tall young virgin *witch* about her, that made the house-dog men shy off. She might metamorphose into something uncanny before you knew where you were.

This made her lonely, in spite of all the courting. Perhaps the courting only made her lonelier.

Leo, who was a sort of mastiff among the house-dogs, returned after his dance, with fresh cheery-o! courage.

'You've had a little think about it, haven't you?' he said, sitting down beside her: a comfortable, well-nourished, determined sort of fellow. She did not know why it irritated her so unreasonably, when he hitched up his trousers at the knee, over his good-sized but not very distinguished legs, and lowered himself assuredly on to a chair.

'Have I?' she said vaguely. 'About what?'

'You know what about,' he said. 'Did you make up your mind?'

'Make up my mind about what?' she asked, innocently.

In her upper consciousness, she truly had forgotten.

'Oh!' said Leo, settling his trousers again. 'About me and you getting engaged, you know.' He was almost as off-hand as she.

'Oh that's *absolutely* impossible,' she said, with mild amiability, as if it were some stray question among the rest. 'Why I never even thought of it again. Oh, don't talk about that sort of nonsense! That sort of thing is *absolutely* impossible,' she reiterated like a child.

'That sort of thing is, is it?' he said, with an odd smile at her calm, distant assertion. 'Well, what sort of thing *is* possible, then? You don't want to die an old maid, do you?'

'Oh I don't mind,' she said absently.

'I do,' he said.

She turned round and looked at him in wonder.

'Why?' she said. 'Why should you mind if I was an old maid?'

'Every reason in the world,' he said, looking up at her with a bold, meaningful smile, that wanted to make its meaning blatant, if not patent.

But instead of penetrating into some deep, secret place, and shooting her there, Leo's bold and patent smile only hit her on the outside of the body, like a tennis ball, and caused the same kind of sudden irritated reaction.

'I think this sort of thing is awfully silly,' she said, with minx-like spite. 'Why, you're practically engaged to – to – ' she pulled herself up in time – 'probably half a dozen other girls. I'm not flattered by what you've said. I should hate it if anybody knew! – Hate it! – I shan't breathe a word of it, and I hope you'll have the sense not to. – There's Ella!'

And keeping her face averted from him, she sailed away like a tall, soft flower, to join poor Ella Framley.

Leo flapped his white gloves.

'Catty little bitch!' he said to himself. But he was of the mastiff type, he rather liked the kitten to fly in his face. He began definitely to single her out.

6

The next week it poured again with rain. And this irritated Yvette with strange anger. She had intended it should be fine. Especially she insisted it should be fine towards the weekend. Why, she did not ask herself.

Thursday, the half-holiday, came with a hard frost, and sun. Leo arrived with his car, the usual bunch. Yvette disagreeably and unaccountably refused to go.

'No thanks, I don't feel like it,' she said.

She rather enjoyed being Mary-Mary-quite-contrary.

Then she went for a walk by herself, up the frozen hills, to the Black Rocks.

The next day also came sunny and frosty. It was February, but in the north country the ground did not thaw in the sun. Yvette announced that she was going for a ride on her bicycle, and taking her lunch as she might not be back till afternoon.

She set off, not hurrying. In spite of the frost, the sun had a touch of spring. In the park, the deer were standing in the distance, in the sunlight, to be warm. One doe, white spotted, walked slowly across the motionless landscape.

Cycling, Yvette found it difficult to keep her hands warm, even when bodily she was quite hot. Only when she had to walk up the long hill, to the top, and there was no wind.

The upland was very bare and clear, like another world. She had climbed on to another level. She cycled slowly, a little afraid of taking the wrong lane, in the vast maze of stone fences. As she passed along the lane she thought was the right one, she heard a faint tapping noise, with a slight metallic resonance.

The gipsy-man was seated on the ground with his back to the cart-shaft, hammering a copper bowl. He was in the sun, bare-headed, but wearing his green jersey. Three small children were moving quietly round, playing in the horse's shelter: the horse and cart were gone. An old woman, bent, with a kerchief round her head, was cooking over a fire of sticks. The only sound was the rapid, ringing tap-tap-tap! of the small hammer on the dull copper.

The man looked up at once, as Yvette stepped from her bicycle, but he did not move, though he ceased hammering. A delicate, barely discernible smile of triumph was on his face. The old woman looked round, keenly, from under her dirty grey hair. The man spoke a half-audible word to her, and she turned again to her fire. He looked up at Yvette.

'How are you all getting on?' she asked politely.

'All right, eh! You sit down a minute?' He turned as he sat, and pulled a stool from under the caravan for Yvette. Then, as she wheeled her bicycle to the side of the quarry, he started hammering again, with that bird-like, rapid light stroke.

Yvette went to the fire to warm her hands.

'Is this the dinner cooking?' she asked childishly, of the old gipsy, as she spread her long, tender hands, mottled red with the cold, to the embers.

'Dinner, yes!' said the old woman. 'For him! And for the children.'

She pointed with the long fork at the three black-eyed, staring children, who were staring at her from under their black fringes. But they were clean. Only the old woman was not clean. The quarry itself they had kept perfectly clean.

Yvette crouched in silence, warming her hands. The man rapidly hammered away with intervals of silence. The old hag slowly climbed the steps to the third, oldest caravan. The children began to play again, like little wild animals, quiet and busy.

'Are they your children?' asked Yvette, rising from the fire and turning to the man.

He looked her in the eyes, and nodded.

'But where's your wife?'

'She's gone out with the basket. They've all gone out, cart and all, selling things. I don't go selling things. I make them, but I don't go selling them. Not often. I don't often.'

'You make all the copper and brass things?' she said.

He nodded, and again offered her the stool. She sat down.

'You said you'd be here on Fridays,' she said. 'So I came this way, as it was so fine.'

'Very fine day!' said the gipsy, looking at her cheek, that was still a bit blanched by the cold, and the soft hair over her reddened ear, and the long, still mottled hands on her knee.

'You get cold, riding a bicycle?' he asked.

'My hands!' she said, clasping them nervously.

'You didn't wear gloves?'

'I did, but they weren't much good.'

'Cold comes through,' he said.

'Yes!' she replied.

The old woman came slowly, grotesquely down the steps of the caravan, with some enamel plates.

'The dinner cooked, eh?' he called softly.

The old woman muttered something, as she spread the plates near the fire. Two pots hung from a long iron horizontal bar, over the embers of the fire. A little pan seethed on a small iron tripod. In the sunshine, heat and vapour wavered together.

He put down his tools and the pot, and rose from the ground.

'You eat something along of us?' he asked Yvette, not looking at her.

'Oh, I brought my lunch,' said Yvette.

'You eat some stew?' he said. And again he called quietly, secretly to the old woman, who muttered in answer, as she slid the iron pot towards the end of the bar.

'Some beans, and some mutton in it,' he said.

'Oh, thanks awfully!' said Yvette. Then, suddenly taking courage, added: 'Well yes, just a very little, if I may.'

She went across to untie her lunch from her bicycle, and he went up the steps to his own caravan. After a minute, he emerged, wiping his hands on a towel.

'You want to come up and wash your hands?' he said.

'No, I think not,' she said. 'They are clean.'

He threw away his wash-water, and set off down the road with a high brass jug, to fetch clean water from the spring that trickled into a small pool, taking a cup to dip it with.

When he returned, he set the jug and the cup by the fire, and fetched himself a short log, to sit on. The children sat on the floor, by the fire, in a cluster, eating beans and bits of meat with spoon or fingers. The man on the log ate in silence, absorbedly. The woman made coffee in the black pot on the tripod, hobbling upstairs for the cups. There was silence in the camp. Yvette sat on her stool, having taken off her hat and shaken her hair in the sun.

'How many children have you?' Yvette asked suddenly.

'Say five,' he replied slowly, as he looked up into her eyes.

And again the bird of her heart sank down and seemed to die. Vaguely, as in a dream, she received from him the cup of coffee. She was aware only of his silent figure, sitting like a shadow there on the log, with an enamel cup in his hand, drinking his coffee in silence. Her will had departed from her limbs, he had power over her: his shadow was on her.

And he, as he blew his hot coffee, was aware of one thing only, the mysterious fruit of her virginity, her perfect tenderness in the body.

At length he put down his coffee-cup by the fire, then looked round at her. Her hair fell across her face, as she tried to sip from the hot cup. On her face was that tender look of sleep, which a nodding flower has when it is full out. Like a mysterious early flower, she was full out, like a snowdrop which spreads its three white wings in a flight into the waking sleep of its brief blossoming. The waking sleep of her full-opened virginity, entranced like a snowdrop in the sunshine, was upon her.

The gipsy, supremely aware of her, waited for her like the substance of shadow, as shadow waits and is there.

At length his voice said, without breaking the spell, 'You want to go in my caravan, now, and wash your hands?'

The childlike, sleep-waking eyes of her moment of perfect virginity looked into his, unseeing. She was only aware of the dark, strange effluence of him bathing her limbs, washing her at last purely will-less. She was aware of *him*, as a dark, complete power.

'I think I might,' she said.

He rose silently, then turned to speak, in a low command, to the old woman.

And then again he looked at Yvette, and putting his power over her, so that she had no burden of herself, or of action.

'Come!' he said.

She followed simply, followed the silent, secret, overpowering motion of his body in front of her. It cost her nothing. She was gone in his will.

He was at the top of the steps, and she at the foot, when she became aware of an intruding sound. She stood still, at the foot of the steps. A motor car was coming. He stood at the top of the steps, looking round strangely. The old woman harshly called something, as with rapidly increasing sound, a car rushed near. It was passing.

Then they heard the cry of a woman's voice, and the brakes on the car. It had pulled up, just beyond the quarry.

The gipsy came down the steps, having closed the door of the caravan.

'You want to put your hat on,' he said to her.

Obediently she went to the stool by the fire, and took up her hat. He sat down by the cart-wheel, darkly, and took up his tools. The rapid tap-tap-tap of his hammer, rapid and angry now like the sound of a tiny machine-gun, broke out just as the voice of the woman was heard crying, 'May we warm our hands at the camp fire?'

She advanced, dressed in a sleek but bulky coat of sable fur. A man followed, in a blue great-coat; pulling off his fur gloves and pulling out a pipe.

'It looked so tempting,' said the woman in the coat of many dead little animals, smiling a broad, half-condescending, half-hesitant simper, round the company.

No one said a word.

She advanced to the fire, shuddering a little inside her coat, with the cold. They had been driving in an open car.

She was a very small woman, with a rather large nose: probably a Jewess. Tiny almost as a child, in that sable coat she looked much more bulky than she should, and her wide, rather resentful brown eyes of a spoilt Jewess gazed oddly out of her expensive get-up.

She crouched over the low fire, spreading her little hands, on which diamonds and emeralds glittered.

'Ugh!' she shuddered. 'Of course we ought not to have come in an open car! But my husband won't even let me say I'm cold!' She looked round at him with her large, childish, reproachful eyes, that had still the canny shrewdness of a bourgeois Jewess: a rich one, probably.

Apparently she was in love, in a Jewess's curious way, with the big, blond man. He looked back at her with his abstracted blue eyes, that seemed to have no lashes, and a small smile creased his smooth, curiously naked cheeks. The smile didn't mean anything at all.

He was a man one connects instantly with winter sports, skiing and skating. Athletic, unconnected with life, he slowly filled his pipe, pressing in the tobacco with long, powerful reddened finger.

The Jewess looked at him to see if she got any response from him. Nothing at all, but that odd, blank smile. She turned again to the fire, tilting her eyebrows and looking at her small, white, spread hands.

He slipped off his heavily-lined coat, and appeared in one of the handsome, sharp-patterned knitted jerseys, in yellow and grey and black, over well-cut trousers, rather wide. Yes, they were both expensive! And he had a magnificent figure, an athletic, prominent chest. Like an experienced camper, he began building the fire together, quietly: like a soldier on campaign.

'D'you think they'd mind if we put some fir-cones on, to make a blaze?' he asked of Yvette, with a silent glance at the hammering gipsy.

'Love it, I should think,' said Yvette, in a daze, as the spell of the gipsy slowly left her, feeling stranded and blank.

The man went to the car, and returned with a little sack of cones, from which he drew a handful.

'Mind if we make a blaze?' he called to the gipsy.

'Eh?'

'Mind if we make a blaze with a few cones?'

'You go ahead!' said the gipsy.

The man began placing the cones lightly, carefully on the red embers. And soon, one by one, they caught fire, and burned like roses of flame, with a sweet scent.

'Ah lovely! lovely!' cried the little Jewess, looking up at her man again. He looked down at her quite kindly, like the sun on ice. 'Don't you love fire! Oh, I love it!' the little Jewess cried to Yvette, across the hammering.

The hammering annoyed her. She looked round with a slight frown on her fine little brows, as if she would bid the man stop. Yvette looked round too. The gipsy was bent over his copper bowl, legs apart, head down, lithe arm lifted. Already he seemed so far from her.

The man who accompanied the little Jewess strolled over to the gipsy, and stood in silence looking down on him, holding his pipe to his mouth. Now they were two men, like two strange male dogs, having to sniff one another.

'We're on our honeymoon,' said the little Jewess, with an arch, resentful look at Yvette. She spoke in a rather high, defiant voice, like some bird, a jay, or a rook, calling.

'Are you really?' said Yvette.

'Yes! Before we're married! Have you heard of Simon Fawcett?' – she named a wealthy and well-known engineer of the north country. 'Well, I'm Mrs Fawcett, and he's just divorcing me!' She looked at Yvette with curious defiance and wistfulness.

'Are you really!' said Yvette.

She understood now the look of resentment and defiance in the little Jewess's big, childlike brown eyes. She was an honest little thing, but perhaps her honesty was *too* rational. Perhaps it partly explained the notorious unscrupulousness of the well-known Simon Fawcett.

'Yes! As soon as we get the divorce, I'm going to marry Major Eastwood.'

Her cards were now all on the table. She was not going to deceive anybody.

Behind her, the two men were talking briefly. She glanced round, and fixed the gipsy with her big brown eyes.

He was looking up, as if shyly, at the big fellow in the sparkling jersey, who was standing pipe in mouth, man to man, looking down.

'With the horses back of Arras,' said the gipsy, in a low voice.

They were talking war. The gipsy had served with the artillery teams, in the Major's own regiment.

'*Ein schöner Mensch!*' said the Jewess. 'A handsome man, eh?'

For her, too, the gipsy was one of the common men, the Tommies.

'Quite handsome!' said Yvette.

'You are cycling?' asked the Jewess in a tone of surprise.

'Yes! Down to Papplewick. My father is rector of Papplewick: Mr Saywell!'

'Oh!' said the Jewess. 'I know! A clever writer! Very clever! I have read him.'

The fir-cones were all consumed already, the fire was a tall pile now of crumbling, shattering fire-roses. The sky was clouding over for afternoon. Perhaps towards evening it would snow.

The Major came back, and slung himself into his coat.

'I thought I remembered his face!' he said. 'One of our grooms, AI man with horses.'

'Look!' cried the Jewess to Yvette. 'Why don't you let us motor you down to Normanton. We live in Scoresby. We can tie the bicycle on behind.'

'I think I will,' said Yvette.

'Come!' called the Jewess to the peeping children, as the blond man wheeled away the bicycle. 'Come! Come here!' and taking out her little purse, she held out a shilling.

'Come!' she cried. 'Come and take it!'

The gipsy had laid down his work, and gone into his caravan. The old woman called hoarsely to the children, from her enclosure. The two elder children came stealing forward. The Jewess gave them the two bits of silver, a shilling and a florin, which she had in her purse, and again the hoarse voice of the unseen old woman was heard.

The gipsy descended from his caravan and strolled to the fire. The Jewess searched his face with the peculiar bourgeois boldness of her race.

'You were in the war, in Major Eastwood's regiment!' she said.

'Yes, lady!'

'Imagine you both being here now! – It's going to snow – ' She looked up at the sky.

'Later on,' said the man, looking at the sky.

He too had gone inaccessible. His race was very old, in its peculiar battle with established society, and had no conception of winning. Only now and then it could score.

But since the war, even the old sporting chance of scoring now and then was pretty well quenched. There was no question of yielding. The gipsy's eyes still had their bold look: but it was hardened and directed far away, the touch of insolent intimacy was gone. He had been through the war.

He looked at Yvette.

'You're going back in the motor car?' he said.

'Yes!' she replied, with a rather mincing mannerism. 'The weather is so treacherous!'

'Treacherous weather!' he repeated, looking at the sky.

She could not tell in the least what his feelings were. In truth, she wasn't very much interested. She was rather fascinated, now, by the little Jewess, mother of two children, who was taking her wealth away from the well-known engineer and transferring it to the penniless, sporting young Major Eastwood, who must be five or six years younger than she. Rather intriguing!

The blond man returned.

'A cigarette, Charles!' cried the little Jewess, plaintively.

He took out his case, slowly, with his slow, athletic movement. Something sensitive in him made him slow, cautious, as if he had hurt himself against people. He gave a cigarette to his wife, then one to Yvette, then offered the case, quite simply, to the gipsy. The gipsy took one.

'Thank you, sir!'

And he went quietly to the fire, and stooping, lit it at the red embers. Both women watched him.

'Well, goodbye!' said the Jewess, with her old bourgeois free-masonry. 'Thank you for the warm fire.'

'Fire is everybody's,' said the gipsy.

The young child came toddling to him.

'Goodbye!' said Yvette. 'I hope it won't snow for you.'

'We don't mind a bit of snow,' said the gipsy.

'Don't you?' said Yvette. 'I should have thought you would!'

'No!' said the gipsy.

She flung her scarf royally over her shoulder, and followed the fur coat of the Jewess, which seemed to walk on little legs of its own.

7

Yvette was rather thrilled by the Eastwoods, as she called them. The little Jewess had only to wait three months now, for the final decree. She had boldy rented a small summer cottage, by the moors up at Scoresby, not far from the hills. Now it was dead winter, and she and the Major lived in comparative isolation, without any maidservant. He had already resigned his commission in the regular army, and called himself Mr Eastwood. In fact, they were already Mr and Mrs Eastwood, to the common world.

The little Jewess was thirty-six, and her two children were both over twelve years of age. The husband had agreed that she should have the custody, as soon as she was married to Eastwood.

So there they were, this queer couple, the tiny, finely-formed little Jewess with her big, resentful reproachful eyes, and her mop of carefully-barbered black, curly hair, an elegant little thing in her way; and the big, pale-eyed young man, powerful and wintry, the remnant, surely of some old uncanny Danish stock: living together in a small modern house near the moors and the hills, and doing their own housework.

It was a funny household. The cottage was hired furnished, but the little Jewess had brought along her dearest pieces of furniture. She had an odd little taste for the rococo, strange curving cupboards inlaid with mother of pearl, tortoiseshell, ebony, heaven knows what; strange tall flamboyant chairs, from Italy, with sea-green brocade: astonishing saints with wind-blown, richly-coloured carven garments and pink faces: shelves of weird old Saxe and Capo di Monte figurines: and finally, a strange assortment of astonishing pictures painted on the back of glass, done probably in the early years of the nineteenth century, or in the late eighteenth.

In this crowded and extraordinary interior she received Yvette, when the latter made a stolen visit. A whole system of stoves had been installed into the cottage, every corner was warm, almost hot. And there was the tiny rococo figurine of the Jewess herself, in a perfect little frock, and an apron, putting slices of ham on the dish, while the great snow-bird of a major, in a white sweater and grey trousers, cut bread, mixed mustard, prepared coffee, and did all the rest. He had even made the dish of jugged hare which followed the cold meats and caviare.

The silver and the china were really valuable, part of the bride's trousseau. The Major drank beer from a silver mug, the little Jewess and Yvette had champagne in lovely glasses, the Major brought in coffee. They talked away. The little Jewess had a burning indignation against her first husband. She was intensely moral, so moral, that she was a divorcée. The Major too, strange wintry bird, so powerful, handsome too in his way, but pale round the eyes as if he had no eyelashes, like a bird, he too had a curious indignation against life, because of the false morality. That powerful, athletic chest hid a strange, snowy sort of anger. And his tenderness for the little Jewess was based on his sense of outraged justice, the abstract morality of the north blowing him, like a strange wind, into isolation.

As the afternoon drew on, they went to the kitchen, the Major pushed back his sleeves, showing his powerful athletic white arms, and carefully, deftly washed the dishes, while the women wiped. It was not for nothing his muscles were trained. Then he went round attending to the stoves of the small house, which only needed a moment or two of care each day. And after this, he brought out the small, closed car and drove Yvette home, in the rain, depositing her at the back gate, a little wicket among the larches, through which the earthen steps sloped downwards to the house.

She was really amazed by this couple.

'Really, Lucille!' she said. 'I do meet the most extraordinary people!' And she gave a detailed description.

'I think they sound rather nice!' said Lucille. 'I like the Major doing the housework, and looking so frightfully Bond-streety with it all. I should think, *when they're married*, it would be rather fun knowing them.'

'Yes!' said Yvette vaguely. 'Yes! Yes, it would!'

The very strangeness of the connection between the tiny Jewess and that pale-eyed, athletic young officer made her think again of her gipsy, who had been utterly absent from her consciousness, but who now returned with sudden painful force.

'What is it, Lucille,' she asked, 'that brings people together? People like the Eastwoods, for instance? and Daddy and Mamma, so frightfully unsuitable? – and that gipsy-woman who told my fortune, like a great horse, and the gipsy-man, so fine and delicately cut? What is it?'

'I suppose it's sex, whatever that is,' said Lucille.

'Yes, what is it? It's not really anything *common*, like common sensuality, you know, Lucille. It really isn't!'

'No, I suppose not,' said Lucille. 'Anyhow I suppose it needn't be.'

'Because you see the *common* fellows, you know, who make a girl feel *low*: nobody cares much about them. Nobody feels any connection with them. Yet they're supposed to be the sexual sort.'

'I suppose,' said Lucille, 'there's the low sort of sex, and there's the other sort, that isn't low. It's frightfully complicated, really! I *loathe* common fellows. And I never feel anything *sexual* – ' she laid a rather disgusted stress on the word – 'for fellows who aren't common. Perhaps I haven't got any sex.'

'That's just it!' said Yvette. 'Perhaps neither of us has. Perhaps we haven't really *got* any sex, to connect us with men.'

'How horrible it sounds: *connect us with men*!' cried Lucille, with revulsion. 'Wouldn't you hate to be connected with men that way? Oh I think it's an awful pity there has to *be* sex! It would be so much better if we could still be men and women, without that sort of thing.'

Yvette pondered. Far in the background was the image of the gipsy as he had looked round at her, when she had said: 'The weather is so treacherous.' She felt rather like Peter when the cock crew, as she denied him. Or rather, she did not deny the gipsy; she didn't care about his part in the show, anyhow. It was some hidden part of herself which she denied: that part which mysteriously and unconfessedly responded to him. And it was a strange, lustrous black cock which crew in mockery of her.

'Yes!' she said vaguely. 'Yes! Sex is an awful bore, you know, Lucille. When you haven't got it, you feel you *ought* to have it, somehow. And when you've got it – or *if* you have it – ' she lifted her head and wrinkled her nose disdainfully – 'you hate it.'

'Oh, I don't know!' cried Lucille. 'I think I should *like* to be awfully in love with a man.'

'You think so!' said Yvette, again wrinkling her nose. 'But if you were you wouldn't.'

'How do you know?' asked Lucille.

'Well, I don't really,' said Yvette. 'But I think so! Yes, I think so.'

'Oh, it's very likely!' said Lucille disgustedly. 'And anyhow one would be sure to get out of love again, and it would be merely disgusting.'

'Yes,' said Yvette. 'It's a problem.' She hummed a little tune.

'Oh, hang it all, it's not a problem for us two yet. We're neither of us really in love, and we probably never shall be, so the problem is settled that way.'

'I'm not so sure!' said Yvette sagely. 'I'm not so sure. I believe, one day, I shall fall *awfully* in love.'

'Probably you never will,' said Lucille brutally. 'That's what most old maids are thinking all the time.'

Yvette looked at her sister from pensive but apparently insouciant eyes.

'Is it?' she said. 'Do you really think so, Lucille? How perfectly awful for them, poor things! Why ever do they *care*?'

'Why do they?' said Lucille. 'Perhaps they don't, really. – Probably it's all because people say: *Poor old girl, she couldn't catch a man.*'

'I suppose it is!' said Yvette. 'They get to mind the beastly things people always do say about old maids. What a shame!'

'Anyhow we have a good time, and we do have lots of boys who make a fuss of us,' said Lucille.

'Yes!' said Yvette. 'Yes! But I couldn't possibly marry any of them.'

'Neither could I,' said Lucille. 'But why shouldn't we? Why should we bother about marrying, when we have a perfectly good time with the boys who are awfully good sorts, and you must say, Yvette, awfully sporting and *decent* to us.'

'Oh, they are!' said Yvette absently.

'I think it's time to think of marrying somebody,' said Lucille, 'when you feel you're *not* having a good time any more. Then marry, and just settle down.'

'Quite!' said Yvette.

But now, under all her bland, soft amiability, she was annoyed with Lucille. Suddenly she wanted to turn her back on Lucille.

Besides, look at the shadows under poor Lucille's eyes, and the wistfulness in the beautiful eyes themselves. Oh, if some awfully nice, kind, protective sort of man would but marry her! And if the sporting Lucille would let him!

Yvette did not tell the rector, nor Granny, about the Eastwoods. It would only have started a lot of talk which she detested. The rector wouldn't have minded, for himself, privately. But he too knew the necessity of keeping as clear as possible from that poisonous, many-headed serpent, the tongue of the people.

'But I don't *want* you to come if your father doesn't know,' cried the little Jewess.

'I suppose I'll have to tell him,' said Yvette. 'I'm sure he doesn't mind, really. But if he knew, he'd have to, I suppose.'

The young officer looked at her with an odd amusement, bird-like and unemotional, in his keen eyes. He too was by way of falling in love with Yvette. It was her peculiar virgin tenderness, and her straying, absent-minded detachment from things, which attracted him.

She was aware of what was happening, and she rather preened herself. Eastwood piqued her fancy. Such a smart young officer, awfully good class, so calm and amazing with a motor car, and quite a champion swimmer, it was intriguing to see him quietly, calmly washing dishes, smoking his pipe, doing his job so alert and skilful. Or, with the same interested care with which he made his investigation into the mysterious inside of an automobile, concocting jugged hare in the cottage kitchen. Then going out in the icy weather and cleaning his car till it looked like a live thing, like a cat when she has licked herself. Then coming in to talk so unassumingly and responsively, if briefly, with the little Jewess. And apparently, never bored. Sitting at the window with his pipe, in bad weather, silent for hours, abstracted, musing, yet with his athletic body alert in its stillness.

Yvette did not flirt with him. But she *did* like him.

'But what about your future?' she asked him.

'What about it?' he said, taking his pipe from his mouth, the unemotional point of a smile in his bird's eyes.

'A career! Doesn't every man have to carve out a career? – like some huge goose with gravy?' She gazed with odd naïveté into his eyes.

'I'm perfectly all right today, and I shall be all right tomorrow,' he said, with a cold, decided look. 'Why shouldn't my future be continuous todays and tomorrows?'

He looked at her with unmoved searching.

'Quite!' she said. 'I hate jobs, and all that side of life.' But she was thinking of the Jewess's money.

To which he did not answer. His anger was of the soft, snowy sort, which comfortably muffles the soul.

They had come to the point of talking philosophically together. The little Jewess looked a bit wan. She was curiously naïve and not possessive in her attitude to the man. Nor was she at all catty with Yvette. Only rather wan, and dumb.

Yvette, on a sudden impulse, thought she had better clear herself.

'I think life's *awfully* difficult,' she said.

'Life is!' cried the Jewess.

'What's so beastly, is that one is supposed to *fall in love*, and get married!' said Yvette, curling up her nose.

'Don't you *want* to fall in love and get married?' cried the Jewess, with great glaring eyes of astounded reproach.

'No, not particularly!' said Yvette. 'Especially as one feels there's nothing else to do. It's an awful chicken-coop one has to run into.'

'But you don't know what love is?' cried the Jewess.

'No!' said Yvette. 'Do you?'

'I!' bawled the tiny Jewess. 'I! My goodness, don't I!' She looked with reflective gloom at Eastwood, who was smoking his pipe, the dimples of his disconnected amusement showing on his smooth, scrupulous face. He had a very fine, smooth skin, which yet did not suffer from the weather, so that his face looked naked as a baby's. But it was not a round face: it was characteristic enough, and took queer ironical dimples, like a mask which is comic but frozen.

'Do you mean to say you don't know what love is?' insisted the Jewess.

'No!' said Yvette, with insouciant candour. 'I don't believe I do! Is it awful of me, at my age?'

'Is there never any man that makes you feel quite, quite different?' said the Jewess, with another big-eyed look at Eastwood. He smoked, utterly unimplicated.

'I don't think there is,' said Yvette. 'Unless – yes! – unless it is that gipsy' – she had put her head pensively sideways.

'Which gipsy?' bawled the little Jewess.

'The one who was a Tommy and looked after horses in Major Eastwood's regiment in the war,' said Yvette coolly.

The little Jewess gazed at Yvette with great eyes of stupor.

'You're not in love with that *gipsy*!' she said.

'Well!' said Yvette. 'I don't know. He's the only one that makes me feel – different! He really is!'

'But how? How? Has he ever *said* anything to you?'

'No! No!'

'Then how? What has he done?'

'Oh, just looked at me!'

'How?'

'Well you see, I don't know. But different! Yes, different! Different, quite different from the way any man ever looked at me.'

'But *how* did he look at you?' insisted the Jewess.

'Why – as if he really, but *really*, *desired* me,' said Yvette, her meditative face looking like the bud of a flower.

'What a vile fellow! What *right* had he to look at you like that?' cried the indignant Jewess.

'A cat may look at a king,' calmly interposed the Major, and now his face had the smiles of a cat's face.

'You think he oughtn't to?' asked Yvette, turning to him.

'Certainly not! A gipsy fellow, with half a dozen dirty women trailing after him! Certainly not!' cried the tiny Jewess.

'I wondered!' said Yvette. 'Because it *was* rather wonderful, really! And it *was* something quite different in my life.'

'I think,' said the Major, taking his pipe from his mouth, 'that desire is the most wonderful thing in life. Anybody who can really feel it, is a king, and I envy nobody else!' He put back his pipe.

The Jewess looked at him stupefied.

'But Charles!' she cried. 'Every common low man in Halifax feels nothing else!'

He again took his pipe from his mouth.

'That's merely appetite,' he said.

And he put back his pipe.

'You think the gipsy is the real thing?' Yvette asked him

He lifted his shoulders.

'It's not for me to say,' he replied. 'If I were you, I should know, I shouldn't be asking other people.'

'Yes – but – ' Yvette trailed out.

'Charles! You're wrong! How *could* it be a real thing! As if she could possibly marry him and go round in a caravan!'

'I didn't say marry him,' said Charles.

'Or a love affair! Why it's monstrous! What would she think of herself! – That's not love! That's – that's prostitution!'

Charles smoked for some moments.

'That gipsy was the best man we had, with horses. Nearly died of pneumonia. I thought he *was* dead. He's a resurrected man to me. I'm a resurrected man myself, as far as that goes.' He looked at Yvette. 'I was buried for twenty hours under snow,' he said. 'And not much the worse for it, when they dug me out.'

There was a frozen pause in the conversation.

'Life's awful!' said Yvette.

'They dug me out by accident,' he said.

'Oh! – ' Yvette trailed slowly. 'It might be destiny, you know.'

To which he did not answer.

8

The rector heard about Yvette's intimacy with the Eastwoods, and she was somewhat startled by the result. She had thought he wouldn't care. Verbally, in his would-be humorous fashion, he was so entirely unconventional, such a frightfully good sport. As he said himself, he was a conservative anarchist; which meant he was like a great many more people, a mere unbeliever. The anarchy extended to his humorous talk, and his secret thinking. The conservatism, based on a mongrel fear of the anarchy, controlled every action. His thoughts, secretly, were something to be scared of. Therefore, in his life, he was fanatically afraid of the unconventional.

When his conservatism and his abject sort of fear were uppermost, he always lifted his lip and bared his teeth a little, in a dog-like sneer.

'I hear your latest friends are the half-divorced Mrs Fawcett and the *maquereau* Eastwood,' he said to Yvette.

She didn't know what a *maquereau* was, but she felt the poison in the rector's fangs.

'I just know them,' she said. 'They're awfully nice, really. And they'll be married in about a month's time.'

The rector looked at her insouciant face with hatred. Somewhere inside him, he was cowed, he had been born cowed. And those who are born cowed are natural slaves, and deep instinct makes them fear with poisonous fear those who might suddenly snap the slave's collar round their necks.

It was for this reason the rector had so abjectly curled up, still so abjectly curled up before She-who-was-Cynthia: because of his slave's fear of her contempt, the contempt of a born-free nature for a base-born nature.

Yvette too had a free-born quality. She too, one day, would know him, and clap the slave's collar of her contempt round his neck.

But should she? He would fight to the death, this time, first. The slave in him was cornered this time, like a cornered rat, and with the courage of a cornered rat.

'I suppose they're your sort!' he sneered.

'Well, they are, really,' she said, with that blithe vagueness. 'I do like them awfully. They seem so solid, you know, so honest.'

'You've got a peculiar notion of honesty!' he sneered. 'A young sponge going off with a woman older than himself, so that he can live on her money! The woman leaving her home and her children! I don't know where you get your idea of honesty. Not from me, I hope. – And you seem to be very well acquainted with them, considering you say you just know them. Where did you meet them?'

'When I was out bicycling. They came along in their car, and we happened to talk. She told me at once who she was, so that I shouldn't make a mistake. She *is* honest.'

Poor Yvette was struggling to bear up.

'And how often have you seen them since?'

'Oh, I've just been over twice.'

'Over where?'

'To their cottage in Scoresby.'

He looked at her in hate, as if he could kill her. And he backed away from her, against the window-curtains of his study, like a rat at bay. Somewhere in his mind he was thinking unspeakable depravities about his daughter, as he had thought them of She-who-was-Cynthia. He was powerless against the lowest insinuations of his own mind. And these depravities which he attributed to the still-uncowed but frightened girl in front of him made him recoil, showing all his fangs in his handsome face.

'So you just know them, do you?' he said. 'Lying is in your blood, I see. I don't believe you get it from me.'

Yvette half averted her mute face, and thought of Granny's bare-faced prevarication. She did not answer.

'What takes you creeping round such couples?' he sneered. 'Aren't there enough decent people in the world for you to know? Anyone would think you were a stray dog, having to run round indecent couples, because the decent ones wouldn't have you. Have you got something worse than lying in your blood?'

'What have I got, worse than lying in my blood?' she asked. A cold deadness was coming over her. Was she abnormal, one of the semi-criminal abnormals? It made her feel cold and dead.

In his eyes, she was just brazening out the depravity that underlay her virgin, tender, bird like face. She-who-was-Cynthia had been like this: a snow-flower. And he had convulsions of sadistic horror, thinking what might be the *actual* depravity of She-who-was-Cynthia. Even his *own* love for her, which had been the lust-love of the born cowed, had been a depravity, in secret, to him. So what must an illegal love be?

'You know best yourself, what you have got,' he sneered. 'But it is something you had best curb, and quickly, if you don't intend to finish in a criminal-lunacy asylum.'

'Why?' she said, pale and muted, numbed with frozen fear. 'Why criminal lunacy? What have I done?'

'That is between you and your Maker,' he jeered. 'I shall never ask. But certain tendencies end in criminal lunacy, unless they are curbed in time.'

'Do you mean like knowing the Eastwoods?' asked Yvette, after a pause of numb fear.

'Do I mean like nosing round such people as Mrs Fawcett, a Jewess, and ex-Major Eastwood, a man who goes off with an older woman for the sake of her money? Why, yes, I do!'

'But you *can't* say that,' cried Yvette. 'He's an awfully simple, straightforward man.'

'He is apparently one of your sort.'

'Well! – In a way, I thought he was. I thought you'd like him too,' she said, simply, hardly knowing what she said.

The rector backed into the curtains, as if the girl menaced him with something fearful.

'Don't say any more,' he snarled, abject. 'Don't say any more. You've said too much, to implicate you. I don't want to learn any more horrors.'

'But what horrors?' she persisted.

The very naïveté of her unscrupulous innocence repelled him, cowed him still more.

'Say no more!' he said, in a low, hissing voice. 'But I will kill you before you shall go the way of your mother.'

She looked at him, as he stood there backed against the velvet curtains of his study, his face yellow, his eyes distraught like a rat's with fear and rage and hate, and a numb, frozen loneliness came over her. For her, too, the meaning had gone out of everything.

It was hard to break the frozen, sterile silence that ensued. At last, however, she looked at him. And in spite of herself, beyond her own knowledge, the contempt for him was in her young, clear, baffled eyes. It fell like the slave's collar over his neck, finally.

'Do you mean I mustn't know the Eastwoods?' she said.

'You can know them if you wish,' he sneered. 'But you must not expect to associate with your Granny, and your Aunt Cissie, and Lucille, if you do. I cannot have *them* contaminated. Your Granny was a faithful wife and a faithful mother, if ever one existed. She has already had one shock of shame and abomination to endure. She shall never be exposed to another.'

Yvette heard it all dimly, half hearing.

'I can send a note and say you disapprove,' she said dimly.

'You follow your own course of action. But remember, you have to choose between clean people, and reverence for your Granny's blameless old age, and people who are unclean in their minds and their bodies.'

Again there was a silence. Then she looked at him, and her face was more puzzled than anything. But somewhere at the back of her perplexity was that peculiar calm, virgin contempt of the free-born for the base-born. He, and all the Saywells, were base-born.

'All right,' she said. 'I'll write and say you disapprove.'

He did not answer. He was partly flattered, secretly triumphant, but abjectly.

'I have tried to keep this from your Granny and Aunt Cissie,' he said. 'It need not be public property, since you choose to make your friendship clandestine.'

There was a dreary silence.

'All right,' she said. 'I'll go and write.'

And she crept out of the room.

She addressed her little note to Mrs Eastwood. 'Dear Mrs Eastwood, Daddy doesn't approve of my coming to see you. So you will understand if we have to break it off. I'm awfully sorry – ' That was all.

Yet she felt a dreary blank when she had posted her letter. She was now even afraid of her own thoughts. She wanted, now, to be held against the slender, fine-shaped breast of the gipsy. She wanted him to hold her in his arms, if only for once, for once, and comfort and confirm her. She wanted to be confirmed by him, against her father, who had only a repulsive fear of her.

And at the same time she cringed and winced, so that she could hardly walk, for fear the thought was obscene, a criminal lunacy. It seemed to wound her heels as she walked, the fear. The fear, the great cold fear of the base-born, her father, everything human and swarming. Like a great bog humanity swamped her, and she sank in, weak at the knees, filled with repulsion and fear of every person she met.

She adjusted herself, however, quite rapidly to her new conception of people. She had to live. It is useless to quarrel with one's bread and butter. And to expect a great deal out of life is puerile. So, with the rapid adaptability of the post-war generation, she adjusted herself to the new facts. Her father was what he was. He would always play up to appearances. She would do the same. She too would play up to appearances.

So, underneath the blithe, gossamer-straying insouciance, a certain hardness formed, like rock crystallising in her heart. She lost her illusions in the collapse of her sympathies. Outwardly, she seemed the same. Inwardly she was hard and detached, and, unknown to herself, revengeful.

Outwardly she remained the same. It was part of her game. While circumstances remained as they were, she must remain, at least in appearance, true to what was expected of her.

But the revengefulness came out in her new vision of people. Under the rector's apparently gallant handsomeness, she saw the weak, feeble nullity. And she despised him. Yet still, in a way, she liked him too. Feelings are so complicated.

It was Granny whom she came to detest with all her soul. That obese old woman, sitting there in her blindness like some great red-blotched fungus, her neck swallowed between her heaped-up shoulders and her rolling, ancient chins, so that she was neckless as a double potato, her Yvette really hated, with that pure, sheer hatred which is almost a joy. Her hate was so clear, that while she was feeling strong, she enjoyed it.

The old woman sat with her big, reddened face pressed a little back, her lace cap perched on her thin white hair, her stub nose still assertive, and her old mouth shut like a trap. This motherly old soul, her mouth gave her away. It always had been one of the compressed sort. But in her great age, it had gone like a toad's, lipless, the jaw pressing up like the lower jaw of a trap. The look Yvette most hated was the look of that lower jaw pressing relentlessly up, with an ancient prognathous thrust, so that the snub nose in turn was forced to press upwards, and the whole face was pressed a little back, beneath the big, wall-like forehead. The will, the ancient, toad-like, obscene *will* in the old woman, was fearful, once you saw it: a toad-like self-will that was godless, and less than human! It belonged to the old, enduring race of toads, or tortoises. And it made one feel that Granny would never die. She would live on like these higher reptiles, in a state of semi-coma, for ever.

Yvette dared not even suggest to her father that Granny was not perfect. He would have threatened his daughter with the lunatic asylum. That was the threat he always seemed to have up his sleeve: the lunatic asylum. Exactly as if a distaste for Granny and for that horrible house of relatives was in itself a proof of lunacy, dangerous lunacy.

Yet in one of her moods of irritable depression, she did once fling out, 'How perfectly beastly this house is! Aunt Lucy comes, and Aunt Nell, and Aunt Alice, and they make a ring like a ring of crows, with Granny and Aunt Cissie, all lifting their skirts up and warming their legs at the fire, and shutting Lucille and me out. We're nothing but outsiders in this beastly house!'

Her father glanced at her curiously. But she managed to put a petulance into her speech, and a mere cross rudeness into her look, so that he could laugh, as at a childish tantrum. Somewhere, though, he knew that she coldly, venomously meant what she said, and he was wary of her.

Her life seemed now nothing but an irritable friction against the unsavoury household of the Saywells, in which she was immersed. She loathed the rectory with a loathing that consumed her life, a loathing so strong that she could not really go away from the place. While it endured, she was spell-bound to it, in revulsion.

She forgot the Eastwoods again. After all, what was the revolt of the little Jewess, compared to Granny and the Saywell bunch! A husband was never more than a semi-casual thing! But a family! — an awful, smelly family that would never disperse, stuck half dead round the base of a fungoid old woman! How was one to cope with that?

She did not forget the gipsy entirely. But she had no time for him. She, who was bored almost to agony, and who had nothing at all to do, she had not time to think even, seriously, of anything. Time being, after all, only the current of the soul in its flow.

She saw the gipsy twice. Once he came to the house, with things to sell. And she, watching him from the landing window, refused to go down. He saw her too, as he was putting his things back into his cart. But he too gave no sign. Being of a race that exists only to be harrying the outskirts of our society, for ever hostile and living only by spoil, he was too much master of himself, and too wary, to expose himself openly to the vast and gruesome clutch of our law. He had been through the war. He had been enslaved against his will, that time.

So now, he showed himself at the rectory, and slowly, quietly busied himself at his cart outside the white gate, with that air of silent and forever-unyielding outsideness which gave him his lonely, predative grace. He knew she saw him. And she should see him unyielding, quietly hawking his copper vessels, on an old, old war-path against such as herself.

Such as herself? Perhaps he was mistaken. Her heart, in its stroke, now rang hard as his hammer upon his copper, beating against circumstances. But he struck stealthily on the outside, and she still more secretly on the inside of the establishment. She liked him. She liked the quiet, noiseless clean-cut presence of him. She liked that mysterious endurance in him, which endures in opposition, without any idea of victory. And she liked that peculiar added relentlessness, the disillusion in hostility, which belongs to after the war. Yes, if she belonged to any side, and to any clan, it was to his. Almost she could have found it in her heart to go with him, and be a pariah gipsy-woman.

But she was born inside the pale. And she liked comfort, and a certain prestige. Even as a mere rector's daughter, one did have a certain prestige. And she liked that. Also she liked to chip against the pillars of the temple, from the inside. She wanted to be safe under the temple roof. Yet she enjoyed chipping fragments off the supporting pillars. Doubtless many fragments had been whittled away from the pillars of the Philistine, before Samson pulled the temple down.

'I'm not sure one shouldn't have one's fling till one is twenty-six, and then give in, and marry!'

This was Lucille's philosophy, learned from older women. Yvette was twenty-one. It meant she had five more years in which to have this precious fling. And the fling meant, at the moment, the gipsy. The marriage, at the age of twenty six, meant Leo or Gerry.

So, a woman could eat her cake and have her bread and butter.

Yvette, pitched in gruesome, deadlocked hostility to the Saywell household, was very old and very wise: with the agedness and the wisdom of the young, which always overleaps the agedness and the wisdom of the old, or the elderly.

The second time, she met the gipsy by accident. It was March, and sunny weather, after unheard-of rains. Celandines were yellow in the hedges, and primroses among the rocks. But still there came a smell of sulphur from far-away steel-works, out of the steel-blue sky.

And yet it was spring!

Yvette was cycling slowly along by Codnor Gate, past the lime quarries, when she saw the gipsy coming away from the door of a stone cottage. His cart stood there in the road. He was returning with his brooms and copper things, to the cart.

She got down from her bicycle. As she saw him, she loved with curious tenderness the slim lines of his body in the green jersey, the turn of his silent face. She felt she knew him better than she knew anybody on earth, even Lucille, and belonged to him, in some way, for ever.

'Have you made anything new and nice?' she asked innocently, looking at his copper things.

'I don't think,' he said, glancing back at her.

The desire was still there, still curious and naked, in his eyes. But it was more remote, the boldness diminished. There was a glint, as if he might dislike her. But this dissolved again, as he saw her looking among his bits of copper and brasswork. She searched them diligently.

There was a little oval brass plate, with a queer figure like a palm tree beaten upon it.

'I like that,' she said. 'How much is it?'

'What you like,' he said.

This made her nervous: he seemed off-hand, almost mocking.

'I'd rather you said,' she told him, looking up at him.

'You give me what you like,' he said.

'No!' she said, suddenly. 'If you won't tell me I won't have it.'

'All right,' he said. 'Two shilling.'

She found half-a-crown, and he drew from his pocket a handful of silver, from which he gave her sixpence.

'The old gipsy dreamed something about you,' he said, looking at her with curious, searching eyes.

'Did she!' cried Yvette, at once interested. 'What was it?'

'She said: Be braver in your heart, or you lose your game. She said it this way: Be braver in your body, or your luck will leave you. And she said as well: Listen for the voice of water.'

Yvette was very much impressed.

'And what does it mean?' she asked.

'I asked her,' he said. 'She says she don't know.'

'Tell me again what it was,' said Yvette.

' "Be braver in your body, or your luck will go." And: "Listen for the voice of water." '

He looked in silence at her soft, pondering face. Something almost like a perfume seemed to flow from her young bosom direct to him, in a grateful connection.

'I'm to be braver in my body, and I'm to listen for the voice of water! All right!' she said. 'I don't understand, but perhaps I shall.'

She looked at him with clear eyes. Man or woman is made up of many selves. With one self, she loved this gipsy-man. With many selves, she ignored him or had a distaste for him.

'You're not coming up to the Head no more?' he asked.

Again she looked at him absently.

'Perhaps I will,' she said, 'some time. Some time!'

'Spring weather!' he said, smiling faintly and glancing round at the sun. 'We're going to break camp soon, and go away.'

'When?' she said.

'Perhaps next week.'

'Where to?'

Again he made a move with his head.

'Perhaps up north,' he said.

She looked at him.

'All right!' she said. 'Perhaps I *will* come up before you go, and say goodbye to your wife and to the old woman who sent me the message.'

9

Yvette did not keep her promise. The few March days were lovely, and she let them slip. She had a curious reluctance, always, towards taking action, or making any real move of her own. She always wanted someone else to make a move for her, as if she did not want to play her own game of life.

She lived as usual, went out to her friends, to parties, and danced with the undiminished Leo. She wanted to go up and say goodbye to the gipsies. She wanted to. And nothing prevented her.

On the Friday afternoon especially she wanted to go. It was sunny, and the last yellow crocuses down the drive were in full blaze, wide open, the first bees rolling in them. The Papple rushed under the stone bridge, uncannily full, nearly filling the arches. There was the scent of a mezereon tree.

And she felt too lazy, too lazy, too lazy. She strayed in the garden by the river, half dreamy, expecting something. While the gleam of spring sun lasted, she would be out of doors. Indoors Granny, sitting back like some awful old prelate, in her bulk of black silk and her white lace cap, was warming her feet by the fire, and hearing everything that Aunt Nell had to say. Friday was Aunt Nell's day. She usually came for lunch, and left after an early tea. So the mother and the large, rather common daughter, who was a widow at the age of forty, sat gossiping by the fire, while Aunt Cissie prowled in and out. Friday was the rector's day for going to town: it was also the housemaid's half day.

Yvette sat on a wooden seat in the garden, only a few feet above the bank of the swollen river, which rolled a strange, uncanny mass of water. The crocuses were passing in the ornamental beds, the grass was dark green where it was mown, the laurels looked a little brighter. Aunt Cissie appeared at the top of the porch steps, and called to ask if Yvette wanted that early cup of tea. Because of the river just below, Yvette could not hear what Aunt Cissie said, but she guessed, and shook her head. An early cup of tea, indoors, when the sun actually shone? No thanks!

She was conscious of her gipsy, as she sat there musing in the sun. Her soul had the half painful, half easing knack of leaving her, and straying away to some place, to somebody that had caught her imagination. Some days she would be at the Framleys', even though she did not go near them. Some days, she was all the time in spirit with the Eastwoods. And today it was the gipsies. She was up at their encampment in the quarry. She saw the man hammering his copper, lifting his head to look at the road; and the children playing in the horse-shelter: and the women, the gipsy's wife and the strong, elderly woman, coming home with their packs, along with the elderly man. For this afternoon, she felt intensely that *that* was home for her: the gipsy camp, the fire, the stool, the man with the hammer, the old crone.

It was part of her nature, to get these fits of yearning for some place she knew; to be in a certain place; with somebody who meant home to her. This afternoon it was the gipsy camp. And the man in the green jersey made it home to her. Just to be where he was, that was to be at home. The caravans, the brats, the other women: everything was natural to her, her home, as if she had been born there. She wondered if the gipsy was aware of her: if he could see her sitting on the stool by the fire; if he would lift his head and see her as she rose, looking at him slowly and significantly, turning towards the steps of his caravan. Did he know? Did he know?

Vaguely she looked up the steep of dark larch trees north of the house, where unseen the road climbed, going towards the Head. There was nothing, and her glance strayed down again. At the foot of the slope the river turned, thrown back harshly, ominously, against the low rocks across stream, then pouring past the garden to the bridge. It was unnaturally full, and whitey-muddy, and ponderous. 'Listen for the voice of the water,' she said to herself. 'No need to listen for it, if the voice means the noise!'

And again she looked at the swollen river breaking angrily as it came round the bend. Above it the black-looking kitchen garden hung, and the hard-natured fruit trees. Everything was on the tilt, facing south and south-west, for the sun.

Behind, above the house and the kitchen garden hung the steep little wood of withered-seeming larches. The gardener was working in the kitchen garden, high up there, by the edge of the larch-wood.

She heard a call. It was Aunt Cissie and Aunt Nell. They were on the drive, waving goodbye! Yvette waved back. Then Aunt Cissie, pitching her voice against the waters, called, 'I shan't be long. Don't forget Granny is alone!'

'All right!' screamed Yvette rather ineffectually.

And she sat on her bench and watched the two undignified, long-coated women walk slowly over the bridge and begin the curving climb on the opposite slope, Aunt Nell carrying a sort of suit-case in which she brought a few goods for Granny and took back vegetables or whatever the rectory garden or cupboard was yielding. Slowly the two figures diminished, on the whitish, upcurving road, labouring slowly towards Papplewick village. Aunt Cissie was going as far as the village for something.

The sun was yellowing to decline. What a pity! Oh what a pity the sunny day was going, and she would have to turn indoors, to those hateful rooms, and Granny! Aunt Cissie would be back directly: it was past five. And all the others would be arriving from town, rather irritable and tired, soon after six.

As she looked uneasily round, she heard, across the running water, the sharp noise of a horse and cart rattling on the road hidden in the larch trees. The gardener was looking up too. Yvette turned away again, lingering, strolling by the full river a few paces, unwilling to go in; glancing up the road to see if Aunt Cissie were coming. If she saw her, she would go indoors.

She heard somebody shouting, and looked round. Down the path through the larch trees the gipsy was bounding. The gardener, away beyond, was also running. Simultaneously she became aware of a great roar, which, before she could move, accumulated to a vast deafening snarl. The gipsy was gesticulating. She looked round, behind her.

And to her horror and amazement, round the bend of the river she saw a shaggy, tawny wave-front of water advancing like a wall of lions. The roaring sound wiped out everything. She was powerless, too amazed and wonder-struck, she wanted to see it.

Before she could think twice, it was near, a roaring cliff of water. She almost fainted with horror. She heard the scream of the gipsy, and looked up to see him bounding upon her, his black eyes starting out of his head.

'Run!' he screamed, seizing her arm.

And in the instant the first wave was washing her feet from under her, swirling, in the insane noise, which suddenly for some reason seemed like stillness, with a devouring flood over the garden. The horrible mowing of water!

The gipsy dragged her heavily, lurching, plunging, but still keeping foothold both of them, towards the house. She was barely conscious: as if the flood was in her soul.

There was one grass-banked terrace of the garden, near the path round the house. The gipsy clawed his way up this terrace to the dry level of the path,

dragging her after him, and sprang with her past the windows to the porch steps
Before they got there, a new great surge of water came mowing, mowing trees
down even, and mowed them down too.

Yvette felt herself gone in an agonising mill-race of icy water, whirled, with
only the fearful grip of the gipsy's hand on her wrist. They were both down and
gone. She felt a dull but stunning bruise somewhere.

Then he pulled her up. He was up, streaming forth water, clinging to the stem
of the great wisteria that grew against the wall, crushed against the wall by the
water. Her head was above water, he held her arm till it seemed dislocated: but
she could not get her footing. With a ghastly sickness like a dream, she struggled
and struggled, and could not get her feet. Only his hand was locked on her wrist.

He dragged her nearer till her one hand caught his leg. He nearly went down
again. But the wisteria held him, and he pulled her up to him. She clawed at him,
horribly, and got to her feet, he hanging on like a man torn in two, to the
wisteria trunk.

The water was above her knees. The man and she looked into each other's
ghastly streaming faces.

'Get to the steps!' he screamed.

It was only just round the corner: four strides! She looked at him: she could
not go. His eyes glared on her like a tiger's, and he pushed her from him. She
clung to the wall, and the water seemed to abate a little. Round the corner she
staggered, but staggering, reeled and was pitched up against the cornice of the
balustrade of the porch steps, the man after her.

They got on to the steps, when another roar was heard amid the roar, and the
wall of the house shook. Up heaved the water round their legs again, but
the gipsy had opened the hall door. In they poured with the water, reeling to the
stairs. And as they did so, they saw the short but strange bulk of Granny emerge
in the hall, away down from the dining-room door. She had her hands lifted and
clawing, as the first water swirled round her legs, and her coffin-like mouth was
opened in a hoarse scream.

Yvette was blind to everything but the stairs. Blind, unconscious of everything save the steps rising beyond the water, she clambered up like a wet,
shuddering cat, in a state of unconsciousness. It was not till she was on the
landing, dripping and shuddering till she could not stand erect, clinging to the
banisters, while the house shook and the water raved below, that she was aware
of the sodden gipsy, in paroxysms of coughing at the head of the stairs, his cap
gone, his black hair over his eyes, peering between his washed-down hair at the
sickening heave of water below, in the hall. Yvette, fainting, looked too and saw
Granny bob up, like a strange float, her face purple, her blind blue eyes bolting,
spume hissing from her mouth. One old purple hand clawed at a banister rail,
and held for a moment, showing the glint of a wedding ring.

The gipsy, who had coughed himself free and pushed back his hair, said to
that awful float-like face below, 'Not good enough! Not good enough!'

With a low thud like thunder, the house was struck again, and shuddered, and a strange cracking, rattling, spitting noise began. Up heaved the water like a sea. The hand was gone, all sign of anything was gone, but upheaving water.

Yvette turned in blind unconscious frenzy, staggering like a wet cat to the upper staircase, and climbing swiftly. It was not till she was at the door of her room that she stopped, paralysed by the sound of a sickening, tearing crash, while the house swayed.

'The house is coming down!' yelled the green-white face of the gipsy, in her face.

He glared into her crazed face.

'Where is the chimney? the back chimney? – which room? The chimney will stand – '

He glared with strange ferocity into her face, forcing her to understand. And she nodded with a strange, crazed poise, nodded quite serenely, saying, 'In here! In here! It's all right.'

They entered her room, which had a narrow fire-place. It was a back room with two windows, one on each side the great chimney-flue. The gipsy, coughing bitterly and trembling in every limb, went to the window to look out.

Below, between the house and the steep rise of the hill, was a wild mill-race of water rushing with refuse, including Rover's green dog-kennel. The gipsy coughed and coughed, and gazed down blankly. Tree after tree went down, mown by the water, which must have been ten feet deep.

Shuddering and pressing his sodden arms on his sodden breast, a look of resignation on his livid face, he turned to Yvette. A fearful tearing noise tore the house, then there was a deep, watery explosion. Something had gone down, some part of the house, the floor heaved and wavered beneath them. For some moments both were suspended, stupefied. Then he roused.

'Not good enough! Not good enough! This will stand. This here will stand. See – that chimney! – like a tower. Yes! All right! All right. You take your clothes off and go to bed. You'll die of the cold.'

'It's all right! It's quite all right!' she said to him, sitting on a chair and looking up into his face with her white, insane little face, round which the hair was plastered.

'No!' he cried. 'No! Take your things off and I'll rub you with this towel. I'll rub myself. If the house falls then die warm. If it don't fall, then live, not die of pneumonia.'

Coughing, shuddering violently, he pulled up his jersey hem and wrestled with all his shuddering, cold-racked might, to get off his wet, tight jersey.

'Help me!' he cried, his face muffled.

She seized the edge of the jersey, obediently, and pulled with all her might. The garment came over his head, and he stood in his braces.

'Take your things off! Rub with this towel!' he commanded ferociously, the savageness of the war on him. And like a thing obsessed, he pushed himself out of his trousers, and got out of his wet, clinging shirt, emerging slim and livid, shuddering in every fibre with cold and shock.

He seized a towel, and began quickly to rub his body, his teeth chattering like plates rattling together. Yvette dimly saw it was wise. She tried to get out of her dress. He pulled the horrible wet death-gripping thing off her, then, resuming his rubbing, went to the door, tip-toeing on the wet floor.

There he stood, naked, towel in hand, petrified. He looked west, towards where the upper landing window had been, and was looking into the sunset, over an insane sea of waters, bristling with uptorn trees and refuse. The end corner of the house, where the porch had been, and the stairs, had gone. The wall had fallen, leaving the floors sticking out. The stairs had gone.

Motionless, he watched the water. A cold wind blew in upon him. He clenched his rattling teeth with a great effort of will, and turned into the room again, closing the door.

Yvette, naked, shuddering so much that she was sick, was trying to wipe herself dry.

'All right!' he cried. 'All right! The water don't rise no more! All right!'

With his towel he began to rub her, himself shaking all over, but holding her gripped by the shoulder, and slowly, numbedly rubbing her tender body, even trying to rub up into some dryness the pitiful hair of her small head.

Suddenly he left off.

'Better lie in the bed,' he commanded, 'I want to rub myself.'

His teeth went snap-snap-snap-snap, in great snaps, cutting off his words. Yvette crept shaking and semi-conscious into her bed. He, making strained efforts to hold himself still and rub himself warm, went again to the north window, to look out.

The water had risen a little. The sun had gone down, and there was a reddish glow. He rubbed his hair into a black, wet tangle, then paused for breath, in a sudden access of shuddering, then looked out again, then rubbed again on his breast, and began to cough afresh, because of the water he had swallowed. His towel was red: he had hurt himself somewhere: but he felt nothing.

There was still the strange huge noise of water, and the horrible bump of things bumping against the walls. The wind was rising with sundown, cold and hard. The house shook with explosive thuds, and weird, weird frightening noises came up.

A terror creeping over his soul, he went again to the door. The wind, roaring with the waters, blew in as he opened it. Through the awesome gap in the house he saw the world, the waters, the chaos of horrible waters, the twilight, the perfect new moon high above the sunset, a faint thing, and clouds pushing dark into the sky, on the cold, blustery wind.

Clenching his teeth again, fear mingling with resignation, or fatalism, in his soul, he went into the room and closed the door, picking up her towel to see if it were drier than his own, and less blood-stained, again rubbing his head, and going to the window.

He turned away, unable to control his spasms of shivering. Yvette had disappeared right under the bedclothes, and nothing of her was visible but a shivering mound under the white quilt. He laid his hand on this shivering mound, as if for company. It did not stop shivering.

'All right!' he said. 'All right! Water's going down.'

She suddenly uncovered her head and peered out at him from a white face. She peered into his greenish, curiously calm face, semi-conscious. His teeth were chattering unheeded, as he gazed down at her, his black eyes still full of the fire of life and a certain vagabond calm of fatalistic resignation.

'Warm me!' she moaned, with chattering teeth. 'Warm me! I shall die of shivering.'

A terrible convulsion went through her curled-up white body, enough indeed to rupture her and cause her to die.

The gipsy nodded, and took her in his arms, and held her in a clasp like a vice, to still his own shuddering. He himself was shuddering fearfully, and only semi-conscious. It was the shock.

The vice-like grip of his arms round her seemed to her the only stable point in her consciousness. It was a fearful relief to her heart, which was strained to bursting. And though his body, wrapped round her strange and lithe and powerful, like tentacles, rippled with shuddering as an electric current, still the rigid tension of the muscles that held her clenched steadied them both, and gradually the sickening violence of the shuddering, caused by shock, abated, in his body first, then in hers, and the warmth revived between them. And as it roused, their tortured, semi-conscious minds became unconscious, they passed away into sleep.

10

The sun was shining in heaven before men were able to get across the Papple with ladders. The bridge was gone. But the flood had abated, and the house, that leaned forwards as if it were making a stiff bow to the stream, stood now in mud and wreckage, with a great heap of fallen masonry and debris at the south-west corner. Awful were the gaping mouths of rooms!

Inside, there was no sign of life. But across-stream the gardener had come to reconnoitre, and the cook appeared, thrilled with curiosity. She had escaped from the back door and up through the larches to the high-road, when she saw the gipsy bound past the house: thinking he was coming to murder somebody. At the little top gate she had found his cart standing. The gardener had led the horse away to the Red Lion up at Darley, when night had fallen.

This the men from Papplewick learned when at last they got across the stream with ladders, and to the back of the house. They were nervous, fearing a collapse of the building, whose front was all undermined and whose back was choked up. They gazed with horror at the silent shelves of the rector's rows of books, in his torn-open study; at the big brass bedstead of Granny's room, the bed so deep and comfortably made, but one brass leg of the bedstead perching tentatively over the torn void, at the wreckage of the maid's room upstairs. The housemaid and the cook wept. Then a man climbed in cautiously through a smashed kitchen window, into the jungle and morass of the ground floor. He found the body of the old woman: or at least he saw her foot, in its flat black slipper, muddily protruding from a mud-heap of debris. And he fled.

The gardener said he was sure that Miss Yvette was not in the house. He had seen her and the gipsy swept away. But the policeman insisted on a search, and the Framley boys rushing up at last, the ladders were roped together. Then the whole party set up a loud yell. But without result. No answer from within.

A ladder was up, Bob Framley climbed, smashed a window, and clambered into Aunt Cissie's room. The perfect homely familiarity of everything terrified him like ghosts. The house might go down any minute.

They had just got the ladder up to the top floor, when men came running from Darley, saying the old gipsy had been to the Red Lion for the horse and cart, leaving word that his son had seen Yvette at the top of the house. But by that time the policeman was smashing the window of Yvette's room.

Yvette, fast asleep, started from under the bedclothes with a scream, as the glass flew. She clutched the sheets round her nakedness. The policeman uttered a startled yell, which he converted into a cry of: 'Miss Yvette! Miss Yvette!'

He turned round on the ladder, and shouted to the faces below, 'Miss Yvette's in bed! – in bed!'

And he perched there on the ladder, an unmarried man, clutching the window in peril, not knowing what to do.

Yvette sat up in bed, her hair in a matted tangle, and stared with wild eyes, clutching up the sheets at her naked breast. She had been so very fast asleep, that she was still not there.

The policeman, terrified at the flabby ladder, climbed into the room, saying, 'Don't be frightened, Miss! Don't you worry any more about it. You're safe now.'

And Yvette, so dazed, thought he meant the gipsy. Where was the gipsy? This was the first thing in her mind. Where was her gipsy of this world's-end night?

He was gone! He was gone! And a policeman was in the room! A policeman! She rubbed her hand over her dazed brow.

'If you'll get dressed, Miss, we can get you down to safe ground. The house is likely to fall. I suppose there's nobody in the other rooms?'

He stepped gingerly into the passage and gazed in terror through the torn-out end of the house, and far-off saw the rector coming down in a motor car, on the sunlit hill.

Yvette, her face gone numb and disappointed, got up quickly, closing the bedclothes, and looked at herself a moment, then opened her drawers for clothing. She dressed herself, then looked in a mirror, and saw her matted hair with horror. Yet she did not care. The gipsy was gone, anyhow.

Her own clothes lay in a sodden heap. There was a great sodden place on the carpet where his had been, and two blood-stained filthy towels. Otherwise there was no sign of him.

She was tugging at her hair when the policeman tapped at her door. She called him to come in. He saw with relief that she was dressed and in her right senses.

'We'd better get out of the house as soon as possible, Miss,' he reiterated. 'It might fall any minute.'

'Really!' said Yvette calmly. 'Is it as bad as that?'

There were great shouts. She had to go to the window. There, below, was the rector, his arms wide open, tears streaming down his face.

'I'm perfectly all right, Daddy!' she said, with the calmness of her contradictory feelings. She would keep the gipsy a secret from him. At the same time, tears ran down her face.

'Don't you cry, Miss, don't you cry! The rector's lost his mother, but he's thanking his stars to have his daughter. We all thought you were gone as well, we did that!'

'Is Granny drowned?' said Yvette.

'I'm afraid she is, poor lady!' said the policeman, with a grave face.

Yvette wept away into her hanky, which she had had to fetch from a drawer.

'Dare you go down that ladder, Miss?' said the policeman.

Yvette looked at the sagging depth of it, and said promptly to herself: No! Not for anything! – But then she remembered the gipsy's saying: 'Be braver in the body.'

'Have you been in all the other rooms?' she said, in her weeping, turning to the policeman.

'Yes, Miss! But you was the only person in the house, you know, save the old lady. Cook got away in time, and Lizzie was up at her mother's. It was only you and the poor old lady we was fretting about. Do you think you dare go down that ladder?'

'Oh, yes!' said Yvette, with indifference. The gipsy was gone anyway.

And now the rector in torment watched his tall, slender daughter slowly stepping backwards down the sagging ladder, the policeman, peering heroically from the smashed window, holding the ladder's top end.

At the foot of the ladder Yvette appropriately fainted in her father's arms, and was borne away with him, in the car, by Bob, to the Framley home. There the poor Lucille, a ghost of ghosts, wept with relief till she had hysterics, and even Aunt Cissie cried out among her tears: 'Let the old be taken and the young spared! Oh I *can't* cry for the Mater, now Yvette is spared!'

And she wept gallons.

The flood was caused by the sudden bursting of the great reservoir, up in Papple Highdale, five miles from the rectory. It was found out later that an ancient, perhaps even a Roman mine tunnel, unsuspected, undreamed of, beneath the reservoir dam, had collapsed, undermining the whole dam. That was why the Papple had been, for that last day, so uncannily full. And then the dam had burst.

The rector and the two girls stayed on at the Framleys', till a new home could be found. Yvette did not attend Granny's funeral. She stayed in bed.

Telling her tale, she only told how the gipsy had got her inside the porch, and she had crawled to the stairs out of the water. It was known that he had escaped: the old gipsy had said so, when he fetched the horse and cart from the Red Lion.

Yvette could tell little. She was vague, confused, she seemed hardly to remember anything. But that was just like her.

It was Bob Framley who said, 'You know, I think that gipsy deserves a medal.'

The whole family suddenly was struck.

'Oh, we *ought* to thank him!' cried Lucille.

The rector himself went with Bob in the car. But the quarry was deserted. The gipsies had lifted camp and gone, no one knew whither.

And Yvette, lying in bed, moaned in her heart: Oh, I love him! I love him! I love him! The grief over him kept her prostrate. Yet practically, she too was acquiescent in the fact of his disappearance. Her young soul knew the wisdom of it.

But after Granny's funeral, she received a little letter, dated from some unknown place.

'Dear Miss, I see in the paper you are all right after your ducking, as is the same with me. I hope I see you again one day, maybe at Tideswell cattle fair, or maybe we come that way again. I come that day to say goodbye! and I never said it, well, the water give no time, but I live in hopes. Your obdt servant Joe Boswell.'

And only then she realised that he had a name.

THE ESCAPED COCK

THERE WAS A PEASANT NEAR JERUSALEM who acquired a young gamecock which looked a shabby little thing, but which put on brave feathers as spring advanced, and was resplendent with arched and orange neck by the time the fig trees were letting out leaves from their end-tips.

This peasant was poor, he lived in a cottage of mud-brick and had only a dirty little inner courtyard with a tough fig tree for all his territory. He worked hard among the vines and olives and wheat of his master, then came home to sleep in the mud-brick cottage by the path. But he was proud of his young rooster. In the shut-in yard were three shabby hens which laid small eggs, shed the few feathers they had, and made a disproportionate amount of dirt. There was also, in a corner under a straw roof, a dull donkey that often went with the peasant to work, but sometimes stayed at home. And there was the peasant's wife, a black-browed youngish woman who did not work too hard. She threw a little grain, or the remains of the porridge mess, to the fowls, and she cut green fodder with a sickle, for the ass.

The young cock grew to a certain splendour. By some freak of destiny, he was a dandy rooster, in that dirty little yard with three patchy hens. He learned to crane his neck and give shrill answers to the crowing of other cocks, beyond the walls, in a world he knew nothing of. But there was a special fiery colour to his crow, and the distant calling of other cocks roused him to unexpected outbursts.

'How he sings,' said the peasant, as he got up and pulled his day-shirt over his head.

'He is good for twenty hens,' said the wife.

The peasant went out and looked with pride at his young rooster. A saucy, flamboyant bird, that had already made the final acquaintance of the three tattered hens. But the cockerel was tipping his head, listening to the challenge of far-off unseen cocks, in the unknown world. Ghost voices, crowing at him mysteriously out of limbo. He answered with a ringing defiance, never to be daunted.

'He will surely fly away one of these days,' said the peasant's wife.

So they lured him with grain, caught him, though he fought with all his wings and feet, and they tied a cord round his shank, fastening it against the spur; and they tied the other end of the cord to the post that held up the donkey's straw pent-roof.

The young cock, freed, marched with a prancing stride of indignation away from the humans, came to the end of his string, gave a tug and a hitch of his tied leg, fell over for a moment, scuffled frantically on the unclean earthen floor, to the horror of the shabby hens, then with a sickening lurch, regained his feet, and stood to think. The peasant and the peasant's wife laughed heartily, and the young cock heard them. And he knew, with a gloomy, foreboding kind of knowledge, that he was tied by the leg.

He no longer pranced and ruffled and forged his feathers. He walked within the limits of his tether sombrely. Still he gobbled up the best bits of food. Still, sometimes, he saved an extra-best bit for his favourite hen of the moment. Still he pranced with quivering, rocking fierceness upon such of his harem as came nonchalantly within range, and gave off the invisible lure. And still he crowed defiance to the cock-crows that showered up out of limbo, in the dawn.

But there was now a grim voracity in the way he gobbled his food, and a pinched triumph in the way he seized upon the shabby hens. His voice, above all, had lost the full gold of its clangour. He was tied by the leg, and he knew it. Body soul and spirit were tied by that string.

Underneath, however, the life in him was grimly unbroken. It was the cord that should break. So one morning, just before the light of dawn, rousing from his slumbers with a sudden wave of strength, he leaped forward on his wings, and the string snapped. He gave a wild strange squawk, rose in one lift to the top of the wall, and there he crowed a loud and splitting crow. So loud, it woke the peasant.

At the same time, at the same hour before dawn, on the same morning, a man awoke from a long sleep in which he was tied up. He woke numb and cold, inside a carved hole in the rock. Through all the long sleep his body had been full of hurt, and it was still full of hurt. He did not open his eyes. Yet he knew that he was awake, and numb, and cold, and rigid, and full of hurt, and tied up. His face was banded with cold bands, his legs were bandaged together. Only his hands were loose.

He could move if he wanted: he knew that. But he had no want. Who would want to come back from the dead? A deep, deep nausea stirred in him, at the premonition of movement. He resented already the fact of the strange, incalculable moving that had already taken place in him: the moving back into consciousness. He had not wished it. He had wanted to stay outside, in the place where even memory is stone dead.

But now, something had returned him, like a returned letter, and in the return he lay overcome with a sense of nausea. Yet suddenly his hands moved. They lifted up, cold, heavy and sore. Yet they lifted up, to drag away the cloth from his face, and to push at the shoulder-bands. Then they fell again, cold, heavy, numb, and sick with having moved even so much, unspeakably unwilling to move further.

With his face cleared and his shoulders free, he lapsed again, and lay dead, resting on the cold nullity of being dead. It was the most desirable. And almost, he had it complete: the utter cold nullity of being outside.

Yet when he was most nearly gone, suddenly, driven by an ache at the wrists, his hands rose and began pushing at the bandages of his knees, his feet began to stir, even while his breast lay cold and dead still.

And at last, the eyes opened. On to the dark. The same dark! yet perhaps there was a pale chink, of the all-disturbing light, prising open the pure dark. He could not lift his head. The eyes closed. And again it was finished.

Then suddenly he leaned up, and the great world reeled. Bandages fell away. And narrow walls of rock closed upon him, and gave the new anguish of imprisonment. There were chinks of light. With a wave of strength that came from revulsion, he leaned forward, in that narrow cell of rock, and leaned frail hands on the rock near the chinks of light.

Strength came from somewhere, from revulsion; there was a crash and a wave of light, and the dead man was crouching in his lair, facing the animal onrush of light. Yet it was hardly dawn. And the strange, piercing keenness of daybreak's sharp breath was on him. It meant full awakening.

Slowly, slowly he crept down from the cell of rock with the caution of the bitterly wounded. Bandages and linen and perfume fell away, and he crouched on the ground against the wall of rock, to recover oblivion. But he saw his hurt feet touching the earth again, with unspeakable pain, the earth they had meant to touch no more, and he saw his thin legs that had died, and pain unknowable, pain like utter bodily disillusion, filled him so full that he stood up, with one torn hand on the ledge of the tomb.

To be back! To be back again, after all that! He saw the linen swathing-bands fallen round his dead feet, and stooping, he picked them up, folded them, and laid them back in the rocky cavity from which he had emerged. Then he took the perfumed linen sheet, wrapped it round him as a mantle, and turned away, to the wanness of the chill dawn.

He was alone; and having died, was even beyond loneliness.

Filled still with the sickness of unspeakable disillusion, the man stepped with wincing feet down the rocky slope, past the sleeping soldiers, who lay wrapped in their woollen mantles under the wild laurels. Silent, on naked scarred feet, wrapped in a white linen shroud, he glanced down for a moment on the inert, heap-like bodies of the soldiers. They were repulsive, a slow squalor of limbs, yet he felt a certain compassion. He passed on towards the road, lest they should wake.

Having nowhere to go, he turned away from the city that stood on her hills. He slowly followed the road away from the town, past the olives, under which purple anemones were drooping in the chill of dawn, and rich-green herbage was pressing thick. The world, the same as ever, the natural world, thronging with greenness, a nightingale winsomely, wistfully, coaxingly calling from the bushes beside a runnel of water, in the world, the natural world of morning and evening, for ever undying, from which he had died.

He went on, on scarred feet, neither of this world nor of the next. Neither here nor there, neither seeing nor yet sightless, he passed dimly on, away from the city and its precincts, wondering why he should be travelling, yet driven by a dim, deep nausea of disillusion, and a resolution of which he was not even aware.

Advancing in a kind of half-consciousness under the dry stone wall of the olive orchard, he was roused by the shrill, wild crowing of a cock just near him, a sound which made him shiver as if electricity had touched him. He saw a black and orange cock on a bough above the road, then running through the olives of the upper level, a peasant in a grey woollen shirt-tunic. Leaping out of greenness, came the black and orange cock with the red comb, his tail-feathers streaming lustrous.

'O stop him, Master!' called the peasant. 'My escaped cock!'

The man addressed, with a sudden flicker of smile, opened his great white wings of a shroud in front of the leaping bird. The cock fell back with a squawk and a flutter, the peasant jumped forward, there was a terrific beating of wings, and whirring of feathers, then the peasant had the escaped cock safely under his arm, its wings shut down, its face crazily craning forward, its round eyes goggling from its white chops.

'It's my escaped cock!' said the peasant, soothing the bird with his left hand, as he looked perspiringly up into the face of the man wrapped in white linen.

The peasant changed countenance, and stood transfixed, as he looked into the dead-white face of the man who had died. That dead-white face, so still, with the black beard growing on it as if in death; and those wide-open, black, sombre eyes, that had died! and those washed scars on the waxy forehead! The slow-blooded man of the fields let his jaw drop, in childish inability to meet the situation.

'Don't be afraid,' said the man in the shroud. 'I am not dead. They took me down too soon. So I have risen up. Yet if they discover me, they will do it all over again.'

He spoke in a voice of old disgust. Humanity! Especially humanity in authority! There was only one thing it could do. He looked with black, indifferent eyes into the quick, shifty eyes of the peasant. The peasant quailed, and was powerless under the look of deathly indifference, and strange, cold resoluteness. He could only say the one thing he was afraid to say, 'Will you hide in my house, Master?'

'I will rest there. But if you tell anyone, you know what will happen. You too will have to go before a judge.'

'Me! I shan't speak. Let us be quick!'

The peasant looked round in fear, wondering sulkily why he had let himself in for this doom. The man with scarred feet climbed painfully up to the level of the olive garden, and followed the sullen, hurrying peasant across the green wheat among the olive trees. He felt the cool silkiness of the young wheat under his feet that had been dead, and the roughishness of its separate life was apparent to him. At the edges of rocks, he saw the silky, silvery-haired buds of the scarlet anemone bending downwards. And they too were in another world. In his own world he was alone, utterly alone. These things around him were in a world that had never died. But he himself had died, or had been killed from out of it, and all that remained now was the great void nausea of utter disillusion.

They came to a clay cottage, and the peasant waited dejectedly for the other man to pass.

'Pass!' he said. 'Pass! We have not been seen.'

The man in white linen entered the earthen room, taking with him the aroma of strange perfumes. The peasant closed the door, and passed through the inner doorway into the yard, where the ass stood within the high walls, safe from being stolen. There the peasant, in great disquietude, tied up the cock. The man with the waxen face sat down on a mat near the hearth, for he was spent and barely conscious. Yet he heard outside the whispering of the peasant to his wife, for the woman had been watching from the roof.

Presently they came in, and the woman hid her face. She poured water, and put bread and dried figs on a wooden platter.

'Eat, Master!' said the peasant. 'Eat! No one has seen.'

But the stranger had no desire for food. Yet he moistened a little bread in the water, and ate it, since life must be. But desire was dead in him, even for food and drink. He had risen without desire, without even the desire to live, empty save for the all-overwhelming disillusion that lay like nausea where his life had been. Yet perhaps, deeper even than disillusion, was a desireless resoluteness, deeper even than consciousness.

The peasant and his wife stood near the door, watching. They saw with terror the livid wounds on the thin, waxy hands and the thin feet of the stranger, and the small lacerations in the still-dead forehead. They smelled with terror the scent of rich perfumes that came from him, from his body. And they looked at the fine, snowy, costly linen. Perhaps really he was a dead king, from the region of terrors. And he was still cold and remote in the region of death, with perfumes coming from his transparent body as if from some strange flower.

Having with difficulty swallowed some of the moistened bread, he lifted his eyes to them. He saw them as they were: limited, meagre in their life, without any splendour of gesture and of courage. But they were what they were, slow inevitable parts of the natural world. They had no nobility, but fear made them compassionate.

And the stranger had compassion on them again, for he knew that they would respond best to gentleness, giving back a clumsy gentleness again.

'Do not be afraid,' he said to them gently. 'Let me stay a little while with you. I shall not stay long. And then I shall go away for ever. But do not be afraid. No harm will come to you through me.'

They believed him at once, yet the fear did not leave them. And they said, 'Stay, Master, while ever you will. Rest! Rest quietly!'

But they were afraid.

So he let them be, and the peasant went away with the ass. The sun had risen bright, and in the dark house with the door shut, the man was again as if in the tomb. So he said to the woman: 'I would lie in the yard.'

And she swept the yard for him, and laid him a mat, and he lay down under the wall in the morning sun. There he saw the first green leaves spurting like flames from the ends of the enclosed fig tree, out of the bareness to the sky of spring above. But the man who had died could not look, he only lay quite still in the sun which was not yet too hot, and had no desire in him, not even to move. But he lay with his thin legs in the sun, his black, perfumed hair falling into the hollows of his neck, and his thin, colourless arms utterly inert. As he lay there, the hens clucked and scratched, and the escaped cock, caught and tied by the leg again, cowered in a corner.

The peasant woman was frightened. She came peeping, and, seeing him never move, feared to have a dead man in the yard. But the sun had grown stronger, he opened his eyes and looked at her. And now she was frightened of the man who was alive, but spoke nothing.

He opened his eyes, and saw the world again bright as glass. It was life, in which he had no share any more. But it shone outside him, blue sky, and a bare fig tree with little jets of green leaf. Bright as glass, and he was not of it, for desire had failed.

Yet he was there, and not extinguished. The day passed in a kind of coma, and at evening, he went into the house. The peasant man came home, but he was frightened, and had nothing to say. The stranger too ate of the mess of beans, a little. Then he washed his hands and turned to the wall, and was silent. The peasants were silent too. They watched their guest sleep. Sleep was so near death, he could still sleep.

Yet when the sun came up, he went again to lie in the yard. The sun was the one thing that drew him and swayed him, and he still wanted to feel the cool air of the morning in his nostrils, see the pale sky overhead. He still hated to be shut up.

As he came out, the young cock crowed. It was a diminished, pinched cry, but there was that in the voice of the bird stronger than chagrin. It was the necessity to live, and even to cry out the triumph of life. The man who had died stood and watched the cock who had escaped and been caught, ruffling himself up, rising forward on his toes, throwing up his head, and parting his beak in another challenge from life to death. The brave sounds rang out, and though they were diminished by the cord round the bird's leg, they were not cut off. The man who had died looked nakedly on life, and saw a vast resoluteness everywhere flinging itself up in stormy or subtle wave-crests, foam-tips emerging out of the blue invisible, a black and orange cock, or the green flame-tongues out of the extremes of the fig tree. They came forth, these things and creatures of spring, glowing with desire and with assertion. They came like crests of foam, out of the blue flood of the invisible desire, out of the vast invisible sea of strength, and they came coloured and tangible, evanescent, yet deathless in their coming. The man who had died looked on the great swing into existence of things that had not died, but he saw no longer their tremulous desire to exist and to be. He heard instead their ringing, ringing, defiant challenge to all other things existing.

The man lay still, with eyes that had died now wide open and darkly still, seeing the everlasting resoluteness of life. And the cock, with the flat, brilliant glance, glanced back at him, with a bird's half-seeing look. And always the man who had died saw not the bird alone, but the short, sharp wave of life of which the bird was the crest. He watched the queer, beaky motion of the creature as it gobbled into itself the scraps of food; its glancing of the eye of life, ever alert and watchful, overweening and cautious, and the voice of its life, crowing triumph and assertion, yet strangled by a cord of circumstance. He seemed to hear the queer speech of very life, as the cock triumphantly imitated the clucking of the favourite hen, when she had laid an egg, a clucking which still had, in the male bird, the hollow chagrin of the cord round his leg. And when the man threw a bit of bread to the cock, it called with an extraordinary cooing tenderness, tousling and saving the morsel for the hens. The hens ran up greedily, and carried the morsel away beyond the reach of the string.

Then, walking complacently after them, suddenly the male bird's leg would hitch at the end of his tether, and he would yield with a kind of collapse. His flag fell, he seemed to diminish, he would huddle in the shade. And he was young, his tail-feathers, glossy as they were, were not fully grown. It was not till evening again that the tide of life in him made him forget. Then when his favourite hen came strolling unconcernedly near him, emitting the lure, he pounced on her with all his feathers vibrating. And the man who had died watched the unsteady, rocking vibration of the bent bird, and it was not the bird he saw, but one wave-tip of life overlapping for a minute another, in the tide of the swaying ocean of life. And the destiny of life seemed more fierce and compulsive to him even than the destiny of death. The doom of death was a shadow compared to the raging destiny of life, the determined surge of life.

At twilight the peasant came home with the ass, and he said: 'Master! It is said that the body was stolen from the garden, and the tomb is empty, and the soldiers are taken away, accursed Romans! And the women are there to weep.'

The man who had died looked at the man who had not died.

'It is well,' he said. 'Say nothing, and we are safe.'

And the peasant was relieved. He looked rather dirty and stupid, and even as much flaminess as that of the young cock, which he had tied by the leg, would never glow in him. He was without fire. But the man who had died thought to himself, 'Why, then, should he be lifted up? Clods of earth are turned over for refreshment, they are not to be lifted up. Let the earth remain earthy, and hold its own again the sky. I was wrong to seek to lift it up. I was wrong to try to interfere. The ploughshare of devastation will be set in the soil of Judaea, and the life of this peasant will be overturned like the sods of the field. No man can save the earth from tillage. It is tillage, not salvation . . . '

So he saw the man, the peasant, with compassion; but the man who had died no longer wished to interfere in the soul of the man who had not died, and who could never die, save to return to earth. Let him return to earth in his own good hour, and let no one try to interfere when the earth claims her own.

So the man with scars let the peasant go from him, for the peasant had no re-birth in him. Yet the man who had died said to himself: 'He is my host.'

And at dawn, when he was better, the man who had died rose up, and on slow, sore feet retraced his way to the garden. For he had been betrayed in a garden, and buried in a garden. And as he turned round the screen of laurels, near the rock-face, he saw a woman hovering by the tomb, a woman in blue and yellow. She peeped again into the mouth of the hole, that was like a deep cupboard. But still there was nothing. And she wrung her hands and wept. And as she turned away, she saw the man in white, standing by the laurels, and she gave a cry, thinking it might be a spy, and she said, 'They have taken him away!'

So he said to her, 'Madeleine!'

Then she reeled as if she would fall, for she knew him. And he said to her, 'Madeleine! Do not be afraid. I am alive. They took me down too soon, so I came back to life. Then I was sheltered in a house.'

She did not know what to say, but fell at his feet, to kiss them.

'Don't touch me, Madeleine,' he said. 'Not yet! I am not yet healed and in touch with men.'

So she wept because she did not know what to do. And he said, 'Let us go aside, among the bushes, where we can speak unseen.'

So in her blue mantle and her yellow robe, she followed him among the trees, and he sat down under a myrtle bush. And he said, 'I am not yet quite come to. Madeleine, what is to be done next?'

'Master!' she said. 'Oh, we have wept for you! And will you come back to us?'

'What is finished is finished, and for me the end is past,' he said. 'The stream will run till no more rains fill it, then it will dry up. For me, that life is over.'

'And will you give up your triumph?' she said sadly.

'My triumph,' he said, 'is that I am not dead. I have outlived my mission, and know no more of it. It is my triumph. I have survived the day and the death of my interference, and am still a man. I am young still, Madeleine, not even come to middle age. I am glad all that is over. It had to be. But now I am glad it is over, and the day of my interference is done. The teacher and the saviour are dead in me; now I can go about my own business, into my own single life.'

She heard him, and did not fully understand. But what he said made her feel disappointed.

'But you will come back to us?' she said, insisting.

'I don't know what I shall do,' he said. 'When I am healed, I shall know better. But my mission is over, and my teaching is finished, and death has saved me from my own salvation. Oh, Madeleine, I want to take my single way in life, which is my portion. My public life is over, the life of my self-importance. Now I can wait on life, and say nothing, and have no one betray me. I wanted to be greater than the limits of my hands and feet, so I brought betrayal on myself. And I know I wronged Judas, my poor Judas. For I have died, and now I know my own limits. Now I can live without striving to sway others any more. For my reach ends in my finger-tips, and my stride is no longer than the ends of my toes. Yet I would embrace multitudes, I who have never truly embraced even one. But Judas and the high priests saved me from my own salvation, and soon I can turn to my destiny like a bather in the sea at dawn, who has just come down to the shore alone.'

'Do you want to be alone henceforward?' she asked. 'And was your mission nothing? Was it all untrue?'

'Nay!' he said. 'Neither were your lovers in the past nothing. They were much to you, but you took more than you gave. Then you came to me for salvation from your own excess. And I, in my mission, I too ran to excess. I gave more than I took, and that also is woe and vanity. So Judas and the high priests saved me from my own excessive salvation. Don't run to excess now in giving, Madeleine. It only means another death.'

She pondered bitterly, for the need for excessive giving was in her, and she could not bear to be denied.

'And will you not come back to us?' she said. 'Have you risen for yourself alone?'

He heard the sarcasm in her voice, and looked at her beautiful face which still was dense with excessive need for salvation from the woman she had been, the female who had caught men with her will. The cloud of necessity was on her, to be saved from the old, wilful Eve, who had embraced many men, and taken more than she gave. Now the other doom was on her. She wanted to give without taking. And that too is hard, and cruel to the warm body.

'I have not risen from the dead in order to seek death again,' he said.

She glanced up at him, and saw the weariness settling again on his waxy face, and the vast disillusion in his dark eyes, and the underlying indifference. He felt her glance, and said to himself, 'Now my own followers will want to do me to death again, for having risen up different from their expectation.'

'But you will come to us, to see us, us who love you?' she said.

He laughed a little and said, 'Ah yes!' Then he added: 'Have you a little money? Will you give me a little money? I owe it.'

She had not much, but it pleased her to give it to him.

'Do you think,' he said to her, 'that I might come and live with you in your house?'

She looked up at him with large blue eyes, that gleamed strangely.

'Now?' she said, with peculiar triumph.

And he, who shrank now from triumph of any sort, his own or another's, said, 'Not now! Later, when I am healed, and . . . and I am in touch with the flesh.'

The words faltered in him. And in his heart, he knew he would never go to live in her house. For the flicker of triumph had gleamed in her eyes; the greed of giving. But she murmured in a humming rapture, 'Ah, you know I would give up everything to you.'

'Nay!' he said. 'I didn't ask that.'

A revulsion from all the life he had known came over him again, the great nausea of disillusion, and the spear-thrust through his bowels. He crouched under the myrtle bushes, without strength. Yet his eyes were open. And she looked at him again, and she saw that it was not the Messiah. The Messiah had not risen. The enthusiasm and the burning purity were gone, and the rapt youth. His youth was dead. This man was middle-aged and disillusioned, with a certain terrible indifference, and a resoluteness which love would never conquer. This was not the Master she had so adored, the young, flamy, unphysical exalter of her soul. This was nearer to the lovers she had known of old, but with a greater indifference to the personal issue, and a lesser susceptibility.

She was thrown out of the balance of her rapturous, anguished adoration. This risen man was the death of her dream.

'You should go now,' he said to her. 'Do not touch me, I am in death. I shall come again here, on the third day. Come if you will, at dawn. And we will speak again.'

She went away, perturbed and shattered. Yet as she went, her mind discarded the bitterness of the reality, and she conjured up rapture and wonder, that the Master was risen and was not dead. He was risen, the Saviour, the exalter, the wonder-worker! He was risen, but not as man; as pure God, who should not be touched by flesh, and who should be rapt away into Heaven. It was the most glorious and most ghostly of the miracles.

Meanwhile the man who had died gathered himself together at last, and slowly made his way to the peasants' house. He was glad to go back to them, and away from Madeleine and his own associates. For the peasants had the inertia of earth and would let him rest, and as yet, would put no compulsion on him.

The woman was on the roof, looking for him. She was afraid that he had gone away. His presence in the house had become like gentle wine to her. She hastened to the door, to him.

'Where have you been?' she said. 'Why did you go away?'

'I have been to walk in a garden, and I have seen a friend, who gave me a little money. It is for you.'

He held out his thin hand, with the small amount of money, all that Madeleine could give him. The peasant's wife's eyes glistened, for money was scarce, and she said, 'Oh, Master! And is it truly mine?'

'Take it!' he said. 'It buys bread, and bread brings life.'

So he lay down in the yard again, sick with relief at being alone again. For with the peasants he could be alone, but his own friends would never let him be alone. And in the safety of the yard, the young cock was dear to him, as it shouted in the helpless zest of life, and finished in the helpless humiliation of being tied by the leg. This day the ass stood swishing her tail under the shed. The man who had died lay down, and turned utterly away from life, in the sickness of death in life.

But the woman brought wine and water, and sweetened cakes, and roused him, so that he ate a little, to please her. The day was hot, and as she crouched to serve him, he saw her breasts sway from her humble body, under her smock. He knew she wished he would desire her, and she was youngish, and not unpleasant. And he, who had never known a woman, would have desired her if he could. But he could not want her, though he felt gently towards her soft, crouching, humble body. But it was her thoughts, her consciousness, he could not mingle with. She was pleased with the money, and now she wanted to take more from him. She wanted the embrace of his body. But her little soul was hard, and short-sighted, and grasping, her body had its little greed, and no gentle reverence of the return gift. So he spoke a quiet, pleasant word to her, and turned away. He could not touch the little, personal body, the little, personal life in this woman, nor in any other. He turned away from it without hesitation.

Risen from the dead, he had realised at last that the body, too, has its little life, and beyond that, the greater life. He was virgin, in recoil from the little, greedy life of the body. But now he knew that virginity is a form of greed; and that the body rises again to give and to take, to take and to give, ungreedily. Now he knew that he had risen for the woman, or women, who knew the greater life of the body, not greedy to give, not greedy to take, and with whom he could mingle his body. But having died, he was patient, knowing there was time, an eternity of time. And he was driven by no greedy desire, either to give himself to others, or to grasp anything for himself. For he had died.

The peasant came home from work, and said, 'Master, I thank you for the money. But we did not want it. And all I have is yours.'

But the man who had died was sad, because the peasant stood there in the little, personal body, and his eyes were cunning and sparkling with the hope of greater rewards in money, later on. True, the peasant had taken him in free, and had *risked* getting no reward. But the hope was cunning in him. Yet even this was as men are made. So when the peasant would have helped him to rise, for night had fallen, the man who had died said, 'Don't touch me, brother. I am not yet risen to the Father.'

The sun burned with greater splendour, and burnished the young cock brighter. But the peasant kept the string renewed, and the bird was a prisoner. Yet the flame of life burned up to a sharp point in the cock, so that it eyed askance and haughtily the man who had died. And the man smiled and held the bird dear, and he said to it, 'Surely thou art risen to the Father, among birds.'

And the young cock, answering, crowed.

When at dawn on the third morning the man went to the garden, he was absorbed, thinking of the greater life of the body, beyond the little, narrow, personal life. So he came through the thick screen of laurel and myrtle bushes, near the rock, suddenly, and he saw three women near the tomb. One was Madeleine, and one was the woman who had been his mother, and the third was a woman he knew, called Joan. He looked up, and saw them all, and they saw him, and they were all afraid.

He stood arrested in the distance, knowing they were there to claim him back, bodily. But he would in no wise return to them. Pallid, in the shadow of a grey morning that was blowing to rain, he saw them, and turned away. But Madeleine hastened towards him.

'I did not bring them,' she said. 'They have come of themselves. See, I have brought you money! . . . Will you not speak to them?'

She offered him some gold pieces, and he took them, saying, 'May I have this money? I shall need it! – I cannot speak to them, for I am not yet ascended to the Father. And I must leave you now.'

'Ah! Where will you go?' she cried.

He looked at her, and saw she was clutching for the man in him who had died and was dead, the man of his youth and his mission, of his chastity and his fear, of his little life, his giving without taking.

'I must go to my Father!' he said.

'And you will leave us? There is your mother!' she cried, turning round with the old anguish, which yet was sweet to her.

'But now I must ascend to my Father,' he said, and he drew back into the bushes, and so turned quickly, and went away, saying to himself, 'Now I belong to no one, and have no connection, and my mission or gospel is gone from me. Lo! I cannot make even my own life, and what have I to save? . . . I can learn to be alone.'

So he went back to the peasants' house, to the yard where the young cock was tied by the leg, with a string. And he wanted no one, for it was best to be alone; for the presence of people made him lonely. The sun and the subtle salve of spring healed his wounds, even the gaping wound of disillusion through his bowels was closing up. And his need of men and women, his fever to save them and to be saved by them, this too was healing in him. Whatever came of touch between himself and the race of men, henceforth, should come without trespass or compulsion. For he said to himself, 'I tried to compel them to live, so they compelled me to die. It is always so, with compulsion. The recoil kills the advance. Now is my time to be alone.'

Therefore he went no more to the garden, but lay still and saw the sun, or walked at dusk across the olive slopes, among the green wheat, that rose a palm-breadth higher every sunny day. And always he thought to himself, 'How good it is to have fulfilled my mission, and to be beyond it. Now I can be alone, and leave all things to themselves, and the fig tree may be barren if it will, and the rich may be rich. My way is my own alone.'

So the green jets of leaves unspread on the fig tree, with the bright, trans-lucent, green blood of the tree. And the young cock grew brighter, more lustrous with the sun's burnishing; yet always tied by the leg with a string. And the sun went down more and more in pomp, out of the gold and red-flushed air. The man who had died was aware of it all, and he thought, 'The Word is but the midge that bites at evening. Man is tormented with words like midges, and they follow him right into the tomb. But beyond the tomb they cannot go. Now I have passed the place where words can bite no more and the air is clear, and there is nothing to say, and I am alone within my own skin, which is the walls of all my domain.'

So he healed of his wounds, and enjoyed his immortality of being alive without fret. For in the tomb he had slipped that noose which we call care. For in the tomb he had left his striving self, which cares and asserts itself. Now his uncaring self healed and became whole within his skin, and he smiled to himself with pure aloneness, which is one sort of immortality.

Then he said to himself: 'I will wander the earth, and say nothing. For nothing is so marvellous as to be alone in the phenomenal world, which is raging, and yet apart. And I have not seen it, I was too much blinded by my confusion within it. Now I will wander among the stirring of the phenomenal world, for it is the stirring of all things among themselves which leaves me purely alone.'

So he communed with himself, and decided to be a physician. Because the power was still in him to heal any man or child who touched his compassion. Therefore he cut his hair and his beard after the right fashion, and smiled to himself. And he bought himself shoes, and the right mantle, and put the right cloth over his head, hiding all the little scars. And the peasant said, 'Master, will you go forth from us?'

'Yes, for the time is come for me to return to men.'

So he gave the peasant a piece of money, and said to him, 'Give me the cock that escaped and is now tied by the leg. For he shall go forth with me.'

So for a piece of money the peasant gave the cock to the man who had died, and at dawn the man who had died set out into the phenomenal world, to be fulfilled in his own aloneness in the midst of it. For previously he had been too much mixed up in it. Then he had died. Now he must come back, to be alone in the midst. Yet even now he did not go quite alone, for under his arm, as he went, he carried the cock, whose tail fluttered gaily behind, and who craned his head excitedly, for he too was adventuring out for the first time into the wider phenomenal world, which is the stirring of the body of cocks also. And the peasant woman shed a few tears, but then went indoors, being a peasant, to look again at the pieces of money. And it seemed to her, a gleam came out of the pieces of money, wonderful.

The man who had died wandered on, and it was a sunny day. He looked around as he went, and stood aside as the pack-train passed by, towards the city. And he said to himself, 'Strange is the phenomenal world, dirty and clean together! And I am the same. Yet I am apart! And life bubbles variously. Why should I ever have wanted it to bubble all alike? What a pity I preached to them! A sermon is so much more likely to cake into mud, and to close the fountains, than is a psalm or a song. I made a mistake. I understand that they executed me for preaching to them. Yet they could not finally execute me, for now I am risen in my own aloneness, and inherit the earth, since I lay no claim on it. And I will be alone in the seethe of all things; first and foremost, for ever, I shall be alone. But I must toss this bird into the seethe of phenomena, for he must ride his wave. How hot he is with life! Soon, in some place, I shall leave him among the hens. And perhaps one evening I shall meet a woman who can lure my risen body, yet leave me my aloneness. For the body of my desire has died, and I am not in touch anywhere. Yet how do I know! All at least is life. And this cock gleams with bright aloneness, though he answers the lure of hens. And I shall hasten on to that village on the hill ahead of me; already I am tired and weak, and want to close my eyes to everything.'

Hastening a little with the desire to have finished going, he overtook two men going slowly, and talking. And being soft-footed, he heard they were speaking of himself. And he remembered them, for he had known them in his life, the life of his mission. So he greeted them, but did not disclose himself in the dusk, and they did not know him. He said to them, 'What then of him who would be king, and was put to death for it?'

They answered, suspiciously: 'Why ask you of him?'

'I have known him, and thought much about him,' he said.

So they replied: 'He is risen.'

'Yea! And where is he, and how does he live?'

'We know not, for it is not revealed. Yet he is risen, and in a little while will ascend unto the Father.'

'Yea! And where then is his Father?'

'Know ye not? You are then of the Gentiles! The Father is in Heaven, above the cloud and the firmament.'

'Truly? Then how will he ascend?'

'As Elijah the Prophet, he shall go up in a glory.'

'Even into the sky.'

'Into the sky.'

'Then he is not risen in the flesh?'

'He is risen in the flesh.'

'And will he take flesh up into the sky?'

'The Father in Heaven will take him up.'

The man who had died said no more, for his say was over, and words beget words, even as gnats. But the man asked him: 'Why do you carry a cock?'

'I am a healer,' he said, 'and the bird hath virtue.'

'You are not a believer?'

'Yea! I believe the bird is full of life and virtue.'

They walked on in silence after this, and he felt they disliked his answer. So he smiled to himself, for a dangerous phenomenon in the world is a man of narrow belief, who denies the right of his neighbour to be alone. And as they came to the outskirts of the village, the man who had died stood still in the gloaming and said in his old voice, 'Know ye me not?'

And they cried in fear: 'Master!'

'Yea!' he said, laughing softly. And he turned suddenly away, down a side lane, and was gone under the wall before they knew.

So he came to an inn where the asses stood in the yard. And he called for fritters, and they were made for him. So he slept under a shed. But in the morning he was wakened by a loud crowing, and his cock's voice ringing in his ears. So he saw the rooster of the inn walking forth to battle, with his hens, a goodly number, behind him. Then the cock of the man who had died sprang forth, and a battle began between the birds. The man of the inn ran to save his rooster, but the man who had died said, 'If my bird wins, I will give him thee. And if he lose, thou shalt eat him.'

So the birds fought savagely, and the cock of the man who had died killed the common cock of the yard. Then the man who had died said to his young cock, 'Thou at least hast found thy kingdom, and the females to thy body. Thy aloneness can take on splendour, polished by the lure of thy hens.'

And he left his bird there, and went on deeper into the phenomenal world, which is a vast complexity of entanglements and allurements. And he asked himself a last question, 'From what, and to what, could this infinite whirl be saved?'

So he went his way, and was alone. But the way of the world was past belief, as he saw the strange entanglement of passions and circumstance and compulsion everywhere, but always the dread insomnia of compulsion. It was fear, the ultimate fear of death, that made men mad. So always he must move on, for if he stayed, his neighbours wound the strangling of their fear and bullying round him. There was nothing he could touch, for all, in a mad assertion of the ego, wanted to put a compulsion on him, and violate his intrinsic solitude. It was the mania of cities and societies and hosts, to lay a compulsion upon a man, upon all men. For men and women alike were mad with the egoistic fear of their own nothingness. And he thought of his own mission, how he had tried to lay the compulsion of love on all men. And the old nausea came back on him. For there was no contact without a subtle attempt to inflict a compulsion. And already he had been compelled even into death. The nausea of the old wound broke out afresh, and he looked again on the world with repulsion, dreading its mean contacts.

2

The wind came cold and strong from inland, from the invisible snows of Lebanon. But the temple, facing south and west, towards Egypt, faced the splendid sun of winter as he curved down towards the sea, and warmth and radiance flooded in between the pillars of painted wood. But the sea was invisible, because of the trees, though its dashing sounded among the hum of pines. The air was turning golden to afternoon. The woman who served Isis stood in her yellow robe, and looked up at the steep slopes coming down to the sea, where the olive trees silvered under the wind like water splashing. She was alone; save for the goddess. And in the winter afternoon the light stood erect and magnificent off the invisible sea, filling the hills of the coast. She went towards the sun, through the grove of Mediterranean pine trees and evergreen oaks, in the midst of which the temple stood, on a little, tree-covered tongue of land between two bays.

It was only a very little way, and then she stood among the dry trunks of the outermost pines, on the rocks under which the sea smote and sucked, facing the open where the bright sun gloried in winter. The sea was dark, almost indigo, running away from the land, and crested with white. The hand of the wind brushed it strangely with shadow, as it brushed the olives of the slopes with silver. And there was no boat out.

The three boats were drawn high up on the steep shingle of the little bay, by the small grey tower. Along the edge of the shingle ran a high wall, inside which was a garden occupying the brief flat of the bay, then rising in terraces up the steep slope of the coast. And there, some little way up, within another wall, stood the low white villa, white and alone as the coast, overlooking the sea. But higher, much higher up, where the olives had given way to pine trees again, ran the coast road, keeping to the height to be above the gullies that came down to the bays.

Upon it all poured the royal sunshine of the January afternoon. Or rather, all was part of the great sun, glow and substance and immaculate loneliness of the sea, and pure brightness.

Crouching in the rocks above the dark water which only swung up and down, two slaves, half-naked, were dressing pigeons for the evening meal. They pierced the throat of a blue, live bird, and let the drops of blood fall into the heaving sea, with curious concentration. They were performing some sacrifice, or working some incantation. The woman of the temple, yellow and white and alone like a winter narcissus, stood between the pines of the small, humped peninsula where the temple secretly hid, and watched.

A black-and-white pigeon, vividly white, like a ghost, suddenly escaped over the low dark sea, sped out, caught the wind, tilted, rose, soared and swept over the pine trees, and wheeled away, a speck, inland. It had escaped. The priestess heard the cry of the boy slave, a garden slave of about seventeen. He raised his arms to heaven in anger as the pigeon wheeled away, naked and angry and young he held out his arms. Then he turned and seized the girl in an access of rage, and beat her with his first that was stained with pigeon's blood. And she lay down with her face hidden, passive and quivering. The woman who owned them watched. And as she watched, she saw another onlooker, a stranger, in a low, broad hat, and a cloak of grey homespun, a dark-bearded man standing on the little causeway of rock that was the neck of her temple peninsula. By the blowing of his dark-grey cloak, she saw him. And he saw her, on the rocks like a white-and-yellow narcissus, because of the flutter of her white linen tunic, below the yellow mantle of wool. And both of them watched the two slaves.

The boy suddenly left off beating the girl. He crouched over her, touching her, trying to make her speak. But she lay quite inert, face down on the smoothed rock. And he put his arms round her and lifted her, but she slipped back to earth like one dead, yet far too quick for anything dead. The boy, desperate, caught her by the hips and hugged her to him, turning her over there. There she seemed inert, all her fight was in her shoulders. He twisted her over, intent and unconscious, and pushed his hands between her thighs, to push them apart. And in an instant he was covering her in the blind, frightened frenzy of a boy's first passion. Quick and frenzied his young body quivered naked on hers, blind, for a minute. Then it lay quite still, as if dead.

And then, in terror, he peeped up. He peeped round, and drew slowly to his feet, adjusting his loin-rag. He saw the stranger, and then he saw, on the rocks beyond, the lady of Isis, his mistress. And as he saw her, his whole body shrank and cowed, and with a strange, cringing motion he scuttled lamely towards the door in the wall.

The girl sat up and looked after him. When she had seen him disappear, she too looked round. And she saw the stranger and the priestess. Then with a sullen movement she turned away, as if she had seen nothing, to the four dead pigeons and the knife, which lay there on the rock. And she began to strip the small feathers, so that they rose on the wind like dust.

The priestess turned away. Slaves! Let the overseer watch them. She was not interested. She went slowly through the pines again, back to the temple, which stood in the sun in a small clearing, at the centre of the tongue of land. It was a small temple of wood, painted all pink and white and blue, having at the front four wooden pillars rising like stems to the swollen lotus-bud of Egypt at the top, supporting the roof and the open, spiky lotus-flowers of the outer frieze, which went round under the eaves. Two low steps of stone led up to the platform before the pillars, and the chamber behind the pillars was open. There a low stone altar stood, with a few embers in its hollow, and the dark stain of blood in its end groove.

She knew her temple so well, for she had built it at her own expense, and tended it for seven years. There it stood, pink and white like a flower in the little clearing, backed by blackish evergreen oaks; and the shadow of afternoon was already washing over its pillar-bases.

She entered slowly, passing through to the dark inner chamber, lighted by a perfumed oil-flame. And once more she pushed shut the door, and once more she threw a few grains of incense on a brazier before the goddess, and once more she sat down before her goddess, in the almost-darkness, to muse, to go away into the dream of the goddess.

It was Isis; but not Isis, Mother of Horus. It was Isis Bereaved, Isis in Search. The goddess in painted marble lifted her face, and strode, one thigh forward, through the frail fluting of her robe, in the anguish of bereavement and of search. She was looking for the fragments of the dead Osiris, dead and scattered asunder, dead, torn apart, and thrown in fragments over the wide world. And she must find his hands and his feet, his heart, his thighs, his head, his belly, she must gather him together and fold her arms round the re-assembled body till it became warm again, and roused to life, and could embrace her and could fecundate her womb. And the strange rapture and anguish of search went on through the years, as she lifted her throat, and her hollowed eyes looked inward, in the tormented ecstasy of seeking, and the delicate navel of her bud-like belly showed through the frail, girdled robe with the eternal asking, asking, of her search. And through the years she found him bit by bit, heart and head and limbs and body. And yet she had not found the last reality, the final clue to him, that alone could bring him really back to her. For she was Isis of the subtle lotus, the womb which waits submerged and in bud, waits for the touch of that other, inward sun that streams its rays from the loins of the male Osiris.

This was the mystery the woman had served alone for seven years, since she was twenty, till now she was twenty-seven. Before, when she was young, she had lived in the world, in Rome, in Ephesus, in Egypt. For her father had been one of Antony's captains and comrades, had fought with Antony and had stood with him when Caesar was murdered, and through to the days of shame. Then he had come again across to Asia, out of favour with Rome, and had been killed in the mountains beyond Lebanon. The widow, having no favour to hope for from Octavius, had retired to her small property on the coast under Lebanon, taking her daughter from the world, a girl of nineteen, beautiful but unmarried.

When she was young the girl had known Caesar, and had shrunk from his eagle-like rapacity. The golden Antony had sat with her many a half-hour, in the splendour of his great limbs and glowing manhood, and talked with her of the philosophies and the gods. For he was fascinated as a child by the gods, though he mocked at them, and forgot them in his own vanity. But he said to her, 'I have sacrificed two doves for you, to Venus, for I am afraid you make no offering to the sweet goddess. Beware, you will offend her. Come, why is the flower of you so cool within? Does never a ray nor a glance find its way through? Ah, come, a maid should open to the sun, when the sun leans towards her to caress her.'

And the big, bright eyes of Antony laughed down on her, bathing her in his glow. And she felt the lovely glow of his male beauty and his amorousness bathe all her limbs and her body. But it was as he said: the very flower of her womb was cool, was almost cold, like a bud in shadow of frost, for all the flooding of his sunshine. So Antony, respecting her father, who loved her, had left her.

And it had always been the same. She saw many men, young and old. And on the whole, she liked the old ones best, for they talked to her still and sincere, and did not expect her to open like a flower to the sun of their maleness. Once she asked a philosopher: 'Are all women born to be given to men?' To which the old man answered slowly, 'Rare women wait for the reborn man. For the lotus, as you know, will not answer to all the bright heat of the sun. But she curves her dark, hidden head in the depths, and stirs not. Till, in the night, one of these rare invisible suns that have been killed and shine no more, rises among the stars in unseen purple, and like the violet, sends its rare, purple rays out into the night. To these the lotus stirs as to a caress, and rises upwards through the flood, and lifts up her bent head, and opens with an expansion such as no other flower knows, and spreads her sharp rays of bliss, and offers her soft, gold depths such as no other flower possesses, to the penetration of the flooding, violet-dark sun that has died and risen and makes no show. But for the golden brief day-suns of show, such as Antony, and for the hard winter suns of power, such as Caesar, the lotus stirs not, nor will ever stir. Those will only tear open the bud. Ah, I tell you, wait for the reborn and wait for the bud to stir.'

So she had waited. For all the men were soldiers or politicians in the Roman spell, assertive, manly, splendid apparently, but of an inward meanness, an inadequacy. And Rome and Egypt alike had left her alone, unroused. And she was a woman to herself, she would not give herself for a surface glow, nor marry for reasons. She would wait for the lotus to stir.

And then, in Egypt, she had found Isis, in whom she spelled her mystery, she brought Isis to the shores of Sidon, and lived with her in the mystery of search; whilst her mother, who loved affairs, controlled the small estate and the slaves, with a free hand.

When the woman had roused from her muse and risen to perform the last brief ritual to Isis, she replenished the lamp and left the sanctuary, locking the door. In the outer world, the sun had already set, and twilight was chill among the humming trees, which hummed still, though the wind was abating.

A stranger in a dark, broad hat rose from the corner of the temple steps, holding his hat in the wind. He was dark-faced, with a black pointed beard.

'O madam, whose shelter may I implore?' he said to the woman who stood in her yellow mantle on a step above him, beside a pink-and-white painted pillar. Her face was rather long and pale, her dusky blonde hair was held under a thin gold net. She looked down on the vagabond with indifference. It was the same she had seen watching the slaves.

'Why come you down from the road?' she asked.

'I saw the temple like a pale flower on the coast, and would rest among the trees of the precincts, if the lady of the goddess permits.'

'It is Isis in Search,' she said, answering his first question.

'The goddess is great,' he replied.

She looked at him still with mistrust. There was a faint, remote smile in the dark eyes lifted to her, though the face was hollow with suffering. The vagabond divined her hesitation, and was mocking her.

'Stay here upon the steps,' she said. 'A slave shall show you the shelter.'

'The lady of Egypt is gracious.'

She went down the rocky path of the humped peninsula, in her gilded sandals. Beautiful were her ivory feet, beneath the white tunic, and above the saffron mantle her dusky blonde head bent as with endless musings. A woman entangled in her own dream. The man smiled a little, half-bitterly, and sat again on the step to wait, drawing his mantle round him, in the cold twilight.

At length a slave appeared, also in hodden grey.

'Seek ye the shelter of our lady?' he said insolently.

'Even so.'

'Then come.'

With the brusque insolence of a slave waiting on a vagabond, the young fellow led through the trees and down into a little gully in the rock, where, almost in darkness, was a small cave, with a litter of the tall heaths that grew on the waste places of the coast, under the stone-pines. The place was dark, but absolutely silent from the wind. There was still a faint odour of goats.

'Here sleep!' said the slave. 'For the goats come no more on this half-island. And there is water!' He pointed to a little basin of rock where the maidenhair fern fringed a dripping mouthful of water.

Having scornfully bestowed his patronage, the slave departed. The man who had died climbed out to the tip of the peninsula, where the waves thrashed. It was rapidly getting dark, and the stars were coming out. The wind was abating for the night. Inland, the steep grooved upslope was dark, to the long wavering outline of the crest against the translucent sky. Only now and then, a lantern flickered towards the villa.

The man who had died went back to the shelter. There he took bread from his leather pouch, dipped it in the water of the tiny spring, and slowly ate. Having eaten and washed his mouth, he looked once more at the bright stars in the pure, windy sky, then settled the heath for his bed. Having laid his hat and his sandals aside, and put his pouch under his cheek for a pillow, he slept, for he was very tired. Yet during the night the cold woke him, pinching wearily through his weariness. Outside was brilliantly starry, and still windy. He sat and hugged himself in a sort of coma, and towards dawn went to sleep again.

In the morning, the coast was still chill in shadow, though the sun was up behind the hills, when the woman came down from the villa towards the goddess. The sea was fair and pale-blue, lovely in newness, and at last the wind was still. Yet the waves broke white in the many rocks, and tore in the shingle of the little bay. The woman came slowly, towards her dream. Yet she was aware of an interruption.

As she followed the little neck of rock on to her peninsula, and climbed the slope between the trees to the temple, a slave came down and stood, making his obeisance. There was a faint insolence in his humility. 'Speak!' she said.

'Lady, the man is there, he still sleeps. Lady, may I speak?'

'Speak!' she said, repelled by the fellow.

'Lady, the man is an escaped malefactor.'

The slave seemed to triumph in imparting the unpleasant news.

'By what sign?'

'Behold, his hands and feet! Will the Lady look on him?'

'Lead on!'

The slave led quickly over the mound of the hill down to the tiny ravine. There he stood aside, and the woman went into the crack towards the cave. Her heart beat a little. Above all, she must preserve her temple inviolate.

The vagabond was asleep with his cheek on his scrip, his mantle wrapped round him, but his bare, soiled feet curling side by side, to keep each other warm, and his hand lying loosely clenched in sleep. And in the pale skin of his feet, usually covered by sandal-straps, she saw the scars, and in the palm of the loose hand.

She had no interest in men, particularly in the servile class. Yet she looked at the sleeping face. It was worn, hollow, and rather ugly. But, a true priestess, she saw the other kind of beauty in it, the sheer stillness of the deeper life. There was even a sort of majesty in the dark brows, over the still, hollow cheeks. She saw that his black hair, left long, in contrast to the Roman fashion, was touched with grey at the temples, and the black pointed beard had threads of grey. But that must be suffering or misfortune, for the man was young. His dusky skin had the silvery glisten of youth still.

There was a beauty of much suffering, and the strange calm candour of finer life in the whole delicate ugliness of the face. For the first time, she was touched on the quick at the sight of a man, as if the tip of a fine flame of living had touched her. It was the first time. Men had roused all kinds of feeling in her, but never had touched her with the flame-tip of life.

She went back under the rock to where the slave waited.

'Know!' she said. 'This is no malefactor, but a free citizen of the east. Do not disturb him. But when he comes forth, bring him to me, tell him I would speak with him.'

She spoke coldly, for she found slaves invariably repellent, a little repulsive. They were so embedded in the lesser life, and their appetites and their small consciousness were a little disgusting. So she wrapped her dream round her, and went to the temple, where a slave-girl brought winter roses and jasmine, for the altar. But today, even in her ministrations, she was disturbed.

The sun rose over the hill, sparkling, the light fell triumphantly on the little pine-covered peninsula of the coast, and on the pink temple, in pristine newness. The man who had died woke up, and put on his sandals. He put on his hat too, slung his scrip under his mantle, and went out, to see the morning in all its blue and its new gold. He glanced at the little yellow-and-white narcissus sparkling gaily in the rocks. And he saw the slave waiting for him, like a menace.

'Master!' said the slave. 'Our Lady would speak with you at the house of Isis.'

'It is well,' said the wanderer.

He went slowly, staying to look at the pale-blue sea, like a flower in unruffled bloom, and the white fringes among the rocks, like white rock-flowers, the hollow slopes sheering up high from the shore, grey with olive trees and green with bright young wheat, and set with the white small villa. All fair and pure in the January morning.

The sun fell on the corner of the temple, he sat down on the step, in the sunshine, in the infinite patience of waiting. He had come back to life, but not the same life that he had left, the life of little people and the little day. Reborn, he was in the other life, the greater day of the human consciousness. And he was alone and apart from the little day, and out of contact with the daily people. Not yet he had accepted the irrevocable *noli me tangere* which separates the reborn from the vulgar. The separation was absolute, as yet here at the temple he felt peace, the hard, bright pagan peace with hostility of slaves beneath.

The woman came into the dark inner doorway of the temple, from the shrine, and stood there hesitating. She could see the dark figure of the man sitting in that terrible stillness that was portentous to her, had something almost menacing in its patience.

She advanced across the outer chamber of the temple, and the man, becoming aware of her, stood up. She addressed him in Greek, but he said: 'Madam, my Greek is limited. Allow me to speak vulgar Syrian.'

'Whence come you? Whither go you?' she asked, with the hurried preoccupation of a priestess.

'From the east beyond Damascus – and I go west as the road goes,' he replied, slowly.

She glanced at him with sudden anxiety and shyness.

'But why do you have the marks of a malefactor?' she asked abruptly.

'Did the Lady of Isis spy upon me in my sleep?' he asked, with a grey weariness.

'The slave warned me – your hands and feet – ' she said.

He looked at her. Then he said, 'Will the Lady of Isis allow me to bid her farewell, and go up to the road?'

The wind came in a sudden puff, lifting his mantle and his hat. He put up his hand to hold the brim, and she saw again the thin brown hand with its scar.

'See! the scar!' she said, pointing.

'Even so!' he said. 'But farewell, and to Isis my homage and my thanks for sleep.'

He was going. But she looked up at him with her wondering blue eyes.

'Will you not look on Isis?' she said, with sudden impulse. And something stirred in him, like pain.

'Where then?' he said.

'Come!'

He followed her into the inner shrine, into the almost darkness. When his eyes got used to the faint glow of the lamp, he saw the goddess striding like a ship, eager in the swirl of her gown, and he made his obeisance.

'Great is Isis!' he said. 'In her search she is greater than death. Wonderful is such walking in a woman, wonderful the goal. All men praise thee, Isis, thou greater than the mother unto man.'

The woman of Isis heard, and threw incense on the brazier. Then she looked at the man.

'Is it well with thee here?' she asked him. 'Has Isis brought thee home to herself?'

He looked at the priestess in wonder and trouble.

'I know not,' he said.

But the woman was pondering, that this was the lost Osiris. She felt in the quick of her soul. And her agitation was intense.

He could not stay in the close, dark, perfumed shrine. He went out again to the morning, to the cold air. He felt something approaching to touch him, and all his flesh was still woven with pain and the wild commandment: *Noli me tangere!* Touch me not! Oh, don't touch me!

The woman followed into the open with timid eagerness. He was moving away.

'Oh stranger, do not go! O stay a while with Isis!'

He looked at her, at her face open like a flower, as if a sun had risen in her soul. And again his loins stirred.

'Would you detain me, girl of Isis?' he said.

'Stay! I am sure you are Osiris!' she said.

He laughed suddenly.

'Not yet!' he said. Then he looked at her wistful face. 'But I will sleep another night in the cave of the goats, if Isis wills it,' he added.

She put her hands together with a priestess's childish happiness.

'Ah, Isis will be glad!' she said.

So he went down to the shore, in great trouble, saying to himself: Shall I give myself into this touch? Shall I give myself into this touch? Men have tortured me to death with their touch. Yet this girl of Isis is a tender flame of healing. I am a physician, yet I have no healing like the flame of this tender girl. The flame of this tender girl! Like the first pale crocus of the spring. How could I have been blind to the healing and the bliss in the crocus-like body of a tender woman! Ah tenderness! more terrible and lovely than the death I died –

He prised small shell-fish from the rocks, and ate them with relish and wonder for the simple taste of the sea. And inwardly, he was tremulous, thinking: Dare I come into touch? For this is farther than death. I have dared to let them lay hands on me and put me to death. But dare I come into this tender touch of life? Oh this is harder –

But the woman went into the shrine again, and sat rapt in pure muse, through the long hours, watching the swirling stride of the yearning goddess, and the navel of the bud-like belly, like a seal on the virgin urge of the search. And she gave herself to the woman-flow and to the urge of Isis in Search.

Towards sundown she went on the peninsula to look for him. And she found him gone towards the sun, as she had gone the day before, and sitting on the pine-needles at the foot of the tree, where she had stood when first she saw him. Now she approached tremulously and slowly, afraid lest he did not want her. She stood near him unseen, till suddenly he glanced up at her from under his broad hat, and saw the westering sun on her netted hair. He was startled, yet he expected her.

'Is that your home?' he said, pointing to the white low villa on the slope of olives.

'It is my mother's house. She is a widow, and I am her only child.'

'And are these all her slaves?'

'Except those that are mine.'

Their eyes met for a moment.

'Will you too sit to see the sun go down?' he said.

He had not risen to speak to her. He had known too much pain. So she sat on the dry brown pine-needles, gathering her saffron mantle round her knees. A boat was coming in, out of the open glow into the shadow of the bay, and slaves were lifting small nets, their babble coming off the surface of the water.

'And this is home to you,' he said.

'But I serve Isis in Search,' she replied.

He looked at her. She was like a soft, musing cloud, somehow remote. His soul smote him with passion and compassion.

'Mayst thou find thy desire, Maiden,' he said, with sudden earnestness.

'And art thou not Osiris?' she asked.

He flushed suddenly.

'Yea, if thou wilt heal me!' he said. 'For the death-aloofness is still upon me, and I cannot escape it.'

She looked at him for a moment in fear, from the soft, blue sun of her eyes. Then she lowered her head, and they sat in silence in the warmth and glow of the western sun: the man who had died, and the woman of the pure search.

The sun was curving down to the sea, in grand winter splendour. It fell on the twinkling, naked bodies of the slaves, with their ruddy broad hams and the small black heads, as they ran spreading the nets on the pebble beach. The all-tolerant Pan watched over them. All-tolerant Pan should be their god for ever.

The woman rose as the sun's rim dipped, saying, 'If you will stay, I shall send down victual and covering.'

'The lady your Mother, what will she say?'

The woman of Isis looked at him strangely, but with a tinge of misgiving.

'It is my own,' she said.

'It is good,' he said, smiling faintly, and foreseeing difficulties.

He watched her go, with her absorbed, strange motion of the self-dedicate. Her dun head was a little bent, the white linen swung about her ivory ankles. And he saw the naked slaves stand to look at her, with a certain wonder, and even a certain mischief. But she passed intent through the door in the wall, on the bay.

But the man who had died sat on at the foot of the tree overlooking the strand, for on the little shore everything happened. At the small stream which ran in round the corner of the property wall, women slaves were still washing linen, and now and again came the hollow chock! chock! chock! as they beat it against the smooth stones, in the dark little hollow of the pool. There was a smell of olive-refuse on the air; and sometimes still the faint rumble of the grindstone that was milling the olives, inside the garden, and the sound of the slave calling to the ass at the mill. Then through the doorway a woman stepped, a grey-haired woman in a mantle of whitish wool, and there followed her a bare-headed man in a toga, a Roman: probably her steward or overseer. They stood on the high shingle above the sea, and cast round a rapid glance. The broad-hammed, ruddy-bodied slaves bent absorbed and abject over the nets, picking them clean, the women washing linen thrust their palms with energy down on the wash, the old slave bent absorbed at the water's edge, washing the fish and the polyps of the catch. And the woman and the overseer saw it all, in one glance. They also saw, seated at the foot of the tree on the rocks of the peninsula, the strange man silent and alone. And the man who had died saw that they spoke of him. Out of the little sacred world of the peninsula he looked on the common world, and saw it still hostile.

The sun was touching the sea, across the tiny bay stretched the shadow of the opposite humped headland. Over the shingle, now blue and cold in shadow, the elderly woman trod heavily, in shadow too, to look at the fish spread in the flat basket of the old man crouching at the water's edge; a naked old slave with fat hips and shoulders, on whose soft, fairish-orange body the last sun twinkled, then died. The old slave continued cleaning the fish absorbedly, not looking up: as if the lady were the shadow of twilight falling on him.

Then from the gateway stepped two slave-girls with flat baskets on their heads, and from one basket the terra-cotta wine-jar and the oil-jar poked up, leaning slightly. Over the massive shingle, under the wall, came the girls, and the woman of Isis in her saffron mantle stepped in twilight after them. Out at sea, the sun still shone. Here was shadow.

The mother with grey head stood at the sea's edge and watched the daughter, all yellow and white, with dun blonde head, swinging unseeing and unheeding after the slave-girls, towards the neck of rock of the peninsula: the daughter, travelling in her absorbed other-world. And not moving from her place, the elderly mother watched that procession of three file up the rise of the headland, between the trees, and disappear, shut in by trees. No slave had lifted a head to look. The grey-haired woman still watched the trees where her daughter had disappeared. Then she glanced again at the foot of the tree, where the man who had died was still sitting, inconspicuous now, for the sun had left him; and only the far blade of the sea shone bright. It was evening. Patience! Let destiny move!

The mother plodded with a stamping stride up the shingle: not long and swinging and rapt, like the daughter, but short and determined. Then down the rocks opposite came two naked slaves trotting with huge bundles of dark green on their shoulders, so their broad, naked legs twinkled underneath like insects' legs, and their heads were hidden. They came trotting across the shingle, heedless and intent on their way, when suddenly the man, the Roman-looking overseer, addressed them, and they stopped dead. They stood invisible under their loads, as if they might disappear altogether, now they were arrested. Then a hand came out and pointed to the peninsula. Then the two green-heaped slaves trotted on, towards the temple precincts. The grey-haired woman joined the man, and slowly the two passed through the door again, from the shingle of the sea to the property of the villa. Then the old, fat-shouldered slave rose, pallid in the shadow, with his tray of fish from the sea, and the women rose from the pool, dusky and alive, piling the wet linen in a heap on to the flat baskets, and the slaves who had cleaned the net gathered its whitish folds together. And the old slave with the fish-basket on his shoulder, and the women slaves with heaped baskets of wet linen on their heads, and the two slaves with the folded net, and the slave with oars on his shoulders, and the boy with the folded sail on his arm, gathered in a naked group near the door, and the man who had died heard the low buzz of their chatter. Then as the wind wafted cold, they began to pass through the door.

It was the life of the little day, the life of little people. And the man who had died said to himself: Unless we encompass it in the greater day, and set the little life in the circle of the greater life, all is disaster.

Even the tops of the hills were in shadow. Only the sky was still upwardly radiant. The sea was a vast milky shadow. The man who had died rose a little stiffly, and turned into the grove.

There was no one at the temple. He went on to his lair in the rock. There, the slave-men had carried out the old heath of the bedding, swept the rock floor, and were spreading with nice art the myrtle, then the rougher heath, then the soft, bushy heath-tips on top, for a bed. Over it all they put a well-tanned white ox-skin. The maids had laid folded woollen covers at the head of the cave, and the wine-jar, the oil-jar, a terra-cotta drinking-cup, and a basket containing bread, salt cheese, dried figs and eggs stood neatly arranged. There was also a little brazier of charcoal. The cave was suddenly full, and a dwelling-place.

The woman of Isis stood in the hollow by the tiny spring.

Only one slave at a time could pass. The girl-slaves waited at the entrance to the narrow place. When the man who had died appeared, the woman sent the girls away. The men-slaves still arranged the bed, making the job as long as possible. But the woman of Isis dismissed them too. And the man who had died came to look at his house.

'Is it well?' the woman asked him.

'It is very well,' the man replied. 'But the lady your mother, and he who is no doubt the steward, watched while the slaves brought the goods. Will they not oppose you?'

'I have my own portion! Can I not give of my own? Who is going to oppose me and the gods?' she said, with a certain soft fury, touched with exasperation. So that he knew her mother would oppose her, and that the spirit of the little life would fight against the spirit of the greater. And he thought: Why did the woman of Isis relinquish her portion in the daily world? She should have kept her goods fiercely! –

'Will you eat and drink?' she said. 'On the ashes are warm eggs. And I will go up to the meal at the villa. But in the second hour of the night I shall come down to the temple. O, then, will you too come to Isis?' She looked at him, and a queer glow dilated her eyes. This was her dream, and it was greater than herself. He could not bear to thwart her or hurt her in the least thing now. She was in the full glow of her woman's mystery.

'Shall I wait at the temple?' he said.

'O, wait in the second hour, and I shall come.' He heard the humming supplication in her voice, and his fibres quivered.

'But the lady, your mother?' he said gently.

The woman looked at him, startled.

'She will not thwart me!' she said.

So she knew that the mother would thwart the daughter, for the daughter had left her goods in the hands of her mother, who would hold fast to this power.

But she went, and the man who had died lay reclining on his couch, and ate the eggs from the ashes, and dipped his bread in oil, and ate it, for his flesh was dry: and he mixed wine and water, and drank. And so he lay still, and the lamp made a small bud of light.

He was absorbed and enmeshed in new sensations. The woman of Isis was lovely to him, not so much in form, as in the wonderful womanly glow of her. Suns beyond suns had dipped her in mysterious fire, the mysterious fire of a potent woman, and to touch her was like touching the sun. Best of all was her tender desire for him, like sunshine, so soft and still.

'She is like sunshine upon me,' he said to himself, stretching his limbs. 'I have never before stretched my limbs in such sunshine, as her desire for me. The greatest of all gods granted me this.'

At the same time, he was haunted by the fear of the outer world. 'If they can, they will kill us,' he said to himself. 'But there is a law of the sun which protects us.'

And he said again to himself: 'I have risen naked and branded. But if I am naked enough for this contact, I have not died in vain. Before, I was clogged.'

He rose and went out. The night was chill and starry, and of a great wintry splendour. 'There are destinies of splendour,' he said to the night, 'after all our doom of littleness and meanness and pain.'

So he went up silently to the temple, and waited in darkness against the inner wall, looking out on grey darkness, stars, and rims of trees. And he said again to himself: There are destinies of splendour, and there is a greater power.

So at last he saw the light of her silk lanthorn swinging, coming intermittent between the trees, yet coming swiftly. She was alone, and near, the light softly swishing on her mantle-hem. And he trembled with fear and with joy, saying to himself: I am almost more afraid of this touch than I was of death. For I am more nakedly exposed to it.

'I am here, Lady of Isis,' he said softly out of the dark.

'Ah!' she cried, in fear also, yet in rapture. For she was given to her dream.

She unlocked the door of the shrine, and he followed after her. Then she latched the door shut again. The air inside was warm and close and perfumed. The man who had died stood by the closed door, and watched the woman. She had come first to the goddess. And dim-lit the goddess-statue stood surging forward, a little fearsome, like a great woman-presence urging.

The priestess did not look at him. She took off her saffron mantle and laid it on a low couch. In the dim light she was bare-armed, in her girdled white tunic. But she was still hiding herself away from him. He stood back in shadow, and watched her softly fan the brazier and fling on incense. Faint clouds of sweet aroma arose on the air. She turned to the statue in the ritual of approach, softly swaying forward with a slight lurch, like a moored boat, tipping towards the goddess.

He watched the strange rapt woman, and he said to himself: I must leave her alone in her rapture, her female mysteries. – So she tipped in her strange forward-swaying rhythm before the goddess. Then she broke into a murmur of Greek, which he could not understand. And, as she murmured, her swaying softly subsided, like a boat on a sea that grows still. And as he watched her, he saw her soul in its aloneness, and its female difference. He said to himself: How different she is from me, how strangely different! She is afraid of me, and my male difference. She is getting herself naked and clear of her fear. How sensitive and softly alive she is! How alive she is, with a life so different from mine! How beautiful, with a soft, strange courage of life, so different from my courage of death! What a beautiful thing, like the heart of a rose, like the core of a flame. She is making herself completely penetrable. Ah, how terrible to fail her, or to trespass on her!

She turned to him, her face glowing from the goddess.

'You are Osiris, aren't you?' she said naïvely.

'If you will,' he said.

'Will you let Isis discover you? Will you not take off your things?'

He looked at the woman, and lost his breath. And his wounds, and especially the death-wound through his belly, began to cry again.

'It has hurt so much!' he said. 'You must forgive me if I am still held back.'

But he took off his cloak and his tunic, and went naked towards the idol, his breast panting with the sudden terror of overwhelming pain, memory of over-whelming pain, and grief too bitter.

'They did me to death!' he said in excuse of himself, turning his face to her for a moment.

And she saw the ghost of the death in him as he stood there thin and stark before her, and suddenly she was terrified, and she felt robbed. She felt the shadow of the grey, grisly wing of death triumphant.

'Ah Goddess,' he said to the idol, in the vernacular. 'I would be so glad to live, if you would give me my clue again.'

For here again he felt desperate, faced by the demand of life, and burdened still by his death.

'Let me anoint you!' the woman said to him softly, 'let me anoint the scars! Show me, and let me anoint them!'

He forgot his nakedness in this re-evoked old pain. He sat on the edge of the couch, and she poured a little ointment into the palm of his hand. And as she chafed his hand, it all came back, the nails, the holes, the cruelty, the unjust cruelty against him who had offered only kindness. The agony of injustice and cruelty came over him again, as in his death-hour. But she chafed the palm, murmuring: 'What was torn becomes a new flesh, what was a wound is full of fresh life, this scar is the eye of the violet.'

And he could not help smiling at her, in her naïve priestess's absorption. This was her dream, and he was only a dream-object to her. She would never know or understand what he was. Especially she would never know the death that was gone before in him. But what did it matter? She was different. She was woman: her life and her death were different from his. Only she was good to him.

When she chafed his feet with oil and tender healing, he could not refrain from saying to her, 'Once a woman washed my feet with tears, and wiped them with her hair, and poured on precious ointment.'

The woman of Isis looked up at him from her earnest work, interrupted again.

'Were they hurt then?' she said 'Your feet?'

'No no! It was while they were whole.'

'And did you love her?'

'Love had passed in her. She only wanted to serve,' he replied. 'She had been a prostitute.'

'And did you let her serve you?' she asked.

'Yea.'

'Did you let her serve you with the corpse of her love?'

'Ay!'

Suddenly it dawned on him: I asked them all to serve me with the corpse of their love. And in the end I offered them only the corpse of my love. This is my body – take and eat – my corpse –

A vivid shame went through him. – After all, he thought, – I wanted them to love with dead bodies. If I had kissed Judas with live love, perhaps he would never have kissed me with death. Perhaps he loved me in the flesh, and I willed that he should love me bodilessly, with the corpse of love –

There dawned on him the reality of the soft warm love which is in touch, and which is full of delight. – And I told them, blessed are they that mourn, – he said to himself. Alas, if I mourned even this woman here, now I am in death, I should have to remain dead, and I want so much to live. Life has brought me to this woman with warm hands. And her touch is more to me now than all my words. For I want to live –

'Go then to the Goddess!' she said softly, gently pushing him towards Isis. And as he stood there dazed and naked as an unborn thing, he heard the woman murmuring to the goddess, murmuring, murmuring with a plaintive appeal. She was stooping now, looking at the scar in the soft flesh of the socket of his side, a scar deep and like an eye sore with endless weeping, just in the soft socket above the hip. It was here that his blood had left him, and his essential seed. The woman was trembling softly and murmuring in Greek. And he, in the recurring dismay of having died, and in the anguished perplexity of having tried to force life, felt his wounds crying aloud, and the deep places of his body howling again: I have been murdered, and I lent myself to murder. They murdered me, but I lent myself to murder. –

The woman, silent now, but quivering, laid oil in her hand and put her palm over the wound in his right side. He winced, and the wound absorbed his life again, as thousands of times before. And in the dark, wild pain and panic of his consciousness rang only one cry: Oh, how can she take this death out of me? How can she take from me this death? She can never know! She can never understand! She can never equal it! . . .

In silence, she softly rhythmically chafed the scar with oil, absorbed now in her priestess's task, softly, softly gathering power, while the vitals of the man howled in panic. But as she gradually gathered power, and passed in a girdle round him to the opposite scar, gradually warmth began to take the place of the cold terror, and he felt: I am going to be flushed warm again, I am going to be whole! I shall be warm like the morning. I shall be a man. It doesn't need understanding. It needs newness. She brings me newness –

And he listened to the faint, ceaseless wail of distress, of his wounds, sounding as if for ever under the horizons of his consciousness. But the wail was growing dim, more dim.

He thought of the woman toiling over him: she does not know! she does not realise the death in me. But she has another consciousness. She comes to me from the opposite end of the night.

Having chafed all his lower body with oil, having worked with her slow intensity of a priestess, so that the sound of his wounds grew dimmer and dimmer, suddenly, she put her breast against the wound in his left side, and her arms round him, folding over the wound in his right side, and she pressed him to her, in a power of living warmth, like in the folds of a river. And the wailing died out altogether, and there was stillness, and darkness in his soul, unbroken dark stillness, wholeness.

Then slowly, slowly, in the perfect darkness of his inner man, he felt the stir of something coming: a dawn, a new sun. A new sun was coming up in him, in the perfect inner darkness of himself. He waited for it breathless, quivering with fearful hope . . . 'Now I am not myself – I am something new . . . '

And as it rose, he felt, with a cold breath of disappointment, the girdle of the living woman slip from him, the warmth and the glow slipped down from him, leaving him stark. She crouched spent at the feet of the goddess, hiding her face.

Stooping, he laid his hand softly on her warm, bright shoulder, and the shock of desire went through him, shock after shock, so that he wondered if it were another sort of death: but full of magnificence.

Now all his consciousness was there in the crouching, hidden woman. He stooped beside her and caressed her softly, blindly, murmuring inarticulate things. And his death and his passion of sacrifice were all as nothing to him now, he knew only the crouching fullness of the woman there, the soft white rock of life . . . 'On this rock I built my life' – The deep-folded, penetrable rock of the living woman! the woman, hiding her face. Himself bending over, powerful and new like dawn.

He crouched to her, and he felt the blaze of his manhood and his power rise up in his loins, magnificent.

'I am risen!'

Magnificent, blazing indomitable in the depths of his loins, his own sun dawned, and sent its fire running along his limbs, so that his face shone unconsciously.

He untied the string on the linen tunic, and slipped the garment down, till he saw the white glow of her white-gold breasts. And he touched them, and he felt his life go molten. – Father! he said, – why did you hide this from me? – And he touched her with the poignancy of wonder, and the marvellous piercing transcendence of desire. – Lo! he said. – This is beyond prayer. – It was the deep, interfolded warmth, warmth living and penetrable, the woman, the heart of the rose! – My mansion is the intricate warm rose, my joy is this blossom! –

She looked up at him suddenly, her face like a lifted light, wistful, tender, her eyes like many wet flowers. And he drew her to his breast with a passion of tenderness and consuming desire, and a last thought: – My hour is upon me, I am taken unawares –

So he knew her, and was one with her.

Afterwards, with a dim wonder, she touched the great scars in his sides with her finger-tips, and said, 'But they no longer hurt?'

'They are suns!' he said. 'They shine from your touch. They are my atonement with you.'

And when they left the temple, it was the coldness before dawn. As he closed the door, he looked again at the goddess, and he said: 'Lo, Isis is a kindly goddess; and full of tenderness. Great gods are warm-hearted, and have tender goddesses.'

The woman wrapped herself in her mantle and went home in silence, sightless, brooding like the lotus softly shutting again, with its gold core full of fresh life. She saw nothing, for her own petals were a sheath to her. Only she thought: I am full of Osiris. I am full of the risen Osiris! . . .

But the man looked at the vivid stars before dawn, as they rained down to the sea, and the dog-star green towards the sea's rim. And he thought: How plastic it is, how full of curves and folds like an invisible rose of dark-petalled openness, that shows where dew touches its darkness! How full it is, and great beyond all gods. How it leans around me, and I am part of it, the great rose of Space. I am like a grain of its perfume, and the woman is a grain of its beauty. Now the world is one flower of many-petalled darknesses, and I am in its perfume as in a touch.

So, in the absolute stillness and fullness of touch, he slept in his cave while the dawn came. And after the dawn, the wind rose and brought a storm, with cold rain. So he stayed in his cave in the peace and the delight of being in touch, delighting to hear the sea, and the rain on the earth, and to see one white-and-gold narcissus bowing wet, and still wet. And he said: This is the great atonement, the being in touch. The grey sea and the rain, the wet narcissus and the woman I wait for, the invisible Isis and the unseen sun are all in touch, and at one.

He waited at the temple for the woman, and she came in the rain. But she said to him, 'Let me sit awhile with Isis. And come to me, will you come to me, in the second hour of night?'

So he went back to the cave and lay in stillness and in the joy of being in touch, waiting for the woman who would come with the night, and consummate again the contact. Then when night came the woman came, and came gladly, for her great yearning too was upon her, to be in touch, to be in touch with him, nearer.

So the days came, and the nights came, and days came again, and the contact was perfected and fulfilled. And he said: I will ask her nothing, not even her name, for a name would set her apart.

And she said to herself: He is Osiris. I wish to know no more.

Plum-blossom blew from the trees, the time of the narcissus was past, anemones lit up the ground and were gone, the perfume of bean-fields was in the air. All changed, the blossom of the universe changed its petals and swung round to look another way. The spring was fulfilled, a contact was established, the man and the woman were fulfilled of one another, and departure was in the air.

One day he met her under the trees, when the morning sun was hot, and the pines smelled sweet, and on the hills the last pear-bloom was scattering. She came slowly towards him, and in her gentle lingering, her tender hanging back from him, he knew a change in her.

'Hast thou conceived?' he asked her.

'Why?' she said.

'Thou art like a tree whose green leaves follow the blossom, full of sap. And there is a withdrawing about thee.'

'It is so,' she said. 'I am with young by thee. Is it good?'

'Yea!' he said. 'How should it not be good? So the nightingale calls no more from the valley-bed. But where wilt thou bear the child, for I am naked of all but life.'

'We will stay here,' she said.

'But the lady your mother?'

A shadow crossed her brow. She did not answer.

'What when she knows?' he said.

'She begins to know.'

'And would she hurt you?'

'Ah, not me! What I have is all my own. And I shall be big with Osiris . . . But thou, do you watch her slaves.'

She looked at him, and the peace of her maternity was troubled by anxiety.

'Let not your heart be troubled!' he said. 'I have died the death once.'

So he knew the time was come again, for him to depart. He would go alone, with his destiny. Yet not alone, for the touch would be upon him, even as he left his touch on her. And invisible suns would go with him.

Yet he must go. For here on the bay the little life of jealousy and property was resuming sway again, as the suns of passionate fecundity relaxed their sway. In the name of property, the widow and her slaves would seek to be revenged on him for the bread he had eaten, and the living touch he had established, the woman he had delighted in. But he said: Not twice! They shall not now profane the touch in me. My wits against theirs.

So he watched. And he knew they plotted. So he moved from the little cave, and found another shelter, a tiny cove of sand by the sea, dry and secret under the rocks.

He said to the woman, 'I must go now soon. Trouble is coming to me from the slaves. But I am a man, and the world is open. But what is between us is good, and is established. Be at peace. And when the nightingale calls again from your valley-bed, I shall come again, sure as spring.'

She said: 'O don't go! Stay with me on half the island, and I will build a house for you and me under the pine trees by the temple, where we can live apart.'

Yet she knew that he would go. And even she wanted the coolness of her own hair around her, and the release from anxiety.

'If I stay,' he said, 'they will betray me to the Romans and to their justice. But I will never be betrayed again. So when I am gone, live in peace with the growing child. And I shall come again; all is good between us, near or apart. The suns come back in their seasons: and I shall come again.'

'Do not go yet,' she said. 'I have set a slave to watch at the neck of the peninsula. Do not go yet, till the harm shows.'

But as he lay in his little cove, on a calm, still night, he heard the soft knock of oars, and the bump of the boat against the rock. So he crept out to listen. And he heard the Roman overseer say, 'Lead softly to the goat's den. And Lysippus shall throw the net over the malefactor while he sleeps, and we will bring him before justice, and the Lady of Isis shall know nothing of it . . . '

The man who had died caught a whiff of flesh from the oiled and naked slaves as they crept up, then the faint perfume of the Roman. He crept nearer to the sea. The slave who sat in the boat, sat motionless, holding the oars, for the sea was quite still. And the man who had died knew him.

So out of the deep cleft of a rock he said, in a clear voice, 'Art thou not that slave who possessed the maiden under the eyes of Isis? Art thou not the youth? Speak!'

The youth stood up in the boat in terror. His movement sent the boat bumping against the rock. The slave sprang out in wild fear, and fled up the rocks. The man who had died quickly seized the boat and stepped in, and pushed off. The oars were yet warm with the unpleasant warmth of the hands of slaves. But the man pulled slowly out, to get into the current which set down the coast, and would carry him in silence. The high coast was utterly dark against the starry night. There was no glimmer from the peninsula: the priestess came no more at night. The man who had died rowed slowly on, with the current, and laughed to himself: I have sowed the seed of my life and my resurrection, and put my touch for ever upon the choice woman of this day, and I carry her perfume in my flesh like essence of roses. She is dear to me in the middle of my being. But the gold and flowing serpent is coiling up again, to sleep at the root of my tree.

'So let the boat carry me. Tomorrow is another day.'